The Everything Bagel

with a Side of Milk and Honey

The Word is Our Bread of Life.
If you have the Word, you have
Everything you need to survive the perils of this life.
We wait on Messiah for our Sabbath rest in the Land of Milk and Honey.

Sandra Henley

First Edition

PAGE PUBLISHING, INC.
New York, NY

First originally published by Page Publishing, Inc. 2017

ISBN 978-1-64027-733-5 (Paperback)
ISBN 978-1-64027-734-2 (Digital)

Printed in the United States of America

Yeshua is our Bread of Life. He is our Everything Bagel.
King David said in Psalm 34:8, "Oh, taste and see that the Word is good."
The Apostle John tells us that in the beginning, the Word was with
God and the Word is God. The Word came down from heaven,
took on mortal flesh, and did dwell among us (John 1).
To each of us is given the seed of faith so that we might believe
and, through him, we have eternal life with God.

Sandra Henley

Contents

FOREWORD

After years of intensive biblical research and with great eagerness to share the mysteries of God with the world, *The Everything Bagel* was birthed. In an effort to maintain journalistic integrity, sensationalism is limited and factual evidence is presented based on biblical doctrine. In a genre of prophecy- and conspiracy-themed literature dominated by males, the author and female prophecy team did embrace a difficult challenge to present a worldview of the coming apocalypse.

Author Sandra Henley is my mother, friend, and confidant. She has a heart and thrust to understand God's Word and biblical prophecy for as long as I can remember. Her Christian walk and relentless quest to study the scriptures has been the catalyst in my pursuit to answer the call of ministry and to teach the Gospel with simplicity over the past twenty-two years. I obtained my undergrad in biblical studies and MBA. Needless to say, I too feel as if my personal knowledge of biblical prophecy and end-time world events is limited at best. *The Everything Bagel* will enlighten and bring clarification to biblical stories, mysteries, and prophecies congruent with current world events.

Whether you belong to an organized Christian denominations or stand somewhere in between, one thing remaining constant is the infallible Word of God, and the Word will surely come to pass. History reveals that the God of Abraham is the same yesterday, today, and forevermore. He has watched over his Word, performing every promise, command, and judgment without fail. So ask yourself, as you read this book, Would God suddenly divert from fulfilling his original plan of salvation in the twenty-first century? Today many congregations enjoy messages that encourage and promote prosperity and empowerment. Rarely are heard lessons touching biblical mysteries and what to look for in world events leading to the Second Coming of Christ. If you conclude that God's Word stands that test of time, then we must realize that Second Thessalonians 2:1–3 referencing God's judgment, Christ's return, and the persecution of those who believe is inevitable:

> *As to the coming of our Lord Jesus Christ and our being gathered together to him, we beg you, brother and sisters, not to be quickly shaken in mind or alarmed, either by spirit or by word or by letter, as though from us, to the effect that the day of the Lord is already here. Let no one deceive you in any way; for*

that day will not come unless the rebellion comes first and the lawless one is revealed, the one destined for destruction.

Form your own opinions, and ask God to reveal truth and understanding so that you will not be caught off guard as the world catastrophes manifest. I believe and pray that you will walk away from reading this book with greater clarification and increased desires to be about God's work to spread the Gospel of Jesus Christ.

God bless you,
Elder Shirley Rankine

Introduction

The contents within *The Everything Bagel* hold the Bible as the basis for all truth and understanding. It offers a deeper analysis of the treasures found throughout the scriptures. We believe the treasures of God are given to us as mysteries that we are to search out to discover the deeper things of God. The objective of this book is to gather together the best research sources and commentaries of everything Yahweh, beginning with Genesis through to Revelation, presenting complex matters into an easy format for understanding. Scholars have written on various themes, which require the truth seeker to read volumes in order to have an intellectual and spiritual understanding of these very special nuggets. *The Everything Bagel* provides a condensed view on topics, such as, who is God, his creation, angels, giants, our Judaic roots, Frankenstein technology, New World order, Antichrist and the false prophet, understanding the book of Revelation, the Second Coming of Christ, and his millennial kingdom.

Between these covers, one will find various subjects that may not have been discussed in traditional church settings. For instance, this research presents the Resurrection in four stages and clears up centuries of misunderstanding. We provide an overview of religions whose doctrines do not line up with the Bible, such as Mormonism and Islam.

There are many mysteries and messages that have been buried throughout the centuries, and some have been intentionally kept from the world. Knowledge was given to mankind for his understanding, growth, and survival throughout the millenniums. The fallen angel, Satan, influenced the first people to look into the sacred knowledge, to know good and evil and to become as God. Throughout time, mystics, illuminati, and secret societies go to great lengths to discover the secrets of immortality, wealth, and power. All secret societies have an inner core of mystery, which may cloak God's truth and present an unholy doctrine to deceive their adherents. *The Everything Bagel* provides an overview of secret societies, such as the Masonic order.

Isaac Newton said, "There are still more mysteries to be discovered. Many before me laid the foundation, and I have built upon it, so I hope others will proceed higher until the work is finished." Based on that statement, we also stand on the shoulders of great thinkers who have come and gone. We also embrace the wisdom of Saint Paul, who clearly states that God will destroy the wisdom of the wise and bring to nothing the understanding of the prudent. Therein, we come not with excellency of speech or in our wisdom but declaring the testimony of Yeshua and him crucified. We who are in Christ Jesus, God has given unto us wisdom, righteousness, sanctification, and redemption (1 Corinthians 1).

This book is the compilation of thirty years of study and research endeavoring to bring biblical subjects together in a concise, panoramic view of all things Yahweh. History does repeat itself and through data mining, we can look for markers that give us warning of present or near future events. It will give a glimpse into a time before the creation of the earth, connecting the dots from the fall of man, leading up to the Day of the Lord and culminating into the tribulation period. The markers we look for are wars and rumor of wars, technological advancement, the one-world order agenda, social upheaval, disruption of the natural order of all things, extreme climate worldwide, and as the balance of nature is upset through pestilence and plagues, epidemics will be unleashed upon mankind. Throughout *The Everything Bagel*, Satan's agenda is exposed as he has deceived many through religion, racism, secularism, immorality, and hatred.

We consider this book to be a companion to the scriptures as well as a tutorial in guiding many through the end-times holocaust. It is our desire that people will come into a deeper truth of everything Yahweh and his truth will survive after the Internet is classified as a national security risk, taken over by the United Nations, and alternative media sites shut down. The Bible may be burned and destroyed by the one-world religion and replaced with a generic book that removes all things God. *The Everything Bagel* presents God as Creator of everything in heaven, upon the earth, and under the earth. This book might just be the book that is left behind when the saints are caught up. It might survive the coming chaos to be a light in a dark and bleak world.

I grew up in a household that believed in God. My mother took my sibling and me to church every Sunday. She dressed us up in classy outfits even though our family was struggling to make ends meet. Sometimes my father went to church with us as we walked a few blocks to Penn Memorial Baptist Church in West Philadelphia. I still remember when I got baptized, wearing a white gown and being submerged in the baptismal pool. Baptism to me was a church tradition and expected for children coming to the age of twelve. I liked our pastor, Rev. Mitchell, and his wife. My mother would invite them over for fried chicken dinner. The sights and smells of my childhood were, for the most part, pleasant.

Somewhere along the line, my mother decided to take us to the tent meeting revivals. We sat for hours listening to A. A. Allen, R. W. Shamback, and others. It seemed my mother had become hungry for the things of God. However, my father was at odds with her for her growing love of our Lord and Savior, and he moved farther away from Jesus. When we were teenagers, he left his family and took up with another woman. They stayed together for thirty years. I visited with him a few days before he died, and he asked me if my mother was still a Christian.

My mother took my brother and I out of public school and put us into parochial elementary school. Well, what a culture shock: nuns adorned in habits that covered them from head to toe, priests wearing long tunics, and children dressed in school uniforms. So I began a three-year journey in Catholicism. The church was huge with statues everywhere. On Sundays, we sang in Latin, having no understanding of what we were singing. The priest conducted the mass in Latin, and we had no concept of what he was saying. We prayed the rosary, and it was a repetition of "Hail Mary" and "Our Father." The glass beads were lovely. My first Holy Communion was fun. We wore pretty white dresses and veils like a princess. We learned all the rituals of Catholicism and were taught the catechism in school. I remember the nuns were very strict and would slap our faces or crack our hands with a ruler. To ingratiate myself with the nuns, I scrubbed the convent floor on hands and knees. However, it didn't help because I clearly remember leaving the convent one evening and was accosted by three bad boys who taunted and spit on me. I looked up at the convent window, and the nun was looking at it all and said nothing. By the time I was in sixth grade, my perspective of Catholicism began to change. It just didn't sit right with me that I had to go before the priest and confess my sins. I thought, *Why should I confess my sins to a man?* I knew the Ten Commandments. Thou shall make no graven images, and I considered all the statutes in the church. I wondered why we had to kiss old relics. I thought it could not be a good thing that the priest smokes and drinks liquor. My father drove a taxicab part time. I heard him tell my mother that he took priests to meet prostitutes, and he heard of skeletal remains of babies buried in the church. As knowledge of certain practices make their way into the public domain, we wonder if these children were sacrificed.

It was the end of the school year; within a week, we would be on summer vacation. One of my classmates was leaving school early to go on a trip with her relatives. As she passed by my desk, I had an immediate premonition of them in an accident, and I saw three coffins. It came to pass. Our class attended the funeral of our classmate and her two relatives. That was the first time I had such a vivid premonition. I wondered, why me, there was nothing I could do to prevent the tragedy.

My maternal great-grandmother was Cherokee, and my great-grandfather was of European ancestry. My grandfather was Native American, Black Foot tribe, and African ancestry. He married my grandmother, who was Cherokee and European. Therefore, I am a combination of European, African, and Native American ancestry. It is said that the Cherokee Indians experience dreams and visions. I know my grandmother could see things in the spiritual realm. My mother had plenty of dreams and visions. She became an intercessor in prayer and received messages from the Holy Spirit for her family and friends.

At the time my daughter Shirley received the anointing of the Holy Spirit, she and my mother were in prayer. My mother began to speak in her prayer language, and the Holy Spirit showed her a vision of a chandelier that was dripping drops of fire over my daughter. At the same time, my daughter said the anointing was so great she felt like she was on fire. Later that night, she was awakened by the presence of the Lord, who said, "Read 2 Timothy 4:2, and go preach, go and evangelize." From that time for thirty days, the Holy Spirit was with her, teaching her, and she was hungry for the things of God. She devoured the Word. She was called to preach, lay hands on the sick, and rebuke evil spirits. Contrary to some church belief, women are also called by God. She has been in the ministry for over twenty years.

My grandfather gave my mother land in the suburbs outside of Philadelphia, and my mother built a house on the land next door to his house. We moved out of city and back to the suburbs, which held many of my fondest memories of time with my grandparents. When I was young, they had chickens running around, a vegetable garden, an old model T Ford that had a hand crank on the front. Before my grandfather built his permanent house, they lived over a garage, and the toilet facilities were in the outhouse. In the permanent house, there was a spirit that also took up residence in it. I always sensed something weird, but as a child, we cannot explain spiritual things. My aunt, an "old maid," always lived at home with my grandparents, and she was born with a veil over her face. She also could see things in the spirit realm. She saw the spirits of dead people, or so we were told. My mother, myself, and my daughter were sensitive to the presence of spirits as well as having visions and premonitions.

After my grandparents died, I allowed a couple from our church, who was from Brazil, to stay in their house. They told me there was a spirit in the house. This is the same spirit I sensed when I was a child. At this point in time, some members from our church had invited Sam Sweg—a minister from the Midwest—to come for a few services. He had a gift. He would preach the Word, and then he would ask anyone to come before him. He would be able to see physical abnormalities or psychological concerns. We never met Sam Sweg before, so it was not rigged. Anyway, I asked him to visit my mother, who was homebound, and pray with her. When he was finished with her, we asked him if he would go next door to my grandparents' home and pray. We all waited outside, and he went in by himself. When Sam returned, he said there was an Indian spirit in the house, and it had been invited by my Cherokee grandmother. Sam told the spirit it had to leave. After that intervention, the house felt clear of a spiritual presence.

Following my experience in Catholicism, I attended a variety of churches from Methodist to Pentecostal. I got invited to study with Jehovah's Witness, visited the Watchtower in New York, and attended their Sunday meetings at the Kingdom Hall. After studying with them for a year, I had enough previous Bible knowledge to know that the 144,000 spoken of in Revelation was not them as they claimed and Jesus was not Michael the Archangel.

I came across Hal Lindsey's book, *Late Great Planet Earth*, and it was the most exciting book I had ever read. After reading it, I had a great desire to understand Bible prophecy; and lo and behold, I received a brochure about a prophecy seminar for a week at a local hotel. The presenters gave out colorful literature with pictures of seven-headed beast and a huge statue of gold, silver, bronze, and iron—which represented ancient kingdoms. The second week of the seminar was held at a Seventh-Day Adventist church. I attended their Saturday services for about a year. There was something not right, especially with the credence they gave to Ellen G. White and her book, *The Great Controversy*. Their interpretation of Bible prophecy did not sit well in my spirit. I knew this was not the right congregation for me.

My mother and I were attending a small storefront Pentecostal church, and the pastor was a female. One day I walked into the church, and I immediately noticed that the atmosphere in the church was thick and seemed electrically charged. I went and sat down, and I felt a tingling on my legs, and I said, to myself, "Is this Satan?" Then I thought, *Lord, do you really touch people?* About that time, the preacher went to the pulpit to preach and was slain in the spirit, and she just lay on the floor. We had not started praise or worship. We had not done anything to invite the presence of the Spirit. The holy presence of the Lord was already there. I went over to my mother and said, "I think I feel the Holy Spirit." She and a few ladies gathered around me, and they prayed, and then I began to experience a heat on my hands. The gift of tongues came later. What a wonderful, holy experience and one I will never forget.

In my neighborhood, Suburban Bible Institute provided a formalized Bible training program, in which I enrolled. A course on the Holy Spirit was taught by a minister who did not believe the Holy Spirit was for the church today but only for that onetime event of Pentecost. Through my own personal experiences, I knew his position was incorrect. The gifts of the Holy Spirit are prevalent from the first century to the twenty-first century.

When you are excited about the Word of God, you want to share it with others. I was attending another little Pentecostal church and asked the pastor if I could put on a prophecy seminar, and he agreed. It was going to require a lot of preparation because I was always thinking, *I don't know enough*, but the Holy Spirit said, "Go." My mother and I decided to go on a Christian retreat in the mountains. I thought this would be a good time to get some study accomplished for the seminar. At the retreat, they had a praise-and-worship service. We didn't know anyone else there, but we joined in with the praise and were singing, hands raised, when I felt the Holy Spirit come on me like a cloak. I looked at my mother and said, "Do you feel the Holy Spirit?" and she didn't respond. All of a sudden, the praise-and-worship leader all the way up front stopped singing and playing music and said, "Someone here is heavy with the anointing." Well, no one moved, and neither did I because I was too shy to bring any attention to myself. I wonder, to this day, what would have happened if I had gone up to the front.

Still having a great desire to understand Bible prophecy, I attended Noah Hutchings, Southwest Radio Church prophecy seminars for a few years. Then I heard about Perry Stone and attended his seminars. The Lord opened up an opportunity for me to travel to Israel with Perry Stone's tour group in 2006. It was a wonderful experience to set my feet in Israel, the City of God. To see the Sea of Galilee, stand on the Mount of Olives, to put my prayers in the Western Wall, to walk on the Temple mount and to put my feet in the Dead Sea. My visit to the Holocaust museum, also called Yad Vashem, left me in tears. Overall, the trip was very memorable and enhanced my understanding of the relationship of Israel with the body of Christ. Yeshua came first to the Jew and then to the Gentile. Together we are one new man in Christ, as Sid Roth always says. A majority of our subject matter would not be possible if it were not for great minds such as, J. R. Church, Gary Stearman, Donald Perkins, Chuck Missler, Tom Horn, Jack Van Impe, Gary Kah, and many, many more.

I was led to read all I could find on unlocking the keys to understanding Bible prophecy. Many years were spent in studying the writings of Daniel, other prophetic scripture, and grasping the messages revealed in the book of Revelation. The greatest challenge we have is to apply the scripture to unfolding events that fulfill prophecy in these last days.

As I continued to study, I began to understand that the revelation of Jesus is the spirit of prophecy. I met my Jewish Messiah and fell in love with Israel. That opened up another door of understanding for me because in all my church attendances, I cannot recall most pastors speaking about the Jewish Jesus and Israel. Jesus was always presented from a Christian point of view, and our Judaic roots were obscure. One day a friend of mine told me about a Messianic fellowship she thought I would like. It was Shalom Assembly of God, led by Pastor Michael Goldbloom, a Messianic Jew. After a few services, I knew I had found a church home, and I stayed there for twenty years. I grew spiritually and could share many spiritual encounters on this journey. I will share two Holy Spirit experiences. One of our church members, by the name of Vince, had asked for prayer for his sister who was very ill and hospitalized. As the church body went before the Lord, I had a vision of Jesus standing at her bedside. He wore a long white robe with his head covered and face not seen. It was not given to me whether she would be healed or go to be with the Lord. I shared this with a couple of people at church. Our church member came back to our next service and told the congregation that his sister had seen Jesus standing by her bedside. She did not speak English, she spoke Italian, and she had never visited our church before.

The scriptures give an account of Stephen the first martyr who, before dying, looked up and the heavens opened and he saw Jesus standing by the Father. One Sunday we were praising the Lord, and I said, "Lord, you are Aleph and Tav." Immediately, I felt the presence of the Holy Spirit, who then allowed me an open vision of heaven. I saw Jesus standing there, and he was dropping manna out onto the earth. I said, "I do not know what this means," but I shared it with the congregation. After church, I went home for lunch, began to read the *Pentecostal Evangel* magazine, and came to an article regarding Revelation 2:17:

> *He that has an ear, let him hear what the Spirit said unto the churches: To him that overcomes I will give to eat of the hidden manna and will give him a white stone and in the stone a new name written, which no man knows save he that receives it.*

This is a deep passage for our average understanding, but it confirmed the vision and the manna I saw. The manna is the Word, our bread of life, which fills our soul.

Years later, I went outside one day and saw a white stone in the yard that had not been there previously. Meditating on this verse gave me a little revelation that believers are given a symbolic white stone; our rock is Jesus, who helps us overcome the world. I had separated myself from Christendom and am a member of the one and only body of Christ. One day, Jesus will give me a new name.

My husband of many years was diagnosed with lung cancer. He was a United States Marine who served in Vietnam and was exposed to Agent Orange. This poison is slow-moving and took thirty years to develop into a disease. My husband believed in Jesus but was not on fire for the Lord and didn't have a daily relationship with Jesus. I had to beg him to go to church at least a few times a year. He was a nice person, but that will not get you into heaven. One evening, I spoke to him through the urging of the Holy Spirit that he was under my Christian covering and one day he was not going to be under that covering. Shortly after that, he began to develop symptoms. The Veterans' Administration misdiagnosed him over and over. By the time the cancer was prominent, they had given him six weeks to live. Many prayers went out for him. The church members visited and prayed with him. I sat with him, reading scriptures and asking Jesus to heal him. There are times when people are near death that they have an encounter with the Lord, and I would ask him if he had any dreams. The night before he died, he called me back to the hospital and told me he had a dream. In the dream, he was walking with a man wearing a head covering. They passed through an area that looked war-torn, and he saw soldiers dressed in Israeli uniforms (he never knew what Israeli uniforms looked like). He and the man sat down and had a meal together. My husband said he had never felt so much peace. I told him the dream was of he and Lord Jesus and walking through a war-torn area was like his life, desolate of Jesus. The meal they shared was like our taking of the bread and wine, fellowshipping with Jesus until the time we sit with him at the banquet feast in heaven. The peace he felt was the peace that only Jesus can give to us. My husband on his deathbed made his peace with Jesus, and I know I will see him again.

The year is AD 2016, and we are in the seventh millennium of human history. Jesus said he would return in the third day. A thousand years is as a day to the Lord. It has been two thousand years or two days since the birth of Jesus, and the third day, the seventh millennium has arrived.

From this vantage point, we can look back over history and begin to see that a distinct pattern has been woven throughout history. What we will realize is that the hand of Yahweh has intervened in the affairs of mankind since the creation, and so has the hand of his adversary, Satan. We now live in an era that rejects the Triune God. Scripture tells us that a day of famine is coming.

> *Behold the days come said the Lord God that I will send a famine in the land, not a famine of bread or a thirst for water, but of hearing the words of the Lord.* (Amos 8:11)

Scripture tells us that people will run to and fro. In these last days, terrorism has caused people to run to and fro, seeking refuge and safety. During these time, they will seek the Word of the Lord. Perhaps the contents of this book may be a beacon in a dark, dark world. We applaud the ministries that are on the front battle lines getting the Word out and blessing the hungry, thirsty, sick, and homeless by way of radio, newsletters, multimedia sites, and boots on the ground. Christian Broadcasting Network's *700 Club* is to be commended for their Operation Blessing outreach. *Israel News Now*, airing on Daystar, brings vital information so we can stay abreast of major developments in and around Israel. These as well as other ministry and alternative news programs are providing us with current world events.

Through the pages of this book, our journey begins with the Almighty, I Am, and a time before the creation of earth. We pray the Holy Spirit will open our eyes and understanding to peer into a dimension that is unlike anything that we could imagine.

> *For now we see through a glass darkly, but then face to face, now I know in part, but then shall I know even as also I am known … When that which is perfect is come then that which is in part will be done away.* (1 Corinthians 13:10, 12)

Yahweh has given us some insight into his spiritual realm. God is spirit, and to enter into his realm of knowledge, we must come to him through his Spirit.

Writers of the biblical scriptures did so under the guidance of the Holy Spirit.

> *Knowing this first, that no prophecy of the scripture is of any private interpretation, for the prophecy came not in old time by the will of man, but holy men of God spoke as they were moved by the Holy Spirit.* (2 Peter 1:20)

What we see can be applied to the present time that the writers lived in or a future time that we can measure when those prophetic events are fulfilled or to project the reader to a time yet to be fulfilled. Since God dwells outside of time in a dimension we call eternity, he has the ability to see the complete time line of human events—past, present, and future. He knows the end from the beginning, and he will guide us into all truth and understanding if we so seek. Through prophecy given in the Bible, we can know God's future plans for mankind.

In these last days, Yahweh came in the form of man to guide humankind around traps set by Satan and to defeat the works of the devil. Yeshua came to teach and heal the people. He came to be the perfect sacrifice for the redemption of his people. He took all our disease and sin upon himself. Yeshua came to demonstrate his authority over death through his Resurrection, and those who believe in Yeshua will become joint heirs and inherit the kingdom of God forever. While you still have breath today, invite the Lord Jesus into your heart.

> The testimony of Yeshua is the spirit of prophecy. (Revelation 19:10)

CHAPTER 1
I AM YAHWEH

Chapter Overview
- The Ineffable Name
- Who Is God Almighty?
  - Yahweh Is Spirit
  - Yahweh Is the Ancient of Days
- Yahweh's Character and Attributes
  - Omniscient
  - Yahweh Sits Outside of Time
  - Omnipresent
  - Omnipotent
  - Holy
  - Divine
  - One God
  - His Glory
  - Love
  - Wisdom
- God's Nature

Chapter 1

I Am Yahweh

The Ineffable Name

Imagine while driving, your mind wanders, thinking about the things of this world. Abruptly, a voice disrupts your thoughts, and it seems to be coming from outside of your mind; but seemingly, it is in your head. As you refocus on this voice, it simply says, "I Am God." Your heart begins to pound as you try to comprehend what just happened. Was it your imagination playing tricks? Suddenly, you are encompassed by a bright light, and the voice said, "Follow me, and do my work." You notice the atmosphere within your car is static, and instinctively, you sense the presence of the Holy God. The light fades, and the voice ceases to speak. You realize your car is not on the highway but is stopped in the pull-off lane. This supernatural encounter has left you shaken as you attempt to analyze what just happened. The message begins to loop through your thoughts: "I Am God, follow me and do my work." Weakly, you whisper, "Yes, Lord, your will be done."

Almost two thousand years ago, Saul was on the road to Damascus engaged in persecuting the Christians. Suddenly, there shone around him a light from heaven, and he fell to the ground and heard a voice saying to him, "Saul, why do persecute me?" In a state of confusion, Saul asks, "Who are you, Lord?" God answers, "I Am Yeshua." Saul was trembling and astonished and said, "Lord, what will you have me do?" Saul became Saint Paul, and in the name of Yeshua, he did great and mighty works (Acts 9:3–4).

Our Creator is called by many names, but there must be a name that stands out from the many. What is that ineffable name? He told Saul, "I Am Yeshua."

Exodus 3:14, "*I Am that I Am.*" "I Am Yahweh" is the purest expression of the name. Yet he is called by other descriptive names, which allows us to comprehend his deity and eternal existence, which has no beginning and no end.

The Hebrew writings provide us with a deeper understanding of the name above all names. YHWH or YHVH—these four letters are referred to as a *tetragram*, meaning "a word with four letters similar to OMG." These four letters (*Yod*, *Heh*, *Vav*, *Heh*) represent the ancient Hebrew name of God. The name was considered too holy to be spoken; thus the word *Adoni*, *Hashem*, or *Lord*, was substituted. To avoid taking the name of God in vain, Hebrew customs pronounced the name as Hashem and writing the name as Adoni.

Yeshua teaches us in John 8:23, "*I Am from above, I Am not of this world.*" Yeshua or Yeshayah is *Yod* (*Y*), *Heh* (*H*), *Vav* (*W* or *V*), *Heh* (*H*), YHVH. Hallelu-**Yah** is the universal expression for "Praise God," wherein the **Yah** is thought to be a shortened form of YHVH. Who is the Savior of mankind? Clearly, to the Jew or Gentile with a tiny bit of understanding, it is Yeshua who saves. The summation and finality of the matter, Yeshua is our saving Messiah.

I even I Am Adoni and beside me there is no savior. (Isaiah 43:11)

There is no other name in all of the heavens, the earth, or under the earth that man can call on and be saved. Yeshua.

In the opening passage of Genesis 1, it states, "In the beginning, God created the heavens and the earth." In Hebrew, it is read, "B'reshiyt bara **Elohim** Eht hashamayim vaeht ha-eretz." *Elohim* refers to the masculine plurality of God. It also reveals the Triune nature of God the Father, God the Word, and God the Holy Spirit. Further, in Genesis, we see Elohim said, "*Let **us** make man in **our** image.*" Secular cultures using the word *elohim* use it to refer to polytheism, or many gods. Rabbis used a secondary form of *Elohim* shortened to *El* as in *El Shaddai*, God Almighty. The *El* is used to distinguish God's attributes, such as, *El Shalom*, God of Peace herein; we can understand that Yeshua is our Prince of Peace.

The use of *Adoni* gave rise to the hybrid form Jehovah in the English translation. Thus the name Jehovah became widely used in other religions. Certainly, this does not negate the name Jehovah since one can see the similarity between Jeh-o-vah and Jah/Yah/YH-o-Vay/vah/VH. [1]

---

1 R. J. Zwi Werblowsky, Geoffrey Wigoder, *The Encyclopedia of the Jewish Religion* (New York, NY, Holt, Rinehart and Winston, Inc., 1965) p. 160

Who Is God Almighty?

"Who is God?" is a question asked throughout the ages. It has been pondered and considered across all cultures and religions. We cannot rely on a truthful answer to be found in philosophy, science, or various religions. There is only one source that provides an answer that all of mankind can accept, and this question is answered in the Holy Scriptures—a source tested and true.

Yahweh Is an Eternal Spirit, Having No Beginning and No End

God clearly tells us in Isaiah 43:10, 13 …

> *I am He, before me there was no God formed, neither shall there be after me … before the day was I AM He, and there is none that can deliver out of my hand: I will work and who shall let it?*

God is referred to as the "Father of Spirits" in Hebrews 12:9, and in the writings of Enoch, God is called the "Father of Spirits."

> *God is spirit and they that worship him must worship him in spirit and in truth.* (John 4:24)

God is spirit. His essence is spirit; his core is Word. The Word came forth as utterance, and the power of his Word manifested through his Holy Spirit, creating and upholding all things. His Spirit came forth to overshadow the virgin, and the Word became God in flesh.

Yahweh Is the Ancient of Days

> *The Ancient of days did sit, whose garment was white as snow and the hair of his head like the pure wool, his throne was like a fiery flame …* (Daniel 7:9)

Yeshua is the Word and the Ancient of Days.

Religion attempts to define *Yahweh* within man's parameters. God is above and beyond every god; therefore, he must be understood outside of religious constraints. His ways are not our ways, and his thoughts are beyond our thoughts. One need not possess a doctorate in theology to understand the relationship between our Creator and his created. God extends an invitation to all people to come to him with a humble heart and a contrite spirit.

Yahweh's Character and Attributes

Yahweh Is Omniscient

He has perfect knowledge of all things because he created all things. We use limited earthly terminology in our understanding of Yahweh. The word *omniscient* can only apply to God; there is no being in heaven or earth that is omniscient. Humankind must acknowledge, our understanding is meager and flawed. Who can reason with God? He knows things that humankind has yet to discover. The wisdom of God is flawless without dispute. The following scriptures show our insignificance in fomenting our understanding of God.

> *Remember the former things of old, for I am God and there is none else, I am God and there is none like me declaring the end from the beginning and from ancient times the things that are not yet done saying My counsel shall stand and I will do all my pleasure.* (Isaiah 46:9)
>
> *The eyes of the Lord are in every place, keeping watch on the evil and the good.* He is invisible to the human eye. John 6:46 *Not any man has seen God the Father, save he which is of God, he has seen the Father.* (Proverbs 15:3)
>
> *O Lord, you have searched me and you know me. You know when I sit down and when I rise up and you understand my thoughts from afar. You compass my path and when I lay down and you are acquainted with all my ways. For there is not a word on my tongue, but you Oh Lord know it altogether. You have hemmed me in from the back and the front and laid your hand upon me. Such knowledge is too wonderful for me; it is high, I cannot attain unto it.* (Psalm 139:1–6)

There is no place we can go to hide from his face.

> *Oh, the depth of the riches both of the wisdom and knowledge of God, how <u>unsearchable</u> are his judgments and his ways past finding out. For who has known the mind of the Lord or been his counselor?* (Romans 11:33–34)
>
> *For my thoughts are not your thoughts, nor are your ways my ways, says the Lord. For as the heavens are higher than the earth so are my ways higher than your ways and my thoughts than your thoughts.* (Isaiah 55:8–9)

TIME AND SPACE		
PAST	**PRESENT**	**FUTURE**
Creation- 4000 BC	AD 2015	Christ Reigns
YAHWEH sits outside of time.		

God sits outside of space and time and is able to see past, present, and future all at once.

> *Then Job answered the Lord and said, I know that you can do everything and that no thought can be withheld from you. Who is he that hides counsel without knowledge? Therefore have I uttered that* <u>*I understood not, things too wonderful for me which I knew not.*</u> (Job 24:1)

Yahweh Is Omnipresent

Hebrew scholars frequent the name HaMakom, meaning "the place," and explain God is the place of the world but the world is not his place and is translated as "the omnipresent." His divine presence is *Shekinah* [2] translated as "glory."

God is everywhere and is not relegated by the physical boundaries he created. He occupies eternity and is able to see past, present, and future all at once.

The divine revelation is to understand the absolute existence of Yahweh without distinction of past, present, future. Yahweh is above, before, and beyond all things that he created. He is the beginning and the end.

Psalms 139:7–18, written by King David, points to the all-knowing, all-seeing, ever-present Yahweh:

> *Where shall I go from your spirit? Or where shall I flee from your presence? If I ascend up into heaven, you are there, if I make my bed in hell, behold, you are there. If I take the wings of the morning and dwell in the uttermost parts of the sea, even there shall your hand lead me and your right hand shall hold me. If I say, surely the darkness will cover me; even the night shall be light about me. Yes, the darkness hides not from you but the night shines as the day: the darkness and the light are both alike to you. For you have possessed my reins* [formed my inner most parts]. *You have covered* [overshadow] *me in my mother's womb* [formed me]. *I will praise you for I am fearfully and wonderfully made: mar-*

---

2 *The Encyclopedia of the Jewish Religion*, 161

velous are your works and that my soul knows right well. My substance [my frame] *was not hid from you when I was made in secret and curiously wrought in the lowest parts of the earth. Your eyes did see my substance, yet being imperfect* [unformed]: *and in your book all my members were written which in continuance were fashioned, when as yet there was none of them. How precious also are your thoughts to me, Oh, God, how great is the sum of them. If I should count them, they are more in number than the sand; when I awake, I am still with you.*

In portions of the above passage, King David supernaturally points to the time of the Immaculate Conception. At that time, we see that the Holy Spirit overshadows Mary and forms the Son of God in her womb.

Yahweh Is Omnipotent

God is all-powerful and almighty.

But our God is in the heavens, he has done whatsoever he has pleased. (Psalms 115:3)

He is strong and can renew our strength, and he never gets weary.

Great is our Lord and of great power, his understanding is infinite. (Psalm 147:5)

He calls them all by names [stars] *by the greatness of his might, for that he is strong in power and not one fails.* (Isaiah 40:26)

Yahweh Is Holy

God alone is holy, completely pure and without iniquity. Wherever his presence manifest is holy. Moses was told, "Take off his shoes, for the place you stand is holy ground" (Exodus 3:5) God's presence in the temple transformed it into a holy place.

For thus said the high and lofty One that inhabits eternity, whose name is holy and who dwells in the high and holy place … (Isaiah 57:15)

God calls Israel *holy*, a people who were to come from out of the world and consecrate themselves to holiness.

> *For I am the Lord your God, you will sanctify yourself, and you will be holy for I am holy. Neither will you defile yourselves with any manner of creeping thing that creeps upon the earth.* (Leviticus 11:44)

Yahweh Is Divine

God's deity as defined in *Webster's Dictionary* as, "heavenly, sacred, holy, excellent, glorious, beautiful, prophesy."

Yahweh Is One God

> *There are three that bear record in heaven, Yahweh God the Father, the Word Yeshua God the Son and Ruach ha Kodesh, God the Holy Spirit and these three are one.* (1 John 5:7)

- God the Father—no man has seen God.
- God the Son—you have seen me; you have seen the Father.
- God the Holy Spirit, the Comforter, God's truth and power.

Yahweh's Glory

God's glory is manifested in his creation.

> *The heavens declare the Glory of God …* (Psalms 19:1)

His power is transcendent and perfect. In earthly description, his glory is splendor, awesome, and fearsome. His glory is as a consuming fire (Hebrew 12:29).

Yahweh reveals himself to mankind so we can follow and worship him. Moses, Aaron, Nadab, Abihu and seventy elders saw the glory of God, and under his feet was a paved work of sapphire stone and as it were the body of heaven in his clearness. This is the splendor of his glory. The glory of the Lord abode on Mount Sinai as a cloud. God spoke out of the cloud, and the sight of the glory of the Lord was like devouring fire on the top of the mount. The people heard the voice of God and saw his glory. He is awesome and fearsome (Exodus 24:9–17).

Moses, in the glorious presence of God, is commanded to hew out two stones to replace the first set Moses broke. God met Moses on the top of the mount, and he descended in the cloud and stood with him and proclaimed the name of the Lord. Moses was in the presence of God for forty days without food or water. When Moses came down from the mount, his face was radiant as a testimony that he had been in the presence of the Ancient of Days (Exodus 34).

God's glory was manifested in the wilderness tabernacle as a cloud.

> *Solomon had made an end of praying, the **fire** came down from heaven and consumed the burnt offering and sacrifices; and the **Glory of the Lord** filled the house and the priest could not enter because of the **Lord's Holy presence.*** (2 Chronicles 7:1–2)

In Solomon's temple, the glory cloud filled the temple, and the presence of God was so great the priest could not stand in his presence.

> *Then the glory of the Lord went up from the cherub and stood over the threshold of the house and the house was filled with the cloud and the court was full of the brightness of the Lord's glory.* (Ezekiel 10:4)

During the second temple era, the presence of God was displayed.

God's glory was seen at the transfiguration of Jesus on the mount with Moses and Elijah (Matthew 17). After his death, Resurrection, and ascension, the glory of God appeared as wind, fire, and power on the Day of Pentecost. We earthlings know we are in his presence; it can be felt as well as seen. His glory has a weightiness. Standing in the presence of God is holy, electrifying, overpowering, too awesome for human expression. You know that you know you are in his presence.

Yahweh Is Love

Humankind cannot fully understand the depth of godly love. We can look at all that God has created for the benefit of mankind. He made a beautiful, perfect dwelling place for all his creatures. Man was created a little lower than the angels. Angels were fascinated with man. God desired to have fellowship with his creation. He wanted them to love him, enjoy their dwelling place, tend to it, and keep all the animals.

> *Let us hear the conclusion of the whole matter; fear God and keep his commandments for this is the whole duty of man.* (Ecclesiastes 12:13)

God's love is patient. God's love is kind. God's love is slow to anger so that none should perish but all would come into his saving grace.

A summary of God's love as seen in Psalms 103

- He is our provider.
- He forgives us.
- He heals our diseases.

- He redeems us from eternal destruction.
- He crowns us with love and mercy.
- He renews our youth as an eagle.
- He gives righteousness and judgment to the oppressed.
- He called out a chosen people.
- He is merciful.
- He loves his children like a father.
- He remembers we are frail humans as dust.
- He will reward all who keep his commandments.

God loves mankind, but he hates their sin, rebellion, and disobedience. Many ask, Why does God allow for the slaughter of people as we read in the Old Testament? The answer is that God is holy, righteous, perfect, and he must judge wickedness. Wickedness unchecked would have destroyed the entire planet and everything therein.

God Is Wisdom

> *The Lord possessed me in the beginning of his way, before his works of old. I was set up from everlasting from the beginning or ever the earth was. When there were no depths, I was brought forth, when there were no fountains abounding with water. Before the mountains were settled, before the hills was I brought forth, while as yet he had not made the earth, nor the fields, nor the highest part of the dust of the world. When he prepared the heavens, I was there when he set a compass upon the face of the depth. When he established the clouds above, when he strengthened the fountains of the deep, when he gave the sea his decree that the waters should not pass his commandment, when he appointed the foundations of the earth. Then I was by him, as one brought up with him and I was daily his delight, rejoicing always before him, rejoicing in the habitable part of the earth and my delights were with the sons of men. Now hear me oh you children for blessed are they that keep my ways.* (Proverbs 8:22–32)

The above passage is speaking of "wisdom." In Hebrew, the word for *wisdom* is Hokhmah.[3] A masculine or feminine pronoun can be used to express things or concepts depending on the gender of the noun to which it refers. The concepts of wisdom are many—such as, love, truth, justice, peace. Is God male or female? God is not defined by gender. God created male and female so that mankind could procreate. It is commonplace to visualize and associate God as male. God decided to come as a male to be born of the woman. Wisdom is used in the

---

3 *The Encyclopedia of the Jewish Religion*, 403

feminine form but is not that of a female character. Wisdom is presented as a foreshadowing of Christ who is himself wisdom.

King Solomon rightly asked God for wisdom and the ability to understand the ways of God. The first principle is to fear the Lord, and that is the beginning of wisdom, and the knowledge of the holy is understanding. Proverbs 9:10

A wise person seeks wisdom and understanding for relationship with God and for practical living in the following areas:

- Instruction, reproof, correction, chastening.
- Grace, peace, joy, hope.
- Discretion, avoid wickedness.
- To fear God is to acknowledge, respect, and honor him.
- Dwell safely, hedge of protection.
- Be righteous, live upright and perfect.
- Love one another and be helpful.
- Wise will inherit glory and receive a crown.

The spirit of wisdom speaks. She cries out to get attention. Wisdom stands in high places. She asks men to hear the excellent things from her lips, which are righteous and truth. Wisdom is better than gold and jewels. Counsel is mine for sound direction. I am understanding. I have strength and by me men rule. I love them that love me. Those that love me, I will cause them to inherit substances and I will fill their treasures. Those that seek me early shall find me. Riches and honor are with me (Proverbs 8).

In God's wisdom, he will judge righteously. He will avenge and punish evil in his time frame. At the end of the age, during the tribulation, the full wrath of God will come against wickedness.

God's Nature

God's nature is the essence of all things. He is the life of the universe and everything therein. God has a mind; he sees, speaks, touches, appears, walks, has arms, feet, a back, and yet is spirit. God has sensitivities. He has emotions, such as, love, anger, jealousy, compassion. We look at ourselves, and we look at the many references of God's character, and we can begin to understand God's nature. We can also see that man's nature is contrary to God's holy nature. It dawns upon us that we are made in his image yet we are imperfect and sinful. Our earthly bodies house our spirit man, and we are to present our bodies as holy, living vessels, to be sanctified for God's Holy Spirit to dwell within those who believe.

God Is Clothed

O Lord my God, you are very great, you are clothed with honor and majesty. (Psalms 104:1)

I saw the Lord sitting upon a throne high and lifted up and his train filled the temple. (Isaiah 6:1)

The Ancient of days did sit whose garment was white as snow. (Daniel 7:9)

The Word of God, the Creator, was a mystery of whom God revealed to mankind. Emanuel became flesh and was born of a virgin. Yeshua is a light in a dark world showing the path back to God. The Word of God became that perfect sacrifice acceptable to the Father. Yeshua became the Passover lamb, and through his death and Resurrection, all our sins from Adam to the present were taken upon himself, and through his shed blood on the cross we were forgiven, covered in his righteousness and sanctified until the time Yeshua will restore all things.

Without controversy, he is called by many names. His name is Yeshua in Hebrew. Jesus in English. Isa in Arabic. Yesu in Korean. I'sous in Greek. Jaysus in Portuguese, and in the tongues of mankind, he is Yahweh.

Chapter 2
In the Beginning

Chapter Overview

Chapter 2

In The Beginning

In the Beginning, God Created the Heavens and the Earth
B'reshiyt Bara Elohim Eht Hashamayim Vaeht Ha'eretz

In this chapter, we again look at the opening verse of Genesis 1. In chapter 1, we considered the name **Elohim.** Now we look at the words ***B'reshiyt Bara***, which is Hebrew for "*in the beginning.*" Hebrew holds the key to unlocking the mysteries of God and allows mankind deeper insight into various levels of understanding. Hebrew provides three levels of spiritual understanding: (1) Remez is hint; (2) Drosh is regal; (3) Sohd is secret.

> *We speak the wisdom of God in a mystery, even the* ***hidden wisdom which God ordained before the world*** *unto our glory.* (1 Corinthians 2:7)

Wisdom is revealed to mankind from Yahweh. Wherever is God's dwelling place, so are his unattainable mysteries. God has given us keys to unlock things not initially revealed. These keys are the twenty-two primary letters of the Hebrew alphabet. Within this sacred language, we can unlock the hidden wisdom and mysteries of Yahweh. The combination of the letters of *Aleph* and *Tav* form the essence of the Word of Creation, ***Eht***, found in the first verse of Genesis 1.

What is understood about the creation did not come out of existing phenomena but was spoken by the Word of God.

> *Through faith, we understand that the worlds were framed by the Word of God, so that things which are seen were not made of things which do appear.* (Hebrews 11:3)

These *things* are invisible particles, which are discussed in detail in chapter 3.

As we continue to segment and analyze the first verse of Genesis, we are given a glimpse into the eternal dimension before the creation of the universe.

In the Beginning (before) the Creation of Earth

In this first declaration, there is a wealth of nuggets to be uncovered. *It is God's glory to conceal and man's glory to uncover.*

God declares he inhabits eternity. His domain is timeless. The essence of invisible things are retained by God in his eternal domain. It is beyond human comprehension that God brought forth the invisible and gave it birth within the physical universe. We begin to understand that God from his eternal platform simply spoke and creation took on visibility. God calls those things that are not yet as though they are. It is unfathomable to ponder the expanse of worlds and heavenly bodies that God stretched out with the flick of his hand. We can only imagine the perfection, splendor, and beauty of it all.

Through the guidance of the Holy Spirit, we peek into God's dwelling place.

> *For thus said the high and lofty One that* ***inhabits eternity****, whose name is Holy, I dwell in the high and holy place …* (*Isaiah 57:15*)

Yahweh's dwelling place or the kingdom of heaven has a foundation.

> *It is he that builds his stories in the heaven* [tall building]. (Amos 9:6)
> *He lays the beams of his chambers in the* [heavenly] *waters.* (Psalms 104:3)

Yahweh has told us that he dwells in eternity:

- A dimension having no beginning and no end, infinity.
- A dimension that is beyond our physical universe and is timeless.
- It is invisible to the human eye except when Yahweh allows a look-see.
- It is a place where God, Word, Holy Spirit, and angelic hosts exist
- It is holy and divine beyond human understanding because God's ways are higher than mankind.

The beginning of our understanding of this spiritual dimension is by observing creation.

> *For the invisible things of him from the creation of the world are clearly seen being understood by the things that are made even his eternal power and Godhead, so that they are without excuse.* (Romans 1:20)

This poignant message allows us insight and understanding that God brought forth the invisible so we can declare the glory of his creation.

> *Because that which may be known of God is manifest in them for God has showed it unto them.* (Romans 1:19)

God has revealed himself throughout the ages and has given some a glimpse into his domain. Some were taken alive; while others experienced what it is like through visions and dreams. In the book of Enoch, he was taken bodily into the heavenly realm and told to record all he experienced in books. The Old Testament prophet Job provides his discourse with God, having much to say about the majesty of creation. Ezekiel and Isaiah see Lucifer. Stephen the first martyr looks up, heaven opens, and he sees Lord Jesus at the right hand of the Father. In the New Testament, John tells us in Revelation 1:10: "*I was in the Spirit on the Lord's day …*" John in a vision sees into the heavenly realm, and all that he sees becomes the book of Revelation. Revelation 1:11. . . "*What you see write in a book.*"

In a vision, Eziekiel 1:22-28 describes the third heaven. The following scripture is paraphrased due to its lengthiness:

> The firmament above appeared to be the color of a large crystal. In the firmament was a throne having the color of a sapphire stone [blue].
>
> Within the throne was the likeness or appearance of a man. Surrounding the throne and image was brilliant amber shimmering as it were fire radiating from his loins even upward and downward. There were many colors appearing as a rainbow around the throne, and this was the appearance of the glory of the Lord.

Following, we provide excerpts from the writings of Enoch ("The Ancient Book of Enoch," commentary given by J. R. Church, *Prophecy in the News*, 2009).

Enoch's experience in God's heavenly realm predates Ezekiel and does not contradict scripture.

> *And they lifted me up into heaven and I went until I approached near a wall which was built with crystals and a tongue of fire surrounded it and I was afraid. I approached near a large house which was built of crystals and the walls and the floor inlaid with crystals … the ceiling was like the course of the stars*

> *and lightning and Cherubim of fire were between them and their heaven was as water* ... (Enoch 14:9–11)
>
> *And I looked and saw therein a high throne, its appearance was like the hoarfrost and its circuit like a shining sun and voices of the Cherubim. And from under the great throne came streams of flaming fire and it was impossible to look at it. And he who is great in majesty sat thereon, his garment shone more brilliantly than the sun and was whiter than any hail. None of the angels were able to enter, nor any flesh to look upon the form of the face of the Majestic and Honored One.* (Enoch 14:18–21)

In Isaiah's vision he also sees the majesty of God.

> *I saw the Lord sitting upon a throne, high and lifted up and his train filled the temple ... above it stood the Seraphim and each one had six wings ... and one cried to another and said Holy, Holy, Holy is the Lord of hosts, the whole earth is full of his glory ... the house was filled with smoke.* (Isaiah 6:1–4)

In the throne room of God, there is smoke emanating from the burning coals that are on the altar and around the throne. This fire and smoke are supernatural elements.

John hears the voice of Yeshua, and in his vision of heaven, he sees a menorah having seven golden candlesticks.

> *I am Aleph and Tav, the first and the last and what you see write in a book and send it unto the seven churches which are in Asia ... And I turned to see the voice that spoke with me and being turned I saw seven candlesticks, one like unto the Son of man, clothed with a garment down to the foot and girt about the paps with a golden girdle* [like the bands of Orion] *His head and his hairs were white like wool ... and his eyes were as a flame of fire ... His feet like fine brass burned in a furnace and a voice sounding of many waters.* (Revelation 1:11–15)

John describes the throne in heaven.

> *And behold a throne was set in heaven and one sat on the throne ... He looked like jasper (green) and sardine stone and there was a rainbow around the throne like an emerald ... out of the throne came lightning, thunder and voices ... before the throne was a sea of glass like crystal and around the throne were four beast full of eyes ...* (Revelation 4:2)

Hebrews 12:22, "*You are come unto mount Zion and unto the city of the living God, the* ***heavenly*** *Jerusalem and to innumerable company of angels.*" Moses was given instructions by God to fashion the tabernacle after a heavenly type or pattern (Hebrews 8:5). "*Who serve unto the* ***example and shadow of heavenly things*** *as Moses was admonished of God when he was about to make the tabernacle; God said, you make all things* ***according to the pattern showed*** *to you in the mount*" (Exodus 25:40). In the future, New Jerusalem will descend upon the earth at the beginning of the millennial reign.

In summary, there is a heavenly city. We are reminded that Jesus said he was going to prepare a place for us, a place having many mansions. There is a temple, the heavenly ark, large throne, and surrounding the throne is the glory of God in many colors. We are told the colors are blue, green, and a rainbow of colors. Amber is the color that surrounds God's likeness. There are a hierarchy of angels and four creatures surrounding the throne praising God, crying, "Holy, holy, holy." The scriptures tell us there is a heavenly choir, seals, vials, trumpets, inkhorns, books, horses, chariots, altars, incense, and streets of gold. Now seated in heaven, following the Resurrection of Jesus, there are twenty-four elders and innumerable souls of the saints.

Cloud formations that are seen in earth's atmosphere possess physical elements. However, there are supernatural clouds that may not at times be visible to the human eye. Hebrew 12:1, "*We are encompassed about with so great a cloud of witnesses.*" These clouds are usually unseen in the physical realm and may allude to angels and the souls of the saints. Jesus ascended in clouds, and those who witnessed the event could see the clouds. We will be caught up to meet him in the air in the clouds. At the time of the Rapture, it will occur so quickly that left-behind humans will not witness this event.

Perhaps these supernatural clouds are a bridge between earth and the kingdom of heaven and the holy city. God connects his heavenly domain with his earthly domain. Isaiah 66:1 "*The Lord said, the heavens are my throne and earth is my footstool.*" God enters our earthly domain in various forms. In the following passage, Enoch touches on clouds as a bridge between heaven and earth.

In Enoch 16 he sees the earth from above and the foundations of the planet along with its *corner stone,* winds, mountains, and underworld. He uses the term *four winds* as a reference to north, south, east, west, and explains that they lead down the course of the sun. Winds create the atmosphere, which fills the surface of the planet, creating clouds, which are like pillars that hold up and connect heaven and earth's atmosphere. This passage is correlated in Job 38:6: "*Whereupon are the foundations thereof fastened? Or who laid the cornerstone ...*" Reference to this stone could be the mountain of Moriah, situated in the middle of the world in Jerusalem.

We have touched on several areas that simply scratch the surface of Yahweh before the creation of the universe. Mankind was not present during the first five days of creation. Our only clues into the time before humankind are found in whom it has been revealed. God gave knowledge and revelation to those who preceded us—such as, Adam, Enoch, Job, Ezekiel, Isaiah.

God Created Heaven

The statement "God created the heaven and the earth" piques our curiosity and challenges our intellectual understanding of all things God. How can the finite mind comprehend the infinite? To come to a minute understanding of God's creation, we must first believe and receive wisdom in faith. Many are unable to receive this knowledge. They see, hear, and cannot understand—thereby interjecting theories such as evolution that circumvent creation.

> *He has made the earth by his power, he has established the world by his wisdom and has stretched out the heaven by his understanding.* (Jeremiah 51:15)
>
> *And God said, let there be a firmament in the midst of the waters and let it divide the waters from the waters. And God made the firmament and divided the waters which were under the firmament from the waters which were above the firmament and it was so. And God called the firmament* ***Heaven.*** (Genesis 1:6–9)

This water/firmament/heaven was separated. It is a reference to earth atmosphere as well as pointing to the whole universe. The Hebrew word for *heaven* is *Hasha**mayim,*** and ***mayim*** refers to unattainable waters above and earth reservoirs below. In Jeremiah 51:16, we get a better understanding: "*When he uttereth his voice, there is a multitude of* ***waters in the heavens*** *and he caused the vapors to ascend from the ends of the earth …*" Further understanding in 2 Peter 3:5: "*That by the Word of God the* ***heavens were of old*** *and the earth standing out of the water and in the water.*" Peter confirms that the expanse of the *heavens* (plural) existed well before the restoration of the earth and its atmospheric heaven. God distinguishes between other heavens and earth's heaven.

The above analysis allows us to know the **waters in the heavens** is like a cosmic bowl of soup that contains all the planets, stars, galaxies, and earth is but a speck. It is the immeasurable universe.

Mankind looks upward and realizes the vastness of our solar system dubbed the Milky Way. We can see the movement of the celestial objects and understand our galaxy is spinning at an incredible speed of 490,000 miles per hour. Scientific speculation states the galaxy makes one rotation every two hundred million years. That is an astounding revelation, but more so is the knowledge that over one billion other galaxies exist in the universe and still counting.

In exploring the mystery of heaven, we understand that heaven is directional. It is up. Elijah was caught up; Jesus ascended up into heaven; and Stephen looked up. There are lots of ups.

There is a region referred to as the sides of the north. Job 26:7, "*He stretches out the **north** over the empty place and hangs the **earth** upon nothing … by his **spirit** he has garnished the heavens … his hand has formed the **crooked serpent*** [Satan]." It also lets us know that earth, sun, moon, stars are stationed in the universe where God commanded them to be. There is also a reference to Satan—a created being and the first to destroy God's creation. Revelation 20 … "And I saw an angel come down from heaven having the key of the bottomless pit and a great chain in his hand." There is the dimension of hell, which is down. Jesus, after his death, went down into hell to set the captives free.

Understanding the link between heaven and earth, God has given man the gift of faith, which allows our mind to go beyond human reasoning and enter into the realm of God. We can spiritually begin to discern the mysteries of God.

> *Faith is the substance of things hoped for and the evidence of things not seen. For by faith the elders obtained a good report. Through faith we understand that the worlds were framed by the Word of God, so that things which are seen were not made of things which do appear.* (Hebrew 11:1–3)

God Creates the Earth

Our study of the first utterances in Genesis 1 brings us to the word ***Ha'eretz*** and is the Hebrew word for *earth.* God singled out earth from among the billions of stars and planets and prepared it for his future inhabitants. God set the little blue planet in the midst of his galaxies. We believe there are indeterminate periods of time between "in the beginning" and the first day of creation.

The primary description of the earth is likened to a watery sphere. God said the earth was without form, void and dark. From this statement, we may consider that at another time, the earth was pristine and bright. Did the earth become void and dark due to a celestial impact? Satan and his followers had lost their privilege and high esteem in the heavenly domain wherein God dwells. For their rebellion, they were cast out of God's heavenly realm, wherein is God and the holy angels. Once being cast out, where did they go? They entered into a lower dimension later called the "high place," wherein dwells principalities, powers, and wickedness.

Before the first day of creation, there was a cataclysmic impact upon the earth, causing it to become void and dark. We believe it was Satan and his legions that caused chaos upon the earth rendering it in supernatural darkness. Perhaps God, knowing the intent of Satan, decided to contain the evil to one location so as not to contaminate the entire universe. God knew one third of his angelic host would follow Satan. God knew that humankind would give in to the wiles of Satan, and for this reason, humans are relegated to live on one planet.

God calls for light to appear. God calls for the waters to separate. He called for the atmospheric particles—such as, nitrogen, oxygen, argon, and carbon dioxide—gases/vapors to arise and surround the planet, and this firmament was the earth's atmosphere. We call it *air*. Scientists claim our air is exclusive to earth.

> *Whatsoever the Lord pleased, that did he in heaven, and in earth in the seas and all deep places. He caused the* ***vapors to ascend*** *from the ends of the earth …* (Psalms 135:6–7)

The waters below, seas and oceans, were gathered unto their boundaries; and land did appear, allowing the vegetation, trees, and flowers to spring forth.

Curious minds began to ponder: Why does God have such an expansive and seemingly limitless universe? No one has a definitive answer, so we speculate. God created life on one tiny planet. God allowed for mankind to have knowledge of his environment and the proximity of our atmospheric heaven. God placed a message for mankind in his arrangement of the celestial bodies. God has allowed man the exploration of the moon. He has allowed man to view Mars and various planets in outer space to a degree. God knew man would become obsessed with the outer limits looking for other gods, aliens from other planets, and desiring to leave earth to live on another planet. God knew that man would destroy his earthly environment. God knew that man would embrace evolution and dismiss his creation of all things. In summation, God knew mankind would embrace Satan and all things wicked. Now we see the negative impact Satan and his followers had on the earth and its inhabitants. With the vastness of the universe, God has limited man's ability to travel beyond a certain expanse. Man is cursed and relegated to live on one planet. In the eons of time, evil persisted. God promises that the *heavens* (plural), including earth, will exist until the day of judgment.

> *But the heavens and the earth which are now by the same* ***Word are kept in store,*** *reserved unto fire against the day of judgment and perdition* (destruction) *of ungodly men.* (2 Peter 3:7–10)

Saint Peter explains that during the final days, the celestial bodies and the earth, which have been kept in their place by Jesus the Word, will pass away with a great noise; and the elements will melt with fervent heat, the earth also, and the works that are therein will be burned up.

> *Looking for and hasting unto the coming of the Day of God, wherein the heavens being on fire shall be dissolved and the elements shall melt with fervent heat.* (2 Peter 3:12)

This scenario may be the result of nuclear war combined with the judgment of God as spelled out in the book of Revelation. God must purge the firmament of every trace of wickedness.

The Heavenly Hosts

The first of God's created being were angels. He created legions of angels and referred to them as the heavenly hosts. We can only envision the millions of angelic beings created for his service. Why did God create these angelic beings? God is love, so he created and surrounded himself with angelic creatures capable of loving, worshipping, holy, obedient, and understanding the will of God. He gave them free will. God made distinctions within the angelic host. For instance, some of the angels have animal features; some have the features of humankind; and some have features of both animals and humans.

The first reference to angels is found in Genesis 1:26: "*Let us make man in our image, after our likeness …*" The Triune Godhead was not talking to himself. We can speculate, "in our image, after our likeness" included angels. Earthly creatures (humans, animals, birds, insects) are mirror images of God's angelic host yet made lower than the angels.

The second reference to an angel is found in Genesis 3:1. Satan in the likeness of the serpent enters the Garden of Eden and seduces Eve. Here we see Satan as a mirror image of the serpent. Genesis 3:15 parlays with Satan in the garden and his future demise. Genesis 3:24, God placed at the east of the garden of Eden cherubim and a flaming sword, which turned every way to keep the way of the tree of life … Thereafter scriptures make references to angels.

Holy angels are referred to by other names as expouned upon by Don Stewart, "*What are some of the names given to angels*,"[4] They are called angels in heaven, angels of God, mighty angels, host of heaven, sons of God, holy ones, watchers, flames of fire, rulers, and morning stars.

According to the writings of first-century Bible scholar Dionysius, the Areopagite of Athens, *The Celestial Hierarchy*[5] placed angels in the following orders:

---

4 Don Stewart, What are some of the Names Given to Angels, Blue Letter Bible, online, December 2007

5 Dionysius, The Celestial Hierarchy

- the highest triad—seraphim, cherubim, thrones
- the middle triad—dominions, virtues, powers
- the lowest triad—principalities, archangel, angels

Angelic Characteristics

In the above text, we see the presence of God and his glory as a cloud. The cherubim are mentioned numerous times. Let us look at the features of these creatures:

- Have the appearance of a man, called sons of God.
- Four faces on each (man, lion, eagle, ox), God may have assigned them to watch over each created species and Lucifer may have been assigned over reptiles.
- Four wings, sometimes six wings, and some no wings.
- Feet like a calf foot, straight leg and straight foot.
- Sparkle like brass and colorful hues.
- Hands like a man under wings.
- Voices may sound like rushing water, thunder, trumpets, singing.
- Praise God.
- Connected to a celestial chariot with wheels, eyes in the wheels, and vehicle able to move in various directions fueled by fire and the spirit of the angels.
- Some are very tall, thirty-five feet
- None look like little babies.
- They wear clothing.
- Their countenance is bright or projecting light.
- They are spirits some holy, some evil.

Saint Paul makes a clear distinction regarding physical and spiritual bodies:

> *But God gives it a body as it has pleased him and to every seed his own body. All flesh is not the same flesh but there is one kind of flesh of men, another flesh of beast, another of fishes, another of birds. There are also celestial bodies and bodies terrestrial, but the glory of the celestial is one and the glory of the terrestrial is another.* (1 Corinthians 15:*38*)

This scripture goes on to describe Adam as a man of the earth and the second man was the Lord from heaven. The living bears the image of the earthly, and when the spirit/soul is released at the time of death, we will bear the image of the heavenly; we will be spiritual beings like angels but not angels.

Celestial Chariots

The Bible makes reference to celestial vehicles. As we examine these supernatural conveyors, they may offer an explanation of the so-called UFOs seen throughout millennia. Scripture provide various accounts of God, angels, and a few humans traveling in celestial vehicles. Ezekiel 1:4–5,16–19 … they come like a whirlwind out of the **North**, in a cloud, with fire flashing like lightning, bright like amber, they move as a unit, the spirit of the creatures was in the wheels (like a driver controlling a car), supernatural fire in the midst of the vehicle, appears as burning coals of fire, fire which went up and down between them, wheels had very high rims, full of eyes (could be windows). The four creatures rode on this … The appearance of the wheels and their work was like unto the color of beryl (green), and the four had one likeness, and their appearance and their work was as it were a wheel in the middle of a wheel; and when they went, they went upon their four sides and they turned not when they went. As for their rings (rims), they were so high that they were dreadful, and the rings were full of eyes round about them four … Where the creatures went the wheels went with them; when they were lifted up from the earth, the wheels were lifted up; when they stood, the wheels stood … This is a picture of four beings riding in an unidentified flying object propelled by fire.

> *There appeared a chariot of fire and horses of fire and parted them both asunder and Elijah went up by a whirlwind into heaven.* (2 Kings 2:11)
>
> *Behold the Lord will come with fire and with his chariots like a whirlwind to render his anger with fury and his rebuke with flames of fire.* (Isaiah 66:15)
>
> *The chariots of God are twenty thousand, even thousands of angels the Lord is among them* … to him that rides upon the heavens of heavens which were of old, he does send out his mighty voice … (Psalm 68:17, b33)
>
> *And God rode upon a cherub and did fly, yes, he did fly upon the wings of the wind* … (Psalm 18:10)
>
> *His throne was like the fiery flame and his wheels as burning fire, a fiery stream issued and came forth from before him.* (Daniel 7:9)
>
> *And Elisha prayed and said, "Lord I pray thee open the eyes [of my servant] that he may see … " and he saw the mountain was full of horses and chariots of fire around Elisha.* (2 Kings 6:17)

Angelic Activity

Yahweh created legions of angels. Millions. A number we cannot count. We know they praise God continually and they do the will of God. The activities of the heavenly host appear throughout the scriptures. In modern times, there are countless testimonies of angels in the affairs of men. There will be a great deal of angelic activity during the tribulation period.

Flavius Josephus in his *Discourse Concerning Hades* sees that angels are assigned over the souls of men. At the time of death, the just are escorted to paradise, and the unjust are escorted to the lower regions of hell. Following, we highlight a few examples of angelic activity.

Psalm 104:4, "*God makes his angels spirits and his ministers a flaming fire.*" They are the servants of God. They may bring messages, visions, healing, musical sounds, assistance, protection to all those who shall inherit the blessings of the Almighty. They are the end-of-days reapers and will carry out judgment.

Psalm 91:11–12, "*For he will give his angels charge over you to keep you in all your ways, they will bear you up in their hands lest you dash your foot against a stone.*" We have guardian angels who assist us in times of trouble and watch over the heirs of salvation.

Angels around the throne of God, Isaiah 6:2:

> *Above the throne stood the Seraphim each one had six wings with two that covered his face, two that covered his feet and two he did fly. And one cried unto another and said, Holy, holy, holy is the Lord of Hosts and the whole earth is full of his glory. Woe is me for I am undone, a man of unclean lips. My eyes have seen the King, the Lord of Hosts. One Seraphim flew to him with a live coal in his hand which he had taken with tongs from off the altar and laid it upon my mouth and said, this has touched your lips and your iniquity is taken away and your sin purged.*

Daniel had been waiting for twenty-one days for an answer to prayer. Daniel 10:2 … "*I was sitting by the River Hiddekel* [Babylon] *and I looked and saw a man clothed in linen, loins girded in gold, his body was like the beryl,* [bluish green], *face like lightning, eyes like lamps of fire, arms and feet like color of polished brass and voice of his words like the voice of a multitude.*" Only Daniel sees the vision those with him flee because the earth quakes. In the presence, Daniel becomes weak, goes into a deep sleep, face on the ground; a hand touched him and set him up on his knees and upon the palms of his hands. The visitor speaks and tells him to stand because he was sent expressly to Daniel. "*I am come for thy words but the prince of Persia withstood me for twenty-one days but Michael one of the chief princes came to help me.*" Daniel hears message and cannot speak, face back to the ground, "*Behold one like the son of man touched my lips and then I could speak.*" Daniel is in the presence of a holy angel. Humans in the presence of holiness can have a sensual experience or physical reactions—such as, falling, fainting, enter trancelike state, or cause weeping, moaning, utterances. There are various reactions in the presence of holiness.

> *I saw in a vision upon my bed and behold a watcher and a holy one came down from heaven ...* [to bring him a message]. (Daniel 4:13, 17)

Ezekiel has an encounter with men (angels).

> *And behold, six men came from the way of the higher gate which lies toward the* ***north*** [descending from heaven) ... *and every man a slaughter* ***weapon*** *in his hand; and one among them was clothed with linen, with a writers* ***inkhorn*** *by his side* [similar to pen and ink). *They went in and stood beside the brazen altar* [in the earthly temple). *The Glory of the God of Israel was gone up from the Cherub* [the Ark of the Covenant] *whereupon he was, to the threshold of the house. The Lord spoke to the man dressed in linen with the inkhorn and told him to go through the city of Jerusalem and* ***set a mark upon the foreheads*** *of the men that cry for all the abominations that be done in their midst.* (Ezekiel 9:2–4)

And the other men with the weapons were told to go and kill all who have not the mark. This particular **"mark"** is the sealing by the Holy Spirit. We first see a mark placed on Cain so that others would not kill him. During the tribulation period, 144,000 Jews will be sealed and the judgment of God will not fall upon them. Revelation 7:4—in this passage, we see angels with weapons, items that can mark, and angels that make contact with humans.

Ezekiel continues to see the hand of God and his holy angels.

> *Then I looked and saw the firmament* [heaven] *that was above the head of the cherubim there appeared over them the color of sapphire as the appearance of the likeness of a throne. And God spoke to the man clothed with linen and said go in between the wheels, under the cherub and fill your hand with coals of fire from between them and scatter them over Jerusalem.* (Ezekiel 10:1-2) Then Ezekiel sees their presence in the earthly realm.
>
> *Cherubim standing on the right side of the house, man in linen went in and the cloud filled inner court and the* <u>*glory cloud*</u> *lifted from the cherub and stood over the threshold of the house and the house was filled with the cloud and the court was full of the* <u>*brightness of the Lord's glory*</u>*. And the sound of the cherubim wings was heard even to the outer court as the voice of the Almighty God when he speaks. The man clothed in linen is told by God to take fire from between the*

wheels and cherubim and he stood beside the wheels. One cherub stretched forth his hand from between them into the fire and took and put it into the hands of the man who took it and went out. And there appeared in the cherubim the form of a man's hand under their wings. I saw four wheels by the cherubim one wheel by each one and the wheels were the color of beryl.

And as for their appearance, they four had one likeness as a wheel in the middle of a wheel. When they went, they went upon their four sides and they turned not as they went. Their whole body and their backs and hands and wings and the wheels were full of eyes round about … everyone had four faces; one like a cherub, one like a man, one like a lion and one like a eagle. Ezekiel 10:3-14

In the following scripture, Ezekiel accounts his experience with an angelic spirit and the Holy Spirit. Ezekiel 11:1, "*Moreover the spirit* [angel] *lifted me up and brought me to the east gate of the Lord's house* … [to look upon wicked men]." Ezekiel 11:22, "*Then did the Cherubim lift up their wings and the wheels beside them and the glory of the God of Israel was over them above." Verse 23, "And the Glory of the Lord went up from the midst of the city and stood upon the mountain which is on the east side of the city.*" Ezekiel was again lifted up by the spirit and the Holy Spirit of God shows him a vision of the captives in Chaldea, Babylon.

Michael and Gabriel are the most common names found in scripture. Daniel 12:1, Michael is called the great prince who is the defender of Israel. In Revelation 12:9, he is also the warrior who throws the great red dragon, Satan, and his angels out of heaven. Gabriel is in charge of paradise and the cherubim who guard the Gate of Eden and now assume the duty of watching over the reptile kingdom, which was once Satan's responsibility.

Enoch provides additional names sometimes called watchers and can apply to holy or evil angels. Chapter 6 provides additional angel names:

Angelic Proper Names

- Uriel, the angel of thunder and trembling (weather systems)
- Raphael, angel of the spirits of men (records the thoughts and prayers)
- Raguel, angel of vengeance on the earth and luminaries (earth, sun, moon, planets)
- Saraqael, over the evil spirits of the children of men who induce them to sin

Books in Heaven

As we have examined things in heaven and earth, let us explore the possibility of a heavenly library wherein God retains all history.

> *Behold a hand was sent unto me and lo a roll/scroll of a book was therein and he spread it before me and it was written within and without and there was written lamentations, mourning and woe.* (Ezekiel 2:9–10)

Ezekiel is told to eat the scroll.

> *Let them be blotted out of the book of the living and not be written with the righteous.* (Psalm 69:28)

This book contains the names of all the souls of men from Adam to the last soul. In the following scripture, Moses complains to God regarding the sin of the people and the making of gods of gold: *Exodus 32:33, "And the Lord said unto Moses, whosoever has sinned against me, him will I blot out of my book."* Revelation 3:5 explains that the righteous or those who overcome will be clothed in white and God will not blot their name out of the book of life. Revelation 22:19, "If any man will take away from the words of the book of prophecy, God will take away his part out of the book of life..."

Enoch 39:2—in those days, Enoch received books of zeal and of anger and books of disturbance and of expulsion ... (book of life and book of death).

Malachi 3:16 ... "*And a book of remembrance was written before him for them that feared the Lord and thought upon his name.*"

Psalms 139:16, Before we were formed, God saw our substance and in the book all my members were written.

Revelation 5:1. . . "*And I saw in the right hand of him that sat on the throne a book written within and on the backside, sealed with seven seals.*"

Revelation 13:8 ... "*All that dwell upon the earth shall worship him* (Antichrist) *whose names are not written in the book of life of the Lamb slain from the foundation of the world.*"

Daniel 7:10 ... the judgment was set and the books were opened.

Revelation 20:12 ... "*And I saw the* ***dead****, small and great stand before God and the books were opened and another book was opened which was the book of life, and the dead were judged out of those things written in books according to their works.*"

This is the great white throne judgment which occurs at the end of the millennial reign.

We may conclude that God has recorded all history in times past, having preserved the deeds of angels, mankind, and events in heaven and on earth in books.

Chapter 3
The Word

Chapter Overview

CHAPTER 3

THE WORD

The Language of God

Hebrew, a Sacred Language

In a mysterious, sacred language, Yahweh spoke. Many biblical scholars believe a form of Hebrew to be the oldest language. *A Dissertation Concerning the Antiquity of the Hebrew Language, Letters, Vowel Points and Accents* by John Gill, DD[6] tells us that early scholars were convinced that Seth, son of Adam, developed the Hebrew alphabet, which was given by God.

Genesis 4:15—after Cain killed his brother Abel, God placed a mark upon Cain, which some believe to have been the letter *Tav*, appearing as a cross, or *X*. The frozen remains of an ancient man was found with that letter on his leg. It is a logical position that from Adam to Noah, communication with God and each other was one language. Enoch was caught up into the heavenly realm, and all that he experienced, God commanded him to write in books. Enoch would have written in the language familiar to him. God did not need Enoch to record creation events and the actions of fallen angels for himself but for revelation and knowledge for mankind. Enoch returned to earth and shared this knowledge with his family before his final translation. When the old world was destroyed by the flood, the books of God and the animals were safeguarded by Noah for future generations.

Hebrew is unlike any other spoken language. It is a living language. It is the divine hand of God. The first letter of the Hebrew alphabet is the *Aleph*. It is composed of two yods

---

6 John Gill, A Dissertation Concerning the Antiquity of the Hebrew Language, Letters, Vowel Points and Accents (London, England 1767)

Aleph – Beit

א	1	Aleph	Creator, creation, link between heaven & earth Genesis
ב	2	Beit	House (tabernacle) duality, (man/woman) division between good/evil, blessing/curses
ג	3	Gimel	God's loving kindness. God is the head. Nourish until ripe spiritually, set apart for holiness, leads to victory.
ד	4	Dalet	Door – leading to the way of redemption. Wilderness to entrance into the promise land or heaven.
ה	5	Hay	Breath, Holy Spirit the Ruah, leads us to eternity
ו	6	Vav	Nail, redemption through Jesus and transformation
ז	7	Zayin	Struggle, trials, Jesus sustains us and we rest in Him
ח	8	Chet	Newness of life through Grace. New beginnings.
ט	9	Tet	Attacks from the world, satan but which God intends for good as we look towards the millennium
י	10	Yod	Hand of God, spiritual growth from physical into the world of metaphysical and the divine. Yod is part of each Hebrew letter
כ ך	11	Kaf	God's crowning accomplishment to bring sinners into His righteous kingdom. The kneeling Kaf shows humility The elongated Kaf shows standing before God in His glory
ל	12	Lamed	Learning and teaching. Christ ascension, followed by the Holy Spirit who teaches. Highest letter.
מ ם	13	Mem	Revelation. Brings people to everlasting understanding of their place in God's plan. Open mem /accessible, ordinary waters our oceans, seas Closed mem-soffit in final form/inaccessible, waters of Creation above firmament inaccessible

ן נ	14	Nun	Temporary setbacks but faithful will be restored. Downfall & emergence. Kneeling in humility/standing before God perfected.
ס	15	Samech	God's divine presence in the center of the closed samech. As in the Holy of Holies. Symbolizes support, protection Memory.
ץ	16	Ayin	Insight – believers will receive. Hebrew for eye. Secular man's insight is futile. A wise man see God's purpose for for his life. Fear God & keep His commandments.
ף פ	17	Peh	Begin to understand the plain statements (the Word of God) Hebrew for mouth. Make public confession of God. Closed/open mouth, speech & silence
ץ ע	18	Tzaddit	Righteous becomes ingrained. Humility, kneeling with hands raised or standing
ק	19	Koph	Holiness and dedication to the Lord becomes ingrained into the saints. Spiritual growth cycles.
ר	20	Resh	Last traces of wickedness are removed. Jesus will judge wicked.
ש	21	Shin	Divine Power realized
ת	22	Tahv	Believers will fully ascend to God's realm – the world of truth and perfection under the King of Peace. Into eternity.

Theme of righteousness ties Tzaddi, Koph, Resh together pointing to catching away of the Tzaddi (righteous) by Koph (Holy One Christ) who will come to judge Resh (the wicked).

divided by a vav (,); the *Aleph* symbolizes God's oneness and mastery. The yod above is the hand of the Father in heaven; the vav represents the Messiah who will descend. The Word that connects heaven and earth and the yod below represents the hand of the Holy Spirit. We see the Triune Godhead. *Tav* is the last letter of the Hebrew alphabet, and it represents God's realm of eternity and truth. As mentioned, the combination of letters *Aleph* and *Tav* form the essence of the Word of creation, ***Eht.*** This word has no translation into English or another language.

After the Jews were dispersed to the four corners of the earth and over time lost their Hebrew language, God promised he would restore the language to the people. Zephaniah 3:9, "*I will return to the people a* ***pure*** *language that they may all call upon the name of the Lord to serve him with one consent.*" God had laid it on the heart and mind of Ben Yehuda to restore the Hebrew language to Israel. This prophecy was fulfilled when the Jews began to return to their homeland. A few scholars think the pure language was given at the Day of Pentecost when they spoke in the tongues of men. The problem with this view is that they were not speaking in a supernatural language, they were speaking in the dialects of the many nations represented in Israel at the time of Passover. The gift of tongues given by the Holy Spirit remains utterances in human dialects. We may agree that the pure language given by God will be spoken during the millennial reign of Christ.

Revelation within the Hebrew Alphabet

From the twenty-two letters in the Hebrew alphabet, each letter has a numeric value; each written letter forms a symbol; and each letter has a heavenly meaning. The original Hebrew language possessed mysterious insight into the creation. The magnification of the Word explains the wisdom of God, the existence of all things, and is the creative power of the Word. The letters of the Hebrew alphabet are the building blocks of creation.

Psalms 119 is divided into the twenty-two sections, which correspond to the twenty-two Hebrew letters. For instance, Psalm 119:30 is associated with *Dalet*, meaning "door": "*I have chosen the way of truth ...*" Jesus is the door to the way, the truth, and the life. The book of Revelation has twenty-two chapters, which tie into the twenty-two letters of the Hebrew alphabet. For instance, Revelation 1:8, "*I am the beginning and the end* [Aleph and Tahv]." There is great power in this declaration by Yeshua. The overall theme of this book brings to the forefront all things Yahweh from the beginning, the journey of mankind throughout millennia, and finally, entrance into eternity.

These twenty-two letters divided into four groups give a divine message:

(1) *Aleph* through *Zayin* is the plan of redemption through creation, the fall, the Crucifixion, Day of Pentecost, and the coming of the Holy Spirit.

(2) *Chet* through *Nun* show the ministry of Yeshua during his first coming. *Chet* refers to the newness of life through grace. *Tet* refers to attacks from the world and Satan, which God turns for good. *Yod* refers to the hand of God, spiritual growth. *Kaf* is God's crowning accomplishment to bring sinners into his kingdom. *Lamed* refers to teaching and learning. *Mem* refers to Revelation, bringing believers to an everlasting understanding of their place in God's plan, and *Nun* refers to temporary setbacks, but the faithful of God will be restored.

(3) *Samech* through *Shin* show the work of the Holy Spirit and prophecies leading to Christ's Second Coming as in the events pertaining to the day of the Lord.

(4) *Tahv* moves us into eternity. Believers will fully ascend to God's realm, and it is not given to us to see beyond.

The letter *Tzadi* refers the righteous of God becoming ingrained.

The letter *Koph* refers to holiness and dedication to God.

The letter *Resh* refers to the last traces of wickedness to be removed.

The theme of righteousness ties *Tzadi*, *Koph*, *Resh* together pointing to the catching away of the *Tzadi*, "righteous" by the *Koph*, "holy one," who will come to judge the *Resh*, "wicked."[7]

After the flood, language and writing continued through Noah's sons. Their descendants continued to develop language and writing forms. In Egypt they developed hieroglyphics using pictures and symbols. The Asians used lines and circles as their written expression. Assyrians and Babylonians used lines and pictures to express their thoughts. Native Americans drew pictures of animals, people, and tools on the walls of caves. In each language, there are traces of the ancient Hebrew letters.

God Spoke All Things into Existence

Yahweh was shaking up the heavens. His voice did roar from on high. There was war in heaven, and Satan was cast out of God's heavenly domain. Satan caused havoc and chaos in the heavens and upon the earth. When we join in at the creation, the **earth was without form** (without distinction). We then learn that God was transforming the earth; it was becoming discernable, and he was forming it. God was bringing forth order from chaos. The earth was **void** (lacking holiness, perfection). **Darkness** (mysterious darkness) **was upon the face of the deep** (abyss). Literally, there was no light. Then God gathered the primeval water on the surface and subterranean chambers under the earth. These same water sources came

---

[7] J. R. Church, Gary Stearman, Mysteries of the Hebrew Alphabet, (Oklahoma City, OK: PNTN/video)

forth during the flood of Noah's day. The Hebrew letter *Mem* refers to the waters above and below.

The Spirit of God moved upon the face of the waters. A picture of the Spirit hovering over the waters is described in Deuteronomy 32:11: "*As an eagle stirred up her nest, flutters over her young, spreads abroad her wings, takes them, bears them on her wings.*" Psalm 24:2, for he has founded it (earth) upon the seas and established it upon the floods. He stirred up his Spirit and the power of the Spirit moved upon the face of the deep and best described in John 1:1: "*In the beginning was the Word and the Word was with God and the Word was God. The same was in the beginning with God. All things where made by him and without him was not anything made that was made.*" His Word came forth and birthed all things into existence.

God said, "Let there be light." Light came forth, illuminating, becoming visible, glorious. This light is wonderful, mysterious, and ethereal. God is clothed in light. God's dwelling place is illuminated by his light, and not sunlight. His angels appear as beings of light. His presence radiates light. Adam and Eve were clothed in light. Moses's face was shining after being in the presence of God, and Jesus was glowing at the transfiguration. This light is beyond our natural sources of light and may represent a pause before God moved on to take this primal light and divide it between the day and night.

The spectrum of earthly light has seven basic colors. Like a menorah, the servant lamp (middle) represents green. The significance of green is hope of eternal life. Green is the glory of God around the throne. Blue radiates from the throne reflective of the heaven, and the floor in the throne room is clear as the crystal. Red represents the fire of God and the brightness of the sun, which we need to sustain life on the planet. Red is the color of Adam and the earth. The hues in the heavenly dimension are brilliant as seen through the Hubble Telescope. Colors here on our cursed earth are muted.

Job 38:19, "*Where is the **way** where light dwells?*" Mankind has been fascinated with light since the dawn of time. God tells Job that light does not dwell in a place but is established over a **way,** or waves. As scientific study indicates, the property of light is a stream of minute particles (electrons) without magnitude (measureable) but having inertia (staying in place or moving). Speed of light can travel at 186,000 miles per second. Light is an electromagnetic wave. It oscillates through space. It includes radio, infrared, visible light, ultraviolet, X-ray, gamma ray, cosmic ray waves. Our sun is ninety-three million miles from earth. One light-year is the distance that light can travel in a single year. The speed of light is 186,282 miles per second × 31,556,926 seconds in a year (5.88×10^{12}) would equal 5.88 trillion miles. It takes the light of the sun approximately 8.3 minutes to reach the earth.

Before the days of creation, God and his heavenly host existed in a timeless dimension. It is impractical to attempt to assign a time frame to this period. From the first day of creation, wherein God did separate the dark from the light and called it the first day, is a literal twenty-four-hour period.

God divided the light from the darkness and called the light day; the darkness, he called night. Psalms 139:12, "*Darkness cannot hide from God but the night is as the day; dark and light are both alike to God.*" The absence of light is darkness. Total darkness is similar to conditions of a black hole where light is totally absorbed and nothing can escape this black vacuum. The darkness that fell upon Egypt could be felt. Evil hides under a cloak of darkness. The lower regions of the earth are dark, and evil angels are confined in chains of darkness. And the evening and the morning were the first day. The first day became our Sunday, wherein God introduced time to govern the planet.

And God said, "Let there be a firmament [heaven] in the midst of the waters." As mentioned, the Hebrew letter *Mem* is associated with water. The letter in its open form refers to the accessible waters as under the firmament, lakes, seas, oceans, which man can explore. The closed form of the letter *Mem* refers to the inaccessible waters of creation.

> *And God said let there be a firmament in the midst of waters and let it divide the waters from the waters. And God made the firmament and divided the waters which were under the firmament from the waters which were above the firmament and it was so. And God called the firmament Heaven and the evening and the morning were the second day.* (Genesis 1:6–8)

The second day is our Monday.

Psalms 119:89, "*Forever O Lord, your Word is established in heaven.*" When God said, "Let there be a firmament," his word still resonate through the universe, and it is still established in the heavens. Should God remove his Word, the heavens would roll up like a scroll and melt with fervent heat (Isaiah 34:4). Heaven and earth will pass away but my words will by no means pass away (Matthew 24:35).

Mystery of Particles

Scientists want to unlock the secrets of the universe. Space travel has allowed researchers to secure rock samples from the moon and Mars. Objects from outer space colliding onto the earth's surface are studied. They study and investigate the physical properties of the earth, and findings reveal all things are a composition of particles that gather to form a molecular structure. In order to see particles smaller than a molecule—classified as subatomic particles—one must look through a microscope or highly advanced equipment, and then the invisible becomes visible.

Evolutionary theory concludes life evolved from a rock. In contrast to that position, creation scientists believe the factual evidence of how the universe came to be are written in the pages of a divinely composed textbook, the Bible.

It is plausible that the building blocks of creation are found in the unseen or invisible realm. The challenge for both the evolutionist and the creationist is how to access this knowledge from the inaccessible realm. Evolution theorists have discoveries and endless research data. Creationists have the "Word," and it confirms the revelations of creation throughout the heavens and the earth. The planets, stars, moon, and sun remain in their designated places because the "Word" has commanded it to be so.

The inquisitive nature of mankind drives us to investigate our "self" and our environment. Not satisfied, we then desire to delve into the invisible realm, something we instinctively know exists outside of our physical nature. Is there a God? If so, how did God manifest the invisible things into corporality, allowing the created to see God's magnificent handiwork being the evidence that there is a Creator? Those who do not believe in God as Creator have to dig around in God's dirt to analyze its composition or sample the molecules found in God's atmosphere or fill up buckets with water fishing for answers.

Let us surmise that before the creation of the physical world, God's domain is timeless, endless, and beyond human comprehension. Within God's domain exist invisible particles for his greater purpose. Within his power, he did command them to become the fabric of reality, which in turn became his creation. He programmed each tiny particle with a speck of divine consciousness, and when Yahweh spoke, the invisible came forth and become visible. Romans 1:20, "*For the* ***invisible things*** *of him from the creation of the world are clearly seen being understood by the things that are made, even his eternal power and Godhead . . .*" How did God do that? Bible scholars taught that God called forth his creation from nothing. But the scriptures clearly tell us the preexistent came into being through his spoken Word. We can conclude that God spoke and the "invisible things" took on visibility.

God has allowed mankind to peer into the mysterious world of particulates, invisible but can be seen as God put them together to form things. We can see an ant or a grain of sand. Can an ant see a giant human? By investigating the mystery of these invisible particles, we hope to come to a deeper understanding of "from the invisible" came forth the visible things. The world consists of physical properties—things that can be seen, measured, calculated, and explained. In the metaphysical unseen world, scientists relentlessly search for understanding. Life begins with the acknowledgement that consciousness or the spiritual essence is the thing that connects with physical reality. Under girding both realities is a single consciousness we call God.

For centuries, the genius of the scientific community have come to the realization that the number of particles identified make up only 5 percent of the mass and energy of the universe; therefore, a category called dark matter was developed to fill the void. They believe dark matter constitutes 27 percent of the universe. David Spergel, astrophysicist, said, "From our experiments, the periodic table, which comprises the atoms or normal matter that are said to make up the entire universe, actually covers only 4.5 percent of the whole." The periodic table has a new addition: number 113, Uut 286. The element is unstable and emits radioactive waves. Mankind has only an inkling of the universe as they continue to discover it contains billions of universes. God said man's wisdom is foolishness to him.

According to Professor Kyle Cranmer, New York University, "Dark matter has never been seen, and that leaves a huge gaping hole in our understanding of how the universe formed and exists today." Albert Einstein stated that dark matter is invisible but it acts on matter by its gravitational pull, influencing the rotation of galaxies.

Antimatter is rare in the known universe. It has the same mass as its matter counterparts but possesses an opposite charge. It seems to possess the ability to flit in an out of existence in cosmos rays, solar flares, and particle acceleration as discussed in the use of the Large Haldron Collider. Perhaps a greater understanding of antimatter may lead to a deeper understanding of celestial matter. God created celestial particles and combined them together to form an angel. Celestial entities (elemental spirits) are invisible to humanity, having the ability to flit in an out of dimensions. Spiritual composition acts different than terrestrial particulate matter, but yet they may share some commonality. When particles combine, their disposition or primal intelligence instructs it to form an atom—which builds to become a cell and further determines if they are to become eyes, heart, muscle, bone, or a brain. Same thing occurred when celestial DNA came together to form the features of angels.

The study of invisible particles begins at the subatomic level. Each atom is composed of living energy of which both celestial and terrestrial entities search for ways to harness or change this energy for purposes not ordained by God. For example, one cell converting glucose into energy is 50 percent greater than energy created by a gas engine. Fallen angels understood how to mix various particulate matter to create hybrids by observing God at work. The fallen angels understood that the essence of DNA found in all living organisms is composed of trillions of cells. They began to understand that the mysterious substance of blood was composed of millions of cells and is the life force of terrestrial beings. They discovered how to tap into this life force, through the mixing or mingling of DNA found in the various species. They discovered they could create hybrids or entities not approved by God. In other words, they could counterfeit God's creation.

We as physical living beings are limited. We cannot pass through solid walls. On the other hand, spiritual entities can pass through solid structures. Since the earth's gravitational field does not affect celestial beings, they can impact, affect, intermingle, and manipulate human molecular structure—allowing the earth life form to defy gravity, levitate, and pass through obstacles. In this altered state, the human can be conducted through the earth field to some other location. For instance, Satan, a celestial entity, was able to take Jesus from one location to another. In the Bible, Phillip disappeared after speaking with the Ethiopian. Time is applicable to our biosphere and is different or nonexistent in another dimension. Abductees claim to have lost time. A celestial entity can enter into a physical body. They can affect earthly matter. An example recorded in the Bible—when Peter was in jail and shackled, an angel came; and without touching the chains, they fell off, the jail door opened, and the guards were caused to sleep. The concept of space and time remains a mystery.

All life forms are composed of particles. They communicate with each other, such as white blood cells congregate to attack foreign intruders. Lower forms, such as bacteria or virus, reveal they have a form of intelligence or consciousness. Trillions of invisible bacteria find human or animal host. Viruses have the ability to mutate and develop resistance to antibiotics. Bacteria develop resistance to pesticides. We now understand that bacteria or virus particles thriving in their own microscopic domain have the ability to survive, mutate, or grow independent of human intervention. Stephen Hawking said, "There is no physical law precluding particles from being organized in ways that perform even more advanced computations than the arrangement of particles in the human brain ..." Hawking is addressing the ability of scientists to manipulate brain matter for greater performance, but the particulate matter may have a mind of its own.

Quantum physics is an abstract science still evolving, but it deals with physical phenomena on a nanoscopic scale (a nanometer is one-billionth of a meter) where the action is on the order of the Planck constant (describes the energy or movement). Quantum physics provides a description of dual particle-like and wavelike behavior as it interacts with high speed energy or its reaction to extreme temperatures and other experiments (Wikipedia, "Quantum Mechanics").

Professor Howard Wiseman, director at Griffith University, Center for Quantum Dynamics, published a paper in the *Physical Review X* journal suggesting the foundations of quantum science with a radical new theory based on the existence of and interactions between parallel universes. The realization of parallel universes began in 1957. The team proposes that parallel universes really exist and influence one another by a subtle force of repulsion. Their theory suggests this interaction could explain everything that is bizarre about quantum mechanics, and quantum theory is needed to explain how the universe works on microscopic level and how it interacts with all matter. It is understood that the smaller the particle becomes causes it to lose its locality in the earthly dimension, but it regains its locality in another dimension.

In very elementary terms, we see God's ability to bring forth from an invisible dimension the things that are seen in the earthly dimension. Secularists are just now catching up.

The Large Haldron Collider was built twenty-seven kilometers underground beneath the Franco-Swiss border outside of Geneva. It was created by the European Nuclear Research organization, CERN. The purpose of the Large Haldron Collider is to conduct experiments to find the "God particle." This would allow them to have a better understanding of life on earth and in the universe. It was first activated December 17 to 21, 2012, which coincided with the Mayan calendar for the end of the age, December 21, 2012. The LHC generates massive amount of energy as the particles collided. They observed a form of communication between particles; some call it quantum entanglement. The collision of particles created a torsion field that manifest from the electromagnetic interactions, and this, coupled with the notion of dark matter, could possibly be the key to open a portal, or as Professor Wiseman claimed, interactions between parallel universes.

Before Its News, November 27, 2012, article provided additional information as to the function of the Large Haldron Collider. Particles of protons and lead ions are circulated around a track at incredible speed, causing these particles to collide. Some particles were observed moving away from collision. Scientists then study this behavior as they seem to communicate directionally or change from muon particle to electron as well as displaying colors, which were produced by proton lead becoming liquid-like wave. This particle interaction or behavior could be on the edge of discovering another dimension. Looking deeper into the proton, they have found quarks and gluons. Quarks are the smallest known particle. They bind together to form protons and neutrons, which make up the nucleus of an atom. Scientists desire to combine molecules/particles that can self-organize, metabolize, grow, reproduce, and evolve. From our point of view, particles are already capable of this behavior.

Josh Peck, author of *Quantum Creation,* provided updated information, July 2015, reporting that scientists at CERN, Large Haldron Collider, discovered the Pentaquark. Under examination, the particle displays an inner design of five specks arranged like a pentagram. "This is something that has never been confirmed to happen in nature before." Peck shares the comments of Gonz Shimuro, researcher blog called CERN Watch who associates the Pentaquark portal with elemental spirits. Peck reports the finding was published in the Physical Review Letters. Comment by Guy Wilkinson, "The Pentaquark is not just any new particle, it represents a way to aggregate quarks, namely the fundamental constituents of ordinary protons and neutrons in a pattern that has never been observed before in over fifty years of experimental searches. Studying its properties may allow us to understand better how ordinary matter from which we are all made is constituted."

Tom Horn points out the symbolism embedded in the LHC apparatus. It has a design of seven Atlas rings each weighing seven tons. The word *Atlas* stands for A Torodial LHC Apparatus. It is designed like a pagan wheel of time. Atlas was a mythological god required to hold up the heavens. Atlas was a Titan at war with the Olympians. He lost and his punishment was to hold up the heavens to prevent him from mating with Gaia, Mother Earth. Horn's explanation connects to Bertolucci's announcement, "The Haldron Collider may create or discover previously unimagined scientific phenomena or unknown dimensions. Out of this door might come something, or we might send something through it," said Sergio Bertolucci, Director of Research and Scientific Computing at CERN.

Scientists believe the universe functions within four energy fields: (1) strong nuclear/magnetic pull, (2) weak nuclear forces/radioactive, (3) electromagnetic forces, (4) gravity. According to Cranmer, the scientific world is not content with four fields; they are looking to discover more complex matter, "but deep down, these forces are just manifestations of one great force that permeates the universe." Cranmer believes the LHC may help scientists identify new particles, find new forces, or learn something really deep about the nature of space and time.

The results of the experiments performed by the LHC are tracked by a computer system that is able to process fifteen petabytes of data per minute. This system is called Worldwide Large Haldron Collider Computing Grid (WLCG). The computer system has a global infrastructure. Data can be accessed by partners by way of the international grid located in forty countries having numerous computing centers and employing hundreds of thousands of technicians.

As scientists continue to observe and report their findings, possibly believing they are on the cutting edge or revolutionizing how science considers the insights into the origin of mass, nature of dark matter, antimatter, gravity weakness, and symmetry structure of the universe, etc., it may bring them full circle as they realize the majesty of creation has a Creator. All of reality is composed of God's particulate matter, which forms magnetic or gravitational fields maintaining our earth, moon, sun, and planets in their respective place.

Scientists discovered that the neutrino particle has the ability to travel faster than light. This particle is moving beyond our ability to see it, but by technological advancement, its presence is known. We have two unusual particles, and if combined, the question becomes, Are the invisible particles part of another dimension? From the Christian worldview, we believe all things were manifested in a dimension wherein dwells our Creator. Scientific research comes from the material world that can be seen and touched; however, some are beginning to see that there may be another realm of existence leading to the threshold of discovering another dimension.

Someday a certain group of people will be transported from the earthly dimension faster than the speed of light, and in the twinkling of an eye, God changes their earthly forms into immortal forms, allowing them entrance into a heavenly dimension.

Nanotechnology is relatively new in the scientific world. A material found at the 9-11 site in New York called nanothermite was a combination of nanoparticles, iron oxide, and aluminum compound used in an explosive developed by DARPA. The agencies activities are covert and for years has been experimenting with material not common to earth. This discovery was made by Neil Harris Copenhagen, US Geological Society.

Nanoparticles are smaller than atoms, protons, and are being engineered to develop tiny robots that can be programmed to flow through the bloodstream and regulate body functions or destroy malignant cells while protecting healthy tissue. Most impressive, there are no side effects as is common with traditional treatments using chemicals and radiation therapy. April 11, 2014, *International Business Times*' Mary Ann Russon reported that scientists at Harvard University and Bar Ilan University in Israel have successfully injected tiny living nanobots into live cockroaches to deliver drugs directly into the insects' cells.

Several reports claim carbon nanotubes were on microchips implanted in people claiming to have been abducted by aliens. Covert government operatives would have a greater understanding of nanofunctionality. There have been some reports of particles falling like rain mixed with blood cells. This could be the residue or DNA waste matter from earth entities subjected to experiments on a craft in the atmosphere outside of our visibility. Not so science fiction since there are space stations in outer space.

The *Washington Post* reported researcher Xiang Zhang, Berkley University, used gold nanoantennas to create a cloak of invisibility. It is designed to react with light and scatter it.

Physicist William A. Tiller has been researching a level of physical reality undetectable with conventional measurement instruments. *Epoch Times*, March 2014, says, "Two kinds of substances exist. First are the electric atom/molecule, which can be observed with traditional instruments because they are electric-charge based. Second, are the magnetic waves particles not easily observed but existing in the physical vacuum or empty space between the fundamental electric particles that make up our normal electric atoms and molecules." Tiller claims that within this vacuum or empty space lies great power and seems to be affected by human thought or consciousness. Observations can only be detected when these particles interact with the electric molecule/atom particles and human consciousness spurs this interaction. "The consciousness can in a way affect or interact with a power greater than anything conventional instruments have been able to measure thus far."

We understand this line of thought can be applied to God's consciousness or essence wherein God thought, God spoke, and it was. God created man in his image and gave man the ability to think, speak, and create. God is spirit, and he placed within man an invisible soul. The soul is the seat of human consciousness, and within this domain every human knows there is one greater than himself. The soul retains the knowledge of Yahweh, our self-awareness and our memories.

In this realm, physicists or scientists cannot explain consciousness. At the time of death, the soul departs its physical house, moving into its eternal dimension. Until that time, we are connected to God in this life with the ability to link our consciousness to God through communication and, in turn, activate supernatural power greater than all of man's wisdom. Working within God's parameters, man has been allowed to perform great miracles and supernatural events.

At the time of death on the cross, the spirit of Jesus was freed from his physical body. His body was placed in the tomb, where it remained until his spirit reunited with his physical body for the Resurrection. The physics of the Resurrection left residual evidence or particles on the shroud or cloth he was wrapped in for his burial. He was changed from mortal physical man to a composition not of this world. His changed body allowed him to pass through solid objects. He was able to appear and disappear. He could eat food. He was able to go into another dimension we call hell and in another instance be in the heavenly realm.

As long as mankind is allowed to act on his ideas and imagination, he will continue to delve into the outer limits. Man has learned to manipulate DNA, as did the fallen angels before the flood. The time has come that man can replicate a human through cloning. Man can now counterfeit God's creation of man. Scientists began using stem cells to grow human parts. Fetal tissue from aborted babies or stem cells is now used in food and medicine. The demand is so great fetal farming will soon be public knowledge. After all, salmon fish are being genetically altered and are grown on farms. Human fetal farms would allow cloned tissue or eggs to mature in artificial wombs and would be the source for growing organs for transplant recipients or other Frankenstein experiments. Biologist Lee Silver of Princeton, a cloning and human enhancement enthusiast, wrote *Remaking Eden*, "Without cloning, genetic engineering is simply science fiction, but with cloning, genetic engineering moves into the realm of reality."

And God said, "Let the dry land appear," and God called the dry land earth. At this time, the earth was covered in water, and God gathered the waters, and the earth did arise. He established boundaries for the oceans and seas. He saw that it was good. God called for the earth to bring forth grass- and herb-yielding seed and fruit trees after its kind whose seed is in itself. And God saw that it was good, and the evening and the morning were the third day. This is our Tuesday.

God provided the plants and herbs of the field fully grown in the earth. He knew that in a few days, there would be birds and beast requiring sustenance. God mentions that he had not caused it to rain nor was there a man to till the ground but caused a midst to come up from the earth and water the ground (Genesis 2:5–6).

God said, "Behold, I have given you every herb-bearing seed, which is upon the face of all the earth, and every fruit-yielding; tree to you it shall be for meat. To every beast, fowl, and creeping things, I have given green herb for their meat." During the millennial reign animals will eat grass and green plants.

Note that God had specifically created the fruit trees after their own kind and the seed was in itself. You will begin to see how Satan corrupted everything that God put in order. Under Satan's deception, man began to alter what God had intended. This is called genetic modification, the science of creating hybrid plants by splicing, mixing, mingling of seeds producing new types of crops that do not yield seeds. It is totally unhealthy and is one reason why mankind has so many diseases.

The Nature of Time

God instituted time as a compass to guide mankind. He gave man twenty-four hours in a day, four seasons, and originally, the year consisted of 360 days. According to ancient calendars developed by the Assyrians, Chaldeans, Egyptians, Hebrews, Persians, Greeks, Phoenicians, Chinese, Mayans, Hindus, Carthaginians, Etruscans, Teutons, and others—their calendars were based on twelve thirty-day months. Sometime in the eight century BC, the Romans added five days per year. The only constant we can trust is that the evening and the day are twenty-four literal hours as ordained by God and has continued throughout millennia.

Time is the fourth dimension. People have presumed that time is linear and absolute. A linear view is established by our frequent resort to "time lines," having a beginning and an end. Through modern physics, it has been discovered that time is not linear and absolute because it varies with mass, acceleration, gravity, and location.

It was the insight of Albert Einstein in considering the nature of our physical universe that we live in more than just three dimensions. This led to his famous Theory of Relativity and the discovery that time is part of our physical reality. He said, "People like us, who believe in physics, know that the distinction between past, present, and future is only a stubbornly persistent illusion." We ponder the plausibility of Einstein's statement and consider that time can be distorted within certain variables. God promised, at the end of the age, he would shake things in heaven and earth. What if the earth is shaken to such a degree it is no longer positioned on its axis, affecting the meridian time zones and the time of day cannot be determined, as in "no one knows the day or the hour"?

Through the centuries, men have manipulated and changed times. One such instance is "daylight saving time." This practice is used in some nations. In the spring, the hour moves forward. In the fall, the hour moves back. Primitive man did not use daylight saving time. He regulated his life between daytime and nighttime. When he was hungry or thirsty, his body prompted him to satisfy his needs. His internal clock awakened him in the morning, and his body rested in the evening. Animals cannot tell time, but they can sense the time for hunting or hibernation. Simply looking at a clock, one could not tell if it were daylight saving time or standard time because habits regulate schedules. To add to the illusion of time, we have Eastern, Central, Mountain and Pacific time zones. Traveling abroad, one would also encounter different time zones.

To demonstrate the fact that people are hindered in their concept of time is clearly seen by observing the reaction of a person confined in a room without a clock for an extended period of time. The individual would lose their sense of time. If they are placed in a windowless room, they would lose their sense of day or night. The nature of time remains a mystery that the scientific community endeavors to understand.

In understanding the nature of our physical universe, it is determined that there are three dimensions, which are length, width, height/depth, and the fourth dimension is time and space. The dynamics of time and space calls for more research to uncover the mysteries therein. On an elementary level of understanding, time and space could be demonstrated as the time it takes to throw a ball and the space the ball occupies while moving in earth's environment. Apply this same exercise in outer space, and the results would be different. Removing our physical limitations, we could extend our arm into space infinitely. Since time is not absolute, we can alter time with acceleration or gravity. Instead of taking ten minutes to walk from point to point, if you run, you will arrive sooner. If you ride a bike, it will increase your ability to arrive at your destination in less time; however, the distance between point A and B remain constant. These elementary exercises lead scientists to delve deeper into the possibility of traversing space and time. Astronauts landing on the moon was a giant step for humanity. Space travelers of the future would be weaving their path in and out of time and space. Their craft could accelerate to cover millions of miles in light-years in outer space where Earth time ceases to exist. Upon returning to Earth, many years may have passed and they have not aged but the Earthlings have aged.

In our physical reality, we understand the concept of past, present, and future. We exist in the present, yet we are in constant movement toward the future. Our space travelers would be moving forward in time and space while in a state of present time. What happens to the past?

We leave the past behind though we have the ability to access our past through our memories and history. If we are seated in a chair for two hours, our perception would be that we have not moved, but we have moved in time and space as the planet rotates. Reading a book for an hour, we can rely on our memory to tell us we have read the previous pages in the past few minutes, but we cannot physically travel back in time to do anything. We can turn the pages back and forth as we involuntarily move forward in time. Though we are always moving forward in time, most people cannot actually see what is ahead of us in the future. We entertain the possibility that within the next few minutes, we will still be reading our book. But what if that were incorrect and thirty seconds from that thought, a bolt of lightning struck exactly where we were seated and we were immediately killed? This is the illusion of time and space.

We may have some latitude in predicting the future. Prophecy is given for a future event. Some people are given precognition or forewarnings of eminent danger. These "other" sensibilities are not clearly understood or controlled. There are many examples of men in the Bible who were given visions or forewarnings of things to come. Our emotions, memories, are retained in our physical brain as well as in the spiritual place of our soul. Once our physical body ceases to exist, the soul and spirit of mankind exists eternally. Researchers trying to find the "God particle" may be led to discover a bridge between the fourth and fifth dimensions. Our spiritual essence may be the bridge that leads us into the realm of the fifth dimension, and if this is true, the bridge between our physical dimension and the spiritual dimension can only be accessed in an altered state. It appears we must vacate our physical body to come into God's dimension. At the time of our death, God will allow our soul/spirit to transcend from the physical to spiritual.

And God said, "Let there be lights in the heavens to divide the day from the night and let them be for signs and for seasons, for days and years." God made two great lights—the greater, called the sun, and the lesser, called the moon—and he made the stars and set them in the firmament (Psalms 147:4). He tells the number of the stars, and he calls them by their names. God is truly awesome. God saw that it was good, and the evening and the morning became the fourth day. This is our Wednesday.

From Enoch's ancient viewpoint, it appeared to him as if the sun were rotating around the earth. Later astronomers would come to the realization that the earth rotates around the sun. Enoch's perception is no stranger than those who thought the earth was flat. Out of habit, we claim the sun is rising and setting, but it is stationary.

The Celestial Message

God created stars, moon, sun so that man could observe weeks, months, seasons, and signs. The days of the week are named after the luminaries. Sun is Sunday, the moon is Monday, and five planets of which Mars is Tuesday, Mercury is Wednesday, Jupiter is Thursday, Venus is Friday, and Saturn is Saturday.

Man has discovered that there are other infinite, multiple galaxies, but God has given us limited access within our galaxy. Man dreams of exploring other galaxies and traveling light-years to reach another planet. This may be achievable if the technology can accomplish the task.

Before the written Word was popular, man read the signs and movement of the constellations. The study of astronomy has allowed mankind to see a message in the stars. God's message is about his plan for the redemption of mankind through the coming Messiah. The constellations also provide insight into the conflict between God, Satan, and humankind. God allows us to understand that Satan and the fallen angels existed in the heavens and came upon the earth before man was created. God created the luminaries on the fourth day. Man and animals were created on the sixth day. The celestial message encompasses Genesis to Revelation.

Astronomy was part of early civilizations beginning with Adam. "Seth, the son of Adam, invented peculiar wisdom regarding the heavenly bodies and their order," said Flavius Josephus, Jewish historian. Astronomy was incorporated into the writings of the Egyptian, Assyrian, and Chaldean religious beliefs. Egypt has a depiction of the constellations. The study of the stars led the Magi to visit the child Jesus. These men were associated with the priesthood of Zoroaster before the capture of Jews through to the time of the birth of Jesus.

The book of Joel 2 points to signs in the heavens that will be given at the end of the age. God said, "*I will show wonders in heaven above and signs in the earth beneath: blood, fire, and vapor of smoke. The sun will be turned into darkness and the moon into blood before that great and notable Day of the Lord come.*"

The book of Job is the oldest book in the Bible dated around 2150 BC. Job reveled at God's handiwork in the heavens. Enoch is mentioned in the book of Genesis as a righteous man taken into the heavenly realm by God. The writings of Enoch were at one time included in the Canon but around AD 300, Enoch's writings were deleted as part of scripture. Enoch's writings predate the book of Job. In Job 26:13, he understands that by the spirit of God, he has garnished the heavens and his hand has formed the crooked serpent and these are parts of his ways. God has revealed to Job his ancient enemy, Satan; the serpent desires to test him. Many of the expressions given in the Psalms written by King David spoke often of the glory of God seen in the heavenly bodies.

Data found in Wikipedia credit, "The ancient Babylonians charted many of the stars visible to the naked eye and assigned stars to various constellations. The Greek writer Ptolemy recorded lists of these formations of which many are retained in the modern configuration."

In modern times, men are still fascinated with the heavenly bodies using powerful telescopes to see their movements. Rev. E W. Bullinger was a highly respected man of the cloth, and he published his work on the ancient star charts and its understanding by early civilizations in the late 1800s. The International Astronomical Union divided the sky into eighty-eight specific constellations in AD 1922, assigning Latin names for the traditional ones with the exception for those named for Greek mythological figures. The current sky map is based mostly on the work of Benjamin Gould in AD 1895 and Eugene Delporte in AD 1930.

God has arranged the constellations within our galaxy, and God maintains their parameters throughout the universe.

Twelve Major Constellations

Following is a review of twelve constellations found in our galaxy, which give us the Gospel in the stars. WARNING—do not interpret the following scientific review as astrology. Using astrology as a medium to tell the future is a ploy by Satan to corrupt all things that are holy and sacred. The fallen angels taught the practice of fortune-telling and looking at the stars for false future predictions. This practice turned around the original intent of divine wisdom to superstition. Every pagan culture and religion brings forth a perversion of the original story told in the constellations.

Beginning with the constellation of Draco, the dragon curled around the north polar star, whose tail covers a third of the circle of heaven—it portrays Satan as a dragon, who attempted to take control of the north where the throne of God is positioned and who took a third of the angels in his rebellion (Ezekiel 28:13).

The constellation of Cetus is Leviathan, or sea dragon. Job 41:1–34, "*Can you draw out Leviathan with a hook? Or his tongue with a cord which you let down?*" This whole chapter is about Leviathan who is then spoken of as Satan having reptilian features. *"Upon earth there is not his like, who is made without fear, he beholds all high things, he is a king over all the children of pride."*

The constellation of Hydra is seen as a many-headed dragon whose tail covers a third of the ecliptic path of the sun and is moving away from the lion (Jesus) who pounces on its head, birds eats his flesh, bowl of wrath poured out on it. Again this portrays Satan, the dragon, and one third of the fallen angels. Genesis 3:15, "*And I will put enmity between thee and the woman and between your seed and her seed; it shall bruise your head and you will bruise his heel.*" This same multiheaded beast is seen in Revelation 13:1 as arising out of the sea, having seven heads and ten horns. Genesis 3:15 prophecy is twofold. First part is when Jesus will crush the head of the serpent/dragon/Satan at the time of his Second Coming. The second part of this scripture refers to the seed of Satan. Satan did not stop with the corruption of just one snake or two people in the Garden of Eden but has influenced evil entities throughout the ages. Satan does not have literal seed or offspring; those who follow Satan are his seed by adoption. We believe the ungodly followers of Satan produce the spiritual fruit of wickedness. Throughout the history of mankind, mythological records and architectural renderings point to beings that look like reptiles, gargoyles, and other giant monstrosities. This hypothesis is discussed further in this book.

Several theories suggest that Satan, knowing the Genesis 3:15 prophecy, moved to corrupt the Messianic lineage. How did Satan know this since Bible scholars credit the writing of Genesis to Moses around 1400 BC? Perhaps Satan could see the celestial message set in the heavens before the creation of man.

Virgo is the seed of the woman as in Genesis 3:15. Women do not have seed, but this is a foretelling of the virgin birth and is associated with Nazareth, home of Jesus. The ancient Hebrew name for Virgo was Bethula, of which *beth* means house.

Scorpio is the seed of the serpent who points to the Antichrist. This arrangement also points to the scorpion who tries to extinguish the light and steal the northern crown, who is restrained by Ophiuchus, the seed of the woman. Revelation 9 speaks of a hoard of demonic locust being released from the bottomless pit with tails like scorpions during the tribulation.

Leo is seen as the conquering lion who destroys Hydra, the many-headed dragon as symbolized in Daniel and Revelation. Jesus is the lion of the tribe of Judah. The name Leo came from the Egyptian people who worshipped the lion among other creatures. Later the Greeks maintained the name Leo for this constellation.

Taurus, a raging bull, deals with the judgment of the Day of the Lord. God refers to Pleiades and Orion both found in the constellation ofTaurus (Job 38:31). It hints at Arcturus as ash (burning coal) and to the chambers of the south points to hell. This ties in with Satan-like fire being cast out upon the earth and turning to ash.

Orion returns to judge the world. Jesus is pictured as having his waist girded, and Orion is the picture of Jesus with invincible bands; no one can lose the bands of Orion. Jesus is returning to judge the world.

Pleiades and its seven stars could refer to the seven churches of Asia as defined by John in Revelation (Job 38:31). Can you bind the sweet influences of Pleiades or loose the bands of Orion? Can you bring forth Mazzaroth in his season? Or can you guide Arcturus and his sons? (Mazzaroth and Arcturus refer to Satan.)[8]

The twelve major constellations are divided into three groups of four constellations each:

1. Virgo, Libra, Scorpio, Sagittarius represent the first advent of Christ.
2. Capricorn, Aquarius, Pisces, Aries represent the church age.
3. Taurus, Gemini, Cancer, Leo represent the second advent of Christ.

It is interesting to note that the twelve tribes are each associated with the twelve constellations:

1. Zebulon	Virgo
2. Levi	Libra
3. Dan	Scorpio
4. Asher	Sagittarius
5. Nephtali	Capricorn

8 J. R. Church, Celestial Message in the Stars, Prophecy in the News article.

6. Reuben	Aquarius
7. Simeon	Pisces
8. Gad	Aries
9. Joseph	Taurus
10. Benjamin	Gemini
11. Issachar	Cancer
12. Judah	Leo

King David was of the tribe of Judah as well as Mary the mother of Jesus. Therefore, Jesus is the lion of the tribe of Judah.

We previously discussed the eternal domain of God and the initial formation of the heavens. From the Genesis chronicles, we understand that on the first day, God called for light. On the second day, God divided the heavenly firmament. On the third day, God called for the dry land to appear, bringing forth grass, trees, and herbs. God placed the stars, moon, sun in the heavens to define the day from the night and for signs, seasons, days, and years, and this was the fourth day.

Before speaking about the fifth and sixth days of creation, let us interject thoughts of physicists, scientists, and astrophysicists on a superior designer of creation. Fred Hoyle, British astrophysicist, said, "A common sense interpretation of the facts suggest that a super intellect has monkeyed with physics, chemistry, and biology and that there are no blind forces worth speaking about in nature." Michael Turner, astrophysicist at the University of Chicago and Fermilab, said regarding the precisions and fine-tuning of the universe, "the precision is as if one could throw a dart across the entire universe and hit a bull's-eye one millimeter on the other side."

Robert Jastrow, director of NASA's Goddard Institute for Space Studies—referring to himself as an agnostic—wrote a book: *God and the Astronomers.* In the final chapter, he said, "For the scientist who has lived by his faith in the power of reason, the story ends like a bad dream. He has scaled the mountains of ignorance, he is about to conquer the highest peak. As he pulls himself over the final rock, he is greeted by a band of theologians who have been sitting there for centuries" (Kerby Anderson, Point of View, October 7, 2014).

<u>And God said, "Let the waters bring forth sea life and fowl that they may fly above the earth."</u> God created great whales and every living creature that moves, which the waters brought forth abundantly after their kind, and God saw that it was good and blessed them, saying, "Be fruitful and multiply, and fill the waters in the seas and let fowl multiply in the earth," and the evening and the morning were the fifth day. This is our Thursday.

And God said, "Let the earth bring forth living creatures."

Genesis 2:19, "*And out of the ground the Lord God formed every beast of the fields and every fowl of the air. God commanded the earth to bring forth the living creatures after his kind, cattle and creeping things and beast of the earth after his kind.*" God saw it was good. Job 40:15, "Behold now behemoth which I have made with thee, he eats grass as an ox"; his strength is in his loins, and his force is in the navel of his belly. He moves his tail like a cedar, and the sinew of his stones are wrapped together. His bones are as strong pieces of brass; his bones are like bars of iron … He drinks up a river … His scales are his pride shut up together as with a close seal, and no air can come between them. By his neesings, a light does shine and his eyes are like the eyelids of the morning. Out of his mouth go burning lamps and sparks of fire leap out. Out of his nostrils goes smoke. This is a literal description of a giant dinosaur or dragon with the ability to release fire out of its mouth. It is proof they roamed the earth same time as mankind.

Animals have a life source given to them by God. We have a connection with other living things and our physical commonalities set aside evolution. Humans have eyes, nose, mouth, and animals have the same things. Humans can reproduce using their genitals to transmit sperm, and animals have reproductive organs as we do. Humans can love one another, and we believe animals can experience deep emotional attachments to each other and to humans. We have a heart, lungs, and blood, and so do animals. God created both animals and humans from the earth. In order for the lump of clay to become a living being, God breathed life into their body, and they became living souls. The question often asked is, Do animals have souls? And we believe they do. However, the Spirit of God may be for humankind only. Do animals go to heaven? First we consider that once the animal dies, its life force goes somewhere. In modern times, many people have had near-death experiences, and they have seen heaven. In their accounts, they do not mention seeing animals in heaven. It is possible that the souls of the animal kingdom exist in another reality. We cannot answer these questions with assurance, but what we do know, there are horses in heaven. All of God's creation is relative and special because God saw it was good. When Jesus sets up his millennial kingdom, there will be a place for animals to dwell in safety (Hosea 2:18).

And God Said, "Let us make man in our image and after our likeness."

> *God created man in his own image in the image of God created he him, male and female created he them and God blessed them and God said unto them be fruitful and multiply and replenish the earth and subdue it and have dominion over the fish of the sea and over the fowl of the air and over every living thing that moves upon the earth … and God saw everything that he had made and*

> *behold it was very good and the evening and the morning were the sixth day.* (Genesis 1:27–28)

This is our Friday.

The only way to interpret the above passage is literally. "Let us make man in our image," of which we believe is the likeness of God or to look like our counterparts in heaven. After death, we enter into a spiritual realm teaming with life, God the Father, God the Son, God the Holy Spirit, the Old Testament patriarchs including the saints, angels, animals, trees, golden streets, pearly gates, mansions,and more. The appearance of these things will be similar but more spectacular in comparison to the muted things we are accustomed to seeing on earth. Our understanding of God is that his essence is spiritual. The Word of God came forth from his essence. Jesus said, "*If you have seen me, then you have seen the Father, for <u>we are one</u>.*" At the end of the age, the Word took on a flesh nature, becoming both God and Man. The immortal became mortal.

We who are made in his likeness have been given intelligence and knowledge. God gave Adam the gift of free will, and to balance this, he placed within him a moral compass. Romans 1:19 … that which may be known of God, he did manifest it within mankind. We can retain the knowledge of God and prosper or reject him and receive a reprobate mind.

Creation of man is unique. Yahweh touched the clay mass to form himself a <u>body.</u> He gently molded his face, arms, torso, legs, and feet from the very earth that he created to give life. He formed man's inner parts. He allowed the mysterious substance of blood to flow through his veins. He touched his heart, and it began to beat in rhythm with Yahweh. He caressed his beloved. He blew his holy breath, the Ruach, <u>the spirit</u> of life into his nostrils. The body houses the Nephesh, our <u>soul,</u> wherein the spiritual essence resides. The human is a body, soul, and spirit. God said he knew man before he was formed in the womb. The unborn baby is known of God. God gave man life, and we should cherish all life. At the end of our life, we will be changed from mortal to immortal. We will continue our eternal existence in the presence of God or in the absence of his presence.

Adam opened his eyes and looked into the loving eyes of his Creator. Yes, Adam did see the face of God. Genesis 2:7, "*And the Lord God formed man of the dust of the ground and breathed into his nostrils the breath of life and man became a living soul.*" The writer of Hebrews asks the question: What is man that you are mindful of him? It is summed up in Hebrews 2:7–8: "*You made him a little lower than the angels, you crowned him with glory and honor and did set him over the works of your hands. You put all things in subjection under his feet.*"

The spirit of Yahweh became one with Adam. The celestial DNA became integrated into God's creation. Adam's brain became the receptor of the knowledge of God. Adams' brain was a mini universe; it was complex, limitless in its abilities, and all his memories and emotions would be retained in his soul. Adam would forever remember the touch and love of his Almighty God and Creator. Yahweh taught Adam and walked with him in the Garden of Eden. From time forward, we see that Yahweh in sundry times and divers' places spoke to man, guiding him, teaching him, loving him, dying for him all to bring mankind back to himself. Our response to Yahweh is to obey and love him; this is the conclusion of the whole matter.

Creation Versus Evolution

In the six literal days of creation, God spoke all things into existence. Yet the created of God question their origin. The "where and when" opened the study of the origin of creation. The big bang theorists believe there was a great expansion thirteen billion years ago. Others believe mankind came from other star systems and populated the earth. There is no clear consensus within the evolutionist camp as to when the creation began. They present an improbable theory that over billions of years, man developed from primordial ooze into a complex, living, breathing soul. The statistical odds that one protein molecule formed by chance would be 100^{160} according to Sir Fred Hoyle, Cambridge University, and originator of the Steady-State Theory of the Universe. Hoyle said, "The notion that not only biopolymers but the operation program of a living cell could be arrived at by chance in a primordial organic soup here on earth is evidently nonsense of the highest order."

Dr. Paul leMoine, editor of *L'Encyclopedie Francais* said, "Evolution is a fairy tale for adults."

Over time evolutionists would present various theories—such as, dinosaurs roamed the earth millions of years before the existence of man. That notion is debunked in that footprints of both dinosaurs and man were found together.

They attribute the extinction of the dinosaurs to a large meteorite sixty-five million years ago. In the aftermath of this catastrophe, the planet experienced incineration and was left in total chaos. They are halfway on the right track, assessing something impacted the planet and rendered it "void and dark." They are on the wrong track by assuming the earth is sixty-five million years old.

The creation of living things began approximately 6,500 years ago. The dinosaurs, other animals, and humans were created by God on the sixth day. The extinction of the dinosaurs may have been caused by a natural disaster or the infiltration of the fallen angels and their hybrid giants who ate them.

Another theory was, primitive man did not have fire. This is debunked because the fallen angels taught mankind regarding the working of metals, which required heating using fire, and Enoch saw chariots with wheels of fire. Evolutionists suggest man did not have the ability of the wheel for hundreds of years, and this is also debunked in that early man was able to build an ark to house animals, people, food, and float for a year. So the wheel in comparison is elementary.

All are entitled to their theories, but one must remember that God sits outside of time and space. Scientists still seek answers as to the creation of all things. These answers can be found in God's spiritual realm, which are unattainable using man's scientific tools. Astronomers peer as far as the telescope allows, and they are beginning to understand that the physical universe is unmeasurable. They see the spectacular beauty of the galaxy, and some come to realize that Yahweh is the divine architect of creation.

On the extreme opposite, the atheists reject God's creation. Stephen Hawking, astrophysicist and atheist, says, "Science offers a more convincing explanation for the origins of the universe and that the miracles of religion are not compatible with scientific fact." In his 1988 book, *A Brief History of Time,* he wrote, "Scientists would know the mind of God if a unifying set of scientific principles known colloquially as the theory of everything were discovered."

Undecided contemplation on God's creation, Charles Darwin wrote, "But I may say that the impossibility of conceiving that this grand and wondrous universe with our conscious selves arose through chance seems to me the chief argument for the existence of God, but whether this is an argument of real value, I have never been able to decide. I am aware that if we admit a first cause, the mind still craves to know whence it came and how it arose. Nor can I overlook the difficulty from the immense amount of suffering through the world. I am also induced to defer to a certain extent to the judgment of the many able men who have fully believed in God; but here again I see how poor an argument this is. The safest conclusion seems to be that the whole subject is beyond the scope of man's intellect, but man can do his duty." The Bible makes clear that in order to believe, we must first come in faith.

Who or what could have birthed the theory of evolution, specifically apes evolving into men, in blatant contradiction with God as Creator? The who, may begin with Darwin as we follow his imagination, moving away from the observation of the natural order of species to something a bit sinister. Darwin's *Origin of Species* introduces a trend of thought and study that opens a portal suggesting the possibility of animals evolving into a different species. Darwin makes a cloaked statement, "As many more **individuals of each species** are born than can possibly survive, and as consequently there is a frequently recurring struggle for existence, it follows that any being—if it vary however slightly in any manner profitable to itself, under the complex and sometimes varying conditions of life—will have a better chance of surviving and thus be naturally selected. From the strong principle of inheritance, any selected variety will tend to propagate its new and modified form … from so simple a beginning endless forms most beautiful and most wonderful have been and are being **evolved**."

Judge Braswell Dean noted the writings of Darwin were somewhat racist with the full title of his famous 1859 volume, *On the Origin of Species by Means of Natural Selection or the Preservation of Favored Races in the Struggle for Life.*

Reaction to Darwin's book was a mix of reviews, satires, caricatures. One review likened it to "a creed of the men-from-monkeys idea form vestiges." His supporters began to float the idea of supernaturally guided evolution and the church of England considered "natural selection" as an instrument of God's design. Cleric Charles Kingsley saw it "as just as noble a conception of deity." What we have is the birth of evolution, racism, and doctrinal fallacy in denying God and his creation.

Colin Patterson, senior paleontologist and curator of the British Museum of Natural History (which has the greatest collection of fossils in the world), said, "There is no scientific evidence of transitional life forms" (*Hope for the World*, summer 2014, Dr. Dennis Cuddy, "The Theory of Evolution").

Life Is in the Blood

Adam's life was in the blood that Yahweh created, something unusual and mysterious.

Blood is found in the fowl of the air, the fish of the sea, in the smallest insect and the largest mammal. Angels do not have blood. Only through the shedding of blood can there be an acceptable sacrifice to Yahweh. Satan in his quest to be God, figured out how to use the DNA in blood to corrupt God's creation. He deceived mankind to shed blood to pagan gods, an abominable act. God commanded the people not to drink blood, and kosher practices were put in place. Satan turned ungodly people to drink blood, creating a bloodlust culture. The bloodlust is picked up in the final chapter of the Bible. In Revelation, we find a symbolic depiction of the woman riding the beast, holding a cup full of the blood of the saints, a cup full of abominations of which the ungodly nations drink from this cup.

Bone of My Bone

Adam did not have a mate. God said it is not good for man to be alone.

> *And the Lord God caused a deep sleep to fall upon Adam and he slept and he took one of his ribs and closed up the flesh instead thereof and the rib which the Lord God had taken from man, he made a woman.* (Genesis 2:21–23)

God took his rib and it became part of the woman's body from which God formed Eve from the earth as he did the animals and Adam. God brought Eve to Adam and he said, "*This is now bone of my bones and flesh of my flesh, she shall be called woman because she was taken out of man. They were both naked the man and his wife and they were not ashamed.*" Now keep this in mind, before they disobeyed God, they were not ashamed of their nakedness. When our sin is exposed, we are naked and ashamed before our all-knowing God.

Another unique aspect of the creation of man was that the female was part of the man as the man was a part of God. Both Adam and Eve came forth as fully grown adults. When they began procreation, they became one flesh. It is a bit curious that God told them to replenish the earth and subdue it. Does this mean that there were inhabitants on the earth before Adam? There is no biblical evidence that indicates people existed before Adam and Eve. The word *replenish* means "fill," and *subdue* means "to bring under subjection." Adam now had the responsibility to fill the earth with people. Adam had to subdue the earth; perhaps this means that the vegetation was growing, and he had to do some landscaping.

Adam had to name all the animals without the aid of a computer. Apparently, Adam had the ability to remember huge quantities of data. God designed the brain to accommodate unlimited knowledge. The scientific world has yet to figure out all there is to know about the complexities of the brain. Why do some autistic people with obvious disorders operate with extraordinary talents? Many possess mathematical genius, photographic memories, musical talent. Twins have a psychic connection.

Scientists are greatly baffled in attempting to understand the nature of man's essence, which encompasses his soul, consciousness, and intellect. It is said the soul has substance or weightiness. Those who possess extrasensory skills, intuition, or telepathy are unique, or perhaps it is a remnant of original man retained in each of us. Over millennia, these capabilities have been diluted or diminished to such an extent mankind is vaguely aware of their inherent primal abilities. All these attributes could be classified under the Father's attributes, which he transferred to Adam.

At the time of the incarnation, Jesus indirectly received the blood of his mother, Mary. Therefore, Jesus did not have her sin nature imputed to him. Human babies receive the blood type of the father. Herein, God the Father imputed his divine attributes to his son, who would be the unblemished perfect sacrifice acceptable to God for the remission of sins.

As you think on these things, factor in that God the Creator of all things has made us in his image. God is multifaceted, and he implemented a side or a portion of his image to his creation. For example, the cherubim could be classified as multifaceted, displaying the face of man and several animals also having wings and feet. We barely touch the level of omniscience that belongs to God, and that being said, God has programmed mankind to know that he has a Creator and has given man the ability to communicate with our Creator.

Mankind's time on earth is finite.

> *He knows our body and remembers we are dust. As for man, his days are as grass as a flower of the field, so he flourishes, the wind passes over it, and it is gone and the place shall be known no more.* (Psalm 103:14–16)

At the time of our death, our bodies deteriorate and return to the dust from which it was formed, but God remembers each soul.

Eternal Life Is in the Spirit

Angels are spiritual beings. Their essence emanates light. They are encompassed by God's celestial glory. Mankind was created a little lower than the angels and crowned with terrestrial glory. Adam and Eve in their purity emanated light. If this concept seems foreign, consider the body emanates heat, which can be seen by heating seeking equipment. The person appears to be a glowing ember.

Zechariah acknowledges that God stretched forth the heavens, laid the foundations of the earth, and formed the spirit of man within him (Zechariah 12:1).

The soul is the seat of our emotions, desires, personality. While we are alive, our brain houses our memories. When we die, our memories remain with our soul. In the depth of our soul, we desire God, and with our spirit, we seek God (Isaiah 26:9). He puts his spirit upon us as well as in us (Isaiah 42:1). Our spirit connects with the spirit of God. After we invite the Spirit of the living God to dwell in us, the Holy Spirit will guide us into all truth and show us things to come (John 16:13). When we plug into the spirit, we are connected to God's database of knowledge. Only through this connection can we access the storehouse of knowledge, allowing us to discern the things of God (1 Corinthians 2:14).

The work of the Holy Spirit is to empower the saints for our earthly ministry through his anointing. He brings wisdom, understanding, and discernment. There are various gifts of the spirit. Chapter 14 discusses the gifts of the Spirit. Our spoken word has impact on our thoughts and physical reality. We can speak blessings or curses and observe results. Speaking with the gift of tongues, the Spirit can move quickly. For instance, we speak over the dead, and they will live again. We speak over our situations, and the will of God is activated.

> *The Spirit also helps our infirmities for we know not what we should pray for as we ought but the Spirit itself makes intercession for us with groanings which cannot be uttered. He that searches the hearts knows what is the mind of the Spirit because he makes intercession for the saints according to the will of God.* (Romans 8:26–27)

Our eternal journey begins when our ethereal spirit and soul are released to inhabit eternity. The Word of God is powerful and able to divide between the soul and the spirit, and only God will determine if the soul of man will dwell in heaven or hell. Adam was made a living soul. Jesus was made a quickening Spirit and the source of eternal life (1 Corinthians 15:45).

Saint Paul helps us to understand the work of the Holy Spirit in the living and how the Spirit guides us to our eternal destination.

> *There is now no condemnation to them which are in Christ Jesus who walk not after the flesh but after the Spirit. For the law of the Spirit of life in Christ Jesus has made me free from the law of sin and death.* (Romans 8:1–2)

This passage tells the believers in Jesus that they are no longer condemned to eternal death in hell because they have crucified their sin nature and are striving for sanctification, holiness, righteousness through the things of the Spirit.

> *For to be carnally minded is death but to be spiritually minded is life and peace. The carnal mind is enmity against God … They that are in the flesh cannot please God.* (Romans 8:6)

True believers think on the things of God and truly desire to be obedient to the ways of God and avoid the lust of the flesh and the lure of the world.

> *They that are in the flesh cannot please God, but we are not in the flesh but in the Spirit and if so, the Spirit of God dwells in us and if any man have not the Spirit of Christ he is none of his.* (Romans 8:8–9)
>
> *If Christ be in us, the body is dead because of sin but the Spirit is life because of righteousness.* (Romans 8:10)
>
> *The Spirit of him that raised up Jesus from the dead dwell in us, he that raised up Christ from the dead will also quicken your mortal bodies by his Spirit that dwells in us.* (Romans 8:11)

As we meditate on these passages, we can begin to see how life is in the Spirit and how the believers will be taken from death into the presence of the Lord for eternity.

> *For as many are led by the Spirit of God, they are the sons of God … but we have received the Spirit of adoption whereby we cry, Abba Father.* (Romans 8:14)

On the Seventh-Day God Ended His Work and Rested

Thus the heavens and the earth were finished and all the host of them, and on the seventh day, God ended his work that he had made, and he rested on the seventh day from all his work, and he blessed the seventh day and sanctified it because in it he had rested from all that he created (Genesis 2:1). When Jesus finished his work on the earth and hung on the cross, he said, "It is finished." This is the same concept as God resting on the Sabbath, and not because of fatigue but because his work was finished.

The creation of the earth and all that is therein was created in six literal twenty-four-hour days.

Some proclaim each day was a thousand years in length. God separated the light from the dark and said the evening and the morning were the first day. That truth is very clear.

If each day was a thousand years long, perhaps one side of the planet would burn from the constant sun and the other side would freeze from lack of sun. A thousand years of vegetation growth would have made it hard for Adam to maintain the garden, especially without a lawn mower.

Ed F. Vallowe, *Biblical Mathematics*,[9] documents his research on the number 7 and its very important significance:

- The word *created* is used seven times in connection with God's creative work.
- In the book of Revelation, there are seven churches, seven seals, seven vials, seven trumpets judgments.
- There are seven dispensations, seven days, seven musical notes.
- Aaron and his sons were consecrated for seven days before their priestly ministry.
- Joshua marched around the City of Jericho seven times.
- There are seven Jewish feast days.
- The menorah has seven branches.
- Solomon built the first temple in seven years.

The seventh day is the Sabbath, which is our Saturday. God blessed it and sanctified it. The fourth commandment says, "Remember the Sabbath, and keep it holy." Therefore, throughout history, the Sabbath has been observed. Jesus kept the Sabbath. He is the Lord over the Sabbath, and he did not do away with it. The number 7 refers to completeness and spiritual perfection. We have entered into the seventh millennium, and the Lord will fulfill his promise to establish his millennial kingdom. We will soon enter into our rest.

---

9 Ed F. Vallowe, *Biblical Mathematics* (Forest Park, Georgia: Ed F. Vallowe Evangelistic Assoc., 1992)

Age of the Earth

Creation proponents believe that mankind's history is approximately six thousand years old. Commentaries based on the Septuagint range from 3754 BC to 5500 BC. Creationists estimate the creation of the earth and all that is therein began 4004 BC, and this time frame aligns with the Masoretic Text. James Ussher and Isaac Newton both accept this premise. We do not know how long Adam and Eve remained in the garden until they were expelled from it. From the fall of Adam to Noah's flood is approximately a thousand years bringing us to 3000 BC. After the flood to the time of Abraham is approximately a thousand years. Abraham was born around 2100 BC. From the time of the Jews in Egypt to the Exodus was 430 years. Jews entered the promised land around 1406 BC. King Saul began to reign 1050 BC. Babylonian captivity of the Jews 586 BC. Herod the Great begins to rule 37 BC. Jesus's birth estimated 3–2 BC. From creation to AD 1 is approximately four thousand years plus from AD 1 to AD 2000 is two thousand years totaling approximately six thousand years of human history. The dawning of the twenty-first century brings us to the seventh millennium or the next one thousand years of humanity.

Evolutionist Theories Vary on the Age of the Earth

James Hutton, scientists, AD 1795, said earth was eighty thousand years old. By 1900, they thought it was two billion years old. At the beginning of the twenty-first century, it jumped to 4.6 billion years old; and of late, they decided the earth came into existence with a big bang, twenty billion years ago. Dr. Harold G. White, a physicist and advanced propulsion engineer working at NASA, 2013, said the big bang took place 13.7 billion years ago. The problem in presenting various theories may arise from them equating the age of the earth with the age of the universe. It is humanly impossible to date the universe.

Starry Night Pro is an astronomy algorithm computer program with a week-by-week calendar, which can calculate the beginning of creation, the birth date and Crucifixion of Jesus, and can date lunar eclipse, full moon, planet alignment. It calculates the creation to be around six thousand years ago.

Evidence of a Young Earth

Research provides some clues as to the age of the earth based on the accumulation of moon dust. The lunar surface is exposed to direct sunlight and strong ultraviolet light, which can destroy the surface layers of exposed rock and reduce them to dust at a rate of ten-thousandths of an inch per year. But even this small amount during the age of the moon could be sufficient to form a layer several miles deep. Raymond A. Lyttleton, 1911–1995, a British mathematician and theoretical astronomer said that "astronauts from the USA found only a thin layer of dust."[10]

Carl Friedrich Gauss in 1835 measured the strength of the earth's magnetic field, and his calculations suggest the earth is less than ten thousand years old. His theory is that the magnetic field half life is calculated based on measurements taken from 1835 to 1965. His findings indicated the magnetic field has decayed about 10 percent over the last 150 years. If extrapolated back twenty thousand years, the joule heat generated would liquefy the earth. [11]

Mississippi River delta deposits approximately three hundred million cubic yards of sediment into the Gulf of Mexico each year. Analysis of the volume and rate of accumulation and dividing the weight of the sediment deposited annually, the age of the delta appears to be about four thousand years old.[12]

Examination of fossil DNA indicates they are less than ten thousand years old. DNA evidence would have disintegrated over 250 million years. The remains of Lucy in Africa were dated to be approximately six thousand years old.[13] Carbon-dating is not an accurate science. Some archeologists date the remains of dinosaurs to be millions of years old while footprints of man and dinosaurs were found to exist together in some regions. These great animals were created on the sixth day as was man.

Clifford L. Burdick found evidence of dinosaur and human footprints together in the Paluxy River. Someone asked if the dinosaurs were on Noah's ark, and we speculate, they may have been eaten by the giants and were extinct by the time of the flood.

Salinity of the oceans—the uranium, sodium, nickel, magnesium, silicon, potassium, copper, gold, molybdenum, and bicarbonate concentrations in the oceans—are much less than would be expected if these elements and compounds were being added to the oceans at the present rate for millions of years. Nitrates and uranium do not break down or recycle like salt.[14]

Radio halos—primordial polonium 218 has been found in mica and fluorite. Polonium 218 has a half-life of only three minutes. This is evidence of an instantaneous crystallization of the host granite concurrent with the formation of the polonium. This speaks to an instantaneous creation.[15]

---

[10] Chuck Missler, *Book of Genesis* (Coeur d'Alene, Idaho: Koinonia House, 2004) Video series

[11] Ibid

[12] Ibid

[13] Ibid

[14] Ibid Chuck Missler

[15] Ibid

The above analogies work toward providing an idea of the age of the earth. Scientists speculate the universe to be billions of years old based on the discovery of distant stars and other galaxies. The heavens and the host therein were created in eternity past, which is not measurable with quaint human technology. We established in our chapter 2 that the wisdom of God was before the world was called into existence and only God inhabits eternity past. There is no human ability to accurately comprehend the preexistent God or possess tools to enter into his domain.

Critical discoveries—(a) we have in our possession an integrated message system, (b) 66 separate records in the Bible, (c) written by forty different individuals over thousands of years, (d) the records show detail is anticipated by deliberate, skilled design and thus demonstrates that its origin is from outside of our domain.[16]

[16] Ibid

Chapter 4
The Rise and Fall of Lucifer

Chapter Overview

- Lucifer's Special Effects
- Angelic Features Replicated within Earth Species
- First War in Heaven
- Flawed Character
- Name Change
- Satan's Master Plan
    - Satan's Hierarchy
- God, Job, and Satan
- What Can Angels Do?
- The Ability of Evil Spirits
    - Possession
    - Binding
    - Vexing
    - Affect Weather
    - Attack
    - Manifestation
- Second War in Heaven

CHAPTER 4

THE RISE AND FALL OF LUCIFER

This chapter brings us to one of God's most unique creatures before the creation of man. God called his name Lucifer.

Lucifer's Special Effects

His name means light bearer, or angel of light. He was the anointed cherub who covers, son of the morning. He was created as the ultimate musician, "the workmanship of your tabrets and your pipes was prepared in you in the day that you were created." Pipes are wind instruments, and tabrets are percussion instruments. He possessed "viols," which are associated with string instruments, such as violin, Isaiah 14:11. His vocal range was deep base to high soprano as he led the heavenly choir in praise. Lucifer was covered in "every precious stone: sardis, topaz, diamond, beryl, onyx, jasper, sapphire, emerald, gold" (Ezekiel 28:13). He was part of God's original perfect creation. God exalted Lucifer to a lofty position.

Take a moment to visualize what Lucifer was and his appearance before his fall. Also, keep in mind he is of a spiritual nature not made of flesh and blood. It is difficult to comprehend and visualize this being. We allow our imagination to form an image of Lucifer. If we visualize him as human in appearance, that may be partially correct since he can transform himself. However, there exists the possibility that Lucifer may appear as a winged reptile or flying dragon more than as a human. This image may be appalling to some, but this is the creature that God created, and to him, he was beautiful. The Bible presents Lucifer as a winged reptile based on the description given in Revelation 12:3: "*There appeared another wonder in heaven and behold a* ***great red dragon*** *having seven heads, ten horns, seven crowns upon his head. And* ***his tail*** *drew the third part of the stars of heaven.* Over time, caricatures depicted Satan as a red half human half beast with horns and a tail. Some people categorize him as a mythological creature, and society certainly presents a plethora of strange creatures with the appearance of winged dragons, aliens, gargoyles, and all the monster features found on stone carvings, statues, art, and historical records. Fiction mirrors reality, and in this case, Satan is real.

Angelic Features Are Replicated within the Earthly Species

Cherubim or seraphim are described as having wings, animal features, bodies of colored hues, and appearing as giantlike humans. We arrive at this understanding because it is based on biblical facts. God created angels first, and these distinguishing features are replicated in the features of God's earthly creation. God created the living creatures before he formed man from the earth. Looking at the animal species, there are many that have horns and a tail. Some in the dinosaur family had horns, tails, and were classified within the reptilian species. Looking at a human, we have a nose, which is a small horn, and we have a shortened tailbone. We all share similar characteristics with birds, sea creatures, animals, and insects. God created each entity after its own kind, and within each specie, there are hundreds of variations. Herein we can understand that humans did not evolve from apes. However, as Charles Darwin observed the various species, he noticed that the white man was hairy; and viewing his own reflection, he saw his large head resembled the shape of an ape's head. From this observation, his theory of evolution took root.

The mind of God is incomprehensible to humankind. We can imagine the architect of the universe, sitting at his drawing board. When his designs were formed and made manifest, God said, "It was good." God designed complex and unique species. He could look at serpents, lizards, frogs, and bats as beautiful. The complexity and uniqueness of humankind was God's ultimate achievement. He created man in his likeness, or image. God incorporated into man some of the features of angels and the animal species. This may be the reason angels are fascinated with the creation of terrestrial beings.

First War in Heaven

The Bible tells us there was a war in heaven.

> *And there was war in heaven, Michael and his angels fought against the dragon and the dragon fought and his angels … and the great dragon was cast out that* ***old serpent called the Devil and Satan*** *which deceives the whole world.* (Revelation 12:7)

We believe this event occurred before the creation of man. This heavenly war was between angels, which resulted in Satan and one third of his fellow angels being expelled from a higher place in the heavenly realm. Scripture describes Satan as falling from heaven, and we may consider he and his angels fell into lower dimension outside of Earth's atmosphere. In this thought, Satan became the prince over the powers of the air. Satan and his followers would dwell in a place some call the second heaven.

Impact

The angelic rebellion had a devastating impact in the heavenly realm as well as on planet Earth. Satan and his fallen angels swarmed into Earth's atmosphere and impacted Earth. They were likened to fiery objects or similar to lightning heralding toward the earth. The impact would be tantamount to an asteroid strike equivalent to detonating a thousand nuclear bombs all at once and over time cooling fragments become ash. This supernatural phenomena caused a void and darkness to descend upon the earth. Before God spoke and called for the light to come forth was a time that cannot be determined.

Out of the millions of planets in the universe, why Earth? It is possible that Satan and his fallen angels targeted earth, causing a great cataclysmic event, rendering the earth to become void and dark because they knew God was going to form his creation upon the Earth. If this is the case, we have a hint that God had preordained the great red dragon as a watcher or protector over the coming reptilian species that would be created during the six days of creation.

After the creation of man, God placed Adam in the garden, and we find Satan lurking in the Garden of Eden. Satan had chosen to mingle with the serpent because it was subtle and appealing. Genesis 3:1, "*Now the serpent was more subtle than any beast of the field which the Lord God had made.*" The serpent was crafty, intelligent, alluring, and walked upward. Satan, having a reptilian makeup, could find it convenient to extend himself with the serpent—enhancing its ability to speak the words given it by Satan. The celestial DNA of Satan had intermingled with terrestrial DNA of the serpent. This interaction appears to be a possession of the serpent. However, Satan did not possess Adam or Eve; he tempted them into disobedience. The other fallen angels had witnessed this mingling, and some of them vowed amongst themselves to follow suit, leading to something sinister that would be carried out as told in Genesis 6. We explore this abomination along with the writings of Enoch on the subject of intermingling celestial entities with terrestrial beings to create hybrid species called as discussed chapter 7.

Flawed Character

Yahweh created all things good, perfect, excellent. God gave angels and man free will to choose to do good or choose to be disobedient. Yahweh had given Lucifer the ability to be holy, obedient, and faithful. He exercised his God-given right of free will. As the sin of pride dominated Lucifer, he began to influence other angels to join his dark kingdom, wherein he would plot to usurp the kingdom of God. God knew Satan's heart, and he permitted Satan to carry out his goal of destruction until the time God brings all evil to an end. Perhaps in God's domain, Satan had six days to accomplish his evil deeds. We hear the phrase, Satan knows his time is short. To humankind, it seems never ending over a period of six thousand years.

Ezekiel had a vision of Lucifer:

> *Thou has been in* ***Eden the garden of God,*** *every precious stone was your covering … workmanship of your tabrets and pipes … thou are the anointed cherub that covers and I have set thee so, you were upon the holy mountain of God and have walked up and down in the midst of the stones of fire [angels]. You were perfect in your ways from the day that you were created until* ***iniquity*** *was found in thee. Because of the multitude of your merchandise [beauty and superiority] they have filled the midst of you with* ***violence*** *and you have sinned, therefore I will cast you as profane out of the mountain of God* [in the sides of the north] *and I will destroy you, O covering cherub from the midst of the stones of fire* [angels]. *Your heart was lifted up because of your beauty* **[pride]** *you have corrupted your wisdom by reason of your brightness. I will cast you to the ground, I will lay you before kings that they may behold you. You have defiled your sanctuaries by the multitude of your iniquities, by the iniquity of your traffic, therefore will I bring forth a fire from the midst of thee, it shall devour thee and I will bring you to* ***ashes*** *upon the earth in the sight of all them that behold you. All that know you among the people will be astonished at you, you shall be a terror and never shall you be anymore.* (Ezekiel 28:13)

In exploring Ezekiel 28, we see the following:

- Lucifer is first seen as an exalted being in the midst of God and the other angels.
- God found iniquity, rebellion, pride, and disobedience within Satan's nature.
- It took a war to cast Satan out of the highest echelon of heaven wherein God resides
- It tells us in a future second war, Satan will be cast out upon the earth for all to see.

- He was so filled with rage that he and his followers caused chaos in heaven and on earth. In Luke 10:18, Jesus said, "I beheld Satan as lightning fall from heaven"; this event occurred before man was created.
- Satan had been in the Garden of Eden before Adam and Eve. He checked out the lay of the land where God would place his ultimate creation.
- He is a formidable foe against mankind.
- Eventually, God would diminish his attributes and his exalted position. His privilege to come before God in the midst of the holy angels would be limited.
- His light and beauty would be dimmed, his persona changed, and the fire within him would slowly be extinguished.

Name Change

Lucifer began to be referred to as Satan. In Hebrew, he is Helel or Hilail, meaning "bright one and crescent moon." 2 Corinthians 6:15, Paul calls Satan Belial. In Greek, Belial is associated with the number 666. He is also known as the serpent, dragon, devil, Beelzebub, Lord of the Flies, deceiver, Father of Lies, Accuser of the Brethren, Ruler of this World, Prince of the Power of the Air, God of This Age.

Satan's Master Plan

Satan has knowledge of time, space, and our earthly domain. Since he can straddle between dimensions, he was able to plan his move for the destruction of God's creation, utilizing the levels of corruption in his hierarchy of principalities, powers, rulers of darkness, spiritual wickedness in high places, thrones, and dominions. Satan's master plan is exposed:

> *For you have said in your heart, I will ascend into heaven, I will exalt my throne above the stars of God, I will sit also upon the mount of the congregation in the* ***side of the north.*** *I will ascend above the heights of the clouds, I will be like the most High.* (Isaiah 14:13–14)

In our literal galaxy, we are surrounded on three sides by bands of star clusters, and there is an open space in the northern side, suggesting God's domain, of which Satan desired to control.

The chessboard was set up. The players are God and Satan. Satan's strategy is in place, and as seeds grow, he believes his plans will come to fruition. Satan would allow for the corruption of the human genome in an attempt to render mankind unredeemable. However, God had a better strategy in place: he would come himself to redeem mankind.

Satan would try to prevent the birth of Jesus by allowing Herod to kill the baby boys. He would plot the Crucifixion and death of Jesus, believing that would put an end to the kingdom of God being fulfilled. Satan would deceive all of mankind until the time of the end. The scriptures confirm Satan during the final years of the tribulation period desperately trying to kill Israel.

> *She* [Israel] *is nourished for a time and times and half time from the* ***face of the serpent.*** (Revelation 12:14)

Obviously, Satan did not know or anticipate what God would do to hinder his plans. As we look back through the biblical record, we can know what God did do, and we have a general understanding of what God plans to do as future events unfold. God is sovereign and still in control. In his final station, Satan will be cast out upon the earth. The fire in the midst of Satan will be diminished, and he will be reduced to ashes, metaphorically. He will no longer be a terror. He will stand before Jesus, and he will be condemned to spend one thousand years in the bottomless pit.

Satan is an eternal spirit who has abilities that humans do not possess. These angelic entities have supernatural power; they have the ability to integrate with elements of air, earth, animals, and mankind. From the fall to the <u>present time</u>, Satan and his angels occupy a spiritual dimension beyond human visibility. This dimension is lower than God's temple in the heavens. In Ezekiel 28, Satan is cast out of <u>the mountain of God, or the north side</u> of heaven. Satan has command of a part of the heavens where he established a hierarchy composed of principalities, powers, rulers of darkness, and spiritual wickedness in high places.

<u>Satan's Hierarchy</u>

Legions of angels decided to follow Satan in his rebellion against God.

> *For I have seen the angels of punishment going and preparing all the instruments for Satan.* (Enoch 53:3)
>
> *For we wrestle not against flesh and blood but against principalities, against powers, against the rulers of darkness of this world, against spiritual wickedness in high places.* (Ephesians 6:12)

Through his hierarchy, Satan commands legions of evil angels, evil spirits, and evil people who fight against all things holy. His tendrils have infected governments, religions, societies reaching into every facet of humanity and nature. Saint Paul said we are not fighting against flesh and blood, and our weapons must be spiritual for the pulling down of strongholds. Satan's hierarchy is as follows:

Principalities of the air are princes over other angels and demons. Satan gives his minions authority over dominions, kingdoms, nations.

Powers and spiritual wickedness in high places are spiritual entities existing in an unseen world in the heavens that influence world governments, religions, and society.

Rulers of darkness, princes of darkness, rule over mankind in whom darkness and evil becomes manifested through the wicked deeds of men.

Emphatically stated, Satan is the god of this world. He rules over his hierarchy, and he influences mankind. Ephesians 2:2, "*Wherein in time past you walked according to the course of this world, according to the* ***prince*** *of the* ***power*** *of the* ***air****, the* ***spirit*** *that now works in children of disobedience.*" Prince is a ruler, commander, chief, or leader. Power is given to influence. Air is the atmospheric region or dimension where they exist. Evil spirits are vicious enemies of humankind coming for the purpose to torment, deceive, and destroy.

Ezekiel 28:1, the king of Tyre was influenced by Satan. The kings' allegiance to Satan was rewarded with wealth through trade. The king of Tyre exalted himself to be god, as did Satan. Evil spirits are the **powers of darkness** as indicated in Luke 22:53—when Judas betrays Jesus and Jesus said to him, "This is your hour and the **power of darkness**," meaning Satan's powerful attempt was to cut off the Messiah from the land and remove Satan and his evil angels from God's future judgment.

The writer of Romans presents an interesting summary of wickedness applicable to fallen angels and evil men. Roman 1:21–32, "*When they knew God, they glorified him not as God neither were thankful but became vain in their imagination and their foolish heart was darkened, professing themselves to be wise, they became fools.*" Both angels and mankind knew God, but being on a downward spiral into sin, they rejected God. There is no limit to what their evil imaginations can conjure, and they became fools. *They changed the glory of the incorruptible God into images made like corruptible man, birds, beasts, and creeping things.* They replaced the one true God with images made of stone or wood, formed by the hand of man. The fallen angels were seen as gods. Mankind worshipped their images, and they became the false gods of old, such as, Zeus or Diana. In Colossians 2:18, "Let no man trick you into worshipping angels," looking into the realm of angels and things you do not understand.

The universal war is between God and his holy angels versus Satan and his evil angels. To the victor is a priceless prize: the soul of mankind. God has allowed Satan to have the power of death and the title deed to earth. Satan will continue to fill up the caverns of hell with the souls of the unsaved wicked. The battle for the soul is played out in the following record.

God, Satan, and Job

Let us look at the interaction between God, Satan, and Job. In the book of Job 1:1, Job was from the region of Ur in Mesopotamia as was Abraham. We can place a maker in time around the year 2000 BC. The scripture lets us know that Job was a godly man and greatly blessed of God. Coming to verse 6, we are introduced to an unusual encounter between God and Satan:

> *Now there was a day when the sons of God came to present themselves before the Lord and Satan came also among them. The Lord said to Satan, where comes you? Then Satan answered the Lord and said from going to and fro in the earth and from walking up and down in it.*

There are a few interesting things we should consider:

- Who was present to record this conversation?
- Angels are called sons of God as in Genesis 6.
- Satan came into the presence of God with the other angels.
- Satan caused rebellion, and in his fallen state, God allows him to converse with him.
- Apparently, the wrath of God against Satan was temporary, and his love for him was toward forgiveness or at least presented him with an opportunity to repent.
- God also allows fallen, sinful mankind to come before him for repentance.
- Angels have the ability to traverse between the heavenly domain and earth.
- God is all-knowing but questioned Satan perhaps to give him the opportunity to lie or tell the truth.

> *And the Lord said to Satan, have you considered my servant Job that there is none like him in the earth a perfect and upright man one that fears God and avoids evil.* (Job 1:8)

- God initiates the conversation with Satan.
- We believe God may have selected Job as a godly example to chastise Satan, reminding him that he should be holy, perfect, upright, and avoid evil

> *Then Satan answered the Lord and said, does Job fear God for nought* [nothing]? (Job 1:9)

Has not God made a hedge about him and his house and all that he has on every side?

You have blessed him, but if you put forth your hand now and take what you have blessed him with, he will curse you to your face. God gave Satan power over all that Job had: his children, servants, and animals.

- Satan does not humble himself and repent but challenges God by pointing out that Job fears God because of his material blessings.
- Satan knows that God has placed a hedge of protection around Job and uses that reason to tell God that if it is removed, then Job would curse God.
- Only with God's permission could Satan attack Job.

Job 1:20–22, then Job arose and tore his clothes and shaved his head and fell down upon the ground and worshipped saying, *"Naked came I out of my mother's womb and naked will I return there, the Lord gave and the Lord has taken away, blessed be the name of the Lord." In all this, Job sinned not nor charged God foolishly."*

- First, God knew that Satan would not repent even after proving him wrong.
- Job shows Satan up by accepting this attack by worshipping God and acknowledging God is our provider.

The scriptures tell us that Satan came before God again. Job 2:1–3 is exactly the same as the first event, except God tells Satan … *"And still Job holds fast his integrity although you moved me against him to destroy him without cause."* Satan smote Job with boils, and his wife said, "Do you still retain your integrity? Curse God and die."

- Again God holds up Job in comparison, showing Satan lacks integrity.
- Here we see that Satan speaks through Job's wife, using the words he said before God, *integrity* and *curse God.*

Once again, Job proves himself faithful before God and acknowledges that we receive good from God and evil will also come. This ancient lesson is timeless. It lets us know that Satan has been given authority to test us, bring affliction and suffering. Job said, "Though you slay me, I will trust you." Jesus tells us, we will have trials and tribulations, but he would deliver us from them all. Bad things happen to good people, and throughout Jobs' testimony, he proclaims his righteousness and good deeds—giving to the needy, helping the widows, etc. Was Job righteous in his own eyes? Are we righteous in our own eyes? In God's eyes, all of our righteousness is as filthy rags.

There are other interesting things we should consider in the final chapters in the book of Job. First we know that Job had four friends to visit him. Three of the elders engaged Job in regard to why these terrible things have come upon him and question him if he had sinned. In chapter 32, the fourth man speaks after the first three have exhausted their conversations. His name is Elihu. We see he is annoyed with Job because he spent a great deal of time justifying himself. He is annoyed with the other three men because they spent their time in condemnation of Job.

Elihu waited out of respect for the elders to finish, and he begins by stating, "*I am young and you are very old.*" Elihu says, "Because of your combined ages, you should teach wisdom and from the spirit of God that indwells man, the Holy Spirit gives understanding. But you great, old men are not always wise and lack understanding." Elihu began to speak with authority, and they were amazed and spoke no more. He told them he was so filled with the spirit that if he did not speak, he would burst. Chapter 33—he will speak to them under the anointing. His words will be upright from his heart, and he will speak knowledge from the inspiration of the Holy Spirit. Elihu begins by reminding Job of his complaints: "I am clean without transgression, I am innocent, there is no iniquity in me, yet God counted me his enemy, what man is like me who drinks up scorning like water, who goes in company with the workers of iniquity, God said it profits a man nothing that he should delight himself with God." Then Elihu tells Job, "In this, you are not just."

God is greater than man, and he needs not give an account to any regarding his matters. God speaks one or twice, and man perceives it not. Elihu begins to site many instances of God's involvement with humankind. In the end, God wants man to confess he has sinned and perverted that which was right, and then God will deliver his soul from hell. Chapter 34, Elihu defends God. He tells Job he has spoken without knowledge and his words were without wisdom, like that of wicked men. He tells Job he thinks his righteousness is more than God's. Chapter 37, Elihu continues to exalt God and his greatness and finally tells Job to stand still and consider the wonderful works of God.

Chapter 38, God himself speaks to Job out of the whirlwind. God let Job know his error was to contend with the Almighty, instruct and reprove him. Further, God said, "Will you also disannul my judgment and condemn me so that you may be righteous?" He asks Job where was he when he created all things and, in summary, can Job be God.

Chapter 40, God tells Job to "gird up your loins like a man." Job repents by acknowledging he is vile. He admits that God can do everything and no thought can be withheld from Him. He admits that he did not understand and "the things of God are too wonderful for me, which I did not know." He repents in dust and ashes.

Chapter 42, God deals with Job's friends Eliphaz, Bildad, and Zophar. God said, "My wrath is against you because you have not spoken of me the thing that is right as my servant Job. Go and sacrifice before Job, and he will pray for you. From him will I accept, lest I deal with you after your folly." Before God restores all things to Job, God gave an overview of creation—including the largest of animals, Behemoth. God also describes one who may be Satan, in the character of Leviathan.

The Behemoth was large like a dinosaur. There are no supernatural overtones applied to Behemoth; however, in chapter 41, God begins to speak of Leviathan. As we read through this chapter, we see unusual characteristics:

- He cannot be snared with a hook.
- He can speak.
- He can reason.
- His shell is tough; his scales are his pride; they are fitted together tight and cannot be penetrated.
- His heart is hard as a stone.
- Iron and brass are as straw or wood to him.
- His eyes shine with as morning light.
- Out of his mouth goes forth fire; out of his nose goes smoke.
- He is pleasant to look at.
- He is powerful; he cannot be wounded with a weapon.
- He can cause the deep to boil.
- There is none on earth like him.
- He has a connection with principalities and things in high places.
- He is king over all the children of pride and sin.

What Can Angels Do?

Our understanding of spiritual beings is limited. What we do know is presented through searching the scriptures, personal accounts, and extrabiblical commentaries. In general, angels do not possess animals or humans. From research, it appears that evil spirits or demons have the ability to possess entities.

It is rare to find a scriptural reference wherein angels possess people. We found references in Luke 22:3, "*Then entered Satan into Judas Iscariot …*" and John 13:27, "*And after the sop Satan entered into Judas.*" Whether this is a possession or a temptation, Judas had succumbed to temptation and betrayed Jesus. In the account of Satan's attack on Job, he does not possess Job. Satan did not possess Jesus when he tempted him in the wilderness for forty days. The future Antichrist will be empowered by Satan. After the Antichrist is killed, there may be a possibility that Satan will physically possess him while he is dead and resurrect him back to life.

Third-century philosophers knew: "The immense space which lies between earth and heaven has inhabitants far nobler than any earthly creatures … The air is full of innumerable multitudes of beings …" (Plato).

<u>Angels Can Engage with or Battle Other Angels</u>

Another example of Satan's authority over the powers of the air is Daniel 10:13 ... Daniel's prayers had been held up for twenty-one days by the prince of the kingdom of Persia (a spiritual entity). Angel Gabriel required assistance from Angel Michael.

<u>Appearances.</u>

Angels can manifest themselves in different forms. They can cross over into our physical dimension. We are told in Hebrews 13:2: "*Be not forgetful to entertain strangers for thereby some have entertained angels unawares.*" The writer of Hebrews is speaking about visits from holy angels but who can discern between a holy or evil angelic visitation? In Psalm 78:49, in God's indignation and wrath, he sent <u>evil angels</u> among them. Satan himself appeared to Jesus and tempted him.

Holy angels bring messages of good tidings as well as warnings. It could be given in a vision, dream, or appearance. Good angels can help people in times of tragedy, but God receives the glory. Evil angels and demons can also come in a vision or dream. They can cloak themselves as benevolent. They come to bring a message of deception contrary to the Bible. For instance, the founder of Mormonism was visited by the angel Moroni, who brought to him a message of deception, and the false religion of Mormonism took root.

Revelation 9:14–15 foretells of four angels bound in the Euphrates will be released and kill one third of mankind. Are these the fallen angels that were bound before the flood? They influence evil men to carry out this slaughter for one year, one month, one day, and one hour.

As we learn more about these spiritual beings, take a moment to be encouraged and not fear.

> *Who shall separate us from the love of Christ? ... Neither death, nor life, nor **angels, nor principalities, nor powers**, nor things present, nor things to come, not height, not depth, not any other **creature*** (hybrids) *shall be able to separate us from the love of God which is in Christ Jesus our Lord.* (Romans 8:35, 38–39)

The Ability of Evil Spirits

Shortly before the flood event according to the writings of Enoch, the fallen angels were confined under the earth for their sin. The offspring of the fallen angels were giants, hybrids, or Nephilim, and their physical bodies drowned in the flood, but their spirits continued to exist as evil spirits/demons/devils invisible and given permission to torment mankind. They were given the ability to flit in and out of Earth's dimension and are capable of changing forms.

The following discussion is not about the souls or spirits of dead humans. In the book of Job, he makes the distinction that the "spirit of the dead return no more" and is a reference to the spirits of the nonredeemable hybrids created by the fallen angels and earth women.

Evil Spirits Can Possess Humans

A demonic possession is probably the most destructive and devastating of all attacks by evil spirits. People under the influence of a demonic spirit exhibit similar behavior. When a possession takes place, the human may exhibit maniacal behavior, exceptional strength, incoherent, speaking with a demonic voice, causing physical harm to themselves or others, and eating flesh or drinking blood. They have the tendency to commit horrible atrocities. These actions could support evidence these monsters walk amongst us clothed in human form but are demons hiding within. We hear current reports regarding Islamic terrorists group, ISIS burning people alive, crucifying, beheadings, torture, rape of men, women, and children. They have no mercy. These reports are worldwide and may be a sign of the end of the age when demonic activity will increase as predicted in the book of Revelation. We discuss this phenomena in chapter 16.

Many people have never seen a demonic spirit. Others have seen fleeting shadows or sense their presence. Some animals can see spirits, which are invisible to humans. Those who have had near-death experiences say they have seen demons in hell. In our minds, we have a preconceived image of monsters and demons; and for the most part, these images have been implanted into our subconscious by Hollywood. The biblical scriptures do not portray images of monsters roaming the earth with the exception of giants who were human like. Job 41:1 briefly mentions Leviathan, a large fire-breathing creature. Jesus cast out a legion of demons, but he did not describe their appearance. The descriptions given of monsters in the book of Revelation are symbolic.

The Bible relates numerous accounts of demonic possession. How does a possession occur? Those who meditate for the purpose of communicating with spirits provide a portal for visitation and demonic activity. Spiritual possession is directed through the mind. Some claim that messages have been received directly from an evil entity. This message may stir up the imagination to act out some ungodly deed. Many times we hear people say "The devil made me do it," or "I heard voices."

People who delve into the occult, witchcraft, voodoo, and Eastern practices such as yoga, necromancy, or channeling spirits may resort to consuming mind-altering drugs, chanting, meditating, conducting rituals to obtain an altered state—therein resulting in opening their subconscious mind to demonic influence. Those who practice the black arts call themselves clairvoyant, divinators, readers, or psychics. Props such as tea leaves, tarot cards, candles, incense, and globes can be used to fabricate information about a person or place. A successful contact with the other side is welcomed, and they tout their psychic phenomena as gifts.

Those who profess extrasensory perception, precognition, remote viewing, telekinesis may be aided by an invisible presence. Some claim to have the ability to move objects. Edgar Cacey, a seer, dubbed the Sleeping Prophet, claimed to receive supernatural insight into a person's illness while asleep and someone wrote down what he said. Remote viewers are those who claim to be able to describe a scene some distance away in which they are not physically present. Ingo Swann professed to be a remote viewer and a psychic. He wrote a book *The Question of Extraterrestrials and Human Telepathy*, wherein he states that he was contacted by nonhuman entities in the guise of space aliens.

Other people who may not knowingly invite evil spirits can be possessed because they are unsaved and have not the indwelling of the Holy Spirit. These evil spirits are malevolent and malicious, having the ability to seduce (appearing benevolent), vex, injure, or possess humans and other creatures. It has been recorded that people who are attacked in their sleep by demons may awaken to find physical evidence of the occurrence, such as scratches or teeth marks in the flesh.

Academia and religious bodies have studied demonic possession and the exorcising of demons.

We reference the work of Dr. Patrick McNamara, Boston University School of Medicine and author of *The Science and Solution of Those Frightening Visions During Sleep*, 2008. Dr. McNamara conducted clinical research into dreams and nightmares. He associates nightmares with the presence of demonic spirits and claimed spirit possession is much more common than most people think. "Nightmares very often involve supernatural characters … such as monsters, creatures, demons, scary animals that attack or target the dreamer in some way. The person escapes unscathed only if it refuses to look at or engage with the entity. When the person engages the monster, all kinds of ill effects ensue, specifically demonic or spirit possession." When a Christian is attacked, we call on the name of Jesus and rebuke it in his name.

In our studies, we rely on the biblical record of demonic activities to authenticate secular reports. The Bible has many references of demonic possession and we site several:

Then was brought unto Jesus one possessed with a devil, blind and dumb, and he healed him insomuch that the blind and dumb both spoke and saw. Matthew 12:22

Luke 11:14 … Jesus cast out a devil, and it was dumb. And it came to pass; when the devil left him, the dumb man spoke. When the unclean spirit is gone out of a man, the spirit walks through dry places, seeking rest, and finding none, returns to the host he left and finds it clean and brings seven other spirits more wicked than itself.

Mark 5:1 ... Jesus and his disciples came to the country of the Gadarenes ... *There met him out of the tombs a man with an unclean spirit. He lived among the tombs, and no one could bind him with chains because he would break them off. No man could tame him, and always night and day, he was in the mountains and the tombs, crying and cutting himself with stones. When he saw Jesus, he ran and worshipped him and cried with a loud voice, saying, "What have I to do with thee, Jesus the Son of the Most High God? I adjure you by God that you not torment me." Jesus said, "Come out of the man, you unclean spirit. What is your name?" and the spirit answered, "My name is Legion for we are many."*

Following is a summary of evil spirits/demonic abilities:

- Evil spirit can cause inability to speak.
- It can bring multiple spirits to possess one person.
- They are not hindered by space or physicality.
- Demons can render supernatural strength.
- Demons can inflict pain and cause self-injury.
- The demons could see Jesus coming, and they knew him to be God the Son.
- The demons could have a conversation.
- They knew that one day they would be bound in hell.

Mark 1:23-27 ... A man in the synagogue with an unclean spirit cried out, "*Let us alone, what have we to do with thee Jesus of Nazareth, are you come to destroy us, I know who you are, the Holy one of God.*" Jesus commanded the spirit to hold their peace and come out him. The spirit tore the man and cried with a loud voice and came out of him. The witnesses were amazed and asked, "What is this? Is it a new doctrine?" With authority, Jesus commanded the unclean spirits, and they obeyed. Jesus is God, and he had told them, "The kingdom of God is among you." Jesus is more powerful than demons.

In Luke 11:14. . . Jesus cast out a spirit of muteness. The spirit spoke after it was loosed. The observing crowds said, "Jesus cast out the devil through Beelzebub, chief of the devils." Jesus said, "If Satan be divided against himself, how shall his kingdom stand?" Jesus knew that Satan's hierarchy would stand until the end of the age. He let them know that what they had witnessed was of God and that the kingdom of God has come.

In the writings of Italian Franciscan theologian and exorcist Sudovico Maria Sinistrari (1622–1701) on sexual sin with demons records in his *De daemonialitate, et incubis et succubis* that incubi a demon appearing as male and succubi a demon in female form could copulate with humans. Saint Cecilia said to Valerian, "There is a secret, Valerian, I wish to tell you, I have as a lover an angel of God who jealously guards my body." [17] She misunderstands it is not an angel but a demon.

Augustine, in his classic, *De Civiatete De* (City of God), spoke of entities as forest sylvans and fauns, which are incubus "made wicked assaults upon women and satisfied their lust upon them and that certain devils called duses by the Gauls are constantly attempting and effecting this impurity is so generally affirmed, that it were impudent to deny it." [18]

Jesus empowered his twelve disciples with the Holy Spirit to be able to cast out unclean spirits. Believers can also call on the name of Jesus, and the demons will flee.

> *And when he had called unto him his twelve disciples, he gave them power against unclean spirits to cast them out and to heal all manner of sickness and all manner of disease.* (Matthew 10:1)

Demon possession or oppression can bring physical ailments as well as mental disability. Early Bible scholars and latter-day scientists have learned that possession can alter a person's DNA, causing antisocial or criminal behavior. It also may contribute to genetic abnormalities at birth, such as children born with a turtle-like shell growing on their back or people growing limbs that look like tree branches. Altering human DNA may be the cause of these deformities. Chapter 7 explains the connection between fallen angels, evil spirits, and demonic possession.

Evil Spirits Can Possess Animals

Mark 5:11–13 … Jesus cast out the legion of demons from the man in Gadarenes, and he commanded the demons to enter into swine … and the unclean spirits went out and entered into the swine, and the herd ran violently down a steep place into the sea; around two thousand were drowned. The first account of animal possession is Satan and the snake in the Garden of Eden.

Evil Spirits Can Bind

Luke 13:11–17 … A woman was bound by Satan with a spirit of infirmity for eighteen years. Jesus saw her, called her to him, spoke to her, "Woman thou are loosed from your infirmity," laid hands on her, and she was immediately healed. Evil spirits themselves can be bound with chains of darkness.

---

[17] Chris Putnam & Tom Horn, *Exo Vaticana* (Crane, MO: Defender Publishers, 2013) p 529

[18] Ibid

Evil Spirits Can Torment or Vex

They can bring fear, infirmity, depression, suicidal thoughts, or cause perversion. Vexation is not a possession but an external annoyance, such as noise, movement, touching, can cause temporary immobility.

> *And they that were vexed with unclean spirits were healed.* (Luke 6:18)
>
> *There came a multitude … bringing sick folks and them which were vexed with unclean spirits and they were healed everyone.* (Acts 5:16)
>
> *A woman of Canaan came … and cried unto him, Have mercy on me, O Lord, thou son of David, my daughter is grievously vexed with a devil.* (Matthew 15:22)

Spirits Affect Weather

Mark 4:39 … Jesus rebukes the wind (stirred up by evil spirits). Twenty-first century governments of the world have advanced technology to control or manipulate weather with the help of satanic technology.

Evil Spirits Attack Humans

The Bible gives us an account of two men who attempted to cast unclean spirits from a person using the name of Jesus. The evil spirit spoke to them, left the possessed man, and attacked them, tearing them to shreds (Acts 19:13–16). In the book of Revelation, a spiritual element will be released from out of the earth and manifest their ability to attack humans. The scriptures describe them as a hoard of locust that stings mankind.

Manifestations

Evil spirits can appear as shadows, sulfuric smell, room temperature changes, can hit or move objects, make sounds, bite or scratch people, and at times appear as monsters.

What are the weapons of our warfare against unseen forces of evil?

> *Finally my brethren, be strong in the Lord and in the power of his might. Put on the whole armor of God that you may be able to stand against the wiles of the devil. For we wrestle not against flesh and blood but against principalities, against powers, against the rulers of the darkness of this world, against spiritual wickedness in high places. Wherefore take unto you the whole armor of God that you may be able to withstand in the evil day and having done all, to stand. Stand therefore, having your loins girt about with truth and having on the*

> *breast place of righteousness, and your feet shod with the preparation of the gospel of peace, above all taking the shield of faith, wherein you will be able to quench all the fiery darts of the wicked, take the helmet of salvation and the sword of the Spirit which is the Word of God, praying always with all prayer and supplication in the Spirit and watching there to with all perseverance and supplication for all saints.* (Ephesians 6:10)

Believers in the one true God are told to protect themselves by putting on the armor of God. Put on the helmet of salvation to protect our mind from seducing spirits and spiritual attacks. The sword is the Word of God. We must learn to use the Word against the enemy. Use the shield of faith to deflect the attacks of the enemy. As in any battle, stand our ground against the enemy. If we are killed by the enemy, we will be with the Lord, and great is our reward for dying for our Lord and Savior.

Demonic possession has been ongoing from the time of the flood and will continue until the end of the tribulation period when Jesus returns and puts down all wickedness. At the Second Coming, Jesus the Word is seen riding a white horse with a two-edged sword in his mouth. Jesus has given to the believers the sword of his Word.

> *For the Word of God is quick and powerful, sharper than a two-edged sword, piercing even to the dividing asunder of soul and spirit and joints and marrow and is a discerner of the thoughts and intents of the heart.* (Hebrews 4:12)

A Second War in Heaven

Planet Earth is a battleground between the forces of good and evil. Mankind would be completely destroyed by the powers of evil if God had not leveled the playing field by preparing his people for battle.

The first heavenly war was recorded in Ezekiel 28. There will be another war in heaven foretold in Revelation:

> *And there was war in heaven, Michael and his angels fought against the dragon and the dragon fought and his angels and they prevailed not, neither was their place found anymore in heaven. And the great dragon was cast out, that old serpent, called the devil and Satan which deceives the whole world. He was cast out into the earth and his angels were cast out with him.* Revelation 12:7

In this passage we are to understand Satan and his angels are permanently cast out of the heavens to the earth. His invisibility will be removed; he will be seen as he really is—like a serpent, dragon, reptile; and finally, Satan and his angels will be cast into the lake of fire.

The battle lines were drawn eons ago. Satan took on Yahweh. He was permitted of God to be tested to its bitter end from his fall in eternity past to his six thousand years of reigning terror upon the earth, until he is brought down into the abyss for one thousand years. At the end of this time, Satan will be released. We ask, Why? God has told us that he will use evil to judge those who are disobedient. People born during the thousand-year millennial reign will need to be tested before they are allowed to enter into eternity.

From where does evil originate? God answers,

> *I am the Lord and there is none else, there is no God beside me. I strengthened thee though you had not known me. That they may know from the rising of the sun from the west that there is none beside me … I form the light and create darkness, I make peace and create evil, I the Lord do all these things.* Isaiah 45:5-7

In chapter 5, we see the thread of evil as it binds Adam and Eve.

Chapter 5
The Fall of Adam and Eve

Chapter Overview

Chapter 5

The Fall of Adam and Eve

The Garden of Eden

Angels have knowledge that transcends our finite understanding of ourselves and our universe. They were created eons before God created Adam and Eve. The angels witnessed creation. They saw father God preparing good gifts for his soon to be children. Yahweh gave Adam and Eve his love and their life. He placed them in a beautiful, serene environment. The climate was comfortable in that they had no clothes. They had no shelter because it did not rain or snow. Fruit, vegetables, herbs were their healthy sustenance. There were no carnivorous pests to bite them, so they did not require repellants. The animals were meek and need not be feared.

Scripture speaks of the four corners of the earth—being, north, south, east, west, and God created a delightful garden in the eastern area of Eden. *Eden* means "delight." The circumference of the earth is around twenty-five thousand miles, and Eden was situated in the center of the world between Assyria and Africa. The land of Canaan, present-day Israel, is in the center of the Garden of Eden.

God refers to this elevated region as his holy mountain called Mount Zion.

God's throne is thought to be on a heavenly mountain in the north side of the universe. In Jerusalem, there are historical mountain ranges. Several are Mount Ophel, Mount of Olives, Mount Nebo, Mount Zion, and Mount Moriah. God placed a marker in the center of Eden, and we believe this is Mount Moriah, upon which Abraham was going to sacrifice Isaac. It is the site of the first and second temples in Jerusalem. In Psalm 87:1–2, "*God's foundation is in the holy mountains. The Lord loves the gates of Zion more than all the dwellings of Jacob. Glorious things are spoken of these, O city of God.*"

It is said that Eden mirrors the dimensions of the future heavenly Jerusalem that will be established in Israel during the millennial reign. Zechariah 8:3, "*Thus said the Lord, I am returned unto Zion and will dwell in the midst of Jerusalem and Jerusalem shall be called a city of truth and the mountain of the Lord of Hosts, the holy mountain.*"

Genesis 2 (summarized). The Lord God planted a garden eastward in Eden. A river went out of Eden to water the garden, and then it parted and became four tributaries. One is called Pishon, which encompassed Havilah (Arabia) where there is gold, bdellium, and onyx. The second river is Gihon (Nile), and it encompassed the whole land of Ethiopia, and its head waters flow through Jerusalem under the Temple Mount. The third river is Hiddekel (Tigris), flowed toward the east of Assyria, and the fourth river is the Euphrates in the region of Shinar, Mesopotamia. These four rivers give us markers as to where God established the boundaries of the garden. Some believe it was located in Babylon (Iraq) because on a map, we see the Euphrates and Tigris Rivers. The river begins east of Turkey and flows south for 1,700 miles and empties into the Persian Gulf. It is the main source of water for Syria and Iraq. The boundaries of Eden may have been 1,500 square miles, from Iraq to Africa. If this is the case, the following theories may have some credence.

Some believe the birthplace of man was located in Africa. The Gihon, which is Egyptian for Nile, flows from Egypt, Sudan, to Ethiopia. Nile is the Greek name for the river, which means "arises from the east," which would correlate with it beginning in Mesopotamia, flowing through Canaan into Africa. Archeologists found a bone fossil, dated it to be thirty thousand years old in Africa, named it Lucy, and concluded this is Eden. Why not call her Eve? Lucy was more like a chimpanzee than a human. However, they do not factor in that during the flood monuments, bones, and artifacts were displaced by the ferocity of the flood waters.

The Pishon River was in *Havilah* (Hebrew word, means "sandy and gold"), which is Arabia and is now a dry riverbed under sand. In the *Biblical Archeological Review* 1996, the article showed satellite images of the area, indicated jagged seams of limestone rock that was part of a river channel now hidden by sand dunes. In 1932, a gold mine was discovered and thought to be King Solomon's mines (1 King 9:26). In Genesis 10:7, there is mention of the tribe of Shemites and Hamites, of which Solomon was descendant of Shem and Queen of Sheba from the descendants of Ham. Today that mine produces five tons of gold per year and is located adjacent to the dry riverbed.

Genesis 2:7–9, God had formed man from the earth. God knew Adam needed something to eat, and out of the ground God made to grow every tree that is pleasant to the sight and good for food. In this same sentence, we see a casual mention that God also placed the tree of life and the tree of the knowledge of good and evil in the garden.

Before the serpent enters the scene, Father God continued a relationship with Adam. He talked with Adam, and when we talk back to God, we call this prayer, communion, worship.

Since the beginning of God's relationship with mankind, the prayers of the saints are precious and kept in heavenly containers.

God walked with Adam. This walking with Adam set a precedent for our future relationship with God. Deuteronomy 23:14, "*For the Lord thy God walks in the midst of thy camp to deliver you …* In this present day, God still walks with his people. He is with his people always, even unto the end of the age. What a marvelous fellowship we have with our Creator.

God brought the animals and birds to Adam to see what he would call them, and whatsoever he called them, that was their name. God gave Adam the responsibility of tending the garden. How long did Adam walk in the garden before God created Eve? It may have been long enough for him to get the lay of the land and to understand the heart of God before he took a wife. God gave Adam the law before he created Eve. "*God commanded Adam, saying, "Of every tree of the garden you may eat freely but of the tree of the knowledge of good and evil you shall not eat of it for in the day that you eat thereof you shall surely die*" (Genesis 2:16–17). Adam knew firsthand what God required of him, and it was his responsibility to give Eve this knowledge and understanding. Both Adam and Eve knew God had forbidden them to eat of the fruit of the tree of knowledge, warning it would bring death.

People of Light

Is it possible God had planned for them to be immortal? Adam and Eve were more ethereal than earthly. They were covered in light or encompassed by the glory of God. They were innocent and pure. Untainted by sin, they enjoyed being in the presence of God. Unlike Moses, God covered him in the cleft of a rock and allowed him to see his hind quarters, Adam and Eve had full access to God. They could walk and talk with their Creator. God intended for them to live a very long time and to enjoy the beauty and perfection of the earth. However, God wanted to be sure his new people would be faithful to him. It seemed God decided to test his new people. Oddly enough, God factored in his fallen angel, the earthly serpent, and some special trees as part of the test.

Before each temptation, God allows a way of escape. God gave the first people the gift of free will. Adam and Eve made a choice to disobey God, and choices carry consequences. Our nature looks to blame others for our actions. We ask the hard questions. Why does God allow all the wicked and horrible things to continue on the earth for thousands of years? Why does he allow man's inhumanity to man? Why such harm to the animal kingdom and the ecosystem? Why does God allow Satan to rule this earth?

God may answer. All things were in perfect order for man to live, multiply, prosper, and dwell freely in the earth. I gave man free will so he could choose to make life or death decisions. I do intervene in the affairs of men only when I will to do so. I gave my angelic host free will. I gave them the heavenly realm to dwell therein. I gave them specific assignments, and I asked them to worship me, the one true God.

In both instances, angels and man chose the path they would travel. Satan's rebellion caused him to lose his heavenly position and all the wicked angels that followed him. Adam and Eve chose to disobey God's commandment, and they forfeited the pleasure in the Garden of Eden. God must judge sin, and all the generations of Adam and Eve would suffer under the curse.

<u>The Serpent</u>

Genesis 3:1–5, "*Now the serpent was more subtle than any beast of the field which the Lord God had made.*" Let us look closely at this scripture and understand from it that the serpent was classified as a beast. It apparently had the ability to walk upright, and it could speak. Adam and Eve were not shocked that it could speak. Once the serpent was possessed by Satan, it could reason with Eve regarding the trees that they could eat from. Eve confirmed they could eat from all the trees except the tree that is in the middle of the garden. She told the serpent (Genesis 3:3) … "*God said, we shall not eat of it or touch it lest <u>we die.</u> And the serpent said you shall not surely die.*" Once again, the serpent could easily counter her concerns and tell her she would not die but they would have <u>wisdom and be as</u> <u>gods,</u> knowing good and evil. They would gain supernatural awareness.

The concept of death had to be alien to Eve since there were no other humans at that time. They would experience a spiritual change, if not immediate death. This path would lead to physical death, returning them to dus; and their spirit would return to God, who gave them life. We know that when we disobey God and sin, we are separated from him spiritually. The consequence of our sin is spiritual death. Our sin is exposed, and we stand naked before God. Sinners cannot stand in God's holy presence unless we are forgiven and covered in his righteousness.

Genesis 3:5, "*For God knows that in the day you eat of the tree, your eyes shall be opened and you shall be as gods knowing good and evil,*" said the serpent. The serpent distracted Eve from thinking upon all the wonderful things God had done for her and Adam. They had it all, but then she wanted something more. She wanted to look into what God had forbidden. She wanted to savor the forbidden fruit.

Why would God create this strange creature having the ability to speak and reason unlike any other beast of the fields? How is it that the serpent referred to <u>wisdom and other gods</u>? This may be our first clue that Satan is in the mix of all this mess because there is no specific mention of Satan between Genesis chapter 1 to 3. Only an angel would be cognitive of the hidden wisdom that defines good and evil, and only Satan knew that he wanted to be god.

God knew the outcome of his test and acknowledged the ramifications in Genesis 3:22:

> *The Lord God said, behold the man is become as one of **us** to know good and evil and now lest he put forth his hand and take also of the tree of life and eat and live forever.*

If God did not want Adam and Eve to know good and evil, why put those other-than-natural trees there in the first place? The life of humanity was not sustained by eating the fruit of the tree of life. God sent Cherubim to guard the tree of life. Why did God require an angel to protect the tree? God could just remove it as easily as he put it there in the first place. God has not given mankind all the answers, but he promises we will have understanding when we come into his heavenly domain. Revelation 2:7 tells us that somewhere in God's realm is the tree of life. During the millennial reign, this tree of life will be returned to earth for the healing of the nations.

There must be more to this thing with trees than we understand. We notice that throughout the scriptures, there is the mention of various types of trees. Noah was told to build the ark using gopherwood. Solomon was told to use cedar for the temple. Jesus was hung on a tree. Mankind has a fascination with trees. Trees have been a part of pagan rituals. The idols in many instances are placed in "groves" of trees. In California, the Bohemian club conducts their rituals in a grove of trees. Nature worshippers hold trees in high esteem.

Giving man the gift of free will, God asked Adam to obey one commandment: do not eat from the tree of knowledge of good and evil. God, knowing all things, knew that Adam and Eve would be disobedient and fall under the temptation of the serpent. In preparation for their fall, God made a plan of redemption to bring mankind back to himself. We follow the plan of redemption throughout the scriptures and see God work in many ways, shapes, and forms.

The Curse and Genesis 3:14–15

God questions Adam and Eve as to why they are hiding and gives them an opportunity to confess and ask for forgiveness. However, they blame others. For their disobedience, God punishes them, as we read in Genesis 3:14: "*And the Lord God said unto the serpent, because you have done this, you are cursed above all cattle and above every beast of the field, upon your belly you will go and dust will you eat all the days of your life.*" It would seem the serpent was an unwilling victim. We may understand this to mean that they did the crime together, and both are penalized.

Usually, when we come in contact with a snake, we try to crush its head while the snake tries to bite our feet. Genesis 3:15 connects Satan to the woman: "*I will put enmity between thee and the woman and between your seed and her seed, it will bruise your head and you will bruise his heel."*

We understand Genesis 3:15 points to a time future. It predicts that God in flesh will be crucified. Satan thought he had won, thus bruising the heel of Jesus. However, the shed blood of Jesus was for the atonement of sin and his Resurrection was for life eternal. Someday, Jesus will redeem the earth and will crush the head of Satan at his Second Coming.

Understanding the "Seed" in Genesis 3:15

- Satan's seed are those who follow him instead of God, be it angels or mankind. Satan did not beget other angels, nor did he beget humankind. Therefore, Satan's seed is not literal.
- There will be enmity, hostility, and hatred between Satan, fallen angels, demons, and wicked men against God's creation. The enmity of Satan continued by allowing the fallen angels to corrupt the seed of the woman before the flood. Women do not have seed; this is a reference to the descendants of Adam and Eve.
- "Her seed" points to a future time that God will plant a seed in Mary.
- After the flood, the corruption of mankind continued. At the time of the birth of Jesus, the enmity between Satan's seed and the seed of woman ramped up with many trying to destroy Emanuel, God with us.

Genesis 3:15–19, the punishment of the woman would be that her sorrows would be greatly multiplied and she would have pain in bringing forth children, painful menstrual cycle, and her desire shall be to her husband, and he shall rule over her. To Adam, because he listened to his wife and disobeyed God, the ground from which he was formed would be cursed, and in sorrow he would eat of it all the days of his life. There will be thorns and thistles, and by the sweat of man's brow will you get bread. Before the flood, they genetically modified the fruit of the vine to grow extremely large as well as genetically engineering the fruit of the womb, producing giant hybrids.

Satan had fallen because of pride and rebellion. Eve fell because of pride, lust of the eye, lust of the flesh, disobedience, and she wanted Adam to sin with her, of which he did not object. She desired to be like God and listened to the voice of Satan instead of God.

> *And when the woman saw that the tree was good for food and that it was pleasant to the eyes and a tree to be desired to make one wise, she took of the fruit thereof and did eat and gave also to her husband with her and he did eat. And the eyes of them both were opened and they knew that they were naked and they sewed fig leaves together and made aprons.* (Genesis 3:6–7)

Rebellion began with God's angelic host and that activity influenced the first humans towards disobedience.

Adam and Eve made aprons to hide their sin. Aprons became a symbol of rebellion adopted in Mormons and Masonic rituals.

The wrath of God had reached its boiling point and overflowed. The wrath of God is more than we can bear. God's preordained plan of redemption began with the making of coats of skin to cover Adam and Eve's nakedness and sin. Through the shed blood of animals, their sin was covered. God's plan would stand through many generations; it would endure the angelic assault upon the earth, a worldwide flood, and the spilled blood of living creatures that could fill oceans. For almost three thousand years after the flood, the earth and all therein would reel from the wrath of God. Before the foundations of the earth were formed, God knew he would come to earth and take on the form of man. He knew that only a perfect sacrifice could redeem fallen mankind. From the time of the incarnation, mankind would wait on God for two thousand years and counting to cleanse the earth from all wickedness and usher in a time of peace and healing for the world.

> *For since the beginning of the world, men have not heard, nor perceived by ear, neither has the eye seen, O God, beside thee, what he has prepared for those that wait for Him.* (Isaiah 64:4)

At this point, we are reminded that Satan had already staged his rebellion against the Holy God and was banished from his presence. The heavenly host both holy and fallen angels were witness to all of God's creation. Satan decided to corrupt God's creation, beginning with the first people and then their children. God allowed this abomination to come upon the earth as we read in Genesis 6. The fallen angels taught mankind forbidden knowledge, and the people would begin to exalt the fallen angels as gods.

We take the occurrence between God, Satan, Adam, and Eve too lightly and do not fully understand the seriousness and the implication that it had on the future of mankind. Satan and his fallen angels are the epitome of evil, having no conscience. Satan and his fallen angels have followed the same agenda from the Garden to the cross, from the cross to the end of the age, until Satan is banished to the lake of fire. The satanic agenda is to kill, steal, destroy, and deceive mankind, and Satan's reward is your soul.

Life Outside of the Garden of Eden

To add insult to injury, Adam and Eve were driven from the garden.

> *Therefore, God sent him forth from the garden to till the ground from where he was taken. So he drove out the man; God places Cherubim and a flaming sword which turned every way to guard the way of the tree of life.* (Genesis 3:23–24)

Mankind Begins to Multiply upon the Earth

Adam and Eve would have hundreds of years to contemplate all that they loss due to their disobedience.

Adam was at least a hundred years old when he left the Garden around 3,900 BC.

> *And Adam knew Eve his wife and she conceived and bore Cain and she said, I have gotten a man from the Lord. She again bore his brother Abel.* (Genesis 4:1)

In Adam's genealogy, the firstborn Cain and his brother, Abel, are not listed. Since Abel was physically deceased, perhaps Cain was also spiritually dead because of his dastardly deed. Adam was 137 years old when Seth was born. Seth begat Enos at 105 years old and died at age of 912 and had additional children. Enos begat Cainan at age ninety and died at 815. Genesis 4:3, "*And in process of time …*" This scripture allows us to know that a time period passed wherein Adam and Eve had more children, and they in turn reproduced, and the earth had people living here and there for almost a thousand years up to the time of the flood around 3000 BC.

Adam and Eve had invited evil to come upon mankind. It entered into the mind of Cain to kill his brother Abel. Genesis 4:8, "*And Cain talked with Abel his brother, and it came to pass when they were in the field, that Cain rose up against Abel his brother and slew him.*" This is the first murder recorded in the scripture. God asked Cain, "Where is your brother?" and he said, "I know not, am I my brother's keeper?" The first lie recorded in scripture. Cain's descendants followed the way of wickedness.

Before we move on, we found the following passage of interest in Genesis 4:10:

> *God said, what have you done? The voice of your brother's blood cries unto me from the ground. And now you are cursed from the earth which has opened her mouth to receive your brother's blood from your hand …*

Life is in the blood, and eternal life is in the spirit/soul. Is there a connection between shed blood and its ability to cry out from the earth? This could be a metaphor, except that in Enoch 22:1–7, it appears that this question may have a literal meaning. The angel had shown Enoch a place where the souls of men are assembled awaiting the great judgment. As in the story of the beggar, the rich man, and Abraham's bosom, there is a gulf between the place of containment for the righteous souls and the place of condemnation for the wicked souls. Enoch is able to see these souls, and he hears their cry, which reaches up to the heaven. Enoch then sees the soul of Abel, whose lamentation reaches to heaven. The angel clarifies that the spirit that proceeded from Abel, whom Cain killed, it laments on his account till his seed be destroyed from the face of the earth and his seed disappeared from among the seed of men. Humans who follow the way of disobedience and wickedness are associated with the spiritual seed of Satan.

Before the birth of Seth, Cain killed Abel. By God's own declaration, judgment must be passed upon Cain. Genesis 4:14, "*Behold God has driven me out this day from the face of the earth* ..." It is an odd expression that Cain uses the term "banished from the face of the earth." We know that he was still on the earth because he goes to the land of Nod, east of Eden. He took a wife, which would have been one of Adam and Eve's descendants. He called his son's name Enoch, which is not the same Enoch born of the line of Seth. Adam was alive at the time Cain was banished from the colony.

Unto Seth at age 105 was born Enos, ***then began men to call upon the name of the Lord.*** Genesis 4:26—the Bible does not give us any additional information on Seth, but from this passage, we can understand that his lineage would represent those who would follow a godly way. The preflood era is referred to as the Dispensation of Conscience. God placed a conscience in all of mankind to know the difference between right and wrong. From the time of Seth to the time of Noah, people believed in God their Creator. However, more people followed the ungodly example of Cain. They rebelled against their Creator. Seth lived to see the incursion of the fallen angels and their evil activities vexed the righteous of God. They lived by what was right in their own eyes. Traditional religions had not been established. There were no Jews, Christians, or other Gentile denominations established until after the flood.

At this point in time, we can begin to follow the lineage of Cain and the lineage of Seth.

The Bible lists the children of Cain, Genesis 4:17–24. There are some interesting things to see in this listing. The scriptures may not have listed all of Cain's offspring, but the Bible gives us a hint of a few things. Some of the names listed are the same as the names of the children of Seth. Genesis 4:25–26 list the descendants of Seth. Genesis 5:1–32 list the names of Adam's descendants beginning with Seth.

After the birth of Enoch, Cain builds a city. In various myths, this city was named Atlantis. Cain probably lived to be around nine hundred years old. Following is a list of Cain's children:

Enoch begat Irad.

Irad begat Mehujael.

Mehujael begat Lamech.

Lamech had two wives, Adah and Zillah; Lamech commits murder.

Jabal (son of Adah) was the father of tent dwellers and husbandry.

Jubal was the father of harp and organ instruments.

Tubal-cain (son of Zillah), he was instructor/artificer in brass and iron.

Evolutionists fabricated a scenario that early man was ignorant, lived in caves, and would have the gullible belief that primitive man did not have fire. As we just read, brass and iron cannot be made into various objects without fire. During this period of time, men became builders, tent dwellers, cattle herders, developed musical instruments, worked with brass and iron, and they may have had some extraterrestrial help. Chapter 7 explains the activity of the fallen angels.

> *And Lamech said unto his wives, Adah and Zillah, listen, I have slain a man and if Cain should be avenged sevenfold then I, Lamech, should be avenged seventy and sevenfold.* (Genesis 4:23)

These conversations are recorded in the book of Genesis. Who wrote these things down? Perhaps people kept personal journals. There is no exclusive answer, but we do have clues. God had given mankind the ability to communicate through verbal expression, artistic renderings, architectural planning, and record keeping. Enoch wrote of the angelic incursion when the two hundred fallen angels came to Mount Hermon and taught them forbidden knowledge.

People who lived before the flood knew the descendants of Seth to Jared. They knew that Jared's son Enoch had been taken into the heavenly realm and told by God to record all that he saw. After the flood, knowledge continued through the eight survivors and their descendants. Historians believe the first written language was developed by Sumerians or Babylonians, who spoke Akkadian. However, before the flood we have record of language, writing, record keeping, which is accredited to Seth, implemented by Enoch and continued after the flood by Noah and his sons. As people multiplied, so did their dialects; and from the one sacred language given by God, hybrid languages developed after the dispersion at Babel.

In the twenty-first century, we are able to better understand the link between heaven and the creation as recorded in Job and Enoch because God has given man the gift of faith, which allows our mind to explore the things of God. We spiritually begin to discern and understand the mysteries of God. Faith is the substance of things hoped for and the evidence of things not seen. Through the lineage of Seth would come the chosen people, who would produce the future Messiah. The genealogy from Adam, Seth to Noah, and the meaning of their names as listed in Genesis 5.1–23 gives us a message of God's future plan.

Adam	Man
Seth	Appointed
Enosh	Mortal
Kenan	Sorrow
Mahalalel	The blessed of God
Jared	Shall come down
Enoch	Teaching
Methuselah	His death shall bring
Lamech	The despairing
Noah	Rest or comfort

Man (is) appointed mortal sorrow, (but the) Blessed God shall come down teaching (that) his death shall bring (the) despairing rest. Here is God's plan of redemption hidden here within the genealogy:

"The blessed of God did come down teaching, and his death did bring redemption."

The above acronym is shared by many in the Christian community.

Chapter 6
The Testimony of Enoch Pleased God

Chapter Overview

- Enoch Pleased God
- Historical Background on Enoch
- The Books of Enoch
- Enoch's Understanding Is Opened
- Tour of the Universe
- The Unrighteous Versus the Righteous
- Fallen Angels and Earthly Women
- Angels Teach Forbidden Knowledge
- God Judges Wickedness
- Postflood to the Millennial Reign
- Description of Heaven and Hell
- Word of Wisdom
- Final Day of the Lord
- Messiah, Son of Man

Chapter 6

The Testimony of Enoch Pleased God

> *By faith, Enoch was translated that he should not see death and was not found because God had translated him, for before his translation he had this testimony that he pleased God.* (Hebrews 11:5)

Many scholars consider the book of Enoch and want to know what his testimony was. These writings predate scripture and provide insight into the things of God and the account of the fallen angels. The writings of Enoch are a must-read, providing additional insight into the days of Noah. We know that some of the text was corrupted from transcribing it over the centuries, but from our research, we can excerpt those things that tie into the Bible and do not contradict it. The Bible tells us that other prophets were given visions by God, taken into the heavenly realm, and told to write what they saw in a book. John in Revelation 1:11 is instructed, "*What you see, write in a book.*" Daniel is told to seal up the book until the end of days.

Creation is suggested at 4004 BC. Genesis 5 gives the genealogy of the descendants of Adam, providing us with a thousand-year perspective from Adam to Noah. We skip to Jared, who was born at the time the fallen angels had descended onto Mount Hermon. Jared was 162 years old when Enoch was born, estimated to be around 3400 BC. Enoch was sixty-five years old when his son Methuselah was born, and Methuselah was 187 years old when Lamech was born, and Lamech was 182 years old when Noah was born. Adam died at the age of 930, and Enoch was then 310 years old. Enoch and others were alive at the time when the Nephilim roamed the earth. Enoch witnessed all the corruption and wickedness that had encompassed the earth.

Enoch's name means "teaching," herein we understand that Enoch has valuable insight for us to glean. Enoch was sixty-five years old when he experienced his first trip to heaven in a celestial vehicle. Enoch 12:1, "*and previous to all these things, Enoch was hidden and not one of the children of men knew where he was hidden ...*" In this passage, Enoch said he was taken into the heavens and was not accessible to those on earth. We cannot determine the time spent in the heavenly realm. God took him alive and gave him the knowledge of creation, the future flood, the Second Coming of Messiah with ten thousands of his saints. All that he witnessed, God told him to write in books. When God returned him to earth, Enoch 37 confirms that he was given time to share God's revelation with his relatives prior to the flood: "*Three parables were given to me and I commenced to relate them to those who dwell on the earth.*"

Genesis 5:23, Enoch was permanently taken by God at the age of 365 years old and found no more on the earth. This was his final trip to heaven, and Enoch missed the flood. This is a type of the Rapture. Today the faithful listen for the sound of the trumpet and the voice of the archangel to be caught up in the clouds to meet the Holy and Great One, Jesus. He will save us from the day of wrath as he saved Enoch—by translation, the righteous through death before the flood and Noah from the wrath of the flood. Noah was the last of his generation and safeguarded the books of Enoch within the ark. Enoch 68:1, Noah mentions that the secrets in the book were given to him by Enoch.

> *And I Enoch was praising the great Lord and the King of the world and behold the watchers [holy angels] called to me and said to me: Enoch thou scribe of justice ...* (Enoch 12:3)

In this writing we want to point out that Enoch was considered a scribe—meaning, he could read and write with the ability to use the *Aleph* and *Tav*, language of God. The Book of Jubilees reports that Enoch taught others to read and write the sacred language. It is our contention that Adam and his descendants were literate and God had given them wisdom as well as the ability of language, writing, and reading.

Historical Background on Enoch

We must provide historical background on Enoch and his writings. In 1948, several fragments of Enoch's writings in Aramaic were discovered with the other dead sea scrolls at Qumran in Israel. The books of Enoch were widely known and read for many centuries after

Christ. Enoch's writings were thought to be more Jewish in theology than Christian. His writings were copied, studied for their prophetic insight and historic value.

Early church leaders studied, quoted, and read to their congregations the writings of Enoch. First century AD 44 epistle of Barnabas refers to Enoch: "*For this end the Lord has cut short the times and the days that his beloved may hasten and he will come to the inheritance.*" Tertullian, AD 160 to 230, called the book holy scripture. The Ethiopic church added Enoch's book to its canon. The Hasmonians believed in Enoch's writings. Jesus quoted from the book of Enoch. Early church leaders—such as, Justin Martyr, AD 180, Irenaeus, Origen, Clement of Alexandria, and Bishop of Rome, AD 100, Minucius Felix, Commodianus, Ambrose of Milanalso, Tatian, Lactantius, Methodius of Phillip—all made use of the book of Enoch. There are over one hundred phrases in the New Testament that find their precedent in the book of Enoch. Justin Martyr ascribed all evil demons to be offspring of fallen angels and earth women from Enoch's writings. Athenagaros, AD 170, in his writing titled *Legatio*, refers to angels that violated both their own nature and human nature. He goes into detail about the nature of fallen angels, which comes from the book of Enoch. After the Council of Laodicea around AD 700, Enoch's writings were discredited and became obscure. This period in time was known as the Dark Age. Books were burned; the Rapture was dismissed as well as the controversial encounter of angels and women in Genesis 6.

How could any ancient writing survive before the flood and be passed down through the generations? We apply the same credence given to other ancient writings. The verbal record of creation and written accounts in the book of Genesis seem to have survived preflood and postflood. Of course, we ascribe that the books in the Bible were divinely inspired and God-given to the writers of the Old Testament. Moses is credited with writing the first five books around 1,500 BC. The book of Job is said to be the oldest book in the Bible. If we accept these statements as credible, then we can apply the same logic to other ancient writings. There would be oral tradition, divine inspiration, and written accounts. Enoch's writings predate Job; it predates the Exodus; and it existed before Moses wrote the Torah. One clue we find in Enoch's account is the Jewish ritual for the Day of Atonement—wherein Azael, the scapegoat, is laden with the sins of Israel and thrown off the mountain. The writings of Enoch are credible.

At the end of the Protestant Reformation, interest in the book of Enoch was renewed. In the late 1400s, rumors began to spread that a lost copy may exist. Three copies of the manuscript were found by explorer James Bruce in AD 1773, who had spent six years in Abyssinia, Ethiopia. He took them to Europe, and they were translated. An ancient Greek manuscript also surfaced, corroborating the accuracy and authenticity of the Coptic language editions. In 1821, Richard Laurence published the first English translation of the book of Enoch, titled, *The Book of Enoch, the Prophet,* an apocryphal production. The book is in the Bodleian

Library, Oxford. In 1976, J. T. Milik, a Catholic scholar, compiled a complete history of the Enochian writings—including translation of the Aramaic fragments found with the dead sea scrolls. He was considered a respected expert on Enoch's writings.

Books that are not canonical are categorized as pseudopigrapha writings that claim to be by a Bible character or apocrypha, meaning hidden or secret.

The Books of Enoch

Three books exist and are compiled as follows: 1 Enoch—Ethiopian is the oldest; 2 Enoch—Slavonic and in Egypt it is referred to as the Book of Secrets; and 3 Enoch. The Books of Enoch consist of an ancient collection of five scrolls divided into twenty sections.

Why do we want to investigate these writings? Because they shed additional light on our understanding of God, angels, fallen angels, things in heaven, creation, and a message to this generation. A great deal of the writings correlates to existing Bible scripture. Corrupted text will be avoided. There may have been up to thirty books by Enoch. What is available of the writings is about 108 chapters. Following is a division of chapters:

Chapters 1–36	Book of Watchers
37–71	Book of Similitudes or Parables
72–82	Book of Astronomical Writings or Luminaries
83–90	Book of Dreams and Visions
91–105	Book of the Epistle of Enoch
106–107	The Birth of Noah
108	Another Book by Enoch

Let us see what Enoch experienced in heaven and if we may gain a deeper understanding of all things Yahweh from his experience. Buckle up, and let's take a journey. The Book of Watchers opens with a message to the future generation of Jews and Christians that would exist with Christ after the Rapture and see the events of the tribulation unfold from heaven. Enoch speaks in the third person then transitions to the first person.

The following commentary of Enoch is titled *Book of Watchers,* chapters 1 to 36:

> *The words of the blessing of Enoch wherewith he blessed the chosen and just who will exist on the day of tribulation when all the wicked and impious shall be removed. And then answered and spoke Enoch, a just man, whose eyes were opened by God so that he saw a holy vision in the heavens which the angels showed to me and from them I heard everything and I knew what I saw but*

> *not for this generation but for the far off generations which are to come.* (Enoch 1:1–2)

We want to point out that this message is for this generation, and it makes reference to the righteous of God who will be alive at the onset of the tribulation. We are currently experiencing the birth pains of the beginning of the tribulation period. We are also to understand that the purpose of the tribulation is to bring judgment upon the wicked.

Enoch's Understanding Is Opened

> *Concerning the chosen I spoke and conversed concerning them with the Holy and Great One who will come from his abode, the God of the world. And from there he will step on the Mount Sinai and appear with his hosts and appear in the strength of his power from heaven. And all will fear and the watchers will tremble and great fear and terror will seize them to the ends of the earth.* (Enoch 1:3–5)

In this section we note that Enoch is having a conversation with God and is told that God will leave heaven and step on Mount Sinai accompanied by his angels. Those watching this event will tremble with great fear. During the time of Moses and the chosen in the wilderness, God left his abode and appeared on Mount Sinai. At a future time, God will leave his abode and step onto the Mount of Olives; every eye will see him. Those witnessing this event will experience great fear. Luke 21:26, "*Men's hearts failing them for fear and looking after those things which are coming on the earth for the powers of heaven shall be shaken …*"

During the last days, Enoch predicts catastrophic events will take place in heaven and on the earth.

> Enoch 1:6–8 *And the exalted mountains will be shaken and the high hills will be lowered and will melt like wax before the flame and the earth will be submerged and everything that is on the earth will be destroyed and there will be a judgment upon everything and upon all the just. But to the just, he will give peace and will protect the chosen and mercy will abide over them and they will all be God's and will be prosperous and blessed and the light of God will shine for them.*

At the end of the age, persecution, suffering, and death will be experienced by both the just and unjust, but God will give peace to his people who are called by his name.

The following Old Testament writers reflect on Enoch's writings:

> *Lift up your eyes to the heavens and look upon the earth beneath for the heavens shall vanish away like smoke and the earth shall wax old like a garment and they that dwell therein shall die in like manner …* (Isaiah 51:6)

The book of Psalms 97:5 speaks to *the hills melted like wax at the presence of the Lord …*

> *Then the earth shook and trembled, the foundations also of the hills moved and were shaken because of his wrath, there went up a smoke out of his nostrils and fire out of his mouth devoured coals were kindled by it, he bowed the heavens also and came down and darkness was under his feet.* Psalms 18:7

These catastrophic events are a combination of earthquakes leveling mountains and volcanoes erupting like melting wax. The heavens will appear as swirling tornadoes; the sky will be dark and extreme weather will ensue; and some of these conditions will be caused by a nuclear catastrophe.

Many living in Israel and other nations will perish during the tribulation. In the middle of the tribulation, Yeshua will protect the chosen from the wrath of Antichrist. A remnant of the chosen will flee into Jordan, which borders the mountains of Mount Sinai.

> *And behold he comes with myriads of the holy to pass judgment upon them and will destroy the impious and will call to account all flesh for everything the sinners and the impious have done and committed against him.* (Enoch 1:9)

This ties into Jude 1:14–15:

> *And Enoch also, the seventh from Adam prophesied of these saying, behold the Lord comes with ten thousands of his saints to execute judgment upon all and to convince all that are ungodly among them of all their ungodly deeds which they have ungodly committed and of all their hard speeches which ungodly sinners have spoken against him.*

Both Enoch and Jude prophesy about the Second Coming of Christ with his saints at the end of the Tribulation Period. At that time, Jesus will separate the wicked from the righteous in the great harvest.

<u>Tour of the Universe</u>

> *I observed everything that took place in the heavens … the luminaries [sun, moon, stars] do not depart from their path and their laws. See the earth and observe the things that are done on it from <u>the first to the last</u> and no work of God*

> *is irregular in appearing. See the summer and the winter how then the whole earth is full of water and clouds and dew and rain rest over it.* (Enoch 2:1–3)

Snow, rain, wind

> *For he said to the snow, be thou on the earth likewise to the small rain and to the great rain of his strength … Out of the south comes the whirlwind and cold out of the north by the breath of God frost is given and the breadth of the waters is straightened.* (Job 37:6)
>
> *Has thou entered into the treasures of the snow? Or have you seen the treasures of the hail, which I have reserved against the time of trouble, against the day of battle and war?* (Job 38:22)

God uses hail to fall as judgment.

Trees

> *I observed and saw how then all the trees appeared as if withered and all their leaves are shaken off, except fourteen trees whose leaves … abide for two to three years.* (Enoch 3:1)

This is a description of the fall season and the leaves falling except for evergreen trees.

Enoch 5:1 speaks of the trees bearing fruit and knows that "*he who lives forever has made all these for you.*" He acknowledges the works of God year after year, and his creation serves him, and God has ordained everything to take place.

Seasons

> *I observed the days of summer, how the sun is then above it* [the earth] … *but you seek cool and shady places on account of the heat of the sun …* (Enoch 4:1)

Curse upon Ungrateful and Unrighteous People

Enoch 5:4–6 chastises mankind because they "*have not persevered and have not done the commandment of the Lord but have transgressed and have slandered his greatness with high and hard words from your unclean mouths, you hard hearted, will have no peace.*" These will bring a curse upon themselves; "*you will curse your days and the years of your lives perish, the everlasting curse will increase and you will receive no mercy.*" Man's heart is continually evil, and those that reject God and are unthankful will have no peace of heart or mind; they curse their days, and with the passing of time, the curse increases.

Reward for the Righteous

> *But for the chosen, there will be light and joy and peace and they will inherit the earth … Wisdom will be given to the chosen and they will all live and not continue in sin, neither through wickedness nor through pride but they in whom thee is wisdom will be humble without continuing in sin. They will not be punished all the days of their lives and will not die through plagues or judgments of wrath but the number of the days of their lives will be completed and their lives will become old in peace and the years of their joy will be many in everlasting happiness and peace for all the days of their lives.* (Enoch 5:7–8)

We have peace and joy in the midst of turmoil. We have the promise of long life, and when this life is over, we receive the inheritance promised to the heirs of salvation.

Fallen Angels and Earthly Women

Enoch 6 correlates to Genesis 6, and it speaks of the angels who came down onto Mount Hermon, bound themselves with an oath and took wives to themselves and produced giant offspring. In Enoch 6, we see he has listed the leaders of the fallen angels. We also point out that in Enoch 53:3, Satan is identified as the leader of all fallen angels: "*For I have seen the angels of punishment going and preparing all the instruments for Satan.*" Further discussion on fallen angels and humankind is found in chapter 7.

And it came to pass after the children of men had increased in those days, beautiful and comely daughters were born to them. And the angels, the sons of the heavens saw and lusted after them and said one to another, behold we will choose for ourselves wives from among the children of men and will beget for ourselves children. And Semjaza who was their leader said to them, I fear that perhaps you will not be willing to do this deed and I alone will suffer for this great sin. Then all answered him and said, we all will swear an oath and bind ourselves mutually by a curse that will not give up this plan but will make this plan a deed. Then they all swore together and bound themselves mutually by a curse and together they were two hundred. And they descended on Ardis which is the summit of Mount Hermon and they called it Mount Hermon because they had sworn on it and bound themselves mutually by curse. And these are the names of their leaders: Semjaza who was their leader, Urakibarameel, Akibeel, Tamiel, Ramuel, Danel, Ezeqeel, Saraqujal, Asael, Armers, Batraal, Anani, Zaqebe, Samsaveel, Sartael, Turel, Jomjael, Arazal. These are the leaders of the two hundred angels and the others all were with them. (Enoch 6:1–8)

For comparison purposes, we quote Genesis 6. Moses is credited with writing the first books of the Bible while he was alive. We believe that with the help of divine guidance as well as the available scrolls of Enoch and others, Moses had a good understanding of the corruption of the fallen angels with earthly women.

> *And it came to pass when men began to multiply on the face of the earth and daughters were born unto them that the sons of God saw the daughters of men that they were fair and they took them wives of all which they chose. And the Lord said, My spirit will not always strive with man for that he also is flesh yet his days will be a hundred and twenty years. There were giants in the earth in those days and also after that when the sons of God came in unto the daughters of men and they bare children to them the same became mighty men which were of old, men of renown. And God saw that the wickedness of man was great in the earth and that every imagination of the thoughts of his heart was only evil continually, and it repented the Lord that he had made man on the earth and it grieved him at his heart. And the Lord said, I will destroy man whom I have created from the face of the earth both man and beast and the creeping thing and the fowls of the air for it repenteth me that I have made them. But Noah found grace in the eyes of the Lord.* (Genesis 6:1–8)

God passes judgment on the terrestrials and in the writings of Enoch God also bound the fallen angels, destroyed their offspring, and their spirits would be evil spirits or demons.

The similarities between Enoch 6 and Genesis 6:

- The angels were attracted to earthly women.
- They desired to produce offspring.
- Fallen angels manage to corrupt the human seed through the intermingling of celestial and terrestrial DNA.
- The offspring were giants/mighty men.
- Enoch identifies the leaders of the angels.
- God must destroy all the wickedness of angels, humans, animals.
- After the flood, giants would again be on the earth.
- The battle between God and Satan will continue for thousands of years until Satan is finally thrown into the lake of fire.

Enoch 7 through 10 continue to discuss the wicked deeds of the fallen angels, and God sends his holy angels to begin to deal with the evil in the earth before the flood.

> *And they took unto themselves wives and each chose for himself one and they began to go into them and* ***mixed*** *with them and taught them charms and conjurations and made them acquainted with the cutting of roots and woods. And they became pregnant and brought forth great giants whose stature was three thousand ells. These devoured all the acquisitions of mankind till men were unable to sustain themselves. And the giants turned themselves against mankind in order to devour them. And they began to sin against the birds and the beasts and against the creeping things and the fish and devoured their flesh among themselves and drank the blood thereof. Then the earth complained of the unjust ones.* (Enoch 7:1–5)

We should consider these activities:

- "They mixed" this is something other than a sexual union. The Holy Spirit overshadowed Mary, and we do not interpret that to mean a sexual union.
- The angels taught them the art of magic/witchcraft—specifically, conjuring (summoning something dark and foreboding), cutting roots (drugs), using charms. The mixing of genetic material and forbidden knowledge caused the females to become pregnant (similar to artificial insemination or cloning).
- The offspring grew to be giants with insatiable appetites. The giants began to eat the people. The fallen angels began genetic manipulation against birds, beast, fish to create giant hybrids for food for their giant children, which the giants devoured as well as drinking their blood.

Angels Teach Forbidden Knowledge

> *Azael taught mankind to make swords, knives, shields, coats of mail and taught them to see what was behind them and their works of art: bracelets and ornaments and the use of rouge and the beautifying of the eye brows and the dearest and choicest stones and all coloring substances and the metals of the earth. And there was great wickedness and much fornication and they sinned and all their ways were corrupt. Amezara taught all the conjurers and root cutters, Armaros the loosening of conjurations*, Baraqal, Temel and Asradel taught astrology. *And in the destruction of mankind, they cried aloud and their voices reached heaven.* (Enoch 8:1–4)

God condemned all those things. In chapter 8, we see how certain things came to pass:

- The angels taught mankind war and weapons to kill one another.

- They taught them how to use mirrors to see behind them.
- The angels taught how to make jewelry.
- The angels taught the people to wear makeup to be seductive.
- The angels taught them the value of gemstones and precious metals.
- The lifestyle was one of fornication and debauchery.
- The angels taught astrology.
- They taught using blood in rituals.

Enoch 9:1–11 relates a discussion between the archangels, Michael, Gabriel, Surja, Urjan, who have watched the events taking place and the great amount of bloodshed. They see the earth is filled with wickedness. They hear the cry of mankind for help and turn to God, reminding him that he has made all things and all power is with him and all things are open before him. They tell him that the fallen angel Azael has revealed the secrets of the world, which was prepared in the heavens, teaching mankind forbidden knowledge. They tell God that Semjaza has made known conjurations. They tell God that the angels have mixed with the women and produced giants. Verse 11, "*Thou knows everything before it comes to pass and thou knows this and their circumstances and yet thou does not speak to us. What shall we therefore do in regard to this?*" We will read God's answer in the following chapters.

God Judges Wickedness

> *Then the most High, the Great and Holy One spoke and sent Arsjalaljur to the son of Lamech [Noah] and said to him: tell him in my name, hide thyself and reveal to him the end which is to come. For the whole earth will be destroyed and the water of the deluge is about to come over the whole earth and what is upon it will be destroyed. And now instruct him that he may escape and his seed remain on the whole earth. And again the Lord spoke to Raphael, bind Azazel hand and foot and put him in the darkness, make an opening in the desert which is in Dudael and put him there. And lay upon him rough and pointed rocks and cover him with darkness that he may remain there forever and cover his face that he may not see the light. And on the great day of judgment he will be cast into the fire. And heal the earth which the angels have defiled and announce the healing of the earth that I will heal it and that not all the sons of men shall be destroyed through the mystery of all the things which the watchers have spoken and have taught their sons. And the whole earth was defiled through the example of the deeds of Azazel to him ascribe all the sins.* (Enoch 10:1–8)

Analysis of the Above Verses

- Noah is warned that destruction is coming upon the whole earth. It came a hundred years later. The ark took a hundred years to build. God promised to spare Noah, and his seed would replenish the earth.
- Azazel, or Azael, is bound as in chains of darkness and placed under the earth, such as in hell. He will remain there until the great white throne judgment, and then he (and all the fallen angels) will be cast into the lake of fire with Satan, Antichrist, false prophet, and unrepentant wicked people.
- There will be a healing of the earth. Probably, the earth was purged by the flood, and after the waters receded, the earth became fruitful.
- The flood destroyed mankind, who had received forbidden knowledge from the angels; however, after the flood, these same things became prevalent once again because spiritual entities are eternal and did influence postflood humanity.
- Azazel was charged with defiling the earth, and all sin was placed on him. This became symbolic during the time of Moses that the sin of the nation was placed on the scapegoat, Azael.

We continue with the narrative of Enoch 10:9, which will deals with the offspring of the fallen angels:

> *And God said to Gabriel, Go against the bastards and those cast off and against the children of fornication and destroy the children of fornication and the children of the watchers from among men; lead them out and let them loose that they may destroy each other by murder for their days will not be long. And they will all supplicate thee but their fathers will secure nothing for them although they expect an everlasting life and that each one of them will live five hundred years. And God said to Michael, announce to Semjaza and to the others who are with him who have bound themselves to women to be destroyed with them in all their contamination. When all their sons shall have slain one another and they shall have seen the destruction of their beloved ones, bind them under the hills of the earth for seventy generations till the day of their judgment and their end, till the last judgment has been passed for all eternity. And in those days they will be led to the abyss of fire in torture and in prison they will be locked for all eternity. And then he will burn and be destroyed and they will be burned together from now on to the end of all generations. Destroy all the souls of lust and the children of the watchers because they have oppressed mankind.*

There are a few interesting things to consider in the above text:

- God sends Gabriel to round up the bastards/offspring of the fallen angels as well as human fornicators and their children.
- The giant hybrids will kill each other.
- The fallen angels will ask for mercy for their offspring, but they will get nothing for them.
- They expected to live at least five hundred years and then live for eternity.
- God sends his messenger, the Angel Michael, to the fallen angels, who bound themselves to women and all their corruption and contamination; and after they witness the destruction of their offspring, they will be bound and placed in the lower regions of the earth for seventy generations.
- J. R. Church states, "If we calculate the seventy generations and then add the seventh generation from Adam to Enoch we have a total of seventy-seven generations until the judgment of fallen angels, their wives and children. According to Luke's gospel, Jesus was the seventy-seventh generation from Adam. Christ's death signaled the coming doom of these "sons of God."
- At the time of Jesus's Resurrection, he descended into hell and took the keys of death and hell, and he preached to the captives—some to damnation and some to Resurrection.
- What we see is that the fallen angels are bound under the earth; their half-human and half-celestial hybrid children would destroy each other; and their spirits would roam the earth to torment mankind. The wicked humans would die in the flood, and their souls sent to hell until the white throne judgment.
- All this satanic activity is defined as the oppression of mankind. Later, we will see the beginning of demonic possession.

Linking together Enoch 10 and 12 ties together the discussion between the angels and Enoch who petition him to speak in their behalf.

> *Enoch thou scribe of justice, go announce to the watchers* [fallen angels] *of heaven who have left the high heaven and the holy eternal place and have contaminated themselves with women and have done as the children of men do and have taken to themselves wives and are contaminated in great contamination upon the earth but upon the earth they shall have no peace nor forgiveness of sin for they will not enjoy their children. They will see the murder of their beloved ones and they will lament over the destruction of their children and will* <u>*petition to eternity but mercy and peace will not be unto them.*</u> (Enoch 12:4–6)

> *And Enoch departing said to Azazel, thou will have no peace a great condemnation has come upon you and Raphael* [holy angel] *will bind thee.* (Enoch 13:1)

Enoch has departed from being hidden in heaven and delivers a message of judgment to the fallen angels. No mercy will be given unto them for their sin. They were afraid; fear and trembling seized them. They ask Enoch to write a petition to God in their behalf to attain forgiveness and carry their message before God in heaven because they could no longer speak with God or raise their eyes toward heaven from shame on account of their sins. It appears Enoch is given the capability to observe heavenly events as well as the location of the fallen angels that were on earth. Enoch wrote a memorial/petition as he sat near the waters of Dan near Mount Hermon. He read it over until he fell asleep. While asleep, a vision came for an understanding of the fallen angels' condemnation and rejection of their petition from God.

Enoch tells the angels about his visions:

> *This writing is the Word of Justice* [reference to Jesus] *and the admonition of the watchers who are from eternity as the Holy and Great One commanded it in this vision. I saw in my sleep what I now will relate with a tongue of flesh and with my breath, which the Great One has given to the mouth of men that they might converse with it and understand it in their hearts. As he has created and given to men the power to understand the Word of Knowledge* [reference to Holy Spirit] *thus also he has created me and given to me the power to upbraid the watchers, the sons of heaven. I have written your petition and in my vision it appeared to me thus, that your petition will not be granted in all the days of the world and that judgment has been passed over you and nothing will be granted unto you. And from now on you will not ascend into heaven to all eternity and upon earth, it has been decreed they shall bind you for all the days of the world. But before this, you will have seen the destruction of your beloved children and you will not be able to possess them but they shall fall before you by the sword. Your petition for them will not be granted unto you, nor the one for yourselves and while you are weeping and praying you cannot speak a single word from the writing which I have written.* (Enoch 14:1–7)

Here again is another encounter between God, a human, and angels. Pointing out a few things in the above passage are the following:

- Angels are from eternity past, created before humans.
- God has given breath to man for life, conversation, and understanding.

- God has given men the ability to understand the word of knowledge.
- Fallen angels were able to convince Enoch to write a petition for them.
- God gave man the power and authority to rebuke angels (power to upbraid).
- These fallen angels could no longer go before God in heaven for eternity.

God speaks to Enoch,

> *And he answered and spoke to me with his word: hear and fear not, Enoch you are a just man and scribe of justice, approach here and hear my words. Enoch 15:1*

The fallen angels had asked Enoch to write a petition for them. When he fell asleep, God told him to tell them their petition would not be granted. In the following passage, we see that God now tells Enoch directly to "tell the watchers of heaven who have sent you to petition for them but you should instead petition for men and not men for you." Through Enoch, God condemns them.

> *Why have you left the high, holy and everlasting heaven and lain with women and defiled yourselves with the daughters of men and taken wives unto yourselves and acted like the children of earth and begotten giants as sons?* (Enoch 15:3)

<u>Post Flood to the Millennial Reign</u>

Enoch 11:1–2 sees the blessing of God after the flood:

> *And in those days I will open the store rooms of blessing which are in heaven, in order to bring them down upon the earth upon the deeds and labor of the children of men … peace and rectitude will become associates in all the days of the world and in all the generations of the world.*

This passage correlates with Malachi 3:10 …

> *I will open the windows of heaven and pour you out a blessing that there shall not be room enough to receive it.*

The remaining verses of Enoch 10:16–22 address a time after the destruction of wickedness that the <u>plant of justice and righteousness will appear</u> and deeds will become a blessing … We take this as a reference to the millennial reign. Jesus is the root or the branch of justice, and he is our righteousness. Then all the just will bend the knee, and they will remain alive during the thousand-year Sabbath rest. The New Testament speaks to the time when Jesus returns, that every knee will bow.

> *And in those days the whole earth will be worked in justice and will all be planted with trees and will be full of blessing. And all the trees of desire will be planted on it and vines will be planted on it the vine planted on it will bear fruit in abundance and all the seed sown on it one measure will bear ten thousand and one measure of olives will make ten presses of oil.*

We can certainly correlate this with the millennial reign where the tree of life will produce twelve different fruits each month. And in general, the whole earth will be fruitful. God tells Enoch that during the millennial reign, "*All the children of men will become just and all the nations will worship me as God and the earth will be cleansed of all corruption and all sin and all punishment and all torment and I will never again send a flood upon it from generation to generation, to eternity.*"

The scene now shifts to Enoch in a vision being transported back to heaven:

> *And the vision appeared to me thus, behold, clouds in the vision invited me and a fog invited me and the course of the stars and lightning drove and pressed me and the winds in the vision gave me wings and drove me. And they lifted me up into heaven and I went till I approached near a wall which was built of crystals and a tongue of fire surrounded it and it began to cause me fear …* (Enoch 14:8)

In the above passage, Enoch makes reference to clouds as a form of transportation. In Exodus 19:9, God tells Moses he is coming in a thick cloud. In 2 Kings 2:11, Elijah is taken to heaven in a whirlwind riding in a chariot of fire. Ezekiel 1:4, he is taken in a whirlwind and cloud formation, lightning within it. Daniel 7:13, he sees the Son of Man coming in the clouds of heaven. From scripture, Enoch's testimony is credible.

If you are traveling in a craft from earth to heaven, you should see stars, experience centrifugal force and air movement like wind blowing. In providing an explanation of a vision, dream, or life encounter, it could help if we think of ourselves in a movie theater watching a 3-D film. With 3-D glasses, the characters on the screen appear to come out of the screen into our face. Some theaters have a wraparound screen, and as the camera soars toward the heaven or splashes down in the ocean, we get the sensation we are traveling even though we are in a fixed seat. Enoch, Elijah, Paul, John, and others had out-of-this-world encounters where it is difficult to understand if they were actually transported to another dimension or if they were still in a fixed place.

Description of Heaven

Back in the heavenly dimension, Enoch sees a wall-like crystal surrounded by fire. Enoch 14:9–25, he was able to walk through the fire and came to a large house also constructed of crystal. He saw something like consoles monitoring luminaries and the cherubim of fire were in control. He then finds himself in a chamber that was hot like fire and cold like ice, and there was nothing pleasant and no life in it. He said fear came upon him, and he began to tremble and shake and fell down on the floor. Then he is transported to another house much larger with open doors and surrounded with tongues of fire. He said it excelled in grandeur and magnificent in size, beyond his description. The floor and ceiling both were as fire. He now sees a high throne, like frost and shining as the sun, with streams of flaming fire. It was so bright he could not look at it. He heard the voices of the Cherubim, and there were ten thousand times ten thousand before him. He who is great in majesty sat upon the throne dressed in a brilliant, white garment brighter than the sun. None of the angels were able to enter nor any flesh to look upon the form of the face of the Majestic and Honored One. Enoch had a veil covering over his head and face, and the Lord called to him with his own voice and said, "Come hither, Enoch, and to my Holy Word." God caused Enoch to arise, and he went to the door bent over in humility.

Enoch's experience is similar to the reports of Isaiah, Ezekiel, Daniel, and John, who saw it for themselves.

- God is clothed in brilliant white garments (Psalms 104:1) … Clothed in honor and majesty (Isaiah 6:1), I saw the Lord sitting upon a throne, high and lifted up and his train fills the temple (Daniel 7:9) … The ancient of days did sit whose garments are white as snow.
- God's throne was fiery (Ezekiel 1:26) … The likeness of a throne, the appearance of fire, brightness all around, and the appearance of the likeness of the glory of God (Daniel 7:9). His throne was like the fiery flame and his wheels as burning fire; a fiery stream issued and came forth from before him, thousand, thousands ministered unto him …
- Enoch, a human, could feel cold and heat—unlike those who dwell in the spiritual realm, who may not have human sensitivities

In our chapter 2, we discussed the heavenly host and their celestial nature. Following, we look again at these beings:

- Angels are spiritual, eternal.
- God did not reveal all secrets to the angels, but they knew illegitimate mysteries of which they taught mankind forbidden knowledge.
- Because they are spirits, God did not make wives for them; they had no need to reproduce as it is humans who die and need to continue the race.
- Angels defiled themselves with women. It is hard to conceive how they had the ability to procreate.
- They were able to use human DNA blood through a process of mingling to create children.
- They lusted after the blood of men because they don't have blood.
- Blood is a mysterious substance; the life of living creatures is in the blood.

Hell

Angel Raphael shows Enoch a place that the souls of the dead are assembled:

> *And from here I went to another place and he showed me in the west a great and high mountain chain and hard rocks and four beautiful places. Beneath them there were places deep and broad and entirely smooth as smooth as if a thing were rolled and deep and dark to look at. And this time, Raphael one of the holy angels who was with me answered and said to me, these beautiful places are intended for this that upon them may be assembled the spirits, the souls of the dead for they have been created that here all the souls of the sons of men might be assembled. These places have been made their dwellings till the day of their judgment and to their fixed period and this period is long till the great judgment will come over them. And I saw the spirits of the children of men who had died and their voices reached up to heaven and lamented. At this time, I asked Raphael who was with me and said to him, whose soul is that one whose voice reaches to the heaven and laments: and he answered and said to me, that is the spirit that proceeded from Abel whom his brother Cain slew and it laments on this accounts till his seed be destroyed from the face of the earth and his seed disappear from among the seed of men.* (Enoch 22:1)

Enoch ask for clarification as to the separation of these regions and is told there are three apartments made in order to separate the souls of the dead from the souls of the just. This passage aligns with many references in the scriptures as to the region of hell and the separation by a great riff or valley. Paradise, a place where the righteous souls were assembled until Jesus set the captives free.

In Enoch 26, he sees the middle of the earth and saw a place blessed and fruitful, containing a special tree, a holy mountain, and water flowing toward the south. Enoch sees future Jerusalem, tree of life, Mount Moriah, and the waters of the brook of Siloam that flow beneath. He sees another mountain we call the Mount of Olives. Between the two mounts, he sees the Valley of Hinnom, or Gehenna, which he described as sterile and cursed. The angel explains to Enoch that in the "latter days," the unsaved will be gathered in this place for judgment. This is picked up in Joshua 15:8, where it is called the valley of the son of Hinnom and was also called the valley of the giants. This location had a history of idolatry and a place where children were sacrificed to Molech. Chronicles 28:1–3 speaks to the burning of incense in the valley of the son of Hinnom and King Ahaz, who burnt his children in the fire.

Enoch 29 to 32 is given a view of mountains with various trees. He sees the trees of frankincense and myrrh, which are native to Arabia and India. He also sees the cinnamon trees, which produce a pleasant fragrance, and aloe trees with hard bark for perfume. Enoch sees the tree of wisdom that was in the Garden of Eden and the angel Zutel who may have been guarding the entrance into Eden. The Angel Raphael takes him above the Persian Gulf:

> *And I came into the garden of justice and I saw the mingled diversity of those trees many and large are planted there, beautiful and magnificent and also the tree of wisdom, eating of it one learns great wisdom. It is like the carob tree and its fruit is like the grape, very good and the fragrance of this tree goes out and is spread far. I said this tree is beautiful and pleasant to look at. Then the holy angel Raphael who was with me answered and said this is the tree of wisdom from which they old father and they aged mother who were before thee ate and they learned wisdom and their eyes were opened and they learned that they were naked and were driven out of the garden.* (Enoch 32)

Enoch 33—the Angel Uriel takes over from the Angel Raphael and gives Enoch a view of the four corners of the earth. In Genesis, the account of creation is brief. By reading Enoch, we broaden our view of the complexity of God's creation. In summary, Enoch is taken to view the twelve portals of the wind as it blows directionally.

> *And from here I went toward the north to the end of the earth and there I saw a great and magnificent wonder … I saw three portals of heaven open in the heavens from each of them proceed north winds when one of them blows there is cold, hail, frost, snow, dew and rain and out of one of the portals it blows for good but when it blows from the two other portals it blows with power* [hurricanes] *and there is misfortune upon the earth and they blow with great power.* (Enoch 34)

In Enoch 35 and 36, he is shown the west, south, and east portals of the wind. After looking upon the majesty of creation, Enoch gives God his glory:

> *I blessed the Lord of glory who had made the great and glorious wonders to show the greatness of his work to the angels and to the souls of men that they might praise his work and that all his creatures might see the works of his might and praise the great work of his hand and bless him to eternity.* (Enoch 36)

Word of Wisdom

This section begins Enoch's *Book of the Parables,* chapters 37–71, and details his second vision. He opens by accounting his lineage back to Adam and states that this is the beginning of the words of wisdom that he will relate to those who dwell on the earth.

> *Hear ancestors and see descendants the holy words which I will speak before the Lord of the spirits. It is proper to name the former first* [Adam] *but from the descendants* [all people throughout history to the Second Coming] *too we will not keep back the beginning of wisdom and up to the present time there was not given from before the Lord of the Spirits the wisdom which I have received according to my knowledge, according to the pleasure of the Lord of the spirits by whom the portion of life everlasting was given to me. Three parables were given to me and I commenced to relate them to those who dwell on the earth.* (Enoch 37)

A brief summary of the above passage confirms Enoch's relationship to Adam: that the knowledge given to Enoch was not known previously to others and he understands that he will receive life everlasting. Wisdom is a woman who found no place to dwell among mankind because the wisdom of God is rejected by people. Proverbs 8:27 … wisdom is seen as living in heaven when the heavens were created before the earth. Wisdom is later seen as the tree of the knowledge of good and evil. Enoch 33, "*This is the tree of wisdom from which thy old father and thy aged mother who were before me ate and they learned wisdom …*"

Enoch 42 continues to define wisdom:

> *Wisdom did not find a place where she might live and a dwelling place was given to her in the heavens. Wisdom came to dwell among the children of men and found no dwelling place: wisdom returned to her place and took her seat among the angels. And injustice came forth from its repository whom it did not seek them it found and dwell with them like the rain in the desert and like dew in the thirsty land.*

In chapter 33, Enoch associates the tree of wisdom with the tree in the Garden of Eden, where it would have remained had not Adam and Eve disobeyed God. Therefore, it was returned to heaven. In its place the roots of injustice and evil sprung forth.

Enoch 38 is extraordinary in its future prophetic projection looking toward the Day of the Lord and the coming of Messiah with his saints.

> *When the congregation of the just* [the saints] *shall appear and the sinners are condemned because of their sins and expelled from the face of the earth and when the Just One* [Yeshua] *will appear in the presence of the just who are chosen whose deeds hang on the Lord of the spirits and the light* [shekinah glory] *shall appear to the just and to the chosen who dwell on the earth, where will be the habitation of the sinners and where [are] the resting places of those who have denied the Lord of the spirits? It were better had they not been born.*

Jesus used the phrase "It were better had they not been born" when speaking about his betrayal by Judas (Matthew 26:24).

Final Day of the Lord

Enoch 38 ties in a bit with Ezekiel 38 leading into and through the tribulation period when *the sinners will be judged and the impious will be expelled from the presence of the just and chosen.* It brings us to the great harvest when the wheat and tares will be separated. At the end of the tribulation, Satan and "*those who hold the earth will not be powerful and exalted nor will they be able to behold the face of the just for the light of the Lord of the spirits is seen on the face of the holy and just and chosen.*" Enoch further expounds that, "*The mighty kings will perish at that time and will be given over into the hands of the just and holy. And from that time on no one can ask for mercy from the Lord of the spirits for their lives have ended.*"

Enoch 39 proclaims that the saints will descend from the high heavens and they will dwell with the redeemed who came through the tribulation as one people. This passage foresees the Second Coming of Yeshua with the saints who will be with Yeshua as he sets up the millennial kingdom. After this revelation, Enoch is taken in *a cloud and a whirlwind from the face of the earth and carried into the end of the heavens.* From this vantage point, Enoch sees those have passed from death to eternity dwelling with God and the angels who cry "holy, holy, holy," and the saints also are praising the Lord. Enoch 39:6 … "*And in those days my eyes saw the place of the chosen of justice and of faith and how justice will be in their days and the just and chosen without number before him to all eternity.*" He sees the future time that Jesus will resurrect the Old Testament saints and looks toward a time that Jesus will gather together all in Christ.

Enoch 40:2, 9 gives us greater insight into the ministry of angels:

> *I looked, and on the four sides of the Lord of the spirits, I saw four faces, different from those standing and I learned their names which the angel* [of peace] *who came with me announced to me and showed me all the secrets.*
>
> *And he said to me the first is the holy Michael, merciful and slow to anger, the second is Raphael, who is over all sicknesses and over all the wounds of the children of men, the third is Gabriel who is over all the powers and the fourth is Phannuel who is over penitence and the hope of those who inherit everlasting life. And these are the four angel of God, the Most High ...*

Enoch 41:1 ... Enoch comments on the *secrets of heaven* by reiterating the ecosystem of the planet Earth and its heavens as written earlier. In this chapter, he sees the *kingdom as it is divided* and may allude to a coming renewed kingdom headed by Jesus. Enoch has wisdom to understand that before the millennial kingdom is established, Jesus must deal with the wicked, stating ... "*The deeds of men are weighed upon scales and the sinners were cast from there, they who had denied the name of the Lord of the spirits and they are dragged away and there is no rest for them because of the punishments which proceed from the Lord of the spirits.*" Egyptian history uses a picture of scales for the weighing of the soul. His heart is placed on one side and a feather on the other. In Babylon, Belshazzar's saw the handwriting on the wall, which said, "*Thou are weighed in the balances and are found wanting.*" In America, we see the symbol of justice blindfolded holding the balances.

Following in chapter 41, Enoch tells us that the weather during the Messianic Age will be stable or *steadfast*. He sees the *dwellings of the chosen and the dwelling of the holy*. Jesus has promised his bride many mansions. He sees that during the great harvest at the end of tribulation, *all the sinners were cast from there*, and these would be those who took the mark of the beast and worshipped it.

> *I saw lightning and the stars of heaven and he called them all by their names and they heard him. The stars were weighed on scales of justice according to their light, and according to the width of their places and the day of their appearance and their course. One flash of lightning produces another and their course according to the number of angels and their fidelity and they preserved among themselves ... What are these? And he said to me, The Lord of the spirits has showed thee a picture of them these are the names of the just who dwell in the earth and believe on the name of the Lord of the spirits to all eternity.* (Enoch 43)

After reading this passage, you get the impression that Enoch is not talking about the literal stars in the heavens. We think of the redeemed as shining brightly like the stars. When we stand before Jesus at the Bema Seat, he will reward us for the light or the Gospel we shared in a small or mega ministry. Then Enoch gives a little sidebar that is a reference to angels who were faithful and kept themselves holy. He then sees the names of the just or redeemed on the earth, who cannot be numbered like the stars.

> *Is the second parable concerning those who deny the name of the dwelling place of the holy and the Lord of the spirits. They will not ascend to heaven and will not come on the earth; such will be the portion of the sinners who deny the name of the Lord of the spirits who are thus preserved to the day of suffering and sorrow. On that day the chosen One* [Messiah Jesus] *will sit upon the throne of glory and will choose among their deeds and places without number and their spirit will be strong in them when they see my Chosen One and those who have called upon my holy and glorious name. And on that day, I will cause my Chosen One to dwell among them and will transform heaven and make it a blessing and a light eternally. And I will transform the earth and make it a blessing and will cause my chosen ones to dwell thereon and those who have committed sins and crimes will not step on it. For I have seen and satisfied with peace my just ones and have placed them before me but for the sinners there awaits before me a judgment that I may destroy them from the face of the earth.* (Enoch 45)

Here in this passage, Enoch is describing the beginning of the millennial reign where the Chosen One will sit on his throne and he will dwell with the redeemed. The earth will be renewed from the devastation of wickedness and the tribulation judgments. The temple of God will be transformed as it descends upon the earth and Jesus will be the source of its light. The wicked will not be permitted to enter into the millennial kingdom because they have denied the name of the Lord and they will be preserved to the day of suffering and sorrow. They will wait in hell for the great white throne judgment, and Jesus will condemn them forever.

Messiah, Son of Man

In Enoch 46:1 he begins to record:

> *And there was one who had a head of days* [ancient] *and his head was white like wool and with him was a second whose countenance was like the appearance of a man and his countenance was full of agreeableness* … I asked one of the angels who is this? *This is Son of man who has justice, and justice dwells in him and all the treasures of secrecy he reveals because the Lord of the spirits* [Father

> God] *has chosen him and his portion overcomes all things before the Lord of the spirits in rectitude to eternity. This Son of man … will arouse the kings and mighty from their couches* [thrones] *and the strong from their thrones … and will break the teeth of the sinners … because they do not exalt him and praise him and acknowledge him … these are they who raise their hands against the Most High and on earth all their doings is injustice … and their power is in their riches and their faith is in gods which they have made with their hands …*

We find confirmation of Enoch's testimony in Daniel 7:9, 13, 14:

> *I beheld till the thrones were cast down and the Ancient of days did sit, whose garment was white as snow and hair like pure wool … I saw one like the Son of man came with the clouds of heaven and came to the Ancient of days … and there was given him dominion, glory and a kingdom … that all nations should serve Him.*

The remainder of the books of Enoch provides many nuggets of wisdom of the end-times. We suggest readers order the complete series of the Book of Enoch from *Prophecy in the News*, from which the above analysis has been shared.

People who do not believe the literal understanding of the Genesis 6 account will be unable to explain God's words to Enoch. If they say the Book of Enoch was written after Genesis, we still have the same Genesis account of angels mixing with human women and producing the Nephilim, or giants. The Bible is true. The so-called church fathers omitted these writing from being included in the Old Testament due to their controversial nature. Bible printers of today, such as Wycliffe, are deleting and changing Bible text for their own personal reasons.

Chapter 7
Fallen Angels and the Nephilim

Chapter Overview

Fallen Angels Descend onto Mount Hermon
Fallen Angels Corrupt Earth's Life Forms
Fallen Angels Teach Mankind Forbidden Knowledge
Commentary on the Fallen Angels and Giants
Bloodlust
The Wrath of God
Satan's Plans Post Flood

CHAPTER 7

FALLEN ANGELS AND THE NEPHILIM

Fallen Angels Descend onto Mount Hermon

Woe to the inhabitants of the earth and of the sea, for the devil is come down unto you, having great wrath. Satan's time frame is from the fall of Adam and Eve up to the Second Coming of Yeshua, at which time he will be defeated and cast into the lake of fire for one thousand years. Until that time, the inhabitants of planet Earth will be under attack by fallen angels, evil spirits, and evil people who do Satan's bidding.

It began in the Garden of Eden. God forbade Adam and Eve to open the portal of the knowledge of good and evil. They were enticed with the promise of knowledge and immortality, therein disobeying God. When Adam and Eve ate of the fruit of the tree of knowledge of good and evil, their eyes were open to see hidden knowledge. They already knew the goodness and holiness of God; now they were going to see and experience the other side of the coin. They would see unspeakable wickedness. They would see the corruption of humankind through angelic mingling with the seed of man. Their action caused a literal breach, or tear, between dimensions, allowing for a hoard of two hundred fallen angels to descend onto Mount Hermon. Scholars refer to Mount Hermon as a portal or star gate and discovered that Roswell, New Mexico, is on the thirty-third parallel with Mount Hermon. There is a connection between evil entities and current-day aliens.

In modern times, the United Nations has an established an outpost on top of Mount Hermon bordering Lebanon and Syria.

At the time of the angelic descent, Adam was approximately 460 years old. Jared, the sixth from Adam, was said to be sixty-five years old when Enoch was born. Jared lived to be 962 years old. Enoch was 310 years old when Adam died at the age of 930. Many preflood people witnessed the corruption of mankind caused by the fallen angels. Methuselah's death at age 969 would be the last of the living righteous, and his death was the sign that the flood was coming marking the time period to be around 3,000 BC.

All life, terrestrial or celestial, is composed of various elements, or particles, mostly in line with their species. That said, a rock has its own elemental composition of various minerals or metals. A trace quantity of mineral compound is found in the cellular composition of humans and animals having been formed from the earth. Celestial beings, such as angels, are composed of celestial matter, which is different than terrestrial matter. Saint Paul points out in 1 Cornthians 15:39–40: "*All flesh is not the same flesh but there is one kind of flesh of men, another flesh of beast, another of fish and another of birds. There are also celestial bodies and bodies terrestrial but the glory of the celestial is one and the glory of the terrestrial is another.*" The fallen angels moved to defy God's commandment that each species reproduce after its own kind, and herein they began to mingle different species.

Fallen Angels Corrupt Earth Life Forms

Enoch 6 and Genesis 6 provide our foundation for understanding the activities of the two hundred fallen angels. Enoch calls them Watchers. In Genesis 6, they are called *b'nai ha elohim*, meaning "sons of God." The scriptures distinguish between men, women, and angels. The majority of the Old Testament refers to angels as the **sons of God**. Job 1:6, "*Now there was a day when the* ***sons of God*** *came to present themselves before the Lord and Satan came also among them.*" In the New Testament, the term *sons of God* refer to mankind. Believers in Yeshua are the sons of God through adoption. This distinction is relevant since some Bible scholars believe the Genesis 6 account was between human men and women.

Enoch 6 given before the flood and Genesis 6 parallel each other:

> *And it came to pass after the children of men had increased in those days, beautiful and comely daughters were born to them. And the angels, the sons of the heavens saw and lusted after them and said one to another, behold, we will choose for ourselves wives from among the children of men and will beget for ourselves children. Semjaza, who was their leader, said to them, I fear that perhaps you will not be willing to do this deed and I alone shall suffer for the great sin. Then all answered him and said, we all will swear an oath and bind ourselves mutually by a curse, that we will not give up this plan but will make this plan a deed. Then they all swore together and bound themselves mutually by a curse and*

> *together they were two hundred. And they descended to Ardis which is the summit of Mount Hermon and they called it Mount Hermon because they had sworn on it and bound themselves mutually by a curse. And these are the names of their leaders: Semjaza was their leader, Urakibarameel, Akibeel, Tamiel, Ramuel, Danel, Ezeqeel, Sarqujal, Asael, Armers, Batraal, Anani, Zaqebe, Samsaveel, Sartael, Turel, Jomjael, Arazjal, these are the leaders of the two hundred angels and the others were with them.* (Enoch 6:1–8)

Compare the above scripture with Genesis 6:1:

> *And it came to pass, when men began to multiply on the face of the earth and daughters were born unto them, that the sons of God saw the daughters of men that they were fair and they took them wives of all which they chose … There were giants in the earth in those days and also after that when the sons of God came in unto the daughters of men and they bare children to them, the same became mighty men* [Gibborim] *which were of old, men of renown. And God saw that the wickedness of man was great in the earth and that every imagination of the thoughts of his heart as only evil continually.*

In case the reader missed the implication in the first verse, God says it again:

> *There were giants in the earth in those days* ***and also after*** **that** when *the sons of God came in unto the daughters of men and they bare children to them the same* <u>*became mighty men which were of old,*</u> <u>*men of renown*</u>. (Genesis 6:4)

This alludes to the preflood offspring of angels and humans that produced giant hybrids. This description of something *mighty, old, and renown* suggests mighty strong giants and angels of old—both of which earned a great reputation. As we mentioned, if this had been a union between men and women, God would not have sent a flood. Men and women engaged in sexual perversion after the flood, and God has not destroyed the earth.

The scripture says "*and also after that*," which means after the flood, wickedness would return; and Satan, fallen angels, and joining with them, evil spirits would continue to corrupt mankind. This abomination would follow throughout earth history, forming the basis for pagan worship and the subjugation of mankind. Jesus confirms this in Matthew 24 that at the end of the age, there will be a repeat of the "days of Noah."

Fallen Angels Teach Mankind Forbidden Knowledge

> *You* [angels] *have been in heaven and though the secrets were not yet revealed to you, still you knew illegitimate mysteries and these you have in the hardness of your hearts related to the women and through these mysteries women and men increase wickedness over the earth.* (Enoch 16:3)

> *And they took unto themselves wives, and each chose for himself one and they began to go in to them and mixed with them and taught them charms and conjurations and made them acquainted with cutting of roots and of woods* [as in black magic and witchcraft]. *They became pregnant and brought forth great giants whose stature was three thousand ells* [from ten to thirty-feet feet tall]. (Enoch 7:1)

Consider carefully how it could be possible for fallen angels to mingle their celestial DNA with human or animal DNA. Angels have a spiritual nature; they do not have flesh and blood. They would not need genitalia or sperm for the purpose of procreation as well as for bodily elimination. God declared they would not marry or reproduce. Angels did witness the creation. They observed God forming animals and man from the elements of the earth. They were very interested in the mysterious substance of blood. They knew that the spirit of God entered Adam by way of God's breath. God had created a man that possessed both earthly elements as well as spiritual essence. They saw Satan mingle with the serpent. They knew the reproductive elements of the male and female and, through observation of procreation of animals and humans, understood the egg of the female and the sperm of the male. They began to understand the complexity of DNA and began to use the building blocks found in blood to clone a hybrid.

We are told they selected the women and then went into them. Once the angels were with the women, we do not have a clear explanation of how they accomplished their plan. If this were the case of natural mating habits between men and women as God intended, then these passages would not be indicative of something highly peculiar and unnatural before God. Enoch points out they went into them and **mixed/mingled** with them and taught them the use of charms, conjurations, cutting roots, and they became pregnant. This is an early accomplishment of genetic manipulation.

According to Enoch 8:1, certain angels were responsible for the following:

- Azazel taught the art of war; making and using swords, knives, shields, breast plates; becoming knowledgeable of earths metals; also making jewelry, antimony for the coloring of eyelids, dyes and formulas, and precious stones; and seeing what was behind them (mirrors).

- Semyaza taught cursing as in a spell, root cutting (drugs).
- Armaros taught cure lifting.
- Baraqiyael taught star signs (astrology).
- Kokabel taught star patterns and signs.
- Ezeqeel taught cloud lore.
- Araquiel taught land signs.
- Shamsiel taught sun signs.
- Sariel/Asradel taught moon pathway.
- Kasdey taught the (Yeladim-A'am?) evil strickings of unclean ruachim (spirits). He showed them the dashing of the embryo in the womb so it would die (abortion).
- No Name taught the summoning or conjuring of spirits to reside in the mind.

Let us factor in the angelic ability to teach mankind all kinds of things that God called "forbidden knowledge." Mankind was taught how to delve into alchemy, necromancy, demonology, rituals, cutting of roots, and more. Aristotle identified metaphysical elements of mercury, sulfur, salt, alchemy associated with drugs/pharmaceutical. They taught mankind how to make weapons using metal. They taught how to extract properties from plants and how to conduct genetic manipulation and how to abort the fetus. We can imagine they had ancient laboratories for their experiments. Perhaps these labs were located on celestial vehicles.

The abilities that mankind learned was passed on to others. We can observe in modern labs technological advances involving DNA manipulation, mingling of materials, splicing and cloning the knowledge first taught by superior beings. This is confirmed in the book of Jasher 4:18: "*Then the sons of men began teaching the mixture of animals of one species with the other in order to provoke the Lord.*"

There is a possibility that preflood people were compromised against their will. It could be similar to modern-day reports of "alien abductions." People seem to be taken for the purpose of extracting genetic material such as blood, tissue, sperm, eggs from humans as well as animals to create hybrids. The commonality associated with these ungodly actions is the obsession with blood and sexual reproduction. In "alien abductions," these entities have the capability to overpower humans. In some instance, humans became agreeable in exchange for something valuable. World governments made deals with the "aliens," allowing them to use humans and animals in exchange for knowledge and power. From these experiments, a new generation of hybrids may have been spawned.

Commentary on the Fallen Angels and Giants before the Flood

Stories and legends can be found in many ancient civilization accounts of "gods" who descended from heaven and materialized in corporeality. Gilgamesh lived in Erech. His written account alludes to gods descending and mingling with terrestrial creation. The writings of Enoch influenced the Akkadian Epic of Creation in their understanding of Tiamat, a Satan-like being who brought chaos through serpents, dragons, hairy men, half men half beasts, scorpion men, demons, fish men, bull men. Other mythological accounts refer to nonhuman entities as fairies, elves, devas, brownies, leprechauns, gnomes, sprites, pixies, banshees, goblins, dryads, mermaids, trolls, griffins, and more as pointed out in Tom Horn's research in *Exo-Vaticana.* Horn unearthed notables who believed in the union of angels and humans.

Jewish historian Flavious Josephus gives this commentary on Genesis 6:

> For many angels of God accompanied with women and begat sons that proved unjust and despisers of all that was good on account of the confidence they had in their own strength; for the tradition is that these men did what resembled the acts of those who the Grecians called giants. But Noah was very uneasy at what they did and, being displeased at their conduct, persuaded them to change their dispositions and their acts for the better; but seeing they did not yield to him but were slaves to their wicked pleasures, he was afraid they would kill him, together with his wife and children and those they had married, so he departed out of that land.

The following passages address the relationship between people and angels:

1 Corinthians 11:10 … the man was not created for the woman, but the woman was created for the man, and "*for this cause, ought the woman to have power on her head* [to cover her head] *because of the angels.*" This tiny reference to angels has a deeper meaning and may suggest that the curiosity of some angels led to their lust for human women.

Early church leader Eusebius commentary:

> "And they begat human beings with two wings and others with four wings and two faces and one body and two heads … still others with horses' hooves and others in the shape of a horse at the rear and a human shape at the front; they also made bulls with human heads and horses with dog's heads as well as other monsters with horses heads and human bodies then all kinds of dragon like beings." Eusebius clearly describes hybrid monsters, and some of these hybrids became giants called Nephilim, which were the

children of the angels. Others picked up the notion that the hybrids had wings."

Church leader Irenaeus commentary on Genesis 6:

> And for a very long while, wickedness extended and spread and reached and laid hold upon the whole race of mankind, until a very small seed of righteousness remained among them and illicit unions took place upon the earth, since angels were united with the daughters of the race of mankind; and they bore to them sons who for their exceeding greatness were called giants. And the angels brought as presents to their wives teachings of wickedness in that they brought them the virtues of roots and herbs, dyeing in colors and cosmetics, the discovery of rare substances, love potions, aversions, amours, concupiscence, constraints of love, spells of bewitchment, and all sorcery and idolatry hateful to God by the entry of which things into the world evil extended and spread while righteousness was diminished and enfeebled."

Book of Jude, chapter 1, points out that certain men crept in unawares who were before of old (angels) ordained to this condemnation and ungodly men (humans), turning the grace of God into lasciviousness (sexual abomination). This alludes to the union of corrupt humans and fallen angels. Jude further highlights the two hundred angels that kept not their first estate but left their own habitation were confined in everlasting chains of darkness prior to the flood. Jude makes reference to the sexual fornication in Sodom and Gomorrah, specifically, human men were going after strange flesh (angels). Also the filthy dreamers defile the flesh, despise dominion, and speak evil of angels (mankind does not fully understand the angelic realm). They speak of those things that they know not but what they know naturally as brute beast, in those things they corrupt themselves.

> *"And injustice increased upon the earth and all flesh corrupted its way, man and cattle and beasts and birds and everything which walks on the earth. And they all corrupted their way and their ordinances and they began to eat one another. And injustice grew upon the earth and every imagination of the thoughts of all mankind was thus continually evil."* (Jubilees 5, 7)

This speaks to preflood corruption. The giant hybrid/Nephilim were fierce, and the humans could not grow enough food or animals to keep them fed. The animals were genetically altered to become giant animals to accommodate the appetites of the giants. When there were hardly any animals left, the Nephilim began to eat the people. Conditions were so dire before the flood that the people cried out to God and he saw their condition and decided to bring a flood to destroy all except a remnant.

> *And the giants turned themselves against mankind in order to devour them. And they began to sin against the birds and the beast and against the creeping things and the fish and devoured their flesh among themselves and drank the blood thereof.* (Enoch 7)

Then the earth complained of the unjust ones. Before the flood, the living people were distressed; the souls of the dead and the earth cried out to God as related in the following passage:

> *Then Michael and Gabriel and Surjan and Urjan looked down from heaven and saw the great amount of blood which had been spilled on the earth and all the wickedness which had been committed over the earth. And they said to one another, the emptied earth reechoes the sound of their cries up to the gates of heaven. And now to you, O you holy ones of heaven, cry the souls of men, saying, secure us judgment before the Most High. And they spoke to their Lord to the King, O Lord of lords, God of gods, King of kings, the throne of thy majesty is among all the generations of the world, and thy name, holy and glorious, among all the generations of the world. Thou are blessed and praised … see then what Azazel has done, how he has taught all wickedness on the earth and has revealed the secrets of the world which were prepared in the heavens* [forbidden knowledge]. *And Semjaza to who thou has given the power to be chief of his associates has made known conjurations and they have gone together to the daughters of men and have slept with them, with those women and have defiled themselves and have revealed to them these sins … And the women have brought forth giants and thereby the whole earth has been filled with blood and wickedness … And now behold the souls which have died cry and lament to the gates of heaven and their groans ascend and they are not able to escape from the wickedness which is committed on the earth. And thou knows everything before it comes to pass and thou knows this and their circumstances and yet thou does not speak to us. What shall we therefore do in regard to this?* (Enoch 9:1)

God's answer to this grave situation is to destroy all living things in the earth by flood. Also, in this end of the age, the righteous cry out to God to bring judgment upon the wicked.

The giants ate man and beast. There is some evidence that giant animals such as dinosaurs lived before the flood. Archeologists claim to have discovered a beaver skull belonging to an animal ten feet long and the skull of a buffalo belonging to an animal ten times larger than modern buffalos. In Iraq tombs, bones of giant people were discovered measuring thirty-four feet tall. The possibility that animals and food were genetically manipulated is found in the Bible account of the spies of Israel who went into the promised land and reported a cluster of grapes were gigantic, having to be carried by two men.

From our discussion, we certifiably believe giant Nephilim existed before the flood. A reference to the term Nephilim found in Genesis 6 in Hebrew is *naphil*, meaning "to fall," and is associated with fallen angels and hybrids. The Greek translation for giant is *gigantes*, which means "earthborn." The *Anchor Bible Dictionary* also makes reference to Nephilim as giant offspring. The understanding is that fallen angels corrupted humankind, creating giant earthborn offspring called Nephilim.

The word *Rephaim* (dead ones) is mentioned postflood and seems to suggest that the disembodied spirits of the Nephilim would become evil spirits or demons (book of Jubilee 7:21).

After the flood, approximately a thousand years transpired before the Bible mentions giants in the land. In the book of Jude, it addresses the possibility that the men of Sodom were engaging with strange flesh, and this abomination did not produce giants. It appears postflood giants became commonplace and are different than preflood Nephilim.

Bloodlust

We briefly mentioned that blood is a mysterious substance. It is the life of the flesh. Celestial beings watched the creation. They were curious about man and especially his blood. The call for sacrificial blood was first instituted by God. After the fall, God shed the blood of animals and made coverings for Adam and Eve. The next incident in the scriptures tells us about Cain killing Abel, and his blood cried out to God from the earth. Perhaps, Satan influenced Cain to commit the first murder because he witnessed God sacrificing animals, and their blood spilled upon the earth as did Abel's. Following this Bible account, we see the invasion of earth by the fallen angels. Their hybrid creatures ate the animals, the people, and had a great desire to drink blood. This reminds us of the tale of *Jack and the Beanstalk*. When Jack climbed the stalk into the heavens, he found the giant who discovered his presence because he smelled the blood of an English man.

When the waters receded following the flood, Noah built an altar and sacrificed an animal. God tells Noah and his family they can now eat the animals but not the blood. Abraham's covenant called for the blood sacrifice of the ram. Circumcision was instituted as a blood covenant. The Mosaic Law called for the sacrifice of animals for everything. Jesus shed his blood, which is said to have been collected and taken to heaven. Jesus left DNA on his shroud (the shroud of Turin). Jesus said, "Eat my flesh and drink my blood." Those who heard this declaration were confused and astonished that Jesus would suggest something so bizarre. Many left following him. Today biblical scholars understand this was not a literal suggestion but a comment having deep spiritual overtones. The Catholic ritual of communion is associated with crucifying Christ again, and though it is done figuratively, it is as literally eating of the body and drinking of the blood of Christ. In other denominations, it is a symbolic ritual in breaking of bread (his beaten body) and drinking of wine (his shed blood) to commemorate the death and Resurrection of our Lord Jesus.

We have a horrific picture of what transpired before the flood for hundreds of years and all generations have followed suit thereafter. The Old Testament confirms this in Ecclesiastes 1:9 … "*What has been will be again, what has been done will be done again, there is nothing new under the sun.*" Early pagan rituals called for the sacrificing of animals and people to idols. Some rituals required the drinking of blood and eating flesh. Today there remains an insatiable thirst for blood. Modern-day high priests practice the ritual of killing the unborn. Aborted fetuses are used in food and research. False religious practices call for ethnic cleansing and shed blood flows in the streets.

God speaks through Enoch to the fallen angels and condemns their sin:

> *While you were spiritual, holy, having eternal life, you defiled yourselves with women and with the* ***blood of flesh*** *have begotten children and have* ***lusted after the blood of men*** *and have produced flesh and blood as they produce who die and are destroyed. Therefore, I have given them wives that they might impregnate them and children be born by them as it is done on earth. You were formerly spiritual, living an eternal life without death to all the generations of the world. Therefore, I have not made for you any wives for spiritual beings have their home in heaven.* (Enoch 15:4–7)

In this passage, we are to understand that angels are eternal spirits and their nature is unto holiness. This group fell from grace, and they lusted after blood; and through genetic engineering, they produced children as did humans. God turned his angels over to a reprobate mind. We believe God allowed the hybrid offspring to reproduce. God goes on to emphasize that the angels were not given wives to procreate because they are spiritual beings of heaven.

At the beginning of the first century AD, the followers of Jesus were cognizant of the ungodly behavior of humans and angels. In their understanding … "*God gave them up to uncleanness through the lusts of their own hearts to dishonor their own bodies between themselves. They changed the truth of God into a lie and worshipped and served the creature more than the*

Creator who is blessed forever." It is important for us as followers of Jesus to understand the implication of this passage in that sexual perversion would be rampant in the last days as it was preflood. People in all ages would worship something or someone other than God the Creator, and … "*For this cause, God gave them up unto vile affections, for even their women did change the natural use into that which is against nature,*" and this clearly points to women having sex with nonhuman entities, beasts, or same-sex unions … "*And likewise also the men, leaving the natural use of the woman, burned in their lust one toward another, men with men working that which is unseemly and receiving in themselves that recompense of their error which was meet.*" Men had left the natural affection for the woman and instead lusted for sodomy and receiving semen into themselves from other men. Homosexuality was rampant during the days of Lot as it is a pandemic today, and … "*they did not like to retain God in their knowledge, God gave them over to a reprobate mind to do those things which are not convenient … who knowing the judgment of God, **they which commit such things are worthy of death** not only do the same but have pleasure in them that do them.*" There will be a consequence for sin … "*to them that are contentious and do not obey the truth but obey unrighteousness, indignation and wrath, tribulation and anguish upon every soul of man that does evil to the Jew first and also the Gentile*" (Romans 2:8–9).

The Wrath of God

First God deals with his celestial beings:

> *For if God spared not the angels that sinned but cast them down to hell and delivered them into chains of darkness, to be reserved unto judgment.* (2 Peter 2:4)
>
> *And the angels which kept not their first estate but left their own habitation, he has reserved in everlasting chains under darkness unto the judgment of the great day.* (Jude 1:6)

Enoch 10–12, the fallen angels will remain buried in the sands for seventy generations.

The wrath of God destroyed the physical body of the Nephilim in the flood. God condemned their spirits to roam the earth. This supports the increase in demonic activity postflood.

> *And of the death of the giants, when the spirits have proceeded from the bodies their flesh shall decay without judgment thus they shall be destroyed on that day when the great judgment* [flood] *over all of the great world shall be completed over the watchers* [angels] *and the impious.* (Enoch 16:1)

And …

> *The giants who have been begotten from body and flesh will be called evil spirits on earth and their dwelling places will be upon the earth.* (Enoch 15:8)

The spirit of the Nephilim left their physical body at the time of death. Because the Nephilim were the product of angelic beings from above, their spirits will roam the earth and their physical body will decay in the grave. Enoch explains further that the spirits of the giants tried to save themselves by casting themselves upon the clouds but did fall to the earth. They will battle and cause destruction on the earth and do evil. They will take no kind of food. They will not become thirsty. They will be invisible. And these spirits will rise up against the children of men and against the women because they have proceeded from them. The spirits of the giants would torment and possess mankind until Jesus begins the millennial reign.

In summary, the spirits of the Nephilim are the following:

- The spirits of the giant Nephilim are now called evil spirits.
- They are earthbound.
- When the giants die, their flesh will rot, but their spirits will continue on the earth.
- These evil spirits will cause destruction, and they will rise up against humans.
- As spirits, they will not eat or drink.
- They will be invisible.
- God's creation of angels will dwell in heaven.
- Earthborn entities will exist on the terrestrial plain.
- Wicked angels, evil spirits/demons, and unsaved mankind will be judged at the end of the thousand-year reign.

The wrath of God came against unrepentant humans. They rejected God and rebelled against him. God gave them over to their lust.

> *For the wrath of God is revealed from heaven against all ungodliness and unrighteousness because that which may be known of God is manifest in them for God has showed it unto them.* (Romans 1:18–19)

Satan Continues His Plan Post Flood

In chapter 8, we continue our discussion of a time before the flood and how the fallen condition of mankind will continue after the flood. We pick up a clue in Daniel 2:43 … "*They shall **mingle** themselves with the seed of men but they shall not cleave one to another even as* *iron is not mixed with clay.*" Are we to understand that celestial beings will once again mingle themselves with humans? With assistance of wicked people, Satan, and his fallen angels, the preflood abominations will be repeated. Hybrids will intermingle with mankind once again, leading all unbelievers to suffer the wrath of God.

We are able to look back through the annals of time and see the diabolical impact upon God's earthly creation. As the god of this world, Satan increased his abilities. Satan became the ultimate representative of evil and dark power. He perfected his ability to transform himself into various forms. With limited restrictions, he could manifest himself anywhere of his choosing. Fueled by his hatred for God, he and his fallen angels would never be satisfied with their criminal achievements in times past or future. Given the title of Destroyer, Satan conspired to destroy the earth through fierce weather, earthquakes, and pollution. He destroys mankind through corrupt rulers, wars, famine, pestilence, abortion, drugs, disease, and sin. Satan will use every deception to turn mankind away from God. Satan's ultimate prize is the soul of man. We also know that postflood people were drawn into wickedness in every aspect of life. As in the days of Noah, so will it be before the coming of the Son of Man. God's judgment this time will be as never before or ever again.

Throughout this book, we present again and again the goals and plans Satan carries out against this world. We continue to give hope that God has sent his holy angels as messengers to warn mankind and to offer blessings for obedience. Repeatedly, mankind rejects truth and embraces the lie. Satan has deceived man by changing the truth of God into a lie. They rather worship the created instead of the Creator of the universe. Following are highlights of Satan's goal:

- He comes to kill, steal, destroy; he wants your soul.
- Through deception, like sheep, they are led astray for the slaughter.
- He destroys all that our holy God has created.
- He is a counterfeiter.
- He wants power to control the population, wealth, natural resources, your mind.
- He wants to enslave mankind physically, mentally, spiritually as in connection with the demonic world, to force mankind to accept demons under any guise (UFO, angelic appearance, witchcraft, occult).
- He wants you to take his mark so your soul will belong to him.
- He wants to kill humans via abortion, war, genocide, famine, pestilence, drugs.
- At the end of the age, he will vaccinate, poison your air, food, water, set up police states, take away your privacy, and drones will monitor your life.
- He will use one against another in violent crimes, torture, murder across all cultures, religions, and nations.

Trying to wrap our heads around these extraordinary circumstances that befell earth people before the flood, we hope the evidence provided will be a wakeup call. History does repeat itself. Knowing this, we need to have a better understanding of the nature of the spiritual realm and how the spiritual realm interacts with each person.

Daily Mail, April 18, 2016, by Corey Charlton reported, "Mystery body possession epidemic sweeps through Malaysian schools, causing staff and students to collapse while being pinned down by evil spirits." Students report visions of demons, and Teacher Norlelawati Ramli said she was physically pinned down by a spiritual entity while trying to help a student. Clergy were asked to come in for an intervention.

Above, we highlighted Satan's goals and how he uses evil as a weapon against us. If we deny the power of Satan or just don't care, we are targets for attack. Genesis 3:15, we see the seed of Satan at war with the seed of the woman. Again we are reminded that Satan's plan was to prevent the future Messiah from coming to fulfill the Genesis 3:15 prophecy.

Chapter 8
As in the Days of Noah

Chapter Overview

The Birth of Noah
- Days of Noah before the Flood
- God Warns Noah
- Fallen Angels Are Bound
- Fallen Angels Ask for Mercy
- Seventy Generations
- The Waters Cover the Whole Earth
- Holy Angels Heal the Earth
- God's Covenant
- Noah Was Naked
- Historical Evidence of the Flood

The Rebirth of Mankind
- Genealogy of Noah's Sons
- Anthropology and Migration
  - Exhibit: Map of Nations
- Racism Divides Humankind
  - Exhibit: Faces of Humanity

The Legend of Nimrod
- Tower of Babel
- Commentary on Nimrod
- Was Nimrod a Giant Nephilim?
- Giants and Evil Spirits, Post Flood
  - Exhibit: Ruins of Nimrod

Growth of Kingdoms Give Rise to Paganism
- Zoroastrianism
- Sumerian Empire
- Assyrian Empire
- Babylonian Empire
- Persian Empire
- Egyptian Empire
- Greek Empire
- Roman Empire

Identification of Pagan Gods

Chapter 8

As in the Days of Noah

The Birth of Noah

Genesis 5:28, Lamech was 182 years old when his son Noah was born. His name means "comfort." Noah was five hundred years old when Shem, Ham, Japheth were born (Genesis 6:10).

Noah may have had other children before the birth of these three sons, but scripture does not list all births and deaths.

Genesis 6:8–9 … Noah found grace (God's favor) in the eyes of the Lord. Noah was a just man (following the ways of God). Noah walked with God, and in Genesis 5:24, we see his close relative, Enoch, also walked with God. Noah was perfect in his generations, and this may allude to Noah not being contaminated with corrupted celestial DNA during his lifetime.

From Adam to Noah

Adam + Eve
Cain, Abel, Seth,
Seth
Enos
Cainan
Mahalaleel
Jared
Enoch
Methuselah
Lamech
Noah + wife
|
Shem, Ham, Japheth

Cain + wife
Enoch
Irad
Mehujael
Methusael
Lamech + Adah + Zillah
Adah: | Jabal, Jubal
Zillah: | Tubalcain, Naamah

Days of Noah before the Flood

> *The earth was corrupt before God and the earth was filled with violence. And God looked upon the earth and behold it was corrupt for all flesh had corrupted his way upon the earth.* (Genesis 6:11–12)

The scriptures explicitly state that it was a time of corruption and violence. Remember, Adam and Eve opened the portal of evil and chose Satan over God. This allowed an evil so great and malevolent to invade the earth, covering it like a thick darkness—something so heinous it is difficult for humankind to comprehend. We can only piece together a picture of this time before the flood through Genesis, Enoch, Jubilees, and Peter. Enoch and Noah were alive during the invasion by the fallen angels. Noah does not provide us with his account of the time before the flood.

> *And God saw that the wickedness of man was great in the earth and that every imagination of the thoughts of his heart was only evil continually.* (Genesis 6:5)
>
> *And injustice increased upon the earth and all flesh corrupted its way, man, cattle, beasts, birds, and everything that walks on the earth. They all corrupted their way and their ordinances and they began to eat one another.* (Jubilees 5:2)

The writer of Jubilees understood that the flesh of living beings had been corrupted by the fallen angels. This mingling produced giants who had an insatiable appetite, and they ate man and beast.

Noah Is Warned about the Impending Judgment

Genesis 6:13, and God said unto Noah, "The end of all flesh is come before me, for the earth is filled with violence through them [giants], and behold I will destroy them with the earth." God declares his judgment would destroy the whole earth and all flesh (human, hybrid, and animals). It is sobering to consider that God allowed humankind and his other created beings to be corrupted to the extent that only Noah and his family were worthy to be saved. Is this what we can expect at the end of days when the wrath of God is poured out upon the earth?

> *Then the Most High, the Great and Holy One spoke and sent Arsjalaljur to the son of Lamech* [being Noah] *and said to him: tell him in my name, hide thyself and reveal to him the end which is to come for the whole earth will be destroyed and the water of the deluge is about to come over the whole earth and*

> *what is upon it will be destroyed. And now instruct him that he may escape and his seed remain on the whole earth.* (Enoch 10:1–15)
>
> *By faith Noah, being warned of God of things not seen as yet moved with fear, prepared an ark to the saving of his house by which God condemned the world and Noah became heir of the righteousness which is by faith.* (Hebrews 11:7)

At this time in history, before the incarnation of God, men who were faithful and obedient in the ways of God, it was accounted unto them as righteousness. Today believers in Christ who are faithful and obedient are covered in his righteousness because man's righteousness is as filthy rags.

God gave Noah instructions to build an ark when he was five hundred years old. He began by gathering gopherwood and making pitch. It was to be three stories tall with a door on one side and one window at the top. The ark was approximately the size of one and a half football fields, and it was six times longer than it was wide. Modern shipbuilders use this same ratio.

When the ark was finished and all the animals were onboard, food, all the seeds for replanting, barrels to catch rainwater for drinking, and the written records passed from Enoch to Noah, then God shut the door.

God Commands the Fallen Angels Be Bound under the Earth

> *And again the Lord spoke to Raphael, bind Azazel hand and foot and put him in the darkness, make an opening in the desert which is in Dudael and put him there … and lay upon him rough and pointed rocks, and cover him with darkness that he may remain there forever and cover his face that he may not see the light. And on the great day of judgment, he will be cast into the fire.* (Enoch)

This group of fallen angels also called watchers defined in our chapter 7 had descended upon Mount Hermon were the first to be cast into hell a place God prepared for Satan and his fallen angels. Satan and the other fallen angels remained free to continue to deceive mankind. Chapter 4 provided summary of spiritual entities.

Gabriel Is the Angel OverPowers

God tells Gabriel to destroy the bodies of the giant Nephilim:

> *God said to Gabriel, go against the bastards and those cast off and against the children of fornication and destroy the children of fornication and the children of the watchers from among men. Lead them out and let them loose that they may destroy each other by murder for their days shall not be long.* (Enoch)

It appears God is dealing with fallen angels and their children, the Nephilim hybrids, amongst whom he will cause derision to kill each other.

The Fallen Angels and Their Offspring Ask for Mercy

> *They will all supplicate thee but their fathers will secure nothing for them, although they expect an everlasting life and that each one of them will live five hundred years. God said to Michael, announce to Semjaza and to the others who are with him, who have bound themselves to women to be destroyed with them in all their contamination. When all their sons shall have slain one another and they shall have seen the destruction of their beloved ones, bind them under the hills of the earth for seventy generation till the day of their judgment and of their end, till the last judgment has been passed for all eternity. And in those days, they will be led to the abyss of fire, in torture and in prison they will be locked for all eternity. And then he will burn and be destroyed and they will be burned together from now on to the end of all generations. And destroy all the souls of lust and the children of the watchers because they have oppressed mankind.* (Enoch)

The above passages from Enoch provide information that is summarized as follows:

- Four good angels—Arsjalaljur, Raphael, Gabriel, Michael—God tells the good angels to heal the earth and send the hybrids to destroy each other.
- Hybrids thought they would live forever. God gave them five hundred years or up to the time of the flood. Their bodies would be destroyed by killing each other and the remnant in the flood; their spirits would roam the earth to torment mankind.
- Fallen angels who mingled with humans would be bound under the earth for seventy generations.
- At the day of judgment, they will be led to the abyss of fire, tortured and imprisoned for all eternity.

In the book of Jubilees 10:7–9, there is given an account of a flurry of activity before the flood. Satan, whom the writer refers to as Mastema, chief of the spirits, asks God to allow him to keep a tenth of the fallen angels:

> *O Lord, Creator, leave some of them before me and let them obey my voice and let them do everything which I tell them because if some of them are not left for me, I will not be able to exercise the authority of my will among the children of men because they will be corrupted and led astray before my judgment because*

the evil of the sons of men is great and let a tenth of them remain before him but let nine parts go down into the place of judgment.

These passages also support the testimony of Enoch, who understands the fallen angels will be bound under the earth. We also have a glimpse of the relationship Satan has with God. Adam and Eve lost their title deed to the earth. The new landlord is Satan, who will carry out his will until he is cast into the lake of fire. From the passages in Jubilees, writings in the Bible, and the personal testimonies of humankind, Satan apparently was allowed to retain an innumerable host of fallen angels to carry out his will and desires.

Seventy Generations

Enoch 10:12 has told us that this group of fallen angels would be bound for seventy generations. The generations from Adam to Enoch were seven. From Enoch to Noah and sons may be seven generations, or approximately a thousand-year period. We estimate from Shem, Ham, Japheth born a hundred years before the flood, to Abraham, may have been fourteen generations—approximately a thousand-year period. In Matthew 1:17, we are told there were fourteen generations from Abraham (born 2100 BC) to David born (1040 BC), approximately thousand-year period. From David up to the Babylonian captivity, fourteen more generations, a period of five hundred years. From the captivity to Jesus, another fourteen generations (the life span was decreasing and more children born in a shorter time frame), a period of five hundred years. We calculate approximately seventy generations from time of flood to present day, AD 2015—approximately 4,900 years. We fall short by 115 years but can be adjusted based on approximations and not actual time. How many generations have passed in the last two thousand years? If a generation is around seventy years, then approximately twenty-eight generations have passed; seventy plus twenty-eight gives us ninety-eight generations from the time Enoch predicted the captivity of the fallen angels. This brings us to the statement made by Jesus in Matthew 24:34: "*This generation will not pass until all these thing be fulfilled.*" First we may note that Jesus could be defining these two thousand years from AD 1 to AD 2015 as a generation of events and not of particular births. Second, we are wondering about those angels that were bound preflood for seventy generations. Will they be released during the tribulation period?

Enoch tells us that the fallen angels who sinned with humankind would stay bound for seventy generations, and this brings us to the time of Jesus. God told Enoch that the evil spirits of the Nephilim would roam the earth and torment men. In the book of Revelation, we read that during the tribulation, these evil spirits will be unhindered to wreak havoc upon the earth. This may point to an increase in demonic activity nearing the end of the age. We pause for a moment to reflect upon the wickedness and lawlessness of people worldwide in the twenty-first century. It certainly appears those evil spirits have been loosed.

The Waters Cover the Whole Earth

God makes a way of escape for those he chooses, and he chose to save a remnant of all life forms. Entering within the protection of the ark were the representatives of humankind, other species, seed, and the records of creation. Tucked away in the ark from the wrath of God, seven days later, the rain began on the second month, seventeenth day. The waters springing forth from the deep and raining down from heaven continued for forty days. The whole earth was covered in water as it was in the beginning of creation. When the waters receded, the ark had settled upon the mountains of Ararat in Anatolia on the seventeenth day of the seventh month of Nisan. Genesis 8:4, having spent about a year on the ark, God opened the door on the second month, twenty-seventh day, and they all went forth.

The worldwide flood destroyed every breathing, living thing on the face of the earth. Some sea creatures may have been able to survive the raging waters. It can be speculated that the storm was so powerful and devastating that existing archeological records, monuments, landmarks were destroyed and transported by violent tidal waves to distant locations. If there were any human remains of those who lived before the flood, it would be rare. Geologists and archeologists discovered dismembered beasts, birds, reptiles, and fish tangled within fossil or in sediment in the Arctic Circle. In this region, trees and bushes do not exist; however, the remains of elephants and other large beasts were interspersed within the remains of uprooted and broken trees. The earth's land mass broke apart, forming future continental plates.

The ark rested close to regions previously occupied by Noah's ancestors, near the Rivers Tigris and Euphrates. Interestingly, they returned to the cradle of civilization in the upper region of Eden. Repopulation began in what is called the Fertile Crescent. As time passed, the region was referred to as the land of Shinar, the regions of Nimrod, Asshur, Mesopotamia, Chaldea, and Ur.

Noah and his people were the only ones who had firsthand knowledge of the first world—a world of wonders that included city states, technological marvels, and the gods who descended from heaven. Noah's descendants retained knowledge of the one true God from oral records and the writings of Enoch, which passed down from generation to generation.

Who or what was left to be regenerated after the flood? All those on the ark and Satan, his other fallen angels, and the evil spirits of the Nephilim were present. Apparently, Satan was able to make viable the evil spirits and demons for his use. We see this trinity of ungodliness opened another portal for demonic activity. The forbidden knowledge taught to mankind by the first group of angels resurfaced after the flood through the practices of idolatry and delving into areas that God had forbidden. Lord Jesus said just as it was in the days of Noah moral decline, ungodliness and wickedness would again provoke the wrath of God at the end of days.

God Tells the Holy Angels to Heal the Earth

> *Heal the earth which the* [fallen] *angels have defiled and announce the healing of the earth that I will heal it and that not all the sons of men shall be destroyed through the mystery of all the things which the watchers* [fallen angels] *have spoken and have taught their sons.* (Enoch)

God's Covenant

One of the first things Noah did upon leaving the ark was to build an altar and sacrifice animals as an offering to God. Being pleased with Noah, Genesis 8:21, "*And the Lord God smelled a sweet savor* [like barbecue] *and said in his heart, I will not again curse the ground anymore for man's sake for the imagination of man's heart is evil from his youth. Neither will I again smite anymore everything living as I have done.*" In this covenant, God promises to bless Noah and his sons, their seed, and to bless every living creature, including birds and beasts (Genesis 9:9–10).

God also confirms that as long as the earth remains, there will be seedtime and harvest, winter and summer; day and night shall not cease. God blessed Noah and his sons and told them to be fruitful and multiply and replenish the earth. These eight souls would represent the new birth. Here is a good place to interject that the practice of homosexuality is abnormal and the repopulation of the earth would have been impossible between same-sex unions who cannot, through natural means, produce children. Modern man is devising methods to create embryos that can be implanted into an artificial womb, therein eliminating the need for a female to give birth. God acknowledges that the imagination of man's heart is evil from his youth and the lifespan of man would gradually decrease to about 120 years.

Summary of the Noahic covenant as established in Genesis 9 between God, man, and living creatures:

- God will not again flood the entire earth.
- The animal kingdom will flourish.
- Mankind can now eat the animals.
- Man is forbidden to consume blood.
- Capital punishment for murder.
- Be fruitful and multiply.

As a sign of this covenant, God displayed a rainbow in the clouds. A rainbow is likely chosen because it is seen as the colors emanating around the throne of God. This was probably the first ever to be seen. God remembered his love for all living beings, and his covenant extended to the animal kingdom as well as to humankind.

God had shown mercy and grace toward the eight survivors. The number 8 represents new beginnings for Noah and his family and all the animals. It now was Noah's and his sons' responsibility to remember the goodness of God and to pass this knowledge to all generations. It can be speculated that Noah could read and write. He could read the books of Enoch because God returned Enoch to the earth and instructed him to share his testimony with his family and then give the books to his son Methuselah, who in turn passed them to Lamech, who passed them to his son Noah, who passed them to Shem, Ham, Japheth. There are no written records attributed to Noah, Shem, Ham, or Japheth. They had knowledge of the events before the flood. They were witnesses to the flood. After the flood, they lived for hundreds of years. Noah lived another 350 years after the flood. Noah died at the age of 950 years. A small percentage of the birth and death of most of their offspring were recorded. In all that we can gather, Shem, Ham, and Japheth leave no record of giants in the land before or after the flood.

Noah Was Naked

The scriptures tell us that Noah became a husbandman and grew vineyards. After drinking the fruit of his vine, he fell asleep naked. Ham saw his father's nakedness, and Noah cursed his grandson Canaan. God had blessed the sons of Noah and their offspring. Noah's curse could not nullify God's blessing. There are some who say Ham sodomized his father. However, in this writing, we do not believe this to be the case. Nakedness is synonymous with shame. Visit the account of Adam and Eve in the Garden of Eden. They were naked. It was only after they listened to Satan then ate from the tree of knowledge did they become aware of their nakedness or shame. When God found them hiding, they said they were naked. They were ashamed to stand before God because they had disobeyed God. We all stand naked before God. Our sin nature is fully exposed to God, who sees our innermost deeds. We cannot hide our sin from God.

In Habakkuk 2:15, we find evidence to support this theme that nakedness is associated with shame: "*Woe unto him that gives his neighbor drink, that puts the bottle to him and makes him drunken also that you may look on their nakedness.*"

Other supporting scriptures are Revelation 3:18 (to the church of Laodicea) … "gold that has been tried in the fire, clothed in white raiment so that the **shame of thy nakedness** does not appear …"

Revelation 16:15, Jesus said, "Behold I come as a thief, blessed is he that watches and keeps his garments, lest he walk **naked and they see his shame**."

Ezekiel 23:29–30 (in regard to Israel), they shall deal with you hatefully and will take away your labor and will **leave you naked and bare ...**

Nakedness has to do with the shame we feel when our sin has been exposed. Noah got drunk. Ham looked upon his drunken, naked father. God commands us to avoid strong drink and not to be overcome with drunkenness. Noah became aware that Ham found him inebriated and naked, and because of Noah's shame, he cursed Ham's son, Canaan. The sin nature was imputed unto all mankind after the fall of Adam and Eve.

Historical Evidence of the Flood

Mankind did not lack intelligence after the flood. *Primitive* does not mean "dumb" but refers to "earliest or ancient origins." The chosen people were notable for their record keeping, and God watched over his Word. The story of the flood was passed down from Noah through the ages and is found in various cultures.

The original record of God and creation became distorted, and mythological stories took on a life of its own. Over two hundred flood stories of a worldwide flood and fallen angels producing offspring with earthly women are found in the histories and myths of various cultures.

Evidence of a worldwide flood can be found in fossilized remains of sea creatures discovered in the mountain ranges of Mount Everest and other regions. The descendants of Noah's sons would give birth to folklore we find in the Babylonian, Mesopotamia, Sumerian, Assyrian, Persian, and Egyptian artifacts as well as the narratives that followed others as they migrated to further locations on the globe. Plato, in his writing, *Critia*, recounts the great flood and the destruction of the fabled Atlantis. Ancient Chinese history has a record of the flood. Accounts of the flood are found in Peruvian, Mexican, and Native American Indian folklore—who all share genetic heritage.

Some historical findings are maintained in Cambridge University Library. The writings of Sir James Frazer published in 1918 included 137 accounts of the great flood before the Gospel was preached in those nations. Satan influenced people such as Charles Darwin, Nicolas Steno, Georges Cuvier, Charles Lyell, to introduce other theories that the flood was not worldwide but local. If that was the case, God would not have instructed Noah to build an ark to house animals, seed, and humans. If it were local, life would have moved to higher ground. If it were local, then the Word of God would be a lie that the flood was not a judgment for wickedness throughout the world.

The Rebirth of Mankind

Creation of man was approximately 4000 BC, and leading up to the flood brings us to approximately 3000 BC. We estimate a thousand years transpired before the flood since Methuselah, the oldest living person, would die before the flood. He was the last of the patriarchs in Noah's lineage, dying at age 969 BC. It took Noah a hundred years to build the ark. At the beginning of the work, Methuselah was living; and near the completion of the ark, Methuselah died. After the flood, approximately another thousand years transpired, because Abraham was born around 2100 BC in a region called Ur in Mesopotamia.

God created only one race, and that is the human race. After the flood, the whole of humanity descended from Noah's three sons: Shem, Ham, Japheth. His sons were a hundred years old when they began to produce offspring. We can look at the distinguishing features of people today and logically deduce that is what people looked like after the flood. Within the human race, we have various characteristics. For instance, our complexions range from dark to fair; there are more facial features than we can identify; and the texture and color of our hair vary. Apparently, Ham's complexion was dark; Shem's complexion was brown; and Japheth's complexion was fair. If each couple gave birth to one or two children once a year, it would take at least thirteen years for the males and females to come of age to reproduce. The parents probably would have given their sons and daughters to marry their cousins. God did preordain interbreeding. Genesis 10:1, "*Now these are the generations of the sons of Noah, Shem, Ham, and Japheth, and unto them were sons born after the flood.*"

Their offspring **reproduced, intermarried, replenished** the earth and migrated throughout the world, forming the nations. Genesis 10:32, "*These are the families of the sons of Noah after their generations, in their nations and by these were the nations divided in the earth after the flood.*"

We should point out that after the flood, there were no Hebrews or Israelites. There were no traditional religions. People were either godly or ungodly. The godly lineage from Seth to Noah is continued through Shem. The chosen people would come through the bloodline of the Gentile Abraham. God began to instruct Abraham in his ways. Their lineage continues through Isaac and his son Jacob, who became the father of the twelve tribes of Israel. It would continue with Moses, who was born and raised in Egypt, Africa, who would bring the Hebrew Israelites out of Egypt into the land of Canaan. Finally, through the tribe of Judah would come Messiah.

The seed of Jacob would be as numerous as the sand. For future identification of those associated with the twelve tribes, God sealed them and placed a specific DNA marker in them, and this is confirmed by modern DNA testing. The Hebrew Israelites are a classic representation of our ancestors, Shem, Ham, Japheth. The diversity of humanity is reflective in their facial features, range of complexions from dark to pale, physical distinctions as short to tall and various hair textures such as wavy/curly, straight/fine, or coarse/thick. We can conclude that in modern times, people look as they did thousands of years ago.

The book of 1 Chronicles 1 begins with a brief overview of human genealogy beginning with Adam. The Bible record follows the descendants of Shem, Abraham, Isaac, and Ishmael—listing the twelve sons of Ishmael and the twelve sons of Jacob. The Bible follows Jacob's descendants to Salma, who begat Boaz, to Jesse and his son, David, future king of Israel. A few examples of intermarriage are listed: Judah, the son of Jacob, had children with Shua, a **Canaanite.** David's sister, Abigal, had children with Amasa, an **Ishmaelite.** Caleb, the son of Hezron, had children with his wife, Azubah, and with his concubine Jerioth. When his wife died, he had a son with Ephrath, named Hur. He had sons with his concubine Maachah. Continuing with Sheshan, he had no sons but gave his daughter to Jarha, his **Egyptian** servant. The son of Ezra, Mered, had sons with Bithiah, the daughter of **Pharaoh.** In brief, Solomon and David had many wives and concubines. It would have been impossible to keep a family record of all those offspring, but we can factor in secular history to follow the relationship between Shem, Ham, and Japheth's descendants.

Genealogy of Noah's Sons

Genesis 11:10 … Shem was a hundred years old when he begat Arphaxad, two years after the flood. Shem lived five hundred years after the flood and died six hundred years old, approximately 2500 BC.

Arphaxad was thirty-five when he begat Salah and begat more sons and daughters; he died at age 438.

> Salah was thirty years when he begat Eber/Heber (Hebrew). Salah died at age 433.
> Eber was forty-three years when he begat Peleg. Eber died at age 464.
> Peleg was thirty years when he begat Reu. Peleg died at age 239.
> Reu was thirty-two when he begat Serug. Reu died at age 239.
> Serug was thirty-two when he begat Nahor. Serug died at age 230.
> Nahor was twenty-nine years when he begat Terah. Nahor died at age 148.
> Terah lived seventy years and begat **Abram**, Nahor, and Haran.
> Haran begat **Lot**. Haran died before Terah in Ur. Terah died in Haran at age 205.

Genesis 11:29, Abram marries Sarai, and Nahor marries Milcah. Genesis 10, Shem's descendants continue in Elam, **Asshur,** Lud, and Aram. Aram begat Uz, Hul, Gether, Mash.

Eber begat Joktan. Joktan begat Almodad, Sheleph, Hazarmaveth, Jerah, Hadoram, Uzal, Diklah, Obal, Abimael, Sheba, Ophir. Havilah is associated with Arabia and Jobab. (Thirteen sons came from Joktan.)

Genesis 10:30, "*And their dwelling was from Mesha as you go unto Sephar a mount of the* ***east.***" Their roots began in Mesopotamia.

Shem's descendants would become

Arphaxad, also Chaldeans
Joktan—Arabia
Elam—Babylon, Persians, Midian, Chaldeans, Sumerians
Asshur—Assyrians
Eber or Heber—Hebrews, Samaritans
Aram—(Syria) his sons: Uz (founder of Damascus), Hul (Armenia), Gether, Mash
Lud—Lydians
Edom—Ammonites, Moabites
Ishmalites

Ammonites and Moabites, offspring of Lot, and his daughters are associated with Jordan.

Genesis 10:31, "*These are the sons of Shem, after their families, after their tongues, in their lands, after their nations by these were* *the nations divided in the earth after the flood* (no mention of complexion).

Ham's sons were Cush, Mizraim, Phut, and Canaan.

Canaan begat Sidon, Heth, Jebusite, Amorite, Girgasite, Hivite, Arkite, Sinite, Arvadite, Zemarite, Hamathite.

Cush begat Seba, Havilah, Sabtah, Raamah, Sabtechah, **Nimrod.**

Raamah begat Sheba and Dedan.

Mizraim begat Ludim, Anamin, Lehabim, Naphtuhim, Caphtorim.

Pathrusim, Casluhim (out of whom came **Philistines**).

Ham's descendants represent

Egyptians/Ethiopians	Canaanites
Philistine/Casluhim	Mizraim
Amorites	Put—Libya
Hittites	Jebusites
Hivites	Girgashites
Prizzites	Babylonians
Chinese/India/Asians	Phoenicians

Genesis 10:19, "*And the border of the Canaanites was from Sidon to Gerar to Gaza to Sodom, Gomorrah, Admah, Zeboim, Lasha.*"

Japheth, the elder of the three (Genesis 10:21), he begat Gomer**, Magog**, Madai, Javan, Tubal, Mesheck, Tiara.

Gomer begat Ashkenza, Riphat, Togarmah.

Javan begat Elishah, Tarshish, Kittim, Dodanim.

Japheth's descendants became the following nations:

Madai—Medes	Lud/Lydia	Kittim
Magog—Russia	Thracians	Anatolia/Asia/Turkey
Tubal/Iberians	Scythians	Spain/Portugese
Mesheck	Romans	England/Scotland
Tiras	Askenaz	Goths
Gomer/Galls	Togarmah	Germans
Javan/Greek	Thracians	Huns

Genesis 10:5, "*By these were* ***the isles*** *of the Gentiles divided in their lands, everyone after his tongue, after their families, in their nations.*"

Some names and regions may overlap. The study makes suggestions in some areas and lists accurate data in other areas. The study provides us with an overview of our first ancestors. The map allows us to imagine the initial passages of migration into other parts of the world.

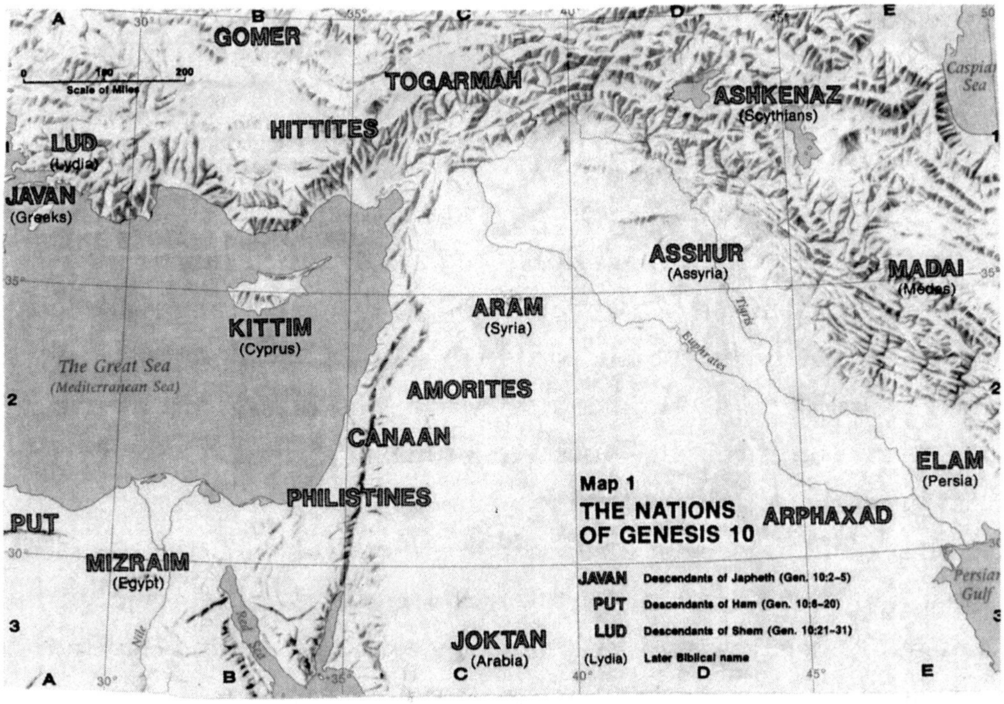

Exhibit: Map of Nations

> *God has made the world and all things therein, seeing that he is Lord of heaven and earth, dwells not in temples made with hands, neither is worshipped with men's hands as though he needed anything, seeing he gives to all life and breath and all things. And he has made of one blood all nations of men for to dwell on all the face of the earth and has determined the times before appointed and the bounds of their habitation.* (Acts 17:24–26)

The descendants of Shem, Ham, Japheth are of one blood. We are all their descendants, and we are all related. Even though humankind has experienced homogenous activity, it is interesting to note that the distinct characteristics of each of Noah's sons was preserved in future generations. For example, many of the Hamites retained their dark complexion and features as did Japheth's descendants, who retained their fair complexion.

God loves all of his people. It is never too late to change the way you think on things and how you perceive God's truth the only light in a dark world.

<u>Anthropology</u>

The study of anthropology allows us to look at distinctions and characteristics within humanity. This area of study has made some interesting discoveries that support ancient human lineage from Noah's family. Researchers of this discipline **vary and disagree** on their findings, the age of artifacts, and its relationship to a particular group of people. For example, anthropologists date humanity from 10,000 to 900,000 BC; while others exaggerate it to be four million years ago.

An article published in *Live Science* by Charles Q. Choi, December 19, 2013, online provide some observation regarding "a forty-thousand-year old Neanderthal woman's genome reveals <u>unknown human lineage</u>. DNA results of her <u>toe bone</u> indicated <u>inbreeding</u> may have been common among her recent ancestors in that her parents were closely related such as half siblings or another relative." **Our comment**, we have discussed inbreeding was a common practice as far back as Adam and Eve, and it is unlikely there exists any viable forty-thousand-year-old human DNA available for comparison.

Human remains found from Siberia to Africa support evidence that humanity bred humans and debunks the theory that apes were primal humans. Even though there is no scientific data to support humanity evolved from apes, some anthropologists continue to cling to an evolutionist point of view. In the developing theory of evolution, people were labeled as Neanderthal, Homo erectus, Cro-Magnon, or Denisovan. European academia began to classify Asians and Native Americans as originating from a Denisovan classification and having <u>interbred with an unknown human lineage.</u> Some may ask, What is an unknown human lineage? An evolutionist could believe it is a reference to apes evolving to humans; creationists could be referencing interbreeding between Noah's three sons, or it could be a cloaked reference to the intermingling of celestials and humans as in the days of Noah. Those who believe the Bible record is true can agree that from one blood came all humanity.

Rasmus Nielsen, biologist of University of California, said, "The study really highlights that **no race of people on earth belongs to one ancestral group;** rather we all have proportions of ancestral groups, and we can begin to contemplate the fact that we are all connected to other species—extinct smart bipeds." **Our comment**—God created each after its own species, and the human connection with other species is that we are all terrestrial life forms.

Migration

Let us consider that primal humanity lived on one land mass surrounded by water. Adam and Eve gave birth to the human race beginning in the region of Mesopotamia. After hundreds of years, the population expanded and advanced. Herein we could interject the legend of the highly advanced civilization of Atlantis, which appears to have been formed on one land mass. As the population grew, people began to migrate to other regions.

After the great flood, land mass separated, dividing into the five continents. If you study a world map, one could push the continents back together again. For instance, North and South America would fit together like a puzzle with Africa.

Evolutionists theorize that humans began to diverge from each other around a million years ago.

Creationists believe the "divergence" was due to a catastrophic event—namely, the great flood approximately five thousand years ago. The survivors of the flood migrated from the mountainous regions of Ararat (Anatolia/Asia/ Turkey) onto the plains of Shinar near the Rivers Euphrates and Tigris, also referred to as the Fertile Crescent. Later the region was called Mesopotamia, and here the rebirth of mankind began. After the flood, another catastrophic event took place in the region of Mesopotamia called the Tower of Babel event. Here God caused the universal language to become many languages. God dispersed the people to other regions, and the people congregated together by language (not complexion).

Linguistic research classifies languages with its parent or original language. Within the diversity of languages, some words can still be associated with the original language. One major language group is classified as Indo-European, which covers Europe to India. In this group, Latin, German, English, Scandinavia, Sanskrit share a relationship. Note, Hebrew is not listed—which we believe is the original language.

People multiplied and migrated throughout the planet. As they settled various regions, they gave names to their nations, which are synonymous with the ancient nations of Assyria, Babylon, Persia, Canaan, and Egypt. Movement of people contributed to intermingling, and from this activity various ethnicities and cultures emerged. Nations rose up against nation, conquering land and people. Conquering forces destroyed historical records and documents, leaving blank spaces in tracing the migration of Shem, Ham, and Japheth descendants. We work from our current time period, tie in biblical facts and historical records, and move back in time to trace the movement of our ancestors.

Shortly, we will analyze the roots of racism. Shem was brown, Ham was dark, and Japheth was fair. Speaking in general, some of Shem's and Ham's descendants remained in the region of Mesopotamia, while many moved toward Canaan and Africa. Japheth's and Shem's descendants found their way into the northern regions we now call Russia, Alaska, Canada, North and South America, as well as toward Asia settling in China, India, Indonesia, Australia.

Following migration patterns, we found the indigenous people referred to as Indians, Native Americans, Eskimos began settling the regions called Alaska, Canada, and the Americas around 2000 BC. Author Tom B. Underwood, *The Story of the Cherokee People,* 1961 Cherokee Publication, makes mention of tribes living in Siberia moved across the Bering land bridge between Russian and Alaska and settled in the Great Slave Lake region of Canada, eventually migrating south toward North America.

The Iroquoi first called Kanata, the region now called Canada. Some of the tribes occupying Canada and Alaska called themselves Iroquoi, Inuit, Metis, Tlingit, Haida, Tsimshian, Yup'ik, Alutiiq, Sugpiaq, Gwichin, Inupiat. Later the Europeans referred to them as Eskimos. The regions we call Alaska and Canada saw the incursion of people from Russia, Britain, Spain, France between AD 1400 through the 1800s. The colonist purchased Alaska from Russia in 1867 for $7.2 million. One of the first English colonies was called Saint John's Newfoundland. Portions of the population have an English accent. The French established a colony in 1600 called Port Royal and Quebec City. Portions of Canadians speak French. Beginning in 1825, migrants from Ireland and Scotland found their way to Canada.

Millions of Natives settled the entire continent of North America, including the regions called Mexico, Arizona, California, Texas. Wikipedia source lists hundreds of tribes recognized by US government Indian Affairs, and we name a few: Apache, Agua Caliente, Blackfeet, Caddo, Cayuga, Cherokee, Cheyenne, Choctaw Cree, Crow, Hopi, Iowa, Inaja, Lummi, Kickapoo, Kewa Pueblo, Mewuk, Wampanoag, Miccosukee, Mojave, Mohegan, Mohawk, Navajo, Ottawa, Omaha, Pawnee, Potawatomi, Sioux, Seminole, Zuni, Winnebago.

Native Americans living in the region of Mexico were referred to as Mexicans. The remainder of their land was conquered during the Mexican American wars beginning in 1910 under President William Taft. Conflict continued to push some tribes southward into South America. People settling this southern region were an extension of "Mexican" tribes calling themselves Olmec, Toltec, Teothuacan, Zapotec, Maya, Aztec. The Mayans and Aztecs are famous for their step pyramids and the long-count calendar ending their cycle in 2012.

After the Christopher Columbus conquest of some regions in South America, other Spaniards invaded South American territory around AD 1519. One such Spaniard was Hernan Cortes. The Spanish introduced smallpox, which killed millions of natives. The survivors were enslaved, sexually exploited, natural resources confiscated, and exported to Spain. The region was under Spanish rule for three hundred years and introduced to Spanish language, culture, and interbreeding. During the Spanish regime, Portuguese, English, French, and Dutch captured other regions. The Natives won their independence in AD 1821 from Spain. Reviewing the migration of the Native Americans, Shem's descendants, over thousands of years, we observe their appearances remained similar.

Ham's complexion was dark. Remnants of Ham's descendants remained in Mesopotamia, Assyria, Babylon regions while others migrated into Arabia, Canaan, modern-day Israel, and moved throughout Africa. Psalm 78:51 … smote Egyptians firstborn … **tents of Ham.**

The Mediterranean Sea allowed access to the Atlantic Ocean. Ancient Egyptians were shipbuilders and learned to navigate the seas from the African coast to North and South America as well as the Caribbean Islands. Ham's descendants migrated eastward into India, China, Indonesia, to Australia, where we find the Australian Aborigines. European explorers found the Egyptian culture was well advanced, and they could not come to a reasonable explanation that dark-complexioned people had arisen to such great accomplishments. Therefore, they began to portray Egyptians as fair-complexioned people, and Egypt was separated from Africa major in geography textbooks. The Europeans invaded Africa and began to plunder its natural resources. South Africa fell to the Europeans, who conquered that region for its beauty and wealth. The aboriginals were displaced, and apartheid was instituted.

Observing modern-day facial features of people living in these regions, many have broad noses, full lips, and complexions of brown to dark brown. Their hair texture was a mix of curly, wavy, straight, and coarse—which is associated with Ham, Shem, and Japheth descendants. The drawings found in the tombs of the Pharaohs portrayed people as fair- to dark-complexioned and having facial features as described.

From the above analysis, it is a misconception to categorize dark or brown complexions living in geographical regions outside of Africa as indigenous to Africa. As noted, Ham's descendants also settled in areas outside of the continent of Africa.

Japheth was fair in complexion. Japheth's descendants moved to the Northern regions. The ancient regions may have been called Anatolia, Togarmah, Gomer, Magog, and later called Asia Minor, Turkey, and Russia. Modern-day Turkey is a peninsula surrounded by the Black, Mediterranean, Aegean, and Bosphorus Seas and the Sea of Marmarna. It borders Russia. The mountain range of Ararat encompasses early Armenia, modern-day Turkey, and where the Ark landed. During the time of Jesus, the seven churches were in this region.

The Bible confirms the migration of Japheth's descendants. Genesis 10:5, "*By these were **the isles** of the Gentiles divided in their lands, everyone after his tongue, after their families, in their nations*" makes reference to land further northwest surrounded by water. Japheth's descendants migrated to the "isles" regions that border the Mediterranean Sea, such as England, Ireland, Scotland. From the modern classification of Europe proper came an influx of people from the regions of Poland, Germany, Norsemen who made up tribes called Visigoths, Vandals, Saxons, Angles, Lombards, Franks. A later reference to people from England and Germany was the term Anglo-Saxons.

Japheth's descendants migrated further North into the region we call Russia. Ancient names associated with this geographical location are Magog and Tubal. Another reference to Japheth's descendants is the term *Caucasian*, or *Caucasoid*, associated with people from Caucasus mountain regions of Russia, Turkey, Armenia. Most people think of Caucasian as a reference to whites, but the indigenous to Turkey, Armenia, and Greece have a range of complexions.

Turkey shares borders with Syria, Greece, Iran, Iraq, Armenia, Russia, and its historical culture is an influence of Greek during the Greek and Persian Wars around 499 BC, the conquest of Alexander the Great in 334 BC, and Romanized to the Byzantine Empire 324 BC. Later the Ottoman Empire's influence of Islam removed most other cultural history, even to renaming regions with Islamic names.

Greeks are associated with Japheth. Migration placed Greeks in Southern Italy to the Caucasus communities. We find they also migrated to North Africa, such as Morocco. Greeks became master shipbuilders, navigating the Mediterranean Sea under Alexander the Great. After the fall of Greece, its culture was merged with Rome, labeled the Greco-Roman period. Greeks spoke Greek, and Romans spoke Latin.

Thor Heyerdahl was born in Norway in 1914. His field of interest was ethnography. We reference his research in plotting the migration of ancient people in his book, *The Ra Expedition*, which explores the possibility of ancient civilizations capable of navigation. From Egyptian tomb reliefs, a history of shipbuilding and sailing is recorded. The world's oldest boats were crafted from papyrus reed. Other African groups sailed from various locations off their west coast. Heyerdahl was able to recreate the voyage in reed crafted boats. He and crew reached Canary Isles, Caribbean Islands, and landed in the outskirts of South America.

What we can garner from his research is that Ham's descendants were able to reach other continents and intermingle with Shem's descendants, or the indigenous people thousands of years before Columbus. By the time Columbus reached South America, he discovered people of dark and brown complexions. Columbus and his crew exploited and killed the natives. Those that survived were sexually assaulted by Japheth's descendants. Some of the native language was replaced by Spanish and Portuguese.

Thor Heyerdahl's book, *Kon Tiki Expedition*, provides an account of his test run in 1947 sailing from Peru, five thousand miles across the Pacific to Polynesian Island Tuamotu with five other people on a raft to prove that ancient people could have made the trip. He interjected the possibility that dark-complexioned people from Africa could have sailed to South America. He found fair-skinned people living in South America partly a result of the Spanish invasion of South America and Caribbean Islands.

There is a myth that the leader of the fair-skinned people named Kon Tiki, or Con Tici Viracocha, was in a battle with Cari of Coquimbo Valley on the Island of Lake Titicaca. Cari massacred the fair-skinned, bearded people. Later historical records tell that the Spaniards (fair-skinned, bearded people) came to Peru. The Incas told them that the colossal monuments that stood deserted were erected by a race of white gods who had lived there before the Incas themselves became rulers. The Incas described these white gods as wise, peaceful instructors who had originally come from the north in the "morning of time" and taught the Inca forefathers architecture, manners, and customs. They were unlike other Native Americans in that they had white skin, long beards, and were taller than the Incas. According to the Incas, they left traveling westward across the Pacific. Jakob Roggeveen discovered Easter Island in AD 1722 and noticed that some of the natives were fair-skinned and retained knowledge of their ancestors back to the time of Tiki when they first came from a mountainous land in the east scorched by the sun (could be Africa).

Heyerdahl said when the Europeans first came to the Pacific Islands, they were astonished to find some natives to have light skins and beards, hair color red to blond. Other Polynesians were described as having brown skin, black hair, and broad noses. Heyerdahl documented his research in his book, *Aku Aku: Secrets of Easter Island.* As a point of clarification, the Europeans began to classify people into racial categories based on complexion and facial features, as such is in contradiction with the biblical record.

Anthropologists claim that physical and cultural evidence suggests that Polynesia was settled by people migrating from the Asian mainland. DNA testing found the Polynesians are similar to people from Southeast Asia, such as, the land of Japan, China, and the Pacific Islands. Their facial features resemble the indigenous people found in the Americas as well as Africa.

Japheth's descendants were traced in Heyerdahl's research in Azerbaijan, Russia. Examining a rock carving that they date back to 10,000 BC located at Gobustan are related to ships designed in Norway. He spoke about a Nordic king called Odin—a Scandinavian god who came to the North with his people from a country called Aser. History confirms that Japheth's descendants became shipbuilders, as did Ham's descendants. They migrated from the East, westward and northward through Saxony, Denmark, Sweden. Modern Azerbaijan is east of the Caucasus Mountains and the Black Sea.

From Heyerdahl studies, we can ascertain that fair-skinned people, descendants of Japheth, migrated from Mesopotamia near East region toward the northern parts of Russia, Scandinavian countries, Rome, and other European settlements. Also, we can determine that fair-skinned people migrated across the Atlantic Ocean and came to North and South America. Once reaching these regions, they copulated with the indigenous people. Archeological records provide evidence of Spaniards in Peru. French and English arriving in North America both copulated with the indigenous people. We find French-speaking people in New Orleans and Canada. The descendants of Shem and Ham migrated South toward Arabia, Canaan, and into Africa—as well as migrating eastward toward India, Asia, settling in the Pacific Islands and into Australia. They also migrated through the north into Canada, Alaska, and into the Americas. We also keep in mind that the global topography after the flood was altered but still connected in places, allowing people to move throughout the world crossing over the land masses.

God created the Garden of Eden in the middle of the world. This is the cradle of civilization where God created man. God consecrated this region, which spans 1,500 square miles from the Mediterranean Sea to the Persian Gulf, up to the mountains of Ararat down to the desert of Arabia and into Africa. God said, "Jerusalem is my holy city." When God came to earth, he was born in the land of Jerusalem. The migration of people interconnect with the land coming from Africa, Arabia, Syria, Persia, Babylon, Turkey, Rome; and to the outer most parts of the world, all will come to Israel.

We are told in Isaiah 11:11–12:

> *And it will come to pass in that day, that the Lord will set his hand again the second time to recover the remnant of his people which will be left from* ***Assyria*** *and from* ***Egypt*** *and from Pathros and from* ***Cush*** *and from Elam and from* ***Shinar*** *and from Hamath and from the* ***island of the sea.*** *And he will set up an ensign for the nations and will assemble the outcasts of Israel and gather together the dispersed of Judah from the four corners of the earth.*

From this passage, the pure in heart will understand that God will bring the descendants of Shem, Ham, and Japheth together in the last days. In modern times, all nations are taken up with the land and people of Israel. People are making aliyah from China, Africa, and Europe. The dispersed are being gathered back to their promised land. At the end of the tribulation, scriptures tell us that **all nations** will come up to Jerusalem to worship the King.

Racism Divides Humankind

The formation and institution of racism has no scientific merit. God said, "From one blood came all nations." Before the flood, our first parents were Adam and Eve. After the flood, our ancestors came by way of Noah's three sons. From them, all nations and ethnicities came to be. Human characteristics, culture, and language distinguish one group from another and should not be the basis to separate people by a perceived racial construct. The Bible tells us, God is not a respecter of man, be he Jew or Gentile, rich or poor, black or white, male or female; but he is Creator of all. Put away hatred one for another, and obey God's command to love one another as God loves us.

Every diabolical plan Satan conceived caused dissention among all the inhabitants of the earth.

It was a satanic plan to influence a few ill-reputed people to devise a plan to divide humanity by pseudo races. The family feud began between Cain and Abel, and Satan stoked hatred within family relationships from times past to the present. Jesus predicted this flaw in humankind would turn parents against siblings and children against parents. Evidence of this can be seen in the feud between Jews and Arabs, who are related through Isaac and Ishmael.

Satan created social division between the poor and wealthy. We cannot fully begin to comprehend the devastation Satan initiated within the religious community. His crowning achievements were to instigate regional wars, and finally, he devised a plan to create dissention based on complexion, culture, and ethnicity.

As we study early empires of Assyria, Babylon, Egypt, Greece, and Rome, battles were carried out to conquer land, wealth, and people. Conquered people were held as slaves but not based on complexion. It does not appear, for instance, that Alexander the Great instituted racism within the lands he conquered.

When the Roman Empire emerged, it seemed concerned about military conquest, wealth, secularism, and paganism more so than the various complexions of humankind. Satan would use religion as a ploy to allow wicked people to control, oppress, enslave, and kill others in the name of God or in opposition to a particular religion. The Romans crucified Jesus because of his doctrine and not because of his complexion. The Romans fed Christians to the lions, hung them on spikes, and set them on fire and crucified them regardless of their complexion. From the time of the formation of the Holy Roman Empire around AD 390, religious battles were carried out between various beliefs and not based on complexion. Strife and division came from a mix of Roman dominion, paganism, Jewish Orthodoxy, and the growth of Christianity.

FROM ONE BLOOD

CAME ALL NATIONS

As Catholicism and Protestant missionary movements began to emerge throughout Europe, America, and in other lands, the idea of racism was transported to the rest of the world as well.

As we enter into the complex vortex of race, we state there is no such thing as a black, white, red, yellow, or a brown race of people. Literally, white is devoid of pigmentation, and true black would be a combination of all colors. Who has ever seen a person who is the color of a white sheet of paper as well as a person black as coal? Dip a paint brush in yellow, and it could become a lovely yellow flower. Bypassing rationale, Johann Blumenbach in 1775, advocating polygenism, divided the world's population into five groups according to skin color. Anders Retzius disproved Blumenbach's polygenism had any fundamental merit in demonstrating that neither Europeans nor different nations are one pure race but of mixed origins.

A few hundred years later, the theory of race took another form by classifying people into three general categories (Rand McNally, 1970, World Atlas, Races of the World, 262–263).

- Caucasian (Whites)—Asians, Australia/Aborigines, Semites, Arabs
- Mongoloid (Browns)—Indians, Eskimos, Malayans
- Negroid (Blacks)—Sudanese, Bantus, Papuans, Hottentots,

In a brief analysis of the above categories, one can see a few problems. Caucasoid includes dark-skinned Australian aborigines, brown-skinned Semites, Arabs, and Asians. Mongoloids do have varying degrees of brown to dark complexions. Finally, the Negroes all come from Africa, and there is no scientific designation for the word "Negroid."

Looking at all of humanity is like admiring hundreds of flowers having different colors, shapes, and forms.

Satan introduced the theory of evolution to replace belief in God as Creator. In the nineteenth century, Charles Darwin began to assert that man evolved from apes and his concept grew like wildfire. The racist mind-set decided to expand this theory to apply to people with dark complexions primarily hailing from Africa. They were called apes, savages, Negroes, and classified as partially human.

In the sixteenth and seventeenth centuries, some explorations were sanctioned and financed by the British government to record and catalogue their findings of the known world. This was done in preparation for colonization. Interestingly, when they began to explore the ancient remnants found in Egypt, they were amazed at their advancements in math, chemistry, science, embalming, medicine, and the creation of huge statues and buildings. As they began to interpret hieroglyphics and study the relief paintings on the walls of tombs and pyramids, they could hardly believe these were people of dark complexion. The British began to excavate the wealth of Egypt.

With the spread of colonialism, the oppressors became aware that the world outside of Europe was populated by people of various hues. The colonialists began classifying people by geographical regions and complexion and forming their platform for racism. From this realization, it became the catalyst to endorse the practice of oppression, enslavement, and inhumane treatment of other people. The colonialists developed a mind-set that other people were inferior, backward, uneducated, and in need of an overseer. Once their perception and practices became commonplace, there was no contrition in further confiscation of the national resources, wealth, or enslavement of people in other nations.

We find an excellent example of European oppression, enslavement, and murder in the history of Christopher Columbus. He and his crew were given permission, money, and ships to find India. In AD 1492, Columbus ended up in South America what he called the West Indies. The natives called themselves Arawaks. He and his crew were treated kindly, and he set up an outpost called *Navidad*, Spanish for "Christmas." On his second journey in 1493, he came to Cuba, Jamaica, and Haiti (Hispaniola). On his third journey in 1498, with seventeen ships and 1,200 colonists, he ended up in Trinidad, Tobago, Grendada, Venezuela. In all his travels, he never reached North America.

In these various regions, Columbus established ruthless slavery, demanding the natives work in their own gold mines. Within two years, 125,000 people were dead because of brutal mining conditions. Columbus and his men forced nine- to ten-year-old girls to serve as sex slaves. The Spaniards introduced disease uncommon to the indigenous population. Natives who resisted had their nose and ears cut off, mauled by dogs, skewered with pikes, or shot. Reprisals were so severe many natives committed mass suicide and women practiced abortion so their children would not be enslaved.

Father Fray Antonio de Montesino, a Dominica priest in AD 1511, stated that Columbus left a "cruel legacy, Columbus and the colonists in the genocide of the native people … by what right or justice do you hold these Indians in such cruel and horrible servitude, on what authority have you waged such detestable wars against the people who dealt quietly and peacefully on their own lands … wars in which you have destroyed such infinite numbers of them by homicides and slaughter never heard of before."

Haiti had a population upward to three million. Within a short period after the Spanish occupation, almost every native had been murdered.

AD 1875, Father Bartolome de Las Casas, in his book, *History of the Indies*, stated, "Slaves were a primary source of income for Admiral Columbus. Columbus and his men were driven by insatiable greed, killing, terrorizing, afflicting, torturing native people with the strongest and most varied methods of cruelty …" Parents were separated, exhausted, depressed, and the birth rate dropped; newborn children died early because mothers were forced to work and produced inadequate milk to feed them, or mothers drowned babies out of sheer desperation. Casas saw in Cuba seven thousand children die in three months. Men and women were worked to death.

The king and queen of Spain learned of Columbus and his brother Diego's crimes against humanity, had them arrested on August 23,1500, placed in chains only to be imprisoned for six weeks. Columbus died at the age of fifty-five, but the reign of European terror would continue. As the colonists moved toward North America, the practice of slavery followed. Columbus was not remembered for his crimes against humanity, but he became a symbol of American independence, a symbol of liberty.

AD 1828, Washington Irving wrote *A History of the Life and Voyages of Christopher Columbus.* Within its pages, Columbus was romanticized, presented as bringing "superior culture and blessings of Christianity." Japheth's descendants in North America made Columbus an idol in their monuments, libraries, cities as in the District of Columbia, paintings, and historical myth. AD 1937, Franklin D. Roosevelt made Christopher Columbus a national holiday (Good Gopher, online August 1, 2015).

King Leopold of Belgium enslaved people in the Congo region under brutal conditions to extract rubber from trees in that region. The practice of slavery was to instill fear in those who were enslaved, and this was accomplished through beatings, dismemberment, and death. For fifteen years, Leopold carried out inhumane atrocities on the Congolese people, resulting in the death of approximately ten million people. When his crimes were exposed worldwide, only then did he retreat from that region.

In the above narrative, European colonialism was highlighted. However, Satan's scheme of pitting brothers against brothers was carried out within Africans, Native Americans, Arabs, and European clans who in turn brutalized, tortured, raped, and killed their own people. Yet the institution of slavery and racism transcends tribal uprisings.

Webster's Dictionary uses the term *xenophobia* to describe intense dislike or fear of people from other countries. The people captured from Africa and transported to America were intensely hated based on their country of origin and because of their dark complexion. The passage from Africa to the Americas was brutal and inhumane as hundreds of Africans were chained to the floor of ships for weeks or months. Millions died on the voyage. Those who survived reached destinations to be sold into slavery. Punishment for dissidents ran the gambit of drowning, hanging, tar and feathering, boiling in a pot, cutting off genitals, beating to death, and dismembering. The colonialists were apathetic to the treatment of other humans.

American racism gave birth to discrimination and segregation. It became the mechanism to distance the superiors from the inferiors. Segregation was instituted in every aspect of society. It played out in housing, employment, schools, churches, public swimming pools, restaurants, hospitals, and even the military at one time was segregated. Racism sat on the front pew in church congregations. Ministers used their pulpits to embolden racial segregation and to promote political propaganda for legalizing slavery. Ministers introduced another gospel, which was not love your neighbor. Many church leaders hid behind white hoods as their darker brothers and sisters were lynched, burned, and raped in the name of "white supremacy." Church leaders preached a segregated heaven and presented a European image of God.

Racism on another level is the classification of the Jews as a race. If they are seen as a race, then others may move toward their elimination as undesirable humans. Under the Nazi regime, Jews were herded onto trains and transported to concentration camps suffering humiliation, enslavement, beaten, and murdered. Even a blind man could see the similarity between slavery and the Holocaust. A holocaust is the systematic destruction of a massive number of people because of their religious beliefs or ethnic designation. There are the righteous among us who know right from wrong and attempt to reach out to help the oppressed and downtrodden. They are the light of the world. When we stand before our Creator, his hue will be brilliant; he will appear as a rainbow of color; he will emanate love; and those things that separated people on earth will not be found in heaven.

It is a monumental task to classify people into a racial construct based on complexion. The institution of racism was dogmatic in its efforts to achieve such designations. Regardless of no scientific evidence or logical deduction, their conclusion was that dark-complexioned people are of the Negroid "black race" from Africa; fair-complexioned people are of the European "race"; brown-complexioned people could be of the Hispanic "race"; Asians are of the "yellow race"; and Native Americans were classified as the "red race." We believe the majority of people are a combination of Noah's three sons, and some people of mixed heritage can state their ancestry from Shem, Ham, and Japheth. Based on the pseudoracial construct, how would persons presenting with DNA from all three sons be classified? They were classified as the "mongoloid race." There must be no limit to this unscientific reasoning. In modern times, several other races have been classified. For instance, we now have the reptilian race and the alien race from another planet. Soon there will be a classification for transsexual and transhuman species.

Again, we assert postflood people originated from the region of Mesopotamia and migrated throughout the world. It is erroneous to assert that dark-complexioned people all originated from Africa or fair-complexioned people all come from Europe. People of all complexions can be found in every nation on every continent. Archaeological evidence found in Egyptian tombs and on walls portrays people with various hues. H. P. Steenswby in 1907 confirmed in his research that all humans today are of mixed origins and claimed that the origins of human difference must be traced far back in time and suggested that the purest race today would be the Australian Aboriginals (Wikipedia, *Racism*).

AD 1648, Peace Treaty of Westphalia divided Europe into various empires and kingdoms: Ottoman Empire, Holy Roman Empire, Swedish, France, German, and Russian empires. With the rise of kingdoms, rulers developed a sense of perceived superiority. For example, upper-class wealthy Europeans thought of lower-class "white" people as poor, ignorant, servants, slaves, and serfs. European history is replete with major conflicts between the ruling royals, clans, and the peasants in regard to class, ethnicity, and religion. Conflicts resulted in ethnic cleansing, for example between Serbs and Croatians or religious intolerance, which manifested in conflicts between Irish Protestants and Catholics.

Some Europeans went so far as to classify themselves as members belonging to a difference race, such as, the German race or the French race. Adolf Hitler rose from meager beginnings and struggled with his own identity associated with his Jewish roots. He envied others having wealth and power. He became obsessed with the idea of German superiority and incorporated Aryan ideas from India and Egypt into building a world power. Interestingly, the Aryans were people of brown to dark complexions. Hitler had a bias toward dark-complexioned people. He demonstrated his dislike during the Olympic trials in Germany when "black" athletes competed in track-and-field events. Germany's quest toward racial superiority gave them a green light for ethnic cleansing. Hitler received some inspiration from the American and British Eugenics Records Office. Hitler believed Germany had become weak because of inferior bloodlines and degenerate breeding. He carried out extermination upon those he considered misfits.

Germans believed themselves to be justified in the extinction of other Germans whose appearance was no different than other Germans because they were Jews; they were classified as the Jewish race thus becoming prime targets for elimination.

A sense of perceived superiority infected Asians as well as Europeans because Asians think of themselves as relative to Caucasians. Asian superiority was exhibited by the Japanese, believing they were superior to Koreans. During the war, Korean women were held as sex slaves. North Korea was divided from South Korea because of political ideology, and each country hated the other. China believed its culture superior and closed itself off from the world, but within its border, there was turmoil between religious groups, peasants, and the communist government. A caste system was developed in India to divide the fair-complexioned "superiors" from the dark-complexioned "inferiors." In Africa, based on differing tribal practices, conflicts took place. One tribe believed their way was the right way, and if others did not adhere, they should be eliminated. Today in the Middle East, people having brown complexions are led by Islamic extremists who believe all should convert to Islam or die. There is dissention in Islamic nations, such as the Sunnis, in conflict with the Shi'ites—both believing their position is superior to the other. In these scenarios, people in their regions are similar in complexion and facial features to each other.

From the above narrative, the basis for racism is not valid and lacks logical deduction. Nevertheless, the spectrum of racism leaves psychological scars on blacks and whites. President Lincoln, a Republican, enacted the Emancipation Proclamation Act, and slavery was abolished. Former slaves had to find their identity. They had to fit into a society that did not want them. Could they find healing in philosophy or religion? They had to educate themselves. The promise of a mule and twenty acres did not become a reality. Livelihood came through sharecropping or menial labor. To get a job as a servant, blacks had to be subservient and dare not look the white man in the eye. Some blacks began to emulate whites to be more acceptable, such as straightened hair, which continues to be a fashion statement in the twenty-first century. Emancipated slaves dressed as their former masters. Blacks hid their natural tendencies toward rhythm so as not to be labeled as savages.

Blacks had freedom with strings attached. The strings were segregations and discrimination.

The Democratic administration was divided in regard to civil rights for blacks. Even though legislation was enacted against segregation, the US government still continued its practice of racism against a people struggling to survive. The "colored people" had to fight for voters' rights, and they had to fight against discrimination on public transportation, housing, public schools, the military, eating in white restaurants, drinking from white-only water fountains, and in movie theaters, blacks had to sit in the balcony. Medical care at white hospitals was prohibited, and the list goes on.

Covert racism did target the black community. Poor black neighborhoods became targets for drugs, alcohol, gambling, and tobacco—creating a culture of substance dependence, and crime increased to get money for vices. Cartels sprung up in most cities and took over gambling, drugs, and prostitution. In the early part of the twentieth century, the police departments were predominately white, and they were bigots. In America, a disproportionate number of incarcerated people are black, in a population of approximately thirty million blacks. Some of these people may be school dropouts, grew up in dysfunctional family units, became addicted to drugs or alcohol, and may be prone to criminal activities.

Advertising companies targeted poor neighborhoods with junk food, soda, sweets, greasy foods, and genetically modified food; and as a result, there is a higher percentage of blacks who have diabetes, heart disease, and obesity. Of course, we see obesity and disease in other ethnic groups. The government targeted poor black communities to release viruses, such as small pox had been released to infect and kill off the Native Americans. Forced vaccinations were given to ethnic children, loaded with toxins that caused brain damage and autism.

Black women were targeted for sterilization and abortion, creating a mind-set that black children were a financial burden and hardship. This is confirmed in the following. In 1910, Charles Benedict Davenport, with Harriman, Rockefeller, Carnegie formed the Eugenics Record Office, Cold Spring Harbor, New York, to study heredity in order to eliminate the substandard or socially inadequate. By 1920, the global elite pushed sterilization and experiments that would prevent undesirables from reproducing. Margaret Sanger, founder of Planned Parenthood, was also associated with eugenics and shared her position with the Ku Klux Klan and others. Sanger in 1938 was quoted, "Certain people are human weeds who should never have been born, and birth control should be used to weed out the unfit … We do not want word to get out that we want to exterminate the Negro population."

Many black men were not treated for sexually transmitted diseases, which allowed STDs to spread. The US government decided to experiment on black men with STDs. Unemployment was high, and males abandoned their families for the pleasures of life to forget their problems, which created single female–parent households. The black male role model was convoluted.

Racism gave birth to the institution of slavery. A side effect of racism is bigotry. Bigotry breeds prejudice and discrimination. And then there was the illusion of freedom. As slavery divided families, the illusion of freedom created a chasm in the family unit and the community at large. When we think of racism, the first thing that enters our mind is an evil that was perpetrated against black people, yet other ethnic groups experienced similar problems within their families and communities.

Breaking down the educational barriers, little black children could go to white schools. Yet in the educational environment, textbooks and literature were immersed with bigotry. Demeaning stereotypical attitudes circled children. For instance, they were taught they were from Africa, a place of savages. This programming was enforced by Tarzan of the jungle. Three hundred years of slavery was barely mentioned in schools, and what little came forth did not cast slavery in a negative light. Eventually, black educators broke onto the scene, and the victims of racism could begin to see themselves as achievers, overcomers, and revolutionaries. Even so, the psychological chains of racism are not easily removed.

Many notable people overcame the challenges of racism and attended schools of higher education, becoming doctors, lawyers, educators, and skilled professionals. In our modern day, most universities are liberal. Students indulge in physical vices and intellectual deception. Spring break is an extension of behavior on campus but is acted out in Florida or Mexico. White college student behavior is criminal or disorderly conduct, drug, and alcohol abuse and public lewdness. Black college students may have their Greek holiday in a park wherein thousands attend, and the same behavior is displayed as the white college students. Media reports these events, but one is tampered to appear as just having fun while the other event is reported unfavorably.

In the early 1900s, the entertainment industry was all white. White actors portrayed blacks and Native Americans in stereotypical roles. In early movies, Cleopatra was depicted as white. Elizabeth Taylor became famous from this role. Moses was portrayed as white since the character was played by Charlton Heston. For many unlearned people living in America or Europe, Egypt was not associated with Africa and dark-skinned people. However, Tarzan movies were produced in the backdrop of Central Africa, whose culture was different than Egypt. The tribal people were classified as primitive savages in need of a white savior. Gradually, blacks broke through the color barrier to take on roles as slaves, dumb blacks, or maids. The entertainment industry realized more money could be made if they produced meaningful parts for black actors.

During the Harlem Renaissance, the "Negro" began to emerge and expressed themselves in poetry, writing, music, art, and business. Others sought liberty by embracing communism. Perhaps joining the Marcus Garvey Back to Africa movement was the way toward true freedom and racial equality. Some believed only through revolution could their concerns be addressed and they adopted a stance for freedom through groups, such as, the Black Panthers and the Nation of Islam.

The fight against racism took on a new persona. After hundreds of years of oppression, the oppressed will eventually rise in revolution. Blacks, who for the most part were fighting for equal rights, sought to bring change through civil disobedience. Protest turned into race riots. Rioters were met by police with military force, dogs, water hoses, lynching, racial slurs, and beat downs were the response of white society. South African apartheid was eliminated only through protest and civil disobedience. The American Civil Rights Movement was successful on many fronts but did little to change deep-seated attitudes between whites and blacks. The impact of slavery is comparable to posttraumatic stress syndrome. Suffering a continuous barrage of demeaning actions and calling blacks "nigger," lazy, worthless, or other slanderous names became part of their self-image and self-loathing. Initially, blacks could do nothing about how they were treated; but as time passed, blacks referred to themselves as "niggers," a sign of PSD and self-loathing.

Protests staged in China, Turkey, Korea, Russia, or Iran are met with strong government response. Protests in the United States today are tolerated by government officials, police, or military. During the Civil Rights Movement, people were frustrated and needed resolution. In our current time, some people perceive a problem that may not be factually accurate. For instance, the police shooting of Michael Brown in Ferguson was taken out of context. Why would hundreds of people across the nation rally in support of a thug who had robbed a store, resisted arrest, attacked a police offer, and got himself killed? They perceive white cops are racist. Nonetheless, nationwide, there is a good representation of black, Hispanic, and Asian police officers. The high number of incidents of black-on-black crime is reaching crisis level, but the majority of blacks are not forming rallies or protesting this reality. Perhaps during the Civil Rights protests, the government had not anticipated this uprising. However, in our current time, the government takes advantage of these type of incidents in order to move their agenda forward, such as, disarming citizens based on shooting innocent people in a church or movie theater or to militarize the police forces. The elite direct certain groups to instigate an uprising, such as the Occupy Wall Street Movement, or Black Lives Matter movements. Instigators may use a symbol such as the confederate flag to cause division and uprisings. Others may dishonor the American flag by burning it. Gay right groups bring their rainbow flags.

In pointing out the aforementioned examples, we see a new breed, a cross section of all ethnic groups arising. The faces of Islamic radicals are white, black, and brown. Muslims are recruiting disenfranchised people who may be criminals or have a misguided perception of the glory of Islam. They lack the ability to discern between right and wrong. Operating from their perceived ideology, ISIS and other terror groups maim, destroy, and kill in the name of god.

Regardless of the historical significance of a flag, statue, or banner, we must remember that behind these movements is an evil oligarchy influencing people of all complexions to carry out its global agenda. All nations must be in turmoil. The Asian nations of Japan, Korea, and Vietnam were targeted and crippled by war, bombs, and Agent Orange. Middle East nations need to be in constant turmoil through the so-called "Arab Spring." Their mantra, "By any means necessary," the population must be reduced through the practice of eugenics, abortion, disease, immorality, and war.

From our analysis, there is no scholarly agreement about the concept of race. The United Nations stated, "There is no distinction between the terms *racial discrimination* and *ethnic discrimination*, and superiority based on racial differentiation is scientifically false, morally condemnable, socially unjust, and dangerous and that there is no justification for racial discrimination in theory or in practice anywhere." Ethnicity is dividing humans into classifications based on national origin, physical, characteristics, language, and sometimes religion. Even with the United Nations's position, the global elite believe their logic cannot be challenged and their truth requires no investigation or validation. In this vein, we can see that the mind-set of the one-world order is superiority and power over all mankind regardless of race, ethnicity, or religious affiliation.

Tom Horn, *Beast Tech*, excerpt, "By 1900, ideas presented by Francis Galton, Charles Darwin, David Starr Jordan on 'race' defined 'selection' to weed out people they considered inferior to ensure the birth of superior people." In a book written by David Starr Jordan, *Blood of a Nation: The Study of the Decay of a Nation through the Survival of the Unfit,* he wrote:

> To select for posterity those individuals who best meet our needs or please our fancy and to destroy those with unfavorable qualities is the function of artificial selection. Add to this the occasional crossing of unlike forms

> to promote new and desirable variations, and we have the whole secret of selective breeding. This process called the "magician's wand," by which man may summon up and bring into existence any form of animal or plant useful to him or pleasing to his fancy.

Following are expressions or statements that are characteristic of a racist mind-set:

Early evidence of prejudice and bigotry was found in a Bible dated 1824 published by Kimber and Sharpless, Philadelphia, Pennsylvania. On the index page 749, section the "First Age of the World": "To Noah, aged five hundred years, is born Japheth and, two years after, Shem." Noah's son Ham is totally eliminated. At the printing and publishing of that Bible, it was a time in American history that black people were kept as slaves. The publisher obviously knew Ham was the darker brother. This is one example of many Bible scholars who will portray Ham and his descendants in an unfavorable light.

> Africans sway like leaves in the wind impervious and indifferent to any form of civilization, a people absent from scientific discovery, philosophy, arts. We believe nothing can come out of Africa other than raw materials. (Quote, Owen Shahada, born in Germany, 1973, Muslim, educated in England, and of dark complexion)
>
> I am apt to suspect the Negroes to be naturally inferior to the Whites ... (Quoted by David Hume, Scottish philosopher)
>
> Africa is no historical part of the world. Blacks had no sense of personality, their spirit sleeps, remains sunk in itself makes no advance and thus parallels the compact, undifferentiated mass of the African continent. (Quoted by George Wilhelm Friedrich Hegel, nineteenth-century German philosopher)
>
> A genius has perhaps scarcely ever appeared amongst the negroes and the standard of their morality is almost universally so low that it is beginning to be acknowledged in America that their emancipation was an act of imprudence. (Quoted by Otto Weininger, Austria)

Mankind is deceived on many fronts; evolution and racial hatred are but two. Working to rid the world of racism begins with reeducation, such as found in this commentary. Racism's roots must be exposed and destroyed with truth, and that truth is, there is but one race—the human race created by God. We would be remiss if we did not mention honorable men and women who knew that racism and slavery were wrong in the eyes of God and mankind. People such as the Quakers and Abolitionist provided refugees fleeing from slavery with food, passage, and clothes.

Finally, we address the conundrum of people living in America who are classified by race based on complexion but also separated by a perceived country of origin. Basically, any person of dark or brown complexion is classified as African American. A person of dark or brown complexion born in America is still classified as African American. A fair-complexioned person of mixed heritage is also classified as an African American but may be given additional labels such as "mulatto." The problem with this illogical reasoning is that not all dark-complexioned people are from Africa. Ham's descendants remained in Mesopotamia as well as migrated to other regions. Therefore, many dark-complexioned people hailing from Arabia, Palestine, Iraq, Iran, India, Pakistan could be descendants of Ham now living in America.

How do we fit fair-complexioned people and their country of origin into a racial classification? Fair-complexioned Europeans born in South Africa living in America are not called by their country of birth as in African American but by complexion are called European Americans or Afrikaners. Europeans from other countries such as Italy are classified as Italian American, Irish American, Russian American, Swiss American, etc.

If we use the above analogy, then dark-complexioned people born in Arabia should be called Arab American or born in Iran should be called Persian American. Afghanistan should be classified as Afghanistan American or Pakistani American, Trinidadian Americans, etc.

People who have a brown complexion having "Hispanic" features may be quickly classified as Mexican Americans even if they are from Brazil, Puerto Rico, Cuba. Hawaiians are brown in complexion; if they do not tell you where they were born, how are they to be differentiated from other brown people? They are related to the Native Americans. Native Americans residing in Alaska are classified as Eskimos. In general, Native Indians living in America are correctly classified as Native Americans.

A few problems surface for other people born in America. The Jews are classified as Jewish Americans. Judaism is not a country of origin it is a religion. It is unlikely they will be classified as Israeli Americans since many in America believe Israel is an illegitimate nation. We find a remnant of Jews living throughout the world. They are not commonly referred to by their nation of origin but are called Jews from Iran, Ethiopian Jews, Jews from Syria, Russian Jews, etc. Following this same line of thought, Arab Americans are quickly classified as Muslim American. The term *Muslim* is not a country of origin; it refers to one who is a follower of Islam. Those classified as Arabs but are Christians living in America are unlikely to be called a Christian Arab American. A person born in Saudi Arabia would be classified as Arab. If they were born in Iran and now are American citizens, they want to be classified as Persians and not Arabs. It may be a bit more practical if people were correctly classified by their country of origin. A natural-born citizen of the United States should be classified as American without the distinction of complexion. If they are not natural-born but are in

America as immigrants, then it would be logical to classify them correctly by their country of origin without the distinction of complexion. For example, immigrants from Poland are classified as Polish Americans; people from India regardless of complexion would be classified as Indian Americans; or Mexican Americans if they were born in Mexico.

The above overview is confusing and lacks rational analysis because it was introduced by Satan, the father of lies and chaos, sowed seeds of dissention. Cain killing Abel was just the beginning of sin. Man became hateful of his brother, which is likened to murder. Stronger nations conquered the weaker nations. Ancient history is a broad and complex area of study. Our objective is to allow the scriptures to be our base and guide. The Bible does not record all of world history, so it is necessary to study extra biblical records in order to get a clearer understanding of world events. It is time for the citizens of the world to break the shackles of racism and to embrace God's divine plan for humankind that we should love one another.

God said the imaginations of men's hearts are continually evil, and this is reflective in the descendants of Ham, Shem, Japheth; each contributed to some **ungodliness** in the scheme of the world. Ham, Shem, and Japheth's descendants each embraced idolatry. A combination of Ham, Shem, and Japheth's relatives built the tower of Babel. Shem's descendants gave birth to Ishmael, and the religion of Islam was established in Arabia. The Arabs are descendants of Shem, and they fuel the perpetual hatred of the chosen people. Japheth's descendants are credited with the destruction of many people throughout the world under Greek, Roman, British rule. Japheth's descendants instituted racism, gave us dictators such as Hitler and Stalin, and it was Japheth's descendants who developed the atom bomb.

As pertaining to the above, is it a fair assessment to blame all of the world's woes on the darker brother, Ham, and his sons? Over the centuries, writers have developed theories about the descendants of Ham, one being Nimrod. Following, we will critique the idea that Ham's grandson, Nimrod, was an infamous person.

The Legend of Nimrod

Cush was the father of Nimrod, his sixth son. Nimrod lived in the region of Mesopotamia, having not migrated to other regions. Nimrod represented one of the first of many empires in the beginning of the formation of human governments. Nimrod became a mighty warrior, a political ruler; and as others in his time, he may have been receptive to ancient spiritual wisdom, which came forth from the fallen angels. Satan has tempted all of mankind, even God. Possibly during the life of Nimrod, he could have been among those who decided to build a tower that could reach to the heavens. In the biblical narrative, Nimrod is not specifically mentioned. In response to their rebellion, God did scatter the people, but Nimrod remained in his region in the cities he had built.

According to legend and commentaries, Nimrod's name implies to subdue. It is speculated that he trained leopards to stalk other animals, and he was associated with the swiftness and strength of a leopard. We do not know for sure, but Nimrod could have worn leopard skins. It is myth that Nimrod came to possess the animal skins God gave to Adam and Eve to cover their nakedness. Myth said they possessed supernatural power. The symbol of the leopard became part of the Babylonian mystery religion and priesthood. Other future civilizations would adopt the symbol of the leopard. Egyptian pharaohs adorned the leopard print as seen in wall drawings. In some references, the Greeks called Nimrod, Nebrod. Alexander the Great wore leopard skins. Greece is symbolized as a leopard implying swiftness and strength in conquest. Are there any distinguishable similarities between Nimrod and Alexander? Both acquired land, both where hunters, both wore leopard skins, both became mighty men. We do not see commentaries labeling Alexander the great as a giant, cruel oppressor of men, or archetype of the Antichrist. Modern-day fashions incorporate the leopard print look in clothing, pocketbooks, and shoes. Do our modern-day scholars associate those adorned in such attire to be affiliated with Nimrod?

Before we peel back the layers of commentary on Nimrod and are able to see him as given in the scriptures, we want to provide a little analysis on how the characterization of a person is developed. For instance, the person of Jesus. None of us were alive two thousand years ago, but from the accounts of eyewitnesses, the words of Jesus in the Bible, and a massive amount of commentary—some in line with scripture and some far-fetched as in the book *Paradise Lost*—we have an accurate and credible account of Jesus. He was good. On the other side of the fence, if we are interested in the life of Adolf Hitler, we would research the reports of many people who had firsthand knowledge of his life and activities. Facts were compiled from people who served in the war, from people who had a personal relationship with Hitler, from people who survived the Holocaust, or from people who were involved in the heinous experiments performed on humans. Hitler was evil.

In order to determine what kind of person Nimrod was, we must investigate facts. There is very little given on the life of Nimrod in the Bible. There is only one Bible reference given for our understanding of Nimrod, and that is found in the following verse:

> *Cush begat **Nimrod**. He began to be a mighty one in the earth. He was a mighty hunter before the Lord wherefore it is said, even as Nimrod the mighty hunter before the Lord. And the beginning of his kingdom was Babel, Erech, Accad and Calneh in the land of Shinar. Out of the land went forth **Asshur** and builded Nineveh, city of Rehoboth and Calah and Resen.* (Genesis 10:8–11)

In the above verse, we are told Nimrod's father was Cush, in the lineage of Ham. Nimrod must have been a prominent person to get mentioned in the Bible. He was a hunter before the Lord. Nimrod became mighty because of the regions he developed, and he was ruler over the people in his region. It also says that Asshur went forth and built Nineveh, Rehoboth, Calah, and Resen. Asshur is the son of Shem. From Asshur may have come the name Assyria.

The Tower of Babel

> *And the whole earth was of one language and of one speech. And it came to pass as they journeyed from the east that they found a plain in* ***the land of Shinar*** *and they dwelt there. And they said one to another, go to let us make brick and burn them thoroughly. And they had brick for stone and slime had they for mortar. And they said, go to, let us build us a city and a tower whose top may reach unto heaven and let us make a name lest we be scattered abroad upon the face of the whole earth. And the Lord came down to see the city and the tower which the children of men build. And the Lord said, behold the people is one and they have all one language and this they begin to do and now nothing will be restrained from them which they have imagined to do. Go to* ***let us*** *go down and there confound their language that they may not understand one another's speech. So the Lord scattered them abroad from there upon the face of all the earth and they left off to build the city. Therefore is the name of it called* ***Babel*** *because the Lord did there confound the language of all the earth …* (Genesis 11:1)

We speculate this impressive building was shaped like a ziggurat, similar to an ancient ziggurat found in Ur. Others say it was like a pyramid. In either case, Bible history tells us the people built a structure. The scriptures say little about the Tower of Babel. We analyze the above scripture:

- The scripture tells us the descendants of Ham, Shem, Japheth had migrated into the land of Shinar, later called Mesopotamia, region of Ur, land of the Chaldeans, and it lets us know the people still spoke one language.
- Genesis 9 provides a brief account of Noah after the flood, the covenant, rainbow. Noah planted a vineyard, got drunk naked, and in his shame he cursed Canaan. Genesis 10 provides an account of the generations of Noah and his sons. In verse 8, we are introduced to Nimrod; and in verse 11, we are introduced to Asshur. Genesis 11 tells us the people built a city and a tower and God confounded the language. Genesis 11:10 begins with a genealogy of Shem's descendants, which leads

to Genesis 12 to Genesis 50, which provides an account of Abraham, Sarah, Isaac, Jacob, Esau, and Joseph.

- There is no specific mention of Nimrod in Genesis 11, but there is a tiny reference to the name Babel associated with confusion. Is the kingdom of Babel in Genesis 10 related to the word *Babel* in Genesis 11? In Genesis 10, it points out Babel was the **beginning** of Nimrod's kingdom. We cannot be sure the reference made in Genesis 11 to people building a city and tower is the same as the kingdom built by Nimrod. We cannot be 100 percent sure the kingdom of Babel has the same connotation as the word *Babel* used by God in association with confusion. *Webster Dictionary* spells ***babble*** and is defined as confused, incoherent talk. In the *Encyclopedia of the Jewish Religion*—"etymologically, Babel probably means Bab-ili, Gate of God," derived from the Hebrew root balal "to confuse." *Bab* means "gate," and *el* means "God." We do not know how much time passed from the time the people came into the land of Shinar or even if the person of Nimrod was still alive when they began to build a city and a tower. We have a problem with word associations beginning with the kingdom of Babel and the word *Babel* to infer confusion. Also we do not know if the word *Babylon* is an extension of Babel. We can only consider the multitude of commentaries on various subjects but do not have to accept them as accurate.
- They (more than one person) planned among themselves to build a city and a tower. Normally, there is nothing wrong with building cities and towers, but they had in mind to build the tower to reach heaven, and they would be famous and proud.
- God said to go multiply and go throughout the earth, and they decided they did not want to be scattered. God, knowing the thoughts of their heart, confounded their language, and it is called Babel for this reason.
- God said, "Let us go …" Once again who is *us*? We can assume a reference to the Triune Godhead, or a reference to angels.

If Nimrod was involved in the building of the tower, then it would seem that God put a crimp in Nimrod's kingdom. It says the people stopped building, could no longer understand each other, and were dispersed. We do see divine intervention. We can only speculate that they desired to establish a connection with the gods (fallen angels) and once again delved into forbidden knowledge. If the Tower of Babel was Nimrod's ultimate achievement, why is there no mention of Nimrod in the above text? Where is Nimrod's glory in all of this? Where are the remains of his cities? As it was in the days of Noah, the flood destroyed Cain's cities. The scriptures do not say God destroyed the Tower of Babel and its surrounding cities. There is no further mention of Nimrod or his kingdom of Babel in the book of Genesis. There is a time span of thousand years between Nimrod's Babel and the Babylonian Empire. It is only speculation that Babylon got its name from Babel. The history of Babylon begins around 1800 BC during the reign of Kings.

Several points for consideration—Satan is referred to as the father of rebellion. He desired to ascend to the throne of God. Since Satan can influence behavior, this connection goes back to Adam and Eve, who made a pact with the fallen angel Satan, believing they would be like gods.

It is reasonable to speculate that the people gathered to build a city and a tower because they had acted on the temptation and attempted to ascend to heavenly heights.

We are not certain to the time frame it had taken Nimrod to complete building cities. We know mankind's life span was decreasing. Perhaps Nimrod lived to be three hundred years old, and he died. The Bible does not tell us how many children came forth from his loins. With the increase of people, a pure language no longer existed, and various dialects came forth as people were separated by hundreds of miles, unable to communicate by telephone or e-mail. After God confounded their language, dialects of Semitic, Akkadian (a mix of Babylonian and Assyrian), and Turanian were spoken. They separated into groups by language and not by race. After Japheth's descendants settled into their regions, the Bible does not mention them for hundreds of years until around 1000 to 900 BC. Revolution and regional wars gave way to the rise of the Persian, Grecian, and Roman Empires. The scriptures follow the paths of Ham (Canaan) and Shem (Assyria) through Abraham to the Kings of Israel, the divided kingdoms, the captivity in Babylon, capture by the Assyrians and Egyptians. The Bible path follows Israel returning to their land and the rebuilding of the second temple. In future times, Japheth's descendants would construct Babel-like towers in Rome at the Vatican. In America, we call it the Washington Monument, and it may be the tallest obelisk in the world. Is it a satanic influence on modern man that spurs the building of sky scrappers throughout the world? The knowledge of God was passed from generation to generation and from culture to culture. We have insight into their understanding of God by reading their scriptures and legends. For instance, Hinduism may date back to 2000 BC, and their writings called the Bhagavad-Gita talk about the nature of God the Creator being eternal, omnipresent, one who is not born nor does he ever die. It talks about a battle between the gods and the immortals taking human form. From these various records of events, people in authority, births, deaths, transactions, and wars, we develop a working knowledge of the ancient mind-set. No one man such as a Nimrod or any kingdom could totally displace the knowledge of God. As much effort that Satan and his cohorts put forth, they could not blot out the Ancient of Days. As time passed, Satan's evil activities interjected myth, lies, immorality, evolution, racism, paganism around the knowledge of God. We see the growth of paganism developed in Assyrian, Babylonian, Canaanites, and Egyptian cultures. The kingdom of Babylon became a model for spiritual idolatry and paganism as given in the book of Revelation. God had a plan to separate from amongst them a remnant that would be faithful to safeguard the knowledge of God. Herein, he called Abram from out of them to carry forth to all generations the true knowledge of our Creator.

In our chapter 7, we discussed the fallen angels had taught mankind forbidden knowledge. However, all of man's knowledge did not come from fallen angels. God instilled in the mind of early man, we do have a Creator. God gave mankind knowledge of his environment and knowledge to survive. The Bible mentions that Abel was a husbandman and Cain was a farmer. After Cain murdered Abel, he went out and built a city. God gave Noah skills to build the ark. His sons were almost one hundred years old, and they helped Noah build the ark. Nimrod and Asshur built cities. The hanging gardens in Babylon and the pyramids in Egypt became one of the Seven Wonders of the World. These early kingdoms had knowledge of math, science, medicine, and the ability to build monolith statutes, pyramids, and temples.

Commentary on Nimrod

There is a massive amount of commentary on the man Nimrod. As we present the following commentaries, each writer builds upon the layers and layers of speculation. Their verdict—Nimrod was responsible for everything that went wrong on planet Earth after the flood.

Before Noah and his relatives set foot on dry land, some scholars knew what was in the mind and heart of Ham. Michael Lake, in his book, *The Shinar Directive*, said, "Ham on the ark became a sleeper agent of darkness … infected with the forbidden knowledge … within the mind and heart of Ham were the foundational concepts upon which Babylon and Egypt were built and upon which the kingdom of Antichrist is being built today." Lake associates the event in Genesis 9:20 when Ham looked upon Noah's nakedness, and from this, Lake states that the "seed of the watchers were sprouting in Ham's heart." **Our comment**—Lake loses his credibility by assuming he knows what is in the mind of a man over five thousand years ago even though the scriptures tell us Noah and his generations were perfect and God blessed all of them. Lake tells us that Ham was infected, imperfect, and Ham was the prophet of darkness. We have previously demonstrated that all three of Noah's sons contributed to ungodliness.

Lake states that when Jesus comes, "the esoteric knowledge given by the fallen angels through the bloodline of Ham will not save them from God's judgment. There will be no promise of a Godhead, no immortality, no superhumans, and no Luciferian elite will save them." **Our comment**—Lake now knows who will be saved, and apparently, the descendants of Ham will not be saved.

Lake continues his attack on Ham and his descendants. Lake builds his theory using the commentary of Alexander Hislop, *The Two Babylons.* Following is a breakdown of Hislops comments, which do not line up with the Bible record of Ham's genealogy:

- Babylon mystery religion based on worship of prototype of Antichrist to glorify Nimrod that the whole Chaldean system of iniquity was formed.
- Ham is identified as Hermes in Egyptian for Son of Ham. Hermes was the great original prophet of idolatry, paganism, and interpreter of the gods.
- Ham is Mecury and could interpret the speeches of men/Hermeneutics.
- Ham, or Khem, is the Burnt One.
- Her is Chaldean for Hermes, Son of Her, or Ham.
- Mesh is Mesheh.
- Cush (son of Ham) is Bel, or Belus, also known as Hermes, Mercury, Nebo and associates him to Janus and the Tower of Babel. Bel is the confounder in Jeremiah 1:2. Ovid commentary calls Janus a god of gods; "the ancients call me chaos." Salii commentary calls Janus god of confusion; chaos is Cush.
- Ethiopian is Kuwshiy/Kushites, descendants of Cush. Lake comments, Zephaniah 2:12, "The Ethiopians will be put to death by my sword."
- Nimrod is Ninus.

From our assessment in portions of Lake's book, he portrays Nimrod as the culprit that opened the portal for demonic activity to invade the earth and infect the minds of men for the next five thousand years. We will summarize Lake's characterization of Nimrod:

- Greatest of all demigods in Shinar.
- Prototype of a transhuman/part human and part hybrid.
- A despot
- He is Osiris.
- He is Gilgamesh.
- He is Apollo.
- He is the Assyrian.
- He is the Antichrist.
- The original son of perdition.
- He plotted to devise a plan to enslave humanity through a false religion.

Lake has read many commentaries. We also have read the article in *Prophecy in the News*, by Gary Stearman dated 2001, "Night of the Leopard." And from it and in Lake's own imagination, he has developed a theory on the person of Nimrod: "In the beginning, Nimrod the Assyrian was the spiritual inheritor of the postflood religious apostasy. He is the keeper of the great heritage that began at the Assyrian capital Nineveh whose founder is Nimrod. Genesis 10:8–9 is a conspiracy that would change the world for the worst; knowledge of the watchers found its zenith in Nimrod. Nimrod possessed the strength, cunning, cruelty of the Nephilim before the flood. This change super charged his despotic desires." **Our comment**—Lake's statement is incorrect; Asshur was the founder of Assyria and its city Ninevah and the rest is pure conjecture.

According to Lake, "Nimrod possessed demonic intelligence and supernatural strength that enabled him to enslave people through tyranny and force. No other figure in history or the Bible, not even the pharaohs of Egypt come close to personifying the Antichrist the way Nimrod did. His ruthlessness is documented in most biblical resources [commentaries]." **Our comment**—many adjectives of which none can be proved. Sensationalism is better suited for science fiction.

According to Lake, "Nimrod birthed a religion that is still spreading like cancer in the world today … sacrificing children to Molech. Nimrod is the future Antichrist who comes in the name of mystery religion, it attempts to channel the power of ancient gods through one powerful man Nimrod who became the god." **Our comment**—pure speculation; no records exist that Nimrod sacrificed to Molech, no factual evidence that Nimrod is Antichrist or he is a vessel for Antichrist.

According to Lake, "At the end of times, Nimrod's mystery Babylon will gather to build a new Tower of Babel for Nimrod/Apollo's Second Coming but will be traversed by the end-time here—a triumphant church." Our comment—Bible scholars immediately know that the apostate end-time church will not put down the evil during the tribulations but only Jesus himself. As concerning the building of a new tower, can we distinguish it among the thousands of skyscrapers throughout the world that dwarf the Tower of Babel?

As we review Lake and other commentary, it is interesting to note that their perception of Nimrod comes from a European mind-set. Nimrod was black, and it appears their commentary is laced with racial bias. When we read commentary, keep in mind it is the opinion of another and not necessarily based on facts as presented in scripture or even based on archeological evidence. Lake quotes the position of John Garr on "commentary": "People read their own concepts and cultures into the Bible rather than drawing out of the scriptures the truths that have always been there. When interpreting the Bible in such a way their process introduces one's own presuppositions, agenda, biases rather than [exegesis] explain the text based on careful study and objective analysis but inject their preconceived notions into scripture rather than extracting from the text what it clearly says … the bases of the scriptures has been usurped by nonbiblical, antibiblical, traditional, and even demonic perversion." **Our**

comment: OMG, did Lake not understand this is exactly what he has done in creating a scenario for shock value and book sales?

> Nimrod is a prophetic archetype whose evil motives creep like the stain of spilled ink across the pages of scriptural history ... He represents the coming man of sin who will rule the entire world. In the world of occult he lives on as a shadowy figure of many names and many identities. Nimrod and his followers established the idolatrous pagan cultures that would determine the character of the world for the next four thousand years. Nimrod is both the political and spiritual progenitor of the evil system that places itself between man and God. (Gary Stearman, "Night of the Leopard")

Our comment—in Stearman's report, he has reproduced a picture of the "alleged" ruins of Nimrod on the slopes of Mount Nimrud in Turkey. The head sculptures found in the ruins are "alleged" to be those of Nimrod. Stearman also uses colorful, literary drama to make his report exciting and interesting; but most of it, like the following commentaries, lack factual evidence. If this were CSI, where is the proof connecting Nimrod to paganism? We are pleased Stearman did not portray Nimrod as a giant.

Clementine referred to Nimrod as King Ninus of Assyria. Nimrod was also referred to as King of Shinar, Land of Nimrod, which encompassed Assyria, Mesopotamia, and Babylon. **Our comment**—the original expanse of Eden would have encompassed these areas near the Euphrates and Tigris Rivers moving southward to Arabia and Africa, approximately 1,500 miles. Clementine states, the fallen angels taught men the use of incantations ... After the flood, Ham's descendants taught their sons. This was ingrained into Egyptian, Persian, Babylon culture. Ham died after the Tower of Babel ... Nimrod was handed this knowledge and by it caused men to go away from worship of God. They fell into superstitions governed by signs in stars and the motion of planets. **Our comment**—it is correct to assume that Ham taught his sons, but what he taught them, we do not know. We agree that the evil influence of Satan and his fallen angels continued through the descendants of Ham, Shem, Japheth and is evidenced in the behavior of modern man.

Jasher 9:8–10, "Nimrod turned government into tyranny ... set up twelve idols of wood named after twelve months of the year, each representing a sign of the Zodiac and commanded everyone to worship each idol ..." **Our comment**—is there any archeological evidence?

Flavious Josephus in his *Antiquities of the Jews*, "Nimrod was the first man after the flood to perfect the concept of martial self-discipline and the model of war as an art. Ambition and self-glorification were Nimrod's hallmarks." **Our comment**—we believe the art of war was first taught to man by the fallen angel Semjaza. After the flood, well before the birth of Nimrod, mankind fashioned weapons for protection against beast or tribal conflicts.

James E. Smith, *The Pentateuch,* Smith acknowledges there is **scant information** concerning Nimrod. The region was ruled by non-Shemitic people. Nimrod began … set out to be a mighty one, a gibbor. Nimrod's name means "revolt," and he was a tyrant. Nimrod was ruthless in opposition to all existing order. Mighty hunter of animals and men. Empire builder. **Our comment**—Shem's descendants also lived in Mesopotamia, such as Abraham of Ur, whose father worshipped idols. How does Smith arrive at his conclusion that Nimrod was ruthless?

Adam Clark, *The Syrica Targum*, call him a warlike giant. Babel was built by giants because Nimrod one of the builders is called gibbor, a mighty man or in Septuagint 10:11 giant. Giants sprang up from the earth. He went out of the east, **Asshur who was another of Babel builders.** These giants waged war with the gods because it is said Nimrod was a mighty hunter before the Lord. Other commentary changed it to say a warrior and a rebel against the Lord. **Our comment**—Genesis 11:1 makes absolutely no reference to giants building the tower of Babel. Asshur, son of Shem, built cities. Neither Nimrod nor Asshur were giants. The scriptures do not support any exchange between fallen angels, Nimrod, or Asshur postflood. Where is the archeological evidence of the giants before the flood or during the time of Nimrod?

Finis Dake, "*Nimrod* means 'rebel' in Hebrew. Points to open rebellion against God. He began to be a mighty one, which means bold and daring deeds. Gibbor in Hebrew is mighty warrior, tyrant, champion, strong one." **Our comment**—the highly respected Dake does not say Nimrod changed into giant.

A. W. Pink describes Nimrod as savage, cruel oppressor of men, first to develop open war against God. **Our comment**—blacks in Africa were stereotyped as "savages," and the black Nimrod is characterized as a savage. The racist mind-set habitually labels others in unfavorable terms. Nimrod was not the first to wage war against God. Satan and the fallen angels have the distinction of the first of God's created beings to rebel against him. For hundreds of years before the flood, wicked people were rebellious toward God. Pink states, "Antichrist should arise out of Babylon because Nebuchadnezzar and Antiochus Epiphanes were two monsters who bore down upon the people of God with overwhelming power and destruction. Seeing these ruled in Babylon, the New Testament Antichrist should arise from Babylon … It is appropriate for the nativity of the Antichrist, Babylon is the city of the devil versus the city of God in Jerusalem. Babylon represents the mother and disseminator of every kind of confusion, idolatry, impiety, foul pollution, crime, and perpetual iniquity." **Our comment**—Antiochus Epiphanes was a tyrant in Greek records. We hope Pink can distinguish between the literal Babylon and the spiritual, mystery Babylon—which is a symbol of confusion, rebellion, and false religion. Japheth's descendants have a history of oppression of men. America is the symbolic Babylonian harlot.

Edward F. Murphy, *Spiritual Warfare,* "Again this supports our spiritual warfare interpretation of the sin of Babel leading to God's judgment. The god of the world building on the corrupt flesh of man (his pride) and his worldly ambitions was the spirit behind the Tower of Babel." **Our comment**—we agree with Mr. Murphy that Satan, the god of this world, through the spirit of rebellion did influence mankind on a whole during and after the Babel event.

Wenham, "Throughout scripture Babylon is seen as the embodiment of human pride and godlessness that must attract the judgment of almighty God." **Our comment**—we agree with Mr. Wenham that Babylon during the time of Nebuchadnezzar, through the image he built and demanded the people to worship it, brought judgment against Babylon.

The legion of Nimrod is picked up in European mythology in the fourth century AD, which is evidence that Japheth's descendants migrated north and eastward from Mesopotamia.

Reference in the *Encyclopedia of European Peoples*, the Huns may have been a combination of Asian/Turkic, which may have included people called Hungarians, Azerbaijanis, Turkmens, Uzbeks, Ottoman Turks, and others. Their descendants may have been the Huns, as in Attila the Hun. The Huns were barbarians, who were fierce conquerors slaughtering women, monks, and burning monasteries. This includes Mongolic/Asian people who live in Russian, China, Mongolian regions. Some of these regions would be classified as Europe, and the people dwelling in these regions would be fair to brown complexion. The Ugric people may have records dating back to 2200 BC and are linked to Hungarians. Hungarian legend refers to Nimrod as a giant who built a tower two hundred years after the flood. It says he lived in the land of Evilat with wife Eneh and sons Hunor and Magor, who were great hunters with the bow.

Was Nimrod a Giant Nephilim?

Some scholars believe Nimrod became a giant Nephilim. There is no supporting evidence deeming the birth of Nimrod was a product of fallen angels and human women. If so, where is the archaeological evidence of the remains of Nimrod to present for DNA testing? It is our understanding that this unlawful union between angels and humans created the giant Nephilim before the flood. The Bible clearly states Nimrod was the human son of Cush. He was born to a human father and mother. From Genesis 10:8, there is nothing to substantiate he became a giant Nephilim. So from conjecture, some scholars portray Nimrod as a giant. If he had children, wouldn't his royal descendants be giants also?

We did discuss the Bible verse in reference to Nimrod who *began to be a mighty one in the earth* in Genesis 10:8. Over a period of time, perhaps Nimrod did excel as a mighty warrior, builder, and ruler. The term *mighty one* refers to one possessing strength and authority. In 1 Chronicle 12, the term *mighty men* is used to convey battalions of men ready to engage in military battle. There are no archeological findings of giants within three hundred years after the flood during the life of Nimrod. Similarly, there is no concrete evidence of the City of Atlantis; however, that does not hinder scholars from presenting commentaries on Atlantis.

The fallen angels were thought to be gods, given various names, and were worshipped by mankind. Ancient statues and carvings display images of beast with human heads and the body of animals or animal heads with the body of a human, which may be representative of hybrids existing before the flood. From what we can ascertain from the writings of Enoch, after the physical death of the Nephilim hybrids, their spirits existed as evil spirits or demons. We place our characters into a few categories:

- Fallen angels that had been deified were given names, such as, Apollo, Osiris, Diana, Zeus, These entities were never humans.
- Nephilim hybrids were created by the mingling of fallen angels and earth creatures and existed after the flood as evil spirits and demons.
- Humans have been deified by other humans, being immortalized in statues of pharaohs, emperors, Caesars, kings, queens, presidents, etc.
- Masks created by people are worn by other people to symbolize a variety of entities or deities, such as seen in Egyptian, Native America, African, Mayan artifacts; some mask are grotesque depictions of half human, half monster.
- Grotesque statues made by humans are mythological interpretations of gargoyles, dragons, demons, monsters.

Nimrod may have been deified by the people, having preserved his image in stone creations. In Egypt we find monoliths statues of the pharaohs worshipped by Egyptians. During the time of Nimrod, there are no monolith statues of his image found in Babel, Mesopotamia, Shinar, Babylon. Heads or statues of rulers found in some regions as those remains found in Turkey were suggested to be that of Nimrod, which cannot be verified. In New York City, the giant statue of Liberty symbolizes the Roman goddess Libertas. The seven spikes on its head represent Apollo, the sun god. Are we to believe this is a true representation of the goddess or the fallen angel that man imagined? Applying the same logic to Nimrod, some legends call him the sun god, enlightener, illuminator; these labels do not make him a god.

Daniel of the Bible gives us a greater insight into the Babylonian Empire, of which Nimrod's perceived influence upon paganism is not mentioned. Some scholars characterize

Nimrod as the father of paganism, which is not supported by Bible scriptures. Nimrod the person did not have a great empire no more so than Cain or Asshur. Their influence upon the growth of paganism was minimal. The Babylonian Empire is not exclusive toward paganism since Assyrian and Egyptian Empires were developing at the same time. Paganism became rampant in all the empires continuing in one form or another. Daniel 2 specifies the methods used by pagan practitioners—such as, magicians, astrologers, sorcerers, soothsayers—in order to learn the hidden secrets of the gods and to see what the future holds. King Nebuchadnezzar became well aware that all his wise men could not interpret his dream; only the God of gods reveals the deep and secret things. Though King Nebuchadnezzar acknowledged God Almighty, he continued in his pride, thus creating an image of himself, commanding the people to worship it and him as god. Egyptian culture is replete with human kings who were later deified and placed within the pantheon of gods. Greek and Roman Empires made gods of fallen angels and themselves. Caligula wanted to be more than emperor; he wanted to be a god and sat himself in the temple of Diana. Secret societies adopted pagan rituals, altars, symbols, statues, the wearing of mask and other garb. These practices flourished throughout the Middle Ages and found their way into modern times as we consider the Illuminati, Masons, Satanist, Wiccan, and others that embrace occult and pagan rituals.

Giants and Evil Spirits in the Land after the Flood

In our chapter 7, we discussed the Nephilim was a hybrid as a result of mixing between celestial and biological earth forms preflood. The word *Gibborim* is used to define the physical nature of the Nephilim hybrids as mighty ones who were earthborn.

Following, we discuss the existence of giants in the land after the flood. The reappearance of giants began around 2000 BC as evidenced in folklore, scripture, writings, and archeological artifacts. These postflood creatures were different than the Nephilim. Other historical artifacts discovered on clay tablets, stele, monuments, caves have similar accounts of giants as found in the Torah. Many scratch their heads and wonder how the Genesis account in the Bible could be similar to what is found in these ancient records, which in some instances predate the Bible. As mentioned, the written preflood records were given to Noah. God called Moses forth to give him the understanding found in Genesis through to Deuteronomy. The Torah became a guidepost to the truth of God. Over thousands of years, some truth mixed with mythology emerged. These legends repeat an account of gods who descended, intermingled with existing species to create hybrids. In some writings, these beings are called Ananuki, gods from the planet Nibiru. The artifact called the Epic of Gilgamesh gives the name of Enki, or Enlil, as the creator god, and some commentaries link these names with Nimrod. It speaks of a man taken to heaven to meet the gods. In the Bible there are several accounts of men taken to heaven as well as God coming to earth, as in the giving of the law to Moses. This belief in gods coming down is carried forward into the first century AD. Sumerian images of these space travelers are shown with wings, riding in vehicles, wearing boots and helmets—which is a close description of angels. Some people believe these gods came to earth to extract its precious metals, and mankind was made to mine for them.

Native American folklore records a feathered serpent seen in the constellations. India has a myth of the sky god, who was half human and half serpent. Chinese myth in the fifth century BC speaks of a flying dragon. Others refer to the serpent (Satan) as bringer of knowledge, which ties into the biblical account of Satan in the Garden, deceiving Eve with a promise of knowledge, immortality, and power. The Mayans, Aztecs, Incas of South America believed in a winged god appearing as a feathered serpent who taught mankind wisdom. He was described as a bearded white man who did fly in disks.

Some scholars speculate that during the flood, some of the fallen angels had made an escape for some of their hybrid children. Those who had mingled with sea creatures may have been able to survive in the waters. It was also considered that the fallen angels had celestial vehicles that may have carried hybrid survivors. The Dead Sea scrolls were written thousands of years after the flood, but a small fragment titled *Book of Giants* briefly mentions the pre-flood mixing of species, which produced giants or monster animals. It also alludes to the possibility that some giants could fly like their father, the angels. These records point to the activities of Satan and his fallen angels before and after the flood.

An excellent reference source that documents all things "giant" is Stephen Quayle's *Genesis 6 Giants*; *Master Builders of Prehistoric and Ancient Civilizations.* [19] He provides in over four hundred pages credible evidence, pictures, and history of giants existing after the flood on every continent. Quayle inserts a photo of a fossilized giant, measuring twelve feet two inches tall displayed at Broad Street Station, London, late nineteenth century (page 257). Quayle said, "The remains of giants have been found throughout the world and mostly kept secret." For instance, the Smithsonian Institute received giant bones, and then the evidence is classified "not for public viewing." The Vatican may also have retained remains of some giants.

Quayle and associate Timothy Alberino have amassed records of giants, which are presented in their documentary, *True Legends: Technology of the Fallen Angels*. Many of the giant remains had red hair, six digits, and double rows of teeth. Researchers believe these giants were fierce, cruel, cannibals. Several discovery made by Quayle are presented:

---

[19] Stephen Quayle, Genesis 6 Giants, (Bozeman, MT, End Time Thunder Publishers, 2008)

- 2005 giants were reported in Afghanistan who attacked soldiers. One giant was nine to ten feet tall; he was killed by soldiers and transported to Wright Patterson AFB, United States. This could have been the result of genetic experiments.
- Giant remains found on the Solomon Island, Japan.
- Giant footprints observed in China in 2016 and one seen in South Africa in 1912.
- During the Spanish inquisition in Peru, indigenous people claim giants built houses and dug wells. Estimates of their height ranged from ten to thirty feet tall. People worshipped the giant remains, and the church burned giant bones to dissuade them from paganism.
- The Pawnee Indians showed Buffalo Bill Cody evidence of giant bones, stating the giants were in the land before the natives migrated to the region.
- Samuel Hubbard Jr. reported in the *LA Times*, 1896, that the petrified body of a man preserved in lime or silica in water was found in the Grand Canyon. Hubbard also claimed dinosaur evidence was found, which supports the Bible truth that animals and man existed together. Hubbard also said the body was of a living, breathing man. This supports our claim that the possibility of finding preflood Nephilim DNA is probably impossible.
- Giant remains found in Grand Canyon in 1909 by G. E. Kinkaid in an underground area.
- Eighteen giant skeletons and pyramids were found in Lake Delavan, Wisconsin. Their height ranged from 7.6 feet to ten feet, large skulls, double row of teeth, six digits on hands and feet.
- Newark, New Jersey had large skeletal remains dating back 3,500 years, which would bring us to 1,500 BC.
- On file at the Lincoln Institute, President Abraham Lincoln wrote about giant remains that filled the mounds of America.

Serpent mounds, crop circles, pyramids, and other monolith stone structures have been found on earth surface and under the ocean throughout the world. Some scholars believe the fallen angels developed a grid around the planet marked by pyramids, mounds, and crop circles for unknown purposes. Satan and his fallen angels continued their conquest of the earth after the flood. Other scholars believe these monoliths were the work of the giants.

L. A. Marzulli, author of the *Watchers* video series, has explored the existence of giants after the flood. Marzulli supports the Bible record that giants lived among the Canannite tribes. Marzulli describes the giants had elongated or cone-shaped heads; remnants of hair appeared to be red or blond; some had double rows of teeth and hands with six fingers. Giant remains were found in regions of South America, Iran, Germany, Russia, India. Marzulli shared on Skywatch TV, 2016, that the elongated head of an infant—with yellow and red hair, approximately two thousand years old, found in Peru—had traces of Middle Eastern and European DNA. Marzulli claims this evidence supports the creation of the giant Nephilim. **Our comment**—red hair, six digits, double rows of teeth do not confirm these are the preflood giant Nephilim. Some European anthropologists also claim that African skulls are broad, incorrectly associating them with apes to support their theory of evolution. Red hair is characteristic of fair-skinned Irish people as blond hair was observed among the Aboriginal people of Australia. Given a broader view, modern man has a range of characteristics, some being unusual.

At this point, we cannot find clear evidence to confirm postflood giants are Nephilim. The existence of preflood Nephilim DNA has not been found or confirmed. There is no evidence to confirm that postflood remains of giants were the product of angels and humans. Preflood evidence, such as Noah's ark, has been sighted but not confirmed. The City of Atlantis has not been confirmed. Where are the tools and weapons made before the flood? What has been confirmed is that life existed worldwide and the flood encompassed the whole world.

To find definitive proof that postflood giants are Nephilim hybrids, Marzulli contracted for DNA testing on hundreds of **elongated skulls** found in Paracas, Peru, dated to be three thousand years old. According to the age assigned to these bones, it would place them postflood, around 1000 BC.

Initial DNA analysis performed on the skulls show **minute traces** of other-than-human DNA, and no explanation is suggested at this time. As researchers look for traces of unusual genetic markers, they must factor in abnormalities found in modern people of gigantic or dwarf statures. Pathological studies may factor in the introduction of pathogens from viruses and bacteria. The mention of trace nonhuman DNA may be transmitted from species (animals, fish, plant), carrying viruses or bacteria that were absorbed within the human host.

As we indicated, it is unlikely there exists Nephilim hybrid DNA to compare with the DNA markers discovered in these skulls, and therefore we may not arrive at a solid conclusion that these skulls are associated with Nephilim hybrids. Our conclusion is supported in a recent article seen in the Mysterious Universe, June 22, 2016, by Paul Seaburn, published in Plos One, reported by Dong Hoon Shin (bioanthropologist at Seoul National University, College of Medicine, in Korea, discovered the head of a female associated with the Silla kingdom around 57 BC to AD 935). Shin said, "It is **very rare** to find any preserved skeletons from the Silla kingdom era." The excitement around the find is that the elongated shaped head is believed to be a **natural development** and not that caused by cranial binding. **Our comment**—this skull was not elongated due to Nephilim factors.

During the time of Abraham, he traveled from the Mesopotamia region into Canaan around 2000 BC. In Canaan, he encountered giants. He lived in Hebron near the Anakim giants. It appears Abraham and his family coexisted with the giants, and seemingly they were not hindered as they did prosper. Abraham and Lot prospered so much they could not share the same land space, so they parted ways.

Lot went toward the Jordan valley, near the cities of Sodom and Gomorra, in the location of the Dead Sea. Lot became a resident of Sodom. Here he discovered that the people were depraved and under the power of demonic spirits. Saint Jude in his writings gave an initial warning to beware of "*certain men that crept in unawares, who were before of old ordained to this condemnation, ungodly men, turning the grace of our God into lasciviousness and denying the only Lord God and our Lord Jesus Christ.*"

Jude specifically calls out Sodom and Gomorra and the other ungodly cities of Adman, Zeboiim, Zoar, who gave *themselves over to fornication and went after strange flesh … filthy dreamers defile the flesh, despise dominion, and speak evil of dignities.* Our understanding of this passage indicates that humans had intercourse with other humans and beings of a different nature. These entities are referred to as old and condemned, strange flesh, filthy dreamers, dominions and dignities. Jude continues to expound on these "spots" who are without fear, clouds without water, carried about of winds, fruitless, twice dead, likened to raging waves of the sea, foaming out their own shame, wandering stars, to whom is reserved the blackness of darkness forever. This does not sound like a description of angels or people but may allude to the evil spirits of the Nephilim. Jude makes a reference found in Enoch, who wrote of the spirits of the Nephilim.

During the war of the kings, it seemed that Abraham did not make a big deal about the giants who lived in the regions. Teraphim is associated with spiritualism in Chaldea, and Egypt and has a connection to shape, type, transformation. Spirits can transform themselves. Around this time frame, the word *Rephaim* was associated with the Netherworld as in the spirits of dead things.

In the book of Job 26:5, "*Dead things are formed from under the waters and the inhabitants thereof.*" This could allude to the drowning of the physical portion of the Nephilim during the flood and their spiritual portion continues to exist as Jude makes mention of "twice dead" entities. Job lived not long after the flood and probably knew of the legend of the Nephilim, and this passage could be referring to the spirits of the Nephilim who dwell in the Netherworld.

Genesis 14:5 tells us that King Chedorlaomer and other kings killed the Rephaims in Ashteroth Karnaim. Abraham rescues Lot (Genesis 14:22).

Partial List of Giants

From Anakim came versions as Emims, Zamzummims, Zuzims and may be different terms for the same group of giants.

- Zuzims
- Emims of Moab and Shaveh Kiriathaim
- Anak or Anakim of Hebron,
- Zamzummims, region of Ammon
- Horites of Mount Seir
- Og, king of Bashan (near Sea of Galilee)
- Avvim region of Gaza
- Philistines regions Gaza, Ashketon, Edron, Ashdod
- Goliath of Gath, also called a Gittite

Father of Moses Sees Fallen Angels

A fragment among the Dead Sea scrolls contains an admonition by Amram, the father of Moses, to his children. In a vision, Amram sees the chief angel of darkness, a watcher named Melkiresha, who appeared in a reptilian form. "I saw watchers in my vision … behold two of them argued about me … asking why, they said, we have been made masters and rule over all the sons of men … which of us do you choose, I raided my eyes and saw one of them, his looks were frightening like those of a viper and his garments were multicolored and he was extremely dark … his appearance and his face was like that of an adder …" The biblical record substantiates that Satan contended with Michael for the body of Moses, and this encounter with Amram and angels is credible.

Giants During the Time of Moses and Joshua

God assures the Israelites that they can possess the land because he will go before them as a consuming fire, driving out the occupants. God also emphasized that it is not because of the Israelites' righteousness but it is God's righteousness that he destroys the giants and regular-size people out of the land, because of their wickedness.

Numbers 13:22–33, the spies had been sent into the promised land, and they encountered the children of Anak in the region of Hebron (south of Jerusalem). They described them as giants or men of great stature. We are also told the Amalekites, Hittites, Jebusites, Amorites, and Canaanites dwelled in the region.

> *Hear O Israel, you are to pass over Jordan this day to go in to possess nations greater and mightier than yourself, cities great and fenced up to heaven, a people*

> *great and tall, the children of the Anakims, whom you know and of whom you have heard say, who can stand before the children of Anak.* (Deuteronomy 9:1)
>
> *For only king Og of Bashan remained of the remnant of giants, behold his bedstead was a bedstead of iron … nine cubits was the length and four cubits wide.* (Deuteronomy 3:11)

Recorded in Numbers 21:33, Moses encounters Og, king of Bashan, and "*they smote him and his sons and all his people until there was none left alive and they possessed his land* (land of Bashan is near the Sea of Galilee)."

Joshua killed King Og of Bashan, which was of the remnant of the giants that dwelt in Ashtaroth and at Edrei and reigned in Mount Hermon. Other giants still remained in Gaza, Gath, and Ashdod. Joshua 11:17–23, Joshua 12:4–5, Joshua 15:8 speak of the valley of giants near Jerusalem, associated with the valley of Hinnom.

Joshua encounters giants in the promised land in the area of Mount Halak that goes up to Seir, unto Baal-gad in the Valley of Lebanon under Mount Hermon, and he killed them. Joshua cut off the Anakims from the mountains near Hebron, Debir, Anab, Judah.

> *Anakim which also were accounted giants but the Moabites call them Emims.* (Deuteronomy 2:11)
>
> *That also was accounted a land of giants. Giants dwelt therein in old time and the Ammonites call them Zamzummims, a people great and many and tall as the Anakims but the Lord destroyed them before them and they succeeded them and dwelt in their stead …* (Deuteronomy 2:20)

Zamzummin in Hebrew translates to "buzzers," or whose speech sounds like buzzing.

Giants During the Time of King Saul

> *Now the Philistines gathered together their armies to battle and were gathered at Shochoh which belonged to Judah …* (1 Samuel 17:1)

Saul and the men of Israel were gathered by the Valley of Elah to do battle. The champion of the Philistines was Goliath of Gath, who was about ten feet tall. David killed the giant Goliath of Gath and cut off his head.

Giants During the Time of King David

Around 1000 BC, 2 Samuel 5:18, David encounters the Philistines in the valley of Rephaim and killed them from Geba to Gazer. The Philistines occupied the regions of Gaza,

Ashketon, Ashdod, Ekron, Gath. In 2 Samuel 16, we see David and his men fighting giants. The giant names were Ishbi-benob, Saph, and two unnamed living in the region of Gath.

Goliath was called a Gittite and had a giant brother who had six fingers and six toes. It is interesting to note that the passage says *he also was born to the giant*; there were probably giant women who mated with giant men, producing giant children.

The Bible tells us that giants lived in the promised land from Lebanon to Jerusalem to Jordan.

The above scriptural references to giants in the land do not allude to them as being products of fallen angels and humans. They just might be a freak of nature or not. On the opposite side of the coin, <u>what</u> do we contribute to the abnormality of very small people? As in gigantism and dwarfism, there is a scientific genetic explanation. God created so much variation in the animal kingdom, and perhaps he created variations in the human species.

Growth of Kingdoms Gives Rise to Paganism

<u>Zoroastrianism</u>

We are discussing the worship of false gods, idolatry, and paganism and its influence through the ages. At this juncture, we want to review Zoroastrianism since it ties into Babylon, King Nebuchadnezzar, the Magi, and the Hebrew-Israelite Daniel. This ancient religion leans toward monotheism.

Zoroastrianism has its roots in Persian and Babylonian cultures. It embraces mysticism, esoteric, secret wisdom, ancient mysteries, as is also embraced within the Jewish Kabbala. Its founder, Zarathustra, believed in life on earth, life in the hereafter, immortality of the soul, the Resurrection of the body and one God—the Almighty Creator. Records dating back to 1500 to 1000 BC claim Zarathustra Spitama of royal Persian ancestry was thirty years old, meditating on Mount of Ushidarena, when he received a revelation from Ahura Mazda by way of the angel Vohu Mana, who appeared nine times the size of a man. The angel told him Ahura Mazda was the one true god and he was to be his prophet.

In an article published in Ancient Origins, August 2014, April Holloway shares her insight about activity in the Mesopotamian region and mention of Zoroastrianism. Ruins of a five-thousand-year-old city were discovered in Turkey-Armenia region. Ani was the capital of Armenia located near the Akhuryan River and was known as the City of 1001 places of worship, housing Zoroastrian temples, and the City of Forty Gates. Historians say that Ani at its zenith was as Constantinople, Babylon, and Egypt. The underground cities of Ani were discovered in AD 1880 by George Ivanovic Gurdjieff. These caves led to the discovery of tunnels, water channels, monk cells, currently 823 structures. Gurdjieff found a parchment in a wall niche written in ancient Armenia from one monk to another. The writings referenced the Sarmoung Brotherhood associated with an esoteric school, delving into secret mysteries and associated with Babylon around 2500 BC.

We are interested in Zoroastrianism because it provides a connection with the monotheistic beliefs of Noah to Daniel to Jesus. The majority of Shem's descendants carried on the godly line through Abraham and thereafter. It is reasonable to consider that the concept of monotheism existed before the flood and continued through the survivors of the flood and was later embraced by others as recorded in the history of mankind.

Zarathustra said God revealed himself to humans through six modes—one called Amesha Spenta (holy immortals, or we call them angels). He traveled to the city of Balkh under King of Persia, Kavavishtapa. Dressed in white garments, bearing sacred fire (fire of Empyrean) and a staff made of cypress wood, he told the king about his religious philosophy from Ahura to elevate Aryans/Persians to lofty and intellectual purity of monotheism. The Aryans were living and working in Atropatene near the Capsian Sea (region of Turkey) and may have fallen into polytheism. Zarathustra attempted to remedy this error and tried to turn the people back to worship of Ahura. God is called by many names, and Zarathustra called the Creator in the language spoken during that period and in that region. He promoted piety, religious convictions in conjunction with Judaism. Hundreds of years later, Zarathustra's beliefs were in line with the Gospel. Case in point, the Magi of Babylon were of the order of Zoroaster, of whom King Nebuchadnezzar appointed Daniel overseer. Perhaps the captivity of Israel by this king had a dual purpose. First was the punishment of disobedient Israel, and second could have been to bring enlightenment to the followers of Zoroaster. The Magi had foreknowledge of a king that would come and set up his kingdom on earth. When the sign appeared, they traveled hundreds of miles to see Yeshua the king and to honor him as King of Israel. Their caravan consisted of hundreds of horses, ridden by priests, regally dressed in white, bringing with them great wealth.

All religions experience divisions and branch off into other denominations or sects. Zoroastrianism split between Indo-Iranians (a branch of Aryans dedicated to monotheism called Mazayasnians) versus Daevayasnians (who were polytheist). The Daevayasnians migrated to India and became Brahmins of Hindu, who worshipped hundreds of deities. Later, some Hindus converted to Islam around AD 642 and are called Sikhs.

The above excerpts are taken from S. A. Kapadia, *Teaching of Zoroaster and Philosophy of Parsi Religion*, Inner Temple, London, January 1905.

As kingdoms and empires flourished throughout millennia, God always provided a connection to himself, as was Zoroastrianism in the midst of pagan Babylon. God did determine that there would be a righteous lineage that would be a light to mankind. These were the descendants of Shem, Abram, Jacob, Moses, and others who were called to be the patriarchs of the Hebrew Israelites and the twelve tribes giving birth to the Messiah. These would be a light unto the Gentiles.

The Rise of Paganism

Migration patterns demonstrate that groups formed tribes. Tribal elders became rulers, who in turn formed governments. Some governments became empires. Satan established seats of wickedness and spiritual strongholds over empires. For instance, one reference is to Pergamon in Turkey. Archaeologists discovered the stone heads of a ruler in Turkey as well as two statues guarding the "Gate to Hades." One statute depicts a snake, and the other is a three-headed watchdog; both statutes in mythology are associated with the underworld or hell. Hades was the brother of Zeus. Other remains in Turkey were monolithic structures and the Gobekii Tepe, site in Anatolia having a circular formation with hundreds of *T*-shaped pillars.

Babylon was also a seat of wickedness. Babylonian rulers were partially responsible for creating a portal for evil through pagan religious practices. Egypt was a satanic seat for the promotion of pagan deities, building monolith statues, pyramids, and obelisk symbols of worship to the fallen angels. There continues to be demonic stronghold over regions currently in the form of false religions. These practices continued into the twenty-first century. For example, Hitler established an altar to Zeus in Germany. The United Nations in America houses a statue of Zeus. America symbolizes its allegiance with satanic forces by placing the image of a pagan goddess on its shores. The Statue of Liberty is admired by many nations. Satan worshippers have placed statues of Satan in their temples throughout the United States. Over these seats, Satan places spiritual rulers, such as the king of Tyre or the prince of Persia, who influence the movements of human rulers.

Nations flourished, and belief in the one true God diminished. Coming into the time of Jesus Christ, Saint Peter points out that wicked men and false prophets were spreading lies about the death, Resurrection, and deity of Jesus. They also encouraged all kinds of immoral acts, specifically sexual sin. Saint Peter connects the sin of the angels before the flood and the sexual perversion of Sodom and Gomorrah. Holy angels came to deliver Lot from the filth of the wicked. The men of Sodom and Gomorrah wanted to have intercourse with the angels, and they were not afraid to speak evil of dignities (angels).

> *Whereas angels which are greater in power and might, do not bring railing accusations against them before the Lord. But these as natural brute beasts, made to be taken and destroyed speak evil of the things that they don't understand and will utterly perish in their own corruption.* (2 Peter 2:11–12)

It is less complicated to study the rise of empires when taking into consideration that more than one empire flourished at the same time. Certainly, biblical and secular history tell us that the Assyrian, Babylonian, and Egyptian Empires interacted one with another. The Bible is an accurate compass that provides markers throughout human history. Following these markers, we are able to provide a summary of the earliest empires.

Sumer Civilization

Scholarly dating varies between the creation date, 4004 BC, and earlier theories. We base our study on the creation date with some flexibility. First we did consider the regions that Shem's, Ham's, and Japheth's descendants settled. Then we factor in the biblical account of the regions Nimrod and Asshur settled. People called Sumerians, Assyrians, Babylonians lived during the same time period. They occupied the larger region called Mesopotamia near Euphrates and Tigris Rivers. Other cities associated in this region are Kish, Erech, Ur, Sippar, Akshak, Larak, Adab, Umma, Bad-tibira, Larsa, Calah, Assur, Nineveh, and Babel. Some of these cities are associated with Nimrod—such as Babel, Erech, Accad, Calneh; and other cities are associated with Asshur—such as Nineveh, Rehoboth, Calah, Resen (Genesis 10:8–11). People in these regions interacted with each other through marriage, society, and trade.

People of Sumer were called Sumerians. Other groups of people living in Sumer were called Ubaidians. Ancient Origins writer John Black, online, December 12, 2013, discussed "The Unanswered Mystery of 7,000-Year-Old Ubaid Lizardmen":

> It is accepted by mainstream archaeology that civilization started in … Mesopotamia and at the Ubaid archaeological site, pre-Sumerian artifacts were found of humanoid figurines with lizard characteristics.

The figurines are described as male with genitalia and female with breast, nursing its baby. They are wearing some type of elongated head gear, broad shoulders, narrow torso, lizard-like facial features, slanted eyes, reptile nose, and slit mouth. We cannot at this time reach a conclusion as to what these figurines represent. However, it does not appear that any evidence of physical remains of a hybrid with a lizard head and human body has ever been found.

Researchers note that before the Tower of Babel incident, the language spoken by Sumerians "belonged to no known language family." According to the Bible, all mankind spoke one language before the Tower of Babel incident, then afterward, God confounded their language. Their dialects became bilingual associated with ancient Semitic and Akkadian and became more diverse as people migrated throughout the earth.

A list of Sumerian kings inscribed on a cuneiform tablet was dated around 2900 BC and discovered by Hermann Hilprecht, AD 1900s at Nippur site. The first king of Sumer was Etana. Besides a list of kings, other names may refer to mythical gods. The cuneiform mentions gods coming from the heaven and also mentions the great flood. Many cuneiform tablets, pottery sherds, and other artifacts were found—which offer insight into these ancient civilizations. The names of some of the gods or kings associated with Sumer are also recorded in the Assyrian and Babylonians cultures—such as, Enki, god of earth; Enlil, god of air; Sin, moon god.

The people of Sumer developed math, irrigation, built housing and boats, and common products were traded between regions, such as, agriculture, fishing, farm animals, weaving, leather work, metal work, masonry, and pottery (*Ancient Origins*, April Holloway, January 2014; and Wikipedia, "Sumer").

Assyrian Empire

The Sumerians were eventually absorbed into the Assyrian culture. Assyrians occupied regions identified postflood. Some archeological evidence was found on pottery in Calah, Assur, Nineveh, dated 3000 BC. Assyrians rose up in power around 2500 BC. They amassed territory that ran from Turkey to Mesopotamia to Egypt.

Assyria ruled by king Tudiya 2400 BC, then Sargon of Akkad became Akkadian kingdom. In 2332, BC, King Sargon I of Akkad claimed the remaining territory of Sumer. He made Nineveh the Assyrian capital. It became famous for its culture, technology, libraries, buildings, irrigation system, lush gardens, and overall beauty. Over a period of time, approximately thirty-six kings ruled, including Ninus, son of Belus, to Sardanapalus. Was Ninus Nimrod, as some scholars claim? At the 2500 BC period, Nimrod most likely was dead and the Bible does not list his children. It is recorded that they worshipped Shemach, the sun god; Sin, the moon god; Hadad, the god of thunder. They amassed wealth from the plunder of other nations. They were known for their barbaric and inhumane torture.

Ishme-dagon (1780 BC) was the Assyrian ruler who was contemporary to Hammurabi of Babylon.

The Hebrew Israelites were living in Egypt. Moses was born 1526 BC. Moses received instructions to free his people from Egypt around 1447 BC. Around 1407 BC Israel moved into the promised land. Solomon was king of Israel 970 BC. He built first temple 966 BC.

Assyria ruler Adad-nirari II overthrew the twenty-fifth Egyptian dynasty, 1365 BC. The Assyrian Empire may have conquered territory in Babylon, Elam, Urartu, Media, Persia, Phoenician, Canaan, Aramea, Syria, Arabia, Philitine, Edom, Moab, Samaria, Cyprus, Chaldea, Commagene—involving tribes of the Hittites, Nubians, Kushites, Ethiopians,

Cimmerian, Scythians. Records indicate by 883 BC, Ashurnasirpal II was king followed by his son, Shalmaneser. Coming to 859–824 BC, the Assyrian Empire was under the control of Shalmaneser III, controlling territory toward the Mediterranean Sea. Between 783–754 BC, Shalmaneser IV, Ashur-dan III, and Ashur-nirari served as kings of Assyria. The Bible records ties Jonah into Assyrian history 750 BC when he was in the belly of a whale and then reluctantly preached to the people of Nineveh, capital of Assyria. Jonah became a prophet 793 BC at the time Jeroboam II, king of Israel, ruled.

Tiglath-pileser III (727 BC) was king of Assyria. Israel king Menahem paid him tribute (2 Kings 15:19). Ahaz gave him gifts in exchange for military aid. By 722 BC, Shalmaneser V became king of Assyria. He and Sargon II brought an end to the northern kingdom of Israel. Assyria captured its capital Samaria because King Hoshea of Israel wanted to join forces with King So of Egypt against Assyria. The Israelites were taken captive to Assyria in Halah and Habor by the River of Gozan in the city of the Medes, and many never returned to their homeland (2 Kings 17:6). The prophet Micah 5:5–6 makes reference to the Assyrians coming against Israel.

In 705–681 BC, an angel of the Lord destroyed 185,000 Assyrians soldiers during the reign of Sennacherib, king of Assyria who openly defied God when he came against Judah, Southern kingdom (Isaiah 37:36). Sennacherib had many dealings with Israel king Hezekiah (23 Kings 18).

There is a record, 670 BC, in Isaiah 18 and Ezekiel 30:9 regarding the fate of Ethiopia. God used the Assyrians to invade Egypt, which affected Ethiopia.

During the years 669–633 BC, King Ashurbanipal built up Nineveh as a mighty city with walls a hundred feet high and wide enough that three chariots could ride side by side. The walls encompassed large towers that were a hundred feet higher than the walls. Around the walls was a moat, which was 150 feet wide and sixty feet deep. Coming to the year 612 BC, Nineveh was destroyed by the Medes and Babylonians, who breached the walls when the Tigris River overflowed and destroyed a part of the wall. Under King Nabopolassar, the Babylonians plundered the city and set it on fire.

Nahum the prophet predicted that Nineveh would fall and "be hid," and the city was not discovered again until around AD 1842–1845. Excavation of Nineveh found Library of Ashurbanipal, a cuneiform, and cylinder of Nebuchadnezzar and Sennacherib. Art and reliefs depicted activity of the era. One stone relief showed battles; another showed them in a boat transporting cedar from Lebanon. Kings displayed them on royal palace. Assyrian sculpture of winged bull Lamassu guarded the entrance to king's court. Jewelry was found in royal tombs at Nimrud palace in northern Iraq. An ivory statute from the era of Nimrud VI was preserved as a record of the conquest between the Assyrian Empire, Babylonian, and Median armies who captured the City of Calah.

Akkadian Empire

From the region of Mesopotamia, the City of Akkad emerged around 2334 to 2154 BC. People identified as Sumerians intermingled with the Akkadians. The Akkadian language became the dominate dialect. The first ruler was Sargon of Akkad, followed by his son, Naram-Sin of Akkad. During their rule, they invaded various lands, including Syria and Canaan. After 180 years of dominance, the empire collapsed around 2154 BC. Some scholars believe it was due to a famine and invasion by other groups. This famine had spread from Mesopotamia to Egypt, and it was during the time Abraham and his family traveled to Egypt because of the famine.

Babylonian Empire

The Assyrians interacted with the Egyptians and Babylonians. Babylon became a strong world power more so than Assyria. The Bible tells us Babylon encompassed the regions of Mesopotamia, now modern-day Iraq and Iran. Belief in pagan gods surfaced in Babylon as well as the mother-and-son cult, which continued for hundreds of years to the present. In Babylonian mythology, Ninus was cast as the husband of Semiramis. The story says he died a violent death, torn in pieces, body parts carried to different places; the wife reunites the pieces and, through a series of mystical rites, reanimates her husband; but she holds him in her arms as a child called Tammuz. Those who worshipped Semiramis began to call her Queen of Heaven. Eventually, the worshippers considered Semiramis and Tammuz, mother and son, to be coequal deities.

Beginning our study of the Babylonian Empire, we find no mention of Nimrod in the writings of Daniel. During the time of Nimrod, scriptures references are miniscule. From our overview to this point, we see that Nimrod is not the sole progenitor of paganism.

In 1800 BC, king of Babylon, Sin-Mubalit, passed rule to his son, Hammurabi, born 1792 BC. Under his authority, the cities Borshippa, Kish, Sippar, Eshnunna, Larsa, and Elam were conquered. After the death of Hammurabi, 1750 BC, his son, Samsu-iluna, took over the empire.

We fast-forward to 747 BC, Nabonassar ruled Babylon. Displaced Egyptians fled to Chaldea, bringing with them knowledge of astronomy, astrology, architecture, year calendar. Babylonian and Egyptian cultures and beliefs were intermingled. Chaldeans are a mix of Shem and Ham.

In 715 to 700 BC, Berodach-baadan of Babylon sent letters to King Hezekiah of Israel, who was near death. Hezekiah prayed, and God extended his life fifteen additional years. God also promised Hezekiah he would deliver his city out of the hand of the king of Assyria. The king of Babylon visited Hezekiah, who showed him all the treasures of silver and gold, spices, ointments, and the armory. Hezekiah became prideful and did not give God the glory (2 Kings 20).

Nabopolassar captured Nineveh, capital of Assyria, decreasing the strength of the Assyrians, 612 BC.

In 605–586 BC, King Nebuchadnezzar began his conquest of Jerusalem during the time of King Jehoiakim over Judah, 596 BC. Ezekiel writes Neboaw prophecy. Ezekiel and Daniel were settled near Chebar River, City of Nippur, the religious center of Mesopotamia. By 586 BC, Nebuchadnezzar had completely destroyed the Jewish temple and took the temple vessels to his land, placing them in the temple of his god. What happened to the Ark of the Covenant? Was it taken to Ethiopia, captured by King Nebuchadnezzar, or hidden beneath the Jerusalem temple?

The king told Ashpenaz, master of his eunuchs, to bring certain children of Israel—who were children of the king, in whom was no blemish, possessing wisdom, knowledge, and understanding science. Among them were Daniel, Hananiah, Mishael, and Azariah. Their names were changed. Daniel was called Belteshazzar; Hananiah was called Shadrach; Mishael was called Meshach; and Azariah was called Abed-nego. God gave Daniel and the others favor and tender love with the prince of the eunuchs. God also gave them knowledge, wisdom, and skills. Daniel could interpret dreams, of which God revealed the understanding to him.

During the time Daniel was a captive in Babylon, King Nebuchadnezzar appointed him to oversee the Magi who were of the Zoroastrian priesthood. These are the Magi who visited the child Jesus. After Babylon was conquered by the Medes and Persians, Zoroastrianism was made the state religion. The Bible also gives an account of the captivity of the Jews in Babylon where the Babylonian Talmud was recorded by the Jews.

Nebuchadnezzar had a dream of a huge statue made of gold, silver, brass, iron, representing various future kingdoms (Daniel 1:7 and 2:32). Daniel interprets the king's dream, telling him the head of gold represented his present kingdom but it would be usurped by another. The king fashioned a golden image of himself, ninety feet tall and commanded all to worship it. Since the statue was all gold, perhaps the king thought this would placate future empires represented by lesser metals from conquering his empire and the prophecy would not come to past. The king decreed that whoever did not worship the statue would be cast into the fiery furnace. As the story goes, three of Daniel's companions were taken into custody, having refused to bow, and were thrown into a fiery furnace. They did not burn, and Nebuchadnezzar is quoted as saying he saw a fourth person in the fire, one like unto the Son of Man (Daniel 3:14).

Scripture tell us that Nebuchadnezzar challenged God to save the Israelites from the furnace. Nebuchadnezzar in his pride would fall. God declared he would be as an animal for seven years. After God restored Nebuchadnezzar to his right mind, the king blessed the

Most High and praised and honored him that lives forever whose dominion is an everlasting dominion (Daniel 4).

It appears the king got saved.

In the Babylonia story, there appears an archetypes that points to a future **final** ruler who will have an image of himself created and all will be required to worship the image of the beast.

Babylon would continue as an empire experiencing peaks and valleys throughout the ages. Its empire diminished after the conquest by the Medes and Persians, and its empire will continue through to its prophetic downfall. Isaiah 13:19, "*Babylon, the glory of kingdoms, the beauty of the Chaldees' excellency shall be as when God overthrew Sodom and Gomorrah.*"

In 538 BC, Daniel interprets the handwriting on the wall. Beltshazzar, son of Nabonidus, was king for fifty years after Nebuchadnezzar. He worshipped pagan gods, but he also knew about the God of the Jews. As an insult to God, he decided to use the holy vessels taken from the temple in Jerusalem to drink from them. They did drink wine, and they praised the gods of gold, silver, brass, iron, wood, and stone. In his state of pride, God declares the future of Belshazzar in the handwriting on the wall. That night his kingdom was conquered by Darius the Mede (Daniel 5:30).

Darius, son of Ahasuerus, began to rule over Babylon. At this time, Daniel had the book of Jeremiah the prophet that the captivity of Judah would be for seventy years. Daniel was held in esteem and given responsibility to oversee 120 princes. Those opposed to Daniel plotted his death by getting King Darius to sign a decree that if anyone was found praying to another god, they would be fed to the lions. Daniel was known throughout the kingdom as righteous and a man of the Almighty God. Therefore it grieved Darius to act on the decree he signed. Daniel was put into the lion's den, and Darius prayed that Daniel's God would deliver him, and it was so. God sent an angel to shut the lion's mouth. Darius was happy Daniel survived, and in turn, he cast Daniel's accuser into the lion's den. Darius made a decree in his kingdom that men should fear the God of Daniel. A clay cylinder was discovered with this decree now in the British museum (Daniel 6:25). This brings to mind, when you dig a hole for another, you may fall in it yourself.

The Persian king Cyrus in 535 BC (descendant of Shem) ruled Babylon. Under King Cyrus, the Jews were allowed to return to their homeland after fulfilling seventy years in captivity. Daniel died in the Babylonia region at around age eighty-five. Ninety percent of the Jews stayed in Babylon and did not return to Jerusalem. Others migrated into other regions near to Babylon, such as Iran, Syria, and Turkey. Daniel spoke and wrote Aramaic, as did Jesus. The influence of Judaism continued to leave a footprint of their existence in Babylon/ Iraq (Ezra and 2 Chronicles).

The remnants of the Babylon Empire was conquered by the Achaemenid Empire around 300 BC, later falling under the control of the Grecian Empire of Alexander the Great.

AD 226, Babylon fell to Sassanid Persian Empire. AD 600, it came under Islamic influence. AD 637, the Arabs captured Babylon by defeating the Persians. Later the Persian had their empire in what we now call Iran. Persians are quick to state they are not Arabs. Many Jews and Christians lived in Iran. The Arab Empire established a caliphate under Umayyad. Marwan II ibn Muhammed persecuted the Jews still living in this area and required them to wear yellow patches.

In the twentieth century, Iraq's dictator, Saddam Hussein found the Babylonian cuneiform tablets whose message said, "Whoever finds these, rebuild the temples and palaces." He spent $100 million dollars to rebuild and used sixty million bricks with his name on them. Some of those funds came from the United States.

Persian Empire

Persia is also referred to as Medes, Parsi, Parthian, Iran. Ancient people living in Persia were called either Medes or Persians. The Assyrians were in conflict with their neighbors, the Medes and Persians. The Persian Empire picked up steam under King Achaemenes around 705–675 BC. Cyrus the Great was a descendant of Achaemenid, and we see he conquered Babylon, Media, and Lydia a few hundred years later. After the reign of Cyrus, Darius the Great was first to establish the Persian Navy. Experienced sailors were Phoenicians, Egyptians, Greeks, which made up the Persian Navy.

When the Persians conquered Babylon, the empire extended into portions of Europe, Africa, Middle East regions of Iran, Iraq, Syria, Jordan, Jerusalem, Palestine, Lebanon, Libya, Turkey, Armenia, Georgia Central Asia, Afghanistan, Arabia, Pakistan. It controlled approximately 44 percent of the population living in these regions (Esther 1:1)

During the time of King Ahasuerus (Xerxes), 486 BC, being the fourth Persian ruler after the fall of Babylon, he established his kingdom in Shushan, which is in the region where the Euphrates and Tigris Rivers meet before emptying into the Persian Gulf. In the third year of Ahasuerus's reign, he held a feast for all to display the power and riches of Persia and Media. Vashti, his wife, refused to join her husband, the king, at the royal celebration. She was deposed, and the king sought a new wife in the kingdom. Esther, also called Hadassah, was Mordecai's uncle's daughter, whose parents were dead and he took her as his own daughter. Mordecai was a Jew, son of Jair, son of Shimei, son of Kish a Benjaminite. Esther received favor from all, and the king placed his crown upon her head. She became queen. She heard of a plot by Haman to kill the Jews, and she was able to foil the plot and save the Jews. To this day, Jews honor Esther with the Feast of Purim (book of Esther). The books of Ezra and Nehemiah were written during the rule of Artaxerxes I, 457 BC.

Egyptian Empire

The Egyptians were primarily descents of Ham but intermarriage with the offspring of Shem and Japheth had occurred. Observing the complexion of Egyptians in their historical hieroglyphics show fair- to dark-complexioned people.

Ham's grandson Canaan settled in what is referred to as Palestine, our modern-day Israel. Mizraim moved further into Egypt on the African continent. The Egyptians became a vast civilization around 2500 BC. Their territory extended from Africa to Syria. They had conflict with other nations. The Babylonians had attempted to conquer Egypt during king Nebuchadnezzar's reign.

They developed knowledge of astronomy, astrology, architecture, annual calendar. They discovered how to use papyrus as parchment for writing. These people developed a written language we call hieroglyphics, which were primarily symbols. A picture can communicate a message to another who does not speak the same language. Modern scholars eventually deciphered the code through the discovery of the Rosetta stone, which exhibited three different scripts: hieroglyphic (old Egyptian) and demotic (new Egyptian) and the third inscription was in Greek. Many hieroglyphic drawings and symbols on relics were found in the tombs of the pharaohs and at other archeological sites. From this history, we can understand the Egyptian culture.

The African continent is rich in precious metals, gold and diamonds, which were extracted for use by the pharaoh's. Most of the Egyptian beliefs were steeped in idolatry and paganism. They deified animals. The bull was revered and feared. They thought the gods had made them. When a bull died, its bones were broken and placed into huge stone coffin with lids that weighed 3500 pounds to ensure that they could not come back into the world of the living. Horses were domesticated in Egypt.

In 925 BC, a report in 2 Chronicles 12, in the fifth year of King Rehoboam, King Shishak of Egypt came against Jerusalem with 1,200 chariots, thirty thousand horsemen, and many people—including Lubims, Sukims, Ethiopians. The Egyptians fashioned bows and arrows for war and hunting.

By 600 BC, Babylon defeated the Egyptian armies. Civilizations in turn are conquered by other empires. Some regions are conquered totally, and their history and culture are destroyed or assimilated into the new regime and other times history is partially retained. The Egyptians were conquered by the Persians in 525 BC. Later Egypt was conquered by the Greeks under Alexander the Great. The Greeks are the descendants of Japheth. Intermingling of people within these nations continued under the various occupations. The majesty of Egypt is retained in its pyramids, tombs, monoliths.

Greek Empire

The first Olympics were held in 776 BC, dedicated to Greek god Zeus, celebrated every four years. Greek history is steeped in mythology—such as the creation of the moon goddess Artemis and her twin Apollo born on Mount Kynthos, a region held by the Greeks. Titan mythology produced giant offspring called Olympians from the story the Battle of the Giants.

Daniel 7:6, Daniel had a vision of a leopard with four wings and the beast had four heads and dominion was given to it, which indicate military prowess and swiftness. This was a prophecy of the coming Greek Empire. The empires of Babylon and Greece fought for years. Greece overthrew Medes and Persians and took control of Babylon around 330 BC. Alexander the Great had in four years conquered most of the known world. The Greek Empire is symbolized as bronze and ties into Nebuchadnezzar image of gold, silver, bronze, iron with bronze representing Alexander's empire. Its language is referred to as Hellenistic, associated with Greek language. When Alexander died, 323 BC, his kingdom was divided between his four generals: Cassander, Lysimachis, Ptolemy (Egypt), Seleucus (would birth Antiochus IV, Epiphanes, who would desecrate the Temple in Jerusalem, proclaim himself to be god, and set up Greek system of pagan worship around 175 BC). Paganism influenced many, including the Jews. Paganism gave birth to various practices, and one such is the priesthood of Baal, goddess worship, and mother-and-child worship which became part of the Holy Roman Empire. Jerome in AD 385 translated Greek to Latin in post-Roman world.

Roman Empire

Daniel 2:40 begins to predict the coming Roman Empire: "*And the fourth kingdom will be strong as iron forasmuch as iron breaks in pieces and subdues all things … it shall break in pieces and bruise.*" Daniel goes on to predict that the kingdom will be divided into two, and then it will be revived as in ten toes. In Daniel 7:23, he tells us, "*The fourth beast will be the fourth kingdom upon earth which will be diverse from all kingdoms and will devour the whole earth and tread it down and break it in pieces. And the ten horns out of this kingdom are ten kings that will arise …*"

We do not have a good time line of Roman events, so we punctuate historical records with a few notable people. Rome may have received its name after Romulus in 53 BC. Julius Caesar was assassinated 44 BC, and his son Octavian Augustus succeeded him. Caligula was assassinated 41 BC. Story of Mark Antony and Cleopatra is associated with the battle of Actium, 31 BC, ending in Roman annexation of Egypt and Palestine. Herod the Great was in authority approximately thirty years up to AD 1.

Rome was symbolized by iron, which is associated with Nebuchadnezzar's vision of an image having two iron legs. They became a great military power. They were pagans. Their rulers were called Caesar or Emperor. Aureus of Augustus is recorded as the first Roman emperor.

The Roman Empire was certainly prominent at the turn of first century AD. During the time of Christ, the Jewish priests were in cooperation with their Roman rulers. By AD 30, there were major uprisings between Jews, Christians, and Romans and the controversial Crucifixion of Jesus. Nero ruled Rome for fourteen years and was sentenced to death for setting fire to Rome and blaming it on the Christians around AD 68. He escaped and committed suicide at age thirty-one.

AD 70, the Romans turned on the Jews and destroyed the Jewish Temple. From AD 70 to 135, Roman persecution increased, forcing many Jews and Christians to flee Roman territory. This was different than the Babylonian captivity, which lasted about seventy years; the Jewish dispersion would last almost two thousand years. Could this punishment have been in response to their rejection of Messiah? Small numbers of Jews began returning to Israel in the 1800s and joined those who never left. The Roman Empire began to call the land of Canaan "Palestine," as an insult to the Jews. At the decline of the Roman Empire, it was divided between the western and eastern regions.

Western Region:

Carthage in Africa was the capital. Tenth Roman legion consisted of Turks, Syrians.

Latin was the main dialect primarily spoken by Italian, French, Spanish, Portuguese, Romanian. General Octavian received regions of Italy, France, Belgium, Spain. Lepidus received minor province of Tunisia. There was ongoing conflict between rulers. AD 285, Diocletian divided the empire and promoted Maximian to emperor to control western regions. AD 306, Constantine the Great became emperor and controlled Britain. AD 379, Emperor Valentinian accepted Christianity, but his son, Gratian, refused to wear the mantle of Pontifex Maximus; but he did remove pagan altar from Roman Curia. Later, Theodosius decreed a ban on native paganism, further enforcing Catholicism as the official state religion. He ruled a short time, died AD 395. His son, Honorius, inherited region until his death in AD 423. AD 444, Attila the Hun claimed west and marched on Italy AD 452, at the time of Pope Leo. AD 455, the Vandals sacked Rome. AD 475, Charlemagne, king of the Franks and Lombards, was crowned emperor of the west by Pope Leo III.

Under Germanic rulers, Catholicism grew. The Catholic church maintained Latin until 1969. In the early 1200s, Pope Innocent III headed the Catholic church. In 1309, Pope Clement V moved the papacy from Rome to France, where it remained for seventy years.

It was moved back to Rome in 1378, by Pope Gregory XI. Catholic bishop Saint Ambrose of Milan and Saint Germanus of Auxerre were influential in law and civil administration, bringing government and religion together. Many Europeans converted to Catholicism. AD 1517 was the famous Martin Luther act, where he posted his ninety-five theses in protest of changing doctrine. AD 1585, Pope Sixtus installed an obelisk in Rome.

<u>Eastern Region:</u>

Greek influence and language—Byzantine, capital, renamed to Constantinople by Constantine AD 324. Constantine recognized Christianity and made it the state religion. His mother, Helena, converted to Christianity and had the Church of the Nativity built around AD 326 in the region of Bethlehem. Around the middle of the fourth century, various people conquered parts of Rome. Some were called the Visigoths, who settled in Balkans AD 376. AD 533 Emperor Justinian was in power, and by the seventh century, the region came under the Persians and Arabians control. Sassanid of Persia had taken control, and the Greek/Roman influence lost Egypt, Syria, Greece, and Turkey. Islam was created in AD 620, and their strength increased greatly over fifty years. Damascus was taken by Muslims in AD 660, and Constantinople fell to them in AD 674. Different factions of Muslims fought over the same territory. The Seljuk Turks had control of Constantinople after the Battle of Manzikert in AD 1071. Finally, Constantinople, now present-day Istanbul, was sacked around AD 1261 and held by Ottoman Turks for approximately four hundred years.

During the hundreds of years of activity within the divided Roman Empire, by the ninth century, other parts of Europe were becoming distinguishable—such as, Harald Fairhair became king of Norway, AD 872. Gorm the Old became king of the Danes, AD 883. Burik, a Norseman, became the founder of Russia, AD 862. Polish dukes came into power around this same period. Boris I became czar of Bulgaria, AD 852. Alfred the Great, a Saxon, established Britain, AD 871. France and Germany came into existence by the Carolingian Empire, Ruler Louis III, AD 899 (J. R. Church, *Guardians of the Grail*, 42.)

Identification of Pagan Gods

In the above overview, we attempted to demonstrate how early cultures were punctuated with some form of paganism that was mingled with a one God theosophy. People created mythological entities from their perception based on accounts of the actual account of fallen angels who came down and mingled with humans. Captured in stone, metal, or wood, these creatures took on a persona of their own. God warned mankind not to make any graven images because they would in turn worship it. A diabolical partnership between evil people, evil spirits, Satan, and the fallen angels would continue to corrupt mankind throughout the ages. Evidence of paganism is found in ancient empires whose mythology passed to Greek and Roman cultures, continuing into China, India, Arabia, Africa, Canaan, and the outer parts of the world.

Supporting this statement, the chosen people, the Hebrew Israelites, fell into paganism during various periods in time. They came out of Egypt bringing with them the effects of the gods Molech and Remphan. Acts 7:43, they built altars to gods. In Ezekiel, 8:12–14, God showed him the Israelites worshipping the pagan god Tammuz at the temple. They also worshipped Baal. Saint Paul and the other apostles constantly encountered people who believed that gods came down in the likeness of men and the people deified these entities. Acts 14:11, "*And the people saw what Paul had done* [a healing miracle]; *they lifted up their voices saying in the speech of Lycaonia, the gods are come down to us in the likeness of men.* They called Barnabas, Jupiter, and Paul, Mercurius.

The Roman culture deified many gods. Zeus was a major deity. His perceived image was placed in temples. The god of Chaos—then Gaia for earth—married Uranus, who was heaven, produced Titan gods, including Kronos, who married his sister, Rhea, and gave birth to Zeus. When Rome became Christianized, emerging as the "Holy" Roman Empire, remnants of paganism were grafted within the first formalized denomination. Catholicism retained some pagan beliefs throughout its existence, such as the Queen of Heaven associated with the goddess Diana. Painting eggs and hiding them comes from the tradition of the goddess Istar, which is popularly called Easter. Mary the mother and Jesus the son are coequals to be worshipped and adored, as in Bacchus (son) and goddess Ceres (mother), later forming the Orpheus priesthood. All Hallows Eve is associated with Halloween acknowledged by churches, occults, and spiritualists. Gaia is celebrated as the goddess of earth. Celebrating pagan rituals is one example of how false beliefs were introduced into Christendom.

The promotion of paganism is a billion-dollar industry called science fiction. An entire mystique can be formulated around a fictional scenario, such as aliens from another planet. High level government officials, the Vatican, Hollywood, and numerous cults have given life to the aliens' scenario. In the movie *ET*, the alien was adorable. Zeus, Poseidon, Hercules, Apollo were cast as superhero gods. In the modern era, Superman, Batman, Captain America became the present-day superhuman heros in movies, video games, comic books. Those who are conformed to worldly imaginations accept fiction as their reality. The true church of God is not conformed to this world, knowing the difference between fiction and reality, because God has warned his people to not be deceived.

A panacea of false gods exists worldwide. These gods of old, given other names and face makeovers, were assimilated as compatible deities within world societies. It is challenging to condense history to allow the reader to understand the growth of paganism. We provide a partial overview of false deities:

- Zeus is Jupiter/Fortuna—Roman.
- Zeus took on form of white bull and seduced Europa.
- Zeus took on form of eagle and kidnapped Ganymede, Trojan prince.
- Poseidon, god of the sea and brother of Zeus.
- Apollo, son of Zeus/Satan, Greek chief god of the sky.
- Apollo sun god, god of light and prophecy.
- Apollo's twin sister is Artemis; their mother, Leto. Artemis is associated with the goddess Hecate, a luminary god who controlled the access to portals in the spirit world.
- Aeus and his niece, Leto, gave birth to twins, Apollo and Diana/Artemis.
- Oracle, or sibyl at Delphi, a spiritual adviser to Apollo's—like shaman, witch doctor, medium heard from fallen angels and demons.
- Saturn, Satan or sons of Satan.
- Abaddon, a reference to the underworld or hell, is Hebrew for *Apollyon*.
- Hades, god of the underworld and brother of Zeus.
- Diana, sister of Apollo, goddess of fertility (many breasts). Temple of Diana built over crucifixion site, a temple located in Ephesus (Acts 19:24–35), Romans worshipped, symbol of the bee incorporated into Merovian cult.
- Istar, Astarte, Baal. In celebration of Istar, they would paint eggs and hide them. Also Canaanites' god.
- Semiramis Diana, Artemis, wife of Nimrod, and her son, Tammuz/Babylon (reincarnated Nimrod); Mithra, son god.
- Ra, the sun god, and Osiris is Bacchus son of Isis/Ceres—Egypt and Greek.
- Osiris Egyptian god of the dead; Isis, his wife.
- Horus, Egyptian, eye of.
- Nebo, or Mercury, version of Thoth god of writing and illumination.
- Ashtoreth, goddess of Zidonians and worshipped by King Solomon 1 Kings 11:5.
- Milcom of the Ammonites.
- Chemosh, god of Moab.
- Molech, god of Ammonites. An altar called tophet built in the Valley of Hinnon to sacrifice children, and so did the Jews (2 Kings 23:10).
- Baal worshipped by Israel's King Ahab and wife, Jezebel, 874 BC.
- Queen of Heaven, worshipped by Jews in Egypt, Jeremiah 44:17.
- Brahma, a four-armed Hindu god recognized as the creator.
- Vishnu, Hindu god, as preserver the image shown with his consort Lakshmi.
- Shiva, a four-armed Hindu god of death and reproduction.

Research commentary by J. R. Church, *Prophecy in the News*, *The Dragon and the Beast*, July 2012 provided some of the names of pagan gods.

Numerous legends and mythological facades come together to form our perceptions of fallen angels deified. The activities of fallen angels created hybrid children who may have appeared as half man and half animal. Multicultures captured these images in various mediums, such as in masks, paintings, and sculptures for posterity as well as to build upon their misconceptions and false doctrines. Evidence and examination of masks and other artifacts were found in Africa, the Americas, and elsewhere—portraying images made in the likeness of animals, birds, humans, and lizards. Some bizarre masks combine horns with huge eyes as seen in the "all-seeing eye of Horus"; while others are displayed with exaggerated facial expressions. Native Americans, Incas, Mayans, and others used mask as headdress and to build tall totem poles. As we consider these images carved in stone or wood, some scholars believe the mask were the actual head of a half human or half animal called a chimera.

In chapter 17, we provide a clearer understanding of the roots of paganism and idolatry. A false religion or cult may incorporate bits and pieces of truth found in the Bible and mold it into a half-truth or outright lie. God warns us to be aware of the doctrine of devils and false prophets. We also discuss the plan for a one-world religion and the false prophet. The reader will see how the Luciferian doctrine came to the shores of North America cloaked in the Masonic Order.

Chapter 9
Abraham and Melchizedek

Chapter Overview

- Life of Abraham
- War between the Kingdoms
- Melchizedek
- Ishmael and Isaac
- The Rite of Circumcision
- God Tests Abraham
- Esau and Jacob
- Genealogy of Abraham
- Twelve Tribes of Israel

Chapter 9

Abraham and Melchizedek

Life of Abraham

The estimated time of the birth of Abram was around 2166 BC. Abram was a descendant of Noah's son, Shem. He was born in the City of Ur, near the River Euphrates, also referred to as Ur of the Chaldees in Mesopotamia. His father was Terah; brothers, Nahor and Haran, plus other brothers and sisters. Haran was Lot's father. He took to wife, Sarai. We follow the biblical account of Abraham, a Gentile who had beginning in Genesis 12.

When Abraham was seventy-five years old around 2091 BC, God spoke to him, telling him to leave his land. This exchange between Abraham and God was the first step in separating out a peculiar people from amongst the nations. Not knowing where he was going but in faith, Abraham gathers his family and leaves Ur with Sarah, Lot, Terah, his father, and others. They came to the City of Haran, near the land of Syria. Here they lived for a while. Abraham's father, Terah, died in Haran at the age of 205 years old. Leaving the region of Haran, Abraham and his family reached Shechem in Canaan. As we follow the movement of Abraham's family, we begin to see the distinct hand of God preserving and preparing them for their future role. Abraham would become the father of many nations through Isaac, Ishmael, and the children he fathered after the death of Sarah. Abraham, as a beacon of light, followed the ways of God, and many followed the example of Abraham. This group would become the first representatives of a traditional religion that believed in the one true God and Creator.

Some of the descendants of Ham had become a large nation, residing in the region called Canaan, after the person of Canaan. The Canaanites had become idol worshippers, and they were wicked before God. God appears to Abraham and tells him, "Unto your seed will I give this land." Abraham builds an altar to God and calls the place Bethel, meaning "House of God," located in the area of Canaan. In Hebrew, *Beth* means "house" and *el* means "God."

God spoke to Abraham again and promised to make a great nation from his seed even though he had no heirs. God said, "I will bless them that bless Abraham and curse them that curse Abraham." In Abraham, all the families of the earth will be blessed. Abraham was referred to as Hebrew in Genesis 14:13, which means "one from beyond." Later the term *Israelites* would be associated with Jacob and the twelve tribes. These families are the offspring of Shem, Ham, and Japheth; thus Abraham became the patriarch of the called-out ones who became the chosen people, the Hebrew Israelites.

There was famine in the land, and Abraham and his family went into Egypt. Before entering into Egypt, he tells Sarah to say she is his sister (she is his half sister) because of her beauty and his fear that he would be killed and Sarah taken. We can imagine that Sarah had beautiful dark hair, brown eyes, and copper complexion. Abraham and all those with him were received into Egypt because they blended in with the descendants of : Ham having brown to dark complexion.

When the pharaoh saw Sarah, he took her into his house, treated Abraham well, and gave him gifts and servants. However, God sent plagues against the pharaoh, and he understood that Sarah was Abraham's wife. Thereafter, Abraham, his family, and their servants—some of whom were Egyptians—left Egypt, returning to Bethel.

By this time, the families, herds, and wealth of Abraham and Lot had grown. Lot moves to Jordan where Sodom and Gomorrah are. Abraham goes to Canaan, where lived his cousins, the Canaanites and Perizzites. God said, "Look north, south, east, west, and all the land you see, I will give it to you and your seed forever." Abraham makes permanent residence in Mamre, which is Hebron, near Jerusalem, and he built an altar unto the Lord (Genesis 13:10–18). Hebron is the second holiest site to Jews, and the temple mount is the first.

War between the Kingdoms

War breaks out among the kingdoms. Those involved are King Amraphel of Shinar, King Arioch of Ellasar, King Chedorlaomer of Elam, King Tidal of nations, King Bera of Sodom, King Birsha of Gomorrah, King Shinab of Admah, King Shemeber of Zeboiim, King Bela of Zoar, and people from Siddim near the Dead Sea. They began to kill the Rephaims in Asteroth, Karnaim, Zuzims in Ham and the Emims in Shaveh Kiriathaim, Horites in Mount Seir near Elparan by the wilderness, Enimishpat of Kadesh, Amalekite, Amorites near Hazezontamar. Some of the participants were said to be giants.

Abraham was notified that Lot was taken by one of the invaders. He takes his men and rescues Lot. When he returns victorious, he is met by King Melchizedek of Salem.

Melchizedek

> *For this Melchizedek, king of Salem, priest of the most high God ... without father, without mother, without descent* [no children] *having neither beginning of days nor end of life but made like unto the Son of God abides a priest continually.* (Hebrews 7:1–3)

As we consider the personage of Melchizedek, the scriptures immediately acknowledge him as different from other biblical characters.

- He is both king and priest.
- He is Shalom (peace).
- He has no biological children.
- He had no beginning or end.
- He is eternal.
- He is the Son of God.

We believe Melchizedek was the preincarnate Jesus our King and High Priest, from whom all blessings flow. Genesis 14:18, "*Melchizedek, king of Salem brought forth bread and wine and he was the priest of the most high God ... he blessed Abraham.*" The Levitical priesthood would not come into existence until the time of Israel in the wilderness and called forth by Moses. Hebrews 9:11, "*Christ being come a high priest of good things to come ...*" presented himself in times past as high priest. The bread and wine become a foreshadow of the body and shed blood of Jesus. Hebrews 9:26 ... "*But now once in the end of the world has he appeared to put away sin by the sacrifice of himself.*" In the form of Melchizedek, Jesus brought forth bread and wine, a shadow of Passover. Hundreds of years later, Passover would commemorate the sacrificial lamb and the atonement for sins. At the last supper, the breaking of bread and drinking of wine would begin the traditional celebration of the death of Jesus, his shed blood, and Resurrection to life.

Abraham gave tithes to Melchizedek and received a blessing from him. We give our tithes to the Lord, and he is faithful to bless us.

Melchizedek and Abraham were strangers, or had Abraham had other encounters with a type of Melchizedek, a type of the Son of God? Genesis 18:1, "*And the Lord appeared unto him in the plains of Mamre as he sat in the tent door in the heat of the day.*" As it is told in scriptures, there were three that appeared to Abraham, but he addressed one as Lord. After the two angels departed to Sodom and Gomorrah, Genesis 18:22 ... "*Abraham stood yet before the Lord.*" Abraham continues his conversation with the Lord regarding these cities and would the Lord spare any if at least ten righteous could be found. Genesis 18:33, "*And the Lord went his way as soon as he had left communing with Abraham and Abraham returned to his place.*"

The king came to Abraham, and Jesus came to mankind to be born of a virgin. What Abraham had in common with Melchizedek is that they both worshipped the one true God, maker of heaven and earth. The king said, "Blessed be the Most High God, which has delivered your enemies into your hand," and the king blessed Abraham. In the New Testament, Jesus always gave glory to God the Father.

A pattern of discord and hatred continued between relatives. Abraham's sons, Isaac and Ishmael, were at odds with each other. Isaac followed the ways of God, while Ishmael cohabitated with unbelievers who practiced idolatry. God knew that through Ishmael, he and his descendants would be at enmity with everyone. Discord would also follow Isaac's sons, Esau and Jacob.

Ishmael and Isaac

God appeared to Abraham and said, "*I am your shield and your exceeding great reward.*" Abraham reminded God he has no heir. God confirms that an heir will come forth from his loins. Abraham asked God for confirmation. God tells him to sacrifice several animals. God caused him to sleep and gave him a message: the future Hebrews would live in a strange land, not theirs, and serve them and be afflicted by them for four hundred years (Genesis 15:13). That land (Egypt) God will judge, and the Hebrews would leave the land with great wealth. It is interesting to note that Noah had cursed the son of Ham, Canaan, saying his descendants would serve the other two brothers; but in this verse, we see that Shem's offspring would serve Ham's descendants in Egypt for four hundred years. This could be a future prediction of Ham's descendants being taken from the land of Africa to America and being enslaved for almost four hundred years. If so, then we must consider the Hebrew Israelites having lived in Africa for hundreds of years and did intermarry producing a blend of offspring; some of whom became followers of Yahweh.

God told Abraham that the land inheritance is from the Nile in Egypt to the River Euphrates in Babylon. The land was occupied by Kenites, Kenizzites, Kadmonites, Hittites, Perizzites, Rephaims, Amorities, Canaanites, Girgashites, Jebusites. Genesis 15, it is noted that Abraham lived amongst these tribes. At times there was peaceful coexistence as well as conflict. Some of these people were associated with giants while others were identified as pigmies.

Around 2080 BC, Sarah is impatient to wait on the promise of a child. She sent Abraham into her Egyptian servant, Hagar, and Ishmael was conceived. Abraham was eighty-six years old when Ishmael was born. Genesis 16 ... Sarah despised Hagar and caused her to run away.

An angel of the Lord told Hagar to return to her mistress and submit to her. The angel told her that her son would be called Ishmael and he would be a great nation. He would be blessed as was Isaac, but Isaac would be the rightful heir, from whom a great nation would come forth. The angel predicted that Ishmael would be a wild man; his hand would be against every man and every man's hand against him. He became a skilled archer and hunter. Later Isaac's son, Esau, would be like Ishmael. Ishmael was brought up in the ways of Yahweh, and he had an understanding of the way of the Hebrews, as did Esau. God blessed the seed of Ishmael, and twelve future princes would come from his lineage (Genesis 25:12).

As Ishmael's descendants increased, he moved toward the land of Havilah unto Shur associated with Arabia (Genesis 25:18). It appears that Ishmael kept in touch with Abraham and Isaac. They both buried Abraham (Genesis 25:9). Later we see that Esau, son of Isaac, married the daughter of Ishmael. Today we refer to those hailing from Arabia as Arabs. During that time, many in Arabia had fallen into idolatry, and some of them were the descendants of Ishmael. Ishmael died at the age of 137 years old.

We believe Ishmael knew of the one true God, Yahweh, and it is incorrect to assume that Ishmael is the father of Islam. The time frame between Ishmael and Muhammad is more than a thousand years. Around AD 570, Muhammad was born in the land of Arabia during a time that hundreds of deities were being worshipped. Muhammad established Islam AD 620 and destroyed all pagan gods except for the false god Allah. There had been an Israelite Hebrew presence in Arabia back to the time of Abraham and Ishmael. The Bible record tells us, even to the time of the disciples preaching Christianity in Arabia, there was a Jewish presence. When Muhammad created Islam, Jews lived in Arabia, as noted in the historical account of Muhammad, who met with them on various occasions. It is well to remember that Muhammad adopted doctrine from both the Old and New Testament writings, corrupting scripture with pagan beliefs, and incorporated them into his Koran. He had heard the stories of Abraham and Ishmael, and he mixed them with his Islamic doctrine, as he did with Mary and Jesus. The Jesus of the Jews and Christians became a fabricated person of Islam.

Abraham and Sarah were impatient; their faith waned; and they were operating in unbelief of the promise of an heir to be provided by God. The promised son of Abraham and Sarah was born around 2066 BC, and they named him Isaac. Isaac represents the son of promise, spiritually ordained of God, and would be the ultimate test of Abraham's faith. Galatians 3:19, "*God gave the law to Abraham by promise until the seed should come to whom the promise was made and it was ordained by angels in the hand of a mediator, God.*"

When Abraham was ninety-nine years old, God appears to make a covenant:

- God will give the land of Canaan to his seed.
- Every man will be circumcised, the covenant sealed with blood.

- God will give him the promised son.
- The covenant will be established with his seed, Isaac, forever.

The Rite of Circumcision

Genesis 17:23—Abraham, aged ninety-nine; Ishmael, aged thirteen; and every male were circumcised in obedience to God. From Abraham through the bloodline of Isaac, Jacob, Joseph, Moses, Joshua, David stayed true to the covenant made by Yahweh. They worshipped Yahweh and did not turn to idolatry, though many among them did so.

Israel practiced circumcision while living in Egypt, and some Egyptians also practiced circumcision depicted in papyrus drawing and engravings on walls. Historical records indicate that other African tribes, as well as Aboriginals in Australia, Aztec, and American Indians performed circumcision as a rite of passage on males coming of age at twelve years old. The Hebrew Israelites kept this practice as a visible sign of the covenant between them and God. It became the custom to perform this on eight-day-old infants. The uncircumcised were to be cut off from the people and regarded as covenant breakers. During New Testament times, the Jewish followers of Christ attempted to misconstrue the spiritual meaning of circumcision and began using it against non-Jews as a requirement for salvation. Peter and Paul both corrected the church's position that Gentile converts need not be circumcised to be saved.

Romans 2:25–29 discusses the spiritual aspects of circumcision. The bottom line is … "*For he is not a Jew which is one outwardly, neither is that circumcision which is outward in the flesh, but he is a Jew which is one inwardly and circumcision is that of the heart in the spirit and not in the letter whose praise is not of men but of God.*"

God Tests Abraham

> *It came to pass after these things that God did tempt* [test] *Abraham* and said … *take now your only son Isaac whom you love … and go into the land of Moriah* [Mount Moriah, present-day temple mount] *and offer him there for a burnt offering upon one of the mountains which I will tell you.* (Genesis 22)

In obedience, he leaves Beersheba and travels about fifty miles to Mount Moriah in Salem (Jerusalem). Abraham was prepared to sacrifice Isaac as a burnt offering to God.

"*And* ***the angel of the Lord*** *called unto him out of heaven and said, Abraham, Abraham* [answering he said] *here am I.*" He is told not to harm the lad … "*I know that you fear God and have not withheld your only son from* ***me.***" We can know this to be an accurate interpretation: this was God Yeshua himself speaking through the voice of an angel. God states, "*You have not withheld your son from* ***me.***"

The Bible account states God provided a lamb for the sacrifice. Abraham called the name of that place Jehovah Jireh, "God provides." An archeological figure of a ram in a thicket was found in a cemetery in Ur.

> *And **the angel of the Lord** called unto Abraham out of heaven a second time and said,* by *myself have I sworn, said the Lord because you have done this thing and have not withheld your son … I will bless you and multiply your seed as the stars of the heaven and as the sand upon the sea shore* **…**

Esau and Jacob

Genesis 23, "*And Sarah was 127 years old … she died in Kirjatharba, which is Hebron in the land of Canaan …*" Abraham purchased a field and cave for her burial from Ephron, a Hittite, for four hundred shekels of silver. Sarah died before Isaac married Rebekah. Genesis 26 tells us that after the death of Sarah, Abraham took another wife named Keturah, who gave birth to six sons (Genesis 25:7).

Genesis 24, before the death of Abraham, he sent his servant to the land of his birth to seek a wife for Isaac. Rebekah came to give water to the servant and his camels, and by doing this, she fulfilled his requirement. He gives her gold for her service. She is the daughter of Bethuel, the son of Milcah, which she bore unto Nahor, Abraham's uncle.

Abraham died at the age of 175 years old. His sons, Isaac and Ishmael, buried him in the cave of Machpelah with Sarah—also the burial place for Isaac and Jacob. Rachel is buried at Ephratha, which is Bethlehem; a marker was placed there by Jacob (Genesis 35:19)

Isaac and Rebekah had two sons, Esau and Jacob, twins born around 2006 BC. After praying, God opened Rebekah's womb to conceive. The babies struggled together in her womb. She asked the Lord why, and she was told that "two nations are in your womb, and two manners of people will be separated from your bowels, and the one people shall be stronger than the others, and the elder will serve the younger." As was in the case of Isaac and Ishmael, one followed the ways of Yahweh, and the other followed the lust of the world. This pattern would be repeated in the lives of Jacob, who would follow the ways of Yahweh, while Esau would do the opposite.

When it was time for her delivery, the first child came out red and hairy and was named Esau, which means "hairy." The color red symbolizes a man of the earth. The name Adam means red, and red-colored earth can be found in various locations. The second child followed with his hand on the heel of his brother, and he was named Jacob, which means "heel catcher." In Hebrew, his name refers to a pious man who finds pleasure at home. Esau became a hunter and a man of the fields, and Jacob was a plain man dwelling in tents.

It had been prophesied that Jacob, the younger, would be the lineage that Messiah would come through and not the lineage of Esau. In Malachi 1:2–3, the Lord declares his love for Israel represented in Jacob, and the Lord said, "I hated Esau," representative of the future Edomites, descendants of Lot and Esau. God did not hate the individual Esau, but God knew that the seed of Esau would be sinful.

> *And I hated Esau* [who would] *lay his mountains and his heritage waste for the dragons of the wilderness. Whereas Edom/Esau said, we are impoverished but we will return and build the desolate places and the Lord of hosts said, they will build but I will throw down and they will call them the border of wickedness and the people against whom the Lord has indignation forever. And your eyes will see and you will say, the Lord will be magnified from the border of Israel.* (Malachi 1:3)

This prophecy has been fulfilled. Looking at the Esau/Edomites/Palestinians people today, their hatred for the descendants of Jacob/Israel fuel their activities. Palestinians focus their energy and attention on the destruction of Israel and have forsaken to build up their land and have laid it to waste, crying, "We are poor refugees."

Jacob received the blessing from Isaac under a deceptive ploy. Jacob told Esau, if he gave him his birthright, he would give him the red stew he had made. Isaac's blessing,

> *Therefore God give thee of the dew of heaven and the fatness of the earth and plenty of corn and wine, let people serve you and nations bow down to you, be lord over your brothers and let your mother's sons bow down to you cursed be every one that curses you and blessed be he that blesses you.* (Genesis 27:28)

Esau traded his birth right to Jacob for food. The Bible says, "Man should not live by bread alone but by every word that precedes from the mouth of God."

When Esau discovered he has been tricked from receiving his father's blessing upon the firstborn, he was angry. In rebellion, Esau decided to align himself with unbelievers and married Canaanite women to displease his father. He went to Ishmael, son of Abraham, and took his daughter Mahalath, Genesis 28:9, and his daughter Bashemath, Genesis 36:3. During Esau's disappointment, he continued to ask Isaac for a blessing, and Isaac prayed: "*Behold thy dwelling shall be the fatness of the earth and of the dew of heaven from above; and by thy sword will thou live and will serve thy brother and it shall come to pass when you shall have the dominion that thou shall break his yoke from off your neck*" (Genesis 27:39–40).

Jacob followed the ways of God. Jacob was obedient, and he did not marry outside of those whose God is Yahweh. On his way to visit his uncle Laban, he camps for the night in

Haran, near a city called Luz. Jacob has a dream of a ladder set up on the earth, and the top of it reached to heaven and angels of God, ascending and descending on it. He saw the Lord above it, who said, "*I am the Lord God of Abraham your father and the God of Isaac, the land whereon you lie, to thee will I give it and to your seed which will be as the dust of the earth and all the families of the earth will be blessed*" (Genesis 28:12). Jacob acknowledges the presence of the Lord and builds an altar, which he calls Beth-el. Jacob promised to keep the way of the Lord, and all that the Lord provides for him, of that he gave the Lord a tenth.

Jacob retreated to the area of Padan-aram and fell in love with Rachel, daughter of Laban. Laban is referred to as a Syrian. It appears that he was an idol worshipper. Jacob's uncle tricked him into working for him for seven years on the promise he would receive the hand of Rachel. Laban tricked him into marrying the oldest daughter, Leah. Jacob had to work another seven years to marry Rachel. Jacob tricked Esau, and Laban tricked Jacob. Through it all, the favor of God remained with Jacob. After serving Laban, Jacob takes his family to return to the land of his father and encounters the angel of God, who would protect Jacob from future trouble (Genesis 32:1).

Esau left Canaan and settled in the land of Seir, which is ancient Edom, now called Jordan/Arabia. Standing on Mount Seir, one can see the city fortress of Petra built by the Edomites. Mount Seir is also called shaggy or hairy. In Hebrew, Seir refers to a hairy he-goat, as in Jacob deceived Esau by placing a hairy skin on his arm for Isaac to touch. Genesis 36:8, "*Thus dwelt Esau in mount Seir. Esau is Edom and these are the generations of Esau father of the Edomites.*" Genesis 36:1–43 list the generations of Esau. The Moabites and the Edomites are both descendants of Lot and his two daughters.

Many years had passed since Jacob received his father's blessing. Esau may have continued to harbor resentment toward Jacob. These Edomites had become a mighty people full of pride. Esau had set out to meet Jacob with about four hundred men. Jacob was traveling from Leban and was returning to his father's land. Jacob feared for his life. He prayed for protection, and he offered Esau many animals as a peace offering (Genesis 32:14).

Before encountering Esau, Jacob encounters the Angel of the Lord, who wrestled with him until the breaking of day, touched the hollow of his thigh, and changed his name from Jacob to Israel. The Lord said, "For as a prince has thou power with God [wrestling] and with men has prevailed [Jacob did not give up until he received a blessing]" (Genesis 32:25–28).

Jacob and Esau meet, and they embrace. All is well. Esau will return to Seir. Jacob will travel to Succoth and build a house. Jacob will travel further to Shalem, a city of Shechem in the land of Canaan, where he camped at Padan-aram. He purchased land from Hamor, Shechem's father, for one hundred pieces of money. Later Dinah, the daughter of Leah and Jacob, was raped by Shechem. He asked his father, Hamor, to speak to Jacob for his daughter in marriage. This meeting did not go well. In the end, Dinah's brothers, Levi and Simeon, killed all of Hamor's men and took their women, children, animals, and wealth to Jacob. Jacob was upset with the action of his sons for fear of reprisal from the Canaanites and Perizzites (Genesis 34:30).

The bad blood between the relatives of Ishmael and Esau continue throughout history. Scripture backs up this statement. Esau/Edom refused to allow Moses and his people to cross their land at the border in Kadesh. The Edomites sent out men to fight (Numbers 20:14).

Amalek is the grandson of Esau (Genesis 36:12). His descendants would oppose Israel for hundreds of years. Amalek fought with Israel in Rephidim. Moses told Joshua to choose men and go out and fight Amalek. This is the account where Moses held up his arms and Israel prevailed. When he let down his arms, Amalek prevailed. Moses proclaims that the Lord has sworn that they will have war with Amalek from generation to generation (Exodus 17:8–16) What is seen in this action will follow a pattern of continual conflict between the Edomites and Amalekites attack upon the Israelites. Deuteronomy 25:17, "*Remember what Amalek did unto you by the way, when you were come forth out of Egypt, how he met you by the way and smote the hindmost of thee, even all that were feeble behind thee when you were faint and weary and he feared not God.*" The Edomites would suffer conquest by the Nabataeans from Arabia. Genesis 36:7, many would find refuge in Judah. Once in the land of Israel, they changed their name to Idumean. Herod the Great was an Idumean and descendant of Esau. Modern-day Palestinians claim Herod was their ancestor.

The prophet Samuel told King Saul to destroy the Amalekites in their entirety. It was around 1050 BC, and Saul disobeyed. He allowed the people to take spoils, which they were going to sacrifice to God at Gilgal. In 1 Samuel 15:19–21, God punished Saul by removing him as king and anointing David to be king. Since the Amalekites line continues, we see it rising in the story of Haman in **Persia,** who plotted to kill the Jews. In 486 BC, Haman was son of Hammadatha, descendant of Agag, king of the Amalekites. They are descendants of Amalek, grandson of Esau (Esther 3:1–6).

In the future, all of Edom will be judged for its treatment of Israel. In other words, the descendants of Esau will be judged for its treatment of their kinfolks, the descendants of Jacob. Many of the descendants of the Edomites, Ammonites, Amalekites, etc., had fallen into idolatry, would later put away polytheism but adopt the false religion of Islam. Islam calls for the death of Jacob's descendants, Israel.

> *For the day of the Lord is near upon all the heathen and as you have done, it will be done unto you, your reward will return upon your own head ... on Mount Zion will be deliverance and there will be holiness and the house of Jacob will possess their possessions and the house of Jacob will be a fire and the house*

of Joseph a flame and the house of Esau for stubble … there shall not be any remaining of the house of Esau for the Lord has spoken it. (Obadiah 1:15)

From Jacob came the twelve tribes of Israel:

Reuben, whose name means "gifts are given" or "behold a son."
Simeon's name means "God has heard my cry, heard."
Judah means "praise the Lord."
Issachur, "burden bearer."
Zebulun, "emanated living."
Dan means "judge."
Naphtali, "wrestling."
Gad, "troop."
Asher, "happy."
Joseph, "God has added"—counted as two: his sons, Manasseh and Ephraim.
Benjamin, "son of my right hand."
Levi's name means "adjoined to one," not counted as a tribe but a priestly order.

Genealogy of Abraham

Sarah	Hagar
|	|
Isaac and Rebekah	Ishmael and Egyptian wife
|	
Born 2006 BC, Jacob and Esau	

|

Wife of Esau, Bashemath, daughter of Ishmael
Son, Reuel, and his sons, Nahath, Zerah, Shammah, Mizzah

Wife of Esau, Adah, daughter of Hittite Elon
Son, Eliphaz, and his sons, Teman, Omar, Zepho, Kenaz, Amalek, Gatam

Wife of Esau, Aholibamah, daughter of Hivite Zebeon
Sons, Jeush, Joalam, Korah
Esau genealogy, Genesis 38, Esau moves to Mount Seir, region of Jordan

Jacob leaves Beersheba to Haran, renamed city Luz to Bethel
|

Wife of Jacob, Rachel, daughter of Laban his mother's brother
Son's Joseph (DOB 1915 BC) and Benjamin
Leah wife, daughter of Laban

Son's Reuben, Simeon, Levi, Judah, Issachar, Zebulun, Dinah
Zilpha, Leah's servant
Sons, Gad and Asher
Bilhah, Rachel's servant
Sons, Dan and Naphtali

Abraham remarried after death of Sarah Genesis 25:1
|
Keturah, wife
Son's Zimran, Jokshan, Medan, Midian, Ishbak, Shuah
Jokshan's sons, Sheba, Dedan
Dedan's sons are Asshurim, Letushim, Leummim
Midian's sons are Ephah, Epher, Hanoch, Abidah, Eldaah

Ishmael sons are called princes Genesis 25:13
Nebajoth, Kedar, Adbeel, Mibsam, Mishma, Dumah, Massa,
Hadar, Tema, Jetur, Maphish, Kedemah

Ishmael lived to be 137 years old. He lived in Havilah unto Shur—that is, before Egypt toward Assyria. Both he and Isaac lived to see Abraham's death

By following the movement of the twelve tribes, we have a record of their interaction with other nations throughout history. They spent hundreds of years in Egypt. After the death of Solomon, the twelve tribes split into two kingdoms: northern kingdom of Israel represented by ten tribes and the southern kingdom of Judah represented two tribes. We understand from the Bible that the tribes were taken into captivity first by the Assyrians in 726 BC and later by the Babylonians in 586 BC. After the diaspora, the majority of the chosen people were found in almost every nation in the world. Others chose to stay in Jerusalem. After suffering persecution in these foreign lands, they began to return to their land. Chapter 12 tracks the regions from which the Hebrew Israelites left in their effort to reach Israel.

Chapter 10
Joseph, Jacob, and Moses in Egypt

Chapter Overview

- The Favorite Son
- Joseph's Journey
- Four Hundred Years in Egypt
- The Birth of Moses
- Moses's Transition from Egypt to Midian and Back to Egypt
- God Brings Plagues against Egypt

Chapter 10

Joseph in Egypt

Joseph the Favorite Son

Joseph was born around 1915 BC. He was at that time the youngest of Jacob's sons. Jacob loved him because he was the son of his beloved Rachel. Jacob loved Rachel above his other wives. She had been barren for so long, and finally, she was pregnant with Joseph, her first-born. Because of this favoritism, his brothers hated him.

He and his family lived in Canaan, a region that had been settled by Ham's descendants. Joseph was seventeen years old when his brothers plotted to sell him. Joseph took food to his brothers tending the sheep in Shechem and up to Dothan, which was a trade route into Egypt. His brothers put Joseph into a pit. Midianite merchants passed by and pulled him out and sold Joseph to the Ishmaelites for twenty pieces of silver. They in turn sold him to Potiphar, an officer of Pharaoh's guard. When Joseph's brothers returned to the pit, he was not in it. They decided to fabricate a tale that Joseph has been killed by a wild beast. They gave Joseph's bloody coat to their father, who tore his clothes and mourned for his son many days (Genesis 37).

Potiphar lived in Egypt on the continent of Africa, and we place Joseph in this setting around 1898 BC. He saw that there was something very special about Joseph. He discerned that God was with Joseph. God prospered all that Joseph did while living as a slave in Potiphar's house. Because of Joseph, all of Potiphar's house and fields prospered. Potiphar's wife, being tempted by Satan, compelled Joseph to lay with her, but he refused time and time again. She then decided to say that Joseph tried to rape her. Her husband put Joseph in jail. The Lord was with Joseph, and he found favor with the guards and prisoners (Genesis 39).

Pharaoh's butler and baker had offended him, and he cast them into prison. While in prison, they both had a dream. Joseph interpreted their dreams. The butler would be restored to his position, and the baker's head would be severed (Genesis 40).

Joseph is still in jail, going on three years. The pharaoh of Egypt had a dream that troubled him. He called for the counsel of his magicians and wise men. They could not interpret the dream. The butler finally remembered Joseph could interpret dreams. Joseph is brought before pharaoh. Joseph tells him only God can give the interpretation then proceeds to tell him that there will be seven years of plenty and seven years of drought. Joseph advised the pharaoh to make plans for the upcoming drought. Joseph is then elevated in status to rule over the land of Egypt. Joseph is given pharaoh's ring and fine linen to wear. The people were ordered to bow their knee and respect all that Joseph did in the land. Pharaoh recognizes the Spirit of God was upon Joseph. Pharaoh gave Joseph a new name, Zaphnathpaaneah; and the daughter of Potiphar, Asenath, became his wife.

It was around 1885 BC, and Joseph was thirty-four years old when the pharaoh, king of Egypt, made him a coregent. Joseph and Asenath had two sons, Manasseh and Ephraim. Then famine came over the face of the earth. People living in other regions came into Egypt to buy grain (Genesis 41:56).

The famine had reached Canaan, and Jacob sends his ten sons to Egypt to buy grain. As the story goes, Joseph's brothers do not know he is their brother. They bow before Joseph just as he had dreamed they would do many years ago. Joseph accused them of being spies, and they would have to prove they are not by returning to Canaan and bringing Benjamin back with them. He kept his brother Simeon in jail until they came back. Over the complaints of Jacob, he finally agreed to send Benjamin and gifts for Joseph. This time, Joseph now saw his brother Benjamin, son of his mother, for the first time. He is overcome with joy and turned away to weep. He fed all the men and gave more to Benjamin.

The other Egyptians would not eat bread with Hebrews for that was an abomination. Why did they consider them an abomination? It was not because of "race," since they were all dark- and brown-complexioned people. If they had been fair complexioned, the darker Egyptians would have thought they suffered from leprosy. We believe it was because of their religious beliefs and their garments were in contrast to the Egyptian culture.

After the meal, Joseph ordered his brothers' sacks to be filled, returned their money, and put a silver cup in Benjamin's sack. Joseph was deceitful with them again. By the time they reached the city limits, Joseph's men stopped them and charged them with theft. The silver cup was found, and they were taken back to Joseph. He threatened to keep Benjamin. They appealed to Joseph, telling him if they did not bring Benjamin back to Jacob, it would surely kill him. Joseph finally revealed who he is to his brothers.

Joseph explained to them to not be sorrowful for selling him into slavery but that it was the hand of God that could foresee the famine to come and had placed Joseph in a position that he would be able to help his people. He told them to go get Jacob and all their possessions and move to Egypt in the land of Goshen, and he would take care of them through the remainder of the famine. Pharaoh approved of the plan and sent wagons with goods to bring the people back to Egypt. Joseph gave Benjamin clothes and silver, and he sent to his father ten mules laden with supplies. Jacob's sons told him that Joseph was alive and was the governor of Egypt. Jacob had been so downhearted since the loss of Joseph, but now hearing the great news, his spirit was revived. He said, "I will go and see him before I die." Approximately 1883 BC, Jacob and his household, around seventy-five people, traveled to Egypt (Genesis 42–45).

The story of Joseph has some similarities to Jesus:

- His father loved him dearly—God the father loves the Son.
- A shepherd of his father's sheep—Jesus is our shepherd.
- Sent by the father to his brothers—Jesus came to the Jews first.
- Hated by brothers—Jesus was hated and rejected by the Jews.
- Tempted by Potiphar's wife—Jesus was tempted by Satan.
- Taken to Egypt—Mary and Joseph took Jesus to Egypt.
- Joseph's robe is taken—Jesus garments are taken.
- Sold and betrayed for silver—Jesus was betrayed for silver.
- Falsely accused—Jesus was falsely accused by the Pharisees.
- In prison with two others, one saved and the other lost—two men on cross, one saved and the other lost.
- Both thirty years old at the beginning of public ministry.
- Forgave those who wronged them.
- Saved their nation.
- Every knee shall bow.

Four Hundred Years in Egypt

Genesis 46 records the story of Jacob and his family of eleven sons, wives, and children coming into Egypt around 1883 BC. When Jacob and his family first went into Egypt, they were treated kindly by the pharaoh. As they multiplied, the pharaoh allowed them to dwell in the land of Goshen. Genesis 47:6 … "*In the best of the land make your father and brothers to dwell in the land of Goshen.*" At that time, the region of Egypt under Pharaoh Ramses extended to the Mediterranean Sea. Looking at ancient maps, people could cross from Egypt onto the Sinai Peninsula, and they could travel by land up to Jerusalem. As well, they could travel by land or boat and come into Jordan and proceed into Arabia.

Joseph brought Jacob to the pharaoh, and Jacob blessed the pharaoh, and Jacob tells him that he is 130 years old. Jacob lives in the land of Egypt for seventeen additional years, and he dies at the age of 147. The body of Jacob is taken back to Canaan for burial in the cave with Abraham (Genesis 47:7–9, 28). Rachel dies and is buried in Ephratha, Bethlehem.

Before Jacob died, he gave a prophecy for the last days over his sons (Genesis 49):

- Reuben, unstable as water, you will not excel, you defiled my bed.
- Simeon and Levi, cruel murderers, fierce anger divide and scatter them.
- Judah, you will be praised, your hand will be on your enemies' necks, they will bow down to you, a lion's whelp, the scepter will not depart from Judah, or the lawgiver from between his feet until Shiloh come.
- Zebulun, he will dwell by the sea and be a haven of ships, his border is to Zidon.
- Issachar, strong ass couching down between two burdens, saw the land was pleasant and became a worker unto tribute.
- Dan will judge his people as one of the tribes of Israel, a serpent, an adder that bites the horses' heels.
- Gad, a troop will overcome him, but he will overcome at last.
- Asher, his bread will be fat, and he will yield royal dainties.
- Naphtali is a hind let loose, he gives good words.
- Joseph is a fruitful bough by the well whose branches run over the wall, his enemies grieve him, he is strong by the hand of God.
- Benjamin will be as a vicious wolf.

Joseph and all his brothers died in Egypt. Joseph died at the age of 110 around 1805 BC. He was embalmed in the Egyptian way and placed in a sarcophagus (Genesis 50:26). His remains stayed in Egypt for four hundred years, and then his bones were taken to the promised land at the time of the Exodus.

Hundreds of years passed; many of Jacob's descendants had gotten very comfortable in Egypt and adopted the pagan practices of the Egyptians. This human activity could be expected due to the intermingling of the descendants of Ham and the descendants of Shem. Coming to the four-hundred-year maker, the Hebrew Israelites began to be treated harshly by the current pharaoh. He began to enslave them as he also enslaved the Egyptians. The only way that the people of God get out of their comfort zone is through persecution.

Exodus 1 brings us to approximately one hundred years or so before the Hebrew Israelites would exit Egypt. The story begins with a new king who knew not Joseph, and he said to his people, "Behold the people of the children of Israel are more and mightier than we." If they join forces with our enemies, they will overcome us. Let us get them out of our land. He set taskmasters to afflict them with their burdens. As slaves, they built for Pharaoh treasure cities, Pithom and Raamses. No matter what hardship he placed upon the Israelites, they still continued to multiply. He told the Hebrew midwives to kill the male babies, and they did not do so.

The Birth of Moses

During the affliction of the Hebrew Israelites, a Levite named Jochebed and his wife, Amram—who lived in Egypt on the African continent—gave birth to Aaron, Miriam, and Moses. The birth of Moses is dated around 1526 BC (Numbers 26:59). They saw that Moses was a special child. His mother hid the baby for three months since the pharaoh's people were seeking to kill the male babies. The mother made an ark of bulrushes or papyrus reeds and sealed it with slime and pitch. She placed it near the riverbanks, while Miriam, his sister, kept watch. The daughter of the pharaoh came and had it withdrawn from the river. She saw the baby boy and knew from his clothes he was of the children of Israel, but she had compassion on him. Moses's sister suggested to the princess that a Hebrew woman nurse the baby. When Moses was weaned, his mother took him to the princess, and he became her son and called his name Moses, which means, "I drew him out of the water." This Egyptian princess could either have been Hatsheput married to Pharaoh Thutmose II. Some think the princess was the daughter of Ramses II. In either case, the princess was barren, and this child was a gift from the gods and heir to the throne. Moses lived in the pharaoh's palace for forty years, and during this time, he saw the harsh treatment of his people. The children of Israel cried, and God remembered his covenant with Abraham (Exodus 2).

Transition from Egypt to Arabia and Back to Egypt

Moses traveled to the region of Midian, which is Arabia, north of Jordan. The populous was diverse. People referred as Arabs, Africans, Hebrews lived in this area. Their complexions ranged from dark to brown. Upon Moses's arrival in Midian, he met the daughters of Reuel. Moses helped them water their flock. He became a shepherd, married Zipporah, had children, and stayed in Midian for forty years, bringing us to 1486 BC.

Moses Hears from God

One day while Moses was tending sheep near a mountain in Horeb, Arabia, he hears from God and gets his marching orders. At first Moses does not feel adequate to accomplish this enormous task. To encourage Moses, God demonstrates a few miracles. First he turns the staff into a snake, and second, he turns the brown hand of Moses white and then brown again. God approves Aaron the Levite, the brother of Moses, to help him accomplish the assignment.

Moses Returns to Egypt

Empowered by God, Moses (eighty years old) and Aaron (eighty-three) returned to Egypt to do as God commanded. It may have been around 1447 BC when they gathered their wives, children, and animals for the long trip back to Egypt. After arriving, Moses and Aaron spoke to the people, telling them their deliverance was at hand. They convinced the people with the signs that God had done with Moses. The people believed and bowed their heads and worshipped (Exodus 4:30).

Moses and Aaron met with Pharaoh and told him the God of the Hebrews said, "*Let my people go so that we may sacrifice unto the Lord our God lest he fall upon us with pestilence or the sword*" (Exodus 5:1–3).

God Brings Plagues against Egypt

According to the scriptures, the pharaoh would not let the people leave Egypt, and God hardened his heart against them. We will highlight the plagues that God brought upon Egypt (Exodus 7 to 12):

- Aaron's rod becomes a serpent; the rods of pharaoh's magic men became many serpents, but Aaron's one serpent swallowed them up.
- Aaron's rod smites the river, and all the waters turns to blood, fish die, and it stinks for seven days.
- Aaron stretched forth his rod, and frogs came up from the waters into all the land, houses, and upon the people. They died and were gathered into heaps and did stink.
- Aaron strikes the dust of the land, and it turned to lice, which came upon man and animals.
- Swarms of flies came upon the land, houses, and people. The flies do not attack Israel.
- The cattle, horses, oxen, sheep were killed by God, but he spared the animals of Israel.
- God brings boils upon man and beast.
- Moses stretched forth his rod toward heaven, and there was thunder and great hail with fire that rained up the earth, crops, man, and beast. The people of Israel were spared.

- Locusts covered the land and devoured trees, herbs, and crops.
- Darkness that could be felt came upon Egypt for three days. Israel had light.
- Death came upon the firstborn of man and animals at midnight but not upon Israel.

God prepares Israel to leave Egypt. They did apply the blood of a lamb over their doorposts so the angel of death would pass over. They did eat their last supper fully dressed in clothes and shoes, for in the morning, they would leave Egypt. They were to attain silver, gold, and jewels from the Egyptians. God directed them to take a route that would bypass Philistine territory and not have to encounter the threat of war (Exodus 13:17). God demonstrated his power over the earth and water by parting the Red Sea to allow his people to pass from Egypt into the wilderness of Sinai. Egypt was left desolate after all the plague judgments. From that time to the present, Egyptian splendor and glory has declined. However, Egypt left behind an archeologist's treasure trove. There remained a great deal of history from the drawings on the walls, pyramids, giant statues, and various artifacts covered in hieroglyphics. Were all traces of the Hebrew Israelites time in Egypt vanquished? We think not. One major archeological find was the remnant of Egyptian chariot wheels found at the bottom of the Red Sea.

Chapter 11
Moses: Fight or Flight

Chapter Overview

- The Role of Moses
  - Moses as Prince, Shepherd, Deliverer
  - Route to Midian? Exhibit: Map
  - The Burning Bush
  - The Passover
  - Forty Years in the Wilderness
  - Moses's Father in Law Visits
  - Come Up to the Mountain
  - Ten Commandments
  - Mosaic Covenant
  - The Tabernacle
  - Ark of the Covenant
  - High Priest Garments, Urim and Thummin
  - Pillars of Clouds and Fire
  - The Desert Rock
  - The Bronze Serpent
  - Moses Sees the Promised Land
- Death of Moses

Chapter 11

Moses: Fight or Flight

Over four hundred years in Egypt, the chosen people would be led out of Egypt by Moses. During that time, they numbered over a million people. Included in this multitude were Egyptian Gentiles who left Egypt with the Jews. Having lived in Egypt for a time in freedom and prosperity, they became complacent and relied on the provisions of Egypt. Exodus 1:7, "*And the children of Israel were fruitful and increased abundantly, multiplied and waxed exceeding mighty and the land was filled with them.*" God took away their comfort and allowed a great hardship to come upon them. The last hundred years in Egypt were spent as slaves under harsh overseers who demanded of them to make bricks. Exodus 1:8 "*There rose up a new Pharaoh … he made their lives bitter with hard bondage … and the king spoke to the Hebrew midwives to kill the male babies.*"

Moses had grown up in the luxury of Egyptian royalty. As he began to see the plight of the Hebrew Israelites, he was moved with compassion. The story tells us Moses killed an Egyptian and he had to quickly leave Egypt for fear of his own death. Returning to Egypt forty years later, Moses tells the people to prepare to leave Egypt. Even under hardship, many Hebrew Israelites wanted to stay in Egypt, and they did. On the other hand, people who were not Hebrews left Egypt in the exodus. The Hebrew Israelites and others living with them would experience supernatural sights and sounds over the next forty years in the Sinai. In this region, they were not persecuted from outsiders but were plagued by internal problems of disobedience to God and disrespect of Moses. God gave Moses and the people hundreds of laws for everything imaginable. Even so, they relapsed many times and decided to make a golden idol. In God's wrath, many of them died. At the end of the forty-year period, around 1406 BC, God gives Joshua and Caleb the order to take the remnant into the promised land.

The land would need to be purged of idolatry and ungodliness. For seven years, Joshua and his military cleansed the land.

The Role of Moses

Prince, Shepherd, Deliverer

The Hebrew Israelites had a presence in the land of Egypt from the time of Joseph, his father, Jacob, and sons. The parents of Moses lived in Egypt, and he was born around 1526 BC. Moses lived his first forty years of life as a **prince** in Egypt. His mother kept the God of Abraham before Moses, even though he was well educated in the ways of the Egyptians. As an adult, Moses had free range throughout Egypt. He began to see the abuse of his people. Moses rebelled, and he left Egypt to escape the wrath of Pharaoh.

Exhibit: Map to Midian

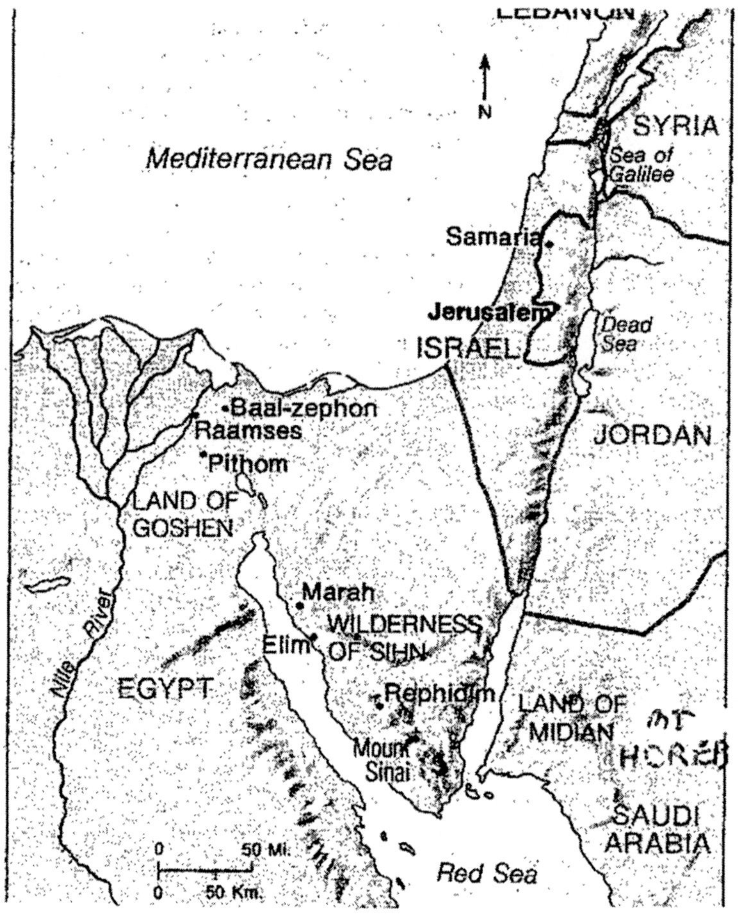

Route to Midian

Let us first consider that Moses knew the regions of Egypt, the Sinai, and the territory of Arabia. In order to travel from Egypt to Midian in Arabia, Moses had a few options. Moses was royalty in Egypt, so he had access to a boat. He may have sailed the Red Sea. Looking at a map, one route would be to sail down the Red Sea, around the Sinai Peninsula, and up the other side to debark near to Midian. From that point, he and his entourage would travel by land to Midian.

Moses may have assembled a caravan of horses and camels in Upper Egypt, traveled across the Sinai peninsula, then headed south through Arabia to Midian. Either route was four hundred to five hundred miles. Moses would have to take supplies and servants to accompany him on his long journey.

The scriptures open with Moses resting by a well in Midian (Exodus 2:16). Here he encounters the daughters of a Midian priest named Reuel/Jethro, and Moses helps them to water their sheep. They told their father an Egyptian had helped them water the flock. Jethro and his people knew Egyptians. Moses was still dressed in his customary Egyptian garb. The timing is around 1487 BC, and Moses is around forty years old. Making his home in Midian, Moses married Zipporah, Reuel's daughter. They had a son and called him Gershom. Moses spent the next forty years as a **shepherd** in Midian.

The Burning Bush

Approximately 1448–7 BC, Moses, being eighty years old, God appeared to him in a burning bush on the mountain of God, also called Mount Horeb in Midian in Arabia. Exodus 3:1–6, "*An angel of the LORD appeared unto him in a flame of fire out of the midst of the bush.*" Moses desires to investigate the burning bush, and with an audible voice coming forth from the midst of the bush, God warns Moses not to approach. Moses could not enter into the presence of God because he was not covered. God tells him to take off his shoes for the place where he is standing is holy ground. Moses realizes he is in the presence of God and covers his head, removes his shoes as an act of reverence and conveying his own lack of righteousness. Moses hears God speak: "I AM the God of your father, the God of Abraham, Isaac and Jacob."

> *And I am come down to deliver my people out of the hand of the Egyptians and to bring them up out of that land into a good land … flowing with milk and honey* (Exodus 3:8)

God told him to return to Egypt to free his people. His brother, Aaron, was in the region of Midian, where they did rendezvous (Exodus 4:14). We come to a bit of insight that tells us Hebrew Israelites lived in various locations outside of Egypt proper. Sometimes we think that all the Hebrew Israelites lived in Egypt for four hundred years. Joseph and his relatives multiplied in Egypt. Before Jacob was born, Abraham's people settled in Shechem area of Cannon. His people traveled into Africa as well as other locations throughout the Middle East. After God promised land to Abraham, it seems that God began to gather his people from various regions, directing them into the area of Cannon. They came out of Egypt, Sinai, Arabia, Turkey, Persia, and Mesopotamia. We keep in mind that not all the Hebrew Israelites left their regions to congregate in the promised land. In the fullness of time, God is directing the Hebrew Israelites to return to Jerusalem; even so, not all the Jews dispersed around the world will make Aliyah.

Moses understood the magnitude of the assignment. He had to trust God. He then became the **Deliverer.** Through faith, Moses carried out God's plan for the chosen people. He had retained the oral tradition of God's Word. He may have had the written records handed down from Enoch to Noah to Abraham. Exodus 24:4, "*And Moses wrote all the words of the Lord ...*" verse 7, "*And he took the book of the covenant and read to the people.*" This is pointed out because God carved the Ten Commandments on tablets of stone, but here we see Moses writing and reading from parchment scrolls. We pick up a confirmation that there existed scrolls as indicated in Hebrews 9:19, "*For when Moses had spoken every precept to all the people according to the law, he took the blood of calves and of goats with water and scarlet wool and hyssop and sprinkled both <u>the book</u> and all the people.*" After four hundred years in Egypt, we can be certain records were maintained within the Jewish community.

During the last forty years of the life of Moses, he was known as the **lawgiver.** The Torah, or first five books of the Old Testament, were credited to Moses. God instructed Moses to record the history of man's beginning in what is titled the Genesis Chronicles. God told him to record all the events that led up to the Exodus. Through the giving of the Ten Commandments to the establishing of the Levitical laws, the book of Leviticus was written. The book of Numbers was compiled after the numbering of the chosen people in the wilderness of Sinai and a second census before entering the promised land. Deuteronomy wraps things up since Moses would die before officially entering the land of Canaan. He had some last instructions for Joshua and blessings over the people. After Moses died, Joshua and the scribes were responsible for continuing the written account of the Hebrew Israelites history.

<u>The Passover</u>

This feast is a reminder of the blood of a lamb over the door to protect against the angel of death. Believers still know that there is power in the shed blood of Jesus. On the tenth day of Nisan/Abib, a lamb will be sacrificed, there will be a holy convocation, and the eating of unleavened bread to observe the exodus from Egypt. As a reminder of what the Lord did to bring them out of Egypt, he told the Israelites to wear a band around the hand as a reminder of the Lord's strength and wear frontlets on the forehead to remember the law (Exodus 13:6, 9).

Forty Years in the Wilderness

We come to the year 1446 BC. In the third month after Israel left Egypt and came into the wilderness of Sinai, settling near the mount of Sinai, God commanded Moses to come up onto the mount. Moses is instructed to remind the people of what God had done for their release from Egypt.

> *You have seen what I did unto the Egyptians and how I bare you on eagles wings and brought you unto myself. Now therefore, if you will obey my voice indeed and keep my covenant then you will be a peculiar treasure unto me above all people for all the earth is mine. And you shall be unto me a kingdom of priest and a holy nation.* (Exodus 19:4)

God knew that the people had been exposed to polytheism, and he would need to purge them of their pagan mind-set. God told Moses to tell the people to obey him and keep the covenant. If so, they would be set aside, would be a peculiar treasure above all people, be a kingdom of priest and a holy nation. The people said we will do all that the Lord has spoken. Moses returned the words of the people to the Lord. Then God said, "I will come unto you in a thick cloud. The people will hear my voice and believe." God tells Moses to sanctify the people. Exodus 19:10, "*And the Lord said unto Moses, go unto the people and <u>sanctify them today and tomorrow</u>* [two days] *and let them wash their clothes.*" The two days symbolizes that after the blood atonement and forgiveness of sins through the death of Jesus on the cross that for the past two thousand years (two days), the people of God are being sanctified, purified, and awaiting to be dressed in white robes. We are to **be ready** to meet him. We are to listen for the voice of God, **sounding** like the blowing of the trumpet.

A future prophetic word in Exodus 19:11: "*And **be ready** against the third day for the third day the Lord will **come down** in the **sight of all the people**.*" The twenty-first century is the beginning of third day. At the Second Coming, Jesus will **come down** at the **blowing of the seventh trumpet**. He will make his triumphal entry, and **all the people will see him.** There will be lightning, clouds, the angelic hosts, and the saints of Jesus riding horses will accompany him. The earth will tremble; there will be smoke and fire, and the scene will be amazingly spectacular as they behold his glory. Exodus 19:16, "*And it came to pass on the third* *day in the morning there was thunder and lightning and a thick cloud upon the mount and the* ***sound of the trumpet*** *exceeding loud so that all the people that was in the camp trembled.*"

Returning to the scene at the base of the mountain, God required Moses to set a boundary around the base of the mountain and warn the people not to come close to the mountain and not touch the mountain, neither man or beast, or they will be killed. They would hear the sound of the trumpet, see thunder, and lightning, and the presence of God would descend in smoke and fire. The vibrations of the mountain reverberated through the people, the land, and they would be fearful. God commands Moses to come up and tells him to go back and warn the people not to break through the boundaries lest they perish. God tells him he can bring Aaron back when he returns to the top of the mountain (Exodus 19:17–24).

Exodus 20 tells us God spoke in an audible voice regarding his commandments for the people.

It was his priority that they begin to understand there is one God and they will not make any graven images or worship them. They will learn to exalt Yahweh and reverence his name. God said, "Rest on the Sabbath, and keep it holy." Exodus chapters 21 through 23 are the laws regarding people, animal, property, and ethics.

Exodus 24:4, "*And Moses wrote all the words of the Lord ...*" Moses made many trips up to the top of Mount Sinai and back down to instruct the people. Moses then built an altar, erected twelve pillars, and men were selected to sacrifice animals. Moses separated the blood and sprinkled the blood over the altar and the people. He took the book of the covenant and read to the people.

After their sanctification, sacrifice, sprinkling of blood, and hearing the Word, God called Moses, Aaron, and his leaders to come into his presence. Exodus 24:10, "*They saw the God of Israel and there under his feet as it were paved a work of sapphire stone and as it were the body of heaven in his clearness ...*" What a marvelous experience.

God was satisfied. Moses and his leaders had come into his presence. They did worship, celebrate, eating, and drinking on a lower level of the holy mountain. This points to the time the saints will be in heaven at the banquet feast with the Triune Godhead (Exodus 24:12–18). After the celebration, God told Moses to come up to the top of the mount and he would give Moses the tablets of stone, the law and commandments that God had written with his hand. Moses left Aaron and Hur in charge. Moses ascended to the top of the mount, wherein the glory of God abode. He remained there for six days. Exodus 24:17, "*And the sight of the glory of the Lord was like devouring fire on the top of the mount ...*" On the seventh day, God spoke to Moses out of the midst of the cloud. Moses ascends further into the cloud, where he stayed in the presence of God for forty days and forty nights. He did not eat or drink. In the future, Jesus would be taken into the wilderness for forty days and forty nights.

Exodus 32, during the time Moses was in the presence of God, the people decided he was not returning. They went to Aaron and demanded he make them an idol. He told them to gather their gold, and after melting it, they fashioned it into a golden calf. Aaron built an altar, and they offered sacrifices to the golden calf. God, seeing all things, said to Moses, "Arise, get you down quickly from here, for your people which you brought forth out of Egypt have corrupted themselves, turned away from that which I commanded them, and they have made a molten image." Moses left the presence of God with the two tablets of stone God had prepared and returned to the people. Moses heard the noise coming from the camp and at first thought it was war then realized it was a celebration. Joshua met with Moses, and they come to the camp and saw the golden calf and the dancing and singing. Moses was so angry he threw the tablets and broke them. He took the calf and burned it, grounding it to powder, throwing it into the water, and told the people to drink it.

God was angry that the people had turned aside so quickly, and he desired to destroy them and blot out their name from under heaven. Moses interceded for the people before the Lord, asking that he not destroy them because they are his people and his inheritance.

Aaron gives an account of his actions. Moses then calls for those who are on the Lord's side to gather with him, and the sons of Levi did so. Apparently, not all the people did come to worship the golden calf. Moses tells the Levites to go through the camp and kill the offenders. They killed about three thousand men. To the rest, Moses told them to consecrate themselves and be blessed. Moses chastised the people for their sin and said he would return unto the Lord and make atonement for their sins.

Looking beyond our human faults and failures, we should keep our minds focused on the marvelous works of the Lord. The Hebrew Israelites were reminded of the many miracles that God did in Egypt, to the parting of the Red Sea and all the miracles recorded during the forty years of wondering.

Out of the forty years, we do not know how many years were spent in the Sinai region. Eventually they moved into Arabia. Moses led them to a place God had identified, which is mount Horeb in Arabia (Exodus 32:6). The angel assigned to watch over Israel did go before them. In this location, Moses set up a tent outside of the camp (Exodus 33:7–10). When he went to the tent, the people stood in respect of Moses as he passed by. The glory of the Lord did descend as a pillar of cloud and remained at the door. Seeing the glory of God, the people remained at their doorways, worshipping God.

Exodus 33:13, Moses desired another meeting with the Almighty. He begins his request by reasoning with God: "*I pray thee if I have found grace in thy sight, show me now thy way …*"

> *I beseech thee, show me your glory …* God said, *I will make all my goodness pass before you … you cannot see my face, for there shall no man see me and live.*

> And the Lord said, *Behold there is a place by me and you will stand upon a rock and it will come to pass while my glory passes by that I will put you in a cliff of the rock and will cover you with my hand … and I will take away my hand and you will see my back parts but my face will not be seen.* Exodus 33:18-23

Exodus 34:29, Moses prepared another set of stone tablets, and God wrote on them. After being in the presence of God, the face of Moses shone. The people saw the glory of God upon Moses, and they were afraid to come near him. He covered his face with a veil. Being in the presence of God is life-changing and physically apparent. We can feel his presence; the Spirit may radiate from our eyes. At times, others can sense we have been in his holy presence.

<u>Ten Commandments, Exodus 20</u>

1. I am the Lord your God … You shall have no other gods before me.
2. You will not make any graven image or likeness of things in heaven or in the earth, and you will not bow down or worship them.
3. You will not take the name of the Lord your God in vain.
4. Remember the Sabbath day, and keep it holy and do no work.
5. Honor your father and mother so your days will be long upon the land.
6. You will not kill.
7. You will not commit adultery.
8. You will not steal.
9. You will not lie.
10. You will not covet you neighbor's house or wife.

Tracing the footprints of the Hebrew Israelite through the scriptures from Mesopotamia, Canaan, Egypt, Arabia, making their way back to the land of Canaan—many artifacts, testaments in stone, wood, metal, or scrolls have been left in these regions as a witness to their existence. Kings David and Solomon built the House of the Lord in Jerusalem. The temple did house the Ark of the Covenant as the Ark housed the tablets of stone. Preflood people learned to build ships and did navigate the globe. Postflood people continued to build ships and navigate the globe. For instance, King Solomon had a fleet of ships. "*And king Solomon made a navy of ships in Ezion-geber which is beside Eloth on the shore of the Red Sea in the land of Edom.*" 1 Kings 9:26 As captives, the Hebrew Israelites were transported back to Mesopotamia to the regions our ancestors Shem, Ham, Japheth resided after the flood while repopulating the earth. From the text in 1 Kings, we can surmise ancient people could sail from the Mediterranean Sea to the Atlantic Ocean into the Caribbean Sea to the Gulf of Mexico, making their way into South and North America, leaving monuments and traces of their presence in the land. An eighty-ton boulder was found in Los Lunas, New Mexico. The stone was inscribed in the language of paleo-Hebrew, which is an older form of Hebrew, listing the Ten Commandments. Archaeologists date the stone to be around the time of King Solomon, 900 BC.

Mosaic Covenant, Exodus 19

- Obey and keep the laws.
- You are a peculiar treasure above all people.
- You are a kingdom of priests and a holy nation.

The Tabernacle, Ark, Priesthood are discussed in the following chapters of Exodus 26, 35, concerning the preparation and construction of the Tabernacle.

Moses constructed the tabernacle after the heavenly pattern. Exodus 26:1 speaks of the four coverings of the Tabernacle:

- The inner material was made of fine linen curtains housing the Holy Place and the Holy of Holies. Veil or curtain dividing the two rooms symbolized how the people were separated from God. At the cross, the veil was torn in half, making way for our access to God through Jesus.
- The middle covering was made of goat's hair (Exodus 26:7).
- The outside covering was made of ram's skins dyed red (Exodus 26:16).
- Curtains to the entrance of the Tabernacle were made of four colors: blue for heaven, purple for royal, red for blood, and white for purity.

Exodus 25, 27, 38 concern the details for the construction of the Table of Shewbread, Lampstand, Altar. The significance of these items:

- Table of Shewbread in the holy place was to symbolize the bread of the presence. Jesus is the bread of life. Twelve loaves represented each tribe of Israel, and God provides spiritual nourishment.
- The golden lampstand in the Holy Place was designed with seven lamps, which we know as the menorah and the middle lamp is the servant lamp. Jesus left his lofty throne to come to earth as a humble servant.
- Altar of Incense in the Holy Place is symbolic of our prayers that rise before the throne as a sweet smell.
- Bronze altar for the burnt offerings may symbolize the Old Testament practice of maintaining a relationship with God. In the New Testament, Jesus became our

sacrifice once and for all eliminating the need to shed the blood of animals for an acceptable relationship with God.

- Basin outside of the tabernacle symbolizes our need for purification. Water baptism symbolized the old life is washed away and we are baptized into a new life with Jesus.
- Anointing oil was always present to anoint the priest and objects in the tabernacle. It also signifies the Holy Spirit anointing us with gifts to carry out his work.

Exodus 25, 37 addresses the Ark of the Covenant. Moses selected Bezaleel, the son of Uri, the son of Hur of the tribe of Judah, to fabricate the Ark. God anointed him with wisdom, understanding, knowledge in all manner of workmanship. The ark contained the tablets of stone, a pot of manna, and Aaron's staff. The word *manna* means "what is it." God provided their daily bread. The manna was sweet and pure. Like Jesus, we should taste and see that the Lord is good. The people tired of the manna and complained for the things of Egypt. Our words have impact, and the manna changed in color; it was no longer white but became dull. The manna changed from delicate to tough, and it tasted bland. Exodus 25:10 provides an overview of the materials used for the construction of the Ark:

- The name Ark of the Covenant pertains to the relationship between God and Israel. It is covered in gold symbolic of our works tried in the fire.
- Mercy Seat is the lid of the Ark and symbolizes the presence of God among his people and is the place where the glory of God would be manifested. If anyone other than the priest touched the ark, they would die.
- Two Cherubim placed over the Mercy Seat represent the angelic order that is before the throne of God continually in worship. Some angelic creatures appear to have four faces representing lion, man, ox, and eagle, and four of the twelve tribes will have an ensign representing these features—Judah, a lion; Reuben, a man; Ephraim, an ox; Dan, an eagle.

The Ark accompanied the chosen people through the wilderness into the promised land. Eventually, the first temple would become home for the Ark of the Covenant.

Exodus 28, 39 define the Priesthood and their garments. God gave Moses clear instructions on these garments. First we note that the craftsmen were filled with the spirit of wisdom so that the garments could be consecrated and that Aaron may minister unto God. The garments consisted of a breastplate, ephod, robe, broidered coat, mitre, girdle arrayed in gold, blue, purple and red. The ephod did contain two onyx stones engraved with the twelve tribes of Israel encased in gold to be worn by the high priest. The breastplate would contain twelve various stones, each carved with a tribe of Israel. Exodus 28:30–38, "*And you will put in the breastplate of judgment the* Urim [light] *and the* Thummin [perfection] *would be worn by Aaron when he goes in before the Lord and Aaron would bear the judgment of the children of Israel upon his heart before the Lord continually.* Recently, it was reported by Sky Watch TV, September 15, 2016, that the Urim and Thummin stone was found in South America, and Israel has offered $200 million for it. Aaron wore a mitre on his head engraved with the words "Holiness to the Lord" to signify that he may bear iniquity and that the Israelites may be acceptable before the Lord (Leviticus 8:31–36). Before Aaron and his sons entered their priestly work, they were consecrated for seven days.

Pillars of Clouds and Fire

After all things were completed, in Exodus 40:34, "*Then a cloud covered the tent of the congregation and the glory of the Lord filled the tabernacle.*" So great was the presence of the Lord no one could enter into the tent until the glory cloud lifted. Exodus 13:21, "*And the Lord went before them by day in a pillar of a cloud to lead them the way and by night in a pillar of fire to give them light ...*"

The Desert Rock

Wondering around in the desert, the people were thirsty and complained to Moses. God told Moses to go before the people with the elders and take his rod. God said he would stand before him upon the rock in Mount Horeb, Arabia. The rock was a giant boulder. Moses struck the rock once, and a flood of water came forth. There were approximately two and half million people and cattle, and the water was plentiful. The rock split, creating a fissure down the middle. Moses named the place Massah (proof) and Meribah (contention) because of chiding Moses and not believing God or giving him the glory (Exodus 17:3–7).

The next time the people became thirsty, they complained to Moses again. He and Aaron prayed at the Tabernacle, and the glory of the Lord appeared unto them. God told Moses to take the rod, gather the assembly, and speak to the rock before their eyes and it shall give forth water. However, Moses was angry with the people, and he struck the rock twice, which was not what God told him to do. The water came forth again. God told Moses and Aaron because they did not trust the Lord and give him glory, they would not go into the promised land.

Today a large rock with a split stands in Saudi Arabia and may be the rock of the Bible. The Arabs that occupy this region acknowledge that the Israelites had a presence in the land.

Wandering around for forty years, the people came into various regions. Moses led the people to Mount Pisgah and asked King Sihon of the Amorites to pass through their land.

Instead he sends his army to attack them. Israel defeats them and takes their land, which covered the territory from Jahaz, Heshbon, to Edrei on the east of the Jordan (Numbers 21:23–26).

Moses led the people into the land of Bashan, and their king was Og, who was a giant.

God tells them, do not fear him, for he will deliver him, his people, and his land into the hands of Israel. We want to point out that Moses is in the promised land. Bashan is a short distance from the Sea of Galilee.

The Bronze Serpent

Moses had led the people to the area called Hormah, and here they encountered King Arad of the Canaanites. He fought against them, but they sought the Lord, and he gave them favor. After this the people complained, and God sent fiery serpents who bit the people, and many died. Seeing their error, they sought Moses to pray to God to take away the serpents. God instructs Moses to make a bronze serpent and put it on his staff, hold it up, and all who looked upon it would be healed and live. The serpent represents the curse of sin. The metaphor in this is that in lifting up Jesus on a cross, he will take away the curse of sin, crush the head of the serpent, and all who look to Christ will be saved from eternal death in hell.

> *And as Moses lifted up the serpent in the wilderness, even so must the Son of man be lifted and whosoever believes in him should not perish but have eternal life.* (John 3:14–15)

Moses Sees the Promised Land

> *Moses went up from the plains of Moab unto the mountain of Nebo to the top of Pisgah that is over against Jericho. And the Lord showed him all the land of Gilead unto Dan, and all Naphtali and the land of Ephraim and Manasseh and all the land of Judah unto the utmost sea and the south and the plain of the valley of Jericho, the city of palm trees unto Zoar. And the Lord said to him, this is the land which I sware unto Abraham unto Isaac and unto Jacob saying, I will give it unto your seed. I have caused you to see it with your eyes but you will not go over there.* (Deuteronomy 34:1–4)

The word *Nebo* is associated with prince Nebo/Mercury/Thoth, god of writing and illumination. Hebrew, association with Nebo-aw, is understood as written prophecy. From this vantage point on Mount Nebo in Jordan, Moses can see to the Mediterranean Sea and all the land that God promised the chosen people. We pointed out that Moses was in the promised land, and as there can be no contradiction in the scriptures, we believe that the short time Moses was in the promised land is not the same as bringing all the souls out of the wilderness and putting down permanent roots.

Moses Speaks His Last Words to the Congregation

> *Gather unto me all the elders of your tribes and your officers that I may speak these words in their ears and call heaven and earth to record against them. For I know that after my death, you will utterly corrupt yourselves and turn aside from the way which I have commanded you and evil will befall you in the latter days because you will do evil in the sight of the Lord to provoke him to anger through the work of your hands. And Moses spoke in the ears of all the congregation of Israel the words of this song, until they were ended.* (Deuteronomy 31:28–30)

The Death of Moses

After seeing all the land that God promised to Abraham's seed and knowing that God said he and Aaron would not go into the promised land, Aaron, the first high priest, died upon Mount Hor near the land of Edom (Jordan). God appoints his son, Eleazar, the next high priest (Numbers 20:23–29).

Moses died in the presence of God around 1406 BC.

> *So Moses the servant of the Lord died there in the land of Moab according to the word of the Lord and* ***he*** *buried him in a valley in the land of Moab over against Beth-peor but no man knew of his sepulcher unto this day. And Moses was 120 years old when he died and his eye was not dim nor his natural force abated and the children of Israel wept for Moses in the plains of Moab for thirty days …* (Deuteronomy 34:5–8)
>
> *Michael the archangel when contending with the devil he disputed about the body of Moses, did not bring against him a railing accusation but said, the Lord rebuke thee.* (Jude 1:9)

To our limited understanding, this is an unusual confrontation between a good angel and an evil angel over the body of the man Moses.

Yahweh redeemed his people. He snatched them from the grip of Satan. Through the supernatural power of God, the obedience of Moses, and through the blood of the Passover lamb, the chosen people made a significant move from worldly lusts and pagan influence to life in the wilderness to be purged, refined, and sanctified for their responsibility as the chosen people. Our sin nature is like a roller coaster; sometimes we are up with God, and other times we are down in the muck and mire.

After living for hundreds of years in the promised land and under the rule of judges or wicked kings, Israel fell into idolatry. These wicked kings killed their people, and in response to Israel's disobedience, God allowed them to be taken into captivity by the Assyrians, 700 BC. By 586 BC, others were taken into captivity by the Babylonians. Many Israelites died at the hands of their captors. At the end of the seventy-year captivity, they were free to return to their homeland, but the majority remained in Babylon.

Chapter 12
Israel in the Promised Land

Chapter Overview

- City of God, Jerusalem

- Burial Site of Adam, Eve, and the Patriarchs
- Coming to the Promised Land
- The Israeli Conquest
- Land Covenant
- Judges, Kings, Prophets
- The Divided Kingdoms

- The Regathering
- Centuries of Historical Events
- Israel in the Twenty-First Century
  - A Land of Milk and Honey
  - A Cup of Trembling
  - In the Hearing of the Rabbis

- Temples
  - Exhibit: Tabernacle (Page 233)
  - King Solomon's Temple
  - Ark of the Covenant
  - Restored Temple
  - Conquest for the Temple Mount
  - Tribulation Temple

Millennial Temple
Blood Moons Phenomena
Seven Feast of Israel
Hebrew Calendar
Blowing of the Shofar
Light at the End of the Tunnel

Chapter 12

Israel in the Promised Land

City of God, Jerusalem

Yahweh, Creator of heaven and earth, chose Jerusalem as his holy city. God established this point in the center of the world to be his connection between the heavenly realm and the earthly dimension. Ezekiel 5:5, "*This is Jerusalem, I have set it in the midst of the nations and countries that are round about her.*" This is eternal Zion. Israel was charged with the responsibility of being the custodians of God's Word, and through the lineage of David, the whole world could be saved in Yeshua.

<u>Burial Site of Adam, Eve, and the Patriarchs</u>

Historical and legendary accounts mention that in Hebron, a short distance from Jerusalem proper, may be the burial site for Adam and Eve. This is extraordinary. In all places in the world, the first people were placed in the region of the City of God. This would be center within the boundaries of the Garden of Eden. Abraham, Sarah, Isaac, Jacob, Leah, Rebecca also find their resting place in Hebron, cave of Machpelah. Jacob's wife, Rachel, died during the birth of Benjamin, and she is buried in Bethlehem. Biblical records indicate that Moses brought the bodies of Jacob and Joseph out of Egypt, and their final resting place is in the promised land: Canaan, later called Palestine, modern-day Israel. Miriam, the sister of Moses, died and was buried on the upper side of the Sinai Peninsula in the area called Kadesh. In 1967, Israel took back control of the patriarchs' resting place from the Muslims.

One can begin to understand why this place is special to Yahweh, because he walked in the Garden of Eden and then he placed his first people in that Garden. After the flood, God would direct the steps of Abraham, bringing the chosen people into the original region. This real estate is special to God, and Satan continues his designs to destroy the region. Nearly every campaign that has come against Jerusalem, God has broken the teeth of the enemy. The Gentiles have trampled upon Jerusalem for centuries and expelled the chosen people from their God-given land. The battle between good and evil rages on, but one day, God will finally destroy the works of Satan and establish his throne in Jerusalem.

One of the first tasks given to the chosen people coming into the promised land was to wipe out the pagan nations as judgment against them for their wickedness. God tells Israel to separate themselves from the wickedness of other nations:

> *And you shall not walk in the manners of the nation which I cast out before you for they committed all these things and therefore I abhorred them. But I have said unto you, you shall inherit their land and I will give it unto you to possess it, a land that flows with milk and honey, I am the Lord your God which have separated you from other people.* (Leviticus 20:23)

Israel is the wife of God. Hosea 2:19–20, "*And I will betroth you unto me forever, yes I will betroth you unto me in righteousness, judgment, loving kindness and mercies. I will even betroth you unto me in faithfulness and you will know the Lord.*" The Jews are the apple of God's eye (Zechariah 2:8).

Coming to the Promised Land

At the end of the forty years in the wilderness and shortly before entering the promised land, the Bible record tells us that the people continued to complain about lack of water, food, and saying they should have stayed in Egypt. Moses and Aaron lost their privilege to enter into the promised land because of their contentious people. Joshua in their stead would lead the people through treacherous terrain and through enemy territory into the promised land. The king of Edom, relative of the Israelites, would not let them pass through his land, so they had to detour to Mount Hor.

The book of Deuteronomy completes the five books of the Torah. After the death of Moses, Joshua would lead the people.

> *Now after the death of Moses the servant of the Lord, it came to pass that the Lord spoke unto Joshua the son of Nun, Moses minister, saying, Moses my servant is dead, now therefore arise, go over this Jordan, you and all this people into the land which I do give to them even the children of Israel. Every place that the sole of your foot shall tread upon that have I given unto you as I said to Moses. From the wilderness and this Lebanon even unto the great river Euphrates, all the land*

of the Hittites and unto the great sea toward the going down of the sun shall be your coast. (Joshua 1:1)

The promised land was initially called Canaan, wherein dwelled the descendants of Ham and others. The Canaanites were relatives of the children of Shem. The Canaanites were wicked in the sight of the Lord, having turned to idol worship, and God would deliver their land into the hands of the Israelites. This included the land of the Hittites, Hivites, Perizzites, Girgashites, Amorites, Jebusites, Joshua 3:10 The region of Lebanon was occupied by the tribe of Dan. Modern-day Lebanon is occupied by people referring to themselves as Palestinians and in constant conflict with Israel.

The Amorites and Moabites were the descendants of Lot and worshipped the false god called Chemosh, god of war (Numbers 21:29). Since Israel with all its faults still at that time worshipped the one true God, all other gods must come under his feet, and God showed favor to Israel over their enemies.

Jordan borders Israel and Arabia. Esau, son of Isaac, and his descendants lived in this region. They were called Edomites, Moabites, Ammonites. Esau is the patriarch of the Edomites. Approximately four hundred years before the Israelites moved into the promised land, Edom was a great power who encompassed the Dead Sea on the north and the Gulf of Aqaba on the south. During the reign of Kings Saul and David, Edom continued to be a sworn enemy of Israel. Jordan plays a role in the end-time. We see that Antichrist does not conquer Jordan and believe that during the tribulation, the persecuted of God will find refuge from the Antichrist in Petra, Jordan.

Those who settled in Judea were called Idumeans. During the time of Christ, Judea was ruled by Herodian (Jews), dynasty of Idumeans/Edomites. The Idumeans had a powerful alliance with Rome, strengthening the consolidation of power by the Caesars. Antipater, an Idumean, was the father of Herod the Great. Caesar Augustus made Herod the Great governor of Israel in 63 BC. His son, Herod Agrippa, in 37 BC served as the final ruler. In 19 BC, he began construction of the second temple, which was destroyed in AD 70 by the Romans. Jesus was born during the era of cooperation between Jews and Romans. However, Herod attempted to kill the male babies to eliminate the threat of a new king of the Jews. The alliance between Rome and the Herodian Dynasty continued with Drusilla, daughter of Herod Agrippa I. She married Felix, the Roman procurator of Judea around AD 52. Political marriages took place for a period of time. Bernice, Herodian princess, aged thirteen, while visiting Caesarea with her brother Agrippa II had been given in marriage to Roman nobility, Marcus, son of Tiberius, Julius Alexander. These unions give us historical data that Jews and Gentiles intermarried. Jewish commentary refers to Edom as Rome, or a metaphor for the Gentile world system. Through Roman royalty came European royalty. Roman citizenry was a conglomeration of cultures, religions, and ethnicity. For example, we know the Apostle Paul was a Jewish Roman citizen. The architects of the new world order are made up of descendants of Israel and Rome. Rome, Europe, America represent the revived Roman Empire and controlled by the forces of darkness known as the spirit of mystery Babylon.

Approximately 1406 BC, the Israelites began their journey from Acacia in the land of Jordan by crossing over the Jordan River. God caused the river to stop flowing from the City of Adam near Zaretan. The priest and the Ark stood firm on dry ground in the middle of the river, allowing the nation to cross on dry ground.

They camped at Gilgal on the other side of the Jordan River for a year. God told Joshua to pick twelve men, one from each tribe, to carry a large stone to be put in the middle of the Jordan River—to be a memorial to Israel forever—and the stones remain there to this day (Joshua 4:9). More important was the memorial of Passover. Since manna had ceased, the Passover was celebrated with unleaven cakes, corn, and fruit. Joshua circumcised the men that had survived the wilderness as a sign that their reproach had been taken away and continued within the blood covenant called for by God.

The Israeli Conquest

Joshua made war plans to attack Jericho. He sent out spies who found safety with Rahab. Joshua 2:9–11 Rahab said to the spies,

> *I know that the Lord has given you the land and that your terror is fallen upon us and all the inhabitants of the land faint because of you. For we have heard how the Lord dried up the water of the Red sea for you when you came out of Egypt and what you did unto the two kings of the Amorites that were on the other side Jordan, Sihon and Og whom you utterly destroyed. As soon as we heard these things, our hearts did melt neither did there remain any more courage in any man because of you for the Lord your God he is God in heaven above and in earth beneath.*

Later, Joshua assembled forty thousand men for war from the tribes of Reuben, Gad, and Manasseh.

The angel of the Lord visits:

> *And it came to pass when Joshua was by Jericho that he lifted up his eyes and looked and behold there stood a man over against him with his sword drawn in his hand and Joshua went unto him and said unto him are you for us or for our adversaries? And he said no, but as captain of the host of the Lord am I now*

> *come and Joshua fell on his face to the earth and did worship and said unto him what says my lord unto his servant: And the captain of the Lord's host said to Joshua, loose your shoe from your feet for the place whereon you stand is holy …* (Joshua 5:13)

God gave Joshua his marching orders to conquer the City of Jericho. Joshua 6:3, "*And you shall compass the city all your men of war and go around about the city once for six days.*" The daily procession lineup was the warriors first followed by the seven priests with the ram's horn, then the Ark, and last were the people. After each day, they would make camp for the night. Joshua instructed them not to speak, but on the seventh day, all shall walk around the city seven times and the priest will blow the trumpets. When they heard a final long blast, the people were instructed to shout because God had given them the city and the walls around the city would fall. It may boggle the mind how the walls of Jericho could fall, besides a miracle from God. Consider a million people walking around the city fourteen times, blowing the shofar and then all shouting; the walking caused vibrations in the earth, weakening the walls; and the shout sent sound waves into the walls, causing them to crumble.

God commanded the Israelites to utterly destroy all that was in the city—both man and woman, young and old, and ox and sheep with the edge of the sword save Rahab and her family. God allowed them to take the gold and silver then burn the city. Joshua said, "Do not take the accursed things associated with idolatry," and he speaks a curse, saying, "Cursed be the man before the Lord that rises up and rebuilds the City of Jericho, a curse will be upon his firstborn."

There is usually one rotten apple in the crate. The people were commanded not to take any spoils. Achan of the tribe of Judah took a Babylonian garment, idols of silver and gold, and buried them in his tent (Joshua 7:21). When they had gone up against the City of Ai, which is in Beth-aven, they lost the battle. Joshua tore his clothes and fell to the ground before the Ark and sought God's wisdom. God told him Israel had sinned and had taken the accursed things and God would not be with them until all associated with it were destroyed. Achan's sin was discovered. He and his household and animals were stoned to death then burned. A heap of rocks covered them. The place is now called the Valley of Achor.

If sin is not dealt with, it is likened to a little yeast that will affect the whole loaf. Give the enemy an inch, and he will take a yard. It is better to obey than to suffer punishment even to the death.

Joshua's second conquest against Ai was successful because they followed God's command to the letter. It appears that the people of Ai were dwelling peacefully in the land, but God came against them; they were all killed by the Israelites. This time, God told them to take the animals and the spoils then burn the city.

Moving roughly twenty miles north, they come to Mount Ebal and built an altar unto God. Joshua carved the law on this altar. They made burnt offering and sacrificed peace offerings. Half of the congregation stood in Mount Gerizim and the other half at Ebal (Joshua 8:30).

The reputation of Israel preceded them throughout the land. The people of Gibeon made a peace treaty with Joshua. The kings of Jerusalem, Hebron, Jarmuth, Lachisch, and Eglon conspired together to come up against Gibeon for making a peace treaty with Israel. Joshua is warned of the plot, but the Lord God said, "Fear not, I have delivered them into your hand." Two miracles occur during this battle. Joshua asked God for additional day light, and it appeared the sun stood still, and great hailstones killed more of the enemies than Israel did by the sword (Joshua 10:1–15).

After destroying the five cities, Joshua moves to Makkedah and killed the king and the people. He continued to destroy those in the southern regions. The kings of the north formed an alliance to come against Israel. Kings of Hazor, Madon, Shimron, Aschshaph, Chinneroth, and the remnants of Canaanites, Amoritres, Hittite, Perizzite, Jebusite, Hivite—they gathered at the waters of Merom. Their numbers were as the sand at the seashore. Again God tells Joshua to not be afraid, and he will deliver them (including the giants) into his hand. Joshua 17:15 mentions the giants. These giants were present among the Philistines and other tribes, continuing to the time of King David. Please note that not all of the tribal members were giants; there were regular-size men also.

As Joshua continues to sweep through the cities, he came to Lebanon at the foot of **Mount Hermon,** the site where the fallen angels descended. Here the Anakim giants were destroyed. The giant King Og of Bashan and others at Ashtaroth and Edrei were destroyed. However, there remained a remnant of giants in the land. Some giants where found in Gaza, Gath, and Ashdod (Joshua 11:21–22). Joshua 12 lists the kings and cities conquered by Joshua. After seven years of battles, Israel rest in the land.

Joshua and the congregation assembled at **Shiloh**, where they set up a tabernacle and placed the Ark therein (Joshua 18:1). They lived in this area for 350 years until they began to worship idols. During this time period, Israel was ruled by judges. The Lord sent Jeremiah to warn the people to repent or be judged. By this time, Samuel hears from the Lord, and the Lord revealed himself to Samuel in Shiloh (1 Samuel 3:21). Time period approximately 1057 BC.

<u>Land Covenant</u>

The enemies of Israel reject the historical fact that Israel has a right to their land. The historical records of the Abrahamic, Mosaic, and Davidic land grants are numerous. In the final chapters of Joshua 13 through 22 record the division of land between the tribes of Israel. We make mention of the land appointed to Manasseh was a portion in the area of Bashan, which is today's Golan Heights (Joshua 13:29–31). God gave Caleb the area of Hebron, which is the oldest Jewish community, which Abraham purchased in Genesis 13.

Abraham came through the promised land around 2100 BC, approximately seven hundred years before the children of Israel would possess the land. Genesis 12:7, "*And the Lord appeared unto Abram and said, unto your seed will I give this land and he built* [Bethel] *an altar unto the Lord who appeared unto him.*" God appeared to Abraham to establish a binding and immutable land agreement that could never be broken.

Abraham purchased land in Canaan from Ephron, the Hittite son of Zohar, for four hundred shekels of silver. Sarah died at 127 years old, and Abraham buried her on this land (Genesis 23:1–20). Abraham was to sacrifice Isaac upon Mount Moriah, which is the rock under the dome on the temple mount. King David purchased Mount Moriah from Ornan for six hundred shekels of gold, and later King Solomon built the first temple on that site. When Abraham died, both Isaac and Ishmael buried him in the cave at Machpelah.

Jacob and his sons lived in the land of Canaan. Jacob's wife, Rachel, died in Canaan, and she was buried in Ephratha, which is Bethlehem and the future site of the birth of Jesus.

Judges, Kings, Prophets

After about thirty years in the promised land, the period of judges began around 1375 BC and lasted over three hundred years. These people where leaders of the twelve tribes and were burdened with the Israelites falling into apostasy. Fourteen people served as judges beginning with Othniel, who was also Caleb's brother. Deborah was the only female to serve from 1209 to 1169 BC. At this time, Deborah would have to deliver them out of the hand of King Jabin of Canaan, who oppressed them for twenty years. Samson was the last judge, around 1075 to 1055 BC. Samson was from the tribe of Dan, and he married the Philistine Delilah from the land of Gaza. She would be his downfall. At the time of Samson, the Israelites had been oppressed by the Philistines for forty years (Judges 1–6).

Saul was appointed the first king between 1050–1045 BC. He was from the tribe of Benjamin. Preceding the first king, the prophet Samuel had chastised Israel for following false gods Baalim and Ashtaroth, and because of their disobedience to God, he allowed their continued oppression by the Philistines. God subdued the Philistines, and they returned land taken from Israel, from Ekron to Gath (1 Samuel 7:13–14). Saul would make his way to Samuel, who was called a seer (1 Samuel 9:19). Samuel anointed Saul (1 Samuel 10:1). The next man to serve as king was David, around 1010 BC. David's son, Solomon, 970 BC, served as king. He and the queen of Sheba, Africa, had a son. The only female queen was Esther, 479 BC.

The Divided Kingdoms of Israel

After the death of King Solomon, the nation split into two kingdoms around 930 BC, becoming the kingdom of Israel and the kingdom of Judah.

Northern kingdom of Israel composed of ten tribes—capital cities, Shechem, Tirzah, then Samaria, ruled by King Jeroboam 930 BC. The northern kingdom lasted for 208 years and was ruled by a total of nineteen kings—all who were evil in the sight of the Lord.

The southern kingdom of Judah, capital Jerusalem, represented by two tribes—Benjamin and Judah—ruled by king Rehoboam 930 BC. Total number of kings was twenty, and only eight considered righteous:

> *And it came to pass when Rehoboam had established the kingdom and had strengthened himself, he forsook the law of the Lord and all Israel with him. It came to pass in the fifth year of king Rehoboam, Shishak, king of Egypt came up against Jerusalem because they had sinned against the Lord. He came with twelve hundred chariots, thousands of horsemen and the people were without number that came with him out of Egypt, the Lubims, the Sukkims and the Ethiopians.* (2 Chronicles 12)

Shishak of Egypt took the fenced cities and came into Jerusalem. He took away the treasures from the house of the Lord, including the gold shields Solomon had made. The prophet Jeremiah proclaimed to King Rehoboam that they had forsaken the Lord, and they were given into the hand of Shishak. Israel humbled themselves, and the Lord turned back from destroying them. They would be punished to be servants of Shishak. Here is another inference that Shem's descendants would be servants to the descendants of Ham and is in contradiction with Noah's curse that Ham's descendants would serve Shem.

Archeological record of this invasion was found on a stone in Egypt, which says that Shishak's army penetrated as far north as the Sea of Galilee.

In 874 BC, Ahab became king of Israel, and at that time Israel was worshipping Baal and Ishtar. Ahab was Israel's most evil king, allowing his people to continue in idolatry (1 Kings 16:31). He married Jezebel the Phoenician (associated with Philistines, a people strong in commerce). Ahab represented false religion, and Jezebel represented corrupt government as a prelude to the future one-world government and a one-world religious system. Jezebel's father was Sidonia, king of Ethbaal, grandson of Hiram, king of Tyre.

A record of Jehu, 841 BC, commander of King Jehoram's army, his father was Jehoshaphat. Jehu was anointed king over Israel by Elisha. Jehu killed Ahab the wicked king; his wife, Jezebel; and all his children and servants. He killed Kings Joram of Israel and Ahaziah of Judah. He killed all the worshippers of Baal and destroyed its temple and images. This is mentioned because the feats of Jehu were carved on a black obelisk stone by King Shalmaneser III of Assyria. (2 Kings 9 to 10). Herein is a connection with Israel and the Assyrians.

After King Hezekiah, 700 BC, the next king would be wicked. King Manasseh, son of Hezekiah, is recorded in 2 Kings 21. He built up again the high places which Hezekiah his father had destroyed. He reared up altars for Baal and made a grove and worshipped all the host of heaven and served them (Satan and fallen angels). He set up altars in the house of the Lord. He sacrificed his son in the fire. He observed times (astrology) and used enchantments and dealt with familiar spirits and wizards. Herein the scriptures are explicit as to Manasseh's wickedness. Because of Israel's wickedness, they were taken captive by the Assyrians around 722 BC and later by the Babylonians. As we follow the time of Daniel in captivity, he chose to follow the ways of God and not to succumb to paganism.

Around 650 BC, the Babylonians captured the southern kingdom of Judah and sacked Jerusalem due to continued disobedience and worshipping false gods. The Jews were severely punished by God and taken into captivity by the Babylonian Empire 586 BC, six hundred miles from Jerusalem.

> *They provoked him to jealousy with strange gods, with abominations provoked they him to anger. They sacrificed unto devils, not to God, to gods whom they knew not, to new gods that came newly up, who your fathers feared not. Of the rock that begat thee thou art unmindful and has forgotten God that formed you.* (Deuteronomy 32:16–18)

The prophet Daniel was among the captives taken to Babylon in 586 BC. The prophet Zechariah was born in Babylon. In 538 BC, Daniel interpreted the handwriting on the wall when Belshazzar was king. After seventy years of captivity, King Cyrus of Persia issued a decree giving the Hebrew Israelites permission to return to their homeland. The profit Haggai left in 520 BC. For hundreds of years during the period of judges, kings, and captivity, God called out his prophets to warn his people. The first notable prophet would have been Samuel, around 1100 BC, followed by Elijah, 875 BC continued by Elisha after Elijah is translated. Amos, Hosea, Micah, and Isaiah began their ministries mid-750 BC. Jeremiah, Ezekiel, Daniel, Ezra, Nehemiah covers a period between 600 to 400 BC. Nehemiah gave the record of the land grant from Abraham.

> *You are the Lord the God who did choose Abram and brought him forth out of Ur of the Chaldees and gave him the name Abraham and found his heart faithful before you and made a covenant with him to give the land of the Canaanites, the Hittites, Amorites, Perizzites, Jebusites and Girgashites to give it, I say to his seed and has performed the words, for you are righteous.* (Nehemiah 9:7)

During the ministry of Ezekiel, he did prophesy 570 BC to a future time when Israel would be in conflict with its enemies in the twentieth century, and it has come to pass. Many covet the land, primarily Christendom and Islamic factions. Ezekiel 37, "*Because the enemy has said against you, Aha, even the ancient high places are ours in possession … they have made you desolate and swallowed you up on every side that you might be a possession unto the residue* [other nations] *of the heathen.*" God speaks "*against all of Idumea* [descendants of Edom] *which have appointed my land into their possession with the joy of all their heart with despiteful minds, to cast it out for a prey.*"

Sometime in the seventh millennium, God will make Israel one nation again:

> *Thus said the Lord God, I will take the children of Israel from among the heathen, wherever they be gone and will gather them on every side and bring them into their own land. I will make them one nation in the land upon the mountains of Israel and one king will be king to them all and they will be no more two nations neither will they be divided into two kingdoms anymore.* (Ezekiel 37:21)

The last of the Old Testament prophets was Malachi 430 BC, and then there was a four-hundred-year period of silence between the end of Old Testament prophets and the beginning of the New Testament.

The Regathering

The sin nature is the condition of all mankind, regardless of Jew or Gentile. But to whom much is given, much is required. Israel was chosen by God. They were to be an example to the rest of the world. Unfortunately, their disobedience levied a hefty judgment upon them. They found themselves captives in Babylon, Assyria, Persia, Egypt; and in these distant lands, they made for themselves a living, and they did prosper. Due to their ability to prosper, a remnant of Jews remained in the lands of Africa, Syria, Lebanon, Turkey, France, Russia, Germany, India, Pakistan, and the Americas.

During the Roman occupation of Jerusalem, AD 135, Emperor Hadrian decided to erase a connection with the Jews to the land by renaming the region to Syria Palaestina. After the division of the Roman Empire, an ethnically diverse population made up the Roman citizenry. Regardless of who controlled Jerusalem—such as the Templars, the Ottomans, British—there was a continual presence of Jews living in Jerusalem.

Somewhere in time, someone always attempted to scatter and kill the Jews. Russian historian Leo Tolstoy, 1828–1910, said, "What is the Jew? All the rulers of the nations of the world have disgraced, crushed, expelled, persecuted, and yet they continue to live and flourish."

After almost two thousand years of being scattered throughout the world, the Jews began returning to their homeland. The time frame has come to pass: "*In the latter years you will come into the land that is brought back from the sword and is gathered out of many people against the mountains of Israel which have been always waste but it brought forth out of the nations and they shall dwell safely all of them.*"

- The land was barren until Israel restored agriculture.
- AD 1800, Jordan/Edom was to be divided between Muslims on the west of the Jordan River and for Israel on the east. Israel agreed, Muslims rejected.
- AD 1917, the Arthur Balfour Declaration was signed partitioning land for the Jews.
- Israel became a nation in AD 1948, took back land from Arabs.
- The Jews have returned to Israel from many nations.
- Israel is in the land dwelling in some relative safety.

> *Then it will happen on that day that the Lord will again recover the second time with his hand the remnant of his people who will remain from Assyria, Egypt, Pathros, Cush, Elam, Shinar, Hamath and from the islands of the sea. And he will lift up a standard for the nations and assemble the banished ones of Israel and will gather the dispersed of Judah from the four corner of the earth.* (Isaiah 11:11–12)

God has been regathering the Jews and bringing together all of the twelve tribes in the last day. In fulfillment of scripture, they will come from the north, south, east, and west. Jews from the tribe of Manassa of the Bnei Menashe of Manipu, India, are making aliyah. The Lema Jews in Africa were DNA-tested by Orthodox Jews and have the Kohen markers of the high priests of the Levites, and their DNA genetic marker is 70 percent higher than other Jews of the diaspora.

A group of Chinese Jewish women made Aliyah in 2006 and completed their conversion. According to a report in the *Jerusalem Connection* online February 27, 2013, it is said six Chinese Jews from Kaifeng China completed the Judaic ceremony of immersion for purification before three rabbis. One man's name is Yaakov Wang. They said their ancestors settled in Kaifeng in the eighth-century during the Song Dynasty. They were Sephardic Jewish merchants from Persia, traveling along the silk route. They were accepted by the emperor and enjoyed tolerance and acceptance unlike some other regions that Jews migrated to. In AD 1163, they built a synagogue. During the Ming Dynasty, 1368 to 1644, the number of practicing Jews was around five thousand. It is recorded that during the seventeenth century, Jews had high rank in the Chinese Civil Service. Their last Rabbi died early part of ninteenth century. The synagogue was destroyed by floods in 1840s. Presently, around a thousand Jews remain in this area of China. The younger Jews want to learn more about their heritage and reclaim their Jewish roots.

> *Therefore, behold the days come said the Lord that it will no more be said, the Lord lives that brought up the children of Israel out of the land of Egypt but the Lord lives that brought up the children of Israel from the land of the north and from all the lands whither he had driven them and I will bring them again into their land that I gave unto their fathers.* (Jeremiah 16:14)

In 1769, explorer, James Bruce located around one hundred thousand Jews identified with the tribe of Dan living in Ethiopia. These people would have been descendants of King Solomon, who had many wives and children. Israel had a good relationship with Ethiopia until around 1973, under Arab pressure, Ethiopia cut its ties with Israel and outlawed Judaism by 1980. Operation Moses was established in 1984 and brought seven thousand Jews back to Israel. As of September 2013, all of the Ethiopian Jews have been brought back to Israel.

By the 1800s, Jerusalem had become a desolated region, yet thousands of Jews remained in their homeland regardless of the circumstances. Mark Twain, 1835–1910, wrote about the desolation he found in 1866 in his book, *Innocents Abroad*: "It is a blistering naked, treeless land … Palestine is a hopeless dreary heartbroken land … sits in sackcloth and ashes … it is desolate and unlovely." In 1897, Twain was quoted in *Harper's Magazine*, "The Jews represent a small part of humanity and everyone has heard of the Jew … They have made major contributions to the world of science, medicine, literature, and art."

Wherever the Jews resided, God blessed them to prosper. Success and wealth led some to become liberal and secular. For instance, Jews who lived in Germany may have believed the government was equitable toward all its citizens. When Hitler came into power, he wanted a superior Germany. Disillusioned Jews believed his hype for a better Germany and did align with Hitler's ideology, unaware they were his target for elimination.

As it was in days of old, so is it prevalent in the twenty-first century: liberalism cuts across all denominations, creating an apostate mind-set—which severs our relationship with God, be it Jew or Gentile. Because God loves his people, it is he that reaches out time and again to snatch them from the jaws of the enemy. As the prophet Amos declares once, the Jews have returned to their land, they will not be removed again, and the land will prosper.

> *Behold the days come said the Lord that the plowman will overtake the reaper and the treader of grapes him that sows seed and the mountains will drop sweet wine and all the hills will melt. And I will bring again the captivity of my people of the Israel and they will build the waste cities and inhabit them and they will plant vineyards and drink the wine thereof they will also make gardens and eat the fruit of them and I will plant them upon their land and they will no more be pulled up out of their land which I have given them, said the Lord thy God.* (Amos 9:13–15)

AD 1920, Yehoshua Hankin purchased the Jezreel Valley—which was a desolate land filled with swamps, mosquitoes, and areas of barren land. He migrated to Israel from Russia. In 1936, the Hankins began building on the northern side of the Gilboa Mountains overlooking the Jezreel Valley. He had a cordial relationship with Arabs and Bedouin people, who also lived in the area. His wife, Olga, died in 1942, and he built a tomb for his wife, which is located inside Ma'ayan Harod National Park. During the time of Judges in Israel, Gideon's army was divided at Ma'ayan Harod (Judges 7:1).

The King of Assyria placed the Israelites into bondage and put them in Halah, Habor, by the river of Gozan in the cities of the Medes 2 Kings 18:11 . The region once occupied by Persians and Medes in modern times is called Afghanistan. It was home to twenty-five thousand Jews with a synagogue since AD 632. The people are known as Pythons, also refer to themselves as children of Israel. These remnants of Jews associate themselves with the tribe of Benjamin. In keeping with Jewish tradition, they have side locks, beards, blue eyes, keep laws, circumcision, marriage canape, prayer shawls, mitvah bath, kosher, Sabbath, Yom Kippor, Mezzuah, recite the Shama, and pray toward Jerusalem.

Jonathan Bernis, *Jewish Voice Ministries*, developed a world map that spotlights the nations where Jewish people presently reside. We will summarize these areas:

- Canada, 373,000
- United States, 6,500,000
- Mexico, 49,000

- South America, 343,000
- Argentina, 184,500
- Africa, 78,000
- Spain, 12,500
- France, 492,000
- Israel, 8,000,000
- Russia, 228,000
- India, 1,500,000
- China, 1,500
- Australia 103,000
- Yemen, 90

Unknown numbers of Jews live in Iran, Turkey, Syria, Hungary, Romania, Ukraine, Turkmenistan, Myanmar, Yemen, and other regions.

Identification within the twelve lost tribes are the following:

- Issachar and Naphtali regions of Uzbekistan, India, Afghanistan, China.
- Ephraim, Reuben, Gad, Simeon, Benjamin regions of Afghanistan.
- Manasseh regions of Nepal, Manipur, India.
- Asher region of Tunisia.
- Dan region of Ethiopia. Beta Avraham and Beta Israel are associated within the region of Ethiopia.
- Levi region of Zimbabwe and Ethiopia consist of Lemba and Gefat tribes.

Other groups associated with Israel are the following:

- Children of Israel, Yibir tribe (means "Hebrew") region of Hargeisa, Somaliland.
- Jews from region of Madagascar, one hundred, entered into the covenant of Abraham, May 2016. In 1 Kings 9:28, King Solomon makes reference to importing items from Ophir, which is associated with Madagascar.
- Calling themselves the Jewish Kingdom of West Africa, King Francois Ayi of the Republic of Togo asked Israel to recognize them as a lost tribe, stating his ancestors came from Israel two thousand years ago via Egypt to Morocco.

Centuries of Historical Events

AD 1492 is a significant date. The Jews that settled in Spain began to be persecuted and killed under the Spanish inquisition. The king and Queen Isabella gave them fourteen days to leave Spain or convert to Catholicism. The Jews' wealth was taken by the ruling government. What they managed to keep, they hoped to find a new homeland. During this period, there were four blood moons.

Oliver Crumwell in the 1700s allowed Jews to return to England. AD 1798 Joseph Levi converted to Christianity. Other Jews converted: Joseph Wolff, Ridley Haim Herschell, Philip Hersfeld, Michael Solomon, Alexander. Alexander became the first Anglican bishop in England. He began a Zionist movement called the London Society for the Promotion of Christianity amongst the Jews.

Entering the nineteenth century, Jerusalem was still called Palestine as it had been named by the Romans, and this equated to the Jewish presence in the region.

AD 1809 began a Christian movement to adopt the Jews as they realized these are the chosen people. By 1835, the movement had gained momentum. Charles Simeon said God intends to glorify his people, and the Restoration of Israel movement grew. Others involved were William Wilburforce, Duke of Devonshire, Duke of Kent, and seven earls.

AD 1841, came the archbishop of Cantebury, and the Episcopalians supported Zionism—also Charlotte Elizabeth; Marian Evan, aka George Elliott; Anthony Ashley Cooper, president of London Jewish Society for three decades.

AD 1881, thirty thousand Jews left Russia because of persecution and returned to Palestine. AD 1904, thirty-two thousand Jews left Russia for Palestine.

AD 1897, concerned people came together in Switzerland and formed the First Zionist Congress to work toward a homeland for the Jews in Palestine.

AD 1917 Balfour Declaration

World War I was going on when Dr. Chaim Weizman discovered acetone used in manufacture of explosives, which allowed Britain's war effort to advance. They being grateful, British Foreign Secretary Arthur Balfour issued a declaration written to Walter Rothschild, leader of British Jewish community, in support of a homeland for the Jewish people and their right to Palestine.

This was later reaffirmed by the League of Nations at the San Remo Conference, Italy. The League of Nations became the United Nations, who voted to accept Israel as a United Nations member nation.

League of Nations established State of Israel; they divided the land into two states: west of Jordan River for Jews and east of Jordan River called trans-Jordon for those identifying themselves Arabs and being followers of Islam. Arabs living in this region objected to Jews returning to their homeland and began to attack the Jews.

AD 1918 Gen. Edmund Allenby under British rule conquers Palestine from the Ottomans of Turkey. At that time, Arabs outnumbered the Jews. Britain's Mark Sykes and

France's Charles Picot agreed to divide the Ottoman territory. Sykes took Palestine, and Picot took Syria, Golan Heights, which belonged to the tribe of Manasseh (Elaine Durbach, January 8, 2014, *New Jersey Jewish News*, quotes).

"Dr. Mordechai Kedar regarding Palestinians claim to Jerusalem is based on false Arab claims. Kedar is an expert on Islamic and Arab culture in a report to *New Jersey Jewish News* and to Al-Jazeera TV that Palestinians' insistence on having Eastern Jerusalem as their capital has absolutely no historic justification. Jerusalem was never, not even for one day in history the capital of any Arab or Islamic entity. No king, caliph, emir or sultan governed from Jerusalem. So what do they base their claim to Jerusalem? Kedar has addressed the Knesset and US Congress."

The Arabs and Jews are kinfolks. January 3, 1919, an agreement was made between the Arab kingdom of Hodjaz. Royal Highness the Emir Faisal ibn Hussein bin Ali al-hashemi, who was once king of Syria in 1920 and later king of Iraq, member of Hashemite Dynasty, agreed with Dr. Chaim Weizmann, Zionist Organization, and first president of Israel for unification and recognition of the racial kinship and ancient bonds that existed between Arabs and Jews. Faisal's father, the Shafif of Mecca and king of Hodjas, endorsed Balfour Treaty then reneged under pressure. The Palestinians may come through the line of Esau, son of Isaac, son of Abraham, a follower of Yahweh.

AD 1922, Winston Churchill throws Israel under the bus. Britain, caved into the Arabs, demands against the Jews. He declined to rescind the Balfour Declaration, but to appease the Arabs, he took back land allotted to the Jews. The Arabs were reallotted 76 percent of land east of the Jordan River, and 24 percent of land west of Jordan River to Mediterranean Sea was for the Jews. The Arabs continued to attack the Jews.

AD 1924, seventy-eight thousand Jews from Poland made Aliyah to Palestine.

AD 1930, Britain sets limits on number of Jewish immigrants to once again appease the violent Arabs who claimed Jews were taking their jobs. The opposite is true. Wherever the Jews live, they prosper and benefit non-Jews living with them. Britain was a world power, having colonized other people's land. After turning their back on Israel, territories held by Britain were lost, and Britain diminished in power.

AD 1933, over 230,000 Jews fled German persecution and returned to Palestine.

AD 1937, the Peel Commission, in an effort to end the Arab violence, Lord Robert Peel pushed for a two-state solution, which was rejected by both Jews and Arabs.

AD 1939, World War II, Czechoslovakia was one of the first countries Hitler and the Nazis took over at the beginning of World War II and one of the first places Jews were deported to the death camps. Approximately 250,000 Jews lived there at that time, and thousands were murdered during the Holocaust. Mid-1900s Czechoslovakia was under communism and intolerance of Jews. Today the Czech Republic is a strong friend to Israel.

The Jews begin going through the Holocaust and need a safe place to live. Britain decided to only allow ten thousand Jews a year to return to their land. The Jews were being attacked in Palestine and slaughtered by the Nazis. The United Nations did not rescind the Balfour Declaration but took away Judea and Samaria. With their head in the lion's mouth, the Jews settled for less land and immigration limits. The United States joined with others to support the establishment of a Jewish state but not without a great deal of infighting in the Harry Truman administration. Surprisingly, not all American Jews were supportive of a Jewish state or the right of return. Some American rabbis protested Zionist efforts by forming the American Council for Judaism. Within a few years, the council had approximately fourteen thousand members. Once again, Jews in America had gotten complacent and prosperous in the movie industry, media, business, and medical arena and considered a Jewish state a threat to their comfortable lifestyles.

During the growth of Nazism, ninety-five thousand Jews left Europe between 1941–1948. In 1941, Hitler began his campaign against the Jews living in Germany. He confiscated their wealth and rounded them up for slaughter. Even after Allied forces began bombing Germany, they did not bomb the train tracks that led to the gas chambers. Hitler killed the Jews for as long as he was able. This was a God-ordained judgment against the Jews and served as a catalyst to cause the Jews to return to their homeland. Israel had come through the Holocaust suffering the loss of six million people. Hitler was a type of Antichrist. He killed approximately ten million people. We contemplate why God would allow such a holocaust and offer this thought. This tragedy in history was a precursor for the great devastation that is coming upon the earth during the reign of the final Antichrist. Certainly, history repeats itself, and is God warning our future generation to repent and follow Jesus so we can avoid the wrath to come?

May 14, 1948, is a milestone in Israel's history. Isaiah 66:8, "*Who has heard such a thing? Who has seen such a thing? Shall the earth be made to bring forth in one day? Or shall a nation be born at once …*"

The United Nations voted for Israel's statehood under Resolution 181 and 213. This passed with thirty-three yeas, thirteen nays, and ten abstains. Britain abstained. Mr. David Ben Gurion, 1886–1973, first prime minister of Israel, went into the art museum in Tel Aviv to announce to the waiting crowd that Israel had been granted statehood approved by the United States and British prime minister Winston Churchill. Ben Gurion said, "In order to be a realist, you must believe in miracles."

The following day, the Muslims invaded Israel. With a poor army and with God on their side, Israel pushed the invaders back to Jordan West Bank. Since no "so-called" Palestinian refugee people existed, Israel had the right to reclaim land. The CIA was surprised Israel could win with such a small army. There were four blood moons observed from 1948 to 1950.

The Invented People

Often, people are confused by the term *Philistines* and believe they are associated with Palestinians who may be associated with the Phoenicians. We know from history, the Philistines migrated to the land called Canaan and were enemies of Israel. There is no connection between these two groups of people. The term *Syria Palaestina* replaced the name Jerusalem in the first century AD during the Roman occupation of Jerusalem. At that time, Islam did not exist. People referred to themselves as Arabs, Persians, Syrians, Jordanians, Egyptians, etc. These groups were not interested in establishing a Palestinian state, but their constant goal was the destruction of the Jews. People who call themselves Palestinians would become synonymous with the region mislabeled Palestine. The term became prominent after Yasser Arafat formed the Palestinian Liberation Organization around 1964. Arafat and his people occupied the region called Lebanon. Syrian dictator Hafez Al Assad stated to Yasser Arafat, "Never forget this one point, there is no such thing as a Palestinian people, there is no Palestinian entity. Palestine is part of Syria." Saudi Arabia representative at the United Nations in 1956 stated, "It is common knowledge that Palestine is nothing but southern Syria". Arafat developed a theme of Israeli occupation and Palestinian refugees. The region of Jordan, the West Bank, had been set aside under the British Mandate for Arabs. Currently, 80 percent of "Palestinians" live in Jordan.

Muslim historian Awni Abdul Hadi stated before the Peel Commission 1937, "There is no such country as Palestine, it is a term the Zionist invented." **Our comment**—Hadi is incorrect since history tells us the term *Palestine* was given by the Romans in the first century.

Prime Minister of Israel Golda Meir, June 15, 1969, stated, "There is no such thing as the Palestinian people. It is not as if Israelis came and threw them out and took their country, they didn't exist." Meir's statement is confirmed by Christian Broadcasting Network, Jordan Robertson, in a documentary on the roots of the so-called Palestinians, which clears up a great deal of misinformation and ignorance.

The "Palestinians" were a regional group of Arabs/Islamists having no cultural or national distinctive traits separating them from Syrians, Lebanese, and Jordanians. They came into the land of Israel in the late nineteenth century. Palestinian nationalism is a reinvented version of Arab nationalism, and it is difficult to distinguish between Islam and nationalism. Arab assaults from 1948 to 1973 had nothing to do with Palestinians. Jerusalem is not mentioned in the Koran.

The PLO is now led by Mahmoud Abbas cofounder of Arafat's Fatah Party. He received training from the KGB. He continues to push for a two-state arrangement, with him taking over Jerusalem. In a highly irregular move, the biased voting majority of the United Nations allowed the Palestinians who are not indigenous to Israel, had no functioning economy, no legal system, many are terrorists, teach hatred, and have no formally elected president were allowed United Nations recognition. After demonizing Israel, endless claims for a divided Jerusalem and recognition as a state came before the United Nations once again to apply for statehood. Statehood was denied, but eventually they were granted observer status in 2014. Again in 2015, Abbas submitted to the United Nations' request for statehood, which was denied.

AD 1967 Marks the Miracle of the Six-Day War

Hebron, eighty thousand Muslims lived there in 1967, and the Jews were willing to coexist with them. Egypt controlled Gaza; Syria controlled Golan Heights; Jordan controlled West Bank; they attacked Israel. In retaliation, Israel took back Gaza, along with the Sinai Peninsula, to Suez Canal, West Bank, Golan Height—which is Judea and Samaria. The City of Jerusalem and the temple mount were back in Jewish hands after 1,897 years. The Muslims surrendered to Rabbi Shlomo Goren, Israel Defense Force. In victory, Rabbi Shlomo Goren blew a shofar at the Western wall and proclaimed, "We have taken the city of God, we are entering the Messianic era for the Jewish people."

1973 Yom Kippur War

While Israel celebrated a holy day, Muslims attacked. Israel turned them back and could have taken Cairo and Damascus. God has plans for both those regions in the near future.

United Nations got involved, stopped Israel, and required both sides to sign a cease-fire, not a peace accord or not to distinguish borders.

Israel in the Twenty-First Century

A Land of Milk and Honey, Exodus 3:8

Modern-day Israel is home to people from all over the world, especially those making aliyah. The population reported in 2016 is 8.5 million. The chosen people are a blessing to many throughout the world. Nations have benefited from Israeli technology. Israel creates joint ventures in Palestinians regions; one such project was teaching them the science of dairy production.

Israel has installed their drip water irrigation system in drought-stricken regions in nations, reversing the results and allowing farmers to raise crops.

The Ariel University is operated in the West Bank, Samaria, by Jews. The fifteen thousand students who attend the university are from Islamic, Arabic, Jewish backgrounds.

The Soda Stream plant is located in the West Bank. It hires a thousand employees, of which 50 percent are Palestinians. All employees, Jews from Iran, Druze from Galilee, Israelis, and Palestinians work together for good pay in a safe work environment. Muslims are allowed to pray on-site. CEO Daniel Birnbaum says he is building bridges for peaceful relationships (*Israel Now News*, July 11, 2015). Because of pressure from the BDS movement, Soda Stream company withdrew from the region, and hundreds of Palestinians and others lost their jobs.

It was reported, June 16, 2015, gold was discovered in the mountain region of Eilat. Rabbi Yehuda Glick and Yehoshua Friedman have received permits from the government to explore beginning January 2015 to December 2016 for the gold reserves estimated at one billion dollars.

Israel is blessed and highly favored. Israel is self-sufficient. They do export produce and flowers. The nation is rich in oil and gas reserves. Christian organizations and individuals have blessed Israel for years, such as *Christians United for Israel* having donated millions to Israel. We were delighted to come across a list of prominent Jewish billionaires who bless Israel: Haim Saba raised $31 million for Friends of Israel Defense Forces from various celebrity guest at his November 12, 2015, fund-raiser. Some notable attendees were Simon Cowel, Mark Wahlberg, Jason Alexander, Antonio Banderas, Live Schreiber, Jason Segel, Steve Tisch. Others who honor Israel are the following:

Michael Bloomberg, New York mayor
Larry Ellison, Oracle, computer software
Sheldon Adelson, Casino's
Michael Dell, Dell Computers
Leslie Wexner, Victoria Secrets
David Green, (Christian) Hobby Lobby
Sam Zell, Equity Group Investments
Robert Kraft, owner of Patriots
Ira Renner, investments
Donald Trump (Christian), real estate; daughter Ivanka converted to Judaism
Isaac Perlmutter, CEO Marvel
Daniel Gilbert, owner, Cleveland Cavaliers and Quiken Loans
Lynn Schusterman, Oil and Gas
Leon G. Cooperman, investments
Ronald Lauder, Estee Lauder Cosmetics
Bernard Marcus, Home Depot
Henry Samueli, Broadcom semiconductors

Daniel Abraham, Slim Fast
Paul Singer, Investments

A Cup of Trembling

> *Behold I will make Jerusalem a cup of trembling unto all the people round about, when they shall be in the siege both against Judah and against Jerusalem. And in that day, said the Lord, I will make Jerusalem a burdensome stone for all people; all that burden themselves with it shall be cut in pieces, though all the people of the earth be gathered against it.* (Zechariah 12:3)

As the only democratic nation in the Middle East, Israel tolerates all religious practices. Jews, Christians, and Muslims coexist. Israel does allow abortion but are not as enthusiastic about it as America. They also tolerate homosexuality. Approximately one quarter of Israel's population are secular. Recent reports suggest secular technological companies in Israel may be moving toward the implantation of RFID chips in its citizens. This technology will be seen initially in smart cards, iPhones, national ID cards, passports (reference, RFID Journal).

As the world moves closer to the end of days, Israel will again come under severe attack from their enemies. Eventually, one of the terrorist nations will launch a nuclear attack. Israel will be isolated and surrounded by their enemies. There will be great devastation, and many will run to a place of safety that has been provided by God. Perhaps 50 percent of the Jewish population are looking for Messiah to come and save them. There is a small community of Christian Jews who know that Yeshua is Messiah, and they will be caught up being saved from the day of wrath.

Various treaties and agreements did not bring peace. Israel desires to live safely in the land at all costs. They gave up portions of the land to Muslims in exchange for peace. AD 2005, Israel pulled out of Gaza, and Hamas took over. Gaza is now a haven for Hamas terrorists. It has continued to target Israel with missiles up to the present day. AD 2014, Hamas leader Khaled Mashaal claims all of the land of Israel belongs to him. AD 2015, Hamas recently attacked Israel, and Israel's response called Pillar of Cloud hit back fast and hard. Over a thousand die in Gaza and less than fifty in Israel. United Nations threatens Israel with war crimes.

From 2000 to the present, Muslims launched missiles from Lebanon west bank. Israel killed 5,800 militants before they would stop their attack, and 1,053 Jews died. Hezbollah terrorists have a stronghold in Lebanon. Israel built a buffer zone for security. The Christians in Lebanon fought with Israel against the terrorists. Hezbollah was being funded and equipped by Iran and Syria. President Abbas continues to call for Palestinians terrorism against Israel. Abbas declares no future peace treaty with Israel.

The United Nations told Israel to withdraw and Hezbollah to disarm. Israel withdrew; Hezbollah did not disarm but continued to grow. They now have forty thousand rockets, which they can use against northern Israel.

The Arab, Persian, and other Islamic representative membership in the United Nations have increased to almost the majority vote. Their strategy is to use political propaganda and blatant lies against Israel to influence anti-Semitism in the world. "Palestinian" leader Abbas has gotten the United Nations to recognize them as nonmembers as they push for Palestinian statehood. Dividing the Holy Land with the Gentiles again will be devastating for Israel.

AD 2009, US pressures Israel to divide the land for a two-state solution. Obama is anti-Israel, and this will cause judgment to come upon America. United States will cease to be a world empire, as did Britain. AD 2013, Secretary of State John Kerry continues to pressure Israel to accept an agreement with the Palestinians. United States pushes to allow Palestinians to have Jerusalem as their capital and swap territory, which would create Palestinian states in Judea, Samaria, Lebanon, and Gaza. No Jews would be allowed in Palestinian areas. Kerry had influenced Europeans to boycott Israel. The United Nations' UNRWA, Iran, and the United States fund terror cells found in Gaza, Syria, and Lebanon.

Missiles from Syria land in Golan Heights. AD 2015, Russia setting up military base in Syria, with support of Iran and China.

Kerry has been relentless in pushing for an agreement with Iran and its nuclear program against the concerns of Israel. Iran has consistently threatened they will destroy Israel. AD 2015, we are pleased to report that after meeting with Iran's foreign minister Mohammad Javad Zarif, Kerry broke his leg while riding his bike. July 2015, an agreement was made between Britain, Russia, China, Germany, United States, to allow Iran to continue working toward nuclear devices. Israel was not allowed participation in these negotiations.

The United States and few European nations are strong, arming Israel not to build homes in their territory in Jerusalem. November 2014, clashes are increasing on and around the temple mount. Islamic militants have become increasingly hostile toward Jews, praying on the temple mount, including the western wall. Islamic terrorists are using vehicles to run into Israel citizens, causing death and injury. Abbas called for Muslims in Israel to take knives, guns, vehicles, and attack Jews.

Prime Minister of Israel was invited by members of the US Congress to address the assembly, 2015. The Obama administration protested the PM's visit, declaring it was political; yet on too many occasions, Obama used any public gathering to campaign for the Democratic party. Obama is anti-Semitic and would like to displace Netanyahu with another who is more amenable to dividing Israel. Obama and his administration and about thirty congressmen refused to attend. News coverage of the event showed a full house and enthusiasm for Israel.

March 2015, Benjamin Netanyahu successfully was reelected for another four years as prime minister. Obama had sent staff to Israel to derail Netanyahu's campaign. During this time in Israel, it is important to show a cohesive government. Netanyahu again declares his position that Jerusalem will not be divided.

In the Hearing of the Rabbis

Rabbi Yitzhak Kaduri

Once two become one, all Israel may be saved and is presently being fulfilled. Jew and Gentile in Yeshua become one new man. As God's plan for the restoration of Israel moves forward, there is no doubt that the beginning of that time has begun. The scales of blindness are falling from their eyes, and many Jews recognize Yeshua as their Messiah. One specific example is that of Rabbi Yitzhak Kaduri who was born in Iraq in the late 1800s. His family migrated to Israel at the turn of the twentieth century. He died in 2006 and may have been around 108 years old. He lived his life as an Orthodox Jew well versed in Judaism and kabbalah. He had a great desire to know Messiah. During his time in Israel, he lived through World War I and II and witnessed the rebirth of the nation of Israel. Before his death, he had a visitation from Messiah. His son David said that after that experience, all he talked about was Messiah. Since Kaduri was well known in Jewish circles, many Orthodox Jews were astonished to hear him reveal who is Messiah. He wrote Messiah's name on paper and sealed it in an envelope with instructions to open one year after his death. In 2007, the contents were revealed to the media, and the message said, "Yehoshua/Yeshua." In the note, it also said that when former Prime Minister of Israel, Ariel Sharon, passes, Jesus told Kaduri that his coming would be very soon and he would appear to Israel. Sharon died January 11, 2014.

Pastor Carl Gallups heard of Kaduri and his message. Gallups wrote a book, *The Rabbi Who Found Messiah*, and it became a great evangelical tool to the Jews. The book features a picture of the famous Kaduri on its front cover. Gallups tells us many Orthodox Jews knew Rabbi Kaduri, and when his message was revealed that Yeshua is Messiah, they attempted to discredit the statement and shut down the media. God will have his glory. Hundreds of the book and movie were given away in Israel. Kaduri's students are on record, stating they are born-again Christians. Gallups gives a testimony of one Israeli man named Zev Porat, who accepted Yeshua as savior while surfing a Christian website. He became an evangelist to the Jews. He knew of Kaduri and prayed for God to provide material on Kaduri. There was a knock at the door, and a man from the United States was there with a box of the books and movie about Kaduri. The man said, "God says you need this stuff." Zev later reported that there was a Kaduri revival in Israel.

The nation of Israel on a whole has not and will not accept Yeshua until he returns at the end of the tribulation. At that time, every eye will see him and every knee will bow. They will look upon his pierced hands and feet, and they will mourn for him. Israel will repent and be saved (Romans 11:25).

Israel's history is far from complete. According to scripture, Israel has a time coming that is unlike any time in the history of mankind. Presently, Israel is surrounded by Islamic nations that threaten her very existence. We watch for the unfolding of prophecies in Psalm 83, Isaiah 19, and Ezekiel 38. Our chapter 19 discusses the end-time events surrounding Israel and leading up to the tribulation period.

Rabbi Amran Vaknin, June 12, 2015, received a message from the Prophet Elijah. He and sixty Jewish men and women were gathered praying for Israel at the cave of Elijah. He fell out in the Spirit and, while in the Spirit, received a decree from heaven from Elijah. "War will start in the south of Israel, move to the north and continue inside of Israel. Thousands will die" (*Breaking News Israel*, June 12, 2015, by R. Adler).

Rabbi Matityahu Glazerson, June 17, 2015, researcher of Bible codes said he found a message that ISIS will be destroyed between 2015–2016 by Mashiach Ben Yosef. Words found around the letters were *Daesh for ISIS, Keitz, end of days, Mashiach* for "rise up," *Ben Yishai* for "son of Jesse," *Ben David* for "son of David," and *Mashiach Ben Yosef*, "Messiah, son of Joseph."

He believes the beginning of the new Shemita year, 5776 or September 2015, is associated with the arrival of Messiah and ties into Daniel 12:4 prophecy: "*until the time of the end*," meaning now and the arrival of Messiah, son of David (*Breaking News Israel*, June 17, 2015).

R. Adler., October 2015, Russia, Iran, Turkey, and United States began military strikes against ISIS. Nearing the end of 2016, ISIS remains a global threat.

Rabbi Glazerson announced a discovery found in the Torah codes in Deuteronomy, September 15, 2016, regarding the health of Hillary Clinton. Sick ... Hillary Clinton ... Mainstream media reported Clinton had pneumonia. Glazeron also said torah codes predicted a Trump victory, (Sky Watch TV).

Rabbi Jonathan Cahn has opened the eyes of millions with his book on the *Harbingers.*

Rabbi Jonathan Bernis for over thirty years has reached out to the lost tribes of Israel with medical help and the Gospel.

These predictions coming from various sources line up with Malachi 4, wherein God warns Israel of coming judgment ... "*The Sun of Righteousness arise with healing in his wings ... You will tread down the wicked under the sole so your feet in the day and I will do this said the Lord of hosts ... Behold I will send you Elijah the prophet before the coming of the great and dreadful day of the Lord, and he will turn the heart of the fathers to the children ...*" Elijah is one of two witnesses that will proclaim the Day of the Lord at the beginning of the tribulation period.

An eight-hundred-year-old Jewish commentary called Yalkut Shimoni speaks to the threat of Iran. "Paras will be the dread of humanity. The world leaders will be frustrated in their futile efforts to save what they can but to no avail. The people of Yisrael will also be petrified by the impending danger and Hashem will say to us, Why are you afraid? All of this I have done in order to bring you the awaited redemption and this redemption will not be like the redemption from Egypt which was followed by suffering. The redemption will be absolute, followed by peace."

Israel's future glory is predicted in Isaiah 60:1–22:

> *Arise, shine for they light is come and the glory of the lord is risen upon these. For behold, the darkness shall cover the earth and gross darkness of the people but the Lord shall arise upon these and his glory shall be seen upon thee. And the Gentiles shall come to your light and kings to the brightness of your rising. Lift up your eyes round about and see, all they gather themselves together, they come to you; your sons shall come from far and your daughters will be nursed at your side. Then you will see and flow together and your heart will fear and be enlarged because of the abundance of the sea will be converted unto you, the forces of the Gentiles will come unto you. The multitude of camels will cover you … they will bring gold and incense and they will show forth the praises of the Lord … They shall come up with acceptance on mine altar and I will glorify the house of my glory. Who are these that fly as a cloud and as the doves to their windows? Surely the isles shall wait for me and ships of Tarshish first to bring your sons from far, their silver and gold with them unto the name of the Lord thy God, and to the Holy One of Israel because he has glorified you.*
>
> *In my wrath I smote you but in my favor have I had mercy on you. Your gates will be open continually, they will not be shut day or night … for the nation and kingdom that will not serve you will perish, yes those nations will be utterly wasted. The glory of Lebanon will come unto you, the fir and pine tree together will beautify the place of my sanctuary and I will make the place of my feet glorious. The sons that afflicted you will come bending and they that despised you will bow themselves down at the soles of your feet and they will call you the City of the Lord, the Zion of the Holy One of Israel. Whereas you have been forsaken and hated so that no man went through you, I will make you an eternal excellency, a joy of many generations. You will take the milk of the Gentile*

kingdoms and you will know that I the Lord am your Savior and your Redeemer, the mighty One of Jacob. For brass I will bring gold, for iron I will bring silver, for wood brass, for stones iron and I will also make your officers peace and your extractors righteousness. Violence will no more be heard in your land, wasting or destruction within your borders but you will call your walls Salvation and your gates Praise. The sun will be no more your light by day or for brightness of the moon but the Lord will be unto you an everlasting light and your God your glory … The days of your mourning will be ended. Your people will be righteous and they will inherit the land forever, the branch of my planting, the work of my hands, that I may be glorified. A little one shall become a thousand and a small one a strong nation, I the Lord will hasten it in his time.

God has wonderful plans for Israel. Following, we point out some of these blessings:

- The glorious light of Messiah Yeshua will remove the darkness/evil.
- The Gentile nations will see the light and come to Jerusalem.
- Israel will be astonished to see them coming from afar, sons and daughters.
- They will come in ships and airplanes and bring wealth.
- Jerusalem will be an open city day and night.
- Nations that refuse to serve Israel will perish.
- Messiah Yeshua will rule from Jerusalem, and his sanctuary will be elaborate.
- All who despised and hated Israel will bow before them in the City of the Lord, Mount Zion.
- Jesus will make Israel excellent and a joy forever.
- The days of their mourning will end and no more violence in the land.
- Israel will be righteous and will inherit the land.

SOLOMON'S TEMPLE
960–586 B.C.
Solomon's Temple was a beautiful sight. It took over seven years to build and was a magnificent building containing gold, silver, bronze, and cedar. This house for God was without equal. The description is found in 2 Chronicles 2–4.

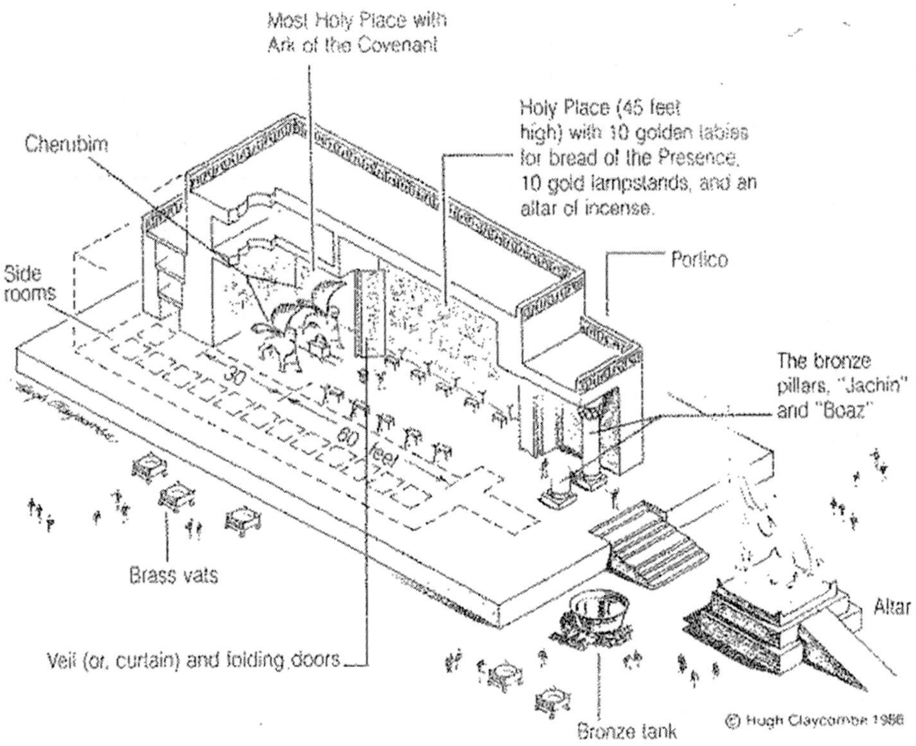

FURNISHINGS

Cherubim: represented heavenly beings, symbolized God's presence and holiness (gold-plated, 15 feet wide)

Ark of the Covenant: contained the Law written on two tablets, symbolized God's presence with Israel (wood overlaid with gold)

Veil: separated the Holy Place from the Most Holy Place (fine linen of red and blue, embroidered with depictions of angels)

Folding doors: between Holy Place and Most Holy Place (wood overlaid with gold)

Golden tables (wood overlaid with gold), *golden lampstands* (with seven lamps on each stand), and *altar of incense* (wood overlaid with gold): instruments for priestly functions in the Holy Place

Bronze pillars: named Jachin (meaning "sustainer") and Boaz (meaning "strength")—taken together they could mean "God provides the strength"

Altar: for burning of sacrifices (bronze)

Exhibit: The Tabernacle

Temples

The first archetype of a temple was the tabernacle constructed in the Sinai by Moses under the direction of Yahweh. He did all that God required for this edifice. Its primary purpose was to house the Ark of the Covenant where God's glory would be centralized. Its secondary function was for the high priest offering of sacrificed animal blood for the atonement of sin once a year, and its general purpose was for prayers, feasts, and ceremonies. From the time Israel entered the promised land, a period of over four hundred years would transpire before Israel would build a permanent temple in the promised land.

Both the tabernacle in the wilderness and the first temple in Jerusalem were constructed from plans provided by Yahweh. The sanctuary would consists of three parts. Holy of Holies, on the west containing the Ark, then the Holy Place containing the Altar of Incense, the Table of Shewbread, the seven branched Menorah, and the court on the east containing the sacrificial altar. The outer court for the people is not part of the sanctuary.

Solomon's Temple

King David purchased the land, including the region of the temple mount. God gave King David architect plans for the building of the Temple around 966–959 BC. The land tract was approximately thirty-two acres, and the location is Jerusalem, the site of Mount Moriah, the place where Abraham was to sacrifice Isaac. King Solomon built the temple and placed the Ark of the Covenant in the temple. He prayed for the glory of the Lord to fill the temple, and God's presence was manifested. For four hundred years, Israel enjoyed the benefits of a temple.

Ark of the Covenant

In 586 BC, Babylon attacked and destroyed the temple, taking many Israelites into captivity for seventy years. They also took the temple treasures. What happened to the Ark? Speculation continues to shroud the location of the Ark. According to Apocrypha writings, 2 Maccabee 2:4 Jeremiah, the prophet hid the Ark and other temple artifacts in a cave at the base of Mount Nebo—a mountain range in Jordan where Moses saw the promised land. He closed the entrance, and it was unseen. "It shall remain unknown until God regathers his people and the glory of God shall appear as the cloud …"

Some claim that the Ark is buried under the temple mount. The Knight Templar's headquarters was on the temple mount during the crusades, and they may have discovered its treasures. During British control of Palestine, 1884, archeological exploration under the temple said some temple treasures were seen there during excavations.

Ethiopians said the Ark was in Axum, Egypt, bought there by King Solomon and Queen of Sheba's son, Prince Menelik I. It was said that the original Ark was taken to Ethiopia and a decoy left in its place. Solomon knew dissention was coming and that the kingdom would be divided between Judah and Israel. 1 King 11:9, Solomon knew God would be taking the kingdom from him because of his sin with Gentile wives and worshipping pagan gods. His heart no longer was turned to Yahweh.

Second Temple

Cyrus issued an edict permitting the rebuilding of the temple, encouraging the exiled Jews to return to their homeland. History refers to this as the second temple, but it is the restoration of the first temple. It began around 530 BC by Zerubbabel and completed by 516 BC. There would be no Ark placed in the Holy of Holies, just a stone slab where the high priest would place the censer. Some refer to it as Zerubbabel's temple. It would be a place of contention up to AD 70 and beyond.

In 168 BC, Antiochus IV Epiphanes, a Greek, desecrated the temple by placing a statue of Zeus there. This caused the Maccabee revolt, which did purify and rededicate the temple.

Judas Maccabee and his brothers battled Antiochus to restore temple worship and retake Jerusalem.

In 63 BC, Pompeii ended Greek rule and captured Jerusalem, making way for the growth of the Roman Empire. Pompeii desecrated the temple by entering into the Holy of Holies.

Under King Herod's rule around 47 BC, he enlarged the temple and built walls around the city. Before the turn of the century, King Herod restored the temple at great expense. Herod also decided to have the Roman government appoint the high priest as long as they were loyal to Rome and later paid taxes. Herod died between 2–1 BC.

Herein the authority of the Pharisees increased, and on behalf of the Jews, they did compromise in order to continue in their temple practices. Also by the time Jesus came on the scene, Jews had become tax collectors, such as Matthew.

A story in the Jerusalem Talmud speaks about the middle lamp (Jesus) on the Menorah in Herod's temple was extinguished around the time of the Crucifixion, and up to the time of the destruction of the temple in 70 AD, the middle lamp could not be relit.

Jesus had been crucified and risen when the Roman emperor Caligula came to Jerusalem around AD 40. He had made arrangements to have an image of himself placed in the temple. This led to an uprising of the Jews against Rome, which ended with Titus destroying the temple in AD 70. The temple had survived for over five hundred years between Zerubbabel and AD 70.

When the Romans under General Titus Vespasian were ordered to sack and burn the Temple, there was not one stone left upon another as Jesus predicted. The vessels and artifacts were taken by the Romans. The Arch of Titus depicts Romans carrying the menorah and parading Jewish captives. The destruction of the temple would be the sign of increased persecution of the Jews by the Romans in Palestine. Historical records estimate the slaughter of one million Jews. The Jews had to escape into other nations for survival. Jews resettled in Rome during a time that Christians were being persecuted by Emperor Nero. As time progressed, Jews were absorbed into the Roman Empire and given the right to become citizens. Many still wonder what happened to the temple treasures taken by Rome. The Roman Empire adopted Christianity and referred to themselves as the Holy Roman Church, morphing into a formidable religious organization. Eventually, the temple treasures could have been retained by the Vatican.

New Testament writers began to understand that the law was a foreshadow of things to come, and the offering of yearly sacrifices was unable to perfect a person. Each year the ceremony for atonement brought to remembrance sin. It was not possible for the blood of animals to take away sins. God had no pleasure in burnt offerings. Jesus said he came not to take away the law but to fulfill it.

> *But this man, after he had offered one sacrifice for sins for ever sat down on the right hand of God, from henceforth expecting till his enemies be made his footstool … the Holy Ghost also is witness to us for after that he had said before, this is the covenant that I will make with them after those days … I will put my laws into their hearts and in their minds will I write them and their sins and iniquities will I remember no more, now where remission of these is there is no more offering for sin.* (Hebrews 10:12–17)

Jesus became that Passover Lamb, the perfect sacrifice for the redemption of all mankind. In him all things were complete and finished. The atonement for sin by Jesus would be the acceptable sacrifice to God once and for all, and the temple had to go. The temple had become the center of religiosity, and within this framework, they rejected their Messiah. Once the temple was destroyed, the sacrificial practices were finished.

The Jordanian Waqf over the temple mount prohibits any archeological digs, but digs do occur. They have sealed the east side gates to the temple and have a Muslim cemetery located outside of the gates to prevent Messiah from coming through the gates at the end of the tribulation period. His feet will touch the Mount of Olives, and from there, Yeshua will come through that eastern gate.

> *Son of man, the place of my throne and the place of the soles of my feel, where I will dwell in the midst of the children of Israel forever and my holy name, shall the house of Israel no more defile ...* (Ezekiel 43:7)

Some of the rubble from the temple walls remain to this day. The western side of the temple also referred to as the wailing wall is most holy to modern-day Israel, who daily worship God at this site.

This location is under increasing assault from Islamic sects and Christian sympathizers who wish to claim the temple mount for themselves. A group called the Islamic-Christian Commission is intent on doing away with Israel history specific to the region in order to strengthen the Palestinians' claim that Israel is the occupier. Fabrication, lies, and changing historical truth has helped Palestinians to get a seat in international agencies like UNESCO and to be heard at the United Nations. They also draw sympathy from the ignorance of those in the United States and around the world who excite anti-Israel sentiments in protests and other actions.

Third Temple

This coming temple will not be acceptable unto God. God will allow it to be built since it will fulfill the prophecy of the coming third temple. Jews believe the temple will bring the awaited Messiah. They are waiting for a sign from God to begin building.

Conquest for the Temple Mount

Third temple adherents calling themselves the Temple Faithful propose to build the temple on the temple mount on top of the remains of the second temple. They have ready the cornerstone. (Yeshua is the cornerstone that the builders rejected.) All the artifacts and high priestly garments are ready in anticipation of the third temple. The rumor is that the Ark is in Jerusalem, awaiting the building of the third temple. We cannot substantiate this claim. Sacrifice will be reinstated.

In Revelation 11, we see that the two witness are empowered by God to prophesy during the first half of the tribulation. They will be in the vicinity of the third temple area. God has instructed that the outer court will not be part of the temple but will be given unto the Gentiles, and they will tread upon the holy city for three and a half years. This could mean that the third temple could be built on the temple mount alongside of the al Aqsa mosque. The courtyard area would still be accessible to the Gentiles.

> *The people of the prince that will come will destroy the city and the sanctuary and the end thereof will be with a flood and unto the end of the war*

desolations are determined and he will confirm the covenant with many for one week and in the midst of the week he will cause the sacrifice and the oblation to cease and for the overspreading of abominations he will make it desolate even until the consummation and that determined will be poured upon the desolate. (Daniel 9:26–27)

The people of the prince have come and are in place, diligently working to destroy Israel.

Around AD 690–700, the Muslims were in control of the temple mount and built the Al Aqsa Mosque on top of the remnants of the second temple ruins. In 746, an earthquake destroyed the mosque. Muslims rebuilt it around 754. An earthquake in 1099 partially destroyed the mosque. During this time, the crusaders took back control over the temple mount and used the mosque as a palace, calling it Solomon's Temple, and the dome of the rock was used as a church. By 1119, the Knights Templars were involved in oversight of the mount. The Muslim Saladin recaptured the mount in 1187 through to the Ottoman occupation in 1517 to 1917. The British took control of Jerusalem up to the establishment of the nation of Israel. Several earthquakes occurred year 1927 and year 1937, involving the temple mount. The structure called the Dome of the Rock reflects Byzantine architecture, while the al Aqsa mosque reflects Islamic architecture. The Dome of the Rock sits over Mount Moriah, upon which Abraham would have sacrificed Isaac. Muslims claim, Muhammad ascended to heaven on a white horse from this rock, which is a fairy tale (Wikipedia online, Al Aqsa Mosque, June 2015).

AD 1924, Muslims published a booklet regarding the Temple mount, calling it *Al-Haram Al-Sharif*, indicating, "It is the site of Solomon's temple and is beyond dispute … This too is the place according to universal belief, David built there an altar unto the Lord." Today the site is a reminder of Gentile domination and the ongoing desecration of the holy site. Muslims desecrate the temple mount while eating, littering, and allowing Muslim children to play ball on this holy land (YouTube video).

Muslims attack Jews who attempt to come onto the temple mount. Some Jewish high officials have gone onto the site but not without controversy from the Muslims. Other visitors can go onto the temple mount without any obvious religious items. Israel courts have recently ruled that all people can go onto the temple mount. It will be interesting to see how God will allow for the building of this temple.

The Dome over the Rock has a golden tone, which reflects the sun, allowing it to be seen from afar. We could think of it as a beacon that marks the location of the New Jerusalem and the coming of King Jesus.

In Matthew 24:15–22, we read that after the desecration of the temple, Jesus warns the Jews to prepare to leave:

> *When you see the abomination of desolation spoken of by Daniel the prophet stand in the holy place, then let them which be in Judaea flee into the mountains. Let him which is on the housetop not come down to take anything out of his house, neither let him which is in the field return back to take his clothes and woe unto them that are with child and to them that give suck in those days, but pray that your flight be not in winter or on the Sabbath day. For then will be great tribulation such as was not since the beginning of the world to this time no nor ever will be, and except those days should be shortened there should no flesh be saved but for the elect's sake those days will be shortened.*

This passage could have been applied to those living before the AD 70 destruction of the temple, but we know it points to the future third temple, desecration by Antichrist, the killing of the two witnesses who are seen ascending into heaven, followed by a great earthquake destroying a tenth of the city and killing seven thousand. After these things, the great tribulation will occur, a time not since the beginning of the world. God will shorten those days so that there will be a remnant of Jews and Gentiles.

Following are a few current reports regarding the temple:

A report coming from Arutz Sheva, August 22, 2013, reporter Elad Benari, "Area near Al Aqsa Mosque collapses." There is concern that the mosque is in danger. Will some sort of natural disaster destroy the mosque making way for the temple?

Recent updates on Israel reestablishing full sovereignty over the temple mount as activists stand their ground to access the mount. Israel government calls for equal rights to temple mount.

Yehudah Glick of the Temple Mount Heritage Foundation went to Istanbul, Turkey, during Ramadan to meet with Muslim leaders to promote dialogue and peace. His goal is that the temple mount be a house of prayer for all nations (*Breaking Israel News*, July 2, 2015).

Palestinians cause riots when Christians or Jews come to the mount. Jordan now joins Palestinians in claiming right to east Jerusalem and the mount. Will Israel take back sovereignty over the temple mount?

May 2015, researcher and archeologist Robert Cornuke claims that Solomon's temple is located in the City of David and not on the temple mount area. He is associated with Bible Archeology Search Exploration Institute, BASE, Colorado Springs, Colorado. He believes that the Temple Mount Institute could begin building the third temple in the City of David region and that would end the conflict in building the temple next to the mosque. As always, we will watch and see.

Muslim support for the third temple does exist. Some believe the freedom of worship is an essential issue to Jews, Christians, and Muslims because God has said this is to be a house of prayer for all nations. All who call on God should be able to offer prayers on the temple site in peace. To cast believers out from such a place, to prevent worship that is an offense and cruel policy not only to men but to Islam. God himself condemns anyone who forbids worship. Will the Vatican, Muslims, and Christendom come to an arrangement regarding the temple mount?

June 22, 2016, Muslim Adnan Oktar, Istanbul, Turkey, hosted representatives from Israel, Muslims, and Christian to gather during Ramada to support the restoration of the Temple.

The Millennial Temple

The final temple spoken of in the scriptures will not be built with human hands because it is not a temple but a city built by God. Hebrews 8:1–2 … "*We have such a high priest who is set on the right hand of the throne of the Majesty in the heavens. A minister of the sanctuary and of the true tabernacle which the Lord pitched and not man.*" Over three thousand years ago, Moses built the tabernacle in the wilderness after the likeness of the example and shadow of the heavenly tabernacle.

Revelation 11:1, 19, John sees the heavenly temple of God and the altar, also those who worship there. "*And the temple of God was opened in heaven and there was seen in his temple the Ark of his testament*" (Ark of the Covenant). Two thousand years ago, John sees the heavenly temple, and from other scriptures, we know this heavenly city will descend to earth.

Haggai 2 opens with the rebuilding of the second temple and later alludes to the New Jerusalem temple:

> *Yet once, it is a little while and I will shake the heavens and the earth and the sea and the dry land and I will shake all nations and the desire of all nations will come and I will fill this house with glory, said the Lord of hosts … the glory of this latter house will be greater than the former said the Lord of hosts and in this place will I give peace said the lord of hosts.*

The world awaits the arrival of Messiah. His feet will touch the Mount of Olives; and it will split in two. A massive earthquake will change the landscape in Jerusalem, causing the mountain of the Lord to rise to a higher elevation. Micah 4:1–2, "*In the last days, it shall come to pass that the mountain of the house of the Lord will be established in the top of the mountains and it shall be exalted above the hills and people will flow to it.*" We also see that the house or New Jerusalem will encompass the land of Israel. From this domain, Jesus will teach the nations his way, and the law will go out of Zion in Jerusalem. Jesus will judge the people and rebuke strong nations afar off, and they will turn their weapons into farming equipment. War will be vanquished. People will live in peace. All of nature will flourish.

Ezekiel 37, "*The hand of the Lord was upon me and carried me out in the spirit of the Lord ...*" All the tribes of Israel will become one. "*And I will make them one nation in the land upon the mountains of Israel and one king will be king to them all ...*" At the beginning of the millennial reign, King Jesus will rule from the land of Israel. He will continue the everlasting covenant of peace with Israel. "*And I will set my sanctuary in the midst of them forever and my tabernacle also will be with them, I will be their God and they will be my people.*" At that time, the presence and glory of the Lord will fill the earth.

Ezekiel 47 foresees waters that come forth from under the threshold of the temple mount, which accumulate into a river and along its bank trees grow. The waters flow to the desert and flow into the Dead Sea, of which a portion will be restored to life, and fish will be abundant again out of the Dead Sea. "*But the miry places thereof and the marshes will not be healed but will continue to be salty. The trees are for food whose leaf* [will be for medicine] *will not fade or will the fruit thereof be consumed, it will bring forth new fruit according to his months because the waters come from out of the temple.*

Revelation 22, John foresees the future river of life coming from the throne of God and the Lamb. In the middle of the street on either side of the river was the **tree of life,** which bear twelve manner of fruits and yielded her fruit every month and the leaves of the tree were for the healing of the nations.

The Blood Moon Phenomena

Mark Bilitz is to be credited with extensive research in the appearance of the blood moons.

J. R. Church and John Hagee also researched the blood moons, and others have provided insightful teachings on the coming four blood moons.

In the past, celestial signs in the sky were evident during times of persecution and deliverance of Israel. The blood moon is a complete lunar eclipse, when the earth is between the sun and the moon. They have occurred throughout time, but we are interested in those that align with an event in Israel. Many believe these celestial wonders are omens.

In 1948, Israel became recognized as a nation. A blood moon appeared between 1949 and 1950. Four blood moons made their cycle, which coincided with the six-day war in 1967. With the help of God, Israel took back Jerusalem, Judea, and Samaria, their rightful land.

AD 2014 Blood Moon

A blood moon made an appearance around April 2014 on Passover. Also a blood moon appeared in October 2014 between Yom Kippur and the Feast of Tabernacles. These luminary events are recorded by NASA. There was a solar eclipse on March 20, 2015, Adar 29/ Nisan. This event falls in the middle of the blood moon, which occurred April 3, 2015, the beginning of Passover. Rabbi commentaries believe that a solar eclipse is a bad omen for idolaters or the world system and a moon eclipse is a bad omen for Israel. Either way, judgment is coming. As told in the book of Joel, we see judgment came to Israel and their enemies. We can apply this same scenario to events occurring in the twentieth and twenty-first centuries in fulfillment of the Day of the Lord:

- Evil envelopes the world as a cloak of darkness, gloom (Joel 2:2).
- The meat is cut off as in the killing of forty million chickens; drought conditions prevent the seeds from growing; the corn is withered; the barns are desolate; the cattle, horses, sheep are perplexed because they have no pasture (Joel 1:16).
- Fire burns round about as in the eruptions of volcanoes, forest fires, and the denotation of missiles and bombs around the world (Joel 2:3).
- The noise of military battalions coming whose armies are strong, and they are not stopped by any obstacles (Joel 2:4–9).
- This gathering is so great, the earth quakes, the heavens tremble, the sun and moon are dark, and no stars can be seen (Joel 2:10). Could refer to the gathering for the battle of Armageddon.
- He will cause to come down for you the former rain and the latter rain. This is a reference to actual rain and also a spiritual reference to the outpouring of the Holy Spirit (Joel 2:23).
- It will come to pass that I will pour out my spirit upon all flesh; your sons and daughters will prophesy; men will have dreams and visions (Joel 2:28).
- I will bring the twelve tribes back into the land of Israel (Joel 3:1).
- I will show wonders in the heavens and in the earth, blood, fire, and pillars of smoke. Then the sun will be turned into darkness and the moon into blood before the great and terrible day of the Lord (Joel 2:31).
- In these days, whosoever will call on the name of Jesus will be delivered (Joel 2:32).
- Jesus will roar out of Zion, Jerusalem (Joel 3:16). Jesus shouts before his great, innumerable army. His Word is strong, for the day of the Lord is great and very terrible and who can abide it (Joel 2:11).
- At the end of the tribulation, Jesus will call the nations to come to the valley of decision or the valley of judgment (Joel 3:14). This may be Armageddon leading up

to the great harvest, put in the sickle for the harvest is ripe … for their wickedness is great (Joel 3:13).

- Nations will war no more; they will beat their swords in to farming equipment.
- Looking forward to a time of peace and plenty (Joel 3:18).

Presently, Israel is being threatened by hostile Islamic nations vowing to wipe Israel off the face of the earth. The year of 2016 begins with significant signs such as a nuclear Iran and Russian military intervention in Syria.

Seven Feast of Israel

1. Passover, Pesach,

This is a four-day feast that celebrates God's deliverance of his people, Israel, from the tenth plague (death) in Egypt—which was the death of the firstborn. Each Jewish family had to apply the blood of a lamb over their doorpost, and the death angel would pass over it, sparing them from the plague. Moses told the people to kill a lamb for their evening meal. They were also to make bread without yeast. It also commemorates the escape from Egypt and the freedom from bondage. This festival is the start of the Jewish New Year. Exodus 12, it begins 9/10th of Nisan to 13/14th of Nisan.

The recitation of the Haggadah is read to remember and teach future generations of God's deliverance from Egypt. Yeshua is our rabbi/teacher. In fulfilling the scriptures, Yeshua presented himself to Israel for examination. He rode into Jerusalem on a donkey, and the people cried, "Hosanna." Before the people, he offered himself as the ultimate Passover Lamb. We remember his sacrifice through the sacraments of Communion. The bread without yeast represents the sinless life of Jesus, and wine represents his shed blood for the atonement of our sins. He is the perfect, sinless, unblemished Lamb of God.

2. The Festival of Unleavened Bread

This is the second of the seven festivals mentioned in Leviticus 23. It commemorates the hastily baked bread without yeast/leaven. It is called the bread of affliction. Jewish observers use matzah bread, taking three pieces and placing them in a cloth. At the beginning of the sader meal, the middle matzah is removed and hidden. At the end of Passover, it is retrieved and presented as the afikomen, which means dessert morsel. In Greek it means, "He comes." The deeper understanding is that the hidden Messiah once concealed is now revealed. His body is the piece broken for our sins.

3. First Fruits, or the Omer

During the forty years in the wilderness, part of this ceremony was marked by the priest waving a sheaf of barley grain as the First Fruits of their harvest. The spring wave offering lasted fifty days, which ends at Pentecost. Yeshua became the First Fruits of the Resurrection from the dead, and the Holy Spirit was given on Pentecost for the empowering of the saints.

4. Pentecost, *Shavuot*, or Feast of Weeks

Jews celebrate this feast on Sivan 6 and associate it with the giving of the Law at Mount Sinai. Both Noah and Abraham received their covenants from God around this date. It also marks the end or fiftieth day of the grain harvest or First Fruits celebration. Jews remember the marriage contract between God and Israel through the reading of the book of Ruth. Israel is the wife of Yahweh. The early church was empowered by the Holy Spirit on the Day of Pentecost. The church is the bride of Christ. Pentecost introduced the dispensation of grace, which we are presently under.

5. The Feast of Trumpets is the blowing of the shofar. Its future significance is that the sound of the trumpet will be heralded before the coming of Messiah (1 Thessalonians 4:16). "*For the Lord Himself will descend from heaven with a shout, with the voice of an archangel and with the trumpet of God*" (Numbers 29:1). On the first day of the seventh month, hold a sacred assembly and do no regular work. It is a day for you to sound the trumpets. We wait for the sound of the trumpet, the beginning of the tribulation and the Messianic kingdom.

6. *Yom Kippur*, or Day of Atonement

This day is observed on the tenth of Tishri, the final Day of Awe. On a personal level, each person would examine themselves regarding good deeds and sinful practices. They will rest and fast. Originally, *Yom Kippur* was focused upon the actions of the high priest as he entered into the Holy of Holies once each year to sprinkle the blood of sacrifice upon the mercy seat for himself and the sins of the people.

Prophetically, this day looks forward to Israel's national repentance, which will come forth during the tribulation period. This period is a time of purging the chaff of the world. It prepares those Jews who have had the scales of their eyes removed and have been given a heart of flesh to accept their Messiah. It is a time of preparation for the righteous Jew or born-again Gentile to enter into the Kingdom of God.

7. Feast of Tabernacles, or *Sukkot*

The *sukkot* is a small shelter or hut outdoors, without any modern comforts. Some will decorate their *sukkot* with fruit or vegetables. It is a time for sharing and reading scripture. It may be to symbolize the fall of man living in a cursed world but looks toward the redemption of man living in the kingdom of God on earth. It is celebrated on the seventh and final day of *Sukkot*.

It is symbolic of the final defeat of the evil world system, and mankind will tabernacle or have their Sabbath rest with God forever.

Israel celebrates other festival besides the seven listed above. *Rosh Hashanah* is a major festival, which is the celebration of the Jewish New Year. The Ten Days of Awe are initiated on *Rosh Hashanah* through *Yom Kippur*. This holiday commemorates the reaffirmation of faith and significant events throughout history. Some of these events are Adam and Eve created on Rosh Hashanah; the sixth day of creation; the first day of Tishri; the first day of the opening of Noah's ark; Abraham was going to sacrifice Isaac this day; the exodus; Mount Sinai; and receiving of the Ten Commandments and the Torah, in association with the building and destruction of the temples, return of Jews to their homeland, growing cycles.

The above seven feasts have a prophetic pattern woven through them. The seven feast form a menorah design. The feast of Pentecost is the middle lamp, which is referred to as the servant lamp. Jesus came as a humble servant. Three lamps on each side represent the three spring festivals, and on the opposite side the three lamps represent the fall festivals.

The Shemitah

God required Israel to rest the land every seventh year is referred to as the Shemitah cycle. A Sabbatical year began September 2015 ending September 2016. There are approximately six million Jews living in the United States which is around the same number living in Israel. Some events seem to correlate with the Shemitah cycle. For instance, at the start of a seven year cycle in 2001 saw the 9-11 attack and the stock market fell losing $1.4 trillion. In 2007-2008, the US housing market crash occurred. Coming to of the end of the Shemitah cycle world economies are unstable such as Greece and Venezuela. Statistical analysis project an economic collaspe in the United States tetering on a $19 trillion debt threshold. If the United States experiences an economic collapse, this may be the catalyst to cause many Jews to return to Israel. The 2015 date also coincided with a blood moon phenomena around September 28, which will be seen in Israel and is the Feast of Tabernacles. Some scholars are wondering if Israel will regain dominion over the temple mount. We are also watching to see if 2016 signals the start of the tribulation.

Hebrew Calendar

The Hebrew calendar is biblically based from the time of creation and ties into the cycles of the moon. Each of the twelve months begins with the new moon. Each month is twenty-nine to thirty days long, and periodically an extra month, Adar, is added to catch the lunar calendar up to the cycles of the sun. In AD 1582, Pope Gregory XIII changed the calendar to a solar cycle based on 365 days per year and is called the Gregorian calendar.

Month	Today's Calendar	Bible Reference	Israel's Feast Days
Nissan/Abib (7)	March–April	Exodus 13:4	Passover Unleavened Bread First Fruits
Iyar/Zif (8)	April–May	1 Kings 6:1, 37	
Sivan (9)	May–June	Esther 8:9	Pentecost
Tammuz (10)	June–July		
Av (11)	July–August		
Elul (12)	August–September	Nehemiah 6:15	
Tishri (1)	September–October	1 Kings 8:2	Trumpets Day of Atonement Tabernacles
Cheshvan (2)	October–November		
Chisleu (3)	November–December	Nehemiah 1:1	Dedication
Tebeth (4)	December–January	Esther 2:16	
Shevat (5)	January–February	Zechariah 1:7	
Adar (6)	February–March	Esther 3:7	

The Jubilee Year

The Jubilee represents the fiftieth year after seven Shemitah cycles. At the end of the forty-ninth year and the beginning of the fiftieth year, celebratory shofars are blown throughout the land, celebrating the new Jubilee year. It is sacred, a time of freedom, a time to free slaves and to return land or forgive debts. Through the sounding of the shofar, human breath resonates from deep within our souls as we cry out to God. It can be related to the Day of Pentecost, when the Holy Spirit came in as a mighty rushing wind (breath of God) and tongues of fire set upon each person and the Holy Spirit gave them utterance in other tongues.

Blowing the Shofar

The shofar is fashioned from a ram's horn. It is also called a trumpet. This practice of blowing the shofar is to sound the call to arms, sound the alarm for danger, to signal the assembly for community business, or to call in obedience to God. Most notable is the sound of a silver or gold trumpet, the voice of God calling Moses and the people to Mount Sinai. Many are the miracles of God associated with the sounding of the shofar. Today there are claims that people are hearing sounds from heaven, comparing it to the sound of trumpets perhaps heralding the soon coming of the Lord. There are three or more distinct sounds from the shofar: a simple blast called *tekiah*, staccato *teruah*, galloping *shevarim*, and long, wailing *tekiah gadolah*.

God's voice is likened to the sound of a trumpet:

> *And it came to pass on the third day in the morning that there were thunders and lightnings and a thick cloud upon Mount Sinai and the voice of the trumpet exceeding loud so that all the people that was in the camp trembled.* (Exodus 19:16)

At the time of the Rapture, 1 Thessalonians 4:16, "*For the Lord himself will descend from heaven with a shout, with the voice of the archangel and with the trump of God …*"

Joshua and the battle for Jericho. Scriptures define God's instructions regarding the blowing of the *shofar*, or trumpet. Israel would march around Jericho seven times, and the priest would blow the *shofar*; and on the seventh day—when the people heard the last long blast, the tekiah gadolah—they would shout in praise to God (Joshua 6:4–5).

King Solomon fashioned trumpets made of silver.

Rabbi Shlomo Goren blew the Shofar at the Western Wall and in Hebron in 1967 when Israel succeeded in regaining Jerusalem and other territory.

The *shofar* is blown to announce the beginning of the Jubilee year:

> *You shall number seven Sabbaths of years unto thee, seven times seven years; and the space of the seven Sabbaths of years shall be unto you forty-nine years. Then you shall cause the trumpet of jubilee to sound on the tenth day of the seventh month in the day of atonement* [Yom Kippur] *and shall you make the trumpet sound throughout all your land. And the fiftieth year will be holy and you will proclaim liberty throughout all the land …* (Leviticus 25:8–10)

In our present day, true believers watch, pray, and listen for the shout of Yeshua with the voice of the archangel and with the trump of God to call us up to meet him in the air.

Light at the End of the Tunnel

We have followed the many encounters experienced by the Hebrew Israelites throughout the scriptures, and we end in the Old Testament book of Malachi, which brings us to around 430 BC. The prophet Malachi reminded God's chosen nation of their disobedience, beginning with the priesthood. They again fell into idolatry and led others astray. They broke God's laws and sinned, becoming prideful and arrogant. Evil was called good. They robbed God of tithes and offerings. If there was no turning from sin and repentance, God's judgment was coming. Malachi 2:9 … "*I have also made you contemptible and base before all the people according as you have not kept my ways but have been partial in the law.*" To whom much is given, much is required. The chosen people had been given much, and God required their allegiance and obedience above all the people in the earth. Malachi 4:1, "*For behold that day comes that shall burn as an oven and all the proud, yes and all that do wickedly shall be stubble and the day that comes shall burn them up said the Lord of hosts that it shall leave them neither root nor branch.*" This passage looks toward the Day of the Lord and the great tribulation.

Throughout history, there is always a remnant who love and honor God. These are blessed in this life or in the hereafter.

> *And they that feared the Lord spoke often one to another and the Lord hearkened and heard it, and a book of remembrance was written before him for them that fear the Lord and that thought upon his name. And they shall be mine, said the Lord of hosts in that day when I make up my jewels and* ***I will spare them*** *as a man spares his own son that serves him.* (Malachi 3:16)

Take note, God will remember the righteous either in life or death; they will be spared from judgment that will befall the whole earth.

Malachi encourages the faithful through these words:

> *But unto you that fear my name shall the Sun of righteousness arise with healing in his wings and you shall go forth and grow as calves of the stall.* (Malachi 4:2)

Jesus is our light. He will arise, and we shall go forth to be with him forever.

> *Behold I will send Elijah the prophet before the coming of the great and dreadful day of the Lord. He shall turn the heart of the fathers to the children and the heart of the children to their fathers …* (Malachi 4:5)

This future prophecy is a sign for Israel. They will see Elijah and another witness during the first half of the tribulation period before the second half, which is called the great tribulation. Israel will begin to turn back to God.

All the writers in the Old Testament, where Hebrew Israelites and whatever was to be included in the scriptures was completed around 400 BC. At that point in time and looking forward to the beginning of the year of our Lord was like seeing a dim light leading the way to the arrival of Messiah. Between the Old Testament book of Malachi and the New Testament beginning with Matthew, there is a four hundred-year gap referred to as the silent years. We can pick up the history during those silent years in the writings of the Apocrypha.

The Bible is exclusive above all other religious books. The difference between the Bible and other writings is that the Bible was given by God, and its words are interwoven with prophecy. Prophecy reveals God's plan in advance and is the missing element in other religious writings. No other religion can make the claim that their predictions, if any, can be proven to have been fulfilled specifically, nor do they have any corroborating evidence or witnesses. No prophecy is found in the Koran, Hindu Veda, Book of Mormon, Buddha, Ellen White, to name a few. Hundreds of prophecies are in the Bible, and two thirds of them have already been fulfilled. Therefore the Bible is credible, reliable, and true. Other religions have taken from our biblical scriptures and added bits and pieces from it to their own writings. They plagiarized the Bible and rendered half-truths and distortions. The book of Mormon is a good example of taking from the Bible. Mormom founder Smith added whatever he thought sounded good to him, and nothing can be corroborated. The Koran is a mixture of Judaism, Christianity, and paganism. All other religious books pale in comparison to the Bible. Nostradamus was well versed in biblical scriptures and especially prophecy. He was able to extrapolate Bible prophecies and then give them his personal touch.

Chapter 13
God Comes to Earth

Chapter Overview

Chapter 13

God Comes to Earth

In Genesis, God is seen coming from his heavenly abode, fellowshipping and walking with Adam in the garden. After the fall of man up to the flood, God's interaction with mankind came by speaking to him from heaven or reaching down to bring man up into the heavens. After the flood, God continued to intervene in the affairs of mankind. He made various appearances throughout scripture. God came as a pillar of fire, a glory cloud, burning bush, and clothed in flesh. He spoke through his angels also referred to as ministering spirits; he spoke through the prophets and carried out his will through his Spirit. In our chapter 3, we define the abilities of angels. Angels can appear and intermingle with humankind. Sometimes it is difficult to distinguish between the appearance of God or angels. Some false doctrines portray Jesus as an angel.

<u>Angel of the Lord</u>

> *Being made* [the incarnation] *so much better than the angels, as he has by inheritance obtained a more excellent name than they. For unto which of the angels said he at any time, you are my Son, this day have I begotten thee? And again, I will be to him a Father and he shall be to me a Son? And again, when he brings in the first begotten into the world, he said, and let all the angels of God worship him. And of the angels he said, who makes his angels spirits and his ministers a flame of fire.* (Hebrews 1:4–7)

This passage gives us credible evidence that Jesus is not an angel. It also differentiates between the deity of Jesus Christ, God the Son, and his created beings.

- In the beginning, God created Adam, a little lower than the angels. Jesus, the second Adam, was physically created a little lower than the angels for his suffering.
- God became man for a short period. Jesus became the first begotten of the Father. On earth Jesus was God and man. He did not stop being God.
- Jesus is above the angels, and they are commanded to worship the Son.
- At no time did God command any angel to become flesh and become his Son. Angels are referred to as sons of God but as created beings.
- The name of Yeshua is above all names.

We are going to interject a few nuggets for thought where we see God speaking and acting through his angelic host. Throughout the scriptures, in some instances, the appearance of the angel of the Lord is thought to be Jesus. Let us examine 2 Kings 19:35:

> *And it came to pass that night that the angel of the Lord went out and smote in the camp of the Assyrians a hundred eighty-five thousand …*

In 2 Kings 19:35, the angel's mission was to actually kill the Assyrian Army. If this is Jesus in person, then it sends a strange message that God becomes one of his own warring angels. This is an angel. The false religion of Mormonism puts Lucifer and Jesus together as angelic brothers. They know that Lucifer is an angel, and to blend with their doctrine, Jesus is transformed into an angel. The Jehovah's Witnesses label Jesus as Michael the Archangel. Other people believe the falsehood that when they die, they become angels. We do not believe Jesus becomes an angel but being God chooses to make appearances, speak, or act through his angels. He chose to speak through Baalam's donkey or to speak to Moses out of a burning bush. Jesus had an encounter with Saul as a bright light and audible voice. We are careful to give God the glory and not to glorify angels:

> *And the angel of the Lord called unto him out of heaven and said, Abraham … lay not your hand upon the lad … And the angel of the Lord called unto Abraham out of heaven the second time and said, by myself have I sworn said the Lord for because you have done this thing and have not withheld your son … I will bless you.* (Genesis 22:11–15)

In the above passage, it is clear that the angel's mission was to deliver a message speaking with the voice of God.

There are times when God makes a personal appearance:

> *And the **LORD** appeared unto Abraham in the plains of Mamre as he sat in the tent door in the heat of the day. And he lifted up his eyes and saw three*

> *men ... and when he saw them he ran to meet them from the tent door and bowed himself toward the ground and said, my* ***Lord****, if now I have found favor in your sight ...* (Genesis 18:1)

This is an appearance of Jesus (LORD is all caps) and two angels. Abraham bows before God and acknowledges only one Lord. If these were three angels, they would have told him not to bow or worship them. Following this scripture, Jesus and Abraham discuss his future son and the destruction of Sodom and Gomorrah. In Genesis 19:1, "*And there came two angels to Sodom at evening ... Lot bowed himself and he said behold now my* ***lords*** *...*" This passage picks up on the two angels who were with Abraham and Jesus, then they departed to visit Lot, who in turn shows them respect and refers to them as (lowercase) lords.

In Daniel 10:4–21, he is visited by an angel clothed in linen with loins girded with fine gold of Uphaz; his body was like the beryl; and his face as the appearance of lightning—eyes like fire, arms and feet the color of polished brass, having the appearance of a man and the voice of multitude. Daniel became weak in his presence; at the sound of his words, Daniel was in a trance. The angel touched Daniel. Reasons why this is an angel and not Jesus are the following: (1) he was sent, angels are messengers sent by God; (2) he and Michael had to fight with the principality of Persia; (3) Jesus would not have required the help of an angel to fight prince of Persia; (4) Daniel refers to as lord (lowercase); (5) the angel touched his lips like the angels touched the coals upon the lips of the prophet; and (6) angels have been recorded as saying, "Fear not."

From Genesis to Revelation, we find many accounts of angels on mission from God.

The Preeminence and Deity of Christ and the Triune Godhead

We look to Yahweh, God the Father, and through the Father, we can know the Word, the person of Jesus Christ, the Son of God, who is unveiled by the person of the Holy Spirit. There is but one God who operates through his Word and through the power of his spirit. Understanding this relationship can be perplexing; therefore it should be internalized that the deity of Christ cannot be separate from deity of the Father and deity of the Holy Spirit.

The Triune Godhead has baffled many and been rejected and misunderstood by Christians and other religions. There are numerous scriptures that support the Triune Godhead as well as the deity of Christ incarnate. We first see the Triune God in the opening verse of Genesis 1, where the person of the Holy Spirit moves upon the face of the waters. The Holy Spirit is associated with water, outpouring, refreshing, power. Then we see God speak his Word, which burst forth as, "I came forth from the Father." There was darkness over the earth, which we associate with evil; and the Word, the light of the world, came forth and dispelled the darkness.

All things were created by Yeshua, the Word of God.

> *In the beginning was the Word and the Word was with God and the Word was God. The same was in the beginning with God. All things were made by him and without him was not anything made that was made.* (John 1:1–2)
>
> *Yeshua is the image of the invisible God the firstborn of every creature. For by Him, all things were created that are in heaven and that are in earth, visible and invisible, whether they be thrones or dominions or principalities or powers, all things were created by him and for Him. He is before all things and by him all things consist.* (Colossians 1:15–17)

This passage seems to define the Triune Godhead before the creation of angels as God brought forth his Word. Then we see that by the Word, all things were created in heaven—including the invisible angels, which would later become principalities and powers in high places, and finally the creation of earth and all that is therein.

> *And without controversy, great is the mystery of godliness: God was manifest in the flesh, justified in the Spirit, seen of angels, preached unto the Gentiles, believed on in the world, received up into glory.* (1 Timothy 3:15)

In this passage, we understand that in the fullness of time our God, Yeshua, would be manifested in the flesh.

> *All things are delivered unto me of my Father and no man knows the Son but the Father neither knows any man the Father save the Son and he to whomsoever the Son will reveal him.* (Matthew 11:27)
>
> *I and my Father are one.* (John 10:30)
>
> *Now Father glorify me with thy own self with the glory which I had with you before the world was.* (John 17:5)
>
> *I am from above, you are of this world, I am not of this world.* (John 8:23)
>
> The Messiah *was foreordained before the foundation of the world but was manifest in these* ***last times*** *for you.* (1 Peter 1:20)
>
> *For* ***God*** *is my witness whom I serve with my* ***spirit*** *in the gospel of his* ***Son,*** *that without ceasing I make mention of you always in my prayers.* (Romans 1:9)

In this passage, Saint Paul acknowledges the Triune Godhead.

History in the Scriptures

We have visited four thousand years of human history through the writings in the Old Testament.

Hebrew Israelites immersed themselves in the study of the Torah, continued in temple rituals, as well as keeping the feasts. All the Old Testament writings were compiled by 200 BC. The Torah and Talmud refer to the teaching and study of written and oral law for eight hundred years BC, including the Babylonia captivity. Talmudists began to produce copies of the Old Testament in Hebrew during the first century AD, a task so sacred that they worked in full Jewish dress and washed their entire body before copying a single word. Every scroll was made of particular materials and penned in special ink. Not a single word could be written from memory. The original scrolls no longer exist. We have copies from that time period, which have been verified to be accurate.

At the end of the fourth millennium, around 4–3 BC, before the beginning of the first century AD, God came to earth. His visitation was during the rule of King Herod of the Roman Empire.

The Romans were the descendants of Japheth. Jesus came at a time when the descendants of Japheth were at enmity with the descendants of Shem, Hebrews, Moabites, and descendants of Ham, Canaanites. King Herod was deceased by AD 1 at the beginning of the fifth millennium.

The fifth to the seventh millennium could be considered the day of the Lord. Scribes began to compile the teachings of Jesus and others twenty years after his death. Along with scriptures in Hebrew, there existed scriptures written in Aramaic. This language was spoken in Galilee, Jerusalem, Damascus, Antioch, Edessa, Armenia, etc. The New Testament was written in Greek between AD 49 to AD 95. The book of Revelation written by John on the Island of Patmos was the last book of the New Testament work. The scriptures were translated into Latin and used by the Roman Catholic Church. Jesus spoke in Aramaic, Hebrew, Greek. He could speak all languages because he is God the Creator.

Innumerable Orthodox Jews and Messianic Jews were killed by the pagan Roman Empire. We know from scripture that around AD 70, the Jewish temple was destroyed. Jews, Christians, and Gentiles were forced to leave the area and scattered throughout the world. Some stayed in Israel.

After the destruction of the Temple, the Masoretic period of copyists began. The copyists of that period took great care to enumerate every letter. This group was responsible for dividing the words, books, sections, paragraphs, verses, and clauses. They fixed the spelling, pronunciation, and cantillation (accents/sound). During this period, the change from the old Hebrew script to the square type of the Hebrew alphabet was developed. The Masorah copyists also paid attention to textual data or halakhic and aggadic (legends) interpretation. They recorded full and defective spelling, as well as orthographic (accepted standard of spelling) grammatical abnormalities, and enumerated the letters, words, and verses by use of the words (Hebrew) *kerei*, "to be read"; (Hebrew) *ketiv*, "to be written"; and (Hebrew) *sevirin*, "of an opinion." And in all this, the text itself was left unchanged since it was forbidden to add to holy writ[20] (Deuteronomy 13:1). The term *Mishnah* refers to the law divided into sections concerning agriculture, festivals, marriage, and divorce, civil and criminal law, temple and holy things, and purity laws.[21] The word *Pentateuch* refers to the first five books of the Bible. The Septuagint is the Old Testament translated into Greek by seventy scholars.

The Dead Sea scrolls were discovered in 1947 in Qumran, the region of Sodom and Gomorrah. They are referred to as the Dead Sea because no living thing can survive in its water. It is rich in mineral content and a source for natural healing. Scriptures predict that during the end of the age, the Dead Sea will support life. Presently, freshwater ponds have been springing up near the shores of the Dead Sea. Most Dead Sea scrolls were written around 150 BC and confirmed the Old Testament texts were reliable. Included in this discovery were original writings classified as *Pseudepigrapha* (Greek for "false title"): Psalms of Solomon, Testament of the Twelve Patriarchs, Book of Jubilees, Apocalypse of Baruch, Book of Enoch, Assumption of Moses, Ascension of Isaiah, and Sibylline Oracles. The order of the Essenes (a Jewish sect) may be responsible for the Pseudepigrapha writings.[22]

Other writings known as *Apocrypha* (Greek for "hidden") in Hebrew or Aramaic included themes of prophetical, historical, legendary, and apocalyptical literature. They included Edras, Tobit, Judith, Esther, Wisdom of Solomon, Ecclesiasticus, Baruch, Susanna, Bel, and the Dragon, Maccabees.[23] These books were popular for three hundred years during the time of Jesus and thereafter. Christians preserved these writings. The original Hebrew and Aramaic texts were lost. The copies that survived were translated into Greek, Latin, Armenian, Coptic, Ethiopian. These books were included in the Septuagint and Vulgate (Latin) but not in the Hebrew Bible. Eleven of the books were declared canonical by the Catholic Church and remain a part of their Bible to this day. The Ethiopian Jews retained the writing of the Books of Enoch as part of their canon. Around the destruction of the second temple in AD 70, some of the artifacts from the temple may have been relocated by Solomon's descendants to Ethiopia for safekeeping.

---

[20] R. J. Zwi Werblowsky and Geoffrey Wigoder, The Encyclopedia of the Jewish Religion (New York, NY: Holt, Rinehart and Winston, 1965) p 253

[21] 22 Ibid, Talmud, p 373

[22] Ibid, p 36

[23] Ibid, p 36

The rabbinical order rejected these Jewish writings because they lacked canonical authority and for the most part were not biblical interpretations or commentaries. Also, they were rejected on the basis of being too eschatological. Perhaps the thought of angels and women was too risqué. More so, the arrival of Messiah could displace their coveted positions in the hierarchy of Judaism, causing a divide between the Orthodoxy and new converts to Christianity, which could upset their place within the Roman Empire. Later, rabbis did incorporate some writings in the Talmud. In AD 1240, the Jewish Talmud is burned in France because they thought its writings contained blasphemies against Jesus. The books were also burned in Italy and Poland.

The Word of God in the Old and New Testaments are full of types and shadows pointing to Yeshua. We understand he is the preexistent, Ancient of Days. In the extensive study of the Bible, no one could miss the prophetic writings that confirm who is Messiah.

The Coming Word Prophesied

The biblical symbolism of the Jewish Messiah and Redeemer of the world has been a mystery to mankind, but the good news is that God has given us the keys to understanding the things that are hidden. Revelation of God's truth is reserved for those who have ears to hear and eyes to see those things concealed in the shadows of scripture that point to Yeshua. We see this symbolism in the Hebrew letters *Aleph* to *Tav*, which reveals a message from God. The hand of God, bridged by the Holy Spirit, are connected by Messiah, who leaves heaven and comes to earth. This image of the Triune God depicts the mastery of the Ancient of Days over all of creation. It is the revelation of truth, perfection, and completion. Yeshua is our truth. He is was our perfect sacrifice hung on a cross. His last words, "It is finished." Combining the *Aleph* and *Tav* reveals that Yeshua is the beginning and the end.

> *Now to him that is of power to establish you according to my gospel and the preaching of Jesus Christ, according to* ***the revelation of the mystery which was kept secret since the world began****, but now is made manifest and by the scriptures of the prophets, according to the commandment of the everlasting God made known to all nations for the obedience of faith.* (Romans 16:25–26)

Seven Hundred-Year-Old Prophecy of the Messiah

Isaiah 53 is the most astounding Messianic chapter, worthy to be read in its entirety:

> *Who has believed our report? And to whom is the arm of the Lord revealed? For he shall grow up before him as a tender plant and as a root out of a dry*

ground, he has no form or comeliness and when we will see him there is no beauty that we should desire Him. He is despised and rejected of men, a man of sorrows and acquainted with grief and we hid as it were our faces from Him, he was despised and we esteemed him not. Surely he has borne our grief and carried our sorrows yet we did esteem him stricken, smitten of God and afflicted. He was wounded for our transgressions, he was bruised for our iniquities, the chastisement of our peace was upon him and with his stripes we are healed. We all like sheep have gone astray, we have turned everyone to his own way and the Lord has laid on him the sins of us all. He was oppressed and he was afflicted yet he opened not his mouth. He is brought as a lamb to the slaughter and as a sheep before her shearers is dumb, so he opened not his mouth. He was taken from prison and from judgment. Who shall declare his generation? For he was cut off out of the land of the living for the transgression of my people was he stricken. He made his grave with the wicked and with the rich in his death because he had done no violence, neither was any deceit in his mouth. Yet it pleased the Lord to bruise Him, he has put him to grief when you shall make his soul an offering for sin, he will see his seed, he will prolong his days and the pleasure of the Lord will prosper in his hand. He will see of the travail of his soul and will be satisfied by his knowledge will my righteous servant justify many for he will bear their iniquities. Therefore will I divide him a portion with the great and he shall divide the spoil with the strong because he has poured out his soul unto death and he was numbered with the transgressors and he bare the sin of many and made intercession for the transgressors.

An overview of Isaiah 53 predicts that Jesus would suffer for the sins of all people—that God would come as a humble suffering servant. His appearance was not attractive. He would be rejected by the Jews. He would be the sacrificial lamb for the sins of the people. He would be hung on a cross between two criminals; he would be buried in a rich man's tomb; and he would ask the Father to forgive them because they know not what they do.

Five hundred years before the birth of Christ, Zechariah 9:9 prophecy of the Messiah will come:

Rejoice greatly oh daughter of Zion … behold your King comes unto thee; He is just and having salvation; lowly and riding upon an ass.

Many prophecies and eyewitness accounts were rejected by the Jews. They could not see the hand of God before them. Their judgment was partial blindness until the day of the return of Jesus, and then they will look upon the one they crucified and mourn for him.

The revelation of Jesus was known by those who studied the Old Testament scriptures. Some of these prophecies are seen in the books of Micah, Daniel, Isaiah, Psalms, and other writings. King Herod of the Jews knew of the prophecy and attempted to eliminate the promised one by killing the male babies in Bethlehem. The Pharisees all knew that God would send the promised Messiah, King of the Jews. When the time came, they rejected the one that they waited upon. The writings in the book of Isaiah precede the coming of Christ approximately seven hundred years. Yet in darkness they had seen a great light, and the light shone upon those in the shadow of death. They knew that a future child would be born and the government would be on his shoulders, and his name would be called Wonderful, Counselor, the Mighty God, the Everlasting Father, Prince of Peace. His government would be everlasting, and the throne of king David, he would sit upon (Isaiah 9:2, 6–7).

The Word Becomes Flesh

The Holy Spirit revealed the coming Messiah to the Old Testament prophets, and even the angels were curious to see God become man.

> *Which things the angels desire to look into.* (1 Peter 1:12)
>
> *Who being in the form of God thought it not robbery to be equal with God.* (Philippians 2:6)
>
> *I came forth from the Father and am come into the world again. I leave the world and go to the Father.* (John 16:28)
>
> *But made himself of no reputation and took upon him the form of a servant made in the likeness of men and being found in fashion as a man, he humbled himself and became obedient unto death, even the death of the cross.* (Philippians 2:7–8)

Christ emptied himself. He could not cease to be God but chose (voluntarily) to set aside the outward manifestation and attributes of his glory. Jesus did allow for his supernatural power to manifest when he walked on water and at the transfiguration (Luke 9:29). He operated in his supernatural abilities when performing miracles, raising some from the dead and knowing the thoughts of men. When they came to arrest him, he said, "I AM"; and power of God came forth, causing them to fall backward.

Jesus Christ Fulfills the Promises and Prophecies of the Old Testament.

> *God during many times and in different manners spoke in times past unto the fathers by the prophets. He has in these last days spoken unto us by his Son, whom he has appointed heir of all things and by whom also he made the worlds,*

> *who being the brightness of his glory and the express image of his person and upholding all things by the word of his power, when he had by himself purged our sins, sat down on the right hand of the Majesty on high.* (Hebrews 1:1–3)

- God speaks through the prophets in the Old Testament.
- God speaks to us through his Son, Jesus, in these last days.
- Jesus made the worlds and upholds all things by himself.
- Jesus is the heir of all things.
- The radiant brightness of Jesus is his glory and his image.

Virgin Birth

God would give Israel a sign of the coming King. A virgin will conceive and bear a son and will call his name Immanuel (Isaiah 7:14). When the appointed time had come, the Almighty God stepped out of his dwelling place to become a man four thousand years after the creation of Adam and Eve.

The Angel Gabriel brings God's message to Mary. The Holy Spirit will come upon Mary, and the power of the Highest will overshadow Mary (Luke 1:35) God the Holy Spirit overshadowed Mary as he did in the beginning of creation by overshadowing/hovering over the waters. The Word of God is the spiritual seed. Women do not have seed or sperm. Since there was no intercourse, as is between humans, the Holy Spirit would plant the seed into Mary's egg. Mary's egg was fertilized by the "seed." Fetal development began, and the Word became flesh. God's DNA and Mary's DNA merged. God took on humanity. In Genesis 3:15, we were introduced to this concept of "the seed of the woman." God created man from earth, blew breath into him, and he became a living soul; therefore, it is not inconceivable to picture the supernatural impregnation of the virgin. God can bring forth from the invisible particulate matter.

God the Father provided twenty-three chromosomes, and Mary, the mother of Jesus, produced twenty-three chromosomes. Since it was predetermined that the baby would be male, God contributed the Y chromosome. The baby Jesus grew in Mary's womb. This physiological process allows the embryo to attach itself to the uterine wall. The placenta membrane is formed from the embryonic chorion (sack) and the maternal uterine tissue to protect the embryo, provide food, and waste removal and oxygen. The fetus is surrounded by amniotic fluid. The rapid growth of the chorion forms villi, which becomes vascularized as the embryonic circulation develops. This growth destroys some endometrium tissue (uterus), including small blood vessels, allowing small amounts of blood oozing from these vessels to form pools around the villi (part of placenta). The umbilical cord develops, connecting the embryo with the placenta, which consists of chorion together with the uterine tissue between the villi that contains maternal capillaries and small pools of maternal blood. Blood from the villi returns to the embryo through the umbilical vein, which passes through the umbilical cord. The placenta brings maternal blood close to the blood of the fetus, but the two circulatory systems are separate from each other. Oxygen and nutrients pass from the maternal blood through the placental tissue and diffuse into the embryo's blood, which then transports these materials to the developing tissues of the embryo's body. Two umbilical arteries pass through the umbilical cord and connect with a network of capillaries, developing within the chorionic villi.[24]

Human cells are composed of blood and genetic material. Jesus received his humanity through the blood of his mother. When it was time for his birth, he was born in the manner of humanity.

Joseph was Jesus's stepfather. In order for Jesus to be associated with his blood lineage through the tribe of Judah, it must be on his mother's side. In Luke 3:23, the writer lists the ancestors of Joseph. In Matthew 1:1, he lists the generation of Jesus beginning with Abraham; and in verse 1:16, he lists Joseph, the husband of Mary, of whom was born Jesus.

At the time of the Messiah's birth, there were several belief systems: those who believed the prophecies, those who rejected the truth of the scriptures, and those that fell into Roman idolatry. Those who heard the good news of Messiah's birth and received the seed of truth planted in good soil, and the Word grew in their hearts. The shepherds tending their sheep at the time of Jesus's birth heard the message of the angels and were the first to see the baby Jesus, and they believed. Simeon and Anna had waited many years at the temple to see the Son of God. On the eighth day, Jesus was brought to the temple for circumcision, and when they saw him,they believed. The Magi from a distant land traveled to see the child Jesus, who at that time was a toddler. They brought him gifts, and they believed. Herod knew the prophecies of the coming king. He allowed Satan to influence his mind and put forth a decree to kill all babies from the age of two and under. Satan set out to kill Jesus in order to prevent the fulfillment of prophecy.

Luke 2:1–20, "*It came to pass in those days there went out a decree from Caesar Augustus that all the world should be taxed.*" This was the first census and tax taken while Cyrenius was governor of Syria. And everyone was on his way to register for the census, each to his own city. Joseph also went up from Galilee from the city of Nazareth to Judea to the city of David, which is called Bethlehem, because he was of the house and family of David, in order to register along with Mary—his wife being with child. While they were there, the days were completed for her to give birth. And she gave birth to her firstborn son, and she wrapped

---

24 Eldra Solomon, P. William Davis, *Human Anatomy & Physiology*, (Philadelphia, PA: Saunders College Publishing, 1983), 712

him in cloth and laid him in a manger because there was no room for them in the inn. This fulfills Micah 5:2; he would be born in Bethlehem Ephrata and be ruler of Israel (this second part of the prophecy will be fulfilled in the millennial reign).

In the same region, there were some shepherds out in the fields and keeping watch over their sheep by night. And an angel of the Lord suddenly stood before them, and the glory of the Lord shone around them, and they were terribly frightened. But the angel said to them, "Do not be afraid, for behold, I bring you good news of great joy, which will be for all the people for today in the city of David. There has been born for you a Savior who is Christ the Lord. This will be a sign for you, you will find a baby wrapped in clothes and lying in a manger." And suddenly there appeared with the angel a multitude of the heavenly host, praising God and saying, "Glory to God in the highest, and on earth peace among men with whom he is pleased." When the angels had gone away from them into heaven, the shepherds began saying to one another, "Let us go straight to Bethlehem then and see this thing that has happened what the Lord has made known to us." So they came in a hurry and found their way to Mary and Joseph and the baby as he lay in the manger. When they had seen this, they made known the statement that had been told to them about this child. And all who heard it wondered at the things that were told them by the shepherds. But Mary treasured all these things, pondering them in her heart. The shepherds went back, glorifying and praising God for all that they had heard and seen, just as had been told them (Luke 2:8). The shepherds were the first witnesses to the birth.

Luke 2:25–32, Mary and Joseph bring Jesus to the temple in Jerusalem for blessing. Simeon, a just and devout man having the Holy Ghost with him, waited for the consolation of Israel. It was revealed unto him by the Holy Ghost that he should not see death before he had seen the Lord's Christ. He held the Messiah in his arms and blessed God, saying, "Now let your servant depart in peace, for my eyes have seen your salvation, a light to the Gentiles and the glory of your people Israel."

Another group of people called Magi were from the priestly order of Zoroaster among the Persians and Babylonians visited the young child Jesus. These Magi from the east were adept in study of the constellations. They saw the unusual star, and it was beyond natural but a divine manifestation used by God to indicate the place of the Messiah's birth. They knew by the alignment of the stars and one bright star that the King of the Jews was to be born. Why would the Magi be interested in the Jewish Messiah? We understand that the order of Zoroaster predating the time Israel was taken into Babylonian captivity. The prophet Daniel had been assigned to oversee the Zoroaster priesthood, and through Daniel, they began to understand the wisdom of God. The Jewish presence in Babylon had influenced many. By the time the large caravan made their way to Jerusalem to see the baby king, Jesus may have been a year old because Herod was still alive. When Magi spoke with Herod, he also knew the prophecy of the sign in the sky and the bright star was a fulfillment of the coming King of the Jews. Following the star, they found the child Jesus, now living in a home in Bethlehem, and they rejoiced exceedingly. The Magi worshipped him and presented him with gifts of gold, frankincense, and myrrh (Matthew 2). From the biblical record, Joseph, Mary, and Jesus were not poor as many claim. Also, during Jesus ministry, he would state that he came first to the Jew. Herein we see the first Jews to witness the birth were the shepherds. The Magi were representative of the Gentiles and the second to see Jesus, first to the Jew and then to the Gentiles.

The angel of the Lord appears to Joseph in a dream and tells Mary and Joseph to take Jesus to Egypt to prevent Herod from killing Jesus. They were told to stay in Egypt until after the death of Herod. When the word came, they could then return to their home in Nazareth (Matthew 2:13).

Jesus was born in September, around 3–2 BC. The Bible tells us that Jesus was baptized by John in AD 28 at age thirty. Jesus began his ministry when he was thirty years old. Jesus's ministry was about three to three and half years long. He was crucified at the age of thirty-three in April AD 30/31.

The Kingdom of God is the Kingdom of Heaven

God the Father looks forward to the time God the Son will inherit the eternal kingdom:

> *But unto the Son he said, Thy throne O God is forever and ever, a scepter of righteousness is the scepter of your kingdom. You have loved righteousness and hated iniquity, therefore God, even your God has anointed you with the oil of gladness above your fellows, and you Lord in the beginning had laid the foundations of the earth and the heavens are the work of your hands; they will perish but you remain and they all will wax old as does a garment and as a vesture will you fold them up and they will be changed but you are the same and your years will not fail. But to which of the angels said he at any time, sit on my right hand until I make your enemies your footstool?* Are they *not all ministering spirits sent forth to minister for them who shall be heirs of salvation* (Hebrews 1:8–14)

- God the Father and God the Son share the throne.
- The coming kingdom is one of righteousness.
- God the Father acknowledges God the Son, anointing him with oil (Holy Spirit).
- God the Father acknowledges God the Son before his incarnation and before the foundations of the earth were laid, and the heavens are the work of his hands. The earth will wax, old, and perish, but God the Son is forever.

- God reaffirms that he did not command any angel to sit at his right hand.
- Angels are to minister to the heirs of salvation—all who believe on Jesus, the Son of God.

John the Baptist first announced the kingdom of heaven is at hand (Matthew 3:1).

Jesus is the Kingdom of Heaven on earth. From that time forth, the spiritual kingdom dwells within each believer until Jesus establishes his literal kingdom on earth. As we recite in the Lord's Prayer, "*Our Father who are in heaven, holy is your name, your kingdom come your will be done on earth as it is in heaven,*" We are tasked to understand the mystery of the kingdom of heaven. Jesus said he would speak things that had been kept secret from the foundation of the world (Matthew 13:35).

Unbelievers will not be able to hear, see, or understand the principles of the kingdom, and many will be deluded in believing everyone is going to heaven. Paul makes it clear that the works of the flesh are adultery, fornication, uncleanness, lasciviousness, idolatry, witchcraft, hatred, variance, emulations, wrath, strife, seditions, heresies, liars, envyings, murders, drunkenness, reveling, and such of which I tell you ... they which do such things will not inherit the kingdom of God (Galatians 5:19–21).

We find illustrations and parables concerning the kingdom in Matthew 13:24: kingdom of heaven is a field (our heart) where good seed (Word of God) was sowed, but Satan sowed tares in with the wheat. The tares (unbelievers) and wheat (believers) grow together until the harvest. Yeshua will tell the angels (reapers), "Gather first the tares and bind them to burn and gather the wheat into my barn." Jesus will send forth his angels, and they will gather out of his kingdom all things that offend and sin and shall cast them into a furnace of fire; there will be wailing and gnashing of teeth. Then shall the righteous shine forth as the sun in the kingdom of their Father

Summary of the Kingdom of God (Matthew 13:24):

- The field is the world, and the soil is our heart.
- Jesus sowed the good seed, which became the believers.
- The good seed grew into wheat (children of the kingdom) in the earth.
- Satan came in a sowed tares, who are the children of the wicked one.
- Bad seed grew into tares (unbelievers) in with the wheat.
- The believers and the unbelievers exist together on the earth.
- Now in the end of the age, it is becoming discernable who are the wicked and who are the righteous.
- Harvest time is end of the world; the angels (reapers) will identify and separate the believers from the unbelievers.

- The unbelieving sinners will be gathered together and cast into hell.

People hearing the Gospel is likened to a seed that falls by the wayside and the birds eat it; or some seed fell upon stony places, grew, but had no deep roots, and the sun scorched it; other seeds fell among thorns and grew, but the thorns choked the seed; and best of all, the seed fell into good ground and brought forth fruit (Matthew 13:1–8)

In this passage, it explains the parable of the seeds and soil.

> *When one hears the word of the kingdom and understand it not then comes the wicked one and catch it away that which was sown in his heart. This is he that received the seed by the side. He that received the seed into stony places, the same is he that hears the word and with joy receives it yet he has no root in himself but endure for a white for when tribulation or persecution arise because of the word, by and by he is offended. He also that received seed among the thorns is he that hears the word and the cares of this world and the deceitfulness of riches choke the word and he became unfruitful. But he that received the seed into the good ground is he that hears the word and understands it which also bears fruit and brings forth some a hundred fold, some sixty, some thirty.* (Matthew 13:19–23)

Summary of Mathew 13:19–23

- The seed is the Word.
- The soil is the heart.
- Those who do not understand the Word, Satan takes it away.
- Seeds fell upon rocks, grew up, scorched by the sun (persecution) and weak roots withered away (worldly cares). Jesus said, "These that hear the Word receive it joyfully, but it does not take root, when tribulation or persecution arise they become offended."
- Seed fell among thorns and were choked by the thorns. Jesus said they hear the Word but because of the cares of this world and deceitfulness of riches choke the word, and he is unfruitful.
- Seed fell on good ground and brought forth fruit. These are they that heard the word, understand it, and bring forth fruit.

Summary of the parable of the mustard seed—the kingdom of heaven is like a grain of mustard seed (Matthew 13:31–32)

- The Word as a tiny seed in good ground can produce strong roots, grow into a large tree, and bring forth good fruit.

Parable of the Kingdom of Heaven is like unto a certain king who made a marriage for his son (Matthew 22:1). He sent out his servants to invite the guest to the wedding, but they would not come. Again he sent out his servants to tell the guests that all things are ready and come to the marriage. They went their ways, tending to the cares of this world. They treated the servants spitefully and killed them. The king was angered and sent out his army to destroy the murderers and burn their city. The king says the wedding is ready, but they who were invited are not worthy. He tells the servants to go into the highways, and as many as they find, bid them to the marriage. They found both good and bad, and the king came in to see the guests, and there was one who had not on a wedding garment. The king asked, "How is it that you came here and have not a wedding garment?" and the man was speechless. The king told the servants to bind him hand and foot and take him away and cast him into outer darkness where there shall be weeping and gnashing of teeth. Many are called, but few are chosen.

Summary of the parable of the Kingdom of Heaven and the marriage.

- Father God has prepared for Jesus, his Son, the marriage of the believers for thousands of years. The ceremony will take place when the saints are all gathered together in heaven.
- His servants—the apostles, prophets, preachers, teachers—went out to invite many to come into a saving relationship with the Son, and they rejected such a great invitation.
- Jesus came first to the Jew. He was rejected. The father sent his wrath upon the Jews, destroying the temple in 70 AD, and scattered them throughout the world.
- Jesus extended the invitation to the Gentiles from the four corners of the earth. Those who are good need to accept the invitation of salvation, and bad sinners need to repent and accept the invitation. "Many are called but few are chosen."
- Except a man be born again, he cannot see the kingdom of heaven (John 3:3).
- When Jesus calls his bride to meet him in the air, they will be changed and adorned in white robes
- The king saw a man without wedding garments. This is like those who are shut out from entering the kingdom but are saying, "I had fellowship with Jesus, I heard his Gospel, I had a mega church, and I gave to the poor." It is like those who have a form of godliness but deny the truth. Only thing Jesus can say is, "I know you not."

- Those who are left behind and must endure the tribulation have one final chance to get right with God. The marriage supper of the Lamb will take place near the end of the tribulation period in heaven before Jesus returns with his saints. At that time, Jesus will bind the unrepentant, like the reapers who bind the tares, and they will be cast into outer darkness, where there is weeping gnashing of teeth, the place of hell.

Who Will Inherit the Kingdom?

John 3:3 … except a man be born again, he cannot see the kingdom of God.

Jesus gives this summarized parable:

When the Master of the house has risen up and has shut the door and you stand outside of the door and knock, crying, "Lord, Lord, open unto us," and the Lord will say, "I know not who you are." They will say, "But, Lord, we have eaten and drank in your presence, and we know you have taught in our streets." The Lord will say, "I know not where you are, depart from me, all you workers of iniquity." There will be weeping and gnashing of teeth when you will see Abraham, Isaac, Jacob, and all the prophets in the kingdom of God and you will not be there. The believers will come from the east, west, north, south and will sit down in the kingdom of God. The last will be first, and the first will be last.

Matthew 24:50—those who are not ready, not watching, sinful living, he shall cut them asunder, appoint them their portion with the hypocrites who are in hell.

> *If we sin willfully after that we have received the knowledge of the truth, there remains no more sacrifice for sins, but a certain fearful looking for of judgment and fiery indignation which shall devour the adversaries he that despised Moses' law died without mercy under two witnesses. Of how much sorer punishment suppose you will be thought worthy, who has trodden under-foot the Son of God and has counted the blood of the covenant wherewith he was sanctified, an unholy thing and has done despite unto the Spirit of grace. Vengeance belongs unto me, I will recompense says the Lord and the Lord will judge his people.* (Hebrews 10:26)

Once we have received the knowledge of the truth, there remains no more sacrifice for sins. If we willfully sin and reject such a great gift of salvation, there is no way for that person to be saved. We become an enemy of God. Rejection of the Holy Spirit is an unpardonable sin. The punishment is much worse for those who trample upon the Son of God and consider his shed blood unholy.

Now the works of the flesh are manifest which are these: adultery, fornication, uncleanness, lasciviousness, idolatry, witchcraft, hatred, variance, emulations, wrath, strife, seditions, heresies, envying, murders, drunkenness, revellings and such like of the which I tell you before, as I have also told you in time past, that they which do such things shall not inherit the Kingdom of God. (Galatians 5:19)

Know you not that the unrighteous will not inherit the kingdom of God? Be not deceived, neither fornicators, idolaters, adulterers, nor ***effeminate*** [homosexuals], *nor abusers of themselves with mankind, nor thieves, covetous, nor drunkards, nor revilers nor extortioners shall inherit the Kingdom of God.* (1 Corinthians 6:9)

Fornication, all uncleanness, covetousness, let it not be once named among you as becomes the saints. Neither filthiness, nor foolish talking nor jesting which are not convenient but rather giving of thanks. For this you know, that no whoremonger, nor unclean person, nor covetous man who is an idolater has any inheritance in the kingdom of Christ and of God. Let no man deceive you with vain words, for because of these things comes the wrath of God upon the children of disobedience. Be not partakers with them. For you were sometimes darkness but now are you light in the Lord, walk as children of light. (Ephesians 5:3)

Six things the Lord hates and seven an abomination unto him: a proud look, a lying tongue, and hands that shed innocent blood, a heart that devises wicked imaginations, feet that be swift in running to mischief, a false witness that speaks lies and he that sows discord among the brethren. (Proverbs 6:16)

The Ministry of Yeshua

Jesus began his ministry around AD 28, when he was thirty years old, and continued for three and a half years to around AD 31–32.

John Baptizes Jesus, Matthew 3

John the Baptist's message was to repent, for the kingdom of heaven is at hand. On this particular day, a crowd gathered, including the Pharisees and Sadducees. Orthodox Jews believed in the sacrament of baptism, but John called them religious hypocrites—a *generation of vipers.* And in their hearing, John clearly stated that *I indeed baptize you with water unto repentance but he that comes after me is mightier than I whose shoes I am not worthy to bear and he will baptize you with the Holy Ghost and with fire …* These Jews knew the prophetic scriptures were being fulfilled in their presence. Then came Jesus, the kingdom of God, to John at the Jordan River. It appears that John the Baptist acknowledged the Messiah's arrival and, knowing this, considered it not proper to baptize Jesus who was sinless. Jesus said, "*Suffer it to be so for thus it becomes us to fulfill all righteousness* [fulfill prophecy]."

At the time of Jesus's baptism, his ministry began. We also see the Triune God, Spirit of God (his anointing) descending as a dove upon Jesus, and the voice of God said, "*This is my beloved Son in whom I am well pleased* (his confirmation).

Hundreds of years before this event, Isaiah 42:1 predicts, "*Behold my servant whom I uphold, mine elect in whom my soul delights, I have put my spirit upon him; he will bring forth judgment to the Gentiles.*" The Son becomes the suffering servant. He will be the perfect sacrifice. The Spirit in the form of a dove rested upon Jesus. He has brought salvation to the Jew and the Gentile.

Water baptism represents the death, burial, and Resurrection of Jesus. For believers, the ritual of baptism is unto repentance—an outward sign of our death to sin. Water baptism represents the Crucifixion of our old sin nature. Believers are submerged in water, which symbolizes our death to sin. We are raised into a new eternal life in Jesus. No longer will sin have dominion over us, for we are not under the law but under grace (Romans 6:1–14).

The Temptation of Jesus, Matthew 4

Jesus was transported to the wilderness by the Spirit. Where was this wilderness? We consider this supernatural event. In times past, men of God were transported by the Spirit into the realm of God. With some it was bodily, and with others it was in the spirit. John said he was in the spirit on the Lord's day when he received the visions recorded in the book of Revelation. In this instance, Jesus probably disappeared and reappeared at his given coordinates. Time was altered. One second Jesus was in our physical, earthly realm; then moving through time space continuum, his molecular structure was reassembled back in the physical realm in a new location. This happened to Phillip, who after baptizing the Ethiopian eunuch, disappeared or was transported by the Spirit to another location.

This God-ordained time alone in the wilderness was for what purpose? Truly, Jesus did not feel lonely or abandoned. The host of angels were always present. He could see them. God was with him.

Jesus decided to fast for forty days. Jesus may have put himself into suspended animation for forty days. He was hungry at the end of the forty days because his humanity kicked in. Why did Jesus fast in the first place? After his Resurrection, a length of forty days is given before his ascension.

The number 40 is associated with trials and testing. For instance, Moses was on Mount Sinai for forty days, receiving the law at the same time the people were making a golden idol.

Elijah, fleeing from Jezebel, went into the wilderness and was there forty days in Horeb. The angel of the Lord brought him food for forty days.

At the end of the forty days, Satan pays Jesus a visit. Satan, as the god over the earth, having been running to and fro throughout the earth, was told by his minions that Jesus, Son of God, is in the wilderness. Satan was very familiar with the weakness of humanity, and perhaps seeing God in the form of man, Satan considered there may have been vulnerability in Jesus he could exploit. However, we know Jesus was fully God, fully man and sinless. Jesus was not going to allow his created fallen angel Satan to cause him to sin. Yet Satan, like a wild animal, came looking for weakness he could attack. Satan knew Jesus was hungry, and he began goading Jesus to turn stones into bread to fulfill the lust of the flesh. Jesus said, "*Man will not live by bread alone but by every word that proceeds out of the mouth of God.*"

Satan was not so easily put off and supernaturally transported Jesus to another location in Jerusalem onto the pinnacle of the temple. Thinking about sitting on a pinnacle would seem uncomfortable unless we take into consideration that Satan is a spirit and Jesus, God, is spirit. Here they are outside of our time-space domain, invisible, and are spiritually encompassed in the vicinity of the temple pinnacle. Satan begins with a challenge to Jesus: "*If you be the Son of God, cast yourself down for it is written, he will give his angels charge concerning thee and in their hand they will bear thee up lest at any time you dash your foot against a stone.*" Satan quotes a portion of Psalm 91. Jesus responds, "*It is written again, you will not tempt the Lord your God.*" This temptation is referred to as the lust of eye. As we ponder this exchange between God the Creator and his created, what was Satan's frame of mind? Certainly, he knew Jesus was all-powerful, so much so he could save himself.

Lastly, Satan transported Jesus up to a high mountain and showed him all the kingdoms of the world and the glory of them. Humans do desire the lure of worldly things, and this is referred to as the pride of life. Satan said, "*All these things will I give you if you will fall down and worship me.*" Jesus rebukes Satan, "*Get thee hence Satan for it is written, you will worship the Lord your God and him only will you serve.*"

In considering Satan's exchange with Jesus, it seems we are looking at a scene in the theater of the absurd. In this play, the thief stole your gold then tells you he will return your gold if you accept his offer and honor him.

Jesus is the Creator of all things. Jesus in his power upholds all of creation. Jesus knows the end from the beginning. Satan deceived himself, believing he could tempt the holy God to sin against himself. The Bible presents this scene in the wilderness and its related temptations as a lesson to angels and to mankind. The God of creation now in this world is above all that he created.

Jesus Gives the Invitation

Jesus began his ministry by inviting people to follow him. He first invited the disciples who gave up their worldly goods and followed him. The first twelve disciples were Peter, James, John, Andrew, Philip, Bartholomew, Matthew, Thomas, James, Thaddaeus, Simon the Canaanite, and Judas Iscariot (Mark 3:13–19). Jesus ordained them to preach. Jesus did empower them through his Holy Spirit to perform miracles to heal all manner of disease and infirmities, to cast out demons, and to raise the dead. As it was in those days and throughout the church age, Jesus still calls upon many to share the Gospel. Through the first twelve and millions later, the masses of humanity were invited to come into the kingdom of God.

Healing the Multitudes

Jesus healed all manner of disease and cast out demons (Matthew 4:23). Jesus went throughout Galilee. The people came from Syria, Decapolis, Jerusalem, Judea, Jordan, and beyond for healing and to free of demons. All the works of Jesus cannot be contained in one book (Hebrews 3:7).

Today if you will hear his voice, harden not your hearts as in the provocation (Israel in the wilderness). They saw all God did for them. He delivered them out of Egypt; they saw miracles; and he provided for them for forty years. Yet they grieved the Lord by not taking heed, and their hearts became evil in their unbelief. God allowed many of them to die in the wilderness. They forfeited the promise of a land flowing with milk and honey.

The above passages tell the account of the Israelites in the wilderness thousand of years ago. The message illustrates a problem facing many who fill our churches today. They know about Christ, but they do not know him personally. When we hear the Word, we should listen and draw near to him and not harden our hearts and reject him. We must study the Word, for it is the bread of life for our spiritual well-being. For his promise is the blessed hope that we have eternal rest in him.

> *For the Word of God is quick and powerful and sharper than any two edged sword, piercing even to the dividing asunder of soul and spirit and of the joints and marrow and is a discerner of the thoughts and intents of the heart. There is not any creature that is not manifest in his sight but all things are naked and opened unto the eyes of him with whom we have to do.* (Hebrews 4:12–13)

The Word of God Jesus is alive, able to change lives as it (the Spirit) works in us from the physical to the soul. It penetrates the core of our moral and spiritual life and discerns what is within us both good and evil.

Do This in Remembrance of Me

I invite all my beloved saints to keep the Passover with me. I will not break bread with you again until we sit together at the marriage supper. Until that time, remember me and all that I did for you by celebrating my death and Resurrection. Breaking bread together as a symbol of my body that was beat and spit upon. Drink this cup, which symbolizes the blood that I shed for the forgiveness of your sins and the healing of your diseases. Remember the first Passover and the blood of the lamb that was shed for your protection and deliverance. The one that betrayed me, sat with me, and took the bread and the wine unworthily. Remember, you are all unworthy; therefore be faithful to repent. No one can be good enough or holy enough, but through my blood, you are covered in my righteousness. I have forgiven all that have betrayed and forsaken me. I leave my grace, and you may enter into my fellowship. You may sit and commune with me. Remember, because of my death, you are overcomers and have victory over death (1 Corinthians 11).

Will You Tarry with Me for One Hour

> *As he prayed the fashion of his countenance was altered and his raiment was white and glistening. There talked with him two men which were Moses and Elias who appeared in glory and spoke of his decease which he must accomplish at Jerusalem.* (Luke 9:29–36)

Peter, James, and John awoke in time to see the supernatural transfiguration of Jesus and the spirits of Moses and Elijah … "*There came a cloud and overshadowed them and they feared as they entered into the cloud and there came a voice out of the cloud saying, this is my beloved son, hear him.*"

Jesus said, "My hour is near, and knowing the agony I must suffer, I need to come before the Father for strength. Watch with me while I pray. Yes, I am disappointed that you could not stay with me for one hour. I know your spirit is willing but your flesh is weak. After I return to the Father, spend time with me in prayer. You will receive the power of the Holy Spirit, and though I no longer walk with you in the flesh, we are connected through my Holy Spirit. I love you and will be with you always."

First and foremost, Jesus came to offer himself as the perfect sacrifice for the sins of all mankind (Luke 22:43). On the Mount of Olives in the garden of Gethsemane, Jesus understood the suffering he would endure, and there appeared an angel unto him from heaven, strengthening him. Jesus did die for sinners while we were without strength, in unbelief, destined to life without God. All he asks is that we spend one hour with him.

This invitation is timeless. It is for the Jew, Christian, Muslim, Hindu, and all mankind. We must first believe on who is Jesus, and through the Holy Spirit our mind and heart is touched.

Belief in Jesus leads to faith in Jesus. Faith strengthens our trust in Jesus who gave us his peace, comfort, or assurance to see us through the tribulations of this world. As we go through tribulation, we stand in the grace of Jesus, his favor, and look to Jesus—our blessed hope—to deliver us from all evil. Trusting and investing in these things, we now have the strength to glory in our tribulation; we can give praise to God in our circumstance because Jesus did promise to deliver us from them all even unto death (Romans 5:1–5).

<u>The Love of God Transcends Human Comprehension.</u>

> *For God so loved the world that he gave his only begotten son and whosoever will believe on him will not perish but have everlasting life.* (John 3:16)

This is a promise to all the people in the world. He loves the sinner but hates the sin. We begin to understand Agape love.

> *Hereby perceive we the love of God because he laid down his life for us and we ought to lay down our lives for the brethren.* (1 John 3:16)
>
> *For the Father himself loves you because you have loved me and have believed that I came out from God.* (John 16:27)

Before the foundation of the world, the Triune God knew the Word would become man and die once in the end of the world, ushering in the era of grace.

<u>Jesus, the Perfect Sacrifice</u>

Hebrews 9:11–28, Jesus Christ becomes our High Priest of good things to come by a greater and more perfect tabernacle not made with hands—that is to say, not of this building, neither by the blood of animals; but by his own blood, he entered in once into the Holy Place, having obtained eternal redemption for us. How much more shall the blood of Christ who through the eternal Spirit offered himself without spot to God to purge your conscience from dead works to serve the living God? For this cause, he is the mediator of the New Testament that by means of death for the redemption of the transgressions that were under the first testament, they which are called <u>might</u> receive the promise of eternal inheritance. For where a testament is, there must also of necessity be the death of the testator. For a testament is of force after men are dead; otherwise it is of no strength at all. Under Moses, the Day of Atonement was dedicated with animal sacrifices, red wool, water, hyssop, all sprinkled on

the book and the people. The people were ceremonially cleansed on the outside. These practices pointed toward the coming one whose shed blood is more acceptable than the blood of animals. Through the shed blood of Christ, we are transformed and cleansed on the inside. Without the shedding of blood, there is no remission for sin. Christ has not entered into the Holy Place made with hands but into heaven itself to appear in the presence of God for us. He offered himself once in the end of the world to put away sin by the sacrifice of himself. It is appointed unto men once to die but after this the judgment. Believers go before Christ at the Bema Seat and the unrepentant stand before Christ at the white throne judgment.

The Crucifixion of Jesus

The Old Testament predicts the death of the Son of God.

> *And I will pour upon the house of David and upon the inhabitants of Jerusalem the spirit of grace and of supplication and they will look upon me whom they pierced and they shall mourn for him.* (Zechariah 12:10)

Some Jews at the time of his death did mourn him. At the end of the tribulation, they will mourn him as a nation when he returns and Israel will be redeemed and spiritually regenerated.

Psalm 22 is often called the song of the cross. It points beyond David's time to the suffering and death of the Messiah. This Psalm begins with, "My God, my God, why have thou forsaken me?" words uttered by Jesus on the cross. Psalm 22:14–18 describes the excruciating pain of the Crucifixion, his thirst, the piercing of his hands and feet, parting his garments, and casting lots for them.

Daniel 9:25–26 is a prophecy that foretells that Messiah will be cut off (crucified) but not for himself.

People play the blame game on who was responsible for killing Jesus. We know some of the Jewish leaders called for his death. The Romans nailed him to the cross, and the Christians ran away or stood by as spectators. Even if the Christians had taken up arms to protect Jesus, it would not have prevented the Crucifixion. It was preordained by God that his son would die for us.

> *My Father loves me because I lay down my life, that I might take it again. No man takes it from me, but I lay it down of myself. I have power to lay it down and I have power to take it again.* (John 10:17)

Jesus was famous. Many had heard of him. Thousands had been healed by him. Others had received their salvation by believing on his Word. There was a great gathering that watched the events at the time Jesus was arrested until the time he died on the cross. There are numerous supernatural events that took place on that day, such as darkness, earthquake, and the veil in the temple was torn. Jesus hung on his cross between two sinners. The sinner hanging on the cross on his left was the embodiment of the unrepentant sinner. He mocked Jesus. While the sinner on the right side of Jesus had heard the message of salvation and eternal life and asked Jesus to save him, Jesus said, "Today, you will be with me in paradise." This is a reminder that Jesus does not want anyone to perish but all to come to salvation. The grace of Jesus was there for either man to come to him or to reject him.

The Resurrection of Jesus

If you like supernatural thrillers, the Resurrection is the mother of them all. Jesus said, "*Father into thy hands I commend my spirit.*" At the instant, Jesus died; his body still on the cross, his spirit left his physical body. While in the spirit, the following scripture tells us that Jesus initiated several actions: Psalm 68:18, "*Thou hast ascended on high, thou has* [descended] *led captivity captive, thou has received gifts for men, yes for the rebellious also, that the Lord God might dwell among them.* It does appear that Jesus ascended into the heavenly realm to the Father, and he may at this time have taken his blood to the mercy seat. We also know that Jesus descended into the lower regions to set the captives free and take the keys of hell and death.

> *But now is Christ risen from the dead and become the* ***First Fruits of them that slept*** [dead]. *For since by man came death, by man came also the resurrection of the dead.* (1 Corinthians 15:20–21)

This is a testament to all the righteous who died from Adam to the thief on the cross; their souls would be taken from Abraham's bosom to be with Jesus in the heavenly domain. A deeper understanding of the Resurrection is found in chapter 15.

> *He had promised afore by his prophets in the holy scriptures concerning his son Jesus Christ our Lord which was made of the seed of David according to the flesh and declared to be the Son of God with power according to the spirit of holiness by the resurrection from the dead by whom we have received grace and apostleship for obedience to the faith among all nations for his name, among whom are you also the called of Jesus Christ.* (Romans 1:2–6)

Jesus came to earth and put on humanity to redeem his creation who had lost their way by following Satan. His Resurrection was the First Fruits for souls of the righteous from captivity, gathered together with Jesus in heaven.

There are some preachers who put forth a false concept that Jesus was not crucified on Friday and it was not possible to get a third-day Resurrection out of this time frame. One pastor reasoned that in Matthew 27:62, it tells us that the next day (Saturday) following the preparation (preparing Jesus body on Friday), the Pharisees came to Pilate and said, "We remember that the deceiver said while he was yet alive, '**After** three days, I will rise again.'" These preachers chose to take the word ***after*** and reason unto themselves this is to be interpreted as more than three days. People who adhere to the truth of the scriptures would not take the words spoken by the Pharisees as credible in that they called Jesus a "deceiver" and then ignoring prophetic scriptures foretelling of Messiah's Resurrection on the third day.

April 2014, Joel C. Rosenberg's blog discussed the belief that the third-day Resurrection was a Jewish concept that predates Jesus. He quotes Dr. Israel Knohl, professor and Dead Sea scrolls expert at Hebrew University, "Death and third-day Resurrection of Messiah is in fact a distinctly Jewish concept that predate Jesus." His proof is a three-foot-tall tablet with eighty-seven lines of Hebrew predicting the coming of Messiah who would arise from the dead in three days. Archaeologist and scholars have named the tablet "Gabriel's Revelation" because it suggests that the angel Gabriel was instructed by God to direct that the Messiah be raised from the dead on the third day. Dr. Knohl has written extensively on this precept. Rosenberg references 1 Corinthians 15:1–5: Paul preaches that the believers stand on the Word that Jesus died for our sins, was buried, and raised on the third day.

Some confusion could be eliminated if people are able to consider the three days not as twenty-four-hour literal days but apply the events as given in the scriptures. On Friday he died, day one. On Saturday his body was in the tomb, day two; and on Sunday his body and soul reunited and he left the tomb, day three. We are reminded that God sits outside of time and is not relegated by time. Time was given by God for man's benefit. Once the spirit of Jesus departed his body while hanging on the cross, he entered into his spiritual domain where time is not literal.

On the third day, the angel of the Lord rolled back the stone, announced that Jesus had risen, and the tomb was found empty. The burial clothes remained. At the moment of the Resurrection, when spirit was reunited with body, an energy signature was left on the burial clothes. This was a physiological reaction of energy concentrated in particulate matter that responded to the supernatural power of God and a testimony to the truth of the Resurrection. The imprint on the grave cloth, known as the Shroud of Turin, has been viewed and tested for its authenticity.

Perry Stone, *Secrets from Beyond the Grave*, Charisma House, 2010, suggests that at the time of death, when the soul vacates the body, "There is an extremely powerful surge of electricity in the body or some type of electromagnetic activity" (p. 119). Stone said that people who have had near-death experiences say their watches stopped at the exact time of their death or that the magnetic strips on their bank cards demagnetized. In regard to the Resurrection of Christ, Stone said, "The only explanation would be that the power of the Resurrection was so great that the energy around Christ's body was imprinted in the cloth in the same manner that light passing through a lens of a camera would imprint the image on photo film" (p. 120).

Jesus appeared to Mary outside of the tomb and said, "Handle me not, for I have not yet ascended," which pointed to his literal ascension forty days later in the sight of angels and witnesses.

Jesus, Our High Priest

Hebrews 3:1–6, Jesus Christ is the Head and High Priest of our profession. Jesus is greater than Moses, whom he called out. All glory to God the Son who has built all things. Christ is head over his church, whom we are, and we will hold fast the confidence and the rejoicing of the hope firm unto the end.

Forty Days on Earth, New Body, New Suit

Leaving those grave clothes behind, Jesus was instantly arrayed in garments not of this world. During this time, Jesus first appeared to Mary Magdalene and others; then Jesus walked with two of his disciples and joined others to break bread. After doing so, they recognized Jesus, who instantly disappeared. In his glorified body, Jesus could manipulate time and matter. The next day, he appeared in the midst of the disciples, who thought he was a ghost. Jesus said, "Look at my hands and feet, a spirit has not flesh and blood." He ate fish and honeycomb with them, and still they wondered; afterward he opened their understanding to the scriptures. Jesus breathed on them and said, "Receive you the Holy Ghost." In the book of John 21 is an account of Jesus appearing to the disciples who were fishing but caught nothing. Jesus called to them, saying, "Cast the nets on the right side," then the nets were full with a fish count of 153. They met Jesus on the shore who gave them bread and fish. Jesus gives them a final message that they are his witnesses and to go into all the world and preach the Gospel. Jesus instructed them to wait for the power from on high to come forth from his Holy Spirit. One hundred and twenty souls gathered in the upper room awaiting the comforter.

The Ascension

As he blessed them, he was parted from them in a cloud, carried up into heaven out of their sight. They joyfully worshipped him. As they looked steadfastly, two men stood by them in white apparel and said, "*You men of Galilee why stand gazing up into heaven, this same*

Jesus which is taken up from you into heaven will so come in like manner as you have seen him go into heaven" (Acts 1:10).

The Age of Grace

Looking back over the dispensations of time, at the beginning of the fifth millennium, AD 1, God ushered in the age of grace. This gift of grace was given to us in Christ Jesus before the world began but is now made manifest by the appearing of our Savior Jesus Christ, who has abolished death and has brought life and immortality to light through the Gospel (2 Timothy 1:9–10).

Number 5 is associated with grace. It is also the fifth letter in the Hebrew alphabet, *Heh*, which means "breath of God." Breath gives life, and Jesus is the way of life. At the dawning of the fifth dispensation or fifth millennium, God breathed his grace upon fallen mankind, who would be doomed to eternal death without a savior. Grace is God's favor; it is a gift that cannot be purchased.

> *For if by the one man's offense* [Adam] *death reigned through the one, much more those who receive abundance of grace and of the gift of righteousness will reign in life by one, Jesus.* (Romans 5:17)
>
> *Even so at this present time also there is a remnant according to the election of Grace and if by Grace then it is no more of works, otherwise Grace is no more Grace but if it be works then it is no more of Grace otherwise work is no more work.* (Romans 11:5–6)

The word *grace* is used five times in the above scripture. Man cannot work out his own salvation; we need the grace of Jesus.

Day of Pentecost

The age of grace became tangible on the Day of Pentecost, which was the beginning of the church age. On the Day of Pentecost, they were all on one accord, waiting as instructed when there came a mighty rushing wind (the breath of God), tongues of fire (Holy Spirit), and they began to speak in other languages (tongues is one of the gifts of the Holy Spirit). They spoke in the tongues of the people assembled in Jerusalem for the feast of Passover. Those people heard the Gospel spoken in their language. Thousands were saved. This is God's mercy and grace showering his favor upon the baby church. It is only through his grace that he plucks the sinner from the muck and the mire, washes away our sins, anoints us with power, and sets us on a path to carry out his will. Paul sums this up in 1 Corinthians 15:9–10:

> *I am the least of the apostles and not fit to be called an apostle because I persecuted the church of God. But by the Grace of God, I am what I am and his Grace was bestowed upon me not in vain, but I labored more abundantly than they all, yet not I but the Grace of God with me.*

The anointing of the Holy Spirit was given in times past. Ezekiel 11:5. . . "*The Spirit of the Lord fell upon me*" (this is the Holy Spirit as the anointing to prophecy comes upon Ezekiel). King David, Daniel, and others throughout the Old Testament received the anointing of the Holy Spirit. The Day of Pentecost signaled from that time forward the Holy Spirit would be poured out as the former and latter rain throughout millennia. The body of Christ will be indwelt with the Holy Spirit.

At the time of the Crucifixion, Satan was celebrating his short-lived victory. He had bruised the heel of Jesus. For the next fifty days, Satan observed God-ordained events unfold. He may have anticipated the Resurrection, but he was caught unawares of the significance of the Day of Pentecost. He saw the Spirit of God come as wind and fire; he saw the empowering of the saints; and he heard the Gospel preach and the power of the Word draw the people to salvation in Jesus. Satan then began to plot his course of deception to corrupt the Gospel of our Lord and God, Jesus. First he created doubt amongst the people by saying, "These people are drunk." He whispered, into itching ears, Jesus is not the son of God. God has no son. He began to cause dissention among the people by using the Jews and the Romans to persecute the new Christians. He began to sow heresy and ungodliness throughout the places of worship. Satan has thrown Islam into the mix to come against both Jews and Christians. Satan has used secularism, atheism, and all forms of ungodliness against the people of God and what these cannot destroy, the apostate church in the last days will accomplish. Satan has continued with his goal to destroy the body of Christ, but Jesus said the gates of hell shall not prevail.

It brings to mind that many pastors claim the outpouring of the Holy Spirit as a onetime event. Even though commonsense allows us to see that since the beginning of the church age, two thousand years ago, billions have come to Christ and they do so through the work of the Holy Spirit. The gifts of the Spirit were active then and are for today until Jesus removes the Holy Spirit.

> *For <u>the promise</u>* [outpouring of the Holy Spirit] *is unto you and to your children and to all that are afar off even as many as the Lord our God will call.* (Acts 2:39)

> *And it shall come to pass in the last days, said God, I will pour out of my spirit upon all flesh and your sons and your daughters will prophesy and your young men will see visions and your old men will dream dreams …* (Joel 2:28)

Jesus is appearing to many in dreams. This supernatural encounter may be likened to a near-death experience. It could be associated with Muslims who are given a revelation about Jesus as the way of salvation. Jesus may come to those he is calling for a special purpose.

Yeshua came through the tribe of Judah. Followers of Christ understand he came through the Jews to bridge the gap between Jew and Gentile. That gap was sealed on the Day of Pentecost. Since the death and Resurrection of Christ in these last days, we can begin to see the miracle of Jews and Christians coming together. The Jews hold to the Old Testament, while Christians embrace both the Old and New Testament written by Jewish followers of Christ. Satan has caused division among God's people pitting one against another.

> *By Jesus we have received grace and apostleship for obedience to* ***the faith among all nations*** *for his name. Among whom are you also the called of Jesus Christ, to all that be in Rome … that I might have some fruit among you also, even as among other Gentiles. I am debtor both to the Greeks and to the barbarians, both to the wise and to the unwise … for I am not ashamed of* ***the gospel of Christ*** *for it is the power of God unto salvation to everyone that believes, to the Jew first and also to the Greek* [Gentiles] *for* ***therein is the righteousness of God*** *revealed from faith to faith as it is written* ***the just shall live by faith.*** (Romans 1:5–7)

A message from the Jewish Messiah, through his Jewish disciple Paul, to all Jews and Gentiles.

Many have been called to proclaim the Gospel and to carry out all those needs for the community. We are to love one another and to provide for the widows and orphans. We are to feed the hungry, give drink to the thirsty, and shelter to the homeless. We are to visit the sick and those in prison. Throughout the centuries, the faithful have done these things. Some people may be able to help a few, while God has blessed mega ministries to do great works for those who are hurting and for the needy worldwide. Before we discuss the apostate church, we certainly acknowledge those who have gone the distance and followed the commands of Jesus.

New Covenant

Throughout the millennium, God established covenants with those he called out from amongst the people. God provided a blood covenant with Adam and Eve by shedding the blood of an animal to cover their nakedness. During the first millennium, God established a covenant with Noah, which promised he would not destroy the whole earth by water again. Noah sacrificed an animal, whose blood bound this covenant between God and Noah. God promised to bless Noah and his sons to replenish the earth. During the second millennium, God established a covenant with Abraham through the rite of circumcision. Sealing this agreement in blood, God promised to multiply his seed and gave him the promised land. In the third thousand year after creation, Moses was called by God to live as a prince in Egypt, dwell as a shepherd, and be a deliverer of his people. God gave Moses the Law, and the covenant was kept through the sacrificial rituals in an earthly tabernacle. During the fourth thousand-year period, God established a covenant with David as king, planning for the first temple and to be the ancestor for the coming Messiah. This brings us to the year of our Lord, the fifth- and six-thousand-year period wherein we have a better covenant than all the previous. Herein, God shed his blood for mankind, and it does not get any better than that.

"Upon this rock, I will build my church, and the gates of hell shall not prevail against it." Jesus is the rock and foundation of the church. This is the blood covenant between our Savior, who shed his blood, and through his grace salvation came to the Jews and Gentiles.

The agreement within this covenant provides unmerited favor for the believers. It allows for the Holy Spirit to dwell in a consecrated vessel. It provides a peace to the believers that pass all understanding. It brings forgiveness of sin and redemption. This new covenant allows us to have a relationship with God and access into the Holy of Holies. It is our blessed hope that we will be with our Lord and Savior for eternity in the world to come.

> *The Holy Spirit this signifying, that the way into the holiest of all was not yet made manifest, while as yet the first tabernacle was yet standing which was a figure for the time then present in which were offered both gifts and sacrifices that could not make him that did the service perfect as pertaining to the conscience, which stood only in meats and drinks, divers washings, carnal ordinances imposed on them until the* <u>*time of reformation.*</u> (Hebrews 9:8–10)

The time of reformation would be the new and better way by Jesus. We have entered the seventh millennium awaiting our Sabbath rest.

> *But Christ being come a high priest of good things to come by a greater and more perfect tabernacle, not made with hands that is to say not of this building,*

> *neither by the blood of goats and calves but by his own blood he entered in once into the holy place* (heaven) *having obtained eternal redemption for us … how much more will the blood of Christ through the eternal Spirit offered himself without spot to God, purge your conscience from dead works to serve the living God? And for this cause he is the mediator of the* ***new covenant*** … (Hebrews 9:11–15)

Before the new and final covenant was presented by Jesus, the shedding of the blood of animals was necessary for the remission of sins. It was necessary that those things patterned after the heavenly things (tabernacle, ark, table of show bread, etc.) needed to be purified by the blood of animals.

> *But the heavenly things themselves were better sacrifices than these* [earthly] *for Christ is not entered into the holy places made with hands which are the figures of the true but into heaven itself now to appear in the presence of God for us … but now once in the end of the world has he appeared to put away sin by the sacrifice of himself … He bore the sins of many and to them that look for him will he appear the second time without sin unto salvation.* (Hebrews 9:23–28)

The final covenant …

> *This is the covenant that I will make with them after those days said the Lord, I will put my laws into their hearts and in their minds will I write them and their sins and iniquities will I remember no more. Now where remission of these is, there is no more offering for sin.* (Hebrews 10:16–17)

This new covenant moves believers away from the sacrificial rituals of shedding blood for the atonement of sin. By this covenant of grace, believers receive an inheritance. Through the death of Jesus, we became joint heirs with him. We understand that we have obtained this inheritance in earnest or installments. The first advance on our inheritance is that we are redeemed from eternal death in hell and sealed by the Holy Spirit; we have a future place in heaven and have the riches of his grace. We receive our final portion of our inheritance at the dispensation of the fullness of times when Jesus will gather together in one all things in Christ—both which are in heaven and which are on earth. We will receive our immortal body, rule with Christ through the millennial reign, and be with him for eternity (Ephesians 1).

Chapter 14
The Church Age

Chapter Overview

- The Church Age
  - Empowered Church
  - Gifts of the Holy Spirit
    - Tongues and Interpretation of Tongues
    - Word of Wisdom
    - Word of Knowledge
    - Gift of Faith
    - Gift of Healing
    - Working Miracles
    - Gift of Prophecy
    - Discerning of Spirits
    - Apostles, Teachers, Helpers, Administration

- Body of Christ
  - The Gospel Proclaimed in All the World
  - Ten Commandments
  - Sin, Salvation, Rewards

  - Church under Persecution
    - Standing on our Biblical Foundation
    - Early Church Leaders
    - Practices Leading to Apostasy

  - Apostate Church
    - Emergent Church
    - Statistics
    - Gnostics
    - Replacement Theology
    - Chrislam
    - Heresy and False Doctrine
    - Self-Righteous and Worldliness
    - Tolerance and Carnality

- Message to the Seven Churches
    - Specifics of the Message
    - Promise to the Church
    - Warnings to the Church
  - Dispensations
  - In the Fullness of Times

Chapter 14

The Church Age

The church age is also referred to as the dispensation of grace. Jew and Gentile believers in Christ flourished as wheat and were dubbed Christians. The true church is the body of Christ and is not made up of brick and mortar but is a spiritual congregation made up of spiritual lively stones. The chief cornerstone of the church is Jesus. This spiritual congregation envelopes the whole world from the highest mountains, to the outer regions, and in the inner cities. There is no distance in prayer; and true believers, wherever they may be located, are bound together through their love for Jesus and fellowship one with another through the Holy Spirit. Before the death of Jesus, he said to Peter, "Upon this rock I build my church, and the gates of hell will not prevail against it." Peter was not the sole proprietor of the church but only one representative of the millions of followers that would come into the true body of Christ. Jesus also told Peter that Satan desired to sift him as wheat, and in hindsight, this is was a prophetic statement that the church would be persecuted for two thousand years but would remain as a cornerstone.

After the Crucifixion and Resurrection, many more became believers in Jesus. The ascension of Christ drew others into the fold. The outpouring of the Holy Spirit on the Day of Pentecost came as a mighty rushing wind, with tongues of fire over each person, and they began to speak in other tongues. Those believers received the baptism of the Holy Spirit. They were empowered to share the Gospel and to operate in the gifts of the Spirit. Multitudes of people had come up to Jerusalem from various parts of the Asia, Rome, and Africa and heard the Gospel spoken in their language. Thousands of people that day were saved and followed the teachings of Christ. In Acts 8:26, we see that the angel of the Lord directed Phillip to meet with the Ethiopian man who was with Queen Candace of Ethiopia who had come to Jerusalem to worship. A Jewish remnant continued in Ethiopia from the time of King

Solomon, and evidence of that fact is seen here in that the queen was a believer, and so was her servant. Ethiopian believers would follow Jesus and continue into our modern era.

The Empowered Church

The outpouring of the Holy Spirit on the Day of Pentecost opened our understanding of the person of the Holy Spirit. This is the Spirit of God, our comforter, teacher, and guide. It is the Holy Spirit that draws people to Christ. When we feel this tugging on our heart, we can invite the Spirit into a relationship with us, or we can reject the Holy Spirit. Once we accept Jesus into our lives, there will be a change. People have various experiences at this juncture. With some it is gentle and peaceful. Others weep. People may fall prostrate in the holy presence of God. Some people speak in tongues. We refer to this experience as the baptism of the Holy Ghost, and through this baptism, believers become a vessel for the indwelling of the Holy Spirit. When people have a physical encounter with God, we refer to this as the anointing of the Holy Spirit. The anointing gives power to the believers to overcome the works of Satan. It is a battle not easily won. Satan has been spiritually defeated, but his authority over the earth is ongoing and will continue until Jesus returns, and then he will be cast into the lake of fire.

As it was in the days of the early church, believers today are empowered to share the Gospel and to operate in the gifts of the Holy Spirit. In these last days, the outpouring of the Holy Spirit is active throughout the world. For instance, Iran is hostile to Christianity and persecute or kill those who convert from Islam to Christianity. Presently, in Iran, there has been a 19 percent increase in those accepting Jesus compared to 1 percent in the United States. A convert to Christianity, Hormoz Shariat, has been likened to a Billy Graham in Iran, boldly preaching the Gospel in the face of danger.

> *But the manifestation of the Spirit is given to every man to profit withal ...*
> *and the Spirit gives to every man individually as he wills.* (1 Corinthians 12:7)

Before we examine the gifts of the Spirit, let us clarify that all who come to Christ are spiritually baptized into one body. The Spirit of the Lord dwells in each believer. As we examine the diversity of the gifts of the Holy Spirit, it is important to understand no one person receives all the gifts. People are saved, and some have not received the gift of speaking in tongues, but they are still a member of the body of Christ. People are saved, who have not undergone water baptism. In 1 Corinthians 12, Saint Paul clarifies this doctrine in its entirety.

Third Person of the Trinity, God the Holy Spirit

Humankind is first introduced to the Triune God, the Word, and the Holy Spirt in the beginning of creation. We enter the scene in Genesis 1. God established the heavens and has turned his attention to planet earth, which appears without form, void, and darkness was upon the face of the deep. "*And the Spirit of God moved upon the face of the waters.*" From this action, we have the concept of a bird hovering over the water. The movement of a bird creates wind, and wind creates power. At the time of the baptism of Jesus, the Holy Spirit is seen as a dove descending over Jesus. Jesus blew on his disciples, and they received power of the Holy Spirit, or the anointing. When the Day of Pentecost came, they first heard something that sounded like a mighty rushing wind, which filled the room. The power of the Holy Spirit came as wind. The manifestation of the power of the Holy Spirit formed as tongues of fire over each person, and they were filled with the Holy Spirit. The outward sign of the presence of God was the utterance of tongues given by the Holy Spirit (Acts 2:14). The Holy Spirit makes intercession between God and man through his breath, utterances, and groaning. Romans 8:26, through the power of the Holy Spirit, Jesus was raised from the dead. The Holy Spirit indwells the believers. Through our breath, our groaning and in our prayer language, the power of the Holy Spirit manifest in healings, raising the dead, and other gifts of the Spirit given to the believers. In summary, the Holy Spirit can manifest as wind, breath, living waters, fire as in the anointing. The Holy Spirit is the witness, and our testimony is confirmation of the work of the Triune God.

Gifts of the Holy Spirit

Gift of Tongues—Jesus did not speak in tongues because the gift was given to mankind from the Holy Spirit to assist man in communicating with the Triune Godhead. The gift of tongues was given on the Day of Pentecost. Saint Paul tells us in 1 Corinthians 13:1: "*Though I speak with the tongues of men and of angels and have not Love, I am become as sounding brass or a tinkling cymbal.*" Paul lets us know not to be judgmental about who has a certain gift or not but rather you have love. Paul lets us know that the gifts of tongues will cease *when that which is perfect is come, then that which is in part will be done away* (1 Corinthians 13:10).

Interpretation of tongues is needful because he that speaks in an unknown tongue speaks not unto men but to God, and no man understands him except he that interprets so the church may receive edifying (1 Corinthians 14:2, 5).

Word of Wisdom, Word of Knowledge and Faith are gifts of the Spirit.

Gift of Healing and Working of Miracles—the works of Jesus are so numerous they cannot be contained in one book. Jesus anointed his disciples to go out and do the works that he performed. For instance, multitudes were healed by Peter's shadow (Acts 5:15). Stephen the first martyr was empowered by the Holy Spirit to heal and preach the good news. The apostles were put into prison by the religious leaders. The angel of the Lord opened the prison doors and freed them. The officers found the prison doors still locked, yet the apostles had been transported through walls and placed in the temple.

Gift of Prophecy is for the purpose of edification, exhortation, comfort, and warning for the church. Prophecy is beneficial to the hearing of the unbelievers or the unlearned in his hearing he is convinced of all, be judged of all, and thus are the secrets of his heart made manifest; and so falling down on his face, he will worship God and report that God is in you of a truth (1 Corinthians 14;3,5,24).

Discernment is a gift that we may identify wickedness in its various forms.

The continuation of the church is on the shoulders of apostles, teachers, helpers, and church administrators.

There would be harmony in the body of Christ if we remember to think not of ourselves more highly than we ought to think (Romans 12:3). The Gifts of the Spirit were mentioned and are given to each member of the body of Christ as the Spirit wills. Romans 12 goes on to define that the diversity gifts are given according to God's grace and our faith.

The Body of Christ

The body of Christ began with the twelve Jewish disciples. They were Simon Peter; Andrew, his brother; James, son of Zebedee; his brother, John; Philip; Bartholomew; Thomas; Matthew; James, the son of Alphaeus; Thaddaeus; Simon, the Canaanite; and Judas Iscariot, the betrayer. There were friends and associates such as Luke. He was a Greek Gentile and physician. As a Christian and eyewitness to the works of Jesus, he wrote the books of Luke and Acts (Matthew 10:2). Jesus commanded them to go first to the house of David. Jesus empowered them to preach, heal, and cast out demons. John Mark, a Roman Jew, wrote the first book of the Gospel of Mark, and he was not one of the original disciples. The first martyr was Stephen, stoned to death because of his bold declaration for Jesus Messiah. In his final hour, the heavens opened, and he saw Jesus. Saul witnessed the death of Stephen. Later he is converted, and Paul becomes tireless in his work proclaiming Jesus.

The body of Christ is diverse embracing converted Jews, Romans, Arabs, and Gentiles from other nations. All believers who follow Jesus Christ are called Christians. But not all who call themselves Christians are so. Only God knows the heart of man; if it is evil, Jesus will tell them, "I knew you not." True believers will follow Jesus without compromise. Many say they are the true believers, but Jesus tells us to look at their fruit. The fruit of the Spirit is love, joy, peace, long-suffering, gentleness, goodness, faith, meekness, temperance, and holiness—having crucified the flesh of sin and temptation (Galatians 5:22).

Religious organizations say, "Our way is the right way," yet they deny the deity of Christ, his incarnation, virgin birth, and deny he is the Son of God. They dismiss Israel, the wife of God. The blood atonement is reduced to nonessential. Those who adopt the doctrine of devils are of the seed of Satan and are not of the body of Christ.

Jesus is the head of his body, and we who are followers are embraced by Jesus as one of his. He said, "My sheep know my voice" because we are in tune with the mind of Christ. Having the mind of Christ is not the New Age "Christ consciousness" or some universal spiritual connection. The body of Christ is made up of all those who have come to Jesus, whether they are Jew or Gentile. Jesus said his church will have love one for another, and through love we will know each other. We are forgiven of our sins by his shed blood and death for us on a cross. We will have eternal life with Jesus because he is risen from the dead, and we will rise from the dead also. The body of Christ is of (one) spirit and that being the Holy Spirit who dwells in the believers, and he leads us into all truth. Christians are of one mind, one body, and one spirit (Ephesians 4:4–5).

Jesus establishes his church by saying to Peter, Matthew 16:18, "*Upon this rock I will build my church and the gates of hell will not prevail against it.*" Peter as well as the other disciples represent the church. They are one of many foundation stones that would build up the church for the next two thousand years. Jesus has given his church the keys of the kingdom of heaven for spiritual warfare, as in the gates of hell shall not prevail against the church.

The spiritual church of Jesus is not built of earthly stone, brick, and mortar but is made up of lively stones of which Jesus is the chief cornerstone in Zion. This is a church not built with hands but a living temple composed of living parts. We are the living stones that are built upon Jesus Christ, our rock and our foundation. We are a chosen people, a royal priesthood, a holy nation, a peculiar people, and we praise the one who has called us out of the darkness into his marvelous light. We don't offer blood sacrifice but spiritual sacrifices, which are pleasing and acceptable to God (1 Peter 2:4–9).

> *He that has an ear let him hear what the Spirit said unto the church, the body of Christ: to him that overcomes, will I give to eat of the hidden manna and will give him a white stone and in the stone a new name written which no man knows save he that received it.* (Revelation 2:17)

Jesus is the bread (manna) of life and is nourishment to our souls. Jesus is our foundation, and to each who receives his salvation, we become as living stones, which have our new names imprinted on them. In the life to come, we will have a new body and a new name.

Jesus clearly demonstrates his gift of grace in the life of Saint Paul. Years after the Resurrection, Jesus called Saul to his ministry. He was a Roman citizen and a Pharisee. After his conversion, he became a zealot for Jesus. The Holy Spirit anointed Paul with gifts of healing, visions, discernment, prophecy, tongues, and preaching the Gospel. Paul tells us in Ephesians 2:19–20:

> *Now therefore you are no more strangers and foreigners but fellow citizens with the saints and of the household of God and are built upon the foundation of the apostles and prophets, Jesus Christ himself being the chief corner stone.*

God allowed Satan to put a thorn in Paul's side to buffet him and to remind him that all that he is and all that he has is because of the grace of God.

> *And lest I should be exalted above measure through the abundance of the revelations, there was given to me a thorn in the flesh, the messenger of Satan to buffet me lest I should be exalted above measure. For this thing I besought the Lord three times that it might depart from me. And he said unto me, my grace is sufficient for thee for my strength is made perfect in weakness.* (2 Corinthians 12:9)

God allows Satan to bring sickness and persecution for his glory, for in our times of tribulation and in our weakness, we find our strength in Christ. We see this example was taught to Job. God allowed Satan to take away his possessions, his family, and his health. This was like a thorn in his side. Job understood that all that he was blessed with was provided by the Lord. He also knew that through his suffering, the grace of God would be sufficient. "*Though you slay me, I will trust you.*" The grace of God would deliver him from the hand of Satan. Jesus said we will have tribulations, and through them we will grow in patience. Jesus promises to deliver us out of all our trials and tribulations. Saint Paul reminds us "*that the sufferings of the present time are not worthy to be compared with the glory which will be revealed in us*" (Romans 8:18).

The Gospel Proclaimed in All the World

> *And this gospel of the kingdom will be preached in the whole world as a testimony to all nations and then the end will come.* (Matthew 24:14)

With the advent of radio, television, cell phone, satellite, Internet, the Gospel has been preached to all nations. There are groups of people in some regions that may not have heard the Gospel. These people are judged by their enlightenment or by their knowledge of right and wrong. Jesus does not want anyone to perish but all to come to salvation. However, the Gospel message to the saving of the soul through Jesus has gone forth for almost two thousand years. Many have heard and rejected this wonderful gift. Through wars, calamities, disease, and other judgments, some will awake and believe; while others will hear and reject. God has given mankind every opportunity for repentance and salvation. Even when the horrors of the tribulation come upon the earth, many will curse God, while others will cry out to him.

The chosen people (Jews) called out by God have been good stewards of watching over the sacred writings. In the historical account, the chosen ones became remiss in sharing **the faith** with the rest of the world. To correct this omission, Yahweh came into the world as a light. He made new disciples of all that would come and believe.

At the beginning of the first century AD, three beliefs systems were active: Judaism, idolatry, and Christianity. Judaism had been in place for thousands of years. Idolatry had passed from Gentile kingdoms throughout millennium. Now what had been promised thousands of years ago had come to pass. Messiah had come. Many converts to Christianity were Jews who left Orthodox Judaism and Romans and other Gentiles who rejected idolatry. Pagan beliefs were intermingled with Christianity. The apostles were constantly rebuking those who would bring in damnable heresies. Constantine was instrumental in converting Roman paganism to Christianity; however, pagan influence continued. While he stared at the sun, he saw the form of a cross, and this caused him to convert to Christianity. Constantine initially worshipped the sun god, "Sol Invictus," meaning the "invincible sun," and from this influence, he declared "*dies Solis*" as Sun-day, changing the Sabbath day to Sunday as the official day of rest on AD March 7, 321. Constantine decided to celebrate the birth of Christ on the pagan celebration of the sun, December 25.

Jesus as the light of the world tells us the way to heaven is like a narrow path leading up to the strait gate where we may enter into eternal life with Jesus. Only few will walk this straight and narrow path. Jesus tells us that the path toward worldly pleasure is wide and leads to destruction, and many will take that path (Matthew 7:13–14).

Summary of the Strait Gate, Luke 13:24–30

- Narrow is the path that leads to eternal life with God, and few will follow the way of holiness. At the end of the path is a gate, and many will try to enter and will not be allowed.
- Jesus for two thousand years has knocked on the door of our hearts. Some did open their heart for the Lord while many did not. After the Rapture, Jesus will shut the gate. Many will seek to enter but will be turned away, rejected because of sin. They will say we had fellowship with you. We prophesied in your name, cast out devils, and done many wonderful works. Jesus will say, "I never knew you, depart from me, you workers of iniquity" (Matthew 7:21–23).

- The destination for sinners is hell, where there is weeping and gnashing of teeth. Just as the rich man could see Abraham; apparently, those in hell can still see others as a reminder that they could have chosen Jesus and the heavenly rewards.
- The saved will be from every corner of the earth in the kingdom of God, and those who got saved at the last minute will be given the same honor as those who have lived godly lives for many years or those such as Abraham, who were part of the First Fruits' Resurrection.

Those who do enter into the kingdom of heaven are those that do the will of the Father, which is in heaven, those who believe and live in faith of the promised hope. *Know you not that the unrighteous will not inherit the kingdom of God …* (1 Corinthians 6:9).

> *Verily I say unto you I have not found so great faith no not in Israel and I say unto you that many shall come from the east and west and will sit down with Abraham and Isaac and Jacob in the kingdom of Heaven but the children* [unbelievers] *of the kingdom* [Satan's domain] *will be cast out into outer darkness where is weeping and gnashing of teeth* [hell]. (Matthew 8:10–12)

Religion will hinder many from having faith in Jesus—be it Judaism, Islam, pagan religions, or Christendom. Jesus sent his twelve disciples out and told them to preach the kingdom of heaven is at hand; in other words, their Messiah is here (Matthew 10:7).

Sin, Salvation, Rewards

Most Bible students understand God's laws were given to Moses on Mount Sinai. We believe the Ten Commandments were written on the tablets of stone, and hundreds of others laws followed during their forty years in the wilderness. The purpose of the Ten Commandments is to give notice that we are to obey them. They are like a signpost. It signals us to stop following sin. We see the warning, and the wise will turn from their wicked ways.

Ten Commandments

"(1) I Am the Lord your God, you will have no other gods before me." (2) You will not make any graven images"—refers to statues and tattoos (Leviticus 19:28). You shall not make any cuttings in your flesh for the dead, nor print any marks upon you.

(3)You will not take the name of the Lord in vain.

(4)You will remember the Sabbath and keep it holy. The Sabbath is Saturday, the seventh day of the week. God has not dismissed worship on the Sabbath. The fourth commandment, "Remember the Sabbath and keep it holy," is difficult to practice. Jesus broke the Sabbath laws by healing on this day in order to teach the Pharisees "that the Son of man is Lord also of the Sabbath." Jews have tried to keep the Laws of Moses, and they were unable to do so. Outside of Judaism, mankind cannot keep ten laws. Jesus said he came not to do away with the law but to fulfill it. The Mosaic laws and church rituals take the focus off of Jesus. Like Elizabeth and Mary, one was focused on her kitchen duties while the other was washing the feet of Jesus.

Early Christians met on Sunday to honor Jesus's Resurrection and the Day of Pentecost. This became a traditional day of worship for Christians who know that our new covenant with Jesus is not law but grace. Jesus is looking for his true worshippers, those who know that we have a twenty-four-hour, seven-day relationship with Jesus. We can worship God in truth and spirit on any day of the week.

(5) Honor your father and mother that your days may be long upon the earth.

(6) You will not kill and this applies to the shedding of innocent blood.

(7) You will not commit adultery (Proverbs 6:32). Whosoever commits adultery with another lacks understanding, and he that does it <u>destroys his own soul</u>. A wound and dishonor will he get, and his reproach will not spare in the day of vengeance.

(8) You will not steal.

(9) You will not lie.

(10) You will not covet your neighbors' goods, such as in envy or jealousy.

The commandments reveal that in our flesh nature, dwells no good thing. Herein we see our constant struggle between our spirit, which may be willing to obey, but our flesh is weak. Who will deliver me from this body of death (Romans 7:7–25)?

<u>Our Sin Nature</u>

Every human on the face of the earth has sinned. Sin passed into the world through the disobedience of Adam and Eve. Romans 5:18, "*Therefore as by the offence of one* [Adam] *judgment came upon all men to condemnation.*" They devolved from perfect beings living in a perfect world to fallen sinners living in a cursed and dying world. Their offspring carried the burden of sin like a yoked ox (first ancient letter of Hebrew looks like an ox). Mankind became bound by Satan and his demons. Excellent health was taken, and in its place came disease, addiction, depression, self-loathing, death.

In the fullness of time, God came. Yeshua, the Jewish Messiah, came first to the house of Israel then to the world. Romans 5:18, "*By the righteousness of one* [Jesus], *the free gift came upon all men unto justification of life.*" He came to free us from the burden of sin and disease. He took the yoke upon himself and gave us the gift of salvation. Ephesians 2:8–9, "*For by grace are you saved through faith and not of yourselves it is the gift of God not of works, lest any man should boast.*" Grace is undeserved favor, faith is what we believe, salvation is a gift and cannot be earned. Romans 6:14, "*For sin will not have dominion over you for you are not under the law but under grace.*" There is no name on earth or in heaven that we can call upon except the name of Jesus for salvation and healing. The invitation is offered to all to come to repentance because all have sinned. As to any that come to Jesus, he is faithful to forgive them of their sins.

Some theologians make statements that may not line up with scripture:

- Once saved, always saved.

  Know you not that you are the temple of God and that the Spirit of God dwells in you, If any man defile the temple of God, him will God destroy for the temple of God is holy, which temple are you. (1 Corinthians 3:16)

- Christians must be baptized by water, or they will not be saved.

  Water baptism is an outward sign that the old sin nature is washed away through the blood of Jesus. A new convert who dies before the church sets up its monthly water baptism does not lose their salvation. A soldier on the battlefield has just given his life to Christ and is shot dead before undertaking water baptism is still saved.

- When a Christian is saved, they must speak in tongues, or they are not really saved.

  The Holy Spirit gives gifts to people as he decides. Paul says he speaks in tongues more than others, but the greatest gift is love. Tongues will not exist forever. If a believer does not speak in tongues, they are still saved. Jesus judges the heart and not an outward appearance.

- Since we live under grace, we can sin, and we will automatically be forgiven.

  A person who is truly born again is convicted by the Holy Spirit to stop sinning. In their heart, they want to please Jesus. Jesus does give the sinner many opportunities to turn from sin and live a holy life. Forgiveness can only be given if a person asks to be forgiven. If there is no repentance, eventually, Jesus may turn them over to a reprobate mind and a seared conscience. We see in 1 Corinthians 5:5 that Christians who continue to sin could "*be deliver such a one unto Satan for the destruction of the flesh that the spirit may be saved in the day of the Lord Jesus.*"

Following are scenarios that we can consider to measure our place in Christ:

- There was a man who spent his money on alcohol. He was drunk most of the time and arrested a few times for public drunkenness and disorderly conduct. On occasion, he would manage to get himself together and go to church on Sunday. His breath usually reeked of old whiskey. The pastor would share the Gospel and make an altar call for any who wanted to repent or receive Jesus as their Lord. This man would make his way to the altar and confess with his mouth the Lord Jesus. He said he believed that Jesus was the Son of God, died for his sins, and rose again. He received the usual accolades from the pastor and a few church members. When church was over, the man would go straight to the VFW for drinks, food, music, and camaraderie.
- A woman for many years was plagued by demonic lust. She had gone to church from her youth and continued in church. She was like the woman at the well who had four or five husbands and was living with a man. She was in and out of relationships, looking for Mr. Right. She met Jesus and believed in Jesus. But she still struggled with promiscuity.
- A successful businessman went to church when he could find time from his busy schedule. He was loud and boisterous and had no problem in telling people he loved the church, gave money to the church sometimes, and he loved God. He was full of pride. His life was based on lies, sexual sin, and materialism.
- A well-known pastor had a TV ministry and a mega church. He preached the Gospel for others, but in his private life, he was a homosexual. When his secret life was exposed, there was never a public statement of repentance. He continued as pastor.
- Those who have abortions are murderers. This woman had three abortions. She attended church regularly and asked God to forgive her. When it was time to vote, she always put her support behind those who are proabortion.
- The president of the most powerful nation said he was a Christian. He spent time in a dead church. When he spoke at a Christian university, he asked that all religious symbols be covered, and he mocked the Bible scriptures. He endorsed same-sex marriage and supports abortion.
- A teenager had just given his life to Christ. He had spent years on drugs and was rebellious. He left church that night filled with the Spirit. Shortly he was killed in a car accident. He had not been water-baptized or received the gift of tongues.
- Christian immigrants from Europe had no problem in kidnapping and enslaving millions of Africans. Some of the Africans were introduced to Christianity, though they were forbidden to learn to read the Bible. When slavery ended, churches were segregated.

- There was a godly woman who went to church regularly, and her outward appearance showed that she loved Jesus. She had been water-baptized, but even though she asked for the gift of tongues, she never received it.
- Judas Iscariot betrayed Jesus. Judas had a bad attitude, and he mismanaged the treasury. He knew Jesus up close and personal. Judas broke bread with Jesus and kissed him. Later Judas felt so guilty he killed himself. What happened to the soul of Judas. Is he in hell or heaven?
- A successful Anglican priest took up the sword to promote anti-Semitism in America and had the audacity to set up a theology center in Jerusalem to continue his anti-Semitism campaign. He creates division between Jew and Gentile.

We ask our readers to consider the above examples and apply a litmus test based on scripture. How do the above examples line up with our biblical understanding? We present a few scriptures that may help us to see clearly on the position of God in all areas of humanity.

> *For if after they have escaped the pollutions of the world through the knowledge of the Lord and Savior Jesus Christ, they are again entangled therein and overcome, the latter end is worse with them than the beginning. For it had been better for them not to have known the way of righteousness than after they have known it to turn from the holy commandment delivered unto them.* (2 Peter 2:20–21)
>
> *Now the works of the flesh are manifest which are these: adultery, fornication, uncleanness, lasciviousness, idolatry, witchcraft, hatred, variance, emulations, wrath, strife, seditions, heresies, envy, murders, drunkenness, reveling and such like of the which I tell you before as I have also told you in times past that <u>they which do such things will not inherit the kingdom of God.</u>* (Galatians 5:19–21)
>
> *Six <u>things God hates</u> and seven is an abomination unto Him: a proud look, lying tongue, shedding of innocent blood, wicked imaginations, feet that run to mischief, false witness that lies and sowing discord among the believers.* (Proverbs 6:16)
>
> *Know you not that <u>the unrighteous will not inherit the kingdom of God</u>? Be not deceived neither fornicators, idolaters, adulterers, effeminate or abusers of themselves with mankind, not thieves, nor covetous, drunks, revilers, extortionist will inherit the kingdom of God.* (1 Corinthians 6:9)

In the above passage, we understand that we all sin and come short of the glory of God. However, true followers of Christ will turn from sin and ask to be forgiven. Many times we cannot seem to stop sinning, and that person must pray and ask Jesus to deliver them. Jesus is very patient with mankind. He said to forgive seventy times seven. Forgiveness is given when the sinner asks to be forgiven. So we are given 490 times to fall short, to stumble, to backslide. Since we cannot keep count, only Jesus knows what fate or judgment will befall the sinner. Only Jesus knows the heart of man.

> *Whosoever abides in Jesus sins not. Whosoever sins has not seen him or known him … let no man deceive you, he that does righteousness is righteous even as Jesus is righteous. He that commits sin is of the devil, for the devil sinned from the beginning. For this purpose the Son of God was manifested that he might destroy the works of the devil. Whosoever is born of God does not commit sin for his seed remains in him and he cannot sin because he is born of God.* (1 John 3:6)

Ezekiel 33:9–15, the wicked are warned in advance to turn and repent; if they do not turn from wickedness, they will die in their iniquity. God said, "As I live, I have no pleasure in the death of the wicked but that the wicked turn from his way and live." Ezekiel speaks in general to all sinners, and all who repent and make restitution, they shall live. God tells Ezekiel to tell the people that their (self) righteousness will not deliver them in the day of their transgression. As for the wickedness of the wicked, he will not fall; thereby in the day that he turns from wickedness, neither shall the righteous be able to live for his righteousness in the day that he sins. When I will say to the righteous, he will surely live. If he trust to his own righteousness and commit iniquity, all his righteousness will not be remembered; but for his iniquity that he has committed, he will die for it. If the wicked restore the pledge, give again that he has robbed, walk in the statues of life, without committing iniquity, he will surely live and he will not die.

The above passage was mostly directed to the Israelites who were captives in Babylon and Assyria. This was their punishment for being disobedient, unholy, and unrighteous.

They had the commandments, yet they sinned. Today we have the same commandments, yet we sin. Living righteous and holy is what God required of them and requires of us today.

Sin separates us from the presence of God because our covering is removed and our sins are laid bare before the Lord. When King David sinned, he did repent and asked God not to take his Holy Spirit from him.

Salvation

If the wages of sin are death and separation from God, then repentance and obedience must be life eternal with God. What happens to a person if they die in their sins? Ezekiel said the unrepentant will be condemned. If death is not instantaneous and the person has a few minutes to ask for forgiveness, we believe he is then saved from hell's fires. The Bible says, "Call on the name of Jesus, and you will be saved." Being careless and sinful puts a person's soul in danger. It is not wise to test the Lord. So live a holy and obedient life while there is time because tomorrow is not promised.

Today, if you hear his voice, repent. Call on the Lord Jesus, and believe in your heart and mind that he is God, died, and resurrected, and you will be saved from eternal damnation.

> *Confess with your mouth the Lord Jesus and believe in your heart that God raised him from the dead and you will be saved. In the heart, man can believe unto righteousness and with the mouth confession is made unto salvation.* (Romans 10:9)
>
> *Therefore if any man be in Christ, he is a new creature, old things are passed away, behold all things are become new.* (2 Corinthians 5:17)

Our sins are forgiven.

Revelation 3:5 Jesus promises "*that he who overcomes will be clothed in white raiment and I **will not** blot his name out of the book of life but I will confess his name before my father and the angels.*" There is a reward for those who overcome the sin nature, the lure of the world, and who crucify the old nature, stop sinning, and live a holy life. At the time of the Rapture, those who are Christ's will be given a white robe like the one Jesus had at his Resurrection. Most importantly, those who come to Christ will have their names written in the book of life. It does appear that continuing down the path of unrighteousness, taking on a reprobate mind, and having a seared conscience, those may have their name removed from the book of life. "Once saved always saved" could not be applied if your name can be blotted out of the book of life.

Rewards

We are colaborers with Christ. We all build on the foundation laid by Jesus. He commanded us to go out into all the world and preach the Gospel as well as to heal, feed, and minister to those in need. When we leave the world of the living and arrive at the Bema Seat judgment (John 5:22), the believer will be judged on the works he did for the glory of Jesus. Rewards will be given for works of gold, silver, precious stones that are not burned up in the fire.

Now if any man build upon this foundation gold, silver, precious stones, wood, hay, stubble, every man's work will be made manifest for the day will declare it because it will be revealed by fire and the fire will try every man's work of what sort it is. If any man's work abide which he hath build thereupon he will receive a reward. If any man's work will be burned he will suffer loss but he himself will be saved yet so as by fire. (1 Corinthians 3:12)

Works of wood, stubble, and hay—which were done for personal glory or recognition—will be burned in the fire. If we suffer loss of rewards, we are still saved. How will Jesus look at the overall person? The scripture references provided should give us a good basis for understanding where we stand in Christ. We should measure ourselves by the Word of God and perhaps be skeptical of man's viewpoints and opinions, which can be misleading or deceitful.

Church under Persecution

Jesus warns his followers that they will be persecuted, delivered up in the synagogues, imprisoned, and accused before the rulers (Luke 21:12). Persecution for righteousness sake has been going on since mankind began to multiply upon the earth. In the New Testament, Luke states that the Jews persecuted and killed the prophets who pointed to the coming of the Just One, Jesus (Acts 7:52). Stephen is recorded as the first martyr. After hearing the Gospel, the Jews were cut to the heart and grit their teeth. Stephen, being full of the Holy Ghost, looked up into heaven and saw the glory of God and Jesus standing at the right hand of God and told them what he saw: they were so filled with evil that they cried out with a loud voice and stopped their ears and ran as a mob to cast Stephen out of the city and to stone him (Acts 7:54–58). One of these persecutors was Saul of Tarsus, who was on a trip to Damascus when he had a radical experience with the risen Christ. He heard the voice of Jesus; he saw him in the bright light; he was physically overcome with blindness. Saul changed his name to Paul and became a zealot for Christ, preaching the Gospel to many.

At the time of outreach by the apostles and followers of Christ, Jerusalem was under pagan Roman authority. The Apostle John was persecuted by the Romans and sent to the Island of Patmos. What Satan deems for evil, God will turn it around for good. While being exiled, John was able to receive the most incredible vision of the Revelation of Jesus. It began with a clear message to the seven churches.

The Roman Empire controlled much of the known world. The empire was pagan. Opposed to paganism were the Orthodox Jews, Pharisees, Sadducees, Essenes, Christian Coptics, and other sects. Contention among these various religious groups and the position of the Roman Empire led to the formation of the Holy Roman Empire around AD 300. Constantine, under the influence of his mother, called for Christianity to be the state religion around AD 315. It is alleged that his mother found the three crosses assumed to be Christ and the two thieves. She ordered the enshrinement of Jesus's tomb, now called the Church of the Holy Sepulcher.

The concept of universalism was already a basis of Roman philosophy, and the ideology of Catholicism blended well within the morphing Holy Roman Empire. Early Christian congregations sprung up in Syria, Persia, Egypt, Ethiopia, Tunisia, Algeria, Arabia, Rome, Spain, France, Greece, Turkey, and to the outer most parts of the world. AD 301, Armenian Christians were established in Jerusalem. The nation of Georgia established their Orthodox church during this time frame, and it has remained a constant during times of persecution. Currently, Georgia has a healthy body of Christian believers. The Orthodox Coptic congregation was strong in Egypt.

The Holy Roman Empire appointed a pope as the head of the state-sanctioned church. This would begin the growth of Catholicism, a religion that would be at enmity with the early Christian church. The pope took the position of God on earth. He became the intercessor between man and God. The priest served in place of Jesus in the forgiveness of sins. This is in contrast to Christian doctrine that Jesus is our intercessor and no man comes to the Father except he comes through the Son. Only through the atoning blood of Jesus can we receive forgiveness of sin. Christians protested this different doctrine, and it became the catalyst for the protestant reformation. For hundreds of years Catholics, and Protestants would be at odds with each other to the extent of death. Islam would join the fray and rain its jihad upon all.

In these last days, we see a few developments. First, the Catholic church has extended their hand to all religions, offering peace and unity, especially toward the Muslims. Yet on the other hand, persecution has ticked up against Christians, Jews, Muslims, or just plain folks set upon by Islamic radicals. Attacks are widespread, causing millions to flee in search of safety. The exodus is extensive in Middle East regions with a mix of Christians, Muslims, and secular people relocating to Israel, Canada, South America, United States, Germany, Australia, England, and other nations. In the midst of persecution, rape, and murder, many people remain in their countries regardless of the threat to life. Though their numbers have diminished, we find Christians in Egypt, Gaza, Lebanon, Iran, Syria, Kurdistan, and Turkey to name a few, trying to survive. Finally, we see something extraordinary occurring around the world in the center of the chaos. Revival.

Under the repressive regime in Iran, 2016 reports that upward to a million have converted to Christianity. In communist China, the underground church is growing into the millions. Brazil had a revival, and hundreds of thousands attended. In the United States, there are regions that are experiencing a great outpouring of the Holy Spirit.

All the atrocities and genocide we hear about are weighing heavily on believers who have not experienced that level of persecution. We pray for our brothers and sisters in Christ, and we ask, "How long, Lord, will you allow your bride to be singled out like sheep for the slaughter?" The Lord said, "They are with me now as, one day, all believers must be changed from mortal to immortal in order to be with me for eternity."

Standing on our Biblical Foundation

> *For as the body is one and has many members and all the members of that one body being many are one body so also is Christ. For by one Spirit are we all baptized into one body whether we be Jews or Gentiles, whether we be bond or free and have been all made to drink into one Spirit.* (1 Corinthians 12:12)

In this passage, we can understand that the spiritual church is united by the Spirit and unwilling to compromise with Satan's agenda. Therefore, some church members are breaking away from their national church organization. One such group is the Menlo Park Presbyterian, San Francisco, and where Condoleezza Rice is a member. Pastor John Orlberg and his members voted 93 percent to leave Presbyterian main body. The Presbyterians have compromised on the teaching of the scriptures by accepting the homosexual agenda and allowing them to serve as pastors. They have also taken a strong stand against Israel, calling for boycott, divestment, and sanctions in favor of the Muslims claiming to be refugees entitled to the land of Israel.

In order to stand firm in the face of adversity, we need to know the Word. Rev. Clarence Larkin, 1920, wrote, *Rightly Dividing the Word*, clearly explaining,

> The Holy scriptures are not a systematic treatise on theology, history, science or any other topic. They are a revelation from God of his plan and purpose in the ages as to the earth and the human race. They were given to us piecemeal, "at sundry time and in divers manners." While the Bible has been complied in the manner described, it is not a heterogeneous jumble of ancient history, myths, legends, religious speculations, and apocalyptic literature. There is a progress of revelation and doctrine in it. The Old and New Testaments cannot be separated. You cannot understand Leviticus without Hebrews, or Daniel without Revelation. The Bible and its supernatural origin is seen in the fact that it can be translated into any language and the language of the scriptures is figurative, symbolical, and literal. While the Bible was written for all classes of people for our learning, it is not addressed to all people in general. Part is to the Jews, to the Gentiles, and to the church.

All scripture is profitable for (our) doctrine, for (our) reproof, for (our) correction, for (our) instruction (2 Timothy 3:16).

During the church age, men provided their own interpretation and opinion of the intent or meaning of the scriptures. The self-proclaimed "church fathers" are not the final authority on scripture. The scriptures clearly state: there is no private interpretation. Following, we mention a few of those considered to be "church fathers," and some of their comments:

Early Church Leaders

Polycarp—a disciple of Apostle John, bishop of Smyrna and burned at the stake.

Philo of Alexandria studied under Paul.

Erasmus claimed that if hating Jews is Christian, then all of us are exceedingly Christian.

Ignatius, Bishop of Antioch, early second century, began to introduce the concept of "Catholicism or universal."

AD 100–165, Justin Martyr claimed that God ordered the circumcision of the Jews so that they might suffer the afflictions that they deserved.

AD 120–202, Irenaeus, disciple of Polycarp, Pastor Lyons, France.

AD 200–258, Cyprian, bishop of Carthage.

AD 150–220, Clement of Alexander believed that the dead could be sanctified and made pure in purgatory, a position of Catholicism.

AD 150–225, Tertullian, father of Latin theology, Carthage, Africa, introduced the concept of the Trinity and believed in prophecy and the writings of Enoch. He believed in praying for the dead, and this practice was adopted by the Catholic church

AD 160, Melito, pastor of Sardis.

AD 170, Hippolytus, pastor of the church in Rome, disciple of Irenaeus.

AD 240–320, Lactantius, Latin rhetorician.

AD 260–339, Eusebius, Christian historian of Caesarea.

AD 325, the Council of Nicea taught many questionable doctrines. They taught the doctrine of angels in AD 343 was idolatry. The Council of Nicea believed the church is Israel and the covenant made between God and the Jews now belong to the church called Reformed Covenant Theology. False priest Marcion taught there should be a break between Old Testament and New Testament by severing all ties between Judaism and Christianity. This heresy was adopted by the Council of Nicea and by Augustine. This became a theological axiom by Catholicism and belief now entrenched in Protestant denominations.

AD 350–430, Augustine promoted that people could be made pure and righteous through suffering in the afterlife (purgatory). Augustine said, "How I wish you would slay the Jews with your two-edged sword." Israel had no place in his view. Augustine denied a future millennium reign. He envisioned a thousand-year church age, and when that time had passed, much of his work was discredited. His writings gained acceptance in the medieval church, later picked up by the Roman Church and followed suit with reformed churches. Today groups as the Islamic Christian Committee embrace Augustine's beliefs, especially where it applies to Jerusalem as the capital of the Gentiles.

AD 540–604, Gregory was a bishop of the Roman church and became pope in AD 590. He furthered developed the unbiblical doctrine of purgatory—a place between heaven and hell where the dead could suffer and be made pure before entering heaven. People would pay the church for prayers or a mass dedicated to the soul of the dead.

Practices Leading to Apostasy

The pope calls for May 13, AD 600, to commemorate dead saints called All Hallows Day and was embraced by Protestants. They promoted the false belief that the souls of the dead could revisit their homes for warmth, walking around and looking for food or treats. Later, the day was labeled Halloween, between October 31 to November 1, and was a commemoration to Beltane and Samhain for changing of autumn to winter. Dark forces also roamed the night: demons, hobgoblins, and witches wanting to carry out acts of mischiefs or tricks. Occult, witchcraft, and Satanist rituals continue to embrace pagan practices celebrated on Halloween in the summoning of demons and dressing as ghost, devils, vampires, werewolves, and monsters. To those who continue to promote Halloween or disguise it, calling it a Harvest Festival, as an innocent and fun holiday are deceived.

Martin Luther of Germany is partially famous for posting his 95 dissertation on the church door around AD 1522. Luther was born 1483, died 1546. He was a German priest, living in Eisleben, Saxony, under the Holy Roman Empire. He split with the Catholic church during the time of Pope Leo X around AD 1520. In brief, he disagreed with the church position on salvation, that it cannot be earned through good deeds but through grace and faith in Jesus. He translated the Bible from Latin to German. He was married and had children. Gradually, he developed animosity toward the Jews, which he wrote in his book, *On the Jews and Their Lies.* We list some of his antagonistic beliefs regarding the Jews: their homes destroyed and synagogues burned; their money confiscated and liberty curtailed; they are no longer the chosen people but the devil's people; they are violent and have a vile language. Three days before his death, Martin Luther gave a sermon in Eisleben to expel Jews from German territory, "Drive the Jews bag and baggage from their midst, they are our public enemies, unless they convert to Christianity." Luther was admired and considered a prophet. He did influence others toward hatred, stirring up riots to expel Jews from German Lutheran states. Anti-Jewish rhetoric contributed to the rise of anti-Semitism, which played out 1930s to 1940s, creating a platform for the Nazi's attack on the Jews. The *Third Reich*, writings referenced quotes from Martin Luther. Heinrich Himmler admired Luther. Excerpts from Luther's book were displayed under glass at Nuremberg.

Bishop Martin Sasse, Protestant, applauded the burning of synagogues to celebrate Martin Luther's birthday, November 10, 1938, calling him the greatest anti-Semite. December 17, 1941, seven Protestant churches agreed to forcing Jews to wear yellow badges (Wikipedia online, July 13, 2015, Martin Luther).

AD 1547, Council of Trent was put in place by the Roman Catholic church to counter Protestant Reformation by Pope Paul III.

We can see how the mind-set and practices of the early church leaders led into apostasy, and such continues into our modern era. Many pastors cherry-pick through the scriptures and bypass the whole Word of God. Some pastors lack belief in the power of God's Word. They need to eat the Word and taste and see that the Lord is good. They need to digest the Word, and the Word will be down on the inside like fire shut up in their bones.

Some may avoid teaching prophecy because they lack knowledge and spiritual guidance to handle the prophetic scriptures. Others may say they don't have the time to devote to prophecy. The fear of being labeled a prophecy nut or fear monger may be a reason for steering clear of prophecy. Many preachers avoid the doctrine of sin, judgment, and hell. Having a conservative and proper appearance became more important than pleasing God. They will be held accountable for not sounding the alarm and warning the people.

Where there is a spiritual vacuum of the Word, the void is filled with false doctrine, wrong interpretation, and misunderstanding of the Word of God. Following are a few modern-day sentiments:

- One such supporter is Rowan Williams, archbishop of Canterbury, who said, "Christians and Muslims have a common agenda, both faiths believe in the living image of a community raised up to God's call to reveal to the world what God's purpose is for humanity." According to Islam, all the world should submit to a false doctrine.
- Also at the meeting with Williams, Fouad Tawl, Latin patriarch of Jerusalem, protested that there are half a million Israelis living in East Jerusalem and the West Bank, and they are a growing threat to the sacred sights. Tawl, being blind with anti-Semitism, must have forgotten that the Islamic radicals consistently desecrate the holy places of Jews and Christians.
- Another protester is the Vatican's former archbishop of Jerusalem, Michel Sabbah, who called upon the United States and Europe to stop the Hebrewzation of Jerusalem.

- Greek Orthodox archbishop of Jerusalem, Atallah Hanna, is an activist who publicly denounces the Israeli occupation and supports the establishment of a Palestinian identity. Hanna is quoted as saying, "The suicide bombers who carry out their activities in the name of religion are national heroes."
- Newt Gingrich appropriately referred to the Palestinians as an "invented" people.

Christendom has existed for almost two thousand years, and since its inception, it has continued in a spiritual decline, morphing into something the apostles may not recognize. It is important to remind the reader that this condition of apostasy didn't begin two thousand years ago but was orchestrated by Satan before the flood. It is also important to remind the reader that the beginning of the church age was an outgrowth of Judaism. Jesus our Messiah is the bridge between Judaism and Christianity.

From early church leaders to modern-day leaders, the disease of apostasy is a falling-away from God-given truth. The condition of apostasy was grievous for Israel. We thank God that in both Judaism and Christianity, God always set aside a remnant. God calls out those who will remain faithful and will not compromise with Satan's agenda. The true body of Christ is not confined to buildings but is spiritual in nature.

Judaism and Christianity both have been plagued by ungodliness and unbelief. Both blame the other for the state of world. As we focus on the spiritual condition of the apostate church from the time of the apostles, the Roman church, Protestant reformation, and its offshoots had an appearance of godliness but were moving away from biblical doctrine and the tenants of the faith.

The scriptures warn us to be aware of those that have a form of godliness but deny the truth. Beware of those who preach another Jesus, have another spirit and a different Gospel (2 Corinthians 11:4). The scriptures warn us of false prophets, deceitful workers, transforming themselves as apostles of Christ … For Satan himself is transformed into an angel of light and his ministers also be transformed as the ministers of righteousness (2 Corinthians 11:14–15).

Once these counterfeit workers creep into the church body, they have little difficulty finding those who have itching ears to hear the doctrine of devils.

> *The time will come when they will not endure sound doctrine but after their own lusts will they heap to themselves teachers, having itching ears, they will turn away their ears from the truth and will be turned unto fables.* (2 Timothy 4:3)

Apostate Church

The body of Christ is distinct from those who embrace Christendom, which has an outer appearance of godliness but are as whitewashed tombstones. Apostates have fallen away from biblical truth, bringing forth false prophecy and doctrinal heresy.

> *But there were false prophets also among the people, even as there will be false teachers among you who privately bring in damnable heresies, even denying the Lord that bought them and bring upon themselves swift destruction. And* ***many*** *will follow their shameful ways by reason of whom the way of truth shall be evil spoken of …* (2 Peter 2:1)

Ancient false prophets denied the true God, and in his place they followed false gods such as Baal, Osiris, Zeus, Mithra, Dagon, and others (Matthew 7:15). Jesus warns us to beware of false prophets, who come to you in sheep's clothing but inwardly they are ravening wolves. We must rely on the gift of discernment to test "a word of prophecy" and see if it aligns with the Word of God. Then we look at the credibility of the "prophet" and see if he is living a holy life. Signs and wonders can be performed by demons. If we follow false prophets, then shame, spiritual depravity, and moral corruption will follow suit. The consequence of false prophecy is that the false prophet himself receives death and destruction (Jeremiah 28:16).

The symptoms of the apostate church is an overall falling-away from biblical truth and following the doctrines of devils. A few signs that demons are occupying the pews are disruption, attention seeking, gossips, secret sins, embracing homosexuality, and abortion.

We should know the Word of God and be able to test the spirit by the spirit.

> *Now the Spirit speaks expressly, that in the latter times, some shall depart from the faith giving heed to seducing spirits and doctrines of devils speaking lies in hypocrisy, having their conscience seared with a hot iron …* (1 Timothy 4)

Emergent Church

A booklet titled *Emergent Church* written by Dr. William R. Goetz explains how allowing false doctrine and mystical beliefs into the church give birth to the apostate church. He highlights a gathering in 2008 of the National Pastors' Convention, sponsored by emergent friendly Zondervan Publishing and Inter Varsity Press. The convention included a number of emergent speakers, featured yoga and Nooma films, as well as prayer labyrinths and instructions by spiritual directors. It was sold as a safe place to be honest about the challenges of spiritual leadership, to experience spiritual rhythms of solitude, meditation, and understanding that this experience flows from one's "authentic self" (not flowing from the Holy Spirit). Here we see the exaltation of "self." These things can be subtle and appealing. This view is a symptom of a sick church. The emergent church is a spiritual condition brought on by embracing false doctrine.

The booklet gives a description of the emergent church as seen by one of its founders, Mark Driscoll, who is no longer following the path of the damned.

- Evangelicals who believe in at least the basic Christian doctrines, but though they are fairly conservative theologically, they are culturally liberal in the way they do church.
- House church evangelicals, still basically doctrinally conservative, who form little house churches or in smaller settings like a coffee shop in opposition to mega churches.
- Evangelical reformers who embrace reformed theological traditions, but they try to find ways to make church relevant, accessible, and culturally connected.
- Liberals who call into question fundamental Christian doctrine, "Do you need Jesus to go to heaven?" or "Is adultery and homosexuality really sinful?"

<u>Statistics (Estimates)</u>

In 2011, 19 percent of pastors do not believe Jesus is coming back, and 30 percent of membership.

In 2011, 50 percent of pastors read the Bible; only 6 percent believe it is literal.

Year 2013, removed *In Christ Alone* from their hymnal. In 2010, 35 percent believe Jesus is the only way to salvation; 65 percent of Christian churches worldwide promote replacement theology. In 1965 there were 4.25 million Presbyterian members and by 2013 there were 1.84 million in US churches, all denominations, have around 340,000. Assemblies of God, 12,595 churches. Worldwide Christendom is around two billion.

<u>Gnosticism</u>

This is Greek for *knowledge*. Gnostics believe that all physical matter is evil and spiritual enlightenment is good. Only the intellectually enlightened could enjoy the benefits of religion. They derived knowledge from other cultures, including Judaism, Christianity, Greek, Roman, Oriental records, and mythology. Therefore, it was not accepted that Jesus was both divine and human. The deity of Christ, God in the flesh, was rejected. The scriptures are clear that those who deny the Father and Jesus the Son are liars and Antichrist (1 John 2:22).

Replacement Theology Is the Belief the Church Has Replaced Israel

Since many pastors do not understand prophetic truth, they believe the church has replaced Israel. They ignore the hundreds of scriptures that attest to the fact Israel has an everlasting covenant with God. The fulfillment of prophecy they ignore is the regathering of Jews into the land. In their thinking, the church is destined to create the spiritual platform that will pave the way for the Lord's return, and the church will be instrumental in establishing the kingdom of God on earth. They will work to eliminate Israel, and on this premise, anti-Semitism takes root. Some have called America the New Jerusalem.

Sometimes we need to be aware of the small innuendos spoken from the pulpit. One small church pastor would make comments that were anti-Semitic. "I support Israel but not if they are saying or doing something foolish." "The legions of demons were cast out of the man at Gaderene and went into the swine, which were owned by the Jews." "The New Jerusalem that comes down has twelve gates with the apostles' names on them." Those who love Israel know that we love them unconditionally. Jews have kosher laws, forbidding the eating of pork. The twelve gates of pearl have the names of the twelve tribes, but the twelve foundations have the names of the apostles. Other pastors absolutely believe Israel are the occupiers, oppressors of the "refugee" Palestinians, and are apartheid.

Present-day Protestant denominations—namely, Methodist, Presbyterian, Lutheran—join with the National Council of Churches to petition Congress to cut off funding to Israel.

On a good note, the Episcopal Church in the United States met in Salt Lake City, July 2, 2015, and rejected an action to boycott, divest, sanction BDS Israel. They received appreciation from the World Jewish Congress on their pro-Israel action. Episcopal membership is 1.8 million.

The Mennonite church in the United States voted at their Kansas conference to put on hold action to move on BDS until 2017.

Christ at the Check Point, 2012, conference held in Israel in occupied Bethlehem was attended by Arabs and church leaders opposed to Israel in the land.

Replacement theology holds to the false belief that the New Covenant replaces the old Mosaic Covenant, and the church has inherited the promises made to Israel. They begin with the idea that Israel is forever lost in sin and never to be redeemed. On the contrary, Romans 11:11,

> *I say then, have they stumbled that they should fall? God forbid but rather through their fall salvation is come unto the Gentiles for to provoke them to jealousy. Now if the fall of them be the riches of the world and the diminishing of them the riches of the Gentiles, how much more their fullness.*

In support of scriptural position on Israel, John Nelson Darby presented the Gospel as given by the apostles that the return of Christ is imminent and national Israel is at the center of prophetic fulfillment. Israel is God's prophetic time clock. We must always watch unfolding end-time events with Israel as a barometer. In the dispensations of time, true believers understand that the age of grace is associated with the church and in no way usurps Israel's central place in the fulfillment of Old Testament prophecy.

Zephaniah 3:9–17 looks to a future time when Israel has returned to the land: "I will return to the people a pure language that they may all call upon the name of the Lord … I will bring my suppliants, even the daughter of my dispersed from beyond the rivers of Ethiopia" … In that day, God will take away out of the midst of them the shame of their transgressions … God will remove those who were prideful, haughty, and rejoice in themselves … a remnant of Israel can look to a time when God will take away their iniquity, cast out their enemy, take away judgment, and they will live in peace … singing, "Oh, daughter of Zion, shout, oh, Israel be glad and rejoice with all the heart for the king of Israel, even the Lord is in the midst of you, and you will not see evil anymore" … He will save, he will rejoice over you with joy; he will rest in his love (Israel); he will joy over you with singing.

Chrislam

The one-world religion embraces all religions. The concept of Chrislam is introduced where the god Allah and the God of the Bible are considered the same. Some scholars said this idea originated in Nigeria thirty years ago between an Iman and a Christian pastor. They agreed to compare commonalities in each religion. In 2011, the idea took root in the United States, bringing together church and Muslim leaders to read the Koran and the Bible side by side. This was in a church building. However, this would not be allowed in the mosque. No Iman is going to bring a Bible into his mosque and read it or allow a Christian to come in and talk about Jesus. Muslims are just going along with the farce where Christians are being conciliatory or kind by saying we worship the same god. Pastors such as Rick Warren—Saddleback Church, having a congregation of over six hundred thousand people—goes a step farther in believing the church has replaced Israel. Warren began his antibiblical movement, mingling Islam and Christianity, which he popularized by calling it Chrislam.

Heresy and False Doctrine

Even though the signs of the times are falling around us like bricks, some pastors cannot associate prophecy with current events. They are afraid to let people know the real works of Satan, and in doing so, God's warnings are ignored. Seminary professors admonish students to steer clear of prophetic teachings except to gloss over the terminology for basic understanding.

Some seminary professors do not believe in the literal creation and inject the myth of evolution as a reality. The fact that in the book of John, it clearly states Jesus is God and Jesus created the world and all that is therein.

There is a growing number of biblical scholars that misinterpret the Word of God as it applies to the church and its relationship with Israel. Justin Martyr thought the church is spiritual Israel. Hippolytus said the Jews have been darkened in the eyes of the Lord forever. Origen and Martin Luther held to the belief that the Old Testament prophecies once intended for the Jews were now to pertain to the church.

Seminary promotes ungodly teachings. One comes to mind where professors introduce the idea that Jesus and Mary Magdalene had children. In defense of the scriptures and the Word of God, there is not one bit of evidence that point to that heresy.

In the scheme of things planned by God before the formation of the earth, God would come and be born of a virgin. The virgin birth firmly states that God was not born of the seed of sinful man but of the Holy Spirit. Jesus was the sinless, unblemished Lamb of God to take away the sins of the world. If Jesus had sex with Mary, he would have been guilty of the sin of fornication. He would no longer qualify to be that unblemished, sinless sacrifice to die for the sins of mankind. Now, let's just say, if it was God's plan to allow Jesus our God to marry and have children, this in itself is not a sin; and if that was the case, why would it have been a secret throughout all the scriptures? It is not a hidden secret or mystery because all mysteries in scripture give us a hint or clue to search the scriptures for deeper understanding. Why would Jesus want to have biological children in the first place? The Word in the beginning is God our Jesus, Creator of all things. The first children of God were Adam and Eve; they disobeyed God, and the whole world was cursed and fell into sin. Later, fallen angels found a method to mingle with earth women and created monsters that God had to wipe from the face of the earth. After the flood, Noah's descendants repopulated the earth, and the majority of these children were wicked and ungodly forward to the present time. God could see firsthand that humans are disobedient and sinful. If God had sex with Mary, a sinner, then his offspring would have been sinners. There is no logical reason for God to have biological children. Once we accept the atoning death and Resurrection of Jesus, we become adopted into the household of God. We become joint heirs with Jesus. We are the spiritual children of the Most High God.

Catholics come up with the misconception that Mary the mother of Jesus was a virgin forever. They totally dismiss the children she and Joseph produced after the birth of Jesus. Mary becomes their center of worship and their Queen of Heaven. The woman described in Revelation with the twelve stars about her head is Israel.

The early church was beleaguered with doctrinal impurity and outright error, and the same dogma is evident in present times. False doctrine can be implemented through Bible colleges, church training organizations, and church leadership. There is usually some program to reach out to the lost, but there must be a gimmick to attract them. Sometimes a struggling church will take the council of some who appears to be a Christian. They have a spiritual aspect to their philosophy, but it is influenced by mysticism. Some believe God is in everything, and everything has a divine spark. God and man are one, which all higher religions share. These people have no problem embracing Buddhist or New Age sympathizers.

Opening the occult portal, churches are being deceived and will make way for the end-time prophecy, "the great delusion." When the Rapture occurs, many church people will be left behind. The new age doctrine subtly creeps into church. It will promote the idea of the new spirituality, which embraces a worldview. It joins with all the world calling for peace. The Antichrist will deceive many under the guise of peace, and then he will destroy many. It teaches that we are all one because God is in everyone and God is in everything. The Sprit of the Holy God cannot dwell in a dirty, sinful temple (John 2:24). Jesus did not commit himself to men because he knew what was in men. Was God in Hitler? We believe not, because Hitler was obviously of the seed of Satan.

The church in the modern era says old biblical doctrines need to be questioned and challenged. "Truth cannot be known with certainty." A millennial view such as, "the kingdom of God has come and is operating now upon the earth"—to support that position, the church would need to embrace all religions to bring about peace and harmony upon the earth. All spiritual vehicles are acceptable because everyone is connected and we are all gods. Environmental concerns would require involvement to save the planet, recycle, save the animal species.

The Self-Righteous and Worldliness

Many are quick to label themselves as rabbis, reverends, bishops, prophets, apostles and are far removed from Jesus and his Word. They desire to be exalted and to have others serve them. Jesus speaks to this mind-set in Matthew 23:2–35. The religious leaders bid you observe and do, but do not you after their works for they say and do not. They bind heavy burdens to bear on men's shoulders, but they themselves will not move them with one finger to help. All their works, they do for to be seen of men, and they make broad their phylacteries and enlarge the border of their garments. They love the uppermost rooms at feast and best seat in the synagogues. They love to be greeted in public as rabbi or bishop. Jesus said do not call yourself rabbi or greater because all have one Master, even Christ; and all are brothers and sisters, equal in the faith. He that is greatest among you will be your servant. Whosoever will exalt himself will be humbled, and he that will humble himself will be exalted.

Jesus calls the religious leaders blind guides, who strain a gnat and swallow a camel—which means they were meticulous regarding cleansing the outer and assuring their intake was free of pollutants while they had lost their perspective of inner purity. You Pharisees make clean the outside of the cup and the platter, but within, they are full of extortion and excess. Clean first that which is within, and the outside will be clean also. You are like white sepulchers, which appear beautiful outward but within full of dead men's bones and all uncleanness. You appear outwardly righteous, but within you are full of hypocrisy and iniquity.

Woe unto you, Pharisees, for you shut up the kingdom of heaven against men, for neither go in yourselves neither suffer you them that are entering to go in. Woe unto you, Pharisees, for you devour widows' houses. For a pretense you make long prayer, and therefore you will receive the greater damnation. You pay tithes of mint, anise, and cumin and have omitted the weightier matters of the law, judgment, mercy, faith. Woe unto you, hypocrites, for you compass sea and land to make one convert, and when he is made, you make him twofold more the child of hell than yourselves.

You serpents, you generation of vipers, how can you escape the damnation of hell? You have killed the prophets, and because of this all, their righteous bloodshed upon the earth—from Abel to Zacharias—be upon you (Matthew 23).

Jesus addressed the religious leaders of his day, but this is also relevant for those in the ministry in current times. There are many who don themselves with titles but do not live up to the calling.

For instance, the right Rev. Al Sharpton in April 2014 was cited as being involved with the mob and turned FBI informant on the mob to avoid jail. He is head of National Action Network and Obama supporter. Simply listen to his speech, and a Christian should be able to discern his ungodliness.

Rev. Jesse Jackson, a man who is an adulterer, has a following of ignorant people who do not know the scriptures. He loves the limelight.

TV minister Bishop Eddie Long was accused of homosexual relations with teenage boys yet his church members continue to fellowship with him. Long is a millionaire and is unrepentant. He did not step down from leadership but was seated in an elaborate chair, lifted up and carried around the stage.

Mega churches bring in millions, and the ministers live lavish lifestyles, such as Fred Price and Joel Osteen. Creflo Dollar asked his congregation for $65 million to buy a new jet. Kenneth Copeland boasted his ministry took in over a billion dollars. Copeland has a plush mansion and owns an airfield with many planes.

Faith Chapel Christian Center, Wylam Alabama, recently held an open house to celebrate the opening of its $26 million, six-dome entertainment center on 137-acre campus funded by 6,400 members' tithes and offerings. Other entertainment features at the church are a twelve-lane bowling alley, basketball court, fitness center, banquet hall, café, teen dance club, and adult night club. Michael Moore, member of the church, wrote a book, *Rich Is Not a Bad Word*. He said, "We believe we can really meet the needs of the low-income community and bridge people from the world to the kingdom."

In regard to the above example of mega churches that appear more worldly than obeying the command of Jesus, we reiterate scripture:

> *Then said one unto the Lord, are there few that be saved? And he said unto them, strive to enter in at the strait gate for many, I say unto you will seek to enter in and will not be able. When once the master of the house is risen up and has shut the door and you begin to stand without and to knock at the door saying, Lord, Lord, open unto us and he will answer and say unto you, I know you not where you are. Then will you begin to say, we have eaten and drunk in your presence and you taught us in our streets. But the Lord will say, I tell you, I know you not where you are, depart from me all you workers of iniquity. There will be weeping and gnashing of teeth when you will see Abraham and Isaac and Jacob and all the prophets in the Kingdom of God and you yourselves thrust out.* (Luke 13:23)

Some churches include Eastern ancient practices to induce altered states of consciousness. The "silence" is rooted in mysticism, but for the Christian audience, it is touted as the way to truly know God through "contemplative spirituality." This becomes contemplative or centering prayer; the goal is to arrive at a state of complete stillness or mindlessness in order to hear God's voice. One is taught to choose a word—*Jesus* or *Father*—and focus. Repeat the word silently for a while until inner self seems to be repeating the word; take deep breaths, concentrate, relax, stop the flow of talking going on in your head until it stops. Yoga is being included in churches and speaking chants to some pagan god.

On the other side of the world, China may plan to nationalize Christian theology. According to Wang Zuoan, director of the State Administration for Religious Affairs, he said, "The construction of Chinese Christian theology should adapt to China's national condition and integrate with Chinese culture." China's state media said, "National theology will encourage more believers to make contributions to the country's harmonious social progress, cultural prosperity, and economic development." Communist China has not been a friend of

Christians in the past, forcing them into underground churches and removing crosses from existing churches.

Tolerance and Carnaltiy

The Vatican's position on tolerance and inclusion was clearly set November 1986, at the invitation of Pope John Paul II, when he invited twelve religious leaders to a convocation to pray to their "god" to bring peace to the world. The Dalai Lama was present, and his followers believe he is god. The pope believes all prayers rise up to the same god. In December 2000, in another message to Catholics, the pope said, "All who live a just life will be saved even if they don't believe in Jesus and the Roman Catholic church and all that is needed for salvation is a sincere heart."

The Vatican's stance in protecting pedophiles is carnal. Also an abomination to the Lord would be the breach of the second commandment: "Thou shall not make any graven images." Many statues adorn the church. Chapter 18 discussed idolatry, which says the formation of an idol from stone, wood, metal is the physical representation of a false god. The image of this god is worshipped. Catholics worship Mary the mother of Jesus. She is called the Queen of Heaven. Is there a difference in the many statues and idols found in Hindu or Buddhist temples between the statues found in the Catholic church?

Catholic archbishop of Wales said, "The church needs to evolve and change as it responds to the world around it or risk being seen as homophobic" (*Wales Online*, April 23, 2014, Sion Morgan reporter).

Satanic influence has penetrated the church. We only need to look at the rotten fruit coming from Christendom. It is embracing carnality in the areas of abortion and sexual sin.

Abortion

The Presbyterian church is committed to abortion since 1970 to the present time. Other churches do not preach about the sin of murdering the unborn and are complicit through silence.

Presbyterian denomination voted **no** on their motion protecting the life of children born alive during botched abortions. The group was asked to (1) reflect on the plight of children unwanted by society, born and unborn, and to seek to enter the pure worship of God by offering aid, comfort, and the Gospel to those responsible for the care of our most desperate orphans, parents, siblings, church, and community leaders and the medical profession; and (2) direct the moderator of the General Assembly and the Stated Clerk to issue statements that denounce the practice of killing babies born alive following an abortion procedure, such as was revealed in the Kermit Gosnell clinic in Philadelphia (*Breitbart News Roundup*, Dr. Susan Berry, June 25, 2014).

Homosexuality

It is Satan who undermines the commitment to the truth of the Gospel. To appeal to the masses, the apostate church must be innovative. The church may want to avoid appearing intolerant or bigoted toward the homosexual agenda or prochoice woman who wants to abort her child. All sexual sin is sin regardless of its category: adultery, pedophilia, homosexuality, fornication, etc.

In 2011, Presbyterians endorsed homosexuals as pastors and deacons. This abomination is found in other congregations as well. By 2014, the top legislative body of the Presbyterian church voted to endorse same-sex marriage as part of their church constitution. Other denominations are also allowing this abnormal lifestyle.

Christian publisher, Waterbrook Press for Multnomah books, supports author Matthew Vines, *God and the Gay Christian: The Biblical Case in Support of Same-Sex Relationships*," as a beginning to discuss controversial, cultural issues. The archbishop of Wales agrees with Multnomah, "We should never quote God's word on homosexuality because we have moved beyond **his outdated opinion**" (*Christian Post*, April 24, 2014, Stoyan Zaimov).

Christian singing group Jars of Clay also support same-sex marriage. Lead singer Dan Haseltine referenced the biblical interpretation of marriage and could not understand conservatives who use scripture to deny same-sex couple equal rights and also for the LGBT rights in general (*Huffington Post*, "Gay Voices," April 25, 2014, James Nichols).

Episcopal Church House of Bishops approved 2012, by gay Bishop Gene Robinson, to allow transgender people the right to become ministers according to their nondiscrimination clause in its canon. A transgender priest was scheduled to preach at Washington National Cathedral. Episcopalians will perform same-sex weddings.

United Church of Christ will perform same-sex marriage and pushes for divestment in Israel.

Anglican Church of England approves gay priest.

Some pastors speak out against the apostate church. John MacArthur, pastor, Grace to You Baptist Church, condemns churches who condone same-sex marriage, calling them apostate and Satan's church. Satanist Temple of America calls same-sex marriage as one of its sacraments.

World Council of Churches is a conglomerate of humanism, secularism, and false doctrine and is a perfect umbrella for the false prophet and the one-world religion.

Message to the Seven Churches

Near the end of the life of the Apostle John, a Messianic Jew, he received a vision from Yeshua, the Jewish Messiah, which he recorded in the book of Revelation. It is a message to the Jewish converts in the churches of Asia and applicable for all Christians throughout history. In his salutation, John makes reference to the seven spirits that are before God's throne. This is an acknowledgment to the Holy Spirit. The number 7 symbolizes completeness and perfection. Seven Gifts of the Spirit are given for the church. These are the gifts of miracles, healing, diversity of tongues and interpretation, apostles, prophecy/discernment, teaching,, and service (1 Corinthians 12:28). The Jewish followers of Christ operated in the Gifts of the Spirit. At the time of the writing of the book of Revelation, around AD 90, many of the churches were made up of Jews and Gentiles. After the message to the seven churches given in Revelation 1 to 4, the church is not mentioned further. Revelation 5 and thereafter reveals events dealing with Israel, the Antichrist, false prophet, mystery Babylon, battle of Armageddon, and judgment upon the Gentile nations, Israel, and the Second Coming of Christ.

Message to the Seven Churches, Revelation 1 to 3

Jesus selected these seven churches in this particular order to prophetically suggest the major trends in church history (Elmer Towns, commentary on the Seven Churches):

- Ephesus is the apostolic church forming during Pentecost to AD 100.
- Smyrna represents the persecuted church, AD 100–316.
- Pergamos is the world church, AD 316–800.
- Thyatira is the Medieval church, AD 800–1517.
- Sardis represents the rise of the state church, AD 1517–1750.
- Philadelphia is the missionary church, AD 1750–1900.
- Laodicea is the end of the age apostate church, AD 1900–2015.

These seven churches foreshadow a spiritual condition that the church would undergo during the two thousand years of the church age. These spiritual conditions are not just for the church body but also point to the strength and weakness of every believer. There is a prophetic message given to each church in part, and when the messages are combined, we can see the gifts that God has planned for those who love him. We can also see the warning that God has given to the church and the body. In the Revelation given to John, he focuses on the church from chapters 1 to 3. After chapter 3, there is no further mention of the church until Revelation 22. The church has been removed from the earth before the great and terrible Day of the Lord, as predicted in Revelation.

Specifics of the Messages

The message to the church of Ephesus, which means, "desirable" (Revelation 2:1)

- Faith, patience, doctrinal truth.
- Hates evil, exposes false apostles.
- Have continued in the faith and not given up.
- Rebuke—you have left your first love, Christ.
- Promise—I will let you eat of the Tree of Life.

The message to the church of Smyrna, which means, "myrrh" (Revelation 2:8)

- Suffering tribulation and poverty.
- Exposed those who say they are Jews but are the synagogue of Satan.
- Persecution and martyrdom.
- Rebuke—have no fear in the midst of tribulation.
- Promise—I will give you a crown of life.

The message to the church of Pergamos, which means, "elevation of power" (Revelation 2:12)

- Worldly alliance.
- Location identified as the Seat of Satan.
- Rebuke—in their midst are those that hold to the doctrine of Balaam, causing the children of Israel to stumble and eat things sacrificed unto idols and to commit fornication; also in their midst are false teachers. Repent, or else I will come unto you quickly and will fight against them with the sword of my mouth.
- Promise—I will give you hidden manna and a white stone with a new name.

The message to the church of Thyatira, which means, "sweet smell" (Revelation 2:18)

- Good works of charity and service.
- Faithful and patient.
- Rebuke—has in their midst Jezebel, a false prophet who leads astray the followers to eat things sacrificed to idols, indulge in fornication and false doctrine.
- Promise—I will give you power over the nations and the morning star.

The message to the church of Sardis, which means, "prince of joy" (Revelation 3:1)

- Dying faith, having the appearance of a lively body but are dead.

- Your works are imperfect before God.
- Hold fast to the knowledge you have received, repent.
- Rebuke—if you are not vigilant and watchful, I will come on thee as a thief, and you will not know what hour I will come. There are some among you that have not defiled their garments, and they will walk with me in white, for they are worthy.
- Promise—he that overcomes will be clothed in white raiment, and I will not blot out his name out of the book of life, but I will confess his name before my father and his angels.

The message to the church of Philadelphia, which means, "brotherly love" (Revelation 3:7–13)

- Evangelism—I have set before you an open door, and no man can shut it.
- You have a little strength and have kept my word and not denied my name.
- Promises—I will make them of the synagogue of Satan, who say they are Jews and are not but do lie, and I will make them to come and worship before your feet and to know that I have loved you.
- Promises—because you have kept the word of my patience, I also will keep you from the hour of temptation (tribulation), which shall come upon the world to try them that dwell in the earth.
- Behold, I come quickly. (When we see the unfolding of the end-time signs, then we know his coming is near.)
- Hold fast to truth (do not be deceived), so no man will take thy crown. (Jesus will bring our rewards with him, and it appears we will receive these crowns after the Bema Seat.)
- Promises—he that overcomes (apostasy and temptation) will I make a pillar in the temple of my God, and he shall go no more out, and I will write upon him the name of my God and the name of the city of my God, which is New Jerusalem, which comes down out of heaven from my God, and I will write upon him my new name. We will dwell with God in the New Jerusalem, which comes down out of heaven during the millennial reign.

The message to the church of Laodicea, which means, "laypeople" (Revelation 3:14).

- Blinded by material riches and spiritually shameful. You boast that you have need of nothing, and you know not that you are wretched, miserable, poor, blind, and naked.
- You are neither cold or hot but lukewarm, and I will spit you out.

- Buy gold that has been tried in fire so you may be spiritually rich, then you will be clothed in white raiment, and the shame of your nakedness will be covered. Anoint your eyes with salve that you may see.
- Jesus will rebuke and chasten those he loves, so they will repent. He will knock on the door of their heart, and if any may hear my voice and open the door, I will come in and fellowship with him and he with me.
- In his patience, Jesus continues to extend an opportunity for repentance.
- The spiritual condition of this apostate end-time church has put aside the truth of the Word and embraced feel-good theology, tolerance philosophy, no longer serious about repentance and salvation, reject the power of the Holy Spirit. There is now a door open for repentance before the Rapture.
- Promise to them—overcoming apostasy and the lure of the world, then Jesus will grant to "sit with me in my throne, even as I also overcame and am set down with my Father in his throne."

Promises to the Church

Review of the promises that Jesus has made to his body, the true believers who overcome the temptations of the world:

- I will set before you a tree of life. This is the tree that was in the Garden of Eden. It will be available during the millennial kingdom. It represents eternal life with Jesus, and its fruit is for the healing of the nations (Revelation 2:7).
- I will give you a crown of life. Overcomers will be rewarded with many crowns. This particular crown is for those who were martyred because of their faith. Overcomers will not be hurt by the second death, which is associated with the white throne judgment at the end of the millennial reign (Revelation 2:10–11).
- I will give you hidden manna and a white stone with a new name. Jesus is the bread of life; he is the chief cornerstones, and we are living stones. We will have immortal bodies and given a new name (Revelation 2:17).
- Those who are faithful and true believers, Jesus will keep from the hour of temptation (tribulation period), which shall come upon all the world (Revelation 3:10).
- I will give you power over the nations and the morning star. At the end of the tribulation, Jesus will rule over the nations with his saints. The morning star may refer to spiritual insight or discernment. At the time of the Rapture, we will be changed. We will have new bodies, new clothes, new name, rewards, and gifts of intellect and understanding of all the ways of God (Revelation 2:26–28).

- I will dress you in white raiment and confess your new name before my Father. An innumerable number of saints dressed in white, congregated in heaven during the tribulation, will be introduced to the Father. Jesus will write upon us his new name. We will see the glory and magnificence of Father and Son (Revelation 3:4–5).
- I will make you a pillar in the house of God. Heaven has no boundaries; millions will stand as pillars before God in the New Jerusalem, which will come down out of heaven (Revelation 3:12).
- Jesus will allow us to sit with him on his throne. This is no ordinary throne. It is surrounded by angels, lightning, and fire. It can transport through the heavens (Revelation 3:21).

Warnings to the Church

Let us study the warnings to the church, which address its decline in the things of God and because of ungodliness has created a spiritual vacuum, which is filled by false doctrine and occult practices.

- Revelation 2:4, "I have somewhat against you, because you have left your first love. Remember from where you are fallen, repent, and do the first works, or else I will come unto you quickly and will remove your candlestick."
- Revelation 2:9, "You have suffered tribulation, behold the devil will cast some of you into prison and persecution."
- Revelation 2:14, "You have taken the doctrine of Balaam and the Nicolaitanes which thing I hate, repent, or else I will come unto you quickly and will fight against them with the sword of my mouth."
- Revelation 2:20, "I have a few things against you because you entertained the woman Jezebel, who calls herself a prophetess, leading my servants into fornication and eating things sacrificed to idols. Repent, or I will send great tribulation, kill her children, and all will be judged according to your works."
- Revelation 3:2, "You are not perfect before God. Remember the Word you received, hold fast to it and repent. If you are not watchful, I will come on you as thief, and you will not know what hour I come."
- Stay strong, hold onto the word so no man can take your crown. I will keep you from the hour of temptation, which will come upon all the world."
- Revelation 3:16, "You are lukewarm, and I will spit you out of my mouth. You think you are rich and have need of nothing but you are wretched and miserable, poor, blind, naked. Repent and anoint your eyes so you may see. Those I love I rebuke and chasten."

Dispensations

Dispensational time frame covers a span of six thousand years. Robert Dean Jr. provides an excellent summary on dispensations:

> Dispensational theology enables us to correctly understand God's prophetic timetable for humanity. It provides an interpretive key that unlocks the pages of scripture and allows us to understand prophecy and orients our thinking about God's blueprint for human history. Three principles form the foundation of dispensational theology: (1) the Bible should be consistently understood literally; (2) God has a distinct plan for national Israel and a distinct plan for the church; (3) human history is the outworking of an eternal plan of God that will bring maximum glory to himself. Through each dispensation, God's truth and principles are constant."

The seven dispensations are listed:

1. The Age of Innocence
   From Creation to the fall of Adam and Eve.
2. The Age of Conscience
   From the fall to the flood is the age of conscience. The time frame from creation to the flood is approximately a thousand years.
3. The Age of Human Government
   From the flood to Abraham is approximately a thousand years.
4. The Age of Promise
   From Abraham to Moses is approximately a thousand years.
5. The Mosaic Law
   From Moses to the Cross, approximately a thousand years, the change from law to grace.
6. The Church Age
   From the Day of Pentecost to the present time is referred to as the church age or age of grace, over approximately two thousand years and during the fifth and sixth milleniums. Ephesians 3:2, "*If you have heard of the dispensation of the grace of god which is given me to you.*"
7. The Kingdom Age
   The beginning of the seventh millennium takes us into the millennial reign, also referred to as kingdom of God a time period of a thousand years. At the end of the kingdom age, God will move all to a state of eternity.

The Seven Feast of Israel also correlates with the seven dispensational periods, which point to the fulfillment of prophecy in the New Testament.

1. Passover, Jesus, the sacrificial lamb, shed his blood.
2. Unleavened bread represents the sinless nature of Jesus and his body on the cross.
3. First fruits is the Resurrection of Jesus and the dead from Noah to the thief on the cross.
4. Pentecost or Feast of Weeks is equivalent to the church age.
5. Feast of trumpets is the Rapture.
6. *Yom Kippur* is the tribulation.
7. Feast of Tabernacles is the millennial reign.

Other cultures have a dispensational belief. For instance, the Hopi Indians have a verbal tradition that promotes the idea of four worlds. They lived in North America for thousands of years. The first world was destroyed by fire; the second world was destroyed by ice; and the third world was destroyed by the flood. Their traditional beliefs say that the fourth world will undergo a great purification. They foresaw the white skin man coming to their land, followed by the "iron snake," railroad, spinning wheels, cars, and giant spiderweb streets and highways.

In the Fullness of Times

> *In the dispensation of the fullness of times he might gather together in one all things in Christ, both which are in heaven and which are on earth, even in him.* (Ephesian 1:10)

As the church age comes to an end we see the gathering together of Jew and Gentile. In Romans 11:25, Paul gives us another tidbit that when the fullness of the Gentiles come, the blindness of Israel would dissipate. Many Jews have accepted Yeshua as Messiah.

Fifteen years into the seventh millennium, Satan is still causing a great division between the true believers and world religions. The line in the sand is clear. Those who are for Jesus are not compromising with the ungodliness permeating the world. Even with the threat of backlash and persecution, they are holding up the banner.

We salute those ministries that are remaining faithful to Jesus and the Bible. For instance, the Southern Baptist Convention has taken a stand to uphold traditional values. At their annual convention, they voted against transgender people, saying, "God's original design did create two distinct and complimentary sexes. Gender identity should be determined by biological sex and not one's self-perception." The report was opposed by other counterfeit Christians condemning the position as intolerant, such as, Rachael Held Evans said, "There are people and churches ready to welcome you with the open arms of Christ."

Dr. Ronnie Floyd, pastor of Cross Church in Arkansas and newly elected president of the Southern Baptist Convention, calling for prayer for a third great awakening in America. He said, "Now is the time we take aggressive action by calling out to God together in prayer, at the same time we must take the needed strategic actions to change our trajectory as a convention of churches. We need extraordinary prayer for the purpose of revival personally, revival in the church, and spiritual awakening in America ..."

Billy Graham's daughter, Anne Graham Lotz, is speaking out for a broad-based revival in the church and the spread of the Gospel. Lotz served as chair for the 2014 National Day of Prayer and spoke from the book of Joel: the Day of the Lord is at hand. She believes that judgment is coming to America and called for a seven-day prayer vigil, July 7, 2014. We are to pray for protection and deliverance from evil, renewal to magnify Jesus in our church, our lives, and to pray for the Holy Spirit to fall on us in a fresh way, compelling repentance, and return to faith in Jesus.

Until the earth receives her full redemption, even nature and animals wait for the manifestations of the sons of God. For even the creature itself will be delivered from the bondage of corruption into the glorious liberty of the children of God. All creation groans and travails in pain together, not only them but ourselves, also waiting for the adoption and the redemption of our body (Romans 8:19–23).

<u>Time before Christ Is Noted as BC or BCE Time before the Christian Era</u>

Creation, 4004 BC
Flood, 3000 BC
Abraham, 2000 BC
Moses and promised land, 1000 BC
Herod died around 1 BC
Birth of Jesus, 3–2 BC
<u>Year of our Lord is noted as AD or CE Christian Era</u>
Death of Jesus, AD 30
Day of Pentecost through the church age, or age of grace, 30 AD to the present

Day of the Lord includes Rapture, tribulation, Second Coming, millennial reign will begin sometime during the seventh millennium.

Chapter 15
Death, Resurrection, and the Afterlife

Chapter Overview

Chapter 15

Death, Resurrection, and the Afterlife

Is Death a Mystery?

A prudent person plans for future occurrences by having insurance for various unforeseen events. These people will have homeowners insurance against fire or flood disasters. They will have health insurance. Business owners should have liability insurance. A pilot must have aviation insurance. A law-abiding person will have auto insurance to protect their vehicle and other drivers. It is therefore logical to have assurance for the end-of-life event. A wise person will have life insurance to take care of their shell/body and leave children or spouses with money to help them continue on. Yet so many people have not taken out insurance for their various needs. There is a final form of insurance that God tells us we need to provide for our soul in the afterlife. We take out a policy with Jesus, who gives us assurance that after we pass from this life into eternity, he has prepared a place for us. The unwise have not taken advantage of this free offer, and to their utter demise, their soul will spend eternity in hell.

God has given us details to understand the nature of death. Dying is a process. We could think of it as crossing a bridge, where one side connects the physical life and spans over to the spiritual realm. A dying person leaves their physical self on one side of the bridge, while the soul and spirit of man moves forward into the spiritual dimension. As King Solomon portrays in Ecclesiastes 12:5–7, at the time of death, we do fear the unknown spiritual world that we will all enter. After death, every physical life form will decay in the dirt or dissolve in the water. Those who have died in Christ, their souls go to be with the Lord. At the Rapture Resurrection, Jesus will reunite their souls with their disintegrated bodies. Those of us who are alive at the Rapture are immediately changed from an earthly corruptible body to an eternal, incorruptible body. These people pass from the physical life to the spiritual life in a split second. They cross the bridge at warp speed.

Job gives us a clearer understanding of the promise we have that our bodies will be changed. Job 14:14, "*If a man die, shall he live again? All the days of my appointed time will I wait, till my change come.*" Job understood that his physical body would return to dust while his eternal soul would be held in Abraham's bosom until the first fruit Resurrection and his soul would be transitioned into the heavenly realm, and Job also knew that at the time of the Rapture Resurrection, his body and soul would come together, and all will be given new bodies that are incorruptible and immortal.

The average person does not witness the process of dying often. However, there are various experiences that happen during the dying process. Here we relate an actual personal experience with a dying person. The family had requested prayer for this individual who was comatose. We could not with certainty say he was saved. During our first visit, we prayed and put headphones on his ears and played worship music. We had a follow-up visit the next day and were asked to stay in the waiting room so that the nurse could clean him up. While sitting there, we attempted to read scripture, and it seemed to be a burden for the Word to come forth. Entering the patient's room, we again prayed and played worship music. Shortly, the atmosphere in the room changed; we sensed his spirit had left his body and was hovering. At that time, we decided to leave, and a presence of heaviness came over us, leaving us with a sensation that our legs were made of lead. In the early hours of the next morning, he was pronounced dead.

In our past experiences, sometimes we are given an inclination that someone we know will be passing on. Personally, I have felt a heaviness in my chest; other times we smell flowers that are not present, or we had thoughts of this person. What we glean from the process of dying and death is that it cannot be put in a box; there are variables. At another time, we were at the bedside of a person who had never given his life to Christ. This man was semiconscious, and we asked him to call on the name of Jesus. We sensed there were demonic spirits hovering over his bed as he appeared to be in torment with writhing and moaning. We again encouraged him to call on the name of the Lord Jesus; finally, he said, "Jesus." We cannot know what happened to his soul as he passed from this life into eternity.

Angel of Death

Is there an angel of death? This angel is seen as bringing death upon the firstborn of Egypt and would bypass the Israelites' homes that had the blood of a lamb over the doorposts.

Encyclopedia of Jewish Religion, page 31[25], defines, "Angel of Death as the most terrible of the destroying angels is the Malakh Ha-Mavet, the Angel of Death who waits at the bedside of the sick. At the tip of his sword hangs a lethal drop of venom. Like other angels, he also personified a function of the divine will, but gradually he acquired a wicked individuality. He is linked and at times identified with Satan."

Job 38:17, "*Have the gates of death been opened unto thee? Or have thou seen the doors of the shadow of death?*" Sometimes spirits appear in our visibility as shadows.

Perhaps there is more than one angel associated with the task of the dying. In Luke 16:22, the beggar Lazarus at the time of death was carried by the angels into paradise. From this passage, we can declare that the angels accompany the saved into the presence of the Lord while the lost souls are escorted into hell.

Near-Death Experiences

The scientific arena is interested in phenomena related to near-death and immortality. The Immortality Project at the University of California, Riverside, had received $5 million in funding for research into the possibility of man-made immortality.

Jesus brought people back to life, and prophets raised the dead. At the time of death, the silver cord will be broken, allowing the spirit to return to God (Ecclesiastes 12:6).

The new age guru Shirley Maclaine spoke about a silver cord connecting the body and the soul. When a person has a near-death experience and floats up and passes through the ceiling into the atmosphere, as long as the cord remained intact, the person could return to the body.

When does death occur? People who have been pronounced brain-dead can be kept alive by life-giving machines. Has the soul moved on at that time? People who are in a comatose state are alive, and their soul probably is still attached. There is a difference between being pronounced brain-dead and being in a coma. In some situations, people recall their spirit self leaving their bodies. Apparently, during these out-of-body experiences, they can see, hear, smell, and recall family members or routines performed by medical staff. Perhaps at this time, their spirit/soul could have the ability to appear to another family member.

In these instances, a person is hovering between life and death. They are standing on the bridge, and only God knows their outcome. There are thousands of documented accounts of near-death experiences. Terry James, a Christian author of *Heaven Vision: Glimpses into Glory*, shares his experience of dying on April 22, 2011. He was suffering severe chest pains, and then he heard a blip; and in the next moment, he saw many vibrant young people. Terry succumbed to blindness at age thirty-five in 1993. One thing this revelation confirms is that

---

25 *Encyclopedia of Jewish Religion*, p. 31

once we leave this physical plain, we also leave behind our infirmities. We can visualize that our broken bodies are made whole. Saved individuals are comforted in knowing that their souls will have peace with God. The unsaved will have no peace but eternal torment in hell. [26]

L. A. Marzulli, in his video "Watchers 4," reports the experience of an atheist who died in a hospital in France. He had not been seen by medical staff for nine hours. Unable to cling to life, he let go. In the spirit realm, he was summoned by people to follow them, and they walked for what seemed like a long time when he realized he was not in the hospital corridor but some place dark and sinister. Those with him who had at first the appearance of people changed, becoming vicious and attacked him, biting and beating him and doing horrible acts upon him. Demons await the souls of the lost and drag them down into hell. Crouched in a heap on the floor, overcome with great fear, he remembered a song he had learned as a child in Sunday school: "Jesus loves me, this I know, for the Bible tells me so." He sang and sang until the demons began to leave him alone and he saw a light shining from above into the darkness. The appearance of a man came to him, and he knew it was Jesus. Jesus told him he loved him and began to clean him up, and he held him. They talked for what seemed like hours, and Jesus told him it was time to return. He didn't want to leave. He found himself back in the hospital, and apparently, they had performed surgery. His wife was there, and he wanted to tell her what happened, but he could hardly speak. A few days later, he began to unravel his experience. Today, he is a pastor." [27] An encounter with God can change one's life drastically.

On January 8, 1991, Angie Finimore committed suicide. When she became aware that her spirit had left her body, her life flashed before her. She sensed she was moving into darkness, into another realm, and found herself surrounded by other tormented souls who had committed suicide. She felt their despair, which was the same emotion she felt. Then she heard a voice, "Is this what you want?" A small light grew, and she knew the light was God. God told her she cannot take life but must go through tribulation. She felt love, compassion, and his pain. She was in the presence of Jesus, who suffered for us. She was returned to her body.

With the assistance of Rabbi Rami Levy, Natan, a fifteen-year-old living in Israel, recounts his experience when he was dead for fifteen minutes, September 2015. He was from a secular background and had no learning in Torah. At the time of death, he felt his soul depart. He floated up over his body and further up that he could see planet earth. He sensed being drawn into a swirling tunnel, saw other souls, and the formation of bright light. The closer he came to the light, he felt safe, and the light source telepathically communicated with him.

---

26 Terry James, Heaven Vision: Glimpses into Glory

27 L A Marzulli, Watchers 4

He was asked, "Do you want to die?" He was told that if he crossed through the boundary, further into the light, he could not return. He was ushered into the appearance of a very large hall and saw many people dressed in fine clothes; he noticed his clothes were dirty and tattered. The people were happy to see him. He recognized a few, such as Rabbi Ovadia Yosef. Upon a large stage, there were three sources of light. His life flashed before him, and he knew all the bad things he had done in life and good. From this place, he was directed to the place of Gehenna, where he felt fear, heard screams, and saw fire.

He was firm in his position that he was given an understanding of future events. Natan said the battle of Gog and Magog began September 11, 2015. News sources report that Russia officially entered the war in Syria on this date. (Our update—November 2015, Russia fully engaged in war in Syria.) He was to understand that there would be conflicts within the region between Muslims and all coming against Israel. He said Obama was Gog, and he would be instrumental in starting the war. Natan said it would begin in two months. He saw the death of millions of Israelis. He said something catastrophic was going to occur. Things would escalate to a very big war, and the whole world will be involved. Rabbi Levy asked who would be involved, and he said the United Nations, United States, Russia, Korea, and seventy nations. He believed Messiah would come soon and stand on the Mount Olives, which would split in half. He said Messiah would reveal himself, and many would be surprised to see who he is. From an Orthodox Jewish viewpoint, salvation comes by reading the Torah, repentance, and doing good works (*Breaking Israel News*, November 22, 2014, by Rivkah Lambert Adler).

We presented a few examples of near-death experiences. Then we came across a study reported by *Natural News*, November 6, 2014, by David Gutierrez: "*Life after death is real, concludes scientific study of two thousand patients.*"

> In the largest study ever conducted, researchers have found evidence that consciousness continues even after brain activity has ceased, according to researchers at the University of Southampton. The study was written by Jerry Nolan and published in the journal *Resuscitation.* According to Dr. Sam Parnia, out of patients who have gone into cardiac arrest, 40 percent of those revived said they recalled experiencing some form of awareness. The study is called AWARE, Awareness during Resuscitation, and its goal is the investigation of NDE, near-death experience, and OBE, out-of-body experiences. The study involved 2,060 subjects in fifteen participating hospitals in Austria, United Kingdom, and the United States. Researchers found that 39 percent had some awareness following cardiac arrest; 2 percent described

OBE (observing conditions outside of the body); and 9 percent described NDE (feelings of warmth, seeing light, or unpleasant experiences).

In these cases, consciousness and awareness continued after cardiac arrest.

The Tunnel

Some people that have reported near-death experiences say they were transported through a tunnel toward a light at the end. People report seeing family members along the way. This occurs when the holy angels escort that redeemed soul into heaven, where they are met by familiar faces. Then they meet Jesus.

Perry Stone, in his book, *Secrets from Beyond the Grave*, equates entering a wormhole like a "space tube where movement is faster than light, connects the distances between time and space, and serves as a shortcut in time-space travel" in near-death experiences. Once you enter the bottom from our galaxy, you would exit it at about the same moment you entered it.[28]

Are There Such Things as Human Ghosts?

Matthew 14:22, Jesus walks on water, and his disciples perceive it is a ghost. Jesus tells them it is he that they see. God the Son has authority over the elements.

From what belief system did the disciples arrive at the conclusion that they were seeing a ghost walking on water? They clearly were aware that the spirit/soul of the deceased go into the recesses of the underworld. In their Old Testament writings, Job 26:5 speaks regarding Abaddon—a region for the damned in Sheol or hell—and the disciples were cognizant of the writings of Enoch who saw hell.

From the following few examples, the disciples knew there was a placed called hell. They knew there were occasions where the souls of the deceased were allowed to materialize for God's purpose, such as in the transfiguration. Shortly before the Crucifixion, Elijah and Moses came from the afterlife and appeared with Jesus. This type of event is rare and God ordained, as it was when Jesus called Lazarus to arise from the grave. The disciples also knew that outside of human visibility existed a world of evil spirits and demons, who at times could manifest themselves to humans.

Isaiah 29:4 makes mention of a familiar spirit with the ability to speak from the earth. We understand this is a demonic entity. There is given a scenario of King Saul, who seeks the help of a demon-possessed medium to contact the soul of Samuel found in 1 Samuel 28:6 because God was silent. In this account, Saul in disguise asks the medium to contact

[28] Perry Stone, *Secrets from Beyond the Grave*

the spirit of Samuel. She contacts a spirit who is able to tell her she is dealing with the king. Saul does not see Samuel and ask her to describe his appearance. She said he is an old man wearing a robe. As Saul is lying prostrate, a dialogue between the two begins. A spirit posing as Samuel asks, "Why have you disturbed me by bringing me up?" Saul states his concern about a conversation he had with the prophet before his death.

What can we take from this rare encounter recorded in our scriptures? Do we accept this as a literal encounter between the deceased and a medium-, witch-, or demon-possessed person? Has God turned from his own commandment, wherein he has forbidden mankind to communicate with the dead? Taking into account people who are possessed by an evil spirit seemingly are given abilities from that evil spirit to conjure up other spirits or to give information to a human only an evil spirit could access. With much consideration, we believe this encounter with King Saul, in his unrighteousness, he sought out the services of a demonically possessed medium to contact the dead, and she conjured up a spirit counterfeiting as Samuel.

In the case of the rich man and Lazarus, the rich man had requested that someone from the spirit world go and tell his brothers that hell is for real. His request was denied.

After his Resurrection, Jesus supernaturally appears unto the disciples. They thought he was a ghost. He tells them, "Touch me and see, a ghost does not have flesh and bones." Jesus asked for food and did eat (Luke 24:36–39). We emphasize Jesus is God over elements and the spiritual world. What Jesus could do may be allowed on a limited basis. In the first stage of the Resurrection, we discuss the passage of scripture that deals with the bodies of the dead appearing to many in the city. These were not ghosts but had bodies as the risen Christ. The occurrence of reuniting body and soul and the ability to become visible to others was God-ordained and a rare occurrence. Were these people able to keep their new bodies? Did they ascend in the clouds with Jesus forty days later?

There may be the possibility of a human spiritual appearance after death—during the time, the soul hovers between our earth and another dimension. This could explain the ability of that soul to appear to a loved one. After the deceased has been dead for a period of time and someone claims to have seen this person, we believe that supernatural manifestation is of nonhuman origins referred to as a spirit, apparition, phantom, or ghost. These entities roam the earth, some having the ability to become visible. The TV series *Ghost Whisperer* is a parade of the souls of the dead working out relationships that had been left undone before their death. After these "ghosts" had resolved their problems, they were drawn into the light and were no longer visible to others. Though this TV show is fictional, it conditions people to believe that the souls of humans are in a transitional state until they move on by their own will. The souls of humans cannot manifest themselves at will; and if this were the case, all dead people would desire to be with their loved ones, and no one would be in the afterlife. A case in point, C. S. Lewis, *A Grief Observed*, wherein he mourned the loss of his wife so deeply that he believed her ghost was appearing to him. Certainly, Lewis saw an apparition, but it could have been a familiar spirit appearing as his wife. The demonic forces come as lying signs and wonders to deceive the living.

The Resurrection in Four Stages

Stage 1 is First Fruits. First Corinthians 15:20, "*But now is Christ risen from the dead and become the First Fruits of them that slept.*" This first stage of the Resurrection involves all God-fearing **souls** who died from Adam to the Resurrection of Jesus. First Corinthians 15:22, "*For as in Adam all die, even so in Christ shall all be made alive, but every man in his own order, Christ the First Fruits and **afterward** they that are Christ at his coming,*" refers to the Rapture, second stage of Resurrection.

In his final departing breath, Christ uttered, "Father, into your hands I commend my spirit" (Luke 23:46). At the instant of Christ's death, the spirit of the Lord left his physical shell and was in the presence of God the Father. Psalm 68:18, "*Thou has ascended on high* [and] *thou has led captivity captive ...*" The spirit of Jesus ascended to the Father, perhaps to present his blood to be placed on the altar or mercy seat of the Ark in heaven.

> *Wherefore he said, when he ascended up on high, he led captivity captive and gave gifts unto men. Now that he ascended what is it but that he also **descended first** into the lower parts of the earth? He that descended is the same also that ascended up far above all heavens that he might fill all things.* (Ephesian 4:8)

In both Psalms and Ephesians, we read that Christ did ascend into the heavenly realm and descended into the lower regions to set the captives free, thus bringing the righteous dead with him. "*Being put to death in the flesh but quicken by the spirit by which he went and preached unto the spirits in prison...*" (1 Peter 3:18-19) Who were these spirits in prison? They represented the righteous and the wicked—all the souls of those who died from Adam to the last person who died coinciding with Christ's death on the cross. It could be that death was put on hold for a few days until Jesus delivered his message to the dead, conquered the last enemy's death, and took the keys of hell and death.

> *Who will give account to him that is ready to judge the living and the dead. For this cause was the gospel preached also to them that are dead ...* (1 Peter 4:5–6)

In the region of the underworld, the righteous were gathered in Abraham's bosom, and the wicked were separated from them in other sections. After his death, Jesus took on the role of king and judge. As judge, the sinners would remain in hell, and the righteous were taken out of Abraham's bosom to heaven, where Jesus gave them gifts. He brought a message for all those souls. He preached the good news that he is king of kings and death has been defeated.

There are a few scholars who believe the Old Testament saints were not resurrected during the First Fruits Resurrection and will not be resurrected until the end of the tribulation period. To address this concern, let us understand that in Luke 9:29, Jesus is transformed—wherein his countenance becomes bright and glowing—and he is joined in this glorious meeting by Old Testament saints, Moses and Elijah. In this passage, we understand that Moses died and Elijah was translated alive, yet both appear together. Moses's soul would have been in paradise or Abraham's bosom. Their conversation may have been about the imminent death and Resurrection of Jesus and the soon-to-be released souls from Abraham's bosom to join him in the heavenly dimension. Jesus states, "Many will come from the east and west (faithful believers) and will sit down with <u>Abraham, Isaac, and Jacob in the kingdom of Heaven.</u>" We could understand this to mean that from Adam to the thief on the cross and for all-time future, the dead in Christ will join with those who now reside in the presence of God, Jesus, and the angels in the heavenly kingdom.

When Luke wrote his book, Jesus had been crucified. Luke quotes the future prediction made by Jesus.

> *But they which will be accounted worthy to obtain* ***that*** *world and the resurrection from the dead neither marry or are given in marriage, neither can they die any more for they are equal unto the angels and are the children of God being the children of the resurrection.* ***Now that the dead are raised, even Moses showed at the bush when he called the Lord the God of Abraham, Isaac and Jacob for he is not the God of the dead but of the living*** … (Luke 20:35–38)

In this passage, Jesus addresses (1) those that are counted worthy to obtain the heavenly world; (2) have been resurrected and no longer have need to marry, they are now immortal and equal as the angels, called the children of God; (3) speaking of the First Fruits of the Resurrection points to Moses who recognized Jesus as God in the afterlife; (4) Jesus is not the God of the dead but the living, and in this declaration, we can understand that the souls of the Old Testament saints are resurrected.

> *What be these two olive branches which through the two golden pipes empty the golden oil out of themselves? And he answered me and said, knowest thou not what these be? And I said no my lord. Then said he, these are the two anointed ones that stand by the Lord of the whole earth.* (Zechariah 4:12)

We believe this passage is pointing to the two witnesses who will prophesy to the nations during the tribulation period. Elijah, Enoch, or Moses will return for their earthly ministry. Jesus will have outfitted them in bodies that can die just as Jesus was given a body of flesh for the purpose of his death. The return of the Old Testament saints proves they would have been resurrected before the end of the tribulation.

No one can enter into the Kingdom of God in the flesh. Enoch and Elijah were translated alive and changed from corruptible to incorruptible. 1 Corinthians 15:50 … "*Flesh and blood cannot inherit the kingdom of God neither dose corruption inherit incorruption.*" The scriptures do not allude that these two men were sent to wait in Abraham's bosom. At the time of the First Fruits Resurrection, the righteous were united with Enoch and Elijah. After the ascension of Jesus, John wrote Revelation around 95 AD, and he attested to seeing an innumerable crowd gathered in heaven. This gives further credence that the Old Testament saints had been resurrected during the First Fruits and were in heaven already when the souls of the apostles arrived, having died after the visible ascension of Jesus. The angelic host and others rejoice over each saint, coming into heaven at the time of their death. For almost two thousand years, they witnessed the arrival of millions.

> *I know that my redeemer lives and that he will stand at the later day upon the earth and though after my skin worms destroy this body yet in my flesh will I see God, whom I will see for myself and mine eyes will behold and not another though my reins be consumed within me.* (Job 19:25)

In the oldest book of the Bible, Job began to understand that at the time of death, his body would rot in the grave but his spiritual self would see Jesus. Job saw Jesus with his own eyes when he descended to set captivity free. Job and the souls of the righteous dead would dwell in Abraham's Bosom until the time of First Fruits, when Jesus would transfer their souls to the heavenly domain.

Daniel 12:13, "*But go your way until the end be for you will rest and stand in your lot at the end of the days.*" Daniel had been in Babylon captivity for most of his life, and he understood that he would die in captivity. Before his death, God assured Daniel that though he will not be given the understanding of future end-times, he will stand with the other Old Testament saints at the time of the Resurrection. The end of days, last day, or the Day of the Lord, include the Lord's death and Resurrection as well as the future Rapture and Second Coming of Christ.

Jeremiah 30:9 … "*They will serve the Lord their God and David their king whom I will raise up unto them.*" Jeremiah's ministry was during the time that the tribes of Israel and Judah would be taken captive by the Assyrians and Babylonians. Jeremiah predicts that during the time of "Jacob's Trouble," which is a reference to Israel during the tribulation period, God would save Israel. At the time of this writing, King David had been dead for hundreds of years, but in the following passage, we see that David knows he will be resurrected with the Holy One.

> *For you will not leave my soul in hell nor will you suffer your Holy One to see corruption.* (Psalm 16:10)

King David understood that the Holy One's (Jesus's) body would not be allowed to decay in the grave, and David understood that his body would rest (in the grave) in hope of a future Resurrection while his soul would be kept in Paradise/Abraham's bosom until the time of the First Fruits when his spirit would be taken into the heavenly realm accompanied by Jesus. Herein, we have additional evidence that the souls of the Old Testament saints were raised up out of Abraham's bosom and transferred into the heavenly realm at the time of the First Fruits Resurrection.

Jesus was only dead once. Jesus was the fulfillment of the Old Testament saints who waited for the promise of the Resurrection. If the Old Testament saints are not resurrected until the end of the tribulation as some believe, they will have to be mixed in with the unrighteous dead, the unrighteous survivors, the remnant of Israel, and those who did not take the mark of the beast. Post-tribulation people are a different group, and Jesus has a different plan for them. They will be separated or divided in the great harvest, as in separating the wheat from the tares. If the Old Testament saints were not resurrected until the end of the tribulation, they would have missed the Bema Seat judgment, the marriage supper of the Lamb, and the banquet—which takes place in heaven while the tribulation period rages on. At the end of the tribulation, without that preparation, how can they join with the saints, who accompany Jesus back to earth in their purified bodies, dressed in white, and married to the Lamb? Oh, yes! Jesus could say, "Wait a minute, I forgot about the Old Testament saints, let's back up and get them prepared."

Saint Paul refers to a time when he was caught up into heaven (2 Corinthians 12:1–4). Paul could not determine if he was having an out-of-body experience or a vision, but he knew he had been caught up to Paradise, where he heard unspeakable words that were unlawful for him to speak. At the time of Paul's experience, it appears that Paradise was no longer in the confines of another dimension but had been elevated to the heavenly dimension, wherein dwells the Father and the Son on their throne.

> *The graves were opened and many* ***bodies*** *of the saints which slept arose and came out of the graves after his Resurrection and went into the holy city and appeared unto many.* (Matthew 27:52)

We do not have the impression that all the souls were allowed to appear in the streets. This is a strange occurrence. It seems that their bodies were dust and their souls in Abraham's bosom were reunited for a purpose that we can only speculate about. Was it to be further evidence of the Resurrection of Christ? They were allowed to go into the holy city and appear unto many. Perhaps this manifestation was given to prove that one day, all bodies and souls would be reunited. We can reason this was done to show that in the future, we will have the same body as Christ, one that can be seen and touched and could speak, eat, appear, and disappear. In the power of his Resurrection, Jesus demonstrated authority over life and death.

Jesus did not ascend permanently back to the Father until forty days after his Resurrection. What happened to those who were seen in the streets? It is logical to believe that they ascended into the heavenly realm with Christ. Christ ascended in a cloud, which the writer of Hebrews 12:1 tells us, "*We are compassed about with so great a cloud of witnesses.*" These witnesses may have included angels and the souls of the righteous dead. We can wonder, at the time of the ascension, did their physical bodies return to dust to await the future Rapture, where souls will be reunited with their bodies? Or when they were changed from corruptible to incorruptible to walk the streets, did they retain those incorruptible forms?

Perhaps the last person to be included in this first stage of Resurrection is the thief on the cross who Jesus told, "Today you will be with me in paradise." We can also assume that this man's soul joined together with the other recently resurrected souls to transcend into the heavenly realm. His body will remain in the grave until stage 2 of the Resurrection. At that time, Jesus will bring their souls to reunite with their bodies, and the dead bodies will arise first, to meet Christ in the air.

For the past two thousand years until the time of the Rapture, those who die in Christ join the First Fruits souls in heaven. After the Rapture, those who repent and die, their souls go to be with Jesus and their bodies remain in the grave until the Second Coming—when the great harvest will take place at the end of the tribulation period.

Stage 2, Rapture/Resurrection is twofold. The first part, the **bodies** of the righteous **dead**—all who died from Adam to the time of the Rapture—will be reunited with their **souls**, which Christ brings with him. Isaiah 26:19, "*The dead men will live together with my dead body shall they arise, awake and sing you that dwell in the dust, the earth will cast out the dead.*" It appears that Isaiah is referring to Old Testament patriarchs, prophets, kings, etc., whose bodies will be reunited with their souls during this stage of the Resurrection. In the following passage, 1 Thessalonians 4:14, "*For if we believe that Jesus died and rose again, even so them also which sleep in Jesus will God bring with him,*" confirms that Jesus will bring their souls with him at the time of the Rapture, reuniting dead bodies with their souls. This supernatural act removes that which is corruptible, mortal, decaying, and replaces it with that which is incorruptible and immortal.

> *So also is the resurrection of the dead, it is sown in corruption, it is raised in incorruption, it is sown in dishonor, it is raised in glory, it is sown in weakness, it is raised in power, it is sown a natural body, it is raised a spiritual body.* (1 Corinthians 15:42)

The second part applies to those who are **alive** at the time of the Rapture will be translated instantly from physical life to immortality. Saint Paul said, "Absent from the body, present with the Lord."

> *We which are alive and remain unto the coming of the Lord will not prevent them which are asleep, for the Lord himself will descend from heaven with a shout, with the voice of the archangel, with the trump of God and the dead in Christ will rise first, then we which are alive and remain will be caught up together with them in the clouds to meet the Lord in the air and so will we ever be with the Lord.* (1 Thessalonians 4:15)

At the time of the Rapture, our bodies will be changed from mortal to immortal, so aptly declared in 1 Corinthians 15:51–58:

> *Behold, I show you a mystery, we will not all sleep but we shall all be changed in a moment in the twinkling of an eye, at the last trump* [not the tribulation trumpet] *for the trumpet will sound and the dead shall be raised incorruptible and we* [who are alive] *shall be changed. For this corruptible* [mortal] *must put on incorruption* [immortality] *... when this is brought to pass the saying that is written, Death is swallowed up in victory ...*

We must be changed in order to enter into the heavenly realm.

The most important aspect of the bodily Resurrection of all believers is that it includes (1) the bodies of the Old Testament saints; (2) those who died after the Crucifixion and Resurrection of Yeshua; (3) the souls of the dead in Christ will return with Christ and be reunited with their bodies; and (4) all those who remain alive at his coming will be changed.

Time of Regeneration

Christ became flesh, suffered, and died. After his Resurrection, he shed mortality and was regenerated to receive a glorified body and a spirit filled life to rule and reign forever.

> *And Jesus said to them, verily I say to you, that you which have followed me in the* ***regeneration*** *when the Son of man will sit in the throne of his glory, you*

> *also will sit upon twelve thrones, judging the twelve tribes of Israel.* (Matthew 19:28)

Jesus was speaking to those who followed him to the cross and witnessed his Resurrection and ascension, and they too would be with him in heaven. We that have been followers of Jesus can also be assured that we are now seated in heavenly places, for the kingdom of heaven is within us; and when our change comes, we will see him as the glorified savior and king. Jesus used the word *regeneration*, which has a mysterious undertone that leads to a deeper understanding. *Webster* defines it as "spiritual rebirth, to bring into existence again, completely reformed, reconstituted." What kind of people will we be after the change? The human body of flesh will be reformed, reconstituted, and then regenerated to immortality. We will be made whole. Those missing limbs or blind in life will have be restored.

> *We are the children of God and it does not appear yet what we shall be but we know when he will appear, we will be like him for we will see him as he is.* (1 John 3:2)

The Bible says that this body or the seed must first die before it can be changed into immortality. There is no contradiction. We who are alive at the time of the Rapture seem not to have undergone death, but in the twinkling of an eye, the corruptible is changed. We die and are changed so quickly it cannot be comprehended as we understand the process of dying and death. In John 5:24, Christ assures us that those who believe the Word and the Father that sent him will have everlasting life and will not come into condemnation <u>but is passed from death unto life.</u>

> *All flesh is not the same flesh but there is one kind of flesh of men, another flesh of beasts, another of fishes and another of birds. There are also celestial bodies and bodies terrestrial but the glory of the celestial is one and the glory of the terrestrial is another.* (1 Corinthians 15:39–41)

God has said we all have our glory, such as angels, humankind, animal kingdom, and the sun, moon, stars have their glory. Only after the physical change can the glory of the spiritual body come into its gloriousness.

> *We have born the image of the earthly, we will also bear the image of the heavenly.* (1 Corinthians 15:49)

Jesus answers the Sadducees regarding the Resurrection and would there be marriage in the afterlife. He tells them that the children of the (physical) world marry, but those that will be accounted worthy to obtain that (spiritual) world through the Resurrection from the dead neither marry or are given in marriage; neither can they die anymore; they are equal unto the angels and are the children of God.

Jesus Returns on the Third Day

Jesus said he would return in the third day. Our study in Exodus 19 gives us a scenario that Moses was told to prepare the people for God's visitation. They were to be sanctified and wash their garments for two days, and on **the third day**, God would come down to the Mountain. The people were ready to receive God, and it was signaled by thunder, lightning, and the very loud sounding of a trumpet whose vibrations shook the base of the mountain and the people round about. God came in a cloud and told Moses and Aaron to come up to him. To apply this archetype to our present day, we are reminded that a thousand years is as a day unto to the Lord as discussed, and we are living in the last day, the seventh millennium, the third day.

The people of God have had two thousand years, which are **two days**, to be holy and sanctified. We are now in **the third day**, awaiting the sound of the trumpet. We are awaiting the voice of the Lord to call us up to meet him in the clouds.

Pretribulation Rapture

No one knows the day or the hour when Jesus will call us up from the earth, but throughout the scriptures, God has given signs that point to his timing. It will be during a time of trouble as Satan orchestrates world events closer to the start of the tribulation. The world is in chaos, and Christians are being persecuted and killed. God has promised to save us from the day of wrath, but how much more will believers contend with before we are snatched out of this wicked world? As we watch, pray, and speculate as to the nearness of the Rapture, we discern two prominent signs: (1) revival is spreading in the midst of (2) perilous times. Of course, we are anxious to get out of here, but we realize the Lord is patient and long-suffering, desiring that none perish.

> *And this is the will of him that sent me that everyone which sees the Son and believes on him may have everlasting life and I will raise him up at the last day.* (John 6:40)
>
> *No man can come to me except the Father which has sent me draw him and I will raise him up at **the last day.*** (John 6:44)

In the last/third day, Muslims are having visions of Jesus and turning to Christianity. The Iranian Christian population is around a million, and the underground church in China has exploded with millions coming to Jesus. The Holy Spirit is being poured out, and our Lord has cast out his net, and it is filled. He is saving millions from the wrath that will be poured out during the tribulation, a time that has never been before or ever will be again (Joel 2:28). When the Holy Spirit is removed, wickedness will be unprecedented.

Many Bible scholars believe the Rapture may occur before the tribulation period. The majority of scholars support the hope that those in Christ will not experience the wrath of God during the tribulation and the judgment to condemnation. Isaiah 26:20, "*Come my people enter into my chambers and shut the door, hide yourself for a little moment until the indignation be over.*" Now that we see persecution has increased, we need to adjust our thinking that believers may experience the beginning of the tribulation, but God will deliver his people from the time of the great tribulation. Jesus said that the signs would be like the days of Noah. The whole world was wicked, and the people would not heed the warnings of Noah. When the door of the ark was shut and Noah and his family were safe, destruction came (Matthew 24:37). The tribulation is a seven-year period on earth, and once we are with Christ in the heavenly realm, earth time is not applicable in heaven. In Isaiah's passage above, he may also be warning modern-day Israel that God will save a remnant of Jews. He will prepare a place of refuge for them.

Ancient writing found in the Kabbala, Book of Splendor, predicted the coming of the Messiah would be during the Hebrew year 5773, or September 16, 2012, to September 4, 2013.[29] Though this prediction is incorrect as to the return of Jesus, it could point to the arrival of Antichrist and false prophet. Another sign, according to scripture, Israel will accept a false Messiah.

Others referred to as "date setters" have incorrectly predicted the Rapture event. Nevertheless, the Bible does encourage us to study the signs of the times that provide clues to the nearness of the Rapture. The Rapture of the body of believers has always been held as imminent—meaning, there will be no global announcement, no any specific signs, and it could occur without warning. Its timing will correlate with global corruption and ungodliness. Like Sodom and Gomorrah, immorality had hit rock bottom. God allowed for Lot and his family to leave before judgment was meted out. The Rapture event will be instantaneous and global.

We believe we are in the end of days as we witness the apostasy of the church, persecution of God's people, worldwide wickedness, and the unfolding of Bible prophecy before our eyes. God is warning this secular generation that judgment is coming, but the warnings are not heeded. The world is standing at the gate of the tribulation. Many are looking for specific signs, such as the signing of a seven-year covenant with Israel or the rebuilding of

---

[29] Kabbala, Book of Splendor

the third temple. These would be indicators that time is short and the Rapture could occur at any moment. Whenever the Rapture occurs, life on earth will continue, and the end-time events could drag on for five or ten more years. Those who are left behind can know the final judgments will go into overdrive.

Jesus warns us to watch and be ready. We are to be living holy lives and occupying our time with the things of God until he returns. If the righteous scarcely be saved, where will the ungodly and sinner appear (1 Peter 4:18)?

- Watch, for you know not when the Lord comes (Matthew 24:42).
- Be ready, for when you think not, Jesus will come (Matthew 24:44).
- Be faithful; Jesus finds faith on the earth (Luke 18:8).
- Occupy until he comes (Luke 19:13).
- Watch and pray that you may be accounted worthy to escape all these things (Luke 21:3).

The apostle Peter said we have a sure word of prophecy, which is a guiding light in a dark world until <u>the day dawn and the day star arise in our hearts</u> (2 Peter 1:19). This may indicate that those who are alive just before the return of Christ for his church will be given a spiritual unction from the Holy Spirit that the time is at hand. Simeon prayed that he would not die until he saw the Messiah. Joseph and Mary brought Jesus to the temple for blessing as many parents had done for years. The only way Simeon could know that the Messiah was physically at the temple was that the Holy Spirit gave him spiritual enlightenment. He held the baby Messiah in his arms and praised God for granting him the desire of his heart.

Revelation 2:28, "*And I will give him the morning star.*" Christ is called the morning star, which appears just before dawn, when the night is coldest and darkest, when the world is at its bleakest point. So it is possible that such a spirit of anticipation may spring up in the hearts of the believers just before Jesus shouts, "Come up here."

Following are scriptures that suggest the saints may be caught up before the tribulation or shortly thereafter. We must keep in mind, Christians are being presently slaughtered, and the tribulation has not officially started:

"*Wait for his son from heaven, who will deliver us from the **wrath** to come.*" 1 Thessalonians 1:10.

"*When they shall say peace and safety then sudden destruction, but this day will **not take us unawares.***" 1 Thessalonians 5:3

"*God has **not** appointed us to **wrath** but salvation.*" 1 Thessalonians 5:9

"*Live holy so we will be considered **worthy** to be Raptured*". 2 Thessalonians 5:9

"*We, being saved by the blood, will be **saved from wrath***". Romans 5:9,

"Let no man deceive you by any means, for **that day will not come except there is a falling away first and the man of sin is revealed,** son of perdition." 2 Thessalonians 2:3

"*And now you know what withholds, that he might be revealed in his time, for the mystery of iniquity does already work (spirit of Antichrist); only he who now lets will let until he be taken out of the way (Holy Spirit restrains evil until he is taken out of the way) and then will that wicked be revealed, whom the Lord will consume with the spirit of his mouth and will destroy with the brightness of his coming.*" 2 Thessalonians 2:6–8,

"*God will* ***rescue*** *us from tribulation and judge the persecutors*". 2 Thessalonians 1:7,

Stage 3—the great-harvest Resurrection is for those who died **after the Rapture.** At the time of the Rapture, only the righteous were resurrected. This stage of the Resurrection deals with the unrepentant dead who rejected Jesus or took the mark of the beast and worshipped it. It also deals with those who rejected the Antichrist and accepted Jesus as savior and died. Before the revelation was given to John, Daniel foresaw time at the end of the tribulation when the dead will arise some to everlasting life and some to shame and everlasting contempt.

> *And many of them that sleep in the dust of the earth will awake, some to everlasting life and some to shame and everlasting contempt.* (Daniel 12:2)

In the following passage, John confirms Daniel's vision:

> *Marvel not at this for the hour is coming in which* ***all*** *that are in the graves shall hear his voice and will come forth; they that have done good unto the resurrection of life and they that have done evil, unto the resurrection of damnation.* (John 5:28–29)

We are given a clue that this Resurrection is after the Rapture and before the white throne judgment because it deals with a body of people who have done good and **all** (good or evil) are called forth. This third stage of the Resurrection is likened to a **harvest**, when the wheat and the tares are separated. The wheat are the saved, and the tares are the unsaved. The saved (dead or alive) will be ushered into the millennial kingdom. The unsaved (dead or alive) will be sent to hell. Similar to the Rapture event, those living at the end of the tribulation will be changed to enter into the millennial kingdom or hell. While this is taking place on earth, John is given a message in Revelation 20:4:

> *And I saw thrones and they sat upon them and judgment was given unto them and I saw the souls of them that were beheaded for the witness of Jesus and for the word of God and which had not worshipped the beast or his image, nei-*

> *ther had received his mark upon their foreheads or in their hand they lived and reigned with Christ a thousand years.*

This passage allows us to understand that those who died before or during the tribulation would be judged to live again in the millennial kingdom.

Stage 4—Great White Throne Resurrection occurs at the end of the thousand-year millennial reign and is the final judgment.

> *The rest of the dead lived not again until the thousand years were finished ... Blessed and holy is he that has part in the first resurrection on such the second death has no power but they will be priests of God and of Christ and will reign with him a thousand years.* (Revelation 20:5)

This passage explains that the righteous were resurrected during the first, second, and third stages of the Resurrection and will rule and reign with Christ for one thousand years. At the time of the great white throne judgment, they have nothing to fear of a second death. Throughout time, the bodies of the wicked remained in the grave and their souls in hell. At the end of the thousand-year period, all the unredeemable souls will be summoned before the great white throne.

Those who will stand before Jesus at the great white throne include the following:

- Those who died because they aligned themselves with Satan in the rebellion against God at the end of the thousand years
- All the ungodly who remained in hell since the creation of man
- The unrighteous living during the millennial reign

> *And I saw the dead, small and great stand before God and the books were opened and another book was opened which is the book of life and the dead were judged out of those things which were written in the books according to their works, and the sea gave up the dead which were in it and death and hell delivered up the dead which were in them and they were judged every man according to their work. And death and hell were cast into the lake of fire. This is the second death. Whosoever was not found written in the book of life was cast into the lake of fire.* (Revelation 20:12–15)

God the Son is judge.

> *For the Father judges no man but has committed all judgment unto the Son.* (John 5:22)

The Spiritual Prison

Once a soul has been condemned to this godforsaken place we call hell and escorted through its gates, there is no escape. It is a place of eternal darkness and torment. Those in hell know they are separated from God their Creator. Hell is referred to by various names, of which theologians debate; but the bottom line, it is still hell. The following terms apply to the region of hell:

- Sheol is grave, pit, place of the dead.
- Hades is hell, grave, underworld.
- Tartarus is a lower chamber of hell.
- Bottomless pit or abyss.
- Lake of fire, associated with the place of final punishment for the Antichrist, false prophet, Satan, fallen angels, and wicked unredeemed people (Revelation 20:10).
- Gehenna is associated with the Valley of Hinnom, a place where garbage was dumped, smoldered, and smelled.
- Abaddon—a place of destruction, hell, the abyss.
- Hell, a place where the fire is never quenched or where the worm never dies (Mark 9:43–44). Hell will deliver up all its dead at the white throne judgment at the end of the millennial reign (Revelation 20:13).
- Purgatory is a Catholic theory that souls can be held in a place between heaven and hell and through prayers of the living may be released to enter heaven. According to the Bible, after the death and Resurrection of Jesus, the souls of the righteous go to be with him in heaven. Souls of sinners are retained in hell until judgment.

There probably have been literal explorations that attempted to access hell. According to geologists, the core of the earth is hollow and filled with molten gases. Actual drilling events have uncovered chambers at various depths, and they may have experienced foul smell and fire, seen strange images, and heard unnatural sounds. The center of the earth has no gravity. There would be a loss of direction and inability to distinguish between up or down. It is a true abyss, or bottomless pit. People are limited to explore beyond a certain depth because of inadequate equipment, fire suits that are unable to withstand extreme heat, and physical extremes that man cannot endure. In the physical realm, mankind cannot drill their way into the recesses of inner earth and find the dimension of hell.

We can now determine there is a place called hell. First, we know that God refers to a place of eternal torment for spiritual entities. God said he prepared hell for Satan and his evil angels. Before the flood, we know that some of the fallen angels were imprisoned under the earth in another dimension. Also, there have been witnesses who have been to hell and by the grace of Jesus were snatched out of the clutches of hell.

Enoch Sees Hell

Enoch was the first to see this place and write about it.:

> *And I Enoch alone saw this vision, the ends of all and no man has seen them as I have seen them.* (Enoch 19)

Enoch was given a tour of the underworld.

> *And I went around to a place where not one thing took place. And I saw there something terrible, no high heavens, no founded earth, but a void place, awful and terrible. And there I saw seven stars of heaven* [fallen angels], *tied together to it like great mountains and flaming as if by fire. At that time I said, on account of what sin are these bound and why have they been cast hither? And then answered Uriel, one of the holy angels, who was with me conducting me and said to me, Enoch, concerning what does thou ask, and concerning what does thou inquire, and ask and are anxious? These are of the stars who have transgressed the command of God, the Highest and are bound here till ten thousand worlds, the number of the days of their sins shall have been consummated. And from there, I went to another place, which was still more terrible than the former. And I saw a terrible thing, a great fire was there which burned and flickered and appeared in sections; it was bounded by a complete abyss great columns of fire were allowed to fall into its extent and size I could not see and I was unable to see its origin. At that time answered Uriel, one of the holy angels who was with me and said to me, Enoch, why such fear and terror in thee concerning this terrible place and in the presence of this pain? And he said to me this is the prison of the angels and here they are held to eternity.* (Enoch 21:1–10)

We summarize Enoch's experience:

- Prison of the fallen angels (Enoch sees it before human incarceration).
- It is a portal that extends into a spiritual realm.
- It is an abyss (vastness beyond description).
- There is a great gulf (to prevent passage from one section to the other).
- It has sections.
- There is fire.
- Seven stars are evil angels.

After the flood, the reality of hell expanded. This understanding comes through scriptures and the testimony of humans who can only access hell through death. Their soul would then see the spiritual horrors of hell and its immeasurable abyss. Some were allowed to return to life to tell others that hell is for real.

Abraham's Bosom

There is another section of hades/hell referred to as Abraham's bosom, or paradise, separated from the place of torment by a gulf or valley. We understand this to be so from scripture, and we must keep in mind that this is a spiritual dimension. From the time of Adam and Eve, to the righteous before the flood, up to all the Old Testament saints at the time of their death—their souls were retained in Abraham's bosom, a special place. The Bible provides us with the story of the rich man in hell, a place of torment, in contrast to Lazarus in Abraham's bosom, a pleasant and comfortable place.

> *And it came to pass, that the beggar died and* was *carried by the angels into Abraham's bosom: the rich man also died and was buried; and in hell, he lifted up his eyes, being in torments and seeing Abraham afar off and Lazarus in his bosom and he cried, father Abraham have mercy on me and send Lazarus that he may dip the tip of his finger in water and cool my tongue for I am tormented in this flame.* (Luke 16:22–24)

Flavious Josephus, Jewish historian wrote that paradise was in a subterranean place but was delightful and comfortable.

There is one descent into this region at whose gate we believe there stands an archangel with a host, which gate when those pass through that are conducted down by the angels appointed over souls. They do not go the same way but the just are guided to the right hand are led with hymns sung by the angels appointed over that place into a region of light in which the just have dwelt from the beginning of the world; not constrained by necessity but ever enjoying the prospect of the good things they see and rejoice in the expectation of those new enjoyments, which will be peculiar to every one of them and esteeming those things beyond what we have here with who there is no place of toil, no burning heat, no piercing cold, nor are any briars there; but the countenance of the fathers and of the just, which they see always smiles upon them, while they wait for that rest and eternal new life in heaven which is to succeed this region. This place we call the Bosom of Abraham. [30]

In certain situations, God has allowed some to see into the caverns of hell. A similar situation will be allowed according to the message given in Isaiah 66:24:

---

[30] Flavius Josephus, Discourse Concerning Hades

> *And they shall go forth and look upon the carcasses of the men that have transgressed against me for their worm shall not die, neither shall their fire be quenched and they shall be an abhorring unto all flesh.*

This verse uses the terms *a place where the worm does not die* and *where there is unending fire,* and this description is associated with hell. This verse implies that the resurrected saints will be able to look into the chasm of hell and see the wicked who are being tormented in hell for all eternity.

The Bible tells us that after the death of Jesus, yet being in his spiritual essence, he descended into hell to set the righteous captives free. There was no further need for Abraham's bosom to be confined in a dimension of hell. Christ reunited with his body and took all those souls into the realm of the Father in a heavenly dimension. They ascended into the heavens, as did Jesus. The forgiven thief on the cross was told by Jesus, "Today you will be with me in paradise."

Another account given by Flavius Josephus, first-century AD historian, in his *Discourse Concerning Hades* regarding sinners after their death:

But as to the unjust, they are dragged by force to the left hand by the angels allotted for punishment, no longer going with a good will but as prisoners driven by violence to whom are sent the angels appointed over them to reproach them and threaten them with their terrible looks and to thrust them still downwards … those angels that are set over these should, drag them into the neighborhood of hell itself; who when they are hard by it, continually hear the noise of it and do not stand clear of the hot vapor itself, terrible and exceeding great prospect of fire, they are struck with fearful expectations of a future judgment and in effect punished thereby and not only so, but where they see the place [Abraham's bosom] of the fathers and of the just even hereby are they punished for a chaos [gulf] deep and large is fixed between them, insomuch that a just man that hath compassion upon them cannot be admitted, nor can one that is unjust if he were bold enough to attempt it, pass over it.[31]

Our comment—in Josephus's understanding, he believes those who died after the death and Resurrection of Jesus, condemned to hell, were still able to see souls in Abraham's bosom; but we believe that assessment may not be correct, being Jesus released the captives from the place referred to as Abraham's bosom.

Hesiod, a Greek mythology writer of *Theogony,* describes the place of imprisonment for the Titan gods that once ruled the world: "And there, all in their order, are the sources and ends of gloomy earth and misty Tartarus and the unfruitful sea and starry heaven, loathsome and dank which even the gods abhor. It is a great gulf, and if once a man were within the

---

31 Ibid Josephus

gates ... in front of it the son of Iapetus stands." **Our comment**—Hesiod is describing hell, and Iapetus is but one of Greece's pantheon of gods/fallen angels, who rightly would be standing at the gate of hell.

Dante's Inferno, a work of fiction written around AD 1300 by Dante, defines hell as having nine circles of suffering, beginning with an outer ring and culminating with inner levels that descends to the core of the earth. Dante believed in the Bible, and sinners were to be punished based on the degree of sin. The story begins with his arrival at the gate of hell with a sign that reads, "Abandon All Hope, You Who Enter Here." He is accompanied on his journey with the Roman poet Virgil. The first area they arrive at is on the shores of Acheron—a mythological river in Greece, also called the River of Pain, leading to the underworld, then called the River of Hades (or Tartarus, meaning the pit, abyss, dungeon of torment and suffering). The souls on this first level are people who did neither good or evil but had not accepted Jesus as their savior, and they were tormented with hornets and maggots. This is also the area from which the souls of people who did worst are taken across the river by Charon, the ferryman of Hades, who requires a coin. In real life, some cultures put coins on the eyes of the deceased for that payment. The ferryman did not want to take Dante because he was alive, but Virgil insisted.

Dante's work is lengthy and is summarized for our reading. Upper hell has five circles for all those who lived a self-indulgent life without Jesus. The regions are limbo, lust, gluttony, greed, and anger—all with associated torments. Middle hell consists of level 6 for heresy, such as those who say soul dies with body and are then trapped in flaming tombs; and level 7 are for those who committed violent sins, who are submerged in boiling blood; and these include suicides, sodomites, blasphemers. The lowest level, level 8 is for malicious sinners, fraud, sorcerers, false prophets, astrologers, corrupt politicians, hypocrites, sowers of discord, falsifiers. Level 9 is for those who are treacherous and the area that houses giants, Cain, and Judas Iscariot.

Lastly, Satan is seen as a giant beast with three faces—one red, one black, one pale—and he has wings, and he is trapped in frozen liquid up to his waist. He is able to chew on the others and strip the skin off their backs. Dante and Virgil leave hell by climbing down Satan's back and exiting at the opposite end of the earth.[32] Dante's writing and the artist rendition of hell is impressionable. **Our comment**—in reality, Satan is not presently in hell but running to and fro throughout the earth.

Contemplating our eternal existence after death, if we do not make it into the heavenly realm then you are destined to spend eternity in hell. A place where the dammed are tormented by demons, scorpions, snakes, buzzards tearing flesh and a place where the worm

[32] Dante's Inferno

doesn't die The bible also confirms a realm where demons and evil spirits exist. These entities will arise from the abyss to torment humankind during the tribulation period. Revelation 17:8 At the end of the tribulation and after the battle of Armaggedon we see that evil spirits, Satan, false prophet, Antichrist and wicked people will be cast into the lake fire, a region of hell.

This chapter highlighted disturbing future events and the realization there is an eternal dwelling place for all of mankind. We end this chapter with good news. Sometime before the tribulation, the saints will be taken from the earth. While the tribulation events take its toll, we will be in heaven for seven years.

Chapter 16
The Day of the Lord

Chapter Overview

Last Days and End of the Age

Jesus Foretells the Signs, Matthew 24
1. Apostasy, Deception, Ungodliness
2. Anti-Semitism, Anti-Christianity, and Death to Apostates
3. Shedding of Innocent Blood
4. Amoral, Perilous Times, Lawlessness
5. Technological Advancement
    - Transhumanism, Artificial Intelligence, Geoengineering
    - Harnessing the Environment
6. A Strong Delusion
    - The Vatican on Aliens
    - Lady of Fatima
    - Alien Legends
    - Alien Craft
    - Alien Abductees
    - Experimentations on Humans by Other Humans
    - Animal Mutilations
    - Crop Circles
    - Full Disclosure
    - Can We Identify the Hybrids amongst Us?
    - Zombies, Cannibals, Vampires

Underground Bunkers and Seed Vaults

Did 2012 Mark the Beginning of the End?

Day of the Lord
- Signs in Heaven and Earth
- Solar Eruptions
- Four Blood Moons
- Trumpet Sounds and Booms
- Naturally Occurring Organisms
- Vaccinations a Toxic Cocktail
- Monsanto, Agent of Death

A Beacon of Light in a Dark World

CHAPTER 16

THE DAY OF THE LORD

By now, we have a better understanding of the mystery of iniquity that has engulfed the whole world in wickedness and ungodliness. There are a few major events that need to come to pass to complete the fulfillment of the Day of the Lord. These events would be the (1) Rapture of the body of Christ, (2) the seven-year tribulation, (3) the second return of Christ, (4) the battle of Armageddon, and (5) the kingdom of God on earth and Christ will usher in a new age, a new beginning, wherein righteousness will reign. The curse will be lifted, and the earth will be purged of wickedness. Yeshua will bring peace upon the earth and restore all things. We look forward to a renewed ecosystem for the benefit of man, animal, and marine life. Yeshua, King of Kings and Lord of Lords, will rule and reign. Until that time, what current-day indicators allow us to know the culmination of the Day of the Lord is at hand?

Last Days and End of the Age

Doomsday prophets stand on street corners with signs that read, "The end is here, repent." There is merit in the message, and we need to understand terms such as *end of the age*, *end-times*, or *last days*; but it does not mean the world will end. We are that end-time generation, and God has warned mankind of events that would come to pass. Hebrews 1:2, "*God in these last days has spoken unto us by his Son whom he has appointed heir of all things.*" Matthew 24:34, "*This generation shall not pass till all these things be fulfilled.*" It can be confusing to some, and others are simply not interested if these messages have any prophetic significance. God's time is not man's timing. His ways are above man's ways. God is supreme above all in this life and the life hereafter.

Another end-time indicator is the church age, or the age of grace, slowly being replaced by the apostate church and will formally end with the Rapture of the body of Christ. In place of the body of Christ or the true church, a one-world religious system overseen by a one-world religious leader will deceive the secular world. With the global influence of the Vatican and the pope, the foundation for a one-world religious system is in place.

Another sign this generation will witness is an explosion of unprecedented evil.

This reality is reported by mainstream media, alternative news sites, and movies sensationalizing malevolent themes of zombies, demons that rise from the depths of hell, ungodly experiments to create humanoids, or aliens descending to earth from other planets. Our subconscious minds have been inundated and haunted with images of vampires, demon-possessed, serial killers, and evil spirits. The entertainment industry has provided us with scenarios of worldwide destruction from earthquakes, tsunami, pandemics, and nuclear war. Other themes such as *Hannah* prepare our minds for the reality of cloning and the development of superhumans. Movies present situations of the collapse of governments taken over by terrorists or a world with food shortages leading to the "*Hunger Games*."

Our perception of this imaginary realm becomes real, and well, it should, because Satan, his fallen angels, and their demonic hybrids have superior abilities. Under certain circumstances, these entities may appear as demonic monsters in the summoning of demons from the deep recesses of some other domain. In chapter 3, we discuss the ability of fallen angels, and demons usually invisible to the human eye are able to manifest in our earthly dimension. Even though they have this ability, we do not find Hollywood-type monsters roaming the streets. People possessed by evil spirits appear to us as humans. ISIS, lone wolf shooters, rapists, murderers, and thieves are human in appearance.

As previously mentioned, humankind has entered into the seventh millennium since the creation of the earth. It is year 2016 of the twenty-first century. These sixteen years may be a prelude or a short space of time before the final events go into full force. Or this time frame is an adjustment for the original 360 days per year, which had been changed by Rome to 365 per year.

Jesus said, "In three days, I will return." Hosea 6:2–3, "*After two days will he revive us in the third day he will raise us up and we shall live in his sight.*" The fifth and sixth millenniums represent two thousand years or two days since the death and Resurrection of Jesus, AD 30. The twenty-first century is the beginning of the third day. We do not know the day or hour when Jesus will revive us and raise us up, but we can certainly study the signs and have an idea of the nearness of his return as we see the days grow increasingly wicked. His Second Coming is in two stages: the first is the catching away, or Rapture of the saints to heaven, and the second stage is at the end of the tribulation period, when he returns with his glorified saints to put an end to wickedness, bring the heavenly kingdom to fruition, and establish his millennial reign.

In the past years, the world system has been experiencing its final death throes evidenced by world events that have seen an increase in ungodliness, chaos, and death. There is a divisive spirit moving throughout the world. Families are divided, churches are divided, nations are divided. As we see the days grow dark, knowing the signs of the times were commanded by Jesus saying, you can analyze the clouds and the wind to know there will be a storm. You hypocrites, why can't you analyze this present time ? (Luke 12:51) Israel had the Old Testament prophecies about their Messiah, but many rejected him. Modern man has the New Testament prophecies and the Gospel but have also rejected Jesus.

The world is deceived and blinded on every front hindered with the inability to align scriptural prophecy with current events. The masses are limited in knowledge due to doctrinal error, or the teaching of end-time prophecy is avoided. We hope this book will help seekers to connect the dots in order to have a better understanding of these end-times, lest we be caught unawares.

We are called to watch and pray. Jesus has given us signs to watch as indicated in Matthew 24. One of the signs would be an era of "perilous times," and the world has entered into that era. These perilous times are likened to a woman in travail; the birth pains increase until the birth. In this context, the world has always been subject to peril, but the warning is that events will get worse up to and through the tribulation, culminating with the battle of Armageddon. The loss of life worldwide will be unprecedented, and to prevent all flesh from destruction, Jesus will shorten the days to save Israel. Once we understand the signs, we will have a deeper understanding of God's end-time plan.

A major fulfillment of prophecy and a significant sign is the regathering of the Jewish people back to the land of Israel.

> *And it shall come to pass in that day, that the Lord shall set his hand again the second time to recover the remnant of his people which shall be left from Assyria, Egypt, Pathros, Cush, Elam, Shinar, Hamath and from the islands of the sea. He shall set up an ensign for the nations and shall assemble the outcast of Israel and gather together the dispersed of Judah from the four corners of the earth.* (Isaiah 11:11–12)

The house of Israel is returning to their homeland from across the globe. The land of Israel was barren during the absence of the Jews, and now it is an agricultural phenomena; this and the revival of the Hebrew language are both a fulfillment of prophecy.

Jesus said in Luke 21:24, "*Jerusalem will be trampled on by the Gentiles until the times of the Gentiles are fulfilled.*" In 1967, which is called the six-day war, Israel took back Jerusalem, their capital from the Gentiles, and is another fulfillment of prophecy. Seemingly the nations of the world are against Israel as God puts a hook in them, drawing them into a final conflict. This is being fulfilled as hostilities towards Israel increase within Iran, Gaza, Lebannon. anti-Semitic European nations, America and the United Nations.

An end-time sign is that the whole world will be under stress, fear, perplexity, anxiety, and hardships. Citizens fear a tyrannically corrupt government. We all worry about attacks from nuclear, electromagnetic, biological, or chemical weapons. We are perplexed that our region may be impacted by earthquakes, floods, fires, tsunami, pestilence, or plagues. Will we be able to survive if shelter, food, medicine, and water are not available? We are anxious that criminals will rob and kill our families as reported on the news daily. So we ask, Why? We find the answer in Matthew 24 to 25, where Jesus has warned us that perilous times would come and these situations would usher in the last days.

Jesus Foretells the Signs

Jesus describes the signs that are symptoms of the end-times: Matthew 24 is referred to as the Olivet Discourse, which outlines the signs of the latter days, the tribulation, and the Second Coming of Christ.

- Destruction of the second temple (fulfilled AD 70).
- Be aware of false Christ and false prophets (ongoing).
- Wars and rumors of wars (ongoing).
- Nations against nations (ongoing).
- Famine (ongoing).
- Pestilence, toxic air, polluted water and food (ongoing).
- Earthquakes (increasing).
- Hatred of Jews and Christians (escalating).
- Jews returning to Israel from the four corners of the earth (ongoing).
- Betrayal (commonplace).
- Iniquity so great, there is no mercy or compassion (ongoing).
- Shedding of innocent blood (abortion).
- Preach the Gospel in all the world (fulfilled and ongoing)
- The seven-year covenant with Israel (in the works).

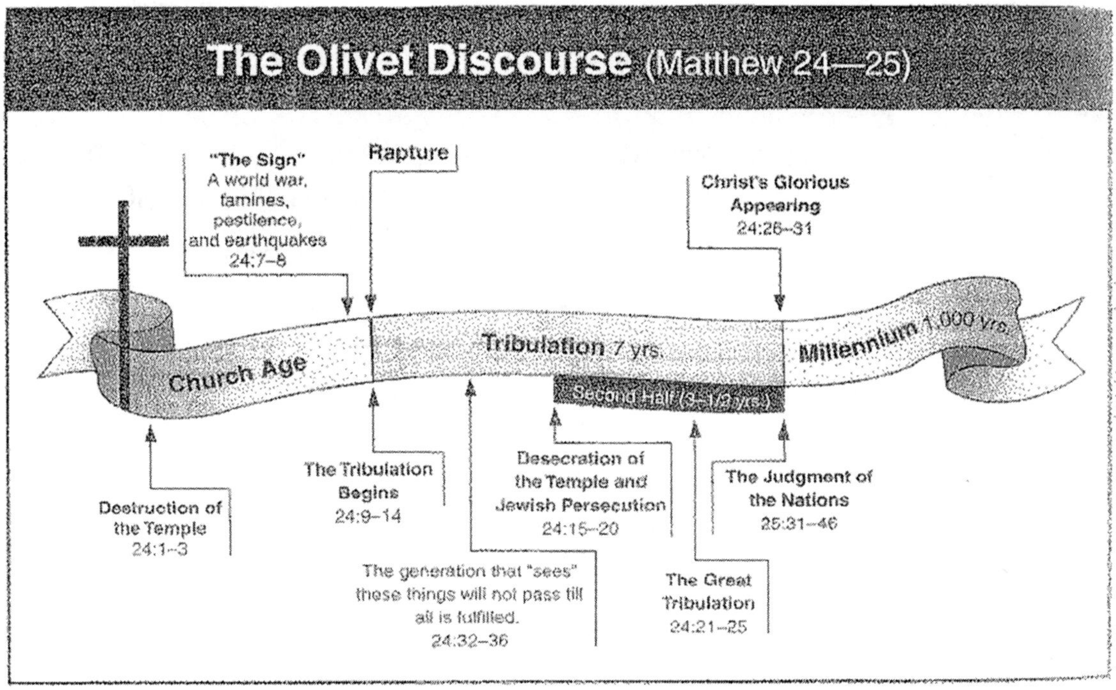

Exhibit: Mathew 24 and 25

- Abomination of desolation (future desecration of the third temple).
- False prophet coming with great signs and wonders (very near).
- If in Judea, flee to the mountains for safety (future).
- Great tribulation as was not since the beginning of the world.
- Jesus's Second Coming will be seen as lightning from east to west (future).
- During the tribulation, the birds will eat the flesh of the dead (future).
- After tribulation, the sun will be dark, no moonlight and stars will fall, and powers of heaven will be shaken (future).

Scriptures have given numerous warnings of the impending judgment to befall the earth in the last days, or end of the age. God is preparing mankind for this imminent doom that the wise man can discern and avoid being caught unaware. Many of the signs spoken of in Matthew 24 and 25 have been developing for over two thousand years; as birth pangs intensify, so have these events increased in the world.

Israel has endured many past wars, and more are on the horizon. Several regional wars in the Middle East will escalate and come against Israel. On this precipice, we watch Israel closely to see the Gog of Magog war come to pass as a fulfillment of Ezekiel 38 and 39. Russia is associated with Gog of Magog and has set itself up in the region of Syria, near Israel's border. China, 2016, has decided to send troops to Syria. The United States has military presence in the region and is aligned with Turkey. ISIS is likened to the four demons released from the Euphrates River. As chaos erupts in and around Israel, this will set the stage for the one-world leader to introduce a seven-year covenant, which will mark the beginning of the seven-year tribulation period.

The key to understanding the importance of ongoing events is to measure the frequency of events and correlate it with prophecy. Having a biblical understanding of the scriptures from Genesis to Revelation is necessary in order to marry world events with scripture. We will highlight five primary symptoms that are significant signs for this present time: (1) apostasy, deception, ungodliness; (2) anti-Semitism, anti-Christianity, and death to apostates; (3) shedding of innocent blood; (4) smoral, perilous times, lawlessness; (5) technological advancement; (6) strong delusion.

(1) Apostasy, Deception, Ungodliness

Apostasy

Webster Dictionary defines *apostasy* as "abandoning a belief once held in faith, religion, a cause, or a principle." For example, people who once believed in the sanctity of marriage between a man and a woman have become apostate, turning away from God-ordained truth to compromise their beliefs with this new age of sexual freedom. In chapter 14, we discussed the apostate church. Herein, we apply apostasy to a broader spectrum as it pertains to a dysfunctional world. Let us consider the mind-set of Islamic extremists who believe anyone who does not adhere to the dictates of the Koran is an apostate and should be killed. Islam is not the only religion who has carried out holy war in the name of their god. Unfortunately, history provides accounts—such as the Crusaders, who killed others, labeling them apostate from Christendom. Bosnians killed millions of Muslims because they were of a different ideology. The church has been remiss in speaking out against the ongoing atrocities toward Christians around the world as well as taking a position against Israel. It is through persecution that the plan of God is carried forward. By divine intervention, we are seeing the coming together between Jews and Christians and this being the fulfillment of God's plan for "one new man." Apostasy is a sign.

Behind all insurrections is Satan leading mankind into a world of deception. Satan begins by attacking our godly beliefs.

Deception

One of the signs given by Jesus was to be aware of deception.

> *Take heed that no man deceive you for many shall come in my name saying I am Christ, and shall deceive many and many false prophets shall rise …*

> *deceiving many ... then if any man shall say unto you, lo, here is Christ, or there, believe it not. For there shall arise false Christ and false prophets and shall show great signs and wonders, insomuch that, if it were possible they would deceive the very elect.* (Matthew 24:4–5, 11, 24)

Warnings given in the above scripture applied to the early church age but forecast the course of events for two thousand years, bringing us into the twenty-first century. Seeds of deceit have been planted in every facet of global society, and the fruit of deceit was harvested by false Christs and workers of iniquity.

The church was to be a light unto the world. The light dimmed when the apostate church would mingle God's Word with the doctrines of false religions. For instance, some are embracing Islam—a religion that denies the deity of Jesus Christ, the Son. Other church bodies align itself with secular authorities to amass wealth and materialism. Many church leaders are full of pride, and prestige is their god. They measure their success on huge church buildings, mega congregations, and personal wealth. On the extreme, some churches have embraced pagan rituals, such as the celebration of the Easter bunny and Halloween, calling it a harvest festival, and including Eastern meditation and yoga. Then there are those bodies that are outright satanic, such as, Anton Lavay and Alester Crawley, members of Church of Satan. Atheists who deny God in his entirety are opening atheist churches or freedom from religion churches.

Deception gives way to accepting false doctrine, immorality, and sin. The secular world calls it tolerance, and tolerance becomes the norm in the acceptance of Islam, homosexuality, and abortion. Those within the church that condone immorality and sin are an abomination unto God. Those who are deceived are given a warning in 2 Peter 2 of false prophets and teachers who bring into the church damnable heresies, even denying the Lord and bringing upon themselves destruction. The church became a conduit for deception, and deception leads to destruction.

Ungodliness

Global powers are under Satan's control; his venom has seeped into all religions; and the powers of darkness have influenced every aspect of society. When the church embraced deception, it opened the door to satanic darkness. God commands us to be holy as he is holy. Only God knows the heart, but the fruit of the Spirit is evident. Ministers who are engaged in immorality are evil shepherds deceiving their flock. There are people who attend church yet shun the light of the Gospel, not allowing it to shine into the darkness of their inner man. They decline a true relationship with our savior because they have to repent or believe in God's way. Another warning is given to them in 2 Peter 2:20, to those who knew the Lord and Savior Jesus Christ (the church body) then abandoned the true faith to become entangled in the mire of ungodliness; for them it will be worse in the end than it was in the beginning. It would have been better for them not to have known the way of righteousness than after they have known it to turn from the holy commandments.

God Bless America

Was America founded upon Christian values? Perhaps a few of the founders of the government embraced godly principles as set forth in the constitution and bill of rights. Did "all men are created equal" apply to African slaves, Native Americans, Jews, Catholics, and Asians? The faith of some of the architects of America made its way onto a cornerstone of morality and godly values. However, the majority of the founding fathers were steeped in occult, idolatry, witchcraft, and secularism upon which the basis of Americanism gave way to discord and hatred.

Americans are not remiss in voicing the mantra, "God Bless America." How can Yahweh bless a nation that has forgotten God? It no longer wants the name of God spoken in public forums. Those who dare speak for godly values are lambasted, vilified, and killed. Sexual immorality is now an acceptable lifestyle. Abortion is the choice, displacing "thou shall not kill." Corruption, greed, murder, and lies begin at the highest levels of government. Where is the income equality promised by our leaders? The average citizen is suffering various hardships. Our veterans are denied care, are homeless, and are dependent on soup kitchens, handouts, and government subsidies. America is guilty on all counts.

From the first to the current president has embraced a satanically controlled one-world government ideology. This nation's god is money and power. President Obama has served his master well by taking a national stand for homosexuality, same-sex marriage, and forcing states to allow transgender people to use the opposite-sex bathrooms. Abortion is a mainstay, and the sale of baby parts is profitable. The military, Boy Scouts, and churches must embrace the homosexual lifestyle. Obama is not a friend of Israel and Christians. Chaplains and military personnel cannot speak the name of Jesus, display Bibles, or post scripture. He promotes liberation from religious icons such as the cross, the Nativity scene, or Ten Commandments displayed in state facilities. The deceived label themselves liberals as they move farther left and out of the will of God.

Liberalism in this country is the individual right to feel good through music, alcohol, cigarettes, drugs, sex, gambling, and entertainment. Those who oppose them are vilified. Celebrities are worshipped. Obama is worshipped as the savior to bring hope and change to America. After eight years, what does hope and change look like? People have been lulled into a state of complacency that big government will take care of them. If you are hungry, you can get food stamps. If you are homeless, you can get a section 8 subsidy or a FEMA trailer. If you are unemployed, you can get temporary unemployment benefits. If you need health care, there is Obamacare. If you need an abortion, the way is made easy and affordable to kill the unborn. Citizens do not need to own guns because the local police and military will protect them.

National sin is a reproach unto God, as it was in Sodom and Gomorrah. Only a few in those wicked nations remained faithful and obedient unto God. In the midst of darkness, they sparkle like beacons of light. God looks upon those who call upon the name of the Lord and commands them to separate themselves, keep their garments white, and continue to sound the alarm: judgment is coming.

(2) Anti-Semitism, Anti-Christianity, and Death to Apostates

This category regards religious persecution. History tells us that at one time or another, each religious organization persecuted another religion. For instance, the Jews persecuted the Christians. The Romans persecuted the Jews and the Christians. Then Christendom persecuted the Jews. Islam persecuted everyone. Those on the left and not of the true body of Christ will continue hatred and discord among the people of the world. These tyrants have worn many hats, and notably, Hitler's regime was one of the worst times in history. Little is said that some Jews sided with Hitler during the annihilation of their own people. When we speak of the Holocaust, we should also remember that Hitler killed Christians, Gypsies, and others he classified as inferior. Under Stalin and Mussolini, many Europeans were killed. In Africa, tribes turned on other tribes, and millions have been killed. In the Muslim community, Islamic sects turn on each other, and thousands have been killed. Once again, we see the rise of Islamic terrorism against everyone. Historians often overlook the persecution and murder of Natives in North and South America, including the African slaves in America. Prejudice against these people has continued for centuries. The Ku Klux Klan call themselves Christians while murdering people of various ethnicities.

At the start of 2015, reports of anti-Semitism and anti-Christianity grabbed headlines and became a global concern. Currently, Islamic factions are the major cause of religious intolerance joined by uninformed, ignorant people. False doctrines found in Islam and apostate Christendom are the fodders that fuel hatred against God's people. Of course, we are all God's creation, but as the evil angels rebelled against God and were rejected from his presence, the same goes for evil people who reject God are not the children of God but the children of Satan. The enemies of God are out to destroy the people of God. *Israel Now News*, February 2015, report by Raymond Ibrahim—Egyptian-born author of *Crucified Again* addressed the increase of religious persecution toward Christians by Islamic terrorists.

Since the inception of Islam, approximately 1,500 years ago, there has been a consistent command to kill Christians, Jews and Muslim apostates. Following is a sampling of Islamic terrorism throughout the world:

Syria

A future prediction for the City of Damascus is destruction (Isaiah 17:1–3, Jeremiah 49:23–27). The prophecies are being fulfilled at this time. Damascus is one of the oldest continuing cities in the world, and it is almost uninhabitable. Currently, Syrian president Bashar Assad takes action against those who threaten to depose his presidency. The opposition is just as bad as the government. Millions have been displaced, trying to find refuge in other nations. ISIS captured some Syrian territory and killed Muslims, non-Muslims, and Christians. Muslims kidnapped thirteen nuns and held them captive for three months until Bashar Assad agreed to release 150 female prisoners. In 2011, the Christian population was two million; by 2015, there remained five hundred thousand. Free Syrian Army overran Christian town of Maalula, where many still spoke Aramaic.

Iran

October 2012, Christians United for Israel reported Iran had arrested over one hundred Christians. It imprisoned Christian pastor Youcef Nadarkahani and Pastor Saeed Abedini; both were jailed for years. During their imprisonment, they were tortured and deprived health care.

Due to the relentless work of the American Center for Law and Justice, both men were released.

These two men are representative of hundreds of others persecuted for their faith. The US administration has been tepid on the persecution of Christians, and with the Iranian nuclear deal on the forefront, the pastors were released. Iranian ayatollahs pursue nuclear weapons to hasten the end of days. They hearken to their coming messiah, the twelfth Iman who will rule the earth. Iran continues to call for the destruction of Israel.

Iraq

Two-thirds of Christians have fled or been murdered in this country in the midst of burning churches, homes, and businesses. Between 2004–2009, many churches were destroyed in Baghdad and Mosul. The archbishop of Mosul was kidnapped and killed in 2008. ISIS has a stronghold in Iraq and carries out persecutions, rapes, tortures, kidnappings, beheadings, and evictions.

Turkey

AD 1453, Muslims burned monasteries and looted, killing monks and raping nuns. Turkey has a long history of anti-Semitism and anti-Christianity. The ancient church Hagia Sofia will be turned into a mosque. Turkey seized six Christian churches, and no mosques have been seized. Mid-2016, reports of terrorism against citizens have increased. The military attempted to remove President Erdogan in a takeover. Some news outlets are reporting that Erdogan will use the uprising to force the nation into Sharia law.

Lebanon/Gaza

Greek Orthodox nuns at a monastery in Bethany asked PLO leader Abbas to do something about increasing attacks on Christians. Palestinian children as young as five years old are taught to hate Israel and the infidels. Children are taught to be martyrs as in suicide bombers. Palestinians lie about being suffering refugees. They receive millions from America, United Nations, Israel, and other countries. Israel allows Palestinians to come into their hospitals and medical facilities for treatment. Israel has joint agriculture and business ventures with Palestinians. However, Jews are denied access to Palestinian territories. Abbas calls for a ban of selling Israeli food products in Palestinian stores. If store owner stock their shelves with Israel products, he has ordered hit squads to destroy those items. Abbas calls for the annihilation of Israel, and Lebanon is home to terrorist group Hezbolla. Iran supplies tens of thousands of missiles to Hezbolla and Hamas in Gaza.

Hamas militants have been launching missiles at Israel for years and up to 2015. They call for the demise of Israel. Israel defended itself by bombing terrorists' strongholds in homes, hospitals, schools. Hamas uses its citizens as human shields.

Israel

Things within Israel are not quiet; over a thousand ISIS supporters gathered at the Temple Mount to show support for ISIS. Protesters were led by the Tahrir Liberation Party in Jerusalem, calling themselves the Palestinian branch of jihad. Israel leaders said they will not tolerate these uprising, and any future attacks will be dealt with harshly. Abbas in Lebanon calls for Palestinians who live in Israel to get knives and vehicles to kill Israeli citizens; some terrorists have followed his call, and reports of these violent acts began in November 2014 and continue presently.

Pakistan

In 2012, Muslim gunmen opened fire on Saint Francis Xavier Catholic Cathedral in Hyderabad, killing twenty-eight. A Christian woman was imprisoned and sentenced to death for being a Christian. October 19, 2014, eighty-five worshippers were killed at All Saints' Church established in 1883 in Peshawar. Islamic terrorists killed 140 students at a military school. In 2016, Bacha Khan University was attacked by terrorists; twenty-one were dead and many others wounded. Pakistan is home for the Taliban terrorists.

Wallid Shoebat, February 26, 2013, reported that in Mandi Farooqabad, Pakistan, local Muslims of Saddiqabad falsely accused Jan Mashih—a Christian under Pakistan blasphemy law—saying he used a cloth sheet on which there is a footprint that showed disrespect for the prophet of Islam. The accuser, Sehar-ul-Zaman, incited other Sunni Muslims to gather around Mashih's home, threatening him. Zaman has a track record of blackmail and harassment of the Christian community. The Christian was exonerated by Haji Rasheed, a Muslim leader whose investigation found Mashih innocent. Wallid Shoebat's organization will be relocating Mashih out of harm's way. These blasphemy laws are being enforced more so in order to persecute the Christian community as in the 2015 case Asia Bibi imprisoned for her faith and sentenced to death over a cup of water.

Pakistani Muslim men living in United Kingdom have been kidnapping white girls as young as nine years old, gang-raping them repeatedly, inserting foreign objects in their anus or vagina; and authorities are turning a blind eye (Walid Shoebat.com).

India

Bangladesh has 90 percent Muslim population. Armed men attacked the Pontifical Institute of Foreign Mission convent. The nuns were beaten and raped (*Front Page Magazine*, August 2014).

Africa

Somalia

Muslims shot sixty-six-year-old nun who had devoted thirty years taking care of those in need.

Nairobi, Kenya

In 2014, seventy people were killed at shopping center by Somali Islamic militant group al-Shabab. They separated Muslims who were set free and killed others.

Nigeria

In 2014, almost a hundred students were killed by Islamist bomber. In 2015, Nigeria, Boko Haran continues to kidnap and slaughter thousands. President Obama is silent on Boko Haran as a punishment upon Nigerian president, a Christian who condemns homosexuality.

Kenya

A 2015 report reports Al Shabab, Islamic terrorists, killed 148 Christians at a school.

Burkina Faso

Hotel Splendid was attacked by al-Qaeda; twenty were killed.

Liberia

Monrovia has a female Christian president. Their government holds prayer meetings. The local churches prayed for the intervention of God in the Ebola crisis. Several African nations rejected homosexuality and same-sex marriage as president Obama attempted to strong-arm them into rejecting godly values and embracing sexual abomination. It appears that those who resist the intentions of Obama become the targets of his wrath.

Egypt

The Coptic Christians are experiencing abductions, rapes, and murders. Many are forced to convert to Islam. Coptic churches and homes have been burned and confiscated. Muslims brutally have been ongoing for hundreds of years. A few examples are in AD 1300, Taqi al din al Marqrizi historian, captured women and nuns for sex; AD 900, Severus ibn Muqaffa said Muslims killed many monks and raped nuns; 2013, a Franciscan school was burned.

The Obama regime supported the overthrow of longtime Egyptian president Mubarick who had peaceful ties with Israel. He was replaced with radical Muslim Brotherhood dictator, Morsi, calling for the demise of Israel and to take Jerusalem for its capital. July 2013, protests in Egypt hold up signs that read: "Obama, your bitch is our dictator" (Morsi); "Obama, stop supporting Muslim Brotherhood Fascist Regime." The Muslim Brotherhood bombed Two Saints Church in Alexandria as well as eighty other churches. Twenty-one Coptic Christians were beheaded by ISIS. A coup overthrew Morsi, and he was replaced by the military. New president al Sisi is tolerant of Israel but is against the Muslim Brotherhood.

Libya

In 2013, Muslim rebels threatened nuns who had been there since 1921 into fleeing the nation. Some Christians were rounded up for sharing the Gospel in 2013.

South Africa

Durban University of Technology students of the Progressive Youth Alliance called for the expulsion of Jewish students.

Guinea

June 2013, a Muslim mob attacked churches, killing ninety-five Christians, 130 wounded and convent burned.

Philippines

Muslims bomb Roman Catholic cathedral in Jolo as well as kidnap priests and nuns. This country has a strong allegiance to Israel.

Indonesia

ISIS killed two and wounded twenty-four in a bomb attack in Jarkata, 2016. Christians have been killed and churches burned by other Muslims.

Vietnam

Christians killed and jailed (Walid Shoebot, August 2016).

Saudi Arabia

In 2013, persecution of Christians is on the increase. Sixty-five Ethiopian Christians were arrested, who live and work in Saudi Arabia—their crime, sharing the Gospel.

Yemen

In 2015, Iran backed Shiite Houthis and killed 120 at a mosque. Terrorists have taken over some cities. The president of Yemen has left, fearing assassination. Saudi Arabia was conducting air strikes against the rebels. Missiles target US ships, October 2016, and United States returns missiles into Yemen.

There are other incidents of anti-Christian or anti-Semitism in other nations. For example, Toronto, Canada, police stop preacher speaking out against gay pride parade.

London, Britain, has seen a 400 percent increase in violent incidents against Jews and Christians. The government operates against godly beliefs when it forced the deputy prime minister to conduct gay marriage.

In Ukraine, Russian Orthodox Church persecutes Evangelical Christians. One reports, the Orthodox took over a church and forced the congregation to vacate; then they allowed the pro-Russian forces to store weapons in the church basement.

France in 2015 saw the killing of twelve at a newspaper that put out a cartoon of Muhammad.

Jews leaving France for Israel are up 289 percent.

United States, 2015, San Bernadino terrorists killed fourteen and wounded others. Boston marathon bombers were associated with Islam, and this is only two of many incidents.

Anti-Semitism and Anti-Christianity from non-Muslim organizations

Persecution is also practiced in the United States. It can be found in government organizations that have the power to demonize citizens who oppose abortion or homosexuality as terrorists.

US military has taken a stand against Christianity. Chaplains are forbidden to say the name of Jesus. Bibles are not allowed to be displayed on desks. Chaplains cannot preach against the sin of homosexuality. Transgenders must be accepted in military. New inductees are briefed at military bases that the new terrorists are Evangelical Christians, Conservatives, Tea Party affiliates, former military, gun owners, and patriots. They are told not to join or contribute to these groups, or they could face punishment. The military does consult with anti-Christian extremists to help formulate its own policies regarding religious freedom American Center for Law and Justice, October 28, 2013.

US Air Force Base, Colorado Springs, spent eighty thousand to build open-air worship center for pagans and Wiccans. The structure is formed like Stonehenge with a center altar. Out of 4,300 cadets, three identified themselves as pagans. This is done in the name of tolerance and political correctness.

A Christian Marine was court-martialed for displaying a Bible verse on her desk: "No weapon formed against me will prosper." Military court said that expressing the Bible is not part of a "religious belief system."

Persecution of Christians in Other Fields

A Christian county clerk was jailed for refusing to sign same-sex marriage license.

American Christian businesses refusing to serve homosexuals based on their religious beliefs are fined, punished, harassed by the gays, and sometimes forced out of business.

Christians who speak out for traditional bible based beliefs are labeled as bigots, haters and despicable. Standing for traditional beliefs, if contrary to secular worldview dictates there will be consequences. Proponents for traditional marriage such as Mozilla CEO Brendan Eich was fired; HGTV hosts David and Jason Benham's show was canceled; a beauty contestant who said she believed in traditional marriage was vilified; and a football player was fined for saying his faith was based on traditional marriage in response to gay player Michael Sam, who kissed his partner on TV.

Anti-Semitism/Christianity on College Campuses

Opposition to Jews and Christians is found on college campuses across the nation.

Sinclair College tells Christians they can't have a rally on college property for their "Stand Up for Religious Freedom" rally. Yet Islamic radicals can have a rally on campus that call for sanctions, divestment, and the destruction of Israel in general. There is not a peep from these groups about the persecution and murder of Christians and Jews in the Middle East.

"There is a disturbing increase of anti-Semitism at colleges and universities where 40 percent of incidents reported involved graffiti, vandalism, hate speech, and violence. Infiltration by the Muslim Brotherhood began in the 1960s on college campuses calling themselves Muslim Students Association. Saudi Arabia funds Islamic movements. Communist and left wing align with Islam. Protest movements are totally hostile and have moved beyond free speech" (Allen West the Next Generation Today, based in Florida via Wallid Shoebat interviews Jewish journalist Lee Kaplan regarding anti-Semitism on college campuses).

Yale University received $10 million from Saudi Arabia to establish an Islamic Law Center at its university.

David Horowitz, Freedom Center 2015, said that 54 percent of Jewish students reported anti-Semitic incidents. We list some colleges who support anti-Semitic rallies on campus: Columbia, Loyola, Portland State, George Mason, University of San Diego, Temple University, UCLA, Vassar.

Princeton University professor and chairman of Commission on International Religious Freedom, Dr. Robert P. George, reports that the administration and society condemns Christian beliefs as bigoted and hateful. Christians United for Israel, founded by Pastor John Hagee, has established regional coordinators throughout the United States to set up pro-Israel clubs on college campuses and to support Israel in its entirety.

Wheaton College took a stand for Christian values based on the Bible in response to a professor who wore a head covering because she upholds the doctrines of Islam.

It is shameful when so-called Christian media and organizations take up the pro-Palestinian, Islamic agenda without understanding the facts. One such Christian publication is *Christianity Today*—a prominent evangelical journal who endorsed the books of pro-Palestinian authors. Proclaiming to be a Palestinian Christian does not give them the right to lambast Israel. Bible publishers are changing the original language in the Bible to accommodate homosexuals and Islam.

The Presbyterian and Methodist churches call for sanctions against Israel as well as divestment because of the perceived "Palestinians oppression" by Israel, which is a lie from the pit of hell.

Rep. Frank Wolf expressed his concerns about the lack of support from the Obama administration for Christians being persecuted around the world. Wolf created a bill for a special envoy within the State Department who would advocate on behalf of vulnerable religious minorities, and it passed the House in September 2013, with a bipartisan vote of 402 to 22. Pressure from the Obama administration and the State Department, the bill is stalled and has not moved to the Senate.

We note that segments of Christendom are anti-Semitic as well as some Jews are anti-Christian. Is it possible that Jews could be anti-Semitic? We recently saw on the Internet a photo of Orthodox Jews burning an Israeli flag. The caption said they were anti-Israel. In 2016, we became aware that Bernie Sanders, US candidate for president, is an atheist Jew.

Jonathan Bernis, *Jewish Voice Today Magazine*, March 2013, takes a look at anti-Semitism from a Messianic Jewish point of view in an article, "The New Face of a Primitive Hatred." The Anti-Defamation League reports that there is a 70 percent increase of anti-Semitism in Europe since 2009. In America, reported incidents of anti-Semitism were 62 percent compared to incidents of anti-Islam, 13 percent.

The historical accounts of hatred and violence over the centuries bring up the question: Why? Anti-Semitism stems from a primitive hatred as old as Satan himself. Satan hates God and all that stand for godly righteousness. Satan knows that the restoration of the Jewish people plays a central role in the return of the Messiah to this earth. He wants to prevent the Second Coming of Jesus. Satan knows his time is short.

John D. Garr gives a perspective in the *Jewish Voice Today Magazine*, March 2013, on *Christian Anti-Semitism: History's Greatest Aberration?* He said, "How could a religion founded by a Jew and perpetuated by Jewish apostles ever have anything but the highest level of love and respect for the Jewish people?"

Our analysis of Mr. Garr's statement is to separate Jewish Christians from Orthodox Jews. Believing in Jesus or not does not remove a person from their ancestry. They are still Jews. According to the Bible, the early Christian Jews did have love and respect for their fellow Jews. History paints a different picture of the Orthodox Jews, Pharisees, and Sadducees in that they hated Jesus and his followers. By the time Jesus was crucified, he had been abandoned by everyone save a few. Orthodox Jews celebrated his death. Pagan Rome was apathetic. Followers of Christ where afraid they were going to be executed and hid themselves.

Mr. Garr continues, "Amazingly, however an indelible blood spattered record of 'Christian' hatred for Jews is strewn across the annals of history, written in the blood of countless Jewish men, women, and children who have suffered violence at the hands of Christians and in the anguish of millions more who have been subjected to unwarranted suspicion, to despicable slurs and to the fear of mayhem all perpetrated in the name of the Christian Jesus."

In response to his comment, we say that hatred comes in all forms, and Satan uses willing evil people to carry out his plan to kill the people of God. History reports that the new Christians were killed by the Jews. Later, pagan Rome killed thousands of Jews and Christians, slaughtering them in the coliseum for entertainment. Catholicism killed millions of Protestants and Jews. Hitler killed millions of Jews but not in the name of Jesus. The rise of Islam perpetrated hatred of Jews and Christians. Millions have died at the hand of Muslims.

Garr's narrative does not apply to the Africans, who were enslaved in America for hundreds of years and suffered the same fate as the Jews. People claiming to be Christians did sanction slavery and murdered millions. Garr's narrative does not apply to the Native Americans, who became nearly extinct at the hand of pseudo-Christians. Jewish people are not the only ones who have suffered at the hands of religious zealots. Not all Christians hated Jews. History records countless acts of kindness shown by Christians toward the Jews, and it continues exponentially today.

Mr. Garr correctly points out that some early church leaders were anti-Semitic. "John Chrysostom's claim that the synagogue is worse than a brothel, the temple of demons devoted to idolatrous cults, a place of meeting for the assassins of Christ, an abyss of perdition. Garr says, Christianity has been among the most insidious and dangerous enemies of the Jewish people."

In response to Mr. Garr's comment, we believe him to be an intelligent individual. Surely he can discern that these people, even if they claim to be Christians, only have a form of godliness and are like white-washed tombs. He knows that the actions of evil people are not what Christianity is all about. Jesus said, "If they hated me, they will hate you." Jesus said to love your enemy and forgive those who persecute you and speak evil about you; turn the other cheek. Where are Mr. Garr's accolades for good, decent, God-loving Christians? There are two sides to a coin: one represents hate, and the other side represents love. Serious scholarship must analyze both sides of the coin and present a balanced summation.

The Jerusalem Connection reported April 4, 2013, on Christian Anti-Zionism. In 1994, Reverend Naim Ateek, an Anglican priest, established the Sabeel Ecumenical Liberation Theology Center in Jerusalem. He believes, "the Palestinian Arabs are victims and equates them to Jesus. In an article in 2005, he said the Gaza strip is like Christ being nailed to the cross. Ateek promotes the idea that Israel insists on repeating the sins of the ancient Israelites as detailed in the Old Testament." With the power of Satan behind him, he has created a powerful international anti-Zionist infrastructure. He promotes anti-Zionism to mainstream American churches and far-left Jewish anti-Zionist. Ateek does not speak against the atrocities committed by Muslims against Israel, or terrorist groups such as Hamas and Hezbollah;

nor does he speak out against the persecution of Christians living in Muslim-dominated nations. The Sabeel organization is actively influencing Christians to be anti-Zionist by conducting "witness trips" to Israel. If they go to visit the Holy Land, they will see that Naim Ateek is a liar. If they visit the Palestinians in Lebanon or Gaza, they will not find refugees but modern infrastructure, and they will see Israelis and Palestinians working together. Israel is not the aggressor.

According to the Pew Forum on Religion and Public Life reports, "Christians suffer persecution, discrimination, harassment, and death in 133 countries."

One of the signs of the end of the age is the increase in persecution of God's people. Anti-Semitism and anti-Christianity go hand in hand. Currently, hundreds of people are martyred for their faith. The believer's peace is not of this world; our peace is in Jesus, who has made both the Jew and the Christian one—who through persecution has broken down the wall of partition between the people of God, and in Jesus the two become one new man (Ephesians 2:14–15).

Is God ramping up persecution to separate the believers from apostate Christendom? Is God increasing duress upon the Jews to fulfill the prophecy that the Jews will return to Israel from the four corners of the earth? Jews had gotten comfortable in their geographic locations, especially in America. Some wealthy Jews in Hollywood, Wall Street, legal or medical professions, seem apathetic toward the dire situation that Israel is facing today.

These situations sum up our case, and it all points to an anti-God movement in these last days orchestrated by Satan who comes to kill, steal, and destroy God's people.

(3) Shedding of Innocent Blood

The shedding of innocent blood is the culture of death and is required by Satan and his minions. Abortion is a holocaust on the unborn. The practice of terminating the life of the unborn began before the flood when the fallen angels introduced the method of killing the fetus. In one form or another, killing of the unborn has been a constant throughout the ages. Perhaps we are beginning to see an eye for an eye. Judgment against abortion is seen in the death of your living children who are dying from multiple diseases, abuse, neglect, and murder.

We have affirmations by Christians, such as John Garr, who demonize Christianity for their treatment of the Jews. Yet these same individuals who represent Christendom have turned a blind eye to sixty million aborted babies in the United States since 1973. Where is John Garr's outrage? If the church body as a whole rose up against abortion, it would not have been legalized in America.

Before abortion became widely acceptable, organization and churches secretly performed abortion. Case in point, it was disclosed that Bon Secours Sisters, a Catholic service for unmarried pregnant women in Ireland had buried the remains of over eight hundred babies under their facility during 1925 to 1961. (Reuters, 2017) The United States of America made a judicial decision to legalize the murder of the unborn in 1973 in the infamous Supreme Court ruling of Roe versus Wade. Since abortion is protected under the law and government funded, mothers can abort their babies at will. Partial birth abortion is inhumane and violent. Live babies are stabbed in the back of the head and killed. Long-term babies are aborted, and the human children—some who survive the procedure—are looked upon by its murderers as something nonhuman. Having no empathy, compassion, or mercy, the child is mutilated and sold for body parts. The remains are used in food additives and some discarded to be used as fuel.

President Obama made known his support for the abortion industry, and the sanctity of life was not even an afterthought. Planned Parenthood is a demonic organization responsible for the murder of millions of unborn babies. President Obama spoke at their April 2013 conference and assured them his support and had the audacity to say, "God bless Planned Parenthood." In pagan cultures and secret societies, animals and children are sacrificed as part of their satanic rituals. They also ate humans. The act of cannibalism was an ancient practice and is still followed by some today.

April 2013 exposed the infamous abortion doctor, Kermit Gosnell, who operated a filthy abortion clinic in Philadelphia. Several women died. He was devoid of conscience. Many infants who survived the abortion procedure were killed by Gosnell, who severed their spinal cords. He kept trophies by cutting off heads and feet, storing baby remains in jars throughout the clinic. Judge Jeffrey Minehart dismissed several murder charges, but after some media pressure, he changed his ruling. The Philadelphia Health Department had not inspected his house of horrors in almost twenty years. Media coverage initially ignored this criminal case. At the last hearing, when Defense Attorney Jack McMahan rested his case, *AP*, *New York Times*, *Wall Street Journal*, Fox News, CNN, *The Blaze*, *Philadelphia Inquirer* were on the scene after prolife activists used social media to get the attention of the public.

Legal under man's government, illegal under God's commandment—"Thou shall not kill and you will not offer your children to false gods." To get around this, those who sanction abortion try to make a case that the unborn fetus is not human, or a nonperson, but God says, "*Before I formed you in the womb, I knew you and before you were born, I consecrated you* (Jeremiah 1:5). By dehumanizing the baby abortion becomes palatable and acceptable.

We may also be reminded that under slavery in America, the Africans were dehumanized by legislating that they were partially human (Dred Scott, 1856). People became desensitized to the brutality and murder of other humans. Under the Fourteenth Amendment, "No person shall be denied life, liberty, property without due process of law," the United States government restricted the application of the law in bias and with prejudice.

> *Six things does the Lord hate, a proud look, a lying tongue and hands that shed innocent blood, a heart that devises wicked imaginations, feet that are swift in running to mischief.* (Proverbs 6:17)

The fortieth anniversary of Roe versus Wade will be celebrated in 2013. The freedom of choice, prochoice, or proabortion advocates will celebrate the death of approximately sixty million children. This is six times the number Hitler killed. Counting the death toll of all the wars fought by Americans from the Revolutionary War, Civil War, World Wars I and II, Korean War, Vietnam War, Iraq, and Afghanistan, abortion worldwide may outnumber the casualties of war.

In a recent article by Claire Chretien, *Life Site News*, August 1, 2016, she shares research and documentation provided by James Studnicki, Sharon MacKinnon, John Fisher, University of North Carolina, Charlotte, in their 2009 study posted in *Open Journal of Preventive Medicine*: Induced Abortion, Mortality and the Conduct of Science, found that abortion is not listed by the US Public Health Department in their statistics as a cause of death. The department states the number one cause of death is heart disease. The researchers found that the leading cause of death of African Americans is abortion at 61 percent and Hispanics at 64 percent; whites, 16 percent. They reported that 3,589,163 million deaths of mothers and babies was 4 percent higher than people who died from heart disease. What we take from this report is that for over a hundred years, the practice of eugenics by way of abortion, sterilization, and death are methods to reduce the general population with emphasis on the minority population in the United States.

Those who stand up and protest ungodliness are attacked and ridiculed. A prolife advocate was beaten by abortionist in front of his children. Another was killed by a proabortion group. These are only two instances out of hundreds. In a few instances out of frustration, prolife advocates have resorted to violence against the abortion industry.

This is truly a holocaust of babies. America is supposed to be the godly role model to the rest of the world. A 2014 TV series called *Lottery* is about women worldwide having lost their ability to become pregnant. No child had been born in six years. A laboratory creation caused worldwide sterility. A scientist finally finds a hundred eggs and fertilizes them. Corrupt government officials and the wealthy want the eggs. Murder and chaos ensue. This would be a great judgment on the world that has no regard for the unborn, and therefore God closes the womb.

China's secular culture is amoral. The government-approved religion is secular and controls all aspects of life. China has a "Rule of One," meaning each family can only have one child. The one-child policy in China has caused innumerable abortions. The Chinese highly favor male babies. If a female is born and the parents desired a male, it is common practice to allow the newborn to live after birth but denying it nourishment, causing death by starvation and exposure.

In China, when a woman becomes pregnant with child 2, she can get an abortion voluntarily. If she refuses, the government can force her to have an abortion up to nine months. If a family does not comply, the government will burn homes, cause loss of jobs, and deny them citizenship. If a second child is discovered, the government can kill the child regardless of age. The government is stationed at hospitals, and when a child is brought in for treatment, the parent must produce a certificate for the one child. If not, the military has the right to inject the child with poison on the spot. In 2015, China relaxed its one-child, policy allowing people to have two and only because of the imbalance of males and females.

America would be hypocritical in pointing a finger at China for human rights violations.

The European Union and the United States are both guilty of baby genocide. Ted Turner said he agrees with China's policy of one child per family, that it is a good model for the rest of the world because of overpopulation.

Now, if all of the above is not bad enough, "fetal soup" is a delicacy in China. The cost for a bowl of baby soup is thirty to forty yen. Aborted fetus is in high demand to be used for medicine, sexual prowess, and food. Some methods are to cremate the remains, ground into a power, and put into capsules. You may remember from time to time, food products imported from China to the United States have been tainted with toxins such as melamine found in **Nestlé** milk in 2008. That year, China sponsored the Olympics, and there was not much media coverage; but there were some deaths, and over two hundred thousand people were sickened from tainted food (Children of God for Life, *ABC News*, and 20/20). Fetal tissue is being used in American food products to enhance flavors and added to rice so that a protein can be extracted for some medical research.

In the United States, there is no outright indignation about using aborted babies in substances that people ingest. **Pepsi** shareholders filed a resolution, petitioning the company to adopt a corporate policy that recognized human rights and employ ethical standards that do not involve using the remains of aborted beings in both private and collaborative research and development agreements. But the Obama administration dismissed this thirty-six-page proposal, deciding instead that Pepsi's use of aborted babies to flavor its beverage products is "just business as usual and not a significant concern." A report dated February 28, 2012, noted the Security Exchange Commission (SEC) approved the use of human embryos for Pepsi Company to enhance the flavor of their drinks. It is called HEK 293—human embryonic kidney. Pepsi paid $30 million to a research and development company called **Senomyx**, 11099 North Torrey Pines Road, La Jolla, California, 92037. It will be listed under ingredients as "artificial flavors" or "natural flavors," but not specifically that it is human embryos. The FDA allows for a certain percentage of animal or dirt particles to be in foods, and this now includes the use of human matter. This is only the tip of the iceberg.

Following are some companies that use aborted babies in their products:

Kraft, Pepsi, Nestlé, Nescafé, KitKat, Nestlé Crunch, Butterfingers, Nesquik, Lean Cusine, Hot Pockets, Buitoni Pasta, Poland Spring Water, Carnation Coffee Mate, Hagen Daz Ice Cream, Cambells soup, Stouffers, Aquafina, Tropicana, Dole, Ocean Spray, Lipton, Quaker Oats, Frito Lay, Cheetos, Cadbury, Honey Maple Log Cabin, Stove Top, Triscuit, Wheat Thins, General Mills, Cheerio, Cinnamon Toast, Bisquik, Fruit Roll Ups, Oscar Meyers, Teddy Grams, Newton, A1 Steak Sauce, Breakstone, Capri Sun, Chips Ahoy, Cool Whip, Cracker Barrel, General Foods, Handi Snack, Honey Maid, Kenco, Lata, Lunchables, Maxwell, Nabisco, Nilla Cookies, Nutter Butter, Onko, Oreo, Philadelphia Cream Cheese, Planters, Premium Cracker, Ritz, Royal, Jell-O, Trident, Dentyne, Halls Cough, Miracle Whip, Miracle Whip Cream.

L'Oreal, cosmetics owned by Liliane Bettencourt, richest woman in France, uses aborted babies in cosmetics. Search the web, and you will find hundreds of sites talking about these atrocities.

Vaccinations are developed, using stem cells obtained from fetal tissue and are combined with toxins and viruses. Coming soon will be human fetal farms similar to salmon farms, where salmon is genetically modified to grow giant fish quickly. Planned Parenthood could be considered a fetal farm, where fetal tissue is harvested and sold. Who having any conscience could think this is acceptable? US suppliers use almost two million baby parts for research and development. The scientists say the best time for the products' viability is twenty-two weeks. Efforts to limit term abortion to twenty weeks were denied by the court.

Mexico is proabortion and also sells aborted babies to companies for research and development.

The government of Hungary recently raided a treatment center where the aborted embryonic tissue concentrations are used for injection into wealthy people who pay $25,000 per shot. We are not certain what benefits are provided (*Life Site News*, April 17, 2013).

One-world order leaders want to reduce the population by six billion, employing various methods. Sterilization and abortion are effective methods. AIDS and the Ebola virus were created, and the African population was targeted initiating a domino effect in the world. The cure for these viruses is vaccination laced with DNA, viruses, and chemicals. The vaccination is used as a biological weapon for a silent genocide—an effective method. Third world countries have been targeted for years, such as India, South America, and Africa, using climate control to create drought and starvation. Global leaders help third world nations with GMO seeds, which are drought resistant but bad for health and the environment. Sickened by a toxic environment, people develop a plethora of disease and illness, and the solution is assisted suicide or mercy killing. At risk are sick children, the elderly, disabled vets, and the mentally challenged. Social Security and Medicare are currently under attack due to fiscal mismanagement. Assisted suicide is an effective method to weeding out the disabled and reducing dependency on Social Security and Medicare.

(4) Amoral, Perilous Times, Lawlessness

Webster's Dictionary defines **amoral** as "those without moral conviction." These people may not be able to distinguish between right and wrong. They are unable to show mercy or feel compassion for another's suffering. In many situations, these individuals have been desensitized through experiences within their environment or ideologies, such as the German citizenry allowed for the slaughter of millions of people during the Holocaust. Amorality has a sexual component, which encompasses the practice of abortion, homosexuality, pedophilia, incest, and sex with animals. God gave man a moral compass. The Bible tells us some have lost their moral compass and have come to possess a seared conscience. For example, an amoral person could rape a three-year-old, cut off their limbs, and have no emotional reaction or guilt. In societies throughout the world, people observe as a baby is dismembered and killed during an abortion procedure. These two examples demonstrate how humans have lost their ability to discern between right and wrong.

In the scriptures, the writer has defined the character of amoral, apathetic, seared-conscience people:

> *This know that in the last days* ***perilous times*** *shall come for men will be lovers of themselves, covetous, boastful, proud, blasphemers, disobedient to parents, unthankful, unholy, without natural affection, trucebreakers, false accusers, incontinent, fierce, despisers of those that are good, traitors, heady, high minded, lovers of pleasure more than lovers of God, having a form of godliness but denying the power thereof … divers lust,. . . ever learning but never coming into the knowledge of the truth …* (2 Timothy 3:1–9)

Deluded and blind to the wiles of Satan, they are unable to realize their fallen nature.

By highlighting characteristics of the amoral nature, we can begin to see the state of unrighteousness. Because of these things, sinners are given over to a reprobate mind and a seared conscience.

- Lovers of themselves (selfish)
- Lovers of pleasure more than lovers of God (lustful)
- Form of godliness but denying God
- Always learning but never coming into the knowledge of truth
- Blasphemers
- Disobedient
- Ungrateful
- No empathy
- Truce breakers
- False accusers, liars
- Incontinent (lack discipline)
- Fierce despisers of those that are good
- Corrupt minds, reprobate
- Traitors

> *God gave them up to uncleanness through the lusts of their own hearts to dishonor their own bodies between themselves who changed the truth of God into a lie and worshipped and served the creature more than the Creator … God gave them up unto vile affections for even their women did change the natural use into that which is against nature and likewise also the men, leaving the natural use of the woman burned in their lust one toward another, men with men working that which is unseemly and receiving in themselves that recompense of their error which was meet and even as they did not like to retain God in their knowledge, God gave them over to a reprobate mind to do those things which are not convenient …* (Romans 1:24)

Unrighteous	Backbiters	Malicious
Haters of God	Implacable	Deceitful
Despiteful	Unmerciful	Full of envy
Fornicators	Gossipers	Murderers
Wicked	Proud, high-minded	Boasters
Covetousness	Inventors of evil things	Covenant breakers
Disobedient to parents	Lack natural affection	

In these perilous times, there will be an increase of unprecedented wickedness and **lawlessness** perpetrated by individuals and government leaders. Any nation whose foundation is built on ungodliness, immorality, and corruption will crumble. These traits target godly values and family. The young nation of America is an archetype of ancient spiritual Babylon, and she is the great harlot who sits on many waters that will be destroyed in one hour, finally reaping the full wrath of God.

The downfall of America began by its declining respect for God and making a mockery of traditional values. We know this to be true based on the actions of heads of government to lone wolfs. America's moral foundation is rotting away. The citizens elected an amoral, ungodly president, and its administration over the past eight years has worked to do away with the last vestiges of morality. America has become the leader of tolerance for all things ungodly. The Obama administration has created a Christian subculture within society. Dissidents against the practice of homosexuality and abortion are vilified, labeled as intolerant, bigots, and haters.

Homosexuality

Under the Obama administration, sexual immorality is now the pinnacle of American society. God ordained sexual relations between man and woman as the natural way for procreation. In June of 2015, the highest court in the land upstaged God and determined that traditional marriage between man and woman is unconstitutional. It ruled that same-sex couples have the right to marry. Supreme Court Justices who were opposed said, "The proponents 5 to 4 were not in the positon to hijack the State's authority to regulate marriage."

The federal government moved quickly to protect the civil rights of the LGBT community at the expense of those who believe in traditional values as set forth by God. The floodgates were opened as a perverse sexual revolution flooded the nation. "Coming out" was celebrated with parades and encouraged others to follow suit.

John Henry Westen, editor of *Life Site News*, May 2016, in several of his speeches sums up the dire situation we are facing as Christians in an immoral society. Under the guise of fighting homophobia, the government employs legislation for the LGBT community to protect them from discrimination. The law is enforced by mandating sex education be taught for elementary children to indoctrinate them in favor of homosexuality and transgender identification lifestyles. The ideology of the LGBT community is imposed on all.

Speaking out one's beliefs may be classified as hate speech and criminalized. This administration will strong-arm the opposition into accepting an ungodly agenda. For instance, Attorney General Eric Holder blatantly overruled Utah's Supreme Court ban on same-sex marriage, stating the DOJ would take matters into its own hands. He offered more than a thousand federal benefits to couples who under state law were not even legally married. Holder said, "I am confirming today that for purposes of federal law, these partnerships will be recognized as lawful and considered eligible for all relevant federal benefits on the same terms as other same-sex marriages." Same-sex unions are reaching epidemic levels. For instance, in Utah, 905 same-sex couples applied for licenses in one day. This is reflective across the nation as support for same-sex unions increase.

There has been some outcry worldwide against homosexuality. Nigeria passed a law that those practicing homosexuality will be imprisoned. Obama threatened to withhold aid to Nigeria because of their position. The Mormon church in Utah said they will not perform same-sex marriage or allow their facilities to be used for such. Christian businesses who take a stand against same-sex marriage are demonized, penalized, and shut down. Russia has taken a stand against homosexuality by disallowing public display, advertising, or rallies. Some Islamic sects will kill homosexuals.

Wesleyan University, formerly a Christian college, has gone to the dark side by offering open housing to alternative sexualities—such as flexural, asexual, polyamorous, bondage, sadism, masochism, LBGT, transsexual, queer. As stated, there is no end to immorality.

Transsexuals

Gaining the right to same-sex marriage, many thought this would appease the LGBT movement, but then they wanted to show tolerance to transsexuals. The federal government is forcing state facilities and public schools to allow males dressed as women to use the female public toilets or school locker rooms. Transsexuality is a psychological identification disorder. The government and other groups will punish anyone offering counseling toward a normal lifestyle because all of "society must not only tolerate but positively accept any kind of sexual orientation. The acceptance of transgenderism proposes that a person's sex is not biologically determined but that it was historically, socially constructed and that individuals should have the choice to determine their own sex or gender. It is a belief system that denies bodily reality and forbids even the consideration of the risk factors associated with abnormal sexual activity" (*Life Site News*, Gabriele Kuby, John Henry Westen).

The Obama administration pushes for radical social policy as evidenced in a position taken by an Oregon judge's ruling in favor of a man to claim his sexual identification as **non-binary.** A Georgia lawyer for the ACLU resigned after her daughters were in the women's bathroom and three transsexual males came into the restroom. These are just two complaints from a growing concern over this insanity.

Following the transsexual push will be the transspecies agenda, meaning people who believe they are animals trapped in a human body. Reported on *Life Site News*, February 1, 2016, a twenty-year-old female called Nano says she is a cat trapped in a human body: "Because of a genetic defect, I am a cat trapped in a human body." Nano wears cat ears and tail, puts on pink paws, speaks in meows, hisses at dogs, hates water, has a good sense of smell, sees in the dark, and hunts mice. YouTube had 1.3 million hits.

Pedophilia

As mentioned, immorality has a sexual component that not only embraces homosexuality but goes beyond that to push for the acceptance of sex with children. Pedophilia will become commonplace. Pedophilia is practiced by people in the highest levels of society, including politicians and royalty. It is predominate in the clergy in Protestant denominations, Catholicism, Mormonism, and Islam. Regardless of their station in life, these diabolical scum prey upon children for the purpose of sexual exploitation, torture, and murder. Society is being desensitized to female teachers who had sex with juveniles, and male teachers seduce and rape minor girls. Children are abducted, kept in captivity for years, raped, and in many instances, killed. Parents are sexually abusing their children. (Missingkids.com reports over eight hundred thousand children are abducted globally each year.)

Fritz Springmeler and David Icke report on global pedophile rings. Their investigation helped to expose criminals such as Jimmy Savile, charged with child sexual abuse. He is associated with BBC and Radio Luxembourg, where he gained access to children through youth programs. He is a regular visitor at Buckingham Palace, Kensington Palace, where Diane and Charles lived and High Grove Estate popular with Prince Charles. Savile got children from orphanages, foster homes, or other children organizations. He was the supplier of children for the perverted. Sian Griffith exposed this criminal activity in the United Kingdom and United States by videotaping the rape of children.

Report by the *Associated Press*—the most recent case in the United States is Jerry Sandusky, Penn State coach. He openly perpetrated sexual crimes against children, and he was protected. Several other Philadelphia pedophiles that got caught were Phil Foglietta and Lawrence Ward, Wharton School professor, now incarcerated.

Australia investigators were looking into churches, state care facilities, schools, children service agencies, and the police hindered the investigation by covering up crimes in the church.

DYN Corporation works to recruit, train, and deploy civilians to work as peacekeepers in eleven countries. They were engaged in child sex. Ben Johnson and Kathryn Bolkovac were fired for trying to stop criminal activity against children. DYN held boy play parties in Afghanistan. US taxpayers fund this corporation. Donald Rumsfeld was trying to explain why the United States support this corrupt corporation. One soldier in Afghanistan was dishonorably discharged for intervening in the rape of a male child. ACLJ took his case, and he was reinstated.

Another sexual component is bestiality. This behavior is pushing its way to the forefront as sex with animals is normalized. Canada, 2016, rules people can have sex with animals. Rich people leave their pets millions of dollars and would not give a dollar to a beggar. Some people care about their animals more than people and want to marry them. Soon they will push for the legalization of marriage to animals. Wildlife preserves are good, and legislation to protect the ball eagle and her eggs is good. Killing animals for fur or ivory is not good. In this picture, animal rights come before the human baby's right to life. All things that are wrong will be right.

Media Bias

The mainstream news media is silent on issues of morality and godliness but are ready to demonize Christians who oppose same-sex marriage, homosexuality, and abortion. As atheists work to remove religious artifacts from public spaces, there is no outcry from the liberal media. *Point of View*, Kirby Anderson, February 22, 2013, reports that the National Religious Broadcasters have been monitoring the censorship of religion on the news media platforms through their John Milton Project for Religious Free Speech. "The free speech liberty of citizens who use the Internet is being threatened. Internet providers such as Apple, Google, YouTube and Facebook have been censoring Christian content." Pastor Chuck Colson who upholds the biblical perspective on life and marriage said Apple pulled their iPhone app for the Manhattan Declaration, caving into pressure from homosexual groups. Lila Rose posted her investigative reports on Planned Parenthood, and it was pulled from YouTube. Facebook pulled a page by former governor Mike Huckabee that called for a Chick-fil-A appreciation day.

The US government is pushing for international control of the Internet, which allows for greater spying and censorship.

Followers of Satan

An Associated Press article by Juan A. Lozano, February 11, 2014, tells of two teenage boys, ages sixteen and seventeen, in Houston who raped and killed fifteen-year-old Corriann Cervantes as a satanic ritual to sell their souls to the devil. They hit her in the head with a toilet tank top, stabbed her in the face with a screw driver, and carved an upside down crucifix on her stomach.

Satanists are erecting statues of Satan throughout the United States. In 2016, we hear they want to introduce a satanic after-school club in elementary schools. Evil is a shroud over a corrupt nation. Conspiracy theorists believe there is a connection between the Sandy Hook School shooting and Aurora movie theater shooting. Both assailants where seeing psychiatrists and taking prescribed drugs. Father of Sandy Hook school shooter was going to testify on Libor scam trials, and the father of Aurora shooting was also to testify on Libor scam. CNBC exec published story on $43 billion banks lawsuit, and his children were killed by nanny. In the *Batman* movie, both Aurora and Sandy Hook were referenced in the movie. Actor puts finger on Sandy Hook and says, "There are no coincidences." A new movie called the *Rise of the Guardians*, the sandman's name is Sandy, who influences children's dreams. Hurricane Sandy happened October 29; *Batman* movie played on November 21. Sandy Hook shootings occurred December 12, 2014. In San Antonio, Texas, December 17, 2012, a shooting near the Santikos Mayan 14 movie theater showing the *Hobbit* where the shooter wanted to shoot his girlfriend who worked at restaurant near the movie. She wasn't there, so he shot and wounded two people and gun-jammed. He was shot by an off-duty sheriff.

United States of America is in its final decline. Rev. Franklin Graham said, "Unless America repents as a nation, God is going to bring quick and swift judgment." What does this judgment entail when the hedge of protection is lifted? Hordes from hell will impact mankind. People have lost their ability of self-discipline; anything goes. There already is an increase in lawlessness and criminal acts. Civil unrest is witnessed in various states. The US economy is on the brink of collapse. Threats from hostile nations and terrorist groups will come to fruition. America will be the recipient of greater natural and man-made disasters. Pestilence, disease, toxic food, water, and environment are killing all living things.

(5) Technological Advancements

Before we explore the scientific world of weird and their ongoing plans for corrupting the natural order of things, let us take to heart and understand the report of the Lord.

> *The wisdom of this world is foolishness with God, for it is written, he takes the wise in their own craftiness, he knows the thoughts of the wise that they are vain, therefore, let no man glory in men.* (1 Corinthians 3:19)
>
> *It is written, God will destroy the wisdom of the wise and bring to nothing the understanding of the prudent.* (1 Corinthians 1:19)
>
> *Judge nothing before the time until Jesus comes who will bring to light the hidden things of darkness and will expose the counsels of their hearts.* (1 Corinthians 4:5)

As we bring to the forefront some extraordinary developments in the world of transhumanism, singularity, artificial intelligence, biometrics now using acronym GRINS (genetics, robotics, intelligence, nanotech, synthetic)—keep in mind that these developments are sensationalized and promoted to the world as an improvement of God's creation. The trend of technological advancements will move beyond the limits of ethics because the imagination of man is continually wicked. Always keep in mind that God is still in charge, and he will expose the hidden things.

Mankind outgrew the need for hunters and gathers by improving upon agriculture methods that were completely transformed by the industrial era, which gave way to the technological era. In the world, Japheth descendants excelled at the expense of life in all its forms and would lead the way for ungodly technological advances discussed herein. Man would not be satisfied with discovering a cure for cancer but would move on to attain godhood and immortality.

During the twentieth century, technological advancements made by German scientists were exported to the United States, Europe, and Australia after World War II. It is well documented that under Hitler's regime, aviation was advanced to another level. Mankind learned to develop weapons of mass destruction, such as the atom bomb. Biological and chemical weapons were developed, and delivery systems were enhanced. The Germans conducted heinous experiments on humans, and the records of these experiments has been guarded but employed. Germany was obsessed with cloning and the mingling of various species as well as mind control and the use of hallucinogenic agents.

Within the past hundred years, technological and scientific advancement would increase exponentially. Twentieth-century technologies rolled over into the twenty-first century. Scientists developed more effective delivery systems for dispensing airborne chemicals using drone vehicles. Boeing engineers did a test flight in Oregon, June 2012, of the Scaneagle drone, which performed like a swarm of insects communicating with each other. The US Navy has been working on their swarm technology, using drones that work together, communicating with each other, surrounding environment like a mobile network of connected robots and coordinating attack. The book of Revelation predicts that during the tribulation period, a swarm of machine-like insects will sting people; the pain will be great; and they will wish for death.

Death by environment is a scheme to recreate certain conditions that can cause an epidemic. For instance, during the time of the Black Death plague a few hundred years ago, severe drought conditions created an environment for rats bitten by fleas to transmit bacteria to humans. Millions died in Europe and other regions. Government programs such as HAARP have mastered creating drought conditions. The Spanish inquisition introduced smallpox throughout North and South America, and millions died. The AIDS virus was created to target Africa, and millions worldwide have died. Never learning from the past, scientists in their covert labs continue to repeat the horrors that unleash these diseases upon the public. Of course, the early invention of vaccines and antibiotics were helpful in some situations; but these same vaccinations were weaponized to deliver lethal toxins into unsuspecting victims, causing cancer, neurological problems, birth deformities, autism, and death. Big pharma calls for vaccinations for everything under the sun. Scientists continue to work feverishly in Frankenstein labs to improve upon viruses, bacteria, toxic combinations, or to create something new that would release a pandemic. Unregulated research programs and experiments are conducted 24-7 to gain an edge on biological or chemical warfare before the competition. This dangerous stuff ends up in the hands of terrorist or rogue governments.

Illegal manufacturing of drugs—such as crack, meth, cocaine, heroin—created in basements, warehouses or garages is now a $350-billion industry responsible for millions of deaths. Statistics reveal the drug trade comes by way of Hawaii, Colombia, Dominican Republic, Mexico. New York is a drug haven for heroin plus. Hawaii has a high number of drug users and is a land of nature worship. Every inner city in the United States is plagued by drug activity. Homosexuals use meth because it gives them a sexual high. Inhibitions have consequences, such as AIDS or other STD. Legal pharmaceutical companies produce drugs for everything imaginable, which also have dire side effects and death.

Scientists are working to develop invisibility. The technology to see through objects has been achieved. The TV series *The Dome* portrayed a city encased in a dome created by advanced technology. In the real world, plasma globes or domes do exist. MI 6 saw a dome over Russia to protect it from gamma rays. Laser or scalar technology is being perfected as a weapon.

Quantum and nanotechnology have excelled in all scientific disciplines. Nanotechnology is being researched by China, Russia, Brazil, United States, and others. South Korea is spending $860 million to research nanomemory device, nanomedical diagnosis, and nanostructured solar cells. Biological warfare is advancing to attack the immune system to disrupt normal body functions (similar to organs dissolving). Psychoenergy can be directed to cause people to kill themselves or others. These are just a few areas of research.

Moving on from drugs, chemical warfare, pandemics, mankind has entered an age of technology that crosses a threshold of morality and ethics. Perhaps delving into the paranormal, mind control, remote viewing is the bridge that leads to the rising of technology not limited in its scope or imagination. What monsters will come forth from genetic enhancement, cloning, quantum physics, and artificial intelligence? In the analysis of these subjects, we will not sensationalize the practice or present it as Hollywood sci-fi. For instance, some reporters will say that genetic engineering will change the human race, and we will no longer be humans. We believe many people will reject and fight against this ungodliness, and God will intervene before the whole of the human race becomes hybrids of various sorts.

Transhumanism

This catchy title involves research that seeks to transform humanity by combining technology, science, and philosophy, fast-forwarding mankind into the age of the hybrids. To avoid public dissention, a propaganda campaign is introduced to promote this ungodly technology as a wonderful way to cure diseases, eliminate aging, and enhance human potential in all areas. Some areas of research are not public knowledge. Case in point, Planned Parenthood provides an endless supply of human tissue from aborted babies. Media propaganda influences people to believe that abortion is acceptable because it is health care for women. The availability of human and animal DNA is essential in advancing their goals to merge or mingle carbon-based forms.

One area of research involves genetic engineering of humans. This gene-editing technology is called CRISPR (Clustered Regularly Interspaced Short Palindromic Repeats), which has the ability to sequence DNA then alter or modify the DNA by rewriting the genetic code.

Further experiments involve splicing or intermingling of genes, allowing for the transfer of genes between species. This includes plant, animal, and human DNA. The practice of genetically modifying vegetation is to alter plants for higher yield and resistance to pestilence. These crops are referred to as GMOs. Animal experiments have been ongoing for years. An animal embryo is injected with human DNA. After the embryo's become viable, their development is observed. In some instances, it can be determined that the forming embryo may appear as a chimera, something that looks part human and part animal. Many reasons are given for this ungodly research—for instance, to enhance animal intelligence, to give humans animal abilities or to extract the animal DNA, to mix with viruses to create vaccines. Scientists also hope to grow organs in animals to be used for human transplants. The end goal of transhumanism is to enhance human ability as in a superhuman or human cyborg being stronger, highly intelligent, disease free, and able to exist for periods without food, water, or sleep—the creators' dream of the newly enhanced body being able to survive the collapse of civilization and protect itself against biological or viral attacks. This also leads into artificial intelligence (AI) research.

Following are comments made by transhumanism and AI advocates:

Arizona State University, September 24, 2014, interview with Michael Crow, president of AZU and J. Craig Venter, biologist and entrepreneur:

> Venter created the first synthetic life form in 2010. This was accomplished by changing or altering human DNA and replacing it with digital DNA. They studied the sequencing of thousands of human genomes and from this data, know precisely what is nature and what is nurture. It will give

> understanding into longevity, disease and race. Will it close the gap between natural science and design science? It will be overwhelmingly tempting for humanity to refrain from using this knowledge to modify our species.

Ted Chu, professor of economics at New York University in Abu Dhabi and former chief economist for General Motors argues:

> Posthumanity is a logical and necessary evolutionary next step for humanity and we need a new heroic cosmic faith for the post human era. The ultimate meaning of our lives rests not in our personal happiness but in our contribution to cosmic evolution a process that transcends the human and yet is integral to who and what we are in the universe.

Chu believes that a new wave of sentient beings, artificial intelligences, and synthetic life forms should be created.

Dr. Peter Diamandis, founder of Singularity University and the X-prize, spoke at *The World in 2050 Conference*, February 2014, saying,

> The world is changing year by year and because of the fast rate of change, companies and individuals should not have a local and linear way of thinking toward the future. The theme is that in ten years or so, robots will replace humans. Robots can think better than humans, translate eighty-five languages, and their intervention will be in every aspect of life, and that time is now.

The TV show *Almost Human* features humanoid robot police officers, which would be a fulfillment of Diamandis's dream.

A report in 2005 said Dr. Ronald Evans, scientist on hormones at Salk Institute of Biological Studies in La Jolla, California, did gene modification research on mice, developing a slow twitch muscle fiber, the type associated with strong cardiovascular muscle with the ability to boost endurance, and no matter what the mice ate, they did not gain weight. Perhaps this will surpass steroid use to boost strength and endurance. Technology is advancing rapidly, and to what end? There will be consequences for corrupting God's creation. In the movie *I Am Legion*, the scientists created a virus that wiped out the majority of people. Those left became mutated zombies.

Warnings against Genetic Manipulation

A documentary titled *Inhuman*, product of Jeremiah Films in association with Tom Horn, released in 2015, addressed the transhumanism agenda. Another one of their productions is titled *Transhumanism: Recreating Humanity* and provides a deeper look into the scientific community gone rogue. It is a documentary that reveals the technological advances that empower governments to create a new, genetically modified, computer-enhanced super soldier. Billions have been spent to develop a new breed of warriors not quite human. Hollywood presents these scenarios as entertainment; however, there is a strong element of truth weaved throughout their stories (*Inhuman* excerpts Sky Watch TV online, August 2015).

July 8, 2015, Dr. Bill Foster, PhD in science, addressed Congress in protest against "human genetic engineering in modifications made to the germ line will affect future humanity as cells from sperm, eggs, or embryo are used to evolve humanity into the next level toward transhumanism." After Forster's warning, scientists and ethicists referred to as the Hinxton Group as well as the Academy of Medical Science reported in favor of gene modification research. The consensus believed that genetically modified babies ... may become a norm and growing better animals, and humans will be unlike any of the versions God made.

US Government Deeply Involved in Experiments

> The Obama Administration is proposing tax funds for research to create half animal, half human being for experimentation. The National Institute of Health announced a proposed change in the ethical limits of federally funded research allowing animals/human cross species called chimera research. (Mark Hodges, *Life Site News*, August 9, 2016)

The US military, scientists, and technologists began covert experiments in the 1940s. At the end of World War II, German scientists were placed in strategic government positions. For instance, Walter Von Broun, a German, was appointed to head up NASA. Other Germans headed up various departments for development and research.

DARPA, Defense Advanced Research Projects Agency, operated by Pentagon, is working on a project to genetically modify humans to create "super soldiers." The characteristics of a super soldier would be like the Alphas, mutants, superheroes. They would be faster, forego food and sleep for days, regrow lost limbs (bionic man), stronger (using exoskeletons like transformers), and be telepathic (using helmets to communicate). The Germans may have achieved some success in creating a superman.

DARPA's, Deep Sea Sleepers', project is to deploy deep-ocean nodes into certain areas years in advance, also called robots or submersible pods, to be used for surveillance and exploration. When the command comes, they could launch to the surface and release waterborne or airborne unmanned systems to disperse chemicals to contaminate people, ecosystems, or atmospheric conditions. The program is called Upward Falling Payload (UFP). DARPA gave an overview to its commanders, January 25, 2013, in Washington, DC. It has been discovered that the Germans were using underwater facilities in the region of the Antarctica to develop highly advanced craft that could be submerged and launched from underwater.

DARPA Pentagon projects four years in the making and desires to boost artificial intelligence systems by building machines that can teach themselves. These robots could evolve, using algorithms to probabilistic programming with the capability to view vast amounts of data and select the best. This reminds us of the movie *I Robot*.

Artificial Intelligence

This area of technology has to do with integrating human DNA with computer hardware and software to create a unit that goes beyond the level of human intelligence, having the ability think for itself to solve complex problems at super speeds, remember billions of computations, and the crowning achievement would be to improve upon its own capabilities. It is linked to singularity, or attaining a successful outcome toward combining artificial intelligence with biological entities to bring about digital surrogates of ourselves. These inhumane units are referred to as Artilects, or AIs.

Inventor Mark Saga developed a program called BabyX, which is a computer-driven simulation of how the human brain sends signals to a digital face that responds to commands, allowing the baby face to adapt, respond, smile, laugh, or cry to human interactions like a real baby. He took computational neuroscience models of how brain works and linked them to biomechanically models of human faces. His goal is to create a machine that thinks the same way as people; it learns, dreams, and adapts to its environment and develops a memory and personality as it grows up. The virtual baby can see because of the built-in camera and can hear sound through the computer system. That means almost giving it some sort of a digital life force or trying to put a soul into the machine (*The Blaze*, Elizabeth Kreft, August 27, 2014). We found this similar scenario on the TV program *Extant*, wherein a robot child is created and programed to learn, develop, express emotions, make decisions, and is treated like a family member. The show also has a theme of an alien entity impregnating a human woman—the intermingling of two species resulting in a superior being.

Singularity

This area of technology brings together the successful accomplishments of transhumanism and artificial intelligence. The new artificial life forms may replace carbon-based, useless humans. These artificial life forms will have the capacity of simulating life, evolving beyond man's knowledge of physics and math, rendering it obsolete and irrelevant. The AIs will be able to build other units greater than themselves. This level of intelligence introduces the singularity hypothesis.

BGI is a Chinese biotech giant. The firm purchased Bay Area Juggernaut Compete Genomics for $117 million in 2012. BGI owns 156 DNA sequences and produces 10 to 20 percent of the world's genetic information. They are currently investigating the genetics of genius. The TV series *Touch* identifies ten savants in the world. Eight had been killed by a deranged zealot doing the will of god. The two remaining genius fight to survive those who wish to use them as lab experiments and to dodge being killed by the hunter.

Robotics

Industrial robots have been around for decades. The modernization of manufacturing practices using a robotic arm replaced the need for human operators. Modern robotics incorporate artificial intelligence, wherein the bionic limb is capable of receiving computer-generated messages from its human counterpart. The realm of robotics is boundless. Driverless vehicles are programmed to carry out their basic functions and to learn from their environment to improve upon its functions.

University of Zurick created Roboy as a tendon-driven robot modeled on human beings. It will be a service robot and share living space. Hopefully, it will be safe and user-friendly. China and Japan are both on the cutting edge of robotics. In the United States, we have introduced the robot vacuum cleaner; but in the Asian countries, they have personal robots that are purchased by individuals to be used for services, including sex.

University of Colorado, Boulder, Professor Nikolaus Correll developed a robotic building block to reproduce complex systems using a swarm of twenty robots, Ping-Pong-size balls called droplets. When they swarm together, they can form a liquid that thinks like nanotheory; together they could contain an oil spill or self-assemble into a piece of hardware after being launched into space.

University of Ganz Artificial Life Lab, Austria, developed robotic drones that operate underwater given the name CoCoRo (Skywatch, October 22, 2015).

Some people have expressed concern about the safety of robots and raise questions if they pose a threat to humankind. Recently, 2014, Angela Kane, United Nations representative on universal weapons and disarmament told Britain's *Telegraph* newspaper that she is concerned about killer robots.

> Robots that can be programed to fire on anyone without being directly controlled by a human and may not be able to distinguish some realities

> on a battlefield should be outlawed and banned. Governments involved in enhancing this technology need to be more transparent about their current programs. Warfare is becoming automated as in pilotless drones and increase risk of citizen casualties.

MAAR-system (The Modular Advanced Armed Robotic Systems), a creation of QinetiQ North America, is one such robot—unmanned ground vehicle that is powerful, modular, and combat ready.

Military weapons, such as drones and hybrids, are controlled by a human, but they are being programmed to function on their own. Major General Mark Milley, Army chief of staff, spoke at Norwich University, ROTC, meeting. He said, "2016 is more complex than previous wars. You will be dealing with hybrid armies and little green men."

Lt. Col. Robert MacGinnis, author of *Never Submit*, said, "Hybrids, drones, private contractors, and little green men from the United Nations or Russia wearing masks and green uniforms but not obvious as military personnel."

Biometrics

This area of research deals with identifying people using fingerprint, palm prints, iris and retinal scans, facial recognition, vein patterns, and DNA. In the not-too-distant past, computers were very large machines housed in air-conditioned rooms. Later the personal computer sat on a desk. Modern laptops are portable, and computers are now incorporated into our iPhones. One day the computer will be very small and implantable.

Biometrics also deals with tracking or monitoring devices to be implanted or tattooed in or on people. Proteus Digital Health Company announces their start-up of ingestible ID chips production factory is located in the United Kingdom. The creation of "smart pills" is supported by Google Advanced Technology and Products Group, Eastern Academic Health Science Network, Northern Health Science Alliance, and Oxford University and its hospitals.

Tech companies are designing wearable computer that adheres to the skin like temporary tattoos or attach to the body like a Band-Aid. University of Tokyo has developed e-skin; it is an electronic skin that sits on top of real skin. It looks like a flexible and stretchable sheet of plastic wrap yet contains data-related sensors. In our chapter 19, we discuss the Mark of the Beast. When the time comes for all to take the mark, millions will do so willingly.

There will be some obvious benefits for interfacing computers with human brains, such as it would be beneficial to a quadriplegic who had no movement below the neck. The procedure to connect the computer to the brain's neuronal receptors, the brain could interpret the commands and translate signals to a robotic arm.

Governments around the world are happy to fund biometric development for the purpose of identification and tracking. The United States spends $1 billion to upgrade its existing criminal database. The public is led to believe these biometric security measures are for the safety of students on college campus or elementary schools. United States schools began using a GPS-tracking device worn external but later could be replaced by an implantable chip. The college student is informed that this is a secure means to conduct transactions and banking. Students are gradually becoming comfortable with this technology as iPhone app can scan fingerprints.

Another example, Saint Mary's School Ascot, in Berkshire, England, is one of 3,500 schools using biometric scanning of the finger as a security precaution for its students (*The Conversation*, January 6, 2016).

In 2012, Saudi Arabia was planning to chip all their women as a method of tracking.

The Vatican clergy and employees may be issued an ID card with RFID chip. Financial institutions are issuing bank cards with RFID chips.

Through these various devices, collected data is being stored in a global database. One such place is located in Geneva, Switzerland. Accenture Corporation has contracts with eighty-nine Fortune 500 companies to set up data collection and security systems to replace cards and PIN numbers. They gross around $32 billion a year.

A new technology called 3-D printing is able to create hybrid organs using other-than-ink compounds. They are adding human DNA to these materials that can be transplanted into humans to replace some organs. Rhiannon William, reporting on *The Telegraph* website, February 11, 2014, said,

> 3-D printed human tissue is created by using modified printer cartridges and extracted cells, sourced from patient biopsies with respect to examining cancer cells or stem cells. They are grown using standard techniques and cultured in a growth medium in dishes, allowing them to multiply. Once enough cells have grown, they are collected and formed into spheroids or other shapes and loaded into a cartridge to create bio ink. The bio ink is loaded into a NovoGen MMX printer along with a cartridge of hydrogel, a synthetic matrix effectively used as a scaffolding for building 3-D layers of cells. The printer prints a layer of the water-based gel, followed by a layer of bio ink cells and so on. The layered cells naturally fuse together as the layers are built upon. Once the desired amount of layers is printed, the printed tissue is left to mature and grow as a structure, during which time the hydrogel is removed. Ethical and moral concerns have been raised over the quality of the organs, who controls the right to produce them, and will this ability

further blur the line between man and machine, giving us the right to play God on an unprecedented scale.

Harnessing the Environment

Harnessing the environment will disrupt the natural rhythm of the planet. Nicholas Tesla tapped into the earth's energy and discovered how to harness this energy source in the 1900s. After Tesla's death, the US government confiscated his research and continued to develop his theories. Scientists discovered how to concentrate energy, and the technology became known as electromagnetic pulse, EMP. They found the EMP could be used as a weapon. The effects of an EMP attack could create massive blackouts, causing disruption of the power grids supplying electric to banks, ATM, gas pumps, grocery stores, computers, and homes. Billionaire Paul Singer of Elliott Management warned his investors of the real possibility of an EMP strike (CNBC, July 29, 2014, Lawrence Delevingne).

Former Secretary of Defense William Cohen under Clinton, 1997, said EMP technology using the caloric energy from the earth concentrated through scalar transmitters could alter climate, cause volcanoes, earthquakes, and can target underground bunkers. Cohen spoke at the conference on terrorism, 1997, *Weapons of Mass Destruction and US Strategy*, held at the Georgia Center in Athens. He discussed the development of weather-related weaponry using techniques to create weather events to support military operations. Cohen said, "Labs were working to develop pathogens that are ethnic specific to eliminate persons of a particular ethnicity; other labs were designing insects that can destroy specific crops, while other labs were focused on ecotype terrorism in that they could alter climate, set off earthquakes, volcanoes remotely using electromagnetic waves (EMP)."

Russia in 1985 developed scalar technology by tapping into the core of the earth to extract iron and nickel and convert it to caloric energy. Some reports say scalar technology has been used to cause earthquakes around the world. They claim a scalar attack at Yellowstone's caldera would set off the magma, causing a volcano. If Yellowstone blows, it will affect the planet, spewing ash clouds, a nuclear winter, blocking the sun and creating an ice age. Some believe the *Challenger* space shuttle was destroyed in 1986 by scalar waves. For clarification, death ray, lasers, EMP, and scalar energy share a common technology. Following, we discuss the government's use of this technology in their HAARP project.

HAARP, High-Frequency Active Auroral Progam

The HAARP project has an impact on weather. Unusual weather phenomena is now called global warming and climate change. HAARP is a joint effort with the US Air Force, Navy, DARPA, and University of Alaska. At one HAARP location, there are 180 antennas covering a span of thirty-three acres with the ability to direct high-frequency radio waves into the ionosphere. These radio waves cause birds to drop dead out of the sky in the areas of transmission. HAARP can disrupt communications over a large portion of the earth, according to Dr. Bermard Eastlund, physicist. One purpose is to study ionospheric impact on weather conditions. It has been reported that it has the capability of creating lightning storms, tornadoes, and earthquakes. Experts say on an average, there should be one 8- or 9-level quake every five hundred years. Seismic monitors reveal, since 2004, there have been eight worldwide. Drought conditions can be simulated, and during 2012, parts of America experienced severe drought levels. Government held back financial aid to farmers losing crops due to drought. United States had no problem giving one billion to Egypt while denying aid to farmers.

Other HAARP locations are in the China, Russia, United Kingdom, Norway, Australia.

The Weather Space organization on May 30, 2013, reported the government was testing tornado experiment on Oklahoma this date and that the frequencies had been turned up to the highest levels and people needed to be aware. Several cities in Oklahoma were devastated by tornados.

When strange and extra-destructive events like mega typhoons hit the Philippines, Katrina in New Orleans, or Hurricane Sandy in New York, curious minds wonder if these are natural or man-made systems. Earth's ecosystem was put in place by God to sustain all life. Man has created or caused ecological disasters—such as, oil spills, radiation leaks, developing and releasing virus and bacteria to our detriment. Experiments involving the release of chemicals in the upper atmosphere may be contributing to the depletion of the ozone layer, which would increase the strength of the sun's rays entering earth's atmosphere.

Geoengineering

Geoengineering is a term that applies to a field of research that conducts experiments to modify or manipulate weather and climate conditions. These experiments could change rainfall patterns, causing droughts and famine, affecting billions of people. Several examples are shading the earth from the sun or soaking up carbon dioxide and releasing aerosol sulfuric particles that will mimic the cooling effect of volcanoes and reduce carbon emissions seen as a solution to global warming. "Despite the risk of catastrophic side effects from geoengineering the study authors believe that research should continue just in case runaway warming leaves no other options" (Piers Forster, Professor at Leeds University in Eco-Business, November 2014). Note—credible scientific research indicates the planet is not warming.

As early as 1947, various governments were involved in conducting test to modify hurricanes. Some of this technology may have been garnered from German scientists after World

War II. General Electric was seeding eye wall of hurricanes by dropping dry ice, causing it to strengthen and change directions. This was Project Cirris, including Army, Navy, and Air Force intelligence.

Witnesses have seen unmarked aircraft at various locations some near Nellis AFB, Mancomp Complex, Tonopah, South Nevada; Dobbins AFB, Marietta, Georgia; Tinker AFB accommodated 30 KC 135 planes; George AFB, Mojave Desert; McGuire AFB, New Jersey.

A report provided by Zach Miller, July 10, 2013, on *Natural News* website, defines this spraying as "geoengineering":

> Stratospheric aerosol geoengineering is a climate modification program being conducted by major world powers. The program is executed by spraying microscopic toxic metal aerosol particles into the atmosphere from aircraft. This spraying occurs above all the continents and has the stated goal of weather control and slowing so called global warming. Aluminum and Barium used in the spray are toxic to living organisms and bioregions ... It also disturbs the hydrological cycle of the planet, shrinks the atmosphere, promotes the proliferation of fungi, drives species to extinction, fills the world's oceans with toxic particulate heavy metals which disturb aquatic ecosystems and destroys our planet's ozone layer, in other words, stratospheric geoengineering is destroying the planet as well as animal and human health.

Wendy Merrill, January 13, 2014, on *Natural News* site reports chemicals containing lithium according to officials is to study certain wind patterns. This chemical has been used in psychiatric and mood-stabilizing drugs for the treatment of schizophrenia and depression. Barium and aluminum particles have been analyzed in the atmosphere. Barium and aluminum, both silvery metals and volatile, must be kept in a controlled environment.

In Chino Valley, Arizona, residents Marie Snow and Cori Gunnels witnessed the flyover of C-130 military transport plane with two escort planes. Then falling from the sky were fifty- to sixty-feet-long gelatin-like clusters landing on fences and bushes. They decided to collect samples of the material. They contacted their local news KPHO/CBS to report the phenomena. The news group sent some of the material to Grand Canyon University Forensic Science Lab, who said it was only biodegradable gauze made of wheat and bacitracin used by cattle farmers. Not satisfied with this explanation, they contacted *IntelliHub* news, who told them to send samples to an independent test facility. They contacted Al DiCicco, involved in the documentary on bioweapons, *SHADE The Motion Picture*, and were also told to get an independent analysis. The test results confirmed the presence of aluminum, barium, and strontium found in compounds used for geoengineering.

Chemtrails Versus Contrails

Chemtrails are seen in the sky as unordinary clouds that linger for many hours. This is geoengineering, another method to disperse toxins upon the unsuspecting masses. These formations are made by airplanes releasing a crisscross pattern of chemicals. Pilots admit releasing their load in a grid formation and are told not to talk about it. The government says these are contrails from airplanes dumping jet fuel, which dissipates quickly, or they are seeding clouds for rain.

World Net Daily reported chemtrails have an adverse effect on people's health. After coming in contact with these particles, some people experience respiratory problems, pneumonia, intestinal distress, fatigue, dizziness, disorientation, headaches, arthritic symptoms, nosebleeds. In extreme cases, people have developed skin lesions called Morgellons disease. The medical profession has no treatment and dismisses cases as psychosomatic.

Michael J. Murphy, in his documentary film, *What in the World Are They Spraying?* Claims that long-lasting chemtrails in the sky are actually the result of secret government spray operations and are part of a geoengineering project, involving injecting large amounts of aluminum into the atmosphere to block the sun's rays and control climate change. According to neurosurgeon Russell L. Blaylock, the nanosized aluminum particles found in chemtrails are contributing to degenerative disease (Nilufer Atik, January 2015, *Billionaires Newswire*).

Contrails

Airplanes release around 570 tons of aviation fuel per year, according to EPA. The fallout contains high levels of lead, halogen, bromial, chlorine, and these toxic chemicals infect crops, water, air, humans, and animals. Unlike chemtrails, contrails evaporate within a short period of time.

Toxic Environment Kills Wildlife

The result of harnessing the environment creates a toxic environment, killing wildlife over the planet. Following is a partial report:

- United States and Mexico—millions of chickens were destroyed due to bird flu.
- Peru—dozens of sea lions, turtles, dolphins, sharks are dead onshore.
- Chile, Strait of Magellan—forty-five whales washed ashore; twenty died.
- US bee and butterfly colonies are dying off; beekeeper had four hundred hives and discovered the bees had disappeared.

- Brace Point, Seattle, 2013—thousands of sea stars die.
- Monterey Bay, California—hundreds of sea lions, pelicans, manatees, dolphins, whales anchovies are washing up onshore.
- Kentucky—five hundred thousand Asian carp dead in Lake Barkley dam.
- Minnesota—tens of thousands of walleye, bass, pike are dead in Grand Lake.
- New Jersey—massive fish die in Shark River.
- Gulf of Mexico—bottlenose dolphins and turtles are dying due to BP oil spill.
- Maryland—seven thousand Atlantic menhaden are dead in Baltimore Harbor.
- Vermont—thousands of alewives are dying annually in Lake Champlain.
- Singapore—160 tons of fish dead.
- Japan—thousands of dolphin killed by hunters.
- Chile—thousands of shrimp, crabs, whales, and squid washed onto shore.
- Lake Erie—thousands of dead fish for twenty-five miles.
- Brazil—five hundred dolphins dead.
- Wisconsin—thousands of hatching may flies caused a massive swarm of the insects that covered streets and building.
- Yellowstone River, August 2016, reported by Sky Watch TV—two hundred miles along river is covered with ten thousand dead fish.

Climate Change and Global Warming

In our discussion, we see how the conduct of man impacts our environment and quality of life.

Some scientists have manipulated data to make it appear the earth is warming. Other scientists provide data that show the earth is not warming. The global warming gurus such as Al Gore, the Vatican, United Nations, President Obama are putting the final touches on their sinister agenda to force people to accept climate change and their global warming mandates. Mother Nature is exalted as goddess; she must be protected from humans. The humans must be sacrificed. May 21, 2015, President Obama said "global warming is the cause of chaos worldwide, and it is the greatest security threat to the nation." There is a hidden agenda in that declaration. We speculate that the elites realize they have gone too far in creating man-made earthquakes, manipulating weather, other diabolical activities in the destruction of the earth, and something catastrophic is heading our way.

What does God declare? He reminds us that the weapons of our warfare are not carnal but mighty through God to the pulling down of strongholds, casting down imaginations and every high thing that exalts itself against the knowledge of God, and bringing into captivity every thought to the obedience of Christ (2 Corinthians 10:4–5). Foremost, true believers will be praying against all wickedness. We trust in God to destroy the strongholds of Satan and to destroy the scientific imaginations that have exalted itself against the wisdom and knowledge of God. Yes, man may plan, but God can destroy those plans.

(6) Strong Delusion

> *Because they received not the love of the truth, that they might be saved and for this cause God will send them* ***strong delusion*** *that they should believe a lie that they all might be damned who believed not the truth but had pleasure in unrighteousness.* (2 Thessalonians 2:10–12)

In this section, we attempt to disclose what the "strong delusion" is. Apostasy is the turning away from God's truth. Absence of God and his truth creates a void, which will be filled with deception. Jesus has told us to be aware of false prophets bringing damnable heresy or deception. Once the mind is deceived, mankind will embrace strong delusions.

> *Even him, whose coming is after the working of Satan with all* ***power and signs and lying wonder,*** *and with all deceivableness of unrighteousness in them that perish because they received not the love of the truth that they might be saved.* (2 Thessalonians 2:9)

This passage is telling us that the Antichrist and false prophet will be empowered by Satan to perform signs and lying wonders, deceiving the unrighteous so they will reject truth, believe a strong delusion, and perish. This secular generation could care less about salvation.

We consider the state of humankind sixteen years into the twenty-first century. What is evidently clear is that evil is increasing and people have rejected the truth of God, believing Satan's deception and lies. In the past, followers of Satan—witches, vampires, and other ungodly groups—did practice their craft in secret. However, in modern times, the tolerance agenda has emboldened them to come out unashamed; and in full force, they are in our face. Jennifer Leclaire, *Watchman on the Wall*, December 16, 2013, shares in her article, "Satanist Demand Equal Time with Jesus as Antichrist Spirits Rise," she gave a factual example wherein the state of Oklahoma decided to allow a Ten Commandment monument be erected on its lawn in 2012. Satanists and Hindus want to erect a statue for their false gods. The Satanists had plans for an interactive display for children alongside of the Ten Commandments. The Hindus want a monkey god placed on the lawn similar to the one President Obama carries in his pocket. Immortalizing pagan imagery in stone is an ultimate action. The state of Oklahoma was in a predicament in that a Christian symbol was allowed; therefore any other pagan religions must be afforded the same consideration. Satan is using legalism to push his Antichrist agenda. Oklahoma has a large Christian community, and satanic forces target areas where Christianity is thriving.

The strong delusion has been on the playlist for eons. The delusion will magnify up to and through the tribulation. Several considerations are provided for the possibility of the strong delusion. It could be the acceptance of fallen angels and demonic hybrids masquerading as alien saviors from other planets. The UFO and aliens from outer space dominate the global consciousness. The Vatican claims these supreme beings are our brothers from another galaxy, bringing up the rear for deception and delusion. At the time of the Rapture, it could be perceived that the disappearance of millions was caused by alien abductions. The Rapture of the believers will be downplayed by those left behind as folly. Through supernatural signs and mind control, people will accept the satanic agenda. They will be deceived into taking the mark of the beast and worship the beast, and by this they will be damned. High on the list from the United Nations to the Vatican to all nations, global warming or climate change takes precedence. This channel connects new agers to the green religion, Gaia worship, forming the axis of idolatry at its forefront. Images, apparitions, and simulations will control the minds of the masses as they enter into the world of virtual reality, smartphones, and tech toys. The commonality within these delusions is that they are inaccessible or not tangible, allowing for manipulation and propaganda to attack the subconscious mind.

Mankind has an ongoing fascination with watching heavenly, celestial bodies. While we were all trained to look up and scan the skies, another realm of activity was ongoing in lower earth. Remember, Satan is the god of this world. His agenda is to counterfeit, corrupt, kill, and destroy God's creation on earth. Satanic tentacles have a strangle hold on the world. His wickedness has seeped into every social reality, technology gone rogue, world powers are in his grasp, and most religions are under his influence—each embracing things that are evil, wrong, ungodly.

The Bible allows us to know that in these end-times, this generation will witness an explosion of unprecedented evil. This reality is reported by mainstream media, alternative news sites, and movies sensationalizing malevolent themes of monsters that rise from the depths of hell or those descending to earth from alien planets. Our subconscious minds have been inundated and haunted with images of vampires, demons and zombies, serial killers, and monsters. Movie themes such as *Hannah* prepare our minds for the reality of cloning and the development of superhumans. Our conception of this "imaginary" realm becomes real, and well. it should, because the fallen angels and their demonic hybrids have superior abilities. An official of Bank of America branch in North Carolina claimed, "We are in a matrix, and reality is a simulation." Others in the scientific arena are beginning to believe we are living in giant hologram.

As discussed in chapter 3, fallen angels and demons usually, invisible to the human eye, have the ability to manifest in our earthly dimension. Even though they have this ability, we do not find Hollywood-type monsters roaming the streets. Nonetheless, we need to prepare ourselves to acknowledge that evil spirits may have taken possession of humans, appearing to others as humans. On rare occasions or under certain conditions, these entities may appear as the alien Greys or alien lizard-like monsters that we have been preconditioned to recognize and associate with the UFO phenomena. All this attention has opened a portal summoning demonic forces from the deep recesses of the earth or some other abode.

We will discuss the deception of UFOs and aliens from outer space. These entities are fallen angels, evil spirits, demons, and hybrids disguised as modern-day space travelers. Sightings of strange vehicles in the sky were seen in ancient times, mentioned in the Bible, and observed early in the 1900s well before the 1947 spectacular event in Roswell, New Mexico. With the mention of Roswell, the reader is transported to the time when an alien spacecraft with alien bodies crashed in that location. From that time to the present, there has been a great deal of interest in UFOs and aliens from other planets. Interest in the alien agenda became the focus of government cover-ups, using code words such as *Collins Elite*, *Majestic Five*, and *Blue Book*.

The UFO agenda found its way into hundreds of books, movies, TV shows. Religious groups and organizations were formed to analyze and develop theories on what this all means.

The Obama administration appointed a UFO Disclosure advocate to his administration. January 2014, John Podesta assumed his role. According to Leslie Kean's research, *UFO's, Generals, Pilots and Government Officials Go On Record* said, Podesta in 2002 pushed for government disclosure saying, "a fascinating phenomenon the nature of which is yet to be determined … it is time to open the books and <u>find out what the truth really is</u> …" The *European Union Times* newspaper, January 22, 2013, reported Prime Minister Dimtry Medvedev, speaking at the World Economic Forum, Switzerland, challenged Obama: "The time has come for the world to know the truth about aliens, and if the United States won't participate in the announcement, the Kremlin will do so on its own." Both statements allude to the unveiling of something sinister that has been concealed from the public. When the delusion is finally revealed, we believe that truth will not be a disclosure of aliens from another planet but an **alliance** with Satan, fallen angels, demons, and hybrids.

<u>The Vatican's Take on Extraterrestrials</u>

The Vatican promotes the delusion that aliens are our brothers and should be offered salvation. The Vatican has taken a stand that God created aliens, and this belief will not challenge the Catholic church's authority. The Protestant church has been silent on the subject.

Based on credible research data, we will provide a balanced and fair overview of this subject. The Vatican is correct that God created angels not of the earth and, therefore, are aliens to the earth. In contrast to the Bible, the fallen angels are not our brothers, and there is no salvation for fallen angels.

Tom Horn and his associates wrote an article, "Mount Graham and the LUCIFER Project." The Vatican's observatory on Mount Graham is maintained by Jesuit priest. "The priests state their research is to pinpoint extrasolar planets and advanced alien intelligence." Jesuit priest Guy Consolmagno is spokesman for the Vatican. His field is astronomy, and he worked at NASA, taught at Harvard and MIT, and travels between the observatory in Arizona and the one located in Castel Candolfa, Italy. His time is spent trying to reconcile science and religion as it relates to the subject of extraterrestrial life and its potential impact on the future of faith. He also said, "Contemporary societies will soon look to the aliens to be the saviors of humankind." He desires to reconcile the wildest reaches of science fiction with the flint-eyed dogma of the Holy See. He speculates about the "Jesus Seed," where other intelligent planets also have a Christ walk across its seas just as Jesus did here on earth at the Sea of Galilee. He considers that they may be morally superior to men and come to Earth to evangelize us. Our comment—God created the science of all things. Man created religion to worship the creation instead of the Creator. The Vatican will lead the way in worshipping fallen angels/aliens who are not moral but are superior to men. They will not evangelize mankind to repent and accept Jesus as savior, but they will elevate Satan above the Son of God.

The mind-set of many serving in the Vatican is contrary to the Bible as noted below:

Dr. Christopher Corbally, vice director for the Vatican Observatory Research Group on Mount Graham, believes, "Our image of God will have to change if disclosure of alien life is soon revealed by scientists and will require a need to evolve from the concept of an anthropocentric God into a broader entity." Corbally is quoted from his writings:

> What if there were other inhabited worlds. While Christ is the first and the last word ... spoken to humanity, he is not necessarily the only word spoke to the universe ... for the Word spoken to us does not seem to exclude an equivalent word spoken to aliens. They too could have had their logos-event. Whatever that event might have been, it does not have to be a repeated death and resurrection. If we allow God more imagination than some religious thinkers seem to have had ... for God, as omnipotent, is not restricted to one form of language, the human.

Father Jose Funes, director for the Vatican Observatory, suggested that "alien life does exist in the universe and are our brothers but will, when manifested, confirm the true faith of Christianity and the dominion of Rome" (the kingdom of Satan).

In the mid-1990s, Monsignor Corrado Balducci—exorcist, theologian, member of the Vatican Curia (governing body at Rome), and friend of the pope—appeared on Italian TV, stating, "Extraterrestrials were not only possible but already interacting with earth and that the Vatican's leaders were aware of it." He said, as an expert demonologist, "Aliens are not demonic, they are not due to psychological impairment, and they are not a case of entity attachment, but these encounters deserved to be studied carefully." The Vatican has been collecting data on UFOs since the 1950s. Balducci said, "I always wish to be the spokesman for these star people, who also are part of God's glory, and I will continue to bring it to the attention of the holy mother church."

Lady of Fatima

Discussing the following appearance of an apparition will assist us in exposing high-tech delusions. The Vatican kept secret the apparitions seen by three children in Fatima, Portugal, in AD 1917 until 2000. Their names were Lucia Santos, Francesco, and Jacinta Marto. They told that an apparition appeared and called itself "lady from heaven." It gave them instructions to meet again the following month on the thirteenth. The apparitions continued for months, then the church told the children to ask for a sign. The speaking apparition agreed that on October 13, there would be a sign for all to see. On that date, thousands gathered in a field at Cova da Iria. They waited in the rain, clouds overhead. Only the children could see the apparition. The crowd then witnessed the clearing of the clouds and saw a shining disk; some believed it to be the sun. The disk began to spin with a display of colors and appeared to be falling toward the earth. The people became fearful, falling to their knees and screaming. Some claimed to have an altered state of consciousness, as in mass mind control, to believe the delusion to be of God. Shortly thereafter, the disk began to climb into the heavens and disappeared. The people soon realized their clothes were now dry. One witness in 1917 said, "It was a globe of light advancing from east to west, gliding slowly and majestically through the air … suddenly vanished." Entering the twenty-first century and after years of study, we believe this is a description of a celestial vehicle operated by fallen angels. This event and the analysis of the message does not align with scriptures. It does reinforce the Catholics' position and doctrine of Mary.

The Vatican decided to strengthen their claim that the apparition was Mary, the mother of Jesus. In 1854, the Vatican evolved the Marian dogma to promoting Mary as a virgin after giving birth to other children, wherein developed the term, *Immaculate Conception*. In 1950, the church came up with the assertion that the body of Mary ascended to heaven, called the Assumption of Mary. In 1965, she was proclaimed the Mother of the Church. The church also proclaims Mary as coredeemer and mediator of all graces and advocate for the people of God. She will be equal with Jesus and mediator between God and man. She is considered sinless, and prayers may be made before her image.

Catholics love miracles, even if they are manifested by other spirits. Pope John Paul II dedicated the world to "Our Lady of Fatima." They also claimed it was a miracle that had occurred with the sun. The Vatican may not have had the modern-day terminology for an unidentified flying object at that time, but they knew this was not the sun. If the sun had actually moved in such a manner, the heat and gravitational effects would have been catastrophic upon the earth. There are no astronomy or observatory records of that anomaly. From this encounter, the Vatican opened the portal to embrace the satanic delusion of "aliens, our brothers."

The apparition gave three initial messages to the children. The full understanding of the message would be meted out over an eighty-year period. The first part of the message was a vision of hell and tormented souls. At this time the world was engaged in World War I. The second part of the message involved a directive to Pope Pius XI to go and consecrate Russia—which he did not do. World War II broke out in 1938. Russia became a communist, atheist nation. In 1944, the message was given to Bishop Jose Alves Correia da Silva. Lucia had asked that the third part of the message be given publically in 1960. Over the years, each incoming pope read the message but did not reveal it. The Vatican kept the third message a secret. During 1960, Cuba and Russia had aligned, and Russia would set up a nuclear base in Cuba. It was defeated by President Kennedy. Russia and the United States entered into a Cold War scenario. Father Joaquin Alonso had privileged conversations with Sister Lucia, and he was the archivist at Fatima for sixteen years. He died in 1981. In 1984, Pope John Paul II decided to finally consecrate Russia, which led to Christianity being practiced in Russia once again. The final message was to be shared and on May 13, 2000. Pope John Paul II read a version of the message.

Cardinal Joseph Ratzinger said, "There is a part of the third secret that has not been published. What has been published is authentic, and the nonpublished speaks to a bad council and a bad mass that would come in the future." Pope Benedict XVI, who vacated the papacy, denies that there is more of the message to be revealed. The full message may point to corruption within the Vatican, apostasy, and demise of the Catholic church and Christendom in general.

Pope Francis seems to be moving away from traditional Catholic doctrine. He is staunch on embracing all religions toward unification under a one-world religious umbrella (*Exo-Vaticana* and History Channel).

Jesuit Malachi Martin—a close friend of Pope Paul VI, a researcher of the Dead Sea scrolls and teacher of scripture—had privileged information on the third secret of Fatima. Father Malachi Martin, who before his death in 1999 hinted at something like imminent extraterrestrial contact, more than once said, "The mentality among those who are at the highest levels of the Vatican and geopolitics know what is going on in space and what is approaching us could be of great import in the next five to ten years." He was speaking of "the mysterious sign in the sky," a comet approaching from the north. On the anniversary of the event at Fatima, October 13, 2013, Pope Francis consecrated the world to the immaculate heart of our Lady of Fatima flying saucer.

The Vatican hosted a conference in 2009 in Rome to mark the 150th anniversary of the Origin of Species, by Charles Darwin's theory of evolution. The Vatican wanted to look beyond entrenched ideological positions, including misconstrued creationism, and reconsider the problem of evolution with a broader perspective. We feel this is their way of resolving the dilemma of aliens who seeded other planets and earth, thereby developing a position to justify linking humans with their alien brothers.

In another segment of Tom Horn's *Exo-Vaticana* book, he documents the findings of Aleister Crowley, who claims to have discovered a portal between dimensions. In 1918, Crowley titled his research the *Amalantrah Working*. He says it was successful when an entity manifested itself, which he called "Lam." His drawing of the entity looks like the "alien Greys." Crowley died in 1947, same year as the Roswell crash. It is reported that Ron Hubbard and Jack Parsons invited a demonic entity to manifest. They called their experiment "Babalon."

UFO researchers listen and look for messages from deep space. Billions have been spent on high powered telescopes. We mentioned the LUCIFER apparatus, which stands for Large Binocular Telescope Near-Infrared Utility with Camera and Integral Field Unit for Extragalactic Research. The equipment is fixed in Stafford, Arizona, next to the Vatican's Observatory on Mount Graham. Mount Graham is a holy site to the Apache Native Americans, who maintain in their folklore the legends of giants and alien visitors.

The UFO culture believes aliens made life. They nurtured evolution, and they are watching over the inhabitants of the earth. They believe that they are more advanced and should have dominion over us. These aliens are then looked upon as gods. From a Christian perspective, the invasion of planet Earth took place when Satan entered the Garden of Eden, later followed by an invasion of two hundred angels that intermingled with earth women. Satan wanted to be God, and he wants to be worshipped as a god. It is the same old lie in a new disguise. Satan has to appeal to the culture of the time. For instance, early man would be influenced by an appearance of the fallen angels who control the elements and fertility simply because agriculture and husbandry was their mainstay. If they need rain, there was a ceremonial ritual to the gods for rain. If they need to be blessed with children, they made sacrifice to the fertility gods.

Rabbis weigh in on aliens. According to Dr. David Weintraub, professor of astronomy at Vanderbilt University, author of *Religions and Extraterrestrial Life: How Will We Deal With It?* "Judaism" is spiritually prepared for little green men, accepting the possibility of extraterrestrial life, since there are no limits on the power of the Creator. The universe belongs to God, and God can do what God wishes to do with the universe. He might choose to guide extraterrestrials along a different path into a worshipful relationship with God, and if that relationship has a different label, mazel tov. The God of Judaism is universal, but Judaism is not. Judaism is for humans on earth" (*Breaking Israel News*, January 26, 2016, Adam Berkowitz).

Legends on Aliens

Ancient civilizations have hundreds of stories etched in stone or impressions found on wall paintings about entities that came from the heavens to the earth. In Greek and Roman legends, there are fables of the gods who came down from the heavens. These entities became the gods of Olympus. Their behaviors resemble the actions of the fallen angels while the accounts of the Titans resemble those of the Nephilim. Greek writings and art speak of monstrosities such as Minotaur, chimeras, and Centaurs, the result of mixing of species of animals and humans producing hybrids of half human, half animal.

Sometime after Noah's flood, abduction and hybridization activities increased. Millions of genetically altered pseudohumans or animals may have been created. Where is the physiological evidence of these beings? Hard evidence of these things is rare, but according to the account of many witnesses, entities are seen in association with alien abductions. As best we can, we must determine if these are anomalies of nature or products of the alien abduction project.

Before Its News, August 22, 2012. The myth tells of spaceships that landed thousands of years ago, and the people on them were called Dropa. In 1938, an archaeologist by name of Chi Pu Tei went to Baian Kara Ula in the Himalayan Mountains of China. In a cave he found stone disks with a circle-shaped hole in the middle, like a phonograph record. There were around 750 of these discs. Under magnification, the disc had a spiral groove etched on it, which had tiny hieroglyphics in an unknown language. The findings remained in Beijing University for years until Dr. Tsum Um Nui began to decipher the code. He was amazed that the writings were tiny and could only be seen under a microscope. The code told of the Dropas coming in spaceships. The indigenous tribes called Ham, or Han, began to kill the Dropas until they understood they were not going to kill them.

Today the inhabitants of this area call themselves Dropa and Han. Anthropologists are unable to categorize them by ancestry. The people are small in size, three feet six inches to four feet seven inches, weigh thirty-eight to fifty-two pounds, have yellow skin, thin bodies, large head, and eyes that are blue in color. Their physical description is unusual—having big heads, small frames, and large blue eyes similar to the description of Grey aliens seen in various accounts. We cannot determine if these features are the product of hybrids.

Prior to the flood, fallen angels did mix with humans and produced giants. The fallen angels also conducted genetic engineering to produce small beings and half human–half animal creatures. During the Middle Ages, there were legends of fairies, genies, gargoyles, ogres, giants, and leprechauns; and at Halloween you can add ghost, devils, goblins, etc.—certainly, the stuff for fairy tales but far from myth. In 1995, a tribe of around 120 small people were discovered living in Sichuan Province near the mountain range of the Dropas. It is called the village of the dwarfs, and their height is two feet one inch to three feet ten inches. Scientists thought they were dwarfs because high mercury was in the soil. Dr. Norbert Felgenhauser, Munich Institute of Toxins, refutes this and said mercury would cause death, not dwarfism. Evidence of another group of small people called Huldufolk, meaning "hidden people," said to live in Iceland by the Saga Foundation. This could be a legend since no one has ever seen one. Small people called pygmies or dwarfs have been found living in Africa and around the world. They should be classified as an anomaly of nature and not thought to be the result of an experiment. In the United States, there is a TV series, *Little Women*, featuring the life of dwarfs.

Other small characters such as fairies, genies, and leprechauns are not similar to small humans. These creatures had magical powers, could become visible or invisible, and were probably demons. We believe there is no physical evidence of these beings. On the opposite end of the spectrum, there is evidence of very large beings or giants. Remains of giants some with elongated heads, fifteen to thirty feet tall, have been found on every continent. Giants lived alongside of normal-size humans. We find giants throughout history. They should be characterized as an anomaly of nature since there is no evidence these are preflood Nephilim hybrids.

Alien Craft

One of the earliest reports of alien craft is found in the Bible discussed in our chapter 2, "Celestial Chariots." We can accept the premise that spiritual beings rode in celestial vehicles, and in a few instances, human beings also rode in celestial vehicles. On the Altar of Visoki Decani Monastery, Kosovo, Yugoslavia, is a Crucifixion scene painted in AD 1350, and seen on each side of the cross are spacecraft with a cutaway showing a person steering the ship. In another fifteenth-century painting of Madonna with San Giovanino, it shows a disc craft to the right of Mary's head, Florence Palazzo Vecchio. These depictions may have come from the Bible accounts of Enoch, Ezekiel, and Elijah—all who had encounters with celestial vehicles.

The use of the term *alien* can be applied to something other than little green men from outer space. The term *UFO* is used because we cannot determine the nature of the craft. Research reveals that there are other accounts of strange craft reported in ancient times. An India legend speaks of vehicles called Vimana or flying machines thousands of years before the development of airplanes. There is an extensive article in *The Times of India: Flight Plan* written by Mukul Sharma. The section titled "Vaimanika Prakarana" deals with vehicles that traveled from place to place, nation to nation, and vehicles that could traverse between planets. These vehicles were highly advanced, dealing with electromagnetism, antigravity, mercury vortex propulsion, and this technology may have been introduced to man before the flood by the fallen angels. India as well as other nations worshipped pagan gods, allowing for spiritual entities to interfere with the development of humanity. Hitler was obsessed with the Aryan/India mystique and their technological advancements. Somehow Hitler and his scientists had acquired advanced technology for flying craft. Before World War II, Germany was conducting experiments in underground locations and had reached some level of success. Their advancements got the attention of other nations, such as Russia and the United States.

Considering UFO sightings before the Roswell incident in 1947, we need to keep in mind that by the mid-1900s, technology had soared. There was a report of a UFO sighting in 1897, Aurora, Texas. The cigar-shaped craft, apparently having mechanical difficulties, flew into a tower located on Judge Proctors farm. People who witnessed the crash site said there was also a body of a dead alien, to which they referred as a "Martian." The story was written up in the local paper; the alien was given a Christian burial; and the debris from the ship was carted off, except for some miscellaneous debris, which were thrown down a water well. After this incident, Aurora experienced a series of unfortunate events such as a major fire, small pox, boll weevil destroyed cotton crop, and the railroad had planned to extend into Aurora but stopped the tracks twenty-seven miles outside of the town. Population of the town dwindled to four hundred people (History Channel, August 9, 2013, *Deep Sea UFOs*). There are a few problems with this narrative. The vehicle had mechanical problems, which may suggest this was man-made. If there was a dead alien body, it should have been preserved as evidence, placed in a museum such as Egyptian mummies, and everyone would want to see it. The incident is suspicious and follows a pattern of tactics to cover up the event and to get people to move out of the area.

In 1945, the *USS Franklin D. Roosevelt* carrier was the first ship to carry nuclear weapons. This drew world attention. Crew members reported seeing a cigar-shaped UFO, changing colors, no sound, windows around the cabin with aliens looking out. It was able to move at speeds unknown at that time. This craft could dive underwater as well as fly in space. Over the years, many sightings were reported from the *USS FDR*, and many reports were kept secret. Again this appears to be man-made, as well as in an aircraft traveling at high speeds, onlookers would be unable to see faces looking out windows. By 1962, crew members reported sightings that moved at speeds hitting 4,000 MPH, left no heat signature, could fly close to their ship, then disappear and reappear in a minute; it also dove into the ocean. The fifteen crew members were sworn to silence, and the event was covered up. It is unlikely that crew members on a ship had the capability of measuring the speed of an object traveling 4,000 MPH.

Reports of the 1947 Roswell crash indicated there were debris from a craft scattered across field land. This material looked like aluminum foil, very lightweight, could be crumpled up and then returned to its former shape. It could not be burned, cut, or destroyed, yet it was in found in pieces. There were parts of the craft that contained alien hieroglyphics, which was later debunked. Various material found at the scene could not be identified, but it does not require jumping to a conclusion that it is something out of this world.

Scientists have only identified a small number of elemental materials common to earth, including some elements left from meteors or comets that are part of our physical universe. We believe there was a crash at Roswell but was probably man-made. Retired Air Force Lt. Col. Richard French was interviewed on *Open Minds TV* and by the *Huffington Post*. He said there were two craft that crashed in New Mexico. A few days earlier, one was downed by United States Air Force out of White Sands, New Mexico, using EMP (electromagnetic pulse). EMP technology was discovered by Tesla in the beginning of the twentieth century, so here is a possibility that scientists have discovered advanced technology. French said that military personnel had gathered pieces of the crash material along with two dead bodies and a survivor. All evidence was taken to Patterson Air Force Base and examined then possibly transferred to Area 51 site. French wrote a book called *Macedonian Gray* about the Roswell UFO event.

Most governments continue to cover up alien phenomena, or most likely, they are covering their covert/black ops programs. It is alleged President Eisenhower made a deal with the extraterrestrials. In 1969, President Jimmy Carter saw a UFO, and he wanted to make public UFO documents. President John Kennedy also wanted to allow the public access to this information, but he was assassinated. President Ronald Reagan said that "if the world encountered alien forces, the world would unite as one." Reagan said, "Aliens are already here." For a short period in 1967, government allowed for study of UFO sightings. Australia released UFO files from their National Archives. Russian interest goes back to 1908, when a meteor or object crashed, causing an explosion around a thousand megatons and impacted a twenty-mile circumference. Russian government covered up this event. In the twenty-first century, Valdimir Putin wants to disclose the alien reality.

According to studies and based on witness accounts (not necessarily true) are some beliefs:

- Aircraft are transferring visitors from another galaxy.
- Realities from a parallel universe.
- Time travelers from our future.
- Craft hidden from civilization in Atlantis, or inner earth.
- They are composed of unknown material.
- Government super secret inventions, black ops, area 51.
- These craft fly at incredible speeds and fly maneuvers no early craft can do.
- They come from another dimension, or transdimensional.
- Come to protect earth from a disaster.

Can we possibly imagine that in another dimension, fallen angels have a factory to construct their travel vehicles? We know that the fallen angels (aliens) taught mankind how to work with metal components found on earth before the flood, so it is plausible that alien technology was provided to man postflood. It would seem that the construction of UFO craft are part of government or commercial advanced technology projects with alien oversight.

In order to navigate in earth atmosphere, any aircraft would need to overcome gravity and operate on a source of fuel or energy. Highly advanced craft may harness Earth's electromagnetic field. We previously discussed the advancement Tesla made in the 1890s with electromagnetic energy. Later, the government was able to harness energy through HAARP. As modern aircraft technology advanced, craft could fly faster, finally breaking the sound barrier. In the past, we could hear it. With today's advance aircraft, we no longer hear supersonic travel. Standing on earth observing the sky, a craft traveling at light speed probably cannot be seen or heard. Those who witness UFO craft say they appear to blink in or out of sight and are quiet. The famous Bermuda Triangle was a magnetic anomaly, where it generated some sort of energy field that caused ships and airplanes to disappear into the ocean deep. Other energy fields are located near Japan and Australia.

Some reports claim governments made a deal with the aliens in exchange for advanced technology. World leaders exercised their will to enter into an alliance with the forces of evil, and a portal was opened. Humans and animals were the bargaining chips. Could world leaders have agreed to share space under the earth for their clandestine operations? We did discuss there is a great deal of activity in extensive underground facilities. UFO crafts have been seen diving into the oceans. Mankind is limited in its ability to investigate deep-sea caverns. Apparently, highly advanced equipment has no problem in descending into the deepest ocean terrains that standard equipment cannot accomplish. An article appeared on News.com.au, April 26, 2016, writes, "The incredible mystery of the alien spacecraft that lies at the bottom of the Baltic sea." Several others have seen this object, such as Swedish treasure hunter Peter Lindgerg. The object looks like a craft and is sixty-one meters wide and eight meters tall, and it interferes with electricity and satellite phones reception. The object has not been proven to be a spacecraft.

It has been well documented for more than seventy years, approximately 150 million witnesses worldwide have seen UFOs. Some sightings were declared hoaxes. Discovery Channel, History Channel, and other media sources have presented documentaries on UFO craft, trace materials, alien entities, and abductions. We are programed to believe these UFOs belong to an advanced civilization. Some speculate that crashes occur for the purpose of providing extraterrestrial materials that can be reverse-engineered by world governments. Alien bodies are provided to support the deception that these are extraterrestrial travelers.

Credible sources, such as Gary Stearman, *Prophecy in the News*, saw an alien craft while he was piloting his plane.

Noah Hutchings, president of Southwest Radio Ministries in Oklahoma for over sixty years and author of approximately a hundred books, saw alien craft.

> In 1939, I lived with my family on a farm in Oklahoma. At the time I was fifteen years old … returning from school I saw an intense bright and glowing object suddenly ascend over the woods into the sky followed by a second and third craft. All three objects, radiating orange, white, and blue lined up to form a triangle in the sky. I watched, waiting to see if they would move. Later I went home, ate dinner, and went back to see if the three objects were still in the sky, but they had gone.

In the mid-1960s, Dr. Walter Martin had taken a picture of a UFO. He was instrumental in the establishment of the Christian Research Institute. His colleagues included Donald Grey Barnhouse, John Warwick Montgomery, Dr. Chuck Missler.

> I possess, and it has been printed in color, a UFO taken at an altitude of eight hundred feet on a clear day in New Jersey hovering near a seminary … It is a circular ship with opaque windows circling it … about fifty to seventy-five feet across and at least fifty feet thick … It made no noise, bluish gray in color. The question in my mind is not what but who.

Dr. Martin went on to explain his belief about the who that is piloting UFOs; he concluded: **"They are demonic agents of deception."**

"I know what they are," said Dr. Josef Allen Hynek, US astronomer, professor, and lead scientific adviser for UFO studies by US Air Force under Project Sign, Project Grudge, and Project Blue Book. The Soviet government knows what they are ... some form of extremely sophisticated aircraft not made by any government occupying territory on our Earth that we know of ...

Dr. Josef Allen Hynek developed a theory of the evolution of UFO encounters:

- Close encounters of the first kind, CEI, involve visual sightings of an UFO.
- Close encounter of the second kind, CEII, include visual plus physical traces, such as burned spots on the ground, radiation, strange markings, wreckage debris.
- Close encounter of the third kind, CEIII, involve sightings of the UFO occupants near the UFO.
- Close encounters of the fourth kind, CEIV, include human abduction by a UFO or its occupants.
- Close encounters of the fifth kind, CEV, developed by Steven Greer's Center for the Study of Extraterrestrial Intelligence (CSETI), joint bilateral contact events produced through the conscious, voluntary, and proactive human-initiated or cooperative communication with extraterrestrials.
- Close encounters of the sixth kind, CEVI, UFO incidents that cause direct injury or death.
- Close encounter of the seventh kind, CEVII, involve abduction for the purpose of mingling human and extraterrestrial DNA to produce hybrids.

There have been reports that correlate UFO appearances with religious activity. In 1978, multiple UFOs appeared in Italy. One was seen over Saint Peter's Basilica, and a beam of green light was seen directed downward to the steeple. This was seen by many and reported in several newspapers. These appearances were associated with the year three popes came under mysterious conditions. Pope Paul VI said this was the smoke of Satan coming into the sanctuary.

Records have shown that since the 1947 Roswell crash, there is an increase in sightings when something of significance is associated within Israel; following are a few examples:

1897 First Zionist Congress convened.
1947 Dead Sea scrolls discovered.
1948 Israel became a nation.
1952 War.

1956 War.
1967 Six-day war and the capture of Jerusalem.

As we reflect on these things, where are these craft constructed? A few possibilities come to mind. They are building craft that have physical components, and they would need a structural base, as in underground facilities, of which many exist. Even though space travel is still limited, constructing platforms in outer space is a reality. Developed nations have built space stations hovering over the earth. It is reasonable to consider a giant space station for their activities. Some abductees reported being taken up into a craft. Telescopes have been mounted on satellites. Hundreds of satellites encompass the earth, possessing various capabilities. Fiber optics can transmit frequencies from earth to a satellite. That particular satellite has the capability to transmit messages and images to millions of receivers on earth. Government spy satellites surveil the circumference of the earth in real time, such as Israel's satellite OFEK-11 recently launched in September 2016. Governments may have developed star wars capabilities to send instructions to drones to destroy enemy targets. Coming soon is a light show in the heavens transmitted from a satellite. An apparition or hologram will be seen. It could simulate the appearance of a messiah in the heavens descending to earth. It will be a great delusion.

Alien Abductions

This overview of abductions barely scratches the surface. There is a parallel between Genesis 6, where the fallen angels abducted women and intermingled celestial and terrestrial DNA. In that caldron, there was a mix of manifestations and abominations. We attempt to present our reports based upon credible resources. Our position is that the "aliens" are fallen angels, demons, and hybrids. Researchers such as Timothy Alberino, Steve Quayle, Tom Horn, and others did the work, and our job is to pass it forward and awaken the people.

We cannot discount millions of people worldwide who have experienced and reported an abduction. It seems that the majority of people abducted are of European descent and hail from the four corners of the Earth. Some research sources indicate many of these people were involved with the occult or had prior dealings with psychics, tarot cards, Ouija boards, consulting the magic 8 ball, horoscopes, and other areas that open a portal of demonic activity. Christians may not have encountered an abduction because they had accepted Jesus as their savior and were sealed by the Holy Spirit. Those not having a saving relationship with Jesus look to every secular outlet, guru, shaman, Wiccan, or Krishna for answers. This deception pulls people away from the one true God, Creator of the universe, and points mankind to false saviors.

Abductions are multipurpose and ongoing stretching the limits of God's patience. According to some abductees, procedures are conducted for the sport of torture and to observe the victim's suffering very similar to activities conducted in German and US laboratories. Animals used in experiments have been subjected to extreme pain and suffering resulting in death. God did not intend for his created to be treated in this manner. Evil scientists, following the bidding of satanic forces, carry out horrible, inhumane experiments on animals and humans. Jesus said that as in the days of Noah, so shall it be before the coming of the Son of man.

What are the experimentations for? Some will say for the advancement of the human race, or humans need to be elevated to the next evolutionary level. In order for the survival of the planet, they must help humans overcome disease and war. Victims are told not to worry; don't be fearful because they are participants in a great cosmic (scheme) evolution that is being carried out on Earth. Victims are told they are special and are needed to spread the word of impending disaster and only a certain number of humans will be rescued, relocated, and then returned when the global chaos is over. Another reason given for abductions is to rejuvenate the alien race.

The purpose for abducting humans and animals is to **extract** genetic material from sperm, ovum, and blood. Human eggs are in demand, and women are paid for their eggs. These eggs will be used to clone other humans or develop something not human. Another purpose for abducting earth species is to **inject** them with alien DNA. When something other than human DNA is injected into a human, it is alien DNA, but it does not refer to aliens from another planet. DNA material may come from created hybrids to **combine** with an existing species. This said, technology has excelled, cloning has been achieved, artificial insemination is a successful procedure, and genetic engineering is on the cutting edge. There is nothing new under the sun, and these practices were performed by the fallen angels thousands of years ago and continued by scientists who follow the same patterns and practices.

As in any abduction or kidnapping, the victims experience fear and terror. Perhaps their experience can be likened to being in the clutches of hell where exists demons, torture, darkness, and foul smells. The aliens are not benevolent beings but are insidious and sadistic. Abductees report seeing beings that look gray in color with large black eyes, reptilian or humanoid. Using mind control, victims are subjected to brainwashing, manipulation, propaganda to indoctrinate them and to keep them involved in the scheme of things. For tracking purposes, some abductees have RFID chips implanted in them. Fear, intimidation, and brainwashing are methods to **control** abductees.

These aliens seem to operate in the shadows, and their secret activities are not fully disclosed to the masses. Let us debunk the notion that abductees are taken to another planet but more likely transported to a ship in the upper stratosphere or to an underground facility.

Heads of world governments know what is going on, but in exchange for alien technology, they cooperate by allowing large portions of the population to be abducted to be used as guinea pigs for experimentation and hybridization. Technology becomes a source of **power** to control others.

Army Lt. Col. Philip J. Corso wrote a book, *The Day after Roswell.* In it he described the US government's knowledge of human abductions and animal mutilations since the 1950s. He said, "It was the UFOs, alien spacecraft thinking themselves invulnerable and invisible as they soared around the edges of our atmosphere, swooping down at will to destroy our communication with EMP bursts, buzz, our spacecraft, colonize our lunar surface and occupy our deep oceans."

John Mack, Harvard psychiatrist and Pulitzer Prize winner, in an excerpt from his writing, *Passport to the Cosmos*, said, "Some abductees feel that certain beings seem to want to take their souls from them. Greg told me that the terror of his encounters with certain reptilian beings was so intense that he feared being separated from his soul, describing that he would cease to exist and that would be the worst thing anyone could do to me." The popular TV series *V* shows the visitors as reptiles housed in human forms. The aliens were interested in experiments to create hybrids and the extraction of the soul of man. Fiction mirrors reality.

A recent article in the *New York Times*, December 2012, by Ellen Barry reported that in Moscow, Russia, in a women's prison, unusual behavior of some women are said to have experienced "collective mass psychosis," so intense that their wardens summoned a priest to calm them down. In another Moscow town, residents stripped shelves of matches, kerosene, sugar, and candles. In Chelyabinsk, Russia, a group were building a large Mayan style archway out of ice. In brief, fear and reaction to the upcoming Mayan end of a cycle on December 21, 2012.

Carla Turner and her family were abducted. She wrote several books detailing her experiences: *Into the Fringe, Taken* and *Masquerade of Angels.* These books can be viewed online.

Research data provided by David Ruffino and Joseph Jordan in their book, *Unholy Communion*, provides insight into the alien agenda from a Christian perspective. In our studies, there is a minority that understand we are dealing with fallen angels, demons, and hybrids. The authors assert that those who call on the name of Jesus may divert or defend against an abduction.

According to Ruffino and Jordan, some of the procedures and brainwashing forced on the victims is dreadful. Following is a summary of procedures people claimed to have experienced:

- They can alter a person's perception of their surroundings. They instruct victims telepathically or use an alien sideshow like a hologram.

- They can control what you think you see; aliens can manifest in various shapes and guises as dead loved ones, celebrities, Jesus, or the pope. They can be invisible, partially visible, or fully visible.
- They can manipulate consciousness, no control over physical body, possess a human with their own entity, and use the person's body before allowing them to return to consciousness.
- The alien procedures can leave marks on the victim's bodies from puncture wounds, bruises, and claw marks. They inflict pain on victims through anal, genital, and navel probes.
- Male and female genitalia are violated and entered. Aliens are very interested in human sexuality in adults and children. They have forced victims to have sex with other aliens or other abductees while they watch.
- They take body fluids from neck, spine, blood veins, joints, and inject unknown fluids into various parts of the body.
- Side effects are illness, death, degeneration of mental capacity, development of strange obsessions.
- People are taken on some kind of craft or inside a facility. People have seen grotesque hybrid creatures, hybrid humanoid fetuses, vats filled with body parts. They have seen humans drained of blood, mutilated, flayed, dismembered, and stacked in piles.
- Alien entitites can come into homes and take children, paralyzing parents and telling them, "The children belong to us."
- A device is implanted into abductees. Dr. Roger Lier has removed many implants. He said they are resistant to cutting, heat, or cold. The host does not reject it. It has magnetic properties. A closer look seems to indicate they are like miniature machines made of carbon nanotubes, 300 gigaherts faster than anything on planet earth, and it is changing the DNA in people. There are other things that are beyond human explanation.

As we consider the above analysis, the majority of details are common to earth procedures and activities. It also appears to encompass an element of demonic behavior.

It is hard to fathom that some people go willingly because they have been told they are special, chosen, doing good, coming into enlightenment, and pride avails. A report on *Before It's News* on August 13, 2012, in an interview with Erica Goetsch, member of the Church of Mabus (new age). She believed the alien reptilian species were from outer space. She said her abduction was a pleasant experience. The aliens were loving and nurturing like a mother and child, when she was in the exam room and they were fixing her. She had nothing to fear. She has come in contact with blue reptilians, short and tall Greys. "People who speak out against these aliens, she said, are psychotic." Goetsch comments tell us she could be demon-possessed. When the Antichrist demands all to take the mark, many people will go without a second thought. There are a few reports of people who have volunteered to get chip implants already.

There are accounts of people and objects that disappear and never return. Some claim entire groups of people just up and disappear, such as the Mayans, or objects sucked into a vortex, such as the Bermuda Triangle. The explanation for this situation can be found in advanced technology, such as in disrupting the molecular structure and reassembling it elsewhere or not at all. It is similar to *Star Trek*, "Beam me up, Scottie," which is an example of molecular dislocation.

Experimentations on Humans by Humans

During the time of Jesus's ministry on earth, evil spirits possessed many people. Jesus spent half his time casting out demons. These same demonic spirits continued to exist and influenced the activities of nations right up to the twenty-first century. Under demonic power, rulers had no empathy and no conscience or mercy, inflicting unbearable pain and suffering on other living beings. It is important to connect our discussion with experimentation of humans under the alien abduction scenario with the experimentation of humans by humans not associated with aliens since there is a great deal of commonality. There is no culture, society, or ethnicity that did not carry out atrocities against others. Herein, we will discuss some of these diabolical experiments conducted in the United States based on experiments conducted by German scientists in cooperation with US government agencies and US scientists over the past seventy years.

We will begin with excerpts provided by Jon Rappoport, *Natural News*, December 11, 2015, *Government Experiments on Humans.* "The USGAO, General Accounting Office, testimony by Frank C. Conohan, Assistant Comptroller General for National Security and Internal Affairs Division before the House of Representative, Legislative and National Security Subcommittee on Government Operations, September 28, 1994. Conohan's subject, *Human Experimentation—Cold War Era Program*" … Use of humans in test and experiments conducted for national security purposes by DOD, Department of Defense, between 1940–1974 involved Army, Navy, Air Force, Defense Nuclear Agency, CIA, Department of Energy, Department of Health and Human Services test involved the use of radiation, chemical and biological agents for their research. Hundreds of thousands of people from the military, unsuspecting citizens, and other nations were subjected to experiments using nerve gas, blister agents, radiation, LSD, Agent Orange, PCP (phencyclidine). Some experiments were conducted in secret; others used test subjects without their consent (adults, children with mental disabilities, prisoners). Subjects suffered acute injuries and health problems that persisted for many years and death.

During the period of 1945–1962, the largest test known was the Atmospheric Nuclear Test program, performed more than two hundred tests on over two hundred thousand people. One of the projects was called Operation Crossroads. Military personnel were exposed to radiation during the Hiroshima and Nagasaki bombings. Also military personnel were exposed to Agent Orange chemical spraying on Vietnam. The Army during 1949 to 1974 sprayed biological chemical over US cities such as Saint Louis, San Francisco, New York Subway, and Washington International Airport.

In the 1940s, during World War II, upward to sixty thousand military personnel were used by Army and Navy to test mustard gas—a product of Lewisite Chemical. Subjects were placed in gas chambers as well a direct skin test. The irritants caused burning, itching, swelling, rash, blister, burning lungs, sneezing, vomiting, pulmonary edema, cancer, and death. The testing of nerve gas continued up to 1975, still observing how it might render incapacity. Later tests were administered at Edgewood Arsenal, Maryland; seven thousand Army and Air Force soldiers were experimented on. Later some testified before Congress that they had not been informed of the risks.

Other experiments were conducted on two thousand volunteers, exposing them to biological pathogens, such as Venezuelan Equine Encephalitis and Tularemia, in order to develop vaccines and antidotes. Today Army Medical Research Institute for Infectious Disease uses volunteers to test vaccines for malaria, hepatitis, and other exotic diseases (Ebola).

Commanders would commend military personnel for their sacrifice for national security. In other words, they were expendable.

Dr. Cornelius Rhoads, in cooperation with the Rockefeller Institute, in 1931 conducted experiments in Puerto Rico, infecting people with cancer cells, causing some deaths. He stated, "Puerto Ricans were dirty, lazy, degenerate, thieves, and worst race to live on the planet. I have done my best to further the extermination … All physicians take delight in abuse and torture of these subjects." Rhoads was appointed to the US Atomic Energy Commission and was vice president of the American Cancer Society.

During World War II, Shiro Ishii of Japan carried out violent experiments on ten thousand prisoners, doing vivisection without anesthesia, meaning they were cut open and their organs removed while fully conscious. He caused pregnant women to abort and induced strokes, heart attacks, frost bite, hypothermia, etc. He was only stopped when Japan was defeated in 1945; at that time he killed all his subjects. General Douglas McArthur struck a deal with Ishii and gave him immunity if he would give the United States his germ warfare database on human experiments.

The United States Condoned Human Torture for the Advancement in Biological Warfare

A plane named Enola Gay dropped the first bomb on Hiroshima and Nagasaki. After the bomb was dropped on Hiroshima and Nagasaki, the United States continued to test thermonuclear bombs in the Pacific. The fallout blew onto people who got radiation sickness, birth defects, cancer. Project 4.1 was to study the effects of the above. In 1958, the US government planned another Project Chariot. They identified a small town in Alaska, planning to detonate nuclear bombs to study the effect of radiation on the people and the environment. There was great outcry from the citizens, and the tests did not happen there, but nuclear testing did continue elsewhere.

During the years 1939–1945, the United States brought together the greatest of scientific minds, including eight Nobel Prize winners. Many of these were Germans who were covertly brought into the United States. Some were placed in a facility in Los Alamos, New Mexico, out of which the Manhattan Project was formed to create a nuclear weapon, using isotopes composed of uranium U2-38/ 35. By smashing or colliding these isotopes into each other, they sought a fission reaction for the bomb. Mankind moved into the development of the hydrogen bomb and nuclear energy, which also threatens civilization. Besides creating these bombs, other experiments were conducted by injecting people with plutonium. At a Massachusetts hospital in 1946, Dr. William Sweet injected eleven victims with uranium.

At the end of World War II, under Operation Paper Clip, the United States gave thousands of Nazi scientists new identification to work in the United States on various projects. One was Dr. Joseph Mengele, aka Dr. Green, came from Auschwitz in 1945. He and other Nazi scientists had conducted the most heinous and inhumane experiments on humans. Whatever their evil imaginations conjured up, they carried it out upon countless of victims, including the unborn, children, women, men. Some of these procedures were to surgically graft twins together, removing nerves without anesthesia, testing explosive effects on people, inserting a hose into the vagina and water pressure would remove internal organs, and making lampshades out of skin. The atrocities were so great the records were classified. President Truman allowed these monsters to live in the United States as free men. Only a few Nazis were condemned for war crimes and went on to infiltrate American society. Such a person was Fritz ter Meer, who had received a five-year prison term for human rights violations. After release, he headed up Bayer Corporation. Bayer was one of a few German conglomerates that developed chemical compound Zyklon B to carry out genocide in Germany. These chemicals were used in the gas chambers to kill Jews.

A research facility was set up on Plum Island in New York. The Nazi mind-set, which is not limited to Hitler, comes through the dehumanization of other people. Hitler viewed the Jews and Christians as nonhuman, and he was able to kill over eleven million people.

In the mid-1900s, the US government experimented on four hundred black men in Tuskegee, Alabama, who were injected with syphilis to study the effects of this disease. No cure was provided for these people. Later President Clinton apologized for a racist government.

Monsanto, Dow Chemical, Johnson & Johnson, and the Army used prisoners for research studying the results on skin exposed to this poison, Dioxidin, and associated injections of poison 468 times regular strength. Maui is one of a few nations that reject Monsanto and Dow to experiment in their land with GMO and pesticides.

During the mid-1990s, the US government under the CIA and Army conducted biological spray test on American cities. This is still being conducted today, known as Chemtrails. These toxins poison vegetation, wildlife, and are causing a skin condition called Morgellons disease. These experiments are to eventually cause and control weather and earthquakes.

The United States government released whooping cough virus on Tampa Bay residents using boats. The Navy sprayed San Francisco residents with bacterial pathogens, giving people pneumonia.

In Savannah, Georgia, and Avon Park, Florida, it was discovered that the Army released millions of mosquitoes to spread yellow fever and dengue fever. People got fevers, typhoid, respiratory problems, and affected pregnancies. Army personnel came later disguised as health workers to chart the affects.

The Army Chemical Corps contracted with universities, state hospitals, and medical foundations from 1950 to 1960 to research the influence of psychochemical agents on troops with LSD and other mind-altering drugs.

Operation Midnight was a CIA project to establish safe houses in New York and San Francisco to study LSD effects. They told people they were brothels. Agents said it was fun; where else could a red-blooded American boy lie, kill, cheat, steal, rape, and pillage with the sanction and bidding of the government? Also, in the 1950s, the CIA's Scientific Intelligence Division initiated Project MKULTRA for the purpose of observing behavior of humans using mind-altering drugs. Test subjects underwent experiments to manipulate mental state, alter brain functions through the use of chemicals, drugs, LSD, hypnosis, sensory deprivation, isolation, verbal and sexual abuse, and torture. Dr. Donald Ewen Cameron was one of many complicit in these experiments, which were conducted in eighty institutions, forty-four universities, hospitals, prisons, and pharmaceutical companies. This same research is being carried out in the twenty-first century. The CIA will not release names of participating organizations. On December 14, 2012, the European Union court ruled the CIA is a torturer.

Mind control practices over fifty years have achieved success. In some instances, people are driven to commit crimes and said they heard voices in their heads telling them to do it.

Mind control can be conducted through psychiatric sessions, occult involvement, television, music, drugs, videos, movies, cell phones, hypnosis, electroconvulsive shock at high levels—all have an impact upon the mental capacity and susceptibility of some people. There are documented studies of people who were programed to carry out heinous crimes and feel no remorse or guilt. Some people have no recollection of their actions.

Operation Gladio, the Pentagon through NATO organized bombing and shootings in the streets of Europe, Italy. One captured terrorist under mind control said he was ordered to kill innocent civilians, women, children. The people would be forced to ask the government for protection called the "strategy of tension," out of this chaos would bring reactionary social and political tendencies. Everyone is expendable to bring their objective to fruition and that being, a new world order. We see that the actions of the past have been put in play as the world watches the path of radical Islamic terrorists.

Satan attacks our minds. Jesus said, to protect ourselves from these attacks, we need to put on the armor of God, the helmet of salvation, and cover our thoughts with the Word. A person walks into a school and kills children or walks into a mall or movie theater and shoots unknown victims. Was that person insane? These random acts of violence can have an explanation. They are the product of satanic influence upon their mind. Throughout history, there have been tyrants and dictators whose greatest goal is to kill and enslave its citizens. They are found on every continent, such as, the US presidents, Mao Zedong, Hitler, Mussolini, Stalin, European nobility, Islamic rulers under a mind-altering religious delusion, and the list could go on and on.

Animal Mutilation

The term *alien* is used since the entity cannot be clearly identified. *Alien* also alludes to a supernatural component. The forces of evil have observed human behavior and see the lack of concern in regard to the brutality and murder of other humans. What has been done to humans gives them a green light to do the same to animals. The vileness of ongoing experiments is shocking. Living creatures are subjected to unspeakable horror and suffering with the approval of world leaders.

Gary Stearman, *Prophecy in the News*, March 2013, in "*Obscene Sacrifices*" discusses cattle abduction and mutilation conducted by aliens. The mysterious deaths of cattle and other animals have been observed around the world. The bodies have been surgically mutilated and totally drained of blood. Reports from ranchlands in the United States have said cattle mutilations are common.

These events are well documented and witnessed by many.

There is a documented case of an Appaloosa horse owned by Berle and Nellie Lewis had become the victim of an alien abduction. The owners found the remains and knew that its death was not caused by any earthly action. "The flesh and hide had been stripped from the shoulders, neck, and head. No blood or bodily fluids of any sort were found anywhere near the body. Incisions on the body were surgically accurate. Some internal organs were missing, and the brain was taken without disturbing the skull … The owners believed their horse was killed by aliens from another world."

Linda Moulton Howe's book, *Glimpses of Other Realities*, documents an account in which Timothy Fint describes his own abduction from a Portland apartment, taken to a field to witness a cattle mutilation. The animal was singled out by the craft, levitated up to the ship, and while dangling there, it was surgically dissected. The cow uttered a series of bloodcurdling screams.

We know that some cult rituals or pagan religions have been able to drain all the blood from an animal before mutilating or killing it. The ability to drain all blood leaving no trace of blood and to surgically remove eyes, tongue, ears, genitalia, and other organs with precision is beyond cultic capability but points to advanced technology.

Law enforcement has been unable to make an arrest in the past forty years over animal abduction and mutilation. These losses are an economic hardship on ranchers as well as fuel popular opinion toward aliens from other planets.

Numerous eyewitnesses, biological samples of hair, footprint ranging up to twenty-four inches, sulfuric odor, sounds, voices, shadows, lights have been documented but do not provide conclusive answers of who is involved and what they are doing. There was a report of a big foot sighting around 125 years ago in Siskiyou Mountains, California. Tall, bulldog head, hairy, was a description found in a frontiersman pamphlet. President Theodore Roosevelt told a story in the *Wilderness Hunter*, 1893, when he saw a beastlike man who killed a human and ate him. Roosevelt said, "The hunter was killed by something half human or half devil." Sounds like a chimera hybrid.

Today we still ask what they are doing with the animal parts and all the blood. Apparently, the human-demon breeding project involves the use of animals. Preflood activity involved mingling various animals, birds, and fish, producing a combination of monstrosities. Postflood hybrids may appear as the Yeti, Himalayas, Bigfoot, Sasquatch in North America, or Lochness Monster in Scotland. Dr. Richard Seed, physicist, Chicago, a proponent of combining human and animal DNA, said, "This is my dream, and we are going to become gods, period."

Jesse Ventura, former governor, did a program on TruTV regarding human and animal hybrid experiments. "Science has made major breakthroughs in transplant technology by creating chimeras, which are human-animal embryo hybrids."

Using advanced technology, the procedure to drain blood, lasers for surgical removal, and even the ability to levitate or pass solid objects through barriers can be explained. Joseph Rose reported in the Oregonian paper, February 17, 2016, on the data gathered by Christopher O'Brien, author of *Stalking the Herd: Unraveling the Cattle Mutilation Mystery* believes, "These mutilations could be part of a covert environmental monitoring process perpetrated by shadowy operations within highly advanced technologies … as far as I am concerned, this could be the greatest unsolved serial crime spree in history."

Crop Circles

Unless you live in a remote jungle, almost everyone has seen a picture of a crop circle. Etching seen over large swatches of land may have existed for millennia. Some ancient designs, which could only be seen from the air, show what appears to be a landing path and figures of insects. Researchers report messages and drawings of pentagram; white horse on hillsides may date back to 2500 BC. Symbols that can be seen from the ground may have been adopted by ancient occult, Celtic, Druid groups. In this segment, we are addressing crop circles that started appearing in this generation. Hundreds have been found in places such as Israel, Germany, Australia, England, Canada, United States, Netherlands. Close examination of some circles disclose they were man-made and not an overnight sensation. However, those designs that seemingly appear overnight are very complex, exhibiting perfect alignment or symmetry. The designs are symbols, geometric formations of galaxies, planetary alignment, wormholes, DNA structure, insects, a menorah, star of David, and alien face within a binary disk accompanied with a message saying, "Beware of the deceivers and not all are evil." The symbols seem to be relative to our galaxy or planet Earth and not something alien. We factor in the possibility that these crop circles could have been created using computer technology that can create an image and then transfer it through a directed energy source. In very simple terms, it could be like taking a heated branding iron and searing it into flesh and, in this case, a wheat field.

Besides crop circles, there are the mysteries of Easter Island statues, Stone Henge monuments, and pyramids in Egypt. No one has a definitive explanation of how these monuments came to be, so we speculate if they were constructed by aliens or giants.

Jesus said to watch the signs in the heavens. Could Satan counter that warning by directing man's attention to signs in the earth? Following are examples of deception directed toward the creation and away from the Creator of heaven and earth:

- Fallen angels/alien entities can interact with earthlings. In exchange for advanced technology, they give their allegiance and soul to the entities of darkness.
- Man desires to capture beautiful and inspiring images on earth and call it sacred art.
- The divine (Satan) operates through sacred art.
- Mother Earth is our god; protecting earth it is holy.
- Geometrical designs are a universal language.
- They are messengers from the gods using crop circles.
- Metaphysical practices will enhance human consciousness and bring about a union/ demonic possession.
- Meditation to indoctrinate that evil beings are really compassionate will help bring the invisible to visible; some report seeing balls of light at crop circles.
- Atmosphere becomes energetically charged.
- They want to be seen on earth.

Full Disclosure

Over eons, Satan has used evil people to propagate methods to delude the masses into accepting his alien agenda, of which UFO signs and lying wonders are but a part. Ungodly governments use propaganda/mind control to bring the masses in line with their idea that evil is good. Tyrants and dictators past and present are able to accomplish murdering millions through philosophy and ideology. Hitler said, "Make the lie big, make it simple, keep saying it, and eventually they will believe it." Indoctrination comes through media, government speeches, and movies targeting the mind through our eyes and ears. The contents in movies in many instances are to indoctrinate the viewers to a certain subject. Fiction mirrors reality. Hollywood began with subliminal suggestion back in the '40s with a variety of space themes and other demonic subjects. Space traveler *Flash Gordon* and *War of the Worlds* opened our mind to UFOs and little green men. The *Frankenstein* movie was to indoctrinate the masses with experiments that change humans into monsters and the likes of Dr. Jekyll and Mr. Hyde where people turn into vampires, werewolvess, zombies, demons. To desensitize people from rejecting the practice of witchcraft, talking to dead spirits, and channeling, media themes incorporated occult practices as entertainment appearing to be innocent in its nature. A good example of being desensitized is the *Harry Potter* books and movies, which celebrate wizards, demons, black magic, and their target audience is youth.

Throughout the contents of this book, the cast of characters remain the same—being, God, the holy angels, Satan, fallen angels, evil spirits are demons, hybrids before the flood, hybrids postflood, and humanity in its variations. Put all the players together with all the various scenarios discussed, and our conclusion is that the alien agenda is satanic.

Over fifty years of abductions have been recorded. In the last few years, there has been no news of abductions. The UFO phenomenon is unresolved. If there will be a full disclosure, it will not be at all what mankind has anticipated. Technology has excelled. Have the perpetrators achieved their goals? The Obama Administration has publically authorized experimentations that combine human and animal DNA. People who are aware know these procedures have been going on for some time. Obama's public announcement could be part of the "disclosure." The government may be preparing the public to accept its end product: an entity walking among us that appears to be human but is not.

Can We Identify the Hybrids Amongst Us?

A researcher by the name of Mary Rodwell wrote a report titled *The New Humans*. She presented her case study of 1,600 people to Leeds at Exopolitics Conference, Great Britain, 2010. Her position is occult and new age. She believes in aliens from another planet. She is prime example of one who is deluded, not understanding her sources are the doctrine of evil spirits and demons.

Rodwell's opening statement—"Extraterrestrial intelligence are preparing human psych to accept their presence on earth." Through case studies, she provides evidence of complex extraterrestrial programs that will enable humans to

- Communicate with extraterrestrials;
- Understand our place in the cosmos
- Download data of our true genetic origin using our psych skills and complex knowledge;
- Manipulate matter, space, and time;
- Astrophysics, beyond light speed;
- Recall being on a space craft, educated on the craft;
- Healing;
- Combine human DNA with spirit for awaking of human consciousness;
- Remember past life when they were not human;
- They have a sense of "mission"; and
- Assist humans to evolve into fully functional multidimensional beings—her term, *HomoNoetics*.

In Rodwell's summary of ongoing alien abductions and activity for many years, from her point of view, the end product of these abductions can be analyzed. She said that these hybrids are referred to as star children, platinum children, *indigols*. They may have been born of human women but have alien DNA, or they may have been cloned. The DNA of star children contain tenfold more information. Whatever procedures, these humans have undergone change through the mingling with alien matter to cause evolution from human to superhuman (transhumanism).

Rodwell used one of her case studies, a female named Tracy Taylor. Tracy said she was taken at three years old onto a spacecraft. At fifteen years old, she possessed healing ability from the extraterretrials. She did psych "writings" and geometric drawings while under control by extraterrestrials. Edgar Cayce was able to communicate while asleep and give healings. He was also given a message that by year 2000, the "Fifth Root Race" would come. This may refer to demons from a spiritual or unseen dimension becoming visible.

Rodwell showed a video of Taylor who had "so-called healing powers." She was communicating with an entity, speaking in an unknown language, moving the energy field with her hands, touching the person. Their explanation of this is called coding in air; energy fields are seen like numbers, dots, and opening a portal listening for sounds, chanting, or directions. Words can influence living entities. She said it was as if somebody else was in her body performing the healing. There is now a clear message or understanding, according to Tracey: "a new race of beings" are on the planet, increasing in number, visually and physically indistinguishable to most humans. They are bringers of light. They are here to guide the awakening of terrestrial consciousness.

Our comment—this is not of God but a demonic counterfeit and opening a portal to demonic activity. This phenomena is global and is part of the "strong delusion." Reports of strange behavior, characteristics, and abilities of children come out of the Himalayas, China, Mexico, Russia, and United States. One source said some Chinese children were born with blue eyes, and this is a genetic anomaly. One boy could see in the dark. This source said there are a high number of pale-complexioned children born to darker-complexioned parents. One photo showed dark-skinned parents with their pale, blond-haired baby. In Africa, pale children (albinos) are being born and killed because they are so different, and there was a photo of a child with dark complexion and very blue eyes. A Brazil couple had twins: one was brown, looked like them, and the other was pale with blond hair.

We came across information provided by Timothy Alberino, Christian researcher, regarding the appearance of children with black eyes and pale complexion, who seem to appear in the presence of people. They have a foul smell, telepathic, speak in monotones, create a sense of fear, and ask for food and blood. Alberino believes these may be the product of years of alien abduction and their hybrid breeding program. They ask to come into the house. Like a horror movie, hopefully, no one will allow them inside.

Following are a list of abilities that these children possess:

- Using unknown sign language

- Geometric drawings, also of spacecraft, strange writings
- Telepathic, intuitive, telekinesis, use of nonverbal concepts.
- Agile, talented, solve problems easily
- Disciplined
- Can see with various parts of the body other than eyes (a recent contestant on *America's Got Talent* could see things blindfolded)
- Can affect DNA molecules with their mind
- Photographic memories

Mary Rodwell shared the experience of a five-year-old. The child said, "I don't mind going through the walls, I learn more on the ships than in school. The extraterrestrials appear as blue orbs or balls of light passing through walls; they float. They come at night, sometimes looking like insect beings." So they won't be afraid, children said they change forms and look like relatives, Teletubbies, or something familiar. The aliens make them feel comfortable and euphoric.

Rodwell provided additional insight from a seven-year-old living in Russia. The child said she was born on Mars, was able to speak at four months old, has an exceptional memory, and remembers past lives. Most interesting is her account on how the pyramids were built. She said the extraterrestrials changed the density of the stones and levitated them into place. They placed a crystal triangle at the top to communicate with their distant extraterrestrials. She said there is a spaceship under the pyramid. She knows these details because she was there. Well, while we have all been trying to figure out who built the pyramids and how, this explanation is as plausible as others.

Obviously, these beings are highly advanced and seem to have knowledge beyond our earthly reality. Summarizing a bit of what Tracey shared, in brief, it involves physics, moving beyond light speed, operating outside our space-time continuums, ability to dematerialize is manipulating matter. According to Tracey, "The universal language are the ancient symbols for communications and are a more accurate representation of an individual—it takes in the vibration of the soul and comes directly from the universal mind [the God conscious], which link all existence together. The symbols [as found in crop circles] hold conceptual keys that trigger reception within the observing mind. There is volume of information and can be absorbed without having to read pages and pages. By merging data through mind meld, telepathy, thought transplanting, a human being can be reschematized." Music or sound waves tie in to harmonics as portrayed in the movie, *Encounters of the First Kind.*

We have now come to a period in time that the veil that separates fallen angels and demons from human visibility is thinning.

Raiders News Update, April 2013, reports the findings of Professor Carol Cleland, philosopher at Colorado University Astrobiology Center, spoke on "desert varnish" (particles that form a layer on rock) as a manifestation of alternative invisible, biological world ... as ethereal dimension, the shadow biosphere. "On earth we may be coexisting with microbial life forms that have a completely different biochemistry from the one shared by life as we know it." She associates this life form with fairies, elves, or shadow entities just outside our visibility. July 2016, L. A. Marzulli and Richard Shaw showed a photo of a small entity with a face, wings, tail stinger, and limbs. They are presently analyzing the remains and have not reached a definitive conclusion. We will classify this under the mystery of fairies. For the purposes of this book, we look at Cleland's secular mind-set and can understand that the manifestation she speaks of are as we reported the activity of demons becoming visible. The TV series *Grimm* depicts visually pleasant humans who have the ability to transform themselves into monsters.

The question is, How do we identify those entities that walk amongst us? One way to identify a demonically possessed person is to witness their sociopathic and antisocial behavior. There also is a possibility that these demons/hybrids can attack outside of a human host (such as biting, scratching, moving objects). We must factor into our analysis that amoral behavior and heinous acts are carried out by individuals but also gangs and mobs under the influence of mind control, drugs, and demonic spirits resulting in a hive mentality. The evidence of groups working as one mind could be applied to Islamic terrorists, Ku Klux Klan, Planned Parenthood, and cults that kill and torture for ritualistic practices, misguided ideology, or scientific research. The sanctity for life is absent in their mind-set. Taking the life of others has plagued mankind in times past and continues in modern times. The nature of fallen mankind has not changed. Reports indicate a range of sites that killing sprees have been carried out such as on college campuses, schools, research labs, abortion clinics, military installations, movies, malls, restaurants, churches, etc. Following, we provide real-life situations of demon-possessed hybrids hiding in plain sight, integrated into all aspects of society:

A Partial List of Incidents Where the Demon-Possessed Prey on Innocent People

October 1, 2015, lone shooter Christopher Harper-Mercer kills nine on Oregon college campus. He was diagnosed with Asperger's syndrome, on prescription meds, committed to psychiatric hospital. He entered the campus carrying six guns (*New York Times*). Online quotes state he claimed to be a dark prince in Lucifer's army and singled out Christians for slaughter.

Dylann Roof, twenty-one years old, entered a black church in Charleston, South Carolina, and killed nine church members because he wanted to start a race war. Roof was a frequent drug user and would be a good candidate for suggestive actions.

Adam Lanza, on Friday, December 14, 2012, at Sandy Hook School, Connecticut, killed twenty children and six adults. Other shooting took place at Columbine School, Virginia Tech, Thurston High School.

Anders Breivik on Friday, July 22, 2011, Norway, killed seventy-seven people while on a rampage, using a bomb blast and shooting spree, mostly killed teenagers.

James Holmes, on Friday, July 20, 2012, Aurora, Colorado, killed twelve wounded fifty-eight in movie theater.

December 2012, approximately sixty rounds were fired inside the Portland, Oregon, mall.

Fort Hood military base shooting by radical Islamist, killed soldiers.

Philadelphia Naval Base shooter said he heard voices. The military are using bioeffects of selected nonlethal weapons, such as people. They transfer radio frequency toward the human target, and it sounds like speech that drive the target insane or to commit violent acts.

A woman was shot in DC for ramming a barricade and running from police; she said she heard Obama's voice in her head. The National Institute of Health report on BRAIN, Brain Research through Advancing Innovative Neurotechnologies. Obama is said to have examined this report. The need to develop electromagnetic modulation using this as a weapon is scientifically possible.

Chris Dorner, former military and police personnel, was disgruntled and killed four people.

People like Charles Manson clearly were demon possessed. Jeffrey Dohmer killed many boys and men in the Wisconsin area. Photos were taken of mangled bodies and partially eaten people. Ted Bundy in the 1970s killed thirty women. Dennis Rader, 1974, Kansas, over a period of thirty years tortured and killed ten people. Donald Harvey, male nurse, Ohio, killed for seventeen years the sick and elderly at a hospital—up to ninety dead. John Wayne Gacy, married, business owner, clown entertainer, killed boys and men. Lonnie Franklin, sanitation worker in Los Angeles, killed hundreds of people. Jared Loughner, Arizona, fired into a group of federal workers, killing many.

Jim Jones, a very persuasive cult leader, convinced approximately one thousand people to leave their homes to relocate to Guyana, South America, and then they were given poison, which killed over nine hundred adults and children.

Domestic crimes in the United States have become an epidemic. Crimes committed by ISIS terrorists now top the list for brutality and killings. The above list is a sampling of demon-possessed people who walk among us.

Zombies

Zombies in Hollywood terminology would be the living dead or the walking dead who want to eat people and presented as fictional entertainment. In the twenty-first century, we have witnessed people with zombielike symptoms who commit heinous acts, such as cannibalism. Some things that may contribute to the development of irrational behavior are mind-altering drugs, obsessions (social media), chemicals in vaccines, GMO, altered food, bacteria, toxic water, as well as not having a relationship with the one true God.

Zombies are the walking dead, a metaphor, but actual zombies suffer from physiological dysfunctions, which may cause an apathetic mental state, decreasing their ability for compassion, mercy, and lack a consciousness between right and wrong. And their condition may create a desire to eat flesh or drink blood.

There is an ongoing battle between species and organisms, such as bacteria or viruses. When organisms attack a living species, the illness is treated with antibodies, pesticides, or other foreign chemicals, which are trying to kill them. In order to survive, bacteria or virus mutates so as to become resistant to antibodies or chemicals. Good bacteria live in or on its host, assisting with fighting bad bacteria, virus or parasites. Researchers have discovered several species of parasites that lodge inside of the human brain. Of these bacteria, several have been identified such as the Naegleria fowleri, which enters by way of the nostrils and goes into the brain, then destroys all brain tissue it can. Another is Toxoplasma gondii—compromises brain function by slowing down reaction time—and one found in the rain forest is the Loa Loa eye worm, which causes cognitive loss, memory problems, and personality changes. By observing the larger species of parasites, scientists are able to create and program microscopic (nanoparticles) to function as a weapon to attack bad bacteria or virus. Treatment using nanoparticles would be rare for the general public. Untreated or misdiagnosed people are literally becoming zombies manipulated by mad scientific cocktails or attacked by brain-eating bacteria.

The United States Army considers the zombie problem serious enough to include training soldiers for any event such as weather, power outages, mobs, and hordes of the undead. New Hollywood movie called *World War Z* portrayed this idea as a reality. Recently obtained documents CONOP 8888 is a zombie survival plan for military planners trying to isolate the threat from various zombie scenarios. US Strategic Command has been tasked to develop comprehensive plans to protect nonzombies from zombies and preserve human life resulting in measures to quarantine the infected from spreading a disease to others. This scenario was depicted in the TV series *Containment.*

US intelligence and military communities are concerned by the evidence presented by the JASONs on the Pentagon's advisory panel, who warned that human enhancement involving genetic alterations by design, accident, or bioweapon represents an existential risk. Genetic technologies indicate that genotypes and phenotypes could experience predictable deviations that revise their original genetic signature, causing a change in behavior. Governments may embrace this as useful for their agenda in creating super soldiers as weapons.

Our preconceived image of zombies is unlikely to present them as monsters, so we look for behavior that fits into that mold (Mike Adams, editor of *Natural News*, online article, September 2, 2013, "Zombie Attacks for Chicken Nuggets").

> "Real-life zombies will maraud through cities, smashing windows, stealing fast-food, threatening to eat people; and lashing out at others was experienced at a fast food chain in Toledo, Ohio, captured on video a woman demanding chicken nuggets. She came out of her car, banged on drive through window, lashed out at the clerk, then she broke the window, and she was screaming, hissing, and making animal sounds. She said, "Don't make me assume my ultimate form, I will f—— wreck you, I'm going eat your f—— face, I'm going to digest it ..."

This behavior fits our mold. They look like people but have a loss of human dignity and lack of control, are apathetic, human life has no value, so they threaten to maim and eat us.

This behavior seems far-fetched but is presenting itself within various situations. Megan Willett provided an article in the *Business Insider*, March 26, 2014, "States Most Likely to Survive a Zombie Apocalypse:

> How to survive a zombie apocalypse ... some say science will save us all, some will rely on math, others are banking on specialty gadgets or buy zombie apocalypse survival kits. Estately Organization prepared a map that determined which US state are best prepared for any zombie-related disaster based on factors such as active military per capita, martial arts enthusiast, survivalists, people with guns, and triathletes to name a few.

Tom Horn and Steve Quayle have provided additional insight into the zombie reality in a six-hour dialogue, 2014, *The Coming Zombie Apocalypse.* They tell us the Bible makes reference to the genetic alteration of people who lived before the flood. The fallen angels and their genetic creation produced soulless creatures called Nephilim. These creatures were amoral and bloodthirsty. Jesus tells us that during the end-times, mankind would witness a return of the activity that happened when Nephilims first walked the earth. Modern-day scientists have created a genetic hazard that could unleash a global pandemic. Through genetic manipulation, they can alter the behavior of people and animals to cause them to exhibit aggressive or antisocial behavior. Scientists want to reprogram people to act abnormal or without inhibitions. Experiments can and do have outcomes not anticipated by the scientists. In the movie *I Am Legend*, the scientists thought he had a cure for cancer, but the vaccination induced rabies, and people turned into zombies. This is no longer a fictional scenario, according to Jonathan D. Dinman, professor in the Department of Cell Biology and Molecular Genetics at the University of Maryland. He says,

> Such a zombie virus almost exists now and could be engineered to fully occur using the very elements depicted in the movie. Infection is nearly 100 percent lethal, and it turns people into the walking dead, and it caused them to change their behavior by reprogramming them to bite other people to spread the infection.

Vampires

Natural News, October 5, 2015, ran an article on vampires by Jennifer L. Reynolds:

> People belonging to a large, authentic vampire community in which consenting adults allow other like-minded people to make small incisions on their chest, at which time they allow the other person to treat their taste buds to some blood-consenting vampire.

The director of social work at Idaho State University, D. J. Williams, studied people who identify as vampires for about ten years. He distinguished between authentic vampires and their lifestyle are made up of conscientious, ethical, successful, and ordinary people, and the practice of sucking blood from others to increase their energy level is normal. Williams said, vampires fear coming out for fear of being misunderstood and labeled, and because of this fear, social workers should treat vampires with dignity and respect as they would with nontraditional energy seekers. He said, vampires are called goths, otherkin, furries, BDSM, and vampires were born that way.

All we can say about this report is that it is demonic in that God said not to drink or eat blood.

Cannibalism

Cannibalism was practiced preflood, where there are accounts of the giants who ate the flesh of humans. Postflood accounts of cannibalism are found in Greek and Roman legends of the gods eating their children. Incidents of cannibalism are found in West Indies, New Guinea, Lesser Antilles, Fiji, Amazon, Congo, Liberia, England, and other regions.

Tracing Egypt's heathen roots, human sacrifice was followed by ritual cannibalism. On the temple of Edifu, carvings picture all lands (Asia, Beduin, Nubians) and pictured under the feet of the pharaoh, four men are bound to be ritually sacrificed; a person hovers over them, reciting the "Book of the Subduing of the Nobility." This practice was part of an annual fertility ritual, which depicted birds, fish, and mortals as representing the enemies of the pharaoh to be eaten for breakfast, lunch, and supper. By consuming the flesh of their enemies, the Egyptians believed that they would absorb their desired qualities.

Cannibalism continued on in Egypt and elsewhere even after the Christian era. One account during the Christian era—Cyril, a deacon of Heliopolis, who despised paganism, was killed, his stomach torn open and they ate his liver.

In AD 1148, Rudwan, a criminal fleeing for his freedom, was caught and slain in front of the palace of the Khalifa. His head was cut off and his body mutilated into little pieces, only for them to be eaten by Egyptian soldiers in their belief that they would absorb the courage of the victim.

Modern-day cannibalism was reported by Wallid Shoebat, January 28, 2013, on his website. As violence escalates in Egypt, Islamists now condone cannibalism. In an interview with Al-Azhar al-Sharif, scholar and founder of Islamic jurisprudence, Egypt:

> We allowed the eating of the flesh of dead humans … under necessary conditions. It must be cooked to avoid Haram [wrongdoing] … and he can kill a murtadd [apostate] and eat him. You may kill an enemy fighter or an adulterer and eat his body. This will be justified through the establishment of committees for promotion of virtue and prevention of vice that will carry out this practice of cannibalism.

In Egypt, there exists an Islamic mafia called Promotion of Virtue and Prevention of Vice Authority—which is the exact name of the moral police in Saudi Arabia. They roam the streets, assaulting or even killing those whom they believe to be apostates. One such incident is reported on November, 2012. These mobsters entered the shop of Ahmed Gharib to use the bathroom; the owner told them that they had to ask for permission before using the restroom; they said, "We do not ask for permission." A few minutes later, thirty bearded men entered the shop to discipline him and attempted to cut off his hand, but he escaped with deep wounds. His brother tried to help, and the mob tried to cut out his tongue, but he escaped.

Under Egyptian President Morsi, the new constitution already established that the nation will be having a Saudi-style Sharia police, which will be implementing not only this sort of violence but the eating of human flesh. President Morsi's coming moral mafia and individuals will be given the power to partake in such barbarism. Morsi said, the constitution will be reviewed by Al-Azhar university scholars. This means cannibalism will be observed in Egypt.

Walid Shoebat wrote that an Egyptian butcher killed his wife, flayed her flesh off the bone, and put it for sale as lamb in his market. Islam is an intolerant, hateful religion, having its foundation in paganism. Islamists have not evolved to embrace empathy and compassion but continue in the mind-set that was demonstrated in Ramallah in which two Israeli soldiers were beaten, tortured to death to the chants of Allah Akbar, and their flesh then chewed by the crowd. In a picture, they held body parts of the Israelis and cried out, "I eat the flesh of my occupier."

Walid Shoebat, August 22, 2016, Shoebat.com, reported that a man in Florida killed two people and began eating the face of one of the dead victims. It took four police, stun gun, and a police dog to get him off the victim. Police say he was growling like an animal.

Dublin, Ireland, report on *Life Site News*, January 14, 2014, said that thirty-four-year-old Savrio Bellante killed prolife activist Tom O'Gorman by stabbing him multiple times and then eating one of his lungs.

A US cop wanted to kill a hundred women and then eat them.

There are numerous accounts of people who eat babies, beat babies to death, rape babies, starve and deprive children of basic necessities, burn their bodies, throw them into dumpsters—an endless list of inhumanity, apathy, no conscience, and lack of mercy.

Students of Bible prophecy are dissecting subjects that were off-limits to the traditional Christian mind-set. As we correlate the scriptures with the unfolding of world events, it is relevant that we understand the realm of the supernatural. The Bible says, "My people perish for lack of knowledge, accepting false doctrine, and embracing immorality." Bible study of prophecy dealt with the usual subjects but bypassed areas concerning the true nature of demonic interference in the affairs of mankind. Specifically, principalities over the world, the UFO delusion, and Frankenstein experiments creating things that God has forbidden. In the past, governments covered up this activity, and religious bodies turned a blind eye. Now we can see the unfolding and coming together of the satanic alien agenda.

> *They shall mingle themselves with the seed of men but they shall not cleave one to another.* (Daniel 2:43)

Alien technology is the mingling of celestial entities, and the seed of man/animals to create hybrids that walk among us. They may be indistinguishable because we have been programmed to tolerate people who appear to have a nice persona yet evil to the core and carry out heinous deeds. End-time signs are these technological and biological advancements that counterfeit God's creation.

Underground Bunkers

Let us surmise that all the fears of mankind are coming upon him such as a nuclear, biological, EMP, or extreme climate events. The Bible said, "Their hearts will fail them because of what they see coming." The Bible also said, "They will try to find refuge from God's judgment." This brings us to the consideration that mankind is making preparation for the Day of the Lord. Some citizens are preparing for all types of calamities, including building underground bunkers.

Mankind fears an alien invasion. The revelation of Area 51 caught our attention, and we began to look upon the earth and what secrets it hides. We became intrigued with the high level of government secrecy regarding underground operations. Very little information has come forth from the government since the creation of Area 51 in the 1950s. Mostly, the government denied the existence of a secret facility. In 2013, the government acknowledged the existence of Area 51 located at Grim Lake, Nevada, desert, occupying 4,700 acres, employing eighteen thousand working in deep underground facilities. Whatever goes on there, American tax dollars have paid for it.

In Annie Jacobsen's book, *Area 51: An Uncensored History of American's Top Secret Military Base*, Jacobsen conducted interviews with former employees from 1940 to 1960—who worked as technicians, pilots, and scientists. The combined information she gathered said Area 51 was involved in the development of nuclear weapons, advanced rockets, and planes. As a cover for government black ops, Area 51 developed into "a conspiracy theory." People who wanted to investigate these activities were discredited, and tales of reverse-engineering of alien craft and the capture of extraterrestrial bodies dead and alive was sensationalized.

The government terminology for underground bunker is *Deep Underground Military Bases*, DUMB. These underground facilities are used for the security of nuclear weapons and bioweapons. Push a red button, and the ground opens and a nuclear bomb ascends.

Other uses for the underground facilities is to maintain secrecy of classified technology and experiments that may include behavior modification, genetic engineering, human cybernetics, and intermingling nonhuman materials. These facilities will be the future home of high-level government officials and the elite. Whatever is going on underground will not be made public. In this atmosphere, government officials can subvert public scrutiny, rule of law, and achieve its goals for the one-world order.

At the end of World War II, allied troops discovered underground facilities in Germany. It was claimed Germany had a Roswell event and given alien technology to develop spaceships and bombs and to conduct human experimentation for the purpose of creating something other than a human. Germany also had covert underground facilities in Antarctica. We have mentioned that after World War II, Russia and the United States took German scientists and their valuable documentation on advanced designs to their respective countries.

The government is preparing for a Black Swan event such as an EMP, nuclear attack, or severe climate incident. They are not preparing for an invasion from outer space. During a catastrophe, only high government officials, their families, and the elite will be allowed in the underground facilities. The president will be taken to a DUMB location to ensure the continuity of government. Local government officials, police, firefighters, citizens will be on their own.

These are not mere holes in the ground but high-tech, secure bunkers having provisions to last for an indefinite period. The government has stocked these sites with food, weapons, ammunition, etc. There may be over two hundred bunkers maintained across the nation and 1,400 worldwide. The US government budgets approximately $500 billion per year to its black ops projects.

Jim Marrs, journalist and author, spoke on the Dave Hodges radio show, December 9, 2012, and provided info that hundreds of bank and Wall Street executives left their position and have gone into seclusion, in preparation for coming bad events. Marrs said that retirees from the CIA, DHS, NSA, and FEMA are relocating to safety enclaves. Marrs predicts that Washington, DC, will become obsolete. Some officials have opted out of using the underground bunkers, believing they will become targets to eliminate the people in the know; "Dead men can't tell secrets."

There is a known bunker located on a parcel of land owned by AT&T in Peter's Mountain, Virginia. This corporation is in cooperation with NSA, conducting surveillance activities. The access road has a sign warning not to enter the area (Sky Watch TV by F. Michael Maloof, September 2015).

Another facility is Cheyenne Mountain complex used by North American Aerospace Command, NORAD, which is the nation's early warning center. The Cheyenne complex is used by the Army and Airforce.

There is a DUMB in Blue Ridge mountains of Virginia called Mount Weather Complex, High Point Special Facility, constructed in 1958 and operated by FEMA. It could accommodate up to a thousand people. There are underground facilities under the Pentagon and the White House.

Some crucial information was divulged by Phil Schnieder, who worked for seventeen years as a government geologist, engineer, and metallurgist. He was directed to take soil samples from deep drilling activities miles underground. One day he and another military man descended into the lowest region ever achieved. There was a pungent smell, and they saw alien hybrids with the appearance of the Greys but taller. As they were observed by the aliens, one sent a laser beam and burned off a few of Schneider's fingers and toes. The Grey was shot and killed. Hybrids can be killed, but demonic spirits cannot be killed. As they retreated, the military agent was killed. Schnieder divulged his experiences from 1994 to 1996 before he was eliminated. He said, advanced technology is used for boring tunnels through the mountains. The units are called subterrenes, working off nuclear reactors. Tunnel debris are incinerated, requiring no need to remove rubble. Some facilities are ten miles deep. There is the Very High Speed Transit, VHST, for the Maglev train that moves at Mock 2 speed, connecting to other underground locations. It can travel from East to West Coast in thirty minutes. It operates in its own rarefied atmosphere in evac tubes, using electromagnetic wave propulsion. Schnieder had evidence of unknown metals used in stealth planes. The government made many attempts on Schnieder's life, and he was eventually assassinated. His research was confiscated. We can learn more from Richard Sauder's book, *Underground Bases and Tunnels.*

Richard Sauder also wrote on under the ocean activities. Recently, Stephen Quayle released his book *Empire Beneath the Ice*, which investigates German facilities under the Antarctica during the 1940s, where they developed advanced technology.

It turns out that Schnieder's report of tunnels is true. *Life Site News* and *Tru News* both reported in June 2016, there was a grand opening ceremony held in Gotthard, Switzerland, for the longest tunnel in the world at fifty-seven kilometers running through the Swiss Alps. This is the achievement of seventeen years of work at a cost of $12.3 billion. Video of the ceremony was attended by European leaders, Angela Merkel, Germany, Francois Hollandle, France, Matteo Renzi, Italy, Adrian Hasler, Liechtenstein, Christian Kern, Austria. The dignitaries and attendees were entertained with a six-hour program of Illuminati-themed symbolism consisting of bizarre costumes representing the image of Baphomet, underwear clad dancers simulating sexual acts and prostrating themselves before the image.

The movie *2012* gave a scenario of the destruction of earth by earthquake and tsunami, and in preparation for this event, the Chinese had constructed mass underground facilities to build arks to save those who could afford a ticket. This is similar to Noah building an ark to save a few people and animals against the flood.

Mankind has been digging holes and tunnels throughout the earth for centuries. It is no wonder that sinkholes are appearing in many places. There have been reports out of Australia, China, and various US locations. According to Randolf Orndorff, director of Eastern Geology and Paleoclimate Science in the United States, said sinkholes are more common in populated areas. We have some insight that a great deal of activity has been conducted under the oceans. Modern man now focuses on black holes in space, always attempting to enter into another realm.

<u>Seed Vault</u>

Years ago, the global elite decided to store every seed on earth in a vault in Svalbard, Norway, in an underground facility. In 2008, the vault became home to 860 thousand seed varieties, totaling around 2.25 billion seeds. Global Crop Diversity Trust oversees the vault. Nations contribute packages of seeds native to their country to be stored in the vault. Recently, Syria requested the return of some of their seeds for replanting in war-torn areas (*Washington Post*, September 23, 2015).

If the elite are preparing for something catastrophic, should we as well? Some people go to extremes in storing food, water, ammunition, and other necessities. We believe that some moderate preparations for survival be in place. If the power grid is disabled, it would be a good idea to have flashlights and candles. With the power grid down, people will be unable to pump gas or get money from ATMs. Therefore, it would be a good idea to keep the gas tank filled and have some money on hand. If the power grid is down, pharmacy and food stores will close in a day or two. Having a portable grill, fuel, and matches on hand will help when you need to heat water and cook; long-shelf-life food, smart people have stored. It would be a good idea to keep some drugs available for insulin, high blood, pain, or first aid provisions for wounds. Public water will not be available to homes if the power grid is down, and in that event, knowing where there is an alternative source of water is wise. Storing up portable water for hygiene, handwashing clothes, or toilets will be a big help. Finally, have guns and ammunition available because when others have no provisions of their own, they are coming after yours.

Did 2012 Mark the Beginning of the End?

A generation may be counted as seventy, fifty, or forty years. Moses and the Israelites were in the wilderness for forty years. Some scholars measure our generation beginning with the establishment of Israel as a nation in 1948 and a fulfillment of prophecy.

> *Who has heard such a thing? Who has seen such a thing? Shall the earth be made to bring forth in one day or <u>shall a nation be born at once?</u>* (Isaiah 66:8)

From 1948 to 2016, sixty-eight years have passed. Israel was in Babylonian captivity for seventy years. Calculating from the six-day war in Israel, 1967 to 2016 is forty-nine years. Every fiftieth year is celebrated as a Jubilee year. In considering the concept of a generation, we look to see if the year 2012 had prophetic significance that aligns mankind with the end-time generation.

In the chronicles and <u>legends</u> of various cultures, such as the Mayan and the prediction of seers like Nostradamus, they speak of a time when there will be an alignment between

Sagittarius and Scorpio in the center of the galaxy. The sun will appear in the center of these two, forming a cross. It is suggested that this alignment occurred around 11,000 BC. Computer simulation anticipates this alignment will occur again around 2012–2013. This could be considered the thirteenth constellation associated with the end of the age.

The Mayan calendar was based on signs in the heaven and predicted that on December 21, 2012, the sun would pass through the galactic plain and align with the moon and planets. The Mayan astrological signs saw the sun arising in Sagittarius symbolic of a centaur with a bow, which coordinates with the book of Revelation, the first horse of the apocalypse and its rider with a bow going forth to conquer. They saw this centaur coming out from the mouth of Leviathan and the sun god rising again, both a reference to Satan and his Antichrist. Inscriptions made in stone by the Mayans found in Tabasco, Mexico, predicted 2012 will see the return of the spirit of Bolon Yokte K'u, the underworld lord who represents the solar system and its nine supporting gods orbiting the sun. The Antichrist may have been crowned in 2012.

The sensationalism of the Mayan calendar for 2012 had some believing it was the end of the world. It was a sign seen by pagans and religious groups that we are entering the end of an age. It was claimed that the world had come to a precipice signaled by the year 2012. The Aztecs and Incas also believed in cycles. They believed celestial cycles were affected by other worldly entities.

The predictions are associated with the sun. Extreme heat in 2015 of 118 degrees and upward killed over 1,800 people in India. In the past few years, the sun has exhibited strong solar eruptions and dark spots appearing to orbit the sun.

The Cherokee Rattlesnake Prophecy made by the Cherokee Native Americans around AD 1812 predicted the serpent constellation will take on a different configuration. The serpent will have head feathers, glowing eyes, and wings, hands and arms holding a bowl of blood, and its tail having seven rattles also glowing. They saw this as the return of a spirit. The serpent is associated with Satan. The book of Revelation gives us symbolism of the beast arising with seven heads. The Cherokee calendar will end with the alignment of Jupiter, Venus, Orion in 2012 followed by the awakening of the Pleiades star system.

Hindu Kali Yuga calendar ties into the Mayan's fifth Baktun cycle, predicting global earth changes following 2012.

Jonathan Edwards in the mid-1700s believed Antichrist would come between 2012–2016. When the United States designed its currency, it incorporated a symbolic pyramid with the all-seeing eye and a list of dates from 1776 to the year 2012, which some scholars believe is the time when the Antichrist will enter the world scene.

In David Flynn's book, *Temple at the Center of Time*, infers the relevance of the year 2012. Flynn calculates that the circle of the earth is 33.33 degrees, or <u>2,012</u> nautical miles.

Mount Hermon, site of the fallen angels, lies 33.33 degrees north, 33.33 degrees east from the equator, and is 2,012 miles from the equator and 2,012 miles from prime meridian location of Mount Hermon. Does the location at Mount Hermon set in time the unveiling of the one-world leader to be in the year of 2012? Flynn associates the UFO crash at Roswell, New Mexico, to be 33 degrees north latitude and 2,012 miles from the equator and is aligned with Mount Hermon. Flynn said this does not appear to be happenstance but a deliberate message from the time of the fallen angels to the Mayan end of their long-count calendar, 2012. David Flynn passed away March 2012.

Rabbi Judah Ben Samuel, died in AD 1217, prophesied that the Ottoman Turks would conquer Jerusalem 1517 for four hundred years up to 1917 when the British took back Jerusalem. Beginning from 1917 to 2017, he believed the Messianic end-times would begin.

The Jewish Kabbalah predicts signs announcing the Messiah will come 2012 to 2013. A messianic figure arriving on the scene at this time will be the arrival of Antichrist.

The 2012 presidential race was entered by Mitt Romney, champion of the Mormons, and their "white horse" prophecy versus Barack Obama, the "sun rising" in the west and his mantra of change. Obama's reelection in 2012 was a sign pointing to the eminence of the Antichrist and the false prophet. Along this same time line, Pope Francis came on the scene.

From 2012 to 2016, prophecy watchers have seen the unfolding of signs and omens. Recently, the Watchman of the Harvest posted the numbers 9 and 23 were an omen having been publicized in movies and events for years by the Illuminati and other occult groups. Around the 9/23 time frame, there would be a Medudeshet consecration of the world in Gehinnom, Jerusalem. It was reported in *Breaking Israel News* that a few Jews, Arabs, and Christians congregated in this region for meditation as part of the AMEN event. What is disturbing about the location is found in Enoch 26, called the Valley of Hinnon, or Gehenna, a place sterile and cursed, and in the latter days, the unsaved will gather in this place of judgment. Joshua 15 calls the Valley of Hinnon a place where Israel sacrificed their children to god Molech.

CERN's Large Haldron Collider was to be activated again on September 23, 2016. As particles collide at incredible speed, the reaction sends ripples into the earth and earth atmosphere.

We have come to the year 2016, or 5776 on the Hebrew calendar, and will continue to watch the unveiling of events.

The Day of the Lord

What is the Day of the Lord? We could picture it as an everything bagel sliced in half. The halves represent God in the beginning and God at the end of time. Sandwiched between are six thousand years of human history. We can look at the physical components of the day of the Lord, but it is a little more difficult to expose the spiritual strongholds that have infested the whole world. There are hundreds of unseen spiritual entities, and we can deduce their activities by what can be observed in our physical world. The world and its people are wicked, and the prognosis for wickedness is judgment. The healing of the earth comes with the finality of the Day of the Lord as in redemption, restoration, and a time of peace. The Day of the Lord could be counted from the birth of Jesus to his Second Advent. Or it could have begun after his Resurrection and the beginning of the age of grace. Perhaps the day of the Lord began with the establishment of Israel in 1948 as a nation.

The Bible makes numerous references to the Day of the Lord as far back as 640 BC in the writings of Zephaniah 1:7 during the reign of King Josiah. Israel had fallen into worshipping false god Molech. They had again taken up the practices of the heathens as modern mankind is plagued with today. Zephaniah is told by God to preach that the Day of the Lord is at hand; turn from wickedness and repent. Hundreds of years after Zephaniah, the apostle Peter admonishes those who mock the return of the Lord but reassures us that the Day of the Lord will come as a thief in the night followed by a great noise, the heavens seem to pass away, and the elements will melt with fervent heat so much so that the earth and the evil therein will be burned up (2 Peter 3:10).

In modern times, there are many voices crying out in the wilderness, sounding the alarm that the Day of the Lord is at hand. Regardless of the time frame of the Day of the Lord, it appears we are now in a time of revival parallel to perilous times, and judgment is looming. The prophecy foretells that in the latter days, there will be an outpouring of the Holy Spirit before the Rapture of the body of Christ. Around the world, people are coming because the Holy Spirit is drawing them to Jesus.

> *It will come to past in <u>the last days,</u> I will pour out my Spirit upon all flesh and your sons and your daughters will prophesy, young men will see visions and old men will dream dreams ...* (Acts 2:17–21)

This same sign was given in Joel 2:28:

> *And it will come to pass <u>afterward</u> that I will pour out my spirit upon all flesh and your sons and your daughters will prophesy, your old men will dream dreams your young men will see visions, and also upon the servants and upon your handmaids in those days will I pour out my spirit ...*
>
> *And he will come unto us as the rain as the <u>latter and the former</u> rain unto the earth.* (Joel 6:3)

The "former" outpouring of the Holy Spirit began on the Day of Pentecost. Since that day, the Holy Spirit has been "poured" out at different times and in various places. One of the signs given for the "latter" day is the outpouring of the spirit being evidenced around the world. The history of the Azusa Street outpouring began April 9, 1906, in California. William J. Seymour was a student of Pentecostal preacher, Charles Parham. Seymour preached in a private home. The presence of God was so great that the small house could not accommodate the crowds. They moved the meeting to 312 Azusa Street, where the manifestation of the Spirit continued for over five years. Believers from Baptist, Mennonite, Quakers, Presbyterian faiths and representative from various ethnic groups—such as, Africans, Europeans, Germans, and Spanish—attended these revival meetings. Another sign of the latter rain is that many Muslims and others have had visions of Jesus. Indonesia is a predominantly Muslim nation. Evangelist Binny Hinn reported that his revival in Indonesia, September 2014, drew 1.6 million people in two days. He said it was sponsored and paid for by the Muslim government. In Iraq, Iran, Syria, and Egypt, Christians are drawing others to Jesus. Pat Robertson reports that the use of their ministry's SuperBook of Bible stories has drawn a significant number of people to Christ in China. Chinese believers in Christ are exploding upward to a hundred million. In these wicked times, the Holy Spirit is working double time to help people get saved before the Rapture.

In our analysis of signs pointing to the Day of the Lord, we need to keep in mind that there is a spiritual component at work. It can be called the spirit of Antichrist, which is contrary or opposite of everything good and holy. These spirits attack the people of God as evidenced in an increase of persecution of Christians and Jews. There are evil spirits associated with sexual perversion and seemingly to have created a sexual epidemic. One instance is the repulsive acts of rape being carried out by Muslims and sex traffickers. Certain government heads are pushing for the spirit of Aphrodite—an entity that is both male and female as in transgenderism, homosexuality, etc. There are spirits that cause dissention in families and nations. Addition to drugs, alcohol, nicotine are driven by evil spirits, and there are spirits that can affect the weather.

We Will See Signs in Heaven and Earth

In the Old Testament, Joel 2:30, and in the New Testament, Acts 2:19 both provide another sign given before the return of the Lord:

> *I will show wonders in heaven above, signs in the earth, blood, fire and smoke, the sun will turn into darkness and the moon into blood before that great and notable Day of the Lord come.*

The book of Revelation pertains to the end of the age, and in Revelation 6:12, we see the prophecy of Joel and the repeat of the prophecy in Acts, telling us:

> *I beheld when he opened the sixth seal and there was a great earthquake, the sun became black as sackcloth of hair and the moon became as blood and the stars of heaven fell unto the earth ...*

These passages speak about the signs that are brought about by God. There will also be signs and lying wonders brought about by Satan to deceive the people.

There are reports of rain mixed with blood and fire, pillars of clouds have been seen, and the sun and moon have been eclipsed on various dates as well as the moon appearing bloodred.

Sign in the Clouds

March 17, 2015, a picture was posted on Facebook of a cross in a cloud formation. If it were Photoshopped or not, it was pleasant to the eye. In 2014, during the war with Hamas, Israel called their defense efforts "pillar of cloud," and a cloud column formation was seen in the sky. Another unusual cloud formation was seen in Norway; here the clouds were forming a perfect moving spiral.

Asteroids and Comets

There is a great deal of debris in outer space, and reports of comets or meteors heading toward earth are frequently made. Recent discovery of the comet Ison is seen moving close to the sun around November 2013, near Jewish festival of Hanukah. It will come close to the sun, causing greater solar flares, which will impact the comet itself. February 2013, an asteroid exploded over Chelyabinsk, Russia, injuring 1,700 people.

Asteroid "Pitbull" passed over Earth at a distance of twenty-one thousand miles. September 7, 2014, debris hit New Zealand, creating a thirty-nine-foot-wide and twenty-five-foot-deep crater in Nicaraguan capital of Managua.

December 23, 2015, Sky Watch TV and *Breaking News Israel*, March 4, 2016, reported three autistic Jews in Israel made nonverbal predictions an asteroid, Nibiru, or Planet X, would make a near Earth pass, and its debris will cause volcanoes, tornadoes, earthquakes, and tsunamis. Rabbi Amnon Yitzchak also believes chunks from the asteroid could hit earth near end of March 2016 or early April. World leaders and Obama have warned that a catastrophe is coming. NASA has gone dark. Zechariah Sitchin, Russian Jew, 1920–2010 believed there was a planet beyond Pluto called Nibiru, or Planet X, passing through our solar system every 3,600 years. Sitchin said fifty years ago, it was close and would cause climate changes and death. He wrote a book in 1991, *The 12th Planet.* Ezekiel 38:22 predicts God will rain down fire and brimstone, and Zechariah 13:8 predicts two-thirds of the population will die.

Solar Eruptions

There are reports that the sun may experience a reversal of its north and south poles by the end of 2013. This phenomena occurs once every eleven years. It may cause greater weather events and geomagnetic storms that will affect the planet. These geomagnetic storms may interfere with satellites and space stations. Winter of 2014 in the United States was extreme. Reported by Stanford University, Wilcox Solar Observatory, March 17, 2015, two solar eruptions made contact with the earth at a force of four (4). March 20, 2015, there will be a solar eclipse.

CME, Coronal Mass Ejection, near miss in July 2012 would have been devastating worldwide. NASA reports the CME was the most powerful solar storm seen in 150 years. NASA reported, August 2014, they are monitoring X class eruptions, which is the most powerful, tagged AR2151. September 10 and 11, 2014, tons of solar material was projected toward the earth at five million miles per hour, arriving in our atmosphere nineteen hours later (NASA, Slooh, Virtual Telescope Project, Goldstone Complex).

End of 2015, the nations of the world are concerned about climate change. Governments will not tell the masses if they are in danger of a catastrophe, such as a CME direct hit on earth or impact by a meteor/comet, which would cause mass extinction, power grid failures, extreme weather. The Bible tells us at the end of the age the earth will be on fire.

Signs in the Earth

July 27, 2015, Russia reported severe lightning and heavy rains, 40 percent increase. A huge fireball exploded over Bangkok. Extreme heat was reported in Israel, Iraq, Iran, India, in the range of 118 to 167 degrees. August to September brought a sandstorm to hit Israel and Syria. Flooding was reported in Israel. Galilee hit by a rare hailstorm. The United States has raging fires in California and flooding in various areas.

Volcanoes

January 2016, approximately ten to seventeen volcanoes erupted within a two=week period. These volcanoes are located within the ring of fire in the Pacific Ocean. Two volcanoes, three thousand miles apart, erupted at the same time. Earthquakes and volcanoes are associated.

Earthquakes

- October 2015, Afghanistan, 7.5
- April 2015, Nepal, India, 7.8
- September 2015, Chile, 9
- Hawaii, over 8.3 magnitude

August 2016—Italy, 6.2, November 2016, New Zealand 7.4

These are a few recent earthquakes. Emergency planners on the West Coast are preparing for the deadly big one. John Vidale, director of the Pacific Northwest Seismic Network at the University of Washington displays a beta version of an early warning system in Seattle. Seismologist say a full rupture of a 650-mile-long offshore fault from North California to British Columbia would result in a tsunami. Lt. Col. Clayton Braun of the Washington State Army National Guard prepares for an emergency military response plan when a tsunami and earthquake occur. The contingency plan and response would include waves of cargo planes, helicopters, ships, and tens of thousands of soldiers, emergency officials, mortuary teams, police officers, firefighters, engineers, medical personnel, and other specialists. This planned response would be superior to that of hurricanes Katrina and Sandy. The plan factors in the devastation caused in 2011 by a 9.0 earthquake and tsunami that hit Japan (*The Atlanta Journal Constitution*, January 24, 2016, AP Terrence Petty).

Floods

God promised not to flood the entire world, but he did promise that a sign of the end of the age would be with the roaring of the oceans.

In the United States, flooding occurred in September 2015 in Utah, April 2016, Texas, Houston, June 2016, West Virginia, and August 2016 in the Louisiana region, causing unprecedented destruction and loss of life. In 2005, this region became famous for the aftermath of Katrina Hurricane and flooding. The Gulf of Mexico experienced devastation from the BP toxic oil spill. Fishing and tourist industry suffered as well as untold death of fish and wildlife. Some contractors benefited from cleanup and providing toxic chemicals for cleanup. EMA and Red Cross received millions in funding and provided meager assistance. Some alternative news sites suggest this region is being targeted to depopulate the coastal regions to develop an energy and trade hub.

In other parts of the world, flooding has occurred.

Sign of the Four Blood Moons

Presently, there is some sensation regarding the four blood moons that appeared between 2014 and in 2015. Some say God is using this as an attention-getter that something catastrophic is coming, and it is centered around Israel.

As of this writing, two blood moons occurred during 2014 and 2015. Did we see any significant events that tie into this cycle? We did see that Hamas bombed Israel for a few weeks. We see that Hezbolla in Lebanon has released a few missiles into Israel. We see that the United Nations is considering war crimes against Israel, and there is a movement to take part of Jerusalem from Israel. ISIS is threatening Israel at the Syrian border. There was an incident at Mecca. The Ebola outbreak began in Africa and is spreading. In our chapter 12, we further discuss the blood moon events as associated with Israel.

People observe planetary catastrophe as well as moral decline and social unrest in fragments. If it does not affect them personally, they could be somewhat apathetic. For instance, a county in the state of Georgia may experience a devastating tornado. Other places in Georgia that had no affects from the storm may feel some sympathy, but for the most part, they are detached from that event. In 2013, people living in the Staten Island area of New York were hit with a powerful hurricane, flooding, and power outage, causing significant devastation. People living in other states may have felt sympathetic, but since they were not impacted, it is business as usual. People will be living their life, believing they are dwelling in peace and safety, then sudden destruction. Two will be working in the field, and one will be taken, and the other left. Woe to the woman who is with child; she will need to find refuge.

Trumpet and Boom Sounds

These could be a supernatural occurrence or results of HAARP experiments.

Loud booms, strange lights in the sky in Michigan, and trumpets heard from heaven, booms from the earth. Bob Powell, the *Truth Is Viral*, a Michigan resident was trying to investigate the nature of the sounds and vibrations (Pakalert Press blog). Booms heard in New Jersey, Connecticut, South Carolina, caused windows to rattle, January 6, 2013. Similar sounds heard in Alaska, Oklahoma, Massachusetts, Indiana. Some claim it could be due to underground facility activity. December 2014, booms heard in Idaho, Illinois, New York. May 2015, reports of trumpet sounds heard. Reports come from various parts of the world. In 2016, reports of unusual sounds heard in Africa, Netherlands, England. One report heard heavenly music in Florida.

We mentioned prominent signs pointing to the Day of the Lord are apostasy, increase in lawlessness, ungodliness, abortion, and immorality as well as the rise of persecution and death of believers. Nations are in distress and chaos rules. The masses are deceived. As all these signs come to a climax; surely, the Rapture, tribulation, and Second Coming are not far off. These signs and events contribute significantly in defining the Day of the Lord and point to the beginning of the end. Chapter 19 provides additional details as the Day of the Lord moves humanity into the tribulation period.

As the Day of the Lord has a component of signs, in some instances, the signs are warnings. Some heed the warning, while others reject them. The prophet Daniel predicted a sign of the time of the end is the increase in knowledge and man running to and fro (Daniel 12:4). Daniel also warns of the coming one-world leader who demands global control. We understand that during the last two hundred years, great technological advancements have been achieved. We also know that with the invention of flight, man has been able to travel the globe. A sign that the warning phase has come to an end is preceded by the fervency of events. For example, millions are evacuating Syria, North Africa, Iraq, and other areas seeking refuge in Greece, Europe, Germany, United States, etc. This sign in Daniel also predicts knowledge will increase.

Organisms Occurring Naturally in Our Environment Can Be Lethal in the Wrong Hands

Radiation

Nuclear plants do emit radiation operating under normal conditions. In the case of the 2011 Japanese nuclear reactors damaged by earthquake and tsunami, it resulted in high levels of radiation fallout. The effects of radiation poisoning are seen in animals with lesions, killing marine life, and humans presenting with a variety of illness. Radiation particles are carried on air and water currents. Governments are maintaining a cap on the actual results of radiation poisoning.

Thomas Henry, *Natural News*, January 12, 2014, reports: US Officials deny that radiation levels from Fukushima pose a threat to American lives in spite of evidence. Russia has rejected Japanese car imports after testing showed radiation contamination. Russia is also checking seafood imports sourced anywhere in the Pacific Ocean. United States, EPA, and FDA are downplaying concerns about radiation contamination while increasing its radiation limits in order to avoid alarming the public. Statements from EPA National Air and Radiation Environmental Laboratory made reassuring claims that it was actively monitoring real-time air quality and detected no elevated levels of radiation in March 2011. An internal audit in 2012 revealed that 20 percent of its 124 real-time monitors were broken, and those functioning were incapable of taking accurate measurements because the filters that should be changed twice per week had gone anywhere from two to ten months unchanged.

Thomas Henry, *Natural News*, January 21, 2014, reports: Radiation levels at Fukushima plant increased 800 percent over government limits. This report comes from the Tokyo Electric Power Company, which eclipses the Japanese government report. Contaminated water, some three hundred to four hundred tons, is leaking daily into the Pacific Ocean. Seventy-one US sailors are suing Tokyo Electric Power Company because they now suffer from brain tumors, thyroid cancer, and leukemia as a result of exposure to radiation three hundred times the safe level.

Personal Liberty Digest, Bob Livingston, reports on radiation danger levels on the California coast in a report from North Pacific Marine Science Organization annual meeting by researchers from Fisheries and Oceans Canada confirm that the radioactive plume from Japan is reaching shores of Canada and United States in the water and air. Recent snow in Saint Louis and Arkansas showed elevated radiation levels. West Coast tuna contaminated with Cesium 134 and 137; herrings are bleeding from their gills, bellies, and eyeballs. *Vancouver Sun* tested Japan fish imports. It showed 73 percent contamination in mackerel; 91 percent in halibut; 92 percent, sardines; 93 percent, tuna; 94 percent, cod; 100 percent, carp, seaweed, shark, and monkfish; and high rate of death among sea lions.

In the 1960s, the Pentagon authorized the treatment of black cancer patients with extreme radiation to allow Department of Defense to study the effects of high levels of radiation.

Dr. Eugen Saenger did this to poor black Americans, exposing them to levels of radiation 7,500 times greater to the chest area, causing intense pain, vomiting, bleeding, and death.

Saint Louis, Missouri, reported a radioactive landfill smoldering for years is leaking into the public water supply due to heavy rains and flooding.

Indian Point, New York, March 2016, media reported radiation was seeping into ground water, increasing toxic level 740 times higher than safe level from a nuclear power plant.

San Fernando Valley, California, October 2015, residents were reported having to relocate and some schools closed due to a natural gas leak into the environment at 110,000 pounds per hour.

Pestilence, Bacteria, Viruses

Laboratories create viruses, such as Zika, and pharmaceutical companies develop chemical aerosols as a deterrent. The AIDS virus was a laboratory creation, requiring pharmaceuticals to develop drugs for treatment. Ebola was designed in a laboratory, and pharmaceuticals develop a vaccine for cure. The bacterial or viral elements in these plagues build up a molecular defense against antibiotic, drug, or chemical compounds, becoming superbugs that resist treatment.

The cycle of disease begins when a microcosm is laden with foreign material, which is then transmitted to other species, who in turn present with a viral or bacterial ailment and are treated with an overuse of antibiotics or vaccines, which compromise the immune system, hindering the body's ability to heal itself, resulting in further contamination of other living organism, debilitating health, and eventually, death. Following are examples of infections:

- Listeria, salmonella, tuberculosis are caused by bacteria.
- Hepatitis and meningitis are caused by a viral infection. Hepatitis attacks the blood, and meningitis attacks the brain.
- Ringworms, athlete's foot, and eczema are caused by fungus.

Carbapenem-Resistant Enterobactgeriaceae, CRE

Mike Adams, *Natural News*, July 17, 2014, reports that drug-resistant superbug infections have reached near-epidemic levels across United States hospitals, documented by Infection Control and Hospital Epidemiology, *Journal of the Society for Healthcare Epidemiology of America*, reporting a 500 percent increase in infections. Dr. Joshua Thaden's research says this dangerous (mutated) bacteria is finding its way into health care facilities nationwide. CRE is fast approaching epidemic levels. WHO (World Health Organization) calls it one of the three greatest threats to human health and is antibiotic resistant.

Big pharmaceutical and research corporations are responsible for most viral or bacteria epidemics, of which they have no effective cure, save for ineffective vaccinations. Center for Disease Control admitted that we are now living in a postantibiotic era, and antibiotic resistance bugs are a reality. The consensus of infectious disease experts report the world is facing an onslaught of outbreaks.

Influenza

US virologist intentionally engineered super deadly pandemic flu virus, as H5N1 avian flu. Researchers do not want their work to be restricted by government regulations or watch groups. According to *Time*, regulatory agencies want precise details about how the labs developed the deadly flu strain, how they infected the public, and why research was allowed to continue at the expense of public health. This may be window dressing (Ethan Huff, *Before It's News*, January 31, 2013).

Recently, Merck made millions on the swine flu vaccine, which was ineffective against the flu. Merck was exposed by whistle-blower who said Merck committed scientific fraud by spiking test subjects' blood with animal antibodies in order to fake the vaccine's efficacy. Some may recall that Merck experimented on the Tuskegee victims and Guatemalan prisoners with syphilis and held back a cure using penicillin.

Zika Virus

Media reported January 2016 that mosquitos carrying the Zika virus had infected millions in South America, Puerto Rico, and was moving into North America. Zika was claimed to cause deformity in the fetus of pregnant women, and there is no scientific testing or proof that it causes microcephaly. There have been twenty-five thousand cases of microcephaly in the United States and was not related to Zika virus. The media was quick to show babies born with small heads and instill fear. This outbreak is suspicious and raises a red flag. South America was reported as ground zero right before the 2016 summer Olympics in Brazil. Could this be an opportunity for big pharma to come up with a vaccination against Zika virus? People in Brazil or traveling to the nation just might want to get inoculated. Revenue would increase for big pharma. Investigators disclosed the Brazil government dumped pyriproxyfen into their public water supply. The warning on the chemical container states: "Toxic to aquatic environment." Avoid release into the environment. Was this due to incompetence or done intentionally? This chemical is manufactured by Sumitono Corporation, a partner of Monsanto.

We are always researching for data to fill in the holes. The Zika virus outbreak is not an epidemic, and this virus has been around for seventy years, affecting upward to 75 percent of the world's population with no reported birth defects, serious illness, or death. South America had completely eliminated Zika during the 1950s. In an earlier consideration of the Zika virus, the CDC said the Zika virus was not very harmful. Once infected, the body will self-immunize against the virus, and no vaccine is required.

The virus was harvested from the rhesus monkey in Uganda in 1947. The Rockefeller Foundation isolated the virus and researched it. During the McCarthy era, the US military began research at Fort Detrick, Maryland, to see if mosquitoes could be used as a biological weapons delivery system. Additional reports indicate these mosquitoes were fed sugar water, blood, and the Zika virus to infect the larva. Hundreds of thousands of A-aegypti mosquitoes carrying the Zika virus were released in Georgia and Florida. The chemical industry profits by developing a pesticide against the mosquitoes.

Natural News reported that regions in South America had been sprayed with a toxin called pyriproxyfen to kill the mosquitoes. This chemical is a growth inhibitor to the mosquito larvae and alters its development. The spraying of the chemical would also affect the nervous system of the neurodevelopment of the human fetus, resulting in deformities in some cases. The above reports confirm that a pesticide contaminate contributed to birth defects (Sarah Laskow, Atlas Obscura and *Natural News*).

Genetically modified organisms can be used to combat malaria and dengue fever carried by other mosquitoes. The Zika mosquitoes were genetically programmed to mate with other mosquitoes, but they came in contact with pesticides, containing tetracyctine, which altered their program, increasing their population instead of decreasing it. CDC and WHO had been downplaying this outbreak until media reported over four thousand babies were born with small heads.

Dr. Francis Boyle, researcher and author on biological warfare, said the release of this genetically modified virus was intentional and the Bill Gates Foundation was involved in funding the research. Boyle said swine flu and Ebola were created to depopulate the planet (Alex Jones, Info Wars, January 2016).

Bill Gates said, "The world today had 6.8 billion people … that's headed up to about nine billion. Now if we do a really great job on new vaccines, health care, reproductive health services, we could lower that by perhaps 10 to 15 percent." Our interpretation of Gates's statement—toxic vaccines cause illness and death; abortion and sterilization will reduce the population.

Other wealthy people such as Ted Turner, Rockefeller, support depopulation efforts.

Professor Erik Pianka, speaker at the 109th conference at Texas Academy of Science in 2006 and a proponent for depopulation said, "The best way to kill 90 percent of the human population is to spread an airborne version of Ebola virus … Humans are destroying the planet and need to be culled in mass numbers." To this statement, the attendees gave an enthusiastic standing ovation (Ethan Huff, *Natural News*, January 29, 2016).

Report by Aaron Dykes and Melissa Melton, writers for *Truthstream Media*, August 2014, "Edible vaccine inventor jokes about culling population with genetically modified virus." Dr. Charles Arntzen, head of Biodesign Institute for Infectious Diseases and Vaccinology and developer of Ebola vaccine tested on mice, was asked if the earth was able to sustain eight billion people and if we should concern ourselves with feeding them or should we allow natural forces to limit population growth. Arntzen's response was, "Has anybody seen *Contagion* [the virus killed one-fourth of the population] that's your answer, go out and use genetic engineering to create a better virus."

Ebola

In 2014, Ebola was released in West African countries of Sierra Leone, Liberia, Guinea. These were the hardest hit with a few reported cases in Nigeria, Senegal, and Mali. The death toll in February 2014 was six hundred, climbed to over ten thousand in October 2014. There were several cases in Spain of a priest returning from Africa and a nurse taking all precautions contracted the virus, October 6, 2014. Several doctors returning to the United States, having worked with the infected, did contract the disease around October 2014.

It was reported on *Natural News*, September 2014 that the United States owns the patent on the Ebola virus and various strains. The virus was collected in 2007 and filed under EboBun. It was deposited in the CDC with clearance to access it whenever needed. Fact-check on Google. There was an Ebola outbreak in November 2007 in Bundibugyo District of Uganda, which is next to Kenya, where Obama's father lived. EboBun is short for Ebola in Bundibugyo. The 2014 outbreak is on the opposite side of the continent from Kenya.

According to the media, treatment for Ebola is experimental, and currently, a few companies have untested vaccine. *Israel Now News* reported they have a firm in Israel, Protalix, which developed a vaccine for Ebola. They said it is made from tobacco plants. The Israeli cure was ignored because the creators of these viruses want to study the impact on civilization. If they created these viruses, it is most likely they have a cure. Holding back on the cure will increase demand, which will generate greater profits when the cure is sold internationally.

Like Ebola, AIDS virus was developed and released on the African continent and was initially spread between homosexuals. This recent Ebola outbreak raises a red flag as to its origins and underlying intentions. If it had developed into a pandemic, investors in the cure would be making a lot of money. FDA had put a vaccine on hold created by Tekmira Pharmaceutical but then released it for testing on humans. Stock went from $14 a share to $24 a share overnight.

Obama appointed Ron Klain to be his Ebola czar, October 2014. His background is attorney-at-law, Washington insider, no medical experience, and served as chief of staff to Joe Biden and Al Gore. Klain commented, "Prepare for next outbreak, need a global squad or international unit."

United States sent three thousand troops to Liberia to set up seventeen treatment centers, allowing the United States to follow through with the establishment of military bases in African countries with the reasoning it is now a global threat. On the surface, it appears to be a humanitarian relief effort but may be a cover for something more sinister.

Mike Adams, *Natural News*, October 3, 2014, states United States may be complicit in the spread of Ebola. According to Dr. Gil Mobley, the CDC is lying or grossly incompetent: "Patient Zero" Thomas Eric Duncan was the first confirmed case of Ebola in the United States. He came from Liberia to United States. Coming from Liberia did not raise a red flag at Washington, DC, or Dallas Fort Worth airports. He was not questioned or screened for health conditions. When his condition worsened, he went to a hospital and was sent home. Few days later, he returned to the hospital and was classified as in critical condition. The apartment where Duncan was staying with four other people had not been professionally sanitized. *New York Times* and Fox News said the infected sheets and towels used by Duncan were still in the apartment. The other people were forced into isolation in the contaminated apartment. One woman, Louise Troh, told reporters she was tired of being locked up and decided to leave. The *Los Angeles Times* reported that officials issued a confinement order, but they did not stay. The US government continued to allow flights into United States from Liberia and Sierra Leone. The United States had no problem canceling flights to Israel during the Hamas bombings. It would seem the US government would take measures to prevent the spread of Ebola. This government's inaction reminds us that the US Southern border remains penetrable.

Middle East Respiratory Syndrome, MERS, is a superbug. It is resistant to medical treatment, antibiotics, vaccines. In Saudi Arabia, 140 cases reported in 2014 and some cases reported in Egypt. Health care workers were exposed and infected. They will transmit the disease to others.

Interovirus EV D-68

September 2014, media report that approximately a thousand children across the United States that had contracted this respiratory virus claimed to have come from South American immigrants. The virus attacks the respiratory systems and causes paralysis in limbs. As of October 1, 2014, forty-eight states had reported cases and five deaths (Fox News). Obama has signed an executive order to push for a mandatory vaccination campaign, allowing the federal government power to force people to be quarantined if they show signs of respiratory illness. Merely coughing in public could get you taken away and placed in a FEMA facility.

Chikungunya has been reported in thirty-five US states as well as Puerto Rico and the Virgin Islands, reported 497 cases. The virus was first reported in South America and moved into the United States.

Bubonic plague outbreak found in a city in China. This plague is spread by rodents. Fleas that bite rats can bite humans, transmitting the disease. Government quarantined entire city. Bubonic plague wiped out millions of people in Europe in the 1300s; it was called the Black Death. Rumor said United States may have dropped a bomb on Korea laden with the bubonic plague.

Small pox viruses were discovered at research center near Washington, DC, that had been forgotten and were improperly stored. Anthrax is supposed to be under control by the US government, but quantities have been released and unaccounted for.

The CDC and other government agencies are careless in the handling and disposal of pathogens.

Report by Ethan A. Huff, July 25, 2014, *Natural News*, said, "Hundreds of vials of freeze-dried exotic pathogens were discovered at a government laboratory, abandoned vials labeled 'Dengue,' 'Influenza,' 'Q fever' were among twelve boxes sitting in the corner of a cold storage room in the National Institute of Health in Maryland. AP said there were around three hundred vials, some labeled 'Smallpox.' FDA is investigating, according to Deputy Director Dr. Peter Marks. This discovery comes as it was recently disclosed that anthrax was released at the CDC in Atlanta. The vials were sent to DHS for safekeeping."

God provided mankind with natural remedies (herbs) and natural antibiotics, such as honey and garlic, to fight against sickness. Traditional medical treatment using drugs, chemotherapy, and radiation decrease the body's immune system to fight back.

Vaccinations, a Toxic Cocktail

Big pharma world has made billions developing vaccines for children and adults to counteract the bacteria and viruses they created. Theirs is a never-ending cycle. Release a virus, develop a vaccine, sell to the medical profession, and make money. We refer to these vaccines as a toxic cocktail because vaccinations contain aborted human fetal tissue, altered DNA material, and viruses according to National Vaccine Information Center. In the 1960s, researchers extracted lung tissue from a fourteen-week aborted baby and developed a cell line known as MRC-5 and developed Varivax vaccine for chicken pox, measles, mumps, rubella. RA27/3 was developed from another aborted human baby and developed MMRII to target measles, mumps, rubella. According to NVIC, vaccines contain fetal cell lines, human albumin from blood and genetically modified yeast. Data tracking the side effects of vaccinations believe it causes autism, allergies, attention deficient, respiratory problems, cancer, neurological, brain damage, and death. One out of four children has developed autism. Infants and young children have cancers, tumors, and other diseases. It has been reported that some doctors inject newborn babies, causing death. The state forces parents to get between eight to twenty-three injections prior to entering public school. These side effects are reaching epidemic levels (Mike Adams, *Natural News*, January 29, 2013). The news media promotes the hype that vaccinations are helpful to prevent chicken pox, measles, mumps, and more. Parents who do not want their children vaccinated are threatened.

Whistle-blower Dr. William Thompson at the CDC admitted to scientific fraud to hide the link between MMRII vaccine and autism. United Kingdom reports reveal that GlaxoSmithKline manufacturer of MMRII knew in the mid-1900s that there were problems with the vaccine, which caused adverse events in children—such as, encephalitis, autism, intestinal problems, seizures, and brain damage. Measles, mumps, rubella vaccinations are not 100 percent effective. At that time the British government withheld information from the public (Child Health Safety Word Press.com).

Pharmaceutical companies use live viruses to manufacture vaccines. Small pox virus used in vaccinations can cause death. With mounting evidence, in the last two decades, multi-vaccine shots have killed up to 145,000 children and injured countless others. A pattern is developing within pharmaceutical companies, UNICEF, WHO, Program for Appropriate Technology in Health, PATH—who were involved in targeting illiterate, uneducated, under-informed, and vulnerable populations worldwide.

Drs. NeetuVashish and Jacob Puliyel, head of Department of Pediatrics at Saint Stephen Hospital in Delhi, reported in *Indian Journal of Medical Ethics* that WHO and Bill Gates allowed for the polio vaccination of 47,500 cases, which caused Nonpolio Acute Flaccid Paralysis, NPAFP, which is more lethal than polio. In Gouro, Chad, Africa, children were injected with polio vaccines and are now experiencing polio-like symptoms affecting their spinal cord and losing the ability to use their arms and legs (Pharmabiz, Ramesh Shankar Mumbai, 2012, and Occupy Corporatism, Susanne Posel).

Reports say a lawsuit has been filed in the India Supreme Court against the Bill Gates Foundation. The case focuses on vaccinations for HPV, Cervarix, developed by GlaxoSmithKline and Gardasil by Merck pharmaceutical. It claims that in 2009, Gates funded trials of Gardasil on sixteen thousand adolescents in Andhra Pradesh, India. After injections, the side effects caused illness, and five died. Gates funded Cervarix trials in Vadodara Gujarat on fourteen thousand children with side effects that caused illness. In many instances, consent forms may have been forged or signed with a fingerprint (*Natural News*, Jonathan Benson, December 10, 2015, and *Health Impact News*). US TV ads in 2016 promote HPV vaccines should be taken by all youth beginning at age ten.

November 16, 2013, in response to a meningitis outbreak at Princeton, all students were required to get a nonapproved vaccine. In Africa, this meningitis vaccine left fifty children paralyzed. Gates was involved in trial test of meningitis vaccine given to children.

Genetically Modified Organism

In 1973, a fictional movie titled *Soylent Green* told of a time in 2022 that the world was overpopulated, natural resources were exhausted, and humans were starving. It was decided to recycle dead humans and make them into loaves of bread called Soylent Green. Sometimes there is an element of truth wound through fictional narratives.

The idea of genetic engineering has been ongoing for decades and applies to living organisms that have been genetically changed. Living organism pertains to food, fish, animals, and humans that have been altered at the molecular level to enhance or fabricate unnatural traits. This area of research into genetic manipulation does produce unforeseen complications or resulting variable.

In 2015, it became public knowledge that humans, animals, fish, and vegetation were being recycled for a variety of things. Aborted human fetuses were added to food and a source of material for research. Genetically modified rice crops were discovered to contain traits of human DNA cultivated from liver cells. This rice is produced by biotechnology company Ventria Bioscience on 3,200 acres in Junction City, Kansas, for the purpose of taking the artificial proteins produced in the Frankenrice and using it in pharmaceuticals with approval from USDA.

Concerned groups have been pushing to have products labeled that use genetically modified contaminates. The US government and their interest groups are pushing back to prevent the labeling of GMO products. US consumers unknowingly ingest more GMOs than other countries. Scotland, Germany, Italy, and Austria are among countries refusing to buy wheat, rice, soy, and corn products from United States. Obama pressures Vietnam to not label GMO food. In India, Monsanto tries to get the ban on GMO products overturned. China refuses to allow GMO rice or corn to be grown.

Industries who push for GMO products claim they are safe and will yield more than natural crops. Independent studies have been ongoing for years, and the findings are disturbing on the domino impact upon humans, animals, food, water, and air.

Following, we highlight a few articles that contradict the GMO industry claim:

Thierry Vrain, a scientist for Agriculture Canada, thought these altered crops were safe. Research reports are now indicating that there needs to be concern about GMO crops and animals. He explained the technology of engineered plants present a protein that is different because they insert a gene into a genome, which damages the proteins. The viral gene is designed to disable their host in order to facilitate pathogen invasion. The reports show that engineered corn and soy contain toxic or allergenic proteins. GMO food weakens the immune system, hindering its ability to fight viral infections and disease (European Food Safety Authority recently discovered the altered virus gene introduced concerns of its long-term effects). They do understand that viral genes are designed to hobble our immune systems so that the viruses can invade cells and flourish. Reports show that eighty-six different processes are being used to insert genes into GMO crops; the virus is present in fifty-four of them.

Bill Gates and Rockefeller are working together to reduce poverty and hunger in Africa with the Alliance for a Green Revolution in Africa, AGRA, donated $180 million in 2006 for a five-year project to provide farmers with Western-style agriculture technology. They were given fertilizers, weed killer, GMO seed. Nine thousand dealers were hired to sell the supplies to the farmers; three thousand inspectors were hired to monitor the soil health. Later farmers reported that the AGRA methods depleted soil nutrients and killed beneficial microbes. Farmers saw this as a flawed attempt to impose industrial agriculture at the expense of more ecologically sound approach to farming. Activists from Zimbabwe, Nigeria, South Africa, Uganda, and Ethiopia came to Seattle, Washington, October 12, 2014, to express their concern to AGRA (*Seattle Times*, Daniel Maingi). **Our comment**—AGRA appears to be philanthropic and beneficial, but in the end, it depletes the soil of natural resources, creates drought, and forces a diet of GMO crops.

Bob Livingston, *Personal Liberty Digest* article, "GMOs Hiding in Plain Sight," August 5, 2013, shares excerpts from the article: GMOs infest almost everything we consume, and most Americans are unaware of GMO-tainted food because they are deceptively hidden as natural in the list of ingredients. Some are hidden in ingredients such as baking powder, corn flour, food starch, fructose, vitamin B12, xanthan gum, ascorbic acid, corn syrup, maltodextrin, sucrose, and others.

Farms around the world and over one billion acres in the United States have been planted with these laboratory-created crops: mostly soy, corn, cotton for cottonseed oil, fast-foods, vitamins, and pet foods. Food producers use Monsanto's herbicide Roundup, which contains glyphosate to kills weeds, and believe their GMO crops will survive the herbicides. Honeybees, butterflies, wildlife, and fish perish from pesticide exposure and contaminated water. Lab results on rats exposed to this indicate damage to their reproductive development and caused infertility and cancer. According to a US Geological Survey, "Eighty-eight thousand tons of Monsanto glyphosate have been used in the United States. EPA classifies it as a Class III toxic substance. Thirty grams can be fatal to humans. Some effects attributed to it are autism, gastrointestinal disease, obesity, allergies, cardiovascular disease, depression, cancer, infertility, Alzheimer's and Parkinson disease, multiple sclerosis, and Lou Gehrig's disease." *GreenMedInfo. com* provides extensive data on Monsanto and GMOs.

Monsanto, Agent of Death

Monsanto is the leading organization pushing for engineered crops, which allegedly produce a greater yield and create transgenic seeds that are resistant to pest and weeds. These crops are negatively impacting the environment and causing diseases. This is a powerful organization that has influenced Congress, EPA, FDA through lobby, lawsuits, misinformation, and propaganda. Monsanto is the creator of Agent Orange used as a chemical weapon by the US military forty years ago, dumping around twenty million gallons on the unsuspecting people in Vietnam. This toxin killed vegetation but also had long-term negative effects on the health of the people. Over the years, many developed terminal illnesses and birth defects. US soldiers were exposed to these chemicals and suffered the same health issues as the people in Vietnam. After years of battling the Veteran's Administration, it was declared that Agent Orange was the cause of leukemia, respiratory cancer, prostate cancer, Parkinson's, heart disease, type 2 diabetes, and spina bifida, to name a few.

As horrific as these chemicals are on the health of humans and vegetation, the Dow industry is pushing the FDA to have Agent Orange used again as 2.4-D (dioxin) in the spraying of crops.

Bayer Crop Science, Germany, received a patent on chemical compounds to be used as aerosols.

A Japanese firm called Ajinomoto manufacture neurotoxins. A popular one is MSG, a flavor enhancer, but the toxin can alter behavior and in extreme behavior may cause a person to kill. They also manufacture a toxin called aspartame, which US Pentagon, 2010, said was a chemical weapon. The Japanese company renamed it to amino sweet.

In a shocking story reported by researchers Joe Ardis and Donna Howell in their book, *Dead Pets Don't Lie*, they expose the pet food industry and exactly what is in the food. The food is made from dead animals killed at shelters, veterinarian clinic, roadkill, diseased chickens, dead farm animals with maggots, expired supermarket meats. These dead animals are collected and recycled, including collars, cellophane, and Styrofoam containers mixed with chemicals and processed for animal consumption. These dead animals are usually labeled on the bag as by-products.

Mike Adams, *Natural News*, February 20, 2014, presented his article, "Battle for Humanity Nearly Lost: Global Food Supply Deliberately Engineered to End Life, Not Nourish It." Research conducted in their *Natural News* Forensic Food Lab arrived at alarming conclusions.

> The food supply appears to be intentionally designed to end human life rather than nourish it. Toxic substances, heavy metals, plastic, and rubber products used in nonedible items are found in our food supply, including vitamins and vaccines. The effects of these toxic additives have caused mental instability, infertility, organ damage, cancer, and learning disability. Humanity cannot survive the mass-engineered poisoning of the food supply. These chemical toxins are found in air, soil, water, crops, and animals. GMO foods grow a deadly toxin inside each grain, which is passed to humans and animals. Food imported from China is heavily polluted, either accidentally or deliberately. Diet sodas are laced with aspartame; processed foods contain nitrites and preservatives. Fluoride and chlorine toxins are found in water and tooth products. Avoid artificial sweeteners, energy drinks, and cheap vitamins—which are laden with chemicals and heavy metals such as aluminum, copper, mercury, and lead. Evidence of people who are ingesting these foods may be listless, weak, sickly, academically inept, poor memory, and prone to violent acts like zombies.

The *Natural News Site* reported, June 2016, that a study conducted by the National Academy of Science concluded GMO farming practices have created pesticide-resistant insects and herbicide-resistant super weeds that contribute to major agricultural problems. Planting GMO crops have required more toxic chemicals, such as Roundup produced by Monsanto, to be used to fight super weeds such as the seven-foot palmers pig weed and to fight pests that have built up a resistance to chemical sprays (such as the pink bell worm, which attacks cotton crops).

Secularists Concerned about the Future of Humankind

Sophie McBain, reporter with the New Statesman, September 23, 2014, stated the Future of Humanity Institute Research Department at Oxford University established in 2005 and a department at MIT, Boston, to study the "big-picture questions" of human life and what the greatest threat to human life is. With the increase in nuclear weapons, advanced robotics, synthetic biology, nanotechnology, chemical and viral delivery systems, weather manipulation bring to the forefront the potential for catastrophic events. When the scientific community is concerned, the onus is not entirely on the back of religious organizations, conspiracy, or doomsday forecasters and the aura of science fiction is diminished—including, Center for the Study of Existential Risk; Jaan Tallinn, cofounder of Skype; Martin Rees, astronomer and author, *Our Final Century*; Stephen Hawking, physicist; Elon Musk, founder, PayPal and SpaceX; Peter Singer, ethicists; Peter Theil, Bitcoins. Physicists, philosophers, biologists, computer techs ponder the future apocalypse.

McBain quotes Martin Rees, astronomer, "When you consider events that have changed the earth dramatically, such as asteroids and volcanic eruptions, something extraordinary has happened in recent decades. Never before have human beings been so able to alter our surrounding and to alter ourselves through advanced biology and computer sciences which open the possibilities of transforming the way we think and live."

Finally, Monsanto is being taken to task by an International Tribunal to be held responsible for its crimes against nature and humankind. The hearing will be held in Hague, October 12–16, 2016. This is also associated with the United Nations International Criminal Court, which was established in Hague in 2002. In brief, Monsanto is accused of illicitly manufacturing their own success by manipulation of the media, lobbying regulation agencies and various governments, financing and falsifying research data, bullying politicians and health policy leaders into bringing GMOs and crop chemicals to the world's markets without any evidence of safety or necessity. Case in point, Monsanto is suing Hawaii for passing legislation to restrict GMOs products (Jonathan Benson, *Natural News*, January 21, 2014).

Nations and various organizations are pushing back. Case in point, Taiwan bans GMOs in school lunches and requires labeling of GMO products. A partial list of concerned organizations are Organic Consumers Association (OCA), headed up by Ronnie Cummins; International Organic (IFOAM) headed up by Andre Leu; Navdanya, Regeneration International; and millions against Monsanto (Ethan Huff, *Natural News*, January 10, 2016).

A Beacon of Light in a Dark World

As mentioned, there are numerous references of the Day of Lord in scripture. This time frame is not as relevant as knowing that God did come to earth and took upon himself flesh, shed his blood for all, arose from the dead, and will redeem those who call on the name of the Lord at the end of days. Hebrews 9:26, "Now once in **the end of the world** Jesus came to put away sin through his sacrifice. It is appointed unto men once to die, then the judgment, and unto them that look for him shall he appear the second time unto salvation."

At the end of days we understand in Ephesians 1:10, "*in the dispensation of the* ***fullness of times****, Jesus will gather together in one all things in Christ both in heaven and earth.*" This speaks to those whose spirits dwell with Jesus already in heaven, to those who will be gathered at the Rapture, and then those saints who die during the tribulation period will be gathered together at the great harvest.

The seventy weeks of Daniel came to an interlude at the sixty-ninth week when Jesus was cut off or crucified. The total fulfillment of the final seventieth week of this prophecy will come to pass during the seven-year tribulation period. The final seven years will see the end of Gentile world domination, Daniel 9:24–25. Jesus will rise up, gather the nations, and pour upon them his indignation and his fierce anger, for all the earth will be devoured with the fire of my jealousy, Zephaniah 1:8.

Satanic darkness has enshrouded the whole world. Evil comes upon us as a tsunami. Scriptures remind us that when the enemy comes in like a flood, God will hold up a standard. In these troubled times, we feel overwhelmed, but our Lord and Savior is a light in the darkness. He is holding up that standard, and we keep our eyes on him that can save us from these tribulations. No matter what we must endure, even to death, nothing can separate us from his love. In life, we are alive in him, and in death we are alive with him forever. Our Comforter will put a psalm in our heart and a song on our lips. When we have done all we can do, we will stand, and we will look up to the hills from where comes our help. Our help comes from the Creator of the heavens and the earth. When we have done all we can do, we will pray and seek his face. We will pray and be reminded that we are the people of God, and it is us who dwells in the secret place of the Most High, and we shall abide under the shadow of the Almighty. We will say of the Lord, "He is my refuge and my fortress, my God, in him will I trust." We put our trust in him only, and in faith, we know that he shall deliver us from the snare of the fowler and from the noisome pestilence. He will protect us as a hen and her chickens. God will cover us with his feathers, and under his wings we will trust. We stand on the truth of the Word, and we will not be deceived. God's truth will be our shield and buckler, and we will not be afraid for the terror by night or for the arrow that fly by day or for the pestilence that walks in darkness, and we will not be afraid of the destruction that comes at noonday. Even though we witness a thousand dying on one side and ten thousands on the other side, we believe the Word of God that it will not come near us. As the world is shaken around us as in a whirlwind of destruction, we see the reward of the wicked. Though we see these things that have come upon the world, we will not be detracted, but we will know without a doubt that our God is our refuge and our habitation. We will stand firm, knowing that no evil will befall us and no plague will come near our dwelling. God has promised to give his angels charge over us and to keep us in all our ways. They will lift us up, lest we dash our foot against a stone. God has given us authority over the works of Satan, and we can trample on the serpent and the roaring lion. We can sing of the love of God because he has set his love upon us, and therefore will he deliver us in times of trouble. He said he will set us on high because we have known his name. His sheep know his voice, and when he calls, we will answer. Once again, be encouraged. God will be with us in times of trouble, and he will deliver us and honor us with long life. God will satisfy us and show us his salvation. (Author's commentary and paraphrase, Psalms 91.)

In the face of wickedness, God's people must stand for righteousness. A current example of someone who took a stand for godly values was CEO Dan Cathy of Chick-fil-A. He was demonized by homosexuals and their proponents who zealously felt that he should not announce he was a longtime Christian, married to one wife, and believed in traditional marriage between man and woman. He was respectful and kind and in no way did he say he would not serve or hire a homosexual. What Satan does for evil, God will turn it around for good. Over six hundred thousand people across the nation came out on August 1, 2012, to support this business. People waited in long lines. At the end of the day, Chick-fil-A had sold all of its chicken nationwide. September 2014, Dan Cathy was taken home to be with the Lord.

Chapter 17
One-World Religion and the False Prophet

Chapter Overview

- The One-World Order and the One-World Religion Are Interconnected
    - The Occult
    - Symbolism — Exhibit: All Seeing Eye
    - Secret Societies
        - Rosicrucian
        - Knights Templar
        - Merovingian
        - Masonic Order Exhibit: Washington, Mason
        - Illuminati
        - Skull and Bones
        - Hitler's Aryan Order
        - Bohemian Club

    - Religion Versus Idolatry
    - Bible Truth in Contrast to False Religion
    - The Rotten Fruit of False Religions

    - Characteristics of a False Religion
        - Nature Worship, Pantheism, Green Religion
        - Witchcraft, Wizards, Vampires, Voodoo
        - New Age
        - Aryan, Hinduism, Buddhism
        - Mayans
        - Scientology
        - Mormons
        - Seventh-Day Adventist
        - Jehovah's Witnesses
        - Atheism
        - Islam
        - Nation of Islam
    - The Rise of Radical Islamic Terrorism

    - The Vatican and the Pope
        - World Religions — Exhibit: World Religions Logo
        - Catholicism Interacts with All Religions
        - Prophecy of the Last Pope
        - Will the False Prophet Please Stand Up
        - Union between False Prophet and Antichrist

Chapter 17

One-World Religion and the False Prophet

The One-World Order and a One-World Religion Are Interconnected

The following overview will demonstrate a connection between a world entrenched with pagan beliefs and practices entangled within a multifaceted religious system. The architects of the one-world system orchestrate their goals through the machinations of world governments.

An idea seeded in ancient times would become fertile through the growth of a revived Roman Empire. The arrival of Europeans to the Western continent brought with them plans to birth their objective. Its offshoot, America, was selected to give life and nourish the new world order agenda. Freemasonry would be the conduit for these ambitious plans because Masonry has ancient roots in the mystery Babylonian religion. Masons believe that Babylon was the City of Atlantis, and the future goal is to resurrect the New Atlantis in the nation of America. The coming utopia will be occupied by superior beings who come down from heaven to live with superior humans. That idea is not so far-fetched. Through DNA manipulation and creation of artificial intelligence (AI), modern technology is working to create superhuman people. All nonessential, useless people will be enslaved or eliminated.

The Masons call God the Great Architect of the Universe. For hundreds of years, the Masons and other occult practitioners have been working to manifest a son, a messiah, a global leader. As Christians believe God the Son came in flesh, died, and was resurrected, Masonic rituals attempt to resurrect something from the dead remains of a special person. Masons believe there is a child, casket, and a **magical stone** from the star Sirius, which can give eternal life and to be the cup of Christ but not Christ. As mentioned, paganism takes bits and pieces from the Bible and corrupts its truth. It is interesting to read in Revelation 2:13, Jesus speaks about the dwelling place of Satan in Pergamos and then speaks against those who hold to the doctrine of Baalam. In Revelation 2:17. . . Jesus promised to give to those who overcome a **white stone** and in the stone a new name written, which no man knows save he that receives it. Note the comparison between the Bible (Jesus is our rock) and in Masonry (masons are men who work with stone), and they have incorporated a stone into their rituals, believing it to be a symbol of power.

George Washington, first president of America, was a high-level Mason pledging his allegiance to the Great Architect of the Universe. From the first president to the last president, all will play a significant role in bringing to fruition the final world leader. George Bush and son were Bonesmen, members of the Skull and Bones secret society as well as members of the Masonic Order. It is interesting to note that Bush (number two) planned to enter the presidential race based on acceptance by the Evangelical church. After receiving their pledge of support, they laid hands on Bush to anoint him for his future role. In the future, Mitt Romney, a Mormon and Mason, would seek the presidential nomination, also having had hands laid on him for his future role. This laying on hands may be a Masonic ritual, more so than the biblical account of "laying on of hands."

January 20, 2001, President George W. Bush at his inaugural address made comments that alerted occult members and new world order affiliates that the time is at hand.

The reference was regarding an "angel that rides in the whirlwind and directs this storm," also called Moriah Conquering Wind by the Illuminati. Five weeks later, February 28, 2001, Congressman Major R. Owens, before House of Representatives, issued a prayer to the "angel in the whirlwind" and that this spiritual force would guide the future and fate of the United States. Twenty-eight weeks later, for a total of thirty-three weeks from the day of the inauguration, nineteen Islamic terrorists flew planes into the Twin Towers on September 11, 2001. Bush took the stage to make an appearance of outrage for public sentiment. In retaliation, Bush decided to attack Iraq under the guise of weapons of mass destruction. Thousands of American soldiers lost their lives and became disabled veterans for a "false flag" war. Author Tom Horn correlates this attack on Iraq with something sinister and covert. Iraq is linked to ancient Babylon. Saddam Hussein claimed to be the reincarnated Nebuchadnezzar. The future (spiritual) Babylon is linked to America. This "divine mission" sent a message to Bush's Bonesmen, neocons, and guardians of secret orders: the cloaked phrase "fire in the minds of men" coded language to usher in the New World Order. Tom Horn said, "A reference to the Promethean faith is understood that neo-Conservatism, and Prometheans could be married in this way in that both doctrines are occult visions of a kingdom of gods on earth established through human endeavor and enlightenment." Prometheus was the mythological Greek titan who stole fire from the gods and gave it to man. When the spirit of Prometheus is incarnated in the human mind as the mystical longing for illumination, it is as "fire in the mind" (Tom Horn, *Zenith 2016*, p. 39–40).

At Bush's second inaugural speech, four years later, he again offered a cryptic commentary saying, "There came a day of fire, by our efforts we have lit a fire as well. It warms those who feel its power, it burns those who fight its progress, and one day this untamed fire of freedom will reach the darkest corners of our world." The phrase "fire in the minds of men" is from Fyodor Dostoyevsky's nineteenth-century book, *The Possessed,* a reference to devils. Dostoyevsky's book is about violent government crackdown on dissidents that sparks civil unrest and revolution marked by public violence. Bush also tied the cryptic message to the Masonic involvement in the American Revolution, "When our founders declared a new order of the ages, they were acting on an ancient hope that is meant to be fulfilled." Bush's second term ended in a firestorm of economic crisis, involving the housing market, auto industry, stocks, and financial markets, but they were too big to fail, and they stood in line to receive billions in taxpayer-funded government bailout. The brunt of the fallout impacted millions of citizens. People were looking for renewed hope, and Obama entered the arena with his platform of hope, change, and "yes, we can." Obama was selected and anointed at the Bilderberg gathering. His presidency is a continuation of the Bush era, and he was primed to fast-forward the goals of the one-world order. Tom Horn clearly connects this time frame that the "elite occultists goal to accomplish a fire burning in the minds of men, fanned by multinational chaos and desperation, resulting in universal entreaty for an inspirational and political demigod, a savior to arise on the global scene promising a one-world order" (Tom Horn, *Zenith 2016*, p 29–37).

Like landing lights at the airport, messages, symbolism, imagery, rituals have paved the way for the coming one. With the world in turmoil, it is poised and ready to accept a false messiah—a man empowered by Satan who will be the ultimate one-world leader. Satan will also empower a man, the false prophet who will unify all religions. Satan knows, Jesus will come and establish his millennial kingdom; but before this occurs, Satan is working to establish his kingdom first.

The All-Seeing Eye on US Currency

The architects of the one-world order embedded their occult message on American currency. The dollar bill has symbolic imagery of a pyramid with the all seeing eye and a list of dates from 1776 to the year 2012, which some scholars believe is the time when the Antichrist will enter the world scene.

The Occult

Adam and Eve opened Pandora's Box and allowed for evil to enter into the world. A group of fallen angels traversed through a portal between dimensions, descending onto Mount Hermon. Once establishing themselves in the earthly realm, they began corrupting and teaching humankind forbidden knowledge; some of which have been identified. Prior to the flood, all flesh with the intrusion of the fallen angels had been corrupted. After the flood, Satan, the fallen angels, and demonic spirits once again enveloped the world in evil. Humankind fell into idolatry and ungodliness. They desired access to forbidden knowledge and summoned the gods of old.

The formation of an occult develops its basic foundation from religious and pagan principles. For instance, in Ezekiel 1:5, he had a vision of four living creatures, called Cherubim, having four distinct faces: one of a man, one a lion, one an ox, and one an eagle. The occult associates the four faces with pagan gods: Imbolc is Diana, fertility; Beltrane is Walpurgisnacht of lust, chaos, fertility, Mayday; Lammas is festival/harvest, Thanksgiving; Samhain is demons and evil spirits, Halloween (Dan Block on Ezekiel).

An occult rejects God's truth and commandments and replaces them with practices forbidden by God. Occults steer mankind away from the one true God, Creator of the heavens and the earth. In God's absence, he is replaced with counterfeit deities. Students of the occult indulge in esoteric forces and dark supernatural powers emanating from the demonic domain. These activities prepare them as receptacles to receive demonic illumination. Practitioners become skilled in the art of meditation, séances, telepathy, and divination. Becoming masters, they conjure demonic entities through various practices such as black magic, alchemy, astrology, necromancy, witchcraft, and channeling. Rituals include blood sacrifice, sexual depravity, cuttings (tattoos), forming images, and idols. Satanist or Wiccans both indulge in rituals of debauchery and sadistic acts carried out on humans or animals, even to the eating of flesh or drinking blood. These are the behaviors of demons and those they inspire. All occults embrace some form of symbolism, which can be traced back to ancient pagan practices.

Every civilization contains reports of despots who go to great lengths to embrace ungodly practices, so there is an unending thread that binds occults, secret societies, and religions together through symbolism. In connection one with another, they form the hub of the architects of the one-world order. The hub is symbolically displayed as an octagon having eight sides. This octagon symbol can be seen as an eight-sided star, as in the I Ching as well as the octagon form of the Dome of the Rock. In modern times, the whole world seems to intersect with the influence of occult visionaries who must leave their message to future adherents in the form of symbols similar to crop circles or megaliths.

Symbolism

Symbols are made of numbers, letters, and pictures used as signposts or markers. Symbolism can be displayed in objects, buildings, and statues as permanent mediums for future associates. Cloaked phrases made in public speeches can depict a meaning or send a message to be understood by certain adherents. Occult practitioners, Satan worshippers, witches, mystics, members of secret societies, fraternities, and pagan religions have a system of knowledge formed within symbolism. For example, the creation of crop circles uses symbols and signs as discussed in chapter 15, "Alien Delusion." A symbol of Islam is the crescent moon; Judaism is recognized by the Star of David; and Christianity is the symbol of the cross. The Bible uses symbols as well. Symbolic descriptions in the book of Revelation are used to give a message pointing to the end of the age and judgment. Throughout scripture, the prophets received symbolic messages in visions or dreams. Daniel's beasts were symbolic of kingdoms. Some of these symbols and relics were believed to hold supernatural powers, such as in the Holy Grail or the Spear of Destiny that pierced the side of Jesus.

Many entertainers align themselves with occult organizations through the use of symbolic imagery as seen on their costumes and display their allegiance with hand signs. We have seen performers such as Rihanna, Beyoncé, Maddona, Lady Gaga use pagan symbolism in their performances. Katie Perry at Super Bowl halftime came out riding a huge beast.

The word *semiotic* means "the ability to hide meanings within symbols." As we research further, we will see this to be an accurate statement.

As mentioned, a relic or object can represent something deeper. Some believe demons have the ability to merge with an object. A myth was created around the chalice or Holy Grail: that it collected the blood of Jesus. It was deemed so special that the order of the Knights Templar came into existence to protect the vessel. A legend surrounded the Spear of Destiny that pierced the side of Jesus. Occults believed it held supernatural power and the one who had the sword had victory over their enemies. Constantine held the spear, and he rose to the throne of the Roman Empire. He declared himself to be the thirteenth apostle. In the eighth century AD, Charles Martel of France was in possession of the sword. In the battle of Tours, he ran the Muslims out of Europe, and Christianity became the dominant religion. The spear passed to Charlemagne, who kept it with him night and day, believing it had magical powers. In AD 800, Charlemagne became known as the Father of the Holy Roman Empire and was crowned emperor. He was also titled the King of France. Frederick Barbarossa possessed the sword, and he ruled Venice from AD 1152 to 1190. He dropped the spear in a stream, and he died in 1190. The spear continued to pass from one hand to another. By AD 1273, Rudolf I of the Habsburgs became the emperor of the Holy Roman Empire, also in possession of the spear. The spear remained in the Habsburg family possession in their Treasure House in Vienna, Austria. In AD 1913, Kaiser Wilhelm was ruler of Germany and wanted the spear for war. He asked to borrow the spear and other treasures from the Hapsburgs for a special exhibition. One of Wilhelm's officers secretly told a Habsburg that Wilhelm was planning to keep them. One year later, June 28, 1914, Archduke Francis Ferdinand and his wife, Sophie, of the Habsburg Dynasty were assassinated, and this sparked World War I. Hitler, before his rise to power, visited the treasure house and would gaze upon the spear for hours.

He had become involved with the occult. While looking at the spear, he went into a trance and saw a demon, and he offered his soul as a vessel for the demon. He came to power in Germany in 1933. By 1938, he had amassed a strong military. They marched into Vienna and took control of the spear. One year later, he invaded Poland and ignited World War II. The Allied forces found the spear and returned it to the Habsburg Treasure House (J. R. Church, *Guardians of the Grail*).

The mystery of the Palladium seems to arise from a wooden image, which supposedly had fallen from heaven and given the name Pallas. It was consider an object of protection. David Flynn, author of *Temple at the Center of Time*, mentions the Palladium. In the writing of Arthur Edward Waite,

> May 20, 1737 … in France the Order of the Palladium or Sovereign Council of Wisdom came into existence … this order is connected by more than its name with the legendary Palladium of the Knights Templars … for a period of sixty years little is heard of the legendary Palladium but in 1801 the Israelite Isaac Long is said to have carried the image and the skull of the Templar Grand master Jacques de Molay from Paris to Charleston in the United States.

In Mark Flynn's book, *Forbidden Secrets of the Labyrinth*, he brings to the forefront the importance of symbols and their impact on various orders. He makes a connection with this relic referred to as the Palladium. Flynn takes us back to Alexander the Great (300 BC) who pledges his allegiance to Achilles and believes his power is bestowed upon him from his warrior ancestors and their taking of the Palladium. After the destruction of Troy, the Palladium was placed in Greece at the Erechteum Acropolis, where it remained for hundreds of years. During the formation of the Roman Empire, the Palladium was placed in the Temple of Vesta in the Roman Forum. Coming to the reign of Lucius Caecilius Metellus around 290–221 BC, the Palladium was rescued from a fire in the Temple of Vesta.

Emperor Marcus Aurelius Antoninus, AD 203–222, incorporated the Elagabalus cult in Rome, which regarded the Palladium as one of their pledges of rule, which guaranteed the republic's continued power and command of the empire. Emperor Elagabalus, AD 218–222, took the Palladium to his temple, which carried the name Elagabalium Palladium. Within the temple was a black conical meteorite they called Heaven Stone, and during the summer solstice the stone was removed from the temple and paraded throughout Rome on a chariot pulled by six horses. In AD 600, a black stone in Mecca would be revered.

Flynn lets us know that Elagabalium considered the Palladium to be representative of the Great Mother, the fire of Vesta, the shields of Salii, and from this we begin to see the image is depicted as hermaphrodite. Over time the Palladium morphed into the image of Baphomet, appearing with horns, wings, intertwined with serpents, pentagram backdrop, and monster face.

During the time of Constantine, around AD 330, he came into possession of the Palladium, where he buried it under the Column of Apollo-Constantine at his forum. Here we see Constantine exalting himself, as did Elagabalium, building a statue of Apollo and Constantine on top of the column. After the fall of Constantinople, the Roman Church became powerful. The Holy See is Latin for "seat," and the word *Vatican* comes from the Roman god Vaticanus—which alludes to foreteller, seer, soothsayer, and to shine or be white as in the pope dresses in white garments.

After the rise of Britain, Flynn speculates as to where the Palladium may be located. He suggests it was held in the Palace of Placentia or Westminster Abbey in England. He also suggests it may still have been in the possession of the Catholic church and under the protection of the Knights Templars.

Research from Tom Horn, *Apollyon Rising, 2012*, gives us further insight into pagan symbolism incorporated within the Vatican. For instance, the obelisk in Saint Peter's Square is a phallus symbol with a pyramid-shaped pinnacle, which could suggest the discharge of seed. It was created in Egypt during the fifth dynasty as a monument to Osiris placed at the Temple of the Sun in Heliopolis, dedicated to the sun god Ra, Osiris, and Isis. Emperor Augustus had the obelisk moved to the Julian Forum of Alexandria. From there, Caligula moved it to Rome in AD 37, where it was resurrected to witness the brutal slaying of Christians and the apostle Peter. Fifteen hundred years later, Pope Sixtus V ordered the obelisk to be installed in Saint Peter's Square. The obelisk was erected to line up with the dome of the Vatican, which is symbolic of a womb. Pope Sixtus V was very much taken in with these pagan symbols and had other obelisk erected in Rome, even to the removing of Christian antiquities in the process. Many medieval images sit atop an obelisk or column, representing an idol or false deity. Sixtus also erected a cross on top of the obelisk in Saint Peter's Square, and he marked the occasion by conducting the ancient rite of exorcism against the symbol. Horn suggests that Pope Sixtus believed that these objects housed a deity, and if not treated properly, evil omens could befall the people. Admiration of this pagan symbol in Saint Peter's Square continues to this present day.

It is said Leonardo da Vinci wrote in his *Codex Urbinas* how those who would adore and pray to the image were likely to believe the god represented by it was alive in the stone. During the tribulation period, many will see this specific event as they are required to worship the image of the beast.

The Bible speaks of ancient towers such as in Ur, Ziggurats, monuments, ancient buildings flanked by columns, statues, and so forth; these objects would be held sacred by religions, secret societies, and cults who are the sentinels that preserve the things forbidden by God throughout all generations. The one-world order stakes its claim through architecture that displays occult messages. These symbols appear in the design of major cities. Tom Horn, in *Apollyon Rising, 2012*, provides examples of pagan symbols incorporated in architect structures:

The capital of the United States displays many symbols, carvings, and statues of pagan gods. In Washington, DC, the "dome" on the capital is in line with the Washington Monument, the "obelisk." This is similar to the symbolism found in Saint Peter's square. DC's obelisk is placed near the west end of the national mall. It was built by Freemasons and dedicated to George Washington. It is the tallest obelisk in the world, reaching a height of 6,666 inches and has a pyramid capstone.

Freemasons Albert Pike and Albert Mackey describe the obelisk/phallic and other symbols as the active and passive principles of the universe that commonly symbolize the generative parts of man and woman. Secret societies or cults usually have a sexual component in their rituals.

In the headquarters of the Scottish Rite Freemasonry, House of the Temple, 17**33** Sixteenth Street, Washington, DC, is a replica of a pre-Christian temple, of King Mausolus (mausoleum), symbolic of the place to be taken after death. The temple is flanked at the entrance by two seventeen-ton sphinxes as common in the Egyptian dynasty. The interior has many ritualistic rooms, halls, vaults, libraries, and a hollow wall with the remains of two human bodies. The supreme 33rd degree council traditionally inducts one who rises to the highest level of masonry in the "raising" ceremony scheduled after the election of the US president. The ceremony includes a retelling of the death epic of the pagan god Osiris. He is bathed in the glory celestial by the Great Architect as in the glory surrounding the all-seeing eye of Osiris above the pyramid. The inductee is charged with the task of finding the body of Hiram Abiff and raising him from the dead, and the great work will conclude when the god (Antichrist) will inhabit the third temple. The message of this symbolism as practiced in Freemasonry is the death, burial, and future resurrection of Osiris. Hiram Abiff was a mason in the construction of Solomon's temple (excerpts, *Petrus Romanus* and *Apollyon Rising 2012*).

The Statue of Liberty in New York was a gift to the American Masons in 1884 from the French Grand Orient Temple of Masons. The statue was designed by Frederic Auguste Bartholdi, a Mason, and built by Gustave Eiffel. It was first called Isis. A design of it can be found on a marble table in Corinth Greece Archaeological Museum. Liberty is the image of the Roman goddess Libertas and associated with the Egyptian goddess Isis. The seven spikes on its head represent sunrays of Greek god Apollo.

Astoni hosted the fourth world congress. Media showed pyramid-structured building having repetitive geometric patterns of 666. Inside the pyramid was a large round table for seating.

Dubai has undertaken a huge project in building a replica of Atlantis and Tree of Life design in the sea.

Nashville capital has seal of Solomon, who conjured seventy-two demons and bound them with symbols.

The Baphomet statue flanked by children was erected in the satanic temple in Detroit in 2015. A similar image was used in the 2015 TV series *Children's End.* In the series, Earth had been invaded by aliens. The overlords looked like Baphomet, and they controlled all the affairs of the world, creating the appearance of a utopia. The children were enhanced hybrids, having supernatural abilities. At the end, children ascended into the air to be with the aliens.

Secret Societies

Occult organizations maintain a level of secrecy, mystery, and their agenda is concealed as also is the agenda within the foundations of secret societies. Since we know the names of some well-known secret societies, why are they labeled as secret? One definition of a secret society is that they keep their inner doctrine and rituals secret while giving the outer pretense of benevolent or good for all mankind hype. They may appear to have a form of godliness, but they are whitewashed tombs. A secret organization usually embraces pagan practices, steeped in symbolism, and may have interrelationships with other societies and religions. Their commonalty is the enthronement of Satan, the practice of rituals to invoke evil spirits who will bring hidden knowledge and power.

There is a connection between various mystic organizations and the families that control them. We provide the following summary on several known secret societies:

Rosicrucian, Knights Templar, Merovingian Society, Masonic Order

The above listed organizations share some commonality. In general, each embraces a philosophy based upon Babylonian, Egyptian esoteric beliefs intermingled with Judeo and Christian doctrine. Those areas involve universe, mysticism, nature, and humanism. They desire to know hidden secrets, and to attain this knowledge, they may knowingly consult with demons.

AD 46, Ormus an Alexandrian (Egypt) Gnostic and his six followers were converted by Mark of the New Testament. Their symbol was said to be a red cross surmounted by a rose, calling it Rosy Cross or Rose Cross, later to be associated with Rosicrucian.

Rosicrucian teaching was established in Germany by Christian Rosenkreuz in the early fifteenth century, having an influence of Christianity, Islam, and Zoroastrian. The order was symbolized by a cross with a rose. First writing to surface was titled, *The Fame of the Brotherhood of RC.*

AD 1530, the cross and rose existed in Portugal in the Convent of the Order of Christ, home of the Knights Templar, also called the Order of Christ.

AD 1561–1626, Francis Bacon born in London was known for his philosophy and literature.

He was called the father of the modern scientific method. Bacon was associated with the Rosicrucian order. He confessed his love for Kabbala and areas that dealt with secret knowledge, mysticism, man deified. He said he had encounters with demons. He was an associate of John Dee, wizard and astrologer to Queen Elizabeth. Bacon was a firm believer in the new Atlantis to arise in America. Bacon also incorporated Rosicrucian beliefs into Freemasonry. It is said he had a New Foundland stamp with his image and 666, which reads, "Lord Bacon, the guiding spirit in colonization scheme." Bacon was influenced by the writings of Plato's *New Republic*—which influenced his ideas for a new Atlantis, a new world order and superhumans. Following is additional discussion on Bacon associated with the Mason.

AD 1710, alchemist Sanuel Ricter continued the influence of the Golden and Rosy Cross in Germany. He published *The True and Complete Preparation of the Philosopher's Stone by the Brotherhood* from the Order of the Golden and Rosy Cross.

Rosicrucian-inspired Masonic rites emerged in the late 1700s called the Rectified Scottish Rite in Central Europe and France, displaying a golden Rosy Cross symbol. Those ascending to the eighteenth degree were called Knights of the Rose Croix. The change from Rosicrucian to Masonry was evidenced around 1641 to 1670 from the writing of Comenius in England before the grand lodge in 1717 England. When the Knights Templar Order phased out, it is believed they became known as Masons (Wikipedia, "Rosicrucian," online August 16, 2013).

Knights Templar, KT

The Knights Templars were organized around AD 1128 by Hugues de Payens, a French nobleman who went to England to raise men and money for the Crusades. The Crusades were military campaigns sanctioned by the Catholic church under Pope Urban II around AD 1095. The church was fighting against the Muslim Turks to guarantee pilgrims access to the holy sites in Jerusalem. Hundreds of thousands of Catholics enlisted in the Crusaders. The Crusaders' objective became the opposite of the Gospel for peace and love and took on the appearance of a Catholic military. Jews were later killed by the Crusaders, known as the Rhineland massacres in the late 1800s. The Vatican still maintains a military component.

Knights Templars were labeled monks called the Order of the Poor Knights of Christ of the Temple of Solomon and generally known as the Knights Templar. Their philosophy was garnered from Old Testament Hebrew, Kabbala, New Testament studies, and Catholicism. Their first mission was to protect Jerusalem from invaders, which they did for many years. They set up headquarters in the al Aqsa mosque and believed their goal was to protect the treasure found in King Solomon's Temple. It is rumored they excavated under Temple Mount and found temple treasure, scrolls, and relics—including the Holy Grail, which they took back to Europe. Their secret purpose was to preserve the Merovingian bloodline in hopes of establishing a one-world religion whose king would be a descendant of Mary Magdalene and Jesus. They are associated with the mystique of holy blood and holy grail as promoted by the Merovingian society.

They grew in power and wealth, answering to no authority. They operated as bankers, merchants, farmers, and builder of cathedrals. AD 1139, Pope Innocent honored Knights Templars with unlimited authority. AD 1150, as bankers, the Knight Templars established a way to protect the resources of the pilgrims traveling to Jerusalem. They would leave their wealth with Knights Templars, receive a paper voucher or check to buy items in Jerusalem from Knights Templars retailers. King Henry II, AD 1154, granted the Knight Templars land in England. They built cathedrals and other buildings in England.

Between AD 1177 to 1244, there were battles between Knights Templars and the Muslims as well as battles between the Knights Templars and Protestants mostly over the control of Jerusalem. By AD 1244, the Turks were in control of Jerusalem up to the 1900s.

AD 1305, King Philip IV of France had assassinated Pope Boniface VIII. King Philip placed his own candidate, archbishop of Bordeaux, onto the papal throne. The new pope took the name Clement V. A few years later, around AD 1307, King Philip IV put his plan into action to destroy the Knights Templar and confiscate the wealth. Jacques de Molay was officiating as the Knights Templars' grandmaster. The king asks Knights Templars to join forces under a false pretense on Friday the 13th, but under the cloak of darkness the Knight Templars were rounded up and charged with blasphemy, homosexuality, devil worship, and desecration. King Philip could not locate the temple treasures. Many Knight Templars were killed or imprisoned along with Molay. Seven years later, Molay and a few others were brought into the public square for their execution. Molay spoke out against the lies brought upon them by the king, and in his final hour, he spoke a curse upon the king and the pope. The pope died thirty-three days later from dysentery, and the king died eight months later in a hunting accident.

Those Knights Templars that managed to escape made their way to Scotland and connected with the Masons, where they met in the Roslyn Cathedral built by the Masons. It is said this building has the exact measurements of Herod's temple in Jerusalem. It displays carvings of faces, statutes with wings, a noose around a neck, blindfold, bare chest, and carvings of maze fifty years before the pilgrims were introduced to maze in North America.

Around AD 1328, they sided with King Robert against the British. They also found refuge in Sweden, where they fought with Vikings against the British. Some made their way to Germany and Austria, where an order of the Templars was established.

A plague carried by rats came upon Europe in 1362, killing over a million people. Some of the Knights Templars made their way to America. Eventually, they went underground and resurfaced as the Scottish Rite of Free Masons. An archeological stone was found in Kensington, Minnesota, with carvings similar to Norwegian cuneiform. It is housed in the Runestone Museum. This artifact is linked to writing found in 1449, Easter Table. Egyptian items were found in a cave in 1982, Little Egypt, Illinois, which are associated with the Knights Templar who may have brought them to America. Some of the writing on the Runestone is connected to Masonic writings (J. R. Church, *Guardians of the Grail and History Channel*).

Merovingian Society

This group perpetuates the fallacy that Jesus and Mary Magdalene were married and had children. The members of this organization commit to the protection of the sacred lineage, later calling themselves Guardians of the Grail. It began at the Crucifixion of Jesus, wherein someone captured the blood of Jesus in a chalice or grail. Herein the theme "Holy Blood, Holy Grail" took root. They venture further with their lie and claim Jesus did not die but escaped the tomb with the help of Mary Magdalene. In AD 70, the Romans destroyed the temple. Mary fled with her children to France and settled in a Jewish community. Her offspring married into the royal Frankish family of Germany. Around AD 400, Merovee was born and became the first in a line of kings of the Merovingian society from AD 447 to 458. King Merovee worshipped the goddess Diana. He consorted in black art and paganism, which followed the lineage of European royalty. His first son, Childeric I, practiced witchcraft and died at age twenty-four. Merovee's son, Clovis I, came to power around AD 496 and adopted Christianity. This line of kings continued to Childeric III, AD 751, who was the last of the Merovingian to serve as king of France.

In AD 1653, King Childerics's grave was opened. He was buried with hundreds of solid gold bees and other occult items. The bees are associated with the rituals of the goddess Diana.

Masonic leader Manly P. Hall, in his writings, *The Secret Teaching of All Ages*, said, "The bee is used as a symbol of royalty by the immortal Charlemagne … those who worship Diana and the spirits that come into the minds of sorcerers and mystics who bring wisdom and power to its practitioners."

The Merovingian line continued through Godfroi de Bouillon, son of Sigisbert III, and branched off into various royal families, including the Habsburgs. AD 1056, Godfroi's sister, Alex, married Emperor Henry IV of the Holy Roman Empire, continuing the Merovingian bloodlines through the Roman Empire. The Priory of Sion was established AD 1099, by Godfroi de Bouillon after his conquest of Jerusalem, and he called himself King of Jerusalem. In brief, the Priory of Sion believed one from the lineage of the Merovingian bloodline should be king of Jerusalem.

The Habsburg Dynasty played a significant role in the revived Roman Empire from AD 1438 to 1806. AD 1508, Claude de Lorraine's daughter, Marie, married James V and gave birth to Mary, Queen of Scots. The Habsburgs of Spain were influential at the time of King Ferdinand I and Queen Isabella of Spain. In the sixteenth century, Charles V, son of Leopold I, his daughter, Marie Teresa von Habsburg, empress of Austria, married Holy Roman Emperor Francis I, bringing Austria into the mix. AD 1765, Charles VI de Lorraine married Eleonore Marie von Habsburg, daughter of Ferdinand III, emperor of the Holy Roman Empire. One of their children was Marie Antoinette von Habsburg, who married Louise XVI, king of France.

Napoleon Bonaparte married Josephine Beauharnis, whom they believe was a Merovingian descendant. When Bonaparte became emperor, he had his royal robe embellished with the golden bees. AD 1806, Napoleon gave little credence to the Holy Roman Empire.

This is a brief overview to exhibit the ruling families of Europe, including popes that are tied to the Merovingian bloodline. With the influence of the popes, the Catholic Crusades promoted the myth of Mary Magdalene. Christianity had been accepted by Constantine in the fourth century, where it impacted Turkey and Italy. It was accepted by Merovee's son, Clovis. Herein the myth of Mary Magdalene's holy bloodline was mingled with Christianity. This led to the term *Holy Roman Empire* in AD 962, sanctioned by the pope.

Dr. John Dee was court astrologer to Queen Elizabeth I, and as in clairvoyants, they must speak to demons to give messages to their adherents. In modern times, Prince Charles claims his lineage to the Merovingian bloodline.

During the twentieth century, Pierre Plantard de Saint-Clair, serving as secretary general of the Priory of Sion and believed to be of the Merovingian bloodline, claimed to a reporter in France that he was knowledgeable as to the location of the temple treasures, and they would be returned to Jerusalem when the time is right.

Masonic Order

The Knights Templars were established around second century AD and preceded the Masonic order. As mentioned, the Knight Templar fled persecution, and some came to

America. The Masonic order is an offshoot of the Knights Templar, and they share similar ideology going back to Nimrod, calling him the Founder of Freemasons, even though the Bible provides very little specifics on the person Nimrod. Nimrod was a builder of cities and could be called a mason. The Knights Templar associated themselves with King Solomon's temple, and their travels took them to Egypt, Jerusalem, Rome, France, Scotland, England. They built many structures in these regions. The Masonic Order, as did the Knights Templar, incorporated the history of King Solomon as it pertains to the construction of the first temple, 900 BC. Solomon's chief architect was Hiram Abiff, who assumed a major persona in Masonry.

After the Knights Templar established roots in America, they reorganized and resurfaced as the Masonic Order. Under the Masonic Order, they could conceal their wealth and incorporate their occult practices in a new nation.

The Knights Templar were Catholic, so as Masons, they had a leeway to influence Catholic universities as well as Protestant denominations. However, they were opposed by the Order of Jesuits in AD 1784, who fought against the Masons because of their mysticism. The Masonic mix of paganism and Christianity did not sit well with some popes.

Perhaps a facade of Masonry was the idea of stonemasons becoming a fraternal organization. As stonemasons, they would establish and regulate stonemason qualifications. They came up with degrees of masonry beginning with guilds, apprentice, journeyman, and master mason. The symbol for Masonry is a square and compass. These degrees were also secret levels to be achieved by freemason members. Occult groups and the Masons value the number 3 in the science of Freemasonry, navigation, and sacred locations. The number 3 is the triangulation on maps to plot latitude and longitude, space and time, and may reveal appointed time of human destiny. The number 33 is highly esteemed in Masonry in that it is a symbol of perfection and illumination. The number 1.414 has sacred geometric significance tying it to deity, math, science, and mysticism. Masonry uses signs, symbols, secret handshake, and moving followers toward the path of the enlightenment. Candidates must declare belief in a deity.

We highlight a few Masonic trailblazers.

Benjamin Franklin was born AD 1706 in Massachusetts and died 1790 in Pennsylvania. During his life, he was an author, printer with works of *Poor Richard's Almanac* and the *Pennsylvania Gazette*. Franklin was a postmaster, scientist, and inventor. He was a politician serving as the sixth president of the Supreme Executive Council of Pennsylvania and as diplomat to France.

He became a Freemason in 1731 and arose to grand master in 1734 at a lodge in Philadelphia and was associated with the Nine Sisters Lodge in France. He published the Masonic book *Constitution of the Free Masons*. His philosophy was toward enlightenment, believing organized religion was necessary to keep men good to their fellow men, but he himself rarely attended religious services. His parents were Puritans and may have influenced his early years. Later, around 1728, he published his beliefs, in which did not mention Christian beliefs on salvation and the divinity of Jesus. He did label himself a deist and thus having faith in a god as the wellspring of morality and goodness in man and a god as the providential actor in history responsible for American independence. The enlightenment belief in deism is that God's truths can be found entirely through nature and reason. Franklin was an enthusiastic supporter of Evangelical minister George Whitefield during the first great awakening, but he did not subscribe to Whitefield's theology. Franklin published his sermons, which boosted the great awakening.

Benjamin Franklin was one of five who drafted the Declaration of Independence in Philadelphia. He was second to George Washington as a champion of American independence. As one of the Founding Fathers, he was the only one to have signed all the original founding documents as the Declaration of Independence, Treaty of Paris, and US Constitution. While the Founding Fathers were proclaiming that all men were created equal, the majority of them had no moral conviction toward the enslavement of humans, owning slaves themselves, and the inhumane treatment of other humans as well as the destruction of the Native Americans. Franklin was elected as president of the American Philosophical Society. Initially, he supported slavery, owning, selling, and posted ads for runaway slaves. He freed his slaves and became president of the Pennsylvania Abolition Society. In 1790, the Quakers and the society petitioned for abolition of slavery to Congress, which was rejected.

George Washington was born AD 1732 and died 1799 in Virginia. He was the first president of the United States from 1789 to 1797. Washington was called the Father of America. Washington was a deist but associated with Episcopalian denomination. He served as a British officer during the French and Indian wars and then fought against the British. His family was wealthy slaveowners operating their tobacco plantation. In later years, he desired to abolish slavery and in his will made provision to free his slaves after his death. His wife Martha was proslavery. He was initiated into Freemasonry in 1752 and achieved a 33rd degree level. He held the Masonic order in high regard and was attracted to its enlightenment principles based on rationality, reason, and fraternalism. He was named Master in the Virginia charter of Alexandria Lodge Number 22.

President George Washington in Masonic Dress

Albert Mackey, born AD 1807, in South Carolina was a physician, journalist, and educator. He became involved with Freemasonry around 1844; and by 1849, he established the *Southern and Western Masonic Miscellany* magazine. Mackey studied Greek, Latin, and Hebrew languages as well as the Bible and Kabbala. He served as secretary general of the Grand Lodge of South Carolina and of the Supreme Council of the Ancient and Accepted Scottish Rite for the southern jurisdiction of the United States. He died in 1881 and is buried at Glenwood Cemetery in Washington, DC. His grave stone is in the shape of a triangle with Masonic symbols engraved on it.

Albert Pike was born in 1809 in Massachusetts. He had a military career, obtaining the rank of general. He wrote poetry, and his first work was *Hymns to the Gods*. He joined the Masons around 1840, became very active, and rose to be sovereign grand commander of the Scottish Rite Southern jurisdiction in 1859. Later he wrote *Morals and Dogma of the Ancient and Accepted Scottish Rite of Freemasonry* in 1871. Pike died in 1891 in Washington, DC, and was buried at Oak Hill Cemetery. Throughout DC, there are statues and memorials to Pike.

In 1944, his remains were moved to the House of the Temple, headquarters of the Southern Jurisdiction of the Scottish Rite located in DC.

Manly P. Hall was born in 1901 in Canada. His parents were Rosicrucian members. Hall became involved in mysticism, Greek philosophy, Hinduism, and reincarnation after moving to California. He introduced his humanistic beliefs to members of the Peoples Church in 1919, where he served as their pastor in 1923. Hall as a 33rd degree Mason believed, "Man is god in the making and as in Egyptian mysticism, man is being molded on the potter's wheel. When man's light finally shines out to lift and preserve all things he receives a triple crown of godhood and joins that throng of Master Masons." He wrote *The Lost Keys of Freemasonry*, published in 1923. A quote from *The Lost Keys of Freemasonry*, "The principles of mysticism and the occult rites … the outcome of the secret destiny is a world order ruled by a king with supernatural powers. This king was descended of a divine race, that is he belonged to the order of the illumined for those who come to a state of wisdom then belong to a family of heroes-perfected human beings." Before Hall was born, we see the same sentiments reflected in the Mayan, Aztec, and Inca cultures—which he embraced. The feathered serpent (Satan) is king over the earth.

After traveling the world to study customs and religions of people in Asia and Europe, Hall published in 1928 *An Encyclopedic Outline of Masonic, Hermetic, Kabbalistic and Rosicrucian Symbolical Philosophy: Being an Interpretation of the Secret Teachings Concealed within the Rituals, Allegories, and Mysteries of All Ages*—which is more commonly referred to as *The Secret Teachings of All Ages*. Hall is quoted in his book *Secret Destiny of America*, "European mysticism was not dead at the time of the founding of the United States, the mysteries controlled the establishment of the new government for the signature of the occult may still be seen on the Great Seal of the United States, the Masonic symbol of the eagle is a phoenix, which is derived of Phoenicians who inhabited the land." The Great Seal of the United States, according to Hall, "is the signature of exalted Masons who designed America for a peculiar and particular purpose." Hall goes on to explain his idea of universal democracy: "Believing this to be so, I dedicate this book to the proposition that American democracy is part of a universal plan." **Our comment**—over the centuries, we see that America's interference in the affairs of other nations is to bring them under a global order via of a democratic system. Hall goes down in the annuals of Masonry as a great philosopher.

The Great Seal of the United States was first initiated by Benjamin Franklin, Thomas Jefferson, and John Adams, in 1776. Others worked on the design—such as, James Lovell, John Morin Scott, William Churchill Houston, and Francis Hopkinson. The rendition was completed in 1782 by Arthur Middleton, Elias Boudinot, Arthur Lee, and William Barton, the final designer/artist.

The dollar bill displays both sides of the seal. The obverse side is portrayed by an eagle holding arrows and wheat with thirteen stars over its head. The reverse side portrays a thirteen step pyramid and a capstone featuring the all seeing eye of the Egyptian god Horus. Symbolism embedded within the seal points to the coming one world order. Robert Hieronimus did extensive research on the great seal. He also believes in Atlantis (Masonic Order, Wikipedia and History Channel, June 14, 2013).

Other notable Masons were James Monroe, James Madison, Theodore Roosevelt, Franklin Delano Roosevelt, Harry Truman, Ronald Reagan.

In summary, the Masonic Order has roots in the ancient mystery religions and was formed on the doctrines of the Rosicrucian and Knights Templars. From the works of Plato, the fabled civilization of Atlantis that existed before the flood and destroyed by the flood had been the home of gods, immortals, superhumans, intellectuals, and giants. Plato's legend continued in the writings of Francis Bacon. Bacon was enthralled with the idea of Atlantis and laid the groundwork for the Resurrection of the new Atlantis. Bacon believed that the "continent of Atlantis," now America, had been previously visited by Phoenicians, Chinese, Egyptians, Tyrians, Europeans. Roman coins dating back to 800 BC were found in Vermont. Knights Templar symbolism was discovered in Canada along with Egyptian artifacts. Some data indicate Peruvians landed on a mysterious island called Bensalem. From the tidbits of history, the founding fathers had a plan for this land as stated by Manly Hall: "The *Order of the Quest* herein claims that all secret societies working together belong to the order of the quest to bring about a perfected social order, the government of the philosopher king in the new Atlantis."

Francis Bacon and his writings on the legend of Atlantis portray a center in this utopia called Solomon's House, wherein the study of science, philosophy, and material benefits of mankind are discussed. Bacon describes the departments and riches of Solomon's House: burials in several underground facilities, high towers (skyscrapers) half mile in height, great lakes, artificial wells and fountains, large baths for the cure of diseases, orchards and gardens, fish pools, bakeries, dispensaries of medicines, mechanical (engine houses, wind, water turbines), electrical devices, perspective houses, precious stones, music houses, perfume house, and mathematical house.

Other legends abound that when the Europeans came to America, they were instructed in the history of the old world (preflood), which reigned supreme. Legends were formed that the preflood people of Atlantis were higher, noble, possessing secret knowledge. Some suggest they had advanced technology, as in genetic labs, industrial plants, lasers, telescope, magnifying glass, firearms and missiles, flying machines, submarines, and holographic projection. This sounds far-fetched but we pick up pieces of legend from other sources that confirm the time before the flood may have been highly advanced. Legends in India speak of flying machines. If we factor in that the fallen angels brought with them advanced knowledge, which they taught to mankind, anything could have been possible.

Freemasonry is embedded throughout the United States. Washington, DC, is especially significant in its display of statues, images, obelisks, and an assortment of pagan imagery. The five-pointed pentagram was designed into Washington, DC, street grid by Pierre L'Enfant, 1791–1792. Manly P. Hall recognized the pentagram as a symbol of occult and magic rituals. Greek philosopher Pythagorean, a mystic, and his Pythagorean theorem was introduced as right triangle symbols. Prime numbers 1, 3, 7, 5, especially 5 points of the pentagram also called pentalpha used in Masonic lodges. The pentagram is symbolically used in Satanism or Wiccan cults.

Euclid was considered the father of geometry, 300 to 200 BC. Living in Alexandria, Egypt, associates him with Egyptian culture. Knowledge of math is a component of Masonry. Egypt was advanced in math. Philosophers Plato and Solon both believed in the legend of Atlantis before the flood. The Masonic order would graft that legend into their philosophy. The US Supreme Court building has a statue of Moses holding the Ten Commandments, flanked by Confucius and Solon.

The god of Masonry is referred to as the Great Architect of the Universe. To placate Christianity, Congress created something reflecting the Christian faith as in the mottos on the currency "In God We Trust," or "One Nation under God" in the Pledge of Allegiance.

AD 1819, Thomas Jefferson, a Freemason, disputes the scriptures and wrote his own version called the Jefferson Bible—where he omits the virgin birth, miracles of Christ, his resurrection and ascension, and the entire book of Revelation was deleted. He called Saint Paul stupid, rogue, impostor, and corruptor of the doctrines of Jesus.

AD 1836, the Washington National Monument Society was formed. It commissioned Freemason Robert Mills to design it, and he incorporated the obelisk as its symbol. It was completed after the civil war by Thomas Lincoln Casey, and in 1884, Chester Arthur dedicated the monument.

Walter Leslie Wilmshurst, a Mason, wrote in his book in 1922, *The Meaning of Masonry*:

> Candidates are being led from an old to an entirely new quality of life. He begins his masonic career as the natural man he ends it by becoming through its discipline a regenerated perfected man. To attain this transmutation, this metamorphosis of himself, he is taught first to purify and subdue his sensual nature then to purify and develop his mental nature and finally, by utter surrender of his old life and losing his soul to save it he rises from the dead a Master, a just man-made perfect. This, the evolution of man into superman, was always the purpose of the ancient mysteries and the real

> purpose of modern Masonry, not the social and charitable purpose to which so much attention is paid, but the expediting of the spiritual evolution of those who aspire to perfect their own nature and transform it into a more godlike quality. This is a definite science, a royal art …

Gene Roddenberry, 1921–1991, creator of *Star Trek*, a 33rd degree Mason, introduced advanced technology in a fictional scenario.

In 2007, when Nancy Pelosi became speaker of the House, the House passed resolution 33, which validated Freemasons throughout the nation. A quote from the resolution reads, "The founding fathers of this great nation and signers of the Constitution most of who were Freemasons provided a well-rounded basis for developing themselves and others into valuable citizens of these United States" (Tom Horn, *Apollyon Rising 2012*).

Illuminati

We have been following the connection between Babylonian and Egyptian mystery religions, secrete doctrines revealed in Rosicrucian and Masonic practices pave the way for rebirth of a new age embraced by. Illuminati established in Europe whose production played out on the American stage. Pilgrims coming to northern shores opened the way for multitudes of people to follow. As we see, some of these individuals had intentions of creating a new Atlantis in America based on the legends that foretold of a city that existed preflood founded on secret doctrine involving genetic engineering between fallen angels and humans. They were in pursuit of bringing about a golden dawn, a new age, and the reincarnation of their god.

May 1, 1776, five men met in a cave in Ingolstadt, Bavaria. One of these individuals was Dr. Adam Weishaupt, who at the invitation of Rothschild banking cartel attended the meeting. Weishaupt is credited with the founding of the Illuminati. His father was a Jewish rabbi. Weishaupt later converted to Catholicism, becoming a Jesuit. He was a professor of canon law at Ingolstadt University in Bavaria, a lawyer and occultist. As Weishaupt had Jewish roots, the Khazars had Jewish origins. They came from a Turkish-Mongolian tribe, which converted to Judaism in the middle of the eighth century. They occupied Russian and European countries and later migrated to North America. Being converts, they were not of direct lineage with the twelve tribes. Weishaupt gained his knowledge from a man named Kolmer, who spent years in Egypt learning secret doctrines found in its literature. He spent time in Kabbalah, searching for the secrets to cast spells and learn the hidden knowledge of God. Weishaupt and Kolmer met in Germany and spent five years together. Later, Hitler became a student of these same occult teachings.

The purpose of the meeting in 1776 was to devise a plan to take over the world and present this plan to their leader and master, Lucifer. The presence of an evil spirit was guiding them in developing the plan and recruiting new members. The organization would be referred to as the Illuminati, and their symbol would be the all-seeing eye or the capstone of the pyramid pictured on the dollar. This symbol can be traced back to Egypt, Pharaoh Amenhotep IV, 1350 BC. The organization would employ the principles of liberalism, socialism, immorality, and godlessness to bring about a one-world order. Its leader would also require a sacrifice, as is symbolically portrayed in Masonic rituals and celebrated at the Bohemian Grove. Their propaganda would infiltrate universities, religions, take over resources, conduct global conflict, and destroy objective dissenters. Under the cover of Masonry, they would recruit the best, brightest, and wealthiest. They would achieve high positions in the political arena from George Washington to the Bushes, Clinton, Obama. A tidbit gives us a link from 1782 between the Illuminati and the Masons established in Virginia and associated with New York Governor Dewitt Clinton.

The Illumed embraced Greek and Roman philosophy, classical authors, and musicians. Through entertainment, the organization could influence the mind-set of the masses. Entertainers who pledged their allegiance to these occult leaders would excel in the field. They used media outlets to announce incidents. For instance, the cartoon series, Family Guy, had a Robin Williams character who was portrayed as depressed and suicidal. Soon thereafter, the real Robin Williams committed suicide because of his depression. Williams could have been a required sacrifice. February 2016, Supreme Court Justice Antonin Scalia was found dead at a hunting lodge in Texas. Once again, predictive programing on the *Family Guy* show, season 5, made a reference to the death of Scalia before it occurred. The character of death carrying a cycle made a reference to Dick Cheney and Hal Burton in a hunting accident, and Scalia's name is mentioned, inferring his death in a hunting accident. Many believe Judge Scalia, a Conservative, was murdered by the one-world order elite to create an opening for a more liberal judge.

James H. Billington's book, *Fire in the Minds of Men*, spoke about revolutionary faith in Bavarian Illuminati. By forming public opinion through philanthropic outreach, beautiful gardens, and wineries in France, giving the appearance of legitimate banking and educational institutions, they wanted to appear as harmless sheep. Propaganda manipulates the masses into obedience and acceptance of conditions that are unproductive, such as homelessness, drug addiction, immorality, high unemployment, and government handouts. The masses cannot discern corruption at high levels carried out by the government and corporate chiefs. The people are conditioned to attack anything or anyone that stands against government dependence, against government-sanctioned abortion, against intolerance of the homosexual agenda, or having a perception that wealth is a reason to protest and riot. Race-batting has been successful in stirring up riots.

The plan then and now is to bring order out of chaos, to deceive many, and to divide and conquer through any means necessary. Since 1776, there have been many revolutions, two world wars and World War III is on the brink. This narrative is not far-fetched but is standard operating procedures for Satan and his followers.

Skull and Bones

Antony Sutton, *America's Secret Establishment*, calls Skull and Bones the brotherhood of death. Their earliest roots tie into Greek, Demosthenes, in 322 BC. It was later organized in 1832 in Germany. The number 322 is important to them. The 32 may refer to the year the organization was established, and the 2 may refer to its chapter. Members undergo extreme initiation rituals and psychological conditioning as well as receiving a new name. The initiation is to ensure members will continue a lifelong allegiance and retain power with an elite group, who follow a planned agenda for a NWO. Some families associated with this organization migrated to America in the 1600s—names such as Whitney, Lord, Phelps, Wadsworth, Allen, Bundy, Adams.

Class of 1878 had William Howard Taft, whose father was Attorney General Alphonso Taft, who cofounded the American branch.

Yale University hosts a Skull and Bones order with notable members, such as, Prescott Bush, father of George H. W. Bush, Bush Jr., John Kerry, Harriman, Rockefeller, Payne, Davison. Over the past century, the order has maintained around twenty-five families who retain their wealth and power. The Skull and Bones order penetrated into society by way of political affiliations, foundations for think tanks, policy making, education, media, publishing, banking, business, industry, and religion. Its infiltration in the protestant sector is to promote secular humanism. Union Theological Seminary is affiliated with Columbia University, New York. This seminary was subject of investigation for Communist activities and was called the Red seminary linked to Skull and Bones. Henry Sloan Coffin Jr. served as professor of Practical Theology at Union from 1904 to 1926. He had established a club for atheist students. Club meetings are held at 64 High Street, referred to as the "tomb," because it is windowless. The club headquarters features a roof with a landing pad for private helicopters.

Hitler's Aryan Order

Adolf Hitler and his followers' interest in the occult are widely documented. The Nazi party began an occult fraternity before it morphed into a political party. The SS was created based on occult beliefs. The Wewelsburg castle was their headquarters, and there they carried out initiation rituals for twelve SS knights modeled on King Arthur's legend. As early as 1935, the Nazis were interested in all things supernatural to be found in treasures, religious relics, telepathy, fairies, and giants. These interests led to the formation of the Ahnenerbe, or Ancestral Heritage Research and Teaching Organization. Psychics and astrologers were employed to attack the enemy based on the alignment of the stars.

Adolf Hitler was attracted to the Aryan philosophy because of its mystical and secret knowledge. He believed it would elevate Germany as a superior worldpower. Hitler adopted Aryanism as part of their master race ideology. His organization sent researchers throughout the world, searching for traces of the original, uncorrupted Aryan race of people. Seeking clues in Tibet, they looked for the Yeti or abominable snowman in the Himalayan Mountains. They searched for the Ark of the Covenant in Ethiopia. In Nuremberg, they searched for the Holy Grail and the Spear of Destiny used to pierce the side of Christ.

In Iceland, they searched for a magical land of telepathic giants and fairies called Thule, whose entrance could be accessed using a secret code hidden in medieval Icelandic saga called *The Eddas*. The Nazis thought Thule might be the location of the origin of the Aryans and from that the Thule Society was formed. If found, they might accelerate their Aryan breeding program and recover the supernatural powers of flight, telepathy, telekinesis, and immortality. Hitler began to promote the belief that Germany was inferior because of inner breeding with lesser races. During World War II, it was discovered the Germans had developed an underground facility in the Antarctica region. It was called Neuschwabenland. The Germans desired to create super soldiers enhanced with supernatural abilities and could be reanimated after the war. Great sums of money were funneled into the Ahnenerbe for research along with hundreds of workers and scientists. Today, the United States DARPA continues to expand on German research toward the development of super soldiers.

By 1943, the artwork referred to as the Ghent Altarpiece was most coveted by Hitler and his followers because it was a famous work with a German artist. The piece had been in Germany until it was returned to Belgium after World War I. Hitler believed the painting contained a coded map to lost treasures held by the Knights Templar—such as the instruments of Christ's Passion, including the crown of thorns, the Holy Grail, and the Spear of Destiny—and if these things were in his possession, they would grant him supernatural powers. The work was created by Jan van Eyck, *Adoration of the Mystic Lamb,* AD 1432, and the painting covers twelve oak panels. Eych painted a hundred figures into the twelve panels based on an elaborate pantheon of Catholic mysticism. At the center of his work is the sacrificial lamb upon an altar bleeding into a chalice, the Holy Grail. It was housed in Saint Bavo Cathedral in Ghent, Belgium, and is approximately 14 × 11.5 feet, weighing two tons. It had been stolen at least six times. The Belgium government had sent it to Chateau de Pau in France for safekeeping. Hitler got hold of the piece and sent it to Castle Neuschwanstein in Bavaria, where it was restored and then stored in a salt mine in the Austrian Alps near Altaussee. At this site, it joined approximately twelve thousand art pieces stolen by Hitler. Hitler planned to build a super museum the size of a city and to display every important artwork in the world. Later the treasures in the salt mine would be recovered by Austrian miners along with Robert Posey and Lincoln Kirstein (Noah Charney, December 21, 2013, *The Daily Beast*, "Hitler's Hunt for the Holy Grail and the Ghent Altarpiece").

Bohemian Club or Grove

The club was established in 1872. Its location is Bohemian Avenue, Monte Rio, California, on 2,700 acres—all male membership of around two thousand men and years-long waiting list. Attendees included US presidents T. Roosevelt, Reagan, Nixon, Hoover, Bush, Clinton; Chief Justice Earl Warren; Henry Kissinger; William Henry Rhodes; CEOs of corporations and banks, oil, military, and Federal Reserve heads; media; international dignitaries; royals; and artists. The majority of members are Masons. Hillary Clinton crashed the club but was escorted off the property. Obama attended in 1995. Collin Powell attended July 2016 as indicated in his hacked e-mails by DC Leaks. The e-mail was sent to Peter Gordon Mackay, Canadian politician, telling him of Powell's planned weekend to the club (New American, C. Mitchell Shaw, September 20, 2016).

A forty-foot tall owl shrine is located in the middle of the grove where the "cremation of care" ceremony takes place. This idol/statute was made by club president Haig Patigian in the 1920s. Later the owl was fitted with electronics to speak a recording and accompanied with pyrotechnics for the ritual. The cremation of care ceremony has a high priest, the spirit of care is slain by the high jinks, and then cremated. The ceremony served as a catharsis for pent-up high spirits and to present symbolically the salvation of the trees (in ancient times idols were placed among a grove of trees) by the club and then developed into the exorcising of the demon to ensure success of the two-week retreat. It is alleged that a sacrificial ceremony at one time may have involved a living person. The program is set up to rid one of their inhibitions. Men freely urinate in the woods, can opt to wear outlandish costumes, and sexual acts between men are encouraged. Another patron statue is of John of Nepomuk dressed in cleric robes with his finger over his lips to symbolize the secrecy kept by the Grove's attendees throughout history. A Satanist by the name of Zackery Cane became a high wizard in the club, and he attended the ceremony for years. He said actual spells were cast before the image.

Phillip Weiss writer for *Spy Magazine* infiltrated the club in 1989. In 2000, Alex Jones of Info Wars managed to sneak in and record activity. He was able to bribe a worker there to film the whole complex. God promises in Micah 5:13 that these idols will be destroyed. Still waiting.

Religion Versus Idolatry

What Is Religion?

Before tackling this question, we should look at the relationship of God and his angels before the creation of man. This relationship was not a religion but the worship of the Holy God by his creation. God created Adam, and their relationship was not a religion but one of honor, respect, and love between Creator and the first human son. After the fall of Adam and Eve, Satan introduced pride and the falsehood that they too could be like God. They turned from their relationship with God and accepted the lie. That act of disobedience had a significant impact on all of creation. Man had relinquished his God-given authority over the earth, and Satan became the god of this world. Satan's ploy was to create division and separate man from God. This was not religion, but it led to a pathway of worship outside of God, thus separating man from God.

God, in his mercy, shed the blood of animals, covered Adam and Eve in animal skins, and sent them into the world. This covering was a covenant and a realization that things would be different for the first people, but God is sovereign. Adam and Eve tried to maintain their relationship with God by building stone altars and offering burnt sacrifices, which was a primitive manner of worship and the birth of a religious system.

Satan continued his evil agenda by creating division between Cain and Abel. The dispute was in regard to who had the better religious sacrificial offering. He caused Cain to commit the first murder. Cain is banished from the area and goes on to practice his own brand of religion. During the preflood era, people began to worship the fallen angels, and this became the foundation of pagan religions. The practice continued postflood and multiplied, developing into a variety of pagan religions. The path to false religion begins with the opening of the occult portal, allowing Satan entry into the hearts and minds of people.

We offer a generic understanding of religion. Hundreds of different religions have been established in the world. "A religion has a system of beliefs associated with its gods, spirits, demons, or angels shrouded in myths of their existence in an unseen world. Around the objects of their beliefs, they develop rituals, temples, priests, writings, and more. The doctrines of that religion would provide the adherents with a belief about their god's image and characteristics. It would provide a belief for the afterlife, heaven, hell, or reincarnation."[33] It is safe to say, man-made religion opens a portal for paganism and occultism. Jesus came to free mankind from religious constraints.

---

33 Lewis M. Hopfe, *Religions of the World* (New York, NY: Macmillan Publishing, 1983) p2

What Is Idolatry?

Idolatry begins with the formation of an idol from wood, stone, metal, and is or could be the physical representation of a false god. The image of this god and the powers they represent are worshipped. The Baphomet statue is a perceived image of Satan and is an idol that is worshipped.

Idolatry began with the worship of fallen angels, who became the persona of Assyrian, Babylonian, Egyptian, Greek, or Roman gods and goddesses. In early records, we find that the Canaanites worshipped the false god Baal, and the goddess Astarte came forth from the Babylonian religious system. Hinduism and Buddhism embrace and worship many idols. Even Christendom surrounds itself with idols, lavish decorations, pomp and various icons associated with their religion. Idolatry can be found in any religion, be it Judaism, Christendom, as well as in paganism.

We can deduce that mankind was introduced to idolatry in the Garden of Eden when they chose to obey the image of the snake rather than Yahweh. Satan said, you shall be as gods, and you will not die. Could the first parents have been fully cognizant of death or immortality? Did they know Satan was a fallen angel who desired to be as God? The Bible alludes to the entertaining of angels unaware. Later on, down the road, the righteous would begin to understand that Satan, the god of this world, came to deceive and destroy mankind. The unrepentant would follow Satan, who lured them with gifts of power, wealth, immortality, and access to forbidden knowledge in exchange for their soul.

Since we understand that religion is man-made, then what idiom would apply for following the one true God outside of a religious constraint? The answer is relationship. We can have a personal relationship with the one true God without man-made contraptions. The Bible points us to the eternal Godhead. Yahweh extends an open hand to come into his presence. Yahweh has embraced his people in a love that passes all human comprehension. Our response to his invitation is, "Yes, I will follow you in obedience, love, and faithfulness." I will not sin against you, and if I do, I will sit at your feet and ask to be forgiven. We must refrain from evil and follow a path of holiness. We walk in the shadow of the Almighty and are covered in his righteousness.

The Bible Truth in Contrast to False Religion

The Bible truth is knowledge and salvation for every person. Paul says in Romans 1:16, "*I am not ashamed of the gospel of Christ for it is the power of God unto salvation to everyone that believes, to the Jew and the* Greek." God's truth is inconvertible, unchanging, and timeless.

> *That which may be known of God is manifest in men for God has showed it unto them. For the invisible things of him from the creation of the world are clearly seen, being understood by the things that are made, even his eternal power and Godhead so that they are without excuse.* (Romans 1:19)

Mankind has no excuse for rejecting God's truth and embracing Satan's lie. God has placed the knowledge of himself in everyone, and they can look upon his creation and see his handiwork.

> *Because that, when they knew God, they glorified him not as God, neither were thankful but became vain in their imaginations and their foolish heart was darkened.* (Romans 1:21)

This passage ties together Satan's lies and false beliefs that move mankind farther from the truth of God. The first patch in this man-made quilt is pride and man believing he is wiser than his Creator.

Cultures who worship creation rather than the Creator span thousands of years, and they are foolish.

> *They changed the glory of the incorruptible God into an image made like to corruptible man and to birds and four footed beasts and creeping things. God gave them up to uncleanness through the lusts of their own hearts to dishonor their own bodies between themselves. Who changed the truth of God into a lie and worshipped and served the creature* (Satan a created being) *more than the Creator, who is blessed forever.* (Romans 1:22–25)

God does not take lightly images made like unto man, birds, beasts, and creeping things. He put it in writing: "I Am the Lord your God, you will have no other gods before me, and you will not make any graven images of stone or wood as well as cravings on your body."

God has given to each person knowledge that he is our Creator. At the time of death, if a person has rejected this basic truth, their soul belongs to Satan. The reason why God came in the form of man was to show us the path to eternal life with God instead of eternal life in hell. Yeshua came to show mankind that through his miracles, his Gospel, and his death, we can have eternal life with the triune Godhead, God the father. Son and Holy Spirit. His shed blood paid for our sins, and in his Resurrection, we have the promise of eternal life with God.

When Yeshua died on the cross, His spirit went into the lower regions of the earth and took the keys of death and hell. He preached to the captives and set the righteous in

Abraham's bosom free. We who are encumbered with chains of sin can be set free by accepting Jesus as our savior.

Satan's agenda has not changed since it began in Genesis. Satan and his followers are hell-bent on counterfeiting God's creation, corrupting the human genome, destroying God's creation, creating false religions, and turning man away from the truth of God. The Luciferian doctrine becomes the basis of all false religions. His doctrine is found in witchcraft and occult practices. Satan and his followers use these methods to pervert the truth of God, and this is why God has forbidden his followers to indulge in them. Entertaining demons and evil spirits allow evil entities to possess people, control and direct people into false beliefs. The result of these practices lead mankind into immoral degradation, debauchery, human sacrifice, and rejection of all things holy. The use of mind control, chanting, ritualistic conditioning, propaganda, promises of rewards and riches are the stitches that connect people and influence them to become receptive to the ploy of Satan.

Satan knew Jesus is God but attempted to use his wiles on Jesus. Satan may have thought that since God was now in the flesh, he was weak and vulnerable. In Luke 4, Jesus is transported to the desert by his Holy Spirit. During his forty days of fasting, he was tempted by the devil. Satan said, "If you are the Son of God, command this stone be made bread," and Jesus said, "It is written that man will not live by bread alone but every word of God." The devil took Jesus into a high mountain overlooking the kingdoms of the world and said, "All this power will I give you and the glory of them, for it is delivered unto me and to whomsoever I will I give it, if you will worship me," and Jesus said, "Get thee behind me Satan, for it is written, you will worship the Lord your God, and him only will you serve." Finally, Satan takes Jesus to the corner of the temple in Jerusalem and said, "If you are the Son of God, cast yourself down from here, for it is written, he will give his angels charge over you to keep you, and in their hand they will bear you up lest at any time you dash your foot against a stone," and Jesus said, "You will not tempt the Lord your God." Satan then departs for a season (Luke 4 paraphrased by author). In these lessons, we are to see that Satan will influence mankind to sin through the lust of the eye, lust for materialism, and the pride of life.

The Rotten Fruit of False Religion

We can compare the fruit of the Spirit with the spirit that operates in false religions.

The fruit of the Sprit is love, joy, peace, patience, gentleness, goodness, and faith. We who are in Christ have crucified the flesh and no longer desire the affections and lusts of the world. If we live in the Spirit, let us also walk in the Spirit. Let us not desire vain glory. Let us not be envious. Let us not provoke one another (Galatians 5:22–26).

Romans 1:26–32, the rotten fruit of false religion is not unto holiness but is unto sin, or as it is opposed to godliness. Following are examples of bad fruit:

- Idolatry.
- Lust, impure thoughts.
- Vile affections, women changed the natural use of their bodies that was against nature (bestiality).
- Men left the natural use of the woman and burned in their lust one toward another, men with men (homosexuality), working that which is unseemly (sodomy) and receiving in themselves (sperm).
- Fornicators (all sexual sin).
- Received a reprobate (depraved) mind, inventors of evil things.
- Without natural affection (toward the unborn, torture of living things).
- Unrighteous, wicked.
- Maliciousness, covetousness, envy, unforgiveness, hatred, jealousy.
- Murder, unmerciful.
- Deceit, liars, malice, despiteful, anger.
- Backbiters, gossipers, complaining, criticizing.
- Hate God.
- Disobedient to parents.
- Proud, boasters.

For doing these things and have pleasure in doing them, know the judgment of God for such things is death.

The satanic agenda is in operation in current times evidenced by the spiritual degradation of mankind. Satan recruits people like Darwin, a man versed in Bible scripture yet rejected the Creator and introduced the theory of evolution, turning many away from the truth that God created all things. Satan was able to recruit people to get the Word of God thrown out of schools and public places. He influenced the judicial system in favor of Roe versus Wade to legalize the killing of millions of unborn babies. He was able to promote the depravity of homosexual practices as a normal lifestyle. Satan seduced an entire culture to be destroyed through drugs, crimes, and prostitution. Society has been deceived and has turned a blind eye to sin. The thread that connects man to Satan's agenda is sewn throughout the fabric of secularism, liberalism, and humanism.

The fallen angels taught man how to make weapons and the art of war. God said we should love our neighbor, but Satan spurred man to hatred. Man's inhumanity played out in atrocities committed by people, while others watch persecution, rape, mutilation, and death.

The Romans made a sport of sending the Christians into the coliseum to be eaten by lions or to be burned alive on stakes. Man lost his sense of conscience, compassion, and mercy.

God is all-knowing. He knew that over the course of time, mankind would continue to turn away from godliness and fall under the occult spell, leading into idolatry, false religions, and wickedness. Yeshua has always been a beacon of light shining in a dark world. When we lose our way, we look for his light in the scriptures, in the light of ministers of the Gospel, and Jesus will guide our path back to himself. The Old Testament is Yeshua concealed, and the New Testament is Yeshua Messiah revealed.

Characteristics of False Religions

As the teachings of Noah faded, people created their own belief system influenced by otherworldly spirits evidenced in symbols and images of false gods depicted in their places of worship. Those involved in false religions embody false doctrines to assuage their beliefs. The Holy Bible is the inerrant Word of God. Yahweh said, "I am God, there is none other." There are three that bear witness: Father, Son, and Holy Spirit, and these are one (1 John 5:7). Anyone who denies the deity of Jesus Christ, God came in flesh, the only begotten of the Father, Son of God, born of a virgin, are Antichrist. Those who reject God crucified, shed his blood for sinners' redemption, resurrected, and sits at the right hand of God are deceived. If anyone perverts the Gospel of Christ, be it an angel from heaven preaching any other gospel than that which has been given through God, is accursed (Galatians 1:8). There is only one way to God, and that is through Jesus, who is the truth and the life; no man comes to the Father except he come through the Son. Anyone who denies this truth is accursed and is Antichrist herein; false religions are in opposition to the divine Word, unable to adhere to biblical truths. False religions have a perverted account of God the Creator, the creation, the flood, and Lucifer. God's truth is rejected, and Satan's lies, "you can be as God," are embraced. The Word of God is usurped by the tenants of humanism, the worship of self, indulgence for the lust of the world, philosophy, science, and much interest in the UFO phenomenon—believing alien spirit children from another planet seeded Earth, nurtured evolution, and are our saviors. They will easily align themselves with the satanic kingdom on earth and reject the heavenly kingdom of God the Creator.

Following, we have highlighted several religions that are in contrast to the aforementioned biblical truth. Some references are taken from Lewis M. Hopfe, *Religions of the World.*

Nature Worship, Pantheism, Green Religion

Early worshippers of Mother Earth called her Gaia and envisioned her as a living female deity. Greek and Roman cultures gave her the credit for their opulent lifestyle and a green light for debauchery. They made altars in groves, under trees, and high places up on hills. Beautiful shrines were erected, where they left offerings and prayed for the nature god to bestow upon them fertility and bountiful crops. Modern man has renewed his interest in the goddess Gaia, the patron of the green religion. Protection of earth from mankind is their priority.

Pantheism

Native Americans expressed their beliefs in the spirit world found in nature, animals, lightning, and rain. They respected all of nature. They carved totem poles to identify their tribe and association with nature. The spirits of dead ancestors were memorialized and included in ritual ceremonies. The great spirit or supreme being in the sky was acknowledged at the time of the sun dance. The powers of nature can be personified, and man will be rewarded with favorable temperatures and good crop growth. Native practices did not call for blood sacrifice, but on occasions, others would be killed to accompany the dead. Pantheism is the belief that God is in everything. The universe is God. The Pantheon was a temple built in 27 BC in Rome to celebrate all gods.

On the African continent, the practice of sacrificing or burying others with the dead to accompany them in the afterlife was part of the Egyptian culture. Throughout Africa, religious practices were similar to those practiced by Native Americans. Like their Native American relatives, Africans carved images of everything; they wore ceremonial garments, masks, and they were polytheistic. As we study other religions, we also discover that European religions practiced idolatry, witchcraft, and held to superstitious beliefs, such as werewolves, vampires, and some European cultures would not bathe so as to ward off evil spirits by their personal stench.

Green Religion

Going green is a Resurrection of nature worship. It is the worship of ancient Gaia, or Mother Nature. Ancient practices have taken on a modern-day appearance. The power in weather, hurricanes, earthquakes, lightning, and rain can be harnessed and controlled by man. God the Creator is taken out of the equation. One group called the National Religious Partnership for the Environment has its goals to integrate green beliefs with our traditional religious beliefs. Nature worship has become big business—going green. Green religion must protect the earth from man, who is seen as the destroyer of nature with high carbon output and they believe is the cause of global warming. Overpopulation is responsible for the proliferation of resources such as water, minerals, food, and should be culled.

Nature worship, new age, and the green religion are interconnected. The green religion is aligned with the United Nations' Agenda 21 initiative and supported by many world leaders. The earth is exalted, and its natural resources are more precious than the inhabitants, and humans must be eliminated in order to save the earth and protect the environment. Worshipping the creation and not the Creator is clearly a false religion. For detailed insight into the new age and green religion, read Russell Chandler, *Understanding the New Age*.[34]

Witchcraft, Wizards, Voodoo, Sangria

Some people believe witches, wizards, and vampires are fairy tales, legends, and myths. Many of us watched the TV series *Bewitched* through to the Salem witch trials. We got drawn into actions of wizards in *Harry Potter*, and the vampire culture has been romanticized for hundreds of years. These practices are real. Witchcraft is pitted against Christianity. Witches believe Christians are ignorant, caught up in mass hysteria, and acted out of fear, burning witches at the stake. The modern incarnation is called the religion of Wicca, whose concept is on the feminine or goddess worship instead of a male image. Their belief system is a mix of nature worship, Eastern mystics, druidism, Celtic lore, and others pagan traditions. It became associated with a countercultural movement as expressed in the hippie culture, new age philosophies, radical feminism, free love, LSD to take one into a higher spiritual awakening. Wicca is an occult using spells, incantations, magic, sorcery, divination in their rituals. Some of these rituals require a blood sacrifice. For example, American rapper, Azealia Banks a practicing witch revealed a small blood stained room where she slaughters chickens in her rituals. Article by Andrew Bieszad on the Walid Shoebat site, December 30, 2016.

Article by Natalina Hansen, A Bubbling Cauldron in Hope for the World. Summer 2015

New Age

New age is a catch all for a variety of practices, including philosophy, Eastern religions, humanism, astrology, witchcraft and worship of Gaia. The principles of Yoga can open the mind to Eastern rituals such as chanting, meditation, visualizing energy moving through the chakras in the spine, and opening oneself up to channel evil spirits.

Dr. David Reagan and Evangelist Nathan Jones, Lamb and Lion Ministries, March 2013, interviewed Warren Smith, author of *The Light That Was Dark.* [35] The book is a testimony of how Warren got involved with the new age movement and was delivered by Jesus.

---

[34] Russell Chandler, Understanding the New Age (Dallas: Word Publishing, 1988) p 17, 33, 43

[35] Warren Smith, The Light That Was Dark (Kingsway Publications, 1993)

The new age teaching got a jump-start from Shirley MacLaine in late 1980s, when she stood on the seashore and proclaimed, "I am god, I am god." MacLaine's celebrity prompted others to jump on the bandwagon.

Marilyn Ferguson, author of *The Aquarian Conspiracy,*[36] debuted on the *Oprah Winfrey Show*, focused on the new age movement. Ferguson's theme was, "We have a great idea, God within and God in everything, in time, we can pull this off by wide publicity, we can have our way." Oprah Winfrey is like the high priestess of the new age movement, inviting many new agers to be on the show. She interviewed M. Scott Peck, author of *Community of the Cosmic Christ*, [37] a proclaimed Christian but influenced by new age philosophy. He said, "We are in crisis, we need to have a new way of looking at things, we need a new worldview, our salvation lies in community." Peck expounds on this idea, "The mystical prophet who is bringing forth this idea of sort of a quantum leap into a new level of understanding was the Catholic Jesuit priest Pierre Teihard de Chardin, the father of the new age movement." Chardin says, "This soul must be a conspiracy of individuals, and God is in every atom." Other well-known new agers are Deepak Chopra, Betty Eadie, and Dr. Mehmet Oz. Dr. Oz was featured on the Oprah show for years until he had his own program. Warren Smith says, "Dr. Oz is probably one of the more dangerous, and I say that carefully, occultists out there." Oz endorsed a book by psychic Ainslie MacLeod, *The Instruction*. [38] The book refers to spirit guides over 175 times, past lives, and promotes meditation to contact spirit guides. Oz promotes transcendental meditation, known as *Reiki*—which invites spirit guides.

Quote from *New Age Journal*, 1992, "Transcendental meditation associates Christianity also with having a form of mantra meditation. The technique is called centering prayer, draws on the spiritual exercises of the Desert Fathers, *The Cloud of Unknowing*, and the famous Jesus Prayer, reliance on a mantra centering device has a long history in the mystical canon of Christianity."

Barbara M. Hubbard wrote *A Course in Miracles*, and Neal Donald Walschi wrote, *Conversations with God*, each promoting new age philosophy. Another popular book that surfaced was William P. Young's, *The Shack*. It was read by Christians and new agers alike. The writer promoted God is in his creation, and we are lesser gods.

A new age leader known as Lord Maitreya promotes the coming of a (false) messiah. Another, Benjamin Creame, was like an evangelist telling people of the coming messiah. He took out newspaper ads, saying, "The Christ is here, and he is waiting to be called forth,"

---

[36] Marilyn Ferguson, The Aquarian Conspiracy (Published by Jeremy Tarcher, 1987)

[37] M. Scott Peck, Community of the Cosmic Christ

[38] Ainslie Macleod, The Instruction (Published by Sounds True, 2007)

and this contradicts the words of Jesus who warns if they say Jesus is here on in the desert, it is a lie.

Aryans, Hinduism, Buddhism

Aryans

Some postflood people migrated from Mesopotamia to the land mass called India around 2500 BC, supported by archaeological evidence located in the Indus Valley early 1920s. Evidence revealed an advanced civilization showing planned cities, streets, drainage systems, agriculture, and a written language. The name *Aryan* in Sanskrit means "noble ones." Aryans may have been related to the Hyksos, who migrated to Egypt and to the Celtics in the "isles" (*Religions of the World*, "The Origins of Hinduism," p. 83–84).

Aryans who did not migrate into India remained in Mesopotamia, which encompasses the ancient regions of Persia and Babylon. Some Aryans/Persians may have been the founders of Zoroastrianism. See chapter 8 for details on Zoroastrianism. As the Persian Empire grew, they named their land Iran, meaning "the land of the Aryans." Their dialect was Indonesian and European, and the term *Indo-European* is used. The Aryan religion was polytheistic, also incorporating false gods of Greece (Zeus) and Rome (Jupiter). Their rituals included animal sacrifices and offerings of agriculture.

Hinduism developed in India and remains their major religion. It has no founder or central leader. Hinduism has thousands of false gods. Their sacred writings are called *Veda*, meaning "knowledge regarding lore, hymns, chants, rituals, and philosophy." Within the Vedas are descriptions and mythology of Aryan gods. Mohandas Gandhi was a well-known Hindu leader working to bring improvement to his people from British rule. Jainism and Buddhism were an outgrowth of Hinduism around 500 BC. Both beliefs rejected sacrificial rituals, the Vedas, and the caste system. They have a common belief of reincarnation, monks, practice chastity, and no injury to animals. Remnants of Judaism and Christianity are found in India, perhaps coming into this region after the dispersion in Rome, first century AD. They predate Islam. In the fifteenth-century AD, followers of Islam invaded India, which gave birth to Sikhism, a combination of Hindu and Islam. Hinduism absorbed their distinctive features into their religious beliefs.

Buddhism is a minor religion in India but has greater followings in other Asian countries as well as infiltrating into Europe and America. Its founder was Siddharth, 560 BC, of the Gautama clan. He was born of royalty, and it was proclaimed he would be a great Buddha or enlightened one. He was raised in a cloistered environment. His father had a harem of women. At nineteen, he married his cousin, and they had a son. Around the age of thirty, he desired to see the world he had never known. He left home and sought enlightenment. It was not his intention to form a new religion but rather to teach about ethics, self-understanding, and salvation through good works. He did not believe in the soul of man housing the emotions and consciousness but was part of an endless cycle of birth, death, and rebirth.

Buddhist monk Thich Nhat Hanh wrote *Living Buddha, Living Christ: Jesus from an Eastern Perspective.*

Mayans, Aztec

Since the discovery of the Mayan long-count calendar predicting the end of the age on December 21, 2012, their culture and pagan beliefs moved to the forefront of discussion. Mayans are relatives of the Native Americans having migrated into Mexico and throughout South America. A large concentration of Maya artifacts was discovered in the Yucatan Peninsula. Social and religious life was led by shamans, kings, or priests.

Complex hieroglyphics present an understanding of their spiritual beliefs and practices. Their knowledge of the universe consisted of the starry heaven ruled by a cosmic lizard-like creature, and its direction was north, or "side of heaven"; the middle world of earth, which flourished only by blood of humans; and the dark waters of the underworld, which was a portal that could be attained while in a trance. The image and belief in a "world tree" with a serpent was to symbolize the directions of the earth and a portal of communication between the human world and the otherworld. Symbols of the "vision serpent" and the "double-headed serpent" were displayed. The trunk of the tree went through the middle world; its roots plunged to the watery underworld; and its branches soared to the zenith in the highest layer of the heavenly region of the "otherworld." Entrance into these portals was opened by bloodletting sacrifices. The "world tree" emerges from the head of the god Chac-Xib-Chac, meaning "evening star," as he rises from the black waters of the portal. The trunk of the "world tree" splits to become the "vision serpent," whose gullet is the path taken by the ancestral dead and the gods of the otherworld when they commune with the king as the forces of nature and destiny. Once brought into the world of humanity, these otherworld beings could be materialized in ritual objects or in the actual body of a human performer. [39]

The Mayan ritual of bloodletting was considered a gift of blood from the body as act of piety. Sacrifices included infants, children, and adults ranging in a few drops to extreme mutilation. The aim of these rituals was the opening of a portal into the otherworld, through which gods and the ancestors could be enticed so that the beings of this world could commune with them. The Maya thought of this process as giving birth to the god or ancestor, enabling it to take physical form in this plane of existence.

---

[39] Linda Schele, David Freidel, *A Forest of Kings: The Untold Story of the Ancient Maya,* (New York, NY: William Morrow and Company, Inc., 1990), p66–70

Aztec and Inca cultures share similar beliefs and practices with the Mayan culture. A common theme is the feathered serpent, bringer of light and illumination. The Maya call this god Kukulkan; the Aztec call him Quetzacoatal; the Inca call him Amaru Muru. Various Native Americans tribes refer to him as the feathered serpent. These are all references to Satan, angel of light, having the appearance of a reptile with wings like feathers, one who brings knowledge.

Scientology

This organization was founded by L. Ron Hubbard, 1911–1986. He incorporated the Church of Scientology in 1953. His published book, *Dianetics*, was his thoughts on self-help remedies.[40] A summary on their beliefs are that Xenu—an immortal ruler of the galactic confederation, which was an extraterrestrial civilization—came to earth seventy-five million years ago, bringing billions of people. He crashed the vehicles into mountains, causing volcanoes to erupt and causing the people to cling and merge with living people. The people are called Thetans, and in the primordial past, they brought the natural universe into being for their pleasure. The universe has no independent reality but derives its apparent reality from the fact Thetans agree it exists. They believe people are immortal, intrinsically good, omniscient, nonmaterial core capable of unlimited creativity—which is their true nature; therefore, rationality trumps morality. They fell from grace when they began to identify with creation rather than their original state of spirituality and purity, causing a memory of their creative powers. Therefore, they are required to study the handling of the spirit in relationship to itself, a god, others, and all life. They now think of themselves as embodied beings.

This belief by Hubbard of aliens coming to earth is similar to data we discussed in chapter 16 regarding a legend of spaceships that landed thousands of years ago in China and the people on them were called Dropa. The Chinese tribes called Ham, or Han, killed the Dropas until they understood they were not going to kill them. Today the inhabitants of this area call themselves Dropa and Han.

The Mormon doctrine also believes that "spirit children," having existed in heaven, were sent by God to earth to populate the earth, including Lucifer and Jesus, also spirit children. Adam and Eve were Elohim, and they began the human race. They will aspire to become gods and return to live on various planets.

Hubbard's philosophy is a mix of paganism, Mormonism, and his own understanding used to developed methods to attain greater spiritual awareness and unlocking of hidden abilities through a progression level to level called Bridge to Total Freedom. Level 1 subject is referred to as a Preclear; next level is called Clear; then move up to Operating Thetan, OTs.

---

40 L. Ron Hubbard, Dianetics (Bridge Publishing Inc. 1981)

Since their true nature has been long forgotten, people are in need of rehabilitation called Auditing. In brief, one must reexperience painful/traumatic events in their past to free self of limiting effects. The process called Assumption, or reincarnation, is to be reborn again and again assuming new bodies.

"The Way to Happiness," a twenty-step program, printed in seventy languages, is a compass to bring happiness, peace, and to unite cultures through the Church of Scientology. The truth is what is true for you. Good works are important, and they have outreach organization—such as Narcon, an anti-drug intervention program; Criminon, working with prisoners toward rehabilitation; and Study Tech, an education program.

Their church symbolism is an eight-pointed cross and double triangles. It is a cross with an *X* through the middle. Lower triangle stands for affinity, reality, communication, ARC; and higher triangle stands for knowledge, responsibility, control, KRC.

Some celebrity members are Nancy Cartwright, Isaac Hayes, Tom Cruise, Charles Manson, Lisa and Marie Presley, John Travolta, etc. Their membership can be found in Italy, South Africa, Australia, Sweden, New Zealand, Portugal, Spain, Canada, France, Germany, United Kingdom, etc. Their headquarters are in Flagland Base, Clearwater, Florida.

Scientology has been labeled as a cult because it charges exorbitant fees for spiritual services and members cannot freely leave the cult. Case in point—in 1995, Lisa McPherson, a member, had a psychotic breakdown; and since the organization does not believe in psychiatric therapy to help with mental disorders, they took her in for Introspection Rundown. She was locked in a room for seventeen days, had a hundred insect bites on her body, and was severely dehydrated and malnourished, causing her death. The State of Florida filed a criminal case against them.

Critics to the organization will be litigated and aggressive tactics are used in pursuing foes, such as in the case of Martine Boublil. In 2007, ex-member Boublil was kidnapped and held for two weeks against her will by four scientologists. She was found half naked and locked in a room full of trash and insects. The group believes in punishment of dissidents; some were thrown overboard into the ocean while on the SEA ORG, fleet of ships Hubbard owned.

In 1979, they developed Operation Snow White, which became the largest theft of government documents in US history. Ms. Hubbard was convicted. In 1993, the IRS took back their tax-exempt religious status, and they had to pay $12.5 million to the IRS ("Church of Scientology," Wikipedia online).

Scientology is based on a bunch of outright unscriptural statements and no belief in Jesus as savior; they have a humanist view, intermingled with Gnosticism, Hinduism mythology, and other pagan beliefs. Therefore, this organization is classified as a false religion.

Mormonism, Latter-Day Saints

Salt Lake City, Utah, is the heartland of the Mormons. The bee is the state symbol for Utah, which connects this organization to the Merovingian philosophy. The official title is Church of Jesus Christ of Latter-Day Saints, established in 1830 by Joseph Smith. Smith was involved in the occult and Freemasonry. He became a Mason in 1842 with over one thousand Mormon followers. Smith began to incorporate Masonic rituals interlaced with Knights Templar philosophy into the Mormon temple practices.

"Mormons believe in a premortal existence as spirit children who lived in heaven and were sent by God to earth to go through trials in bodies of flesh in order to be perfected by the father. When they reach perfection, they will become gods and rule over their own worlds on other planets and be worshipped and served by lesser humans."[41]

They have a one-world government philosophy. They claim a priesthood after the order of Aaron and Melchizedek. America is the promised land, and they are the regathered Israel. Smith believed the Christian church was lost after the death of the twelve apostles and needed to be restored through himself. Mormons believe they will usher in the Second Coming and the kingdom of God.

There are six million followers with 152 sites, and they continue to grow. Smith was said to have built three cities and two temples. The founder had about three years of education and was taught the Bible at home. Mormons practiced polygamy. Some of their church fathers, such as Warren Jeff, were jailed for marrying ten- to twelve-year-old girls. Winston Blackmore had twenty-five wives and a hundred children. Brigham Young had fifty-five wives and fifty-six children.

Following, we provide several excerpts from the Book of Mormon, 1 Nephi, Smith said,

> A Jew named Lehi from Jerusalem built a boat in 600 BC and sailed to the promised land, to a place called Bountiful in America. Before his trip to America, Lehi lived in Jerusalem during King Zedekiah of Judah's reign. His wife is Sariah, they had four sons, Laman, Lemuel, Sam, and Nephi. During prayer, Lehi had a vision of a pillar of fire. He is carried away by the spirit to heaven and thinks he sees God sitting on a throne with many angels, singing and praising God.
>
> In this vision, he sees one descending from heaven followed by twelve brothers. They gave Lehi a book which contained some woes unto Jerusalem, judgment to come, destroyed by sword and taken captive to Babylon. Lehi tried to warn the Jews but was rejected. The Jews try to kill Lehi. The spirit

[41] Tom Horn, *Zenith 2016*, (Crane, Missouri: Defender Publisher 2013)

> tells him to leave his wealth and land, take his family and travel three days to the wilderness. There he will marry the daughter of Ishmael. He is told the lord will lead him to the promised land, a land prepared for you. Before he leaves, he is told to go to the house of Laban and get the records, which were engraved on brass plates having the genealogy of Lehi who was a descendant of Joseph.

These plates were alleged to be the five books of the Torah. There are many fragmented references to various biblical accounts, but for the sake of space, we will stop at this point.

Smith said when he was fourteen years old, God and Jesus appeared to him; therefore he believed that Jesus and God the Father are separate and different and not equal. He claims to have been visited by Apostles John, Peter, and James. Smith said, "By our own righteous acts, we build to get a special kingdom and reach god (as in the Tower of Babel). We must do works to qualify for eternal life and abstain from tea, coffee, and alcohol."

First vision was given for his understanding of the physical nature of God and Jesus. Mormons developed the "Gospel Principles." Lucifer and Jesus are brothers. Lucifer presents a plan to God the Father to subjugate humanity into humility and righteousness. Jesus offered the idea of free will, and God the Father accepted his plan. Mormons believe that God the Father had many wives who bore millions of spirit children. God, Lucifer, and Jesus decided to build planet Earth to allow the children to live there and to take on mortal bodies. Lucifer wanted to be the god over the earth and its savior. God decided to allow Jesus to be the savior. Lucifer rebelled against this decision and convinced one-third of the spirits destined for earth to revolt against God. God's response was that Lucifer became Satan and his followers, demons. They would not receive physical bodies. Those spirits that remained neutral were cursed to be born with black skin. Those who fought on the side of God would be allowed to be born into Mormon families on earth. They would be the lighter-skinned, "delightsome" people. God and one of his wives came to earth to become Adam and Eve. Later God would return to earth and have sex with the Virgin Mary so that Jesus would have a physical body. Mormons introduced the idea that Jesus was married to Mary, Martha, and Mary Magdalene, and they had children. Marriage and children lead to godhood. Good works lead to glorification. Humans will become glorified gods and rule over other planets.

Smith received an ancient record from the angel Moroni on engraved metal plates, which gave the history of the people in America during the time of Jesus Christ. According to Smith, the last keeper of the metal plates was Prophet Mormon, who passed them on to Moroni, who buried them in New York State at the Hill Cumorah. Later Angel Moroni appeared to Smith and led him to the plates. Smith showed the plates to a couple of men. Mormon legend says Smith received glasses from the angel to translate the message on the tablets. He was able to translate the ancient writings in three months, which became the five hundred pages of the book of Mormon, a new revelation, which was <u>another</u> testament of Jesus. He returned the plates to Moroni. According to Smith, the visitation by angels established the churches authority.

Mormon priority would be foremost the Book of Mormon, the Constitution, and lastly, the original writings of the Bible. Smith replaced the truth of the Bible with his Book of Mormon and replaced God with the occult of Masonry.

Later, there was dispute between Smith and President Van Buren. Joseph Smith asked Congress to allow him to establish a place in Nauvoo in Hancock County, Illinois, so he could get federal troops to defend his city. He spoke a few curses in public, and one specifically, "The United States Constitution would hang by a thread and would barely be preserved and saved by a rider on a white horse, a man mighty and strong." Smith pursued a goal to overthrow the government and have it led by the Mormon theocracy with himself as leader of the army of God. Smith and his brother were assassinated. The rider on the white horse is symbolic of the Antichrist, and Jesus is replaced by a Mormon savior.

Counter Cult Apologetics provides the following for understanding:

> Smith claimed to miraculously translate the book of Mormon from gold plates written by a divine hand. This is a one generation translation from plates to Smith's manuscript. One would think or expect the book of Mormon to be sacred scripture of the most direct and pure translation. The insurmountable obstacle for the veracity of the book of Mormon is demonstrated by the fact that when it references passages from the Hebrew Bible, it follows the translated text of the King James almost perfectly. For instance, italicized words in the book of Mormon follow suit. Obviously Smith copied his references from the Bible and not an ancient source as the mythological metal plates.

Saint Paul warns all Christians that if we receive a gospel from an angel or man, which is contrary to the gospel preached by Paul, then they are accursed (Galatian 1:8–9).

According to *Mormon's Temple of Doom*, DVD by Bill Schnoebelen 2011, Mormonism is linked to freemasonry, occult, Lucifer, and witchcraft.[42]

<u>Temple Practices</u>

- Sealing for marriage.
- Saving work can be done for the dead through baptism.

[42] Bill Schnoebelen, Mormon's Temple of Doom, DVD, 2011

- Initiation, involves wearing white shields, which is practiced in witchcraft.
- Wearing an apron with a fig, which is associated with Satan's priesthood.
- Anoint all body openings, required to stand there naked.
- Wear garments stitched with symbols.
- Receive a secret name, husbands know their wife's secret name, so he can raise her from the dead.

Mormon Beliefs

- Seeking secret knowledge to reach a higher plane of existence (agnostic).
- Second Nephi 2:118 be like Eve knowing good and evil.
- Man can become god, their law of eternal progression.
- The color green is associated with Satan, and planet Venus, copper, turns green.
- Zion, the New Jerusalem, will be built upon American continent and not Jerusalem.
- Michael the Archangel is Jesus, and he and Satan are brothers.
- God had literal sex with Mary.
- Salvation is of our own righteous acts as we work to build our special kingdom and reach God in contrast to the Bible, which tells us salvation is a free gift from God.
- Man's self-righteousness is contrary to the Bible; man's righteousness is as filthy rags.

In the formative years of Mormonism, other Christian denominations protested against the LDS and ran them out of various areas. Then Mormons became vindictive and started killing people who passed through their lands. In Nauvoo, Illinois, Smith ran for president of the United States. He was killed at age thirty-eight in 1844.

Brigham Young was leader of LDS from 1847 up to his death in 1877. During his tenure, he was appointed governor of Utah territory and superintendent of American Indian affairs by President Millard Fillmore. Young organized the Mormon Tabernacle Choir. Later he established the Brigham Young University. Young banned African Americans from the priesthood and temple blessings. He said, "Shall I tell you the law of God in regard to the African race: If the white man belongs to the chosen seed mixes his blood with the seed of Cain, the penalty under the law of God is death on the spot" (*Journal of Discourses* vol. 10, p. 110).[43] In 1978, president of the church, Spencer W. Kimball, rescinded that policy. Nevertheless, prejudice toward dark-complexioned people persisted and was picked up by Ellen White in her Seventh-Day Adventist philosophy an offshoot of Mormonism.

---

43 Brigham Young, Journal of Discourses, Vol. 10, p110

The White Horse Prophecy

"In 1843, Joseph Smith called forth the White Horse Prophecy after the white horse in the book of Revelation. He predicted a time when the United States Constitution would be in crisis only to be saved by a member of the Latter-Day Saints." Not taking center stage in Mormonism, this prophecy lived on in the church (Tom Horn, Zenith 2016).

Willard Mitt Romney, born March 13, 1947. His namesake was J. Willard Marriott, the richest Mormon in history. Mitt's father was George W. Romney, a descendant of Parley Parker Pratt, one of twelve Mormon apostles. Romney's father was elected governor of Michigan in 1962. Mitt's mother, Lenore Romney, ran for Senate in 1970. During the time Mitt attended Brigham Young University, he was the president of the Cougar Club, an exclusive white-male club. Mitt did his required missionary work in France, where he also supervised two hundred young men. Romney was a seventh-generation Mormon. He was committed to the Mormon belief that they lived in heaven before birth on earth, became mortal to usher in latter days. They hold to the belief that Joseph Smith was a prophet, Book of Mormon is the Word of God, and church is the one true faith.

Romney married Ann and has five sons. Ann was born in Detroit in 1949 and raised by a wealthy family in Bloomfield Hills. Her father, Edward Davies, a businessman, also served as mayor of Bloomfield Hills. Ann enrolled at Brigham Young University and embraced Mormonism. She attended Harvard in Massachusetts. Mitt was governor of Massachusetts, and eventually, Barack Obama would attend Harvard. Mitt and Barack's paths would cross again.

Michael D. Moody, *Mitt, Set Our People Free,* [44] wrote in 1963, "Harold Brinley laid hands on Mitt and told him he was valiant, true son, preexistent, with important earthly responsibilities to raise his voice in defense of true Mormonism ... Lord would magnify and enhance him in the eyes of his fellow man. His instruction comes directly from Jesus. Moody said his destiny called for him to do duty to the Mormon gods, and he ran for governor to help Mitt lead the world into the millennium."

The Mormons have a political agenda that eventually, one would come forth to fulfill the "white horse prophecy" to save the US Constitution during a time it would be "hanging like a thread" of fine silk and one from the Mormon priesthood would save it. They hold to a theodemocracy where God and people hold the power to conduct the affairs of men in righteousness. Romney had risen to be considered the man most likely to take over the reign of the US presidency. He has been diligent in all the Mormon requirements, such as serving as pastor of a church for ten years, helping the poor, and tithing 10 percent of his income to the church.

---

[44] Michael D. Moody, Mitt, Set Our People Free

Mormonism Offshoot

Rulon Jeffs began his cult after breaking away from traditional Mormonism. He called it Fundamental Church of Jesus Christ of Latter Day Saints. At the time of Rulon's death at age ninety-two in 2002, he had seventy-five wives and over sixty-five children. His son Warren Jeffs assumed leadership of the cult. Warren married all but two of his father's wives. Warren indoctrinated more than ten thousand followers to believe he was a prophet and God speaks directly to him and whatever he says is law. He was the authority over all marriages and assigned wives to husbands. Warren selects men that will go to heaven if they have lived a totally obedient life to his will. If a man is disobedient, Warren will take his wives and children and give them to another man. The cult is housed on 1,700 acres of land far removed from transportation and retail. He controlled land in Colorado City, Arizona, and Hildale, Utah. Warren Jeffs is currently serving a life sentence for pedophilia. He had sex with young girls. Warren kept volumes of "priesthood records," a diary of his sexual encounters and daily activities. The State of Texas is in the process of confiscating his property.

Notable Mormon followers

Dictator Benito Mussolini was made a saint in the Mormon Church.

Glen Beck, Harry Reid, and Orin Hatch are Mormons.

Comments of Those Who Call LDS a Cult

In 1998, Southern Baptist Convention, held in Salt Lake City, Utah, with three thousand attendees, said Mormonism is a great deception in the history of religion. The attendees went door to door to give out the booklet *Mormonism Unmasked.*

In our present time in America, there are not many who speak out against this or any other heresy. Mitt Romney spoke at Liberty University. Jerry Falwell said they had no official position on Mormonism.

Pastor Robert Jeffress, First Baptist Church of Dallas, declared Mormons are a cult and not Christians.

Pastor Joel Osteen believe Mormons are Christians but not in the purest sense.

Seventh-Day Adventist, SDA

This group was founded in 1830 by James and Ellen White of New England and is an offshoot of Mormonism. Ellen claimed to have a spiritual gift of "authority," which is not one of the seven gifts of the Holy Spirit. This group came out of the Millerites, founder William Miller. They believe Catholics are the great apostasy.

In Ellen White's book, *Spiritual Gifts*, volume 3, page 64[45], she gives her theory of amalgamation:

> But if there were one sin above another which called for the destruction of the race by the flood it was the base crime of amalgamation of man and beast which defaced the image of God and caused confusion everywhere and these were destroyed in the flood. After the flood there has been amalgamation of men and beast as may be seen in the almost endless varieties of species of animals and in certain races of men.

Her theory was projected toward people with dark skin, and during American slavery, these people were classified as part human and part animal. As in Mormonism, dark-skinned people were thought to be cursed.

Early Adventist taught the heresy called Arianism, which asserts that Jesus is not God the Son, second person of the Trinity. They teach he is Michael the Archangel. Ellen believed that the death of Jesus also was for the redemption of angels. Jesus cast the demons out of the man at Gadarene, and they sought to possess the herd of pigs, which cast themselves over a cliff, but Ellen states, "Had not Christ restrained the demons, they would have plunged into the sea not only the swine but also their keepers and owners" (Ellen G. White, *The Great Controversy*, p. 515).[46]

Ellen's take on the Rapture of the church—"We all entered the cloud together and were seven days [Bible says we are changed in the twinkling of an eye] ascending to the sea of glass when Jesus brought the crowns and with his own right hand placed them on our heads" (crowns are received after the Bema Seat judgment) (*Early Writings,* p. 16).[47] In this same book, she claims that "there is perfect order and harmony in the Holy City. All the angels that are commissioned to visit the earth hold a golden card, which they present to the angels at the gates of the city as they pass in and out. Satan and his fallen angels did not have a gold card but found a backdoor to travel to and fro through the earth" (Wikipedia).

Jehovah's Witnesses, JWs

This group defines itself as the one true Christian religion and others are occult and pagan. The roots of the Jehovah's Witnesses are steeped in false doctrine. Their founder is Charles Taze Russell, 1852–1916, who came out of Millerism, as did the Seventh-Day Adventist. He founded the Jehovah's Witness around 1870 in Pennsylvania.

---

45 Ellen White, Spiritual Gifts

46 Ellen White, The Great Controversy

47 Ellen White, Early Writings

He knew little about Christianity until he had an encounter with an infidel regarding hell and became a further skeptic. Seeking truth, he studied pagan religions and found no satisfaction. He decided to study the Bible. The Jehovah's Witness bible is a rewritten version called the New World Translation, where we find that Jesus is Michael the Archangel, a created being, and Jesus is not deity or God incarnate. The soul and spirit of the dead remain within the body referred to as a soul asleep until the Resurrection. Christians believe that the body is in the grave but the soul is with Jesus. Jehovah's Witnesses believe the battle of Armageddon began in heaven in 1914 and the millennial reign of peace on earth has begun. The Bible says in Revelation that the 144,000 are Jews from each of the twelve tribes who preach the Gospel during the tribulation period. The Jehovah's Witnesses believe they are the 144,000 who will rule with God in heaven. Only they can partake of the body and blood of Jesus that Christians do in remembrance of Jesus's death. They believe that Jesus returned to earth in 1874 and the Rapture occurred three and a half years later. Jehovah's Witnesses have readjusted their Rapture date many times.

After the death of Russell, Joseph Rutherford took over in 1916. He proclaimed Abraham would rise in 1925, so he built a house for him, but he lived in it. After he died in 1942, the property was sold. Nathan Knorr took over in 1944–1977, and he proclaimed battle of Armageddon would be in 1975 (John Ankerberg, *The Pagan Roots of Jehovah's Witnesses*).[48]

In our position, we believe that before the flood, God gave people a conscience; they knew right from wrong. With the influence of the fallen angels, many turned away from God. After the flood, people still knew right from wrong but chose to rebel against God and make images to worship. Abraham was called by God; he knew right from wrong, and he choose to turn from Jehovah's Witness. Isaac's son Jacob followed God and became the father of the twelve tribes of Israel. Many followed God, and many turned away from God. Joseph was set aside for a time to save his people from the famine. Moses was called by God to bring his people out of Egypt. Many of Moses's people followed the law, and many retained the pagan influence of Egypt. From around 1500 to 1400 BC, the chosen people went through one crisis after another because of disobedience. They became an ensample to the world. Through the Old and New Testament scriptures, Gentiles could see God's love, protection, judgment, and redemption. Based on the Word of God, people can apply a litmus to their life as pleasing to God or not.

Atheism

The atheist has spoken from the deep recesses of his heart and said, "There is no God." In their rejection of God, they have acknowledged him. They display deep hatred for the

[48] John Ankerberg, The Pagan Roots of Jehovah's Witnesses

things of God and his people. A book written by Richard Dawkins in support of atheism, *The Divine Delusion,*[49] writes:

> The God of the Old Testament is arguably the most unpleasant character in all fiction: jealous and proud of it. He is a petty, unjust, unforgiving control freak, vindictive, bloodthirsty ethnic cleanser, a misogynistic, homophobic, racist, infanticidal, genocidal, filicidal, pestilential, megalomaniacal, sadomasochistic, capriciously malevolent bully.

In their rants and actions, it is evident they are obsessed with the one that they vehemently reject.

In modern times, atheists have started churches, which meet on Sunday, and their popularity is growing. One such congregation was highlighted by Peter Foster, *National Post*, August 12, 2014. "From the outside it looks like a church in Nashville, Tennessee." They sing songs and have a motivational message and quiet reflection but not to the glory of God but to their humanist philosophy. David Lyle, founder of the Nashville Sunday Assembly Secular Church, said, "We needed a place for us." Our comment—God loves the atheist, and in his mercy, some have come to believe in him. The evidence of the existence of God rest in the scriptures and especially the hundreds of prophecies made in advance that have been fulfilled in these future times.

Islamic Religion

Islam is the youngest of the world's religions, currently with a billion followers dwelling in every nation. Islamic roots began in the Middle East region of Arabia. Not all people who lived in Arabia were followers of Islam. As in modern times, all Arabs are not Muslims. With the rise of Islamic terrorism, the Koran has been reexamined for its content pertaining to peace and violence. We find it is not a religion of peace. The following suras call for jihad: Sura 4:89, 8:60, 9:5, 9:123, 47:4 (Jack Van Impe Ministries).

This religion was founded by Muhammad around AD 620. Muhammad was born AD 570 into the Hashemite clan of the tribe of Quraysh. His father, Abd-Allah, died before he was born, and his mother died when he was six years old. He was raised by his uncle Abu-Talib, chief of the Quraysh tribe, and his wife, who treated the child harshly. Muhammad had no formal education, and history states, Muhammad was illiterate. While he worked on the trade routes, he came in contact with representatives of various religions and cultures of the world. Traveling through the Arabian Peninsula to Byzantine cities of Damascus and elsewhere, he would have contact with Jews, Christians, and Zoroastrians, who had a one-God

[49] Richard Dawkins, The Divine Delusion

theology. Early Arabs and other pagan religions worshipped many deities. Muhammad was influenced by the stories told by these travelers—especially those holding to monotheistic belief, a Messianic figure, and had an eschatology that taught the world would one day end and the righteous would be rewarded while the evil would be tormented in hell. This concerned him because his people worshipped many gods and the future of humankind would be judged. He had to rely purely on his memory of the things he heard from various sources, and because of his illiteracy, the Koran is a mixture of partial truths and personal perceptions similar to proverbs.

A student of world religions is immediately aware of the similarities in the Muslim belief scenario and those of Zoroastrianism, Judaism, and Christianity. Islam, like other false religions, chose from biblical scripture ideas that appeal to them then add their own human understanding to frame their system of belief yet rejecting the fullness of the Godhead. The passages spoken by Muhammad are referred to as suras. We select from Sura II, the Heifer, section 8:62:

> *Those who believe in the Koran and those who follow Jewish scriptures and the Christians and the Sabians, any who believe in God and the last day and work righteousness shall have their reward.*

This demonstrates Muhammad had some understanding of Old and New Testament scriptures. He acknowledges in section 6:47: "*O Children of Israel call to mind the special favor which I bestowed upon you and that I preferred you to all others for my message,*" that Israel was chosen by God. He saw that Hebrew was read from right to left, and he directed that the Koran follow this same pattern. Islam requires Judeo-Christian doctrine to validate its theology, while the Bible does not need to be validated by any other world belief. In this consideration, we must remember that statements made in the Koran or Hadith are not credible and should never be used as God-given doctrine. We will discuss later the similarities of Islam's messiah and their understanding of an Islamic Antichrist as these figures are compared within a biblical context.

Muhammad met his first wife, Khadija, a wealthy widow, owner of a business in Mecca where he worked. She was forty and he was twenty-five when they married. He only had this one wife until her death. They had two sons and four daughters; all died young except for Fatima. After the death of his wife, he married approximately fifteen wives, including a nine-year-old girl and his cousin Zaynab. He received some criticism from other Arabs who were opposed to incestuous relationships. His reasoning was always, "Allah told me to do it."

In Hadith, Muhammad says, "The revelation does not come to me when I am in the garment of any woman except A'isha."[50] Muhammad at times dressed in women's clothes. *Mukhannatah* is Arabic for homosexual. The Koran promised boy love for jihadists in paradise. Daayiee Abdullah, an openly gay Imam, describes Mukhannathun as "sort of male-female, cross-dressing types. They existed and they also lived and worked in the household of the prophet Muhammad. Aisha, one of the prophets' wives, indicated that there were men who worked in the household that were homosexuals …"

Pre-Islam Muhammad spent time in the hills of Mecca. He stashed his booty in a cave on Mount Hira. While alone, he contemplated how he could have respect, wealth, and power. An idle mind is the devil's workshop. He decided to increase his position in life through religion. During these meditative periods, according to Muhammad, he received a visit from an angel who called himself Gabriel. This counterfeit spirit gave Muhammad the following command from a god:

> Read in the name of thy lord who created, who created man of blood, coagulated. Read. Thy lord is the most beneficent, who taught by the pen, taught that which they knew not unto men.

In our study, we presented evidence that the fallen angels/gods taught mankind forbidden knowledge. Galatians 1:8, "*If we or an angel from heaven preach any other gospel unto you than that which we have preached unto you let him be accursed.*"

Since Muhammad could neither read nor write, it is interesting that the first words from an angel speaks to literacy. Probably, Muhammad did desire the ability to read and write. Muhammad's goal was to teach the uneducated and poor people. He could gain followers by giving them food and goodies. Many came out of paganism but followed Mohammad into a false religion.

Islamic tradition says Muhammad received his revelations through what could be called epileptic seizures. One famous vision was his journey to Jerusalem on a white horse named Barack, and from Mount Moriah he visited heaven. Perhaps this encounter can be associated with the translation of Elijah, who ascended to heaven in a chariot. Muhammad never visited Jerusalem. From memory he committed the visions to writing with assistance of his secretary, Zayd (same name of his adopted son who was married to his cousin Zaynab), who wrote on stones, leaves, bones, or parchment. After Muhammad's death, these writing were collected, arranged by length, some text replaced, and arranged in chapters called surahs, which eventually became the Koran.

---

50 Hadith 2442, Chapter 52

Muslims believe this to be eternal scripture, written in heaven and revealed, chapter by chapter, to Muhammad. Followers of Muhammad made many commentaries on his thoughts and collected them into what they call the Hadith. It also spells out the traditions and interpretations relating to the laws of the Koran,[51] which do vary. In the Hadith, it incorrectly states the mother of Jesus (*Isa* in Islam) was Mary, the sister of Moses. For the record, Moses's sister's name was Miriam, and there were over a thousand years between Moses and the birth of Jesus. Islam denies Jesus is the Son of God, crucified (Suras 4:165, 5:18, 6:101, 17.111, 9:30, 19:38).

Judaism predates Islam by over two thousand years. The inception of Christianity began during the time of Christ. Religious beliefs of the Zoroastrians can be traced back to Babylon, during the time of Jewish captivity. Daniel was appointed head over the Zoroastrian priesthood. The land covenant between God and the chosen people goes back to the time of Abraham, around 2000 BC. The Jews are the rightful inheritors of the land called Palestine. We call the land Israel, and Jerusalem is its capital.

The Jesus, or Isa, of the Koran is not the Jesus of the Bible. Muslims desire to align their version of Jesus with Muhammad. Jesus of the Bible was holy and perfect in all his ways. Muhammad on the other hand would be classified as epileptic, schizophrenic, psychopath, murderer, adulterer, thief, liar, plagiarizer, bisexual, and child molester. Muhammad is the epitome of the sin nature. In 2013, Maqmood Abbas of Lebanon said Jesus was a Palestinian, and Israel defended that Jesus was a Jew. The church was silent. Some Muslims believe Jesus of the Koran will return when their Mahdi arrives and will be a servant to him, renounce Christianity, and kill the infidels (Sura 4:159).

Muhammad convinced himself that there should only be one god, and Muhammad decided his name was Allah. Muhammad declared himself to be the last and the greatest in a series of self-proclaimed prophets. He considered himself greater than Abraham, Moses, and Jesus. According to him, they only had an incomplete revelation of Allah, but he had the complete and final revelation. At Islam's inception, it did not deny the validity of other monotheistic religions but looked at itself as the completion of what others had begun.

According to Islam, Allah became representative of the one sovereign god over all the universe. Islam's mantra, "There is no god but Allah and Muhammad is his messenger … who has not begotten and has not been begotten and equal to him is not anyone." Islam rejects the Triune Godhead of the Bible, the Father, Son, and Holy Spirit, believing this to be polytheistic. Based on this one principle, the denial of Jesus as the only begotten Son of God places Islam in the category of a false religion. Yahweh is not Allah.

---

[51] Koran

Walid Shoebat was a former Muslim who converted to Christianity. In his online study on the word *Allah*, he has said it is associated with an Arabian god, and in another word form, *Allah* is associated with a Babylonian god. The Babylonian god was named Bel, associated with the moon god. Allah is a pre-Islamic name for Bel. This Babylonian god was later worshipped by Rome and Greece. Halial Bin Sahar is associated with Satan, morning, bright star, and crescent moon. Bismillah is Arabic name for Allah associated with the moon god. Islam's symbol is crescent moon and star. Allah is not the God of the Bible. The name Allah cannot be transliterated to Yahweh.

Muslims seeing God alone, they believe he surrounded himself with heavenly figures of angels and jinn. The jinn are a creation between human and angels of fire. Some are good, and the evil ones are demons. The leader of the jinn is a fallen angel called Iblis, who is equal to Satan and caused the fall of Adam. Other Islamic beliefs include a heaven and hell. When a person dies, their body returns to the earth, and the soul sleeps until Resurrection day. At the sound of the trumpet, bodies will rejoin their souls and then be judged by Allah. Christian students can see this is the Islamic version of the Rapture.

Traders had profited on travelers coming to Mecca to worship various idols at the Kaaba (a black cube that covers a rock). When Muhammad sought converts in Mecca, bringing the message of one Allah and he the prophet of Allah, it was not readily received. Around AD 622, Islam advanced into the area called Yathrib (later renamed Medina); delegates from other tribes came to meet with Muhammad and asked him to be the judge between warring clans. Some of these delegates may have been from Jewish tribes, believing Muhammad might be the Messiah.

While in Medina, he sought favor with the Jews and told his followers to pray toward Jerusalem. We point out that Jews lived in Arabia from as far back as their exodus from Egypt. Moses went up to Mount Sinai, which may be in the Mecca area. Arabs say at the *Kaaba*; this is the place where Moses, Aaron, and Jethro came. Saint Paul stayed in Arabia for three years. Archeologists found the carvings of sandals in rocks, which were made by the Jews to mark places they had been.

Conflict continued between secular people of Mecca and Medina, Christians, Jews, and Muslims. Muslims may have gotten as far as Ethiopia. Their practice was to rob the caravans, taking booty and prisoners, enslavement and murder of millions. Today we would call this a mafia, cartel, caliphae or ISIS. Jews, Meccans, Christians and others who fought against Muhammad were decimated. Spurred on by evil spiritual forces, the Islamic reign of terror continues into the twenty-first century. No one was spared. Men, women and children hundreds of years ago suffered these same atrocities carried out by the unmerciful Islamic terrorist today. People from other religions began to leave regions where Muhammad ruled. The final break ocurred when Zainab, a Jewish matron, invited the prophet and his friends to dinner and poisoned the lamb. Muhammad ate a little but suffered the effects the rest of his life.

Around AD 629, Islam had a stronghold in Medina and Mecca. Muhammad destroyed all the idols and images at Mecca and told the people the one new god is Allah. This is an interesting selection for the name of his god after the name of his father, Abd-Allah. He did not want any competition from other gods, and he wanted to control the donations of Muslims making hajj. Muhammad's last trip to Mecca was AD 632. He died in Medina at the age of sixty-two.

Testaments of Muhammad to his followers are the five pillars or obligations of a good Muslim:

- Repetition of the creed, "There is no god but Allah, and Muhammad is his messenger."
- Daily prayer, five times.
- Almsgiving to share with the poor.
- Fasting on Ramadan.
- Pilgrimage to Mecca.
- **Kill the infidels.**

In Islamic culture, a woman has low standing, considered chattel, and owned by the male. She must be covered from head to toe. Muhammad saw Catholic nuns dressed in their habits, which covered them from head to toe, and he probably decided Muslim women should also dress as such. The killing of female babies was exercised and later forbidden. Polygamy is allowed up to four wives. Eat no pork, drink no wine, and gambling is forbidden. Homosexuality is not tolerated, although it is practiced. Pedophilia is practiced on boys and girls. Islam permits lying, called *al-taqiyya*, for the purpose of dissimulation, diplomacy, and deception. It is acceptable to lie to the infidels. Systematic lying is a religious policy justified to further Islamic causes, and Allah will not hold them accountable. In Christianity, we attribute Satan as the father of lies.

Islam is not a religion of peace. Muhammad called for killing, robbery, and rape. Islam is a false, intolerant, and militant religion. In the name of Allah, holy war, or jihad, is commanded to wipe out the infidels on every continent. The Islamic practice of killing non-Muslims was seen as far back to the Ottoman Empire. The resurgence of holy war has taken on a life of its own and now is the terror threatening the civilized world. It goes beyond the killing of non-Muslims; it targets and kills other apostate Muslims they perceive are not true to Muhammad. In 1979, hundreds of Muslim militants attacked worshippers in Mecca, trying to force them to accept one of their own as the Mahdi. Currently, various sects of Islam are at war with each other. The Middle East is in turmoil due to tribal infighting. Militants work to recruit new terrorists and threaten others to convert or die. Even with the rise of Islam, it will not be the dominate religion of the world, but it is a tool used by Satan to bring division and death.

Muslims believe that Islam should dominate the world, recognize no other national barriers, and all Islam should be united under one body. Islam set up shop alongside of Buddhism and Hinduism. Muslims killed millions of Hindus. Indonesia once predominately Hindu is now 60 percent Islamic. Pakistan was divided from India. Islam followers went to Pakistan, and Hindu followers stayed in India. The idea of a global Islamic caliphate could become a reality in some form. Under the rule of Antichrist, radical Muslims may assume the role of executioner for the one-world religious system.

Before the inception of Islam, people of Arabic descent were Jews, Christians, and polytheists. The first caliphs were in the circle of friends of Muhammad and ruled from Arabia. They were upstaged by the first Islam dynasty called the Umayyads around AD 661, who ruled in Damascus. They in turn were upstaged in AD 750 by the Abbasid Dynasty, which ruled from Persia. Later, the Mamelukan Turkish Empire ruled from Egypt, then they were replaced by the Ottoman Turks in the thirteenth century, who made the title *caliph* synonymous with that of sultan of Turkey. Muslims converted the largest church in Constantinople into a mosque. Islam spread to North Africa, India, China, and Russia. After World War I, the Ottoman Empire faded, and British influence spread. The Muslim goal for a global caliphate is hindered by tribal infighting. Yahweh will confound them, and they will turn one against another.

Offshoots from Islam form various Muslim sects, which are prevalent today. As previously mentioned, sayings of Muhammad were up for interpretation and compiled in the hadith. Interpretations of Islamic laws were made by abu-Hanifah, AD 767. Followers of Hanifah occupy Asia, India, Lower Egypt. The Malikites follow the teachings of Malik ibn-Anas, AD 795, and occupy the region of North and West Africa and part of Egypt. The Shafiite group follows the patterns of al-Shafi'I, AD 820, and lives in lower Egypt, Syria, India, Indonesia. The Hanbalites follow Ahmad ibn-Hanbal, AD 855, and live in Saudi Arabia.

Various schools of thought arose in different geographical regions. Following, some are highlighted:[52]

<u>Sunnis</u>

This group makes up the largest percentage of Orthodox Islam. As traditionalists, they follow the path of their religion exactly as established by their prophet, Muhammad. They

---

52 Wikipedia

experienced difficulty in applying his teachings to people living in other regions. Sunnis represent 90 percent of the 1.6 billion Muslims and are represented in Saudi Arabia, Jordan Yemen, United Arab Emirates, Pakistan, Afghanistan, Syria, Turkey.

Shi'ites

Also called Shia, they represent a rupture in the body of Islam. It began as a political dispute over the leadership of Islam after the death of Muhammad. Shi'ites believed the successor should be Ali, Muhammad's cousin. In the eleventh century, the Shi'ites mastered the art of killing and sent assassins out on missions. They also believe that the revelation did not end with Muhammad and the Koran, which contradicts Muhammad's belief that he was the fulfillment of revelation. They believe additional revelations came to figures called "Imams." Majority hold to twelve Imans, with the twelfth disappearing into a well and will come forth in the end-time. This Iman Mahdi, a messiah figure, will appear on earth and will be a world leader. All people will submit to him or be killed. This is the Bible's Antichrist. Shites are in Iran, Iraq, and lesser numbers in other regions. Iran is interested in changing their holy site from Mecca to Carbola.

Both Sunni and Shia have an eschatological view of a coming one-world leader and messiah, who will bring the world to Islam. Further discussion is made on the one-world leader in chapter 18.

Sufi

These followers believed in union with God through mystical experience. They were more concerned with spiritual matters than tradition. One such Sufi was Mansur al-Hallaj, who sought the mystical oneness with God, and he said, "I am the truth." For this offense, his fellow Muslims crucified him in AD 922. This group then practiced their belief underground. In the twelfth century, Sufi's belief resurfaced through the teaching of Abu-Hamid al-Ghazali, a professor of theology at the Nizamiyah School in Iraq. He forsook materialism, his family, and set out to find God in poverty and mystical experiences. The Sufi's became a monastic order, where they emphasized discipline, poverty, abstinence, and celibacy. Their worship became emotional, where they would whirl or spin in circles and got the name *dervish*.

Wahhabi

A group of conservatives standing against change was founded by Muhammad ibin-Abdalah-Wahhab, AD 1744. They opposed European influence. They became associated with the House of Saud, who controlled Arabia. Osama Bin Laden was a Wahhabite.

Regardless of affiliations within various Islamic sects, they all share one ideology and that is to conquer others. William J. Federer, author, What Every American Needs to Know About the Qur'an provides extensive research into the history of Islam.

Nation of Islam in America

One of its most notable leaders was Elijah Muhammad, born 1897 in Georgia as Elijah Robert Poole, died 1975. His father was a Baptist preacher. Elijah went as far as the fourth grade and left school to work as a sharecropper with his parents. When he was sixteen, he left the hardships of the South to work in Northern factories, settling in Michigan. The stigma of racism was deep amongst those who were affected by hundreds of years of slavery, and when he heard a call to black empowerment, he found it appealing, The founder of the movement was Wallace D. Fard who settled in Detroit around 1930 and was recruiting disenfranchised black men to Islam. Fard's background is sketchy. He appears to be a light-skinned Middle Eastern man. He was affiliated with the Moorish Science Temple, a Muslim organization that promotes the belief African Americans are descendants of the Moors in Morocco, Africa. This organization was started by Timothy Drew in Illinois. He later called himself Prophet Noble Drew Ali. As in the Nation of Islam and Moorish teachings, the black man was taught racial pride, identity, and self-sufficiency. Drew taught his followers to face east when praying; regard Friday as their holy day; and call their god Allah and their leader, Prophet. They took on surnames such as Bey, Ali, and El to signify their Moorish heritage. Male members wore a fez head covering, and women wore turbans. The ways of Islam were promoted. Drew did teach that all races need to reject hate and embrace love. His members were taught to reject the derogatory labels created by whites, such as references to "colored, black, Negro."

Elijah Poole joined Fard's movement, received the Muslim name of Elijah Muhammad, rose through the ranks, and became the leader of the Nation of Islam's number 2 temple in Chicago. Elijah also took over leadership of Detroit temple in 1934 when Wallace Fard disappeared. Elijah began to tell his followers that Wallace Fard was Allah on earth and he would return. He also opened temple number 3 in Milwaukee, Wisconsin, and number 4 in Washington, DC.

Followers of Islam have embraced their own doctrines, which are a combination of personal beliefs and fragments of other people's beliefs. In this mind-set, Elijah taught his people blacks were the original human beings and evil whites were an offshoot race that would oppress blacks for millions of years. He preached Christianity was the white man's religion. He instilled black pride and independence to heal the wounds of racism, and in this vein, many young blacks accepted Islam. He was a mentor to Malcolm X, Muhammad Ali, Louis Farrakhan.

Louis Farrakhan descended from the Caribbean Islands, and his mother relocated to Boston, Massachusetts. His birth name was Louis Eugene Wolcott. He excelled in violin, attended Boston Latin School and then English High Schools from which he graduated. He completed three years at Winston Salem Teachers College. His family attended the Episcopal Saint Cyprians Church in Massachusetts. Farrakhan married Betsy Ross, and she later took the name Khadijah.

In the 1950s, Farrakhan started his professional music career recording several calypso albums. While singing in Chicago, Illinois, he was introduced to the Nation of Islam. He was greatly influenced by Malcom X and Elijah Muhammad. He rose up in the ranks and eventually was appointed over several temples. At Elijah's death in 1975, his son Warith Deen Mohammed, also known as Wallace, was the new leader of the Nation of Islam. He changed the organization to traditional Islam and renamed the group World Community of Islam in the West and American Society of Muslims. He rejected the belief that Wallace D. Fard was Allah in person.

Louis Farrakhan rose up to reestablish the Nation of Islam in 1977 to 1979 and currently is its leader. He had a good relationship with civil rights leaders, such as Martin Luther King. After the death of King, the black community consistently sought a messiah. By the time Obama came on the scene, many blacks thought he was their messiah. Even Farrakhan supported Obama's election in 2008. By the time Obama entered his second term in 2012, many black leaders began to disenfranchise themselves with Obama based on his support of homosexuality and other concerns. Louis Farrakhan was most outspoken that homosexuality was unnatural and ungodly.

We listened to a few of Farrakhan's recent speeches, and he quoted from the Bible more than the Koran. He spoke of Jesus as his savior, Jesus as the returning Messiah, every knee will bow, and that the Spirit of Jesus did dwell in him. However, he did misinterpret the concept of the trinity, the deity of Christ, they are the original Jews, and Israel is now America. Farrakhan's youth was influenced by Christianity. Later he set the Bible aside and decided Islam was the way. In 2010, Farrakhan embraced L. Ron Hubbard's Dianetics and engaged the Church of Scientology to Audit the Nation of Islam members. Farrakhan opened his mind up to false religion and occult beliefs. He sets himself up as an expert on the biblical scriptures, but oil and water do not mix. We are grateful that he is not calling for the Nation of Islam to become Islamic terrorists (Wikipedia and Sacred Texts online).

A new film entitled *The Innocent Prophet* by Pastor Terry Jones[53] provides an excellent overview of Muhammad's life, rise to power, and a compelling look at Islam. It can be seen on YouTube (David Reagan and Mark Gabriel of Lamb and Lion Ministries, Nature of Islam;

[53] Terry Jones, The Innocent Prophet, Video

John Ankerberg, *Are Allah and the Biblical God the Same?* John Ankerberg, *How Do Muslims View Jesus Christ?* Walid Shoebat, *Islamic Converts to Christianity*).

The Rise of Radical Islamic Terrorism

Current Islamic terrorism may be the catalyst that unites the world's religious groups all seeking peaceful solutions for the world as well as blending global ideologies, such as preservation of Mother Earth. Some scholars consider Islam in general as playing a major role in end-times as they begin to understand Islamic eschatology. Their goal is destruction and the preservation of earth is not important. The position of pro-Islam advocates initiated the Arab Spring events and in turn incited an increase of Islamic terrorism.

The US occupation of Afghanistan resulted in removing one president and approving another feckless president. The Taliban still has a foothold in Afghanistan, and the country is as unstable today as it was years ago.

The Obama administration believed it was good for the overall Middle East regions to remove Kadafi and destabilize Libya, which is now a haven for Islamic terrorists, and set the stage for the Benghazi event.

The US game plan moved on to Egypt, where the longtime president was removed and replaced with the US approval of Muslim Brotherhood dictator Morsi. The Egyptian military had its own plans and kicked him out, to the dismay of the United States.

United States attempted intervention in Iran but ran into a brick wall. It was decided to use diplomacy with Iranian leaders and cave into their goal for developing nuclear arms. Sanctions against Iran were lifted, and the nation received billions of dollars.

The US intervention in Syria to overthrow the government allowed for the rise of various terrorists groups, resulting in the destabilization of Syria. Stirring up civil unrest may have begun in 2011 or 2012 against Bashar Assad's government when the United States and Turkey decided to unseat Assad. Russia and Iran intervened in behalf of Syria against the United States and Turkey.

In 2004, the United States had initially believed Saddam Hussein was responsible for the 9-11 attack in New York and had weapons of mass destruction. Later intel pointed a finger at Bin Laden hiding in Pakistan. Since that time, we learned that the United States was also culpable in the 9-11 attack and destruction of the towers and surrounding buildings.

The call for an Islamic caliphate ricochets within various sects, but the problem is a lack of unity or support behind one leader. Iran is majority Shiite and quick to say they are Persians. Saudi Arabia is Sunni and correctly refer to themselves as Arabs, the birthplace of Islam. Syria and Lebanon have both Sunni and Shiite sects as well as ancient Judaic roots, which they reject. Jordan is the ancient kingdom of the Hasemites and are predominately

Sunni. Babylon, modern-day Iraq, has a 65 percent Shiite following while the minority are Sunni and Kurds. The Muslim Brotherhood was organized after the post-Ottoman Empire, dating back to the late 1920s. They are committed to the Wahhabis movement of Sunni Islam. Osama bin Laden was a Wahhabite out of Saudi Arabia who traces his lineage to Muhammed. ISIS, Hamas, and others emerged from the Muslim Brotherhood ideology. ISIS leans toward Sunni theology. We factor in the various Islamic terrorist organizations working to make a name for themselves through slaughter and rape, such as the Muslim Brotherhood, Hezbollah, Hamas, al-Qaeda, Taliban, Boko Haram, Nigeria, Al Shabab, Kenya. And other Islamic terrorists throughout Africa are increasing attacks on civilians, schools, hotels, churches, and malls. ISIS has captured the headlines worldwide, reporting atrocities against humanity on a historic scale. ISIS targets men, women, children, Christians, Jews, and those they consider Muslim apostates. Their victims were brutally raped, tortured, beheaded, buried alive, and burned to death, to name a few.

Initially, ISIS was called Jama'at al-Tawhid wal-Jihad and pledged their support to al-Qaeda and its leader, Osama Bin Laden. As Saddam Hussein's government unraveled, Islamic terrorists joined with other Sunnis in Iraq and formed the Mujahideen Shura Council, later called the Islamic State of Iraq. This faction is predominately Sunni Muslims. It was able to establish a foothold due to civil unrest and an ineffective Iraq military; the retreat of US forces allowed Islamic terrorists to gain control of Anbar, Nineveh, Kirkuk. A great deal of US weapons and equipment were seized by terrorists' coalition after the United States retreated. One report said they had confiscated four thousand Humvees, guns, and some tanks. We wonder if the availability of all that equipment was left there intentionally to facilitate the Arab Spring. After the loss of over four thousand US soldiers, one trillion US tax dollars spent training Iraq military and setting up a mock democratic government, it now seems futile.

In 2009, General Ray Odimo, commander of US forces in Iraq, stated that ISIS "has transformed significantly in the past two years." US forces killed ISIS leaders al-Masri and al-Haghdadi in 2010. General Odimo reported that 80 percent of ISIS, forty-two leaders, were killed. The Obama administration stated, ISIS rebels were like junior varsity, JVs, ISIS is contained, and the world should not take them as a serious threat. In 2016, hindsight, Obama's bravado came back to bite him. The international community has deemed ISIS a terrorist organization.

ISIS leader in 2012 released a statement online that the group was returning to the former strongholds, from which US troops had driven them prior to the withdrawal of its troops from Iraq. They declared the start of a new offensive in Iraq, beginning with the freeing of five hundred men held in Iraqi prisons. The loss of its initial militants where reinforced with Ba'athist military officers who served under Saddam Hussein and who were willing to join with the ISIS movement. Coming into 2013, violence in Iraq began to escalate, reporting thousands of deaths in the first month. ISIS captured the towns of Zumar Sinjar and Wana in northern Iraq. Jordan and Saudi Arabia moved their troops to their borders with Iraq after Iraq lost control of some of its territory. United States' intrusion into Iraq has left the nation in just as dire condition as it was under Saddam.

Leader of ISIS, Abu Bakr al-Baghdadi, is Caliph Ibrahim. In June 2014, Baghdadi proclaimed ISIS a caliphate holding claim over religious, political, and military authority over all Muslims worldwide. ISIS's long-term caliphate goal is to establish dominance over Iraq, Syria, Jordan, Israel, Lebanon, Cyprus, Turkey, Sinai, Libya, and Pakistan. He has organized a government with deputy leaders, councils on finance, leadership, military, legal matters, media, all to be ensured under Sharia law. Headquarters are set up in Ar-Raqqah, Syria. ISIS gained significant territory in Syria, such as Idib, Deir ez-Zor, Aleppo, border towns between Turkey and Syria of Atmeh, al-Bab, Azaz, Jarablus, and Trabil near the Jordan-Iraq border.

The United States used this conflict as an opportunity to move against President Assad. The United States began with propaganda claiming Assad used chemical weapons against civilians. Reports in 2015 said ISIS used Sarin gas against the people. In an interview with *CBS News*, CIA Director John Brennan confirmed ISIS used chemical weapons and are working to develop more efficient weapons and delivery systems.

Al-Baghdadi released a statement announcing that Syrian, al-Nusra Front, and the Islamic State of Iraq were merging. This was contested by al-Qaeda leader, al Zawahiri, but ISIS forged the merger. ISIS's goal is to establish rule over conquered territory, while al-Nusra's goal was to topple Assad's government. ISIS sent Iraqi fighters into Syria to fight with the protesters and to support the al-Nusra Front. Some Muslims groups have accepted him and pledged their allegiance. A group of eight hundred radical militants from the Libyan City of Dema pledged their allegiance to al-Baghdadi. The Egyptian militant group, Ansar Bait al-Maqdis, also pledged allegiance to ISIS. Boko Haran in Nigeria pledged their allegiance to ISIS.

Al-Baghdadi and his caliphate do not have the support of all Islamic nations. There are differing positions. Some Muslims may agree with some of his doctrine, and many do not agree with his methods at all. In 2016, Turkey's president claimed he was leader of the caliphate.

The United States funded the antiregime protesters against Assad, such as the Free Syria Army, which included ISIS sympathizers. In the middle of the fray, the United States was not sure whom they were supporting and should have ceased sending weapons from Libya into Syria. US intervention in Syria left the country torn in shreds, thousands dead, and millions of Syrians were forced to leave war-torn regions to find refuge elsewhere. Fleeing Syrians found refuge in neighboring Turkey, Lebanon, and Jordan. There are no reports that the Syrians were allowed into Saudi Arabia or Iran. In the mix of the migrants are ISIS forces making their way into other parts of the world. Nearing the end of 2015, migrants from North Africa joined with migrants fleeing Iraq and Syria and were moving through Turkey, Greece, Germany, France, England, Norway, and other European nations.

The Yazidis of Kurdistan are both Christian and Muslims. Their region borders—Turkey, Syria, and Iraq—were hit hard by ISIS, causing an exodus into the mountain range of Sinjar. The United States sent help to get them off the mountain and to refugee camps. The United States began an aerial assault against ISIS ground forces. The United States did not assist the Yazidis further with weapons to defend themselves. Report 2015, some assistance has been coming to Kurdistan.

ISIS also attacked Shiite indigenous people of Assyria, Chaldea, Armenian, Druze, Shabaks, and Mandeans. Recently, ISIS made a threat to take over Rome, the Vatican, and behead the pope.

They have infiltrated Africa, Europe, South America, and Canada. France reported that 1,800 of its citizens were radicalized in Syria and returned to France to carry out terrorist attacks. A Muslim drove a truck into a crowded walkway in France, killing eighty-four people. Canada has approved twenty-five thousand Syrians into their country, and amongst them will be terrorists, who can easily make their way into the United States.

ISIS calls for lone wolf attacks around the world, using social media, and has recruited thousands online. ISIS message to American Muslims is, "Hurt the crusaders day and night without sleep and terrorize them so that the neighbor fears his neighbor." Some reports claim they have established sleeper cells in every state. Omar Mateem was radicalized online and in 2016 attacked people at an Orlando, Florida, night club killing forty-nine people and wounding others.

ISIS is one facet of Arab/Muslim belief promoting a global caliphate fueled by Islamic end-time eschatology to hasten arrival of Mahdi. Its present leader, Abu Bakr al-Baghdadi, claims lineage back to Muhammad, and as the self-appointed caliph, he demands the allegiance of all devout Muslims according to Islamic jurisprudence. Their goal is to restore Islam to its glory and further the name of Allah. His organization believes the legality of all emirates, groups, states, and organizations become void by the expansion of the caliphates authority and the arrival of its troops to their areas.

Raheel Raza, Sunni Muslim, provided statistics in her article, "By the Numbers: Untold Story of Muslim Opinions and Demographics." In cooperation with the Pew Research Center, *The World's Muslims: Religion, Politics, and Society* data and statistics were produced by the Clarion Project. A survey was conducted within thirty-nine Muslim countries on their position to Islamic terrorists and Sharia law. Following is a sampling of opinions: Egypt, Jordan, Afghanistan, 79 to 86 percent condoned the execution of an apostate and the murder of women for some infraction. Muslims who believe suicide bombings are justified—42 percent in France, 35 percent in Britain, and 26 percent in United States. Raza divided Muslims into three categories: (1) radical, violent jihadist, terrorists; (2) Muslims who support those in category one but do not want to carry out violence themselves; (3) fundamentalists who hold to some beliefs and practices but prefer to make gains through a political system (Christian Broadcasting Network, December 18, 2015).

In general, thousands of Muslims believe Sharia law should be practiced. Moderate Muslims say ISIS does not represent Islam because of its violence but they are very quiet about its atrocities. Muslims who live in Europe or the United States do not fully integrate into the culture of the host country. Islamic attacks against the citizens are on the rise. Imams set up "no-go zones" to keep out non-Muslims. Within these regions, they want to follow Sharia law and bypass the law of the land. Belgium and France are both known for its anti-Semitism. Radical Muslims could see this as approval to attack Jews. ISIS looks for these pockets of dissidents to recruit new fighters. Some mosques encourage radicalism against governments and other civilians. Those who strictly follow the Koran must abide by its doctrines, calling for death to the infidels. The Koran calls for the unification under Allah and his prophet Muhammad. Arab Nationalism is out, and Islamic universalism is in that all should submit.

Sometime in the future, Mecca will not be considered the most holy place for Muslims. The cube covering the rock may be destroyed. Isaiah 34:5 seems to point to a time that the judgment of God will fall upon Bozrah and Idumea associated with Edom and Moab ... "*A great slaughter in the land of Idumea.*" This may encompass the greater area of Saudi Arabia, Jordan, Iraq, Iran, Syria ... "*Their land will be soaked with blood ... for it is the day of the Lord's vengeance and the year of recompenses for the controversy of Zion.*"

With the Isaiah scripture in mind, we can report that a massive crane collapsed on September 11, 2015, damaging the Mecca site. John Kerry said, "We stand with Muslims around the world in the aftermath of this dreadful incident at one of Islam's holy sites." On September 24, 2015, over 1,400 people died in a stampede while making their hajj to throw stones at the devil in their Feast of Sacrifice. Iran is furious with Saudi Arabia and threatened to convene an independent body for future planning and oversight of the hajj pilgrimage (*MSN News* and AFP).

The rich nations' oil fields may burn as occurred during Desert Storm in Iraq.

> *And the streams thereof will be turned into pitch and the dust thereof into brimstone and the land thereof will become burning pitch. It will not be quenched night or day. The smoke will go up forever from generation to generation, it will lie waste none will pass through it forever.* (Isaiah 34:9)

Isaiah 34 tells us that the kings, princes, and their palaces will be inhabited by thorns and wild beast.

Ezekiel 25:1–7 predicts that God will judge the Ammonites, which are also associated with Edom and Moab and occupied the regions of Jordan and Saudi Arabia. Some of these nations are related to Israel and rejoiced at their demise … "*I will deliver you to the men of the east for a possession … I will make Rabbah a stable for animals and you will know that I am the Lord … I will stretch out my hand and will deliver you for a spoil to the heathen …*"

Pentagon insider Robert Macginnis shared his insight on the *Jim Bakker Show*, December 8, 2015, regarding Islamic terrorism. Macginnis worked at the Pentagon for over twenty years. He states that the Muslim Brotherhood has committed to take over America from within. The Obama administration is pro-Muslim Brotherhood, and a number of Muslims hold key positions in the government. Recently, the president claimed there is not a threat to the United States from ISIS even as incidents are occurring in the United States and elsewhere. Another lie by Obama and Clinton—both taking no responsibility for their failed foreign policies, allowing ISIS to rise. They blame responsible gun owners for violence or the police. Reports from the Defense Intelligence Agency said there is a problem. Recently, eight Syrian terrorists were caught on the Mexican border. The security is so bad at the border that 50 percent of immigrants manage to sneak through. FBI report in October 2015 discovered gangs trying to sell radioactive material and ISIS trying to get airplanes to release chemicals over US cities. Macginnis said cyber attacks on the United States occur daily, numbering in the thousands.

Is the one-world order complicit in the Islamic uprising? Could ISIS be the hook that draws others into World War III? What we can see is that Russia, China, North Korea (nations of the northeast) are aligned with Islamic nations of Iran, Iraq, Syria. Turkey is anti-Syria. Russia is making nice with Egypt, conducting joint military drills. August 2016, Russian and Turkey amend their relationship as well as Turkey making truce with Israel.

Bloomberg reported on September 24, 2015: Russia is setting up their base in Syria near Damascus. Russia supports Assad's government, and they are there to help restore order. Russia has begun bombing terrorist sites as well as regions occupied by Turks in Syria. Turkey shot a Russian plane down. Those of us who understand the end-times know these things must be.

Ezekiel 38 prophecy of Gog and Magog now places Russia within striking distance of Israel. Russia is presently extending cooperation with Israel, but eventually, this will not hold true.

Early 2016 began with Saudi Arabia (Sunni) killing Islamic protesters, which included several Shiite clerics. Iran's response to this action was harsh, resulting in both sides rising in demonstrations and closing of their embassies. The dissention between the Prince of Persia and the King of Arabia had been predicted eight hundred years ago found in the Jewish book, *Yalkut Shimoni,* a book of rabbinic commentary. When this sign of this conflict comes to pass, redemption is near, and the Messiah's coming is soon (*Breaking Israel News*, Rivkah Adler, January 2016).

August 2016 news reports China will be sending troops into Syria to train Syrian military (Dave Hodges, *Common Sense Show*, August 19, 2016).

The Vatican and the Popes

Is Catholicism a false religion? In order to answer that question, we must first look at the tenants of Catholicism and its structure. The Vatican is located in Rome, Italy, on approximately 108 acres and is established as the seat of the Holy Roman Catholic Church. The Holy See comes from the Latin word *sedes*, meaning seat, which refers to throne (a seat), and there is a throne in the Cathedral of Saint John. In the Bible, there are references to seats representing regions of authority controlled by Satan.

The Holy Roman Catholic Church came forth from the Holy Roman Empire, which grew out of the Roman Empire. The Roman Empire was known for its pagan beliefs and, in the process of embracing Christianity, incorporated some of its pagan beliefs within Christianity. For example, December 25 is the celebration of Mithras, a god of Persia, and introduced to Rome.

Constantine decided to celebrate the birth of Jesus on December 25. When Constantine and his mother became Christians, he made a decree that the Roman Empire should also embrace Christianity.

The Nicene Creed is a doctrinal statement developed in AD 325 at the first ecumenical council meeting in Constantinople. The Nicene Creed was accepted by the Orthodox and Anglican denominations. Constantine accepted it around AD 381. This first creed is also called the Apostles' Creed, which title became popular around AD 390 and possibly through Ambrose from a council in Milan to Pope Siricius. The Apostles' Creed was incorporated into liturgy by the Catholics as well as Lutherans, Presbyterians, Methodists. It basically acknowledges the tenant of the Christian faith but adds "I believe in the Holy Catholic Church." We once asked an African Methodist Episcopal pastor why they pledged allegiance to the Catholic church. The baffled minister had no answer.

AD 800, Pope Leo III crowned Charlemagne, king of the Franks, as the Roman Emperor on December 25, assuring the continuation of the Holy Roman Empire.

AD 1095, the Crusades began under Pope Urban II for the purpose of restoring Christian access to holy sites predominantly in Israel under Muslim domination. The Vatican gave purpose to a military arm of the church. Thousands of Catholics from Europe joined the

Crusades. Eventually, they were called the Knights Templars. A few hundred years later, the Pontifical Swiss Guard was officially set by Pope Julius II, AD 1506, and continues to the present.

Most battles were fought against Muslims, and caught in the cross fire were the Jews, dying by the thousands; and from their ashes, the Zionist movement gained momentum. Theodor Hertzel was born in Budapest in AD 1860, where a large population of Jews resided. Hertzel moved to Vienna in 1878 and was concerned about the unfair treatment of Jews. He decided to promote the idea that the Jews needed a homeland. He wrote *Der Judenstaat* (*The Jewish State*). The formation of the World Zionist Organization promoted Jewish migration to Palestine. From Hertzel's work, he became known as the Father of Zionism.

An agreement between the kingdom of Italy and the Holy See was established in AD 1929, called the Lateran Treaty. Italy was a fascist government and later became a democratic government. The Lateran Treaty recognized the Vatican as an independent state. The agreement was signed between King Victor Emmanuel III of Italy, by Prime Minister Benito Mussolini, and Pope Pius XI. Italy promised financial support in return for the Vatican's public support.

The Holy See is a sovereign entity, has diplomatic relations in many countries, is a member of various international bodies, and has permanent observer status at the United Nations. It operates like a governmental body with one leader, the pope. He oversees the Roman Curia that regulates the administration of the church, having a secretary of state, a hierarchy of congregations, tribunals, councils, commissions. The Vatican has a bank and controls great wealth.

Some Jews believe the Vatican has their temple vessels and numerous Jewish manuscripts. Recently, the Vatican allowed online viewing of collections in Hebrew, which include the Rambam and Ritva manuscripts. There is no other religious organization that has this international recognition, organizational structure, and is sovereign unto itself.

The Vatican Is Shrouded in Mystery, Secrecy, Mysticism, and Symbolism

There are people within the Vatican that work toward the reign of the god of this world and his kingdom on earth. Catholicism was corrupted when it was infiltrated by priests who were associated with the Masonic and Jesuit orders. Some of these men would have been descendants of the Knights Templar.

Malachi Martin, a Jesuit priest, 1921–1999, exposed the satanic corruption within the Catholic church in his writings, *Windswept House*:[54]

[54] Malachi Martin, *Windswept House*

> As a body, they had sworn the sacred oath of commitment administered by the delegate, then each man had approached the altar to give evidence of his personal dedication with blood drawn by the prick of a golden pin each pressed his fingerprint beside his name on the bill of authorization the life and work of every member of the Phalanx in the Roman citadel was to be focused on the transformation of the papacy no longer was the Petrine office to be an instrument of the nameless weakling [Jesus] it was to be fashioned into a willing instrument of the Prince [Satan] and a living model for the new age of man.

Martin continues,

> Through invocations, they bring unanimity of heart … perfect synchronization of words and actions between target chapel, the living wills and the thinking minds of the participants concentrated on the specific aim of the Prince who would transcend all distance.

The invocation to enthrone the fallen archangel, Lucifer, had been executed.

These observations and statements remind us of the two hundred fallen angels that came to Mount Hermon and swore amongst themselves and bound themselves together to intermingle with humans according to Enoch.

Pope John Paul I learned of the infiltration of Masons as well as sexual corruption and money laundering in the church. He may have been planning to expose these crimes, but he was assassinated thirty-three days after his election to pope. These men are the embodiment of all things wicked, evil, and ungodly.

The Enthronement of Satan

According to Martin in *Windswept House*, "The signal that the availing time had begun and its fulfillment would be a pope taking the name of Paul VI." This enthronement ceremony took place on June 29, 1963, at the ordination of Lorenzo Baldisseri. Some refer to it as the return of Apollo, which is another name for Satan. They envision the prince of darkness coming to possess the person who will serve as the one-world religious leader (false prophet). Some scholars go so far as to say this person would be Nimrod, summoned from the grave and then possessed by Satan. We do not agree with that position. At the same time this ceremony was being conducted in Rome, there was a similar ceremony going on in Charleston, South Carolina, which is on a 33rd degree parallel to Rome. This location is the site of the first supreme council of Scottish Rite Freemasons in United Sates, called Mother Lodge of the World (Tom Horn, *Exo-Vaticana*).

Satan's High Priest

William G. von Peters explains in his commentary, *The Siri Thesis*:

On the manipulation of the selection and election of popes by Freemasonry, most Catholics today simply cannot comprehend why or how such a crime could have been so successfully carried out almost undetected by the outside world, with the active participation of high princes (priests) of the church over the span of a generation. Surely such a long, drawn-out conspiracy would be beyond the ability of even the most evil men. But 130 years ago, Pope Pius IX explained that "if one takes into consideration the immense development which the secret societies have attained, the length of time they are persevering in their vigor, their furious aggressiveness, the tenacity with which their members cling to the association and to the false principles it professes, the persevering mutual cooperation of so many different types of men in the promotion of evil, one can hardly deny that the Supreme Architect, the god of Freemasonry of these associations can be none other than he who in the sacred writings is styled the prince of the world and Satan himself even by his physical cooperation directs and inspires at least the leaders of these bodies physically cooperating with them." [55]

Queen of Heaven

Catholics place Mary on the same level with Jesus. They pray to Mary. They believe she is the Queen of Heaven, perpetual virgin, and bodily ascension into heaven. Pope Benedict XVI believes Mary represents the path of truth, the path of beauty, and the path of love—of which Mary and Jesus took the same path. Biblical scriptures are clear that there is only one path, and that is Jesus. This pope held to the belief that Christ and Mary are inseparable from the beginning. Pope Saint Pius X said, "There is no more direct road than by Mary for uniting all mankind in Christ."

Further belief is that church must be personalized and not seen as a structure but as a person, and it brings forth the emotional component of the sacred heart of Mary depicted in statues where she is holding her heart. Jesus said to Peter, "Upon this rock I build my church." Peter now shares the mother church with mother Mary, and two women carry on the hope that is Christ. Without Mary, there would be no Jesus, and without the church, we cannot go forward. Pope Francis I cites a passage in Revelation 12:1. . . "*The woman was clothed with the sun and the moon under her feet and upon her head a crown of twelve stars and she being with child ...*" For Catholicism, this represents the assumption of Mary into the

[55] William G. von Peters, The Siri Thesis

heavens. **Our comment**—this is a symbolic image of Israel and the twelve tribes and not Mary the mother of Jesus.

Pope Francis pays homage to Mary. In Rome, there is an edifice called Basilica of Saint Mary Major, and the Pope prayed before the statue of Mary for her blessing before his trip to the Holy Land, May 2014. He laid flowers at the feet of the statue. According to *Catholic News Agency*, Pope visited this site eight times since assuming the papacy. The false prophet will tell the people to build a statue in likeness of the image of the Antichrist and worship it (Revelation 13:14). This will not seem odd to Catholics, who are accustomed to many statutes in their church. The Vatican Radio host, Cardinal Santos Abril y Castello, explained that the pope sees Mary as a maternal guide and inspiration for his actions. From the church's position on Mary, we can see how they accepted the apparition of a spirit posing as Mary at Fatima.

Pagan Symbolism

December 2015, on the celebration of the Feast of the Immaculate Conception and the advancement of the United Nations's agenda at the Paris conference on climate change and global warming, the Vatican allowed a light show to be projected onto Saint Peter's Basilica. Before we present the symbolism of the images, we first notice that the light show was sponsored and funded by the World Bank Group, Okeanos (environmentalist) and Vulcan Organization (believes in sins against Mother Earth). The production was orchestrated by a US-based company Obscura Digital and its artist Andrew Jones. Jones admits to using psychedelic drugs to help him portray occult deities accurately, and these deities are actively involved in guiding his hands. Obscura and their associates also did the light show emblazoned on the Empire State Building in celebration of the defeat of the Defense of Marriage Act, 2015. Jones projected an image called Kali, the Hindu goddess of darkness and death. Others referred to the image as Aya, Babylonian goddess associated with the rising sun and sex. The Hindu goddess was pictured with a long red tongue; its name means "black one," promises wealth to those who worship it by satiating her lust for blood by providing human sacrifice. Jones said he "wanted to depict Mother Earth in her fiercest form to draw attention to what might happen if people ignore implications of climate change." **Our comment**—these images do not appear to be coincidental since we understand messages are given in symbols. From this message we see the Antichrist having an affiliation with Hinduism brings darkness and death. The Antichrist, the black one, is associated with the rising sun, and he certainly stands on a platform of sexual abomination. The red tongue tells us he is unrelenting on shedding the blood of the innocent, which is none other than human sacrifice. The

Antichrist is staunch on climate change, which he believes is the greatest threat to the goddess Gaia.

Life Site News presented comments by Cornelia Ferreira—who holds a master of science, international lecture, and writer—exposing the new age movement. She said, "The show is definitely occult and new age depicting many levels of symbolism." She associates the butterflies as a sign of transformation. The large rising sun is used in occult symbolism as representing the rising of a new day dawning upon the masses, a change in direction. Other images of the moon, clouds, sky, water, and burning candles show the four elements worshipped by indigenous people. Animals were projected as endangered species (but not the life of the unborn). There was a swarm of bees that covered the basilica, which is associated with ancient occult practices and the Merovingian society.

Sound effects were metallic—tinkling of crystals, heavy breathing, chanting, nightmare sounds—and the scene was dark, heavy, and foreboding. Sights and sound could influence people to worship earth instead of God the Creator. Ferreira said these light shows are being projected onto buildings around the world. The global elite work to change the consciousness and thinking of the masses to orient them onto a spiritual path toward goddess Gaia, Mother Earth, and save the planet.

Michael Hichbornn of Lepanto Institute studied the occult for twenty years and noticed there were no Christian symbols at the Vatican light show such as the cross. He also contends the light show displayed occult symbols as half of a human face and one eye (the eye of Horus, the all-seeing eye), which is prominent in Masons, Illuminati, and black magic. The doves were flying backward, and he believes that Satan mimics God but does so in reverse, for instance a satanic mass is the reverse of a Catholic mass. Other strange images in the light show were humanlike forms, totem pole-like faces, and glowing eyes.

Bottom line, the Vatican did approve of the project, and Pope Francis watched from his balcony (Louie Psihoyos, one of the show's creators, said the Vatican gave them the green light). These are not isolated events. The forces of evil have been staking claim throughout the United States with statues of Satan; events such as the Burning Man Festival held yearly with hundreds of thousands of attendees celebrating new age, oneness, god, man, and nature are one. Drugs and debauchery are carried out at this event as well as seen in gay pride parades or Dragon Con conventions. This behavior does not honor Yahweh but pays allegiance to Satan.

One-World Religion

As we attempt to demonstrate satanic influence over the creation of hundreds of false religions, like a ball of thread, they will form the basis for the one-world religion and its false prophet. As discussed, the Catholic denomination is infested with paganism, occult, and satanic doctrines. The papacy is the catalyst to bring together world religions under one banner, and it is on the forefront to introduce the one-world religious leader.

What Will Be the One-World Religion?

From the multitude of religions worldwide, Bible scholars considered the Holy Roman Church would represent a universal religion with over a billion followers. The one-world religion is not based on the number of its adherents but on its ability to persuade and influence unity between all religions. *Catholicism* means universal. Pope Francis said, "There are many paths to heaven," which is contradictory to scripture—which clearly says there is only one way to the Father, and that is through the Son, Jesus. The one-world religion will not be one of the established religions but will be a sterile and apostate representation of all organized religions, similar to the order of the World Council of Churches.

Logo of the United Religions Initiative

Catholicism Interacts with All Religions

In order for Catholicism to bring other religions under one umbrella, the church will need to embrace other religions. With arms stretched wide, the Catholic church embraces liberalism and tolerance. Issues that are contrary to the Word of God will be eased into acceptance. Pope Francis has extended a wilted olive branch to atheists and homosexuals. Jesus requires us to love the sinner, but the sin must be condemned and not embraced as acceptable before God.

The people of the body of Christ are called saints. In Catholicism, saints are selected by the papacy and then canonized for sainthood. Pope Francis has identified Junipero Serra a liberal and progressive as a saintly role model of the left.

As the one-world religion coalesce, it is vital to observe how Catholicism interacts with other religions.

Israel and Catholics

Pope Francis as a cardinal reached out to Jews in Argentina, quoting Hanukah as an example of his commitment to his interfaith relations. He lit a candle on the menorah, attended a Buenos Aires synagogue, and remembered the wave of violent attacks against Jews before World War II.

Rabbi Abraham Skorka and Pope Francis were friends in Argentina. The two coauthored a book and did a TV series together.

Israel foreign minister Ze'ev Elkin was in Rome, June 2013, for high-level negotiations with Vatican officials over several outstanding land and building issues revolving around properties owned by Vatican in Israel. Elkin told *Hebrew Daily* that after meeting with Pope Francis, he thought an agreement would be signed by the end of the year, which would pave the way for pope's visit to discuss Vatican request to build two new centers.

October 2013, the pope continued his outreach to Jews, reaffirming a commitment to fighting discrimination and further Jewish-Catholic dialogue.

The pope visited Israel, May 25, 2014, and the Vatican Radio reported comments of William Shomali, saying, "The community in the Holy Land is expecting a lot from this visit, Christians, Jews, and Muslims are counting on this visit to intensify the ecumenical and the interreligious relationships."

During a two-week conference in Rome, April, 2014, Archbishop Cyrille Bustros asserted the Vatican's position: "There is no longer a chosen people—all men and women of all countries have become the chosen people." His position on a promised land is that Israel is occupying Palestinian land and "Christians cannot speak of the promised land as an exclusive right for a privileged Jewish people and this promise was nullified by Christ." In attendance were rabbis and Pope Benedict XVI. Israel called on the Vatican to distance themselves from Bustros's comments, while the Arabs praised his comments.

Former President of Israel Shimon Peres visited the Vatican according to report in *Jerusalem Post*, September 10, 2014. Peres proposed a United Nations for religions called United Religions. The Pope seemed interested. The God of Israel is not interested in embracing all man-made religions.

Muslims and Catholics

Pushing for peace, the Vatican overlooks radical Islam's philosophy and actions. However, with the rise of Islam, having over a billion followers to date, it does appear there is competition between all of Christendom and Islam. Presently, Islam is representative of many sects who are at odds with each other in their common beliefs. Conversion to Islam is through force and intimidation or because Islam offers refuge from destitution, hunger, or war. Islam has its holy sites, such as Mecca and Medina; but unlike Catholicism, they have no central leader or specific location, such as Rome and the Vatican.

During the pope's visit to Turkey, he spoke against "terrorist violence" and called for a stop to unjust aggression, but he stopped short of calling them Islamic terrorists to avoid negative portrayal of Muslims. The pope called for interreligious dialogue to end all forms of fundamentalism and terrorism, which exploits religion.

Some church leaders embrace a movement called Chrislam to bring Muslims and Christians together. We believe that this movement will not gain great momentum to bring all Christians into a doctrine that embraces Islam and rejects the tenants of the Christian faith. More so, Bible scriptures predict that Islam will come against the Lord's chosen people, and they will be destroyed. Ezekiel 39 alludes to the enemies of Israel coming out of the north, which could include Russia, Turkey, Syria, Iran, and four-fifth of them will be killed. The Muslim world is in chaos, yet the one-world religious system is on course.

October 17, 2013, the pope and Palestinian Mahmoud Abbas met. The pope gave Abbas a gift pen and said, "You obviously have many things to sign." Abbas said, he hopes to sign a peace treaty, and the pope said, "Soon, soon." The false prophet aligns with the Antichrist in pushing for a peace treaty not in Israel's best interest. The pope has scheduled another meeting with Abbas, May 2014, wherein Abbas hopes to propagandize the "poor Palestinian refugee" situation and that the pope's visit may contribute to alleviate the suffering of the Palestinian people who aspire for freedom, justice, and independence. During Abbas's term he has gotten rich at the expense of poor Palestinians who live in meager homes while he lives in a palace. May 15, 2015, media reports said Pope Francis gave the PLO its diplomatic approval for statehood, including the dividing of Jerusalem. There will be an election October 8, 2016, involving Palestinians. Abbas will be out, bringing an end to his cronyism. There is talk that the PLO will no longer exist, and in its absence, Hamas is trying to take political control in Palestinians regions of Nablus, Hebron, Samaria, Judea.

The pope visited Amman, Jordan, May 24, 2014, and the royals hope it will mark a significant milestone for brotherhood and forgiveness between Muslims and Christians, moving in the direction of religious unification. The pope was met by Jordan's King Abdullah, Queen Rania, and Prince Hussein at their palace. Through King Abdullah, Jordan is the only Islamic country at this time offering a wilted olive branch to both Christians and Jews. The king stresses a message of tolerance, peace, and coexistence. The king touts Jordan as a land of faith and fellowship. The king reminded the public that Moses died in Jordan, Jesus was baptized in the Jordan River, and in the past, other popes had visited Jordan—which he considers part of the holy land. It is interesting that in the future, Jordan will be spared destruction at the hand of the Antichrist, and many Jews will flee from Antichrist into Jordan.

On June 8, 2014, Pope Francis used the Vatican Gardens as his platform to promote peace in the Middle East. He was accompanied by Israeli President Peres and Palestinian Mahmoud Abbas. Before the pope spoke, an unprecedented prayer event took place with a Catholic reading from the New Testament, a Jew reading from the Old Testament and a Muslim reading from the Koran. This was the first time Islamic prayers were made on Vatican grounds (*Reuters*, June 8, 2014).

September 24, 2015, the pope visited America. In a memorial ceremony held at ground zero 9-11 tragedy in New York, the pope was accompanied by Jewish, Orthodox, and Muslim clergy. The pope addressed the Muslims as his brothers and sisters, acknowledged their feast of sacrifice, and expressed his sentiments in the face of tragedy at Mecca. He said, "My prayers and I united myself with you all in prayer to almighty god, <u>all merciful"</u> (term used by Muslims). In response, Muslim Imam Sayyid M. Syeed said, "Catholics are excited by pope's visit to the United States and American Muslims are more excited, it is more important for Muslims than Catholics, **he is our pope**."

<u>Protestants and Catholics</u>

In Christendom, there are over a billion followers in various denominations, and many are at odds with each other over doctrine, tolerance, compromise, and replacement theology. There already exists organizations that strive to unite all religions under one umbrella, bringing Christendom into a new doctrine that embraces Islam, Buddhism, Mormonism, etc. Pagan religions already worship many gods, so they may readily embrace another false god without much reservation. The one-world religion will have a form of godliness but will be barren, bearing no fruit.

With the 2013 selection process of the pope, the whole world was drawn into the rituals of this tradition. The papacy extended open arms to all religions. A document signed October 2013 agrees to recognize each other's baptism in the *Common Agreement on Mutual Recognition of Baptism.* As Islamic terrorism against Christians and others accelerates, Christendom is quiet as the church was quiet during the Holocaust. Pope Francis was pleased with the various efforts in countries to build better relations between Catholic and Evangelicals, especially the work of the Pontifical Council for promoting Christian Unity and the Theological Commission of the World Evangelical Alliance. Another document, *Christian Witness in a Multi-religious World: Recommendations for Conduct*, might become a motive of inspiration for the proclamation of the Gospel in multireligious contexts. One example is the dilution of the scriptures to appease others (*Hope for the World*).

Make no mistake, there is a prevailing spirit that singles out vulnerable people for deception, seemingly drawing them to the "holy" Roman Church. For instance, we attended a Pentecostal church member's mother funeral held at a Catholic church. It was surprising that the priest gave a wonderful sermon and strong in biblical doctrine. We felt drawn to join the church. In another report, a Swedish minister, Ulf Ekman, founder of the Word of Life Movement had been pondering in his heart for a long time and together with his wife had converted to Catholicism.

John L. Allen Jr., writer for the *Boston Globe*, July 2014, provided further insight into the unification of Catholics and Protestants.

> Christians are fond of preaching peace and brotherhood but are splintered and don't practice that gospel. Leaders on all sides have long tried to mend differences with little success and there has been mounting hope that Pope Francis will be the one to finally move the ball in part because of his long history of friendship with other Christians.

One such friend to the pope was Bishop Tony Palmer of the Communion of Evangelical Episcopal Churches, who thought of the pope as his spiritual father. The late Bishop Palmer was careful to point out, "Pope Francis pulled me up on more than one occasion when I used the expression coming home to the Catholic Church. He said, don't use this term, no one is coming home, you are journeying toward us and we are journeying toward you and we will meet in the middle." Palmer was considered an ecumenical star. In his visit with Pope Francis in Rome, he recorded a video message from the Pope to be viewed at a conference of Pentecostals in Texas hosted by Kenneth Copeland of Word of Faith ministries. The Pope's message was an appeal for reconciliation and friendship. The message begins with "The Catholic and Charismatic renewal is the hope of the church." Copeland's audience cheered. One member said, "I could be Catholic, Charismatic, Evangelical and Pentecostal and it would be absolutely acceptable in the Catholic church, I would like to reconnect to my Catholic roots and culture." One of the Catholic church's agenda is to reconvert protestants back into Catholicism. Bishop Palmer hoped God intended to use their connection to accomplish something big, saying he and Francis had made a covenant to work together for the visible unity of Christians. Shortly thereafter, Palmer was killed in an accident.

The pope met with Orthodox Christian Leader Ecumenical Patriarch Bartholomew in Jerusalem, May 2013. They will celebrate mass at the Church of the Holy Sepulcher.

Pope met with Archbishop Justin Welby of the Anglican Community to broach the subject of unity. The pope said, "The goal of full unity may seem distant indeed, yet it remains the aim which should direct our every step along the way."

Pastor Rick Warren, founder of Chrislam, encouraged Protestants to unite with Roman Catholics under the "holy father," Pope Francis. Warren made comments during his visit to the Vatican, November 2014, for an interfaith conference. Warren did condone Mary worship.

In spite of man's efforts toward a global religion, the work of the Holy Spirit in these latter days is evidenced in the growth of true believers in China, Africa, South America, Iran, Russia, and other nations that are under a demonic stronghold.

September 2015, the pope addressed thousands at Saint Patrick's Cathedral, Manhattan, New York, "We need to remember we are following Jesus and his life, humanly speaking, **ended in failure, the failure of the cross.**" Many Christians were stunned that the pope would dismiss the propitiation of Christ on the cross and claim it a failure (Sky Watch TV).

Mormons and Catholics

Reading Mormon history, this religion does not appear to have an extensive connection with the Vatican, but it may take a strong position for embracing a one-world religious agenda. For many years, fringe Mormons believed that one will arise from within their ranks to save America and its "divinely" inspired Constitution. A few scenarios provide a connection among end-time players such as Obama, Pope Francis, and Mormons. Obama moved to Illinois approximately one hundred years after Joseph Smith, founder of Mormonism, ran for president in 1844, from Nauvoo, Illinois. Obama was born in 1961, at a time when Mormon Apostle Ezra Taft Benson became the thirteenth president of the LDS and said, "The lord told prophet Joseph Smith there would be an attempt to overthrow the country by destroying the Constitution …" Fifty years later, president Obama moves toward declaring the US Constitution obsolete. Benson said, "Will there be some of us who won't care about saving the Constitution, others who will knowingly be working to destroy it? He that has ears to hear and eyes to see can discern by the spirit and through the words of god's mouthpiece that our liberties are being taken."

In 2012, Obama ran for reelection against Mitt Romney, a Mormon. Seemingly, the white horse in Mormon prophecy is out of the gate and running parallel to the rider on a white horse in the book of Revelation is going forth to conquer. This confrontation between candidates points to a convergence of events that were preordained. Romney does not publicly proclaim the white horse prophecy, but others in the Mormon church refer to him as "the One Mighty and Strong," taken from Isaiah 28:2. As we closely watch the unfolding of these events, Mormons hope for their savior to bring about the inheritance of the saints or the Mormon kingdom. According to Mike Moody, candidate for Nevada governor, newsman, and personal friend of Romney, he wrote, *Mitt, Set Our People Free*. It describes how the white horse prophecy motivated him to seek a career in government because he believed that he and other Mormons were directed to expand the Mormon kingdom by helping Romney—whom he says is under a sacred blood oath to the Mormon church to improve the US Constitution in order to advance the goal of a one-world government under Mormon paternalistic priesthood and the political kingdom of god, Smith's version of the kingdom on earth. Moody said, "We were taught that America is the promised land, the Mormons are the chosen people, and the time has come for a Mormon leader to usher in the coming of a political kingdom of god in Washington, DC." In a small way, this relates to Pope Francis's position that Jerusalem and the chosen people no longer refer to Israel but all of Christendom (replacement theology). Mormon prophecy is not infallible, and this prediction may end up in the trash bin. Romney did not enter the 2016 presidential race but made a public announcement against frontrunner Donald Trump. Trump is now an end-time player.

Initially, the one-world religious leader will allow a form of religious practice, but later there will be hindrance to worshipping their god. According to Bible scripture, the false prophet will require all to acknowledge the Antichrist as god and worship this false deity. Currently in play, the spirit of Antichrist rejects the truth of the Bible, rejects traditional beliefs, rejects marriage as a God-ordained union between a man and woman, rejects the sanctity of life, and embraces sexual sin, which is an abomination unto God. It works against any display of Christian traditions, such as the Nativity scene, public prayer, or the cross placed at a military cemetery. The spirit of Antichrist will increase persecution upon Jews and Christians as well as the prosecution of preachers and others who speak out against homosexuality or abortion. Under the false prophet, religions would be deluded to think they still can worship their god.

Catholic and Mormons on the Coming Aliens

As discussed in chapter 16, we present evidence that the world is moving to accept aliens from another galaxy. The Vatican believes that aliens are our brothers. The pope has said they are going to make an appearance. They watch the skies from Mount Graham, Arizona, using a powerful telescope. Mormons believe that aliens seeded earth, and this position connects them to Catholicism. The fallen angels intertwine the false concept of "aliens" within various religions as well as on the general public, directing them to believe in a "strong delusion." The Bible speaks of a great delusion that will come upon the earth, blinding and indoctrinating many toward accepting a satanic system under the authority of the Antichrist and false prophet based on a new alien doctrine. "Religious people may not initially need to renounce their faith in a god but as the formation of a global religion trumps all religions, it will be presented and authenticated as sound doctrine." [56]

Catholics, Atheist, and Pagans

Not wanting to leave any belief group out, Pope Francis met with an atheist group called The Family. Recently, the pope stated in all seriousness: "Atheists can go to heaven if they have a good heart." Why would an atheist be interested in heaven wherein **God** our Creator does exist?

Bill Maher, TV host and atheist, said, "We atheists don't believe in heaven."

Humanist Lucile Green concedes that Buddhism, Hinduism, Taoism, Shintoism, may well differ; but together they portray our world as multidimensional, and through their teachings, the foundations of a one-world religion is built. The fourteenth Dalai Lama whose followers think of him as god and the representative of Tibetan monks believes human survival will come from interfaith cooperation. In May 2010, Dalai Lama and Prince Ghazi bin Muhammad of Jordan joining with others launched the Common Ground Project, of which goal is to nurture spiritual relationships across diverse faith traditions.

Rev. Feargus O'Connor, secretary of the World Congress of Faiths, featured readings from humanist sources that states all religions are thought to share the ethical principle of compassion—which the United Nations, Charter for Compassion, 2009, affirms is the golden rule.

Universalism and Gnosticism

Catholicism is universalism and has a connection with Gnosticism. Gnostics believe they have access to higher knowledge beyond the wisdom of the scriptures. Gnosticism picks up certain ideas from the mystical traditions found in the Kabbala, which lean toward the occult. Universalism promotes we are all children of God and a loving God would never condemn anyone to hell, which is in contradiction to the scriptures. The Gnostic mind-set can be traced back to Greek and Roman philosophers. Universalism also believes all religions provide equal enlightenment and represent valid pathways to God.

Combining traditional biblical principles with universalism mixed with humanism and Eastern philosophies is in contrast to the Word of God. Case in point, January 2014, the World Sabbath of Religious Reconciliation featured an orgy of Hindu dancers, Muslim calls to prayer and Jews blowing shofars. Universalism requires no redemption from sin or atonement for it because all are the children of God, all will be reconciled to him and eventually

[56] Tom Horn, Chris Putnam, Exo-Vaticana

be conformed to divine perfection (*Hope for the World Update*, summer 2014, Debra Rae, "*Emerging Universalism*").

Perhaps Catholicism began as a spark toward igniting a one-world religion, but now it has grown into a fire, consuming the minds of mankind. In the following excerpts from the Parliament of the World's Religions held October 15–19, 2015, Salt Palace Convention Center, Salt Lake City, Utah, reported by Carl Teichrib, *Hope for the World Update*, winter 2016, is compelling evidence that a one-world religion has reached its zenith. Ten thousand representative from fifty beliefs came together to celebrate, *Reclaiming the Heart of Our Humanity: Working Together for a World of Compassion, Peace, Justice, and Sustainability.* Hindu author Vandana Shiva rallied the crowd, "Remember who you are, goddess, mother, Shakti of this earth." Rabbi Amy Eilberg called for them to remember our common humanity ... our collective devotion to the earth. Ojibwe, Mary Lyons, told the multitude, "When you breathe in, you breathe in a breath of Mother Earth, and when you exhale, those are your ancestors." Marianne Williamson, author on spirituality, wowed the crowd with her charisma: "Every woman here who is a teacher is a priestess and sacred femininity ... a divine goddess is not just beautiful she is fierce ..." The audience danced, wept, raised their hands, shouted and whistled, drums pounded in affirmation. President of Union Theological Seminary, Dr. Serene Jones, called for them to be "political actors, rethink the world." Also from Union Theological Seminary was Karenna Gore, director of the Center for Earth Ethics and daughter of Al Gore. A video message was given by Gore, reminding the attendees of the encyclical given by Pope Francis on global action to solve the climate crisis. At another session, emphasis continued on the divine mother within us, moving them past the age of the individual and into the collective ... entering a new chapter in evolution. In their prayer, the ancient goddess spirits were summoned to bless the gathering. Wiccan priestess Phyllis Curott read from the Parliament's *Declaration on Women.*

Climate change was another major theme at the conference, and comments were made by Marc Barasch, founder of the Green World Campaign: "Explore connection between the life of the spirit and the fate of the earth ... We as one stand under the tree of life, calling for oneness with earth and each other." Catholic Archbishop, Bernardito Auza, permanent observer status at United Nations, highlighted Pope Francis's position on the true right of the environment and social justice equals integral ecology. The earth is our sister, mistreated, abused, and is lamenting, and what is needed is ecological conversion. Native American chiefs Arvol Looking Horse and Francois Paulette gave comments in opposition to fracking and the Keystone pipeline ... We are servants to Mother Earth ... Sin is the abuse of Mother Earth.

Author Brian McLaren's *Finding Our Way Again: The Return of the Ancient Practices* declared biblical stories are "destructive and harmful" and need to be rewrapped to express tolerance and inclusiveness (shared by Hillary Clinton).

> Brothers and sisters, earth is speaking to us that people of faith need to tell a new healing story, bigger and better and more gracious, rooted in the diverse riches of our various traditions. This new story would lead us to common and joint action … religions must organize for the common good to create a global passionate dynamic movement of contemplative activists to heal the world and protect all living things … The purpose of the practices is to prepare us for the awakening and to prepare us for the all in one union of our nature with the nature of God.

Representatives from Jainism, Dali Lama, pagan community, Islam king Abdullah bin Abdulaziz, International Center for Interreligious and Intergovernmental Organization of Saudi Arabia, and the Mormon Tabernacle choir sang selections—all coming together to honor the multifaith arena.

We asked if Catholicism is a false religion, and in consideration of their Christian doctrines based on the virgin birth, death, and Resurrection of Jesus intermingled with pagan beliefs, it would seem they are likened to the feet of clay and iron given in Daniel's vision; they do not mix. They have one foot in Christianity and one foot in apostasy, and we will leave it at that.

Prophecy of the Last Pope

The *Prophecy of the Popes* was concealed by the Vatican for hundreds of years. It is said that Pope Malachi O'Morgair in the 1100s had a vision of the last 112–113 popes out of a total of 266. Pope Benedict XVI, next to the last in line, at eighty-five years old, resigned on February 28, 2013. According to O'Morgair's prophecy, the last pope would take the name Petrus Romanus, or Peter the Roman. He will lead the flock during the final persecution of the church.

Other high officials in the church believe in the prophecy of the popes. In an interview conducted by Paul Badde with Archbishop Ganswein, serving Pope Francis as Perfect of the Papal Household and secretary to Pope Benedict XVI, said, "When looking at the prophecy and considering how there was always sound references to the popes mentioned in its history … that gives me shivers … speaking from historical experience, this is a wake-up call."

Nostradamus on the last Pope—Quatrain 6:25—through Mars adverse (a time of war) will be the monarchy, of the great fisherman (the pope) in trouble ruinous, a young black red (a young black cardinal—not complexion) will seize the hierarchy, the predators acting on a foggy day.

Changing of the Guards

A Jesuit by the name of Rene Thibaut predicted the final pope on O'Morgair's list would arrive April of 2012. His prediction was in the ballpark. Unknown to the public, the current pope, Benedict, had planned to resign months in advance in 2012. He made his public announcement February 11, 2013. This was followed by a lightning bolt striking Saint Peter's Basilica.

Pope Benedict XVI called for a new world order on December 3, 2012, in a speech to the Pontifical Council for Justice and Peace. He said, "Construction of a world community with a corresponding authority to serve the common good of the human family … the proposed world government would not be a superpower, concentrated in the hands of a few, which would dominate all peoples, exploiting the weakest. Moral authority that has the power to influence in accordance with reason that is a participatory authority limited by the law in its jurisdiction." This defines Catholicism position in the one-world order and one-world religion. Some excerpts were taken from research done by Tom Horn in *Exo-Vaticana, Petrus Romanus*, and *Zenith 2016.*

Selecting a successor for the outgoing pope should be conducted thirty days after the vacancy. However, the Vatican would make its selection within two weeks for the installation of a new pope. Cardinal Christoph Schonborn, archbishop of Vienna, said, "I noted strong supernatural signs that Francis should be elected." Others claim to have had an impression that this man was the "chosen one." The pope was not on a main list as likely candidates, but after two elections, he came forth as a "little miracle and a sign from the Lord." We assume the reference to Lord is speaking about God the Creator, but it could well refer to Satan, the god of this world.

The new pope was selected on March 13, 2013. Numbers 3, 13, 33 are important within the Masonic Order and other cults. It was announced that Cardinal Jorge Mario Bergoglio of Buenos Aires, Argentina, seventy-six years old, would be the next pope. The Vatican had installed their final pope as predicted. His installation was heralded by lightning, meteors, fiery balls, and signs in the sky. These sightings were reported over Cuba, Canada, Belgium, the Netherlands, Germany, and Kazakhstan. Meteors hit Russia on February 15, 2013. During this time frame, a volcano erupted in Italy.

The final pope was predicted to take the name Peter the Roman. Cardinal Bergoglio took the name Francis of Assisi. The AD 1182 painting of Francis of Assisi is shown with birds. A seagull perched upon the Vatican chimney prior to the announcement of the new pope. Francis of Assisi, an Italian or Roman priest whose original name was Francesco di Pietro (Peter) di Bemardone—literally, Peter the Roman. Tom Horn stated the new pope would select the name Petrus Romanus, but a pope of Italian descent would fulfill the prophecy. Petrus Romanus implies this pope will reaffirm the authority of the Roman Pontiff over the church and will emphasize the supremacy of the Roman Catholic Church above all other religions and denominations and in general over all people of the world (Tom Horn, *Petrus Romanus*).

Background on Pope Francis

- He came in as a lamb, simple, humble.
- Cardinal Jorge Mario Bergoglio served in Argentina.
- He was born in Buenos Aires in 1936.
- His parents were Italian.
- He is the first pope from South America.
- He only has one lung; the other was removed when he was a teen.
- He has a master's degree in chemistry from University of Buenos Aires.
- Attended Catholic seminary in Santiago, Chile, and became a Jesuit.
- He has stated several times that his tenure as pope would be short.
- He speaks like a dragon, with authority, bypassing the Word of God.

Pope Francis is an associate of Jose Gabriel Funes, a fellow Jesuit. Funes is from Argentina, as is Pope Francis. Funes is the director of the Vatican Observatory Research Group. Funes is known for his essay, "The Alien Is My Brother," where he supports accepting extraterrestrials as our brothers. The Jesuits were at odds with the Vatican in that some Jesuits embraced Masonic and occult doctrine. Pope Clement XIV worked to suppress the Jesuits. Order of Jesuits is also called Society of Jesus.

Pope Francis served as Provincial of Argentina for the Society of Jesus. He was then the highest-ranking Jesuit in Argentina. At that time, the country was under the dictatorship of General Jorge Videla, who was responsible for countless assassinations including priests and nuns who opposed military rule. CIA intervention, March 24, 1976, overthrew the regime, and Videla was sentenced to life in prison. The Catholic church hierarchy pushed for the legitimacy of the military junta. Myriam Bregman filed a criminal suit against then-cardinal Pope Francis for conspiring with the military. He was accused of betraying captured priest.[57]

In Argentina in 2012, then-cardinal Bergoglio compared Catholic priest who refused to baptize the children of unwed mothers to the Pharisees of Jesus's day. "These are the hypo-

[57] Tom Horn, Chris Putnam, Peter Romano

crites who clericalize the church. Jesus said to go out and share your testimony, go out and interact with your brothers ... become the Word in body as well as spirit."

Pope Francis's Positions Contradict Scripture

If Pope Francis is the final pope identified in the *Prophecy of the Popes*, we must follow his words and actions closely. He appears to be moving away from strong Christian doctrine by compromising with the things of the world.

Following are some of his comments:

On homosexuality—"Who am I to judge?" As a vicar of Christ, he is to condemn sin.

The pope's tolerance toward homosexuality gained him to be featured in *The Advocate*, a gay rights magazine, calling him the Person of the Year.

On atheism—"Atheists can be saved by obeying their conscience and can go to heaven."

On abortion—the pope is divided on whether professed sinners, such as abortionists, should receive communion—such as Joe Biden and Nancy Pelosi, both Catholic and both proabortionists. The Bible is clear to reprimand those who partake of Communion unless they first confess their sins and repent before partaking of the sacrament unworthily. In a 2016 ceremony, the pope did give praise to a leading abortion proponent, Emma Bonion, who was arrested for performing illegal abortions. Now, as an elected official, she pushes for abortion, euthanasia, and homosexual marriages (*Life Site News*).

On the person of Jesus—"A personal relationship with Jesus outside of the Catholic church is dangerous ... can't seek Jesus alone but through the church, there is no such thing as do-it-yourself Christianity." The pope dismissed the miracle of the loaves and fishes and explained it took place by sharing what was available.

The 2013 *La Repubblica* reported remarks made by the pope: "The most serious of evils that afflict the world is youth unemployment and loneliness of the old. Proselytism is solemn nonsense ... makes no sense.

The 2015 *La Repubblica* reported, the pope said, "No person could go to hell, but if they fully rejected God, they would be annihilated ... The soul would not be punished in a place of hell ... Death is the end of their life. All others will participate in the beatitudes of living in the presence of the Father, and those annihilated souls will not take part in the banquet. No one can be condemned forever because that is not the logic of the gospel."

The pope influenced 3.7 million Lutherans to unite with Catholicism, 2016.

Will the False Prophet Please Stand Up

According to the *Prophecy of the Popes,* the final pope will pasture his sheep during many tribulations; and when these things are finished, Rome, the city of seven hills, will be destroyed and the terrible judge will judge his people. Scriptures tell us this final pope will be active during the tribulation period. Will Rome be destroyed? The false prophet will deceive the people, leading them to make and worship the image of Antichrist and false prophet will cause all great and small to take the mark of the beast. They all will come to their end when Jesus, the terrible judge, returns to put an end to all wickedness.

We will examine several Bible prophecies, prophetic commentaries, and current events to see if the false prophet is currently on the scene. Revelation 13:11 introduces the false prophet … "*And I beheld another beast coming up out of the earth and he had two horns like a lamb and he spoke like a dragon.*" According to Catholic doctrine, the pope is the vicar of Christ, or Christ on earth in his place. As Jesus is the Lamb of God, the pope literally becomes man who would be like a lamb. The pope's miter, or head covering, literally has two horns—also called two-horned miter. He speaks with authority, and the world listens.

Before the death of Saint Francis of Assisi, AD 1226, he prophesied that "at the time of this tribulation a man not canonically elected will be raised to the Pontificate, who by his cunning will endeavor to draw many into error and death … some preachers will keep silent about the truth and others will trample it underfoot and deny it for in those days, Jesus Christ will send them not a true pastor, but a destroyer."

Vatican insider Malachi Martin (1921–1999) and Jesuit Cardinal Augustine Bea had access to classified church documents, including the third secret of Fatima. Before Martin's death, he alluded to the Vatican's plan to install the final pope during a final conclave where the current pope would be forced from office (Pope Benedict XVI stepped down) and replaced by a Jesuit (Pope Francis I), who may bring to fruition the one-world religion.

Martin may also have come to an untimely death after writing his book, *Primacy: How the Institutional Roman Catholic Church Became a Creature of the New World Order.* [58] In these writings, he would disclose the Vatican's bank laundering of mafia money, homosexual practices, and pedophile priests. He was also planning to expose plans of Satan worshippers working to ensure the embodiment in flesh of the spirit of Satan into the final pope. Evil spirits can possess humans. The question is, Can Satan, an angelic being, possess humans?

> *And he does great wonders … making fire come down from heaven … he deceives those that dwell on the earth by the means of those miracles.* (Revelation 13:13–14)

Pope Francis did one miracle, which turned dried blood held in a container to liquefy. We will watch for additional supernatural signs

[58] Malachi Martin, *Primacy: How the Institutional Roman Catholic Church Became a Creature of the New World Order*

Will the false prophet come out of Catholicism? Combining all evidence will help us arrive at a credible conclusion.

Union between the False Prophet and the Antichrist

Union between the false prophet and the Antichrist is strengthened by their agreement and similar positions on various subjects.

Climate Change, Global Warming, Mother Earth

Herein we discuss subjects that both the one-world leader and the false prophet agree on.

We previously listed the Green Religion as the Resurrection of nature worship. It is the worship of ancient Gaia, or Mother Earth. Ancient practices have taken on a modern-day appearance.

At the end of 2015, President Obama and Pope Francis indulged in light shows at the Vatican, New York Empire State Building, and White House, portraying symbolisms that speak to a global order, occult, Mother Earth, and sexuality.

It is a United Nations mandate that calls upon nations to get in line under a variety of scenarios, such as global warming, saving the environment, and going green. In our chapter 18, we provide details on the United Nations's Agenda 21 Sustainability Program.

The 2013 Apostolic Exhortation reported the pope embraces the global position on income equality: that the natural resources and wealth of the world be distributed across the board to the rich and the poor alike. Pope believes two greatest issues that will shape the future of humanity is inclusion of the poor in society, peace, and social dialogue (no mention of salvation through Jesus).

The pope's comments released in his encyclical were also spoken to one million followers in Bolivia, South America, July 8, 2015. The pope stated, "An economic system centered on the god of money needs to plunder nature to sustain the frenetic rhythm of consumption that is inherent to it. The system continues unchanged since what dominates are the dynamics of an economy and financial system that are lacking in ethics. It is no longer man who commands, but money, cash commands." He continues, "The monopolizing of lands, deforestation, the appropriation of water, inadequate agro-toxics are some of the evils that tear man from the land of his birth. Climate change, the loss of biodiversity and deforestation are already showing their devastating effects in the great cataclysms we witness."

Pope Francis visited the United States, September 24, 2015, to speak before a joint session of Congress—being the first time ever a pope has addressed the Congress. Further comments by the pope on the environment,

> It is an obligation to take care of those around us and be a good stewards of our resources ... It should be the new world order. As steward of these riches ... we have an obligation toward society as a whole and toward future generation ... We cannot bequeath this heritage to them without proper care for the environment ... The earth is protesting for the wrong we are doing to her because of the irresponsible use and abuse of the goods that God has placed on her. We have grown up thinking that we were her owners, dominators authorized to loot her. The violence that exists in the human heart, wounded by sin, is also manifest in the symptoms of illness that we see in the earth, water, air, and living things.

His comments on climate change and the reduction of carbon emissions were shared at the United Nations general assembly meeting, September 25, 2015. In an article reported by John Vidal, the pope is seen robust and healthy. The pope met with other faith leaders and lobby politicians at the United Nations meeting to support new antipoverty and environmental goals, population control, and global government. He would also speak in Paris, December 2015, at the conference on climate change.

The pope's comments sound practical and a sincere concern for the environment and its production of economic fruits. What may not be forthright is the pope's embracing of goddess Mother Earth. In the globalist mind-set, humankind is destroying the planet, and they must be controlled through economic redistribution, incorporated into a database, and all will be tracked through a chip or mark in order to buy, sell, or survive in the one-world order (Revelation 13:16–17).

In line with the mind-set of the pope on the environment, John Schellnhuber was selected to speak on climate change. This man is akin with the United Nations Agenda 21 for Sustainability. He favors an earth constitution, global council, and planetary court would hold power over every nation and government on the planet. The earth constitution would transcend the United Nations charter agreement. He mandates for a global council that would assemble persons elected within their national, georegion, religion, culture (rulers over the ten-region confederation). His idea of a planetary court would be a transnational body open to appeals from everybody, especially with violations of the earth constitution. He is propopulation reduction and believes human principles, freedom and dignity, and security comes about by eliminating six billion people. Schellnhuber's ideas are equally appealing to Obama and Francis (Mike Adams, *Natural News* online).

Bishop Marcelo Sorondo, chancellor of the Vatican's Pontifical Academy of Sciences, an Argentinian said, "Our academics supported the pope's influence as crucial decision ... The idea is to convene a meeting with leaders of the main religions to make all people aware of the state of our climate and the tragedy of social exclusion." The pope will publish a rare encyclical on climate change and human ecology urging all Catholics to take action on moral and scientific grounds the document will be distributed to the world's five thousand bishops and four hundred thousand priests, who will distribute to its parishioners.

The pope's position on climate change aligns with Obama's position that climate change is a greater threat to the world than terrorism.

Some prominent Catholics and Evangelicals disagree with the Pope's position on global warming. Former archbishop of Sydney, Cardinal George Pell, overseeing the Vatican's budget is a climate change sceptic who has been chastised for claiming that global warming has ceased and that if carbon dioxide in the atmosphere were doubled, then plants would love it. Calvin Beisner, spokesperson for the Cornwall Alliance for the Stewardship of Creation, had declared the US environmental movement to be unbiblical and a false religion (*The Guardian*, December 27, 2014, John Vidal, tag Pope Francis's edict on climate change will anger deniers and US churches).

Economic and Finance

The overhaul of economies and financial systems will level human inequality, aligning it with ecological goals. In 2010, the church pushed for a central world bank that would be responsible for regulating the global financial industry and international money supply. This would be an authority that would have worldwide scope and universal jurisdiction to guide and control global economic policies and decisions (Andrew Puhanic, *Globalist Report*, December 6, 2012).

We see the leader of the Catholic church expanding his role as head of a one-world religious body, further embracing the global agenda of climate change, wealth redistribution, and tolerance on social issues. His position forwards the goals of global government and unites the global religious agenda in following the same humanistic goals.

Social Issues

Obama sends message to outgoing Pope Benedict, 2013: "Michelle and I warmly remember our meeting with the holy father in 2009, and I have appreciated our work together over these last four years." Archbishop Luigi Negri reported to Rimini 2.0 news that he believes Pope Benedict was pressured to resign by the Obama administraion. Under the Obama administration, the nation was forced to embrace homosexuality, redefinition of marriage, same-sex marriage, and the transgender mess. States such as North Carolina, Minnesota, Texas, Mississippi, Arizona, West Virginia, Utah, Nebraska, and Maine rejected Obamas transgender bathroom bill.

The Obama administration is moving to put into law the government can define who is a minister, redefining freedom of religion, freedom to worship. People who speak out against sin are penalized and demonized. One-world order proponents work to remove any semblance of Christianity from schools, courtrooms, and public places.

March 2014, President Obama met with Pope Francis at the Vatican in a first-time face-to-face meeting. The meeting comes at a time when Obama is fighting various Catholic organizations to provide abortion products to their people through the Obamacare mandate. Obama wanted to discuss income equality, but the pope discussed abortion, freedom of religion, and the right to object practices based on beliefs. The pope gave Obama a copy of his book, *The Joy of the Gospel.* They agreed to work together on human trafficking, while the Obama administration had cut federal grants to the US Conference of Catholic Bishops in 2011 because the group refused to refer pregnant women for abortions. It is an interesting tidbit that when Obama lived in Indonesia, he attended the Catholic school, Saint Francis of Assisi.

The Vatican's position on homosexuality aligns with the Obama's administration promotion for tolerance and acceptance. Currently, the pope is toward traditional marriage; however, his stand is weak. The pope pushes for <u>inclusiveness</u> by pondering if the church is capable of accepting and valuing homosexual orientation without compromising Catholic doctrine on family. Here we see a change in his position as cardinal when he firmly believed in marriage between man and woman. Church doctrine would have to be stretched to infinite tolerance to accomplish that. Homosexual Elton John held a praise-a-thon in support of the popes' position on tolerance and compassion. Pope Francis is culling Catholic officials who speak out against sexual sin by putting them out to pasture or demoted. Catholic bishops disagree that they can speak in true freedom. It appears there is no tolerance for defiance of the new sexual glasnost of the church (World Net Daily, Marisa Martin, November 30, 2014).

It was stated that the Pope said, "Jesus is going to take what has been traditionally thought to be impure or scandalous and turn it into a miracle."

<u>Spiritually Speaking</u>

The influential reach of the pope extends to Washington, DC, where a gathering of Senate Democrats began to discuss spiritual aspects as Senator Bernie Sanders said, "We have a strong ally on our side on this spiritual issue, and that is the pope." Mr. Sanders, a Jew, would invoke the pope to Harry Reid, who is a Mormon, delighted Roman Catholics in the room. Senator Richard Durbin, a Catholic, was joyous that they were contemplating the pope's position on economic justice and tolerance, becoming a topic in Washington's policy debate.

Time Magazine, April 2013, heralded Pope Francis as the "New World Pope." He believes Catholicism should oversee all of Christendom. The new pope says he believes that Muslims worship the one god that he also worships and reiterates that all roads lead to God. The ideology of the one-world religion will be philosophy, inclusiveness, and moral authority based on man's laws. Pope Francis called for a peace meeting between world's three major religions in Rome. Beginning of 2014, he had an 88 percent popularity rating among Catholics. New age guru, Deepak Chopra, hails Pope Francis as the "holy man of the world, 2016."

The timing of the pope's visit to the United States, September 23, 2015, aligns with the ending of one seven-year cycle, the Jewish Shemitah, and the beginning of the new seven-year cycle. It is also the end of the forty-ninth year, marking the beginning of a Jubilee or fiftieth-year cycle. The Jews celebrate the New Year, 5776, in September, and it aligns with another blood moon event.

Obama had a few accolades about the pope, but one comment he made stood out, "It's our [Obama and Francis] job to come up with policies to do something, and what the pope can do is to help mobilize public opinion." According to scripture, it is the job of the false prophet to promote the Antichrist. On *60 Minutes* interview with the pope, Robert Mickens said, "He is an icon, the captain of the ship, and it is up to the rest of the church to get with this challenging program, and any Christian that is not challenged whatever you are, right, left, center, conservative, progressive, if you are not challenged by Pope Francis, you are not listening."

We previously discussed the relationships with other religions that the Catholic Church has nurtured. In this consideration, the pope is respected by other religious leaders. The Jews respect the pope, looking to him to assist with a peace accord. Christendom respects the pope. He offers an olive branch, while Islam demands conversion by the sword. How will these opposing religions be connected for the task ahead? Internationalize Jerusalem. The pope said, "Palestinians have a right to statehood, and the land of Israel should be divided to accommodate them."

The pope may create an atmosphere of trust and brotherhood between Jews, Christians, and Muslims by a common historical thread that all could enjoy worshipping on the Temple Mount; this could be the carrot on the stick. Each religion knew of King Solomon or, by Islam, known as the Prophet Solomon and the building of the first temple. A Muslim would find it acceptable to see the rebuilding of Solomon's magnificent temple. Muslims in their own ideology respect Solomon as well as Abraham, Jesus, and Mary. Obama visited Israel in the past, and Israel rolled out the red carpet. In the future, the Antichrist may also want to set up headquarters in Jerusalem. Therefore, it is crucial that they gain control by taking Jerusalem out of the hands of Israel. Currently, the Temple Mount is under Jordan's authority. With the pope embracing the Palestinians' demands to take Jerusalem as part of their territory, things may be resolved if Rome once again controls Jerusalem. Pope Francis and President Obama did visit Israel to get the lay of the land. In this end-time scenario, have we seen the archetypes of Antichrist and the false prophet in Israel? The book of Daniel 11:45 speaks to a man who will plant the tabernacles of his palace between the seas in the glorious holy mountain … yet he will come to his end. Both world leaders are pro-Islam and push for Israel to divide its land to appease Islamic demands.

Foreign Relations

December 2014, President Obama said that the pope "is a key player in the thawing relations between the United States and Cuba."

Pope Francis continues working with the Palestinians, as did his predecessors. He visited with Palestinian Chairman Mahmood Abbas, May 2014. The pope likened Abbas as champion to the Palestinians as was Che Guevera to South America in support of their struggle and rights. The pope suggested Abbas be an "angel of peace." The pope snubbed Israel by holding mass in Palestinian-controlled Bethlehem, a place where Jews are not allowed and where a majority of Christian residents have been expelled. The Palestinians gave a famous painting to the pope. During the visit, the pope was placed in a position to read a sign posted in the Old City in Jerusalem that read, "La ilaha illa Allah … Jesus said: I am indeed a slave of Allah; Allah is my Lord and your Lord so worship him alone" (Koran 3:51) (Islam-guide.com). The pope did not comment on this blasphemous sign because he is a Christ on earth. Abbas claimed Jesus was Palestinian.

The pope validates the Palestinians by signing a treaty or legal document between the Vatican and Abbas in 2015, officially recognizing them as the State of Palestine. The pope bypasses the statehood process of the United Nations as well as ignoring ongoing peace process negotiations between Israel and the Palestinians. In response to this action, the Israel Sanhedrin moves to put the pope on trial for anti-Semitism and on his position that the Jews have no right to Jerusalem. The pope also states, everyone is chosen people. They expect action by September 20, 2015 (*Breaking Israel News*, Matzav Haruach). July 9, 2015, update, September 9, 2016, we have not heard additional news regarding actions by the Sanhedrin.

The Obama administration in 2015 with other nations reached an agreement with Iran to allow them to continue enriching uranium to build nuclear bombs as well as giving them $150 billion dollars some, which will be used for their nuclear program and to continue funding Islamic terrorists. Iran openly admits to supporting Hezbolla in Lebanon, Houthis in Yemen, and a new terrorist group, Al-Sabireen in Gaza. This is a bad deal for Israel and the world. Obama may consider the threat against Israel as an order of the day. Vatican commented on the Iran deal: "It constitutes an important outcome of the negotiations carried out so far although continued efforts and commitments on the part of all involved will be necessary in order for it to bear fruit" (Father Federico Lombardi, Holy See Press Office). Iran continues to scream death to America, death to Israel. It was recently reported, July 19, 2015, that Obama will not wait sixty days for the Congress to review the agreement with Iran but did submit it to the United Nations for approval. The United Nations Security Council did approve the Iran deal.

In the book of Daniel 9:26, it speaks in regard to a man who will confirm a covenant with many for seven years. Most Bible scholars believe the man to be the Antichrist, but it might also suggest another person, the false prophet. This action aligns false prophet (Rome) with Antichrist (revived Rome), both pressuring Israel for years to accept a deal. Now we have a peace deal of sorts with Iran and a peace deal of sorts with the Palestinians. In both cases, Israel comes out on the bottom. Former and current negotiations threaten Israel with boycotts and delegitimization of Israel as a democratic nation. Israel was also threatened by the United States not to take any military action against Iran and to cease building homes in the settlements of Judea and Samaria, and: The United Nations continues to threaten Israel with war crimes against Hamas. The United Nations with the approval of the United States will bring sanctions against Israel for building in their own region.

The pope speaks out regarding Christian genocide in the Middle East, calling it World War III and a reference to ISIS. He apologized for atrocities committed against indigenous populations in the name of religion. He specifically called out America for their grave sins committed against the native people on the tenants of Christianity. On the other hand, Obama addressed a crowd in Germany, but he did not chastise Germany for its atrocities committed against the Jews and others.

During World War II, the Catholics may have been pro-Nazi. The pope wears a symbolic Malta cross, and the Nazis embellished their garments with the Malta cross. The Catholic church has long-reaching influence, intersecting paths with Obama in Indonesia and again when he worked as a community organizer in Chicago. He was associated with Catholic bishops, who headed a campaign for Human Development under the Archdiocese of Chicago, and they paid for Obama's airfare to a training program on community organizing.

In this section, we attempted to make a connection between the one-world leader, or Antichrist, and one-world religious leader, or false prophet. If the Antichrist is on the scene, then so is the false prophet. They will not be besties, but we need to watch their ongoing relationship. They have separate roles, but together they will fulfill the end-time events. Both leaders have worldwide recognition. The false prophet's ambitions are to bring the world's religions under one umbrella, and the world looks to him as a savior. Of all the religious leaders in the world, certainly Pope Francis stands out foremost to wear the shoes of the false prophet. The Antichrist has authority over global politics and conquest. President Obama has been touted as president of the world, stating that at the end of his presidency, he has other goals to achieve, and it has been rumored he would like to be secretary general of the United Nations. The characteristics of the Antichrist line up with the character of Obama. By their words and actions, both may be contenders for these end-time roles.

While our hearts break seeing what has come upon the land, we cry out to God to help and are reminded of the passage in Habakkuk 1:2–11: "Oh, Lord, how long will I cry and you will not hear, even cry out unto you of the violence and you will not save. Why do you show me iniquity and cause me to behold grievance? Spoiling and violence are before me, and there are those that raise up strife and contention." God's answers: "Behold, you among the heathen, and regard and wonder marvelously, for I will work a work in your days, which you will not believe though it be told you. For I raise up that bitter and hasty nation which will march through the breadth of the land to possess the dwelling places that are not theirs. They are terrible and dreadful ... They come for violence ... They will scoff at the kings and princes, and they are a scorn to them and will deride every stronghold ... imputing this his power unto his god" (Habakkuk 2:1). The prophet will watch and see what God will say and do. God's answer—the vision is for a future time, but at the end it will speak and not lie, though it tarry, wait for it because it will surely come. The just will live by faith and will eventually see his vengeance. In the day of trouble, we will be at rest, when he comes against the wicked. They will not prosper forever, and they will see that the earth will be filled with the knowledge of the glory of the Lord.

Chapter 18
Architects of One-World Order and the Supreme Leader

Chapter Overview

- Architects of the New World Order
  - Rothschild Empire
  - George Soros Legacy
  - House of Morgan
  - The Rockefeller Dynasty
  - Keith Rupert Murdock
  - Bilderberg Organization
  - The One Percent
  - Millionaire US Politicians

- Anatomy of the New World Order
  - From Ancient Times to the Present Day
  - The World Is Interconnected
  - Calling for a New World Order
  - Achieving a One-World Order
  - The Georgia Guide Stones

- The United Nations
  - United Nations Agenda 21 Sustainability Program
  - Taking a Closer Look at the United Nations's Six Goals
    - (1) Religion
    - (2) Population Control
    - (3) Military
    - (4) Individual Freedom Versus Global Citizenship
    - (5) Environment
    - (6) Finance, World Economies
  - United Nations and Global Partners Form a Network of Organizations
    - United States of America's Structure
      - Exhibit: US Pyramid

- Ten-Region Confederation
  - Club of Rome
  - Breakdown of the Ten Regions

- One-World Supreme Leader
  - Possible Candidates for the World Leader
  - Ancient Roots

Chapter 18

Architects of the New World Order and the Supreme Leader

Architects of the New World Order

We are reminded that invisible principalities rule over nations and regions. From the influence of ancient powers over humankind, pagan and occult beliefs took formation, giving birth to secret societies. These groups are driven by invisible forces to tap into mystical knowledge, enabling them to harness supernatural powers. Encompassed with a shroud of demonic and dark powers, they act in unison, having a hive mentality toward global domination. In other words, they are the puppets or tools that Satan uses to bring about his ultimate goal, his kingdom on earth, his global empire. In our present time, Satan will select the one that will arise from the nations to become his one-world leader. Another will arise from the midst of Christendom to become his symbolic head over world religions.

In order to have an educated view of the shape of things predicted to be fulfilled at the end of this age, we evaluate events past and present. Our review of symbolism enshrined in stone or wood allowed our readers a better understanding of the significance of these signs and emblems found throughout the world. We can look at paintings or inscriptions and behold subtle messages. World leaders make public speeches with coded messages to be understood by certain adherents. National leaders may use cloaked phrases, such as "Hope," "Change," "Yes, we can," "Forward," "Meaningful action." The term *meaningful action* may be a code word to create a false flag situation. The shootings that took place in Aurora, Colorado, at the theater showing *Batman* movie had some significant symbolism embedded in it. Both George Bush and Barack Obama's words spoken at the 9-11 memorial service carried a cryptic message, which was identified by Jonathan Kahn, *Harbinger*, "We will rebuild, we will rise and will be stronger." In Kahn's book, he goes into detail to its prophetic significance.

In the overall analysis, we reviewed the purpose of secret societies and their continuation into modern times. This study provided a historical time line from the Knights Templar to the formation of the Masons, whose influence continues to impact world affairs. Freemasonry also became embedded into most aspects of American society. The marriage between religion and secret societies gave birth to a political agenda and the establishment of a one world religion foreign to the word of God. We tracked the advancement of Christendom throughout the world. Historians paint a picture of the Puritans who landed on the North America shores AD 1607 in the region called Virginia. They came in search of refuge from religious tyranny. A cross was resurrected on the site, and this land was claimed in the name of Jesus. Collectively, we believe it was purposeful that the seeds of Christianity could be planted in this land. The Gospel was shared with the indigenous people, and that was good. What God intended for good, Satan turned into evil. Satan came forth to disrupt the move of righteousness among the people. As more pale-faced invaders came to the North American continent from Europe, they brought with them seeds of an ungodly agenda. In order to plant, they needed to uproot the indigenous people. It surely must have been difficult to worship the white man's god when there was so much cruelty and hatred perpetrated against them. Yet God would watch over his word and truth would continue in the midst of wicked rivalry.

Here is a good place to observe the hand of Satan and his impact over humankind. This conflict was between Japheth's descendants (Europeans) bringing division to Shem's descendants (Native Americans), and when slavery was introduced, this brought Ham's descendants (Africans) into the fray. This mix of people became America's melting pot.

America had a covert destiny planned for it from ancient times by ancient powers. America would play a pivotal role in the formation of the kingdom of Satan. From what we can see, America is symbolized as a young lion, which can be traced back to the pagan Roman Empire whose symbol was a lion. Satan is also described as a roaring lion. European nations were an outgrowth of the Roman Empire as America is an outgrowth of Europe. The symbol for the European Union is Europa, a woman seated on a beast, and we find a correlation to that in the book of Revelation. America will become the symbolic harlot riding on the beast.

By 1700, war ensued between Britain loyalist and the new Americans. The indigenous people were caught in the middle and were considered to be the interlopers who needed to be expelled from their land. It took treaties between the Indians and the Europeans just to keep some of their land. The natives then became the target of persecution. Obviously, not all the Christians agreed with the majority rule to take the land from the natives.

By the time George Washington became an adult, his mantra for the new nation was based on virtue and morality, stating these principles "are a necessary spring of popular government, and popular government depended on virtuous citizens, and the religion of Christianity could inspire selfless behavior." Certainly, actions speak louder than words, and after Washington's declaration, he did not move to end the suffering of the Native Americans or to mandate the freedom of all slaves, including his own.

Independence Day, July 4, 1776, declared that all men are created equal and have the right to prosper and be happy in a free democratic republic. Moving from Washington's individual declaration to a national declaration by the government, again there was no action taken that would have brought relief to a large portion of the population. The architects of the new world had begun to mingle another doctrine into the rule of government, and that would be the doctrine of demons. It called for spilled blood. America grew to be a great empire on the sweat, tears, and blood of the masses. It took the Civil War in 1865 to set the slaves free. There was not a great outcry for virtue, justice, and fairness from the newly formed government, and the tentacles of hatred won out over Christian civility. The carpet baggers and Quakers came on the scene to fight for equality and to help Native Americans and black slaves.

Moving into the twentieth century, the Democratic party held to discrimination and prejudice. It took civil action, protest, and death to force the American government to make good on their own declaration of justice and equal rights under the law for all citizens. One hundred years later, we have come full circle. The principles of virtue and morality have taken on a new persona of tolerance for behavior that is contrary to morality. Demonic overlords ramp up their calls for spilled blood, be it the blood of innocent babies, the blood of our military, or from the corrupt actions of a rogue government.

For hundreds of years, the United States has been operating behind a shadow government. Former US Supreme Court Justice, Felix Frankfurter, said, "The real rulers in Washington are invisible and exercise power from behind the scenes." That is to say, these forces have been operating behind a cloak of evil and are drunk with power. The elite put America in place to be a world power, to perform as a global police force, having a superior military, strong economy, and control of global wealth. America has been involved in almost every conquest worldwide. Tom Horn reported that the Worldwide Independent Network and Gallup Poll, 2013, found that sixty nations have animosity toward the United States as world policemen and poses greatest threat to world peace. Every department in the US government is compromised, corrupt, and synergistically works to diminish Christian values, economic equality for all, as well as minimizing national sovereignty. The United States and world nations will be in line with the one-world order agenda.

Entering the twenty-first century, world events are increasingly chaotic. The one-world order is not to bring order literally but to bring chaos in order to accomplish its agenda. The dictates of Satan are still in place, and those in allegiance with him are marching full steam ahead. The year 2009 brought a changing of the guard, signaled a downturn in America's biblical foundation influenced by liberalism. A newly elected president came into power—a man exuding confidence, and through him, the plans for the one-world order accelerated; a man that provoked Christianity while publically proclaiming homosexuality as a normal lifestyle, dismantled the Defense of Marriage Act, demonstrated his lack of compassion for the murder of the unborn by standing shoulder to shoulder with Planned Parenthood, regulated for a decrease in our military, hindered individual freedom, speech, and gun ownership. Obama alienated Israel while embracing the false religion of Islam. Why? He is following Satan's playbook.

Architects of a one-world order hail from a cross section of organizations, religions, secularist people of wealth, position, and power—people such as H. G. Wells, Bertrand Russell, Mikhail Gorbachev, Ted Turner, the Clintons, Ban Ki-moon, and many others who promote a one-world order. We bring to the forefront individuals of influence and wealth who have been instrumental in bringing to fruition their common goal for world domination. On the way to global occupation, the use of reforms, referendums, political manipulation, revolutions, and military interventions are employed. Nations are offered freedom and democracy in return for their sovereignty and resources. If they are agreeable, they receive billions in American aid. The alternative is sanctions, isolation, and military intrusion.

We highlight a few influential people to demonstrate the interconnectivity between their concentrated wealth and the power they weld through governments, commercial entities, and financial institutions.

The Rothschild Empire

The Rothschild clan roots grew out of a Jewish ghetto in Frankfurt, Germany, called Judengasse. Amschel Moses (Bauer) Rothschild was a trader in silk and a money changer. Several of Amschel's clients were royalty. Amshel had five sons, which he sent into five regions of Europe: Salomon to Vienna, Carl to Naples, Nathan to London, James to Paris, and Mayer Amshel Jr. in Frankfurt. The Rothschild legacy continues through their descendants. They have occupied positions as prime minister, governors, finance ministers, and more.

Mayer Amschel Jr., the youngest, was born 1744. Mayer was twelve years old when his father died. He was interested in learning finance and attended Hanover school. Mayer later worked for Wolf Jakob Oppenheimer, who gave credit to royalty and worked in international trade. He liked to trade in gold bullion. The future Oppenheimer name will be associated with the atomic bomb.

AD 1917, Walter Rothschild and Arthur Balford signed an agreement to create a state for Israel.

AD 1916, Edmund Rothschild built his career by pushing the British-Khazar interests in Japan. The Virgin Islands may be owned by Russian Jews, the Khazars. Croatia was largely influenced by Rothschild from Hungary, which formed the foundation for the Khazar Dynasty. It took over oil company INA. Trigranit is big industry in Croatia to build sports arena and develop seaside resorts. T-Mobile is present for telecommunications. In cooperation with Winston Churchill, Edmund founded the British Newfoundland Development Corporation in Canada. Edmund's daughter Catherine married Marcus Egius, president of Barclay's global financial group and head of BBC.

The coat of arms of the City of Frankfurt is the red shield going back to the Khazar Empire. In German, it is *rot schild*, which is Rothschild. Frankfurt is the strongest financial center in the European Union. It is the seat of control over European banks as well as a strong influence over American financial institutions. The Frankfurt stock market is aligned with the Deutsche Borse, owned by the Rothschild via the Children's Investment Trust and Atticus Capital and their branches of Merrill Lynch and Fidelity Investments.

AD 1931, Mr. Evelyn Rothschild married Lynn Forester. In the future, the death of a Forester will be associated with Hillary Clinton. Evelyn was involved with Nathan M. Rothschild & Son Investment Bank, London, First Mark Communication, *Economist* and *Daily Telegraph* papers, DeBiers Diamonds, Field Fresh Food, which is associated with the Mittals, India, and the Great Bharti Group. Lakshmi Mittal is the Indian Deripaska. Mittal Steel Zenica bought over the RZR Ljubija complex of iron ore mines. Some of Evelyn's political associates include George Soros, Norman Lamont, Peter Mandelson, the present commissary of Great Britain, and is close to Labor Party and Tony Blair. Vernon Jordan with Lazard Bank is influential in Democratic Party of USA. He was also adviser to Bill Clinton. Evelyn's wife financed Bill Clinton's presidential campaign. Evelyn is close to the Duke of York, Prince Edward, who is the son of Queen Elizabeth, which shows a connection with British royalty and Rothschild Empire.

AD 1942, David Rene and Eduard Rothschild represent the French connection. Their father was Guy Rothschild (1909–2007). David Rene heads up N. M. Rothschild Bank/ Rothschild & Cie Banque, Investment Bank, London.

AD 1957, Eduard Rothschild is also a member of the Investment Bank of London. He controls French newspaper, *Liberation*. He heads up Imerys, metallurgy company owned by Rothschild since 1880.

AD 1971, Nathan Philip Rothschild is the son of Jacob, inherited innumerable agents and influence over vital political, economic, media, military worldwide.

George Soros Legacy

Rothschild progress in Serbia in mining, energy, food, and media in association with George Soros. Soros is a Hungarian Jew, a Khazar born in Budapest in 1930 named Gyorgy Schwartz. In 1936, his parents changed their name to Sorosz. He was educated in London, and in the 1950s he came to the USA. His mentor was Carl Popper, a Khazar. He began to acquire wealth through financial portals. His investments are worldwide—such as the Quantum Fund, whose financiers are Italian and Swiss, such as Richard Katz, a Khazar and member of Quantum Fund, was head of Rothschild Italia SPA and member of N. M. Rothschild & Sons, bank in London. Soros is associated with James Goldsmith, a Khazar connected to the Rothschild Empire.

Soros organizations span the globe, having roots in Eastern Europe, Russia, and later the United States. In 1990, he formed his network by creating organizations such as the Open Society Fund, Humanitarian Rights Fund, Helsinki Committee, Belgrade Circle, European Movement, Center for Antiwar Action, etc. His foundations appear philanthropic, democratic, and civil but lean to the liberal left as in socialism and communism. Behind their legitimacy lies propaganda used to manipulate the psychological shaping of nations. For instance, by accusing the Serbs of genocide, criminal mentality, collective guilt, non-Serbs are indifferent or desensitized to driving the Serbs out of their land or bringing sanctions against them. In the Serbian/Croatia takeover, Soros moved to drive out the Serbian Orthodox Church and to phase out the Serbian language (the Cyrillic alphabet), their history, and their nationalism.

Soros worked through his Open Society Fund to influence protesting groups such as Occupy Wall Street, DC Rally for Refugees, Black Lives Matter.

Personal Liberty Digest, Ben Bullard, February 25, 2014, reported, "George Soros, billionaire hero to progressive activists … ramped up political spending threefold through his Open Society Policy Center and its financial affiliate in 2013. According to *Washington Post*, his lobbying tripled in 2013 from $3.25 million to $11 million. They gave to grassroots Alliance for Citizenship, an immigration reform nonprofit pushing to get Congress to accept an immigration reform plan in 2013." This is not what it appears to be, concern for immigrants, but an agenda from the pit of hell allowing illegals to register Democratic to sway the presidential election.

May 20, 2015, on the Herman Cain radio talk program, he said that the movement called "Black Lives Matter" is being promoted by the defunct Acorn organization, with which Obama was affiliated and funded by George Soros via his Move On Organization. In

Breaking Israel News, Caroline Glick, August 24, 2016, reported Soros had given $650,000 to BLM. Protesters were promised $5,000 a month. Apparently, they had not been paid and were complaining online. The BLM movement is in response to police shootings of black men. Unbeknown to them is that the government can move forward to militarize the police force since there is a breakdown in law and order cracking down on dissidents.

Many electronic and print media outlets are owned by Soros, which lean toward subversive projects. Some familiar names are *Associated Press and Reuters* owned by the Rothschild since the nineteenth century. Soros controls the "Shutel" television, the Vati and Life radio stations.

Soros has infiltrated cultural and educational institutions—such as, Union University, the Alternative Academic Education Network, Belgrad Open School. His influence encompasses theaters, national library, historical archives—through which he can manipulate his followers.

Other connections between Soros and Rothschild are the Carlyle Group and the International Crisis Group, which is campaigning for an independent Kosovo and is financed by Rupert Murdoch, Goldman Sacks, JP Morgan. Kosovo has reserves in lead, zinc, gold, coal, and Soros has invested a lot of money in an effort of getting hold of Trepca for the Rothschild. They were instrumental in getting Argon Dida elected as deputy minister of energy and mining in Kosovo's government.

At this writing, the alliance is now turning its attention to Vojvodina to bring them in with Croatia, Hungary, and Romania. They have created the Danube project backed by Germany, Austria, and Vojvodina and would be part of this federation of countries in the Danube basin as a European region. This project is carried out through the acquisition of agricultural combines, sugar refineries, dairies, oil, and banks. Croatia is buying agricultural estates and food companies. Austria and Germany are also purchasing refineries in Vojvodina, involving tens of thousands of acres of land. In the Muslim Croatian part of Bosnia, the Mittal group is the leader in the area of mining and metallurgy. It controls the steel plant in Zenica, one of the largest in the Balkans.

Pro-Albania element is being promoted with the aim of completing the project of Greater Albania. Its sovereignty and independence refer to the territory while the economy and resources are undergoing quiet occupation and the people are being promised a better future in the European Union. Soros openly supports Albanian interests. For this purpose, he uses numerous organizations—the Helsinki Committee, the Centre for Multicultural Understanding, the Association for Democratic Initiatives, all dominated by Albanians.

Soros also credited the Macedonian (once part of Yugoslavia) government in 1994 with $25 million dollars. During this same period, he attained great influence with the prime minister and the current president of Macedonia, Branko Crvenkovski. Crvenkovski openly supports Soros and his association with the Macedonian mobile phone company MT via Stonebridge Communications Company. MT is the second largest mobile phone company in Macedonia, indirectly controlled by the Rothschilds through Blackstone Group, a major financial investment group that was founded in 1985 by their agents, Peter George Peterson and Stefan Schwartzman (a Khazar). Both of them had previously made careers in Rothschild branch offices Lehman Brothers and Kuhn Loeb Inc. Blackstone group is the leading stockholder of Deutsche Telekom (T-Mobile), which also incorporates the Hungarian mobile phone company Matav.

The Soros and Rothschild involvement is so extensive we cannot cover it all in this report. However, a pattern that is being worked in Europe is similar to the mechanisms developed in USA. A great deal of business and real estate have been purchased by foreign entities. The top 1 percent control the political arena, major resources, and great wealth. In this vein, Soros is connected to the Clintons. DC Leaks hackers opened Soros e-mails in his Open Society Fund, and it revealed he has contributed $30 million to Hillary Clinton. Soros is cochair for the Hillary Clinton Super PAC for 2016. Birds of a feather flock together.

Summarizing the Soros agenda, his affiliates work to weaken free markets through restrictions, taxes, and financial market control. They fight against conservative political ideologies and replace with their liberal agenda. They push for open borders and influx of immigrants undermining national identity and demographic composition. Opposition to open border is demonized. Israel cannot allow untold numbers of Muslims into their country due to security risks and this decision reaps boycott, divestment and sanctions against Israel. In the United States, anyone wanting to build better security between United States and Mexico are labeled racist and a threat to the Democratic way of life. Countries wanting to limit illegal Islamic groups from entering their regions are also demonized.

The House of Morgan

The Morgan legacy was in finance from Wall Street to Main Street. J. Pierpont Morgan's banking cartel has acted as a quasi US central bank since 1838. J. Pierpont Morgan died in 1912.

In 1892, J. P. Morgan did a joint venture to provide Thomas Edison with capital to develop electricity. Edison created DC (direct current). Nikola Tesla worked for Edison. He resigned after Edison refused to consider AC (alternating current). Tesla then partnered with George Westinghouse, who financed his invention of the induction motor and transformer. Morgan took over Edison and created the General Electric Company.

Westinghouse and Tesla lit up the 1893 World's Fair in Chicago. Tesla went on to research and develop other technological milestones. After his death in 1943, it was reported that the

United States government confiscated his work to use for future research. Tesla's research added to scientific advances made by German scientists working in the United States. During this time frame, Henry Ford contributed to the industrial era by introducing the first affordable auto in 1896 to the middle class, which sold for $900.

The Morgans were connected to Rothschilds. Morgan's activities in 1895–1896 involved selling US gold bonds in Europe in connection with Rothschild. Morgan bailed out US federal government by lending it $100 million. The Morgan financial octopus wrapped its tentacles around the globe. Morgan Grenfell operated in London, Morgan et Ce ruled Paris. The House of Morgan was cozy with the British House of Windsor and the Italian House of Savoy. The Kuhn Loebs, Warburgs, Lehmans, Lazards, Israel Moses Seifs and Goldman Sachs also had close ties to European royalty. The Morgans had a connection with the Astors, DuPonts, Guggenheims, Vanderbilt, and Rockefellers. It financed the launch of AT&T, General Motors, and DuPont. The Rothschild's Lambert cousins set up Drexel & Company in Philadelphia.

Like the London-based Rothschild and Barings banks, Morgan became part of the power structure in many countries. In the 1890s, the House of Morgan was lending to Egypt's central bank, financing Russian railroads, floating Brazilian provincial government bonds, and funding Argentine public works projects.

A recession in 1893 enhanced Morgan's power. That year Morgan saved the US government from a bank panic, forming a syndicate to prop up government reserves with a shipment of $62 million worth of Rothschild gold. By 1895, Morgan controlled the flow of gold in and out of the United States.

Morgan was the driving force behind expansion in the United States, financing and controlling westbound railroads through voting trusts. Cornelius Vanderbilt and Morgan financed New York Central Railroad, giving preferential shipping rates to John D. Rockefeller's budding Standard Oil monopoly, cementing the Rockefeller/Morgan relationship. A *New York Herald* headline read, "Railroad Kings Form Gigantic Trust." J. Pierpont Morgan, who once stated, "Competition is a sin," now opined gleefully: "Think of it, all competing railroad traffic west of Saint Louis placed in the control of about thirty men." Morgan and Edward Harriman's banker Kuhn Loeb held a monopoly over the railroads.

Banking dynasties Lehman, Goldman Sachs, and Lazard joined the Rockefellers in controlling the US industrial base. The first American wave of mergers was in its infancy and was being promoted by the bankers. In 1897, there were sixty-nine industrial mergers. By 1899, there were 1,200. In 1904, John Moody, founder of Moody Investor Services, said it was impossible to talk of Rockefeller and Morgan interests as separate.

In 1903, Banker's Trust was set up by predominately eight influential families such as the Rothschild, Morgan, Rockefeller, Vanderbilt, Chase, Carnegie. Benjamin Strong of Banker's

Trust was the first governor of the New York Federal Reserve Bank. The 1913 creation of the Federal Reserve fused the power of these eight families to the military and diplomatic might of the US government. If their overseas loans went unpaid, the oligarchs could now deploy US Marines to collect the debts. Morgan, Chase, and Citibank formed an international lending syndicate.

These influential men did change the face of America from agricultural to industrial at the expense of the poor working class. To fill their coffers, worker's wages were cut while their hours were increased. They were made to work in poor and unsafe factories, and unionization came into play. People seeking employment were plentiful, and those who expressed dissatisfaction with wages or working conditions were immediately terminated, adding to high unemployment (History Channel, Wikipedia, alternative media sites).

The public usually developed a distaste for the wealthy, especially since money did not filter down into the pockets of the working poor. Some thinking class Americans may have thought of them as traitors working for European old money. Rockefeller's Standard Oil, Andrew Carnegie's first steel plant in Pennsylvania, and Edward Harriman's railroads received financing from banker Jacob Schiff at Kuhn Loeb, who worked closely with the Rothschilds.

Popular preacher William Jennings Bryan was the Democratic nominee for president in 1896. He lost to William McKinley, who received substantial contributions form Rockefeller, Carnegie, and Morgan. It could be said they bought the election. McKinley served during the Great Depression. He did lead the nation back to prosperity and victory in the Spanish American War in 1898. War was profitable for America. Bryan ran against McKinley in his second term in 1900. President McKinley was assassinated, September 6, 1901. Vice President Theodore Roosevelt succeeded McKinley. In 1908, Bryan ran against Roosevelt and was defeated.

However, Bryan's campaign message focused on anti-imperialism of large conglomerates such as the steel, oil, and railroad industries run by Rockefeller, Carnegie, Vanderbilt, and Morgan—who sucked the wealth from the land and paid workers meager wages, creating an environment of serfdom. He also believed that America was falling into a trap of financial servitude to British capital. His message resonated with Americans. Teddy Roosevelt, having to deal with Bryan's sentiment, was forced by the populist to enact the Sherman Anti-Trust Act. He then went after Rockefeller and his Standard Oil Company Trust. The end result is that the monopoly had to be broken up.

In 1912, the Pujo hearings were held, addressing concentration of power on Wall Street. That same year, Mrs. Edward Harriman sold her substantial shares in New York's Guaranty Trust Bank to J. P. Morgan, creating Morgan Guaranty Trust. Judge Louis Brandeis convinced President Woodrow Wilson to call for an end to interlocking board directorates, and by 1914 the Clayton Anti-Trust Act was passed.

Jack Morgan, J. Pierpont's son and successor, responded by calling on Morgan clients Remington and Winchester to increase arms production. He argued that the United States needed to enter World War I. As Charles Tansill wrote in *America Goes to War*, "Even before the clash of arms, the French firm of Rothschild Freres cabled to Morgan & Company in New York suggesting the flotation of a loan of $100 million, a substantial part of which was to be left in the United States to pay for French purchases of American goods."

Senator Gerald Nye (D-ND) chaired a munitions investigation in 1936. Nye concluded that the House of Morgan had plunged the United States into World War I to protect loans and create a booming arms industry. Nye later produced a document titled *The Next War*, which cynically referred to "the old goddess of democracy trick," through which Japan could be used to lure the United States into World War II.

The House of Morgan financed a portion of the US war effort, while receiving commissions for lining up Morgan affiliated contractors like GE, Du Pont, US Steel, Kennecott, and ASARCO. Morgan also financed the British Boer War in South Africa and the Franco-Prussian War.

The 1919, Paris Peace Conference was presided over by Morgan, which led both German and allied reconstruction efforts. America took the land of Puerto Rico and the Philippines.

In the 1930s, populism resurfaced in America after Goldman Sachs, Lehman Bank, and others profited from the crash of 1929. House Banking Committee, Chairman Louis McFadden (D-NY), said of the Great Depression: "It was no accident. It was a carefully contrived occurrence … the international bankers sought to bring about a condition of despair here so they might emerge as rulers of us all."

In 1937, Interior Secretary Harold Ickes warned of the influence of "America's Sixty Families." Historian Ferdinand Lundberg later penned a book of the exact same title. Supreme Court Justice William O. Douglas said, "Morgan influence … the most pernicious one in industry and finance today." Jack Morgan responded by nudging the United States toward World War II. Morgan had close relations with the Iwasaki and Dan families, two of Japan's wealthiest clans, who owned Mitsubishi. When Japan invaded Manchuria, slaughtering Chinese peasants at Nanking, Morgan downplayed the incident. Morgan had a relationship with Italian fascist Benito Mussolini. Morgan Bank had a financial relationship with German Nazi Dr. Hjalmer Schacht during World War II. After the war, Morgan representatives met with Schacht at the Bank of International Settlements (BIS) in Basel, Switzerland (History Channel).

In 1968, Morgan Guaranty launched Euro-Clear, a Brussels-based bank clearing system for Eurodollar securities. It was the first such automated endeavor. Some took to calling Euro-Clear "The Beast." Brussels serves as headquarters for the European Central Bank and for NATO.

In 1973, Morgan officials met secretly in Bermuda to illegally resurrect the old House of Morgan, twenty years before Glass Steagal Act was repealed. Morgan and the Rockefellers provided the financial backing for Merrill Lynch, boosting it into the big five of US investment banking. Merrill Lynch is now part of Bank of America.

The Rockefeller Dynasty

Bank of International Settlements is the most powerful bank in the world, a global central bank for the eight prominent families who control the private central banks of almost all Western and developing nations. The first president of BIS was John D. Rockefeller's banker, Gates McGarrah an official at Chase Manhattan and the Federal Reserve. McGarrah was the grandfather of former CIA director Richard Helms. The Rockefellers like the Morgans had close ties to London.

John D. Rockefeller began his empire in oil. He used kerosene in lamps for lightning. He discovered how to make gasoline to power combustible engines used in motor vehicles. He used his oil wealth to acquire Equitable Trust, which had acquired several large banks and corporations by the 1920s. The Great Depression helped consolidate Rockefeller's power. His Chase Bank merged with Kuhn Loeb's Manhattan Bank to form Chase Manhattan, cementing a longtime family relationship. The Kuhn-Loebs had financed along with Rothschild and Rockefeller to control the oil industry. National City Bank of Cleveland provided Rockefeller with the money needed to embark upon his monopolization of the US oil industry. The bank was identified in Congressional hearings as being one of three Rothschild-owned banks in the United States during the 1870s, when Rockefeller first incorporated as Standard Oil of Ohio.

The Dulles and Rockefeller families are cousins. Allen Dulles created the CIA, assisted the Nazis, covered up the Kennedy assassination from his position on the Warren Commission, and struck a deal with the Muslim Brotherhood to carry out terrorism.

John Foster Dulles presided over the Goldman Sachs trusts before the 1929 stock market crash and helped his brother overthrow governments in Iran and Guatemala. Both were Skull & Bones, Council on Foreign Relations (CFR) insiders, and 33rd Degree Masons.

Among Rockefeller's partners in Standard Oil was Edward Harkness, whose family came to control Chemical Bank. The other was James Stillman, whose family controlled Manufacturers Hanover Trust. Both banks merged under the J. P. Morgan Chase umbrella.

In the insurance business, the Rockefellers control Metropolitan Life, Equitable Life, Prudential and New York Life. Rockefeller banks control 25 percent of all assets of the fifty largest US commercial banks and 30 percent of all assets of the fifty largest insurance companies.

Companies under Rockefeller control include Exxon Mobil, Chevron Texaco, BP Amoco, Marathon Oil, Freeport McMoran, Quaker Oats, ASARCO, United, Delta, Northwest, ITT, International Harvester, Xerox, Boeing, Westinghouse, Hewlett-Packard, Honeywell, International Paper, Pfizer, Motorola, Monsanto, Union Carbide, and General Foods.

The Rockefeller Foundation has close financial ties to both Ford and Carnegie Foundations. Other family philanthropic endeavors include Rockefeller Brothers Fund, Rockefeller Institute for Medical Research, General Education Board, Rockefeller University, and the University of Chicago—which churns out a steady stream of economists as apologists for international capital, including Milton Friedman.

The family owns thirty Rockefeller Plaza, where the national Christmas tree is lighted every year, and Rockefeller Center in New York. David Rockefeller was instrumental in the construction of the World Trade Center towers. The main Rockefeller family estate is a mega complex in upstate New York known as Pocantico Hills. They also own a thirty-two-room Fifth Avenue duplex in Manhattan; a mansion in Washington, DC; Monte Sacro Ranch in Venezuela; coffee plantations in Ecuador; several farms in Brazil; an estate at Seal Harbor, Maine; and resorts in the Caribbean, Hawaii, and Puerto Rico.

The Rockefellers were instrumental in forming the Club of Rome at their family estate in Bellagio, Italy.

John Rockefeller Jr. headed the Population Council until his death. His son is a senator from West Virginia, and his brother, Winthrop Rockefeller, was lieutenant governor of Arkansas and remains the most powerful man in that state. In an October 1975 interview with *Playboy* magazine, Vice President Nelson Rockefeller, former governor of New York, articulated his family's patronizing worldview: "I am a great believer in economic, social, political, military, and total world planning." Bill Clinton's stint as governor of Arkansas gave a boost to the upcoming Clintons who would latch onto Rockefeller influence, following suit in forming their Clinton Foundation. In 2016, Rockefeller hosted a fund-raiser for Hillary Clinton.

At the Rockefeller Pocantico Hills estate, the Trilateral Commission was formed and spearheaded by David Rockefeller. Their global influence grew. Rockefeller defended the Shah of Iran, the South African apartheid regime, and the Chilean Pinochet junta. He was the biggest financier of the CFR, the TLC and (during the Vietnam War) the Committee for an Effective and Durable Peace in Asia a contract bonanza for those who made their living off conflict.

Nixon asked him to be Secretary of Treasury, but Rockefeller declined the job, knowing his power was much greater. Author Gary Allen writes in *The Rockefeller File* that in 1973, "David Rockefeller met with twenty-seven heads of state, including the rulers of Russia and Red China" (History Channel and Wikipedia).

Rockefeller's sentiments toward a one-world order—"We are on the verge of a global transformation, all we need is the right crisis, and they will accept a new world order." Realizing time is running out the agenda needs to be accelerated, and Obama was selected to bring about the final metamorphosis.

Keith Rupert Murdock

It is interesting to note that Murdock was a cheerleader for Obama. Keith Rupert Murdock heads up multibillion-dollar media empire such as News Corporation and the 21st Century Fox. His roots are Australian. He acquired *News of the World*, the Sun Media, and Sky TV in the United Kingdom. He was friendly with Margaret Thatcher, Tony Blair, and Gordon Brown. He immigrated to New York and became a US citizen in 1985. While in New York, he bought *The Times*, *Harper Collins*, *Wall Street Journal*, *New York Post*, *Star* tabloid, Fox TV, Direct TV cable. In 2007, he bought Dow Jones for five billion dollars. Jacob Rothschild served as deputy chairman of Murdock's BSkyB Corporation from 2003 to 2007. Murdock invested in Rothschild Genie Oil and Gas, which did shale gas and oil exploration in Israel. Murdock is pro-Israel. His News Corporation had subsidiaries in Bahamas, Cayman Islands, Chanel Islands, and Virgin Islands. By 2000, he owned eight hundred companies, fifty-eight thousand employees in over fifty countries. His net worth was estimated around $35 billion. In 2011, he was accused of hacking celebrity phones and involved in bribery and corruption. On July 21, 2012, he resigned as director of News International. He endorsed Barack Obama in the *New York Post*: "Yes, he is a rock star. It's fantastic, I love what he is saying about education … He will win Ohio and the election. I am anxious to meet him. I want to see if he will walk the walk." Murdock is a member of CFR. His third wife—Chinese-born Wendi Deng, thirty years old—married Murdock, who was then sixty-eight years old, in 1999. They had two daughters. Wendi was a graduate of Yale School of Management and vice president of Murdock's Start TV. In 2013, they filed for divorce.

Henry Kissinger and Vladimir Putin enjoy a very cordial relationship. Putin placed Kissinger (Democrat) as head of a bilateral working group with former KGB globalist General Yevgeny Primakov on foreign policy. Putin is a puppet, as are other world leaders. Their activities are directed, and they are as pieces on the global chessboard, pitted against other nations in a grand theater designed to distract and divide the masses. Kissinger said, in crisis, there is opportunity. Kissinger may have been involved in the assassination of Aldo Moro, Italy, because he wanted to bring progress to Italy. The elite wanted to bring it in line with the new world order. In court it was reported Kissinger made direct threats to Moro. Kissinger had a strong US influence in Korean, Vietnam, Gulf War, and Middle East conflicts. Kissinger threatened Ali Bhutto, Pakistan, not to get nuclear weapons. Bhutto was assassinated in 1979. Kissinger is a supporter of Barack Obama and Hillary Clinton.

The Bilderberg Organization

Founded by Prince Bernard, Netherlands, 1954. Their goal was to regionalize Europe. The Treaty of Rome established the Common Market, which is now the European Union. With the combined influence of their member nations, international bankers, royalty, and the elite and wealthy, the United Nations' mandates will ensure the one-world global agenda is in place. Bilderberg member Queen Juliana endorsed planetary (global) citizens in the 1970s. Like a hive, they all work together to funnel power and wealth to the United Nations to increase its enforcement powers. "A United Nations army must be able to act immediately anywhere in the world without the delays involved in each country making its own decision whether to participate based on parochial considerations." This concept is similar to NATO. Since the mid-1950s, the presence and influence of United Nations peacekeepers has increased.

President Gerald Ford, 1965, said the Bilderberg organization is so exclusive; you don't belong but get invited. In 1974, Henry Kissinger, David Rockefeller, Walter Levy, and Robert McNamara were invited. The organization is male dominated with a small percent of females. Since the attendees and agenda are kept secret, some leaked information indicated world problems are discussed. Some of these topics could involve the future of cyber warfare and its impact on nations' foreign policy as it touches on economics, terrorism, and technology. There may have been discussion regarding oil production and how to manage the flood of petro dollars. Certain oil-producing countries would be onboard under their control.

Argus Press, 1974, expressed his understanding of the organization: "Purpose to allow the elite in every field the opportunity to speak freely without hindrance because their knowledge and ideas would be criticized by the press." No reporters are invited to the meetings.

Henry Kissinger expressed pleasure "over the Persian Gulf war, stressing that it had been sanctioned by the United Nations at the request of George Bush before approval of US Congress." These scheduled wars work toward developing the right frame of mind for years to come as the United Nations will deal with future incidents (Zenith 2016, Tom Horn).

Bilderberg meetings have been held throughout the world. It was held in Rome in 2012, and coincidentally, Pope Benedict resigned and was replaced in 2013 by Pope Francis. June 2013, the Bilderbergs held their annual meeting in Walford, England. The organization does have influence over the outcome of elections in the United States. For example, in 2008, Hillary Clinton and Barack Obama attended the meeting, and it was decided he would be the next president. Clinton may have been promised the presidency in 2016. Some of the

Clintons' activities are highlighted at the end of this chapter under "The Harlot Riding the Beast".

The One Percent

The wealth and mechanisms of the world are controlled by an estimated 1,800 people globally, whose combined wealth is 40 percent of all global assets. Following is a partial list of billionaires and millionaires (Roll Call and Forbes, 2014):

Top Billionaires (Estimate in Billions)

Alan Rufus	178
Alexander Turney Stewart	90
Alice Walton, Walmart	33
Aliko Dangote, Nigeria	14
Andrew Carnegie	310
Bill Gates, Microsoft	87
C. Vanderbilt	185
Carlos Slim Helu, Mexico	23
Charles and David Koch	85
Jeff Bezos, Amazon	56
Friedrich Weyenhaeuser	80
George Soros	22
Henry Ford	199
Henry, Duke of Lancaster, England	85
Jay Gould	71
John Gaunt	110
John Jacob Astor	121
Keith Rupert Murdock	14
Ingavar Kamprad, Sweden, Ikea	39
Lakshmi Mittal, India	13
Larry Page, Google	38
*Larry Ellison	43
Lika Shing, Hong Kong	33
Mansa Musa, Malian Empire	400
Marshall Field	66
*Michael Bloomberg	42
*Michael Dell	19

Mohammed Al Amoudi, Saudi Arabia	10
Mark Zuckerberg, Facebook	42
Osman Ali Khan, Hyperabad	236
Richard Fitzalan, Earl of Arundel	118
Rockefeller	340
Rothschild	350
*Sheldon Adelson	26
Stephen Girard	105
Stephen Van Rensselaer	68
Sergey Brin, US	37
Tsar Nicholase II, Russia	300
Vladimir Potanin, Russia	15
Warren Buffett	60
William de Warenne, Normandy	146
William the Conquer, England	229
Jack Ma, China	26

*Pro-Israel

Millionaire US Politicians (Estimate in Millions)

Alan Grayson	D-FL 26
Bill Clinton D	68
Chellie Pingree, D-Maine	34
Chris Collins R-NY	22
Claire McCaskill D-Missouri	18
Darrell Issa, R-Calif	200
Diane Feinstein D-Calif	43
Frank Lautenberg, D	57
Gary Millier R-CA	32
Hillary Clinton D	38
James Renacci R-Ohio	28
Jared Polis D-Colo	73
Jay Rockefeller D-W. VA	108
John Delaney D-Md	111
John Kerry D	200
John McCain R-AZ	15
Johnny Isakson R-GA	8

Joseph Kennedy III D-Mass	20
Mark Warner D-VA	95
Michael McCaul R-Tex	200
Mitch McConnell R-KT	11
Nancy Pelosi D-CA	29
Richard Blumenthal D-Conn	80
Roger Williams R-TX	28
Scott Peters D-Calif	45
Suzan DelBene D-Wash	37
Trent Franks R-AZ	11

Susan Rice, ambassador to United Nations, and husband have holdings in Shell, European Union, and EIN, Italy, as well as business dealings in Iran.

From the above partial listing, the war on the wealthy is a farce. Approximately 47 percent of members of Congress are millionaires. According to the Center for Responsive Politics, Sheila Krumholz, "Few Americans enjoy the same financial cushion maintained by most members of Congress or the same access to market-altering information that could yield personal, financial gains." Government is a business that establishes relationships with big business, big labor, big pharma through lobbyists. The average worker in the United States earns around $40,000 per year, and many struggle just to make ends meet.

Anatomy of the One World Order

From Ancient Times to the Present

When we consider the anatomy or structure of an organization, it can be defined as having a head and members that form its body. The head of the one-world order is Satan; the members are the wealthy elite, government officials, heads of large corporations, organizations, and religious leaders.

The idea of a new world order is not new but began its formation when Satan rebelled against God. As the god of this world, he holds the title deed to the earth. In his quest for world domination, Satan established a hierarchy of thrones, principalities, and powers in high places. He assigned dark, foreboding, spiritual wickedness and demonic activity over nations. His generals would be the fallen angels who rebelled against God. His lieutenants would be hybrids, demons, evil spirits; and his minions, or foot soldiers, would be wicked people throughout the annals of history.

Spiritual beings are immortal and have maintained their influence over nations since the fall of Adam and Eve. Satan gave spiritual authority over the nations as in the king of Tyre or the king of Persia. Wicked humans controlled by Satan were given power to rule over the affairs of mankind. Humans are mortal and die, and they are replaced by an endless parade of disciples willing to carry out Satan's agenda.

After the great flood, people began to organize into tribal relationships through intermarriage and language or cultural similarities. They built dwellings, which grew into city complexes. They set up chiefs or leaders over large groups and developed rules for governing every aspect of life. One of the notable cities to come into existence after the flood was Babylon. It was wicked in the sight of the Lord. The Babylonian as well as the Assyrian and Egyptian Empires would forever leave an indelible mark identifying them as the forebearers of false religion and corrupt rulers. The spiritual influence over nations can be traced throughout history. We consider the book of Revelation as key to end-time events in predicting the final destruction of a spiritual Babylonian world system. Refer to chapter 8 to follow the growth of kingdoms.

During the captivity of Israel by the Babylonians, King Nebuchadnezzar had a dream of a large statue made of gold, silver, bronze, iron, and feet of iron and clay. Bible scholars agree that the image in the dream represented world empires that would come to power. The last world power represented by iron is Rome. After the division of Rome, we are left to deal with the implication of the feet of iron and clay. Ten toes will come together as a ten-region confederation of the one-world government, which will be under the control of a world leader:

> *And as the toes of the feet were part of iron and part of clay, so the kingdom shall be partly strong and partly broken. And whereas thou saw iron mixed with miry clay, they shall mingle themselves with the seed of men, but they shall not cleave one to another even as iron is not mixed with clay.* (Daniel 2:42)

This passage in Daniel has an ominous message. What is the meaning of "they will mingle themselves with the seed of men but they will not cleave one to another"? Some scholars think this may be the intermingling of celestial (they) and terrestrial (seed of men). In modern terminology, it refers to the alien hybrid breeding agenda, or transhumanism, as discussed in chapter 16. World scientists are obsessed with the creation of superhumans and have tapped into knowledge beyond our world. Daniel's passage may refer to unprecedented wickedness that divides all of humanity, and we are seeing the world divided over religion, power, and immorality. Perhaps the iron portion of the toes represents kingdoms or nations, and the clay represents people who are the citizens living in the ten regions. The laws of the nation will be a negative impact upon those citizens who hold to traditional values. An example of mingling but not cleaving could be the push to integrate Christianity with Islam. Or a nation pushes for the acceptance of the ungodly practice of homosexuality. Same-sex unions mingle one with another, but they are not biologically compatible.

The World Is Interconnected

Supporting the head of the one-world order is a conglomeration of elites. Through them, the world is woven together with old family money, which finances the growth of empires. Tried and proven methods over the centuries mostly through war and conflict achieve their end results.

From global carnage, the United Nation became the governing body for the world's elite who come together to make treaties and mandates. United Nations officials and the heads of nations mostly from wealthy societies control their nation's laws and social conduct. Each head has designated lower officials who will carry out the edicts of their masters to orchestrate events that serve the interests at the top. The United Nations functions as the hub in the wheel connecting all nations. Through this powerful organization, the one-world order agenda will be accomplished.

Calling for a New World Order

The new world order is the one-world order, one-world government, or global government. Its ancient roots reach as far back to the Babylonian Empire, and its branches are entangled throughout the world. Coming to the time of the Roman Empire, the concept of a one-world government was a constant, whose influence spread throughout the world as the revived Roman Empire conquered the world.

Following are examples of European influence that made way for the conception of a new world order in North and South America:

Leif Ericson is noted here as one of the earliest Europeans to make contact on the North American continent approximately five hundred years before Columbus landed in South America. Ericson was born in Iceland around AD 970–1020. He grew up as a Viking. He and his men traveled from Greenland to Norway. He converted to Christianity and was compelled to share the Gospel. In his travels, he landed in Vinland in the Canadian region, bringing with them European customs and ideology. Calvin Coolidge stated at the 1925 Minnesota State Fair to a crowd of a hundred thousand people that Leif Ericson had been the first European to discover America, and a bill was passed to recognize Leif Ericson day on October 9 (Wikipedia).

AD 1492, Christopher Columbus began his journey with the Santa Maria, Pinta, Nina ships landing in the Canary Islands. Then sailing into the Bahamas, he renamed it San

Salvador. He made his way to the East Indies and called the indigenous people "Indians." A year later, 1493, he landed on the Samana Penisula, and today it is called the Dominican Republic. His second voyage regrouped with seventeen ships landed in Guadeloupe. AD 1494, he arrived in Cuba, bringing to it the Spanish language and culture; from there he made his way to Jamaica. AD 1498, Columbus, with six ships, left Sanlucar, Spain landing in Trinidad then on to Venezuela. By AD 1500, he landed in Hispaniola. Columbus died in 1506, never having reached the North American continent (Wikipedia).

Amerigo Vespucci sailed to North America around 1500, and America may have been named after him. However, the indigenous people called their land by another name.

AD 1620, the title of Pilgrims is associated with those who settled in Plymouth, Massachusetts. They left England to escaped religious oppression.

AD 1607, people from England found their way to North America and called the region Jamestown, Virginia. Here they interacted with the Powhatan tribe. The two groups were initially friendly as the natives provided food for the new comers. Within a few years, the English settlers were at war with the native Americans. Many died on both sides. AD 1622, Indians massacred the settlers at Jamestown, Virginia. Around 1610–1619, indentured servants were transported from Britain and Portugal. The first documented Africans to arrive in Jamestown was around 1619, having been aboard a Portuguese slave ship. When they first arrived, they were treated as indentured servants able to work their way to freedom. Africans, Portuguese, Native Americans, and Europeans did intermingle, bearing children of mixed heritage.

Virginia fully enacted slavery between 1640–1660. Slave labor from Africa increased. AD 1705, Virginia came up with a slave code that defined people imported from nations that were not Christian to be sold to colonists, and this became the basis for "legal enslavement." Slaves were used for farming or harvesting cotton and tobacco in the South and to build infrastructure in the North. The Portuguese, Spanish, French, and British benefited from the slave trade in America.

AD 1750, Georgia authorized slavery to fill the void created by freeing of indentured servants.

By 1760, there were almost two hundred thousand African slaves in America. Some Africans were enslaved in Brazil to produce sugar cane; others were transported to other regions in South America. Britain held slaves but not by law. By 1860, approximately four million Africans were enslaved in America.

AD 1775-1783 the Revolutionary war pitted the British against the thirteen established colonies. President George Washington began to allude to a new world order. AD 1846, America began its official conquest against those we call Mexicans, which are related to those we call Indians. Colonialists captured territories of Texas, New Mexico, California, from people who had lived in those regions for a thousand years before Europeans invaded the land called America.

When Abraham Lincoln became president, the states were divided between the interests of the industrial North and the interests of the agricultural South. The North had paid labor, while the South utilized slave labor. As opposition to slavery grew through some efforts of the abolitionists and religious organizations such as the Quakers, it became entangled with the South pushing for succession and President Lincoln calling for all states to be part of the Union. The Civil War began in 1861. Emancipation Proclamation was effective January 1, 1863 (Wikipedia).

Influential people in Europe and leaders in the United States began calling for a new world order. The plans for the new world order had adapted within each generation, but its vision remained firm. The thread is connected from wealthy upper class through a global governing entity, such as the United Nations, to all nations. In recent times, we view various statements to measure the development of the new world order.

AD 1910, Theodore Roosevelt calls for a world federation to bring international peace and justice.

AD 1919, the independent Labor Party held a meeting in Switzerland with the Socialist International on world peace. The conference called on the League of Nations/United Nations should act as a global agency for world organization.

AD 1947, Prime Minister Winston Churchill called for the creation of an authoritative, all-powerful world order.

Republican presidential nominee Barry Goldwater said in 1964: "The union between politics and religion would be a catalyst for global government." He broke it down into four areas: politics, finance, intellectual, and ecclesiastical. "As the managers and creators of the new system, this power elite would rule the future of mankind." Taken from Goldwater's playbook, he warned political preachers that he would fight them every step of the way if they tried to dictate their religious ideas to all Americans in the name of conservatism. Today we have arrived at this plateau. Christian conservatives and their overall moral values are under attack.

A shout-out was noticed in a statement made by Nelson Rockefeller in the 1970s for a new world order. The mantra was taken up by President Jimmy Carter, stating, "We must replace balance of power politics with world order politics." President George H. W. Bush in the 1980s stated, "The time for a new world order has arrived." Bush followed up by creating a crisis in Iraq. The beginning of strong arming nations to comply to the new world order ideology has gained momentum. President Bush envisioned the specter of a Babylonian-like, one-world government. At his second inaugural address, President Bush said, "When our Masonic founders declared a new order of the ages, they were acting on an ancient hope that is meant to be fulfilled." Others who made public proclamation for a one-world order were Henry Kissinger, Joe Biden, Barack Obama, Pope Francis, Bill Clinton, and others.

January 16, 1991, George Bush—in his address to the nation regarding military action in the Persian Gulf—said, "We have before us the opportunity to forge for ourselves and for future generations a new world order ... a world where the rule of law, not the law of the jungle, governs the conduct of nations. When we are successful, and we will be, we have a real chance at this new world order." John Myers, contributor for *Personal Liberty Digest*, August 6, 2014, brings an analysis for "No World Order." Meyers said, "Bush presumed that the United Nations would help build a world utopia ruled by a benevolent government. Two decades later the new world order elites witness the fracturing of society at the regional, national, and international levels ... World mayhem is far beyond the control of a centralized world government."

Myers's assessment is correct in that the fires of mayhem are everywhere. However, the new world order declares that out of the chaos, they will bring order. It will not be a utopian world where peace and equality is enjoyed by all people but just the opposite. Population will be reduced through wars, disease, and famine. People will be undermined in their desire to carve out a subsistence to survive. Food, housing, and medical care will be regulated and distributed to the masses. The nation will become a police state for one social issue or another. The global elite will watch from their ivory towers or underground refuge sites as the world implodes. We can begin to call this global system the "one-world order."

AD 2014, Defense Secretary, Chuck Hagel states, "The world is experiencing historic defining times that will result in a new world order ... This is a time of global transformation, we are essentially seeing a new world order evolving and being built."

The Bushes, Obama, and the Clintons have been longtime globalists and proponents for the one-world order. There is the liberal left position and the conservative right position; however, both sides work together to bring about a one-world order.

Some people are looking for a neon sign announcing "The global regime is in place." The elite regime has been strategically positioned worldwide. What people fail to realize is the evidence of a global regime can been seen in false flag events. It has been the global elite's mode of operation to create and execute crisis events now tagged "false flag event," and it works toward accomplishing their agenda. One of the first false flag events was the 9-11 crisis. After years of analysis, it was discovered the US government had a hand in it with Saudi Arabia. The event exposed major government coverups, and many concerns went unanswered. The FBI has been known to create false flag situations in order to advance the agenda of the administration. They have also been involved in numerous assassinations. The 9-11 event may have been orchestrated to introduce new laws regarding national security, more regulations, such as the TSA at airports and to tighten up on individual freedom. Congress approved law September 2016 to allow families of the 9-11 victims to sue Saudi Arabia, but Obama promised to veto it.

Vladimir Putin said that he had evidence that 9-11 was an inside job and was going to release it after NATO and the United States staged a coup and false flag attack in the Ukraine. The eruption in the Ukraine and the Russian takeover of Crimea may have been instigated by a false flag attack by NATO and the United States in concert with their puppet regime in the Ukraine. The downing of the Malaysian airliner was blamed on Russia, but reports say two Ukrainian fighter jets shot down the airplane.

Following the 9–11 event, George Bush began the destabilization of the Middle East in Afghanistan and Iraq. The Obama administration continued to destabilize Egypt, Libya, and Syria, tagging it as the "Arab Spring."

Dave Hodges on the Common Sense show July 2016 provided a narrative for a false flag event.

He said the Dallas shooting, which killed five police officers, fit the description. There are patterns and profiles that are common in a false flag event.

1. It is preceded by a drill. *CBS* news reported in nearby Argyle, Texas, on June 29, 2016, that police, fire, and medical personnel practiced for a crisis at the North Texas High School.
2. A direct assassination involves a lone shooter. It will reveal the shooter had a manifesto and Military strategy; their residence will have bomb-making material, arsenal of guns and ammo. The *LA Times* reported Micha Johnson, the shooter, ex-military, had all of the above.
3. The false flag could have been coordinated to deflect attention away from the public regarding other issues. For instance, Hillary Clinton had been chastised by the FBI for her handling of e-mails. Clinton is known to be antipolice, anti-Secret Service, antimilitary.
4. The false flag event may result in a large-scale uprising that brings the nation closer to a police state under Marshall Law. The protest could be about racism, religion, sexual orientation, abortion, or violation of Second Amendment rights. Whatever the reason, it is incidental since all crisis situations will be to benefit the global elite.

The European Union did establish their goal to unify Europe by removing barriers between countries and jumping on the one-world order bandwagon. In an article for the *Sunday Times*, March 2009, Gordon Brown of the United Kingdom said, "It is time for all countries of the world to renounce protectionism and to participate in a new international system of banking and regulations to shape the twenty-first century as the first century of a truly global society."

H. G. Wells, *The New World Order*, said, "When the struggle seems to be drifting definitely toward a world social democracy, there may still be very great delays and disappointment before it becomes an efficient and beneficent world system. Countless people will hate the new world order and will die protesting against it, when we attempt to estimate its promise, we have to bear in mind the distress of a generation or so of malcontents, many of them quite gallant and graceful looking people."

As Christians watching these end-time events unfold, we must always remember our God is sovereign, still in control, and we definitely count on his intervention into the affairs of mankind. Satan's goal for world domination has been thwarted by God many times over. This disruption allows the righteous some form of a level playing field. However, prophecy tells us these things must be fulfilled.

Achieving a One-World Order

It is through the skill of deception that Satan and his minions deceive the masses to bring about his global kingdom.

Brandon Smith, contributor, *Personal Liberty Digest* states, "Wars and economic collapse are instigated for the purpose of achieving psychological transformation. This is the fastest method to achieve full spectrum change in a society's principles and loyalties. War and economic manipulation allows for the trampling of freedoms, the accumulation of wealth and political authority, destabilization of the average person's means of survival [to reduce population] and the desperation of the population leading to the centralization of control in the name of safety and security."

Zbigniew Brzezinski said, "The nation state is gradually yielding its sovereignty ... Further progress will require greater American sacrifices, more intensive efforts to shape a new world monetary structure will have to be undertaken with some consequent risk to the present relatively favorable American position." The greater sacrifice is to die fighting for one's country. Troops are conditioned to believe they are fighting for their freedom against terrorism. With this hype and a pat on the back, they are sent to foreign countries to put down terrorism and establish democracy. The new world order leaders do not want democracy; they want world domination. "No nation is favored and all sovereignty is eliminated. Therein citizens must relinquish individual freedom, independence and self-reliance under the guise that their sacrifice is required so that victory can be achieved."

Labels and titles are often designed to deceive. Wars are named as a propaganda ploy, which in turn conditions the mind-set. For instance, the war in Iraq was titled Desert Storm for the purpose of destroying weapons of mass destruction. The war in Vietnam was to upend communism. Cuban missile crisis was referred to as the Bay of Pigs. The Civil War was fought somewhat for the freedom of slaves, but the greater conflict was the South versus the North for territory. The conflicts throughout the Middle East were titled the Arab Spring for the promotion of democracy. Economic crises are given titles or catchphrases, such as TARP, bailout, economic downturn, QE, quantitative easing. Abortion is promoted as prochoice.

Haile Selassie, religious leader of Ethiopia, said, "Throughout history, it has been the inaction of those who could have acted; the indifference of those who should have known better; the silence of the voice of justice when it mattered most that has made it possible for evil to triumph." This timeless quote can be applied to the present day as we see the inactions of political leaders sworn to protect the people and the constitution. They turn a blind eye and are indifferent to the suffering of the people. The justice system is no longer equitable and has turned away from established principles of the law.

The emerging leadership of the NWO may be in concert with Russia, Germany, United States, and others who will influence nations through war, disease, economics, and finance. *Brandon Smith, Personal Liberty Digest,* analyzes the conflict between Russia and the United States as "pandering to the media to appear as enemies." Both United States and Russia deal with global banks, borrowing billions. Russia and United States both have a relationship with Goldman Sachs.

Paul McGuire, *News With Views*, provides an insightful overview on the new world order agenda. "Year 2013 will bring in a convergence of events, some will be man-manufactured crisis. The global elite dominate world events. Through the combined mind-set came forth the Illuminati, from which we can trace its footprint through symbolism seen throughout the world. Sir Francis Bacon, a Rosicrucian, envisioned America as the new Atlantis and head of the new world order before 1776."

In summary, the one-world order is achieved as follows:

- Deception and propaganda to control the masses
- Manufacture crisis for military intervention
- Creating economic instability
- Removing individual freedoms
- Creating a welfare state
- Reducing population through illness, toxic environment, criminal violence, terrorism, war, abortion
- Removing national sovereignty

The Georgia Guide Stones

We commonly hear the term "it is written in stone," and the Georgia Guide Stones stand as a monument to the testament of the new world order agenda. The Georgia Guide Stones, created in 1979–'80, proclaim that the global population should be five hundred million, and nations should resolve their disputes in a world court. The message on the stele is in Egyptian hieroglyphics, Babylonia, Greek, Sanskrit, English, Spanish, Swahili, Hindi, Hebrew, Arabic, Chinese, and Russian. The ten principles engraved on the stones are following:

- Maintain humanity under five hundred million in perpetual balance with nature.
- Guide reproduction wisely, improving fitness and diversity.
- Unite humanity with a living new language.
- Rule passion, faith, tradition, and all things with tempered reason.
- Protect people and nations with fair laws and just courts.
- Let all nations rule internally, resolving external disputes in a world court.
- Avoid petty laws and useless officials.
- Balance personal rights with social duties.
- Prize truth, beauty, love, seeking harmony with the infinite.
- Be not a cancer on the earth; leave room for nature.

The Creator of the guide stones used the name RC Christian. Those he contracted to cut and engrave the stones were Masons. Adjacent to the upright guide stones is a tablet lying ground level, which gives detail about the dimensions, language, weight, astronomical features, and states a time capsule is buried beneath. In one of the squares, a message says, "Let these be guide stones to an Age of Reason." This monument and its testament may appear benign to the uninformed, but to the enlightened its message may lean toward the occult, new age, green religion, and plans for world domination. When we discuss the United Nations' Agenda 21 Sustainability goals, you will see it blends with the Georgia Guide Stone sentiments.

Forms of Government

The United Nations is the overseer of nations, and it determines how nations will blend with the one-world order agenda. Heads of nations establish a form to govern their people and control the affairs of their nation. Following, we provide examples of forms of government.

After the flood, humans governed themselves within a family structure. As civilizations increased, the ruling class moved to the top of the pyramid, making decisions for others. Throughout the ages, mankind set up some form of government to rule over the people.

Regardless of the type of government control, it seems that the elite become the wealthy rulers at the expense and suffering of others.

A monarchy is ruled by one person for an indeterminate period. Their title could be king, queen, prince, emperor, Caesar, dictator, or the title of a religious figure head. History indicates the majority of rulers were corrupt and took the wealth of the people for themselves.

Dictatorship maintains control over people through intimidation, fear, warfare, and bloodshed. Opponents are eliminated. Atheism is their religion. All other beliefs are oppressed. The people subsist in meagerness and poverty. Rulers maintain their wealth and power by having control over military. Another form of dictatorship is Imperialism as was practiced in Japan.

Marxism—Karl Marx promoted "**change.**" Nelson Mandela was labeled a Marxist. He wanted to use force to overthrow the apartheid South Africa government. Zbigniew Brzezinski is quoted: "Marxism represents a further vital and creative stage in the maturing of man's universal vision. Marxism is simultaneously a victory of the external, active man over the inner, passive man and a victory of reason over belief." Some records estimate Marx killed ninety million people.

Communism is a form of government that prescribes to dictator leadership, such as seen in the USSR, North Korea, China, Vietnam, and Cuba. Propaganda sells itself as providing utopia for the people, equality, fair distribution of goods, and services can only be provided by the wisdom of the government to manage resources and all aspects of life. Russia governed by way of the communist agenda. The Bolshevik Revolution was orchestrated by the global elite pitting the ideologies of socialism and communism against each other. North Korea calls itself a Democratic Republic.

Former communist Mike Vanderboegh said that communism has a public face and tells the masses lies that have a kernel of truth. The next level is not seen by the public, referred to as the private core; and then there is the secret level where plans for the masses are developed. Vanderboegh spoke of the relationship Obama had with Frank Marshall Davis and that Obama is the public face of socialism.

Socialism promotes dependence on government in health care, welfare, food stamps, housing projects, federally funded education, and disarming citizens. It stymies free market and limits economic growth. Fascism is similar to Socialism and was a form of government under Mussolini of Italy.

Brandon Smith, contributor for *Personal Liberty Digest*, states, "Marxism and Socialism are simply philosophical reworkings of the collectivist ideology. Collectivism places the needs of the group or society over the freedoms and prosperity of the individual. Globalists proclaim a benevolent desire to save humanity from itself through the use of collectivist concepts such as interdependency which removes the self-reliance of individuals, sovereign communities, nations and making them subservient to the machinations of a complex supply chain dominated by a central authority." Former president Bill Clinton called for collectivism. "This central authority is a conglomeration or network of global dictates over government, banking, economy, health, etc."

National Socialism—Germany was classified as a national socialist government under a dictator. Hitler began his rise on the theme of "**change**." He introduced NAZI, short for National Socialist German's Worker Party, as an ideology. The German government began to monitor all citizen activity. They created a welfare state by offering entitlements in education, housing, food. Soon the subsidies became very expensive for the government, and they instituted taxation. The government wanted to demote the wealthy and create class warfare between rich and poor. Soon Germany decided to have a government-controlled health care system. Finally, the government decided to have all gun owners register their firearms, and finally, the government decided to ban ownership of firearms. By the time Hitler decided to kill Jews, Christians, disabled, Gypsies, and the opposition, the people could not defend themselves because the government had taken their weapons. There were American and European interests who funded Hitler's regime, gave refuge to Nazi scientists and other notables, and today, America seems to have taken a page out of Hitler's playbook.

Democratic Socialism—the United States was formed as a federal republic. It began with the freedom to practice one's religious beliefs without interference from the government. It resolved that all men are created equal and have the right to live in peace and freedom. It is based upon the electorate of the people, and its representatives serve for the good of the commonwealth. Within the republic, those with liberal and progressive views as well as those maintaining conservative and traditional views should be objectively respected by the government. When the government caters to one opinion more than another, it becomes unbalanced and loses objectivity. US citizens have increased their dependence on government entitlements and subsidies. The United States now functions as a socialist democracy. If the government is not for the people and by the people, it is none other than an oligarchy operating as a tyrannical governmental system.

The United Nations

The United Nations, formerly the League of Nations, is a world-governing seat. Currently, the United Nations is the center or meeting place that has given birth to a global agenda. Behind closed doors, secret meetings are held to weave their initiatives through international organizations. The seat of the United Nations is headquartered in New York, and this aligns it with the seat of the world leader in Washington, DC. Draw a parallel line from New York to Rome, and it connects with the seat of the universal religion, the Vatican.

Each location in common displays pagan and occult symbolism. A statue of Zeus dominates the main lobby entrance of the United Nations, therein honoring a pagan deity; and in the United Nations' meditation area, the group acknowledges the supreme god of the world. There are no emblems of Judaism or Christianity displayed within its walls. In New York, the Statue of Liberty stands as a testament to the Roman goddess Libertas. In Rome, a towering obelisk stands in Saint Peter's square, representative of Egyptian paganism.

The seat of spiritual Babylon is America. In the book of Revelation, Babylon the Great is characterized as a system of idolatry, blasphemes, abominations, and fornication with the nations of the world who have symbolically drunk from the harlot's cup of abominations.

Leaders occupying these global seats take on a persona or role, such as the pope is **father** god on earth and the world's spiritual leader. United Nations' secretary general could represent the head of a one-world government and its supreme leader, the **son** of perdition. All the world has pledged allegiance to a global initiative, the one-world order, and its **bible** is the United Nations Agenda 21 Sustainability Program. In concert, their religion is the **green god,** and Mother Earth is their savior. The enemy of Mother Earth is seven billion people—depleting earth's natural resources, polluting the environment, the cause of global warming, and must be dealt with.

The United Nations has many committees, and one is the Council of Elders, made up of independent globalists. Boutros Boutros Ghali served as sectary general of United Nations from 1992 to 1996, raised in a Coptic Christian family in Egypt. Kofi Annan, born in Ghana, attended a Methodist school and served as secretary general from 1997 to 2007. Current Secretary General Ban Ki-moon was born in Korea and has no religious affiliation. The secretary general is the United Nations' chief administrative officer, duly elected by the assembly with approval of the Security Council, but he has little independent power. The United Nations announced, October 2016, the appointment of Antonia Guterres of Portugal to be the next secretary.

US president Obama presided over a meeting in 2010 of the United Nations Security Council. The council oversees the United Nations military forces, which are a combination of soldiers from various nations and is the only United Nations council that can take decisive actions. First time a US president had addressed this committee. What does it mean symbolically? In Revelation, we see the rider on the white horse carrying a bow and wearing a crown signifying authority. It is the unveiling of the one-world supreme leader, a man with the power of universal military might and having the authority as leader of the one-world order. Daniel 8:24, "*And his power will be mighty but not by his own power …*"

President Obama on September 27, 2015, signed over the sovereignty of the United States to the United Nations in a declaration made in concert with the United Nations' Open Government Steering Committee for the implementation of the 2030 agenda for sustainable development (same as Agenda 21). On paper, the United States became a de facto puppet state of the United Nations (Dave Hodges, *The Common Sense Show*, June 6, 2016).

The United States gives the United Nations an equivalent of money totaling the combined payments from 180 nations annually. The United States is a permanent member, giving it power and leverage within the United Nations. The other four permanent members are Russia, China, Britain, and France. These five have ability to cast vetoes. For instance, Russia is allied with Syria and vetoes any effort to pass resolutions against Syria. Germany and other nations are pushing for permanent status. Some prophecy watchers believe an increase from five to ten members would represent the ten-region confederation. We do not believe this applies since the world has already been divided into its ten regions by the one-world order. For example, Germany, Britain, and France would be lumped together within the European region.

Of the total number of nations participating in the United Nations (193), the majority are Arab and Islamic factions. China, Russia, and the European Union are most likely to vote with the Arab and Islamic representatives. Israel virtually stands alone, with only the support of the United States, Canada, and a few others.

Members and associates of the United Nations have a common mind-set, which is expressed in the United Nations Agenda 21 goals. Some of its notable members are Mikhail Gorbachev, born 1931, in the former USSR and member of Club of Rome. Gorbachev is credited with developing the ten commandments of the new world order.

Ted Turner, born 1938 in Ohio, is known for his ownership of CNN and Turner Broadcasting System, TBS. The media mogul would condone monitoring of citizens by way of the Internet, cell phones, GPS, and smart TVs. He would support media bias and propaganda. He contributed one billion to United Nations and did pay to play. As of 2011, it is rumored that Turner was the largest land owner in United States, where he cultivates bison for his Ted's Montana Grill chain. Turner said that "Americans should have no more than two children, Christians are Jesus freaks, and prolifers are bozos." The liberal mind-set blames Christian, Jews, and conservatives for the world's social problems.

The United Nations Agenda 21 places importance on climate change and the environment, which gave rise to its "Green Religion" ideology. President Obama, a globalist, in his appeal to many interest groups has gotten on the climate change bandwagon along with the Vatican. Obama stated that climate change was a threat to national security. The Vatican believes there is a differential in sharing the earth's resources between the poor and the wealthy, and he calls for the removal of income inequality. The pope did not suggest that the wealth of the Vatican be more evenly distributed to the poor.

Historically, the United Nations has done some good things throughout the world, such as working to end poverty and hunger. The United Nations has helped in providing clean water sources. On the downside, the United Nations claims to have procured 2.71 billion doses of vaccines for a hundred countries in 2014. Vaccines are toxic cocktails of viruses, cancer cells, and human and animal DNA and have detrimental side effects as mentioned in chapter 16. The United Nations has suffered some scandals. Peacekeepers transmitted cholera into Haiti, killing 8,500 people. It was alleged that United Nations peacekeepers and civilians were entangled in sexual child abuse scandals. The United Nations seems quiet on child abuse, rape, and torture going on in Afghanistan.

The United Nations is interconnected to approximately fifteen autonomous agencies, various commissions, and bodies—which led to inefficiency and inaction resulting in no decisions to move forward on certain items. Even if there is gridlock, the United Nations' Agenda 21 will move forward.

United Nations' Agenda 21 Sustainability Program

Six, six, six—similar to a patch work quilt, the United Nations has six primary areas of interest, which set the tone for the rest of the world:

(1) Religion
(2) Population control
(3) Military
(4) Individual freedom versus global citizenship
(5) Environment
(6) Economy

These categories form the foundation for the United Nations's Agenda 21. The plan was first birthed in Rio de Janeiro, Brazil, at the Earth Summit, 1993. The subject of that gathering was United Nations Conference on Environment and Development, UNCED. This would become the framework for the end-time global government reality. Over the years, the United Nations has made adjustments to its goals. The revamped plan was unveiled September 25–27, 2015, at the United Nations' Sustainable Development Summit. During this time frame, many notables did address the conference, including Pope Francis. The emphasis will be on the environment because most human activity is tied into the environment. Topics will include climate change, economics, education, and gender equality. United Nations spokesperson stated, "We commit ourselves to working tirelessly for the full implementation by 2030." This being said, Agenda 21 is also referred to as Agenda 30.

The United Nations' leadership in cooperation with the global elite will ensure the goals are received and implemented currently by each representative nation. Each nation will shape their domestic policies for a common global good and global partnership. The theme is, "Think globally, act locally."

Maurice Strong, official of UNCED, a member of International Institute for Sustainable Development, IISD, explains: "UNCED's environmental initiative was set up as a global initiative to induce global action. By strengthening international law, nations would be forced to comply with initiatives. This creates a path toward global citizenship, which is the first step toward global governance."

The above sentiment could be interpreted as follows:

- Government leaders or civil organizations introduce "social change." Change is needed to face a global crisis (real or perceived), which will bring about global transformation. Today's terminology for transformation may be referred to as inciting a crisis called "false flags."
- The international communities through the United Nations are already networking with each other calling for "action." Example of "action" would be polarizing the world toward the Syrian conflict, Russian intervention in the Ukraine, ISIS, nuclear Iran, or the Israel and Palestinian conflict.
- After the players deliberate, they come up with a social contract, such as a treaty, accord, or sanction. Case in point would be sanctions placed against Iran for their nuclear goals. Iran is a nation of radical hardliners, and they fight against their forceful inclusion in a global agenda, but come they must.
- Problems within a nation would require an action plan with federal executives and state administrators to pressure departments or agencies into implementing the agenda. Regulations are created and enforced through lobbying, lawsuits, political and media campaigns. Funding is released for support of projects many times without a clear understanding of the hidden agenda within legislation. Big corporations and pharmaceutical companies cooperate with federal agencies. One such powerful corporation is Monsanto, a leader in pushing GMO crops and pesticides worldwide. The federal government and Monsanto have a close relationship, and the company is allowed not to alert consumers through labeling that their products may be detrimental to health.
- Pharmaceutical companies are pushing vaccines, which cause major health issues, and federal government has turned a blind eye. Some states are forcing parents to vaccinate children. The EPA is regulating every blade of grass and stream of water, yet it has caused a major toxic spill in a river. Local government soon mirrors federal government directives, which act as the unseen driving force for global change.

- Mark Edward Vande Pol, former Agenda 21 planner for Santa Cruz County, United States, understands this global to local regulatory reality: "You will never see it. You will never vote on it. No matter which path they use, the agencies can pen new regulations under threat of lawsuit, and down the pipe it comes, enforceable administrative rules without legislation." In America, there are many examples—such as, President Obama pushing for universal health care in spite of state opposition, or President Obama pushing executive orders without Senate or Congressional approval.
- Nations report back to the United Nations on their successes and challenges. After reviews and reports, national leaders are required to "pull the load and pay our fair share." America is in debt, yet the United States has pledged to give Africa seven billion for their energy initiatives. Islamic radical nations are receiving billions in US aid for working on "democratic" policies. Obama pledges millions to Planned Parenthood to continue performing abortions because population reduction is a United Nations initiative.

Nations committed to United Nations Agenda 21 have presented their nations like an open book, revealing every aspect of life, such as consumption patterns, health care, poverty, energy, land development, air quality, biological diversity, human population levels, women, children, hazardous waste, environments in the mountains, desert, and urban areas, science and technology, trade unions, agriculture, transportation, education, citizenship, capacity building, financial mechanism, and natural resources reduction.

Developed nations have pledged their finances to the developing nations. United States was required to give $600 billion per year to the United Nations for general Agenda 21 Sustainability Programs and an additional $125 billion per year in technical and economic assistance to other developing nations. This is similar to carbon credits. Developed nations create more carbon output than third world nations. China may be the worst polluter on the planet and may be ignoring the agreement regarding carbon credits. Carbon credits are trading on the stock market (Hope for the World, Natural News, Personal Liberty Digest each source contributed data regarding Agenda 21.)

The United Nations has six primary goals within their Agenda 21 Sustainability program.

(1) Religion

The United Nations is a secular organization and foremost to lead the way for the establishment of Satan's kingdom on earth in cooperation with a one-world religious leader. The Vatican is onboard with developing a one-world religion. The apostate church may fly the United Nations flag, American flag or Christian flag over churches signaling they are inclusive.

May 2014, the Vatican's Pontifical Academies of Science and Social Science convened a four-day workshop on sustainable development as a follow-up on the 2012 United Nations Rio+20 Summit. They called the workshop *Sustainable Humanity, Sustainable Nature: Our Responsibility.* It discussed environment, poverty, food, science, and technology. The emphasis was made on "humanity's interchanges with nature through a triplet of fundamental but interrelated human needs … they seek various pathways that both serve those needs and reveal constraints on nature's ability to meet them. The final statement called for global cooperation to meet sustainable development goals and humanity's relationship with nature need to be undertaken by cooperative, collective action at all levels—federal, regional, and global" ("Hope for the World Update," summer 2014).

It is no secret that the United Nations is anti-Semitic. The United Nations, along with many nations, call for the destruction of Israel. The United Nations canceled an Israeli exhibit documenting 3,500 years of Jewish history in the holy land so as not to give credence to the rightful existence of Israel. Just in this vein, the United Nations appears to be one sided and is not objective or equitable toward Israel. United Nations representative Ann Dismorr posed with a map devoid of any trace of the State of Israel. United Nations approved the Iran nuclear deal, a direct threat to Israel. United Nations supports the claim of Palestinian refugees through their UNRWA, United Nations Relief and Works Agency, a German funded program operating in Lebanon (*Prophecy Today*, May 2013, Jimmy DeYoung).

The outgoing Obama administration delivered a death blow to Israel end of 2016 by abstaining in favor of dividing Israel by claiming the building of settlements is illegal. There has been little outcry from the United Nations in regard to Islamic terrorist killing Christians or Jews.

(2) Population Control

Under this category, the United Nations agenda is to end poverty and hunger, achieve food security, improve nutrition, promote sustainable agriculture, ensure healthy lives, promote well-being, and empower women and girls. Cities should be structured as human-settlements safe, resilient, and ensure sustainable consumption and production patterns. United Nations items 1, 2, 3, 5, 11, 12.

In general, the United Nations Agenda 21 Sustainable Development in its forty-chapter manifesto states, "The growth of world population increases severe stress on life-supporting capacities of our planet and calls for measures to bring about a demographic transition. We clarify their position: take action to reduce the population because humans are the problem, using up resources and destroying goddess Gaia.

Polluted Cities Versus Fresh Air, Springwater, and Organic Food

A relocation mandate would be to move people out of rural and suburban areas into urban settlements. Is this goal something we can observe as occurring? Situations exist wherein the government is threatening land owners with fines, trumped-up regulations, and closing down farms. The government chokes off their ability to be self-sufficient, grow food, catch rainwater, and have cows and chickens. The 2015 chicken virus called for the slaughter of millions of chickens and could have been introduced by the government in order to increase hardship for farmers. The Department of Agriculture may hassle farmers regarding grazing rights, producing organic non-GMO food or raw milk, and strong-arming them to use toxic pesticides. The EPA is diligently working to control all sources of water. Farmers may be fined for watering their crops or catching rainwater. High levels of radiation are drifting into the US atmosphere from Japan, and not a word is mentioned by the Obama administration.

Through the United Nations' alliance for food security and nutrition, the Obama administration has pledged $10 billion in commitments for the international community. Africa has received $1.8 billion to date to end hunger in Africa. People are still hungry and suffering in Africa because the money most likely ends up in the pockets of corrupt government, military, and terrorist groups.

Africa is being used to test the smart grid technology. This may be to develop new energy sources. Africa has received $7 billion from the Obama administration. What happened to Obama's commitment to cleaner energy sources in the United States? The US infrastructure is crumbling.

City Life

Tent cities growing in parks; camps established in abandoned industrial sites, near railroads; and people living under bridges are a few areas where hundreds of homeless people call home. Most cities within the United States have to deal with homeless people living in squalor. How can one of the most influential and wealthy nations in the world condone children, women, men, veterans, disabled, sick, and mentally challenged people living in the street? Case in point—an area in Seattle called the Jungle, where approximately four hundred people are forced to live because of their circumstances due to unemployment, little or no income, addiction, and more. The Jungle is a three-mile stretch under Interstate 5. It has a high crime rate of murder, violence, drugs, and rape. Police and fire personnel do not usually go into this region. Fire Chief Harold Scoggins said, "You step in there, and it's like you are not even in the US." Some politicians want to build an eight-thousand-foot fence to contain the people at a cost of one million dollars (no plans to build low-income housing.) The mayor, Edward B. Murray, declares a state of emergency regarding homelessness and is setting aside a few areas for tent camps overseen by Social Services and government rules of conduct.

Urban settlements are not new if we recall housing projects in low-income districts. Today we have FEMA trailers, which have been provided for families who lost everything due to a natural disaster. The Red Cross would direct people to shelters, offering a sense of safety and well-being. Certainly, a natural catastrophe—man-made or otherwise, causing the loss of life and property—would steer people into refugee centers or government-established FEMA camps.

Currently, there are no reports that people live in the FEMA camps at this time. We could speculate that these camps could become vital during a deadly epidemic outbreak where people seek medical assistance and then would be quarantined in these centers.

If the government declares martial law because of a terror attack or threat of war, people may be moved into urban settlements, "bomb shelters," or FEMA camps. Gun owners could not bring their guns to the gun-free zone. Oversight would be carried out by the military, Department of Homeland Security, Internal Revenue Service, Affordable Care Act, Federal Emergency Management, National Security Administration, Environmental Protection Agency, and an endless list of other government departments.

In these situations, people become compliant and dependent. For the collected good, the government will provide the necessary entitlements, such as subsidized housing, food stamps, welfare, and unemployment compensation. The government oversight of health care is a nightmare. The cost of affordable prescription drugs is a thing of the past. When the entitlements are exhausted, people will be systematically eliminated, beginning with their inability to afford medication.

Under the United Nations' global health initiative, the United States has pledged to assist thirty countries to achieve their targets of the global health security agenda all working together to prevent, detect, and respond to infectious disease threats. This means the United Nations will enforce worldwide vaccinations. Bill Gates is gleefully seen holding a needle and vial of vaccine.

The country of Venezuela, once oil rich, is now in crisis due to a drop in oil prices having a severe impact on its economy. Inflation is 140–200 percent. Import and exports are down. The government devalued its currency. The government operates on socialistic policies, wherein all areas of life are controlled by the government. Under President Nicolas Maduro, the government-controlled news media keeps the people in the dark, and they are not fully aware of their dire situation. The media is not allowed to take pictures of the empty grocery shelves. The people are starving. State-run grocery stores have no food. People wait in long lines. The military rations the food.

China is well ahead of creating urban dwelling. They have built entire cities where no one currently resides. China plans to relocate 250 million people from rural regions into the urban centers by 2026 (Kai Caemmerer, photographer, *Unborn Cities*).

Chorale and Tag Them

The global regime has the whole world in turmoil. We can see the flight of people from terrorism and danger driving them to seek refuge in other nations. The call for immigration regulations and amnesty may be another method to get people documented, registered, vaccinated, implanted with an ID chip, and systematically eliminated. Millions of illegals will overload the national entitlement system. Keep in mind, United States, Mexico, and Canada are to be one region. The UNHCR, or United Nations High Commission for Refugees, has a goal to ID and register all humans by 2030. To channel all this data, United Nations partnered with Accenture to implement biometric ID system for storage and retrieval in a facility in Geneva.

The United States has poor border security, and the influx of immigrants is being approved for citizenship in order to vote in the presidential election. Fox News reported, September 22, 2016, that eight hundred to a thousand immigrants identified for deportation were suddenly approved for citizenship. Federal Immigration Department employees were working overtime to swear in as many new citizen voters before the November election. This action was confirmed in an e-mail to Obama and disclosed to Fox News by Republican Senator Ron Johnson of Wisconsin.

Resources for the Elite

Using the above scenarios, millions of people can be channeled into closer proximity to government facilities for extermination similar to the Nazi method. The globalists have propagandized the idea that the earth is overpopulated. Well-known people, such as Jacque Cousteu, believe depopulation is necessary for sustainable development. The goal is to reduce the population to conserve on natural resources, reduce carbon dioxide emissions, and rid the world of useless eaters and inferior humans. An uptick in criminal activity fast-forward their goal to rid the world of undesirables. Soon the prison overload will be decreased by "natural" death in order to harvest organs; prisoners could be used for experimentation and implanted with mind-control device to carry out some action against unsuspecting civilians.

Eliminate the Middle Class

This United Nations category dictates that every aspect of life will be monitored and controlled by global organizations and national administration. According to the elite, only the superior class of people should rule the population—such as the rich, intelligent, famous, and powerful. Unfortunately, the masses have been deceived by the globalists who have no conscience and have constructed an entire system to strip man, woman, and child of their God-given rights to dwell in the land peacefully and to prosper. For appearances, the United Nations promotes reducing inequality by targeting the middle class. Across America, large corporations are downsizing, and middle management personnel are laid off. These represent our middle class workers. Another way to confiscate wealth is through higher taxes, manipulating stocks, and depleting retirement plans. These actions will create a two-class system: the wealthy and the poor. The poor will be dependent on the government to survive.

Abortion Is a Civil Right

Abortion remains a popular means to reduce future population growth. Regulating reproductive rights is carried out through abortion, sterilization, and homosexuality to limit the natural method of procreation. Planned Parenthood is a murder industry supported by taxpayer money. It provides a plentiful harvest of baby parts and tissue for other purposes. The so-called empowerment of females means to continue with the right to murder the unborn politely called prochoice, or women's health. Abortionists are obsessed with the right of the woman over her body and her right to end her child's life.

Obama appointed John Holdren as his director of Science and Technology Policy. Holdren wrote in 1977 that he favors forcing women to abort; sterilization by putting infertility drugs in public drinking water or food; unmarried women should have babies taken and given to certified couples; welfare recipients or prisoners should have forced abortions and sterilizations; and finally, Holdren declares that a transnational "planetary regime" should assume control of the global economy and also dictate the most intimate details of Americans' lives using an armed international police force.

China is saluted for its one-child policy, which reduces population growth. David Lykken—a professor, psychological scientist, and behavioral geneticist—approved of China's method of population control. He said sterilization should begin in the inner cities by targeting dysfunctional families on welfare and have them sterilized.

Tolerance for Everyone

Pedophiles prey upon children, as in the North American Man Boy Love Association. These people are pushing to legalize sex with children. This depravity is not new upon the earth. It has been widely reported that children who are victims of sexual abuse are psychologically and physically damaged for life. Many commit suicide or become criminals. Child pornography is a thriving industry.

The federal government encourages LGBT lifestyle be introduced in elementary school and elsewhere. Under the United Nations gender equality, gender differences will be eliminated. These positions are castrating masculinity and casting males in roles as effeminate weaklings. The feminine mystique is not toward family, motherhood but are cast as seductive characters to be disrespected and sexually exploited. This combination limits reproduction and decreases natural birth

Mercy Killing

The legalization of euthanasia, or assisted suicide, is growing in popularity. The globalists would find this an acceptable method toward depopulation as it would target the sick, old, and disabled to be put to death painlessly.

Vaccinations are Unhealthy

Many of us contracted measles, mumps, chicken pox, and we suffered until it ran its course. No one died from these viruses. The compositions of modern vaccinations are different than they were fifty years ago. They are a composition of human and animal DNA as well as unimaginable toxins, and viruses, resulting in many health disorders. Children as young as one month have been injected with MMR, mumps, measles, rubella toxic cocktail and died. One side effect is autism, and it is treated with antipsychotic drugs, and 80 percent of children vaccinated with MMR came down with mumps and measles. As indicated, vaccinations can be debilitating and deadly. They can be harnessed as chemical weapons.

Centers for Disease Control posted on their official fact sheet that ninety-eight million doses of polio vaccine contained a cancer-causing virus (Simian Virus 40—SV40). This virus was first discovered in monkeys in 1960 and then was combined with polio virus. These various injectable cocktails have been known to cause leukemia, lung cancer, bone cancer, nonhodgkin lymphoma. National Institute of Health states, SV40 is directly linked to causing tumor formation.

In some individuals, the vaccination caused seizures and paralysis like polio, called nonpolio acute flaccid paralysis, which is twice as deadly as polio. Over forty-seven thousand cases reported.

Flu vaccines are widely promoted by big pharma and have little or no effect on the virus but increases the risk of death and other side effects.

Dr. David Witt, infectious disease specialist at San Rafael, California, Kaiser Permanente Medical Center reported in 2012 that children vaccinated against whooping cough come down with this illness more than unvaccinated children. The DTP, diphtheria, tetanus, pertussis vaccine caused infant mortality and brain inflammation.

Drugs for Everything

Big pharma came up with Gadasil for teens to vaccinate against HPV and in turn is causing serious side effects, fainting, and coma. Billions in taxpayer money is given to push vaccines.

UNICEF, WHO, and Kenya Health Ministry targeted 2.3 million females between the ages of fourteen and forty-nine to be vaccinated with tetanus virus laced with HCG, Human Choronic Gonadotrophn, which causes sterilization, spontaneous abortion, and infertility. Dr. Muhame Ngare, Mercy Medical Center, sent samples of the vaccine to labs in South Africa, which confirmed HCG was present. He said, "This is a coordinated forceful population control, mass sterilization exercise." The Kenyan government aligns itself with the United Nations (*Natural News*, November 2014, Jennifer Lilley; additional details on vaccinations are in chapter 16).

UNICEF, WHO, and the Bill Gates Foundation push various types of vaccinations to third world nations. This is another ploy to reduce the global population. The propaganda hype is used to promote mass vaccinations, pay lobbyists, and attack whistle-blowers who dare expose their real intentions. Big pharma profits come in around $25 billion just for vaccines. Big pharma corporations use TV media to promote drugs. Prescription drugs are profitable, and big pharma provides a list of the side effects that can be experienced by using the various medication.

(3) Global Military

The United Nations has so-called peacekeepers comprised of a broad base of soldiers from most nations infiltrating most other nations. Some US soldiers who swore allegiance to protect the United States have been forced to wear the United Nations insignia. Those who protest are court martialed. The United States has sworn its allegiance to the United Nations in money, land use, and cooperation. US officials will bypass the Constitution and Bill of Rights to comply with United Nations dictates. US military presence is established in the majority of nations, especially after war. Other nations that commit troops to the United Nations, such as Bosnia, has commissioned twenty thousand soldiers to serve. NATO was established so that member nations could supply military and direct their efforts where needed. At this time, NATO seems to be ineffective in response to many uprising worldwide. The European Union has been discussing the possibility of forming a military, which would be in conflict with NATO. The world is in turmoil, yet we do not see a meaningful insurgence by the United Nations or even if they have military wherewithal to put down terrorism.

Local Police

Everything on a global level will be translated to the national, state and city levels.

Communities would be under surveillance, creating an increase in police or military presence at times overstepping the rights of the citizens. Police are being provided with military-grade weapons and vehicles. Electric multifunctional handcuffs may soon be used by police. The *Natural News* site reported that the handcuffs are programmed to give electric shocks, chemical injections, and can be remotely controlled.

The United Nations and the Obama administration have agreed to allow the DOJ to nationalize the police force in the aftermath of police killing black criminals. This could be the reason why enforcement agencies have not called for deterrent measures to stymie the increase in black-on-black crimes or crimes committed by blacks in general. The majority of police try to do their jobs, and some police incidents occur resulting in black criminals being killed. Police actions are classified as overreach, brutality, or racism. Under a consent decree, the civil rights division of the DOJ will file lawsuits against local police districts that are in violation of civil rights or if the actions of the police are clearly in violation of police procedure. This will decrease overall morale and a willingness to protect and serve. On the flip side, tensions continue to grow within communities. People fear the black criminals and the police. In either case, police and the communities they protect versus the criminal elements all work toward strife and chaos, bringing all in line with United Nations dictates.

A United Nations official visited the United States beginning of 2016 and instructed the Obama administration to increase its directive toward this end. Complaints of improper treatment or a violation of civil rights would be expelled quickly or give the appearance of the legal procedures. It was recently reported online that a Chinese woman, Ziaojie Li, who doesn't speak English, was trying to buy cell phones in Apple store in a mall in New Hampshire. She wanted to buy more than two, but store refused, asked her to leave, and ordered a no-trespass. Several days later, she returned to store to buy more phones and was asked to leave; when she did not, two police pushed her to the floor and tasered her. A man was arrested and his dog shot when he videotaped the incident. This is one of many incidents of police overreach.

Citizens' legal rights are easily bypassed, and they could be detained indefinitely under National Defense Administration Act (NDAA). Utah 2015 Bundy ranchers were hassled by the Bureau of Land Management, BLM, regarding grazing rights for their cattle. They were later arrested and fined on trumped-up charges regarding a control burn of weeds, which was reported as arson of federal land. The federal government owns large portions of land. Federal and state laws are aggressively rescinding the right to own guns. The right to freedom of speech or assembly is being dismantled through censorship as in Facebook deleting a blogger's content they did not agree with. Those who speak out against homosexuality may be punished as a hate crime. The right to speak about your religion or disagree with other forms of religion is presently being outlawed under hate speech. Tolerance is the rule.

The United States has been engaged in strange and unusual military preparation on American soil. This means that we are seeing an increase of United Nations armored vehicles, United Nations peacekeepers, German, Russian, and Chinese military on American soil conducting joint training operations. These joint military drills are conducted in other countries with the United States, such as South Korean, Japan, and Israel.

We can report on activity in the United States since we live here. Jade Helm 15 was exposed, April 2015. It is a covert operation and does not directly link to the United Nations Agenda 21, but the activity of Jade Helm 15 is one of the goals of the United Nations (*Personal Liberty News*, July 15, 2015, Stephen Qualye on the *Alex Jones Show*.)

We have picked up on various information sources and will share our findings to date. Coming to the end of 2015, there are no further updates:

- Military spokesman Lt. Col. Mark Latoria, Army Special Ops, spoke to a group of citizens and local government in Texas. He said the name Jade Helm is fictitious. One question—why spend millions on this project while not securing the southern border? One question—what if the citizens reject this program and the judge and the commissioners said it's final (not up for a vote)?
- Jade (China) Helm (United Nations helmets) possible meaning stands for Joint Assistance for Development and Execution, out of DARPA.
- It is a joint military operation and may include Navy Seals, Green Berets, Air Force, and Army Special Ops.
- So far, seven states will be forced to participate: Texas, Utah, South California, New Mexico identified as hostile states; and Arizona, Nevada, Colorado may be cooperative. DHS, EPA have a color-coded list. Those states in the red category are identified as hostile, and primary protesters are gun owners, constitutionalists. Those in the blue column are law enforcement, National Guard, green list are probably those that are cooperative. Other states may be involved: Mississippi, Louisiana, Florida.
- Will carry out covert ops within communities and private land; people will see black helicopters and plain-clothes military personnel interacting with locals.
- Program designed to create action and deployment plans using computer models meant to speed up reaction time during crisis scenario (such as Ferguson and Baltimore riots).
- A citizens group has formed, calling themselves Counter Jade Helm to monitor activities. News media will not be allowed. Report as of July 16, 2015, by the

Tribune News Service and *Personal Liberty Digest* said members did go out into the Bastrop, Texas, area but did not detect any unusual activity. Governor Greg Abbott requested the Texas State Guard to work with Jade Helm organizers and provide a daily report to the governor's office of their activities.

Dr. Jim Garrow, 2009 Nobel Peace Prize nominee, wrote on January 21, 2013: "I have been informed by a former senior military leader that Obama is using a new litmus test in determining who will stay and who must go in his military leaders. Get ready to explode folks. The new litmus test of leadership in the military is if they will fire on US citizens or not. Those who will not are being removed." General James Mattis, Marine Corp, head of US Central Command, was ordered by Obama recently to vacate his office immediately.

(4) Individual Freedom Versus Global Citizens

Under this category, the United Nations agenda is to ensure inclusive and equitable quality education and promote lifelong learning opportunities; promote peaceful and inclusive societies for sustainable development; provide access to justice and build effective, accountable, and inclusive institutions at all levels. United Nations line items 4, 5, 10, 16.

Proponents of the one-world order agree with removing individualism and bringing all under collectivism, where rights and subsidies come from the global overseers. Arthur Slessinger states a new world order comes with blood. Bring about cooperation through bombs or bribes. George C. Lodge believes individualism must be removed, and secret societies must operate more openly, and President Obama believes the best course is diplomacy.

To cripple national sovereignty, the United States Constitution must be dismantled. To take away individual freedom, the Bill of Rights must be eroded. Take away First Amendment rights by attacking freedom of speech, freedom of the press, and freedom of religion. Take away Fourth Amendment rights by disarming law-abiding citizens.

Wards of the State

At the United Nations Population Control Summit, one subject was the "rights of the child." A future goal for parents is, they would have to be certified to raise their child in a home environment or give the child up to be raised by another couple. For instance, the state deems the parents unfit, takes the children, and places them in foster care. Parental right may be challenged.

Scotland introduced a law in 2014 to have the government oversee every child in the nation. Each child would be assigned a "Named Person" to ensure the welfare of the child up to age eighteen and have access to all information, and it may not be available to the parents.

These "Named Persons" could be teachers, school administrators, midwife, social worker, but not the parents.

Opponents to this law are Christian and parental groups who have petitioned the United Kingdom's Supreme Court to review this law as an infringement on parental rights. The philosophy in the law states, "Parents cannot raise children without professional help provided by the state in order for children to grow up to be successful Scottish adults … There must be early intervention by the government because every parent is a potential child abuser and the only way to prevent this is by government intervention" (Steve Weatherbe, *Life Site News*, March 10, 2016).

Global Citizens

As governments worldwide seize control of children over parental rights, children will be subjected to vaccinations, indoctrination, and preparation to be global citizens in a one-world order. In the United States, the federal government wheels control over the public educational system with or without state approval. Public schools have worked to integrate Outcome Based Education, No Child Left Behind, and Common Core principles sanctioned at the federal level that tailors the child to work at lower educational expectations in order to pass test that rewards the teacher, school district, and state board. The presidential administration would offer cash strapped schools millions of dollars in stimulus funds to comply with federal curriculum (*Personal Liberty Digest*, Bob Livingston, *Teaching the Test: Common Core Disaster*, September 30, 2013).

The program does not encourage imagination, creativity, individualism but moving children to a culture of socialism as in the redistribution of economics, social justice, mainstream perverted lifestyles, study of Islam, secular humanism, radical environmental ideals. Common Core will focus on reprograming people to believe the conservatives are the enemy, creating a nation of bigots, racists, greedy capitalists, war mongers, imperialists, anti-immigration, segregationists. These enemies are those who hold to traditional views, believe the constitution is important, hold to national sovereignty, and thus need to be neutralized for the collective good of the liberal left.

The Bill and Melinda Gates Foundation has given $200 million to curriculum program developers, Achieve Incorporated. They developed the Common Core curriculum without input from State Legislators, school boards, teachers, or parents. Gates will benefit in that schools must provide each student with a computer and software. The database will track everything about each child, their families, affiliations, medical and psychological profiles, etc. Perhaps this database will detect lower achievers and identify highly intelligent children who could be essential citizens in the new world order.

Federal curriculum is designed to "dumb down" students, produce citizens that don't question government actions, and create obedient citizens. This plan must have some limitations as we witness youth who are carrying out murder, theft, rape, and total disregard for authority. Was the goal to create a generation of criminals preplanned to carry out havoc and chaos to bring about the goals of the one-world government?

The increase in government intrusion into the educational system will mold a leftist mind-set.

Agenda is designed to remove traditional values and insert curriculum that is offensive and biased. The majority of students will be groomed to function in a global society that is peace-loving, antiwar through diplomacy, diversity-tolerant, and big government is our nanny.

Parents who opt out of public school and seek private or Christian schools may find it increasing financially difficult with tuition cost. Parents who chose to home school must be approved and must follow a state curriculum. Recently, in Germany, children were taken from their parents because of home schooling. They sought asylum in the United States for a period. A judge ruled they should return to Germany, and Obama supported the ruling. Another family in Sweden had their parental rights revoked for home schooling their children. Eventually, the option for home schooling will not be tolerated by the government.

In 1948, Julian Huxley, a member of UNESCO, promoted the idea of education for a global society. Every child is our child, and they should be raised collectively by the state. Similar to that idea, it takes a village to raise a child. The state would exercise authority in the home by abolishing parental control. Plato's *The Republic* states that no parent or child would know each other. Reminiscent of Nazi Germany, young children, were placed in government-controlled schools and indoctrinated. Islam indoctrinates young children to hate and kill the infidels. It also creates a martyr mentality of suicide bombers.

Carl Teichrib, Hope for the World, summer 2014, provides insight into global citizenship, *Mind Bending: Education for Global Activism.* He was first introduced to this concept in 1997 at the Global Citizenship 2000 Youth Congress in Vancouver, British Columbia. Robert Muller, the United Nations' Prophet of Hope, spoke at the youth conference, stating, "The purpose of the gathering was to embed the principles of global citizenship into Canada's educational system … We must create a new mind, a new way of thinking, acting, a change in values and beliefs. This planetary approach was built around the ideology of oneness." We are all interconnected to the earth, to the energy of the universe, to each other was the message. Participants received a global citizenship passport, which read, "A good inhabitant of the planet Earth, a member of the great human family, you are the Earth become conscious of herself … unite global citizens to save and heal planet Earth." Robert Muller is the author of the *World Core Curriculum.* He created eleven United Nations agencies, which were recognized by UNESCO for its educational philosophy: "A new world morality and world ethics, global management all to make each human being proud to be a member of a transformed species, managing the world and advancing humanity's collective evolution to bring about our ascension as universal, total beings." Muller connects the thread between global citizen and his idea of United Religions Initiative, 1993 Parliament of the World's Religions, to the spiritual outlook required to save the planet was to recognize the basic truth as given by Jesus, Mohammad, and emissaries from outer space. The basic truth is the cosmos incarnating itself through our collective divinity. The pope leans toward evolution by stating, "God is not a magician." Muller also connects the thread to the United Nations, becoming the United States of the World, or overseer of the new world order.

MSNBC, September 2016 new TV series, *Global Citizens*—the theme promotes the importance of being a global citizen through helping poor people. The show features interaction with VIPs Jose Diaz Balart, Salma Hayed, Don Francisco, Dennis Haysbert.

Internet Freedom Ending

United Nations World Conference on International Telecommunications in Dubai, December 11, 2012, moves to regulate the World Wide Web. Head of Google warns the open Internet is at high risk. China, Russia, and some Arab nations agree that the United Nations should control the Internet. ISIS is using social media, and this will be used as another reason to control the Internet. According to a post on WikiLeaks, the United Nations would have the following oversight:

- United Nations distribute and assign all e-names.
- Each country would be notified of the IP addresses of each user in their land.
- United Nations would regulate Internet content.
- Each nation could censor website in their land.

Hamadoun Toure is the head of the International Telecommunication Union (ITU) of the United Nations. He was educated at Leningrad Institute, Moscow, and has Vladimir Putin's approval to oversee the Internet (Dick Morris Report, October 2012).

Plans to control the Internet have been moving forward. As of 2016, Google, Facebook, Amazon, Twitter, and several others agree that the Internet should be under global control, and the ICANN (International Corporation Assigned Names and Numbers) should oversee the Internet (Sky Watch TV, September 15, 2016).

(5) Environment

Under this category, the United Nations agenda is to ensure availability and sustainable management of water, ensure access to affordable and reliable energy, combat climate change, conserve use of oceans and marine resources for sustainable development, protect terrestrial ecosystems, manage forest, combat deserts, and halt and reverse land degradation and biodiversity loss. United Nations line items 6, 7, 13, 14, 15.

President Obama signed executive order 13391, Patriot Defense of Liberty Enabler Act; in brief it turns all federal territories over to the United Nations in the event there is civil disobedience in the United States. The president can call in United Nations troops to help US military ("Alex Jones on Dave Hodges," *Common Sense Show*, March 2016).

Albert (Al) Gore was born in 1948 in Washington, DC. After serving as US vice president, he took up the "global warming" mantra. It is not a bad thing to be concerned about the environment, but when it takes over your life, it becomes your god. Al has been referred to as the resident druid. In 1990, Gore pushed for a Global Marshall Plan, wherein industrial nations would help less developed countries grow economically while still protecting the environment. This move introduced the Kyoto protocol, which called for reduction of greenhouse gas emissions and later the payment to third world countries in carbon taxes.

Scientists have provided data that indicate the earth is not warming. Global warming pundits have produced no evidence to support their theory. The environmentalists have moved from their rigid, unfounded global warming position to redefinition "climate change."

Prince Charles weighs in on overpopulation and global warming: "On an increasingly crowded planet, humanity faces many threats but none greater than climate change and global warming which reduces ability to feed, maintain health and safety from extreme weather, manage natural resources, avert humanitarian disaster of mass migration and conflict."

The global elite get together—including Bill Gates, President Obama; President Hollande, France; Zuckerberg, Facebook; Jeff Bezos, Amazon; Jack Ma, Alibaba; Xavier Nell, Internet Free in France—committed to spending billions toward clean energy sources and green agriculture.

Obama, the Clintons, as well as the Bushes are global warming and climate change advocates. President Clinton established the President's Council on Sustainable Development, PCSD, to begin translating the vision of the United Nations's Agenda 21 into US action (Carl Teichrib, contributor to "Hope for the World," spring 2013, on *Anticipating Agenda 21: Framework for Global Governance*).

President Obama uses terms as *urgent* and *alarming* to signal his belief that climate change is a security threat. These are not legitimate concerns but conceal a sinister agenda. He has taken the position of anticoal industry and anti-Canadian pipeline because the globalists believe they are the great polluters that contribute to greenhouse gases. However, the EPA caused an environmental hazard, 2015, by releasing toxic water from a mine that polluted the Animus River and impacted the Native American population in that area. They were not demonized, chastised, or disciplined by the Obama administration.

Obama pushes for green energy sources, and corporations with green energy ideas are funded by the government. For instance, United States funded Solyndra and others who have gone belly-up. Obama pushed for electric-powered cars. They were expensive, and recharging locations were sparse. Obama's alternative energy sources are wind mills, solar energy, and hydroelectricity. There are drought conditions in parts of the United States and under the dictatorship of the EPA water rationing, and sanitation systems will be managed. The average citizen and small farmer can expect to have limited water supply and greater increase in water cost. The EPA will conserve oceans and marine resources for sustainable development. This could translate into a ban on ocean fishing and push people to ingest products from GMO fish farms. Under United Nations agenda and its protection of land restoration and sustainable ecosystems the USDA could ban the use of wood stoves, home gardening, farm animals, and rainwater collection. In other words, self-reliance or living off the land would be criminalized.

During Obama's tenure, he funneled billions into green energy projects in America and abroad.. He has pledged $7 billion to Saharan Africa for the project "Power Africa." "Partnership with nations for growth and the potential for every citizen and not just a few at the top," This is the global initiative of the United Nations Agenda 21 create a level field that all the masses will have equal subsidy (not wealth) but enough to eat, modest housing, and some health benefits. That nation's resources will be under control of the United Nations.

The Telegraph, July 2013, reported Obama's comments to students at Georgetown University: "We don't have time for a meeting of the flat earth society." Obama's goal under the Environmental Protection Agency, EPA, is to limit greenhouse gas emissions from power plants—mostly coal, oil, and electric. Nuclear power plants are dangerous if they leak. Radioactivity is worse than carbon emission. According to Obama, cutting back on emissions and changing the country's infrastructure would protect against extreme weather. This would translate into greater hardship for citizens, such as limiting the use of autos and greater use of mass transportation, bus, trains, planes, and increase in TSA-type intrusion. He blames weather conditions such as Hurricane Sandy, wildfires, and droughts on global warming caused by emissions. Obama and other world leaders hold to these same beliefs that global warming is to blame, even though scientists have proven evidence that the planet is not warming.

The buzz words are "Green and Sustainability." Canada came up with "Environmentally Sustainable Defense Activities: A Sustainable Development Strategy for National Defense."

Maurice Strong, Canadian citizen and advocate for the environment and population control, asserted his position as far back as 1972. Strong purchased the Baca Ranch in Creston,

Colorado, in 1978. He built the New Age Manitou Center for interfaith community to promote the human spirit consciousness and earth sustainability. Currently, millions support the "Green Religion" philosophy, where Mother Earth is deity.

Strong was a member of the Club of Rome and supported its 1972 *Limits to Growth*. They believed that by 2030, the population could not be sustained and drastic measures for environmental protection needed to be adopted. In cooperation with Mikhail Gorbachev, they established the *Earth Charter 2000*, which melds religion and the environment. In 2001, Strong published his book, *Where on Earth Are We Going?* In the book, he continues to assert his belief that two-thirds of the world population would perish by 2031 and would be "a glimmer of hope for the future of our species and its potential for regeneration."

Before his death, Strong was instrumental near the end of the twentieth century to shore up the United Nations' position on global government, carbon taxes, United Nations military, global judicial court, and phase out veto power of the five permanent member nations of the United Nations Security Council. In 2009, Strong opined, "Refine democracy as it regards to citizens voting for candidates but modify process to avoid ballot tampering in order to elect strong officials capable of making difficult decisions as it pertains to safeguarding the global environment." He served as United Nations Secretary on Environment and Development, 2014, out of Nairobi. In this position, he made his position clear: "Current lifestyles and consumption patterns of the affluent middle class involve high meat intake, excessive use of fossil fuels to have air condition suburban homes, which are not sustainable. This mind-set was continued with Pope Francis and President Obama's war on the middle class and income inequality. Strong made his contribution to his goals and died, November 2015, at eighty-six years old (Lianne Laurence, *Life Site News*, December 2, 2015).

Santa Cruz County, California, was the first local government to adopt United Nations Agenda 21 program. They created a locally administered and enforceable ecobureaucracy pushing "green" by prohibitive zoning requirements, set asides, green spaces, extra fees, and permitting stipulations, predetermined public hearing, policies, inspections, fines, and lawsuits. Other localities followed the lead of Santa Cruz and have adopted sustainable development action plans.

The push for climate change was touted at the United Nations by Obama, who said it was a national security concern, allowing to bypass the Constitution and think global. Pope Francis also declared in a rare encyclical a call for action against climate change stating, "Global warming is driving the world to the brink of suicide." Germany's Angela Merkel blames climate change on the migrants.

November 30 to December 12, 2015, hundreds of representatives from various nations gathered in Paris for the United Nations conference on climate change. The United Nations conference in 1972 in Stockholm emphasized a movement toward national population policies. In 1997, the United Nations conference in Rio created the Kyoto Protocol aimed at combating global warming through carbon credits. They were planning on having all nations agree to this commitment, and the time frame ended 2012 but was extended to 2020 by the Doha Amendment. The 2015 Paris conference, COP21 (or 21st Conference of the Partners of the United Nations Framework Convention on Climate Change), the consensus agreed to stop humankind from "warming" the earth one degree through an international climate tribunal, giving it power of enforcement. It was suggested that there were five hundred days to avoid a climate disaster per Bilderberg member, Laurent Fabius, who was seen with John Kerry. Obama gave a cloaked message that the world should be concerned about climate change. Rabbis and others are concerned something catastrophe may come in 2016.

James Hansen, a climate change advocate, believed the goal was "ludicrous." The goal was to have 2 C or 3.6 F warming target over an eighty-five-year period. Every five years, nations would try to do better. Hansen said, "There is no action, just promises" (*Natural News*, December 2015).

In order to achieve the United Nations goal for a universal agreement to reduce global warming to below two degrees Celsius by 2100, based on reduction of greenhouse (carbon) gas emissions by 40 to 70 percent, each nation is to put together a plan to explain how they will achieve this goal. In 2018, a new plan would be required every five years. The problem is that there is no mandate outlining how much each nation must reduce their greenhouse gas emissions or how to implement and measure success. This plan would open the door for manipulation of data to bring about a favorable outcome. As it stands now, it is no more than a quasiagreement until fifty-five countries have ratified it, and those countries must make up 55 percent of the total global greenhouse emissions.

According to Mike Adams, *Natural News*, research of this "questionable data" said the source claimed that 97 percent of scientists are onboard with the global warming is man-made mind-set. His research revealed that data collected by way of e-mail and comments handpicked and discarded data contrary to their position. Obama said (based on false data), it is settled science.

(6) Finance and World Economies

Under this category, the United Nations agenda is to promote sustained, inclusive, and sustainable economic growth, full and productive employment, and decent work for all; build resilient infrastructure, promote inclusive and sustainable industrialization and foster innovation; and strengthen the means for implementation and revitalize the global partnership for sustainable development. United Nations line items 8, 9, 17.

We could interpret this to mean that governments will regulate small business out of existence. Small business will have to accommodate a higher minimum wage, outrageous cost of employee medical insurance, hire homosexuals, and make special privileges for transgender. Anyone who speaks out against government intrusion at any level is a dissenter, troublemaker, war monger, and placed on a government watch list. In China, North Korea, Middle Eastern nations jail and kill dissenters.

Big corporations are the bulwark of the global infrastructure. In the United States, they were bailed out by big banks and the government. We heard they are "too big to fail and at the same time, homeowners went into foreclosure, debts could not be repaid, and unemployment surged." In our worldview, people are suffering throughout the world for one reason or another.

Line item 9, applicable to free markets, will not be so free; but under the confines of global regulation, high taxes, tariffs, environmental issues, and the so-called sustainability of natural resources economies will collapse. Global relationships will be foremost, and the availability for financing large corporate goals is paramount to an unhindered marriage between central banks, governments, and mega corporations. Regulations on exporting toxic food from China, such as rice, having a high arsenic, cadmium, lead, mercury and aluminum composition will not be restricted but tolerated. China is a major player in the global economic big picture. Toward this end, the United States is pushing the Trans Pacific Partnership between Canada, Mexico, Chili, Peru, Singapore, Malaysia, Australia, New Zealand, Japan, Vietnam, and several others—which will represent 40 percent of the world trade.

Spain was pushing to take 75 percent of people's income to bail out the government debt. Instead, they confiscated people's bank accounts who made a certain income per year.

Greek citizens were rioting because the government threatened to take away their austerity/entitlements.

The Oil Game

Oil tycoons own Exxon, Mobil, Royal Dutch/Shell, BP, Amoco, Chevron, and Texaco.

End of 2014, the cost for a barrel of oil dropped from $100 a barrel to $55 a barrel. At the end of 2015, a barrel of oil was below $30. US consumers are pleased. However, there will be some blowback as we watch the unfolding of this situation. The first sign of unrest may come from oil-producing nations. OPEC members such as Saudi Arabia did rely on high oil revenues to fund its extravagant monarchy. Saudi Arabia citizens are dependent on government entitlements. The government will cut social programs first before taking a cut to their overflowing coffers. OPEC members want lower oil prices as a retort against the United

States, whose energy barons want to increase the production of shale. The United States has a surplus of oil reserves.

Venezuela is reeling from the fall of oil prices, and there is a rise in social unrest due to food and basic supply shortages.

Russia produces oil and depends on the sale of its exports to fund the government. With current sanctions placed on Russia for its intervention into the Ukraine, they are beginning to feel an economic downturn as well as the devaluation of their ruble. They increased their prime rate to 17 percent. The United States terminated financial relations between western banks who invest in the ruble, and Wall Street has terminated investment firms dealing with the Russian ruble. At the end of 2015 to midpoint of 2016, Russia is rising again on the world scene.

Iraq depends on its oil resources to float its economy. However, with the ISIS insurgency and the threat to their oil fields, this will be a major blow to their economy.

United Nations and Global Financial Network

Following are a few organizations and institutions that make up the financial global network. As the United Nations is the hub of the one-world order, the financial conglomeration is the hub for the global economy. The financial establishment impacts every facet of life on the planet.

International Monetary Fund, IMF

For decades, there has been a push for a cashless society. More people today use direct deposit, debit or credit card for transactions, and online payment options for monthly obligations. Some people invested in the Bitcoin option. The globalists want to consolidate all currency systems and central banks under the outward control of the IMF and the BIS, Bank of International Settlements. They are pushing to devalue national currencies.

One of the goals of the one-world order is to establish a global currency. The IMF may be in charge of the global economy using special drawing rights, SDR, which becomes the currency. The dollar must lose its world reserve status. The IMF will direct which foreign currency uses the SDR. China issued $25 trillion debt instruments to boost their weak economy and is affected by QE (quantitative easing) in the United States. These financial moves are deliberately engineered in order to lay foundation for massive liquidity spike in the Yuan (China currency). China is in a better position than US, who has greater debt and has been on an economic downturn since 2008. China and Russia have a thirty-year contract for Russia to supply China with gas. They have removed the dollar as the reserve currency in transactions between the two nations. China and Russia may refuse to accept the dollar for payment. China is building its own gold exchange to rival the United States. Russian has established the Eurasian Economic Union, including Kazakhstan and Belarus, which have discovered new oil reserves. Russia annexing Crimea was necessary for water rights to import and export materials. China will be the world's largest economy by 2016. They also wish to trade with Iran.

The IMF was formalized in 1944 at the Bretton Woods Conference, headquartered in Washington, DC. The world was reeling from World War II, and at this time, world leaders gathered in Bretton Woods, New Hampshire, to set up a monetary policy that maintained an exchange rate by tying foreign currency to the US dollar. By 1945, twenty-nine member countries were onboard. Its goal was to assist in the reconstruction of the world's international payment system. Member countries paid into the fund, and the IMF was to bridge temporary imbalances of payments. During this era, the United States had $40 billion in gold reserves. The United States terminated the ability to convert the dollar to gold in 1971, and this brought an end to the Bretton Woods system, and the dollar became fiat currency—which derives its value from government regulations.

By 2010, IMF worth for SDR was approximately $780 billion. Currently, the IMF oversees around 188 countries economic position and sets forth self-correcting policies for improvement in the area of global cooperation, financial stability, international trade, employment, and exchange rate stability as well as making financial resources available to member countries to meet balance of payment needs (Wikipedia, June 2014).

Bank of International Settlements, BIS, is the most powerful bank in the world—a global central bank for the eight prominent families who control the private central banks of almost all Western and developing nations. BIS is under directorship by the Federal Reserve, Bank of England, Bank of Italy, Bank of Canada, Swiss National Bank, Netherland Bank, Bundesbank, and Bank of France.

BIS gave a bridge loan to Hungary in the 1990s to ensure privatization of that country's economy. It served as conduit for certain families funding of Adolf Hitler led by the Warburgs, J. Henry Schroeder, and Mendelsohn Bank of Amsterdam.

It is no coincidence that BIS is headquartered in Switzerland, favorite hiding place for the wealth of the global aristocracy and headquarters for the Italian Freemason's Alpina Lodge.

The IMF and World Bank are central to the one-world order. In 1944, the first World Bank bonds were floated by Morgan Stanley and First Boston. The French Lazard family became more involved in House of Morgan interests. Lazard Freres, France's biggest investment bank, is owned by the Lazard and David-Weill families associated with Genoese banking represented by Michelle Davive. Chairman and CEO of Citigroup was Sanford Weill.

Historian Carroll Quigley wrote in his book, *Tragedy and Hope*, that BIS was part of a plan "to create a world system of financial control in private hands able to dominate the political system of each country and the economy of the world as a whole … to be controlled in a feudalistic fashion by the central banks of the world acting in concert by secret agreements."

The US government in its quest for more control over BIS did lobby unsuccessfully for its demise at the 1944 post-World War II Bretton Woods Conference. Instead, the combined power of the eight families was diminished somewhat with the Bretton Woods creation of the International Monetary Fund. The Federal Reserve only took shares in BIS in September 1994. BIS holds at least 10 percent of monetary reserves for at least eighty of the world's central banks, the IMF, and other multilateral institutions. It serves as financial agent for international agreements, collects information on the global economy, and serves as lender of last resort to prevent global financial collapse.

Federal Reserve System, FR

This cartel was established in 1913 by global elite in a secret meeting on Jekyll Island, Georgia, United States. Rothschild was one of the founders. They understood that to control the world, they must control monetary systems. To bring all under the one-world government, the legal tender of sovereign nations must be devalued. One way to accomplish the devaluation of currency is to print more money. The FR is not part of the US government, it is a privately owned corporation. It functions as the central bank in the United States. The FR has twelve branches in the United States. Some notable globalists serve on their board of directors: Goldman Sachs, Rockefeller, Lehman, Kuhn Loebs, Rothschilds, Warburgs of Hamburg Lazards of Paris, Israel Moses Seifs, Italy, J. P. Morgan Chase, Jacob Shiffs, James Stillman of Citigroup. Do note that some of these directors are also listed as the architects of the new world order, and all are interconnected.

Analyst Brandon Smith, *Personal Liberty Digest*, May 20, 2014, said in his article, "The Final Swindle of Private American Wealth Has Begun": "The Federal Reserve is an entity created by globalists for globalists. These people have no loyalties to any one country or culture. Their only loyalties are to themselves and their private organizations."

The FR is powerful, secret and lacks transparency. Representative Ron Paul, Texas, passed House Bill 1207 to audit the Federal Reserve. The Senate watered down the bill so that a complete audit would not be carried out. Ben Bernanke, Alan Greenspan, and other bankers vehemently opposed the audit and lied to Congress about the effects an audit would have on markets. This was the first audit in a hundred years. Results were posted on Senator Sander's website, September 2012. It revealed that $16 trillion had been secretly given to US banks and foreign banks in France to Scotland from 2007 to 2010 as well as US corporations. FR said it was a loan program, but virtually none of the money has been returned at 0 percent interest. There was no outcry from our elected officials or the public who are usually kept in the dark to find out that the FR bailed out foreign banks while Americans were struggling to find jobs and keep their homes. In 2008, the Toxic Asset Recovery Program bailout bill was passed, and loans of $800 billion were given to failing banks and companies. The amount given out is much higher than reported. Goldman Sachs received $814 billion; Citigroup received $2.5 trillion; Morgan Stanley received $2.4 trillion; Merrill Lynch, $1, 950 trillion; Bank of America, $1.344 trillion; Barclays of United Kingdom, $868 billion; Bear Sterns, $853 billion; Royal Bank of Scotland, $181 billion; UBS, Switzerland, $287 billion; Credit Suisse, Switzerland, $262 billion; Lehman Brothers, $183 billion; BNP Paribas, France, $175 billion; Deutsche Bank, Germany, $354 billion; and other banks received hefty chunks of the $16 trillion. Federal Reserve holds Germany gold reserves, 3,400 tons = $190 billion as well as other foreign companies. Germany requested the return of their gold and has been stonewalled to date.

Notable banking overlords are connected to the US Trust Company formed in 1853, now Bank of America. Former directors of the US Trust Company are Walter Rothschild, Daniel Davison of J. P. Morgan Chase, Richard Tucker of Exxon Mobile, Daniel Roberts of Citigroup, Marshall Schwartz of Morgan Stanley—these and others sit on many boards and may represent the top 10 stockholders of the majority of Fortune 500 companies.

J. W. McCallister, an oil industry insider with House of Saud connections, wrote in *The Grim Reaper* that information he acquired from Saudi bankers cited 80 percent ownership of the New York Federal Reserve Bank (unconfirmed.) The same families associated with the FR with four residing in the United States are Goldman Sachs, Rockefellers, Lehmans, and Kuhn Loebs of New York. The international representatives are the Rothschilds of Paris, London, Berlin; the Warburgs of Hamburg, Amsterdam; the Lazards of Paris; and Israel Moses Seifs of Rome, Italy.

Corrupt banks, for example, HSCB, guilty of money laundering, took $7 billion from Mexican drug cartel; conducted twenty-five thousand Iranian transactions, totaling over $19 billion in one week; and helped Saudi Banks with terror financing for groups such as al-Qaeda. In 2016, Wells Fargo was exposed for creating millions of fraudulent bank accounts and activating millions of credit cards not associated with their customer base.

A deficit results when there is an imbalance between revenue and spending. Overspending results in tax increases and cutting services. Quantitative Easing, QE 1, 2, if QE3 takes place, there will be a domino effect. Brazil president came to United States to say no to QE3 because it would hurt their country.

The FR regulates interest rates. Large banks that borrow from FR may be charged 0 percent interest rate. Banks lend this money to consumers at higher interest rates. If FR raises interest rates, it will weaken the dollar. Actions of the FR have an impact on inflation, recession, and stock market trends.

The FR writes a check for any amount of money to buy government bonds, and the US Treasury prints the money to cover the check. The FR sells the bonds to others for profit.

The US government can print its own money, which was executed by President Kennedy, Executive Order 11110, June 4, 1963. After his assassination, these government printed bills were withdrawn.

The globalists don't want a full-scale revolution in the United States but to use financial instability as a tool to bring it under a one-world order regime. Therefore, toward this end is the need to devalue the US dollar and increase debt, resulting in recession. Other foreign currency such as the Euro in Greece and Ireland are losing its buying power. Central banks buy Greek T bonds as a bailout and then invite them to accept the new world currency. Measures such as this work to collapse existing world currencies, resulting in weakened nations, making them ripe for intervention. There will be some pushback from nations who don't like these measures.

Society of Worldwide International Financial Trade, SWIFT

The global elite uses this organization to transfer money. As mentioned, the one-world order is working to weaken the nations financially. Each nation has millions of low-income people dependent on government entitlements. In the United States, if the system shuts down the ability of people to access their income via of the EBT cards, there will be riots because card recipients are suddenly thrust into an emergency situation. In fact, shutting off the EBT cards is actually one way to initiate a false flag event in America. It would take only a few minutes for a bank to shut down their ATMs. They would blame it on a cyber attack. The crisis would be used to the advantage of the government to institute additional controls over the people from increased law enforcement presence to Internet access.

The government would allow the people to vent before bringing in the National Guard. The media would broadcast the riots, and when things are out of control, the government would mandate martial law. Here in the United States, we have seen some situations develop to a crisis level. In 2012, there was an EBT outage, which could have been a practice run in preparation for a real crisis.

Above we reviewed the United Nations and its six areas of concern. Under category 6, Finance and World Economies, we were able to analyze how this platform connects the world's financial institutions that control all of us globally. Following, we factor in the impact of other global organizations.

United Nations and Global Partners Form a Network of Organizations

As we demonstrated, global organizations are made up of world leaders, the rich and famous. The organizations are structured in a pyramid formation. Satan oversees the affairs of the world from his spiritual seat in high places. Those occupying the pinnacle are the architects of the one-world order. They have no national pride or loyalty to any one nation or culture because they have pledged their allegiance, knowledge, and wealth to Satan. Positioned under this hierarchy of spiritual wickedness are nations and governments who carry out the orders of the elite overseeing the affairs of the world. They operate as a corporate hive to bring their final plans to fruition. Those who exist at the base levels are politicians who run interference between the expendable masses of humanity and their masters.

William Norman Grigg, author and journalist, provides an in-depth look at the United Nations in his book, *The United Nations and the American Citizen.* He emphatically states that the United Nations supports a one-world government.

Advanced societies worldwide will structure their nations to be in line with the United Nations global initiative. Each nation will have a system in place to control or oversee those areas that impact the lives of its citizens—such as, finances, military, surveillance, health, religion, education, and environment. Government commissions and regulatory agencies are created to maintain laws over its citizens. In the United States, the Supreme Court was established to interpret the law based on the constitutional rights of the citizens. However, over the past hundred years, the Supreme Court has not been equitable to all of its citizens based on race, religion, and the right to life of the unborn.

Following Are Several Organizations Working toward a Global Government

World Constitution and Parliament Associates, WCPA—this group wrote a world constitution, *Constitution for the Federation of Earth,* submitted to the world of environmentalist, educators, financial leaders, and Eastern mystics, calling for international monetary system, administration of oceans, seabed, atmosphere, elimination of fossil fuels, redistribution of wealth, disarmament, end national sovereignty, world justice system, and world tax agency. Jesse Jackson, member of WCPA/CFR.

World Economic Forum, WEF, held at the Alpine Village of Davos, Zurich, Switzerland, meets yearly to discuss the status of the world. Twenty-five hundred wealthy elite, politicians, CEOs, actors came together. Some notables were Israel's Netanyahu, Yahoo CEO, Matt Damon, Goldie Hawn, and others paid $55,000 for a membership, and the cost to attend is $30,000. In 2014, the conference title was *Reshaping the World,* and the topics discussed were consequences for society, politics, and business as well as economic disparity, the growing wealth divide, and to identify the gravest global threat, climate change, dwindling water supply, and nation's internal conflict. The United Nations' initiative, setting goals for the nations, and how to measure such goals to see if they translate into desired outcomes. Founder of WEF, Klans Schwab, said, "It's time to push the reset button on the world."

North Atlantic Treaty Organization, NATO

German Marshall Fund ties into NATO (North Atlantic Treaty Organization) CFR formed its policies.

Trilateral Commission, TLC

Founded in 1973 by David Rockefeller and cofounder Zbigniew Brzezinski, a Russian globalist and Marxist. Its goal is to promote a one-world government through international economic order, and this is accomplished by stimulating economic interdependence between North America, Canada, Japan, and Europe. There are approximately 350 members; around eighty-seven live in United States, including George H. W. Bush, Bill Clinton, Dick Cheney, Al Gore, Henry Kissinger. President Carter appointed TLC members: Cy Vance as secretary of state, and Brzezinski as national security adviser. This signaled a surrender of the White House to be under the control of globalists.

Brzezinski stated, "The nation state as a fundamental unit of man's organized life has ceased to be the principle creative force. International banks and multinational corporations are acting and planning in terms that are far in advance of the political concepts of the nation state."

Rockefeller stated, "Some believe we are part of a secret cabal working against the best interests of the United States, characterizing my family and me as internationalists and conspiring with others around the world to build a more integrated global political and economic structure—one-world, if you will. If that is the charge, I stand guilty and I am proud of it."

Barry Goldwater remarked on the TLC, "It represents a skillful, coordinated effort to seize control and consolidate four centers of power being, political, monetary, intellectual, and ecclesiastical. All this is to be done in the interest of creating a more peaceful, productive world community. The Trilateral Commission move to the creation of a worldwide economic power superior to the political governments of the nation states involved. They believe the abundant materialism they propose to create will overwhelm existing difference … they will rule the future."

It is reported that Brzezinski is also an adviser to Obama. Obama appointed eleven Trilateral members to posts in his administration. Several are Tim Geithner, treasury secretary; James Jones, national security adviser; Paul Volker chairman, Economic Recovery Committee; Dennis Blair, director of National Intelligence. Forty years after the creation of the Trilateral Commission, their goal is accomplished: "all nations and people of the world are a single collective." Through propaganda, the population has been indoctrinated to accept control and oversight by global organizations working in unison for a one-world order (Jon Rappoport, *Personal Liberty News*, June 2014).

Council on Foreign Relations, CFR

May 30, 1919, the British, Royal Institute of International Affairs and the American Institute of International Affairs merged. Founder Edward Mandell House brought them together in 1921 to form the CFR. Mr. House was friend of President Woodrow Wilson, whom he influenced to support and sign the Federal Reserve Act. Funds to support CFR came from those involved with the formation of the FR. The United Nations was founded in 1945 by these same people, linking the CFR and FR. The CFR is linked by the same people with the Bilderberg and the Club of Rome founded in 1968. Richard Hass and David Rockefeller served as former chairs of CFR and the membership estimated over three thousand. Henry Kissinger is a CFR member.

Congressman John Rarick 1971, "The CFR establishment has influence and power in key decision-making positions at the highest levels of government to apply pressure from above, but it also announces and uses individuals and groups to bring pressure from below to justify the high level decisions for converting the United States from a sovereign constitutional republic into a servile member start of a one-world dictatorship."

CFR has connections to US president, secretary of state, treasury, defense, and NSA. For instance, Nixon appointed 115 CFR members to positions in government, and George Bush appointed 354 CFR and TLC members to government positions.

United States of America and Its Structure

All governments are structured in a pyramidal formation with the ruler of the government at the top. From the top and downward, various departments and multiple agencies are formed to oversee the affairs of that nation. In the United States, the citizens are controlled and regulated by alphabet soup agencies, which create layers of departments, bureaus, administrations, committees.

US government is made up of the executive branch, judicial, and legislative. In order to have a government for the people and by the people, several documents were created—such as the Constitution, the Bill of Rights, and the Declaration of Independence. From these documents, the government is expected to oversee the affairs of the people fairly, ethically, and to protect the freedom of the people. The following exhibit is a simplified diagram of the US government structure:

United States of America Structure

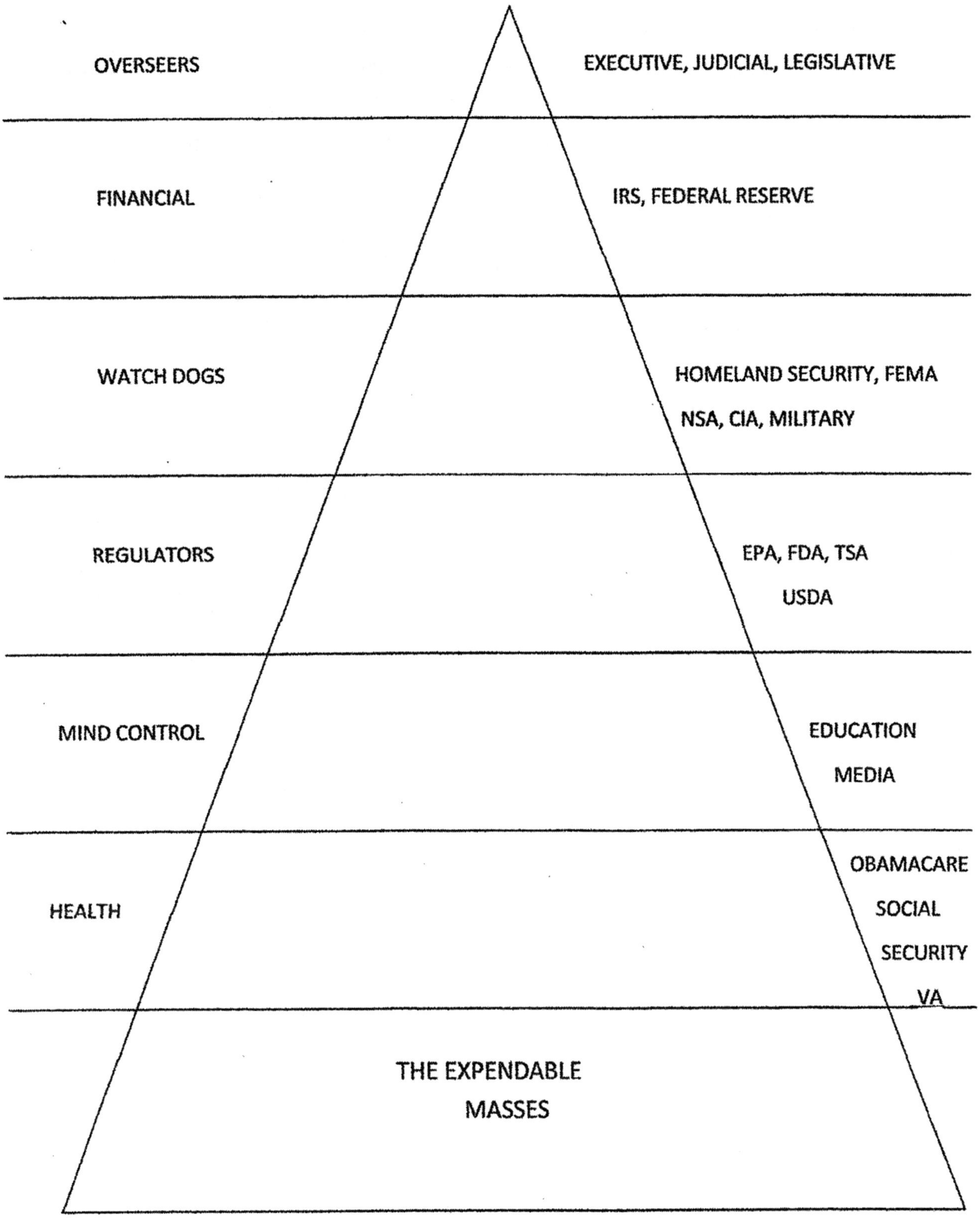

Executive Branch

In 2009, there was a changing of the guards. The new president came on the scene with a platform of "change." At his disposal were a myriad of departments. Obama's first order of business of the new administration was to bail out the failing banks and corporations with the mantra, "too big to fail." Foreign policy was next on the agenda with an apology to the Islamic nations for the ineptitude of American policy. Under the mask of green energy, grants funded by US tax dollars were given to corporations who touted alternative energy schemes. Most companies failed to produce items that they committed to produce, such as affordable electric cars, solar panels, high-tech batteries, etc. Citizens realized an increase in taxes, higher health premiums, penalized for not signing up with Obamacare; the ripple impacted the employment sector, and millions were laid off, causing a spike in national unemployment numbers. Through taxation class, warfare is created, such as the 99 percent against the 1 percent or the middle class against the wealthy. The fallout is hardest on the poor who seem not to have a vested interest in the machinations of the US government. Entitlements for food stamps and welfare tripled, creating a yoke over the citizens. The homosexual agenda advanced while traditional values took a plunge. "Big brother is watching" is a reality. The Arab Spring was the springboard for upheavals in the Middle East. Our only ally in the Mideast, Israel, was given the finger while Iran, and its nuclear ambitions were tolerated.

In 2007–2008, the national debt was published at $9 trillion. Under the Obama administration the published figure in 2016 was $19 trillion but the unpublished figure may be upward to $200 trillion. Under this administration, the nation is divided on every issue and concern such as health care, immigration, the obstruction of First, Second, and Fourth Amendment rights and religious freedom of Christians, and Jews seem to be placated for Islam. America has been complicit in arming drug cartels in Mexico and supplying arms to terrorists in Syria. The United States is funding terrorist activity in the Middle East, such as the Muslim Brotherhood in Egypt and Hamas in Gaza and Hezbollah in Lebanon.

Overseers

United States Supreme Court

The justices of the court are appointed for life. The highest court in the land was designed to carry out the laws based on the Constitution and moral principles, but at times the justices seem to serve at the pleasure of the president. Appointments to the Supreme Court do not place the justices above the law, reproach, or error. The Constitution was in place in the eighteenth century, and the Supreme Court condoned slavery. For hundreds of years, Christianity would flourish unencumbered because religious rights were protected under the Constitution. Even with that in place, Jews and Catholics were alienated, leading to removing God from schools and public places. Native Americans, Asians, Africans, and other immigrants got the short end of the stick as though the principles of the Constitution did not apply to them. Racism, discrimination, segregation abounded throughout the land while the justices sat in their lofty towers in observance. It took civil disobedience to get the Supreme Court to approve laws that ruled out segregation. As moral conscious eroded, the Supreme Court justices ruled in favor of abortion. Continuing on a downward path, the justices ruled in favor of same-sex marriage and eliminated the Defense of Marriage Act as unconstitutional. Sexual preference became a protected class. Here we see the court's bias in the interpretation of laws.

Department of Justice

The legal system must be impartial. Yet under every administration, the DOJ extends the prosecutorial arm of the law over the average citizen unless one is politically connected or rich. Case in point, Hillary Clinton will not be indicted for treason in regard to her handling of sensitive, classified data. Loretta Lynch, attorney general, met with Bill Clinton before July 4, 2016, and a few days later, the FBI made its ruling in the Hillary Clinton case, not guilty. This is impropriety and corruption at the highest levels.

The office of the attorney general is head over the DOJ, which is the chief law enforcement agency in the nation. During the Obama administration, it seems that the DOJ has overreached and directly interfered with positions held by the state. There are times when voters have made their voices heard through the electoral process, and state officials honor the will of the people. Nevertheless, the federal government asserted itself into situations that are one sided. For instance, half of the states in the Union did not want to comply with having to allow transgender people into the opposite sex bathrooms, and in opposition to the states, the federal government made threats. In the case of black criminals who get killed by police, we have seen the DOJ insert itself into the situation and take the side of the criminals, in turn inciting racial tensions.

The FBI was founded by J. Edgar Hoover—a racist and transsexual. During Hoover's reign of terror, blacks were a target. The agency has the responsibility to collect domestic intelligence. Hoover put many people on his watch list as does the current agency. The FBI comes under the jurisdiction of the DOJ. In 2016, James Comey was appointed by Obama to serve as its director. This agency functions as the strong arm of the DOJ. FBI activities were documented by the *New York Times, The Terrorist Factory: Inside the FBI's Manufactured War on Terror.* In our understanding, manufactured war can be associated with "false flag events."

Financial Noose

Federal Reserve Bank

One of the most formidable and influential corporations formed by political operatives and private representatives is the Federal Reserve Bank, which is not a department of the federal government. It functions on an international level. Its formation was previously discussed.

Financial Strong Arm

Internal Revenue Service

IRS formed in 1913, following the adoption of the Sixteenth Amendment to fund the Federal Reserve. The establishment of this branch of the government has been a financial hardship for the average citizen. Due to IRS heavy-handedness, people have lost their property and livelihood. The government believes people should subsist on meager provision. It takes the wealth of the citizens and redistributes it into the coffers of big banks and the pockets of the elite. This method of operation is socialism. Tax revenues are misused to finance terrorism or conflicts in foreign countries. Trillions of tax dollars are wasted, while struggling nonprofit corporation that oppose abortions or homosexuality based on traditional beliefs could lose their 501c3 status and funding. In other words, the IRS tracks conservatives, Christians, patriots, Tea Party members through a highly technological database. After numerous visits to the White House by high-level IRS officials in 2014 and confirmed by the White House sign-in logs, the IRS was authorized to redouble its attack on conservative groups, sending out additional guidance to IRS agents and lawyers in delaying their applications for 501c3 ruling. Some had been waiting for approval for years.

In 1943, the government legislated that income would be hit with a Social Security tax. These taxes would benefit retirees. By 2016, the program was bankrupt due to borrowing by the federal government. President Woodrow Wilson promised Americans that only those earning around $10,000 per year would pay 3 percent of their earnings to the government. Today a person who earns $100,000 per year pays about 36.9 percent of their earnings to the government. People are fearful to complain about the IRS because it will retaliate against them. The government has no right to 40 percent percent of anyone's income, poor or rich. The deduction from the taxpayer bank account goes to the IRS and does not go to the government to pay for its expenditures, as many people believe. The government deficit is $19 trillion and to free up cash, there is the printing of limitless amounts of money, which causes devaluation of the dollar and inflation.

The IRS was authorized oversight of the Affordable Care Act. The passage of HR 4872, titled "Medical Devices," approves for an RFID device to be implanted to track patients' health information. The Obama administration pushes to chip all by 2017.

Department of Treasury

Fort Knox

US bullion depository is located at a US Army post located in Kentucky, occupying 109,000 acres. This is Fort Knox. The US Department of Treasury has maintained the depository since 1937. This was a time when the government confiscated gold from its citizens. Currently, the citizens do not know if there is any gold still in Fort Knox.

US Mint was created by Congress in 1792. Its first director was David Rittenhouse, a very prominent person in Philadelphia. The first mint building was in Philadelphia, where the US capital was located. Today the mint's headquarters are in Washington, DC. The mint is under the control of the Department of Treasury. There are mint facilities throughout the nation today and even one in the Philippines. The mint only produces coinage.

Bureau of Engraving and Printing has the responsibility to print paper money and other security products. It was created in 1862 and headquarters in Washington, DC. It came about during the Civil War to issue paper currency to fund the war. The first money was called "demand notes," meaning payable on demand. Paper currency is printed for the Federal Reserve Bank. In 1987, another facility was built in Fort Worth, Texas.

Watchdogs

Department of Homeland Security, DHS

DHS oversees the Secret Service and interacts with NSA, FEMA, FBI, CIA. They regulate surveillance over streets, highways, monitor Internet, cell phones, data mining, drones, and cameras. In preparation for civil unrest, DHS, according to *Natural News*, December 14, 2012, has funded "Zombie Apocalypse" as part of terrorism training. Planning for any eventual catastrophe, government agencies—such as, Homeland Security, Social Security, USDA, EPA—are being armed with military weapons, ammunition, night-vision goggles, propane cannons costing millions. There have been eyewitness reports of trains transporting tanks and trucks.

Local police are also being militarized and provided with Humvees. Local police will be under the jurisdiction of the DOJ. Are these preparations to defend against civilian disobedience? (Open the Books.com).

As part of controlling the masses, DHS may enforce a National ID Law reported by *Before It's News*, December 26, 2013. "The enforcement steps will be conducted in restricted areas of the DHS headquarters followed by a phased approach with substantial enforcement in 2016. Driver licenses and personal ID cards may be ruled out as unacceptable forms of ID. State governors were notified in 2012 by DHS that a status report on REAL ID compliance be provided. All but Arizona and Pennsylvania provided a response."

Federal Emergency Management Act, FEMA, is under the Department of Homeland Security. The passage of HR 6566 allows for "preparation for mass fatalities." FEMA has been preparing campsites capable of housing millions behind barbed wire fencing as well as millions of body containers stored in various locations. FEMA is stockpiling 140 million meals, blankets, and body bags near the New Madrid Fault zone. One observer said, a FEMA camp was erected near the railroad tracks, reminiscent of Nazi Germany trains to concentration camps. The government is working to disarm, disenfranchise, and create division among the citizens. Those who protest or are uncooperative may be detained in a FEMA facility. Due to prison overcrowding, some nonviolent criminals may be detained in a FEMA camp facility.

National Security Administration, NSA

Its beginnings go back to the early 1900s. President Truman gave it a green light to advance US goals for intelligence gathering, evaluating data, and dissemination regarding national security. The Department of Defense is associated with NSA. The CIA is under NSA in an expanded role of operations, analysis, science and technology, digital innovation, cryptology, surveillance on domestic and foreign entities. John Brennan was appointed as director of the CIA by Obama. NSA is currently building a huge facility in Utah for the purpose of data collection on every individual, organization, and corporation. NSA is one avenue used to track and monitor people in the United States and abroad. Edward Snowden said that five billion cell phone activity are recorded daily by NSA.

Sam Rolley, *Personal Liberty Digest*, online August 5, 2013, article: "God Save the Queen: NSA Paying Brits to Violate US Constitution." A discussion of NSA by whistle-blower Edward Snowden exposed the NSA was invading privacy of Americans. British newspaper, *The Guardian,* August 2, 2013, online revealed that the leaked NSA documents contained information about hundreds of millions of dollars in secret US payments to the UK government communications headquarters over the past three years for the purpose of putting the British intelligence agency on the payroll. US Constitution forbids the government's invasion of citizen's privacy via cell phones or Internet, but the British government is not bound by US Constitution and can spy on Americans. Some staff workers express concern about the morality and ethics of their operational work particularly given the level of deception involved. It was reported that over the past five years, the amount of personal data available on the Internet or mobile traffic has increased by 7,000 percent. Another leaked document reveals that the British value the relationship with the United States and want to deliver on their deal and continue to receive millions in US taxpayers' money. NSA was exposed for spying on Germany, Brazil, Mexico, and France. Washington Blog, *Personal Liberty Digest* online, December 18, 2013, interview with top NSA official, thirty-two years at NSA, Bill Binney, created agency's mass surveillance program. Some comments made by Binney during his interviews with mainstream media is that the United States is close to being a totalitarian state; United States is already a police state engaged in spying on citizens. Personal data collected is shared with federal, state, local agencies—DOJ, FBI, DEA, IRS—and can be used to prosecute crime. All government agencies must intentionally launder the information. NSA data cannot be admitted in court because it was obtained without a warrant. US government also ships information to other foreign countries so they can unmask the information and return it back to NSA. Secret government agency called National Reconnaissance Office performs eavesdropping on phone calls by satellites tied into NSA's space satellite program, Advanced Space & Image Technology.

Regulation Henchmen

Transportation Security Agency, TSA, has a high number of inappropriate incidents—such as, touching, body scanning of extreme exposure, intimidation, detention, and unreasonable demands. One senior citizen was required to take off her diaper for inspection. Recently, Corporal Nathan Kenmitz—Marine Corp, earned a Purple Heart due to war injuries in Iraq—in military dress was traveling to California to receive a honor from his legislative district, Veteran of the Year. At the airport, TSA agents treated him as a terror suspect, ordered him to take off his uniform and raise his arms—which he could not due to injury. Military persons are on the government watch list. Charges were filed against TSA personnel for their treatment of veterans and lack of common sense. Another frequent flyer was detained for twenty hours because of his watch and a health bar. He is filing charges against TSA. In a step forward, US government plans to expand TSA authority to interstate highways, bus, subways, trains, and trucks for stop-and-search for security enhancement. Regulation on government site is titled Highway Baseline Assessment for Security Enhancement (BASE).

Health and the Environment

Department of Agriculture, USDA, Cattle Ranchers
Harassed for Grazing Rights, Pay Fines and Fees.

Food and Drug Administration, FDA

It should ensure the safety of food and drugs. The FDA is complicit in cooperation with big pharma, big food industry, and Monsanto allowing for consumption of unsafe products.

Veterans Administration, VA, exposed for corruption and allowing veterans to wait for months to be seen or receive treatment. Many have died before receiving treatment. Waiting lists were hidden, files lost. Conditions in VA hospitals are poor, and they are a place to go and die. May 2014, head of VA resigned. Obama promised improvement.

Environmental Protection Agency, EPA

The agency issues regulations to crack down on business and individuals. For example, small farmers were harassed to grow GMO crops. The drought in some states may have been caused by HAARP. California is at an 80 percent drought level. Residents are running low on water. In Las Vegas, the Hoover Damn is at its lowest since 1937. EPA released toxins into river, 2015, but will not be held accountable.

National Oceanic and Atmospheric Administration, NOAA

Congress has issued a subpoena to this agency to answer charges of data manipulation regarding global warming. The agency has refused to hand over its data, which supports man-made warming of the planet is not occurring and would be a glaring contrast to the president's position that global warming is the greatest threat to the world and the data is settled science and there is no further need to question its credibility. NOAA ignores years of data that support global temperatures not rising and Artic ice is not melting but expanding (*Natural News*, J. D. Heyes, November 13, 2015).

After the agency was accused of data manipulation in 2015, to make it appear earth surface and ocean temps were rising over the past fifteen years, the NOAA weather satellite was mysteriously destroyed. Government reports claimed that objects were seen around the satellite; it broke by itself, or the battery failed. NOAA added more weight on ocean buoys, adjusted ship-based temps upward, and raised land -based temps (*Natural News*, L. J. Devon, December 10, 2015).

Ten-Region Confederation of Nations

An important piece of prophecy is the formation of a ten-region confederation predicted in the book of Daniel and described as ten toes mixed with iron (government) and clay (people). The revived Roman Empire expanded its global influence through conflict and war. Its consistent goal is destabilization and control under a global regime. As we enter this area of discussion, we provide a short overview of the world at large. The year is 2016. The world has watched the deterioration of Syria. Russia has set up a military base in Syria to assist the current president Assad. China has offered Russia its support. Iran has a nuclear green light. North Korea continues to test its ballistic missiles. Japan and South Korea are upset. Islamic militants continue to spread fear, havoc, and death. Africa is in great turmoil as its people suffer disease, starvation, corruption and terrorism.

The United Nations' alignment with Islamic nations threatens Israel's existence. The United States aligned with terrorist factions moved for the overthrow of the Egyptian, Lybian and Syrian governments. The United States used Benghazi, Lybia as a staging area to send weapons to terrorist in Syria. Vice President Joe Biden spoke at Harvard Business School and confirmed the accusation that Saudi Arabia, UAE, and Turkey played a crucial role in the rise of ISIS in Syria and Iraq. We add also the United States was involved by sending weapons, forces, and money to ISIS to stage a proxy war against President Bashar Assad.

Some clergy believe America has crossed the Rubicon, or the point of no return. Judgment is being meted out against the nation in the form of unusual weather, fires, floods, drought, viruses, blatant immorality, increase in crime, and economic downturn. Preachers call for prayer and revival in America, but the unjust will not turn from their wicked ways and repent.

At this point, we have established the call for a one world order is not a conspiracy theory as some may think but their agenda is a tangible entity that has put in place the ten region confederation from which the antichrist will arise. The formation of the ten-region confederation was predicted over 2,500 years ago. Daniel interpreted Nebuchadnezzar's dream of a giant statue representing kingdoms whose time had come and gone. In Daniel's vision, he speaks to the fall of Babylonian Empire, which fell to the Medes and Persians, whose empire fell to Greece, and its empire fell to Rome. John in Revelation predicts that the seven heads of the beast also refer to seven kingdoms. Specifically, they are the empires of Assyria, Egypt, Babylon, Medes and Persians, Greece, Rome, and revived Rome is the seventh. Daniel points to the greatness of the Roman Empire, which was divided into two regions representative of the two legs of iron. Daniel then provides a prophecy that the ten toes made of iron and clay is the revived Roman Empire, and in the future it would become a ten-region world confederation (Daniel 2:41) The seventh head will be followed by the eighth: the kingdom of Satan.

From the time of Daniel's prophecy in the sixth century BC, God commanded him to shut up the books until the end. Students of prophecy would not have the revelation or understanding of the ten toes until the time of the end. The secular mind-set would also begin to grasp the implication of Daniel's prophecy. Plato was a secular Greek philosopher during the period of 400 BC. Daniel and Enoch's writings may have been available to Plato. In Plato's *Critias*, he states, "I have before remarked speaking of the allotments of the gods that they distributed the whole earth into portions ... and made themselves temples and sacrifices. Poseidon received for his lot the island of Atlantis. He begat children by a mortal woman. He had five pairs of male children ... dividing the island into ten portions for them. His oldest son, Atlas, was made king over the rest." Herein we understand Plato is discussing the legends prior to the flood. The "gods" is a reference to the fallen angels, and in this account, one such being called Poseidon had sired children with a human woman. One of the giant hybrids was called Atlas. Plato described the blessed state of the people of Atlantis who were under the benevolent rulership of ten kings bound together in a league.

The plan for a future ten-region confederation was understood thousands of years ago. These legends were passed to those connected with secret societies. Daniel tells us the time of this ten-region confederation will be before Jesus comes to set up his kingdom. Its time frame would be realized in the twentieth century (Daniel 2:44).

John writes the book of Revelation around AD 90. He allows us to know that the seven heads of the beast in Revelation 17 represent prominent empires: five are fallen, and the sixth one represents Rome. Rome was divided into two regions (two legs). Its two legs combined with its ten toes represent the seventh kingdom, which has encompassed the whole world. Rome in its divided state continued to exist, and we refer to it as the revived Roman Empire. Then John tells us that the other (the eighth) is not yet come, but it will come from the seven. Specifically, we are to understand that the kingdom of Antichrist emerges out of the revived Roman Empire. Students of prophecy should understand the revived Roman Empire is diverse. We should no longer think of the Roman Empire as central to Rome or Europe proper but has a foothold in America, Canada, South America, Africa, Australia, India, China, Russia, and essentially, the whole world.

In summary, Daniel's image and John's beast are referring to former empires, and both point to the ten toes or ten horns as representing a ten-region confederation coming into power during the last days. John gives us insight that the ten horns of the beast represent ten rulers that have no kingdom but receive power as kings for short period of time. One referred to as the little horn will emerge from within the ten (Revelation 17:10, 12).

The above analysis provides our reader with insight into the formation and structure of the ten-region confederation called for by the one-world order—a design birthed in ancient times whose time has arrived. Satan spun his web of deception through religion, secret societies, and nations. Satan has established demonic strongholds over nations, and the Bible refers to them as principalities of the air, seats of authority, and wickedness in high places. Most nations are corrupt and secular. Religious bodies compromise the truth of God with the lies of Satan, making it easy to select recruits for his operation. We highlighted many notable people that in one form or another contributed to the formation of the one-world order. These architects will carry out Satan's agenda to establish his eighth kingdom on earth, which will ultimately collide with the kingdom of God (Revelation 17:11).

At this time in world events, we believe the worldwide ten-region confederation is in place. The heads over each region have been appointed. The identities of these rulers and their activities will not be public knowledge. The elite inner circle is cognizant of the identity of these leaders. The ten leaders know each other. One of these regional leaders will be selected from among the ten to oversee all ten regional leaders and to ensure that their global goals are on track. Prophecy tells us one man—"a little horn, with eyes and a mouth"—will come from out of the ten, and he will be the final Antichrist. We will discuss this one-world supreme leader shortly. There is no past scenario that fits the prophecy of the ten toes and ten horns. The Bible tells us this ten-region confederation has come together at the end of the age and is given a short period to accomplish their evil deeds. We have arrived at the end of the age. Our evidence is biblically based as well as announcements made by national leaders.

The initial ten countries within the European Union were thought to represent the ten regions. Over time, the European Union included other nations, and the number increased to twenty-eight as of 2013. It became difficult to mesh the ten-horn beast prophecy with the European Union. It was reported by Michael Snyder, *Hope for the World*, 2015 that the president of France, Francois Hollande, suggested that the solution to the problems within the European Union would be resolved if all members were to transfer their sovereignty to a newly created federal/global government; essentially, it would be a United States of Europe. In 2016, citizens of England voted to secede from the European Union. These actions have no effect upon the ten-region confederation.

The Asian region is being solidified by China in their development of the Asian Infrastructure Investment Bank, AIIB. Its goal is to fund the development of rail lines, roadways, communications, infrastructure, port facilities for greater trans-Asian trade. Ten member nations of the Association of Southeast Asian Nations, ASEAN, do support China's AIIB, solidifying an Asian regional order.

June 2002 conference, *Toward a North American Community*, convened to discuss the integration of Canada, United States, and Mexico. The conference was held by the Woodrow Wilson International Center for Scholars. This center influences policy making in Washington, being funded by the global elites, Rockefeller Brothers Fund, The Gates Foundation, and George Soros. During the meeting, it was revealed that the elite planned to create a North American Union. In order to accomplish this, representatives from various think tanks agreed that a campaign of social engineering was needed to reshape beliefs about national sovereignty and identity. Representatives came from each of the three nations. Stephanie R. Golob of Baruch College and member of the CFR represented the United States. She said, "The United States is the greatest obstacle to this process of integration into a globalized system. Due to this resistance, <u>integration will have to come from the top down through directives from the US president and his inner circle</u>."

Bruce Stokes, CFR, *National Journal* columnist, Chatham House member, told the conference, "A true North American Community will be forged in the heat of conflict, not through a rational discussion ..." Nancy Pelosi, 2014, stated in response to the immigration influx of children and others, "The United States and Mexico is a community with a border going through it, and this crisis must be viewed as an opportunity." President Obama is probably the unofficial head of the North American Union. He would be one of the kings of the ten-region confederation. It is his responsibility to see that the North American Union comes together as planned. Under the Obama administration, there has been an increase in government intrusion and overreach to ensure the United Nations Agenda 21 mandate fits.

September 2, 2015, reported by Dave Hodges, "Common Sense Show" is an article that provides additional insight into the established North American region. Russian professor Igor Panarin—former KGB analyst, dean of the Russian Foreign Ministry academy—is considered an expert on US and Russian relations and has reported for the past nine years that the United States has been divided into ten military districts. This idea was designed under the Nixon administration and in conjunction with the United Nations. Hodges said it is similar to the *Hunger Games* movie where the United States was divided into twelve districts.

A simulated graph, *Reserve and Corridor System to Protect Biodiversity*, outlines and defines regions as required by the United Nations Convention on Biological Diversity for the wildlands, reserves, corridors, buffer zones, borders, Indian Reservations, military sites, and for habitation. Wildland and reserves will require human depopulation, and this could be the reason there are so many wildfires in California and adjacent regions. Species identified as endangered will take precedence over people.

The Asian region, European region, and North American region provide solid confirmation that three of the ten regions are in place.

The Club of Rome

Fifty-six years ago, the Treaty of Rome was signed by twenty-seven member states. It planned to call this new formation the United States of Europe. The treaty calls for a president to oversee the European Union, which will represent one region of the ten-region confederation. The Club of Rome decided to push forward the concept of dividing the world into ten regions.

The Club of Rome was formed in 1968 in Rome, Italy, by Aurelio Peccei—Italian industrialist, new ager, who believes in world consciousness, humanism, and enlightenment. We call this the Luciferian doctrine. Cofounder was Alexander King, a Scottish scientist. The club described itself as a body of world citizens sharing a common concern for the future of humanity. Its mission is to act as a global catalyst for change through the identification and analysis of crucial problems facing humanity. The club is headquartered in Winterthur, Switzerland. In 1972, *The Limits to Growth,* authored by Donella and Dennis Meadows, Jorgen Randers, and William Behrens III was published and funded by Volkswagen Foundation—selling around twelve million copies. The theme of the book was to address economic stability, population growth, and the impact on dwindling natural resources using the World 3 model to simulate the consequence of interactions between the earth and human systems. Five variables were examined: these were world population, industrialization, pollution, food production, and resource depletion. The data would attempt to predict sustainability through altering growth trends among the five variables. This became the blueprint for the United Nations Agenda 21 Sustainabilty Program. Notables associated with the Club of Rome are Rockefeller, Carnegie, Planned Parenthood Organization, United Nations officials, and others.

In 1974, Eduard Pestel and Mihajlo Mesarovic of Case Western Reserve University developed a model of a ten-region confederation that gave a more optimistic prognosis for the future of the environment, noting many factors were within human control, wherein environmental and economic catastrophe were preventable. Their work was titled *Mankind at the Turning Point* and had the Club of Rome's full support (Wikipedia, "Club of Rome," June 2014).

The ten-region confederation is not for the betterment of mankind. According to Professor Darrell Y. Hamamoto, in comments made to Info Wars, "The illegal immigration is about creating a subservient underclass in America, which will exclude the middle class from higher education and create a new demographic of largely immigrant or foreign national undergraduate population that can be reeducated from the ground up and controlled much more readily" (Daniel Taylor, *Old-Thinker News*, July 13, 2014).

How does the one-world order get people to migrate to another location? Through conflict and war, as seen with the ISIS conflict driving people to migrate from the Middle East into various regions in Europe.

In a quick overview of the world, we can see ten dominate regions. They would be Greenland, North America, South America, Africa, Middle East, Europe, Russia, China, Australia, New Zealand, Antarctica. Islands would need to be combined with larger regions. Israel might not be included as one of the Middle East nations. Japan, Philippines, and Indonesia may be combined as one region.

We are not sure how the elite will divide the world into ten regions. However, Jack Van Impe suggests the following breakdown:

North American Union

America, Canada, Mexico, Alaska, Hawaii, Puerto Rico

Robert Pastor in 2004, developed the model for NAFTA, stated, "The citizens of United States, Canada, Mexico need to be reeducated to view themselves as the North American Union, NAU."

There was talk of NAFTA creating a super highway from Canada to Mexico. Pastor pushed for free trade between the NAU by creating a perimeter for the NAU. Mexico should be funded to strengthen its infrastructure. The dollar and peso should be replaced with the

Amero. There will be no push to secure the border between United States and Mexico. The 2016 presidential candidate Donald Trump is pushing to build a better security wall between the United States and Mexico.

A recent report online by Sam Rolley, *Personal Liberty Digest,* August 5, 2013, article "Feinstein, NSA have built a Dystopian Empire," quoted Dianne Feinstein (D-CA) at the Senate briefing of NSA, Feinstein grouped the United States, Canada, and Mexico together as the "homeland" in her defense of NSA spying activities. She presented a map of aborted terror acts in the world, and the North American continent was colored to include all three countries. A closer look at this segmentation will show it includes Greenland, Honduras, Costa Rica, Nicaragua, Belize, Guatemala, Panama, Cuba, and entire West Indies. Obama in April 2014 moved to repair relations with Cuba. Relations with Cuba were formally established September 2015.

South American Union

Union of South American nations working to integrate the region alongside various other transnationals are the following:

Peru	Paraguay	Argentina
Bolivia	Uruguay	El Salvador
Guatemala	Chile	Colombia

Caribbean Islands

May be linked with the North American Union, the following:

Cuba	Santo Domingo	Bahamas	Haiti	Bermuda
Trinidad	Jamaica	Dominican Republic		

Australia and New Zealand

Could include islands in South Pacific Ocean: Papua New Guinea.

European Union

The European Union represents one arm of the ten region confederation.

West European Union

Ireland	Cyprus	Latvia	Greece
Scotland	Czech Republic	Lithuania	Sweden
England	Austria	Denmark	Spain

France	Estonia	Luxembourg	Belgium
Bulgaria	Hungry	Netherlands	Portugal
Germany	Malta	Romania	Finland
Poland	Slovakia	Slovenia	Norway
Austria	Italy		

BRICS represent Belgium, Russia, India, China, and South Africa working together for trade. This group represents 43 percent of world population and 53 percent of world financial capital.

England

Usually took anti-Israel position. A pro-Israel position was declared by PM David Cameron, March 2014, stating his Jewish roots on his first visit to Israel's Yad Vashem, and he addressed Knesset. Cameron, planning to visit Auschwitz in Poland, pledged to educate children about Holocaust and to fight discrimination and prejudice. He was accompanied by Ben Helfgott, a Holocaust survivor, and some commissioners who will work the new Holocaust commission in Britain. Cameron said, "It is about remembering the long and rightful search of a people for a nation and the right for the Jews to live a peaceful and prosperous life in Israel" (29).

Belgium, France, Germany all have a history of anti-Semitism and a growing presence of Muslims

East European Region

Russia may alone be considered one region.

Russia has an interesting history, and following, we summarize those who shaped its identity.

Joseph Stalin (born 1878, died 1953)—as a youth, Stalin received his education in a Greek Orthodox priesthood school. In his teenage years, he was influenced by Vladimir Lenin and joined the Russian Social Democratic Labor Party, a Marxist group. This association led to Stalin joining the Bolsheviks between 1917–1919, commanded by Lenin, engaging in labor strikes, bank robberies, and assassinations. Under Lenin, millions of its citizens were murdered, religion was banned, and its goal was to establish Communist rule over the entire world. Peasants were forced to fight in World War I, and Lenin confiscated privately owned firearms around 1929.

Joseph Stalin ruled under socialism1941 to 1953. Russians fared no better under dictator Stalin.

Under Stalin, Russia became an industrial power, but in its wake, it regulated grain production, which farmers could not meet, and famine ensued from 1932 to 1933. Starvation and imprisonment resulted in the death upward to sixty million within eight years. Following this death toll, Stalin initiated the "great purge," removing communist party affiliates, government officials, military, and others deemed enemies of the Soviet people—resulting in millions more imprisoned or killed.

In 1939, Stalin entered into a pact with Hitler's Germany, dividing their influence and territory in Europe. This led to the invasion of Poland. Hitler broke the agreement and invaded the Soviet Union in June of 1941. Russia's Red Army pushed back Nazi Germany and captured Berlin May 1945, ending World War II.

Union of the Soviet Socialist Republic, USSR, began in 1918 and ended in 1991, with the fall of the USSR and communism. Russian leaders continued to push for the reunification of Russia and its rise as a world superpower. This would be accomplished through world revolution based on the communist ideology to transform the world into socialist states. Warsaw, Poland, became a target. The city of Lwow (now Lviv, Ukraine) was in their cross fire. Putin moved to take over Georgia. Presently, Russia continues its plans to expand its influence in the Ukraine, as in the annexation of Crimea.

Russian leadership continues to foster relations with China, Cuba, Iran, and North Korea. Tensions between Russia and the United States regarding nuclear arms initiated the Cold War period. After Stalin's death, Nikita Khrushchev became president. United States opposed communism and, under the Cold War premise, went after other communist nations such as Vietnam, Cuba, El Salvador, Korea, and China at the cost of US lives for over fifty years. Antiwar protesters took it out on US cities such as Timothy McVeigh and the Oklahoma bombings and assassination of JFK and Robert Kennedy.

Vladmir Putin, former KGB, joined Kremlin staff under Boris Yeltsin, who promoted him to prime minister and president. Putin was born in Leningrad, 1952. He is Russian Orthodox and Conservative. Russian Orthodox considered themselves czars to protect world's orthodox people in nineteenth century. Vladmir the Great, prince of Kiev, converted pagan Slavs to Christianity. Putin's faith caused him to call United States morally corrupt, weak, and homosexuality was a threat to Russia's birthrate. May 5, 2014, he signed a law restricting profanity in the arts, banning curse words in live performances, and adding warning labels to books, CDs, films. Rock group *Pussy* riot resulted in jail time for performing profane, anti-Putin song at the altar of an Orthodox church in Moscow.

Putin saw the collapse of USSR and loss of Poland, Baltics. United States expanded NATO to include those regions. Putin saw this as a threat and broken promise since Russia supported Germany's 1990 reunification. United States would not expand NATO, which now has military presence in former Soviet territory. Putin was determined to restore Russia's place as a great power. Russia, rich in oil-producing economy, could restore military might. Russia produces more oil than Saudi Arabia. Russia will supply oil to China and accept yuan for payment. Russia may cut oil supply to Europe because of their joint sanctions with the United States against Russia.

Putin's goal was the formation of a new Eurasian union, with Belarus and Kazakhstan. His ally, Dmitri Medvedev, served as president 2008–2012. Putin served as prime minister during Medvedev's presidency (Wikipedia).

Russia has a nuclear weapons arsenal of five thousand missiles. They are planning to modernize their weapons program. September 2014, Russia tested ICBM launched from nuclear sub Vladimir Monomakh. It flew from White Sea near border with Finland to Kamchatka Peninsula, north of Japan—a 3,500–mile distance. Putin thumbs nose at United States and NATO and flies bomber planes near Alaska and Canada.

Russia sells arms and nuclear technology to Iran and has an alliance with North Korea and China. Russia is allied with Bashar Assad of Syria. Russia sold Iskandar and surfaced to air missiles to Syria, sent a message to the United States not to attack Syria, but it could embolden Syria to attack Israel (*World Net Daily*, 2014).

January 17, 2015, China President Xi Jinping and his wife visited Russia. Russia rolled out the red carpet for their visit. This union solidifies their joint cooperation politically, militarily, and economically. Their commonality is that they are both anti-America. Obama invited the China president to United States in September 2015 and rolled out the red carpet.

US and Russian relations were further strained when Russia gave asylum to NSA leaker Edward Snowden. A smidgeon of US retaliation against Russia was the US objection to the annexation of Crimea. United States led media publicity to backfire as a majority of Crimea people wanted to be part of Russia.

Russia gained international attention by hosting the 2014 Sochi Winter Olympics at a cost of $50 billion. United States could only boycott the Olympics by refusing to send high-ranking officials, including the president.

October 2015, Russian military establishes a base in Syria to help the Syrian president defeat terrorists. Russian plane was shot down in Sinai with over two hundred people all dead. ISIS claimed responsibility, but it could be the United States in retaliation for military ops in Syria. Vladimir Putin was ranked by *Forbes* more powerful than Obama.

Asian Nations

Japan	Indonesia
Singapore	China
Mongolia	Philippines
Hong Kong	Thailand, Bangkok

North Korea	Vietnam
South Korea	India

Africa

North Africa

Egypt	Morocco	Mauritania
Lybia	Sahara	Algeria

Africa Major

Sudan	Ghana	Zaire
Chad	Nigeria	Uganda
Niger	Cameroon	Kenya
Mali	Central African Republic	Ethiopia
Senegal	Guinea	Congo
Tanzania	Ivory Coast	Angola
Zambia	Madagascar Island	Somalia

South Africa

Nambia	Zimbabwe	Swaziland
Botswana	Mozambique	South Africa

Middle East

Saudi Arabia	Oman	Afghanistan
Iraq	Yemen	Pakistan
Iran	Syria	Gaza
Turkey	Lebanon	Jordan
Israel	United Arab Emirate	

One-World Supreme Leader

As we connect pieces of the puzzle, the last few pieces will reveal the one-world leader. We have highlighted a few individuals throughout history that were archetypes of a final world leader, the Antichrist. Coming into the twentieth century, German dictator Adolf Hitler, a top general in Satan's army, was an archetype of Antichrist.

(Underlined words are for comparison to the US president.)

Hitler came to the people promising to restore Germany to its glory. He promoted change. Hitler connected with the common man through association by telling them he was poor, worked his way up from meagerness, humble, and a man of moral conviction. His whole persona was based on a lie that would be perpetrated as he climbed his way up through German leadership. Behind the scene, he was enamored (immoral) with teenage girls. His last conquest was Ava Braun, whom he married a few days before the defeat of Germany, and allegedly, they committed suicide.

After writing *Mein Kampf*, the royalties from the book grew, and he was sent a tax bill of over $400,000. He did not want to pay taxes, so he had himself declared tax exempt and had all his tax files sealed. He amassed great wealth from the impoverished citizens and confiscation of Jews' homes and possessions. Hitler enjoyed a life of luxury, and he spent huge amounts of money on himself with no accountability. He took taxpayer funds to build his estates and entertain his elite. To make way for the new Germany, many people were forced to leave their homes, which were demolished for Germany's rise. He marched into Poland, intending to conquer. Germany marched into Austria, Hitler's homeland. Many welcomed the furor but did not realize he was there to take over Austria. Hitler planned to redesign Austria, and he desired a classical museum be established to house classical art, much of which had been confiscated from the Jews whom he, in turn, slaughtered. He sanctioned the Kaiser Wilhelm Estate for the museum. No expense was spared for this project.

In 1938, the Nazis established gun control prior to Hitler's campaign to exterminate the Jews. At the height of World War II, Hitler said,

> A foolish mistake is to allow the subject races to possess arms. History shows that conquerors who allow their subject races to carry arms have prepared their own downfall … to supply arms to the underdogs is door to overthrow any sovereignty. No to native militia and native police. German troops alone will bear the sole responsibility for the maintenance of law and order throughout occupied territories and put into place military strongholds.

The German chancellor's propaganda machine promoted him as a man of the people, a moral man coming to restore honor to Germany. He was beguiling and persuasive, like Satan, appearing as an angel of light. Hitler became a charismatic orator, using the art of speech—intertwining certain buzz words, lies, and deception—until he finally won over the hearts and minds of his followers. The deception was so great that the majority had no problem participating in the mass genocide of other Germans.

In order to move toward perfecting a superior race of people in Germany, ethnic cleansing was mandated to single out Jews and others classified as inferior people living in Germany.

He created a division among the poor, working class, and the German elite. Hitler rewarded those loyal with millions in bonuses. Albert Speer was Hitler's number two man, and he was to oversee the transformation of Germany using slave labor, of whom many were Jews, to create the German utopia without Jews. As the end of days came for Hitler, the German deutsche mark became worthless (economic decline.) The Red Army (Russia) was advancing on Germany in 1945. Hitler hid his master paintings and other trophies underground. Years later, the Nuremburg trials convicted many for the downfall of Germany. Albert Speers received only ten years in jail because he lied and said he did not know the full extent of Hitler's operations. Speers also hid his masterpieces and reclaimed them after his release from prison, profiting on the booty.

Hitler emerged at the beginning of the twentieth century. Obama emerged on the scene at the beginning of the twenty-first century. Following are similarities between Hitler and Obama—both operatives of the revived Roman Empire:

- Both promised "change."
- Both had connection with the little man—poor, humble, moral.
- Both embrace immorality and ungodliness.
- Both are charismatic, good orators, seen as saviors.
- Both rose up from obscurity, dysfunctional family.
- Both wrote books and profited.
- Both changed laws to benefit self and concealed records.
- Both rewarded their faithful with government jobs and money.
- Both enjoy luxury, spending large sums of money on self with no accountability.
- Both were making way for the one-world order by more government control.
- Both admire pagan symbol of Zeus.
- Both stand on the position of gun control and decreasing local police power.
- Both had division among poor, middle class, wealthy.
- Both were pitting ethnic groups against one another.
- Both invaded or intruded into the affairs of other nations.
- Both are Anti-Christian and Anti-Jew.
- Hitler and Obama have Jewish roots; both claimed to be Christians.
- Both control media.
- Hitler pushed for Aryanism while killing millions. Obama pushes for Islamic acceptance in the midst of worldwide Islamic terrorism.

Adolf Hitler came to power through persuasion, political propaganda, entitlements, divisiveness, deception, and murder. His mind-set was secular humanist. Surrounding his death, theories arose that the body of Hitler was a duplicate. Some say he escaped—sort of like the beast was wounded but lived. Currently, Obama appears to admire Hitler. Obama seems to have adopted Hitler's agenda of political propaganda, lies, entitlements, divisiveness, national economic destabilization, gun control, and limiting individual freedoms. Obama openly embraces the false religion of Islam, homosexuality, and abortion—which are an abomination unto God. Obama belittles Conservatives, Christians, anti-Israel, and promotes ungodliness.

The one-world leader will emerge from the revived Roman Empire which is representative of people from Africa, Arabia, Palestine, Asia, and Europe. The one-world leader will be a combination of European, African, and Asian ancestry by blood or adoption. His power will expand and influence every culture, nationality, and ethnic group on earth. As we think on these things, Barack Obama's heritage is African (father), European (mother), and Asian (stepfather). While living in Indonesia, he was introduced to Islam, which connects him with the Arab world.

Before placing the mantle on a particular individual, we need to consider other possibilities.

Possible Candidates for the One-World Leader

Satan, the god of this world, has established his spiritual domain of principalities, powers, wickedness in high places. Under Satan's hierarchy, he did establish his authority in various positions around the globe. Such as Turkey, Iran and Iraq. We can see a concentration of wickedness over America. Obviously. Satan does not require a literal seat on the earth since in his mind, all the earth is his domain. Some scholars have attempted to identify Satan's headquarters as being exclusively in Iraq or Rome as well as suggesting future sites such as Turkey, Israel, Saudi Arabia or New York.

In all probability, he will establish a stronghold in most of these regions. In the following scriptures, we see two events that are associated with principalities, powers, and wickedness.

In Revelation 9, a key is given to an angel who opens the bottomless pit, releases a hoard of demonic locusts, or evil spirits and the name of their king is called Abaddon in Hebrew and Apollyon in Greek. Both these titles refer to Satan. Here we see God opens the bottomless pit, and God allows demons and evil spiritual activity to increase upon the earth.

In Revelation 13, we see a symbolic beast arising from the sea (coming out of the multitudes), and the entity of the beast is a representation of a satanic world system formed over the nations. This system is also called spiritual Babylon. The system includes Satan, the Antichrist, false prophet, and wicked people.

For six thousand years, Antichrist have come and gone. There were archetypes or shadows of the literal, physical man who will assume the role of the final Antichrist. "*Little children, it is the last days and as you have heard Antichrist will come even now are there many Antichrists ...*" 1 John 2:18

These human characters were of the seed of Satan by association, and through their evil works, Satan's plans have been accomplished. Statues of Zeus and other pagan monuments litter the land as a constant reminder that the Prince of Darkness rules over the world. The final world leader, the beast out of the sea will emerge from the satanic world system. The end of the age has arrived, and Satan will select one final man to be his one-world supreme leader. This person will be empowered by Satan and be possessed by an evil spirit.

Many have tried on the glass slipper, but it did not fit. Following, we suggest possible contenders for the one-world leader. Will the Antichrist emerge from Ancient, Arabic, European, or American roots?

Ancient Roots

Will the Antichrist come from ancient roots in the form of the reincarnated and resurrected Nimrod? Sound ludicrous? According to a few scholars, they believe this is the case. We introduce the following overview of a few who make the claim that Nimrod is the literal son of Satan, and he will return as Apollo. This line of thought is presented in Peter Goodgame's book, *The Second coming of the Antichrist.* From our research, the name Apollo is a reference to Satan. Therefore, if Apollo is Satan; Nimrod cannot also be Satan and the son of Satan. If we embrace the concept that Nimrod is Satan's son, then we should believe that evil people in general are the literal seed of Satan. To be the literal seed of Satan, a physical impregnation of a human woman with satanic sperm would need to take place in order for there to be a lineage or children spawned by Satan. First obvious problem is that Satan is spirit, an angel and created not to procreate.

We are unable to find within biblical scriptures a scenario to support the theory that Satan has literal offspring. What we do believe is that evil people who have aligned themselves with the works of darkness are the seed of Satan by association and have opened themselves up to possible possession by evil spirits. People throughout the ages have embraced the work of Satan, desiring to be as gods, a son of Satan, or archetypes of his Antichrist. The Roman emperor Domitian wanted to be recognized as Apollo incarnate. Napoleon's name means Apollo. Emperor Nero was considered an Antichrist. Many despots have wanted to be immortalized as Antichrist. Followers of various religions await the return of someone.

Satan worshippers herald their coming god. They enact rituals to impregnate a female with the seed of Satan, which is a human man having intercourse with a human female. A child is born, and they claim it to be the son of Satan. The Masonic order has a symbolic ritual of the resurrection of Hiram Abiff, their Osiris. Sadam Hussein claimed to be the reincarnated Nebuchadnezzar.

Herein lies the fallacy of resurrected humans outside of God's power. Nimrod, a human, is not Apollo, Zeus, or other mythological god. Those false deities are the fallen angels who were given names and worshipped. Their hybrid offspring were probably worshipped during the preflood era. Satan has been on the earth before the fall of mankind and has seduced many to follow him. Satan will make his final selection of the human despot who he will empower as his Antichrist to serve as his one-world leader. This man will go into perdition, meaning destruction by the coming of our Lord Jesus. Let us surmise that the Antichrist is presently on the scene. Who he is has not been clearly revealed. This person has human parents but by giving his allegiance to Satan, he is, by association, the seed of Satan. In return for his allegiance, Satan gives him power, knowledge, and wealth. Satan has beguiled gullible people to do his bidding in return for his gifts. During the tribulation period, the Antichrist and false prophet, both humans, are given unusual power by Satan. On the other side of the coin, God has empowered his people to fight against spiritual darkness and to show forth supernatural signs and wonders. Satan is a master counterfeiter and attempts to duplicate the works of God.

In Goodgame's book, he presents a scenario where the man of sin, the son of perdition, the final Antichrist will be the literal son of Satan and "paganism ultimate incarnation, the beast of Revelation 13" (Foreword, page 1).

Following the Nimrod is Antichrist mind-set. We consider Goodgame's theory that the final Antichrist is Nimrod now resurrected and whose spirit has incarnated the body of the final Antichrist. What does the Bible say? There is evidence to suggest that all the souls of the unredeemed from creation to the end of the millennial reign have been retained in hell, awaiting to be called forth at the last Resurrection to stand before the white throne judgment, and then all those unredeemed souls will be returned to their place of eternal damnation. Only God knows for sure if the soul of Nimrod is presently retained in hell or heaven.

If we believe the spirit of Nimrod can be summoned by Satan and entered into a physical human, then we must also believe in the false concept of reincarnation. We would also have to concede that Satan has the power and ability to release dammed souls from hell, and if that were the case, he would have released all, including his fallen angels. From our study of evil spirits/demons, the Bible says they have the ability to possess and torment people, but we do not believe the spirit/soul of humans can possess others humans. Therefore, the spirit/soul of Nimrod, a human, cannot possess the body of the Antichrist, who is also human.

Jewish Antichrist from the Tribe of Dan

Some scholars believe there may be a connection with the tribe of Dan and the Antichrist. Will the Antichrist be a Jew, and if so, would he be accepted by Israel as their Messiah? In considering this, we must first go back to the time of Abraham, whose heir was Isaac. Isaac had two sons, Jacob and Esau. Jacob received Esau's blessing, and from that time forward, their families were rivals. Esau married the daughter of Ishmael, Abraham's and Hagar's son. Hagar is of the Canaanite lineage (Genesis 28:8–9).

Jacob traveled to Padan-aram to meet with Laban, son of Bethuel the Syrian and the brother of Rebekah, his mother's brother. Jacob had three wives and twelve sons. His son, Dan, was born of Bilhad, Rachels's handmaid (Genesis 35:25). Jacob had a dream before his twelve sons were born. God confirms the Abrahamic land covenant with Jacob and tells him his "**seed** will be as the dust of the earth, and you will spread abroad to the west, east, north, and south and in thee shall all he families of the earth be blessed." Here in this place, Jacob sets a stone and called it Bethel in the region of Luz (Genesis 28:13–14). Immediately, one must consider how it would be possible to keep track of multitudes of people (seed) living throughout the world, over thousands of years, and tie them into one of the twelve tribes.

Jacob prophesied over his sons and blessed them all. To his son **Judah** called "a lion's whelp" (Genesis 49:9). To his son, **Dan**, he "will judge his people as one of the tribes of Israel and he will be a serpent by the way and adder in the path that bites the horse heels so that his rider will fall backward" (Genesis 49:16–17).

In Deuteronomy 33:22, we find that Moses blessed the twelve tribes before his death. To the tribe of Dan, he said, "**Dan** is a lion's whelp, he shall leap from Bashan." We interjected the descriptions given to Judah and Dan both bearing a referenced as "lion whelps," meaning lion cubs, because scholars attempt to associate this with some foreboding character of Dan like an Antichrist. Each of the twelve tribes had a banner with a symbol. Dan's symbol was a serpent, and the tribe did not like it, so they changed it to an eagle.

As the Israelites moved into the promised land 1406 BC. Joshua was directed to kill the pagans living in the land God had given to Israel. Joshua assigned the twelve tribes their own territories. The Danites were not satisfied with their allotment and left it to take over an inhabited region called Leshem/Laish, region of Bashan/Lebanon, north of Jerusalem. The Danites killed the residents and renamed it the land of Dan (Joshua 19:47–48).

Following the lineage of Dan, we come to a man named Manoah of the Danites. His wife was barren until God blessed her to conceive, and she gave birth to a son named Samson. Samson was blessed of God at his birth for a specific purpose. He was born during the time that God allowed Israel to be under Philistine hardship for their disobedience. Samson was well known for his superior strength; he slew thousands of Philistines with a jawbone, and he killed a lion with his bare hands. Samson became one of Israel's judges around 1070 BC. Samson was a judge, associated with a lion and a warrior, which fulfills Jacobs prophecy over Dan (Judges 13:2, 25).

We find mention of Dan in 2 Chronicles 2:13, during the time Solomon was making preparations to build the temple. He asked Huram, the king of Tyre (region of Lebanon/land of Dan), for cedar and skilled workers. The king first responds by acknowledging the Lord has loved his people and has made Solomon king over them, blessed be the Lord God of Israel that made heaven and earth who has given to David the king a wise son. King Huram tells Solomon he has an intelligent man, who is the son of a woman of the daughter of Dan, and his father was a man of Tyre, having many skills. It seems that these were the descendants of the Danites still living in the region of Lebanon around 960 BC.

The twelve tribes were divided around 930 BC. Ten tribes were classified as the northern kingdom of Israel (including Dan) under King Jeroboam. Two tribes, Benjamin and Judah, were classified as the southern kingdom of Judah under King Rehoboam. The northern kingdom was led into idolatry by the king, setting up idols in Dan's territory and in Bethel. 1 Kings 12:29, Judges 18:27–30 tell us that the children of Dan set up graven images, and Jonathan, son of Gershom, son of Manasseh, were priests to the tribe of Dan until the captivity. Israel as a whole from their time in Egypt until their time in the promised land always fell into idolatry and sin. Why then would those of the tribe of Dan be singled out as the tribe to birth the Antichrist when all twelve tribes did wickedly in the sight of the Lord?

The Assyrian Empire under Shalmaneser conquered the ten tribes, including Dan, in 722 BC, taking them into captivity. Jeremiah began his ministry around 627 to 586 BC. The Babylonian Empire under Nebuchadnezzar conquered the two remaining tribes and took them into captivity, 586 BC.

Other scholars use Jeremiah 8:11–17 as a reference to Dan the coming Antichrist:

> *The snorting of his horses was heard* ***from*** *Dan … the whole land trembled at the sound of the neighing of his strong ones for they have come and devoured the land.*

This passage may be pointing to the Babylonian Empire traveling through various regions, including the territory of Dan. There is no scripture reference that states Dan came to Israel and devoured the land. As in any conquest, some people escaped and remained in Israel as a testimony to these accounts.

There are a few things to consider in the above passages:

- God blesses all of Jacob's twelve sons.
- God tells Jacob his seed will be plentiful throughout the world.

- Jacob tells Dan he will be like a serpent and adder, biting horses' heels.
- Moses blesses the tribe of Dan and defines them as lion's whelp.
- Jacob tells Dan he will Judge Israel.
- Samson of the Danites was a judge, associated with lion, and a warrior (symbolically speaking, as in biting horses' heels to cause rider to fall backward).
- Solomon used the skills of a Danite.
- Twelve tribes divided, and all fell into ungodliness. The descendants of Dan as well as the other tribes were disbursed throughout the land, and it is impossible to identify the remnants from the lost tribe of Dan.
- The time frame of Jacob is far removed from the revealing of the final Antichrist today.
- Though Israel was wicked in the eyes of God, they were blessed, judged, and redeemed continuously.

From the time of Jacob and his twelve sons, we followed their history for hundreds of years. In the biblical passages referenced to Dan or Danites, we could not establish a credible link that the Antichrist will come forth from the tribe of Dan. We will follow other scholarly thought in New Testament times to see if there is a connection with the tribe of Dan and Antichrist. It is like finding a needle (Dan) in a haystack (three thousand years of history) and especially since the ten tribes were absorbed into Turkey, Lebanon, Persia, Babylon, Syria, Jordan, and other regions leaving few traces of their history. James Bruce in AD 1769 discovered people in Ethiopia who were associated with the tribe of Dan.

Other scholars attempt to make the pieces fit by using the quote, "Dan will judge his people as one of the tribes of Israel" and connect it to the Antichrist, the "abomination of desolation," who is used as the instrument of God's judgment. To further the strength of their case that Antichrist is a Danite, Revelation 7:4–8 is used to show that the sealing of twelve thousand from each tribe did not include the tribe of Dan. This is speculation and not fact that the tribe of Dan was excluded because the Antichrist is a Danite. Further review of Revelation 7:4–8, we also see that Ephraim, son of Joseph, was excluded; yet his brother Manasseh is included. Also Dinah, the sister of Reuben, Simeon, Levi, Judah, etc., is excluded. Rachel's children, Joseph and Benjamin, are included, but Jacob's prophecy over Benjamin describes him as a "raven wolf devouring the prey and dividing the spoil." If we use other scholarly considerations, Antichrist could just as well come from the tribe of Benjamin.

A few scholars attempt to squeeze Obama into the Danite tribe by claiming his mother was a Danite. They state his father was of the Tribe of Judah associated with King Solomon and Ethiopian roots or from Kenya. In Zimbabwe/Ethiopia regions, members of the Lemba tribe claim to be associated with one of the twelve tribes. There are no concrete facts to establish this as a credible link to Dan. However, it is interesting that Obama associated himself with Jews: "having a Jewish soul, honorary member of the tribe." *New York Magazine* pictured Obama on its cover wearing a kippah, *First Jewish President.*

Daniel's Visions Points to the Antichrist

In chapter 2 of Daniel, he interprets the dream of King Nebuchadnezzar. The king dreamed of an image with a head of gold representing Babylon; the chest of silver was Medes-Persia; the hips of bronze were Greece; the two legs of iron were Rome. The feet were a combination of iron and clay, representing the revived Roman Empire, from which the final Antichrist would arise.

In Daniel chapter 7, he had a vision of four beast arising from the sea representing four kingdoms, each different from one another. In brief, this correlates with the image in Daniel 2.

1. This beast appeared as a lion with eagles wings, represents Babylon.
2. The second beast was like a bear with three ribs in its mouth, represents Medes-Persia; three ribs represent three nations it will conquer. Daniel 8:3–5 further discusses Medes-Persia as a ram with two horns and a goat representing Greece who defeats the ram.
3. Another beast appears as a leopard with four wings and four heads, represents Greece; four heads represent the division of Greece between Alexander's four generals and also is seen as a goat.
    - Alexander the Great conquered the known world. Daniel's vision tells us that after the death of Alexander, four horns came up, representing the division of Greece between his four generals. The south was given to Ptolemy (Libya, Egypt, Palestine); the west was given to General Cassander, or Antipater (Macedonia, Greece); the north, to Lycimon, or Antigonus (Asia Minor, Turkey); and the east to Seleucus (Assyria, Babylon, Syria, Persia).
4. The fourth beast is dreadful, terrible, strong, with iron teeth—represents the iron legs of the Roman Empire. Its ten horns represent the revived Roman Empire and its future ten-region confederation. It is the fourth empire after Babylon, Medes-Persia, Greece.
    - Daniel 2:40 and Daniel 7:23 point to the fourth beast of iron representing the Roman Empire, which was known as dreadful, terrible, strong, and devouring its enemies; yet it is diverse from all the beast that were before it. The Roman Empire did not fade away but was divided, representing two legs of iron forming the western region and the eastern region.

(a) Western region of the Roman Empire was headed by Romulus Augustulus, including the area of Alexandria, Antioch, North Africa, and spoke Latin, Greek, and Aramaic.

The western region of the Roman Empire made significant historical steps toward the realization of the future Antichrist. Antiochus IV Epiphanes in the second century, 167 BC, attacked the pleasant land, Israel. He overthrew the high priest, looted the temple, and replaced worship of God with Greek idolatry. Antiochus IV Epiphanes was thought to be Antichrist because he desecrated the Jewish temple. He claimed godhood and had an image of himself erected in Jerusalem.

Roman emperor Nero was a cruel ruler who persecuted Christians and Jews. He burned Rome. In AD 68, Nero was condemned to death for his crimes. He escaped to a remote location and killed himself; therein rumors surfaced that he would return to avenge himself upon the Roman world. A myth developed, saying Nero never died and would at some future date be revived and raised to power again. Bible scholars in the twenty-first century would put forth a myth that Nimrod, not Nero, will arise from the dead and embody the Antichrist.

Rome became a global oligarchy out to devour the whole earth, tread it down, and break it into pieces. Britain, part of the revived Roman Empire, set out to capture all the world and colonize it. Rebels who revolted against the crown found refuge and freedom in the Americas, but their roots would still be part of the Roman Empire.

(b) Eastern Byzantine Empire then Constantinople under Constantine then to Ottoman Turks. The eastern leg merged the cultures of Greece and Rome. Later, Rome would assert itself over many regions of the world. The Islamic influence would fluctuate in various regions once controlled by Rome. In these last days, the Middle East regions are under Islamic control.

Chapter 8, "Growth of Kingdoms," provides additional information on divided Rome.

Jew and Gentile Antichrist

Other scholarly interpretation see the Antichrist as a Jew and Gentile. A Jew is someone who associates themselves with the twelve tribes and follow Jewish laws and customs. A Gentile is someone other than a Jew. This combination of Jew and Gentile would be likely when a Jew marries a Gentile. From scripture, we know the Antichrist hates Jews and Christians. History records Jewish parents who had children grow up to hate their Jewish roots. Scholars reference Vespasian, whose descendants intermarried with Herodians/Idumean/Edomites and intermarried with the Seleucid/Greeks descendant of Antiochus IV Epiphanes and intermarried with the Romans/Flavians. Vespasian and Titus are credited with destroying the temple in AD 70.

Hundreds of years later, we find the Kahzars were Gentiles who converted to Judaism. Most Jews from Russia, Germany, or Ukraine are Gentiles who intermarried and converted to Judaism. From this melting pot of Jews and Gentiles, it is speculated they may include the bloodline of Dan. Other scholars connect two thousand years of history from the Romans to the "people of the prince" that will come and confirm the covenant (peace treaty with Israel). In the book of Daniel 7:8, the Antichrist appears to arise from out of the Gentile nations, specifically the revived Roman Empire. There is merit in that line of thought because it was prophesied in Daniel and will be fulfilled in Revelation. The only thing missing is the clear connection between the Antichrist out of Dan and the Antichrist out of the Roman Empire, tying both Jew and Gentile together. Antichrist could well be a Jew or a Gentile. He could have Jewish, European, Middle Eastern, or African roots. Remember, the ten tribes were disbursed throughout the world. Nevertheless, some Bible scholars predict the Antichrist will come from European ancestry, while others believe he will come from the Arabian linage. Either way, they both are part of the revived Roman Empire's two legs and ten toes.

The student of prophecy understands that the nations/kingdoms described in Daniel and Revelation gave way to the <u>divided</u> Roman Empire, which in turn became the <u>revived</u> Roman Empire. The ethnic makeup of the early Roman Empire were people from many nations. During the time of Christ, the Roman Empire controlled a vast majority of other nations. On the Day of Pentecost, around AD 30, people from those nations were in Jerusalem. During the outpouring of the Holy Spirit, those gathered in the upper room began to speak in the tongues of those assembled, being representative of Jews and Gentiles gathered in Jerusalem out of every nation under heaven (Acts 2:4–11) They were Parthians, Medes, Elamites, Mesopotamians, people from Judaea, Cappadocia, Pontus, Asia, Phrygia, Pamphylia in Egypt, Libya, Cyrene, Cretes, Arabians, strangers of Rome, and proselytes (converts).

Some Bible scholars believe the revived Roman Empire was primarily composed of people of European descent (having a fair complexion), and from that standpoint, they develop a European model of the Antichrist. From the list of nations mentioned above, the Roman Empire was <u>ethnically diverse,</u> as is modern-day revived Rome/Europe/America.

Researching historical clues, many antichrists have come and gone. As did his predecessors, this last Antichrist will give his allegiance to Satan. He will also follow an ungodly lineage, having an appearance of righteousness, diplomacy to his constituents, other world leaders, and the uninformed masses. He is lukewarm toward Jews, but they are desperate for peace, causing them to accept a peace deal from the devil. To Muslims, he appears to be a moderate, trying to appease the Islamic world; and in some turn of events, they may consider him Mahdi. Christendom is so divided and apostate they have no qualms aligning with a man who is clearly immoral.

We previously reviewed Antichrist from ancient roots, tribe of Dan, Daniel's prediction of the little horn, and the possibility Antichrist is both Jew and Gentile. Following. we consider Antichrist from three backgrounds being Islamic, European, American.

Islamic Antichrist, the Mahdi

We emphasize that Islamic end-time events are in contradiction to the Bible truth regarding the Antichrist. As Christians, we should consider their doctrine as distortions of the truth. The Koran does not have prophecy and fulfillment of prophecy for its validation as the Holy Bible.

Islam believes the twelfth Imam will be their long-awaited Mahdi, their messiah. This man is not mutually agreed upon within the various sects of Islam. Some claim his name will be Muhammad Ibin Assad Mahdi. A Muslim website, Discoverislam.org, posted that the Mahdi will arrive between AD 2015/2016, and the Islamic Jesus will come in 2022. That is an interesting claim since we believe the Antichrist is present.

Iran's supreme leader, the Ayatollah Ali Khamenei, is a Shiite and fervent believer that the end of days is at hand. They believe the Islamic messiah, the twelfth Imam, or promised one, is coming to conquer and rule the world. Khamenei began tweeting his message in 2009 (same time frame Obama became president). To speed up the coming of their Mahdi, Iran has committed itself to create nuclear weapons that can reach to the United States and Israel, killing the infidels of Allah in a nuclear holocaust.

At the annual United Nations meeting, September 2012, in New York, the Iranian President Mahmood Ahmadinejad's message focused on the coming of a global world order and a one-world leader. He said,

> To voice the divine and humanitarian message … to you and to the whole world. Allah has promised us a man of kindness, a man who loves people and loves absolute justice, a man who is a perfect human being and is named Imam Al-Mahdi, a man who will come in the company of the Islamic Jesus, peace be upon him and the righteous. The Mahdi is the ultimate savior. His arrival on earth will mark a new beginning, a rebirth, and a resurrection. It will be the beginning of peace, lasting security and genuine life. The coming reign of the twelfth Imam [the final one] on earth will

> bring about an eternally bright future for mankind, not by force or waging wars but through thought awakening and developing kindness in everyone.

The Iranian leader did not offer a specific timetable, but he did say the "sweet scent of the Mahdi's global reign will soon reach all the territories in Asia, Europe, Africa and the United States." His statement comes at a time when the acclaimed final pope enters the arena. He is perceived to be a man of kindness, loves people, and has reached out to all the world.

Some of Ahmadinejad's characterizations of his Mahdi do align with the characterization of the anti-Christ as portrayed in scripture. The Iranian leader proclaims his Mahdi comes "not by war" which contradicts their belief that chaos must excel to hasten his arrival. We see an increase in fanatical, apocalyptic Islamic acts of annihilation targeting infidels.

Islamic end-times is the driving motivation for their foreign policy and is a primary objective of the Iranian nuclear project. After Mahdi emerges from a well, his followers believe he will turn all the wars and killing to his advantage in order to establish peace within the caliphate and justice under Sharia.

Following is a summary of the Mahdi and his promises for a one-world leader made by Iranian president at the 2012 United Nations meeting:

- He is kind and loves people, justice, hope, freedom, and dignity to all.
- He will end oppression, immorality, poverty, discrimination.
- He will do away with ignorance, superstition, prejudice by opening the gates of science.
- He is a perfect human being; he is a savior.
- He will come with Jesus.
- He will prepare the ground for the collective, active, and constructive participation of all in a global world.
- He will lead humanity into achieving its glorious and eternal ideals.
- He will come so mankind will taste the pleasure of being human and awakening.
- He will return all children of Adam, irrespective of skin color, to their innate origin after a long history of separation and division, linking them to eternal happiness.
- His arrival is a new beginning, a rebirth, and a resurrection.
- He will bring peace, security, and life.
- He will have a broad forehead and hooked nose.

Islamic eschatology also includes an Antichrist figure. Their theory was developed from portions of Zoroastrianism, Old and New Testament. Passages taken from these sources were embellished and made up, such as "the hour" was associated with the resurrection, judgment, and return of the Islamic Jesus and in the Islamic mind-set not an important event in itself but only as it ties into the arrival of the twelfth Imam, the Mahdi.

Islam's Antichrist is called Dajal, and they believe he will be a Jew born in Iran. His characteristics are as follows and are not accurate to those found in the Bible:

- Has one eye.
- A divine prophet.
- Will deceive many via godliness and miracles.
- Will have an army of seventy thousand Jews and seventy thousand Tartars.
- Will conquer world except Mecca and Medina.
- Written on his forehead is infidel.
- He will be cruel and militaristic.
- Will require all to worship him as god.

Islamic signs for the appearance of their Antichrist are listed:

- Increase in ignorance concerning the faith
- Instability of faith, as in Muslim conversion to Christianity overnight
- Increase in false prophets
- Increase in apostasy as in Muslim's following Jesus of the Bible
- Building of luxurious mosques
- Acceptance of astrology
- Use of alcohol and immorality
- Increase in natural calamities
- Political corruption
- People longing for death due to calamities and wickedness
- Increase in paganism, as in Muslims following lifestyles of non-Muslims
- Increase in war
- The sign of the sun wising in the west

Barack Obama was acknowledged as the fulfillment of the sign of the sun rising in the west according to the Nation of Islam, but Obama is thought more of as a messianic figure or friend to Islam, and they stopped short of claiming he is Mahdi.

The Koran does not provide an overview of end-time events. Islam has taken bits and pieces from the Bible, and their understanding is perverted. Islam speaks of Gog and Magog as two nations with large armies that will invade Palestine from the <u>north.</u> In Arabic, they are called *Yajuj wa-Majuj*. The Islamic understanding of Gog and Magog differ from the Bible's description of these end-time entities. Islam believes Gog is the United States (in the west and not north), and the beast is the president of the United States (and this may be accurate). The Islamic character of Jesus is not the Jesus of the Bible and is a figment of their imagination. They believe when Mahdi comes and during the heat of battle, the Islamic Jesus will cry out to Allah, who will send insects to attack the invaders. Islamic Jesus will say Islam is true, and Christians will convert, and all other religions eliminated, all crosses broken, and all pigs killed. Jesus will rule on earth for forty years, marry, and have children then die and be buried next to Muhammad. Then the righteous will be resurrected.

From an Islamic perspective, the Mahdi is a messiah. From a biblical position, the Mahdi would be a type of the biblical Antichrist but not necessarily the Antichrist per se.

Their Dajal (Antichrist) is a person of Jewish descent, born in Iran, will deceive through religion. The perception of a Jew in Iran is not unusual. Many Jews lived in Persia/Iran. Jews, Persians, Arabs are related through Abraham's sons Isaac and Ishmael and Esau and Jacob.

Perry Stone, *Unleashing the Beast* (p. 172), regarding manuscripts that allude to Greek letters *chi*, *Xi*, and *stigma* being associated with Islam and the mark of the beast. *Chi* is in the form of *X* and is Islamic sign for two swords crossed. Muslims note that *Xi* forms the name of Allah. The letter "*stigma*" looks like a snake and was branded on slaves, cattle, etc. Hold stigma horizontal, Muslims believe it is the name of Muhammad. Stone suggest this could be the mark of the beast. The total of those three letters is 666.

Jordanian Royalty

Another suggestion for an Arabian Antichrist is presented by Pastor Joe Van Koevering, Gateway Christian Church, Saint Petersburg, Florida. In his research, he believed a good candidate is Prince Elhussam Bin Talah of the Hasemite Kingdom of Jordan and heir to the throne. Talah was educated in America and Britain.

Van Koevering points us to Isaiah 14:22: "*For I will rise up against them, says the Lord of hosts and cut off from Babylon the name and remnant and son and nephew says the Lord.*" Referencing "nephew," Prince Talah is the uncle of the king of Jordan. He did not assume the throne when the king died, but it was given to the eldest son. The father said that greater things awaited Prince Talah. So he is yet a prince awaiting a kingdom. The next scripture reference is Isaiah 14:25: "*That I will break the Assyrian in my land . . .*" referencing "Assyrian." The Antichrist will be an Assyrian. The Hasemite kingdom has ancient Assyrian roots. The ancient nations of Assyria and Babylon are associated with Syria, Jordan, Iran, and Iraq.

Some Islamic sects believe the Mahdi must be a descendant of Muhammad through his daughter Fatima. Muhammad was a Hasemite, and Prince Talah is the forty-second descendant from Muhammad.

A characteristic of Antichrist is his charisma. Prince Talah is a globalist and seemingly very pleasant. He served as president of the Club of Rome and speaks six languages, including Hebrew. He is acceptable to Christians, Jews, and other religions. He supports a universal religion as does the Vatican. United Nations named him champion of the earth. He has a broad forehead and pointed nose. He comes from a land with seven hills. Mecca and Rome both had seven hills.

In our consideration of Talah, he does not have worldwide recognition; he is not poised to arise from the ten-region confederation; and there are no omens or prophetic signs surrounding him. He is unlikely the Antichrist.

Other Thoughts on an Islamic Antichrist

Walid Shoebat believes the rise of the Antichrist may be coming out of Turkey. Recep Tayyip Erdogan of Turkey has emerged as the hero to some in the Muslim world. He has recently stated he is god, and touching the hem of his garment is divine. He used a hologram image of himself to be displayed at a meeting where he was not physically present (Anadolu Agency of Turkey). Muslims admired him when he walked out on a meeting with Israeli Perez at the Davos meeting. Erdogan was able to get Hamas to release Gilad Shalit, an Israeli soldier, after negotiations failed from the United States, European Union, and United Nations. The West portrayed him as a perfect broker between Islamists and Israel. Erdogan is committed to taking back Jerusalem, as in the time of the Ottoman Empire. Egypt, Libya, Lebanon also speak about entering Jerusalem triumphantly. Erdogan tells more than fifty Muslim states and the Organization of Islamic Cooperation that Jerusalem is the apple of the eye of every Muslim. Scholars familiar with the Koran will not find this to be true. Jerusalem was considered Islam's third holiest site based on a vision Muhammed had of riding a white horse on Mount Moriah under the dome of the rock.

In 2013, there was an uprising in Turkey. The people want to continue in their secular, democratic government while Erdogan is pushing for Sharia law and a caliphate. Since the uprising, Erdogan has called for the removal of Syrian president Bashar al-Assad, and this has caused a fraction between these two Islamic nations. Turkey does not consider ISIS as a legitimate representative of the Muslim world. United States is trying to hold on to diplomatic relations with Turkey, but it is waning. Turkey shot down Russian plane and is now at odds with Russia.

By the year 2016, there was a military coup in Turkey to unseat Erdogan, but he repealed it and had thousands arrested. Turkey has amended relations with Israel for all its worth.

The region of Turkey has a significant biblical history. The Euphrates River extends to Turkey. Noah's ark rested in the Mountains of Ararat. The seven churches of Asia were in Turkey. The Ottoman Empire was fueled in Turkey and encompassed regions such as Afghanistan, Pakistan, Turkmenistan, etc. The first caliphate was organized in 1924 and associated with Turkey. We do not believe Erdogan encompasses enough of the characteristics to be the Antichrist.

<u>European Antichrist</u>

Prince Charles of Wales was born in 1948, the same year that Israel became a modern nation. His ancestry can be traced back to the Roman Empire and, allegedly, back to the Merovingian bloodline—an order that believes Mary Magdalene and Jesus had children. He is linked to the House of Windsor. The royal family shield visually presents the composite beast made from the body of a leopard, the feet of a bear, and the mouth of a lion with a red dragon. This appears like the description of the beast in Revelation 13:2: "*And the beast which I saw was like unto a leopard and his feet were as the feet of a bear and his mouth as the mouth of a lion and the dragon gave him his power, his seat and great authority.*" The dragon is a symbol on the flag of Wales.

Prince Charles of Wales is more than just a name; it is the title of the heir apparent, or the next in line for kingship. The red dragon dates back to the ancient Romans. Britannia was the head of the western Roman Empire, and the symbol of Roman antiquity was a red dragon. The day that Prince Charles received his title as the Prince of Wales, his name officially changed to Prince Charles of Wales. In celebration, he was surrounded by banners of this red dragon at a castle in Wales.

His power, throne, and great authority have been given to him by a red dragon. The royal family is invested in the European Union and have <u>dominion over many nations</u>.

The royals are figure heads with little power.

The royal family is no stranger to the occult. John Dee served as the queen's astrologer around AD 1600.

Dee's code was 007. They opened a portal for satanic activity.

Does Prince Charles fit the description of the coming Antichrist? *Time Magazine* ran an article written by Catherine Mayer, October 24, 2013, *The Forgotten Prince: Prince Charles, Born to be King but Aiming Higher.* The writer lists his title as his Royal Highness Prince Charles Philip Arthur George, followed by his many pedigrees: Prince of Wales, Earl of Chester, Duke of Cornwall, Duke of Rothesay, Earl of Carrick, Baron of Renfrew, Lord of the Isles, and Prince and Great Steward of Scotland. Queen Elizabeth is eighty-nine years old, and Prince Charles has been assuming additional royal responsibilities. He said, "I feel, more than anything else, it's my duty to worry about everybody and their lives in this country to try to find a way of improving things if I possibly can." Following on his sentiment, Prince Charles purchased the Dumfries House—an eighteenth-century mansion in Scotland for $72 million. The local residents were impoverished due to the closing of mines, and the purchase of this mansion would bring renewed income for the remaining 2,800 residents.

> *Here is wisdom, let him who has understanding calculate the number of the beast, for the number is that of a man and his number is six hundred and sixty-six.* (Revelation 13:18)

The numerical value of "Prince Charles of Wales" is 666, using Hebrew letters, which have a numerical value. The name Charles means "man," and 666 is the number of a man.

Daniel 11 begins with an overview of kingdoms from Darius the Mede through to the kings of the south and north, involving Israel. Coming to verse 16 seems to be addressing the Antichrist, who does according to his own will and none will stand before him, and he will destroy Israel. In verse 18, we see the Antichrist turn his face unto the isles (England, Scotland, Ireland) and will take many, but a prince will cause him to cease. This scripture was inserted to demonstrate that the Antichrist forcibly comes against Israel and comes against England. Prince Charles could not be Antichrist who would come against his own nation.

As we surmise who could be the Antichrist, we must consider the relationship this entity has with Israel. In a report made in the *Jerusalem Connection*, March 13, 2013, *Anti-Semitism: England*, by Victory Sharpe: "Britain's Prince Charles is currently on an official visit to Jordan, Oman, and Qatar. But stepping foot in nearby Israel by any member of the British royal family is officially banned by the British Foreign Office." The royals of Britain do not want to offend their Arab Muslim trading partners or endanger their extensive and lucrative bilateral economic and business ties to the Arab world. In past history, we know that Britain turned their backs on Israel during the Hitler regime and reneged on the allocation of land for the Jewish homeland because of Arab pressure. In 1994, Prince Philip and his sister, Princess Sophie, traveled to Jerusalem to receive Yad Vashem's Medal of Honor of Righteous among the Nations awarded to their late mother, Princess Alice. Prince Philip had to sneak into Israel because of the ban by his government.

In 2011, the Countess of Wessex, wife to Prince Edward, accepted a lavish set of gems and a solid silver and pearl cup from the Bahrain royal family during her visit to the Persian Gulf. The value of the jewels was around $3.5 million. There was an uproar in Bahrain, with demonstrations during the Arab Spring, in which fifty people were killed, others arrested and tortured. Under the circumstances, the extravagant gifts should have been returned, but Buckingham Palace kept the property as part of the royal collection. In 2007, the Duchess of Cornwall was given similar gifts by the Saudi royal family estimated around $3 million.

Here we see that the royals of Britain would rather have ongoing relations with despotic and autocratic regimes of the world while ignoring Israel, the only democratic nation in the Middle East. England consistently aligns itsef with those that hate Israel. Queen Elizabeth, during her sixty years on the throne, has made some 250 visits to Islamic countries and not Israel. England withdrew from the European Union, 2016.

One final scholarly thought sees the Antichrist coming from the divided Roman Empire as it ties into the seven heads and ten horns. The beast that was and is not, even he is the <u>eight</u> and is of the seven and goes into perdition (Revelation 17:8). There have been seven Charles of the Roman Empire. Prince Charles will be the eighth. Historical reports claim that current Prince Charles is a descendant of Charles VI, through the <u>Hapsburg</u> line. We currently do not see the Antichrist arising out of Britain royalty.

<u>American Antichrist</u>

Staying with the above line of thought, the Antichrist will come out of the revived Roman Empire. We have inferred that the US president could be a candidate for the Antichrist. Here is a man for the most part obscure in society, yet he has ascended to the top of the heap. Obama has a very vague but interesting background.

We will examine the current American president, Barack Hussein Obama, more in-depth.

Examining scriptures will allow us to compare similarities between the man Obama and the identification of the Antichrist.

> *A fourth beast dreadful, terrible and strong and it had great iron teeth … it was diverse from all the beasts that were before it and it had <u>ten horns</u> and I considered the horns and behold there came up among them another* ***little horn*** *… in this horn were eyes like the eyes of man and mouth speaking great things.* (Daniel 7:7–8)

Several scholars have suggested that this represents a nation and not a person. Our simple explanation is that every kingdom has a king. This little horn represents a person who appears to emerge out of obscurity and rises to prominence.

> *And of the ten horns that were in the head of the beast and of the other which came up* [little horn] … *and the same horn made war with the saints and prevailed against them until the Ancient of days came* … (Daniel 7:20–22)

From both verses, we are to understand the nature and actions of this fourth beast. Daniel used the terms ten horns, and in Revelation, John used the term ten heads in describing this final kingdom. This is a picture of the final Antichrist arising out of the revived Roman, satanic world system.

- The fourth beast is the initial Roman Empire.
- Revived Roman Empire is identified as ten toes or ten regions.
- Out of the ten arises a world leader, symbolized as a little horn, with eyes like a man and a mouth speaking great things.
- He will subdue three kingdoms (could be Egypt, Libya, Syria, or Iraq).
- The little horn has a fierce countenance.
- This horn/king/Antichrist will do according to his will, exalt himself above every god.
- He will continue till the indignation be accomplished, for that is determined will be done; he will not regard the God of his father, or the desire of women; he will honor the god of forces with gold, silver, precious stones.

From Daniel, we can determine ancient Babylon, Persia, and Greek Empires had risen to prominence then experienced a decline. When we compare the former empires to the nations they represent today, there remains a measure of influence and dominance as can be seen in Iraq, Iran, Greece, revived Rome. The Antichrist will come against or subdues their sovereignty.

> *And out of one of them came forth a little horn which waxed exceeding great toward the south* [Egypt] *east* [Iran/Iraq] *and to the pleasant land* [Israel]. (Daniel 8:9–14)

Two thousand five hundred years ago, Daniel predicted Antichrist will come against nations. Our present time frame is the end of the age.

> *Behold I will make you know what will be in the <u>last end</u> of the indignation, for at the time appointed the end will be.* (Daniel 8:19)
>
> *And in the <u>latter time</u> of their kingdom, when the transgressors are come to the full, a king of fierce countenance and understanding dark sentences will*

> *stand up and his power will be mighty but not by his own power. He will destroy wonderfully and will prosper, practice and will destroy the mighty and the holy people.* (Daniel 8:23)
>
> *And through his policy also he will cause craft to prosper in his hand. He will magnify himself in his heart and by peace will destroy many. He will stand up against the Prince of princes but he will be broken without hand.* (Daniel 8:25)

Daniel symbolically portrays the Antichrist as the little horn. Following are attributes of Antichrist:

- It represents a man.
- Prideful, blasphemous, speaks against the Most High.
- Has a stern look.
- Persecutes the saints, wars against the heavenly host.
- Desecrates the third temple, stops the sacrifices.
- Understands dark sentences could refer to affiliation with secret societies, global elite.
- He causes craft to prosper, and this could be a reference to the occult.
- He changes laws, times, and causes the nation to accept sexual abominations.
- He comes in peace between Islam and Judaism; signing an agreement will bring destruction.
- He will come to his end at the battle of Armageddon.

Selected by the global elite and following, we parity Obama's actions with those of Antichrist:

- No affinity toward the unborn, the shedding of innocent blood, and is steadfast on abortion.
- He has set his will against God's laws, as marriage is between man and woman.
- The act of homosexuality has been championed by Obama as in having a disregard for the desire of women.
- Traditional belief and values are demonized, and the rise of anti-Christianity is of little concern to Obama.
- Obama is not a friend to Israel, and anti-Semitism is rampant.
- The pope and this president see eye to eye on many issues.
- Obama is aligned with big corporations, promoting drugs, GMOs, and vaccinations.
- <u>He will have a fierce countenance, appearing authoritative</u>

- He is articulate and speaks various dialects.
- He can understand dark sentences as in coded messages
- He is powerful but not by his own power.
- He will destroy wonderfully the mighty and the holy people. Obama is not a true friend of Judaism or Christianity
- He comes as a savior. Obama's platform of hope, change, and "yes, we can."
- Through peace, he will destroy many. Obama gives a false impression that he is for peace in the Middle East, but his actions cause dissention.
- Through his policy and craftiness, the elite agenda will prosper. Obama's policies for the United States are to remove sovereignty and individual freedoms. He will say one thing but do another. He is crafty.
- He will magnify himself in his heart. Obama is arrogant and narcissist.
- He will do according to his will. Obama does what he wants to do without regard for the Constitution, Supreme Court, Congress, and the citizens.
- Mystical and paranormal. In the presence of Obama, some felt euphoria, and newsman Chris Matthews said he felt tingling; many were in awe of him.
- Superhuman—Obama has endless energy.
- Exalt himself above every god. Obama takes a position over Judaism, Christianity, favors Islam, and is acceptable of pagan beliefs.
- Speaks marvelous things against the God of gods. Obama has made folly of the Bible, stated America is not a Christian nation, and hinders freedom of religion.
- Speaks like a lion—he is intelligent, persuasive, mesmerizing, and able to convince his listeners that his ideas present the solution to their problems.
- He will prosper until the indignation be accomplished. Obama has managed to win a second term to continue to follow the dictates of the one-world order.
- Controlled by evil power—through his alliance with Satan, he will honor the god of forces (Zeus/Satan). And disregard the God of his fathers.
- He honors a god whom his fathers knew not. Obama embraces the false god Allah.
- He will acknowledge a strange god. Obama accepts Hindu god blessing.
- Appearance is different. Obama is different than any other US president.
- He will stand up against the Prince of Princes, but he will be broken without hand. Obama has already raised his fist up to God, and he will be judged.
- He will set up his palace in the holy mountain in Jerusalem; he will cause the daily sacrifice to cease and will demand to be worshipped as God.

Barack Obama Is a Globalist

The one-world leader must have affiliations with people worldwide. Through his maternal grandmother, he has ties with England, Scotland, Ireland. His grandfather connects him with Germany and a list of US presidents. He seems to have cordial relations with Angela Merkel, chancellor of Germany, 2005. A few facts about Merkel—she holds a PhD in chemistry; first female chancellor of German;, community activist; served onboard of the Free German Youth and secretary of its Agitation and Propaganda Committee. In 1983, she studied Marxism and Leninism. She was a member of Christian Social Union and Social Democratic Party; both lean toward socialistic ideology, embracing immigration, health care reform, moderate energy development, and managing financial crisis in Europe. She was the president of the European Council and is considered the de facto leader of the European Union. *Forbes Magazine* list of the world's most powerful people listed her as number two in 2012 and 2013. In 2016, they rated her most powerful. *Time Magazine* listed her as person of the year in 2015. She is pro-America, Turkey, Russia—pro-Israel with conditions (Wikipedia).

Obama and Merkel share similar backgrounds and ideologies. Obama gave a speech in Berlin, Germany, on July 24, 2008, before the presidential election. His theme was, "The world that stands as one." The speech was mesmerizing to the thousands in attendance. German radio said, "We have just heard the next president of the United States and the future **president of the world.**" The location of the speech was at the Berlin Victory Column, two hundred feet tall, topped by a golden-winged goddess figure sitting in the midst of a 495-acre park. This site is offensive to educated Germans, Christians, and Jews because of its ties to Adolf Hitler and the Nazis. It is a reminder that Hitler had planned to enthrone himself in the Welthapuptstadt Germanania, the new "World Capital," upon winning World War II. Obama saluted the German audience in a way similar to Hitler, and they returned the salute. In his final statement, Obama said, "With an eye toward the future, with resolve in our hearts, let us remember this history and answer our destiny and remake the world once again." This was the sentiment of Hitler, his promise for a new world order in this location. Not far from this site is the great altar of Zeus in the Pergamon Museum, which Hitler had commissioned. It can be interpreted as the altar of Zeus and the seat of Satan, who authorizes powers, thrones, and principalities over nations. Obama's half sister, Auma Obama, studied German at the University of Heidelberg, 1981 to 1987, receiving a PhD. Angela Merkel acknowledged to Obama that she read his autobiography and knew his sister attended German university. Auma's mother, Kezia, was married to Obama Sr.

The followers of Islam have had a long relationship with Germany and Hitler. Obama has ties with the Muslim world through his Kenyan father. *Kenya* means "the abode of the gods." Obama has ties with Saudi Arabia through his Kenyan family. His stepfather connects him with Indonesia and Islam. Obama's college associates were Muslims from Pakistan.

Obama has direct and indirect connections with Russia. In 1992, Tom Fite, a businessman selling IT technology to the Russians, said the future US president will be a black communist.

Henry Kissinger had a good relationship with Russia, stating Obama should be **president of the world**. On January 1, 2009, a quote in the *International Herald Tribune* by Mikhail Gorbachev, former president of Russia, said, "The global clamor for change and the election of Barack Obama was the catalyst that might finally convince the world of the need for global government."

In 2011, Obama was overheard telling the Russian leader, he would have more flexibility after the 2012 election.

He has a positive relationship with Nicolas Sarkozy, France, who is a Greek from Macedonia near Mount Hermon, site of the fallen angels. Obama appears to have a good relationship with former prime minister of England, Tony Blair, who is a proclaimed occultist.

One thing we need to keep in mind is, the world leader will appeal to many through his various global connections; but according to scripture, not all will accept his dictates. Obama has strained ties with the Islamic world. He has alienated himself with Israel due to his pro-Islamic views, and he is steadily alienating himself with Christians. He is not on good terms with Russia, China, North Korea. So who is left that will align with this global leader? He has good relations with France, England, Germany, Canada, Mexico. Some people in Kenya speak of him favorably, but he is viewed unfavorably by other Kenyan leaders who reject Obama's position on homosexuality. He has mended ties with Communist Cuba.

Pastor Robert Jeffress on the O'Reilly show, January 20, 2014, said that "Obama's policies are paving the way for the Antichrist through his position on homosexuality, same-sex marriage, and abortion. Moral laws set by God are replaced by secularism and hedonism. A coming dictator placates the people's civil and human rights." He wages war on God's people, forcing Christians to provide abortion-inducing drugs or to sign same-sex marriage certificates, causing many to compromise their values and principles to tolerate acts that are an abomination unto God. Complaints are met with demonizing the people of faith, legal pressure, and threats to their welfare. The new Americans join the ranks of many before them, who initiated the same methods in removing personal ideals and promoting their ungodly agenda through intimidation, confiscation of wealth, imprisonment, and death.

Besides the above reasoning, the Antichrist will have his hands in world events. It is the goal of Antichrist to disrupt nations to create chaos and death. Nations must be destabilized. Leaders that refuse to cooperate could have sanctions levied against their economy; they could see the infiltration of antigovernment operatives that will undermine the established leadership, and factions will be pitted one against another. Civilians are caught in the middle of civil war, thus suffering fear, loss of life, and possessions. Entire families will be displaced, finding themselves homeless and hungry. A recent example is the destruction of the Syrian and Iraqi governments through US dictates, enabling antigovernment protesters to cause chaos, resulting in a refugee crisis. The Syrian government was on the brink of collapse, but with the help of Iran and Russia, it stands. Within the Syrian crisis, ISIS gained the opportunity to expand. It was monitored by world leaders who did nothing to stymie it, thus unleashing a monster into the world. They are a hoard of demons disguised as humans.

As Britain funded both Hitler and the Allied forces, America also played both sides of the field. They have used al-Qaeda and CIA to bring down governments. They use both Jordan and Turkey in stirring up conflict. The world saw the collapse of Iraq under Saddam Hussein, who was once a US ally. Iraq is still plagued with a government regime, infighting between Islamic tribes and attacks against Christians and others. Iraq is a terrorist stronghold.

The death of Osama Bin Laden attempted to cover the involvement of the Saudi's Wahabite sect and its connection to the 9-11 attack in 2001. The twenty-first century has seen the Arab Spring topple at least ten nations in the Middle East. Gaza and Lebanon are unstable under their rebel leadership.

Canada, North America, and Mexico are classified as one region. Observe Obama's position on immigration. The border is flooded with people coming in from Mexico, South America, Syria, and North Africa. The global elite want to remove borders for free flow between nations. It will be similar to the European Union, where borders were removed between various countries in Europe. Verizon's new ad offers calling to Canada, United States, and Mexico at no additional cost.

The globalist Henry Kissinger on January 5, 2009, at the New York Stock Exchange, told CNBC that "Obama's task will be to develop an overall strategy for America in this period when a new world order can be created." Later, Kissinger stated that "Obama made an extraordinary impact on the imagination of humanity, calling it an important element in shaping a new world order." Kissinger has been a member of the Bilderberg group, Trilateral Commission, Foreign Relations Commission, and Illuminati. Obama's affiliation with Kissinger provides additional insight into whom Obama takes his orders from.

Kissinger made the following statements at the Bilderberg meeting in Evian, France, May 21, 1991:

> Americans today would be outraged if the United Nations/NATO troops entered Los Angeles to restore order; tomorrow they will be grateful. This is especially true if they were told there was an outside threat whether real or promulgated that threatened our very existence. It is then that all

> peoples of the world will plead with world leaders to deliver them from this evil. When presented with this scenario, individual rights will be willingly relinquished for the guarantee of well-being granted to them by their world government.

Obama was handpicked to serve as US president at this time. Joe Biden was handpicked to be Obama's vice president. Biden and Obama had a relationship before his presidential campaign. In 2013, Joe Biden rallies the call for a new world order.

If our reasoning is accurate and things are in alignment—such as the Antichrist and false prophet are on the scene; Gog is in position; the world has been divided into ten regions; the United Nations Agenda 21 is bringing all nations under a global umbrella; the world is in turmoil; the church is apostate; and persecution of Jews and Christians is ongoing—then these facts will allow us to see the fulfillment of the one-world order.

Obama's African Connections

Obama with relatives in Kenya. Sarah, stepgrandmother; Sayid, uncle; and Musa, Ismail cousin.

Obama visited Kenya in 2006, saying, "I am so proud to come home."

After President Obama was inaugurated in 2009, the Muslim side of the Obama family in Kenya became famous overnight. They were considered to be one of the most influential families in western Kenya and even extended their sphere of influence to Saudi Arabia. Sarah

Ogwel Obama was the third wife of Onyango Obama. After his death, she raised his other wife's children—one being Barack Obama Sr. Sarah Ogwel is not a blood relative of president Obama, and we refer to her as his step-great-grandmother. When she decided to go to the hajj, an obligatory pilgrimage to Mecca, with Musa Ismail Obama, they were given royal treatment, welcomed with open arms, and were provided a special escort with full security detail. They were hosted by his Royal Highness Prince Mamdouh bin Abdul Aziz in his palace in Jeddah after the performance at the hajj.

A foundation was started by Sarah Ogwel, known as the Mama Sarah Obama Children Foundation, which raises a majority of its monies primarily from donors in the United States and some from Europe. Several sources is the Catholic Relief Services, The Bill Gates Foundation, and Project Great Lakes Cassava Initiative that provide funds to farmers in Sarah's village to grow cassava a food, which was destroyed by pestilence. These new seeds are genetically modified to resist disease. Monies are solicited as humanitarian aid to make a lasting impact on the lives of the orphans and underprivileged children by improving their housing and education. Also they promote assistance for victims of HIV/AIDS in Kogelo Village by linking them to caregivers and professional health service providers. That's what we're told, but when one peruses the foundation's real activities in Arabic, it reveals a very dark side to the family's involvement.

Musa Ismail Obama, the president's cousin, in an interview with Al-Jazeera TV, explained that 90 percent of funds are used to provide free scholarships to study Islam and Sharia in the Wahabist centers in Saudi Arabia, specifically, Islamic University in Medina, Umm Al-Qura University in Makkah, and the Imam Muhammad bin Saud Islamic University in Riyadh—all of which instill the radical ideas of the Koran. He says his goal is to transform Kenya into an Islamic majority by using President Obama's influence and Mama Sarah's organization to educate the young in Sharia law.

In an interview, Musa was asked about his communications with cousin Barack, and he explained that the president's preferred method of communications was through one chosen conduit that relays messages back and forth with the family in Kenya by going through Uncle Sayid Hussein Obama. This is the man who attended with Mama Sarah in Barack Obama's 2009 inauguration. He also had a run-in with police in the United States.

Islamic ties with Kenya and Saudi Arabia were reinforced, April 18, 2013. After the Boston Marathon bombing, a Saudi national was detained as a suspect. While hospitalized, Michelle Obama visited Abul Rahman Ali Al-Harbi in the hospital. He had been a frequent visitor at the White House. This man was released because there was no evidence to link him to the bombings, but it does continue to make the case that Obama is pro-Islam.

Sayid Hussein Obama, right; Musa Ismail Obama, at Umm Al Qura University
His Highness the Director of Umm Al-Qura University, Dr. Bakri bin Ma'touk A'sas

Musa explains that the lack of proselytization is a catastrophe in Kenya. This is the call for wealthy Saudis to transform Kenya into a Muslim majority. This goal is also expressed by *Al-Arab Newspaper* under the title, "Scholars in Kenya Call Their Brethren to Spread Islam and Teach Arabic." It states, "Muslims in Kenya suffer from the monumental Christianization aided by Zionist expansionism that infiltrates the nation" (Muhammad Lasheeb, *Al-Arab Newspaper*, 8816th edition, published August 1, 2012).

Al-Arab Newspaper expounds on the effort to advance education by the Obama family in Kenya. Under the title "Education First," assistant Mufti of the coastal City of Mombasa Ahmad Bimsallam, chimed in, explaining that "the grand destruction that came upon Muslims in Kenya came from the education and schools that are planted all over the nation by Christian missionary movements."

Al-Arab does not even consider President Obama's conversion to Christianity an issue and included a section entitled, "Obama's Islam," while stating:

> President Obama's Islamic faith was considered a polarizing subject between Muslims and Christians in the Republic of Kenya. It is a center of struggle in the media and continues, as the Anglican Church there attempted to orchestrate a baptismal ordination for his grandmother Sarah in a grand celebration at the Gomokinyata playground in Kizimo, the third largest city

> in Kenya. It was a trick to trap her, pretending to invite her as a guest, as the church sent out information about her conversion and abandonment of Islam. Musa Ismail Obama commented during his interview with Al-Arab that he was with his grandmother during Ramadan in Mecca to do the Umra festivities after she completed her pilgrimage by invitation from the King of Saudi Arabia. Musa Obama who studied Sharia in Medina spoke to us regarding the situation of Muslims in Kenya calling upon the Arab and Islamic states to put more effort toward aiding the Kenyan Muslim brethren, especially since there is much support coming from western nations and western churches, spreading to the rest of Kenyan society from different religions. Musa opined that the situation of Muslims in Kenya is continually getting better, pointing to the village of Barack Obama Sr., Kogelo, which is situated on the shores of Victoria Lake, in western Kenya, for example, had no Muslims except his family. But now, they are increasing because of the kind treatment given by their family and that they have a benevolent institution to raise funds to aid orphans and the poor. It also gives scholarships to study Sharia in Medina. Musa stated despite the fact that Barack Obama had not visited his tribe in Kenya since his election in the United States, there is a continual communication between him and several members of his family and his tribe in Kenya, of which the Kenyan prime minister is also a member. Since that statement, Obama did visit Kenya in 2015. Several members of the tribe came together to celebrate the appointment of one of their tribesmen as president of the United States. Musa clarified that the election of Barack Obama had an impact for the betterment of the Muslim situation in Kenya to a certain degree, despite the attempts of churches to obstruct Muslim demands and rights, especially what relates to segregation and persecution against them in schools, as well as the issue of hijab and the lack of constitutional rights for Muslims in establishing Sharia courts.

Aid from Arab billionaires to finance and develop relationships with minorities in America has been ongoing since the 1970s. It may be that Obama Sr. received aid from this revenue stream and later, Obama Jr. Their agenda would be to further the Arab goal to increase converts to Islam, infect all nations with Islamic Sharia law, and promote the Palestinian state by eliminating Israel.

In America, blacks were the most discriminated against, beginning with slavery, voting rights, equal opportunity for education, employment, and housing. Trotsy quoted in 1939:

> The American Negroes, for centuries the most oppressed section of American society and the most discriminated against, are potentially the most revolutionary element of the population. They are designated by their historical past to be, under adequate leadership, the very vanguard of the proletarian revolution.

His statement rings true in that bigots in high places worked to destroy anyone who would arise to lead the African Americans out of a slave mentality, one who elevates their self-worth and encourages them to pursue an education and a better life. Martin Luther King was assassinated. Malcomb X was assassinated. Angela Davis was vilified. The Black Panther Party was deemed radical terrorist. Any leadership appearing to have the charisma to rally the people were destroyed. The NAACP managed to survive but was infiltrated by government spies who worked to keep the organization as a lesser threat to the establishment of segregation and discrimination.

The Arab contingency could see that black men in America needed help to advance and take positions of power in the government, even the presidency. The Nation of Islam's ideology grew in many American ghettos of Chicago, Philadelphia, Detroit, and especially in the prison system. The Nation of Islam instilled pride in minorities who had been told for years they were dumb and worthless. They helped to develop self-control, self-sufficiency, and a healthy lifestyle in their followers. Where Christianity had dropped the ball, Islam filled the void.

Barack Obama's American Affiliations

Donald Warden, alias Khalid Abdullah Tariq al-Mansour . Warden a black lawyer in San Francisco—developed strong ties with the Saudi royal family to begin the funding of black leaders and minority institutions in America. He converted to Islam and changed his name to al-Mansour. He founded the African American Association in the 1960s. Al-Mansour was a mentor to Black Panther Party leader, Huey Newton, and Bobby Seale as well as an associate of Nation of Islam leader, Louis Farrakhan. It is necessary to provide this background to show how it will tie into Barack Obama Jr. Al-Mansour had developed significant ties with the Saudi royal family since becoming a Muslim. Both al-Mansour and Farrakhan were financial advisers to Saudi royalty, who may have donated money to certain universities in the United States. Al-Mansour had given OPEC Secretary General Rene Ortiz a proposal in 1979 for the special aid program to help American blacks. Al-Mansour may have helped finance the admission of Barack Obama into Harvard Law School in 1988.

Vernon Jarrett

In 1979, Vernon Jarrett was touting the college aid program being funded by OPEC at the same time Obama entered Occidental College in Los Angeles. Vernon Jarrett wrote an article in regard to Arabs funding blacks in America based on information provided by al-Mansour. Vernon is the father-in-law to Valeria Jarrett, who was born in Iran. Valeria Jarret became Obama's adviser. Vernon Jarrett was an associate of Frank Marshall Davis, former Chicago journalist and lifelong communist who moved to Hawaii in the late 1940s and later befriended Stanley and Madelyn Dunham and their daughter, Stanley Ann, the mother of Barack Obama.

Valerie Jarrett

As mentioned above, Valerie was born in Iran. She retained a socialist left ideology, becoming Obama's closest White House adviser. Perhaps her connection with Iran led to the future nuclear deal with Iran. She was CEO of Habitat Company, which managed public housing in Chicago, who received millions of dollars from Illinois state legislature. The public housing was mismanaged and was demolished. Valerie Jarrett also worked for the City of Chicago and hired Michelle LaVaughan Robinson, who later became Mrs. Michelle Obama, who worked for the Sidley Austin Law Firm. Barack Obama got a summer job at Sidley Austin Law Firm and met Michelle. There are no coincidences in the life of Obama, and meeting between Barack and Michelle may have been arranged.

William Ayers

Obama met Bill Ayers, who was known as a 1960s far-left radial revolutionary and cofounder of Weather Underground. Bill's father is Thomas Ayers, who was a friend of Frank Marshall Davis. William Ayers married Bernadine Dohrn. Obama was chair of Chicago Anneberg Challenge in 1999, a project designed to reform Chicago Public Schools. Bill Ayers wrote the grant application for $49.2 million with matching donors. The money was spent, the accounting was shady, and public schools were still poor. Obama's political career began at Bill Ayers home.

Frank Marshall Davis

Davis was a communist sympathizer and activist. He was associated with Chicago defender Vernon Jarrett and Thomas Ayers. Davis was Barack's longtime mentor.

Percy Sutton

Sutton was attorney for Malcolm X, who was associated with Kenya Politician Tom Mboya, who was friend of Obama Sr., who met Malcolm X in Kenya. Percy Sutton was one of the leading black politicians in New York and told an interviewer on Manhattan TV news show that he had been introduced to Senator Obama by al-Mansour, who was raising money for him. Sutton was supporting Senator Hillary Clinton, but he said he thought Obama was nonetheless quite impressive. Sutton said, "I had heard about Obama previously in a letter written by al-Mansour, and I wrote a letter of support for Obama to my friends at Harvard, saying to them I thought there was a genius that was going to be available, and I certainly hoped they would treat him kindly."

Saul Alinsky

Alinsky was born in 1909 to Jewish Orthodox parents in Chicago, Illinois. He did not follow the God of Judaism but embraced an agnostic mind-set. As a pebble cast into a pond leaves ripples, Saul's actions would leave a generation of ripples in society. Saul attended the University of Chicago, where he received his early exposure to Marxist theories on social engineering. He graduated with a degree in philosophy during the 1930s depression. Employment opportunities were sparse, but he obtained employment as a criminologist with the State of Illinois. Shortly, he became involved with the Congress of Industrial Organization in Chicago, a community action program focusing on concerns of poor people.

Alinsky was impressed with the organization of the Catholic church and its outreach programs. Some programs supported abortion, gay rights, radicals, and the defunct Acorn community organization. He began to leverage the church's influence at all levels for his benefit, including the development of multimillion-dollar antipoverty programs. The Catholic bishops of the Chicago Archdiocese under the US Conference of Catholic Bishops campaign for human development. After years of working to improve conditions for the poor, Alinsky founded the Industrial Areas Foundation.

Influenced by Judaism, Marxism, communism, and Catholicism, Alinsky developed a mind-set that was antiestablishment—believing the greatest crimes in history were perpetrated by organized politics, religions, and Nazi genocide. He became radicalized. Alinskiy quotes from "the Prince, Machiavelli for the Haves on how to hold power and in Alinsky's book *Rules for Radicals* is for the Have Nots on how to take it away from those who have." Alinsky was a Marxist and radical agitator. He became adept in social/political warfare, stating, "All effective actions require the passport of morality, you do what you can with what you have and clothe it with moral garments … make the enemy live up to its own rules, moral rationalization is indispensable at times of action." Alinsky wrote the book *Rules for Radicals*, and he dedicated the book to Satan:

> Lest we forget at least an over the shoulder acknowledgement to the very first radical: from all our legends, mythology and history … the first radical known to man who rebelled against the establishment and did it so effectively that Lucifer at least won his own kingdom.

In 1969, shortly before his death, he was involved with Jesuits at the Holy Family Parish in Chicago. Their ideals were established in the formation of the leftist Pacific Institute for Community Organization funded by George Soros. They incorporated Alinsky's methods of creating an enemy to achieve a particular end. The priests considered the Italian mobs the enemy, but Alinsky became friendly with the likes of Al Capone. Alinsky died in 1972, and his desire was to go to hell.

Alinsky's methods would be adopted by the very establishment he opposed. Many years later, Barack Obama would benefit from the Alinsky's Industrial Area Foundation and the Catholic Bishops of Chicago who did sponsor airfare to a training program on community organizing. Obama was a member of Calumet Community Religious Conference associated with the Catholic Bishops of Chicago. As a community organizer, Obama received a $25,000 annual salary, which was funded by a grant from Woods Funds. The Woods family owned Sahara Coal Company, which provided coal to Commonwealth Edison, whose CEO was Thomas Ayers, whose son is William Ayers, who served on the board of the Woods Fund along with Obama.

Rules for Radicals was the inspiration for Hillary Clinton's thesis at Wellesley College. Obama also embraced Alinsky ideology and philosophy. Mike Kruglik said Obama became a master of Alinsky's methods. He was a natural, undisputed master in agitation, and could engage a room full of recruits.

With political aspirations in mind, Obama worked on voter registration drives in Chicago in the 1980s. He worked with leftist political groups like the Democratic Socialist of America and Socialist International, through which Obama met Carl Davidson, who had traveled to Cuba during Vietnam War to undermine US war efforts. Davidson was a member of Committees of Correspondence for Democracy and Socialism, which sponsored a 2002 antiwar rally, at which Obama spoke. The rally was organized by Marilyn Katz, a former member of DSA and a friend of David Axelrod (*Life Site News* and Wikipedia).

David Axelrod

Axelrod was born in 1955 to Jewish parents. His strength is being a political strategist. He was Obama's campaign manager for both runs. After election, Obama appointed him to serve as his senior adviser.

Keith Ellison and Andre Carson

Democrat Socialist of America, DSA, 1996 had grown to be largest socialist organization in United States and tied into affiliates of Socialist International. Ellison is being considered to head up the Democratic National Committee after the 2016 election loss.

Rev. Jeremiah Wright

Wright preached Black Liberation Theology, and his sermons were antiwhite, anti-Jew and anti-American, to a congregation of six thousand plus. Wright began his influence in Chicago after receiving a master's degree from the University of Chicago Divinity School. He became pastor of Trinity United Church of Christ in 1972. He had many connections in the black community. He and Nation of Islam Leader Louis Farrakhan were friends. Wright gave Farrakhan a lifetime achievement award. Rev. Wright says when he met Obama and Michelle, they were not Christians. In 1992, Wright married Michelle and Barack. She wore a traditional wedding ring, and he wore his Islamic ring. Obama was a member of Trinity United Church of Christ for approximately fifteen years, and during that time he made many political connections. Wright and Obama parted ways when Obama began campaigning for president. Ophrah Winfrey was a former member of the church (Wikipedia, September 2014).

Tony Rezka

Obama practice law in Chicago, Illinois. Native American name for Illinois is *Algonquin*, which means "tribe of superior men," or master race. Obama worked as an attorney for Miner, Banhill, and Galland Law firm—which specialized in negotiating state government contracts to develop low-income housing. The law firm was associated with Tony Rezka and his firm, Rezar Real Estate. Tony Rezka, a Lebanese businessman, wanted to build low-income housing. Later, Rezka was under investigation for corruption and, subsequently found guilty, served time in federal prison. Obama may have received political contributions from Rezka. Some news came out that the home Obama was living in was associated with Rezka when Obama was first running for president, but he distanced himself from Rezka.

Rohm Emanuel

Emanuel is former White House chief of staff and now mayor of Chicago. As mayor, he chastised Chick-fil-A CEO for his stand on traditional marriage, calling for a boycott of the business. Instead, thousands of Christian, conservative people nationwide came out to support the business in record numbers, creating a sellout of chicken sandwiches nationwide. Emanuel's grandfather was a Romanian Jew, and Rohm's father was born in Israel.

Obama under the Microscope

Obama's Early Years

Obama was born in Hawaii on August 4, 1961, at Kapiolani Hospital. The doctor that delivered the baby is unknown. The original birth certificate is unavailable. He was named Barack Hussein Obama II. Hawaii is an island in the Pacific region. *Hawaii* means "peace." The AntiChrist will come as a man of peace. *Ha* means "breath," and *wai* means "freshwater," or "water of life." The beast of the one-world order will arise out of the sea.

Obama's grandparents—Stanley Armour Dunham, was born in 1918, he died 1992; and his grandmother, Madelyn Lee Payne, was born in 1922; she died 2008. Stanley and Madelyn married in 1940. During their life, they gave birth to their only daughter, Stanley Ann, November 29, 1942, in Wichita, Kansas. Stanley Ann attended the Mercer Island High School near Seattle, Washington. It is reported that the school had a communistic ideology. In 1960, Ann's parents moved to Hawaii.

Stanley is said to be related to a line of presidents: James Madison, Harry Truman, Lyndon Johnson, Jimmy Carter, and the Bushes. Madelyn's great-great-grandfather was Robert Perry of Wales. Unsubstantiated Internet chatter tells of a meeting, September 26, 1960, with Fidel Castro and Mr. Dunham at the United Nations building, subject of meeting unknown. What they had in common was Communism. Another dark cloud over Stanley was allegations accusing him of selling plans to Germany.

Barack's parents, Stanley Ann Dunham and Barack Hussein Obama Sr., met in a Russian language class at the University of Hawaii in 1959–'60. They shared similar political interests in socialism and communism. Barack Sr. was influenced by Catholicism, Islam, and Anglican religion, but later he became an atheist. Stanley Ann was secular. Ann became an anthropologist, and Barack majored in economics.

Obama's father was a citizen of Kenya, Africa, of the Luo Tribe, born in 1936. Obama Sr. may have been a bigamist, and through his various relationships, Barack Jr. has a few siblings on his father's side. First wife was Kezia Aoko, whom he married in 1954 at the age of eighteen. They had a daughter named Auma Obama, a son Malik, and later other children.

Stanley Ann Dunham became Obama's second wife when they married February 2, 1961. After Obama Jr. was born in 1961, Ann left Obama Sr. and moved to Seattle, where she attended the University of Washington from 1961–'62. They divorced in 1964. Obama Sr. stayed in Hawaii, attending the University of Hawaii, 1961–'62. Then he went to Harvard from 1962–'64. Obama Sr. had children with his third wife, Ruth Baker. Ruth was born in 1937 to Maurice and Ida Baker of Newton, Massachusetts. Their lineage is tied to Lithuanian Jews. After Ruth Baker graduated from Simmon College, Boston, in 1958, she became an elementary school teacher. Somewhere along the line, she met Barack Obama Sr.

After his education, Obama Sr. returned to Kenya in 1964. Ruth followed him, and they married the same year. She was a teacher in Kenya. Ruth and Barack Sr. had two sons: Mark, who claimed his Jewish heritage, and David, who died in a car accident. They divorced in 1973. Here is an indirect connection for Barack Jr. and Jews. After divorcing Ruth, Obama Sr. had a son with Jael Otinyo, named George, in 1982; and when his son was six months old, Obama Sr. died in auto accident in 1982.

Barack's mother, Stanley Ann, married an Indonesian student, Lolo Soetoro, in 1965. Lolo's student visa expired. He returned to Jakarta, Indonesia, 1966. Shortly thereafter, Barack and his mother joined him. Lolo adopted Obama and renamed him Barry Soetoro, and he was then a legal citizen of Indonesia. Between the age six to ten, he was enrolled in Besuki Public School and Saint Francis of Assisi Catholic School in Indonesia. Lolo and Ann had a daughter in 1970, named Maya Soetoro-Ng. Ann and Lolo divorced in 1980, and he remarried had a son, Yusuf Aji, in 1981 and daughter, Rahay Nurmaida, in 1984.

At the age of ten, Barry Soetoro left Indonesia and was sent to live with his mother's parents in Hawaii in 1971. Did his mother or grandparents change his name back to Obama and reapply for US citizenship when he returned from Indonesia? Perhaps it is legal for a person to have duel citizenship, but that could pose a problem for a future president. In 1971, Barack Sr. returned to Hawaii to visit with his young son for a month.

Barack Jr. was enrolled in the Panahou School, Hawaii, a private college prep academy from fifth to twelfth grade. During this period, Barack's grandparents introduced him to their friend, Frank Marshall Davis—a journalist, poet, communist, labor union activist—to be a mentor to Barack.

Davis was born in Kansas in 1905. He moved to Chicago in 1927 and wrote for African American newspapers. He taught jazz history at the Abraham Lincoln School. Near the end of World War II, Davis started his own newspaper called the *Star*. Its goal was to promote a policy of cooperation and unity between Russia and the United States. The *Spokane Daily Chronicle* in 1947 called the *Star*, "a Red weekly because it has the markings of a Communist front publication." In 1948, Davis and his second wife, Helen Canfield (a white woman), moved to Hawaii, where they stayed for over twenty-five years. While living in Honolulu,

Davis wrote a weekly column called *Frankly Speaking* for the *Honolulu Record*, a labor paper published by International Longshore and Warehouse Union. Mr. Davis was on the FBI watch list. Davis died 1987 in Hawaii. We see a few connections between Davis, Dunham, and Obama. Davis and Dunham were both from Kansas. Obama admits knowing Davis in his book *Dreams from My Father*, where he mentions a friend of his grandfather named Frank. Obama remembers Davis: "It made me smile thinking back on Frank and his old black power dashiki self" (Wikipedia, July 23, 2015).

It seems that Barack's mother stayed primarily in Indonesia. His half sister Maya attended the Jakarta International School from 1981 to 1984. In 1981, Barack returned to Indonesia to visit his mother and sister. We assume Ann and Maya returned to Hawaii, where Maya was enrolled in the Punahou High School in Honolulu and graduated in 1988. She attended Barnard College in Manhattan, New York University, and received a PhD from University of Hawaii in 2006. She continues to have a good relationship with Obama and resides in Hawaii.

Stanley Ann acquired her PhD in anthropology and spent many years in Indonesia, doing research and outreach. She returned to Hawaii for treatment of ovarian and uterine cancer. She died in 1995. Janny Scott, author of *A Singular Woman*, wrote a biography on Stanley Ann Dunham.

In 1987–'88, Obama traveled to Europe for a few weeks and then to Kenya, where he stayed for five weeks. He visited Kenya in 2006. He returned to Kenya as the American president, July 25, 2015, to speak with government officials and visit with Kenyan relatives.

Rumors say Malcolm X, or Frank Davis Marshall, could have fathered Barack, but these claims can only be proven through a DNA test. We doubt if anyone will dig up Obama Sr., Malcolm X, or Ann Dunham, nor will Barack Jr. submit to a DNA test. However, we stumbled across something very interesting online, September 2014. The report was made by P. P. Simmons Group, American Thinker, January 2014. Lorretta Fuddy became director of Health Department in Hawaii, 2011, before the computer-generated birth certificate of Barack was released. Stanley Ann Dunham and Lorretta Fuddy, both were members of the Subud Cult, which had influence in occult and Islam. Its founders name was Muhammad Subuh (d) Sumohadiwidjojo of Indonesia. The name *Subud* means "sunrise," or "rising sun." He was born 1901, died 1987. He traveled extensively outside of Indonesia to Europe, Australia, and America. The picture of Subuh and Barack Obama bears a striking resemblance to each other. In his travels, could he and Stanley Ann Dunham have an intimate encounter in 1960? Was her marriage to Obama Sr. a sham? Was her marriage to Soetoro an excuse to live in, of all places in the world, Indonesia, the home of Subud? The name *Barack* means "lightning from heaven," as in Satan was cast out of heaven as lightning, and he is associated with the sun rising.

Obama's Birth Certificate

There has been concern if Obama was born in the United States. In 2008, it was alleged that Obama's grandmother came out on national TV, stating that her grandson was not born in Hawaii but in Africa; and a few days later, she was dead by a stroke. During the 2008 presidential campaign, Hillary Clinton was first to mention the validity of the birther issue. As questions circled, the Obama administration released a copy of his birth certificate online. The birth certificate was believed to have been a forgery, and as national concern grew, Donald Trump offered to give $5 million to Obama if he provided any proof he was born in the United States. In 2016, Trump was running for president, and Hillary Clinton attempted to bring the issue up to portray Trump as racist. Her claim was fact-checked and discovered she was first to leak the birther assertion.

Experts conducted a forensic analysis on the computer-generated birth certificate. They viewed it under twenty-five different protocols and concluded it was a fraud, and it had been altered in at least four places. The Hawaii seal was a fraud. A person by the name of S. Fox said she created the birth document at the request of Deb Addler of the Democratic National Committee. Robert F. Bauer may have initiated actions in keeping Obama's birth certificate, college records, and other records hidden beginning with Philip J. Berg lawsuit in 2008. Bauer was appointed White House General Counsel by Obama. Judith L. Corley of Perkins Cole assisted Obama in procuring the birth document, which is not department policy for an individual to personally request a certified copy of an original birth certificate. Loretta Fuddy, director of Department of Health, said she would make an exception to department policy to accommodate Obama. Fuddy told Corley the copies will be computer generated, but Corley insisted on securing the copies herself. Fuddy released the long form birth certificate. Later, a PDF of the document was available on the White House website in April 2011.

For some thinkers, it was convenient to have Fuddy become director of the Department of Health in Hawaii at the time Obama needed an insider to provide a birth certificate. As the saying goes, "No good deed goes unpunished." Measures were taken to eliminate Loretta Fuddy in a plane crash, where everyone survived with minor scratches—except Fuddy, the only fatality. Fuddy had announced she would be releasing information to the media, and her untimely death wiped out that information. This reminds us that Breit Bart had announced he had some damning information on Obama, and after leaving a conference, he was found dead in the street that same night.

Sheriff Arpaio, 2012–2013, sent Mike Zullo back to Hawaii for more evidence. He spoke with a man named Duncan Sunahara, who had a sister named Virginia, born in Hawaii, August 4, 1961, same day as Obama; however, the next day the baby died. When Duncan requested a copy of his sister's original long form birth certificate, he was denied a copy. He took it to court and was given many excuses why it was too difficult to go back through volumes of documents to pull out one. He was given a computer-generated copy. Upon examination of this form, it was apparent that the birth certificate number was out of sequence with the others babies born on that day. Virginia Sunahara's number was 151-61-11080. The other births were given the following sequence of numbers: Susan Nordyke, 151-61-10637; Gretchen Nordyke, 151-61-10638; Barack Obama, 151-61-10641. Virginia's number is 440 numbers higher, yet it was filed only two days after Barack Obama's. This is strange, and if the Hawaii Department of Health wasn't trying to cover up something, we could get to the bottom of this anomaly (*Prophecy in the News*, September, 2012).

Obama's Social Security Number

Research by Neil Sankey and Susan Daniels, a private investigator in Ohio, researched public databases and found Obama has several Social Security numbers. One was issued by State of Hawaii. But he is using social security number **042-68-4425**, issued from State of Connecticut around 1976–1979 to a resident of Connecticut. Obama has never been a resident of Connecticut. Jerome Corsi, reporter for *World Net Daily*, wrote a book, *Obama Nation*, and he said Obama was using two Social Security numbers. In 1975–1976, Obama worked for Baskin Robbins ice cream in Hawaii while in high school. In 1986, Obama first used the above Social Security number while working in Chicago as a community organizer. He also used that number for his selective service. There are no records of his passport application. These documents are now sealed. A property search in 2010 under the name Barack and Michelle Obama turned up the name of Harrison J. Bonvel of 5046 S. Greenwood Avenue, Chicago. It is alleged that Bonvel's Social Security number is same as Obama's.

The College Years

Obama's ideological position was formed from a mix of Marxism, communism, socialism, and Islam. He transitioned from Hawaii high school to Occidental College in Los Angeles in 1979, having received a Fulbright Foundation scholarship. Some of his instructors were socialists, such as professors Richard Cloward and Frances Piven, who shared their views against a capitalist United States.

If Obama's records were unsealed, you would find he paid little for undergraduate college or Harvard because of foreign aid and scholarships given to poor foreign students like Barry Soetoro.

There is some concern that there are no enrollment records for Barack's time at Columbia University, New York, 1981–1983. He received a Bachelor of Arts in Political Science and International Relations. There are no transcripts available. Wayne Allen Root, a former classmate of Obama at Columbia, said, "Why are the college records of a fifty-year-old president of the United States so important to keep secret? It's not a national secret, so why not release the information? I believe he got a leg up by being admitted to both Occidental and Columbia as a foreign exchange student. It is difficult to transfer into Columbia and graduate in two years, but this fact alone makes what the president did an anomaly."

From Columbia, Obama entered Harvard University. It is reported he studied constitutional law. While there, he became president of Harvard Law Review. Articles written by Barack are unavailable for review, and no college transcripts are available. Obama may have lectured at the University of Chicago School of Law part-time. He was not given professorship.

Academic transcripts are required of presidential candidates, but mainstream media has glossed over this lack of transparency. Other records that should be available for review such as selective service registration, Social Security records, immigration records, and travel and passport records.

It is not difficult to conclude that Obama's ideology and his educational subjects would be an asset in undermining the imperialistic, capitalist, and colonialist America.

Michelle L. Robinson Obama was born January 17, 1964, in Chicago, to Fraser and Marian Robinson. She grew up on Euclid Street and attended a Methodist church. Michelle has a brother, Craig, who was a basketball coach at Oregon State University. In the sixth grade, Michelle was placed in the gifted class at Bryn Mawr Elementary School. She attended the Whitney Young High School, a magnet high school. One classmate was Jessie Jackson's daughter, Sanitita. During her four years in high school, she was on the honor roll and graduated in 1981.

Michelle went to Princeton, majored in sociology, minor African American studies and French language. She graduated in 1985, cum laude, with a bachelor of arts. She entered Harvard Law School and graduated in 1988 with JD. There are several reports claiming Michelle voluntarily surrendered her law license in 1993 (www.iardc.org, Illinois Attorney Registration and Disciplinary Committee).

While working at law firm of Sidley Austin, she met Barack Obama, and they were married in 1992. She gave birth to Malia, 1998, and Natasha, 2001. She served on Chicago Council of Global Affairs. She was employed at the University of Chicago Hospital, earning $273,618. Michelle worked for Mayor Richard Daley.

Real Estate

On the public database, Michelle and Barack Obama's names surfaced with the name of Harrison J. Bonvel of 5046 S. Greenwood Avenue, Chicago, as of 2010. The Obamas are associated with this address but are not the owners. Registered owners are Jane Stevaort, a judge, and Harvey Weinberg, a tax lawyer. The property ID number has had six different numbers in the past six years, but owners stayed the same. This is called multilayer real estate finance transactions. Associated with this North Trust Company was created in 2005 and acquired a loan for $1.3 million from Fannie Mae, and then they did a release the same year, June 2, 2005. There was no index description for the property. There is corruption in Cook County, Recorder of Deeds Department, and an attempt to hide ownership trail. Obama's 2009 income tax under real estate taxes, he paid $22,000 on a million-dollar house. The property ID PIN number was blacked out. His 2010 income tax form for real estate tax, the entire page was missing. Between 2004 and 2009, there are fifty-eight different addresses that show up for Barack and Michelle Obama.

Acorn

In 1994, Obama worked with Acorn training and providing legal assistance for employees. Acorn lost millions in funding due to claims of voter fraud. Obama represented now-defunct Acorn in a suit against Citibank for denying mortgages to blacks (Buycks-Roberson versus Citibank Federal Savings Bank). This was the momentum needed to push banks into approving subprime loans for poor credit risks. This mandate spread nationwide, which resulted in the 2007–2008 housing collapse. This was the lynch pin that propelled Obama to win over McCain.

Author Obama

Obama was given $125,000 to write a book about race relations. He did not write the book but may have used the money to vacation in Bali with Michelle. He received another advance of $40,000 for the book *Dreams from My Father.* The writing style is similar to William Ayers, who appears on the cover of *Chicago* magazine trampling the American flag. In the book, he says while at Occidental, he chose his friends carefully. He was interested in associates who were politically active and shared his interest in Marxism and socialism. Three of his friends were Pakistani: Wahid Hamid, Sohale Siddiqi, and Mohammed Hassan Chandoo. Obama and Hamid went to Pakistan for an extended period. At that time, the United States was not issuing passports to American citizens to travel to Pakistan. At that time, Obama may have been approved for travel to Pakistan because of his Indonesian citizenship.

Senator Obama

In 1996, Obama ran for the Illinois State Senate. He joined the New Party, which promotes Marxism. Obama supporter Dr. Quentin Yong, a socialist, was a proponent for government-run health care. The front-runner for the Democratic seat was Blair Hull, who was forced out of the race after David Axelrod leaked confidential facts about Hull's divorce. Obama then faced Republican candidate Jack Ryan, whose sealed custody records from his divorce were made public, forcing him to withdraw from the race. Obama waltzed into the US Senate. Senator Obama was ranked in 2007 as the most liberal politician. In 2004, Obama was given the opportunity to speak at the Democratic National Convention. At that time, John Kerry was running for president. Many were impressed with Obama's charisma and oratorical prowess. Apparently, the powers to be began to prepare him for greater opportunities.

Reviewing Obama under the microscope, we see the possibility of real estate fraud, stolen identity fraud, insurance fraud, illegal contributions. Many people strongly believe that Obama is not a natural-born citizen and is ineligible to be president. At least twelve civil lawsuits claiming his ineligibility have been filed in courts. In 2010, a Hawaii election official said he was not born in Hawaii. Steven Pidgeon wrote a book, *Obama Error*. In 2008, he wanted to take a closer look at Obama's socialistic background. He also filed a suit to look into his eligibility. Obama's father was a Kenyan citizen, when Kenya was under British colonization. A foreigner married to a US citizen who has a child born on US soil, that child would be a US citizen. If a foreigner married to a US citizen had a child born in their country of origin, the child would be a citizen of that country. An unmarried foreigner who gives birth on American soil, their child is not automatically an American citizen; there are legal requirements that must be pursued. We assume, the American parents' child could run for president, regardless of where he is born.

Immorality, Homosexuality, Abortion

In 2009, Obama signed into law the new hate crime bill, called Local Law Enforcement Hate Crimes Prevention Act. It now protects against speech or action in opposition to sexual or transgender orientation. Pastors who openly speak out against sexual sin as proclaimed in the Bible could be fined or jailed. Churches could be prosecuted for discrimination by not hiring openly practicing homosexuals and lose their 501c3 status. Christians are now labeled as promoting "antisocial hate doctrine"

Christian business owners who elect not to provide services that violate their faith are being harassed and fined if they refuse to comply with the homosexual agenda. Government mandates oppose Christian businesses and the Catholic church who elected not to provide abortion pills, contraceptives, or other services

The Boy and Girl Scouts of America are under attack to allow homosexual persons to work with the scouts.

Obama is an earnest supporter of sexual perversion. Obama celebrates June as LGBT pride month. Obama goes the extra mile and orders schools, businesses, and the military to accept transgender persons. Obama declared the Stonewall Inn as a national monument in memory of the famous riot between homosexuals and police in 1969. We have all seen men dressing up like women, and they look like clowns. Locker rooms and bathrooms will be required to accommodate males in female facilities.

Traditional marriage has been overturned and replaced by same-sex unions. Miss USA Carrie Prejeans said she believes marriage is between man and woman, and she was verbally attacked by liberals, media, and homosexual activists. Obama tells Department of Justice that State attorney generals could ignore state laws protecting marriage. In 2010, Obama began to derail traditional marriage protected under In Defense of Marriage Act, by forcing equal rights to same-sex marriage, and made the first-ever report on US human rights to the United Nations Human Rights Council. The US Supreme Court, 2015, rules in favor of same-sex marriage. Obama administration highlighted the White House in the rainbow colors. The rainbow is a sign of God's covenant, now perverted by the celebration of homosexuality. Since marriage was ordained by God and is holy, to nationally defile it is a desecration.

Obama is the first US president to pose for the LGBT *Out 100 Magazine*.

Obama nominated Eric Fanning to be secretary of the Army and is the first openly gay head of a military branch.

Obama appoints first transgender Amanda Simpson as senior technical adviser to the Department of Commerce.

Obama's Alleged Homosexual Liaisons

Opening this area of discussion, we consider that through Obama's life, there are no reports or pictures of him being in a heterosexual relationship outside of Michelle Obama. Since Obama has been a strong proponent for the homosexual agenda, bits and pieces of news have been surfacing to support the claim that Obama is homosexual. On the Jay Leno show, August 6, 2013, Obama said, "Opposing same-sex marriage violates basic morality, is discrimination of gender, and I have no patience for countries that do not affirm gay, lesbian, transgender persons."

In 1999, Larry Sinclair said he and Obama engaged in homosexual activities and cocaine use in the back of a limousine. At this time, Obama was married to Michelle. Sinclair claims to have been contacted by Donald Young, who was the gay choir director at Rev. Wright's church. Sinclair and Young shared information that could have derailed the Obama presidential campaign, and it could not afford more negative publicity. Shortly after this meeting,

Donald Young was murdered on December 23, 2007. Weeks after, Larry Bland, another gay member of the church, had been murdered.

In a book written by Lawrence Sinclair, 2009, titled *Barack Obama and Larry Sinclair: Cocaine, Sex, Lies & Murder*, Sinclair claims that Obama was involved in the murder of Donald Young, an alleged lover of Obama. His murder occurred weeks before the Democratic 2008 Iowa Caucus. The Chicago police seemed not to properly investigate or arrest a suspect. David Axelrod, Obama's campaign manager, had used Donald Young to contact and seek out information from Sinclair about whom he had told of Obama's crimes and actions. Sinclair claims to have had two homosexual encounters with Obama—on November 6 and 7, 1999, at which time they procured and used cocaine. Obama's team sought to silence Sinclair by using Internet porn king Dan Parisi and Edward Gelb to conduct a rigged polygraph on Sinclair. He passed the polygraph. Mainstream media attacked the National Press Club for allowing Sinclair the use of their facilities for a news conference to present his evidence and allegations to the world media. Vice President Joe Biden's son, Delaware Attorney General Beau Biden, issued an arrest warrant on false and fabricated charges to attempt to discredit Sinclair.

We consider these allegations made by Larry Sinclair and take into account events that have occurred to date that lend credence to his claims:

- Obama's family members are dead, and others who could shed light on Obama's checkered past are dead, missing, or silenced.
- Obama used drugs in college.
- Obama proudly lauds the homosexual agenda.
- Mainstream media is controlled by the White House administration; smear tactics are used against dissidents.
- High-level officials are complicit in covering up for the president. Obama was selected by the elite, and he is shielded and protected.
- No one has come forward to sue Sinclair for defamation.

Obama may be butting heads with other national leaders who oppose homosexuality. Russian President Putin said homosexuals need to keep their relationship private and not an open spectacle. A few African leaders told Obama they outright oppose homosexuality in their countries. Kenyan leaders have sent Obama a letter stating their position against homosexuality and asked that he not broach that subject during his July 2015 visit.

He publically congratulated Jason Collins, basketball player, when he came out. Obama made no mention of Tim Tebow, an upstanding Christian and role model.

Obama honors gay teen Caleb Laieski at White House gay pride dinner. It was reported on November 20, 2013, that Laieski allegedly had sexually abused a minor boy. He met him on Trevor Space, a social media site for children and young adults, thirteen to twenty-four, interested in homosexuality. Laieski is said to have had three-way sex with the boy and adult male, forty-three-year-old Chris Wilson, a Phoenix police officer. Laieski and thirty-five-year-old Casey Cameron sent five thousand e-mails to schools demanding special protection for gay students. He dropped out of high school and went to DC to lobby for the Student Nondiscrimination Act, which is a homosexual provision. October 2015, "If we are truly created equal, then the love we commit to each other is equal."

Abortion

Obama is an enthusiastic advocate for abortion and partial birth abortion. He has no concern for the welfare of the unborn. As a senator, he voted against a law that would have prevented the killing of babies who survived. He pledged his allegiance to giant abortion leader Planned Parenthood, by stating, "God bless their work, I got your back and can count on me to further support with taxpayer funds." Obama is asking the god of this world to bless the murder of children. Certainly, God, Creator of all, would not bless the murder of the unborn. Obama said, proabortion groups are doing God's work. Even after Planned Parenthood was exposed for dismembering human babies and selling their organs, there was no outrage expressed by Obama but still maintained his support for the organization going as far as to threaten the shutdown of the government if funding was cut to Planned Parenthood.

Acceptance of abortion makes way for the acceptance of other immoral practices against children, such as pedophilia. The National Council for Civil Liberties, former Labor Health Secretary Patricia Hewit, 1974–1983, said, "Children are not harmed by having sex with adults if they are between ten to fourteen years old and consent to have sex with an adult." The Pedophile Info Exchange is actively pushing for government acceptance of this offense.

Supreme Court rules to shut down prolife speech in front of abortion clinics (2014). American Center for Law and Justice filed case twenty years ago regarding free speech be protected to save lives.

What Are Obama's Religious Beliefs?

President Obama embraced Islamic fundamentals from his father and stepfather, the Nation of Islam, and his Pakistani college associates.

Barack's early years were influenced by his grandparents, who had an affiliation with East Shore Unitarian Church for a short period of time. His mother does not appear to have been associated with any religion. When his mother married Lolo Soetero, Obama may have been influenced in Islam, Hinduism, and Catholicism while in Indonesia. According to Perry Stone, *Unleashing the Beast: The Coming Fanatical Dictator and His Ten-Nation Coalition*, he reported Indonesia is one of the largest Islamic nations in the world. Over the years, it has forced thousands of Christians to convert to Islam or face death. In 1995, it was reported six hundred churches had been destroyed, and the number of deaths is unknown. In college, his friend was a Pakistani Muslim. In later years, he was associated with the Nation of Islam and Rev. Wright's brand of Christianity. Before we can determine where Obama's faith lies, we must look at the fruit of his labor.

America has been experiencing a cultural and sexual revolution going back to the 'sixties. With the arrival of the twenty-first century, the nation is now entrenched in the homosexual agenda. Obama came on the national scene in 2009 and immediately became the drum major for homosexuality. With his push forward, the LGBT agenda became a household name in the media, entertainment world, workplace, education, and the church. The Obama administration ensured that the homosexual agenda would be a mainstay by passing laws to enforce their so-called civil rights.

We observed the rise of this little-known man and his influence on America and abroad. He promised "change," and he delivered on that promise.

America is a nation that has rebelled against God. God has allowed a fierce ruler to govern. Moral decline of the nation will allow for destruction and demise. Obama made a statement that America is not a Christian nation. At first this is alarming, but when you consider the mind-set of the founding fathers steeped in Masonic occult philosophy, Obama's statement was not far-fetched. Atheists are currently pushing to have "In God We Trust" removed from our currency. Others are pushing to have "One Nation under God" removed from the Pledge of Allegiance. If the reference to "God" in these symbols is not the God of the Bible, our Creator, but is a reference to Satan, the god of this world—we as Christians are not at a loss as atheists and Muslims attack religious symbols that just may refer to the god of the earth. Monuments or plaques of the Ten Commandments also came under attack and removed from public land. A monument of the Ten Commandments was carved by man, and if destroyed or removed, Christians should not be so offended because God said, write his commandments on our hearts.

The Gold Islam Ring and Other Things

During his time at Occidental, Barack began wearing a gold ring on his left hand and has worn the ring ever since. It is believed that he acquired the ring from Indonesia. Upon inspection, the ring has Arabic writing, which is the *Shahada*: "There is no god except Allah."

Obama has been photographed wearing a Masonic ring. He carries a Hindu monkey god statue in his pocket, very popular in Indonesia. The god's name is Hanuman, which is an incarnation of Lord Shiva, another Hindu god. The Hindus presented the president with a two-foot-tall version of the monkey god, which was sanctified in the White House before its presentation to Obama.

People were concerned about the lack of transparency and concealment of much of Obama's background. During his 2008 campaign, liberal mainstream media would report news regarding Obama without question. They were not to question his background. Alternative media would be our source for what is really going on, and we are thankful for brave reporters—such as, Joseph Farah, editor of *World Net Daily*; Gary Kah, *Hope For the World*; Mike Adams, *Natural News*; Kerby Anderson, *Point of View*; Gary Stearman, *Prophecy in the News*; Bob Livingston, *Personal Liberty Digest*; Tom Horn, Sky Watch TV; Walid Shoebat, Alex Jones, Prison Planet, *Breaking Israel News*; and others working to expose the one-world order agenda.

Obama's Relationship with Israel

In an article written by Ben Shapiro, *Front Page Mag*, July 2, 2014, "The Jew-Hating Obama Administration," provides a good summary of Obama's position on Israel:

> Three Jewish boys were found dead, and one youth was an American citizen, murdered by Hamas terrorists … In the interim, Obama said nothing about them publicly. His wife issued no hashtags, his State department maintained that $400 million in taxpayer cash would continue to the Palestinian unity government, which includes Hamas. Presumably, Frenkel, the American citizen, did not look enough like Obama's imaginary son (Trayvon Martin) for him to give a damn. Or perhaps Frenkel hadn't deserted his duty in the military, and therefore his parents didn't deserve a White House press conference (released in exchange for five terrorists). Maybe Michelle Obama was too busy worrying about children's fat thighs to spend a moment tweeting out a selfie to raise awareness. Or maybe Obama didn't care about Frenkel because he was a Jew … When the head of the nation does not bless Israel, it brings curses upon the people."

Obama Says He Is a Christian

We can count on one hand the times Obama has aligned himself with Christianity. He was a member of radical Rev. Wright's church. During the 2008 campaign, he was on Rick

Warren show, the advocate for Chrislam, and said he believed Jesus was his savior. In an interview, he slipped up and referred to his Muslim faith then changed it to his Christian faith. These are the only references we can make. However, his anti-Christian beliefs could fill a book.

Obama's response to Christian businesses or schools in regard to abortion and abortion products under Obamacare is, "Your opposition to forced coverage of abortion pills is not a legitimate religious belief, and our proabortion agenda is far more important than your silly religious beliefs." DOJ attempted to convince the court that forcing Catholic nuns to pay for abortion pills in no way violated their faith because all they had to do was sign a form and let someone else violate their faith for them. Obama's Justice Department argued before Supreme Court that federal government can tell churches and religious organization who they can hire or fire.

Obama has not sincerely aligned himself with godly people. He discouraged Christian programs in the White House but encouraged additional Islamic observances. He spoke at a Christian university and demanded that Christian imagery be covered. While he exalts the Koran, he mocks Bible scriptures. In 2006, in a speech regarding public policy, he used the book of Leviticus to highlight slavery; book of Deuteronomy to highlight the stoning of children; and said the Sermon on the Mount was so radical our own defense department would not survive its applications.

He tolerates Christianity on the surface, but his actions speak volumes to his being anti-Christian. Second-term inauguration committee invited Rev. Louie Giglio to do the benediction. He is pro-traditional marriage and from his pulpit since the 1990s maintains his position on traditional marriage. He speaks out against the sin of homosexuality, and because of his position on the gay agenda, he received backlash from homosexual advocates. He has since declined the White House invitation to pray. Rev. Giglio pastors a church in Atlanta, Passion City Church. One of their ministries is to fight human trafficking. He drew over sixty thousand to Georgia Dome for that particular outreach. Addie Whisenant of the inauguration committee said, "We were unaware of the sermon when we selected Rev. Giglio … We now work to select someone to deliver benediction … We will ensure their beliefs reflect this administration's vision of inclusion and acceptance for all Americans."

At a press briefing, August 2013, Obama was asked by a reporter what is his "red line" for US actions to defend Egypt's Christians from jihad, and he said, "I didn't bring my red pen out with me today." Obama held up a bill introduced by Rep. Frank Wolf and passed the house, 402–22, to create a special envoy in the State Department to help persecuted Christians around the world. This bill must have gotten buried since we hear no outrage from the Obama administration.

In Iran, Americans are imprisoned for their religious belief and other bogus charges. During the Iranian nuclear negotiations, Obama did not ask Iran to free American citizens. Iranian Christians who escaped persecution and came into America through the Mexican border were arrested and detained in prison. Obama has made many concessions for illegals coming into the United States but has ignored the plight of Christian immigrants.

German family received US amnesty from German persecution because family wanted to do homeschooling, which is not allowed in Germany. They believed public education was against their religious beliefs. Germany was going to take away their children. Obama is now working to send them back to Germany. In 2014, a court ruled the family could stay in United States, but Obama continues to fight it.

Survey of Religious Hostility in America recorded six hundred incidents in past ten years. The United States is no better than Islamist radicals who call for destruction of Christians and Jews. This administration demonstrates little concern regarding the persecution and death of thousands of Christians and Jews being killed in Syria, Iraq, Iran, Egypt, France, Nigeria, and other places.

Pro-Islam

In 2003, Mr. and Mrs. Obama attended a dinner in honor of Rashid Khalidi, a former PLO operative, harsh critic of Israel and advocate of Palestinian rights. Publically, Obama denies knowing this Rashid and his wife, Mona. Obama attended the Arab American Action Network (AAAN) where he praised Khalidi. William Ayers was in attendance. This Arab organization received funds while Obama and Ayers were board members of the Woods Fund. Comments from one speaker at the dinner remarked that if Palestinians cannot secure a return to their land, Israel will never see a day of peace. Entertainment at the dinner included a Muslim children's dance, whose performance simulated beheadings with fake swords and stomping on American, Israeli, and British flags. Allegedly, Obama told the audience that Israel has no God-given right to occupy Palestine and there has been genocide against the Palestinian people by the Israelis. *Los Angeles Times* has a videotape of the event but refuses to make it public.

In 2008, Nicholas Kristof, with the *New York Times*, conducted an interview with Obama. He asked him about life in Indonesia. Kristof said, "Obama recited in Arabic the Shahada and said the call to prayer is one of the prettiest sounds on earth at sunset." In another interview, Obama slipped and said his "Muslim faith," and the reporter said, "Muslim?" and Obama quickly changed and said "my Christian faith."

July 2014, Obama celebrated the end of Ramadan with other Muslims at a White House dinner. He said, "Thanking Muslims for their many achievements and contributions to building the very fabric of our nation and strengthening the core of our democracy." Ramadan was celebrated in the White House for the past four years. Obama allowed hundreds of Muslim to pray on the White House lawn as the pope allowed Muslims to pray at the Vatican.

He says Islam is a peaceful religion. Is he aligned to their aspirations for global domination or a worldwide caliphate? That concern was introduced when 2016 presidential contender Dr. Ben Carson was asked if he would support a Muslim in the White House. Dr. Carson said he would not advocate a Muslim as president if the person adheres to the Koran and Sharia law, replacing the US Constitution.

News media are not allowed to associate terrorism with Islam and Muslims but soft-pedal it, calling them radicals or extremists. There are over a billion Muslims, and the majority of Muslims are not jihadist, but they are silent on the barbaric actions and goals of the terrorists associated with Islam. Terrorists number maybe 250 million, and they are moved to carry out their agenda because of their god Allah, prophet Muhammad, and by incitement from their Imam. Any contradiction of this mind-set will be dealt with by death to the apostates and death to the infidels—all of whom will be cast into eternal damnation in hell.

Setting down roots in Chicago, he became affiliated with Rev. Jeremiah Wright—a radical Christian preacher who may have been a former Muslim and black nationalist who had studied at Howard. He may have been affiliated with Hamas. He was a close friend of Louis Farrakhan, leader of Nation of Islam. When Obama first began to campaign for president, the Nation of Islam was elated for him, but Obama's handlers told him to downplay his relationship with the Nation so as not to alienate Americans who were opposed to Islam and especially a Muslim president. Obama was also directed to cut ties with Jeremiah Wright. Muslim nations made comments about Obama, "our brother Muslim Obama." After his winning the presidency, Muslims around the world, blacks in America, and fringe people celebrated.

We spoke about messages conveyed through symbols and speech to certain groups without overtly alerting the masses, and Obama designed a special seal that sent a message to fellow Muslims. The seal was similar to the "Seal of the President of the United States" with changes. The letter *O* for *Obama* had a rising sun within the circle. The masses were told that it represented the sun rising on a new day in America, representing hope, and the mantra was "Yes, we can." In Islamic beliefs, they look for the sign of the "sun rising in the west," and this would mean that the goal of Islam to become dominant in the world had come to America. They had an elected official at the highest level and one who supported the Muslim Brotherhood and its agenda.

The National Day of Prayer held at the White House was canceled because Rev. Franklin Graham spoke on Islamic terrorism on 9-11. Rev. Graham was told that he was intolerant for associating the attack with Islam and, therefore, could not speak.

"The future must not belong to those who slander the prophet of Islam," as per Barack Obama.

When speaking to Islamic groups, he exalts the Koran as "holy," speaks Arabic, and stands on the position that no one should defame the prophet Muhammad, yet there is no outrage when Christianity is attacked. Obama said the *shahida*, the Islam call to prayer, is the prettiest sound.

Obama claimed that portions of the Bible are not for today and there are many paths to God.

Obama no longer speaks of freedom of religion but freedom to worship. He is careful not to speak about Jesus except when it is convenient.

He does not hold to Christian beliefs that homosexuality and abortion are sins.

The Presidential Campaign, Inauguration, and Other Strange Events

Obama became a rising star in Chicago. He was befriended by numerous influential people. After winning the 2008 presidential election, Obama returned many favors. For instance, Valerie Jarrett received the position of adviser to President Obama. If Obama was the recipient of Saudi Arabia money, they might expect him to continue America's advocacy for Islamic interests. Obama's first presidential visit was to Egypt. When Obama visited Saudi Arabia, he did bow before the king.

Obama's presidential campaign received millions and some from foreign sources—such as, $33,000 was donated from Rafah, Gaza, where phone banks were set up to solicit donations.

George Soros, a billionaire and international socialist, donated funds.

Thirteen days before Obama's inauguration (January 7, 2009), four past, living presidents met together at an undisclosed location with Obama. The number 13 is significant to the Masonic organization. Those **five** present were Obama, two Bushes, Clinton, and Carter. These five are globalists with a hive mind-set to bring about the new world order agenda. On May 1, 1776, five men met in a cave to form the Illuminati. Occult organizations use the number 5 as in their five-pointed star—which represents earth, wind, fire, water, and spirit.

The Obama family went on vacation in Hawaii before the inauguration and stayed at a $9 million home. The residence experienced a power outage **11:00** p.m. on Friday night, which coincided with the first Esbat for witches' weekly meeting after Sabat of Yule, meaning "last of the year." The number 11 is significant to the occult, representing the eleventh position in the zodiac, Aquarius.

The latitude of Hawaii is **21.6**, which is associated with 666, $6 \times 6 \times 6 =$ **216**. Obama's date of birth is August 4, 1961, which is the **216**th day of the year. Obama's goal is to divide

Jerusalem between Israel and Palestinians. In Revelation, it alludes to the beast wanting to divide Israel. Twelve thousand from each of the twelve tribes is 144,000, and if divided by 666 equals **216.** The words *messiah Barack* equals 666, the number of a man.

Signs are omens allowing us to see a message or understand something that will come to pass.

Chicago, Illinois, zip code is **60606**. When Mena Lee Grebin was seven years old living in Hyde Park, Illinois, in 1987, she had an open vision. In summary, she saw a man who would come out of Chicago that would destroy the nation of America. She saw riots, war, murder, famine, and chaos, as if watching a TV show. The wind was blowing hard, red sky, people running, saying, "The end has come." She saw newspapers and flyers blowing down the street. At the first newsstand, she saw a picture of George Washington on the paper. The second newsstand, a picture of Abe Lincoln, and the third had a picture of Martin Luther King. The news captions read, "American Freedom Has Been Stripped." In the final part of the vision, she saw a silhouette of a man that would be the future president from Chicago. Her mother and others knew of this vision. In 2004, Jesus told her that the last president of the United States would lead the world into the tribulation. After the 2008 primaries, God told Mena that Obama would win. Mena was given Revelation 6, regarding the opening of the second seal and the rider on the red horse who would take peace from the earth, killing one another with the sword. She saw many people with raised hands, celebrating and chanting to Obama. In 2014, she received a message from Jesus that said, "Death to finance, recession within a recession," and she sees a black horse. April 2015, Mena has a visit from an angel who tells her the countdown has begun and to get supplies (Interview with Rick Wiles, *Tru News*).

In 2008, Rick Wiles of *Tru News* said his daughter Carissa had a vision of a crowd standing with hands raised and she was lifted up over a city and saw zombies across the United States chanting, others around the world, chanting to Obama. In 2014, Carissa was working with orphans in Ecuador. There was a four-year-old girl named Maria who could not speak. Carissa had taught her sign language. Jesus told Carissa to lay hands on Maria for speech; the girl was healed and could speak. She told Carissa, "Maria see Jesus, Jesus come down with fire everything burned up." Maria said Jesus told her to say he comes down with fire. It is difficult to measure spiritual judgment in physical outcomes. However, it was reported by NOAA in 2015, 3,190,000 acres of land burned across Canada, and six hundred fires burned though Alaska, and United States has experienced numerous wildfires.

Obama inscribed on a steel beam at the **9-11** ground zero site. It read: "We remember. We will rebuild. We will come back strong." The *we, we, we* is mankind's rebellion toward God, and God's response to evil is delivered in Revelation 8:13, ending with *woe, woe, woe*—a warning to the inhabitants of the earth. Revelation **9:11**, "*And they had a king* *over them which is the angel of the bottomless pit, whose name in the Hebrew tongue is Abaddon, in Greek Apollyon*"—a clear reference to Satan's dominion over nations and the humans to whom he gives his authority.

The new tower constructed on the 9-11 site was dedicated June 2015. It was important for the architect to add a spiral on the top of the tower, and the spiral mimics a minaret as found in Islam. It was lit up with colors of the rainbow—another sign of mankind's rebellion and abomination. Lightning hit the tower three times.

We are living in the end-times, and the writings in Revelation will be manifested upon the earth. Many will be given visions and have dreams referencing signs and symbols. The prophet Muhammad had a dream about a journey to heaven on a white horse called Barrack. In Arabic, *Barrack* means "lightning from heaven." Revelation 9:1, "*And the fifth angel sounded and I saw a star* [like lightning] *fall from heaven unto the earth and to him was given the key to the bottomless pit.*" This is not a good omen. Jesus said, "I beheld Satan, like lightning fall from heavenly heights." (Luke 10:18, originally written in Greek, but Jesus would have spoken in Aramaic/Hebrew.) Strong's *Hebrew Dictionary* word 1,299 for *lightning* or *cast forth* is *Baraq*. *Strong's Dictionary* word 1,300, *lightning/gleam/flashing sword/bright* is *Baw Rawk*. Isaiah 14:12–19, "I will ascend above the height of the clouds"—as in Satan had fallen from the heights of heaven is Strong's Hebrew word 1116 is *Bam-Maw*. Maw is transliterated *U* or *O* and used as a conjunction ... *Baraq O Bam-Maw* or *Baraq U Bam-Maw* when translated as "lightning from the heights." In Hebrew, Jesus would have said, "I saw Satan as *Baraq O Bam-Maw*" (fall from the heaven). President Obama is not Satan, but the symbolism of his name is a sign or message for these end-times.

Revelation 6:2 refers to the four horsemen of the apocalypse. The first was a white horse whose rider is sent to conquer the nations, and it does represent the Antichrist. Obama gave a speech at the Denver Bronco Stadium, and behind the podium, up high was the statue of a white horse. The Denver Airport displays occult images and strange apocalyptic murals. The Masons dedicated a stone monument dated March 19, 1994, to confirm the location sealed for Satan.

An Obama look-alike character in the mini TV series *The Bible* was portrayed as the devil.

Obama was driven in an armored car called the "beast," which could withstand a terrorist bomb attack. Secret Service code name for him is "renegade," meaning "rebel" or "lawless one."

God is sending warning shots over the bow, but the people of earth are ignoring the warnings. November 17, 2013, eleven tornadoes hit Illinois. The hardest hit community was Washington, with winds up to 190 MPH. Many unusual weather occurrences, economic downturn, increase in terrorist and criminal acts, strange signs in the sky, are a few of the woe, woe, woes God is giving to get mankind's attention.

Flies are an omen of the presence of evil. According to 2 Kings 1:2–3, it is a literal translation of Beelzebub. The plague of flies in Egypt was an omen. January 2013, the Druge Report and several others reported, on four separate instances, flies landed on Obama, and he did not flinch or brush them away.

The theme of Obama's campaign was hope and change. Hitler's campaign theme was similar, promising change, economic recovery, and jobs but resulting in ethnic cleansing.

Obama campaigned on a platform to bring healing to the disenfranchised. People were reeling from the real estate collapse and banks and big corporation bailouts orchestrated by the architechs of the new world order. Obama was their man. He was able to capitalize on the uncertainty of the future. He blamed Bush for everything. Most people could not realize the Republicans and the Democrats are two sides of the same coin.

Obama commissioned the construction of a Greek-columned stage on which he made his acceptance speech for his party's nomination. Ancient Greek temples were built to honor Zeus and were thought to house the spirit of the deity. Obama may have gotten this idea from his recent visit to Germany. The Republicans ridiculed Obama, saying he was playing Zeus of Mount Olympus and the Democrats were kneeling before the temple of Obama. The *New York Post* ran an article on the Democratic convention: "Oh My God: Dems Erect Obama Temple." Others also saw it as a replica of the Altar of Pergamum. Like Hitler, Obama gave honor to Satan in Germany then set up the throne of Satan wherein he accepted his date with destiny.

At the inauguration ceremony, Pastor Rick Warren and member of the Council on Foreign Relations did the invocation. What spirit did he invoke? He has since embraced Islam and promotes a religious following called Chrislam. He also is anti-Israel. Warren was followed by an Episcopal bishop. Gene Robinson, a strong advocate for homosexuality, gave a special prayer. Obama stated, "Praise to the works of our hands, and heaven yield to us." On this platform, there was an absence of true godly people. The inauguration cost $138 million, which was financed by Wall Street—who received bailout money starting in 2007 through 2010.

Obama had to repeat his swearing in ceremony on the Bible. The word *faithfully* was garbled, and his name was given incorrectly by Chief Justice John Roberts. They did a redo the following day in the Map Room of the White House. This time he swore in on the Constitution. This was a signal to the elite. The Masons honored Obama with their first-ever inaugural ball in Washington, DC. The Masons, as it is with other secret societies, esteem rituals, gestures, use of old books, the Bible, and oaths taken by heads of state to be of mystical importance.

Revelation 13 foretells of the rise of the Antichrist. The unknown Obama was heard during his 2004 speech at the Democratic National Convention. The spirit of Antichrist traveled the airwaves, and we were drawn to listen to him. Obama is different from any other US president, and from this platform he will rise to power, and his power will not come from himself but he will receive power from Satan.

Antichrist will speak like a lion. Obama's astrological sign is Leo.

Nobel Peace Prize

Nine months after his presidential term began, Obama received the Nobel Peace Prize, December 10, 2009, in Oslo, Norway. This was a surprise to many. The Nobel committee consisted of representatives of the Norwegian Labor Party, Socialist Left Party, Conservative Party, Right Wing Progress Party. The chairman was Mr. Jagland of the Norwegian Labor Party and Secretary General of the Council of Europe. Mr. Jagland explained that the prize was given for what Obama has done in the past nine months, they liked the speech he gave in Cairo, Egypt, his commitment to nuclear proliferation, promotion of the climate change agenda, and they liked him using the United Nations to pursue foreign policy goals. "No one can deny that the international climate has improved because of Obama, and we want to embrace the message he stands for." Former President Jimmy Carter and Vice President Al Gore received Nobel Prizes. Obama's grandfather Stanley Dunham is related to Jimmy Carter. When we look at this scenario, we believe Obama was rewarded by the global elite. The Nobel committee was composed of socialists. Both Carter and Gore endorse the climate change agenda, as well as worked to remove national sovereignty of nations. Obama is recognized globally as a man of peace. In Daniel 11:24, we are told that the Antichrist will come peacefully into the wealthiest of places, and he will do more than his fathers have done before him.

The Messiah Complex

> *The king will do according to his own will, he will exalt and magnify himself above every god.* (Daniel 11:36)

Another sign we should observe is Obama morphing into a godlike figure. The Antichrist will demand people exalt him as god. It is ironic that during Obama's first term, people around the world were associating him with a messianic figure.

In 2012, an artist by the name of D'Antuono painted Obama poised as crucified Jesus with crown of thorns and arms raised—titled *Truth*—currently displayed at Bunker Hill Community College, Boston.

At the 2012 Democratic National Convention, all the world could see and hear the rejection of God by overwhelming loud nos to allow the name of God be spoken at the convention. They also booed, acknowledging Jerusalem as the capital of Israel. Posters for sale at the convention proudly proclaimed that the Obama presidency was "prophecy fulfilled." After much debate and loud decries against the mention of God or Israel, they decided to allow it. This historical stand against God is on news videos. Harry Reid and Nancy Pelosi are known for their vitriol toward conservatives. Democratic Party Communications Director Allan Brauer told an aide to Senator Ted Cruz, he hoped her children "die from debilitating, painful, and incurable diseases."

Obama sets off on his second term godless and anti-Israel. As in 2011 and again in 2012, Obama left God out of his Thanksgiving prayer.

Actor Jamie Foxx at the Soul Train Awards said, "Giving honor to our lord, god, and savior, Barack Obama."

An Italian artist sculpted figures of Barack and Michelle to be used in a Nativity scene.

The cover of *Newsweek*, January 2013, portrays Barack Obama as *The Second Coming*, which gives him a messianic nod.

Many people around the world see Obama as a messianic figure. Some people have had visions and dreams about this president. In 1971, a man by the name of C. Allen Martin had a dream of twelve houses. Each represented a president beginning with Harry Truman as number 1 through to Clinton, number 10; George Bush, number 11; and Barack Obama, number 12. When Clinton became president, he saw darkness descending upon America. In his vision, he saw president number 12 in position during the blood moon events. Martin said, "This man claims to be god but is the devil." Mr. Martin is deceased and could not know Obama would become president (Rick Wiles, *TruNews*).

At a children's performance, they called Obama Alpha and Omega. No other US president has been likened to a messiah.

One research source in an article by Dan Goodwin, "Palm Sunday, a Prophetic Past-Present-Future" featured in *Prophecy in the News*, April 2015—Goodwin compared the triumphal entry of Jesus Christ, riding on a donkey into Jerusalem, with Obama's messianic image. Daniel 9:25–26 refers to the revelation of the seventy weeks. It predicts that at the sixty-ninth week, 483 years from the decree of King Cyrus to rebuild Jerusalem, Messiah will be cut off and crucified. Beginning on the tenth of Nisan, Palm Sunday—and near the end of his 1,260-day, or three-and-a-half-year, ministry—Jesus rode from the Mount of Olives (the place he will return at his Second Coming) to the Kidron Valley. The multitudes greeted him as their Messiah. Four days later, they would demand his death. Passover is a four-day period from the tenth of Nisan to the fourteenth of Nisan. Moses was commanded to choose a lamb and sacrifice it four days later on Passover.

In our current time period, we may have come to the beginning of the seventieth week. This final week of Daniel's prophecy is associated with the seven-year tribulation. The Antichrist and the false prophet must be on the scene. The year 2012 signaled the changing of the guard. It points to the arrival of a false messiah who must counterfeit the events of the true Messiah. Jesus gave us a clue in John 5:43, "I am come in my Father's name and you did not receive me, if another come in his own name you will receive him." Goodwin correlates Obama's activities beginning on February 2013, when he would be making a trip to Israel. The president arrived in Israel on Thursday, March 21, which is the ninth of Nisan. Friday, March 22, which is the tenth of Nisan, Obama visited the Church of the Nativity in Bethlehem. The president arrived in Israel with the support of the Democratic Party, which has a donkey as its symbol. Jesus was praised when he presented himself to Israel, and Obama received honor and praise upon his arrival. There was an ice sculpture image of him. Jesus entered Jerusalem as the Prince of Peace, and Obama entered as a bearer of false peace, calling the relationship between the United States and Israel an "unshakable alliance." This proclamation is in opposition to God's declaration that he will shake all nations, all in heaven and earth and sea (Haggai 2:6–7).

The Movie *2016: Obama's America*

Chip Wood, *Personal Liberty Digest*, interviewed Dinesh D'Souza for his movie, *2016: Obama's America*, opened in mid-July 2012 in Houston. By August, it was playing on 1,200 screens across the country and then in over two thousand theaters in all fifty states. The movie is based on the book *The Roots of Obama's Rage*, written by D'Souza, who was narrator and codirector of the film. In the interview, D'Souza said that both Liberals and Conservatives make a big mistake when they think Barack Obama has failed to achieve his goals. High unemployment, crippling debt, a weak foreign policy and fading military power are not accidents. According to D'Souza, they are actually the results of the bigger objectives that Obama seeks, specifically the decline of American prosperity and power in the world. Some politicians, regardless of their political affiliation and who are aligned with the one-world order agenda, are amenable with the direction Obama is taking the country.

Obama has to camouflage what he wants to do now that he's in campaign mode by presenting himself as a budget cutter, a friend of Israel, and so on. The globalists depend on the ignorance of the American people not to see through what he says as well as those politicians who are in denial that there is a one-world order agenda. D'Souza said, "All that will change if Obama gets reelected. In the second term, the real Obama will emerge. It will not be a pretty sight.

Chip Wood asked D'Souza to explain a warning he included near the end of his new book, *Obama's America: Unmaking the American Dream*: "The most dangerous man in America currently lives in the White House." D'Souza said, "Obama is dangerous because he subscribes to an ideology that wants to knock this country off its pedestal so we are no longer number one. He wants to transfer wealth away from America to the rest of the world, and he wants to weaken our position in the world."

D'Souza believes Obama's liberal supporters would be shocked if they understood what is really driving our president. At the core of his worldview is a virulent anticolonialism with the United States as the chief culprit. America has more because America has stolen this wealth from others, and Obama believes, "America must now pay it back." D'Souza explains what this means:

> Many of Obama's supporters rail against the top 1 percent, fancying themselves in the lowly 99 percent, and this may be true as far as they are concerned. But it is not true as far as Obama is concerned. When he talks about the 1 percent and the 99 percent, he is using a global basis of comparison. So by Obama's measure, the vast majority of Americans are counted as rich. Obama wants to take their wealth from them and give it to those who he believes deserve it.

"He's doing this in the name of global justice," D'Souza said. Obama will not consider his job finished until the American standard of living is comparable to that of the rest of the world. In other words, Obama thinks of this country as a plunderer and of himself as the messianic leader whose job is to "restore fairness." Obama believes he is destined to be the architect of American decline. He not only wants to see this country lose is superpower status, but he wants to fundamentally transform America so that the shining city on the hill becomes just another shantytown in the global village.

January 2014, Obama administration retaliated against D'Souza with trumped-up charges he received campaign contribution money.

Chip Wood of *Personal Liberty Digest* makes a comparison: "While they are polar opposites politically, D'Souza and Obama share many things in common. A native of Mumbai, India, Dinesh grew up in a different part of the world, just as Obama did. They both were born in the same year, attended Ivy League colleges, graduated in the same year, and married in the same year." D'Souza explains, "Here is the paradox: I am a third world guy who has embraced America, and Obama is an American who has embraced a third world ideology."

Ultimately, D'Souza believes, *2016: Obama's America* isn't just about Obama.

> It's about the American dream itself, the truth is that Obama has a different dream from most of us. It's emblazoned across his book, as he says in the title, it's the dream from his father. He's entitled to have such a dream, if he wishes, but he is not entitled to impose that dream on the American people without their knowledge and consent.

President of the World

The majority of the above data can be verified on government database and alternative news sites. A prudent person will observe the actions of a person and not be taken in by rhetoric. Obama hit the ground running and is steadfastly moving us toward the fulfillment of a global agenda. As a proponent for the one-world order, he must create conditions that confiscate personal wealth and redistribute it into the coffers of the wealthy, greedy, corrupt entities who are the global elite. Therein the middle class became a target. He would make it a priority to attack Judeo and Christian traditional values. Individual freedoms and rights will be hindered. The right to defend oneself will be hindered because the government will bear all the arms and defend the people who cooperate. The right to grow your own food will be punishable by fines and imprisonment. If you don't cooperate, you will be ostracized. The practice of abortion will be promoted to stymie population growth as well as provide embryos for research. Next he would need to disrupt capitalism through economic decline, indebtedness, high unemployment, increase tax on imports, and excessive regulations on business. Obamacare is a burden, money pit, and a means to identify people. A section of the thirty-five-thousand-page law has a provision under the Medical Devices for a national RFID chip by 2017. A welfare mind-set is encouraged and increases number of Americans subsisting on government entitlements. A welfare state allows millions of illegal immigrants into the country, which overwhelm State systems and use illegals to increase the Democratic voter base. Take away State control, and put into place as many federal programs as possible. Take control of the schools, introducing ungodly doctrine and indoctrination through the Common Core Curriculum. Bigger government is supported by Obama. He has hired approximately ninety-five government employees per day for the past four years. Some appointments by Obama are as strange as himself. He hired Jeffrey Immelt, former CEO of General Electric; he served as chair on Jobs and Competitiveness. He said, "China's state-run communism is what got things going. This is a good relationship for the United States to develop a greater consumer-based economy" (*CBS News*, December 10, 2012).

Overwhelm the country with massive spending and debt. Spend billions to protect the planet from global warming while contributing to its destruction through pollution. Keep the United States engaged in world conflicts that result in spending and death. Give more aid to terrorists and radical nations, such as Hamas in Gaza, Syrian protesters, Hezbolla in Lebanon, and Iran to persuade them to cooperate with a nuclear treaty. Control the media to promote himself as an agent of change. Condition the minds of the liberals, and they are willing to accept his lies and agenda. Position himself as a moderate. Hide true intentions by lying and misrepresentation. Demonize his opponents, label them evil, greedy, extreme, radical, terrorist, racist. All that Obama has accomplished in America and his international influence has been observed by the one-world order elite. Is he going to be promoted to president of the world?

Revelation 17:12, ten kings will receive power from the beast in one hour (the ten-region confederation). A day after the inauguration, first day in office, Obama made or received calls from ten heads of nations, including Iran. During his tenure as the US president, he is one of the ten rulers, representing the North American region, which includes Canada and Mexico.

One of the rulers of the ten-region confederation will arise to oversee all ten rulers.

The title President of the World has been bandied around by media and notable people. On several occasions, Obama hinted that after his presidency comes to term, he has other work to accomplish. In keeping with his self-exaltation, he would seek a position with greater power and authority than serving as president of one nation.

Obama addressed the United Nations Security Council.

> *His power will be mighty but not by his own power and he will destroy wonderfully, shall prosper and practice and will destroy the mighty and the holy people. And through his policy also he will cause craft* [deceit] *to prosper in his hand. He will magnify himself in his heart and by peace will destroy many.* (Daniel 8:24)

Placing himself on the United Nations pedestal partially fulfills his goal of power and authority. Receiving the Nobel Peace prize ordains him with the rider on the white horse carrying a bow, wearing a crown, and one who comes peacefully (Daniel 11:24) and will destroy greatly. (Daniel 8:24) The Antichrist will cause great devastation.

Obama's intellectual and oratory assets have been utilized in foreign affairs. His interference in other countries may seem benign as pushing for Democratic rule but covers more sinister actions. Under this president, the Middle East and other nations are in chaos. His administration was covertly responsible for the Arab Spring uprisings, which spread throughout the Middle East. Prior to Obama's presidency, those who served before him authorized the CIA in the disruption of governments worldwide, and herein Obama follows suit.

Obama's administration would not allow the Fort Hood shooting to be labeled a terrorist attack but classified it as workplace violence. The shooter was an Islamic terrorist. Soldiers killed or wounded in that tragedy are not eligible to receive military compensation under workplace violence. Obama vetoed a bill that would award the Purple Heart to those who died at Fort Hood because he deemed it not to be death in combat. How many times has he said he cares about our veterans while the Veteran Administration is derelict in their responsibility of our military veterans?

Foreign Affairs

Egypt

Obama's first presidential speech was made in Cairo, Egypt, declaring a new era between the United States and Muslims. In his proclamation, he apologized for the United States as colonialists who saved Europe from the Nazis and rebuilt the continent through the Marshall Plan. He failed to mention Islamists partnered with Hitler against the Jews. He did not mention the death of millions at the hands of Hitler. He was forthright about his Muslim heritage, lauding the Koran and speaking Arabic. Obama said America is no longer a Christian nation. Is that a cloaked statement saying the United States is now open to Islam?

Having formed an allegiance with the Muslim Brotherhood, Obama set his plan in motion to overthrow the sitting president, Hosni Mubarak, and replace him with Mohammed Morsi. This move would undercut Israeli security, who had a long-term peace agreement with Mubarak.

After Mohammed Morsi became president, he initiated Sharia law and began ethnic cleansing of Christians. Christian persecution increased, including crucifixions, churches burned, Coptic women raped, opposition arrested. There was no outrage expressed by Obama for the atrocities committed by the Muslim Brotherhood.

September 2013, online report said that Obama has been funding Muslim Brotherhood as in bribes. The military has arrested Morsi and other Muslim Brotherhood members on corruption and bribery charges. A document was found as proof of transactions to Muslim Brotherhood up to $850,000 to carry out assassinations, prison escapes, killing demonstrators, spying. The document written in Arabic was translated by Walid Shoebot and published online. Money was channeled through US Embassy in Cairo to Morsi, who distributed payments. This document was printed in Egyptian Almesryoon news. Egypt's attorney general, Hisham Barakat, received complaints about bribes, and the document will be evidence.

Gary Kah, *Hope for the World*, summer 2015, said, "Obama's actions have worked to destabilize conditions across the globe … His speech, 2009, was taken by radical Muslims as a signal to begin revolution. The movement would become known as the Arab Spring. Mideast nations are in far worse shape than before, and the most radical elements of Islam are gaining ground by the day. Mainstream media portrays the Arab Spring as moving nations toward democracy."

Egyptians realized the Arab Spring was not a profreedom movement but an action to destabilize the nation.

Muslim Brotherhood, Deemed Terrorist Organization in Egypt

CNN, Wolf Blitzer, interviewed Egyptian President Mohamed Morsi, who called for the release of the blind sheikh convicted for the 1993 World Trade Center bombing. Morsi is a member of Muslim Brotherhood; and his wife, Najla Ali Mahmoud, is a member of the Sisterhood—who has a relationship with Saleha Abedin, mother of Huma Abedin, Hillary Clinton's deputy chief of staff. The Egyptian connection is tied into the Libya, Benghazi, scandal which is complicit with the uprising in Syria.

Egyptian magazine *Rose El Youssef* published an article, December 22, 2012, that said at least six American Islamic activists were working in the Obama administration. Muslim Brotherhood members are influencing US policy in support of Islam in general. In Obama's pro-Islam position, he appointed Imam Mohamed Magid, president of the Islamic Society of North America in 2011, to be an adviser to the Department of Homeland Security, State Department, and FBI. Also, others, such as, Arif Alikhan, assistant secretary of Homeland Security Policy Development; Mohammed Elibiary, member of Homeland Security Advisory Council; Rashad Hussain, US special envoy to Organization of the Islamic Conference; Salam al Marayati, cofounder of Muslim Public Affairs Council; and Eboo Patel were appointed members of Obama's advisory council on faith-based neighborhood partnerships.

January 24, 2013, Obama administration sent F16 fighter jets and tanks to Egypt. The action was opposed by Congress. Egypt does not have the best relations with Israel, so this was an unwise decision. The Obama administration knows this region is a powder keg. Past US indiscretions have armed both sides of a conflict.

Hamas, Terrorist Organization Based in Gaza

Barack Obama's first term in office, he gave $20.3 million to Muslim Brotherhood affiliates, terrorist group Hamas in Gaza. He obviously knew that the real estate market had crashed, and the ripple effect was foreclosure on millions of homeowners. He knew that big banks and big corporations were lining up for billions in bailout money. He knew that Hamas was consistently launching missiles at Israel and building tunnels to sneak into Israel and kill its citizens. These considerations did not deter him from supporting another terrorist organization.

In support of terrorist group al-Qaeda, June 2014, Obama releases five al-Qaeda leaders from Gitmo in exchange for one US deserter, Bergdahl. At same time, a Marine was still held in a Mexico prison.

Saudi Arabia

President Obama's first meeting with the King of Saudi Arabia began with a bow, prostrating himself before Saudi royalty. He desired to strengthen his relationship with this nation through the oil trade. This nation is hostile toward Christians and women. His Kenyan relatives have a relationship with Saudi Arabia to send boys to their education centers for training in Koran and Sharia law. Between 2015–2016, Obama blocked actions for the victims of 9-11 to sue Saudi Arabia for their involvement in the destruction of the towers. Both the Senate and Congress passed a bill that allowed victims to sue, and Obama vetoed the bill, but both houses overruled Obama.

Thailand

Obama visited Thailand upon hearing that the Asian nations are forming a coalition that excludes United States.

South America

His administration gave millions to Brazil and other South American counties to drill for oil, which they will sell back to the United States at high prices. In the United States, he stopped the Keystone Pipeline and has limited drilling for oil on federally owned lands. He has given billions to companies to produce alternative energy sources, but most of these companies did nothing but file for bankruptcy. Obama does not want the United States to be energy independent.

Libya

Per Iain Begg, professor at London School of Economics, said, "In Libya, it was you push out Moammar Gaddafi, then what?"

Gary Kah, *Hope for the World*, summer 2015, said, "Obama supported the overthrow of Gaddafi, and the nation has spiraled downward … It is a terrorist state and emerging stronghold for ISIS."

In regard to Obama's policies, Valerie Jarrett, senior adviser to the president, said, "There will be payback, if you are not with us, then you are against us, loyalists will be rewarded and the others will get what they deserve. There is going to be hell to pay. Congress won't be a problem for us this time. We have no election to worry about. We have two judges ready to go."

As Valerie Jarrett boasts that the just will get what they deserve, a brewing incident would be a setback for the Obama administration: Benghazi. Some facts that came forth, according to Retired Admiral James Lyons, state, "Obama intentionally conspired with Islamic radicals to stage a bogus attack and the kidnapping of American ambassador Stevens so he could negotiate the release of the blind sheik and bolster his mediocre approval ratings just prior to the 2012 election. The attack on the American Consulate in Benghazi was the result of a bungled abduction attempt, the first stage of an international prisoner exchange that would have ensured the release of Omar Abdel Rahman, the blind sheik."

Hillary Clinton, secretary of state, cut security personnel at the consulate. Navy SEAL's Woods and Doherty disobeyed orders to stand down and were able to save around thirty people, killed some of the attackers, and before saving Ambassador Stevens, were killed themselves. First thing out of Clinton's mouth was, "This uprising was because of a video disrespecting the prophet Muhammad."

John Brennan is Obama's choice for CIA director to replace David Petraeus. Brennan is tied to the Benghazi 9-11 attacks. Anyone with an ounce of common sense can see that Petraeus was set up to be removed as CIA director. The FBI had begun investigation of Petraeus's affair with Broadwell. FBI wanted to close investigation after it was determined there was no illegal activity by Petraeus, showing his confidential schedule. The FBI reported to the Department of Justice, headed by Attorney General Eric Holder, and he knew of the investigation of the CIA director and approved of pushing it forward, probably because Obama wanted him out so he could bring in his man, Brennan. These are old tactics, to get dirt on a person then ask for their resignation.

Benghazi was attacked in retaliation by Islamic militants, Ansar al-Sharia, who had been targeted by covert US special ops to destroy a cache of weapons acquired after the fall of Gaddafi. The report says that John Brennan had been authorizing unilateral operations in North Africa outside of the traditional command structure from the White House. If this report is accurate, then this would mean Obama could be directly accountable for the attacks in Benghazi. Petraeus was furious when he found out he was kept in the dark about the raids being conducted without his knowledge by the Pentagon's Joint Special Operations Command, JSOC. He then realized that he would remain marginalized as long as he was at the CIA and eventually deposed. In all this mess, the United States tried to blame the attack on a video.

We ask: Why was the US involved in the takeover of Libya in the first place? These are the same Islamic terrorists that fought Americans in Iraq. Kaddafi was worth over $200 billion dollars. The Libyan dinaro was backed by gold, unlike the worthless US dollars.

Libya had decided not to use the US currency as a credit. The consulate was not an official classification, and it has been rumored that Ambassador Stevens was recruiting and arming jihadists, involved in gun smuggling into Syria to wage war on the Syrian regime after what Obama called "the success in Libya." Stevens became an expendable liability.

Syria

Obama targets the destabilization of Syria by using the excuse of chemicals released on the people, killing 1,400—of which four hundred may have been children. He called this a "moral obscenity." We consider moral obscenity the killing of sixty million babies in the United States alone. Obama and the elites to whom he answers decided Syrian President Assad must be deposed. Civil unrest was being instigated, and mob violence increased. The military or police threw tear gas and smoke bombs into the crowd to disperse them, just as is practiced in America against unruly crowds.

This brings to mind the position of hypocrisy on Obama's part. Dr. Robert Jeffress, pastor of Pathway to Victory, pointed out on the Mike Huckabee show, September 30, 2013:

> The attempt by President Obama and progressives like Nancy Pelosi to stir up our outrage against Syrian president Assad for gassing several hundred Syrian children would be more effective if the president and his supporters demonstrated the same compassion for the lives of more than a million children in our country whose lives were ended through abortion in 2012. Why is genocide in Syria intolerable while infanticide in our country is not only permissible but considered a constitutional right? By what moral authority do we deny the leader of another nation his freedom of choice to exterminate his own people yet empower our own citizenry to kill their children and even provide millions of tax dollars to abortion industry to carry out the executions?

Life Site News quoted Nancy Pelosi on abortion: "I support Planned Parenthood because I love babies." Need we say more?

Americans voiced their concern that United States should not bomb Syria. Iran and Russia threatened intervention if the United States bombed Syria. Obama backed off but was determined to have his way regardless of the voice of the people. He continued his assault on Assad by arming Syrian rebels in violation of the US prohibitions in section 40 and 40A of the Arms Export Control Act on September 16, 2013. Herein, the provisions make it illegal for our government to send weapons to nations described in another section of the act. Obama is determined to fund al-Qaeda, Hamas Muslim Brotherhood, and others. By 2014, crucifying

Christians in Syria had begun. Shortly thereafter, ISIS began broadcasting the beheading of Christians in Syria and Iraq. October 2015, Russia intervened in behalf of President Assad and set up a military base in Syria to be more affective in bombing ISIS strongholds. China is sending warships to the region. April 6,2017, President Trump authorized the bombing of Syrian military bases as a response to chemical used against civilians.

Iran

Developing news tells us there is more to the Iran deal than the public is aware. Argentina President Christina Fernandez de Kirchner, in her speech at the United Nations, said the United States asked her nation to send enriched uranium for Iran back in 2010. Gary Samore, White House adviser on nuclear issues, met with heads of Argentina, and they declined. The deal was that Iran would ship their low-enriched uranium at 5 percent to Russia, who would enrich it to 19 percent, then ship it to France for further enrichment, then ship it back to Iran for its Tehran research reactor. Iran did not agree to the deal in 2010, and Obama put sanctions on Iran.

December 2013, Obama brokers deal with Iran to give them billions and ease up on sanctions as well as release one prisoner back to them in exchange for a verbal promise to cut back on enriching uranium. Obama as a good faith gesture released an Iranian prisoner. Obama refused to speak to Iran on behalf of imprisoned Pastor Sayeed and other imprisoned Americans.

In 2015, Obama and a few other nations came to an agreement with Iran to allow them to continue enriching uranium and building a nuclear device. Iran will receive $180 billion dollars, and sanctions will be lifted as well as some side deals, such as twenty-four-day notice before international inspections. This deal puts Israel in a dire predicament as Iran continues to call for death to America and Israel. Since the signing of that agreement, Iran is already in violation by testing missiles. January 2016, the media disclosed that Obama had sent a billion in foreign currency to Iran for the release of American prisoners.

Israel

US government made a preference for forcing Israel into conceding to an insatiable anti-Semitic enemy. This agreement legitimizes Iran and its goal for nuclear capability, lessens sanctions, and US threatens to retaliate against Israel if they bomb Iran's nuclear sites. The United States leaked sensitive Israeli national security information four times. Obama administration calls for Israel restraint against hundreds of rockets coming in from Gaza, restraint from avenging the killing of Israel children, and restraint from protecting its citizens.

Obama puts pressure on Israel to release Islamic murderers. He is pressing for Israel to vacate the West Bank, which some believe is occupied territory. The United States threatened Israel to cease from building in their own territory. Obama approves of European Union's boycott of Israel's West Bank and East Jerusalem. God's response is wildfire outbreak on America's west bank, Yosemite Park, including fifty fires burning over acres in California and other western states, costing America $1 billion in loss. Currently, 2015 wildfires rage in California, and severe flooding in South Carolina, Utah, Texas, and the US government were hacked by China.

December 8, 2012, the Obama family made a lukewarm jester, sending Hanukkah greetings to Jews worldwide.

Obama visited Israel, March 20, 2013, which was Nisan 10, the day Jesus made his triumphal entry into Jerusalem. Many see this as Messianic Obama. Israel develops a logo of "unshakeable alliance," showing a combining of Israeli and American flag. Obama's unshakeable agenda is to divide Israel in exchange for peace and the backing of United States against Iranian aggression. He toured important sites in Israel. He forced Prime Minister Netanyahu to apologize to Turkey president in regard to the flotilla incident, and he pushed for peace talks between PLO and Israel. As of 2015, Israel knows Obama is not a true friend and that they must be aware of the wolf in sheep clothes.

Iraq

The invasion of Iraq by the United States has led to the instability of that nation. It cost the loss of life for Americans, Iraqis, Kurds. It cost US taxpayers billions. In the end, ISIS took over US equipment left behind, conquered Anbar, Tikrit, Ramadi, and other cities. The livelihoods of the citizens were destroyed, the wealth of the citizens was confiscated and thousands were killed. Under Saddam, the people had more freedom of religion. Hundreds of militant prisoners were released, including current leader of ISIS, Mohamed al Baghdadi.

Afghanistan

ISIS, the Taliban, and other fringe groups are fighting over regions. US presence is declining.

Turkey

Obama seeks favor with Turkey by forcing Israel to apologize to Turkish government for stopping a terrorist flotilla aimed at suppling Hamas. United States allied with Turkey against Syria.

Cuba

Obama and the pope began to repair relations with Cuba, and this is a good thing. In light of terrorist activities carried out by Islamic radicals, Cuba has been docile for years. Millions of Cubans live in the United States. With the lifting of sanctions, the Cuban citizens will be able to earn a living. The government has relaxed it position on Christianity, and the church is growing.

The above overview is a sampling of US intervention in the affairs of other nations. From this we can summarize that the United States has been instrumental in the death of millions worldwide. The United States put into motion the destabilization of nations, creating a mass exodus of people from war-torn countries. People have loss life, livelihood, wealth, housing, food, medical care, etc. Nations attempting to assist the refugees are now overwhelmed. The United States allowed ISIS to grow as well as its continued support of terrorist groups. The United States has done nothing to stop the brutality of Boko Haran in Africa. US meddling may ignite World War III and the use of nuclear weapons. There is no improvement in US relations with Middle East, Russia, China, North Korea, Africa. Afghanistan is sick of US presence in their nation, but the United States is giving them billions to interfere with their government and military operations. Bottom line, this is the one-world order playbook.

Domestic Concerns

There is a crisis brewing in America. Lawlessness is increasing across the nation, resulting in murder and criminal activities. It involves blacks, Hispanics, whites, and Muslims. It appears the Obama administration is instigating racial unrest by pitting white cops against black criminals. In regard to moral issues, we see more attacks against Christians, Jews, and more pandering to Muslims. Obama aligns himself with the abomination of sexual perverseness. He does embrace the whole spectrum of homosexuality. In regard to abortion, he is 100 percent for the killing and dismemberment of babies. Conservative voices speaking out against this immorality are demonized. He forced Obamacare down the throats of the citizens, and now there is an insurance crisis. Immigration is out of control. The government has no budget and is in trillions of debt; there is no accountability. Obama bypasses Congress and issues executive orders at will, regardless of what the people want. We are being ruled by a tyrant, and he is on target for creating domestic violence, taking away our freedoms, allowing for Islamic terrorists to set up camps in the United States, and diminishing our national sovereignty, moving us into the one-world order United Nations Agenda 21.

There was a high turnover in the Obama administration due to new appointments and resignations. Most of his appointments lean toward the liberal left:

- Zbiznew Brezinsky is a longtime adviser to Obama.
- Secretary of State Hillary Clinton resigned 2012.
- John Kerry was secretary of state after Clinton.
- Sara Horowitz, head of Freelancers Union and Insurance Company, a labor lawyer and community organizer, has been appointed to oversee Obamacare exchanges at a cost of $340 million. She is also former Soros-funded group leader.
- Eric Holder, attorney general, resigns.
- Loretta Lynch was approved April 2015 as attorney general.
- CIA director, General David Petraeus, was forced resignation.
- John Brennan, CIA director, was sworn in at the White House in the Roosevelt Room, March 8, 2013. He chose to reject his swearing in on the Bible, as Obama did, and placed his hand on the Constitution, an older version, which did not contain the Bill of Rights. Brennan served as chief of counterterrorism adviser to Obama. Brennan is rumored to have converted to Islam while stationed in Saudi Arabia in the 1990s. Brennan will be the highest-level Muslim to serve in the White House
- New CIA direction, Comely.
- Chuck Hagel, Defense secretary, pro-Iran, disarming US citizens, and Israel should not retaliate against terrorist attacks. December 2014, Hagel resigns.
- United Nations Ambassador Susan Rice will not be nominated as secretary of state.
- Defense Secretary Leon Panetta resigned.
- Treasury Secretary Timothy Geithner resigned.
- Attorney General Eric Holder will be moving on after several scandals.
- Commerce Secretary John Bryson resigned due to illness.
- Chief of Staff Rahm Emanuel resigned.
- Denis McDonough, chief of staff.
- EPA secretary resigned.
- Energy Secretary Steven Chu.
- Interior Secretary Ken Salazar.
- Securities and Exchange Commission Chair Mary Schapiro.
- Transportation Secretary Ray LaHood.
- Labor Secretary Hilda Solis resigned.
- IRS Director Lois Lerner resigned after scandal.
- Josh Earnest, Press secretary, replaces Carney, 2014.
- Press Secretary Jay Carney replaced Gibbs.
- Robert Gibbs resigned 2011.

US Military

Former Secretary of Defense Robert Gates in his book, *Duty: Memoirs of a Secretary at War*, provides additional insight into Obama's mind-set:

> His administration is more controlling and centralized in national security than other former administrations. Political considerations became a factor in virtually every major national security problem. The military was subjected to micromanagement and operational meddling as well as White House staff calling four-star commanders directly. The president was rarely emotionally involved in most military policy with the exception of Don't Ask Don't Tell policy concerning homosexuals in the military. For Obama, changing the law seemed to be the inevitable next step in the so-called civil rights movement. Obama was deeply suspicious of top general's recommendations and actions. It was not surprising that tensions grew between the president and his military commanders in Iraq and Afghanistan. Joe Biden was added to the 2008 ticket for his foreign policy experience to aid the freshman senator.

Immigration Reform

Obama administration rules to shut down TARS, Tethered Aerostat Radar System, which uses balloons at fifteen thousand feet to monitor low-flying planes and incoming missiles and see illegal activity at the border between United States and Mexico. This would take effect March 15, 2013, and the surveillance system would be taken offline. This action will create a breach in security. There would be less protection for custom and border agents. While the United States spend billions in surveillance, eavesdropping, drone aircraft, and buildup of military on United States, citizens but feel the need to disrupt good surveillance where needed.

Amnesty for millions of illegal aliens comes under Obama's The Dream Act. June 2014, thousands of Mexican and South American children were flooding into United States without their parents. Obama pledged four billion to provide aid to over sixty thousand. Obama mandated they be bused into cities. Local citizens protested, and Obama ordered riot police to come against protesters and to not stop the buses. In 2015, Obama wanted to open the borders to Syrian refugees, and ISIS will be in the mix.

Immigration reform and amnesty for illegal immigrants is another ploy by the government to document and track all people for the North American region.

Fast and Furious

We also are reminded of the devastation caused by the Fast and Furious scandal, whereby the government allowed thousands of weapons to be given to criminals in Mexico. It was after the killing of a border patrol agent that the public became aware of Fast and Furious. Sharyl Attkisson, *Personal Liberty Digest*, October 2011, exposed Eric Holder, attorney general, lying to Congress about this cover-up. Said he didn't know about it. Investigation revealed he was briefed about it June 5, 2010, by Michael Walther, director of National Drug Intelligence center. Valeria Jarrett, Obama's adviser was brought in to spin Holder's statements. Attkisson reported that ATF ran the secret ops under Director Kenneth Melson, who allowed guns provided by the US to move into Mexico and given to drug cartel and gangs so that the guns could be traced to the bad guys. Melson was later reassigned to forensics at the DOJ. The Feds lost track of hundreds of weapons. This kind of activity was repeated in suppling weapons to militants in Syria.

Judicial Watch, nonprofit judicial watchdog, received 1,300 pages of documents provided to the court from the Department of Justice.

Economy

Under the Obama administration, the nation's debt has doubled from nine trillion to nineteen trillion (undisclosed is approximately seventy trillion) high unemployment, more food stamps, and welfare recipients. God said, "Be the lenders and not the borrowers."

Between 2012 to 2015, the number of people on food stamp rose to around seventy million. Unemployment climbed nationwide to 8 percent. Obama bragged when it decreased from 8.1 to 7.8. By end of 2015, it was down to 5 percent. Government reported lower percentage but must factor in those who no longer qualify for benefits and remain unemployed. November 20, 2013, new data says administration ordered the census bureau to lower unemployment numbers in September before the 2012 election. Census employees were deliberately fabricating employment surveys. The Bureau of Labor statistics is corrupt.

How loyal will the reelected commander and chief be to those who voted for him again?

On mainstream TV, December 2012, a councilwoman in Detroit, Michigan, stated that 73 percent of the state voted for him and that they brought home the bacon. Detroit, in bankruptcy, needed Obama to bail them out because they were loyal.

Vacation and Travel

The presidents' vacations, travel, security, staffing, and anything else required for the royal family cost taxpayers around $1 billion per year. Vacations spent in Hawaii cost taxpayers $4 million per visit. The inequity here is, beginning 2013, Social Security recipients will receive a 1.7 percent cost of living increase. Veterans are still homeless, sick, and disenfranchised. Over sixty million people are on food stamps. We are thankful for a few crumbs from the master's table.

Veteran Administration is found guilty of causing vets to wait months for treatment, and many died before treatment. Financial and medical care for veterans is almost as bad as a third world nation. If you are the president, there is no wait time. Obama was hospitalized at Walter Reed Hospital December 7, 2014, received treatment for a sore throat due to acid reflux (NBC, CNN, Fox News).

September 1, 2015, Obama changes the name of Mount McKinley in Alaska to Mount Denali, which means "the high one," or "the great one." President McKinley was assassinated in September 1901. Some thinkers are wondering if there is a symbolic connection in this announcement in the month of September. Certainly, Obama thinks of himself as the great one.

Government Overreach

Bigger government is supported by Obama. He has hired approximately 95 government employees per day for the past four years. Some appointments by Obama are as strange as himself. He hired Jeffrey Immelt, former CEO of General Electric, to serve as chair on Jobs and Competitiveness. He reported, "China's state-run communism is what got things going. This is a good relationship for the United States to develop a greater consumer-based economy" (*CBS*, December 10, 2012).

Obama's ideology is socialism, which conflicts with capitalism, which provides opportunity for people to operate a business and to be independent. Social is the opposite of independent. His administration seems to be waring against livestock farmers, fishers, dairy farmers, homegrown crops through harassment, regulations, fines, taxes—example, BLM against farmers and their grazing rights; government-controlled education and curriculum; home schooling is discouraged; government Common Core Curriculum and preparing youth to be global citizens; government forcing mandatory vaccinations on children.

Gun Control

Obama (if I had a son, he would look like Trayvon Martin) and Justice Department Jesse Jackson, Al Sharpton, spoke out against killing of Trayvon Martin by Zimmerman. DOJ sent workers to Florida to rally protest. But there is no protest from the above on black-on-black crimes. In New York, it was reported a new game called the knockout game involved black youth who randomly target a person, walk up, and punch a person who is not black. Crime is on the rise, and a high percent is committed by black males.

Executive Orders Bypass Congress

President Obama is using his executive privilege to introduce new legislation. In many cases, this means that Obama bypasses the Congress and legislative procedures as mandated by the Constitution to carry out his agenda and those of the shadow government he answers to. Obama also uses executive memos to bring about his agenda. The executive orders are recorded in the Federal Register by Congress. Executive orders allow the president to declare a state of emergency and call for martial law. Through this action, individual rights and the voice of the people are given over to a dictatorship form of governing. George W. Bush passed sixty-two executive orders in eight years; Bill Clinton passed fifteen executive orders in eight years; and one signed May 5, 1994, was to move US troops under United Nations command. Then Clinton signed a new executive order transferring control of the country from FEMA to NSA. Bush Sr. passed three executive orders in four years; Ronald Reagan passed five executive orders in eight years. Carter passed three executive orders in four years; and one was to delegate to FEMA the power to run the entire country.

Following are some of the executive orders signed into law by Obama:

- Executive Order 10990 allows the government to take over all modes of transportation and control of highways and seaports.
- Executive Order 10995 allows the government to seize and control the communication media.
- Executive Order 10997 allows the government to take over all electrical power, gas, petroleum, fuels, and minerals.
- Executive Order 10998 allows the government to take over all food resources, farms, and farm equipment.
- Executive Order 11000 allows the government to mobilize civilians into work brigades under government supervision.
- Executive Order 11001 allows the government to take over all health, education, and welfare functions.
- Executive Order 11002 designates the registration of all persons through the Postmaster General.
- Executive Order 11003 allows the government to take over all airports and aircraft, including commercial aircraft.
- Executive Order 11004 allows the Housing and Finance Authority to relocate communities, build new housing with public funds, designate areas to be abandoned, and establish new locations for populations.
- Executive Order 11005 allows the government to take over railroads, inland waterways, and public storage facilities.

- Executive Order 11049 assigns emergency preparedness function to federal departments and agencies, consolidating twenty-one operative executive orders issued over a fifteen-year period.
- Executive Order 11051 specifies the responsibility of the Office of Emergency Planning and gives authorization to put all executive orders into effect in times of increased international tensions and economic or financial crisis.
- Executive Order 11310 grants authority to the Department of Justice to enforce the plans set out in executive orders, to institute industrial support, to establish judicial and legislative liaison, to control all aliens, to operate penal and correctional institutions, and to advise and assist the president.
- Executive Order 11921 allows the Federal Emergency Preparedness Agency to develop plans to establish control over the mechanisms of production and distribution of energy sources, wages, salaries, credit, and the flow of money in US financial institutions in any undefined national emergency. It also provides that when a state of emergency is declared by the president, Congress cannot review the action for six months.

National Defense Administration Act, NDAA—under this department, citizens can be detained indefinitely without due process. House Bill 6566, 2012, called Mass Fatality Planning and Religious Consideration Act amends Homeland Security Act, 2002. FEMA will provide guidance and coordination for mass fatality planning

We now live in a nanny state. You will be given a treat if you report suspicious activity. The National Association for the Advancement of Colored People asked the United Nations for watchers to be in place during the election to call out voter fraud improprieties. Over the past eight years, there have been numerous corruption and improprieties that surround the voting process, mostly with the Democratic organization attempting to pad voter results. Did the NAACP get a treat? Their reward is to be on the FBI watch list as a terrorist group.

Obama's homosexual agenda applies to institutions of learning. This presidential order makes it illegal to discuss LBGT orientation. In order to receive federal funding under Title IV, schools agree to hire gays and include sex orientation and gender identification in their nondiscrimination policies. Students can only use federal college grants at schools that hire gays. Schools must offer LBGT classes, and transsexuals can use the opposite-sex bathroom. Christian colleges who do not conform may lose their exempt status. Elections in some states had pushed back on the transsexual male to use female bathrooms or locker rooms. Obama, Clinton, Apple, and many other organizations pushed for it.

Obama's newest executive order seeks to "harmonize" US economic regulations with the rest of the world. He also has agreed with the United Nations to allow the United Nations to control the Internet. He is onboard with United Nations Agenda 21 mandates. We recall, Obama studied constitutional law, perhaps for the purpose of dismantling it.

Three were appointed to National Labor Board, 2013, without approval of Congress; while Congress was available to review the Obama's selections. Court rules against Obama as unconstitutional. Recently, June 2014, the Supreme Court ruled 9 to 0 that Obama cannot make appointments when Congress is in recess or not in recess. Overall, he does not have the right to misuse his presidential powers. There are times in the past when Obama thumbed his nose at the Supreme Court. On at least twelve occasions, the administration petitioned the Supreme Court to expand his executive powers, and in each instance, the court unanimously rejected the Obama administration's appeal.

Of late, we hear concerns regarding the violation of our Amendment rights.

First Amendment Rights

Congress will make no law respecting an establishment of religion or prohibiting the free exercise thereof or abridging the freedom of speech or of the press or the right of the people peaceably to assemble and to petition the government for a redress of grievances.

Second Amendment Rights

A well-regulated militia, being necessary to the security of a free State and the right of the people to keep and bear arms, will not be infringed.

Twenty-three (23) executive orders were signed January 2013 to ban assault weapons and require better background checks. During the presidential debates, Obama states he wants to ban weapons of war from the streets of America. After election, Obama calls the United Nations to restart negotiations over the Small Arms Treaty. This action does not seem to take into consideration that law-abiding citizens have the right to purchase arms. There is nothing wrong in wanting better background checks to prevent gun ownership by insane and criminal types. It is a low percentage that documents legal ownership of guns is used in crimes. Another oversight is that criminals have the ability to get guns, which are used in a high percentage of crimes. Somewhere along the line, we need to factor in that the United States is complicit in providing drug lords and terrorists with weapons.

Sandy Hook School shooting, Newtown, Connecticut—December, 2012—this crisis set the stage for gun control legislation. Obama appoints Vice President Biden to head up this reform. The state-sponsored media put forth White House talking points for gun control. Media attacks NRA, or other progun advocates. Senator Feinstein had already drafted gun control legislation a year ago, waiting for the Senate to reconvene.

Third Amendment Rights

No soldier will in time of peace be quartered in any house without the consent of the owner nor in time of war but in a manner to be prescribed by law.

Fourth Amendment Rights

The right of the people to be secure in their persons, houses, papers, and effects against unreasonable searches and seizures will not be violated, and no warrants will issue but upon probable cause supported by oath or affirmation and particularly describing the place to be searched and the persons or things to be seized.

Twenty-Sixth Amendment Rights

There are twenty-six amendments, and for brevity, we will site number 26. The right of citizens of the United States who are eighteen years of age or older to vote will not be denied by the United States or by any State on account of age. The Congress will have power to enforce this article by appropriate legislation.

The Affordable Care Act

Most Americans are asleep. They have been lulled into complacency through propaganda that America is doing great. Unaware of government overreach, people are being documented and tracked through the use of food stamps, welfare, Medicare, medical records, vaccinations, government-provided cell phones that can track and send messages to the holders, GPS systems, driver's license, voter registration, etc. Government-controlled heath care is also used to document and track people.

The unveiling of Obamacare will allow people to see the bondage this program will have on citizens and corporations. Federal government has determined that this program be implemented in all states and is mandatory, but this may not be the case. Many states are refusing to comply. There are more than thirty-five thousand pages of regulations and we thought this book was long. Government bureaucracy will spend $71 billion to mandate Obamacare. The oversight of the program will be handled by the strong arm of the IRS. At this time, it seems as though elected officials are not signing up for Obamacare.

The official launch of the Affordable Care Act on October 1, 2013, was met with across-the-board failures. Thousands of citizens were unable to register for insurance because the software did malfunction. The website crashed on the first day, with approximately six people enrolling. The database asked for all pertinent and private information before allowing people to compare plans and costs. The public was unaware that their private information could be compromised by hackers. Within the month of October, millions of people received notices from their insurance companies that they were being canceled. People were shocked to see how much more they would be paying in yearly premiums. Monthly premiums would surge by 400–500 percent. For instance, a person paying $200 per month would now pay $1,500 per month as well as having to pay outrageous deductibles as high as $5,000.

One month later, November 1, 2013, the Affordable Care Act was still not functioning. The government is now spending millions to fix the site, which is said to have five million lines of code and some code was total jibber or nonsense.

The blowback of Obamacare is higher health care costs across the board, more layoffs, cut employees' hours, tax increases, more regulations, and loss of your doctor of choice and your insurance.

Forcing the American citizens to accept the government mandate is tyranny at its finest. If people refuse, the IRS will levy fines and punishment on individuals and businesses.

By the time people realize the impact of this program, it will be too late to protest. As in the plight of the Jews being herded onto trains, headed to the concentration camps, and then told they will be given a hot shower but instead they are put into the gas chamber—this national health care program is also deceptive. There is an underlying agenda coming to the forefront, which is not apparent to the masses (*Natural News*, November 19, 2013). "*Real purpose of Obamacare is to destroy private insurance,*" according to retired Air Force colonel Tom Snodgrass. "The health care mandate is to intentionally crash the private insurance market in order to replace it with a government-run single payer socialist system." As more details of the failed Obamacare come to light, it appears the administration knew the program was not ready for launch, experiencing technical difficulties with sign-up, the lack of security for private consumer information, and other problems would cause a fallout.

Obama told people that this program was to insure all the uninsured in America regardless of preexisting conditions. The spin continues; if they liked their existing plan and doctor, they could keep them. As millions were notified by insurance companies they were no longer covered, Obama blamed this on the insurance industry. Snodgrass reports, "The mechanism that is a key aspect of the chaotic rollout currently destroying private health care insurance is federal regulatory power that causes the discontinuation of existing private policies by imposing new, high-priced, frivolous requirements (e. g., maternity coverage for young men and old women) that were not in existing plans."

The government created hardship and limited the ability of people to shop for insurance, sign-up, and the loss of private insurance coverage was a blessing in that it caused lawmakers and sleeping Americans to take a look at the imposition of Obamacare and government incompetence.

The cost of Obamacare over a ten-year period will be around $2 trillion. Cost of the health care website, $1 billion. End of 2014 data report thirty-one million people are uninsured, and over 350 employers cut employees' hours because the cost to insure employees will be more expensive.

Some of the fallout is the closing of free clinics throughout the nation, therein depriving poor people medical care. This is a government effort to force the uninsured or underinsured to sign up for Obamacare.

In a report made on *Personal Liberty Digest*, Bob Livingston, November 19, 2012, said, "Obamacare, while being a hardship for average people, the program will benefit and support big pharma, medical programs, and insurance companies. It is a good way to get everyone in the country registered and monitored. Some people think this program is free, but it will cost both the person and the employer."

Pharmaceutical companies are like drug cartels, operating under the pretense of health care. The drugs they push have a deceptive layer of side effects and cause more health problems than help. It is like a revolving door. Medication for one problem leads to more health problems. Doctors write prescriptions based on glowing medical reviews and kickbacks. Sickness is profitable. Government discourages natural remedies, organic foods, organic raw milk, and vitamins. Government is harassing and fining farmers who want to grow organic natural food or provide milk free of additives. Government encourages an unhealthy lifestyle by pushing the drug culture, vaccinations, flu injections, and GMO food.

Bob Livingston, *Personal Liberty Digest*, January 28, 2013, continues his assessment on Obamacare:

"Obamacare is not socialized medicine but is sickness care. Some people believe it is health care, but actually it is to transfer wealth into big business." The cost of this program will bankrupt the treasury. It is to control and track the population as well as single out the elderly and disabled to death panel review boards. One of Obama's insiders, Steve Rattner, wrote an article for *New York Times*, wherein he stated, "We need death panels, well, maybe not death panels exactly, but unless we start allocating health care resources more prudently … rationing by its proper name … the exploding cost of Medicare will swamp the federal budget."

If we liken Obamacare to the Nazi regime, German citizens were shot for treason because they protested the dictator. The wealth of millions was taken by the dictator Hitler, oppression increased, freedom of speech limited, the right to bear arms and freedom of religion were taken away. The military industrial complex promoted war under the pretext of patriotism and superiority of Germany. The right of life, liberty, and the pursuit of happiness was not for the inferior but to be enjoyed by the elite and powerful.

Reminiscence of Nazi Germany, in America there are government directives attacking freedom of speech, freedom to bear arms, and freedom of traditional religious beliefs. The US government is oppressive, and under the cloak of benevolence called health care, people are forced to sign up. Reports of government aggression are surfacing, wherein families who refuse treatment may be taken against their will and forced to ingest any number of debilitating chemicals and drugs. There was a case where the hospital took the parents to court to obtain a court order to allow the hospital to administer chemotherapy against the wishes of the parents to their teenage daughter.

Perhaps less obvious than the NAZI method of genocide, the United States is slowly killing its citizens through the promotion of sickness, dependency on drugs, abortion, pushing for vaccinations of babies to the elderly, creating hardship for the disabled, rationing health care, and tampering with our food. The government is creating a culture of dependency on handouts welfare and food stamps and in many instances are used to buy street drugs.

Nazi Germany used propaganda to desensitize the genocide of millions. America also uses propaganda to fulfill their depopulation goals by dehumanizing sick, elderly, and unborn people. Under Obamacare, medical review boards determine who gets what medical services. The elderly, veterans, or terminally ill are a drain on resources. Medical review boards will argue the quality of life is diminished, and it is time to pull the plug. Euthanasia is called mercy killing. People have been desensitized to abortion by pushing the prochoice right; using the term *fetus* or *not a human until born* is acceptable reasons for abortion, followed by dismemberment and human parts sold to research labs.

In Britain, a forty-one-year-old man, Peter Thompson, was left dying on the corridor floor for ten hours while medical staff ignored him; when he died, his body was dragged away. This was caught on closed-circuit camera. In the United States, there are accounts of people waiting to be seen in the ER for ten hours. Ambulance transport can cost up to $1,000. The cost of prescription drugs has increased 500 percent.

An article on Kerby Anderson's *Point of View* by Lexi Cory, *Wake Up, Millennials, We're the Ones Paying the Bill*, shares problems with this health mandate. Before Obamacare, there was a rational relationship between individual premiums and expected health care costs. The young and healthy were charged less for insurance because they were less likely to consume large amounts of health care … Premiums were fair. Now insurers are required to practice a form of community rating (socialism), in which the healthy and sick are charged the same. The young pay more than they would normally pay in order to cover the cost of the elderly and sick. Premiums are triple the cost or more. People will opt out and perhaps pay the fine, which may be cheaper. Young people coming out of college are now faced with high student loans, poor job prospects, and Obamacare. President Obama on many occasions stated to the American public that they could keep their current health plan if they like it; you can keep your current doctor, and your premiums will be lower. He pushed for the state health care exchange. People who used the exchange are told they were not eligible and must repay the government.

Employers realizing that providing health coverage for their full-time employee would be financially staggering resulted in thousands of people rescheduled to part-time status. Employers said this program will cut into company profits up to 50 percent. Employers are to provide health care insurance for all full-time employees or pay a $2,000 fine per person. Hundreds of employers began layoff proceedings. Following are a few actual instances:

Hobby Lobby, a Christian-owned company, said they objected to providing abortion-day-after pills to their employees. The Supreme Court said they have to do so or be fined over $1 million per day. Later the employer received an appeal, but Obama administration continues to fight them to force them to distribute abortion pills.

David Bar has Taco Bell and Kentucky Fried Chicken franchise, employing 421 people, of which 109 are full-time. He already pays health insurance for thirty—which cost the company $129,000 per year—and the employee pays $995 per year. Under Obamacare, he would have to provide insurance for all 109 full-time employees, which would cost $444,000 per year; a $315,000 increase is more than half of his annual profit after expenses. If he chooses not to provide the insurance, the fine will cost him $89,000 per year.

Darden Foods owns Olive Gardens, Red Lobster, and Longhorn[they will be cutting hours and increasing the cost of the food. Health care will cost $5 million annually.

McDonalds said health care will cost $420 million more, and they will increase prices.

Denny's is adding a 5 percent surcharge and reducing employee's hours.

Walmart raised their health premiums by 36 percent, putting coverage out of reach of employees.

Boeing is laying off 30 percent of personnel.

US Cellular is laying off 980.

Vestas Wind Systems Turbines is laying off three thousand.

Bristol Meyers, New Jersey, is laying off 480.

Lockheed Martin is laying off 123,000.

The Obamacare payroll tax increase is $86.8 billion. The Medicare payroll tax rate on individuals earning $200,000 ($250,000 for couples) will see their payroll tax increase from 2.9 percent to 3.8 percent. This is a direct tax hike on small-business owners, who are liable for self-employment tax.

Medical Device Tax is a $20-billion tax increase. Obamacare imposes a new 2.3 percent excise tax on gross sales—whether the company makes a profit or not. This will increase the cost of medical devices, like pacemakers, prosthetics, and wheelchairs. Within this tax code terminology, there is a subtle clause for implantable devices for medical tracking by 2017.

The Obamacare "Special Needs Kids Tax" is a $13-billion tax increase. It hits thirty to thirty-five million Americans using a work-based Flexible Spending Account (FSA) to pay for basic medical needs by having money removed from their paychecks before taxes, which reduces their taxable income and helps them save on their tax bill. It faces a new cap of $2,500 (currently the accounts have no cap). There are seven million families in America with special needs children who need care that far exceeds the $2,500 cap, and many of them are the working lower-income class.

The Obamacare Surtax on Investment Income is a $123 billion tax increase. This is a new 3.8 percent surtax on investment income earned in households making $250,000 or more ($200,000 for single filer). This will increase the tax on capital gains from 15 percent to 23.8 percent. Capital gains include profits on the sale of a home. In other words, when you sell your house for more than you paid for it, which all homeowners hope to do, you will pay 23.8 percent on the value difference when you sell. It also includes gains made on savings and retirement accounts. The rate paid on dividend income increases from 15 percent to 43.3 percent, as does the rate on other investment income.

The Obamacare "Haircut" for Medical Itemized Deductions is a $15.2 billion tax increase. Currently, Americans facing high medical expenses are allowed a deduction if expenses exceed 7.5 percent of adjusted gross income. The "haircut" raises the threshold to 10 percent. This will mostly harm those near retirement age, modest incomes but high medical bills because of debilitating illnesses.

The bottom line for the average family, according to *Forbes*, is an additional annual cost of $2,000 for the average family, or a diversion of 2.5 percent of the average household's income in taxes alone. This does not factor in the loss of income due to hour reduction or job losses and the rising cost for food and products.

Year 2016, United Health and Aetna are opting out of Obamacare.

When Americans wake up, they will have given up their rights, and the government will have all their personal, financial, and health data. It is no longer a secret the globalists believe the earth is overpopulated and should be culled from seven billion to perhaps one billion people worldwide. When the global population has been tracked and identified, the next step will be to enforce the world to take the mark of the beast in order to buy or sell.

Can We Measure the Promised Change?

Obama came on the scene with a platform of "change." His public facade was caring, charismatic, inclusive, but behind the mask is evil. The real Obama is arrogant, proud, defiant, deceptive, and vindictive. During the past eight years, Obama took power through his executive orders, allowing him to bypass Congress. His rule of law embraces secularism, humanism, hedonism, and socialism. Of course, this ungodly culture has been brewing for hundreds of years, but Obama may be the most prolific president to openly sanction ungodliness and bring it to the forefront, or "in your face." Liberals seem to be less godly and more toward abortion, homosexuality, materialism, entertainment, and pleasure to the extent of, whatever feels good, go for it. Both Liberals and Conservatives support a one-world order.

In 2008, Obama entered into the arena of movers and shakers. What he thought he knew about the one-world order was JV. Throughout his presidency, he was introduced to the dark side of the US government and its world affiliations. As president, he was given a tour of the underworld of secret operations, advanced technology, and he came face-to-face with demons. Yep, all this talk about aliens is real. Once you see it all, you cannot retreat and remain alive. Obama accepted his destiny and sealed it with blood.

2016, the End of a Regime

As Obama term as president ends, we are curious as to his next move. Will he be the one to arise from out of the ten-region confederation and assume the role of president of the world? May 2015, at the Democratic National Convention, Obama made a comment that after 2016, his "project" will continue long after he leaves office, and while he is still in office he will continue to make his policy visions reality. "The project is something that we have to sustain over the long term. The values and ideals that I believe in are ones that I have never expected to realize in just one term or one presidency." Obama did consider being the next United Nations Secretary General. That would have been a crowning achievement. The Antichrist seated on a global throne. At the time of this report, another was selected to chair after Ban Ki Moons term ended. Israel prime minster Netanyahu stated "Eight years of Obama's judgement and marginalizing Israel was not enough, and now he wants to be in a position to cause more trouble on the international forum" After the Democrats lost the 2016 election, Obama stated "If I could run for a third term, I would have won." Obviously many voters felt two terms was enough. Obama has been considering his next move for some time. After the Trump victory. a split in the Democratic party became evident with the hacking of the DNC emails exposing insider corruption, Debbie Wasserman Shultz resigned, CNN's Donna Brazel was caught giving Hillary Clinton pre-debate questions, Democrats lost majority of state governor seats, they lost the House and Senate. After the election, Obama appeared to be gracious and diplomatic calling for the nation to come together and support Trump. However. his public decorum was replaced by hostility aimed at Israel, releasing more Gitmo detainees, denounced the plans to derail Obama care, and he booted Russian diplomats out of the United States. Obama's minions carried out threats and protests. They had temper tantrums and they demeaned Trump and his supporters. If we open spiritual eyes, we can see that this defeat is a spiritual wound to the head of the beast system. The wounded head of the beast recovers. Still enraged, there remains work to be accomplished to bring all under the one world order. The Clintons served their time of usefulness. Hillary lost and it's time to distance himself from the losers. Obama, the community organizer with sharpened skills will initiate a counter-revolution under a shadow government. Obama's sentiments are, "It is time to move forward not only to protect what we have accomplished but also to see this as an opportunity." The liberal left will continue to attack traditional institutions, constitutional rights and individual sovereignty. Their wound is raw seeping fear and hostility and ripe for radicalizing the masses. This crime became worldwide news when a white, mentally challenged man was kidnapped by four hostile blacks who tortured him for two days. They were charged with hate crimes, kidnapping and assault. Hollywood elite call for protests and disruption against the Trump administration. Al Sharpton calls for a racially charged uprising. Nancy Pelosi and Elizabeth Warren pledge the Dems will oppose everything. From these few examples of collected rage a crafty and intelligent man could channel this negative energy into actions. The world has arrived at a critical precipice. The righteous pray asking God for divine intervention. He did intervene in the United Stated election and he will intervene in the affairs of mankind according to his will. Bible prophecy must be fulfilled. Things will get worse.

The Harlot Riding the Beast

We are reminded that the beast in the book of Revelation is ridden by the woman, a harlot holding a cup full of the abominations of the nations—symbolic of corruption, lies, murder, greed, and sin.

During Hillary Clintons' presidential campaign in, 2016, a great deal of the Clintons' dirty laundry was aired by way of leaked emails, exposed in books and movies. Early on both Hillary and Bill realized they had a penchant towards manipulation in order to gain wealth and power. Personal integrity was laid aside as Bill acted on his sexual impulses and Hillary lost her sense of compassion. When Hillary was working for the Rose Law Firm, she defended a man who raped a twelve year old girl so viciously she could never have children. During testimony, Clinton painted the victim as emotionally unstable with an inclination for older men. Clinton got the rapist off, and proud of her accomplishment, she laughingly lauded herself.

Whitewater real estate investment scandal—at this time, Bill was governor of Arkansas. He was involved in several sexual abuse claims. The Clintons hid the Whitewater files for years while under federal investigation. Later the files mysteriously came to light in the White House during Bill Clinton's impeachment hearing in 1999.

Vince Foster and Bill Clinton attended elementary school in Arkansas. Foster became an attorney at the Rose Law Firm in Little Rock, where Hillary was a partner. The Fosters and the Clintons were friends. It is rumored that Vince and Hillary were having an affair. In 1992,

Bill was working his way to the White House. In 1993, Vince Foster was dead by suicide, and his body was found at Fort Marcy Park. Doubt and suspicions surrounded his death. Many people believe murders were committed to cover up the Clintons' scandals. Sky Watch TV 2016 reported files on Vince Foster stored in the National Archives have disappeared.

It has come to light that Mrs. Clinton has close ties with private industries such as the Monsanto Corporation, going back to the time she worked at the Rose Law Firm in Arkansas. The Rose Law Firm represented Monsanto interest. Monsanto lobbyist donated from $500,000 to $1 million to the Clintons. Hillary's top campaign staffer, Jerry Crawford, is a former Monsanto lobbyist.

Currently, the nation is becoming aware of the improprieties and corruption surrounding the Clintons. The Clinton Global Initiative Foundation received billions in donations from private concerns and foreign nations, according to the *Washington Post*, and tax records indicate only 10 percent given to charities. The Clinton Foundation was a depository for donors who would receive favorable consideration from President Clinton and later, Secretary of State Hillary.

Peter Schweizer, May 2015, author of *Clinton Cash*, provides detailed evidence of extensive corruption. How it all works begins with a commercial interest that wants to do business in the United States or internationally. A large donation to the Clinton foundation is expected and is coordinated with a Bill Clinton speaking engagement, of which he will be paid upward to $750,000. Once a financial commitment is made by the commercial entity, Hillary Clinton as secretary of state strikes a deal with that nation. Additional donations are required beyond the speaking engagement fee, especially if the contracts are lucrative.

We will give actual situations that were investigated and reported by Mr. Schweizer. The people, wealth, and natural resources of Africa have been exploited by Europeans, warlords, and dictators for hundreds of years, and in modern times these practices continue. Rwanda president, Paul Kagame, had been documented for human rights violations. Bill Clinton made a speech in his behalf, presenting him with a good citizen award. Sudan dictators are high on the list for human rights violations, and Joe Wilson, vice president of Jarch Capital, wanted to purchase land in Sudan. Secretary of State Clinton was able to broker a deal in his behalf from warlords who controlled the region. Lucas Lindin would reap billions doing business in the Congo. After pledging $100 million to the Clinton foundation, he was on his way.

Nigeria has a 50 percent poverty rate and suffers from government corruption. Nigeria receives US aid based on transparency of how the funds are disbursed. To bypass that requirement, Bill Clinton speaks in Nigeria; receives $750,000 from Mr. Obaigbena—a friend of president Genku; and secretary of Clinton issues a waiver. The Genku administration is reported to have smuggled four to eight billion out of Nigeria and deposited in European banks. In 2001, President Bill Clinton pardoned Marc Rich for money laundering. Rich partnered with Nigerian millionaire Gibert Chagoury, who wanted and received oil drilling rights in Nigeria. According to *Los Angeles Times*, Chagoury made two donations to the Clinton Foundation: $1 million and $5 million.

He has had a long relationship with the Clintons from the 1990s. Chagoury was investigated by the FBI in 2013 for funding the terrorist group Hezbollah. He gave funds to former Nigerian dictator, General Sani Abacha, and to Michael Aoun, Lebanese Army commander, who channeled money to Hezbollah.

Mylan pharmaceutical company purchased the rights to the EpiPen in 2007 and sold it for $57, and by 2016, the cost rose to $600. On August 24, 2016, Hillary Clinton expressed her outrage of another company taking advantage of consumers. She did not mention that Mylan has a history of donations made to the Clinton Foundation. Clinton Foundation records donations in the amount of $100,000 and $250,000. CEO of Mylan is Heather Bresch, who is the daughter of West Virginia senator and Clinton supporter, Joe Manchin. Bresch's salary in 2007 was $2.4 million, and in 2015, $19 million (*Natural News*, David Gutierrez, August 30, 2016).

In 2010, Haiti was devastated by an earthquake that killed over 250,000 people. The country suffered massive infrastructure damage. The international community pledged $13 billion to rebuild. As secretary of state, Hillary made an initial visit to the airport, pledging US support. Bill Clinton was appointed as an envoy to Haiti by the United Nations. Hillary appointed Bill to head up the Haiti Reconstruction Commission. With both Clintons in place, they began to work with disaster capitalists who took advantage of suffering and tragedy. Contractors paid to play promised homes, hospitals, and factories, and the end results fell short. It is estimated only 10 percent of the $13 billion was applied to Haitian relief and rebuilding. Some Haitians complained about the Clinton corruption, but it fell on deaf ears. Denis O'Brien, Ireland, wanted approval to sell cell phones in Haiti. O'Brien arranged for Bill to speak in Jamaica, and Bill received $250,000. Shortly thereafter, O'Brien's contract was approved. Hundreds of thousands of Haitian still live in tents or temporary shelters, but the Clintons, through their contractors, are building luxury hotels. A textile factory was built on the opposite side of the island, away from the earthquake devastation. Clintons promised the factory would hire 1,600 workers. That fell short. Those people employed worked sixteen-hour shifts and were paid .61 cent per hour. The Haitian government had not issued approval for gold mining rights in fifty years, but Tony Rohan received approval to mine for gold. Hillary Clinton's brother sits on the board of directors of Rohan's corporation. Hillary pledged $800 million for a new hospital, and as of 2016, there is no new hospital.

Hillary Clinton calls Donald Trump a racist. If what the Clintons did to the blacks in Haiti is not racism, then what is? Clinton remains friends with acclaimed KKK member

Senator Robert C. Byrd, calling him a hero. Other news report Clinton hired actors to pose as KKK members and pretend to protest her at a campaign function.

When Hillary was appointed secretary of state in 2008, she was opposed to the Keystone XL pipeline. Canada paid Bill an enormous speaking fee, and Hillary changed her position and signed off on the pipeline.

Mr. Ericsson of Sweden wanted to trade with Iran at a time the nation was under US sanctions. Ericsson paid Bill Clinton $750 million, and the secretary of state approved his request.

Frank Giustra of Canada wanted approval to cut trees in the rain forest in Columbia. Giustra, Hillary, and Bill met in Columbia. Over time, Giustra stripped the land, and the trees were shipped to China.

India was pushing for nuclear armament. The Clintons were for disarmament. India paid upward to $1.5 million to Bill Clinton, and sanctions against India were lifted.

The Russian nuclear program is dependent on uranium. Bill was paid $500,000 to speak in Russia. It would cost Russia around $145 million to get 20 percent of US uranium rights. Bill also received a hefty kickback on the deal. Secretary of State Clinton had to sign off on the deal.

Major news reported January 2017 Russia is selling uranium to Iran with the approval of the US and other nations. This comes at a time when many are up in arms over Russia hacking the DNC and Obama expelling Russian diplomats. Saudi Arabia is intolerant of women, Christians, Jews and yet the Clintons received between one to five million dollars in donations from the Saudi's. Nasser Al-Rashid via Forbes and *Breaking Israel News, May 2016*

Fox News, July 8, 2016, reported that Rep. Corrine Brown, D-Fla, was charged with fraud, and federal offenses tied to her fraudulent charity. Brown is charged for the same crimes Hillary and Bill Clinton are guilty of, but they may never be indicted because they are elites.

Hillary spoke in 2014 at the Biotech Convention in San Diego. She was reported as telling the attendees that they need an "image makeover from *genetically modified to drought resistant,* be more careful so you don't raise the red flag too soon" (*Natural News*, June 27, 2015, reporter Daniel Barker; *Politico*; *Daily Mail*; *Washington Times*).

Hanging over Hillary's head and under investigation are the thousands of e-mails sent over a nonsecure server while she was secretary of state. In an attempt to cover up this breach, many e-mails were deleted. Clinton was being investigated for not following protocol, not using a government-approved computer and secure e-mail site. September 7, 2015, according to Edward Snowden, "Secretary of State has the highest level clearance, and Clinton knows how classified information should be handled" (Snowden to *Al-Jazeera News*). Anyone else would lose clearance, job, and face prosecution. The investigation to date revealed that documents transferred from Special Access Program to Clinton's home server contained high-level secret documents, which had to then be moved off electronically or removed out of the secure site physically to an unclassified e-mail system. Lt. Gen. Michael Flynn, Defense Intelligence Agency chief under Obama, said, "Hillary Clinton should quit the presidential campaign to focus on the investigation of her private e-mail server for the good of the country, she should step down and let the FBI investigation play out." Clinton's answers regarding her conduct are on record, and they are full of holes and lies. The FBI concluded its investigation before July 4, 2016. Before FBI director Comley made his ruling, Bill Clinton met clandestinely with attorney general Loretta Lynch on the DOJ's plane on the tarmac. After that meeting, FBI director said he would not file criminal charges against Hillary. This caused an uproar in the Congress, throughout media, and raised concern from citizens. FBI director was called in to testify before congress. During this mess, there was the killing of six police officers in Dallas, Texas, during a protest. The elite may have set this up to misdirect the public's attention away from Clinton, the DOJ, and the FBI. Also Guccifer, aka Marcel Lazar Lehel, from Romania was extradited to the United States for hacking into Clinton's e-mails, which he admits. Reported on the Dave Hodges show, Guccifer was found dead in his cell in Virginia, July 7, 2016.

The Benghazi scandal is unresolved. Clinton wants it to go away, but who can forget "What difference does it make now"? Clinton's improper use of a personal server allowed classified e-mails regarding Benghazi to be sent over an unclassified system. Clinton's IT, Bryan Pagliano, did plead the fifth before the September 10, 2015, committee. Clinton perjured herself before Congress, responding to questions regarding Benghazi that it was the result of a video.

Hillary is not a champion of the downtrodden masses. It is rumored she hates the citizens, and according to Wikileaks, the global elite must "keep Americans unaware and compliant." She dons the hat of a corporatist, whose mission is to further the interest of big business. It was reported that, behind the scene, she states a particular position, and in public, it is the opposite. She was recorded, she wears the hat of a social progressive, and her worldview is toward a global regime. She does play a significant role in the scheme of the one-world order. She entered the presidential race with a statement that should alarm every Christian. At a recent Women's Summit, she said, "Our deep-seated religious beliefs would have to change." No longer will dissenting opinions be tolerated. If laws (structural biases as in the Constitution) then politics will needs to be exercised. Discussion on Glen Beck program, April 29, 2015, analyzed these comments. According to Clinton, the deep-seated cultural codes, religious beliefs, and structural biases have to be changed. This progressive agenda embraces and continues in all the achievements the Obama administration has accomplished. The fundamental transformation of America began a hundred years ago. The Obama administration "slammed it into warp speed, becoming less inclined to bother hiding their efforts anymore. They have become so emboldened that they start saying things that at onetime seemed impossible to believe."

In 2007, Hillary promoted the sanctity of marriage between a man and woman. As a confirmed globalist, she has made a 360-degree turn on that position and is now a proponent of same-sex unions. Same-sex unions reduce the birth rate. She is also proabortion and supports funding Planned Parenthood because they are crucial to women's health. More so than women's health, abortion is one method to reduce the population.

Clinton's comments on the campaign trail, November 2015, regarding Islamic terrorists, "Muslims are a peaceful people," and this could mean, Islamic terrorists are a good resource in reducing the population.

It was reported by Wikileaks that the Democratic National Committee database was hacked. The e-mails exposed the DNC was working to sabotage the Bernie Sanders campaign similar to Watergate, and his supporters were "basement dwellers." The DNC chair, Debbie Wasserman Shultz, resigned. Sean Lucas, attorney, was filing a class-action lawsuit on behalf of Bernie Sanders supporters against the DNC for campaign corruption; he was found dead July 2, 2016. DNC staff person, Seth Rich, was planning to speak with the FBI in regard to the DNC corruption, and he was murdered on July 8, 2016. With all the corruption and accusations plaguing Hillary Clinton, we wonder if she is still the poster child for the one-world order, or has she become a liability?

Hillary has no regard for law enforcement and is disrespectful to her security detail. Christopher Anderson, in his book, *American Evita* (p. 90, "Good morning") (security detail to Clinton) Clinton's response was, "F—— off, it's enough I have to see you shit kickers every day, I'm not going to talk to you too, just do your GD job and keep your mouth shut."

We believe Bill and Hillary's greatest aspiration was for her to be president of the United States in order to further self-serve their ambitions. If the Democrats had succeeded for another term, it will be like the Obama administration on steroids. Actually, the Clinton team is superior to the JV Obama team.

The Clintons threw every conceivable nuance and accusations at Trump to derail his credibility with the help of the leftist media. There was no bar that the Clintons would not go under to steal the election. Donald Trumps victory upset the apple cart. The elitist were wounded. They will revamp in a hail of lying accusations and actions to overthrow Trump. It will be imperative for the elite to position themselves to covertly oversee the Trump administration and to ensure the one world agenda stays on course. It was divine intervention that cleared a path for Trumps victory. In 2007 Pastor Kim Clement (deceased) was given a prophecy that a man "hot blooded will be placed in the highest office, he will build a wall of protection, the economy will change rapidly, he will not be religious but he will go in whispering my name and I will fill him with my spirit, he will be at the helm for two terms." A rabbi also confirmed a Trump win in the Torah codes.

We will watch as events continue to unfold, moving the world closer to the seven year tribulation.

Chapter 19
Celebration in Heaven, Tribulation on Earth

Chapter Overview

Chapter 19

Celebration in Heaven, Tribulation on Earth

Seven Years in Heaven

A growing majority of Christians believe the Rapture will occur before the beginning of the tribulation period. Matthew 24:36, Jesus begins to tell us that no one will know the day or the hour that the Rapture will occur. He advises we watch the signs of the times and cautions that one will be taken and another left behind. In Matthew 25:1–13, Jesus tells us in the parable of the ten virgins wherein five were wise (watching, waiting, and ready) and five were foolish (living and conforming to the ways of the world) and the bridegroom came. The faithful who slept (dead) and those alive heard the announcement (a loud shout) that the bridegroom comes. Those that were ready went in to join the Lord for the marriage, and the door was shut to those who were not ready and missed the Rapture. Messianic Jews, born-again Christian from every walk, will be among those Raptured to join millions who have gone on before to be with Jesus.

Parallel to the tribulation period on earth, the saints will be in heaven during that seven-year period. The earthly tribulation is measured in literal earth time, but the heavenly domain is not regulated by earth time. Heaven is timeless.

Revelation 7 opens with a scene of four angels positioned at the four corners of the earth. They have been instructed to hold back, releasing another judgment until 144,000 from the twelve tribes have been sealed by God. This appears to take place at the beginning of the tribulation, and after the sealing, the scene shifts to the heavenly realm. Revelation 7:9–10, "*After this* [the sealing], *I beheld a great multitude, which no man could number of all nations, and kindred and people and tongues* [representatives of the human race]" stood before the throne and before the Lamb. The saints are dressed in white robes, which is evidence of the body and soul united and changed to immortality. They stand before the throne with palms (represents victory) in their hands, crying with a loud voice, "Salvation to our God, who sits upon the throne and unto the Lamb."

The above scripture provides a perfect picture of the saints assembled in the heavenly realm. These are the souls of the righteous from ancient times resurrected with Jesus two thousand years ago. It also includes those who died between the resurrections up to the time of the rapture. This great multitude is representative of those who die after the rapture and through the tribulation. In Revelation, Saint John describes many wonderful things that we will see, hear, and experience in heaven. While Jesus was on the earth, he told his followers that he was going to prepare a place for them, "*For in my Father's house are many mansions, if it were not so, I would not have told you and I will come and take you.*" The death of the righteous saints, having preceded the living, has been in the presence of God the Father and Jesus the Son. They have seen the angels and all the splendor of heaven, the mansions, the street of gold, and we will be united with those who have gone before us. From this heavenly vantage point, we see the wonders of heaven, the cosmos, and view the tribulation on earth.

BEMA SEAT

REWARDS

Crown of Glory

Elder's Crown

1 Pet. 5:2–4

"Feed the flock of God which is among you, taking the oversight thereof, not by constraint but willingly; not for filthy lucre, but of a ready mind; Neither as being lords over God's heritage, but being examples to the flock. And when the chief Shepherd shall appear, ye shall receive a crown of glory that fadeth not away."

Incorruptible Crown

The Victor's Crown

1 Cor. 9:25

"And every man that striveth for the mastery is temperate in all things. Now they do it to obtain a corruptible crown; but we an incorruptible."

Crown of Rejoicing

Soul Winner's Crown

1 Thess. 2:19–20

"For what is our hope, or joy, or crown of rejoicing? Are not even ye in the presence of our Lord Jesus Christ at his coming? For ye are our glory and joy."

Crown of Life

Martyr's Crown

Rev. 2:10

"Fear none of those things which thou shalt suffer: behold, the devil shall cast some of you into prison, the ye may be tried; and ye shall have tribulation ten days; be thou faithful unto death, and I will give thee a crown of life."

Crown of Righteousness

For those who love His appearing

2 Tim. 4:8

"Henceforth there is laid up for me a crown of righteousness which the Lord, the righteous judge, shall give me at that day: and not to me only, but unto all them also that love his appearing."

Bema Seat

Bema Seat is the judgment seat of Christ where the members of the body of Christ will give an account of their deeds. "*For we must all appear before the judgment seat of Christ, that everyone may receive the things done in his body, according to that he has done whether it be good or bad.*" 2 Corinthians 5:10

After reading this passage, none of us desires to stand before Christ.

We have all done things we are ashamed of, but be encouraged; our life flashes before us in a minute of time. We will still be saved, and then we can look forward to receiving rewards for the good things we did in life in the name of Jesus.

Christians are given gifts from the Holy Spirit to help carry the Gospel forward.

In 1 Corinthians 3, Paul explains that within the body of Christ, one may plant a seed, another may water, but God gives the increase. One may lay a foundation, and another will build upon it. He goes on to say that the one who planted and the one who watered are of one body, but each will receive his own reward according to his own labor. The purpose of the Bema Seat judgment is to try these works in the supernatural fire. If they are as gold, silver, precious stones, they will be accounted worthy; if they are of wood, hay, stubble, they will be burned up in the fire. If any man or woman's work survives the fire, they will receive a reward. If any person's work be burned, they will suffer loss of rewards but will not lose their salvation because salvation is a gift from God.

Paul prepares Christians for the Bema Seat judgment:

> *Every man's work will be made manifest for the day will declare it, because it will be revealed by fire and the fire will try every man's work of what sort it is, if any man's work abide which he has built thereupon, he will receive a reward. If any man's work will be burned he will suffer loss but he himself will be saved yet so as by fire.* (1 Corinthians *13*)

An example of work that will not survive testing is a mega church ministry whose outreach was for selfish gain, prideful recognition, or divisive. Most importantly, the work had not been done for the glory of God but to glorify or exalt self. We need not concern ourselves with who is doing what for Christ because only Jesus can discern the sincere from the wicked. A little storefront church that has a right heart after the Lord will come through the fire as tried gold.

Following the Bema Seat judgment will be the wedding ceremony and the marriage supper of the Lamb.

Marriage of the Lamb

The marriage of the Lamb event seems to occur after the destruction of the Babylonian world system portrayed in Revelation 18. As we read Revelation 19:1, it opens with *and after these things*, which refers to the destruction of the one-world order having taken place, and then the passage immediately transports us to the heavenly realm where John hears the voices of many people praising our Lord God. Revelation 19:2, this great gathering of saints acknowledge that the "*judgments of God are righteous and true, for he has judged the great whore which did corrupt the earth with her fornication* ..."

As we read Revelation 19:7, Jesus has called together all godly people from the time of Adam to those who died during the tribulation period. They are seen in white robes and crowns in preparation for the final union of the true believers and their Lord in an eternal inseparable relationship. The body of Christ has been redeemed and purified, made ready for the marriage and the marriage supper. There is an interlude between Revelation 19:7, the event of the marriage and the marriage supper, and Revelation 19:11–16, the assembling of the saints and the procession from heaven to earth. Revelation 19:11, we first see the heavens opening, and it will be like the gathering of storm clouds. Matthew 24:27 tells us lightning will come out of the east and shine unto the west, so will also the coming of the Son of Man be. While Jesus and the saints are transitioning from heaven to earth, we take time to study the events of the tribulation leading up to the battle of Armageddon.

At the end of the tribulation period, the remnant of humanity will be gathered together for the final battle of Armageddon. Scriptures tell us, Jesus will return to the earth with the saints and destroy all wickedness. This time is the long-awaited Second Coming of Jesus.

> *For as the lightning that lightens out of the one part under heaven and shines unto the other part under heaven so will also the Son of man be in his day.* (Luke 17:*24*)

All will see Jesus descending from the heavens.

As we prepare to study events happening on earth, the focus is on Israel. Since Israel became a nation in 1948, they have endured enemy attacks on every border; but with the help of Yahweh, Israel stands. The following scripture provides an end-time warning:

> *And when you shall see Jerusalem compassed with armies, then know that destruction is near.* (Luke 21:20–24)

Every enemy of Israel has threatened to remove them from their land, but the promise of God to Israel is stated in Amos 9:15:

> *And I will plant them upon their land and they will no more be pulled up out of their land which I have given them said the Lord your God.* All this, *so that the house of Israel will know that I am the Lord their God from that day and forward. Neither will I hide my face any more from them for I have poured out my spirit upon the house of Israel.*

In these latter days, God has been pouring out his spirit. Many have accepted Yeshua Messiah and are saved. During this time of grace, some Jews and Gentiles will still reject God. Their hearts will be hardened just like Pharaoh's, at that time, things got worst in Egypt.

Old Testament Prophecies Reveal End-Time Events

The Day of the Lord has a time line from the birth of Jesus to his Second Coming advent. Following along this time line, prophecies have been fulfilled especially as it relates to Israel. The war of Gog and Magog foretold by the prophet Ezekiel will occur near the start of the tribulation period in the land of Israel, at least a portion of it. Nations will rise up against Israel in a variety of events, continuing through the tribulation, culminating into the final battle of Armageddon.

Mideast regional conflicts will escalate between Islamic nations and Israel before the Russian Gog and Magog incursion. In the last twenty years, there has been unrest and uprisings in Tunisia, Egypt, Libya, Morocco, Algeria, Sudan, Nigeria, Syria, Turkey, Iran, Iraq, Jordan, Saudi Arabia, Kuwait, Yemen, Gaza, Lebanon, and Israel. The Arab Spring, under the Obama administration, accelerated conflict in Islamic nations and provided leeway for the rise of ISIS.

Seventy nations will meet January 14, 2017 in Paris to discuss forcing Israel to give their land away to the Palestinians. This conference follows on the heels of the United Nations vote to sanction Israel for building homes in their land. The United Nations has consistently portrayed Israel as a war criminal. The war drums are beating louder signaling the gathering of nations who threaten Israel's existence making known throughout the world they plot to destroy the people of God. Collectively and in harmony, the United Nations, Muslim nations, European nations, secular society and apostate Christiandom drink from the cup of abominations held by the harlot riding the beast. All are drawn into the conflict as if a hook were placed in their jaw by God. Their enmity towards Israel and his righteous will be their undermining. Before the dust settles, the Lord of hosts will destroy the armies of Satan.

We will analyze passages in Isaiah, Zechariah, Psalms 83, Ezekiel 38, Obadiah, and Habakkuk that provide insight into how God will deal with the nations in these end times:

> *Keep not thou silence O God, hold not thy peace and be not still, O God for lo thy enemies make a tumult and they that hate thee have lifted up the head.*

> *They have taken crafty counsel against your people and consulted against thy hidden one, they have said, come let us cut them off from being a nation, that the name of Israel may be no more in remembrance. For they have consulted together with one consent, they are confederate against thee. The tabernacles of Edom and the Ishmaelites, Moab and the Hagarenes, Gebal and Ammon, Amalek, the Philistines with the inhabitants of Tyre, Assur also is joined with them, they have helped the children of Lot. Do unto them as unto the Midianites, Sisera, Jabin at the brook of Kison which perished at Endor and became as dung for the earth. Make their nobles like Oreb, Zeeb, all the princes as Acebah and Aalmunna. They said, let us take to ourselves the house of God in possession. O my God, make them like a wheel as the stubble before the wind, as the fire burns wood, as the flame sets the mountains on fire. So persecute them with your tempest and make them afraid with thy storm. Fill their faces with shame that they may seek thy name O Lord. Let them be confounded and troubled forever, yes let them be put to shame and perish. That men may know that thou, whose name alone is Yahweh are the most high over all the earth.* (Psalm 83:1–18)

Psalm 83 was written over two thousand years ago; it summarizes ancient enemies that came up against the Hebrew Israelites in the land and points to future judgment against various nations that have conspired against Israel. The scripture allows us to know that there is a future component as it pertains to the end of the age, which references Israel as a nation in 1948:

- Islamic nations surrounding Israel have been plotting her demise.
- United Nations, European, American, and Mideastern nations have taken crafty counsel against the Jews and consulted against my precious ones.
- They said, "Let us cut Israel off from being a nation that the name of Israel may be no more in remembrance" (a constant callout of Lebanon, Iran, and Gaza).
- Edom, Ammon, Moab people in Jordan. Ishmaelites, Hagarenes were native to Arabia
- Togarmah, son of Gomer, Gomer son of Japheth, associated with Russia and Turkey.
- The hostile nations will be confounded, troubled, persecute its people, afraid with the storm, ashamed, and perish.
- They will know the name of Yahweh.

Zechariah 12:2 points to the end of the age as he states, "*Behold I will make Jerusalem a cup of trembling unto all the people round about when they will be in the siege both against Judah and against Jerusalem.*" This prophecy is fulfilled. At this time, Israel and its capital,

Jerusalem, are coveted by the Vatican, America, Lebanon, Hamas, Iran, Syria, Egypt, Turkey, Jordan.

> *In that day, I will make Jerusalem a burdensome stone for all people that burden themselves with it shall be cut into pieces, though all the people of the earth be gathered together against it. In that day, I will smite every horse with astonishment and blindness and his rider with madness.* (Zechariah 12:3)

Currently, nations are in turmoil and are turning against one another.

> *And the governors of Judah will say in their heart, the inhabitants of Jerusalem will be my strength in the Lord of hosts, their God. In that day, God will make the governors of Judah like a hearth of fire among the wood, like a torch of fire in a sheaf and they will devour all the people round about, on the right and left hand and Jerusalem will be inhabited again in her own place, even in Jerusalem.* (Zechariah 12:5)

This prophecy looks at a time when the leaders of Israel will be strong in the Lord God and they will destroy all the people around them with the fire of missiles. Israel took back Jerusalem, its capital, in 1967, and it will not be taken again by their enemies. God says, "It will come to pass in that day that I will destroy all the nations that come against Jerusalem." Currently, Israel has defended itself, but the enemy nations have not been fully destroyed. We watch for something devastating to occur, and this will trigger the Ezekiel 38 and 39 conflict.

We also understand that Israel will suffer great loss during the tribulation, and then they will know Yeshua is Messiah.

> *I will pour upon the house of David and upon the inhabitants of Jerusalem the spirit of grace and of supplications and they will look upon me whom they have pierced and they will mourn for him as one mourns for his only son … in that day there will be a great mourning in Jerusalem.* (Zechariah 12:10)

Israel will see Yeshua.

> *And one will say unto him what are these wounds in your hands? He will answer, those with which I was wounded in the house of my friends.* (Zechariah 13:6)

The sixty-six books of Isaiah begin with the theme of judgment and end in hope at the establishment of the Messianic kingdom. Some scholars say that these sixty-six books are like a miniature Bible and correlate with the sixty-six books of the Bible. Isaiah the prophet paints a morbid scenario of these end-time battles and the hand of God against Israel's enemies.

Egypt, Africa

Isaiah 19 specifically speaks a prophecy against Egypt. God's hand was against ancient Egypt, and God's hand is against present-day Egypt.

> *I will set the Egyptians against Egyptians, and they will fight everyone against his brother, neighbor, city against city ...*

- Islamic factions kill Coptic Christians. Egypt in conflict with other regions in Africa.
- God will destroy their counsel, and they will look to their false religious leaders.
- God will give Egypt over to a cruel lord, a fierce king. This is applicable to Egypt's former president, Morsi, who called for oppression of Egyptians under Islamic law, persecution, and death to Coptic Christians and death to Israel. His battle cry is, "Islam is the answer, and jihad is the way!" but now he sits in jail.
- According to newly released evidence, Obama had been paying Morsi, Muslim Brotherhood, for bribes, assassinations, coordinating prison escapes, killing demonstrators, and spying.
- The economy is in shambles. The Nile River will dry up and will cause fishing industry hardship, especially when the Aswan Dam (towers fall, Isaiah 30:25) is destroyed in the future.
- They will eventually fear Israel, who will take back a portion of Egyptian land.

The new Egyptian administration under al Sisi seems to want to cooperate with Israel. They appear to be maintaining security in the Sinai Peninsula against terrorists. They have on a small-level stabilized attacks on Israel from Gaza and are demolishing tunnels built by Hamas.

Egypt's Future

> *In that day will there be an altar to the Lord in the midst of the land of Egypt and a pillar at the border thereof to the Lord. They will cry unto the Lord because of the oppressors and he shall send them a savior and a great one, he will deliver them. And the Lord will be known to Egypt and the Egyptians will know the Lord in that day ...* (Isaiah 19:19)

This scripture looks back to the time Moses delivered the people. In modern times, God did bring a remnant of people out of Egypt, Ethiopia, and other areas in Africa who claim to be of the ancient Hebrew Israelite linage and bring them into kingdom covenant.

Ethiopia, Africa

Isaiah 18 prophecy refers to the Jews returning from this land to their homeland. In that time shall a present be brought forth unto the Lord of hosts of a people scattered.

- The Day of the Lord would see the fulfillment of the Ethiopian Jews return to Israel. Many believe they had hidden the Ark of the Covenant during the destruction of the first temple and the scriptures point to a "present will be brought forth," and this could be the ark.

Isaiah 30 and 31—in times past, Egypt was a blessing to the chosen people. Genesis 12:10, Abraham leaves Canaan to go into Egypt to escape famine. Joseph, son of Jacob, was sent into Egypt to prepare for the famine to protect his family. Joseph, Mary, and baby Jesus fled into Egypt to escape King Herod.

Isaiah 19:24 points to an interesting alliance after the tribulation:

> *In that day will Israel be the third with Egypt and with Assyria, even a blessing in the midst of the land whom the Lord of host will bless and say, blessed be Egypt* [Ham] *my people and Assyria* [Shem] *the work of my hands and Israel my inheritance.*

Syria

Isaiah 17 specifically highlights a future prophecy against Damascus, which is in Syria. In 2011, civil war erupted; they have been confounded and troubled by internal conflict. Hundreds of thousands have died, many more displaced, and extensive infrastructure damage. The first verse says, "*The burden of Damascus, behold, Damascus is taken away from being a city and it shall be a ruinous heap … Behold at evening trouble and before the morning, Damascus is not.*" Syria continually threatens Israel. Syria had sent rockets into Israeli territory. January 2013, Israel bombed an arms cargo and warehouse in Damascus suspected of housing chemical weapons. Iran had supplied weapons to Syria, also to Lebanon and Gaza, to fuel Hezbolla and Hamas terrorists. September 2013, Obama pushes for a strike on Damascus. Russia intervenes. War in Syria is a threat to Israel borders. Israel shot down one drone coming into its territory. Security operations in the United States, Israel, Europe, and other Middle Eastern countries knew for a few years ISIS terrorists were training militants, gaining weapons, and taking land in both Syria and Iraq.

ISIS took control of oil facilities in Syria. They have sold oil to neighboring Turkey, who is anti-Syrian. The United States did not bomb ISIS-held oil resources because the United States is aligned with Turkey. In recent developments, Russia has a military base in Syria. Russia extended peace toward Israel, which has no substance.

- Damascus is ruined; its cities have been abandoned.
- Multitudes of Syrians left the nation.

<u>Iran/Persia</u>

Iran continues to build nuclear weapons. They threaten to attack Israel for any reason because it is their goal to wipe Israel off the map. They threatened to attack Israel if United States attacks Syria. September 2013, Syrian President Assad and family went to Iran for refuge. Iran is also persecuting Christians, but Christianity is exploding in Iran. United States and other nations made a deal with Iran in 2015 to allow them to continue their nuclear goals. Sanctions were lifted, and Iran received billions to further their nuclear goals.

<u>Iraq/Babylon</u>

<u>Isaiah 13</u>

Present-day Iraq is plagued with civil unrest between Islamic clans. The former glory of Babylon is gone. Prophecy points to the Day of the Lord, and God will destroy the land. Iran wants to take control of Iraq. August 2014, ISIS has taken portions of Iraq, slaughtering the people, beheading, crucifixion, bulldozing and burying people alive. Iraqi Christians and Kurdistan people are fleeing the region. Turkey hates the Kurds. United States sent planes to destroy some of ISIS strongholds and to help set up refugee camps. United States will not get involved to any great extent. ISIS has shown itself to be more brutal than other Islamic terrorists. They destroyed the grave of Jonah.

- Babylon, once the glory of kingdoms and beauty of the Chaldees, shall be as when God overthrew Sodom and Gomorrah.
- At the end of the Day of the Lord, Iraq will not be inhabited for generations but only wild beast, owls, satyrs, dragons will live in the region.

Lebanon

Isaiah 14:28

Isaiah prophecy pertaining to the areas of Gaza and Lebanon—Lebanon supports Hezbolla terrorists and holds influence over Hamas in Gaza. They both support bombing of Israel for a decade or more. They do not want peace. Israel had reached out to help them in all areas, but their hate has blinded them to rationale and logic. Lebanon's president, Abbas, continually calls for Muslims to incite violence against Israel.

- Palestinian cities are dissolved, for there shall come from the north a smoke, and none will be alone in his appointed time. Palestinians adopted the name and will be the recipient of God's wrath for their hatred of Israel.
- The leaders of the nations will know that the Lord has founded Zion.

Jordan

Isaiah 15 and 16 Prophecy Against Jordan

- It will come to pass that God will judge Jordan for its treatment of Israel.
- The glory of Jordan will fade, and the citizens will be small in number and weak.
- And in mercy will the throne be established, and Jesus will sit upon it in truth in the tabernacle of David, judging and seeking judgment and hasting righteousness.

Jordan is the ancient home of Esau, Isaac's brother. Jordan presently oversees the Temple Mount and prevents Jews from worshipping on the mount. It allows Muslims to desecrate the Temple Mount with trash, basketball, and roughhousing. Jordan's king from the Hashemite tribe, a descendant of Mohammad, is providing refuge for Syrians and Iraqis. The king is being threatened by other Islamic sects who want the king deposed because he's is pro-West and peaceful with Israel.

Obadiah 15:21

The prophet Obadiah had a vision of God's judgment against Edom in the end-times:

> *For the **day of the LORD** is near upon all the heathen as thou has done it shall be done unto you. Your reward will return upon your own head. For as you have drunk upon my holy mountain, so shall all the heathen drink continually, yes they will drink and they will swallow down and they will be as though they had not been. But upon mount Zion shall be deliverance and there will be holiness and the house of Jacob will possess their possessions and the house of*

Jacob will be a fire and the house of Joseph a flame and the house of Esau for stubble and they will kindle in them and devour them and there will not be any remaining of the house of Esau for the Lord has spoken it. They of the south will possess the mount of Esau and they of the plain the Philistines and they will possess the fields of Ephraim and the fields of Samaria and Benjamin will possess Gilead. And the captivity of this host of the children of Israel will possess that of the Canaanites even unto Zarephath and the captivity of Jerusalem which is in Sepharad will possess the cities of the south. And saviors will come up on mount Zion to judge the mount of Esau and the kingdom will be the LORD's.

A summary of Obadiah 15–21 addresses several areas:

- The prophecy ties into the end-time events of the Day of the Lord.
- Jordan has control of the temple mount; they have defiled God's holy mountain.
- Mount Zion, including the temple mount area, will be delivered, and holiness will be restored.
- All the land and possessions that had been taken from Israel will be restored.
- Esau/Edom/Jordan people will be a stubble and destroyed. Mount of Esau or Mount Seir will be possessed by Israel.
- The kingdom will belong to Jesus.

Saudi Arabia

The original settlements of Arabia were called Sheba and Dedan. As of September 2013, Saudis are on alert as Russian president threatens to strike in the event United States attacks Syria. November 18, 2013, Saudi Arabia and Israel working on joint defense against Iran. Saudi Arabia hostile to Christians and Jews. Majority are Wahabites and pro–al-Qaeda

Europe and United States

For thus has the Lord spoken unto me, like as the lion and the young lion [Europe and America] *roaring on his prey, when a multitude of shepherds* [political and religious leaders] *is called forth against him, he will not be afraid of their voice, nor abase himself for the noise of them, so shall the Lord of hosts come down to fight for mount Zion and for the hill thereof.* (Isaiah 31:4)

Seemingly, the young lion (America) is involved in every world situation, and it relies on its European roots for direction and support. From this passage, the prophet envisions the future of Europe and its offshoot, America becoming Israel's enemy. The Roman Empire had a long history of animosity toward the Jews, as does the revived Roman Empire.

Over seventy years ago, European nations, Russia, and America came together to stop Germany's advancement but not so much to avenge the deaths of millions of Jews and other citizens but to advance their agenda by arming both sides during World Wars I and II. Hitler was allowed to rise to prominence. Germany became a symbol for socialism. American technology and support were used to construct the German death camps. American financial institutions did launder money for the Nazi regime. Well-known names such as the Rockefellers, J. P. Morgan, Prescott Bush were involved. At the end of the war, Nazi scientists and other important Germans were sent to America and other countries to continue their diabolical research. Currently, Germany is overrun by Muslims who are not willing to blend into German society. Muslims have purchased vacant churches, turning them into mosques and establishing a no-go zone in Germany.

China

Year 2013, year of the snake—China is allied with Iran and Russia. Iran sells oil to China. China sells products to North Korea. China is considered number 1 in world economy. China will be drawn into the end-time conflict through commerce. July 2013 and 2014 news reports China and Russia engaged in joint military exercises. November 4, 2013, China unveils its nuclear submarine and boasts its ability of underwater deterrence against the United States. During the tribulation period, the Euphrates River will dry up to allow the kings of the east passage over land, air, and sea to the battle of Armageddon. Revelation 16:12, a recent report, 2015, indicated that ISIS had stopped the flow of water at a damn in Ramali, Iraq, causing the Euphrates River level to drop.

In times past, it was the hand of God that gathers those that hate Israel to come up against his people at the Valley of Jehoshaphat, named after the king of Judah who was buried in the City of David. In the account given in 2 Chronicles 20, we see that the chosen people were being threatened by a great multitude coming from Jordan. Judah and the people seek the Lord in prayer. He reminds God that he rules over the kingdoms of the heathen and his hand is powerful and mighty so that none can withstand him. He is the God that drove out the inhabitants of the land before the people of Israel and gave it to the seed of Abraham. His people built a sanctuary in the land. When evil comes upon them, they stand before the sanctuary in God's presence and cry unto God in the time of their affliction. Then the Spirit of the Lord came upon Zechariah and the elders. The word of the Lord said, "Do not fear or be dismayed by reason of this great multitude, for the battle is not yours but God's. Go down against them, you will not need to fight but stand still and see the salvation of the

Lord with you." All of Israel fell on their knees before God and worshipped him. The Levites stood up to praise the Lord with a loud voice. When they went out to confront the enemy, they sang unto the Lord in the beauty of holiness, singing praises to the Lord, for his mercy endures forever. God turned the enemies one against another, and they killed each other. King Jehoshaphat and all that were with him saw what the Lord had done, and they began to strip the dead of their wealth. It took three days to gather the booty. Returning to Jerusalem, they played upon the harps and trumpets. The fear of the Lord was upon the Gentile nations when they heard what the Lord had done for Israel. This historical fact occurred around three thousand years ago. A similar scenario came after Israel became a nation in 1948. Arab nation surrounded Israel to attack, and God defeated them and drove them back to their borders. In these last days, we will see the hand of the Lord come against the enemies of Israel because God does not change.

The Ezekiel prophecy for the **latter days** will come to pass at the end of the age, at a time when Israel's enemies have encompassed her. This period of time is different than other events in history. It is a specific time spelled out in scriptures. In Ezekiel 37, 38, 39 an important scenario is presented. Twenty-five hundred years ago, Ezekiel spoke specifically of a ruler called Gog from a region called Magog. Magog was the seventh son of Japheth.

Gog and Magog

Russia

Ezekiel 38:1–3

> *And the word of the Lord came unto me, saying son of man, set your face against Gog, the land of Magog, the chief prince of Meshech and Tubal and prophesy against them say, I am against you Gog the chief prince of Meshech and Tubal.*

The name Magog is associated with the land of Meshech and Tubal, ancient regions of Russia. During the northern migration of Japheth's descendants into modern-day Turkey, the region may have been part of the land of Meshech and Tubal. History associates Magog with the Scythians in the regions of the Black Sea (Russia), Cappadocia (near Haran), Medes (associated with Persia), and Greece associated with Anatolia/Turkey. Gog is the chief prince of the land of Magog. This could have a spiritual overtone in that the "prince" of Meshech and Tubal is a principality or demonic entity who controls leaders. The title Gog may have been applied to a leader in times past and points to a future leader who arises in the end of days leading a mighty army against Israel.

> *And I will turn you back and put hooks* into *your jaws and I will bring you forth with all your army, horses, men, all clothed with all sorts of armor, bucklers, shields, swords. And you will come from the place out of the* ***north*** *parts, you and many people with you … a mighty army.* (Ezekiel 38:4, 15)

Keeping with the perspective of the scriptures, Russia and Turkey are regions to the north of Israel. It seems there will be an initial incursion upon Israel at a time they are enjoying peace and safety. This could be a time when the third temple has been built and Jews are enjoying their new temple. Ezekiel 38:11. . . "*I will go up to the land of unwalled villages, I will go to them that are at rest, that dwell safely* …"

As we watch the unfolding of world events, it will be interesting to observe the interactions between world powers. If Gog is the leader of Russia and the Antichrist is leader of America, both emerging from the revived Roman Empire, it fulfills biblical scriptures that the Antichrist will be upset by rumblings coming from the north.

March 2014, Russia annexed part of the Ukraine, Crimea. America and European leaders were upset, threatening sanctions against Russia. The response from Russia was, "Bring it on," backed up by sending its fighter jets close to American coastal region. Russia threatened to cut the sale of oil to Europe. Russia is not on good terms with Turkey, United States, and Europe since it aligns itself with Syria, Iran, China, and North Korea. Russia has been consistent in its threats toward a nuclear confrontation with America. While the United States was working toward disarmament in the United States and other nations, Russia continued to build their nuclear arsenal and boasts of five thousand nuclear missiles. Iran is also working toward nuclear armament. Forbes reporter James Conca wrote that "America's most pressing concern is complacency." Near the end of 2015, Russia further inflames the ire of the United States by setting up military base in Syria and bombing ISIS strongholds. Russia exposes Turkey for its illegal deal of purchasing oil from ISIS, and the United States was complicit in protecting ISIS oil territory in Syria. As of August 9, 2016, media reported that Russia and Turkey had agreed to work together.

Some may ask, Why are the nations so determined to come against Israel? The scriptures answer:

> *To take a spoil, to take a prey, to turn your hand upon the desolate place that are now inhabited and upon the people that are gathered out of the nations which have gotten cattle and goods and dwell in the midst of the land … are you come to carry away silver and gold …* (Ezekiel 38:12)

And a rich reservoir of natural gas recently discovered in Israel and Israel's agriculture abundance.

Other nations will increase their involvement in the Ezekiel 38 scenario by agreement or disagreement. It may not be that they all come together at the same time but will be in alliance with the Gog and Magog conflict. Ezekiel 38:5,6,13 identify nations playing a role in the initial escalations being Iran, Egypt, Libya, Turkey, Russia, Saudi Arabia, and Europe.

Is Vladimir Putin Gog?

President Vladimir Putin is rising as an international leader demonstrating boldness and arrogance. When his first term as president ended, he manipulated Russian politics to put a puppet president in place until he could become president again. He has the attention of the world as well as prominent world leaders who are disturbed by the Russian leader's speech and actions. Fox News report, October 30, 2013, said that Russian president Putin is now considered the number one world leader, and American president, Obama, is now in second place. Forbes reported Russian president more powerful than Obama as most influential person in the world.

The alliance between Russia, Iran, Syria, China are a threat not only to Israel but to the international community. Russia can influence pro-Russian sentiment; China can influence other communist nations; and Iran can influence militant Islamist. They do not have to operate on sound rationale, but any lame reason can be drummed up to attack Israel. For instance, Putin murmurs that Israel is to blame for the Syrian stockpile of chemical weapons because Israel has WMD. This public statement would inflame other militant Islamist to come against Israel.

In August 2011, the Russian Federation, represented by its secretary, Nikolai Platonovich, met with the Iranian Supreme National Security Council, represented by Secretary Saaed Jalilik—wherein Russia pledged to support Iran if they were attacked by Israel or NATO. Russia will sell Iran antiaircraft weapons and help rebuild their nuclear reactor.

Russian actions and comments inflame the United States and Europe. News headlines in 2013 read as follows: *AP*, "Russia Reemerges as Mideast Player"; *New York Times*, "Putin Shoves Obama aside, and He Seized Syrian Agenda, Sparking Tensions." Putin offers a plan to neutralize Syrian chemical weapons, which removed the threat of United States bombing Syria. *Los Angeles Times*, "Syrian Weapons Deal Help Putin and Assad." Foundation for the Defense of Democracies said, "Putin plans to diminish the United States." Putin said, "America is not special." Putin spoke about ensuring freedom for Christians in Russia. Putin's comment on abortion was, "The Russian population is basically older people, and abortion has prevented a younger population from growing." Putin's comment on homosexuals was, "Russia will not embrace a homosexual agenda. Homosexuals can conduct their relationships in private." Putin's positions on social issues are in contradiction to Obama's position on freedom of religion, abortion, and homosexuality.

The scripture prophesies Russia moving against Israel.

> *And you will come up against my people of Israel as a cloud to cover the land, it will be in **the latter days** and I will bring you against my land that the heathen may know me when I will be sanctified in you O **Gog** before their eyes ... Are you he of whom I have spoken in old time by my servants the prophets of Israel which prophesied in those days many years that I would bring you against them? And it will come to pass at the same time when Gog will come against the land of Israel ... that my fury will come up in my face. For in my jealousy and in the fire of my wrath have I spoken and in that day there will be **a great shaking in the land of Israel.*** (Ezekiel 38:16–19)

- Gog is associated with the head of Russia.
- The incursion will encompass a large portion of Israel.
- This will occur in the latter days, which is now.
- Islamic nations will know the God of Israel.
- This war predicted thousands of years ago.
- When Gog attacks Israel, the wrath of God will be unleashed.

God declares in Ezekiel 38:23, "*I will magnify myself and sanctify myself and I will be known in the eyes of many nations and they shall know that I am the Lord.*" Apparently, the first incursion against Israel was not successful. The unrepentant still curse God and reassemble their armies. God amps up his response, and these judgments tie into the judgments outlined in the book of Revelation during the final years of the tribulation. Revelation 6:12 introduces the opening of the seven seals, which speak of a great earthquake, sun black as sackcloth, blood, the stars fell onto the earth, the heaven departed as scroll, mountains and islands are removed. Many will die.

- There will be a great shaking in the land of Israel. Five earthquakes occurred in Israel during the month of October 2013.
- Sea creatures, birds, beasts, creeping things, and men will shake in the presence of God.
- Earthquakes will cause the mountains to crumble, steep places, and every wall will fall.
- Men will kill each other (confusion).
- There will be pestilence with blood.

- God will rain upon the enemies, hailstones, fire, and brimstone.

Ezekiel 39:1–4

Israel

The opening passage begins with the prophet Ezekiel saying …

Son of man, prophesy against Gog, and say, thus say the Lord God, behold I am against you O Gog, chief prince of Meschech and Tubal and I will turn you back and leave but the sixth [1/6] *part of thee and will cause you to come from the north parts upon the mountains of Israel and I will smite your bow out of your left hand and will cause your arrows to fall out of your right hand … you will fall upon the mountains of Israel, you and all your bands and the people that are with you. I will give you to the ravenous birds of every sort and to the beasts of the field to be devoured.*

This incursion causes death of five-sixth of the invading armies. Their carcass will be eaten by birds and beast. For the past ten years or more, many birds of prey have been gathering in Israel.

Assemble yourselves … that you may eat flesh and drink blood. (Ezekiel 39:17)

And it will come to pass in that day, that I will give unto Gog a place there of graves in Israel, the valley of the passengers on the east of the sea and it will stop the noses of the passengers and there will they bury God and all his multitude and it will be called the valley of Hamon-gog. And seven months will the house of Israel be burying them that they may cleanse the land. (Ezekiel 39:11–15)

Gog and his armies will be buried in graves in Israel. The dead bodies will cause a stink that those passing by will hold their noses. It will take seven months to bury all the remains. People will be hired by Israel to bury the dead. At the end of the seven months, scouts will search the land; and finding a bone, they will place a marker there until the buriers have buried it. The burial site will be called the valley of Hamon-gog in the City of Hamonah.

It will take seven years to burn the weapons and debris.

And they that dwell in the cities of Israel will go forth and will set on fire and burn the weapons both the shields, the bucklers, the bows and arrows, hand-staves, spears, and they will burn them with fire seven years. (Ezekiel 39:9)

There is devastation in Israel and in the enemy territories. God levels the playing field, raining fire upon the Russian homeland and the Europeans nations. February 2013, a meteor hit Russia, raining down fire. This was a precursor.

> *I will send a fire on Magog and among them that dwell carelessly in the isles and they will know that I am the Lord.* (Ezekiel 39:6)

At this juncture, some of the invading armies have retreated and regrouped. A nation from the East, perhaps China, will gather a two hundred million–man army, joining the remnant of enemy armies. According to Daniel, they seem to get involved near the end of the tribulation to coincide with the gathering for the Battle of Armageddon. As we discussed, the Gog and Magog conflict will have a domino effect moving the world toward World War III, culminating into the battle of Armageddon.

The axis of evil with Satan as the general one-world leader, one-world religious leader, Gog of Magog and the Babylonian world system are all aligned and in place. Satan will fight to the bitter end along with the wicked nations. They want to do battle with Creator God, Yeshua Messiah, who will be seen coming with the armies of heaven.

Seven Years of Tribulation on Earth

We discussed incidents leading up to the beginning of the tribulation. Prophecy in many instances is threefold. It may point to a past fulfillment, present or future event to be fulfilled. Events linked to the tribulation may be symbolic or literal. Some events appear to have taken place before certain events that will take place during the seven-year tribulation on earth. There are also events in line with the tribulation but carried out in heaven. This seven-year time frame is also referred to as a week of time as in Daniel's seventieth week. It is a time referred to as Jacob's trouble, or great tribulation. Luke 21:22 refers to it as the days of vengeance, where all things that are written may be fulfilled.

The apostles asked Jesus three questions: When will these things be? What will be the sign of his coming? When will be the end of the world? In Matthew 24:3–14, Jesus provides many signs that point to the <u>beginning</u> of sorrows as highlighted in chapter 16, Day of the Lord.

Now we are seeing the signs of the <u>end of the age</u> and the beginning of the seven-year tribulation period as given in Matthew 24:15–28. In brief, we are seeing world conflict, pestilence, famine, unusual weather, persecution, hatred of all things godly, and the Antichrist and false prophet are in position. We are waiting on the following soon-to-occur events:

- A covenant made with many.

- Ezekiel 38 incursion.
- Appearance of Elijah.
- Building of the third temple.
- Antichrist will desecrate the third temple.
- Antichrist will unleash his wrath against Israel.
- Warning to flee.

The final years of the tribulation will be ushered in by a great earthquake, destroying one-tenth of the city, killing thousands of people. The survivors were frightened and gave glory to the God of heaven.

Old Testament Prophecies Pointing to the Great Tribulation

> *And at that time will Michael stand up and the great prince which stands for the children of thy people and there will be a time of trouble such as never was since there was a nation …* (Daniel 12:1–3)

Israel had been warned thousands of years ago regarding a time of trouble.

> *And it will come to pass that in all the land, said the Lord, two parts therein will be cut off and die but the third will be left therein. I will bring the third part through the fire and will refine them as silver is refined and will try them as gold is tried and they will call on my name and I will hear them. I will say, it is my people and they will say the Lord is my God.* (Zechariah 13:8)

This passage is inclusive of Jews and Gentiles during the great tribulation. It is telling us that many Jews and Gentiles will die. Two-thirds of eight million living in modern-day Israel would be around six million people—a mix of unbelievers, Orthodox Jews, secularists, and others. The remnants could represent those who accepted Jesus as Messiah during the tribulation. If this scripture is making reference to the whole world of people left behind, then only one-third (two billion estimate) of the people did not give their allegiance to Antichrist and will be spared. As the believers' deeds were tested by fire at the Bema Seat, the scriptures tell us the deeds of this remnant will also be tested as in fire, and they will emerge purified.

> *Many will be purified and made white and tried …* (Daniel 12:10)
>
> *But you oh Daniel, shut up the words and seal the book even to the time of the end … And one said to the man clothed in linen which was upon the waters of the river, how long shall it be to the end of these wonders? And I heard the man clothed in linen which was upon the waters of the river, held up his hands unto heaven and swear by him that lives forever that it will be for a time, times*

> *and a half...* [three and a half years] *... Daniel said my lord, what will be the end of these things? He said go your way for the words are closed up and sealed until* the time of the end. (Daniel 12:4–10)

The above passage confirms the time frame of the tribulation will be at the end of the age, which has arrived, and stage 3 of the tribulation will endure for three and a half years.

Books of Daniel and Revelation

By paralleling the writings of Daniel around 535 BC with the writings of John around AD 95, we weave a picture of the tribulation period. Daniel was a captive in Babylon, and John was a prisoner on the Island of Patmos. Daniel was a minister unto God and John, disciple of Jesus, and pastor of church of Ephesus—both holy and faithful unto the Lord.

> *And I saw another mighty angel come down from heaven, clothed with a cloud and a rainbow was upon his head and his face was as it were the sun and his feet as pillars of fire. He had in his hand a little book open and he set his right foot upon the sea and his left foot on the earth. He cried with a loud voice as a lion roars and when he had cried seven thunders uttered their voices. And when the seven thunders had uttered their voices, I was about to write and I heard a voice from heaven saying to me, seal up those things which the seven thunders utters and do not write them. And the angel I saw stand upon the sea and upon the earth lifted up his hand to heaven and swore by him that lives forever who created heaven and earth ... that there should be time no longer.* (Revelation 10:1)

We highlight a few things in Daniel 12 and Revelation 10:

- Both Daniel and John receive a visitation from an angel standing on sea and land.
- Both are told to seal up the writings. God has not revealed all to mankind.
- Daniel asks, "How long will it be until the end?" We can answer his question now because we have the revelation of John.
- John is told that by the end of the tribulation, time is no longer (delayed) and all things are finished. Following passage in Daniel is also associated with time.

> *Blessed is he that waits and comes to the 1335 days.* (Daniel 12:13)

Three and one half years is 1,260 days based on 360 days in a year; add forty-five days is 1,335 days. These forty-five additional days continue after the end of the tribulation. It is a short intermission. Since it is a blessing, perhaps it applies to the saints who died during the tribulation and are awaiting to be called forth in the end-time harvest as indicated in Daniel 12:2–3:

> *And many of them that sleep in the dust of the earth shall awake some to everlasting life and some to shame and everlasting contempt. And they that be wise shall shine as the brightness of the firmaments and they that turn many to righteousness as the stars forever.*

In Matthew 24:31, we pick up this same theme of an end-time harvest. This is stage 3 of the Resurrection, the great harvest.

Three Stages of the Tribulation

> *For these be the days of vengeance, that all things which are written may be fulfilled.* (Luke 21:22)

Jesus tells us that these events are during the end of days. As a marker in time, the second temple was destroyed in AD 70 by the Romans. The destruction of the second temple was a harbinger pointing to the third temple destruction during the tribulation. During the second temple era, Rome ruled and required Christians and Jews to pledge loyalty to the empire of Caesar or die. Many refused to worship the pagan deities, and many died. So will it be during the tribulation period when Antichrist and false prophet will demand worship.

We have divided the tribulation into three stages. Pretribulation events are moving the world into the first three and a half years (stage 1), transitional period (stage 2), and the final three and a half years (stage 3): referred to as the great tribulation. There are a total of twenty-one judgments, of which some overlap. There are seven seals, seven trumpets, and seven vial judgments disclosed in the book of Revelation. The books of Revelation and Daniel are not true to a chronological arrangement, and our commentary is arranged to align with the unfolding events of the tribulation.

The Stage Is Set in Israel

Israel is God's timepiece. It is center stage. As the curtain parts, the whole world is watching Israel. The mind-set of Jews in the twenty-first century can be categorized as secular, orthodox, liberal, messianic, or conservative. Scripture speaks about the evolved mind-set of Israel coming into the time of the end. Romans 11:25, blindness in part, some Jews will see Jesus as Messiah; while others will still have scales on their eyes. National Israel will be confident in itself economically and militarily.

The 2012 presidential election in the United States resulted in a second term for Barack Obama. Statistics indicated that 69 percent of American Jews voted for Obama. This is a real problem. Many Hollywood celebrities are Jewish. Many Democrats such as Bernie Sanders are Jewish. Supporters of Obama such as George Soros are Jewish. Jews living in Israel were hopeful that Obama would save them. This scenario could align with scripture that predicts the Jews will accept a man coming in his own name as a messianic figure. They pledged their allegiance to and put their trust in a man who will betray them. His words declare Israel as an ally, yet his actions are clearly anti-Israel. Specifically, calling for Israel to return to 1967 borders and give up more land to the Palestians. He does not recognize Jerusalem as its capital and calls to partition Jerusalem. Obama signed an agreement with Iran allowing for the completion of their nuclear goals, lifting sanctions against Iran and giving them $150 billion. On several occasions, Obama has snubbed the prime minister of Israel. One instance is when Prime Minister Netanyahu spoke before the United States Congress regarding the Iranian nuclear threat and the Obama administration was livid, refusing to meet with the prime minister while in the United States. In retaliation, Obama threatened to vote for Palestinian statehood at the United Nations. The United States tells Israel not to launch a preempted strike against Iran, who publically states Israel should be annihilated, or the United States would have to intervene in behalf of Iran. October 2014, Obama publically rebuked Israel and suggested his friends to join in the condemnation against them for planning to build 2,600 housing units in Jerusalem as an extension of its Jewish neighborhood. Unlike Muslims in their occupied territory, Jews are restricted from living in Palestinian regions. In Israel, all are welcomed. White House spokesman, Josh Earnest, stated, "This development will only draw condemnation from the international community, distance Israel from even its closest allies, poison the atmosphere not only with the Palestinians but with the very Arab governments with which Prime Minister Netanyahu said he wanted to build relations." These comments and others are an attempt by Obama to reassure Mahmoud Abbas that he would still stand by the Palestinians despite Abbas's hate speech at the United Nations (*EMET News Service*, Isi Leibler).

The United States demands Israel to restrain its attack on Gaza, as if Israel does not have the right to defend its land from hundreds of incoming missiles from Gaza. While taking time embarrassing Israel, Obama's comments regarding ISIS are tepid. Obama refuses to label them as Islamic terrorists. ISIS has killed twelve thousand Yazidis in Iraq. Hundreds of thousands of Christians are targeted and killed by ISIS. ISIS kills Muslims whom they consider apostate. Also under attack are the Mandaeans, a Gnostic following; 90 percent have fled Iraq. Hitler was allowed to kill German Jews, Christians, Gypsies, handicap people. Obama did not condemn Hitler and has himself allowed for the systematic death of millions in the Middle East.

Regardless of US citizens' outcry against funding terrorists, the Obama administration is hell-bent on sending funds to Hamas in Gaza, Hezbolla in Lebanon, the Taliban in Afghanistan, rebels in Syria, as well as the Muslim Brotherhood in Egypt, Turkey, Pakistan, Iran, and Iraq—who are sworn enemies of Israel and call for the destruction of Israel and the United States. Israel's alliance with America is out of desperation.

American Jews have embraced a man who stands against the God of Israel. Obama stands for all things that are an abomination unto God. Many Jews are comfortable in America, having a form of godliness, but their hearts are far removed from Yahweh. Just as Jews got comfortable and confident in Germany, living under the illusion of peace and safety, and then sudden destruction will make the rounds again. The Jews know abortion is murder and is the shedding of innocent blood. Their ancestors sacrificed their children to Moleck. The Jews know that homosexuality is an abomination before God, and for these sins Sodom and Gomorrah were destroyed.

Some Jews may believe Obama is their only hope for peace, and that mind-set may be the precursor for the acceptance of a false messiah who promises peace but brings destruction.

Satan's Future Demise

The beginning of the tribulation also signals the end of the game for Satan. Following the war in heaven (precreation), Lucifer and his evil angels were excommunicated from the heavenly realm wherein the Holy God dwells. God has allowed Satan, a fallen angel, and his followers for the past six thousand years to roam to and fro through the earth and has limited their access into the heavenly domain. Why God has allowed Satan this longtime span to corrupt and destroy his creation is unclear. Satan rebelled against God by creating chaos in the heavenly realm and upon the terrestrial plain. His next act of rebellion was to deceive Adam and Eve. Satan continued his war against God by corrupting the human genome, teaching mankind forbidden knowledge, establishing occultism and idolatry throughout all ages. Satan, the god over the nations of the world, took away peace and gave scientists knowledge to build weapons of mass destruction and create biological weapons that would slaughter millions. Disguising evil spirits as aliens from other planets has created a great delusion that beings on other planets came to earth and created the human race. The practice of sacrificing children to pagan gods in ancient times has continued into the modern-day culture of abortion. The abomination of homosexuality and immorality invade every aspect of society. The introduction of false religions replaces God and makes way for the one-world religion and the false prophet to emerge.

Revelation 12, in summary, speaks about another war in heaven with the dragon and his angels who fight against Michael and his angels, resulting in Satan being cast out of his place in the heavenly domain to the earth for all to see. Matthew 24:29 points to the end of the tribulation … The stars will fall from heaven, and the powers of the heavens will be shaken. Sometimes "stars" are a reference to angels. So what we see here is God shaking the heavens and the angels are falling from heaven to earth. Does this mean Satan's cloak of invisibility will be lifted and all can see him for what he really is? We cannot accurately state when Satan and his angels will be cast upon the earth. However, we were given scripture that tells us Satan and his demons are literally on the earth, yet invisible.

At the end of the tribulation we see that Satan, his regime, and wicked people are destroyed by Jesus with the brightness of his coming.

> *And then will that wicked be revealed whom the Lord shall consume with the spirit of his mouth and shall destroy with the brightness of his coming: even him whose coming is after the working of Satan with all power and signs and lying wonders, all deceivableness of unrighteousness in them that perish because they received not the love of the truth that they might be saved …* (2 Thessalonians 2:8)

As mentioned, the stage is set in Israel; and the primary characters involved with the events of the tribulation will be Satan, the Antichrist, the false prophet, left-behind Gentile nations and left-behind Jews, two Jewish witnesses, and 144,000 Jews who are sealed.

Stage One of the Tribulation

The book of Revelation begins with the revelation of Jesus given to John in a vision of events that <u>must shortly come to pass (because now) the time is at hand</u> (Revelation 1:1–3). The time frame begins with John in AD 90 and into the twenty-first century. Jesus reveals himself to John as the Son of Man, clothed with a garment down to the foot and girt about the paps with a golden girdle. His head and hairs were white like wool … and his eyes were as flames of fire, feet like fine brass and his voice as the sound of many waters … holding seven stars, and out of his mouth went a sharp two-edged sword. His countenance was as the sun … and when I saw Him, I fell at his feet as dead. He laid his right hand upon me, saying unto me, "Fear not I am the first and the last" (Revelation 1:13–17). This event experienced by John was in his present time.

Jesus gives John messages for the seven churches in Asia that existed at that time. John confirms Jesus, *which is, which was, and which is to come.* This speaks to the preexistent Jesus, to the crucified and risen Jesus, and to the Second Coming as King of Kings. John emphasizes Jesus is the faithful first begotten of the dead and the prince of the kings of the earth and his shed blood cleanses us from sin, allowing believers to become kings and priests. We are enthroned with Jesus. We are seated in heavenly places. These Revelation promises were activated at the time of the Resurrection and are prevalent for all believers today.

John is called to come up to the heavenly realm where he will be shown present and future events. In his present time, he sees the throne of God and one who sat on the throne. John sees the risen Jesus in his glory. John sees twenty-four elders clothed in white, wearing gold crowns, and these represent the twelve tribes of Israel and the apostles all who died before John. He sees the four beasts and the host of heaven. Revelation 4 indicates John is in his present time, before his death and while the churches were still in place. John then sees Jesus holding a book with seven seals. Jesus, the lion of the tribe of Judah, the Root of David, has prevailed to open the book and to lose the seven seals thereof. Revelation 5:5—this passage tells us that at that time, **Jesus did open the first four seals,** releasing the four horsemen of the apocalypse.

Stage 1 of the tribulation is preceded by pretribulation events occurring over the past two thousand years, moving toward the beginning of the seven-year tribulation period. These pretribulation events may not be measured in a specific time frame, but their impact has manifested in a limited outcome throughout the earth as a precursor to what is to come. These things spoken of by Jesus in Matthew 24 will increase in intensity up to and through the seven-year tribulation period.

The Witnesses and the 144,000 Servants

The fulfillment of the two witnesses and the 144,000 servants are associated with the beginning of the tribulation. After they are sealed, it appears the 144,000 will still be evangelizing at the time of the fifth trumpet.

Revelation 9:4—the angels are told to hurt only those who have not the seal of God in their forehead. This could also mean that through the ministry of the 144,000, many will come to Christ during the tribulation and will be sealed by the Holy Spirit. It also tells us that unrepentant people will suffer because they took the mark or the seal of the beast instead.

It is possible that the 144,000 individuals have already been identified and are being prepared for their end-of-days ministry. If we understand scripture, these people will go through the first half of the tribulation. It will coincide with the third temple having been completed and then desecrated by the Antichrist. These sealed individuals may be on the scene to help the Jews to accept Jesus before they are slaughtered by the Antichrist.

The 144,000 believers have agreed to be martyrs during the tribulation, knowing their souls will go to be with Jesus.

We summarize a few things that pertain to these people:

- They are sealed by God to do his bidding for a period of time.

- They are virtuous; there was no guile or fault found in them.
- They are Jews from the twelve tribes of Israel.
- They believe Yeshua is their Messiah.

Continuing to follow the events of the 144,000, we see them after their work is completed.

> *And I looked and a lamb stood on Mount Zion and with him a hundred and forty-four thousand having his Father's name written in their foreheads.* (Revelation 14:1)

- They follow the Lamb wherever he goes.
- They are in heaven and singing a song only they know.
- They are seen on Mount Zion with Jesus when he returns to earth.
- These 144,000 will be assigned a high position in the millennial kingdom.

Two Witnesses

We ran across an interesting article and picture taken by *Sagacity News*, March 12, 2013, of a barefoot person—fully bearded, clothed in sackcloth—seen praying in Vatican City in Saint Peter's Square. No one knew who he was or where he came from. He held a wooden staff. He was not attempting to draw attention to himself, and he mysteriously left as he had come. Was this a precursor of one of the two witnesses?

In the book of Zechariah 4:3, he sees two olive trees. He asks, "Who are these?" and in verse 14, he is told they are the two anointed ones that stand by the Lord of the whole earth. We believe this scripture points to the two witnesses who will return at the end of the age.

> *And it came to pass as they still went on and talked that behold there appeared a chariot of fire and horse of fire and parted them both asunder and Elijah went up by a whirlwind into heaven.* (2 Kings 2:11)

We begin our study on the two witnesses by allowing readers to know that Elijah was taken into the heavens, and in the following book, we see Elijah returning.

> *Behold I will send you Elijah the prophet before the coming of the great and dreadful day of the Lord.* (Malachi 4:5)

The Bible has established that Elijah is one of the two witnesses. The other witness is either Moses or Enoch. Some scholars believe it will be Enoch since he and Elijah were the only two people who did not die but were translated alive into the presence of God. Other scholars believe it could be Moses because he turned the waters to blood in Egypt and Elijah held back the rain for three and a half years.

We are given the understanding of the scope of work these two will carry out as stated in Revelation 11:3: "*And I will give power unto my two servants and they will prophesy three and a half years, clothed in sackcloth.*" Their ministry will be during the first half of the tribulation in Jerusalem. We further see they have been empowered by God. Revelation 11:6, "*These have power to shut heaven that it rain not in the days of their prophecy and have power over waters to turn them to blood and to smite the earth with all plagues as often as they will.*" During the first half of the tribulation, the two witnesses will have power to turn water into blood, hold back rain, breathe fire from their mouth, and to bring plagues upon the earth.

In the following scripture, we see that the unholy trio will kill them.

> *And when they will finish their testimony, the beast that came out of the bottomless pit* [Satan, Antichrist, false prophet] *will make war against them and will overcome them and kill them. And their dead bodies will lie in the street of the great city which spiritually is called Sodom* [near the Dead Sea] *and Egypt* [land of Canaan] *where also our Lord was crucified.* (Revelation 11:7)

- They lay dead in the street for three and a half days.
- Jerusalem, once the holy city, is now desecrated and rift with corruption.
- Through media, the world can see the two witnesses lying dead. The world has been desensitized to seeing dead people lying in the street. But for these two, the world is happy to see them killed.
- They supernaturally arise and ascend to join the multitude in heaven

> *And after 3 ½ days the Spirit of life from God entered into them and they stood upon their feet and great fear fell upon them which saw them. And they heard a great voice from heaven saying unto them, come up here. And they ascended up to heaven in a cloud and their enemies beheld them. And at that same hour was there a great earthquake and a tenth part of the city fell and in the earthquake were slain seven thousand and the remnant were terrified and gave glory to the God of heaven.* (Revelation 11:11–13)

We reviewed the ministry of the two witnesses and the 144,000 servants of God, and we introduced the major actors in this play: Satan, Antichrist, and false prophet.

Satan is referred to as the following:

- Dragon, serpent, devil (Revelation 12:9)

- Red dragon with seven heads and ten horns (Revelation 12:3)
- Satan called Abaddon in Hebrew and Apollo or Apollyon in Greek (Revelation 9:11)
- Angel of the bottomless pit (Revelation 9:11)
- Beast of the bottomless pit (Revelation 11:7)

Antichrist is referred to as the following:

- Son of perdition
- Man of sin
- The beast out of the sea (Revelation 13)
- Little horn

False prophet is referred to as the following:

- Beast out of the earth (Revelation 13)

Opening of Seal Judgments

Once again we join John as he describes events in Revelation 5. John sees a scroll/book sealed with seven seals in the hand of Yahweh, God the Father. In the midst of the throne stood a Lamb with seven horns and eyes, which are the seven spirits of God sent forth into all the earth. Yeshua, the Lamb slain at Calvary, took the book out of the Father's right hand. Then the four beasts, the twenty-four elders, angels, and ten thousand times ten thousand of saints fell before the Lamb, crying, "Worthy is the Lamb." The Old Testament saints sing a new song, which reminds us of the song of Moses. At this point in time, John sees the people who were part of the First Fruits Resurrection at the time of Jesus's Resurrection.

Revelation 7:9, 14—John is given a future vision of a great multitude of people standing before the throne of God and is told these are those which came out of great tribulation and have washed their robes and made them white in the blood of the Lamb. This statement distinguishes the persecution, or trials common to mankind, since his creation from those that die during the great tribulation, which will occur at some point in the twenty-first century.

First Four Seals

The first four seals released the four horsemen of the apocalypse. These passages are symbolic and transcend literal time, but the symbolism has manifested throughout the real world. We can go back to 500 BC and find in the writing of Zechariah 6:1–7: a reference to red, black, white, pale grizzled horses. The angel told Zechariah that these are they that the Lord sent to walk to and fro through the earth. Zechariah is told by the angel these are four spirits of heaven sent forth by the Lord and are associated with judgment. Following, we are given the significance of these judgments.

Opening the First Seal

Revelation 6:1, the Lamb opened the first seal; voices of the four beast sounding like thunder said, "Come and see." I saw a white horse, and he that sat on him had a bow (political and military power), and a crown (global authority/victory) was given unto him, and he went forth conquering.

This first horse and its rider represent archetypes of Antichrist prevalent in the world. Throughout the history of mankind, there have been many Antichrists who came and conquered, but we believe the final Antichrist is currently on the scene. The identity of the Antichrist will be known to his followers who have been working toward this crescendo. A foreshadow of the Antichrist will be known to those who understand Bible prophecy. The secular, ungodly masses will be unaware of what is going on, even though for years preachers have proclaimed the Gospel of which they had not ears to hear. They will believe a lie perpetrated by Satan.

Before we jump ahead further in the tribulation period, we need to recall events that led up to the onset of the tribulation. As previously discussed, the enemies of Israel have escalated their campaign as predicted in Psalm 83, Isaiah, Ezekiel 38 and 39. The Antichrist comes to a devastated Middle East region, offering a resolution of sorts. It can no longer be a resolution for peace between Israel and Islam. It cannot be to turn back the hand of a nuclear Iran. At this time, we can speculate it could be about the third temple, of which Antichrist did support and later will desecrate.

> *And he shall confirm the covenant with* ***many*** *for one week* [seven years] *and in the middle of the week he will cause the sacrifice and the oblation to cease.* (Daniel 9:27)

This scripture is two parts: (1) first three and a half years seems to make way for the building of the third temple and between the first half of the tribulation and before the start of the final half; (2) he breaks the covenant in the middle of the seven years and defiles the temple, which causes the rituals to cease. Jesus said in Matthew 24:15: "*When you see the abomination of desolation, spoken of by Daniel the prophet, stand in the holy place, then let them which be in Judea flee to the mountains.*" Jesus warns those in Israel to prepare to take refuge. Antichrist will declare himself god, demand all to worship him; he will speak blasphemies and will set up the image of the beast, and all must take its mark. This will signal the beginning of the third stage, or the final three and a half years of the great tribulation.

Past abominations in the temple occurred. The Romans completely destroyed the temple in AD 70. Following this event, great persecution came upon the Jews and Christians who sought refuge in other nations. The future abomination of desolation will be played out in the coming third temple.

What is the abomination that causes desolation? The Babylonian system referred to as the mother of harlots holds a cup full of the abominations of the nations. The abomination is a cocktail of all ungodliness. The Antichrist is the embodiment of abominations; just his presence in the Temple is defilement. But the Antichrist must do something that is more despicable. Will he sacrifice an unclean animal, or will he set up an idolatrous image? We definitely know there is going to be an image of the beast. This image may be possessed by an evil spirit, or it may be high-tech robotics. It will be able to speak, and it may be able to detect those who do not worship the beast to be killed. The desecration of the temple will be conducted by the Antichrist himself. . . . "*So that he as God sits in the temple of God showing himself that he is God.*" 2 Thessalonians 4

We are not 100 percent sure where the headquarters of the Antichrist will be, but we do see him here in Israel.

Opening Seals Two, Three, Four

Second seal releases the red horse, and the rider was given power to take peace from the earth that they should kill one another, and there was given to him a great sword. This is a symbolic picture associated with wars and strife worldwide (Revelation 6:3–4)

Third seal releases the black horse, and the rider had a pair of balances in his hand. A measure of wheat for a penny and three measures of barley for a penny and see you hurt not the oil and wine. This is associated with the downturn in the world economic systems due to food shortages, famine, and is aligned with the Babylon harlot—a symbol of corruption and greed (Revelation 6:5–6)

Fourth seal releases the pale horse, and the rider's name was Death, and hell followed with him. Power was given to them over the fourth part of the earth to kill with sword, hunger, and with the beasts of the earth. Death has been ongoing for thousands of years, but during the final days, approximately one-fourth of the earth's population will die. If there are eight billion people on the planet, two billion will die by sword, hunger, disease, natural disasters. The book of Revelation tells us that other coming judgments will kill billions more (Revelation 6:7–8).

We tie together the impact of all four seal consequences as having already manifested upon the earth for an unspecified period of time and will intensify as the end of the age comes to a close. The four riders are symbolic of entities that bring about calamity, suffering, and death.

Before proceeding to the opening of the fifth, sixth, and seventh seals, we need to review the person of Antichrist.

Timing of the Final Antichrist

The final Antichrist will come and be revealed at the end of the age and at a time when the one-world order has completed its plans for world domination. That time has arrived. Initially, the Antichrist will not be seen as a tyrant but as a charismatic savior, bringing the solution for world peace; and through peace, he will destroy many. His rise to power comes on the heels of war, economic crisis, depression, famine, and pandemic diseases that ravage the world. These events are already in full swing. In the midst of war, the Antichrist will be on the scene, making agreements with many. Habakkuk 1:11 points to a world leader who breaks a treaty, changes his mind, and makes transgression against God while ascribing this power to his god. In Habakkuk 2:4–19, other inferences are made to Antichrist, whose soul is lifted up and is not upright in him. We know the man of sin will be empowered by Satan. He is full of pride, and his desire is enlarged as hell and is as death. He cannot be satisfied but continues to gather the nations under his control.

As the world enters the tribulation period, the Antichrist will receive supernatural power to influence the nations of the world. He will appeal to the Jews, who may receive him a messianic figure to save them from the end-time persecution and war. Jesus said they rejected their Messiah but will receive one who comes in his own name. To the religion of Islam, he may be their Imam Mahdi. To the apostate Christendom, he will be the Christ spirit. He will be Buddha or Lord Krishna to the pagans. To the new agers, he will be Maitreia.

In 2 Thessalonians 2:1–4, we are given clues to anticipate the general timing of the revealing of the Antichrist:

> *We beseech you brothers by the <u>coming of our Lord Jesus</u> Christ and by <u>our gathering together unto him</u> that you be not soon shaken in mind or be troubled neither by spirit nor by word nor by letter from us. Let no man deceive you for that day will not come except there come a* ***falling away first and that man of sin be revealed, the son of perdition*** *who opposes and exalts himself above all that is called God or that is worshiped so that he as God sits in the temple of God showing himself that he is God.*

In the above passage, Paul tells the believers not to be discouraged because the Lord Jesus would come and gather them together (Rapture) unto himself. Next he tells them that "day," or tribulation period, is not happening at their time in history. Paul then tells them the season leading up to the tribulation would be preceded by a falling away. Many scholars have come to realize that the falling away most likely pertains to apostate Christendom falling away from the Gospel truth, replacing biblical doctrine with the doctrines of demons. Revelation 3:14 speaks to the church of Laodicea, which is representative of the spiritual condition of the apostate church in the end of days. The "day" that Paul spoke of almost two thousand years ago has arrived. This scripture states that **after** the falling away **first**, then the Antichrist will be revealed. We can attest to the signs of ungodliness and heresy we find in the church today. This falling away could also refer to a general worldwide descent into ungodliness as in "perilous times" and "the spirit of iniquity."

Understanding this prophecy is not cut and dry. Considering the Rapture, people are caught up to meet the Lord in the air more so than a falling away. As Christendom continues its downward spiral into apostasy, the man of sin will be revealed. The timing and revealing of the Antichrist will not be a worldwide announcement that Antichrist is on the scene. The final Antichrist will be aligned, involved, or associated with the Middle East chaos: a seven-year covenant and rebuilding of the third temple in Jerusalem, which occurs during the first three and a half years of the tribulation. This final man of sin, son of perdition, having risen from obscurity, is currently a global figure, recognized throughout the world.

Mystery of Iniquity

> *And now you know what withholds that he might be revealed in his time. For the **mystery of iniquity** does already work and only he who now lets will let until he be taken out of the way. And then shall that wicked be revealed whom the Lord will consume with the spirit of his mouth and will destroy with the brightness of his coming.* (2 Thessalonians 2:6–8)

The Antichrist is on a leash. His actions are limited until "*he who now lets will let until he be taken out of the way.*" The Holy Spirit is limiting or restraining the works of Satan and his minions. When the Holy Spirit is taken out of the way, a greater darkness will engulf the world. We cannot accurately predict when the Holy Spirit will be fully taken out of the way, and there is not a promise that the Rapture of the saints will occur before the Holy Spirit is removed, and the Rapture may not occur before the exposure of the Antichrist.

We cannot know how much we must endure before we are caught up. Martyrs for Christ began during John's time and will continue through the tribulation. There is a little encouragement, if we remember the words of Saint Paul: "*None of us lives to himself and no man dies to himself, whether we live unto the Lord and whether we die unto the Lord, we are the Lord's*" (Romans 14:7–8). The Holy Spirit is still drawing many to salvation as in the latter rain now being poured out around the world. Millions are turning to Christ and receiving his gift of salvation. It is Jesus's desire that no one should perish but all come into his amazing grace. Even so, we can still sense the lifting of the Spirit as we witness unprecedented wickedness enveloping the globe.

The scripture tells us the mystery of iniquity is already at work since the fall of Satan, Adam, and Eve. It is defined as a mystery because its relevance had been concealed, but at the end of the age, the mystery is revealed unto us. The combination of both words allows us to know there are wicked spiritual entities influencing mankind, and it will focus on a man of sin, a man of perdition, to carry out ungodliness, abominations, and lawlessness. The wicked trio will not be destroyed until the Second Coming at the end of the tribulation … "*The Lord will consume them with the spirit of his mouth and will destroy with the brightness of his coming.*"

"Man of Sin" will be revealed by specific actions, such as establishing a covenant/peace treaty with Israel, embracing sexual sin and ungodliness, the desecration of the temple and his claim to be God. The man of sin, the Antichrist, will blaspheme God and publically oppose all that is godly or that is worshipped. His greatest hatred is toward Israel and Christians.

Antichrist and false prophet are empowered by Satan to perform signs and lying wonders to deceive the unrighteous, who will perish because they rejected the truth of God, repented not, and rejected God's gift of salvation. Instead God sends a strong delusion, and they believe a lie.

The term "man of sin" is interchangeable with "son of perdition"; both titles allude to a final destruction that will befall all evil persons who reject God and embrace Satan. It is like saying "Jesus is the son of David" or "The saints are the sons of God," therein representing righteousness. 2 Peter 3:7 the term *perdition* suggests judgment and destruction. The "son of perdition" will bring destruction upon himself and unredeemed mankind. Judas Iscariot is referred to as the "son of perdition," and in the end he was destroyed by his own doing. John 17:12, after Judas betrayed Jesus, he hung himself, rope broke, and he fell bursting asunder in Aceldama, the field of blood. Acts 1:18, Hebrews 10:39 use the term *perdition* in relationship to those who had come to the knowledge of salvation but turned back to destruction.

Are There Any Modern-Day Signs Alerting Demonic Activity Is Increasing?

Ungodliness increases demonic activity that results in violence, terrorism and immorality. Daily news reports a steady stream of murders, rapes, assaults, and robberies here in the United States. Added to these are regular reports of government corruption.. The national standard is no longer moral, righteous or godly. Evil has increased exponentially

According to the Vatican's International Association of Exorcists—who met in Rome for their twelfth annual conference October 2014—it reports there is a detectable rise in demonic activity. Conference speaker Dr. Valter Cascioli said a higher number of bishops and cardinals asked to participate in the conference, noting it is becoming a pastoral emergency due to the number of disturbances of extraordinary demonic activity and people falling away from the faith, turning to occult activities. A newTV series titled "The Exorcist" reflects the reality of an increase in demonic activity.

Jesus said it will be a time that has never been seen upon the earth or shall ever be again.

Scriptures tell us that during the final days of the tribulation, demonic spirits will be called forth by the authority of God as will be discussed shortly.

Antichrist Controls the Nations

Under a global umbrella, nations will yield their sovereignty and wealth to the one-world system and its leader. Currently, nations eagerly desire to be a member of the United Nations, pledging their sovereignty and wealth to it. Seated upon his throne of authority, the Antichrist will appeal to many gullible people through deception and delusion.

Not all nations surrender willingly to the Antichrist.

> *And at the time of the end will the king of the south push at him and the king of the north will come against him like a whirlwind with chariots, horsemen, ships* [weapons and ships]. *He will enter into the countries and will overtake them. He will enter also into the glorious land* [Israel] *and many countries will be overthrown. But these will escape out of his hand, Edom, Moab and the chief of the children of Ammon* [Jordan]. *He will stretch forth his hand also upon the countries and the land of Egypt will not escape. He will have power over the treasures of gold and silver in Egypt and Libya, Ethiopia will be at his steps. He will hear reports from the east and the north which trouble him and he will go forth with great fury to destroy and utterly to make away many. He will plant the tabernacles of his place between the seas in the glorious holy mountain* [Israel], *and he will come to his end and none will help him.* (Daniel 11:40)
>
> *But tidings out of the east* [China] *and out of the north* [Russia] *will trouble him* [and Middle East] *and he will go forth with great fury to destroy and utterly to take away many …* (Daniel 11:44)

Just a note of interest, Antichrist will be resisted by nations in the South, East, and North. The United States is referred to as the **West**, and it is not referenced as a region that Antichrist is coming against probably because he is coming from the West.

At this present time, North Korea and China are areas in the Far East, which are uncooperative with the United States. Iran, Syria, Turkey, and other Islamic nations form a Mideast allegiance and are opposed to American meddling. Russia, which is to the North, is uncooperative with the United States. Egypt to the South does not have good relations with the United States because the Egyptians overthrew the Muslim Brotherhood, who has a favorable relationship with the United States.

In chapter 18 we discussed the person of Antichrist as spoken by the prophet Daniel. Following we highlight his words again:

> *And the king shall do according to his will, and he shall exalt himself and magnify himself above every god and shall speak marvelous things against the God of gods and shall prosper till the indignation be accomplished, for that that is determined shall be done. Neither shall he regard the God of his fathers nor the desire of women, nor regard any god for he shall magnify himself above all. But in his estate shall he honor the God of forces and a god whom his father's knew not shall he honor with gold and silver and with precious stones and pleasant things. Thus shall he do in the most strongholds with a strange god who he shall acknowledge and increase with glory and he shall cause them to rule over many and shall divide the land for gain.* (Daniel 11:36–39)

Who does this passage remind you of? Public Policy Poll, April 2011, reveal that one in four Americans believe the current president may be the Antichrist.

Antichrist and False Prophet Working Together

The realization of the one-world government will have a sobering effect as people become aware it is not for benevolent purposes but toward world domination, economic hardship, famine, war, and death. The global government constitution is the United Nations Agenda 21 Program. Its ongoing goal is to decrease the human race by eliminating up to six billion people. As predicted in Revelation, the four horsemen of the apocalypse have shared one common agenda for thousands of years. Death.

In our godless culture, the false prophet has neutralized world religions, bringing mankind under a one-world religion without God, while paying umbrage to the god of this world. Religions are cooperating under a universal false religious system overseen by the false prophet. This milestone will be celebrated with a long-awaited event the world has anticipated for hundreds of years. We can imagine that there will be great fanfare when the Antichrist and his entourage come to the temple in Jerusalem. The false prophet with all his pomp and in cooperation with the Jewish high priest will conduct the opening ceremony and dedication of the third temple. Millions will view this spectacular event. But then something unexpected takes place; somehow the Antichrist causes a desolation to occur in the temple.

The people are horrified, and it signals danger; many look for the exits. There is usually a precursor that occurs prior to the main event. It is possible the Antichrist, the one who is referred to as abominable, has already come to the City of God. He has stood in the holy place, future site of the coming temple. He makes plans for his return visit when the third temple is accomplished.

Daniel 9:24–26 foretold of this event:

> *Seventy weeks are determined upon thy people and upon thy holy city to finish the transgression and to make an end of sins and to make reconciliation for iniquity and to bring in everlasting righteousness … Know and understand that from the going forth of the commandment to restore and to build Jerusalem unto the Messiah the Prince will be seven weeks … After threescore and two weeks messiah will be cut off but not for himself. The people of the Prince, that will come will destroy the city and the sanctuary …*

The seventy weeks include the Crucifixion of Jesus during the sixty-ninth week, or 483 years after the commandment to rebuild the second temple later desecrated by Antiochus. There has been a two thousand–year intermission between the sixty-ninth week and the start of the seventieth week or last seven-year period, which is the seven-year tribulation, and its official start is in line with the building of the third temple to be desecrated by Antichrist and his minions.

The Number of the Beast

Previously, we discussed the characteristics of the Antichrist and false prophet. Both are specifically identified in scripture. Both are involved in a global network and in sync with the United Nations agenda 21 mandate. Both have financial backing and influence from the global elite. The scripture further identifies the Antichrist by a particular number. Revelation 13:18, "*Let him that has understanding count the number of the beast for it is the number of man, and his number is 666.*" David Flynn, *Temple at the Center of Time,*[59] in his research said, "The number of the beast had been put in place at the time Satan tempted Adam and Eve who were temples of God." Flynn associated Greek letters with the mark of the beast and the first act of rebellion of mankind. He displayed an image of a letter *X* and two *S*, serpentine-like letters. The first letter *X* is like unto the ancient Hebrew letter *Tav* and is the symbol of a tree, meaning Satan appeared as a serpent on the tree. Later this would be the symbol of Jesus crucified on a tree formed like a cross. He sees a connection with future temples and 666. In 1 Kings 10:14 refers to King Solomon acquiring 666 talents of gold for the construc-

[59] David Flynn, Temple at the Center of Time (Crane, MO: Defense Publishing, 2012) p. 151–152

tion of his palace while building the first temple. Flynn connects the destruction of the first and second temples by 666 years between the two events.

χξς

Image by David Flynn

During the time of Islamic occupation over the temple mount, there has been continual situations that desecrate the holy site. Flynn is able to connect Islam through the Greek interpretation of "bism Alla in Arabic, in the name of Allah," which numeric value is 666. The Greek letter *chi* (*X*) is a Greek transformation of the Hebrew letter *Tav*, symbolizing crossed sticks; but in Arabic, it symbolized the cross swords. Jews pray toward the temple mount in Jerusalem while Muslims pray toward the black rock, the Kabbah in Mecca, Saudi Arabia. Flynn introduces this scenario so we can see that the distance between Mecca and Jerusalem temple mount is 666 nautical miles.

There is a relationship between the letter form of the mark of the Antichrist written in Greek. The first letter *chi* (*X*) equals 600 and is a Greek transformation of the Phoenician/ Hebrew letter *Tav* (last letter of the Hebrew alphabet) and a symbol of a tree or crossed sticks, which meant a mark: *Xi* equals 60. The stigma (*S*) symbolizes serpent and equal to number 6. The number of the son of perdition/the beast is 666.

Is It Possible for Satan, a Fallen Angel, to Possess Humans?

Some scholars assert that Satan will possess the person of Antichrist based on the statement "will go into perdition". Several believe that spirits of Osiris and Apollo will embody Nimrod who will in turn possess the Antichrist. Their beliefs come from mythological narratives. But were they entirely myth, or did the fable have a thread of truth? We believe they were fallen angels and given names, deified by mankind, manifesting in Babylonian, Egyptian, Grecian, and Roman pagan religious beliefs. Humans deified fallen angels; some of whose names were Semjaza, Akibeel, Ramuel, Asael, Anani, Jomjael, Arazjal, etc. In time, different cultures renamed the fallen angels, who became gods, such as, Osiris, Zeus, Hercules, Diana, Apollo, etc.

During the first century AD, we find this mind-set in Acts 14:11, wherein Paul had performed a miracle and the people said, "The gods are come down to us in the likeness of men, and they called Barnabas, Jupiter, and Paul, Mercurius."

It raises the question, "Can fallen angels possess, embody, or incarnate humans?" We first consider preflood conduct. Satan did mingle himself with the serpent. Two hundred fallen angels descended onto Mount Hermon and mingled with earth life forms. We cannot define this as a spiritual possession. There is no scriptural evidence to support the premise that Satan mated with a human woman. God created the angels, and the angels created the giant hybrids, which were a result of comingling celestial entities with terrestrial species. No one has a 100 percent clear understanding of how fallen angels were able to mingle with humans and produce the giant Nephilim hybrids. There seems to be a distinction between the angelic host who corrupted humankind and evil spirits who are allowed to torment and possess people or animals. Evil spirits/demons/devils are the spiritual entity of the physical Nephilim who were destroyed in the flood. The evil spirits of these hybrids were condemned to roam the earth. In the scriptures, Jesus rebuked entities called evil spirits/demons/devils who possessed people. In conclusion, angels cannot take possession of a human, but evil spirits have that ability. In further consideration, can dead humans possess living people?

Is Antichrist the Reincarnation of Nimrod?

Peter D. Goodgame in his book, *The Second Coming of the Antichrist,* [60] puts forth the notion that the spirit of Nimrod will possess Antichrist. As we ponder this, several considerations arise. First, was Nimrod a type of Antichrist? No. Was he the literal seed of Satan? No. Will the actual spirit of Nimrod be summoned from the afterlife to possess the human Antichrist? No.

Mr. Goodgame uses scripture to support his position (the spirit of Nimrod will possess Antichrist), and in so doing, scripture is taken out of context. In our work, *The Everything Bagel,* we stay true to biblical truth without manipulating it to fit our concepts. Following are a few examples of Goodgame's take on scripture:

- Genesis 3:15 points to the seed of the woman and the seed of the serpent. The foreword in Goodgame's book was written by Tom Horn, page 1, introducing the seed of Satan will be Nimrod who will possess the second seed, also Nimrod, who will be the future Antichrist, having been incarnated, or embodied, by Satan and Nimrod. Our comment—this is not the interpretation of Genesis 3:15, which informs us that the seed of the woman (Jesus) will crush the head of the seed (all ungodly

[60] Peter D. Goodgame, The Second Coming of the Antichrist, (Crane MO, 2012)

angels, demons, and people) of the serpent, who will in turn bruise the heel of Christ at the time of his Crucifixion.

- Revelation 13:1 is used by Goodgame and Horn to support the seed of the serpent will be a man who will not be recognized for what he actually is—paganism's ultimate incarnation, the beast, or Antichrist. Goodgame and Horn assert that Satan once had a son (Nimrod) who is poised to return again as the physical person of the Antichrist.

  Our comment—the first impression, there is a special man coming from the loins of Satan. We believe that Satan has no literal seed but that evil men throughout the ages in association with Satan become his seed as in the sons of Satan. There is no biblical evidence to support this claim that Satan's seed or his literal son was manifest in times past and this entity is poised to return again in a human body. The scriptures tell us, Nimrod's father was Cush. Nimrod cannot be the son of human parents and also the product of a human woman and a fallen angel. There is no evidence to support that after the death of Nimrod, he became an evil spirit with the ability to arise from the dead to possess the future Antichrist.
- Goodgame references a statement from Church Missler, who said, "Could it be that this final world dictator will be in <u>some sense</u> a return of Nimrod?" (Foreword, page 4).

  Our comment—this would be in <u>some sense</u> the spirit of Antichrist will have an evil influence on an evil person, and if you want to call it a Nimrod-like spirit or a Hitler-like spirit, or any of the despots in the past, is acceptable. This spiritual wickedness that permeates the world is not a person, and it cannot support the claim that the spirit of Nimrod is returning to life to possess the final Antichrist.
- Goodgame uses a statement made by Gary Stearman on Nimrod: "He is none other than the spiritual inheritor of the first great postflood religious apostasy. He is the keeper of the great heritage that began at the Assyrian capital, Nineveh, founded by Nimrod. <u>Nimrod is the Antichrist, the future despot, who comes in the name of the ancient mystery religion."</u> He further expounds, "After the flood, Nimrod's rebellion became the foundation of mankind's greatest religious apostasy ... This system of false worship became known as the Babylonian mystery religion" (Foreword, page 5).

  Our comment—we would like to find something in that statement that we could agree on somewhat, but it would be a stretch. We do not agree with the statement "Nimrod is the Antichrist, the future despot, who comes in the name of ancient mystery religion." Stearman would need to give us a deeper understanding of his theory, since no one definitively knows who the end-time Antichrist will be. Nimrod could not even have been a type of Antichrist since the concept of an Antichrist had not been revealed during the life of Nimrod. During the time of the Babylonian Empire, Nimrod was long gone, dead and buried. The idea of an ancient Babylonian mystery religion system could only have been developed through the reigning kings of Babylon, of which Nimrod was not one. It would be more accurate to suggest that Nebuchadnezzar was representative of the Babylonian mystery religion. Stearman has a solid understanding that we are dealing with spiritual darkness in high places. The spirit of mystery Babylon or the spirit of iniquity has been prevalent throughout the ages. The Bible does not elaborate on Nimrod as righteous or wicked. It does not tell us if Nimrod was possessed by demons. The spirit of Antichrist operates in all wicked people as the Holy Spirit operates in the redeemed of Christ. We are not possessed by the Holy Spirit.

- Goodgame uses the above analogy to support his theory that the spirit of Antichrist is "the power of the ancient gods being channeled through the figure of one powerful man, Nimrod, who became that god."

  Our comment—his use of gods is a reference to fallen angels, who corrupted mankind before the flood and were deified by man. According to scripture, all of mankind was wicked. Then after the flood, Goodgame focuses on one person, turning him into a god. Humans want to be like gods/fallen angels, but they are not and cannot be. Goodgame puts forth the analogy that Nimrod (a human) will somehow return, having been embodied by a fallen angel/Satan, and he will, in turn, embody the Antichrist. Of all the despots throughout the annals of history, why do European scholars portray Ham, Canaan, Cush, and Nimrod in such unfavorable light? We explored this concern in our chapter 8 under "Racism." Further, we just do not find biblical support that the spirit of Antichrist is the exclusive person, Nimrod.

It is exciting to study the Books of Revelation and Daniel. These books introduce the beasts arising out of the sea and out of the earth, which represent nations, Satan, Antichrist, false prophet, and introduces the great harlot riding a scarlet beast, representing the Babylonian system of spiritual wickedness. Revelation 13 introduces the beast out of the sea and the beast out of the earth. Revelation 17 introduces the woman, a harlot riding the beast. We place our point of study at this juncture because the Antichrist, false prophet, and Babylonian system exist before the official seven-year tribulation period begins.

Beasts and bottomless pit—all symbolic of something greater. Revelation 17:7 tells us the mystery of the woman is symbolic of spiritual wickedness, and the beast with seven heads and ten horns is symbolic of kingdoms/nations. Revelation 17:8, the beast was, is not, and will ascend out of the bottomless pit and go into perdition, must be correlated with the beast described in Revelation 13.1 … "And I saw a beast rise up out of the **sea**" [multitudes/ nations], having seven heads and ten horns [kingdoms/nations]." We believe Revelation 17:8 is symbolic of seven nations/kingdoms of which five are fallen and one is and the other is not yet come per Revelation 17:10–17. Verse 10 refers to kings, and verse 17 ties the kings into their kingdoms. The beast represents kingdoms or nations, and the beast is also a reference to Antichrist, who in this context will emerge (ascend out of the symbolic bottomless pit). The Antichrist will be a leader of one of the ten horns (ten-region confederation), having authority over a region. Antichrist is also defined as the "little horn," having emerged from one of the seven kingdoms, specifically from the seventh. Rome divided (two legs), and its ten toes became the ten-region confederation, and the eighth, the kingdom of Satan destined for its final destruction. At the peak of dominance, the eighth kingdom, the "little horn" has gotten a promotion and is now the head over the ten-region confederation formed by the Club of Rome in the twentieth century.

The Beast Rising out of the Sea

The beast out of the sea is a reference to a spiritual world system whose king is Satan in cooperation with nations and leaders. Revelation 13:1–10, Daniel 7, Revelation 17:8–18 describe the beast out of the sea. In order to comprehend these passages, we provide a basic overview of the symbolism associated with these entities.

> *And I stood upon the sand of the sea and saw a beast rise up out of the **sea** having seven heads and **ten horns** and upon his horns ten crowns and upon his heads the names of blasphemy. And the beast which I saw was like unto a leopard, his feet were as the feet of a bear and his mouth as the mouth of a lion and the dragon* [Satan] *gave him his power and his seat and great authority.* (Revelation 13:1–2)

- Sand of the sea is a reference to many people.
- Reference to sea, waters, earth is associated with people, multitudes, nations, and tongues.
- Beast comes forth from the multitudes or nations.
- Seven heads, ten horns, ten toes, ten crowns is a reference to kingdoms, empires, nations, authority.
- The beast also represents a blasphemous, wicked system called mystery Babylon, or Babylon the Great.
- The word *beast* or *horn* can be a reference to Satan, Antichrist, or false prophet.

- Satan has given Antichrist headquarters and authority.

Revelation 13:2 correlates to Daniel 7:2–8:

> *And four great beast came up from the* ***sea,*** *diverse one from another ... It had* ***ten horns.*** *I considered the horns and behold there came up among them another little horn ...*

The Beast Is Wounded

> *And I saw one of his heads as it were wounded to death and his deadly wound was healed and all the world wondered after the beast and they worshipped the dragon which gave power unto the beast and they worshipped the beast saying who is like unto the beast who is able to make war with him. And there was given unto him a mouth speaking great things and blasphemies and power was given unto him to continue forty two months.* (Revelation 13:3)

- In this passage, we are to understand that the Antichrist will be wounded, die, and come back to life.
- At some point during the great tribulation (forty-two months, three and a half years), the Antichrist is wounded.
- The unsaved and unsealed followed and worshipped the beast.

Scholars use the scripture passage of "was alive, dead, and lived again" as pertaining to kingdoms or empires that have come and gone. The above passage indicates that one of his head was wounded but it was later revived. As prophecy unfolds, we could insert that the Democrats loss the election to the Republicans and their outcry and rage was as a wounded beast. We also lean toward a literal wounding of the person of Antichrist. The phrase "who was alive is now dead and will live again," generally speaking, that statement could apply to every human. We are alive, and then we die, and our spirit/soul continues to live again in heaven or hell. Jesus was our prototype. He was alive, was dead, and arose again and is alive.

Let us imagine, with satellite TV, people can get news events quickly. The world hears that this famous person was attacked by a dissident and died. The ambulance took him to a hospital. With modern technology, he could be resuscitated, and life-altering situations can be reversed. Antichrist is put on life support machines. He then recovers and is alive and well. World communications followed this situation, and the people of the world now know the one-world leader: the Antichrist is alive. The world would be amazed, curious, and follow after him. Because of this miracle, many will be deceived, whose names are not in the book of life. They worship the dragon/Satan, which gave power unto the beast/Antichrist, and they worshipped the beast, saying, "Who is like the beast and who is able to make war with him?" They take his mark to show their allegiance. The timing of this wound places the Antichrist in the middle of the seven-year tribulation period, or forty-two months.

<u>Daniel's Prophecy of the Beast</u>

Daniel 7:17–24

> *These great beast which are four are four kings which shall arise out of the earth …*
>
> *And of the ten horns that were in his head and of the other which came up and before whom three fell even of that horn that had eyes and a mouth that spoke very great things whose look was more stout than his fellows. I beheld and the same horn made war with the saints and prevailed against them …* (*Verse 20*)
>
> *The **ten horns** out of this kingdom are ten kings that will arise and another will rise after them and he will be diverse from the first and he will subdue three kings.* (*Verse 24*)

Following, we summarize the symbolism in Daniel 7:

- Four beasts represent nations that have come and gone or are revived, such as Rome. They are symbolic representations of evil kingdoms/empires.
- Daniel 7:3, a vision of four beasts from the sea
  (1) lion with eagle's wings, given a man's heart
  (2) bear with three ribs in mouth
  (3) leopard with four wings, four heads having dominion, Greece
  (4) dreadful, terrible, strong, iron teeth, ten-horned beast, Rome
- Daniel 7:17, interpretation of the four beasts
  (1) Four beast are four kings or kingdoms.
  (2) The fourth kingdom, powerful, associated with iron, brass.
  (3) The little horn with eyes and a mouth is Antichrist.
- The revived Roman Empire is described as dreadful, terrible, strong, iron teethed, and devour and break in pieces the other nations. Revelation refers to it as the seventh kingdom, which will morph into the eighth and final kingdom.
- The ten horns (ten-nation confederation) give rise to the little horn: <u>the final Antichrist</u> under satanic control, who gives him power.

From the time Daniel wrote his prophecies to the time John wrote Revelation, a few thousand years had transpired. Revelation portrays the beast as having seven heads and ten horns.

John's Prophecy of the Beast

Revelation 17:7–18 correlates with Revelation 13, and the angel said,

> *I will tell you the mystery of the woman and of the beast which carries her which has the seven heads and ten horns. The beast that you saw was and is not and will ascend out of the bottomless pit and go into perdition and they that dwell upon the face of the earth whose names were not written in the book of life from the foundation of the world when they behold the beast that was and is not and yet is. And here is the mind which has wisdom. The seven heads are seven mountains on which the woman sits. And there are seven kings; five are fallen and one is and the other is not yet come and when he comes he must continue a short space. And the beast that was and is not even he is the eighth and is of the seven and goes into perdition. And the ten horns which you saw are ten kings which have received no kingdom as yet but receive power as kings one hour with the beast. These have one mind and will give their power and strength unto the beast. These will make war with the Lamb and he Lamb will overcome them for he is Lord of lords and King of kings and they that are with him are called chosen and faithful … the waters which you saw where the whore sits are peoples, multitudes, nations and tongues. And the ten horn which you saw upon the beast these will hate the whore and will make her desolate and naked and will eat her flesh and burn her with fire. For God has put in their hearts to fulfill his will and to agree and give their kingdom unto the beast until the words of God will be fulfilled. And the woman which you saw is that great city which reigns over the kings of the earth.*

The above passage introduces the woman riding the beast, which will be discussed shortly. At this juncture, we continue to discuss the beast out of the sea and its references to kingdoms.

- Seven heads represent empires, kingdoms, nations that have come to power and declined yet their influence continues throughout millennia. Britain's family crest is composed of a beast like leopard, feet of a bear, mouth of a lion, and red dragon.

- Revelation 17:8, "*The beast that you saw **was and is not and will ascend** out of the bottomless pit and go into perdition.*" Nations that **"was"** are Assyrian, Babylon, Medes, Persian, and Greek. The nation that **"is not"** was Rome, and the revived Roman Empire is the seventh head, which continues to this day; and from out of it, **"yet to come"** will be the eighth, which is the kingdom of Satan.
- The eighth kingdom has come. Allegorically speaking, Satan and his beast kingdom ascended out of the bottomless pit. The kingdom of the beast was birthed from the time of Satan's fall and ties into pit of hell where he and his are headed at the end of the tribulation. From the pit of hell is portrayed as rising from the depths of wickedness. The essence of spiritual darkness culminates into destruction of God's creation. Satan has empowered his followers for eons, and at the end of days, the literal Antichrist and false prophet will also be empowered to carry out Satan's final agenda.
- Revelation 17:9, "*And here is the mind that has wisdom, the seven heads are seven mountains on which the woman sits.*" The seven heads (kingdoms/empires/nations) and the seven mountains are regions within nations, and the woman represents spiritual wickedness ruling over areas.
- Revelation 17:10, "*And there are seven kings, five are fallen and one is and the other is not yet come and when he comes he must continue a short space.*" Antichrist is on the scene, and he will endure for a short time through to duration of the tribulation.
- Revelation 17:11, "*And the beast that was and is not even he is the eight and is of the seven and goes into perdition.*" This passage tells us that the spirit of Antichrist has been around a very long time, producing despots, and the final despot will emerge from the seventh kingdom (revived Roman Empire.) The term *goes into perdition* refers to the final destruction of Satan's kingdom.
- Revelation 17:12, "*And the ten horns which you saw are ten kings which have received no kingdom as yet but receive power as kings one hour with the beast, they have one mind and will give their power and strength unto the beast …*" Daniel 2:41 also makes reference to ten toes, which are the same as the ten horns.

  Ten horns/toes represent the ten-region confederation organized within the seventh and fulfilled in the eighth kingdom. The "kings" have no kingdom because they are figure heads over the ten regions in the confederation. For instance, the United States, Canada, and Mexico are considered the North American region. From among these ten rulers, one will be selected to rule over all of the ten leaders and their regions. These ten leaders will receive power/authority from the Antichrist for one hour (a short span of time). They have one mind (one-world order) and give their allegiance, military, and wealth to the Antichrist. Since the formation of the United Nations, member nations must pledge their support and money to this organization. Perhaps the Antichrist rules over the nations from the United Nations' headquarters, wherein great power and authority is over the world.

- Revelation 17:16, "*And the ten horns upon the beast will hate the whore, make her desolate, naked, eat her flesh and burn her with fire.*" This confederation will turn against the whore, which is symbolic for one powerful nation: America, Babylon the Great. These other nations will turn against this nation with war and destruction by fire. At this time in modern history, we see that America is still considered the greatest nation on the earth, full of corruption and ungodliness. We also see she is threatened by Russia, China, North Korea, and the militant Islamic nations. One of these nations may succeed in launching a nuclear attack against America.
- Revelation 17:14, besides attacking the whore, which is Babylon the Great, the Antichrist regime will make war with the Lamb (Jesus), and he will overcome them, for he is Lord of Lords and King of Kings and those with him are called the faithful chosen.

As previously discussed, the nation portrayed as a lion was Rome. Rome was divided and is referred to as the revived Roman Empire representing (Rome/Europe/America). Out of the revived Roman Empire, the Antichrist will arise. The one-world order has divided the world into ten regions, and Antichrist will oversee them. He will make war and be in conflict with other nations. Antichrist will persecute and kill God's people, Jews and Christians. The current US president serving from 2009 to 2016 has embraced the idea of president of the world. After his presidency, he has stated that he has more work to do as an international leader.

Symbolism of the Woman Riding the Beast

In Revelation 16, we see the results of the seven vial judgments poured out nearing the end of the tribulation upon the earth and the coming destruction of Babylon the Great. We have discussed the nature of the beast, and now we consider the woman riding on the beast.

Revelation 17 opens with an angel calling John to come see the judgment of the great whore that sits upon many waters. The scriptures alert us that those nations and its inhabitants have committed fornication with the harlot, made drunk with the wine of her fornication and blood of the saints.

Written on the seven heads was the name of blasphemy, which is spiritual wickedness symbolic of the woman on the beast, the Babylonian harlot representing sin, corruption, greed, and ungodliness of nations.

Revelation 17:1–3 … *"I will show unto you the judgment of the great **whore** that sits on many waters … I saw the woman sit upon a scarlet colored beast full of names of blasphemy having seven heads and ten horns."*

Revelation 17:3–6 is a picture of the woman riding a red beast full of names of blasphemy. She is dressed in purple, red, and adorned with gold, precious stones, pearls. She is holding a gold cup full of abominations, fornications, and the blood of the saints. She is drunk with the blood of the saints and martyrs who died for Christ. On her forehead, she is identified as Mystery, Babylon the Great, Mother of Harlots—abominations of the earth.

Let us review the symbolic titles given to the woman:

- Whore—represents a wicked global system that attained wealth through corruption, conquering, persecution, and death of people. It is a system of immorality, such as abortion and homosexuality, and had commercial relations with other nations to obtain power, wealth, dominion.
- Mother of Harlots—the great whore (spiritual wickedness), a great nation sitting on many waters (the world). Holding a gold cup full of blasphemy, fornication, immorality, greed, corruption, murder from which the nations of the world and the unsaved people (ungodly, reprobate, unrepentant, materialistic) have indulged themselves, are deceived (drunk) with the wine (things of this world). It has produced daughters and sons (ancient pagan practitioners) who are workers of iniquity giving birth (to secret societies, occults, false religions).
- Mystery—the woman and the beast represent a marriage made in hell. It symbolizes the union between Satan, Antichrist, false prophet, worldwide ungodliness. It is controlled by spiritual strongholds over the world. God will eventually destroy the spiritual strongholds over nations: *"I am against thee said the Lord of hosts and I will discover thy skirts upon thy face and I will show the nations thy wickedness and the kingdoms thy shame. Your strongholds will be shaken, the fire will devour you and the sword will cut you off."* World governments conduct their affairs in secret.
- Babylon the Great—symbolic ungodly global system but also points to a nation of great influence, imperial, military strength; dressed in royalty and riches; represents wealth, power; and began its formation in the Babylonian, Persian, Greek, Roman Empires and is played out in the revived Roman Empire of Europe, America, and its headquarters the United Nations. The European Union insignia is a woman riding a beast named Europa. Not a coincidence. The European Union parliament building is designed like a ziggurat and has a vacant seat number 666 in anticipation of the coming one-world leader. It is also symbolic of the revived Roman Empire morphing into the eighth kingdom of the beast.

- The revived Roman Empire gave birth to the architects of a one-world order and one-world religion. Other nations of the world have treaties, economic trade, and take billions in aid in exchange for cooperation. These interactions are symbolic of having drunk from her gold cup.
- Abomination of the Earth—she is holding a cup full of abominations, and this symbolism represents false religion, ungodliness, sexual sin, mingling of species, corrupt global government, shedding of blood, and hatred and destruction of every living being. The woman is drunk with the blood of the innocents, saints, and martyrs of Jesus.

A literal example of abominations—in 2016, several US states attempted to pass the Religious Freedom Bill, protecting religious freedom. Homosexual Tim Sweeney spoke of defeating the bill at the Out and Equal Workplace Advocates executive forum. The federal government told states to allow transgender people to use any bathroom regardless if it did not correspond to their biological sex at birth. States that wanted to uphold the religious freedom act and to deny transsexuals men from using the women's bathroom was met with opposition from the corporate world. Eighty companies signed a letter to governor of North Carolina, threatening to boycott the state and they began to take their business to a tolerant state. Some states like Georgia complied with the demand so as not to lose business. This is an example of drinking from the cup of abominations of immorality and ungodliness.

We find archetypes of the woman and the beast in Old Testament passages. Zechariah 5:7 portrays an image of a woman sitting in a basket who is wicked. In verse 11, he is told by the angel that the *ephah*/basket is being taken to the land of Shinar in Babylon where a house or altar will be established as a seat of spiritual wickedness.

In the book of Nahum, we find a reference to Nineveh of Assyria, associated with Babylon, and the time frame speaks to the destruction of Nineveh. The spirit of mystery Babylon was prevalent in Nineveh, and the wicked Queen Huzzab would be taken captive. We see that the ruling class gained wealth from plunder of the poor. Food and provisions were taken from the poor to maintain their luxurious lifestyle. Nahum 3:1–16 describes the wickedness of Nineveh as liars and robbers having a strong military that brings fear and death. "*Because of the multitude of the whoredoms of the well-favored harlot, the mistress of witchcraft that sells nations through her whoredoms and families through her witchcraft, you have multiplied your merchants above the stars of the heaven.*" Many nations hated the rule of the Assyrians but still did envy their power, prestige, wealth, and continued to develop business relationships. The nation of Nineveh was rendered empty, void, and wasted. The time had come for God's judgment to fall, and the people were fearful. Nahum tells them the Lord of host will burn their chariots in the smoke, and the sword will devour their young men, and the voice of God's messengers would be silenced. As these things came upon Nineveh, history repeats, and these things will come to pass on America.

The Fall of Babylon the Great

Mystery Babylon a wicked global system portrayed as a harlot riding a red beast, holding a cup of abominations. Its influence has corrupted all nations, and there are no righteous nations in the world. It is associated with ancient Babylon, or modern-day Iraq. Babylon had its peaks and decline as a nation. With the overthrow of Saddam Hussein, many believed this was the biblical prophecy that declares Babylon will be destroyed. However, Iraq alone is not the system of mystery Babylon, nor will it arise again to be a great empire.

Saudi Arabia is ancient Arabia. The wealth of this nation will come to naught as will their pagan places of worship: Mecca, Medina. The once-great Persian Empire, Iran, will implode upon itself. Egypt is no longer the glory of the pharaohs. Damascus in Syria is promised to become a ruinous heap.

All former empires had their rise and decline. This brings into consideration the Roman Empire and its counterpart, America and Europe, representative of the revived Roman Empire, both wicked unto God. The symbol of America is the pagan Statue of Liberty in New York, standing as a crowning apex of Babylon the Great. The stock market, Wall Street, Federal Reserve represent its financial center. The rich, powerful, and famous covet the lifestyle in New York. Can anything good come out of New York? The Bible singles out a city that rules over the kings of the earth. The United Nations is located in New York, rules over many nations, and is parallel to many waters. The scriptures mention a city on seven hills, and this could be associated to the headquarters of the false prophet in Rome, also destined for destruction. Nations hate America, but they emulate the one they hate, as in drinking from the cup of abominations. It is predicted in Revelation 17:15: the nations will turn against the whore, burn it with fire, make it desolate, naked, and will eat her flesh.

> *For in one hour so great riches is come to nothing, every shipmaster and all the company in ships … as many as trade by sea stood afar off and cried when they saw the smoke of her burning saying what city is like unto this great city … they cried, weeping and wailing saying alas that great city wherein were made that had ships in the sea by reason of her costliness, for in one hour is she made desolate.* (Revelation 18:17)

Could this passage be pointing to America? America is a land of wealth, commerce, trade, and greed. America—a nation given the title of world superpower, intimidating and instigating wars in the name of peace—its evil overshadows its good deeds. America is a nation that has rejected God. The decline and fall of America is predicted because of pride, rebellion, and sin. Other nations will also be devastated during these end-time events.

An angel announces the evil system of Babylon the Great is fallen. This could be the result of nuclear, climate, economic, or worldwide civil unrest, as is seen today but to a greater degree approaching the tribulation period when nations will turn on each other and the wrath of God comes upon the earth. God brings judgment because of the wickedness:

- The world becomes infested by devils, every foul spirit, a cage of every unclean, hateful birds.
- As mentioned, the nations committed fornication with the woman; merchants became rich through the abundance of her delicacies (drug dealers, prostitution rings, abortion industry, sex slaves, pedophilia, etc.).
- A warning is given for the people to come out of her (turn from worldliness) and not partake of her sins, and they will not receive her plagues.
- Reward her as she has rewarded you, and double unto her according to her works in the cup which she has filled; fill to her double. She has glorified herself, lived extravagantly while its people suffered in poverty and death.
- In one day death, plagues, mourning, famine and destruction by fire.
- The merchants will cry and lament for her (worldwide economic collapse) as they see the smoke and know the mighty stock exchange has fallen and national debt is out of control.

The Beast Rising out of the Earth

<u>The False Prophet Has a Major Role in the End-Time Events</u>

> *And I beheld another beast coming up out of the earth and he had two horns like a lamb and he spoke as a dragon. He exercised all the power of the first beast before him and caused the earth and them which dwell therein to worship the first beast whose deadly would was healed. He does great wonders so that he makes fire come down from heaven on the earth in the sight of men and deceived them that dwell on the earth by the means of those miracles which he had power to do in the sight of the beast, saying to them that dwell on the earth that they should <u>make an image</u> to the beast which had the wound by a sword and did live. And he had power to give life unto the image of the beast that the image of the beast should both speak and cause that as many as would not worship the image of the beast should be killed. He caused all both small and great, rich and poor, free and bond to receive a mark in their right hand or in their foreheads:*

> *and that no man might buy or sell save he that had the mark or the name of the beast or the number of his name. Here is wisdom, let him that has understanding count the number of the beast for it is the number of a man and his number is six hundred sixty-six.* (Revelation 13:11–18)

The overview of this scripture introduces the false prophet, who is seen as a beast arising out of the earth, and cooperates with the beast out of the sea:

- He has two horns like a lamb.
- He speaks like a dragon.
- He received power to cause the people to worship the beast/Antichrist.
- He can do miracles, making fire come down from heaven.
- He deceives the people through these false miracles.
- He causes people to worship the image of the beast; if not, then death to them.
- He is given power to cause the image of the beast to speak.
- Demands all to receive the mark of the beast, 666.

False Prophet

In our chapter 17, we discussed the characteristics of the false prophet and who may be a strong contender for the position. His symbolism is likened to two horns (nations), like a lamb (world religion.) For clarification, the false prophet is a counterfeit Jesus on earth and is deceitful as Satan. Satan has given him the same power as the first beast, the Antichrist. He is enabled with power to perform signs and wonders. When he speaks, the whole world listens.

Catholicism has a legacy of documented miracles and supernatural intrigue. The Vatican took the Lady of Fatima event and promoted it as a miracle and thus deceived many to worship Mary instead of Jesus. At the Lady of Fatima event, it appeared as though fire was coming down from heaven and the people fell to their knees. Catholicism and pagan religions have many statues, wherein congregants kneel and pray before the statue. It will not seem unusual to the deceived that the false prophet erects a statue which appears to be animated. There are accounts within Catholicism that statues dripped oil or blood. He will require many to worship this statue. The pope is pushing for income equality, so it would not seem strange that he would strongly require all people to receive a mark in order that they can buy and sell or receive government subsidies.

Scholarly Thoughts on the False Prophet

Father Herman Bernard Kramer in his writing, *The Book of Destiny*, gives commentary on the book of Revelation, chapter 12:

> The sign in heaven is that of a woman with child crying out in her travail and anguish of delivery. In that travail, she gives birth to some definite person who is to rule the church with a rod of iron. It then points to a conflict waged within the church to elect one who was to rule all nations in the manner clearly stated. In accord with the text, this is unmistakably a papal election for only Christ and his vicar have the divine right to rule all nations, but at this time the great powers may take a menacing attitude to hinder the election of the logical and expected candidate by threats of a general apostasy, assassination, or imprisonment of this candidate if elected.

Kramer's interpretation of Revelation 12 is incorrect, and we provide the correct understanding:

- The woman is Israel; the child is Jesus; and the twelve stars are the twelve tribes of Israel
- Kramer sees this passage as that the birth of **another s**pecific person, who was born and is now of the age to fulfill the incarnation of Saint Malachi's prophecy, the final pope.
- He is correct in understanding that the end-time church will have conflict and political manipulation, even to the plotting of assassinations to ensure the false prophet is selected.
- The Catholic mind-set sees the pope as god on earth and only the pope and Christ can rule the nations.

Malachi's prophecy predicts the final pope will come at a time of tribulation. His reign ends with the destruction of Rome, and city of seven hills will be destroyed, and the terrible and fearsome judge will judge his people. See chapter 17, "Prophecy of the Last Pope."

Jewish Kabbalah, the Zohar, a collection of books written in medieval Aramaic seven hundred years ago are not prophecies of the Bible. In volume 3, section 34, "The signs heralding Mashiach," or the coming Messiah (false messiah). The Zohar sets the date for his coming, **2012 to 2013.** This time frame coincides with the Antichrist and false prophet currently on the scene. The Zohar says that the time of Jacob's troubles (the great tribulation), which some Catholic scholars say begins with the election of the final pope, when the "kings of the earth" gather in Rome and are killed by fiery stones or missiles from the sky. The Zohar prophecy is separate from the Catholics' prophecy of the last pope. The Zohar predicts the destruction of Rome 5773 Jewish calendar; our calendar, September 2012 and concludes a year later, 2013. The quote reads, "In the year seventy-three [2012–2013], the kings of the world will assemble in the great city of Rome, and the Holy One will shower on them fire and hail and meteoric stones until they are all destroyed with the exception of those who will not yet have arrived there [threats of terrorism on Rome]." We are now in the year 2016, and Rome still stands.

The Vatican has global influence. House Speaker John Boehner extended a formal and open invitation, March 13, 2014, to Pope Francis to address a joint meeting of Congress; this is unprecedented. No religious leader that serves as head of state has ever addressed Congress. Boehner, who is Catholic, said, "Pope Francis has inspired millions of Americans with his pastoral manner and servant leadership to reflect on matters of human dignity, freedom, and social justice."

At that time, there was no condemnation from the current US administration.

Stage Two, or Midpoint of the Tribulation

Stage 2 represents the midpoint of the tribulation, and it is transitionary. As we study John's revelation, he sees transitions between heaven and earth. It also appears to be a transition between the end of the first half of tribulation and before the beginning of the great tribulation. By the end of the first half of the tribulation, the two witnesses and the 144,000 are gone. Antichrist will break the seven-year agreement, desecrate the third Holy Temple, and set himself up to be worshipped as god. He will begin to require allegiance by all to take his mark and worship an image. The rage of the unholy trio will be unleashed upon Israel (Matthew 24:15–15). God will provide refuge for them in the mountains of Jordan.

Daniel 12:11, "*From the time that the daily sacrifice will be taken away and the abomination that makes desolate set up, there will be 1290 days.*" The desecration of the third temple occurs by the midpoint of the tribulation. Three and one half years, or 1,260 days have passed. An additional thirty days were added and appears to be an interlude before the start of the great tribulation, or final three and a half years. At this point in the tribulation, Revelation 8:1, there is short span of silence in heaven for the space of thirty minutes.

Opening of Seals 5, 6, 7

Opening of the Fifth Seal

Revelation 6:9, John sees the souls of people under the altar who had been killed for the Word of God and for their testimony. They are asking, How much longer before God avenges their death? The persecution and death of martyrs began with the first Christian followers and has been ongoing up to the twenty-first century. During the tribulation, there will be another group of believers who have been persecuted and killed. All those who have died in Christ are given white robes and told to wait a little while until their brothers and fellow servants who also will be killed join them in heaven.

Opening the Sixth Seal

Revelation 6:12—this scripture is moving the world into the beginning of stage 3 of the great tribulation with a great earthquake; the sun becomes black; the moon appears bloodred; stars (meteors) fall from heaven; and the heavens appear to depart as a scroll (storm clouds, tornadoes) rolling together; every mountain and island (volcanoes) were moved out of their places. The kings of the earth and all mankind hid themselves in the mountains (caves/underground bunkers). They said to the mountains and rocks, "Fall on us and hide us from the face of him that sits on the throne and from the wrath of the Lamb for the great day of his wrath is come, and who will be able to stand?" Mankind knows the God of Israel is angry.

Opening the Seventh Seal

Revelation 8, Jesus opens the seventh seal; there is silence in heaven for about thirty minutes. As mentioned, this is an interlude before the next set of judgments befalls the earth, which are seven trumpets and seven vials. During this transition, another angel is given a golden censer filled with live coals taken from the altar before the throne, and incense was poured on the coals. The prayers of the saints are like a sweet smell ascending up to God. Then the angel took the censer, filled it with fire off the altar, and cast it onto the earth. There were voices, thunder, lightning, and earthquake.

In Revelation 8, during the interlude, we see in Revelation 11:13 that the two witnesses, having completed their assignment, then killed, were ascending to heaven during this time. The scriptures tell us in the **same hour** during their ascension: there was a great earthquake in Israel, which destroyed one-tenth of the city, and seven thousand died. Recalling the angel filled the censer with fire and cast it onto the earth, causing earthquakes.

There is a short interlude before the sounding of the seventh trumpet, as there is another interlude before the opening of the seventh seal. During this pause, John sees the twenty-four elders worshipping God. John sees the temple of God open in heaven, and there was seen the Ark of the Covenant. Parallel to the scene in heaven, the nations were angry and unrepentant.

Revelation 11:16–19

John writes about the opening of the little book.

> *I saw another mighty angel come down from heaven, clothed with a cloud and a rainbow was upon his head and his face was as it were the sun and his feet as pillars of fire. He had in his hand a little book open, he set his right foot*

> *upon the sea and his left foot on the earth. He cried with a loud voice as a lion roars and when he had cried seven thunders uttered their voices.* (Revelation 10)

John is ready to write what the voices said, but he is told to "*seal up those things which the seven thunders uttered and write them not.*" John is told to take the book from the angel and eat it, "for you must prophesy again before many people, nations, tongues, and kings." This passage transcends time, taking John back to AD 90 to complete the writing of the book of Revelation. The little book is representative of God's Word, and through the scriptures, many will hear the Gospel.

The passage in Revelation 10 is spiritual in nature. The giant angel and his features are not visible to those on the earth. Whatever the message is at this point, it is not for us to know. This reminds us that the best-laid plans of man can be interrupted by the plans of God. All that we can determine about these end-times is limited in our human scope. So we surmise the what-ifs. What if the demons and evil angels spoken of in the six trumpets were only part of God's plan? What if our suspicions that aliens who are evil angels and their offspring the Nephilim make an appearance on the earth? Revelation 10:6 alludes to this end-time mystery:

> *And the angel which I saw stand upon the sea and upon the earth lifted up his hand to heaven and swear by him that lives forever and ever who created <u>heaven and the things that therein are and the earth and the things that therein are and the sea and the things which are therein that there should be time no longer</u> and in the days of the voice of the seventh angel, when he shall begin to sound, then the mystery of God should be finished as he has declared to his servants the prophets.*

The above underlined is to emphasize that there is a deeper meaning in the things in heaven, earth, and the sea and could apply to things unseen. It does not seem to apply to things we clearly see, but time as we know it to be will be no longer. We clearly cannot comprehend what is beyond our solar system or entities that exist in another dimension. Within our limits, we do not have 100 percent understanding of our own humanity, soul, and spirit, or the innumerable life forms that exist on the earth. We have only a minute understanding of things under the earth as well as things existing in the oceans. Perhaps we are to understand that God will delay no longer, and he will accelerate the fulfillment of all prophecy. The sounding of the seventh trumpet announces the finality of the tribulation judgments.

Stage Three, the Final Three and a Half Years Years

The great tribulation is to continue for three and one half years. This time is signaled by the opening of the sixth seal, Revelation 6:12. It will unleash the full wrath of God with unspeakable catastrophic events upon the earth. The response of the people will be great fear, and they will hide in dens and mountains.

An overview of events that will occur during the last half of the tribulation include the following:

- The Antichrist and false prophet are at their peak, having been empowered by Satan.
- Antichrist is mortally wounded (Revelation 13:3) then revived by satanic power, and the world followed him.
- Antichrist requires all to take his mark and worship him.
- Antichrist has trouble in his kingdom.
- Trumpet and vial judgments.
- Antichrist summons the nations to gather for the battle of Armageddon.
- Antichrist unleashes wrath upon the Jews, who will flee Israel.

Response of the world to the Antichrist

- They are amazed and in awe.
- They worship Satan, who gave power to the beast/Antichrist.
- Those whose names are not written in the book of life will worship the beast.
- They acknowledge his great power over the nations.

Satan's response to the wrath of God is an attack against the Jews. Zechariah 13:8, "*And it shall come to pass that in all the land, said the Lord, two parts therein will be cut off and die but the third will be left therein.*" This passage tells us that two-thirds of Israelis will die. Satan's wrath against Israel will be unprecedented. In the midst of this turmoil, Zechariah 14:2 tells us … "*I will gather all nations against Jerusalem to battle and the city will be taken and the houses rifled and the women ravished and half of the city will go forth into captivity …*" Some Jews will escape to Petra in Jordan, about 176 miles from Jerusalem. Revelation 12:6 tells us that Israel (the woman) fled into the wilderness, where she had a place prepared of God, where they would find refuge for three and a half years during the final half of the great tribulation.

Habakkuk 2:18–19 speaks of a graven image that he has made, the molten image with the ability to speak and is a teacher of lies … Woe unto him that says to the image, "Awake, arise it shall teach." This certainly is a close description of the coming image that Antichrist and false prophet will demand all to worship.

The Image of the Beast

At this point in the tribulation, the unholy trio have fashioned themselves an image. Could it look like the Baphomet statue erected in Detroit? The image will be animated by technology or demonic intervention. With the great technological advances of our day, it will not be considered strange that the image can speak and move. People will see the image by way of television or Internet around the world. Revelation 13:4, "*And they worshipped the dragon* [Satan] *which gave power unto the beast* [Antichrist] *and they worshipped the beast saying who is like unto the beast? Who is able to make war with him?*" People for centuries have worshipped Satan, and during the time of the apocalypse, they will also worship the Antichrist and his image.

For consideration, the image may not be situated in just one location that would require people to travel to it but may be a hologram-type projection beamed to various locations. The projection equipment could be distributed around the world and set up to receive and display a subliminal, awesome, spectacular image—wherever the Antichrist makes his appearance. When the event comes to a town, perhaps the people of that city will be required to pay homage to the image in a large stadium setting. The news media will announce his simulated appearance, and people will be mesmerized and drawn to the event. The Antichrist will not have to make a personal appearance but could seemly appear everywhere.

At this time during the tribulation period, these people will have taken the mark of the beast. They will have been chipped or tagged. Hypothetically speaking, each person entering the stadium will be scanned and documented by their implants. We speculate that the Antichrist will have some means to know who is worshipping him and his image. In modern-day stadiums, facial recognition technology is used to sweep over the crowd. Antichrist minions will be able to determine who is not worshipping the beast and kill them through electrified seats. At the end of the program, the dissidents will be removed by automatic collectors and then incinerated.

In our research, we came across a mystery found once in the Bible in Psalms 139:16, which refers to a Golem as "shapeless mass." The *Encyclopedia of Jewish Religion* defines this as an "embryo." Early Hebrew referred to it in the sense of "formless matter." It later evolved to mean a "robot," or mechanical monster magically created when its master infused life into a clay model by inserting one of the mystic names of God under its tongue. The Golem would then obey its creator.[61] Initially, this anomaly was credited by a mystic. Rabbi Elijah of Chelm, AD 1550–1583, said to have fashioned such a creature. Later, Tzevi, Ashkenazi of Amsterdam, AD 1658–1718, acknowledged that his grandfather, Rabbi Elijah of Chelm, had done such a thing. Tzevi seriously discussed if a Golem might be counted as one in the

---

61 Werblowsky, Wigoder, Encyclopedia of Jewish Religion, P161 Golem

religious quorum of ten, adding that his grandfather said, "R. Judah Low Ben Bezalel of Prague created a Golem. He said it was rendered harmless by removing the source of its animation, the divine name. Ben Bezalel said his Golem acted as his servant."

Wikipedia refers to the Hebrew understanding of Golem as "unshaped form," connoting the unfinished human being before God's eyes. Judaism's earliest stories of Golems were referenced in the Talmud where Adam was initially created as a Golem when his dust was kneaded into a shapeless husk, and like Adam, all Golems are created from mud. Golems could not speak. Further story says that the created Golem was sent to Rav Zeira, who spoke to him, but he did not answer, and Zeira said, "You were created by the magicians, return to your dust."

Following from passages found in the Sefer Yetzirah, *Book of Creation*, it was studied as a means to attain the mystical ability to create and animate a Golem. It was thought by these practitioners that by creating an ecstatic experience with the object through meditation, putting oneself into an altered state of consciousness or reciting rituals and using a token that will connect one with the Golem. In this case, writing the name of God or a Hebrew letter and placing it in the mouth or forehead would cause its animation.[62]

The Jewish Museum in Berlin will exhibit a Golem beginning September 23, 2016. The purpose is to present the Golem within Jewish mystical ritual to its role as a subject in stories and film. The exhibition is a medium to maintain its afterlife in art, digital and verbal expressions of creativity, power, and redemption.

Stories of Golem continue in modern times, mostly in the form of entertainment. However, in the Czech Republic, a small town called Ustek has a Jewish museum with a statue of the Golem at the entrance. We have learned that mythological stories can point to actual situations.

In thinking about a Golem, we can conceive of Satan creating a beast who appears to be alive in defiance of God's commandment not to make graven images. As the Golem took on animation by placing the name of God under its tongue, this future situation is the manifestation of a demon or evil spirit interjecting itself into an object. Throughout the ages, idol worshippers and occultists used statues, images, drawings, humans, and objects speaking rituals and incantations over them to summon the spirits.

When the image of the beast is created by the Antichrist for the purpose of it being worshipped, the power of the spoken word or other supernatural edict will cause it to become animated. In the beginning of creation, we recall that the power of the spoken Word brought forth into the visible, physical realm all things. The angels witnessed the creation, including Satan. Satan counterfeits and corrupts all that God has done.

---

62 Wikipedia, *Golem,* Online access August 27, 2013

We already know that fallen angels are assigned over the affairs of nations. Researchers come to similar conclusions that these principalities can be summoned and then carry out their own agenda. The term *egregore* in Greek means "watcher," which is another name for fallen angels. It is associated with an immaterial entity that is summoned by the collected will of humans through rituals (Wikipedia online September 1, 2013).

The Mark of the Beast

Scripture speaks to this mandate:

> *And he causes all to receive a mark in their right hand or in their foreheads, no man might buy or sell save he that has the mark or the name of the beast or the number of his name … the number of the beast is 666.* (Revelation 13:16–18)

In order for people to work, buy food or other commodities, they will have to take the mark of the beast in their head or hand. This could be a tattoo or a RFID implant that operates wirelessly. March 2015 *Dateline* TV program reported that by 2017, all people will be microchipped. This suggestion is unlikely since millions will not take the chip. Believers are hopeful the Rapture event will take them out of harm's way. Preppers and people living off the grid will still use hard cash or items to barter. Underground black markets will thrive. Doomsday preppers are already getting off the grid, stockpiling and fortifying living facilities. The last group of people who will not be microchipped are those dwelling in remote regions or jungles, have no electricity, TVs, cell phones, and are not aware of the global order of things.

One-world order fanatics will eliminate credit or debit cards and monetary fiat, forcing people to be chipped in order to buy or sell. Personal data will be collected and stored. Years ago, a megalith computer system in England called the "beast" was used to store data. Today's small-in-size computers surpass the antiquated beast. The United States has built the UDC, Utah Data Center. It has the capacity to store all data on each citizen. The computer can store yottabytes and operate at petaflop speed per second, and transmission of data is conducted on laser chips, which increase wavelengths of light at terabyte speed per second.

In our chapter 16, we discuss various prototypes. We do not know what the actual mark of the beast will be at this time. Following are a few samplings of various methods currently being tested.

Scientists are working to perfect a bar code/electronic tattoo called an EES, Epidermal Electronic System, which would dissolve into the skin.

Deborah Dupre, *Before It's News* online, August 5, 2013, article, "1.5 Million Fans Willingly RFID Chipped at Lollapalooza Raises Debate." Article displays picture of a RFID chip compared to a grain of rice. Thousands of young and old alternative music fans lined up to willingly be tracked with RFID microchips at the Lollapalooza in Chi-town, Chicago. They were fitted with nonremovable wristbands with chips to remain in place for the three-day concert. If removed, they would not be admitted and no refunds.

Deluded people are excited to get chipped in order to replace credit cards, keys, IDs. A man named Amai Graafstra, founder of Dangerous Things in Seattle, Washington, had a small RFID implanted in both of his hands. His right hand can download information from a cell phone, and his left hand unlocks his front door, turns on his computer, and start his motor bike. February 2014, at the Transhuman Visions conference in San Francisco, he set up an implantation station offering attendees the chance to be chipped for $50. Using a large needle designed for microchipping pets, he injected a glass-coated RFID tag the size of a grain of rice into each person.

Book by Katherine Albrecht and Liz McIntyre, *Spy Chips: How Major corporation and Government Plan to Track Your Every Move*—"Imagine a world of no privacy, where your every purchase is monitored and recorded in a database and your every belonging is numbered, where someone many states away or perhaps in another country has a record of everything you have ever bought and can be tracked and monitored remotely."

Delivery of the RFID device can be in an ingestible smart pill. Proteus Digital Health of Redwood City, California, won approval to sell a pill that relays information about a person's vital signs via a mobile phone to their doctor.

A company by the name of Kronos has announced updates to its biometric tool, including Cloud and Wi-Fi compatibility and improvements to its data capture software and user interface with its "InTouch" device; it is marketing to employers to replace time clocks.

Google's Motorola Mobility branch made patent application in November 2013 for an electronic skin tattoo for the throat with a built-in microphone that would let someone operate other devices by voice command. Google CEO Larry Page is looking futuristically to implant a device into humans that when they think of a fact, it will just tell you the answer.

MC10 of Cambridge, Massachussetts, is developing a skinlike adhesive bandage-type tattoo with a wireless transmitter to send data regarding the person's health.

Besides maintaining a mega data collection system, world governments have a network of surveillance systems in place. The United States' National Security Administration was exposed for conducting spy ops on citizen through e-mail, cell phones, and the use of drones. When conspiracy theorists exposed government complicity, they were labeled as crazy. Now we know; there are machines that can x-ray through walls and robot insects that can track your whereabouts using GPS technology, facial recognition, and retina scanners. Welcome to the police state (*Raiders News Update*, "Beast Tech," Terry L. Cook and Tom Horn.)

We do not have to imagine a future scenario of the coming mark; we have already entered the realm of no privacy, no individuality, no independent thought. All medical records are on a database; all income and credit reports are in a database; all passport, driver licenses, birth certificates are on a database. Moving from so-called smart cards or mobile devices, which can be stolen and duplicated, the global elite will move to enforce the implantation or marking of every person in the world.

It is mandatory that all receive his mark, or they will be beheaded or struck down by lightning. The form of punishment to be used during the tribulation is beheading. Islamic radicals frequently cut off the heads of the infidels. However, others are pushing for the guillotine to exact punishment. Anyone who takes the mark is eternally doomed to hell. The unmarked will be hunted down and, if found, killed by the Antichrist's global regime.

Seven Trumpets and Seven Vials Judgments

The events coming upon the earth have been foretold thousands of years in advance. In Haggai 2:6–9, "*God said, yet once, it is a little while and I will shake the heavens and the earth and the sea and the dry land, I will shake all nations …*" In modern times, we can measure the predictions made by Haggai. We have seen signs in the sky and meteors falling to the earth. The oceans roar with tsunamis, multiple earthquakes, and volcanoes plague the earth, and there is stress among the nations.

Zechariah 14:12 speaks about a plague that the Lord has sent to kill the people that have fought against Jerusalem. This plague will also kill the animals. He said, "*Their flesh will consume away while they stand upon their feet and their eyes will consume away in their holes and their tongue will consume away in their mouth.*" This sounds like a description of a nuclear plague—a final desperate act by the satanic alliance.

Following, we present the final judgments of the trumpets and vials together to compare their similarities:

Trumpet 1

Revelation 8:6—the first trumpet sounded, and hail, fire, and blood were cast upon the earth, causing one-third of the trees to burn up and all the green grass.

Pouring Out Vial 1

Revelation 16:2, "*And the first angel went and poured out his vial upon the earth and there fell a noisome and grievous sore upon the men which had the mark of the beast and upon them which worshipped his image.*" This could be a reaction to the method of placing the mark on the body.

Trumpet 2

Revelation 8:8—the second trumpet sounded, and a great mountain burning with fire fell into the sea, and one-third of the sea became blood; one-third of the sea creatures died; and one-third of ships in the sea were destroyed.

Pouring Out Vial 2

Revelation 16:3, "*And the second angel poured out his vial upon the sea and it became as the blood of a dead man and every living soul died in the sea.*" The ecological balance of the oceans has been polluted by mankind. Sea creatures are currently dying at an alarming rate. God's final judgment allows the oceans to be toxic as blood and most living things will die.

Trumpet 3

Revelation 8:10—the third trumpet sounded, and a great star from heaven, burning as it were a lamp, fell upon one-third of the rivers and freshwater sources; and its name is called Wormwood. This object caused the water sources to be polluted, and who drank the water died. Some sources of water have already been poisoned by radioactive waste and lead.

Pouring Out Vial 3

Revelation 16:4, "*And the third angel poured out his vial upon the rivers and fountains of waters and they became blood . . . for they have shed the blood of saints and prophets and thou has given them blood to drink.*"

Trumpet 4

Revelation 8:12—the fourth trumpet sounded, causing an eclipse of one-third of the sun, moon, and stars. This created darkness for a part of the day, and the luminaries did not give but a part of their light at night. At this time an angel flies through the midst of heaven, saying, "Woe, woe, woe to the inhabitants of the earth."

Pouring Out Vial 4

Revelation 16:8, "*And the fourth angel poured out his vial upon the sun and power was given unto him to scorch men with fire. And men were scorched with great heat and blasphemed the name of God which has power over these plagues and they repented not to give him glory.*" Earth has experienced intense solar flares and eruptions, but this will significantly increase.

Trumpet 5

Revelation 9:1–11, "*And the fifth trumpet sounded and I saw a star fall from heaven unto the earth and* ***to him was given the key*** *of the bottomless pit.*" When the pit is open, a thick smoke arises enough to darken the atmosphere and block out the sun (similar to a volcanic eruption). From out of the smoke came forth locusts. It was commanded that they should not hurt the grass, trees, or any green thing but only unredeemed people. This is similar to the plagues God sent against Egypt. These locusts have received permission to torment men for <u>five months,</u> and the wound will be like the bite of a scorpion, but they are not to kill them. People are in such torment that they want to die, but death will flee from them. These locusts appear to be demonic.

Revelation 9:11, "*They had a king over them which is the angel of the <u>bottomless pit</u>* [Satan] *whose name in the Hebrew tongue is Abaddon but in the Greek tongue his name is Apollyon.*"

- They are ruled by a king called Abaddon/Apollyon.
- They are demons.
- Shape like a horse outfitted in armor, iron breastplates.
- Crown like gold on their heads.
- The face of a man, long hair, sharp teeth.
- Wings that sound like horses and chariots running.
- Tails like scorpions with stingers in their tails.

After the death of Jesus, he descended and took the keys of death and hell. Two thousand years later, Jesus will give an angel the key to open the bottomless pit, which is also hell. From the "bottomless pit" come forth demonic spirits. Their military leader is Satan. We should not get into a big debate as to who is who in the underworld. These are not humans. It should be no surprise to the reader that evil spirits and fallen angels have been ruling in the affairs of mankind for millennium. Satan and his hoards have the ability to ascend and descend from the lower regions of earth.

Scholarly thought introduced by David Flynn, *Cydonia: The Secret Chronicles of Mars,* suggests that the falling star could be an extraterrestrial ship moving into orbit around earth, carrying aliens/demons. As we discussed, supernatural entities can travel on supernatural vehicles.

A few scholars have come up with the conception that the bottomless pit was a star falling from heaven. An impact upon the earth of a star, comet, meteor would create a crater but not to the extent it would become a "bottomless pit." The Bible also refers to the star as a "him." Reading the scripture clearly indicates the star is an angel who is given the key to open the bottomless pit.

Another scholar thought the bottomless pit existed as another planet. He saw Saturn's moon called Iapetus in 1672, using a small refracting telescope. "There was a great gulf formed by a giant, walled threshold at its equator" (Giovanni Domenico Cassini). This image was later confirmed by NASA in 2005, who reported that the eight-hundred-mile-long and twelve-mile-wide rim had not been seen on other moons. This observation does not lead one into believing a gulf on Saturn is the bottomless pit on earth.

According to scripture, the realm of the bottomless pit is in the lower regions of the earth and is in a spiritual dimension that the living cannot attain unto. Scriptures also tell us that something sinister is coming out of the bottomless pit upon the earth. This region could be a portal, as described in Revelation 9 and also seen in the writings of Joel, who speaks about those things coming upon the face of the earth:

> *Blow the trumpet in Zion and sound the alarm in my holy mountain let all the inhabitants of the land tremble for the day of the Lord has come. A day of darkness and gloominess, a day of clouds and of thick darkness ... a great people and strong, there has not been ever like neither will be any more after it, even to the years of many generations. A fire devours before them and behind them a flame burns. The land is as the garden of Eden before them and behind them a desolate wilderness, nothing will escape them. The appearance of them is as the appearance of horses and as horseman they run.* (Joel 2:2–11)

Combine the descriptions given in Revelation and Joel, and one can get a better understanding of the horror coming forth from the bottomless pit portal.

- Strong, giantlike people, never seen on earth before.
- Fire is emitted around them.
- They look like half horse and half man.
- Dressed in battle array.
- They will run like mighty men, swiftly climb walls and march in unison.
- They will not die from a sword wound.
- They will pass through all the city, enter through windows and none will escape.

The first group described in Revelation 9 is like locust, and God has given them a time period of five months to torment mankind but not to kill them. The entities described in Joel 2 may be literal as we consider that world governments have established underground installations for secret operations. Weapons or missiles have been launched from underground sites accompanied with much smoke. Currently, governments have invested in drone technology.

One term used is Micro Air Vehicles, MAVs, and they have been programmed to swarm like locusts. These units can resemble small aircraft, birds, or insects with or without wings. It was difficult for first-century man to describe twenty-first-century technology. Perhaps the face, hair, and teeth are images of those manning the vehicles, images painted onto the vehicles, or it could be a combination of robotics and humanoid features. Science calls this singularity where man and machine are merged. Technological advances could develop superhuman entities.

Further comparison between Revelation 9 and Joel 2—Joel's monsters do not appear to fly but are strong, giantlike people running swiftly. Throughout history, various empires in their conquests use military forces described as giants, monsters, strong, swift. A current example of this is similar to the rise of ISIS. They are strong and move swiftly. They are like monsters, having no compassion. They are incapable of mercy. The rise of Islamic terrorism is a precursor before the climax of actual events.

Pouring Out Vial 5

> *And the fifth angel poured out his vial upon the seat of the beast and his kingdom was full of darkness and they gnawed their tongues for pain, blasphemed the God of heaven because of their pains and their sores and repented not of their deeds.* (Revelation 16:10)

God brings forth darkness upon the Antichrist and his establishment. Those who are aligned with the Antichrist will experience additional torment of darkness that renders pain and bodily sores. This supernatural darkness came upon pharaoh in the days of Moses and the Exodus.

Trumpet 6

Revelation 9 is a culmination of the fifth and sixth trumpet judgments. Revelation 9:3 releases the locust from the bottomless pit (Revelation 9:13–19). The sixth trumpet sounds, and God commands his angel to loose the four evil angels, which are bound in the great River Euphrates. Enoch spoke of the fallen angels that were bound under the earth. These entities are given one year, one month, one day, and one hour to slay one-third of mankind.

Following the four evil angels are two hundred million horsemen having breastplates of fire, jacinth, brimstone; riding on horses with heads like lions; out of their mouth came smoke and fire. Their power proceeds from their mouth, and their tails are like serpents with heads. John gives a description of this army:

- The riders on the horses wore bright breastplates of fire and colors that resemble jewels of red, blue, yellow.
- The horses had heads like lions, breathing out fire; their weapons of power were in the mouth and tails, like serpents.
- Their weapons are fire, smoke, and brimstone (sulfur).

Looking at this literally, it could be a picture of beings in armored vehicles with multi-colored flashing lights, firing projectiles from the front or rear of the vehicle.

Revelation 9:18, "***By these three*** *was the third part of mankind killed.*" Herein we are to understand as a result of three different incursions identified as (1) the locust which are given 5 months to torment, (2) the four evil angels released from river Euphrates are given a little over a year to kill, and the (3) two hundred million horsemen together with them cause the death of one-third of mankind—all leading to the final battle of Armageddon at the end of the tribulation.

So far, all these horrible judgments did not persuade many to repent.

> *And the rest of the men which were not killed by these plagues yet repented not of the works of their hands that they should not worship devils, idols of gold, silver, brass, stone, wood which neither can see, nor hear nor walk; nor repented they of their murders, sorceries, fornication or their thefts.* (Revelation 9:20–21)

Pouring Out Vial 6

> *And the sixth angel poured out his vial upon the great river Euphrates and the water thereof was dried up that the way of the kings of the east might be prepared. And I saw three unclean spirits like frogs come out of the mouth of the dragon and out of the mouth of the beast and out of the mouth of the false prophet, for they are the spirits of devils working miracles which go forth unto the kings of the earth and of the whole world to gather them to the battle of that great day of God … he gathered them together into a place called in the Hebrew tongue, Armageddon.* (Revelation 16:12)

The Euphrates River is presently drying up. It will be used as a land bridge to bring the two hundred million to Israel for the final battle of Armageddon. The three unclean spirits coming out of the mouth of the dragon (Satan), beast (Antihrist), and the false prophet suggest that Satan is the embodiment of evil, and demonic spirits may have taken possession of the Antichrist and the false prophet. They will work in concert to influence people to believe the great delusion and gather for the final battle.

Seventh Trumpet

Revelation 8:1—returning to Revelation 5, we saw that there was a scroll/book with seven seals. The opening of the seventh seal releases the seven trumpet judgments signaling the final stage of the tribulation is at hand.

> *And the seventh angel sounded and there were great voices in heaven saying the kingdoms of this world are become the kingdoms of our Lord … and the twenty four elders … fell upon their faces and worshipped God … And the nations were angry and the wrath is come and the time of the dead that they should be judged and that thou should give reward unto your servants the prophets and the saints and them that fear your name … and destroy them which destroy the earth.* (Revelation 11:15–18)
>
> *Behold the day of the Lord comes and your spoil will be divided in the midst of you. For I will gather all nations against Jerusalem to battle and the city will be taken and the houses rifled and the women ravished and half of city will go forth into captivity and the residue of the people will not be cut off from the city.* (Zechariah 14:1–2)
>
> Jesus said, *for then shall be great tribulation such as was not since the beginning of the world to this time, no, nor ever shall be and except those days should be shortened, there should no flesh be saved. But for the elect's sake (Israel) those days will be shortened.* (Matthew 24:21)

In this passage, we see that the final three and a half years will be horrific. These end-time events will increase with intensity and will come in like a flood. It is likened to a pregnant woman going into labor and the birth pains increase as the advent of the birth comes to a climax.

Pouring Out the Seventh Vial

> *And the seventh angel poured out his vial into the air and there came a great voice out of the temple of heaven from the throne saying it is done. There were voices and thunders and lightnings and there was a great earthquake and the great city was divided into three parts and the cities of the nations fell and great Babylon came in remembrance before God to give unto her the cup of the wine of the fierceness of his wrath. And every island fled away and the mountains were not found. There fell upon men a great hail out of heaven, every stone about the weight of a talent and men blasphemed God because of the plague of the hail for the plague thereof was exceeding great.* (Revelation 16:17)

With the pouring out of this vial, a loud voice is heard from heaven followed by voices, thunders, lightnings. Upon the earth there was a great earthquake such as was not since men were upon the earth. The great city Israel was divided into three parts; the cities of nations fell; islands disappeared; and the mountains were leveled. Great hailstones weighing a hundred pounds fell upon mankind, and men still cursed God. These judgments are worldwide as it was during the time of Noah; the whole earth was impacted.

In comparing the effects of the trumpets and vials, we see similarities and perhaps overlapping consequences. As these judgments fall, mankind will excuse them as extreme weather patterns, global warming or other pandemic, asteroids hitting earth, radiation leaks kill marine life, sun and moon eclipses.

7 Trumpets	7 Vials
Hail, fire, blood, one-third of trees, grass burn.	Sores come on men who had the mark
Burning mountain fell into sea; one-third turns Water to blood; creatures die, ships destroyed.	Seas become blood, creatures die.
Burning star from heaven, Wormwood, poisons freshwater sources.	Rivers and fountains turn to blood.
One-third of sun, moon, stars darkened; angel announces woe to earth	Sun scorches mankind.
Falling star seen; angel opens bottomless pit, invasion of locust attack and torment mankind for five months; Apollyon leads two hundred million soldiers.	Darkness descends upon the headquarters of the beast; darkness brings pain.
Four angels loosed; two hundred million soldiers kill one-third, tormented for one year, one month, one day.	Euphrates dries up; three unclean spirits, nations gather for Armageddon.

Voices announce Jesus's coming to reign over kingdoms elders worship; dead to be judged; saints receive rewards.	Voices announce it is done; thunder lightning, earthquakes divide city into ;nations fall, islands disappear, mountains leveled, a hundred-

Martyrs for Christ

Millions have been martyred for Christ. Paul gives those being persecuted at this time hope during their time of suffering.

> *Your patience and faith in all your persecutions and tribulations that you endure, which is a manifest token of the righteous judgment of God that you may be counted worthy of the kingdom of God for which you suffer. Seeing it is a righteous thing with God to recompense* [repay] *tribulation to them that trouble you. And to you who are troubled rest with us, when the Lord Jesus will be revealed from heaven with his mighty angels, in flaming fire taking vengeance on them that know not God and that obey not the gospel of our Lord Jesus Christ, who will be punished with everlasting destruction from the presence of the Lord.* (2 Thessalonians 1:4)

This passage pertains to those who are killed for the sake of Jesus before the Rapture and during the tribulation because Jesus will be revealed from heaven only at his Second Coming. It also tells those who were martyred, they will be counted worthy to enter into the millennial kingdom of God.

John sees those who died for their belief in Christ:

> *I saw the souls of them that were beheaded for the witness of Jesus and for the word of God and which had not worshipped the beast, neither his image neither had received his mark upon their foreheads or in their hand and they lived and reigned with Christ a thousand years.* (Revelation 20:4)

John sees a countless number of saints in white robes, and he is told, Revelation 7:14: "*And he said to me, these are they which came out of great tribulation and have washed their robes and made them white in the blood of the Lamb.*" These tribulation saints refused to take the mark of the beast or to worship his image. They repented and accepted Jesus as savior before they were martyred, and their souls go to be with Jesus in heaven. Their body and soul will be resurrected during the great harvest, which is the third stage of the Resurrection.

Daniel 7:20 speaks of the time that the Antichrist will make war with the saints (Israel and tribulation saints) and prevail against them until the Ancient of Days come.

The King Is Coming, Hear the Sound of War Drums

The final days of the tribulation highlight several events. Foremost, the wrath of God has been poured out upon the earth as symbolized in the last trumpets and vials. We can hardly imagine the devastation that has occurred. Land mass has been destroyed by earthquakes and other calamities. The seas and waves will be roaring as in tsunamis. There will be great distress and perplexity of nations. The powers of heaven will be shaken, which refers to Satan and his legions being cast out upon the earth.

> *Whose voice then shook the earth but now he has promised saying, yet once more I shake not the earth only but also heaven. This work signifies the removing of those things that are shaken as of things that are made that those things which cannot be shaken may remain. We receive a kingdom which cannot be moved…* (Hebrews 12:26)

In Israel's final days, they are desperate for God's intervention. Luke 18:7, God will avenge his own elect, who cry day and night unto him, though he bear long with them. God will avenge them speedily. The chosen people have yearned for their Messiah for thousands of years. They have prayed for deliverance from their enemies. The Lord knows that it has been a long time, but when Messiah comes this time, he will destroy and judge the wicked.

> *Behold the Lord comes out of his place to punish the inhabitants of the earth for their evil, the earth shall disclose her blood and shall no more cover her slain.* (Isaiah 26:21)

According to research done by Walid Shoebat, Messiah Jesus will go into Midian in the land of Arabia before coming to the Mount of Olives. There is an archetype recorded in Judges where the role of Gideon is a warrior savior delivering his people out of Midianite bondage. The Ishmaelites/Midianites were of the lineage of Abraham with Hagar and his fourth wife, Katura, around 1160 BC. Following this line of thought, Shoebat directs us to the prophet Habakkuk around 612 BC. In Habakkuk 3:3 we read, "*God came from Teman and the Holy One from mount Paran. His glory covered the heavens and the earth was full of his praise. His brightness was as the light, he had horns coming out of his hand…*" Teman and Paran are associated with Saudi Arabia, and the scriptures point to God, the Holy One, coming out of Teman.

Other scriptures support the coming of Messiah as a warrior:

> *I shall see him but not now. I shall behold him but not near, there shall come a Star out of Jacob and a Scepter shall rise out of Israel and will smite the corners of Moab and destroy the children of Sheth.* (Numbers 24:17)

Further reading specifically calls out the destruction of Moab, Edom, Seir. In Ezekiel 35:15 … "is the destruction of Idumea." Isaiah 25:10. . . "and Moab will be trodden down."

Habakkuk 3:5 describes conditions at the time the Holy One comes out of Teman. Before him went the pestilence, burning coals; the mountains were scattered and made low; as well as the tents of Cush are afflicted along with the land of Midian. Habakkuk is given the understanding that the enemies of his people and the God of Israel are the ancient Chaldeans, Babylonians, Assyrians—inhabitants of the lands of Teman, Dedan, Midian, Arabia, Jordan, Syria, Africa, Canaan. This is applicable to the Roman, British, Ottoman Empires, whose history plagued Israel to this day. Habakkuk 1:5, "Because the nations will march through the breath of the land to possess dwelling places not theirs, God will come out of his place to defend Israel." It has been a very long time, but reading Habakkuk 2:3, "*For the vision is yet for an appointed time but at the end it shall speak and not lie, though it tarry, wait for it because it will surely come*," it will come to pass.

Jesus comes with bloodstained garments, having dealt with the forces of evil.

> *And I saw heaven opened and behold a white horse and he that sat upon him was called Faithful and True and in righteousness he does judge and make war. His eyes were as a flame of fire and on his head were many crowns and he had a name written that no man knew but himself. He was <u>clothed with a vesture dipped in blood</u> and his name is called the Word of God. The armies which were in heaven followed him upon white horses, clothed in fine line, white and clean. Out of his mouth goes a sharp sword that with it he should <u>smite the nations</u> and he will rule them with a rod of iron and he treads the winepress of the fierceness and wrath of Almighty God.* (Revelation 19:11)

At this time, when the residue of nations are gathered for the final battle, they will go into perdition as Jesus brings destruction upon them. Zechariah 14:3, "*<u>Then</u> will the Lord go forth and fight against those nations as when he fought in the day of battle.*" Afterward, Jesus proceeds to the Mount of Olives; it will split in half, and the mountains will move out of their place, creating a great rift or valley. Jerusalem will be elevated.

> *And his feet will stand in that day upon the mount of Olives which is before Jerusalem on the east and the mount of Olives will cleave [split] in the middle thereof toward the east and toward the west and there will be a very great valley*

> *and half of the mountain will remove toward the north and half of it toward the south ... and the Lord my God will come and all the saints with him.* (Zechariah 14:4)

It may help to understand the movements of Jesus in the supernatural realm. We believe that the Second Coming will be observed by everyone in the world. This procession will appear to be moving in slow-motion. What can be seen of this entourage may take some time to literally arrive upon the earth. In the meantime, Jesus alone will move forward to destroy the enemies of Israel. Jesus will appear on the Mount of Olives. Jesus will destroy those gathered for the final battle. At the same time, he will still be visible in the sky. It will seem he is in two places at once. Jesus is not bound by our space and time.

We will review the movements of Jesus as he deals with the nations. Isaiah 25:10 predicts that the hand of the Lord will rest on Mount Zion, but **before** so, Moab/Edom will be trampled by him. This is specifically set forth in Isaiah 63:3:

> *Who is this that* ***comes from Edom*** *with dyed garments from Bozrah ... one who is glorious in his apparel traveling in the greatness of his strength? It is I that speak in righteousness, mighty to save. I have trodden the winepress alone and of the people there were none with me: for I will tread them in mine anger and trample them in my fury and their blood will be sprinkled upon my garments ... for the day of vengeance is in my heart and the year of my redeemed is come.*

This two-thousand-year-old prediction will be fulfilled very soon.

The above passage in Isaiah points to Jesus trampling the nations as in a winepress one tramples grapes, and this alludes to the death of the unrighteous, the unredeemed, and the enemies of Israel. Isaiah 63 is associated with Revelation 14:14–20:

> *Behold a white cloud and upon the cloud one sat like unto the Son of man having on his head a golden crown and in his hand a sharp sickle ... thrust in the sickle and reap for the time is come for you to reap, for the harvest of the earth is ripe ... and the winepress was trodden without the city and blood came out of the winepress, even unto the horse bridles by the space of* [180 miles].

Jesus is wearing garments stained in blood, and this passage is telling us that Jesus will deal with the wicked in his conquest at the battle of Armageddon and before the great harvest begins.

Following, we witness Jesus dealing with his enemies.

> ***These*** *will make war with the Lamb and Jesus overcomes them for he is Lord of lords and King of kings.* (Revelation 17:14)

In Revelation 19:19, we are told that **these** who make war with Jesus are "*the beast* [Satan, false prophet, Antichrist, wicked people], *kings of the earth and their armies gathered together to make war against him that sat on the horse and against his army.*" This passage supports the supposition that all will see Jesus on the horse in the sky with a two-edged sword in his mouth proceeding with the hosts of heaven accompanied by his angels and saints.

> *Behold in those days and in that time, when I shall bring again the captivity* [the Jews have returned from the four corners of the earth] *of Judah and Jerusalem.* [In the near future] *I will also gather all nations and will bring them down into the* ***Valley of Jehoshaphat*** *and will plead with them there for my people and for my heritage Israel whom they have scattered among the nations and parted my land.* (Joel 3:1–2)

The Valley of Megiddo is same as Jehoshaphat. The final battle of Armageddon will be in the Valley of Megiddo. In summary, Jesus will deal with the Islamic nations, and he will deal with the revived Roman Empire nations; and finally, he will gather the remaining factions from Russia, China, Europe, Islamic nations to the battle of Armageddon.

They were destroyed by the brightness of his glory. Millions will be dead.

In the following passage, we see that the Lord has prepared for the cleanup of dead bodies.

> *I saw an angel standing in the sun and he cried with a loud voice, saying to all the fowl that fly in the midst of heaven, come and gather yourselves together unto the supper of the great God, that you may eat the flesh of kings … and the flesh of all men, free and bond, both small and great.* (Revelation 19:17–18)

All Will See the Sign of the Son

After the battle of Armageddon, there will be people alive throughout the world, and they will see the sign of the Son of Man appear in heaven. And all the tribes of earth will mourn, and they will see the Son of Man coming in the clouds of heaven with power and great glory. The sign will at first appear as an anomaly in the heavens. Then Jesus, sitting on a white horse, will become distinguishable. He has prepared himself to judge and make war. His eyes are as a flame of fire; on his head are many crowns; he has a sharp sword in his mouth; and his vesture was stained with blood; written on his thigh, "King of Kings and Lord of Lords." This unfolding scene will now be making touchdown on earth (Matthew 24:30).

Following Jesus are the army of heaven, the host of heaven, thousands and thousands of saints riding white horses and clothed in fine, clean white linen.

Those who could not get plane tickets to this great event will watch on their fifty-inch TVs.

Jesus has redeemed his people; he has defended them. The battle is over. The people will celebrate.

> *In that day I will raise up the House of David that is fallen and close up the breaches thereof and I will raise up his ruins and I will build it as in the days of old, that they may possess the remnant of Edom and all the heathen which are called by my name said the Lord that doeth this.* (Amos 9:11–13)
>
> *And he will speak peace unto the heathen and his dominion shall be from sea even to sea and from the river even to the ends of the earth.* (Zechariah 9:10)
>
> *For they will be as the stones of a crown, lifted up as an ensign upon his land. For how great is his goodness and how great is his beauty …* (Zechariah 9:16)

Following the celebration will be a time to separate the wicked from the just. First one to get thrown into the lake of fire alive are the false prophet and the Antichrist. Satan is chained in the bottomless pit (Revelation 19:20–21).

The Great Harvest

Those who survive the tribulation will be judged by fire. The wicked will be tried by fire and sent to hell. The righteous will be refined as silver and gold. Once purified, they will say, "The Lord Jesus is my God." In that day, the Lord will defend the inhabitants of Jerusalem … and the house of David shall be as God, as the angel of the LORD (Jesus) before them. "And I will pour upon the house of David, the spirit of grace and of supplication, and they will look upon me whom they have pierced, and they shall mourn for him as one mourns for his only son."

In the following passage, it appears that the residue of Jews who are still located outside of Jerusalem, having witnessed the sign of the Son coming, will be gathered to stand before Jesus.

> *Then they will see the Son of man coming in the clouds with great power and glory. And then he will send his angels and they will gather together his elect*

from the four winds, from the uttermost part of the earth to the uttermost part of heaven. (Mark 13:27)

The next passage is general to both the righteous Jew and Gentile.

> *Thy people will be delivered every one that will be found written in the book* [book of life]. *And many of them that sleep in the dust of the earth will awake, some to everlasting life and some to shame and everlasting contemp. And they that be wise will shine as the brightness of the firmament and they that turn many to righteousness as the stars forever and ever.* (Daniel 12:1)

Daniel foresees the third stage of the Resurrection at the end of the tribulation period. Some souls will awake to everlasting life if their names are in the book of life and will live with Christ during the millennial reign. The others will awake to everlasting shame and contempt, and they will be remanded to hell. This is the great harvest. Daniel's prophecy is confirmed in Matthew 13:43:

> *Then will the righteous shine forth as the sun in the kingdom of their Father ...*

After the battle of Armageddon, the Lord will send his reapers to separate the wheat from the tares. In Matthew 13:37–43, Jesus explains that he, the Son of Man, did sow good seed—which is the Word—throughout the world, and the good seed (wheat) represents the children of the kingdom of God. Satan, the enemy, did sow tares (children of Satan) among the good seed.

> *Let both grow together until the harvest and in the time of harvest, I will say to the reapers, gather you together first the tares and bind them in bundles to burn them but gather the wheat into my barn.* (Matthew 13:30)

In this passage, we are to understand that Satan's rule over the earth has ended. The reapers are the holy angels, which will have the task of separating the wheat from the tares or the righteous from the unrighteous. The unrighteous tares are those that worshipped the beast and do iniquity, and they will be gathered, cast into a furnace, and sent to hell to join all the other wicked wailing, torment, and gnashing of teeth.

We get another picture of the great harvest in Matthew 25:32–34:

> *And before him will be gathered all nations and he will separate them one from another as a shepherd divides his sheep from the goats. He will set the sheep*

on his right hand but the goats on his left. The King will say unto them on his right hand, come you blessed of my Father, inherit the kingdom prepared for you from the foundation of the world.

Jesus appears to be dealing with the living worldwide. He will chastise the goats for their hatred and treatment toward Israel, and he will say to "*them on the left hand, 'Depart from me, you cursed into everlasting fire prepared for the devil and his angels.'*"

Transitioning into the Millennial Kingdom

Then come the end when he will have delivered up the kingdom to God, even the Father, when he will have put down all rule and all authority and power, for he must reign until he has put all enemies under his feet. The last enemy that will be destroyed is death. (Corinthians 15:24)

The promise is given when Jesus shall appear in all of his glory; the redeemed saints will be with him (Colossians 3:4). When he shall come, he will be glorified in his saints and he will be admired in all them that believe (2 Thessalonians 1:10).

The coming of Jesus will usher in the acceptable year of the Lord.

To proclaim the acceptable year of the Lord and the day of vengeance of our God, to comfort all that mourn. To appoint unto them that mourn in Zion to give unto them beauty for ashes, the oil of joy for mourning, the garment of praise for the spirit of heaviness that they might be called trees of righteousness, the planting of the Lord that he might be glorified. (Isaiah 61:2)

There will be a time of cleansing at the onset of the millennial reign.

In that day there will be a fountain opened to the house of David and to the inhabitants of Jerusalem for sin and for uncleanness. (Zechariah 13:1)

Jews and Gentiles who did not worship the beast and survived the tribulation period will be purged of their unrighteousness. Jesus will remove objects that are offensive.

Zechariah 14:6, and it will come to pass in that day that the light will not be clear or dark, but it will be one day that will be known to the Lord … It will come to pass that at evening time, it will be light. Living water will go out from Jerusalem, half toward the former sea and half toward the hinder sea (Dead Sea and Mediterranean Sea). And the Lord will be king over all the earth; in that day there will be only Lord and his name one.

Zechariah 14:10–11, all the land will be turned as a plain from Geba to Rimmon, south of Jerusalem, and it will be lifted up (elevated) and inhabited in her place from Benjamin's gate to the place of the first gate to the corner gate and from the tower of Hananeel to the king's winepress, and men will dwell in it, and there will be no more utter destruction, but Jerusalem will be safely inhabited. This passage is telling us that all of the land covenant given to Israel will be restored, and the Holy City will descend to occupy the land. When all things are purified and made ready, Jesus will sit on his throne in Jerusalem, ruling and reigning for a thousand years.

Chapter 20
I Am Aleph and Tav
The Beginning and the End

Chapter Overview

Ushering in the Millennial Kingdom
Healing of the Nations
The Curse Is Lifted
Entering the Sabbath Rest
Jesus Rules and Reigns
Ruling with Jesus for a Thousand Years
New Jerusalem
End of the Thousand Years
Standing Before the Judge of the World
Satan Goes Back to Hell
New Heaven and New Earth

Chapter 20

I Am Aleph and Tav
The Beginning and the End

Ushering in the Millennial Kingdom

The compilation of this book began with the first book in the Bible, Genesis, and traversed throughout millennia, culminating with the last book, Revelation. The world has entered into the seventh millennium. We are looking up and listening for the trumpet of God. We await the catching away of the saints. The Day of the Lord will end with a spectacular panoramic view of the heavens rolling away with a great noise and the elements melting with searing heat. The world awaits the arrival of Messiah Yeshua to establish his kingdom where peace and righteous will reign.

> *Even so, come Lord Jesus.* (Revelation 22:20)

The scriptures portray a heavenly image of twenty-four elders seated on twenty-four thrones. Exalted in the midst of them is Jesus.

> *You who follow me in the regeneration when the Son of man will sit in the throne of his glory …* (Matthew 19:28)

Scholars comment on who these elders are and come to a consensus that twelve are representatives of ancient Israel. The remaining twelve thrones are occupied by the twelve apostles. After the tribulation, Jesus has informed them they will rule with him for a thousand years.

Healing of the Nations

You may recall that a passage in the book of Enoch speaks to a time prior to the flood that God brought judgment upon all wickedness, and then he told the angels to heal the earth.

Here in the following passages, we find God healing the nations, tearing down walls that separate, removing hearts full of hatred, giving leaves from the tree of life and the water of life for healing.

> *In that day the living waters will go out from Jerusalem … And the Lord will be king over all the earth. In that day will there be one Lord and his name one.* (Zechariah 14:8)
>
> *And he showed me a pure river of water of life, clear as crystal proceeding out of the throne of God and of the lamb. In the midst of the street of it and on either side of the river was the tree of life which bear twelve manners of fruit and yielded her fruit every month and the leaves of the tree were for the healing of the nations.* (Revelation 22:1–2)

The Curse Is Lifted

In Genesis 3:14, a curse was placed on the earth due to the fall of man. Finally, the curse will be lifted during the millennial reign. Revelation 22:3, "*And there will be no more curse …*" The earth will be purified so that the Holy One, God the Son, can dwell among mankind once again. We will see his face, and his name will be on our foreheads.

> *I heard a great voice out of heaven saying, behold the tabernacle of God is with men and he will dwell with them and they will be his people and God himself will be with them and be their God.* (Revelation 21:3)
>
> *For he is our peace, who has made both one and has broken down the middle wall of partition between us, having abolished in his flesh the enmity, even the law of commandments contained in ordinances for to make in himself of two, one new man so making peace.* (Ephesian 2:14–15)

Plain and simple, the Jew and the Gentile will be one new man in Christ.

> *Thus said the Lord of hosts, it will yet come to pass that there will come people and the inhabitants of many cities. The inhabitants of one city will go to another saying let us go speedily to pray before the Lord and to seek the Lord of hosts … yea many people and strong nations will come to seek the Lord of host in*

Jerusalem and to pray before the Lord ... In those days it will come to pass that ten men will take hold out of all languages of the nations, even will take hold of the skirt of him that is a Jew saying, we will go with you for we have heard that God is with you. (Zechariah 8:20–23)

We look toward a time when the inhabitants from many nations whose names are written in the Lamb's book of life will walk in the light of the living God.

And there shall be no night there and no need for candles, nor the light from the sun for the Lord God gives light and they will reign forever. (Revelation 22:5)

This refers to the city of God that will descend from heaven.

Entering the Sabbath Rest

Hebrews 4:1–11, the Gospel was preached to all, but the Word preached did not profit them, having no faith. For we who have believed shall enter into his rest. This place of rest was established from the foundation of the world. God spoke in a certain place of the seventh day, and God did rest; all creation was complete. This seventh millennium will become our future rest, and in this place (the kingdom of God on earth) we shall enter into his rest. There remains a rest for the people of God. For he that is entered into his rest, he also has ceased from his own works as God did from his. This rest is a foretaste of our eternal joy in the Lord, when creation is renewed and restored, when every mark of sin has been removed and the world is perfect once again. True believers understand that we are spiritually seated with Christ in heavenly places now, and at the onset of the millennial kingdom, all promises will be fulfilled. The animal kingdom will enjoy rest.

The wolf will dwell with the lamb, they will not hurt in my holy mountain for the whole earth will be full of the knowledge of God. (Isaiah 11:6–9)

Jesus Rules and Reigns

A prophecy is given in Zechariah 6:12–13:

Behold the man whose name is the Branch and he will grow up out of his place and he will build the temple of the Lord [New Jerusalem]. *Even he will build the temple of the Lord and he will bear the glory and will sit and rule upon his throne and he will be a priest upon his throne.*

Twenty-five hundred years later, this prophecy is fulfilled, and Jesus is seated in his temple on his throne. This heavenly temple will come to earth.

> *Thus said the Lord, I am returned unto Zion and will dwell in the midst of Jerusalem and Jerusalem will be called a city of truth and the mountain of the Lord of hosts the holy mountain.* (Zechariah 8:3)

Ruling with Jesus for One Thousand Years

The saints have received their immortal bodies; all are gathered together from the three stages of the Resurrection together with all the heavenly host. These have participated in the Bema Seat judgment and the marriage celebration with Jesus in heaven and have proceeded with Jesus to earth to enjoy his millennial reign as given in Revelation 20:4:

> *And I saw thrones and they sat upon them and judgment was given unto them and I saw the souls of them that were beheaded for the witness of Jesus and for the Word of God and which had not worshipped the beast, neither his image, neither had received his mark upon their foreheads or in their hands and they lived and reigned with Christ for a thousand years.*

Revevelation 21:4, "*God will wipe away all tears from their eyes and there will be no more death, or sorrow, or pain for the former things are passed away.*" For clarification, "no more death" pertains to those who have died in Christ, received their immortal bodies, and will live forever.

The second group of people who survived the tribulation without taking the mark of the beast will be ushered into the millennial kingdom. They will be blessed with length of days as it was before the flood when people lived to almost a thousand years of age, but they will die. If one dies at a hundred years old, they are considered young, or dying at one hundred would be looked upon as one who is cursed. Isaiah 65.20, "*There will be no more an infant of days, or an old man that has not filled his days, for the child will die a hundred years old but the sinner being a hundred years old will be accursed.*" This group is not immortal. There will be birth, death, and sin during the millennial reign. It appears they will stand before the White Throne judgment at the end of the millennial reign.

New Jerusalem

We incorrectly refer to a fourth temple as the millennial temple built by God, but the scriptures tell us in Revelation 21:22, there is no temple for the Lord God Almighty, and the Lamb are the temple of it. New Jerusalem is much more than a temple. The scriptures provide a wonderful view of the millennial city descending from heaven to Israel. Revelation 21:2–3, John sees the holy city, New Jerusalem, coming down from God out of heaven prepared as a bride adorned for her husband. And I heard a great voice out of heaven saying, "Behold, the tabernacle of God is with men and he will dwell with them, they will be his people, and God himself will be with them and be their God."

Revelation 21:11, New Jerusalem reflects the glory of the Triune Godhead shining like many precious stones of jasper and crystal. There is no need of the sun or moon, for the glory of God did lighten it. The rest of the world will receive its light from the sun, stars, moon as usual.

When the nations come to pay homage to King Jesus, the city will shine brightly and be seen from a great distance. The land mass of Israel will be greatly increased and elevated. The Kingdom of God will oversee all the nations in the world.

New Jerusalem has high walls. The height, length, and width were equal and approximately 1,200 square miles high and long. It may be shaped like a pyramid. It is surrounded by twelve gates of pearl, which have the names of the twelve tribes of Israel. The walls of the city had twelve foundations with the names of the twelve apostles. It was adorned with jasper, sapphire, chalcedony, emerald, sardonyx, sardius, chrysolyte, beryl, topaz, chrysoprasus, jacinth, amethyst. The city and streets are like pure gold (Revelation 21:12–21).

New Jerusalem is foretold in Micah 4:1–3.

> *But in the last days it will come to pass that the mountain of the house of the Lord will be established in the top of the mountains and it will be exalted above the hills and people will flow unto it. Many nations will come and say come, let us go up to the mountain of the Lord and to the house of the God of Jacob and he will teach us of his ways and we will walk in his paths for the law will go forth out of Zion and the Word of the Lord from Jerusalem. And Jesus will judge among many people and rebuke strong nations afar off and they will beat their swords into plowshares and their spears into pruning hooks; nations will learn war no more*
>
> *And it shall come to pass when you be multiplied and increased in the land in those days, said the Lord, they will say no more, the ark of the covenant of the Lord, neither will it come to mind, neither will they remember it neither will they visit it neither will that be done anymore.* (Jeremiah 3:16)

There will be no Ark of the Covenant placed in an earthly tabernacle. The high priest used to sprinkle the blood of a sacrificed animal over the ark in a ritual that cleansed the nation from sin. Once and for all, Jesus became the blood atonement for all mankind. There will be no need to shed blood in the New Jerusalem.

All of the universe with its infinite dimensions and the realm of heaven will continue as it was in the beginning, and from his domain God will remain enthroned while the Word of God comes to earth to rule and reign.

End of the Thousand Years

After the thousand years have been accomplished, unfortunately, there will be another Gog and Magog.

> *And when the thousand years are expired, Satan will be loosed out of his prison and will go out to deceive the nations which are in the four quarters of the earth, Gog and Magog to gather them together to battle, the number of whom is as the sand of the sea. And they went up on the breath of the earth and compassed the camp of the saints about and the beloved city and fire came down from God out of heaven and devoured them.* (Revelation 20:7–9)

Why? Many people born during the thousand-year reign had not made a declaration of faith to accept Jesus. They have a sin nature and will have sinned. When Satan is loosed again, it will be as a time of testing. Mortals will have to make a decision to follow God or fall prey to the wiles of satanic influence who will lead them to go up against the beloved city and come against the saints. The saints are immortal, and Satan will have no influence upon them. God allows this interaction for a short period of time. At the end of the thousand years, the Lord will call for the white throne judgment to commence.

Standing before the Judge of the World

Revelation 20:5, "*But the rest of the dead lived not again until the thousand years were finished.*" The souls of the wicked dead from the time of Adam to the end of the millennial reign will be raised in the **fourth and final stage** of the Resurrection to stand before Jesus at the white throne for their final judgment. They will be sentenced and banished to hell a place of eternal fire, brimstone, and torment.

Revelation 20:7–10, those living during the millennial reign will be separated. The faithful whose names are written in the book of life will continue with Christ, receiving their immortal bodies at that time. The unfaithful who aligned themselves with the satanic rebellion will be sentenced to eternal damnation.

> *And I saw a great white throne and him that sat on it from whose face the earth and heaven fled away and there was found no place for them and I saw the dead, small and great stand before God and the books were opened and another book was opened which is the book of life and the dead were judged out of those things which were written in the books according to their works. And death and hell were cast into the lake of fire. This is the second death and whosoever was not found written in the book of life was cast into the lake of fire.* (Revelation 20:11–15)

Job 21:30, "*That the wicked is reserved to the day of destruction and they will be brought forth to the day of wrath.*" This ancient passage confirms that all the wicked dead will be gathered from the time of Adam to the last soul during the millennial reign to stand before Jesus.

Satan Goes Back to Hell

> *And the devil that deceived them was cast into the lake of fire and brimstone where the beast and the false prophet are and will be tormented day and night forever.* (Revelation 20:10)

Antichrist and false prophet were cast into the lake of fire at the end of the tribulation. Satan, who was bound in the bottomless pit, was loosed for a season. Afterward, Satan will be cast into the lake of fire where he and his cohorts will remain forever.

New Heavens and Earth

At the end of the millennial reign, God will remove the heavens and the earth with fire, and a new heaven and earth will be established. Isaiah 65:17, "Behold, I create new heavens and a new earth, and the former will not be remembered nor come into mind."

> *I saw a new heaven and a new earth for the first heaven and the earth were passed away and there was no more sea.* (Revelation 21:1)

We close with this thought. Coming to the end of the millennial reign, the white throne judgment, and afterward, a new heaven and earth, God is silent.

Hope to See You on the Good Side of Eternity

REFERENCES

Bernis, Jonathan. *Jewish Voice Today.*

———. *Types and Shadows of Yeshua in the Old and New Testament.*

Bible (King James Version)

Church, J. R. *Enoch.*

———. *Gospel in the Stars.*

———. *Guardians of the Grail.*

———. *Nimrod.*

Cloud, Bill. *The Messiah Revealed.*

Eade, Alfred Thompson. *Expanded Panorama Bible Study Course.*

Federer, William, *What Every American Needs to Know About The Qur'an: A History of Islam and the United States*

Flynn, David. *Cydonia.*

———. *Temple at the Center of Time.*

Gansky, Alton. *Uncovering the Bibles Greatest Mysteries.*

Goetz, William R. *The Emergent Church.*

Goodgame, Peter. *Second Coming of the Antichrist.*

Grigg, William Norman. *United Nations and the American Citizen.*

Hoppe, Lewis M. *Religions of the World.*

Horn, Thomas, *Apollyon Rising 2012.*

Horn, Tom, and Cris Putnam. *Exo-Vaticana.*

Jeffress, Robert. *Outrageous Truth.*

Josephus, Flavius. *Antiquities of the Jews.*

Kah, Gary H. *Hope for the World.*

Law, Terry. *The Truth about Angels.*

Missler, Chuck. *Cosmic Codes* and *Hidden Treasures in the Bible.*

Pember, George Hawkins. *Earth's Earliest Ages.*

Quayle, Stephen. *Genesis 6 Giants.*

Reagan, David R. *Christ in Prophecy.*

Rudge, Bill. *Not Our Father's Faith.*

Ruffino, David, and Joseph Jordan. *Unholy Communion.*
Shelley, Bruce L. *Church History in Plain Language.*
Stone, Nathan. *Names of God.*
Stone, Perry. *Rapture Revelation.*
———. *Secrets beyond the Grave.*
———. *Unleashing the Beast.*
Underwood, Tom B. *Story of the Cherokee People.*
Vallowe, Ed F. *Biblical Mathematics.*
Zwiwerblowsky, R. J., and Geoffrey Wigoder. *Encyclopedia of the Jewish Religion.*

Online Sources

Adam, Michael. *Natural News.*
Anderson, Kerby. *Point of View.*
Baklinski, Pete. *Life Site News.*
Before It's News
Blue Letter Bible
Breaking Israel News
Breitbart News
Church, J. R., *Prophecy in the News.*
Dante
DeYoung, Jimmy. *Prophecy Today.*
Fox News
Hal Lindsey Report
Horn, Tom. *Sky Watch TV.*
Horn, Tom, and Cris Putnam. *Petrus Romanus: The Final Pope.*
International Fellowship of Christians and Jews, Rabbi Eckstein
Israel Now News, Daystar
Jones, Alex. *Infowars.*
Jerusalem Connection
Last Trumpet Ministries
Livingston, Bob. *Personal Liberty Digest.*
Reagan, David. Lamb and Lion Ministries.
Sacred Text
Shoebat, Walid. Shoebat.com.
Wiles, Rick. *TruNews.*
Wikipedia

MULTIMEDIA

Christian Broadcasting Network, *MYATL TV*
Church, J. R., and Gary Stearman. *Mysteries of the Hebrew Alphabet.*
Horn, Tom. *Transhumanism Documentary.*
Marzulli, L. A.. *Watchers Series, 1, 2, 3.*
Stearman, Gary, and J. R. Church. *Ancient Books of Enoch.*
Stearman, Gary, L. A. Marzulli, Tom Horn. *Alien Agenda.*
Stone, Perry. *Fallen Angels, Giants and Evil Spirits.*
———. *Manna Fest TV.*
———. *Rapture Revelation.*

EXHIBITS

All Bible quotes are from the King James Version. Underscore, bold print, parentheses, italics are used by the author.

About the Author

Born in Pennsylvania, author Sandra Henley is retired CEO of Genesis Community Development Center and former co-owner of Henley Computer Systems. She was president of NAACP, Willow Grove branch, chaired the Good News Jail and Prison Ministry and was deacon at Shalom Assembly of God, Willow Grove, PA. Henley served on the boards for the Willow Grove Bank, Willow Grove Senior Citizen Center, Abington Township Citizen and Police Together and Community Action Development Commission of Montgomery County. She spent her life serving others and received community service awards from the Optimist Club of Lower Montgomery County, Henry Ford Community Service Award, Presidential Award for Legacy of Service to the NAACP as well as citations from Congressman Jon Fox and Governor Tom Ridge of Pennsylvania.

email: sneldahenley@outlook.com

CPSIA information can be obtained
at www.ICGtesting.com
Printed in the USA
LVOW09s1922220218
567564LV00022B/256/P

9 781640 277335